JOSEPH CONRAD

JOSEPH CONRAD

Selected Works

HEART OF DARKNESS

LORD JIM

THE SECRET AGENT

UNDER WESTERN EYES

GRAMERCY BOOKS
NEW YORK • AVENEL

Introduction
Copyright © 1994 Random House Value Publishing, Inc.
All rights reserved

This 1994 edition is published by Gramercy Books,
distributed by Random House Value Publishing, Inc.,
40 Engelhard Avenue,
Avenel, New Jersey 07001.

Random House
New York • Toronto • London • Sydney • Auckland

Printed and bound in the United States

Library of Congress Cataloging-in-Publication Data

Conrad, Joseph, 1857-1924
[Selections. 1994]
Joseph Conrad, selected works
p. cm.
Contents: Heart of Darkness—Lord Jim—The secret agent—
Under Western Eyes.
ISBN 0-517-10125-4
I. Title
PR6005.04A6   1994b   93-44690
823'.912—dc20   CIP

10 9 8 7 6 5 4 3 2 1

CONTENTS

INTRODUCTION

Of all the great twentieth-century English novelists, Joseph Conrad is unique in a significant way—he was born and raised in Poland. He did not begin to learn English until he was twenty-one, when he shipped out on a British steamer as a seaman, and for the rest of his life he spoke the language of his adopted country with a heavy accent. Conrad began writing his first novel while he was still a sailor; much of his work reflects his experiences at sea, and, consequently, during his lifetime he was considered a sea writer. His artistry as a novelist was often hidden under the surface aspects of his stories—the foreign and exotic locales, the life and death situations, and the rough-and-tumble characters would not be out of place in a standard adventure yarn. But as with the man himself, the novels have a complexity and depth that are lost in a superficial appraisal.

Józef Teodor Konrad Korzeniowski was born on December 3, 1857, in Berdichev, Poland, at a particularly turbulent point in the country's history. At the time, Poland was controlled, occupied, and ruled with oppressive and cruel force by Russia. Although the Polish aristocracy persisted with revolutionary activities in noble but futile attempts to overthrow Russian dominion, they were repeatedly and brutally quelled. Conrad's father, Apollo, was one of these revolutionaries, and in 1865 he was exiled to Volgoda, Russia, because of his insurgent activities. As a result of the journey and the harsh living conditions in Volgoda, Conrad's mother, Evelina, died at the age of thirty-four. Father and son returned to Warsaw, but Apollo died soon after, in 1869, and Conrad went to live with his maternal uncle, Thaddeus Bobrowski. Apollo had been an intellectual and romantic idealist who dissipated his fortune in his vain dream of Polish independence. His brother-in-law, on the other hand, was a pragmatic man who had mastered business affairs and had, finally, been supporting Apollo.

Conrad's father was a literary man, a minor poet who translated Shakespeare and Hugo into Polish. He passed his love for literature on to his son. Conrad's childhood, especially during the family's exile, was a lonely one and he found solace in books. His favorite reading included Charles Dickens, the sea-adventure tales of James Fenimore Cooper, James Bruce's *Travels*, and Victor Hugo's *Travailleurs de la Mer*. Through his reading, young Conrad developed a romantic notion of the sea, and a desire to travel and escape Poland, which he came to see as tragically fated in its futile dream of freedom. When he announced his wish to become a sailor, his uncle and the rest of his family were aghast; this was not a profession for a member of the Polish gentry. When it became evident that Conrad would not be diverted from this course, the always pragmatic Thaddeus persuaded him to take it seriously as an occupation. On October 14, 1874, two months before his seventeenth birthday, Conrad left for Marseilles, where he would ship out on French ships to the West Indies as well as to Central and South America.

Conrad tried to live out his youthful and fanciful dreams of a life at sea. He soon became involved in gunrunning for the Carlists—supporters of Don Carlos, the pretender to the Spanish throne. It was a dangerous and romantic undertaking, which was probably the reason Conrad became mixed up in the affair, for he was not committed to the cause. The endeavor ended disastrously with the loss of the ship that Conrad had bought for the enterprise. Still supported by his uncle, he also ran up heavy gambling debts in Monte Carlo, where he also, it seems, had a failed romance with an unidentified mysterious lady. This phase in his life ended in 1878, when he attempted to commit suicide by shooting himself through the chest. He survived and his uncle paid his debts.

Thereafter, Conrad single-mindedly pursued a career as a seaman. On April 24, 1878, after spending four years in the French merchant marine, Conrad—although he barely understood the language—joined the British merchant service and shipped out on the *Mavis*, an English steamer bound for Constantinople. Two years later, he passed the examination for third mate. By 1886, the year he became a naturalized English subject, he was certified to be a master of a ship. He often had trouble finding the command positions he wished for, however, and had to take posts below his qualifications. In 1889, during one of these lulls in employment, Conrad, primarily out of boredom and not an urge to start a career as a writer, began what was to become his first novel, *Almayer's Folly* (published in 1895).

Conrad's next post was on a steamer on a voyage up the Congo River. It was a traumatic trip that would forever stamp Conrad's life and imagination, and marked a major turning point in his life. His health was permanently undermined by the malarial fever he contracted there, but it was the emotional suffering that transformed him. The critic G. Jean-Aubrey wrote, "It may be said that Africa killed Conrad the sailor and strengthened Conrad the novelist." While he recuperated he began to record his experiences in the Belgian Congo in what was to become the basis for *Heart of Darkness* (published in serial form in 1899 and as a book three years later), considered to be one of the great works of twentieth-century fiction. After 1894, although he continued to look for a command, he never went to sea again, and began his career as a writer.

Heart of Darkness is a book that can be read on several levels. It can be appreciated simply as an entertaining adventure yarn set in an exotic and perilous locale, filled with dangerous swarms of armed natives, suspenseful attacks, and hair-raising escapes. Or it can be read as a political critique of Western imperialism as exercised by the Belgians, who more or less raped the Congo of its resources while brutalizing the country's people and making them slaves of unbridled capitalistic avarice. It can also be read as a description of the clash of modern Western civilization and indigenous cultures, and the traumatic disturbances, on both sides, wrought by their interaction.

The book works best, however, as the depiction of a personal ordeal. As Conrad himself wrote, "*Heart of Darkness* is quite . . . authentic in fundamentals . . . it is experience pushed a little (and only a little) beyond the actual facts of the case." But, of course, it is not merely a colorful travelogue. The book has been variously interpreted by critics as a portrayal of a modern descent into hell, as an updating of the quest for the Grail, and as a journey into the unconscious realm of the mind.

In the book, Marlow—Conrad's fictional stand-in—years after the event, is telling a group of men about his trip to find Kurtz, a trading company's agent, who became isolated far in the interior of the Congo. On the surface the story is simple and is told vividly. The descriptions have a concrete realism and Conrad truly evokes the heat and humidity and insects of the African jungles. His ability to capture reality is, indeed, one of the hallmarks of his art. But the greatness of the story lies elsewhere. As the novelist E. M. Forster wrote of Conrad's fiction: "There is a central obscurity, something noble, heroic . . . but obscure! Obscure! Misty in the middle as well as at the edges, the secret cask of his genius contains a vapor rather than a jewel." A mystery pervades the book: Who is Kurtz and why is Marlow so fascinated with him and so intent on talking with him?

It is through Conrad's genius that he never has to explain why. As he wrote, "One writes only half a book: the other half is with the reader." As Marlow continues the narrative, the images and scenes build into a powerful nexus of meaning. Conrad's method of writing is essentially poetic, the images presented live not only as images, but as resonating symbols and metaphors that weave a tapestry of allusions that climax with Kurtz's mysterious and ambiguous words: "The horror! The horror!"

For Marlow it is a revelatory moment. He has met and talked with a man responsible for "unspeakable" evils, who has killed an untold number of men and ravaged the countryside. Kurtz, before he came to the Congo, was said to be a paragon of European civilization, motivated by the highest liberal ideals and with greater goals of doing good. But the trip into the depths of the Congo changed him. For Conrad the jungle represents nature in its primal and most dangerous state. A trip into its heart represents, symbolically, traveling back to man's beginnings. Kurtz is a man who has stripped himself of all of Western society's moral and ethical restraints. He has re-created himself into a horrifying demigod and built a truly evil empire.

To Marlow, Kurtz is a man who has fulfilled humanity's potential for evil, who has sunk to the lowest depths of depravity. In the nightmarish and surreal experience of the journey, Marlow undergoes an existential moment of enlightenment and understanding. Why did Kurtz descend to the hellish depths of corrupted and malignant avarice? Why did he, Marlow, not do the same? At one point he wonders: What is it that is stopping his crew of cannibals, who are very hungry, from eating him and the rest of the outnumbered white men? Restraint, he finally answers. Most people go through life without ever being tested. They live safe lives of hypocrisy, greedily vying with one another within the rules of civilization. But as Marlow realizes, the Christian "love thy neighbor" ethos of Western civilization is a flimsy illusion unless it is truly believed. Here in the jungle it is almost worthless. There is nothing to stop you; it is Darwinian survival of the fittest. All the other company officials Marlow meets on the trip are as greedy as Kurtz, but they are cowardly hypocrites who hide behind their civilized masks, who jealously say they do not approve of Kurtz's "unsound methods." Marlow respects Kurtz because he is not a hypocrite and has fearlessly, at enormous cost, stripped himself of all of civilization's illusions.

When Marlow returns to the streets Brussels he resents the people he sees dreaming "their insignificant and silly dreams" because they "could not possibly know the things I know." Through his unique experience Marlow understands that to survive, the illusion of civilization *is* necessary. Man must have rules and order, and must honor and live by them—or perish. Marlow feels that, perhaps, he alone among them is able to appreciate how tenuous life really is. He is offended by "the bearing of commonplace individuals going about their business in the assurance of perfect safety," because in his view it is "like the outrageous flauntings of folly in the face of a danger it is unable to comprehend."

Conrad wrote, "Those who read me know my conviction that the world, the temporal world . . . rests, notably, on the idea of Fidelity." This a running theme through most of his books. As a sailor he learned that to survive, every crewman did the job he was assigned, and that the survival of the ship, and, therefore, the community, depended on each man doing his duty. He realized that his romantic dreams of the sea were illusions, that the day-to-day life of a seaman was prosaic, but in that simple existence there was a kind of honor and dignity that would see a person through if he followed it faithfully. Marlow represented the archetypal seaman who knew his duty and had a strong moral center, though he might lack imagination.

To Conrad, imagination can be very dangerous, as he demonstrates in his next book, *Lord Jim*—published in 1900—where again Marlow is the narrator. Here, again, he is telling a tale to a group of friends. This time he is relating the life of a curious man he met in southeast Asia. Jim is almost six feet tall and strong, "clean-limbed, clean-faced, firm on his feet, as promising a boy as the sun ever shone on." Throughout the book his appearance and his actions are at odds. Like the youthful Conrad, Jim romanticizes his life. His illusions of being a hero tragically collide with reality.

Marlow repeatedly refers to Jim as "one of us," by which Conrad indicates a universal identification with Jim's predicament. In life one's image of oneself, the ego-ideal, never perfectly aligns with one's actuality. In Jim's case, after the *Patna* incident—in which he betrays his code of honor and his duty as a seaman—he is driven by loss of face to prove that he is the hero of his dreams and that all he needs is a chance to begin again with a "clean slate." But that is impossible: in every port his past catches up with him and induces memories and guilt that are at odds with his illusion of himself as a fearless "master of his fate."

The trader Stein, a romantic himself, albeit a successful man of action, gives Jim a chance to redeem himself by sending him to a trading post rarely visited by white men. Jim becomes the virtual ruler of the domain and falls in love with a native girl, Jewel. He almost fulfills his desire to be a hero, but again there are repercussions from the past from which Jim believes he cannot escape. The romantic illusion that has kept him spiritually alive finally destroys him. Jewel tells Marlow that "he had been driven away from her by a dream."

It is clear that as a seaman Jim is guilty of gross dereliction of duty. The rules that govern conduct at sea, as Marlow—and Conrad—are well aware, are almost inviolable, for they exist to ensure the safety and survival of the ship.

Again, there is the question of why Marlow is fascinated by Jim. Jim always has the best of intentions; he is not evil. Although he may want to be a hero for his own self-gratification, that is not uncommon. What is tragic is that Jim was fated to suffer for his illusion. Had the *Patna* not been struck by catastrophe, Jim would probably have gone through life peacefully. But his loss of honor drives him to an alienated search for redemption that he can never find. As Marlow says, "A clean slate, did he say? As if the initial word of each our destiny were not graven in imperishable characters upon the face of a rock?"

It is evident that Conrad is a fatalistic pessimist, perhaps as a result of his upbringing in Poland, where he saw his father and mother destroyed by the romantic dream of Polish independence, and a whole country mired in what he considered tragic futility. But that is the tragic flaw of the human race, to aspire to what it can never be, as Marlow's friend, the trader Stein, says in comparing man to the nonsentient and happy butterfly: "He wants to be a saint, and he wants to be a devil—and every time he shuts his eyes he sees himself as a very fine fellow—so fine as he can never be. . . . In a dream. . . ."

Throughout the novel, Conrad compares Jim to other characters who personify his concept of fidelity, men who do their duty without thought, like the French lieutenant or the Malaysian helmsman, who are incapable of disobeying orders and have no inclination to romantic action. They do what *must* be done, without question. They would never be in Jim's position because they lack the imagination—and thus are wanting of a certain dimension, and perhaps are closer to the butterfly.

At the center of the book we find Conrad's own ambiguous feelings. There is a combative duality at work that represents the influence of Conrad's two father figures: his romantic and idealistic father, Apollo, and his pragmatic business-minded Uncle Thaddeus, who stayed clear of Polish revolutionary politics. While Conrad obviously has the utmost respect for people like Uncle Thaddeus and the representatives of the type who populate his fiction, he is emotionally drawn to the romantic Jim, or Kurtz, who even for all his evil is essentially a figure of Faustian romanticism. Conrad explores, in Stein's modified paraphrase of Hamlet, "How to be?"

For people without imagination, life is essentially uncomplicated: they do what they do. Life is difficult for those who have imagination, especially when Fate and reality collide with their fantasies. Jim can be compared to such tragic heroes as Oedipus or Hamlet, since, like them, he is at odds with Fate, trying to prove that he has free will and responsibility for his own actions. But Jim, perhaps like Conrad's father and unlike the classic tragic hero, goes to his end without learning the error of his ways. Jim, despite all his suffering and the suffering he causes, is no different at the end of his story from what he was at the beginning. He is under the same romantic illusions when he faces his chosen fate sending "right and left at all those faces a proud and unflinching glance." He retains the image of himself as a hero.

The people affected are those around Jim—Jewel, Stein, and Marlow. For steady old Marlow, Jim represents a fascinating mystery or puzzle that illuminates his—and Conrad's—tragic and pessimistic view of human existence. By the end of the book, Stein, because of Jim, "has aged greatly." Many readers mistakenly identify Stein's beliefs with Conrad's own, especially as expressed in this well-known passage:

> A man that is born falls into a dream like a man who falls into the sea. If he tries to climb out into the air as inexperienced people endeavor to do, he drowns—*nicht wahr?* . . . No! I tell you! The way is to the destructive element submit yourself, and with the exertions of your hands and feet in the water make the deep, deep sea keep you up?

Although this ambiguous passage can be interpreted in various ways, it is essentially romantic. But Jim's failure shows the inadequacy of Stein's view of life. Stein finally realizes his own illusion is faulty and perceives the bleak futility which underlies existence. As Marlow says in the final lines of the book that, "He is 'preparing to leave all this; preparing to leave, . . .' while he waves his hand sadly at his butterflies." Conrad is underscoring his own belief in the hopelessness of romantic notions—no matter how attractive—and pessimistically sees all grand human aspirations as essentially useless before an indifferent Fate.

This bleak pessimism is brought even further to the fore in *The Secret Agent*, published in 1906. It was Conrad's first novel to be set in an urban landscape, London. A political novel, it revolves around the efforts of Verloc, a seedy double agent, to bomb the Greenwich Observatory. It is Conrad's only novel that can be called a comedy, albeit a black comedy. Conrad uses the landscape of the city of London to create a hostile world that is gloomy and dirty, populated by tired and hungry people and dreary shadows. It is a place as hazardous as the jungle of the Congo, filled with mediocre people with virtually no romantic notions at all, who do what they must do to survive.

Verloc runs a shop that sells pornographic literature as a cover for his covert activities on behalf of the Russians. He and his wife, Winnie, live in quarters behind the shop with her retarded brother, Stevie. When Winnie's mother retires to an almshouse, she believes she has left her children in the secure financial hands of Verloc. Winnie, who knows nothing of Verloc's true work, married him because he seemed capable of providing a home for her mother and brother.

It is Conrad's ultimate irony that the only character to have a firm moral nature and good spirit is Stevie, whose ineffectualness is superbly handled by Conrad in the scene where the boy tries to save an old and tired horse from being beaten by its owner. Paradoxically, it is Stevie, deceived by Verloc into believing that he is going to help people, who is used as the means to place the bomb at the observatory.

The other characters in the novel are anarchists, the police, and Russian spies. The anarchists, who are supposedly idealistically motivated in revolt against tyranny, lead a comfortable existence. The martyred Michaelis, for example, who was imprisoned for his revolutionary activities, becomes a hero to the cause and is supported by a rich liberal widow upon his release. The English police, typified by Inspector Heat, are as morally corrupt as the anarchists they are keeping track of. The police and the anarchists are the opposite sides of the same coin. Each needs the other to exist—anarchy cannot continue without forces of order, and order is impossible without the opposing elements of anarchy.

In *The Secret Agent*, Conrad again demonstrates that the tragedy of the world is the blindness of men and women who cannot see themselves or others as they really are. Their deceptions, both intended and unconscious, cause a shallowness in the fragile human relationships where trust is almost impossible. Conrad's London is marked by the absence of love and communication, where the only result is the betrayal of oneself.

Conrad's next novel, *Under Western Eyes*, published in 1910, is also a political novel, but one of very different character from *The Secret Agent*. His characteristic pessimism is evident, but this story is concerned with personal redemption. It is a book that was particularly hard for Conrad to write and he suffered a nervous breakdown after completing it, reportedly holding conversations with the novel's characters. He was successful in being objective and impartial, and was particularly gratified, especially considering his virulent anti-Russian feelings, at its acceptance in Russia, where it went through several printings.

Many critics have noted some striking parallels of this novel with *Crime and Punishment* by Fyodor Dostoyevsky, a writer whom Conrad supposedly detested. In both novels, the central characters, Razumov in *Under Western Eyes* and Raskolnikov in *Crime and Punishment*, are Russian students who commit crimes believing they are destined for greater things and are the intellectual masters of their consciences. In both cases, they are almost driven insane by hallucinations and masochistic self-torment fueled by remorse, and finally, after revealing their guilt, find redemption in a forgiving woman.

In *Under Western Eyes*, however, Conrad is also exploring the destructive power of the Russian autocracy upon human individuals. Razumov, the unrecognized illegitimate son of a Russian aristocrat, is a man who is without family or society, who "was as lonely in the world as a man swimming in the deep sea. The word Razumov was the mere label of a solitary individual." He is just "a man with a mind" who has placed all his hopes in becoming part of the Russian totalitarian bureaucracy. His moral character is tested when Victor Haldin, a fellow student of slight acquaintance, comes to his rooms asking for his help. Haldin, a revolutionary, has just killed a hated ministry official. Razumov immediately fears that his hopes of a career will be ruined if the police find out that he helped a terrorist.

Razumov's ensuing decision results in his involvement with the czarist government's counterrevolutionary activities spying on Russian revolutionaries in Geneva, where he is accepted and hailed as the friend and fellow conspirator of Haldin. But his deception begins to unravel when he meets Haldin's sister, Nathalie, with whom he falls in love.

In Razumov, Conrad is again focusing on an individual, like Kurtz, who has broken away from human society, which is represented not by governments but by personal relationships and trust between people. By embracing and working for the oppressive Russian regime he has forsaken his bond to his fellow man. He becomes alienated and feels the spiritually destructive "naked terror . . . of true loneliness," as reflected in his confession to Nathalie: "It is simply because there is no one anywhere in the whole great world I could go to. . . . Do you conceive the desolation of the thought—no-one-to-go-to?" By the end of the novel Razumov realizes that in his betrayal of another human being, "It's myself whom I have given up to destruction. . . ." But it is not a "happy" ending, for his redemption and reconnection to human society come at a very high price.

While Conrad was writing his best books, the works included in this volume—*Heart of Darkness*, *Lord Jim*, *The Secret Agent*, and *Under Western Eyes*—and others, including *Nostromo* (published in 1904 and considered to be one of his finest novels), he was barely making enough money to support his wife, Jessie, an Englishwoman whom he married in 1895, and their two sons. *Chance*, published in 1913, finally brought him public acclaim and financial security, but it also marked the beginning of a decline in his creativity. After his death in 1924, despite the recognition of his achievements by such renowned writers as Ernest Hemingway and F. Scott Fitzgerald, his books slipped from public memory. It was not until after World War II that his reputation revived and his accomplishments as a novelist were ranked alongside those of James Joyce and D.H.

Lawrence. The distinguished critic H. L. Mencken wrote of Conrad: "He transcended all the rules. There have been, perhaps, greater novelists, but I believe that he was incomparably the greatest artist who ever wrote a novel."

CHRISTOPHER MOORE

New York
1994

Heart
of
Darkness

I

The *Nellie*, a cruising yawl, swung to her anchor without a flutter of the sails, and was at rest. The flood had made, the wind was nearly calm, and being bound down the river, the only thing for it was to come to and wait for the turn of the tide.

The sea-reach of the Thames stretched before us like the beginning of an interminable waterway. In the offing the sea and the sky were welded together without a joint, and in the luminous space the tanned sails of the barges drifting up with the tide seemed to stand still in red dusters of canvas sharply peaked, with gleams of varnished sprits. A haze rested on the low shores that ran out to sea in vanishing flatness. The air was dark above Gravesend, and farther back still seemed condensed into a mournful gloom, brooding motionless over the biggest, and the greatest, town on earth.

The Director of Companies was our captain and our host. We four affectionately watched his back as he stood in the bows looking to seaward. On the whole river there was nothing that looked half so nautical. He resembled a pilot, which to a seaman is trustworthiness personified. It was difficult to realize his work was not out there in the luminous estuary, but behind him, within the brooding gloom.

Between us there was, as I have already said somewhere, the bond of the sea. Besides holding our hearts together through long periods of separation, it had the effect of making us tolerant of each other's yarns—and even convictions. The Lawyer—the best of old fellows—had, because of his many years and many virtues, the only cushion on deck, and was lying on the only rug. The Accountant had brought out already a box of dominoes, and was toying architecturally with the bones. Marlow sat cross-legged right aft, leaning against the mizzen-mast. He had sunken cheeks, a yellow complexion, a straight back, an ascetic aspect, and, with his arms dropped, the palms of hands outwards, resembled an idol. The Director, satisfied the anchor had good hold, made his way aft and sat down amongst us. We exchanged a few words lazily. Afterwards there was silence on board the yacht. For some reason or other we did not begin that game of dominoes. We felt meditative, and fit for nothing but placid staring. The day was ending in a serenity of still and exquisite brilliance. The water shone pacifically; the sky, without a speck, was a benign immensity of unstained light; the very mist on the Essex marshes was like a gauzy and radiant fabric, hung from the wooded rises inland, and draping the low shores in diaphanous folds. Only the gloom to the west, brooding over the upper reaches, became more somber every minute, as if angered by the approach of the sun.

And at last, in its curved and imperceptible fall, the sun sank low, and from glowing white changed to a dull red without rays and without heat, as if about to go out suddenly, stricken to death by the touch of that gloom brooding over a crowd of men.

Forthwith a change came over the waters, and the serenity became less brilliant but more profound. The old river in its broad reach rested unruffled at the decline of day, after ages of good service done to the race that peopled its banks, spread out in the tranquil dignity of a waterway leading to the uttermost ends of the earth. We looked at the venerable stream not in the vivid flush of a short day that comes and departs forever, but in the august light of abiding memories. And indeed nothing is easier for a man who has, as the phrase goes, "followed the sea" with reverence and affection, than to evoke the great spirit of the past upon the lower reaches of the Thames. The tidal current runs to and fro in its unceasing service, crowded with memories of men and ships it has borne to the rest of home or to the battles of the sea. It had known and served all the men of whom the nation is proud, from Sir Francis Drake to Sir John Franklin, knights all, titled and untitled—the great knights-errant of the sea. It had borne all the ships whose names are like jewels flashing in the night of time, from the *Golden Hind* returning with her round flanks full of treasure, to be visited by the Queen's Highness and thus pass out of the gigantic tale, to the *Erebus* and *Terror*, bound on other conquests—and that never returned. It had known the ships and the men. They had sailed from Deptford, from Greenwich, from Erith—the adventurers and the settlers; kings' ships and the ships of men on 'Change; captains, admirals, the dark "interlopers" of the Eastern trade, and the commissioned "generals" of East India fleets. Hunters for gold or pursuers of fame, they all had gone out on that stream, bearing the sword, and often the torch, messengers of the might within the land, bearers of a spark from the sacred fire. What greatness had not floated on the ebb of that river into the mystery of an unknown earth! . . . The dreams of men, the seed of commonwealths, the germs of empires.

The sun set; the dusk fell on the stream, and lights began to appear along the shore. The Chapman lighthouse, a three-legged thing erect on a mud flat, shone strongly. Lights of ships moved in the fairway—a great stir of lights going up and going down. And farther west on the upper reaches the place of the monstrous town was still marked ominously on the sky, a brooding gloom in sunshine, a lurid glare under the stars.

"And this also," said Marlow suddenly, "has been one of the dark places of the earth."

He was the only man of us who still "followed the sea." The worst that could be said of him was that he did not represent his class. He was a seaman, but he was a wanderer too, while most seamen lead, if one may so express it, a sedentary life. Their minds are of the stay-at-home order, and their home is always with them— the ship; and so is their country—the sea. One ship is very much like another, and the sea is always the same. In the immutability of their surroundings the foreign shores, the foreign faces, the changing immensity of life, glide past, veiled not by a sense of mystery but by a slightly disdainful ignorance; for there is nothing mysterious to a seaman unless it be the sea itself, which is the mistress of his existence and as inscrutable as Destiny. For the rest, after his hours of work, a casual stroll or a casual spree on shore suffices to unfold for him the secret of a whole continent, and generally he finds the secret not worth knowing. The yarns of seamen have a direct simplicity, the whole meaning of which lies within the shell of a cracked nut. But Marlow was not typical (if his propensity to spin yarns be excepted), and to him the meaning of an episode was not inside like a kernel but outside, enveloping the tale which brought it out only as a glow brings out a haze, in the likeness of one of these misty halos that sometimes are made visible by the spectral illumination of moonshine.

His remark did not seem at all surprising. It was just like Marlow. It was accepted in silence. No one took the trouble to grunt even; and presently he said, very slow:

"I was thinking of very old times, when the Romans first came here, nineteen hundred years ago—the other day. . . . Light came out of this river since—you say Knights? Yes; but it is like a running blaze on a plain, like a flash of lightning in the clouds. We live in the flicker—may it last as long as the old earth keeps rolling! But darkness was here yesterday. Imagine the feelings of a commander of a fine—what d'ye call 'em?—trireme in the Mediterranean, ordered suddenly to the north; run overland across the Gauls in a hurry; put in charge of one of these craft the legionaries—a wonderful lot of handy men they must have been too— used to build, apparently by the hundred, in a month or two, if we may believe what we read. Imagine him here—the very end of the world, a sea the color of lead, a sky the color of smoke, a kind of ship about as rigid as a concertina—and going up this river with stores, or orders, or what you like. Sandbanks, marshes, forests, savages—precious little to eat fit for a civilized man, nothing but Thames water drink. No Falernian wine here, no going ashore. Here and there a military camp lost in a wilderness, like a needle in a bundle of hay—cold, fog, tempests, disease, exile, and death—death skulking in the air, in the water, in the bush. They must have been dying like flies here. Oh yes—he did it. Did it very well, too, no doubt, and without thinking much about it either, except afterwards to brag of what he had gone through in his time, perhaps. They were men enough to face the darkness. And perhaps he was cheered by keeping his eye on a chance of promotion to the fleet at Ravenna by and by, if he had good friends in Rome and survived the awful climate. Or think of a decent young citizen in a toga—perhaps too much dice, you know coming out here in the train of some prefect, or tax-gatherer, or trader, even, to mend his fortunes. Land in a swamp, march through the woods, and in some inland post feel the savagery, the utter savagery, had closed round him—all that mysterious life of the wilderness that stirs in the forest, in the jungles, in the hearts of wild men. There's no initiation either into such mysteries. He has to live in the midst of the incomprehensible, which is also detestable. And it has a fascination, too, that goes to work upon him. The fascination of the abomination—you know. Imagine the growing regrets, the longing to escape, the powerless disgust, the surrender, the hate."

He paused.

"Mind," he began again, lifting one arm from the elbow, the palm of the hand outwards, so that, with his legs folded before him, he had the pose of a Buddha preaching in European clothes and without a lotus flower—"Mind, none of us would feel exactly like this. What saves us is efficiency—the devotion to efficiency. But these chaps were not much account, really. They were no colonists; their administration was merely a squeeze, and nothing more, I suspect. They were conquerors, and for that you want only brute force—nothing to boast of, when you have it, since your strength is just an accident arising from the weakness of others. They grabbed what they could get for the sake of what was to be got. It was just robbery with violence, aggravated murder on a great scale, and men going at it blind—as is very proper for those who tackle a darkness. The conquest of the earth, which mostly means the taking it away from those who have a different complexion or slightly flatter noses than ourselves, is not a pretty thing when you look into it too much. What redeems it is the idea only. An idea at the back of it; not a sentimental pretense but an idea; and an unselfish belief in the idea—something you can set up, and bow down before, and offer a sacrifice to. . . ."

He broke off. Flames glided in the river, small green flames, red flames, white flames, pursuing, overtaking, joining, crossing each other—then separating slowly or hastily. The traffic of the great city went on in the deepening night upon the sleepless river. We looked on, waiting patiently—there was nothing else to do till the end of the flood; but it was only after a long silence, when he said, in a hesitating voice, "I suppose you fellows remember I did once turn freshwater sailor for a bit," that we knew we were fated, before the ebb began to run, to hear about one of Marlow's inconclusive experiences.

"I don't want to bother you much with what happened to me personally," he began, showing in this remark the weakness of many tellers of tales who seem so often unaware of what their audience would best like to hear; "yet to understand the effect of it on me you ought to know how I got out there, what I saw, how I went up that river to the place where I first met the poor chap. It was the farthest point of navigation and the culminating point of my experience. It seemed somehow to throw a kind of light on everything about me—and into my thoughts. It was somber enough too and pitiful—not extraordinary in any way—not very clear either. No, not very clear. And yet it seemed to throw a kind of light.

"I had then, as you remember, just returned to London after a lot of Indian Ocean, Pacific, China Seas—a regular dose of the East—six years or so, and I was loafing about, hindering you fellows in your work and invading your homes, just as though I had got a heavenly mission to civilize you. It was very fine for a time, but after a bit I did get tired of resting. Then I began to look for a ship I should think the hardest work on earth. But the ships wouldn't even look at me. And I got tired of that game too.

"Now when I was a little chap I had a passion for maps. I would look for hours at South America, or Africa, or Australia, and lose myself in all the glories of exploration. At that time there were many blank spaces on the earth, and when I saw one that looked particularly inviting on a map (but they all look that) I would put my finger on it and say, When I grow up I will go there. The North Pole was one of these places, I remember. Well, I haven't been there yet, and shall not try now. The glamour's off. Other places were scattered about the Equator, and in every sort of latitude all over the two hemispheres. I have been in some of them, and . . . well, we won't talk about that. But there was one yet—the biggest, the most blank, so to speak—that I had a hankering after.

"True, by this time it was not a blank space anymore. It had got filled since my boyhood with rivers and lakes and names. It had ceased to be a blank space of delightful mystery—a white patch for a boy to dream gloriously over. It had become a place of darkness. But there was in it one river especially, a mighty big river, that you could see on the map, resembling an immense snake uncoiled, with its head in the sea, its body at rest curving afar over a vast country, and its tail lost in the depths of the land. And as I looked at the map of it in a shopwindow, it fascinated me as a snake would a bird—a silly little bird. Then I remembered there was a big concern, a Company for trade on that river. Dash it all! I thought to myself, they can't trade without using some kind of craft on that lot of fresh water—steamboats! Why shouldn't I try to get charge of one? I went on along Fleet Street, but could not shake off the idea. The snake had charmed me.

"You understand it was a Continental concern, that Trading Society; but I have a lot of relations living on the Continent, because it's cheap and not so nasty as it looks, they say.

"I am sorry to own I began to worry them. This was already a fresh departure for me. I was not used to get things that way, you know. I always went my own road and on my own legs where I had a mind to go. I wouldn't have believed it of myself; but, then—you see—I felt somehow I must get there by hook or by crook. So I worried them. The men said, 'My dear fellow,' and did nothing. Then would you believe it?—I tried the women. I, Charlie Marlow, set the women to work—to get a job. Heavens! Well, you see, the notion drove me. I had an aunt, a dear enthusiastic soul. She wrote: 'It will be delightful. I am ready to do anything, anything for you. It is a glorious idea. I know the wife of a very high personage in the Administration, and also a man who has lots of influence with,' etc. etc. She was determined to make no end of fuss to get me appointed skipper of a river steamboat, if such was my fancy.

"I got my appointment of course; and I got it very quick. It appears the Company had received news that one of their captains had been killed in a scuffle with the natives. This was my chance, and it made me the more anxious to go. It was only months and months afterwards, when I made the attempt to recover what was left of the body, that I heard the original quarrel arose from a misunderstanding about some hens. Yes, two black hens. Fresleven—that was the fellow's name, a Dane—thought himself wronged somehow in the bargain, so he went ashore and started to hammer the chief of the village with a stick. Oh, it didn't surprise me in the least to hear this, and at the same time to be told that Fresleven was the gentlest, quietest creature that ever walked on two legs. No doubt he was; but he had been a couple of years already out there engaged in the noble cause, you know, and he probably felt the need at last of asserting his self-respect in some way. Therefore he whacked the old nigger mercilessly, while a big crowd of his people watched him, thunderstruck, till some man—I was told the chief's son—in desperation at hearing the old chap yell, made a tentative jab with a spear at the white man—and of course it went quite easy between the shoulder blades. Then the whole population cleared into the forest, expecting all kinds of calamities to happen, while, on the other hand, the steamer Fresleven commanded left also in a bad panic, in charge of the engineer, I believe. Afterwards nobody seemed to trouble much about Fresleven's remains, till I got out and stepped into his shoes. I couldn't let it rest, though; but when an opportunity offered at last to meet my predecessor, the grass growing through his ribs was tall enough to hide his bones. They were all there. The supernatural being had not been touched after he fell. And the village was deserted, the huts gaped black, rotting, all askew within the fallen enclosures. A calamity had come to it, sure enough. The people had vanished. Mad terror had scattered them, men, women, and children, through the bush, and they had never returned. What became of the hens I don't know either. I should think the cause of progress got them, anyhow. However, through this glorious affair I got my appointment, before I had fairly begun to hope for it.

I flew around like mad to get ready, and before forty-eight hours I was crossing the Channel to show myself to my employers, and sign the contract. In a very few hours I arrived in a city that always makes me think of a whited sepulcher. Prejudice no doubt. I had no difficulty in finding the Company's offices. It was the biggest thing in the town, and everybody I met was full of it. They were going to run an oversea empire, and make no end of coin by trade.

"A narrow and deserted street in deep shadow, high houses, innumerable windows with venetian blinds, a dead silence, grass sprouting between the stones, imposing carriage archways right and left, immense double doors standing ponderously ajar. I slipped through one of these cracks, went up a swept and ungarnished staircase, as arid as a desert, and opened the first door I came to. Two women, one fat and the other slim, sat on straw-bottomed chairs, knitting black wool. The slim one got up and walked straight at me—still knitting with downcast eyes—and only just as I began to think of getting out of her way, as you would for a somnambulist, stood still, and looked up. Her dress was as plain as an umbrella cover, and she turned round without a word and preceded me into a waiting room. I gave my name, and looked about. Deal table in the middle, plain chairs all round the walls, on one end a large shining map, marked with all the colors of a rainbow. There was a vast amount of red—good to see at any time, because one knows that some real work is done in there, a deuce of a lot of blue, a little green, smears of orange, and, on the East Coast, a purple patch, to show where the jolly pioneers of progress drink the jolly lager beer. However, I wasn't going into any of these. I was going into the yellow. Dead in the center. And the river was there—fascinating—deadly—like a snake. Ough! A door opened, a white-haired secretarial head, but wearing a compassionate expression, appeared, and a skinny forefinger beckoned me into the sanctuary. Its light was dim, and a heavy writing-desk squatted in the middle. From behind that structure came out an impression of pale plumpness in a frock coat. The great man himself. He was five feet six, I should judge, and had his grip on the handle-end of ever so many millions. He shook hands, I fancy, murmured vaguely, was satisfied with my French. *Bon voyage.*

"In about forty-five seconds I found myself again in the waiting room with the compassionate secretary, who, full of desolation and sympathy, made me sign some document. I believe I undertook amongst other things not to disclose any trade secrets. Well, I am not going to.

"I began to feel slightly uneasy. You know I am not used to such ceremonies, and there was something ominous in the atmosphere. It was just as though I had been let into some conspiracy—I don't know—something not quite right; and I was glad to get out. In the outer room the two women knitted black wool feverishly. People were arriving, and the younger one was walking back and forth introducing them. The old one sat on her chair. Her flat cloth slippers were propped up on a foot-warmer, and a cat reposed on her lap. She wore a starched white affair on her head, had a wart on one cheek, and silver-rimmed spectacles hung on the tip of her nose. She glanced at me above the glasses. The swift and indifferent placidity of that look troubled me. Two youths with foolish and cheery countenances were being piloted over, and she threw at them the same quick glance of unconcerned wisdom. She seemed to know all about them and about me too. An eerie feeling came over me. She seemed uncanny and fateful. Often far away there I thought of these two, guarding the door of Darkness, knitting black wool as for a warm pall, one introducing, introducing continuously to the unknown, the other scrutinizing the cheery and foolish faces with unconcerned old eyes. *Ave!* Old knitter of black wool. *Morituri te salutant.* Not many of those she looked at ever saw her again—not half, by a long way.

"There was yet a visit to the doctor. 'A simple formality,' assured me the secretary, with an air of taking an immense part in all my sorrows. Accordingly a young chap wearing his hat over the left eyebrow, some clerk I suppose—there must have been clerks in the business, though the house was as still as a house in a city of the dead—came from somewhere upstairs, and led me forth. He was shabby and careless, with ink-stains on the sleeves of his jacket, and his cravat was large and billowy, under a chin shaped like the toe of an old boot. It was a little too early for the doctor, so I proposed a drink, and thereupon he developed a vein of joviality. As we sat over our vermouths he glorified the Company's business, and by and by I expressed casually my surprise at him not going out there. He became very cool and collected all at once. 'I am not such a fool as I look, quoth Plato to his disciples,' he said sententiously, emptied his glass with great resolution, and we rose.

"The old doctor felt my pulse, evidently thinking of something else the while. 'Good, good for there,' he mumbled, and then with a certain eagerness asked me whether I would let him measure my head. Rather surprised, I said Yes, when he produced a thing like calipers and got the dimensions back and front and every way, taking notes carefully. He was an unshaven little man in a threadbare coat like a gaberdine, with his feet in slippers, and I thought him a harmless fool. 'I always ask leave, in the interests of science, to measure the crania of those going out there,' he said. 'And when they come back too?' I asked. 'Oh, I never see them,' he remarked; 'and, moreover, the changes take place inside, you know.' He smiled, as if at some quiet joke. 'So you are going out there. Famous. Interesting too.' He gave me a searching glance, and made another note. 'Ever any madness in your family?' he asked, in a matter-of-fact tone. I felt very annoyed. 'Is that question in the interests of science too?' 'It would be,' he said, without taking notice of my irritation, 'interesting for science to watch the mental changes of individuals, on the spot, but . . .' 'Are you an alienist?' I interrupted. 'Every doctor should be—a little,' answered that original imperturbably. 'I have a little theory which you Messieurs who go out there must help me to prove. This is my share in the advantages my country shall reap from the possession of such a magnificent dependency. The mere wealth I leave to others. Pardon my questions, but you are the first Englishman coming under my observation . . .' I hastened to assure him I was not in the least typical. 'If I were,' said I, 'I wouldn't be talking like this with you.' 'What you say is rather profound, and probably erroneous,' he said, with a laugh. 'Avoid irritation more than exposure to the sun. Adieu. How do you English say, eh? Goodbye. Ah! Goodbye. Adieu. In the tropics one must before everything keep calm.' . . . He lifted a warning forefinger. . . . *'Du calme, du calme. Adieu.'*

"One thing more remained to do—say goodbye to my excellent aunt. I found her triumphant. I had a cup of tea—the last decent cup of tea for many days—and in a room that most soothingly looked just as you would expect a lady's drawing room to look, we had a long quiet chat by the fireside. In the course of these confidences it became quite plain to me I had been represented to the wife of the high dignitary, and goodness knows to how many more people besides, as an exceptional and gifted creature—a piece of good fortune for the Company—a man you don't get hold of every day. Good Heavens! and I was going to take charge of a two-penny-half-penny river-steamboat with a penny whistle attached! It appeared, however, I was also one of the Workers, with a capital—you know. Something like an emissary of light, something like a lower sort of apostle. There had been a lot of such rot let loose in print and talk just about that time, and the excellent woman, living right in the rush of all that humbug, got carried off her feet. She talked about 'weaning those ignorant millions from their horrid ways,' till, upon my word, she made me quite uncomfortable. I ventured to hint that the Company was run for profit.

"'You forget, dear Charlie, that the laborer is worthy of his hire,' she said brightly. It's queer how out of touch with truth women are. They live in a world of their own, and there had never been anything like it, and never can be. It is too beautiful altogether, and if they were to set it up it would go to pieces before the first sunset. Some confounded fact we men have been living contentedly with ever since the day of creation would start up and knock the whole thing over.

"After this I got embraced, told to wear flannel, be sure to write often, and so on—and I left. In the street—I don't know why—a queer feeling came to me that I was an impostor. Odd thing that I, who used to clear out for any part of the world at twenty-four hours' notice, with less thought than most men give to the crossing of a street, had a moment—I won't say of hesitation, but of startled pause, before this commonplace affair. The best way I can explain it to you is by saying that, for a second or two, I felt as though, instead of going to the center of a continent, I were about to set off for the center of the earth.

"I left in a French steamer, and she called in every blamed port they have out there, for, as far as I could see, the sole purpose of landing soldiers and custom-house officers. I watched the coast. Watching a coast as it slips by the ship is like thinking about an enigma. There it is before you—smiling, frowning, inviting, grand, mean, insipid, or savage, and always mute with an air of whispering, Come and find out. This one was almost featureless, as if still in the making, with an aspect of monotonous grimness. The edge of a colossal jungle, so dark green as to be almost black fringed with white surf, ran straight, like a ruled line, far, far away along a blue sea whose glitter was blurred by a creeping mist. The sun was fierce, the land seemed to glisten and drip with steam. Here and there grayish-whitish specks showed up clustered inside the white surf, with a flag flying above them perhaps—settlements some centuries old, and still no bigger than pinheads on the untouched expanse of their background. We pounded along, stopped, landed soldiers; went on, landed customhouse clerks to levy toll in what looked like a Godforsaken wilderness, with a tin shed and a flagpole lost in it; landed more sol-diers—to take care of the customhouse clerks presumably. Some, I heard, got drowned in the surf; but whether they did or not, nobody seemed particularly to care. They were just flung out there, and on we went. Every day the coast looked the same, as though we had not moved; but we passed various places—trading places—with names like Gran' Bassam, Little Popo; names that seemed to belong to some sordid farce acted in front of a sinister back-cloth. The idleness of a pas-senger, my isolation amongst all these men with whom I had no point of contact, the oily and languid sea, the uniform somberness of the coast, seemed to keep me away from the truth of things, within the toil of a mournful and senseless delu-sion. The voice of the surf heard now and then was a positive pleasure, like the speech of a brother. It was something natural, that had its reason, that had a meaning. Now and then a boat from the shore gave one a momentary contact with reality. It was paddled by black fellows. You could see from afar the white of their eyeballs glistening. They shouted, sang; their bodies streamed with perspiration; they had faces like grotesque masks—these chaps; but they had bone, muscle, a wild vitality, an intense energy of movement, that was as natural and true as the surf along their coast. They wanted no excuse for being there. They were a great comfort to look at. For a time I would feel I belonged still to a world of straight-forward facts; but the feeling would not last long. Something would turn up to scare it away. Once, I remember, we came upon a man-of-war anchored off the coast. There wasn't even a shed there, and she was shelling the bush. It appears the French had one of their wars going on thereabouts. Her ensign dropped limp like a rag; the muzzles of the long six-inch guns stuck out all over the low hull; the greasy, slimy swell swung her up lazily and let her down, swaying her thin masts. In the empty immensity of earth, sky, and water, there she was, incomprehensible, firing into a continent. Pop, would go one of the six-inch guns; a small flame would dart and vanish, a little white smoke would disappear, a tiny projectile would give a feeble screech and nothing happened. Nothing could happen. There was a touch of insanity in the proceeding, a sense of lugubrious drollery in the sight; and it was not dissipated by somebody on board assuring me earnestly there was a camp of natives—he called them enemies!—hidden out of sight somewhere.

"We gave her her letters (I heard the men in that lonely ship were dying of fever at the rate of three a day) and went on. We called at some more places with farcical names, where the merry dance of death and trade goes on in a still and earthy atmosphere as of an overheated catacomb; all along the formless coast bordered by dangerous surf, as if Nature herself had tried to ward off intruders; in and out of rivers, streams of death in life, whose banks were rotting into mud, whose waters, thickened into slime, invaded the contorted mangroves, that seemed to writhe at us in the extremity of an impotent despair. Nowhere did we stop long enough to get a particularized impression, but the general sense of vague and oppressive wonder grew upon me. It was like a weary pilgrimage amongst hints for nightmares.

"It was upward of thirty days before I saw the mouth of the big river. We anchored off the seat of the government. But my work would not begin till some two hundred miles farther on. So as soon as I could I made a start for a place thirty miles higher up.

"I had my passage on a little sea-going steamer. Her captain was a Swede, and knowing me for a seaman, invited me on the bridge. He was a young man, lean, fair, and morose, with lanky hair and a shuffling gait. As we left the miserable little wharf, he tossed his head contemptuously at the shore. 'Been living there?' he asked. I said, 'Yes.' 'Fine lot these government chaps—are they not?' he went on, speaking English with great precision and considerable bitterness. 'It is funny what some people will do for a few francs a month. I wonder what becomes of that kind when it goes upcountry?' I said to him I expected to see that soon. 'So-o-o!' he exclaimed. He shuffled athwart, keeping one eye ahead vigilantly. 'Don't be too sure,' he continued. 'The other day I took up a man who hanged himself on the road. He was a Swede, too.' 'Hanged himself! Why, in God's name?' I cried. He kept on looking out watchfully. 'Who knows? The sun too much for him, or the country perhaps.'

"At last we opened a reach. A rocky cliff appeared, mounds of turned-up earth by the shore, houses on a hill, others with iron roofs, amongst a waste of excavations, or hanging to the declivity. A continuous noise of the rapids above hovered over this scene of inhabited devastation. A lot of people, mostly black and naked, moved about like ants. A jetty projected into the river. A blinding sunlight drowned all this at times in a sudden recrudescence of glare. 'There's your Company's station,' said the Swede, pointing to three wooden barrack-like structures on the rocky slope. 'I will send your things up. Four boxes did you say? So. Farewell.'

"I came upon a boiler wallowing in the grass, then found a path leading up the hill. It turned aside for the boulders, and also for an undersized railway track lying there on its back with its wheels in the air. One was off. The thing looked as dead as the carcass of some animal. I came upon more pieces of decaying machinery, a stack of rusty rails. To the left a dump of trees made a shady spot, where dark things seemed to stir feebly. I blinked, the path was steep. A horn tooted to the right, and I saw the black people run. A heavy and dull detonation shook the ground, a puff of smoke came out of the cliff, and that was all. No change appeared on the face of the rock. They were building a railway. The cliff was not in the way or anything; but this objectless blasting was all the work going on.

"A slight clinking behind me made me turn my head. Six black men advanced in a file, toiling up the path. They walked erect and slow, balancing small baskets full of earth on their heads, and the clink kept time with their footsteps. Black rags were wound round their loins, and the short ends behind waggled to and fro like tails. I could see every rib, the joints of their limbs were like knots in a rope; each had an iron collar on his neck, and all were connected together with a chain whose bights swung between them, rhythmically clinking. Another report from the cliff made me think suddenly of that ship of war I had seen firing into a continent. It was the same kind of ominous voice; but these men could by no stretch of imagination be called enemies. They were called criminals, and the outraged law, like the bursting shells, had come to them, an insoluble mystery from the sea. All their meager breasts panted together, the violently dilated nostrils quivered, the eyes stared stonily uphill. They passed me within six inches, without a glance, with that complete, deathlike indifference of unhappy savages. Behind this raw matter one of the reclaimed, the product of the new forces at work, strolled despondently, carrying a rifle by its middle. He had a uniform jacket with one button off, and seeing a white man on the path, hoisted his weapon to his shoulder with alacrity. This was simple prudence, white men being so much alike at a distance that he could not tell who I might be. He was speedily reassured, and with a large, white, rascally grin, and a glance at his charge, seemed to take me into partnership in his exalted trust. After all, I also was a part of the great cause of these high and just proceedings.

"Instead of going up, I turned and descended to the left. My idea was to let that chain gang get out of sight before I climbed the hill. You know I am not particularly tender; I've had to strike and to fend off. I've had to resist and to attack sometimes—that's only one way of resisting—without counting the exact cost according to the demands of such sort of life as I had blundered into. I've seen the devil of violence, and the devil of greed, and the devil of hot desire; but, by all the stars! these were strong, lusty, red-eyed devils, that swayed and drove men—men, I tell you. But as I stood on this hillside, I foresaw that in the blinding sunshine of that land I would become acquainted with a flabby, pretending, weak-eyed devil of a rapacious and pitiless folly. How insidious he could be, too, I was only to find out several months later and a thousand miles farther. For a moment I stood appalled, as though by a warning. Finally, I descended the hill, obliquely, towards the trees I had seen.

"I avoided a vast artificial hole somebody had been digging on the slope, the purpose of which I found it impossible to divine. It wasn't a quarry or a sandpit, anyhow. It was just a hole. It might have been connected with the philanthropic desire of giving the criminals something to do. I don't know. Then I nearly fell into a very narrow ravine, almost no more than a scar in the hillside. I discovered that a lot of imported drainage pipes for the settlement had been tumbled in there. There wasn't one that was not broken. It was a wanton smash-up. At last I got under the trees. My purpose was to stroll into the shade for a moment; but no sooner within than it seemed to me I had stepped into the gloomy circle of some Inferno. The rapids were near, and an uninterrupted, uniform, headlong, rushing noise filled the mournful stillness of the grove, where not a breath stirred, not a leaf moved, with a mysterious sound as though the tearing pace of the launched earth had suddenly become audible.

"Black shapes crouched, lay, sat between the trees, leaning against the trunks, clinging to the earth, half coming out, half effaced within the dim light, in all the attitudes of pain, abandonment, and despair. Another mine on the cliff went off, followed by a slight shudder of the soil under my feet. The work was going on. The work! And this was the place where some of the helpers had withdrawn to die.

"They were dying slowly—it was very clear. They were not enemies, they were not criminals, they were nothing earthly now—nothing but black shadows of disease and starvation, lying confusedly in the greenish gloom. Brought from all the recesses of the coast in all the legality of time contracts, lost in uncongenial surroundings, fed on unfamiliar food, they sickened, became inefficient, and were then allowed to crawl away and rest. These moribund shapes were free as air—and nearly as thin. I began to distinguish the gleam of the eyes under the trees. Then, glancing down, I saw a face near my hand. The black bones reclined at full length with one shoulder against the tree, and slowly the eyelids rose and the sunken eyes looked up at me, enormous and vacant, a kind of blind, white flicker in the depths of the orbs, which died out slowly. The man seemed young—almost a boy—but you know with them it's hard to tell. I found nothing else to do but to offer him one of my good Swede's ship's biscuits I had in my pocket. The fingers closed slowly on it and held—there was no other movement and no other glance. He had tied a bit of white worsted round his neck—Why? Where did he get it? Was it a badge an ornament—a charm—a propitiatory act? Was there any idea at all connected with it? It looked startling round his black neck, this bit of white thread from beyond the seas.

"Near the same tree two more bundles of acute angles sat with their legs drawn up. One, with his chin propped on his knees, stared at nothing, in an intolerable and appalling manner: his brother phantom rested its forehead, as if overcome with a great weariness; and all about others were scattered in every pose of contorted collapse, as in some picture of a massacre or a pestilence. While I stood horror-struck, one of these creatures rose to his hands and knees, and went off on all-fours towards the river to drink. He lapped out of his hand, then sat up in the sunlight, crossing his shins in front of him, and after a time let his woolly head fall on his breastbone.

"I didn't want any more loitering in the shade, and I made haste towards the station. When near the buildings I met a white man, in such an unexpected elegance of get-up that in the first moment I took him for a sort of vision. I saw a high starched collar, white cuffs, a light alpaca jacket, snowy trousers, a clean necktie, and varnished boots. No hat. Hair parted, brushed, oiled, under a green-lined parasol held in a big white hand. He was amazing, and had a penholder behind his ear.

"I shook hands with this miracle, and I learned he was the Company's chief accountant, and that all the bookkeeping was done at this station. He had come out for a moment, he said, 'to get a breath of fresh air.' The expression sounded wonderfully odd, with its suggestion of sedentary desk-life. I wouldn't have mentioned the fellow to you at all, only it was from his lips that I first heard the name of the man who is so indissolubly connected with the memories of that time. Moreover, I respected the fellow. Yes; I respected his collars, his vast cuffs, his brushed hair. His appearance was certainly that of a hairdresser's dummy; but in the great demoralization of the land he kept up his appearance. That's backbone. His starched collars and got-up shirt-fronts were achievements of character. He had been out nearly three years; and, later, I could not help asking him how he managed to sport such linen. He had just the faintest blush, and said modestly, 'I've been teaching one of the native women about the station. It was difficult. She had a distaste for the work.' Thus this man had verily accomplished something. And he was devoted to his books, which were in apple-pie order.

"Everything else in the station was in a muddle—heads, things, buildings. Strings of dusty niggers with splay feet arrived and departed; a stream of manufactured goods, rubbishy cottons, beads, and brass-wire set into the depths of darkness, and in return came a precious trickle of ivory.

"I had to wait in the station for ten days—an eternity. I lived in a hut in the yard, but to be out of the chaos I would sometimes get into the accountant's office. It was built of horizontal planks, and so badly put together that, as he bent over his high desk, he was barred from neck to heels with narrow strips of sunlight. There was no need to open the big shutter to see. It was hot there too; big flies buzzed fiendishly, and did not sting, but stabbed. I sat generally on the floor, while, of faultless appearance (and even slightly scented), perching on a high stool, he wrote, he wrote. Sometimes he stood up for exercise. When a truckle-bed with a sick man (some invalided agent from upcountry) was put in there, he exhibited a gentle annoyance. 'The groans of this sick person,' he said, 'distract my attention. And without that it is extremely difficult to guard against clerical errors in this climate.'

"One day he remarked, without lifting his head, 'In the interior you will no doubt meet Mr. Kurtz.' On my asking who Mr. Kurtz was, he said he was a first-class agent; and seeing my disappointment at this information, he added slowly, laying down his pen, 'He is a very remarkable person.' Further questions elicited from him that Mr. Kurtz was at present in charge of a trading post, a very important one, in the true ivory-country, at 'the very bottom of there. Sends in as much ivory as all the others put together . . .' He began to write again. The sick man was too ill to groan. The flies buzzed in a great peace.

"Suddenly there was a growing murmur of voices and a great tramping of feet. A caravan had come in. A violent babble of uncouth sounds burst out on the other side of the planks. All the carriers were speaking together, and in the midst of the uproar the lamentable voice of the chief agent was heard 'giving it up' tearfully for the twentieth time that day. . . . He rose slowly. 'What a frightful row,' he said. He crossed the room gently to look at the sick man, and returning, said to me, 'He does not hear.' 'What! Dead?' I asked, startled. 'No, not yet,' he answered, with great composure. Then, alluding with a toss of the head to the tumult in the station-yard, 'When one has got to make correct entries, one comes to hate those savages—hate them to the death.' He remained thoughtful for a moment. 'When you see Mr. Kurtz,' he went on, 'tell him from me that everything here'—he glanced at the desk—'is very satisfactory. I don't like to write to him—with those messengers of ours you never know who may get hold of your letter—at that Central Station.' He stared at me for a moment with his mild, bulging eyes. 'Oh, he will go far, very far,' he began again. 'He will be a somebody in the Administration before long. They, above—the Council in Europe, you know—mean him to be.'

"He turned to his work. The noise outside had ceased, and presently in going out I stopped at the door. In the steady buzz of flies the homeward-bound agent was lying flushed and insensible; the other, bent over his books, was making correct entries of perfectly correct transactions; and fifty feet below the doorstep I could see the still treetops of the grove of death.

"Next day I left that station at last, with a caravan of sixty men, for a two-hundred-mile tramp.

"No use telling you much about that. Paths, paths, everywhere; a stamped-in network of paths spreading over the empty land, through long grass, through burnt grass, through thickets, down and up chilly ravines, up and down stony hills ablaze with heat; and a solitude, a solitude, nobody, not a hut. The population had cleared out a long time ago. Well, if a lot of mysterious niggers armed with all kinds of fearful weapons suddenly took to traveling on the road between Deal and Gravesend, catching the yokels right and left to carry heavy loads for them, I fancy every farm and cottage thereabouts would get empty very soon. Only here the dwellings were gone too. Still, I passed through several abandoned villages. There's something pathetically childish in the ruins of grass walls. Day after day, with the stamp and shuffle of sixty pair of bare feet behind me, each pair under a sixty-pound load. Camp, cook, sleep; strike camp, march. Now and then a carrier dead in harness, at rest in the long grass near the path, with an empty water-gourd and his long staff lying by his side. A great silence around and above. Perhaps on some quiet night the tremor of far-off drums, sinking, swelling, a tremor vast, faint; a sound weird, appealing, suggestive, and wild—and perhaps with as profound a meaning as the sound of bells in a Christian country. Once a white man in an unbuttoned uniform, camping on the path with an armed escort of lank Zanzibaris, very hospitable and festive—not to say drunk. Was looking after the upkeep of the road, he declared. Can't say I saw any road or any upkeep, unless the body of a middle-aged negro, with a bullet-hole in the forehead, upon which I absolutely stumbled three miles farther on, may be considered as a permanent improvement. I had a white companion too, not a bad chap, but rather too fleshy and with the exasperating habit of fainting on the hot hillsides, miles away from the least bit of shade and water. Annoying, you know, to hold your own coat like a parasol over a man's head while he is coming to. I couldn't help asking him once what he meant by coming there at all. 'To make money, of course. What do you think?' he said scornfully. Then he got fever, and had to be carried in a hammock slung under a pole. As he weighed sixteen stone I had no end of rows with the carriers. They jibbed, ran away, sneaked off with their loads in the night— quite a mutiny. So, one evening, I made a speech in English with gestures, not one of which was lost to the sixty pairs of eyes before me, and the next morning I started the hammock off in front all right. An hour afterwards I came upon the whole concern wrecked in a bush—man, hammock, groans, blankets, horrors. The heavy pole had skinned his poor nose. He was very anxious for me to kill somebody, but there wasn't the shadow of a carrier near. I remembered the old doctor—'It would be interesting for science to watch the mental changes of individuals, on the spot.' I felt I was becoming scientifically interesting. However, all that is to no purpose. On the fifteenth day I came in sight of the big river again, and hobbled into the Central Station. It was on a back water surrounded by scrub and forest, with a pretty border of smelly mud on one side, and on the three others enclosed by a crazy fence of rushes. A neglected gap was all the gate it had, and the first glance at the place was enough to let you see the flabby devil was running that show. White men with long staves in their hands appeared languidly from amongst the buildings, strolling up to take a look at me, and then retired out of sight somewhere. One of them, a stout, excitable chap with black moustaches, informed me with great volubility and many digressions, as soon as I told him who I was, that my steamer was at the bottom of the river. I was thunderstruck. What, how, why? Oh, it was 'all right.' The 'manager himself' was there. All quite correct. 'Everybody had behaved splendidly! splendidly!'—'You must,' he said in agitation, 'go and see the general manager at once. He is waiting.'

"I did not see the real significance of that wreck at once. I fancy I see it now, but I am not sure—not at all. Certainly the affair was too stupid—when I think of it—to be altogether natural. Still . . . But at the moment it presented itself simply as a confounded nuisance. The steamer was sunk. They had started two days before in a sudden hurry up the river with the manager on board, in charge of some volunteer skipper, and before they had been out three hours they tore the bottom out of her on stones, and she sank near the south bank. I asked myself what I was to do there, now my boat was lost. As a matter of fact, I had plenty to do in fishing my command out of the river. I had to set about it the very next day. That, and the repairs when I brought the pieces to the station, took some months.

"My first interview with the manager was curious. He did not ask me to sit down after my twenty-mile walk that morning. He was commonplace in complexion, in feature, in manners, and in voice. He was of middle size and of ordinary build. His eyes, of the usual blue, were perhaps remarkably cold, and he certainly could make his glance fall on one as trenchant and heavy as an axe. But even at these times the rest of his person seemed to disclaim the intention. Otherwise there was only an indefinable, faint expression of his lips, something stealthy—a smile—not a smile—I remember it, but I can't explain. It was unconscious, this smile was, though just after he had said something it got intensified for an instant. It came at the end of his speeches like a seal applied on the words to make the meaning of the commonest phrase appear absolutely inscrutable. He was a common trader, from his youth up employed in these parts—nothing more. He was obeyed, yet he inspired neither love nor fear, nor even respect. He inspired uneasiness. That was it! Uneasiness. Not a definite mistrust—just uneasiness—nothing more. You have no idea how effective such a . . . a . . . faculty can be. He had no genius for organizing, for initiative, or for order even. That was evident in such things as the deplorable state of the station. He had no learning, and no intelligence. His position had come to him—why? Perhaps because he was never ill . . . He had served three terms of three years out there . . . Because triumphant health in the general rout of constitutions is a kind of power in itself. When he went home on leave he rioted on a large scale—pompously. Jack ashore—with a difference—in externals only. This one could gather from his casual talk. He originated nothing, he could keep the routine going—that's all. But he was great. He was great by this little thing that it was impossible to tell what could control such a man. He never gave that secret away. Perhaps there was nothing within him. Such a suspicion made one pause—for out there there were no external checks. Once when various tropical diseases had laid low almost every 'agent' in the station, he was heard to say, 'Men who come out here should have no entrails.' He sealed the utterance with that smile of his, as though it had been a door opening into a darkness he had in his keeping. You fancied you had seen things—but the seal was on. When annoyed at mealtimes by the constant quarrels of the white men about precedence, he ordered an immense round table to be made, for which a special house had to be built. This was the station's mess-room. Where he sat was the first place—the rest were nowhere. One felt this to be his unalterable conviction. He was neither civil or uncivil. He was quiet. He allowed his 'boy'—an overfed young negro from the coast—to treat the white men, under his very eyes, with provoking insolence.

"He began to speak as soon as he saw me. I had been very long on the road. He could not wait. Had to start without me. The upriver stations had to be relieved. There had been so many delays already that he did not know who was dead and who was alive, and how they got on—and so on, and so on. He paid no attention to my explanations, and, playing with a stick of sealing-wax, repeated several times that the situation was 'very grave, very grave.' There were rumors that a very important station was in jeopardy, and its chief, Mr. Kurtz, was ill. Hoped it was not true. Mr. Kurtz was . . . I felt weary and irritable. Hang Kurtz, I thought. I interrupted him by saying I had heard of Mr. Kurtz on the coast. 'Ah! So they talk of him down there,' he murmured to himself. Then he began again, assuring me Mr. Kurtz was the best agent he had, an exceptional man, of the greatest importance to the Company; therefore I could understand his anxiety. He was, he said, 'very, very uneasy.' Certainly he fidgeted on his chair a good deal, exclaimed, 'Ah, Mr. Kurtz!' broke the stick of sealing-wax and seemed dumbfounded by the accident. Next thing he wanted to know 'how long it would take to' . . . I interrupted him again. Being hungry, you know, and kept on my feet too, I was getting savage. 'How can I tell?' I said. 'I haven't even seen the wreck yet—some months, no doubt.' All this talk seemed to me so futile. 'Some months,' he said. 'Well, let us say three months before we can make a start. Yes. That ought to do the affair.' I flung out of his hut (he lived all alone in a clay hut with a sort of veranda) muttering to myself my opinion of him. He was a chattering idiot. Afterwards I took it back when it was borne in upon me startlingly with what extreme nicety he had estimated the time requisite for the 'affair.'

"I went to work the next day, turning, so to speak, my back on that station. In that way only it seemed to me I could keep my hold on the redeeming facts of life. Still, one must look about sometimes; and then I saw this station, these men strolling aimlessly about in the sunshine of the yard. I asked myself sometimes what it all meant. They wandered here and there with their absurd long staves in their hands, like a lot of faithless pilgrims bewitched inside a rotten fence. The word 'ivory' rang in the air, was whispered, was sighed. You would think they were praying to it. A taint of imbecile rapacity blew through it all, like a whiff from some corpse. By Jove! I've never seen anything so unreal in my life. And outside, the silent wilderness surrounding this cleared speck on the earth struck me as something great and invincible, like evil or truth, waiting patiently for the passing away of this fantastic invasion.

"Oh, those months! Well, never mind. Various things happened. One evening a grass shed full of calico, cotton prints, beads, and I don't know what else, burst into a blaze so suddenly that you would have thought the earth had opened to let an avenging fire consume all that trash. I was smoking my pipe quietly by my dis-mantled steamer, and saw them all cutting capers in the light, with their arms lift-ed high, when the stout man with moustaches came tearing down to the river, a tin pail in his hand, assured me that everybody was 'behaving splendidly, splendid-ly,' dipped about a quart of water and tore back again. I noticed there was a hole in the bottom of his pail.

"I strolled up. There was no hurry. You see the thing had gone off like a box of matches. It had been hopeless from the very first. The flame had leaped high, dri-ven everybody back lighted up everything—and collapsed. The shed was already a heap of embers glowing fiercely. A nigger was being beaten near by. They said he had caused the fire in some way; be that as it may, he was screeching most horri-bly. I saw him, later, for several days, sitting in a bit of shade looking very sick and trying to recover himself: afterwards he arose and went out—and the wilderness without a sound took him into its bosom again. As I approached the glow from the dark I found myself at the back of two men, talking. I heard the name of Kurtz pronounced, then the words, 'take advantage of this unfortunate accident.' One of the men was the manager. I wished him a good evening. 'Did you ever see anything like it—eh? it is incredible,' he said, and walked off. The other man remained. He was a first-class agent, young, gentlemanly, a bit reserved, with a forked little beard and a hooked nose. He was standoffish with the other agents, and they on their side said he was the manager's spy upon them. As to me, I had hardly ever spoken to him before. We got into talk and by and by we strolled away from the hissing ruins. Then he asked me to his room, which was in the main building of the station. He struck a match, and I perceived that this young aristocrat had not only a silver-mounted dressing-case but also a whole candle all to himself. Just at that time the manager was the only man supposed to have any right to candles. Native mats covered the clay walls; a collection of spears, assegais, shields, knives, was hung up in trophies. The business entrusted to this fellow was the making of bricks—so I had been informed; but there wasn't a fragment of a brick anywhere in the station, and he had been there more than a year—waiting. It seems he could not make bricks without something, I don't know what—straw maybe. Anyway, it could not be found there, and as it was not likely to be sent from Europe, it did not appear clear to me what he was waiting for. An act of special creation perhaps. However, they were all waiting—all the sixteen or twenty pilgrims of them—for something; and upon my word it did not seem an uncongenial occupation, from the way they took it, though the only thing that ever came to them was disease—as far as I could see. They beguiled the time by backbiting and intriguing against each other in a foolish kind of way. There was an air of plotting about that station, but nothing came of it, of course. It was as unreal as everything else—as the philanthropic pretense of the whole concern, as their talk, as their government, as their show of work. The only real feeling was a desire to get appointed to a trading post where ivory was to be had, so that they could earn percentages. They intrigued and slandered and hated each other only on that account—but as to effectually lifting a little finger—oh no. By Heavens! there is something after all in the world allowing one man to steal a horse while another must not look at a halter. Steal a horse straight out. Very well. He has done it. Perhaps he can ride. But there is a way of looking at a halter that would provoke the most charitable of saints into a kick.

"I had no idea why he wanted to be sociable, but as we chatted in there it suddenly occurred to me the fellow was trying to get at something—in fact, pumping me. He alluded constantly to Europe, to the people I was supposed to know there—putting leading questions as to my acquaintances in the sepulchral city, and so on. His little eyes glittered like mica discs—with curiosity—though he tried to keep up a bit of superciliousness. At first I was astonished, but very soon I became awfully curious to see what he would find out from me. I couldn't possibly imagine what I had in me to make it worth his while. It was very pretty to see how he baffled himself, for in truth my body was full only of chills, and my head had nothing in it but that wretched steamboat business. It was evident he took me for a perfectly shameless prevaricator. At last he got angry, and, to conceal a movement of furious annoyance, he yawned. I rose. Then I noticed a small sketch in oils, on a panel, representing a woman, draped and blindfolded, carrying a lighted torch. The background was somber—almost black. The movement of the woman was stately, and the effect of the torchlight on the face was sinister.

"It arrested me, and he stood by civilly, holding an empty half-pint champagne bottle (medical comforts) with the candle stuck in it. To my question he said Mr. Kurtz had painted this—in this very station more than a year ago while waiting for means to go to his trading post. 'Tell me, pray,' said I, 'who is this Mr. Kurtz?'

"'The chief of the Inner Station,' he answered in a short tone, looking away. 'Much obliged,' I said, laughing. 'And you are the brickmaker of the Central Station. Everyone knows that.' He was silent for a while. 'He is a prodigy,' he said at last. 'He is an emissary of pity, and science, and progress, and devil knows what else. We want,' he began to declaim suddenly, 'for the guidance of the cause entrusted to us by Europe, so to speak, higher intelligence, wide sympathies, a singleness of purpose.' 'Who says that?' I asked. 'Lots of them,' he replied. 'Some even write that; and so *he* comes here, a special being, as you ought to know.' 'Why ought I to know?' I interrupted, really surprised. He paid no attention. 'Yes. Today he is chief of the best station, next year he will be assistant-manager, two years more and . . . but I, daresay you know what he will be in two years' time. You are of the new gang—the gang of virtue. The same people who sent him specially also recommended you. Oh, don't say no. I've my own eyes to trust.' Light dawned upon me. My dear aunt's influential acquaintances were producing an unexpected effect upon that young man. I nearly burst into a laugh. 'Do you read the Company's confidential correspondence?' I asked. He hadn't a word to say. It was great fun. 'When Mr. Kurtz,' I continued severely, 'is General Manager, you won't have the opportunity.'

"He blew the candle out suddenly, and we went outside. The moon had risen. Black figures strolled about listlessly, pouring water on the glow, whence proceeded a sound of hissing; steam ascended in the moonlight; the beaten nigger groaned somewhere. 'What a row the brute makes!' said the indefatigable man with the moustaches, appearing near us. 'Serve him right. Transgression—punishment—bang! Pitiless, pitiless. That's the only way. This will prevent all conflagrations for the future. I was just telling the manager . . .' He noticed my companion, and became crestfallen all at once. 'Not in bed yet,' he said, with a kind of servile heartiness; 'it's so natural. Ha! Danger—agitation.' He vanished. I went on to the riverside, and the other followed me. I heard a scathing murmur at my ear, 'Heaps of muffs—go to.' The pilgrims could be seen in knots gesticulating, discussing. Several had still their staves in their hands. I verily believe they took these sticks to bed with them. Beyond the fence the forest stood up spectrally in the moonlight, and through the dim stir, through the faint sounds of that lamentable courtyard, the silence of the land went home to one's very heart—its mystery, its greatness, the amazing reality of its concealed life. The hurt nigger moaned feebly somewhere near by, and then fetched a deep sigh that made me mend my pace away from there. I felt a hand introducing itself under my arm. 'My dear sir,' said the fellow, 'I don't want to be misunderstood, and especially by you, who will see

Mr. Kurtz long before I can have that pleasure. I wouldn't like him to get a false idea of my disposition. . . . '

"I let him run on, this papier-mâché Mephistopheles, and it seemed to me that if I tried I could poke my forefinger through him, and would find nothing inside but a little loose dirt, maybe. He, don't you see, had been planning to be assistant-manager by and by under the present man, and I could see that the coming of that Kurtz had upset them both not a little. He talked precipitately, and I did not try to stop him. I had my shoulders against the wreck of my steamer, hauled up on the slope like a carcass of some big river animal. The smell of mud, of primeval mud, by Jove! was in my nostrils, the high stillness of primeval forest was before my eyes; there were shiny patches on the black creek. The moon had spread over everything a thin layer of silver over the rank grass, over the mud, upon the wall of matted vegetation standing higher than the wall of a temple, over the great river I could see through a somber gap glittering, glittering, as it flowed broadly by without a murmur. All this was great, expectant, mute, while the man jabbered about himself. I wondered whether the stillness on the face of the immensity looking at us two were meant as an appeal or as a menace. What were we who had strayed in here? Could we handle that dumb thing or would it handle us? I felt how big, how confoundedly big, was that thing that couldn't talk and perhaps was deaf as well. What was in there? I could see a little ivory coming out from there, and I had heard Mr. Kurtz was in there. I had heard enough about it too—God knows! Yet somehow it didn't bring any image with it—no more than if I had been told an angel or a fiend was in there. I believed it in the same way one of you might believe there are inhabitants in the planet Mars. I knew once a Scotch sailmaker who was certain, dead sure, there were people in Mars. If you asked him for some idea how they looked and behaved, he would get shy and mutter something about 'walking on all-fours.' If you as much as smiled, he would—though a man of sixty offer to fight you. I would not have gone so far as to fight for Kurtz, but I went for him near enough to a lie. You know I hate, detest, and can't bear a lie, not because I am straighter than the rest of us, but simply because it appalls me. There is a taint of death, a flavor of mortality in lies—which is exactly what I hate and detest in the world—what I want to forget. It makes me miserable and sick, like biting something rotten would do. Temperament, I suppose. Well, I went near enough to it by letting the young fool there believe anything he liked to imagine as to my influence in Europe. I became in an instant as much of a pretense as the rest of the bewitched pilgrims. This simply because I had a notion it somehow would be of help to that Kurtz whom at the time I did not see—you understand. He was just a word for me. I did not see the man in the name any more than you do. Do you see him? Do you see the story? Do you see anything? It seems to me I am trying to tell you a dream—

making a vain attempt, because no relation of a dream can convey the dream-sensation, that commingling of absurdity, surprise, and bewilderment in a tremor of struggling revolt, that notion of being captured by the incredible which is of the very essence of dreams. . . ." He was silent for a while.

". . . No, it is impossible; it is impossible to convey the life-sensation of any given epoch of one's existence—that which makes its truth, its meaning—its subtle and penetrating essence. It is impossible. We live, as we dream—alone. . . ."

He paused again as if reflecting, then added:

"Of course in this you fellows see more than I could then. You see me, whom you know. . . ."

It had become so pitch dark that we listeners could hardly see one another. For a long time already he, sitting apart, had been no more to us than a voice. There was not a word from anybody. The others might have been asleep, but I was awake. I listened, I listened on the watch for the sentence, for the word, that would give me the clue to the faint uneasiness inspired by this narrative that seemed to shape itself without human lips in the heavy night air of the river.

". . . Yes—I let him run on," Marlow began again, "and think what he pleased about the powers that were behind me. I did! And there was nothing behind me! There was nothing but that wretched, old, mangled steamboat I was leaning against, while he talked fluently about 'the necessity for every man to get on.' 'And when one comes out here, you conceive, it is not to gaze at the moon.' Mr. Kurtz was a 'universal genius,' but even a genius would find it easier to work with 'adequate tools—intelligent men.' He did not make bricks—why, there was a physical impossibility in the way—as I was well aware; and if he did secretarial work for the manager, it was because 'no sensible man rejects wantonly the confidence of his superior.' Did I see it? I saw it. What more did I want? What I really wanted was rivets, by Heaven! Rivets. To get on with the work—to stop the hole. Rivets I wanted. There were cases of them down at the coast—cases—piled up—burst—split! You kicked a loose rivet at every second step in that station yard on the hillside. Rivets had rolled into the grove of death. You could fill your pockets with rivets for the trouble of stooping down—and there wasn't one rivet to be found where it was wanted. We had plates that would do, but nothing to fasten them with. And every week the messenger, a lone negro, letter-bag on shoulder and staff in hand, left our station for the coast. And several times a week a coast caravan came in with trade goods—ghastly glazed calico that made you shudder only to look at it, glass beads value about a penny a quart, confounded spotted cotton handkerchiefs. And no rivets. Three carriers could have brought all that was wanted to set that steamboat afloat.

"He was becoming confidential now, but I fancy my unresponsive attitude must have exasperated him at last, for he judged it necessary to inform me he feared neither God nor devil, let alone any mere man. I said I could see that very well, but what I wanted was a certain quantity of rivets—and rivets were what really Mr. Kurtz wanted, if he had only known it. Now letters went to the coast every week. . . . 'My dear sir,' he cried, 'I write from dictation.' I demanded rivets. There was a way—for an intelligent man. He changed his manner; became very cold, and suddenly began to talk about a hippopotamus; wondered whether sleeping on board the steamer (I stuck to my salvage night and day) I wasn't disturbed. There was an old hippo that had the bad habit of getting out on the bank and roaming at night over the station grounds. The pilgrims used to turn out in a body and empty every rifle they could lay hands on at him. Some even had sat up o' nights for him. All this energy was wasted, though. 'That animal has a charmed life,' he said; 'but you can say this only of brutes in this country. No man—you apprehend me?—no man here bears a charmed life.' He stood there for a moment in the moonlight with his delicate hooked nose set a little askew, and his mica eyes glittering without a wink, then, with a curt Goodnight, he strode off. I could see he was disturbed and considerably puzzled, which made me feel more hopeful than I had been for days. It was a great comfort to turn from that chap to my influential friend, the battered, twisted, ruined, tin-pot steamboat. I clambered on board. She rang under my feet like an empty Huntley & Palmer biscuit-tin kicked along a gutter; she was nothing so solid in make, and rather less pretty in shape, but I had expended enough hard work on her to make me love her. No influential friend would have served me better. She had given me a chance to come out a bit—to find out what I could do. No, I don't like work. I had rather laze about and think of all the fine things that can be done. I don't like work—no man does—but I like what is in the work—the chance to find yourself. Your own reality—for yourself, not for others—what no other man can ever know. They can only see the mere show, and never can tell what it really means.

"I was not surprised to see somebody sitting aft, on the deck, with his legs dangling over the mud. You see I rather chummed with the few mechanics there were in that station, whom the other pilgrims naturally despised on account of their imperfect manners, I suppose. This was the foreman—a boilermaker by trade—a good worker. He was a lank, bony, yellow-faced man, with big intense eyes. His aspect was worried, and his head was as bald as the palm of my hand; but his hair in falling seemed to have stuck to his chin, and had prospered in the new locality, for his beard hung down to his waist. He was a widower with six young children (he had left them in charge of a sister of his to come out there), and the passion of his life was pigeon-flying. He was an enthusiast and a connoisseur. He would rave about pigeons. After work hours he used sometimes to come over from his hut for a talk about his children and his pigeons; at work, when he had to crawl in the mud under the bottom of the steamboat, he would tie up that beard of his in a kind of white serviette he brought for the purpose. It had loops to go over his ears. In the evening he could be seen squatted on the bank rinsing that wrapper in the creek with great care, then spreading it solemnly on a bush to dry.

"I slapped him on the back and shouted 'We shall have rivets!' He scrambled to his feet exclaiming 'No! Rivets!' as though he couldn't believe his ears. Then in a low voice, 'You . . . eh?' I don't know why we behaved like lunatics. I put my finger to the side of my nose and nodded mysteriously. 'Good for you!' he cried, snapped his fingers above his head, lifting one foot. I tried a jig. We capered on the iron deck. A frightful clatter came out of that hulk, and the virgin forest on the other bank of the creek sent it back in a thundering roll upon the sleeping station. It must have made some of the pilgrims sit up in their hovels. A dark figure obscured the lighted doorway of the manager's hut, vanished, then, a second or so after, the doorway itself vanished too. We stopped, and the silence driven away by the stamping of our feet flowed back again from the recesses of the land. The great wall of vegetation, an exuberant and entangled mass of trunks, branches, leaves, boughs, festoons, motionless in the moonlight, was like a rioting invasion of soundless life, a rolling wave of plants, piled up, crested, ready to topple over the creek, to sweep every little man of us out of his little existence. And it moved not. A deadened burst of mighty splashes and snorts reached us from afar, as though an ichthyosaurus had been taking a bath of glitter in the great river. 'After all,' said the boilermaker in a reasonable tone, 'why shouldn't we get the rivets?' Why not, indeed! I did not know of any reason why we shouldn't. 'They'll come in three weeks,' I said confidently.

"But they didn't. Instead of rivets there came an invasion, an infliction, a visitation. It came in sections during the next three weeks, each section headed by a donkey carrying a white man in new clothes and tan shoes, bowing from that elevation right and left to the impressed pilgrims. A quarrelsome band of footsore sulky niggers trod on the heels of the donkey; a lot of tents, campstools, tin boxes, white cases, brown bales would be shot down in the courtyard, and the air of mystery would deepen a little over the muddle of the station. Five such installments came, with their absurd air of disorderly flight with the loot of innumerable outfit shops and provision stores, that, one would think, they were lugging, after a raid, into the wilderness for equitable division. It was an inextricable mess of things decent in themselves but that human folly made look like the spoils of thieving.

"This devoted band called itself the Eldorado Exploring Expedition, and I believe they were sworn to secrecy. Their talk, however, was the talk of sordid buccaneers: it was reckless without hardihood, greedy without audacity, and cruel without courage; there was not an atom of foresight or of serious intention in the whole batch of them, and they did not seem aware these things are wanted for the work of the world. To tear treasure out of the bowels of the land was their desire, with no more moral purpose at the back of it than there is in burglars breaking into a safe. Who paid the expenses of the noble enterprise I don't know; but the uncle of our manager was leader of that lot.

"In exterior he resembled a butcher in a poor neighborhood, and his eyes had a look of sleepy cunning. He carried his fat paunch with ostentation on his short legs, and during the time his gang infested the station spoke to no one but his nephew. You could see these two roaming about all day long with their heads close together in an everlasting confab.

"I had given up worrying myself about the rivets. One's capacity for that kind of folly is more limited than you would suppose. I said Hang!—and let things slide. I had plenty of time for meditation, and now and then I would give some thought to Kurtz. I wasn't very interested in him. No. Still, I was curious to see whether this man, who had come out equipped with moral ideas of some sort, would climb to the top after all, and how he would set about his work when there."

II

"One evening as I was lying flat on the deck of my steamboat, I heard voices approaching—and there were the nephew and the uncle strolling along the bank. I laid my head on my arm again, and had nearly lost myself in a doze, when somebody said in my ear, as it were: 'I am as harmless as a little child, but I don't like to be dictated to. Am I the manager or am I not? I was ordered to send him there. It's incredible.' . . . I became aware that the two were standing on the shore alongside the forepart of the steamboat, just below my head. I did not move; it did not occur to me to move: I was sleepy. 'It *is* unpleasant,' grunted the uncle. 'He has asked the Administration to be sent there,' said the other, 'with the idea of showing what he could do; and I was instructed accordingly. Look at the influence that man must have. Is it not frightful?' They both agreed it was frightful, then made several bizarre remarks: 'Make rain and fine weather— one man—the Council—by the nose'—bits of absurd sentences that got the better of my drowsiness, so that I had pretty near the whole of my wits about me when the uncle said, 'The climate may do away with this difficulty for you. Is he alone there?' 'Yes,' answered the manager; 'he sent his assistant down the river with a note to me in these terms: "Clear this poor devil out of the country, and don't bother sending more of that sort. I had rather be alone than have the kind of men you can dispose of with me." It was more than a year ago. Can you imagine such impudence!' 'Anything since then?' asked the other hoarsely. 'Ivory,' jerked the nephew; 'lots of it—prime sort—lots—most annoying, from him.' 'And with that?' questioned the heavy rumble. 'Invoice,' was the reply fired out, so to speak. Then silence. They had been talking about Kurtz.

"I was broad awake by this time, but, lying perfectly at ease, remained still, having no inducement to change my position. 'How did that ivory come all this way?' growled the elder man, who seemed very vexed. The other explained that it had come with a fleet of canoes in charge of an English half-caste clerk Kurtz had with him; that Kurtz had apparently intended to return himself, the station being by that time bare of goods and stores, but after coming three hundred miles, had suddenly decided to go back, which he started to do alone in a small dugout with four paddlers, leaving the half-caste to continue down the river with the ivory. The two fellows there seemed astounded at anybody attempting such a thing. They were at a loss for an adequate motive. As for me, I seemed to see Kurtz for the first time. It was a distinct glimpse: the dugout, four paddling savages, and the lone white man turning his back suddenly on the headquarters, on relief, on thoughts of home—perhaps; setting his face towards the depths of the wilderness, towards his empty and desolate station. I did not know the motive. Perhaps he was just simply a fine fellow who stuck to his work for its own sake. His name, you understand, had not been pronounced once. He was 'that man.' The half-caste, who, as far as I could see, had conducted a difficult trip with great prudence and pluck, was invariably alluded to as 'that scoundrel.' The 'scoundrel' had reported that the 'man' had been very ill—had recovered imperfectly. . . . The two below me moved away then a few paces, and strolled back and forth at some little distance. I heard: 'Military post—doctor—two hundred miles—quite alone now—unavoidable delays—nine months—no news—strange rumors.' They approached again, just as the manager was saying, 'No one, as far as I know, unless a species of wandering trader—a pestilential fellow, snapping ivory from the natives.' Who was it they were talking about now? I gathered in snatches that this was some man supposed to be in Kurtz's district, and of whom the manager did not approve. 'We will not be free from unfair competition till one of these fellows is hanged for an example,' he said. 'Certainly,' grunted the other; 'get him hanged! Why not? Anything—anything can be done in this country. That's what I say; nobody here, you understand, *here*, can endanger your position. And why? You stand the climate—you outlast them all. The danger is in Europe; but there before I left I took care to——' They moved off and whispered, then their voices rose again. 'The extraordinary series of delays is not my fault. I did my possible.' The fat man sighed, 'Very sad.' 'And the pestiferous absurdity of his talk,' continued the other; 'he bothered me enough when he was here. "Each station should be like a beacon on the road towards better things, a center for trade of course, but also for humanizing, improving, instructing." Conceive you—that ass! And he wants to be manager! No, it's——' Here he got choked by excessive indignation, and I lifted my head the least bit. I was surprised to see how near they were—right under me. I could have spat upon their hats. They were looking on the ground, absorbed in thought. The manager was switching his leg with a slender twig: his sagacious relative lifted his head. 'You have been well since you came out this time?' he asked. The other gave a start. 'Who? I? Oh! Like a charm—like a charm. But the rest— oh, my goodness! All sick. They die so quick, too, that I haven't the time to send them out of the country—it's incredible!' 'H'm. Just so,' grunted the uncle. 'Ah! my boy, trust to this—I say, trust to this.' I saw him extend his short flipper of an arm for a gesture that took in the forest, the creek, the mud, the river—seemed to beckon with a dishonoring flourish before the sunlit face of the land a treacherous appeal to the lurking death, to the hidden evil, to the profound darkness of its heart. It was so startling that I leaped to my feet and looked back at the edge of the forest, as though I had expected an answer of some sort to that black display of confidence. You know the foolish notions that come to one sometimes. The high stillness confronted these two figures with its ominous patience, waiting for the passing away of a fantastic invasion.

"They swore aloud together—out of sheer fright, I believe—then, pretending not to know anything of my existence, turned back to the station. The sun was low; and leaning forward side by side, they seemed to be tugging painfully uphill their two ridiculous shadows of unequal length, that trailed behind them slowly over the tall grass without bending a single blade.

"In a few days the Eldorado Expedition went into the patient wilderness, that closed upon it as the sea closes over a diver. Long afterwards the news came that all the donkeys were dead. I know nothing as to the fate of the less valuable animals. They, no doubt, like the rest of us, found what they deserved. I did not inquire. I was then rather excited at the prospect of meeting Kurtz very soon. When I say very soon I mean it comparatively. It was just two months from the day we left the creek when we came to the bank below Kurtz's station.

"Going up that river was like traveling back to the earliest beginnings of the world, when vegetation rioted on the earth and the big trees were kings. An empty stream, a great silence, an impenetrable forest. The air was warm, thick, heavy, sluggish. There was no joy in the brilliance of sunshine. The long stretches of the waterway ran on, deserted, into the gloom of overshadowed distances. On silvery sandbanks hippos and alligators sunned themselves side by side. The broadening waters flowed through a mob of wooded islands; you lost your way on that river as you would in a desert, and butted all day long against shoals, trying to find the channel, till you thought yourself bewitched and cut off forever from everything you had known once—somewhere—far away—in another existence perhaps. There were moments when one's past came back to one, as it will sometimes when you have not a moment to spare to yourself; but it came in the shape of an unrestful and noisy dream, remembered with wonder amongst the overwhelming realities of this strange world of plants, and water, and silence. And this stillness of life did not in the least resemble a peace. It was the stillness of an implacable force brooding over an inscrutable intention. It looked at you with a vengeful aspect. I got used to it afterwards; I did not see it anymore; I had no time. I had to keep guessing at the channel; I had to discern, mostly by inspiration, the signs of hidden banks; I watched for sunken stones; I was learning to clap my teeth smartly before my heart flew out, when I shaved by a fluke some infernal sly old snag that would have ripped the life out of the tin-pot steamboat and drowned all the pilgrims; I had to keep a lookout for the signs of dead wood we could cut up in the night for next day's steaming. When you have to attend to things of that sort, to the mere incidents of the surface, the reality—the reality, I tell you—fades. The inner truth is hidden—luckily, luckily. But I felt it all the same; I felt often its mysterious stillness watching me at my monkey tricks, just as it watches you fellows performing on your respective tightropes for—what is it? half a crown a tumble——"

"Try to be civil, Marlow," growled a voice, and I knew there was at least one listener awake besides myself. "I beg your pardon. I forgot the heartache which makes up the rest of the price. And indeed what does the price matter, if the trick be well done? You do your tricks very well. And I didn't do badly either, since I managed not to sink that steamboat on my first trip. It's a wonder to me yet. Imagine a blindfolded man set to drive a van over a bad road. I sweated and shivered over that business considerably, I can tell you. After all, for a seaman, to scrape the bottom of the thing that's supposed to float all the time under his care is the unpardonable sin. No one may know of it, but you never forget the thump eh? A blow on the very heart. You remember it, you dream of it, you wake up at night and think of it—years after—and go hot and cold all over. I don't pretend to say that steamboat floated all the time. More than once she had to wade for a bit, with twenty cannibals splashing around and pushing. We had enlisted some of these chaps on the way for a crew. Fine fellows—cannibals—in their place. They were men one could work with, and I am grateful to them. And, after all, they did not eat each other before my face: they had brought along a provision of hippo-meat which went rotten, and made the mystery of the wilderness stink in my nostrils. Phoo! I can sniff it now. I had the manager on board and three or four pilgrims with their staves—all complete. Sometimes we came upon a station close by the bank, clinging to the skirts of the unknown, and the white men rushing out of a tumbledown hovel, with great gestures of joy and surprise and welcome, seemed very strange—had the appearance of being held there captive by a spell. The word 'ivory' would ring in the air for a while—and on we went again into the silence, along empty reaches, round the still bends, between the high walls of our winding way, reverberating in hollow claps the ponderous beat of the stern-wheel. Trees, trees, millions of trees, massive, immense, running up high; and at their foot, hugging the bank against the stream, crept the little begrimed steamboat, like a sluggish beetle crawling on the floor of a lofty portico. It made you feel very small, very lost, and yet it was not altogether depressing, that feeling. After all, if you were small, the grimy beetle crawled on—which was just what you wanted it to do. Where the pilgrims imagined it crawled to I don't know. To some place where they expected to get something I bet! For me it crawled towards Kurtz exclusively; but when the steam-pipes started leaking we crawled very slow. The reaches opened before us and closed behind, as if the forest had stepped leisurely across the water to bar the way for our return. We penetrated deeper and deeper into the heart of darkness. It was very quiet there. At night sometimes the roll of drums behind the curtain of trees would run up the river and remain sustained faintly, as if hovering in the air high over our heads, till the first break of day. Whether it meant war, peace, or prayer we could not tell. The dawns were herald-ed by the descent of a chill stillness; the woodcutters slept, their fires burned low; the snapping of a twig would make you start. We were wanderers on a prehistoric earth, on an earth that wore the aspect of an unknown planet. We could have fan-cied ourselves the first of men taking possession of an accursed inheritance, to be subdued at the cost of profound anguish and of excessive toil. But suddenly, as we struggled round a bend, there would be a glimpse of rush walls, of peaked grass-roofs, a burst of yells, a whirl of black limbs, a mass of hands clapping, of feet stamping, of bodies swaying, of eyes rolling, under the droop of heavy and motion-less foliage. The steamer toiled along slowly on the edge of a black and incompre-hensible frenzy. The prehistoric man was cursing us, praying to us, welcoming us—who could tell? We were cut off from the comprehension of our surroundings; we glided past like phantoms, wondering and secretly appalled, as sane men would be before an enthusiastic outbreak in a madhouse. We could not under-stand because we were too far and could not remember, because we were travel-ing in the night of first ages, of those ages that are gone, leaving hardly a sign—and no memories.

"The earth seemed unearthly. We are accustomed to look upon the shackled form of a conquered monster, but there—there you could look at a thing mon-strous and free. It was unearthly, and the men were——No, they were not inhu-man. Well, you know, that was the worst of it—this suspicion of their not being inhuman. It would come slowly to one. They howled and leaped, and spun, and made horrid faces; but what thrilled you was just the thought of their humani-ty—like yours—the thought of your remote kinship with this wild and passionate uproar. Ugly. Yes, it was ugly enough; but if you were man enough you would admit to yourself that there was in you just the faintest trace of a response to the terrible frankness of that noise, a dim suspicion of there being a meaning in it which you—you so remote from the night of first ages could comprehend. And why not? The mind of man is capable of anything—because everything is in it, all the past as well as all the future. What was there after all? Joy, fear, sorrow, devotion, valor, rage—who can tell?—but truth—truth stripped of its cloak of time. Let the fool gape and shudder—the man knows, and can look on without a wink. But he must at least be as much of a man as these on the shore. He must meet that truth with his own true stuff—with his own inborn strength. Principles? Principles won't do. Acquisitions, clothes, pretty rags—rags that would fly off at the first good shake. No; you want a deliberate belief. An appeal to me in this fiendish row—is there? Very well; I hear; I admit, but I have a voice too, and for good or evil mine is the speech that cannot be silenced. Of course, a fool, what with sheer fright and fine sentiments, is always safe. Who's that grunting? You wonder I didn't go ashore for a howl and a dance? Well, no—I didn't. Fine sentiments, you say? Fine sentiments be hanged! I had no time. I had to mess about with white-lead and strips of woolen blanket helping to put bandages on those leaky steam-pipes—I tell you. I had to watch the steering, and circumvent those snags, and get the tin-pot along by hook or by crook. There was surface-truth enough in these things to save a wiser man. And between whiles I had to look after the savage who was fireman. He was an improved specimen; he could fire up a vertical boiler. He was there below me, and, upon my word, to look at him was as edifying as seeing a dog in a parody of breeches and a feather hat, walking on his hind legs. A few months of training had done for that really fine chap. He squinted at the steam gauge and at the water gauge with an evident effort of intrepidity—and he had filed teeth too, the poor devil, and the wool of his pate shaved into queer patterns, and three ornamental scars on each of his cheeks. He ought to have been clapping his hands and stamping his feet on the bank, instead of which he was hard at work, a thrall to strange witchcraft, full of improving knowledge. He was useful because he had been instructed; and what he knew was this—that should the water in that transparent thing disappear, the evil spirit inside the boiler would get angry through the greatness of his thirst, and take a terrible vengeance. So he sweated and fired up and watched the glass fearfully (with an impromptu charm, made of rags, tied to his arm, and a piece of polished bone, as big as a watch, stuck flatways through his lower lip), while the wooded banks slipped past us slowly, the short noise was left behind, the interminable miles of silence—and we crept on, towards Kurtz. But the snags were thick, the water was treacherous and shallow, the boiler seemed indeed to have a sulky devil in it, and thus neither that fireman nor I had any time to peer into our creepy thoughts.

"Some fifty miles below the Inner Station we came upon a hut of reeds, an inclined and melancholy pole, with the unrecognizable tatters of what had been a

flag of some sort flying from it, and a neatly stacked woodpile. This was unexpected. We came to the bank, and on the stack of firewood found a flat piece of board
with some faded pencil-writing on it. When deciphered it said: 'Wood for you.
Hurry up. Approach cautiously.' There was a signature, but it was illegible—not
Kurtz—a much longer word. 'Hurry up.' Where? Up the river? 'Approach cautiously.' We had not done so. But the warning could not have been meant for the place
where it could be only found after approach. Something was wrong above. But
what—and how much? That was the question. We commented adversely upon the
imbecility of that telegraphic style. The bush around said nothing and would not
let us look very far, either. A torn curtain of red twill hung in the doorway of the
hut, and flapped sadly in our faces. The dwelling was dismantled; but we could see
a white man had lived there not very long ago. There remained a rude table—a
plank on two posts; a heap of rubbish reposed in a dark corner, and by the door I
picked up a book. It had lost its covers, and the pages had been thumbed into a
state of extremely dirty softness; but the back had been lovingly stitched afresh
with white cotton thread, which looked clean yet. It was an extraordinary find. Its
title was, *An Inquiry into Some Points of Seamanship*, by a man Towser,
Towson—some such name—Master in His Majesty's Navy. The matter looked
dreary reading enough, with illustrative diagrams and repulsive tables of figures,
and the copy was sixty years old. I handled this amazing antiquity with the greatest possible tenderness, lest it should dissolve in my hands. Within, Towson or
Towser was inquiring earnestly into the breaking strain of ships' chains and tackle, and other such matters. Not a very enthralling book; but at the first glance you
could see there a singleness of intention, an honest concern for the right way of
going to work, which made these humble pages, thought out so many years ago,
luminous with another than a professional light. The simple old sailor, with his
talk of chains and purchases, made me forget the jungle and the pilgrims in a delicious sensation of having come upon something unmistakably real. Such a book
being there was wonderful enough; but still more astounding were the notes pen-
ciled in the margin, and plainly referring to the text. I couldn't believe my eyes!
They were in cipher! Yes, it looked like cipher. Fancy a man lugging with him a
book of that description into this nowhere and studying it—and making notes—
in cipher at that! It was an extravagant mystery.

"I had been dimly aware for some time of a worrying noise, and when I lifted
my eyes I saw the woodpile was gone, and the manager, aided by all the pilgrims,
was shouting at me from the riverside. I slipped the book into my pocket. I assure
you to leave off reading was like tearing myself away from the shelter of an old
and solid friendship.

"I started the lame engine ahead. 'It must be this miserable trader—this
intruder,' exclaimed the manager, looking back malevolently at the place we had

left. 'He must be English,' I said. 'It will not save him from getting into trouble if he is not careful,' muttered the manager darkly. I observed with assumed innocence that no man was safe from trouble in this world.

"The current was more rapid now, the steamer seemed at her last gasp, the stern-wheel flopped languidly, and I caught myself listening on tiptoe for the next beat of the float, for in sober truth I expected the wretched thing to give up every moment. It was like watching the last flickers of a life. But still we crawled. Sometimes I would pick out a tree a little way ahead to measure our progress towards Kurtz by, but I lost it invariably before we got abreast. To keep the eyes so long on one thing was too much for human patience. The manager displayed a beautiful resignation. I fretted and fumed and took to arguing with myself whether or no I would talk openly with Kurtz; but before I could come to any conclusion it occurred to me that my speech or my silence, indeed any action of mine, would be a mere futility. What did it matter what anyone knew or ignored? What did it matter who was manager? One gets sometimes such a flash of insight. The essentials of this affair lay deep under the surface, beyond my reach, and beyond my power of meddling.

"Towards the evening of the second day we judged ourselves about eight miles from Kurtz's station. I wanted to push on; but the manager looked grave, and told me the navigation up there was so dangerous that it would be advisable, the sun being very low already, to wait where we were till next morning. Moreover, he pointed out that if the warning to approach cautiously were to be followed, we must approach in daylight—not at dusk, or in the dark. This was sensible enough. Eight miles meant nearly three hours' steaming for us, and I could also see suspicious ripples at the upper end of the reach. Nevertheless, I was annoyed beyond expression at the delay, and most unreasonably too, since one night more could not matter much after so many months. As we had plenty of wood, and caution was the word, I brought up in the middle of the stream. The reach was narrow, straight, with high sides like a railway cutting. The dusk came gliding into it long before the sun had set. The current ran smooth and swift, but a dumb immobility sat on the banks. The living trees, lashed together by the creepers and every living bush of the undergrowth, might have been changed into stone, even to the slenderest twig, to the lightest leaf. It was not sleep—it seemed unnatural, like a state of trance. Not the faintest sound of any kind could be heard. You looked on amazed, and began to suspect yourself of being deaf—then the night came suddenly, and struck you blind as well. About three in the morning some large fish leaped, and the loud splash made me jump as though a gun had been fired. When the sun rose there was a white fog, very warm and clammy, and more blinding than the night. It did not shift or drive; it was just there, standing all round you like something solid. At eight or nine, perhaps, it lifted as a shutter lifts. We had a glimpse of the towering multitude of trees, of the immense matted jungle, with the blazing little ball of the sun hanging over it—all perfectly still—and then the white shutter came down again, smoothly, as if sliding in greased grooves. I ordered the chain, which we had begun to heave in, to be paid out again. Before it stopped running with a muffled rattle, a cry, a very loud cry, as of infinite desolation, soared slowly in the opaque air. It ceased. A complaining clamor, modulated in savage discords, filled our ears. The sheer unexpectedness of it made my hair stir under my cap. I don't know how it struck the others: to me it seemed as though the mist itself had screamed, so suddenly, and apparently from all sides at once, did this tumultuous and mournful uproar arise. It culminated in a hurried outbreak of almost intolerably excessive shrieking, which stopped short, leaving us stiffened in a variety of silly attitudes, and obstinately listening to the nearly as appalling and excessive silence. 'Good God! What is the meaning——?' stammered at my elbow one of the pilgrims—a little fat man, with sandy hair and red whiskers, who wore side-spring boots, and pink pajamas tucked into his socks. Two others remained open-mouthed a whole minute, then dashed into the little cabin, to rush out incontinently and stand darting seared glances, with Winchesters at 'ready' in their hands. What we could see was just the steamer we were on, her outlines blurred as though she had been on the point of dissolving, and a misty strip of water, perhaps two feet broad, around her—and that was all. The rest of the world was nowhere, as far as our eyes and ears were concerned. Just nowhere. Gone, disappeared; swept off without leaving a whisper or a shadow behind.

"I went forward, and ordered the chain to be hauled in short, so as to be ready to trip the anchor and move the steamboat at once if necessary. 'Will they attack?' whispered an awed voice. 'We will all be butchered in this fog,' murmured another. The faces twitched with the strain, the hands trembled slightly, the eyes forgot to wink. It was very curious to see the contrast of expressions of the white men and of the black fellows of our crew, who were as much strangers to that part of the river as we, though their homes were only eight hundred miles away. The whites, of course greatly discomposed, had besides a curious look of being painfully shocked by such an outrageous row. The others had an alert, naturally interested expression; but their faces were essentially quiet, even those of the one or two who grinned as they hauled at the chain. Several exchanged short, grunting phrases, which seemed to settle the matter to their satisfaction. Their headman, a young, broad-chested black, severely draped in dark-blue fringed cloths, with fierce nostrils and his hair all done up artfully in oily ringlets, stood near me. 'Aha!' I said, just for good fellowship's sake. 'Catch 'im,' he snapped, with a bloodshot widening of his eyes and a flash of sharp teeth—'catch 'im. Give 'im to us.' 'To you, eh?' I asked; 'what would you do with them?' 'Eat 'im!' he said curtly, and, leaning his elbow on the rail, looked out into the fog in a dignified and profoundly pensive attitude. I would no doubt have been properly horrified, had it not occurred to me that he and his chaps must be very hungry: that they must have been growing increasingly hungry for at least this month past. They had been engaged for six months (I don't think a single one of them had any clear idea of time, as we at the end of countless ages have. They still belonged to the beginnings of time—had no inherited experience to teach them, as it were), and of course, as long as there was a piece of paper written over in accordance with some farcical law or other made down the river, it didn't enter anybody's head to trouble how they would live. Certainly they had brought with them some rotten hippo-meat, which couldn't have lasted very long, anyway, even if the pilgrims hadn't, in the midst of a shocking hullabaloo, thrown a considerable quantity of it overboard. It looked like a highhanded proceeding; but it was really a case of legitimate self-defense. You can't breathe dead hippo waking, sleeping, and eating, and at the same time keep your precarious grip on existence. Besides that, they had given them every week three pieces of brass wire, each about nine inches long; and the theory was they were to buy their provisions with that currency in riverside villages. You can see how *that* worked. There were either no villages, or the people were hostile, or the director, who like the rest of us fed out of tins, with an occasional old he-goat thrown in, didn't want to stop the steamer for some more or less recondite reason. So, unless they swallowed the wire itself, or made loops of it to snare the fishes with, I don't see what good their extravagant salary could be to them. I must say it was paid with a regularity worthy of a large and honorable trading company. For the rest, the only thing to eat—though it didn't look eatable in the least—I saw in their possession was a few lumps of some stuff like half-cooked dough, of a dirty lavender color, they kept wrapped in leaves, and now and then swallowed a piece of, but so small that it seemed done more for the look of the thing than for any serious purpose of sustenance. Why in the name of all the gnawing devils of hunger they didn't go for us—they were thirty to five—and have a good tuck-in for once, amazes me now when I think of it. They were big powerful men, with not much capacity to weigh the consequences, with courage, with strength, even yet, though their skins were no longer glossy and their muscles no longer hard. And I saw that something restraining, one of those human secrets that baffle probability, had come into play there. I looked at them with a swift quickening of interest—not because it occurred to me I might be eaten by them before very long, though I own to you that just then I perceived—in a new light, as it were—how unwholesome the pilgrims looked, and I hoped, yes, I positively hoped, that my aspect was not so what shall I say?—so—unappetizing: a touch of fantastic vanity which fitted well with the dream-sensation that pervaded all my days at that time. Perhaps I had a little fever too. One can't live with one's finger everlastingly on one's pulse. I had often 'a little fever,' or a little touch of other things—the playful paw-strokes of the wilderness, the preliminary trifling before the more serious onslaught which came in due course. Yes; I looked at them as you would on any human being, with a curiosity of their impulses, motives, capacities, weaknesses, when brought to the test of an inexorable physical necessity. Restraint! What possible restraint? Was it superstition, disgust, patience, fear—or some kind of primitive honor? No fear can stand up to hunger, no patience can wear it out, disgust simply does not exist where hunger is; and as to superstition, beliefs, and what you may call principles, they are less than chaff in a breeze. Don't you know the devilry of lingering starvation, its exasperating torment, its black thoughts, its somber and brooding ferocity? Well, I do. It takes a man all his inborn strength to fight hunger properly. It's really easier to face bereavement, dishonor, and the perdition of one's soul—than this kind of prolonged hunger. Sad, but true. And these chaps too had no earthly reason for any kind of scruple. Restraint! I would just as soon have expected restraint from a hyena prowling amongst the corpses of a battlefield. But there was the fact facing me—the fact dazzling, to be seen, like the foam on the depths of the sea, like a ripple on an unfathomable enigma, a mystery greater—when I thought of it—than the curious, inexplicable note of desperate grief in this savage clamor that had swept by us on the riverbank, behind the blind whiteness of the fog.

"Two pilgrims were quarreling in hurried whispers as to which bank. 'Left.' 'No, no; how can you? Right, right, of course.' 'It is very serious,' said the manager's voice behind me; 'I would be desolated if anything should happen to Mr. Kurtz before we came up.' I looked at him, and had not the slightest doubt he was sincere. He was just the kind of man who would wish to preserve appearances. That was his restraint. But when he muttered something about going on at once, I did not even take the trouble to answer him. I knew, and he knew, that it was impossible. Were we to let go our hold of the bottom, we would be absolutely in the air—in space. We wouldn't be able to tell where we were going to—whether up or down stream, or across—till we fetched against one bank or the other—and then we wouldn't know at first which it was. Of course I made no move. I had no mind for a smash-up. You couldn't imagine a more deadly place for a shipwreck. Whether drowned at once or not, we were sure to perish speedily in one way or another. 'I authorize you to take all the risks,' he said, after a short silence. 'I refuse to take any,' I said shortly; which was just the answer he expected, though its tone might have surprised him. 'Well, I must defer to your judgment. You are captain,' he said, with marked civility. I turned my shoulder to him in sign of my appreciation, and looked into the fog. How long would it last? It was the most hopeless lookout. The approach to this Kurtz grubbing for ivory in the wretched bush was beset by as many dangers as though he had been an enchanted princess sleeping in a fabulous castle. 'Will they attack, do you think?' asked the manager, in a confidential tone.

"I did not think they would attack, for several obvious reasons. The thick fog was one. If they left the bank in their canoes they would get lost in it, as we would be if we attempted to move. Still, I had also judged the jungle of both banks quite impenetrable—and yet eyes were in it, eyes that had seen us. The riverside bushes were certainly very thick; but the undergrowth behind was evidently penetrable. However, during the short lift I had seen no canoes anywhere in the reach—certainly not abreast of the steamer. But what made the idea of attack inconceivable to me was the nature of the noise—of the cries we had heard. They had not the fierce character boding of immediate hostile intention. Unexpected, wild, and violent as they had been, they had given me an irresistible impression of sorrow. The glimpse of the steamboat had for some reason filled those savages with unrestrained grief. The danger, if any, I expounded, was from our proximity to a great human passion let loose. Even extreme grief may ultimately vent itself in violence—but more generally takes the form of apathy. . . .

"You should have seen the pilgrims stare! They had no heart to grin, or even to revile me; but I believe they thought me gone mad—with fright, maybe. I delivered a regular lecture. My dear boys, it was no good bothering. Keep a lookout? Well, you may guess I watched the fog for the signs of lifting as a cat watches a mouse; but for anything else our eyes were of no more use to us than if we had been buried miles deep in a heap of cotton-wool. It felt like it too—choking, warm, stifling. Besides, all I said, though it sounded extravagant, was absolutely true to fact. What we afterwards alluded to as an attack was really an attempt at repulse. The action was very far from being aggressive—it was not even defensive, in the usual sense: it was undertaken under the stress of desperation, and in its essence was purely protective.

"It developed itself, I should say, two hours after the fog lifted, and its commencement was at a spot, roughly speaking, about a mile and a half below Kurtz's station. We had just floundered and flopped round a bend, when I saw an islet, a mere grassy hummock of bright green, in the middle of the stream. It was the only thing of the kind; but as we opened the reach more, I perceived it was the head of a long sandbank, or rather of a chain of shallow patches stretching down the middle of the river. They were discolored, just awash, and the whole lot was seen just under the water, exactly as a man's backbone is seen running down the middle of his back under the skin. Now, as far as I did see, I could go to the right or to the left of this. I didn't know either channel, of course. The banks looked pretty well alike, the depth appeared the same; but as I had been informed the station was on the west side, I naturally headed for the western passage.

"No sooner had we fairly entered it than I became aware it was much narrower than I had supposed. To the left of us there was the long uninterrupted shoal, and to the right a high steep bank heavily overgrown with bushes. Above the bush the trees stood in serried ranks. The twigs overhung the current thickly, and from distance to distance a large limb of some tree projected rigidly over the stream. It was then well on in the afternoon, the face of the forest was gloomy, and a broad strip of shadow had already fallen on the water. In this shadow we steamed up—very slowly, as you may imagine. I sheered her well inshore—the water being deepest near the bank, as the sounding-pole informed me.

"One of my hungry and forbearing friends was sounding in the bows just below me. This steamboat was exactly like a decked scow. On the deck there were two little teakwood houses, with doors and windows. The boiler was in the fore-end, and the machinery right astern. Over the whole there was a light roof, supported on stanchions. The funnel projected through that roof, and in front of the funnel a small cabin built of light planks served for a pilothouse. It contained a couch, two campstools, a loaded Martini-Henry leaning in one corner, a tiny table, and the steering wheel. It had a wide door in front and a broad shutter at each side. All these were always thrown open, of course. I spent my days perched up there on the extreme fore-end of that roof, before the door. At night I slept, or tried to, on the couch. An athletic black belonging to some coast tribe, and educated by my poor predecessor, was the helmsman. He sported a pair of brass earrings, wore a blue cloth wrapper from the waist to the ankles, and thought all the world of himself. He was the most unstable kind of fool I had ever seen. He steered with no end of a swagger while you were by; but if he lost sight of you, he became instantly the prey of an abject funk, and would let that cripple of a steamboat get the upper hand of him in a minute.

"I was looking down at the sounding-pole, and feeling much annoyed to see at each try a little more of it stick out of that river, when I saw my poleman give up the business suddenly, and stretch himself flat on the deck, without even taking the trouble to haul his pole in. He kept hold on it though, and it trailed in the water. At the same time the fireman, whom I could also see below me, sat down abruptly before his furnace and ducked his head. I was amazed. Then I had to look at the river mighty quick, because there was a snag in the fairway. Sticks, little sticks, were flying about—thick: they were whizzing before my nose, dropping below me, striking behind me against my pilothouse. All this time the river, the shore, the woods, were very quiet—perfectly quiet. I could only hear the heavy splashing thump of the stern-wheel and the patter of these things. We cleared the snag clumsily. Arrows, by Jove! We were being shot at! I stepped in quickly to close the shutter on the land-side. That fool-helmsman, his hands on the spokes, was lifting his knees high, stamping his feet, champing his mouth, like a reined-in horse. Confound him! And we were staggering within ten feet of the bank. I had to lean right out to swing the heavy shutter, and I saw a face amongst the leaves on the level with my own, looking at me very fierce and steady; and then suddenly, as though a veil had been removed from my eyes, I made out, deep in the tangled gloom, naked breasts, arms, legs, glaring eyes—the bush was swarming with human limbs in movement, glistening, of bronze color. The twigs shook, swayed, and rustled, the arrows flew out of them, and then the shutter came to. 'Steer her straight,' I said to the helmsman. He held his head rigid, face forward; but his eyes rolled, he kept on lifting and setting down his feet gently, his mouth foamed a little. 'Keep quiet!' I said in a fury. I might just as well have ordered a tree not to sway in the wind. I darted out. Below me there was a great scuffle of feet on the iron deck; confused exclamations; a voice screamed, 'Can you turn back?' I caught sight of a V-shaped ripple on the water ahead. What? Another snag! A fusillade burst out under my feet. The pilgrims had opened with their Winchesters, and were simply squirting lead into that bush. A deuce of a lot of smoke came up and drove slowly forward. I swore at it. Now I couldn't see the ripple or the snag either. I stood in the doorway, peering and the arrows came in swarms. They might have been poisoned, but they looked as though they wouldn't kill a cat. The bush began to howl. Our woodcutters raised a warlike whoop; the report of a rifle just at my back deafened me. I glanced over my shoulder, and the pilothouse was yet full of noise and smoke when I made a dash at the wheel. The fool-nigger had dropped everything, to throw the shutter open and let off that Martini-Henry. He stood before the wide opening glaring and I yelled at him to come back, while I straightened the sudden twist out of that steamboat. There was no room to turn even if I had wanted to, the snag was somewhere very near ahead in that confounded smoke, there was no time to lose, so I just crowded her into the bank—right into the bank, where I knew the water was deep.

"We tore slowly along the overhanging bushes in a whirl of broken twigs and flying leaves. The fusillade below stopped short, as I had foreseen it would when the squirts got empty. I threw my head back to a glinting whiz that traversed the pilothouse, in at one shutter-hole and out at the other. Looking past that mad helmsman, who was shaking the empty rifle and yelling at the shore, I saw vague forms of men running bent double, leaping, gliding, distinct, incomplete, evanescent. Something big appeared in the air before the shutter, the rifle went overboard, and the man stepped back swiftly, looked at me over his shoulder in an extraordinary, profound, familiar manner, and fell upon my feet. The side of his head hit the wheel twice, and the end of what appeared a long cane clattered round and knocked over a little campstool. It looked as though after wrenching that thing from somebody ashore he had lost his balance in the effort. The thin smoke had blown away, we were clear of the snag and looking ahead I could see that in another hundred yards or so I would be free to sheer off, away from the bank; but my feet felt so very warm and wet that I had to look down. The man had rolled on his back and stared straight up at me; both his hands clutched that cane. It was the shaft of a spear that, either thrown or lunged through the opening, had caught him in the side just below the ribs; the blade had gone in out of sight, after making a frightful gash; my shoes were full; a pool of blood lay very still, gleaming dark-red under the wheel; his eyes shone with an amazing luster. The fusillade burst out again. He looked at me anxiously, gripping the spear like something precious, with an air of being afraid I would try to take it away from him. I had to make an effort to free my eyes from his gaze and attend to the steering. With one hand I felt above my head for the line of the steam whistle, and jerked out screech after screech hurriedly. The tumult of angry and warlike yells was checked instantly, and then from the depths of the woods went out such a tremulous and prolonged wail of mournful fear and utter despair as may be imagined to follow the flight of the last hope from the earth. There was a great commotion in the bush; the shower of arrows stopped, a few dropping shots rang out sharply—then silence, in which the languid beat of the stern-wheel came plainly to my ears. I put the helm hard a-starboard at the moment when the pilgrim in pink pajamas, very hot and agitated, appeared in the doorway. 'The manager sends me——' he began in an official tone, and stopped short. 'Good God!' he said, glaring at the wounded man.

"We two whites stood over him, and his lustrous and inquiring glance enveloped us both. I declare it looked as though he would presently put to us some question in an understandable language, but he died without uttering a sound, without moving a limb, without twitching a muscle. Only in the very last moment, as though in response to some sign we could not see, to some whisper we could not hear, he frowned heavily, and that frown gave to his black death-mask an inconceivably somber, brooding, and menacing expression. The luster of inquiring glance faded swiftly into vacant glassiness. 'Can you steer?' I asked the agent eagerly. He looked very dubious; but I made a grab at his arm, and he understood at once I meant him to steer whether or no. To tell you the truth, I was morbidly anxious to change my shoes and socks. 'He is dead,' murmured the fellow, immensely impressed. 'No doubt about it,' said I, tugging like mad at the shoelaces. 'And by the way, I suppose Mr. Kurtz is dead as well by this time.'

"For the moment that was the dominant thought. There was a sense of extreme disappointment, as though I had found out I had been striving after something altogether without a substance. I couldn't have been more disgusted if I had traveled all this way for the sole purpose of talking with Mr. Kurtz. Talking with . . . I flung one shoe overboard, and became aware that that was exactly what I had been looking forward to—a talk with Kurtz. I made the strange discovery that I had never imagined him as doing, you know, but as discoursing. I didn't say to myself, 'Now I will never see him,' or 'Now I will never shake him by the hand,' but, 'Now I will never hear him.' The man presented himself as a voice. Not of course that I did not connect him with some sort of action. Hadn't I been told in all the tones of jealousy and admiration that he had collected, bartered, swindled, or stolen more ivory than all the other agents together? That was not the point. The point was in his being a gifted creature, and that of all his gifts the one that stood out preeminently, that carried with it a sense of real presence, was his ability to talk, his words—the gift of expression, the bewildering, the illuminating, the most exalted and the most contemptible, the pulsating stream of light, or the deceitful flow from the heart of an impenetrable darkness.

"The other shoe went flying unto the devil-god of that river. I thought, By Jove! it's all over. We are too late; he has vanished—the gift has vanished, by means of some spear, arrow, or club. I will never hear that chap speak after all—and my sorrow had a startling extravagance of emotion, even such as I had noticed in the howling sorrow of these savages in the bush. I couldn't have felt more of lonely desolation somehow, had I been robbed of a belief or had missed my destiny in life. . . . Why do you sigh in this beastly way, somebody? Absurd? Well, absurd. Good Lord! mustn't a man ever——Here, give me some tobacco." . . .

There was a pause of profound stillness, then a match flared, and Marlow's lean face appeared, worn, hollow, with downward folds and dropped eyelids, with an aspect of concentrated attention; and as he took vigorous draws at his pipe, it seemed to retreat and advance out of the night in the regular flicker of the tiny flame. The match went out.

"Absurd!" he cried. "This is the worst of trying to tell . . . Here you all are, each moored with two good addresses, like a hulk with two anchors, a butcher round one corner, a policeman round another, excellent appetites, and temperature normal—you hear—normal from year's end to year's end. And you say, Absurd! Absurd be—exploded! Absurd! My dear boys, what can you expect from a man who out of sheer nervousness had just flung overboard a pair of new shoes? Now I think of it, it is amazing I did not shed tears. I am, upon the whole, proud of my fortitude. I was cut to the quick at the idea of having lost the inestimable privilege of listening to the gifted Kurtz. Of course I was wrong. The privilege was waiting for me. Oh yes, I heard more than enough. And I was right, too. A voice. He was very little more than a voice. And I heard—him—it—this voice—other voices—all of them were so little more than voices—and the memory of that time itself lingers around me, impalpable, like a dying vibration of one immense jabber, silly, atrocious, sordid, savage, or simply mean, without any kind of sense. Voices, voices—even the girl herself—now—"

He was silent for a long time.

"I laid the ghost of his gifts at last with a lie," he began suddenly. "Girl! What? Did I mention a girl? Oh, she is out of it completely. They—the women I mean—are out of it—should be out of it. We must help them to stay in that beautiful world of their own, lest ours gets worse. Oh, she had to be out of it. You should have heard the disinterred body of Mr. Kurtz saying, 'My Intended.' You would have perceived directly then how completely she was out of it. And the lofty frontal bone of Mr. Kurtz! They say the hair goes on growing sometimes, but this—ah—specimen was impressively bald. The wilderness had parted him on the head, and, behold, it was like a ball—an ivory ball; it had caressed him, and—lo!—he had withered; it had taken him, loved him, embraced him, got into his veins, consumed his flesh, and sealed his soul to its own by the inconceivable ceremonies of some devilish initiation. He was its spoiled and pampered favorite. Ivory? I should think so. Heaps of it, stacks of it. The old mud shanty was bursting with it. You would think there was not a single tusk left either above or below the ground in the whole country. 'Mostly fossil,' the manager had remarked disparagingly. It was no more fossil than I am; but they call it fossil when it is dug up. It appears these niggers do bury the tusks sometimes—but evidently they couldn't bury this parcel deep enough to save the gifted Mr. Kurtz from his fate. We filled the steamboat with it, and had to pile a lot on the deck. Thus he could see and enjoy as long as he could see, because the appreciation of this favor had remained with him to the last. You should have heard him say, 'My ivory.' Oh yes, I heard him. 'My Intended, my ivory, my station, my river, my——' everything belonged to him. It made me hold my breath in expectation of hearing the wilderness burst into a prodigious peal of laughter that would shake the fixed stars in their places. Everything belonged to him—but that was a trifle. The thing was to know what he belonged to, how many powers of darkness claimed him for their own. That was the reflection that made you creepy all over. It was impossible—it was not good for one either—trying to imagine. He had taken a high seat amongst the devils of the land—I mean literally. You can't understand. How could you?—with solid pavement under your feet, surrounded by kind neighbors ready to cheer you or to fall on you, stepping delicately between the butcher and the policeman, in the holy terror of scandal and gallows and lunatic asylums—how can you imagine what particular region of the first ages a man's untrammeled feet may take him into by the way of solitude—utter solitude without a policeman—by the way of silence—utter silence, where no warning voice of a kind neighbor can be heard whispering of public opinion? These little things make all the great difference. When they are gone you must fall back upon your own innate strength, upon your own capacity for faithfulness. Of course you may be too much of a fool to go wrong—too dull even to know you are being assaulted by the powers of darkness. I take it, no fool ever made a bargain for his soul with the devil: the fool is too much of a fool, or the devil too much of a devil—I don't know which. Or you may be such a thunderingly exalted creature as to be altogether deaf and blind to anything but heavenly sights and sounds. Then the earth for you is only a standing place—and whether to be like this is your loss or your gain I won't pretend to say. But most of us are neither one nor the other. The earth for us is a place to live in, where we must put up with sights, with sounds, with smells, too, by Jove!—breathe dead hippo, so to speak, and not be contaminated. And there, don't you see? your strength comes in, the faith in your ability for the digging of unostentatious holes to bury the stuff in— your power of devotion, not to yourself, but to an obscure, back-breaking business. And that's difficult enough. Mind, I am not trying to excuse or even explain—I am trying to account to myself for—for—Mr. Kurtz—for the shade of Mr. Kurtz. This initiated wraith from the back of Nowhere honored me with its amazing confidence before it vanished altogether. This was because it could speak English to me. The original Kurtz had been educated partly in England, and—as he was good enough to say himself—his sympathies were in the right place. His mother was half-English, his father was half-French. All Europe contributed to the making of Kurtz; and by and by I learned that, most appropriately, the International Society for the Suppression of Savage Customs had entrusted him with the making of a report, for its future guidance. And he had written it too. I've seen it. I've read it. It was eloquent, vibrating with eloquence, but too high-strung, I think. Seventeen pages of close writing he had found time for! But this must have been before his— let us say—nerves went wrong and caused him to preside at certain midnight dances ending with unspeakable rites, which—as far as I reluctantly gathered from what I heard at various times—were offered up to him—do you understand?—to Mr. Kurtz himself. But it was a beautiful piece of writing. The opening paragraph, however, in the light of later information, strikes me now as ominous. He began with the argument that we whites, from the point of development we had arrived at, 'must necessarily appear to them [savages] in the nature of supernatural beings—we approach them with the might as of a deity,' and so on, and so on. 'By the simple exercise of our will we can exert a power for good practically unbounded,' etc. etc. From that point he soared and took me with him. The peroration was magnificent, though difficult to remember, you know. It gave me the notion of an exotic Immensity ruled by an august Benevolence. It made me tingle with enthusiasm. This was the unbounded power of eloquence—of words—of burning noble words. There were no practical hints to interrupt the magic current of phrases, unless a kind of note at the foot of the last page, scrawled evidently much later, in an unsteady hand, may be regarded as the exposition of a method. It was very simple, and at the end of that moving appeal to every altruistic sentiment it blazed at you, luminous and terrifying like a flash of lightning in a serene sky: 'Exterminate all the brutes!' The curious part was that he had apparently forgotten all about that valuable postscriptum, because, later on, when he in a sense came to himself, he repeatedly entreated me to take good care of 'my pamphlet' (he called it), as it was sure to have in the future a good influence upon his career. I had full information about all these things, and, besides, as it turned out, I was to have the care of his memory. I've done enough for it to give me the indisputable right to lay it, if I choose, for an everlasting rest in the dustbin of progress, amongst all the sweepings and, figuratively speaking, all the dead cats of civilization. But then, you see, I can't choose. He won't be forgotten. Whatever he was, he was not common. He had the power to charm or frighten rudimentary souls into an aggravated witch-dance in his honor; he could also fill the small souls of the pilgrims with bitter misgivings: he had one devoted friend at least, and he had conquered one soul in the world that was neither rudimentary nor tainted with self-seeking. No; I can't forget him, though I am not prepared to affirm the fellow was exactly worth the life we lost in getting to him. I missed my late helmsman awfully—I missed him even while his body was still lying in the pilothouse. Perhaps you will think it passing strange this regret for a savage who was no more account than a grain of sand in a black Sahara. Well, don't you see, he had done something, he had steered; for months I had him at my back—a help—an instrument. It was a kind of partnership. He steered for me—I had to look after him, I worried about his deficiencies, and thus a subtle bond had been created, of which I only became aware when it was suddenly broken. And the intimate profundity of that look he gave me when he received his hurt remains to this day in my memory—like a claim of distant kinship affirmed in a supreme moment.

"Poor fool! If he had only left that shutter alone. He had no restraint, no restraint—just like Kurtz—a tree swayed by the wind. As soon as I had put on a dry pair of slippers, I dragged him out, after first jerking the spear out of his side, which operation I confess I performed with my eyes shut tight. His heels leaped together over the little doorstep; his shoulders were pressed to my breast; I hugged him from behind desperately. Oh! he was heavy, heavy; heavier than any man on earth, I should imagine. Then without more ado I tipped him overboard. The current snatched him as though he had been a wisp of grass, and I saw the body roll over twice before I lost sight of it forever. All the pilgrims and the manager were then congregated on the awning-deck about the pilothouse, chattering at each other like a flock of excited magpies, and there was a scandalized murmur at my heartless promptitude. What they wanted to keep that body hanging about for I can't guess. Embalm it, maybe. But I had also heard another, and a very ominous, murmur on the deck below. My friends the woodcutters were likewise scandalized, and with a better show of reason—though I admit that the reason itself was quite inadmissible. Oh, quite! I had made up my mind that if my late helmsman was to be eaten, the fishes alone should have him. He had been a

very second-rate helmsman while alive, but now he was dead he might have
become a first-class temptation, and possibly cause some startling trouble.
Besides, I was anxious to take the wheel, the man in pink pajamas showing himself a hopeless duffer at the business.

"This I did directly the simple funeral was over. We were going half-speed,
keeping right in the middle of the stream, and I listened to the talk about me.
They had given up Kurtz, they had given up the station; Kurtz was dead, and the
station had been burnt—and so on, and so on. The red-haired pilgrim was beside
himself with the thought that at least this poor Kurtz had been properly revenged.
'Say! We must have made a glorious slaughter of them in the bush. Eh? What do
you think? Say?' He positively danced, the bloodthirsty little gingery beggar. And
he had nearly fainted when he saw the wounded man! I could not help saying, 'You
made a glorious lot of smoke, anyhow.' I had seen, from the way the tops of the
bushes rustled and flew, that almost all the shots had gone too high. You can't hit
anything unless you take aim and fire from the shoulder; but these chaps fired
from the hip with their eyes shut. The retreat, I maintained—and I was right—
was caused by the screeching of the steam-whistle. Upon this they forgot Kurtz,
and began to howl at me with indignant protests.

"The manager stood by the wheel murmuring confidentially about the necessity
of getting well away down the river before dark at all events, when I saw in the
distance a clearing on the riverside and the outlines of some sort of building.
'What's this?' I asked. He clapped his hands in wonder. 'The station!' he cried. I
edged in at once, still going half-speed.

"Through my glasses I saw the slope of a hill interspersed with rare trees and
perfectly free from undergrowth. A long decaying building on the summit was half
buried in the high grass; the large holes in the peaked roof gaped black from afar;
the jungle and the woods made a background. There was no enclosure or fence of
any kind; but there had been one apparently, for near the house half a dozen slim
posts remained in a row, roughly trimmed, and with their upper ends ornamented
with round carved balls. The rails, or whatever there had been between, had disappeared. Of course the forest surrounded all that. The riverbank was clear, and
on the water side I saw a white man under a hat like a cartwheel beckoning persistently with his whole arm. Examining the edge of the forest above and below, I
was almost certain I could see movements—human forms gliding here and there.
I steamed past prudently, then stopped the engines and let her drift down. The
man on the shore began to shout, urging us to land. 'We have been attacked,'
screamed the manager. 'I know—I know. It's all right,' yelled back the other, as
cheerful as you please. 'Come along. It's all right. I am glad.'

"His aspect reminded me of something I had seen—something funny I had
seen somewhere. As I maneuvered to get alongside, I was asking myself, 'What

does this fellow look like?' Suddenly I got it. He looked like a harlequin. His clothes had been made of some stuff that was brown holland probably, but it was covered with patches all over, with bright patches, blue, red, and yellow—patches on the back, patches on the front, patches on elbows, on knees; colored binding round his jacket, scarlet edging at the bottom of his trousers; and the sunshine made him look extremely gay and wonderfully neat withal, because you could see how beautifully all this patching had been done. A beardless, boyish face, very fair, no features to speak of, nose peeling, little blue eyes, smiles and frowns chasing each other over that open countenance like sunshine and shadow on a wind-swept plain. 'Look out, captain!' he cried; 'there's a snag lodged in here last night.' What! Another snag? I confess I swore shamefully. I had nearly holed my cripple, to finish off that charming trip. The harlequin on the bank turned his little pug nose up to me. 'You English?' he asked, all smiles. 'Are you?' I shouted from the wheel. The smiles vanished, and he shook his head as if sorry for my disappointment. Then he brightened up. 'Never mind!' he cried encouragingly. 'Are we in time?' I asked. 'He is up there,' he replied, with a toss of the head up the hill, and becoming gloomy all of a sudden. His face was like the autumn sky, overcast one moment and bright the next.

"When the manager, escorted by the pilgrims, all of them armed to the teeth, had gone to the house, this chap came on board. 'I say, I don't like this. These natives are in the bush,' I said. He assured me earnestly it was all right. 'They are simple people,' he added; 'well, I am glad you came. It took me all my time to keep them off.' 'But you said it was all right,' I cried. 'Oh, they meant no harm,' he said; and as I stared he corrected himself, 'Not exactly.' Then vivaciously, 'My faith, your pilothouse wants a cleanup!' In the next breath he advised me to keep enough steam on the boiler to blow the whistle in case of any trouble. 'One good screech will do more for you than all your rifles. They are simple people,' he repeated. He rattled away at such a rate he quite overwhelmed me. He seemed to be trying to make up for lots of silence, and actually hinted, laughing, that such was the case. 'Don't you talk with Mr. Kurtz?' I said. 'You don't talk with that man—you listen to him,' he exclaimed with severe exaltation. 'But now——' He waved his arm, and in the twinkling of an eye was in the uttermost depths of despondency. In a moment he came up again with a jump, possessed himself of both my hands, shook them continuously, while he gabbled: 'Brother sailor . . . honor . . . pleasure . . . delight . . . introduce myself . . . Russian . . . son of an archpriest . . . Government of Tambov . . . What? Tobacco! English tobacco; the excellent English tobacco! Now, that's brotherly. Smoke? Where's a sailor that does not smoke?'

"The pipe soothed him, and gradually I made out he had run away from school, had gone to sea in a Russian ship; ran away again; served some time in English ships; was now reconciled with the archpriest. He made a point of that. 'But when one is young one must see things, gather experience, ideas; enlarge the mind.' 'Here!' I interrupted. 'You can never tell! Here I met Mr. Kurtz,' he said, youthfully solemn and reproachful. I held my tongue after that. It appears he had persuaded a Dutch trading house on the coast to fit him out with stores and goods, and had started for the interior with a light heart, and no more idea of what would happen to him than a baby. He had been wandering about that river for nearly two years alone, cut off from everybody and everything. 'I am not so young as I look. I am twenty-five,' he said. 'At first old Van Shuyten would tell me to go to the devil,' he narrated with keen enjoyment; 'but I stuck to him, and talked and talked, till at last he got afraid I would talk the hind-leg off his favorite dog, so he gave me some cheap things and a few guns, and told me he hoped he would never see my face again. Good old Dutchman, Van Shuyten. I sent him one small lot of ivory a year ago, so that he can't call me a little thief when I get back. I hope he got it. And for the rest, I don't care. I had some wood stacked for you. That was my old house. Did you see?'

"I gave him Towson's book. He made as though he would kiss me, but restrained himself. 'The only book I had left, and I thought I had lost it,' he said, looking at it ecstatically. 'So many accidents happen to a man going about alone, you know. Canoes get upset sometimes—and sometimes you've got to clear out so quick when the people get angry.' He thumbed the pages. 'You made notes in Russian?' I asked. He nodded. 'I thought they were written in cipher,' I said. He laughed, then became serious. 'I had lots of trouble to keep these people off,' he said. 'Did they want to kill you?' I asked. 'Oh no!' he cried, and checked himself. 'Why did they attack us?' I pursued. He hesitated, then said shamefacedly, 'They don't want him to go.' 'Don't they?' I said curiously. He nodded a nod full of mystery and wisdom. 'I tell you,' he cried, 'this man has enlarged my mind.' He opened his arms wide, staring at me with his little blue eyes that were perfectly round."

III

"I looked at him, lost in astonishment. There he was before me, in motley, as though he had absconded from a troupe of mimes, enthusiastic, fabulous. His very existence was improbable, inexplicable, and altogether bewildering. He was an insoluble problem. It was inconceivable how he had existed, how he had succeeded in getting so far, how he had managed to remain—why he did not instantly disappear. 'I went a little farther,' he said, 'then still a little farther—till I had gone so far that I don't know how I'll ever get back. Never mind. Plenty time. I can manage. You take Kurtz away quick—quick—I tell you.' The glamour of youth enveloped his parti-colored rags, his destitution, his loneliness, the essential desolation of his futile wanderings. For months—for years—his life hadn't been worth a day's purchase; and there he was gallantly, thoughtlessly alive, to all appearance indestructible solely by the virtue of his few years and of his unreflecting audacity. I was seduced into something like admiration—like envy. Glamour urged him on, glamour kept him unscathed. He surely wanted nothing from the wilderness but space to breathe in and to push on through. His need was to exist, and to move onwards at the greatest possible risk, and with a maximum of privation. If the absolutely pure, uncalculating, unpractical spirit of adventure had ever ruled a human being, it ruled this be-patched youth. I almost envied him the possession of this modest and clear flame. It seemed to have consumed all thought of self so completely; that, even while he was talking to you, you forgot that it was he—the man before your eyes—who had gone through these things. I did not envy him his devotion to Kurtz, though. He had not meditated over it. It came to him, and, he accepted it with a sort of eager fatalism. I must say that to me it appeared about the most dangerous thing in every way he had come upon so far.

"They had come together unavoidably, like two ships becalmed near each other, and lay rubbing sides at last. I suppose Kurtz wanted an audience, because on a certain occasion, when encamped in the forest, they had talked all night, or more probably Kurtz had talked. 'We talked of everything,' he said, quite transported at the recollection. 'I forgot there was such a thing as sleep. The night did not seem to last an hour. Everything! Everything! . . . Of love too.' 'Ah, he talked to you of love!' I said, much amused. 'It isn't what you think,' he cried, almost passionately. 'It was in general. He made me see things—things.'

"He threw his arms up. We were on deck at the time, and the headman of my woodcutters, lounging near by, turned upon him his heavy and glittering eyes. I looked around, and I don't know why, but I assure you that never, never before, did this land, this river, this jungle, the very arch of this blazing sky, appear to me so hopeless and so dark, so impenetrable to human thought, so pitiless to human weakness. 'And, ever since, you have been with him, of course?' I said.

"On the contrary. It appears their intercourse had been very much broken by various causes. He had, as he informed me proudly, managed to nurse Kurtz through two illnesses (he alluded to it as you would to some risky feat), but as a rule Kurtz wandered alone, far in the depths of the forest. 'Very often coming to this station, I had to wait days and days before he would turn up,' he said. 'Ah, it was worth waiting for!—sometimes.' 'What was he doing? exploring or what?' I asked. 'Oh yes, of course'; he had discovered lots of villages, a lake too he did not know exactly in what direction; it was dangerous to inquire too much—but mostly his expeditions had been for ivory. 'But he had no goods to trade with by that time,'

I objected. 'There's a good lot of cartridges left even yet,' he answered, looking away. 'To speak plainly, he raided the country,' I said. He nodded. 'Not alone, surely!' He muttered something about the villages round that lake. 'Kurtz got the tribe to follow him, did he?' I suggested. He fidgeted a little. 'They adored him,' he said. The tone of these words was so extraordinary that I looked at him searchingly. It was curious to see his mingled eagerness and reluctance to speak of Kurtz. The man filled his life, occupied his thoughts, swayed his emotions. 'What can you expect?' he burst out; 'he came to them with thunder and lightning, you know—and they had never seen anything like it—and very terrible. He could be very terrible. You can't judge Mr. Kurtz as you would an ordinary man. No, no, no! Now—just to give you an idea—I don't mind telling you, he wanted to shoot me too one day—but I don't judge him.' 'Shoot you!' I cried. 'What for?' 'Well, I had a small lot of ivory the chief of that village near my house gave me. You see I used to shoot game for them. Well, he wanted it, and wouldn't hear reason. He declared he would shoot me unless I gave him the ivory and then cleared out of the country, because he could do so, and had a fancy for it, and there was nothing on earth to prevent him killing whom he jolly well pleased. And it was true too. I gave him the ivory. What did I care! But I didn't clear out. No, no. I couldn't leave him. I had to be careful, of course, till we got friendly again for a time. He had his second illness then. Afterwards I had to keep out of the way; but I didn't mind. He was living for the most part in those villages on the lake. When he came down to the river, sometimes he would take to me, and sometimes it was better for me to be careful. This man suffered too much. He hated all this, and somehow he couldn't get away. When I had a chance I begged him to try and leave while there was time; I offered to go back with him. And he would say yes, and then he would remain; go off on another ivory hunt; disappear for weeks; forget himself amongst these people—forget himself—you know.' 'Why! he's mad,' I said. He protested indignantly. Mr. Kurtz couldn't be mad. If I had heard him talk, only two days ago, I wouldn't dare hint at such a thing. . . . I had taken up my binoculars while we talked, and was looking at the shore, sweeping the limit of the forest at each side and at the back of the house. The consciousness of there being people in that bush, so silent, so quiet—as silent and quiet as the ruined house on the hill—made me uneasy. There was no sign on the face of nature of this amazing tale that was not so much told as suggested to me in desolate exclamations, completed by shrugs, in interrupted phrases, in hints ending in deep sighs. The woods were unmoved, like a mask—heavy, like the closed door of a prison—they looked with their air of hidden knowledge, of patient expectation, of unapproachable silence. The Russian was explaining to me that it was only lately that Mr. Kurtz had come down to the river, bringing along with him all the fighting men of that lake tribe. He had been absent for several months—getting himself adored, I suppose—and had come down unexpectedly, with the intention to all appearance of making a raid either across the river or down stream. Evidently the appetite for more ivory had got the better of the—what shall I say?—less material aspirations. However, he had got much worse suddenly. 'I heard he was lying helpless, and so I came up—took my chance,' said the Russian. 'Oh, he is bad, very bad.' I directed my glass to the house. There were no signs of life, but there were the ruined roof, the long mud wall peeping above the grass, with three little square window holes, no two of the same size; all this brought within reach of my hand, as it were. And then I made a brusk movement, and one of the remaining posts of that vanished fence leaped up in the field of my glass. You remember I told you I had been struck at the distance by certain attempts at ornamentation, rather remarkable in the ruinous aspect of the place. Now I had suddenly a nearer view, and its first result was to make me throw my head back as if before a blow. Then I went carefully from post to post with my glass, and I saw my mistake. These round knobs were not ornamental but symbolic; they were expressive and puzzling, striking and disturbing—food for thought and also for vultures if there had been any looking down from the sky; but at all events for such ants as were industrious enough to ascend the pole. They would have been even more impressive, those heads on the stakes, if their faces had not been turned to the house. Only one, the first I had made out, was facing my way. I was not so shocked as you may think. The start back I had given was really nothing but a movement of surprise. I had expected to see a knob of wood there, you know. I returned deliberately to the first I had seen—and there it was, black, dried, sunken, with closed eyelids—a head that seemed to sleep at the top of that pole, and, with the shrunken dry lips showing a narrow white line of the teeth, was smiling too, smiling continuously at some endless and jocose dream of that eternal slumber.

"I am not disclosing any trade secrets. In fact the manager said afterwards that Mr. Kurtz's methods had ruined the district. I have no opinion on that point, but I want you clearly to understand that there was nothing exactly profitable in these heads being there. They only showed that Mr. Kurtz lacked restraint in the gratification of his various lusts, that there was something wanting in him—some small matter which, when the pressing need arose, could not be found under his magnificent eloquence. Whether he knew of this deficiency himself I can't say. I think the knowledge came to him at last—only at the very last. But the wilderness had found him out early, and had taken on him a terrible vengeance for the fantastic invasion. I think it had whispered to him things about himself which he did not know, things of which he had no conception till he took counsel with this great solitude—and the whisper had proved irresistibly fascinating. It echoed loudly within him because he was hollow at the core. . . . I put down the glass, and the head that had appeared near enough to be spoken to seemed at once to have leaped away from me into inaccessible distance.

"The admirer of Mr. Kurtz was a bit crestfallen. In a hurried, indistinct voice he began to assure me he had not dared to take these—say, symbols—down. He was not afraid of the natives; they would not stir till Mr. Kurtz gave the word. His ascendancy was extraordinary. The camps of these people surrounded the place, and the chiefs came every day to see him. They would crawl . . . 'I don't want to know anything of the ceremonies used when approaching Mr. Kurtz,' I shouted. Curious, this feeling that came over me that such details would be more intolerable than those heads drying on the stakes under Mr. Kurtz's windows. After all, that was only a savage sight, while I seemed at one bound to have been transported into some lightless region of subtle horrors, where pure, uncomplicated savagery was a positive relief, being something that had a right to exist—obviously—in the sunshine. The young man looked at me with surprise. I suppose it did not occur to him that Mr. Kurtz was no idol of mine. He forgot I hadn't heard any of these splendid monologues on, what was it? on love, justice, conduct of life—or what not. If it had come to crawling before Mr. Kurtz, he crawled as much as the veriest savage of them all. I had no idea of the conditions, he said: these heads were the heads of rebels. I shocked him excessively by laughing. Rebels! What would be the next definition I was to hear? There had been enemies, criminals, workers—and these were rebels. Those rebellious heads looked very subdued to me on their sticks. 'You don't know how such a life tries a man like Kurtz,' cried Kurtz's last disciple. 'Well, and you?' I said. 'I! I! I am a simple man. I have no great thoughts. I want nothing from anybody. How can you compare me to . . . ?' His feelings were too much for speech, and suddenly he broke down. 'I don't understand,' he groaned. 'I've been doing my best to keep him alive, and that's enough. I had no hand in all this. I have no abilities. There hasn't been a drop of medicine or a mouthful of invalid food for months here. He was shamefully abandoned. A man like this, with such ideas. Shamefully! Shamefully! I—I—haven't slept for the last ten nights. . . .'

"His voice lost itself in the calm of the evening. The long shadows of the forest had slipped downhill while we talked, had gone far beyond the ruined hovel, beyond the symbolic row of stakes. All this was in the gloom, while we down there were yet in the sunshine, and the stretch of the river abreast of the clearing glittered in a still and dazzling splendor, with a murky and overshadowed bend above and below. Not a living soul was seen on the shore. The bushes did not rustle.

"Suddenly round the corner of the house a group of men appeared, as though they had come up from the ground. They waded waist-deep in the grass, in a compact body, bearing an improvised stretcher in their midst. Instantly, in the emptiness of the landscape, a cry arose whose shrillness pierced the still air like a sharp arrow flying straight to the very heart of the land; and, as if by enchantment, streams of human beings—of naked human beings—with spears in their hands, with bows, with shields, with wild glances and savage movements, were poured into the clearing by the dark-faced and pensive forest. The bushes shook, the grass swayed for a time, and then everything stood still in attentive immobility.

"'Now, if he does not say the right thing to them we are all done for,' said the Russian at my elbow. The knot of men with the stretcher had stopped too, half-way to the steamer, as if petrified. I saw the man on the stretcher sit up, lank and with an uplifted arm, above the shoulders of the bearers. 'Let us hope that the man who can talk so well of love in general will find some particular reason to spare us this time,' I said. I resented bitterly the absurd danger of our situation, as if to be at the mercy of that atrocious phantom had been a dishonoring neces-sity. I could not hear a sound, but through my glasses I saw the thin arm extend-ed commandingly, the lower jaw moving, the eyes of that apparition shining dark-ly far in its bony head that nodded with grotesque jerks. Kurtz—Kurtz—that means 'short' in German—don't it? Well, the name was as true as everything else in his life—and death. He looked at least seven feet long. His covering had fallen off, and his body emerged from it pitiful and appalling as from a winding sheet. I could see the cage of his ribs all astir, the bones of his arm waving. It was as though an animated image of death carved out of old ivory had been shaking its hand with menaces at a motionless crowd of men made of dark and glittering bronze. I saw him open his mouth wide—it gave him a weirdly voracious aspect, as though he had wanted to swallow all the air, all the earth, all the men before him. A deep voice reached me faintly. He must have been shouting. He fell back suddenly. The stretcher shook as the bearers staggered forward again, and almost at the same time I noticed that the crowd of savages was vanishing with-out any perceptible movement of retreat, as if the forest that had ejected these beings so suddenly had drawn them in again as the breath is drawn in a long aspiration.

"Some of the pilgrims behind the stretcher carried his arms—two shotguns, a heavy rifle, and a light revolver-carbine—the thunderbolts of that pitiful Jupiter. The manager bent over him murmuring as he walked beside his head. They laid him down in one of the little cabins—just a room for a bed-place and a campstool or two, you know. We had brought his belated correspondence, and a lot of torn envelopes and open letters littered his bed. His hand roamed feebly amongst these papers. I was struck by the fire of his eyes and the composed languor of his expression. It was not so much the exhaustion of disease. He did not seem in pain. This shadow looked satiated and calm, as though for the moment it had had its fill of all the emotions.

"He rustled one of the letters, and looking straight in my face said, 'I am glad.' Somebody had been writing to him about me. These special recommendations were turning up again. The volume of tone he emitted without effort, almost without the trouble of moving his lips, amazed me. A voice! a voice! It was grave, profound, vibrating, while the man did not seem capable of a whisper. However, he had enough strength in him—factitious no doubt—to very nearly make an end of us, as you shall hear directly.

"The manager appeared silently in the doorway; I stepped out at once and he drew the curtain after me. The Russian, eyed curiously by the pilgrims, was staring at the shore. I followed the direction of his glance.

"Dark human shapes could be made out in the distance, flitting indistinctly against the gloomy border of the forest, and near the river two bronze figures, leaning on tall spears, stood in the sunlight under fantastic headdresses of spotted skins, warlike and still in statuesque repose. And from right to left along the lighted shore moved a wild and gorgeous apparition of a woman.

"She walked with measured steps, draped in striped and fringed cloths, treading the earth proudly, with a slight jingle and flash of barbarous ornaments. She carried her head high; her hair was done in the shape of a helmet; she had brass leggings to the knees, brass wire gauntlets to the elbow, a crimson spot on her tawny cheek, innumerable necklaces of glass beads on her neck; bizarre things, charms, gifts of witch-men, that hung about her, glittered and trembled at every step. She must have had the value of several elephant tusks upon her. She was savage and superb, wild-eyed and magnificent; there was something ominous and stately in her deliberate progress. And in the hush that had fallen suddenly upon the whole sorrowful land, the immense wilderness, the colossal body of the fecund and mysterious life seemed to look at her, pensive, as though it had been looking at the image of its own tenebrous and passionate soul.

"She came abreast of the steamer, stood still, and faced us. Her long shadow fell to the water's edge. Her face had a tragic and fierce aspect of wild sorrow and of dumb pain mingled with the fear of some struggling, half-shaped resolve. She stood looking at us without a stir, and like the wilderness itself, with an air of brooding over an inscrutable purpose. A whole minute passed, and then she made a step forward. There was a low jingle, a glint of yellow metal, a sway of fringed draperies, and she stopped as if her heart had failed her. The young fellow by my side growled. The pilgrims murmured at my back. She looked at us all as if her life had depended upon the unswerving steadiness of her glance. Suddenly she opened her bared arms and threw them up rigid above her head, as though in an uncontrollable desire to touch the sky, and at the same time the swift shadows darted out on the earth, swept around on the river, gathering the steamer in a shadowy embrace. A formidable silence hung over the scene.

"She turned away slowly, walked on, following the bank, and passed into the bushes to the left. Once only her eyes gleamed back at us in the dusk of the thickets before she disappeared.

"'If she had offered to come aboard I really think I would have tried to shoot her,' said the man of patches nervously. 'I had been risking my life every day for the last fortnight to keep her out of the house. She got in one day and kicked up a row about those miserable rags I picked up in the storeroom to mend my clothes with. I wasn't decent. At least it must have been that, for she talked like a fury to Kurtz for an hour, pointing at me now and then. I don't understand the dialect of this tribe. Luckily for me, I fancy Kurtz felt too ill that day to care, or there would have been mischief. I don't understand. . . . No—it's too much for me. Ah, well, it's all over now.'

"At this moment I heard Kurtz's deep voice behind the curtain: 'Save me!—save the ivory, you mean. Don't tell me. Save me! Why, I've had to save you. You are interrupting my plans now. Sick! Sick! Not so sick as you would like to believe. Nevermind. I'll carry my ideas out yet—I will return. I'll show you what can be done. You with your little peddling notions—you are interfering with me. I will return. I . . .'

"The manager came out. He did me the honor to take me under the arm and lead me aside. 'He is very low, very low,' he said. He considered it necessary to sigh, but neglected to be consistently sorrowful. 'We have done all we could for him—haven't we? But there is no disguising the fact, Mr. Kurtz has done more harm than good to the Company. He did not see the time was not ripe for vigorous action. Cautiously, cautiously—that's my principle. We must be cautious yet. The district is closed to us for a time. Deplorable! Upon the whole, the trade will suffer. I don't deny there is a remarkable quantity of ivory—mostly fossil. We must save it, at all events but look how precarious the position is—and why? Because the method is unsound.' 'Do you,' said I, looking at the shore, 'call it "unsound method"?' 'Without doubt,' he exclaimed hotly. 'Don't you?' . . . 'No method at all,' I murmured after a while. 'Exactly,' he exulted. 'I anticipated this. Shows a complete want of judgment. It is my duty to point it out in the proper quarter.' 'Oh,' said I, 'that fellow—what's his name?—the brickmaker, will make a readable report for you.' He appeared confounded for a moment. It seemed to me I had never breathed an atmosphere so vile, and I turned mentally to Kurtz for relief—positively for relief. 'Nevertheless, I think Mr. Kurtz is a remarkable man,' I said with emphasis. He started, dropped on me a cold heavy glance, said very quietly, 'He was,' and turned his back on me. My hour of favor was over; I found myself lumped along with Kurtz as a partisan of methods for which the time was not ripe: I was unsound! Ah! but it was something to have at least a choice of nightmares.

"I had turned to the wilderness really, not to Mr. Kurtz, who, I was ready to admit, was as good as buried. And for a moment it seemed to me as if I also were buried in a vast grave full of unspeakable secrets. I felt an intolerable weight oppressing my breast, the smell of the damp earth, the unseen presence of victorious corruption, the darkness of an impenetrable night. . . . The Russian tapped me on the shoulder. I heard him mumbling and stammering something about 'brother seaman—couldn't conceal—knowledge of matters that would affect Mr. Kurtz's reputation.' I waited. For him evidently Mr. Kurtz was not in his grave; I suspect that for him Mr. Kurtz was one of the immortals. 'Well!' said I at last, 'speak out. As it happens, I am Mr. Kurtz's friend—in a way.'

"He stated with a good deal of formality that had we not been 'of the same profession,' he would have kept the matter to himself without regard to consequences. He suspected 'there was an active ill will towards him on the part of these white men that——' 'You are right,' I said, remembering a certain conversation I had overheard. 'The manager thinks you ought to be hanged.' He showed a concern at this intelligence which amused me at first. 'I had better get out of the way quietly,' he said earnestly. 'I can do no more for Kurtz now, and they would soon find some excuse. What's to stop them? There's a military post three hundred miles from here.' 'Well, upon my word,' said I, 'perhaps you had better go if you have any friends amongst the savages nearby.' 'Plenty,' he said. 'They are simple people—and I want nothing, you know.' He stood biting his lip, then: 'I don't want any harm to happen to these whites here, but of course I was thinking of Mr. Kurtz's reputation—but you are a brother seaman and——' 'All right,' said I, after a time. 'Mr. Kurtz's reputation is safe with me.' I did not know how truly I spoke.

"He informed me, lowering his voice, that it was Kurtz who had ordered the attack to be made on the steamer. 'He hated sometimes the idea of being taken away—and then again . . . But I don't understand these matters. I am a simple man. He thought it would scare you away—that you would give it up, thinking him dead. I could not stop him. Oh, I had an awful time of it this last month.' 'Very well,' I said. 'He is all right now.' 'Ye-e-es,' he muttered, not very convinced apparently. 'Thanks,' said I; 'I shall keep my eyes open.' 'But quiet—eh?' he urged anxiously. 'It would be awful for his reputation if anybody here——' I promised a complete discretion with great gravity. 'I have a canoe and three black fellows waiting not very far. I am off. Could you give me a few Martini-Henry cartridges?' I could, and did, with proper secrecy. He helped himself, with a wink at me, to a handful of my tobacco. 'Between sailors—you know—good English tobacco.' At the door of the pilothouse he turned round— 'I say, haven't you a pair of shoes you could spare?' He raised one leg. 'Look.' The soles were tied with knotted strings sandal-wise under his bare feet. I rooted out an old pair, at which he looked with admiration before tucking it under his left arm. One of his pockets (bright red) was bulging with cartridges, from the other (dark blue) peeped 'Towson's Inquiry,' etc. etc. He seemed to think himself excellently well equipped for a renewed encounter with the wilderness. 'Ah! I'll never, never meet such a man again. You ought to have heard him recite poetry—his own too it was, he told me. Poetry!' He rolled his eyes at the recollection of these delights. 'Oh, he enlarged my mind!' 'Goodbye,' said I. He shook hands and vanished in the night. Sometimes I ask myself whether I had ever really seen him—whether it was possible to meet such a phenomenon! . . .

"When I woke up shortly after midnight his warning came to my mind with its hint of danger that seemed, in the starred darkness, real enough to make me get up for the purpose of having a look round. On the hill a big fire burned, illuminating fitfully a crooked corner of the station house. One of the agents with a picket of a few of our blacks, armed for the purpose, was keeping guard over the ivory; but deep within the forest, red gleams that wavered, that seemed to sink and rise from the ground amongst confused columnar shapes of intense blackness, showed the exact position of the camp where Mr. Kurtz's adorers were keeping their uneasy vigil. The monotonous beating of a big drum filled the air with muffled shocks and a lingering vibration. A steady droning sound of many men chanting each to himself some weird incantation came out from the black, flat wall of the woods as the humming of bees comes out of a hive, and had a strange narcotic effect upon my half-awake senses. I believe I dozed off leaning over the rail, till an abrupt burst of yells, an overwhelming outbreak of a pent-up and mysterious frenzy, woke me up in a bewildered wonder. It was cut short all at once, and the low droning went on with an effect of audible and soothing silence. I glanced casually into the little cabin. A light was burning within, but Mr. Kurtz was not there.

"I think I would have raised an outcry if I had believed my eyes. But I didn't believe them at first—the thing seemed so impossible. The fact is, I was completely unnerved by a sheer blank fright, pure abstract terror, unconnected with any distinct shape of physical danger. What made this emotion so overpowering was—how shall I define it?—the moral shock I received, as if something altogether monstrous, intolerable to thought and odious to the soul, had been thrust upon me unexpectedly. This lasted of course the merest fraction of a second, and then the usual sense of commonplace, deadly danger, the possibility of a sudden onslaught and massacre, or something of the kind, which I saw impending, was positively welcome and composing. It pacified me, in fact, so much, that I did not raise an alarm.

"There was an agent buttoned up inside an ulster and sleeping on a chair on deck within three feet of me. The yells had not awakened him; he snored very slightly; I left him to his slumbers and leaped ashore. I did not betray Mr. Kurtz—it was ordered I should never betray him—it was written I should be loyal to the nightmare of my choice. I was anxious to deal with this shadow by myself alone—and to this day I don't know why I was so jealous of sharing with anyone the peculiar blackness of that experience.

"As soon as I got on the bank I saw a trail—a broad trail through the grass. I remember the exultation with which I said to myself, 'He can't walk—he is crawling on all-fours—I've got him.' The grass was wet with dew. I strode rapidly with clenched fists. I fancy I had some vague notion of falling upon him and giving him a drubbing. I don't know. I had some imbecile thoughts. The knitting old woman with the cat obtruded herself upon my memory as a most improper person to be sitting at the other end of such an affair. I saw a row of pilgrims squirting lead in the air out of Winchesters held to the hip. I thought I would never get back to the steamer, and imagined myself living alone and unarmed in the woods to an advanced age. Such silly things—you know. And I remember I confounded the beat of the drum with the beating of my heart, and was pleased at its calm regularity.

"I kept to the track though—then stopped to listen. The night was very clear; a dark blue space, sparkling with dew and starlight, in which black things stood very still. I thought I could see a kind of motion ahead of me. I was strangely cocksure of everything that night. I actually left the track and ran in a wide semicircle (I verily believe chuckling to myself) so as to get in front of that stir, of that motion I had seen—if indeed I had seen anything. I was circumventing Kurtz as though it had been a boyish game.

"I came upon him, and, if he had not heard me coming, I would have fallen over him too, but he got up in time. He rose, unsteady, long, pale, indistinct, like a vapor exhaled by the earth, and swayed slightly, misty and silent before me; while at my back the fires loomed between the trees, and the murmur of many voices issued from the forest. I had cut him off cleverly; but when actually confronting him I seemed to come to my senses, I saw the danger in its right proportion. It was by no means over yet. Suppose he began to shout? Though he could hardly stand, there was still plenty of vigor in his voice. 'Go away—hide yourself,' he said, in that profound tone. It was very awful. I glanced back. We were within thirty yards from the nearest fire. A black figure stood up, strode on long black legs, waving long black arms, across the glow. It had horns—antelope horns, I think—on its head. Some sorcerer, some witch-man, no doubt: it looked fiend-like enough. 'Do you know what you are doing?' I whispered. 'Perfectly,' he answered, raising his voice for that single word: it sounded to me far off and yet loud, like a hail through a speaking-trumpet. If he makes a row we are lost, I thought to myself. This clearly was not a case for fisticuffs, even apart from the very natural aversion I had to beat that Shadow—this wandering and tormented thing. 'You will be lost,' I said—'utterly lost.' One gets sometimes such a flash of inspiration, you know. I did say the right thing, though indeed he could not have been more irretrievably lost than he was at this very moment, when the foundations of our intimacy were being laid—to endure—to endure—even to the end—even beyond.

"'I had immense plans,' he muttered irresolutely. 'Yes,' said I; 'but if you try to shout I'll smash your head with——' There was not a stick or a stone near. 'I will throttle you for good,' I corrected myself. 'I was on the threshold of great things,' he pleaded, in a voice of longing, with a wistfulness of tone that made my blood run cold. 'And now for this stupid scoundrel——' 'Your success in Europe is assured in any case,' I affirmed steadily. I did not want to have the throttling of him, you understand—and indeed it would have been very little use for any practical purpose. I tried to break the spell—the heavy, mute spell of the wilderness—that seemed to draw him to its pitiless breast by the awakening of forgotten and brutal instincts, by the memory of gratified and monstrous passions. This alone, I was convinced, had driven him out to the edge of the forest, to the bush, towards the gleam of fires, the throb of drums, the drone of weird incantations; this alone had beguiled his unlawful soul beyond the bounds of permitted aspirations. And, don't you see, the terror of the position was not in being knocked on the head—though I had a very lively sense of that danger too—but in this, that I had to deal with a being to whom I could not appeal in the name of anything high or low. I had, even like the niggers, to invoke him—himself—his own exalted and incredible degradation. There was nothing either above or below him, and I knew it. He had kicked himself loose of the earth. Confound the man! he had kicked the very earth to pieces. He was alone, and I before him did not know whether I stood on the ground or floated in the air. I've been telling you what we said—repeating the phrases we pronounced—but what's the good? They were common everyday words—the familiar, vague sounds exchanged on every waking day of life. But what of that? They had behind them, to my mind, the terrific suggestiveness of words heard in dreams, of phrases spoken in nightmares. Soul! If anybody had ever struggled with a soul, I am the man. And I wasn't arguing with a lunatic either. Believe me or not, his intelligence was perfectly clear—concentrated, it is true, upon himself with horrible intensity, yet dear; and therein was my only chance—barring of course, the killing him there and then, which wasn't so good, on account of unavoidable noise. But his soul was mad. Being alone in the wilderness, it had looked within itself, and, by Heavens! I tell you, it had gone mad. I had—for my sins, I suppose, to go through the ordeal of looking into it myself. No eloquence could have been so withering to one's belief in mankind as his final burst of sincerity. He struggled with himself too. I saw it—I heard it. I saw the inconceivable mystery of a soul that knew no restraint, no faith, and no fear, yet struggling blindly with itself. I kept my head pretty well; but when I had him at last stretched on the couch, I wiped my forehead, while my legs shook under me as though I had carried half a ton on my back down that hill. And yet I had only supported him, his bony arm clasped round my neck—and he was not much heavier than a child.

"When next day we left at noon, the crowd, of whose presence behind the curtain of trees I had been acutely conscious all the time, flowed out of the woods again, filled the clearing, covered the slope with a mass of naked, breathing, quivering, bronze bodies. I steamed up a bit, then swung downstream, and two thousand eyes followed the evolutions of the splashing, thumping, fierce river-demon beating the water with its terrible tail and breathing black smoke into the air. In front of the first rank, along the river, three men, plastered with bright red earth from head to foot, strutted to and fro restlessly. When we came abreast again, they faced the river, stamped their feet, nodded their horned heads, swayed their scarlet bodies; they shook towards the fierce river-demon a bunch of black feathers, a mangy skin with a pendent tail—something that looked like a dried gourd; they shouted periodically together strings of amazing words that resembled no sounds of human language; and the deep murmurs of the crowd, interrupted suddenly, were like the responses of some satanic litany.

"We had carried Kurtz into the pilothouse: there was more air there. Lying on the couch, he stared through the open shutter. There was an eddy in the mass of human bodies, and the woman with helmeted head and tawny cheeks rushed out to the very brink of the stream. She put out her hands, shouted something, and all that wild mob took up the shout in a roaring chorus of articulated, rapid, breathless utterance.

"'Do you understand this?' I asked.

"He kept on looking out past me with fiery, longing eyes, with a mingled expression of wistfulness and hate. He made no answer, but I saw a smile, a smile of indefinable meaning, appear on his colorless lips that a moment after twitched convulsively. 'Do I not?' he said slowly, gasping, as if the words had been torn out of him by a supernatural power.

"I pulled the string of the whistle, and I did this because I saw the pilgrims on deck getting out their rifles with an air of anticipating a jolly lark. At the sudden screech there was a movement of abject terror through that wedged mass of bodies. 'Don't! don't you frighten them away,' cried someone on deck disconsolately. I pulled the string time after time. They broke and ran, they leaped, they crouched, they swerved, they dodged the flying terror of the sound. The three red chaps had fallen flat, face down on the shore, as though they had been shot dead. Only the barbarous and superb woman did not so much as flinch, and stretched tragically her bare arms after us over the somber and glittering river.

"And then that imbecile crowd down on the deck started their little fun, and I could see nothing more for smoke.

"The brown current ran swiftly out of the heart of darkness, bearing us down towards the sea with twice the speed of our upward progress; and Kurtz's life was running swiftly too, ebbing, ebbing out of his heart into the sea of inexorable time.

The manager was very placid, he had no vital anxieties now, he took us both in with a comprehensive and satisfied glance: the 'affair' had come off as well as could be wished. I saw the time approaching when I would be left alone of the party of 'unsound method.' The pilgrims looked upon me with disfavor. I was, so to speak, numbered with the dead. It is strange how I accepted this unforeseen partnership, this choice of nightmares forced upon me in the tenebrous land invaded by these mean and greedy phantoms.

"Kurtz discoursed. A voice! a voice! It rang deep to the very last. It survived his strength to hide in the magnificent folds of eloquence the barren darkness of his heart. Oh, he struggled! he struggled! The wastes of his weary brain were haunted by shadowy images now—images of wealth and fame revolving obsequiously round his unextinguishable gift of noble and lofty expression. My Intended, my station, my career, my ideas—these were the subjects for the occasional utterances of elevated sentiments. The shade of the original Kurtz frequented the bedside of the hollow sham, whose fate it was to be buried presently in the mold of primeval earth. But both the diabolic love and the unearthly hate of the mysteries it had penetrated fought for the possession of that soul satiated with primitive emotions, avid of lying fame, of sham distinction, of all the appearances of success and power.

"Sometimes he was contemptibly childish. He desired to have kings meet him at railway stations on his return from some ghastly Nowhere, where he intended to accomplish great things. 'You show them you have in you something that is really profitable, and then there will be no limits to the recognition of your ability,' he would say. 'Of course you must take care of the motives—right motives—always.' The long reaches that were like one and the same reach, monotonous bends that were exactly alike, slipped past the steamer with their multitude of secular trees looking patiently after this grimy fragment of another world, the forerunner of change, of conquest, of trade, of massacres, of blessings. I looked ahead—piloting. 'Close the shutter,' said Kurtz suddenly one day; 'I can't bear look at this.' I did so. There was a silence. 'Oh, but I will wring your heart yet!' he cried at the invisible wilderness.

"We broke down—as I had expected—and had to lie up for repairs at the head of an island. This delay was the first thing that shook Kurtz's confidence. One morning he gave me a packet of papers and a photograph—the lot tied together with a shoestring. 'Keep this for me,' he said. 'This noxious fool' (meaning the manager) 'is capable of prying into my boxes when I am not looking.' In the afternoon I saw him. He was lying on his back with closed eyes, and I withdrew quietly, but I heard him mutter, 'Live rightly, die, die . . .' I listened. There was nothing more. Was he rehearsing some speech in his sleep, or was it a fragment of a phrase from some newspaper article? He had been writing for the papers and meant to do so again, 'for the furthering of my ideas. It's a duty.'

"His was an impenetrable darkness. I looked at him as you peer down at a man who is lying at the bottom of a precipice where the sun never shines. But I had not much time to give him, because I was helping the engine-driver to take to pieces the leaky cylinders, to straighten a bent connecting rod, and in other such matters. I lived in an infernal mess of rust, filings, nuts, bolts, spanners, hammers, ratchet-drills—things I abominate, because I don't get on with them. I tended the little forge we fortunately had aboard; I toiled wearily in a wretched scrapheap—unless I had the shakes too bad to stand.

"One evening coming in with a candle I was startled to hear him say a little tremulously, 'I am lying here in the dark waiting for death.' The light was within a foot of his eyes. I forced myself to murmur, 'Oh, nonsense!' and stood over him as if transfixed.

"Anything approaching the change that came over his features I have never seen before, and hope never to see again. Oh, I wasn't touched. I was fascinated. It was as though a veil had been rent. I saw on that ivory face the expression of somber pride, of ruthless power, of craven terror of an intense and hopeless despair. Did he live his life again in every detail of desire, temptation, and surrender during that supreme moment of complete knowledge? He cried in a whisper at some image, at some vision—he cried out twice, a cry that was no more than a breath:

"'The horror! The horror!'

"I blew the candle out and left the cabin. The pilgrims were dining in the mess-room, and I took my place opposite the manager, who lifted his eyes to give me a questioning glance, which I successfully ignored. He leaned back, serene, with that peculiar smile of his sealing the unexpressed depths of his meanness. A continuous shower of small flies streamed upon the lamp, upon the cloth, upon our hands and faces. Suddenly the manager's boy put his insolent black head in the doorway, and said in a tone of scathing contempt:

"'Mistah Kurtz—he dead.'

"All the pilgrims rushed out to see. I remained, and went on with my dinner. I believe I was considered brutally callous. However, I did not eat much. There was a lamp in there—light, don't you know—and outside it was so beastly, beastly dark. I went no more near the remarkable man who had pronounced a judgment upon the adventures of his soul on this earth. The voice was gone. What else had been there? But I am of course aware that next day the pilgrims buried something in a muddy hole.

"And then they very nearly buried me.

"However, as you see, I did not go to join Kurtz there and then. I did not. I remained to dream the nightmare out to the end, and to show my loyalty to Kurtz once more. Destiny. My destiny! Droll thing life is—that mysterious arrangement of merciless logic for a futile purpose. The most you can hope from it is some knowledge of yourself—that comes too late—a crop of unextinguishable regrets. I have wrestled with death. It is the most unexciting contest you can imagine. It takes place in an impalpable grayness, with nothing underfoot, with nothing around, without spectators, without clamor, without glory, without the great desire of victory, without the great fear of defeat, in a sickly atmosphere of tepid skepticism, without much belief in your own right, and still less in that of your adversary. If such is the form of ultimate wisdom, then life is a greater riddle than some of us think it to be. I was within a hair's-breadth of the last opportunity for pronouncement, and I found with humiliation that probably I would have nothing to say. This is the reason why I affirm that Kurtz was a remarkable man. He had something to say. He said it. Since I had peeped over the edge myself, I understand better the meaning of his stare, that could not see the flame of the candle, but was wide enough to embrace the whole universe, piercing enough to penetrate all the hearts that beat in the darkness. He had summed up—he had judged. 'The horror!' He was a remarkable man. After all, this was the expression of some sort of belief; it had candor, it had conviction, it had a vibrating note of revolt in its whisper, it had the appalling face of a glimpsed truth—the strange commingling of desire and hate. And it is not my own extremity I remember best—a vision of grayness without form filled with physical pain, and a careless contempt for the evanescence of all things even of this pain itself. No! It is his extremity that I seem to have lived through. True, he had made that last stride, he had stepped over the edge, while I had been permitted to draw back my hesitating foot. And perhaps in this is the whole difference; perhaps all the wisdom, and all truth, and all sincerity, are just compressed into that inappreciable moment of time in which we step over the threshold of the invisible. Perhaps! I like to think my summing-up would not have been a word of careless contempt. Better his cry—much better. It was an affirmation, a moral victory paid for by innumerable defeats, by abominable terrors, by abominable satisfactions. But it was a victory! That is why I have remained loyal to Kurtz to the last, and even beyond, when a long time after I heard once more, not his own voice, but the echo of his magnificent eloquence thrown to me from a soul as translucently pure as a cliff of crystal.

"No, they did not bury me, though there is a period of time which I remember mistily, with a shuddering wonder, like a passage through some inconceivable world that had no hope in it and no desire. I found myself back in the sepulchral city resenting the sight of people hurrying through the streets to filch a little money from each other, to devour their infamous cookery, to gulp their unwholesome beer, to dream their insignificant and silly dreams. They trespassed upon my thoughts. They were intruders whose knowledge of life was to me an irritating pretense, because I felt so sure they could not possibly know the things I knew. Their bearing, which was simply the bearing of commonplace individuals going about their business in the assurance of perfect safety, was offensive to me like the outrageous flauntings of folly in the face of a danger it is unable to comprehend. I had no particular desire to enlighten them, but I had some difficulty in restraining myself from laughing in their faces, so full of stupid importance. I daresay I was not very well at that time. I tottered about the streets—there were various affairs to settle—grinning bitterly at perfectly respectable persons. I admit my behavior was inexcusable, but then my temperature was seldom normal in these days. My dear aunt's endeavors to 'nurse up my strength' seemed altogether beside the mark. It was not my strength that wanted nursing, it was my imagination that wanted soothing. I kept the bundle of papers given me by Kurtz, not knowing exactly what to do with it. His mother had died lately, watched over, as I was told, by his Intended. A clean-shaved man, with an official manner and wearing gold-rimmed spectacles, called on me one day and made inquiries, at first circuitous, afterwards suavely pressing, about what he was pleased to denominate certain 'documents.' I was not surprised, because I had had two rows with the manager on the subject out there. I had refused to give up the smallest scrap out of that package, and I took the same attitude with the spectacled man. He became darkly menacing at last, and with much heat argued that the Company had the right to every bit of information about its 'territories.' And, said he, 'Mr. Kurtz's knowledge of unexplored regions must have been necessarily extensive and peculiar—owing to his great abilities and to the deplorable circumstances in which he had been placed: therefore——' I assured him Mr. Kurtz's knowledge, however extensive, did not bear upon the problems of commerce or administration. He invoked then the name of science. 'It would be an incalculable loss if,' etc. etc. I offered him the report on the 'Suppression of Savage Customs,' with the postscriptum torn off. He took it up eagerly, but ended by sniffing at it with an air of contempt. 'This is not what we had a right to expect,' he remarked. 'Expect nothing else,' I said. 'There are only private letters.' He withdrew upon some threat of legal proceedings, and I saw him no more; but another fellow, calling himself Kurtz's cousin, appeared two days later, and was anxious to hear all the details about his dear relative's last moments. Incidentally he gave me to understand that Kurtz had been essentially a great musician. 'There was the making of an immense success,' said the man, who was an organist, I believe, with lank gray hair flowing over a greasy coat collar. I had no reason to doubt his statement; and to this day I am unable to say what was Kurtz's profession, whether he ever had any—which was the greatest of his talents. I had taken him for a painter who wrote for the papers, or else for a journalist who could paint—but even the cousin (who took snuff during the interview) could not tell me what he had been exactly. He was a universal genius—on that point I agreed with the old chap, who thereupon blew his nose noisily into a large cotton handkerchief and withdrew in senile agitation, beating off some family letters and memoranda without importance. Ultimately a journalist anxious to know something of the fate of his 'dear colleague' turned up. This visitor informed me Kurtz's proper sphere ought to have been politics 'on the popular side.' He had furry straight eyebrows, bristly hair cropped short, an eyeglass on a broad ribbon, and, becoming expansive, confessed his opinion that Kurtz really couldn't write a bit—'but Heavens! how that man could talk! He electrified large meetings. He had faith—don't you see?—he had the faith. He could get himself to believe anything—anything. He would have been a splendid leader of an extreme party.' 'What party?' I asked. 'Any party,' answered the other. 'He was an—an—extremist.' Did I not think so? I assented. Did I know, he asked, with a sudden flash of curiosity, 'what it was that had induced him to go out there?' 'Yes,' said I, and forthwith handed him the famous Report for publication, if he thought fit. He glanced through it hurriedly, mumbling all the time, judged 'it would do,' and took himself off with this plunder.

"Thus I was left at last with a slim packet of letters and the girl's portrait. She struck me as beautiful—I mean she had a beautiful expression. I know that the sunlight can be made to lie too, yet one felt that no manipulation of light and pose could have conveyed the delicate shade of truthfulness upon those features. She seemed ready to listen without mental reservation, without suspicion, without a thought for herself. I concluded I would go and give her back her portrait and those letters myself. Curiosity? Yes; and also some other feeling perhaps. All that had been Kurtz's had passed out of my hands: his soul, his body, his station, his plans, his ivory, his career. There remained only his memory and his Intended—and I wanted to give that up too to the past, in a way—to surrender personally all that remained of him with me to that oblivion which is the last word of our common fate. I don't defend myself. I had no dear perception of what it was I really wanted. Perhaps it was an impulse of unconscious loyalty, or the fulfillment of one of those ironic necessities that lurk in the facts of human existence. I don't know. I can't tell. But I went.

"I thought his memory was like the other memories of the dead that accumulate in every man's life—a vague impress on the brain of shadows that had fallen on it in their swift and final passage; but before the high and ponderous door, between the tall houses of a street as still and decorous as a well-kept alley in a cemetery, I had a vision of him on the stretcher, opening his mouth voraciously, as if to devour all the earth with all its mankind. He lived then before me; he lived as much as he had ever lived—a shadow insatiable of splendid appearances, of frightful realities; a shadow darker than the shadow of the night, and draped nobly in the folds of a gorgeous eloquence. The vision seemed to enter the house with me—the stretcher, the phantom-bearers, the wild crowd of obedient worshippers, the gloom of the forests, the glitter of the reach between the murky bends, the beat of the drum, regular and muffled like the beating of a heart—the heart of a conquering darkness. It was a moment of triumph for the wilderness, an invading and vengeful rush which, it seemed to me, I would have to keep back alone for the salvation of another soul. And the memory of what I had heard him say afar there, with the horned shapes stirring at my back, in the glow of fires, within the patient woods, those broken phrases came back to me, were heard again in their ominous and terrifying simplicity. I remembered his abject pleading, his abject threats, the colossal scale of his vile desires, the meanness, the torment, the tempestuous anguish of his soul. And later on I seemed to see his collected languid manner, when he said one day, 'This lot of ivory now is really mine. The Company did not pay for it. I collected it myself at a very great personal risk. I am afraid they will try to claim it as theirs though. H'm. It is a difficult case. What do you think I ought to do—resist? Eh? I want no more than justice.' . . . He wanted no more than justice—no more than justice. I rang the bell before a mahogany door on the first floor, and while I waited he seemed to stare at me out of the glassy panel—stare with that wide and immense stare embracing, condemning, loathing all the universe. I seemed to hear the whispered cry, 'The horror! The horror!'

"The dusk was falling. I had to wait in a lofty drawing room with three long windows from floor to ceiling that were like three luminous and bedraped columns. The bent gilt legs and backs of the furniture shone in indistinct curves. The tall marble fireplace had a cold and monumental whiteness. A grand piano stood massively in a corner; with dark gleams on the flat surfaces like a somber and polished sarcophagus. A high door opened—closed. I rose.

"She came forward, all in black, with a pale head, floating towards me in the dusk. She was in mourning. It was more than a year since his death, more than a year since the news came; she seemed as though she would remember and mourn forever. She took both my hands in hers and murmured, 'I had heard you were coming.' I noticed she was not very young—I mean not girlish. She had a mature capacity for fidelity, for belief, for suffering. The room seemed to have grown darker, as if all the sad light of the cloudy evening had taken refuge on her forehead. This fair hair, this pale visage, this pure brow, seemed surrounded by an ashy halo from which the dark eyes looked out at me. Their glance was guileless, profound, confident, and trustful. She carried her sorrowful head as though she were proud of that sorrow, as though she would say, I—I alone know how to mourn for him as he deserves. But while we were still shaking hands, such a look of awful desolation came upon her face that I perceived she was one of those creatures that are not the playthings of Time. For her he had died only yesterday. And, by Jove! the impression was so powerful that for me too he seemed to have died only yesterday—nay, this very minute. I saw her and him in the same instant of time—his death and her sorrow—I saw her sorrow in the very moment of his death. Do you understand? I saw them together—I heard them together. She had said, with a deep catch of the breath, 'I have survived'; while my strained ears seemed to hear distinctly, mingled with her tone of despairing regret, the summing-up whisper of his eternal condemnation. I asked myself what I was doing there, with a sensation of panic in my heart as though I had blundered into a place of cruel and absurd mysteries not fit for a human being to behold. She motioned me to a chair. We sat down. I laid the packet gently on the little table, and she put her hand over it. . . . 'You knew him well,' she murmured, after a moment of mourning silence.

"'Intimacy grows quickly out there,' I said. 'I knew him as well as it is possible for one man to know another.'

"'And you admired him,' she said. 'It was impossible to know him and not to admire him. Was it?'

"'He was a remarkable man,' I said unsteadily. Then before the appealing fixity of her gaze, that seemed to watch for more words on my lips, I went on, 'It was impossible not to——'

"'Love him,' she finished eagerly, silencing me into an appalled dumbness. 'How true! how true! But when you think that no one knew him so well as I! I had all his noble confidence. I knew him best.'

"'You knew him best,' I repeated. And perhaps she did. But with every word spoken the room was growing darker, and only her forehead, smooth and white, remained illumined by the unextinguishable light of belief and love.

"'You were his friend,' she went on. 'His friend,' she repeated, a little louder. 'You must have been, if he had given you this, and sent you to me. I feel I can speak to you—and oh! I must speak. I want you—you who have heard his last words—to know I have been worthy of him. . . . It is not pride. . . . Yes! I am proud to know I understood him better than anyone on earth—he told me so himself. And since his mother died I have had no one—no one—to—to——'

"I listened. The darkness deepened. I was not even sure whether he had given me the right bundle. I rather suspect he wanted me to take care of another batch of his papers which, after his death, I saw the manager examining under the lamp. And the girl talked, easing her pain in the certitude of my sympathy; she talked as thirsty men drink. I had heard that her engagement with Kurtz had been disapproved by her people. He wasn't rich enough or something. And indeed I don't know whether he had not been a pauper all his life. He had given me some reason to infer that it was his impatience of comparative poverty that drove him out there.

"'. . . Who was not his friend who had heard him speak once?' she was saying. 'He drew men towards him by what was best in them.' She looked at me with intensity. 'It is the gift of the great,' she went on, and the sound of her low voice seemed to have the accompaniment of all the other sounds, full of mystery, desolation, and sorrow, I had ever heard—the ripple of the river, the soughing of the trees swayed by the wind, the murmurs of the crowds, the faint ring of incomprehensible words cried from afar, the whisper of a voice speaking from beyond the threshold of an eternal darkness. 'But you have heard him! You know!' she cried.

"'Yes, I know,' I said with something like despair in my heart, but bowing my head before the faith that was in her, before that great and saving illusion that shone with an unearthly glow in the darkness, in the triumphant darkness from which I could not have defended her—from which I could not even defend myself.

"'What a loss to me—to us!'—she corrected herself with beautiful generosity; then added in a murmur, 'To the world.' By the last gleams of twilight I could see the glitter of her eyes, full of tears—of tears that would not fall.

"'I have been very happy—very fortunate—very proud,' she went on. 'Too fortunate. Too happy for a little while. And now I am unhappy for—for life.'

"She stood up; her fair hair seemed to catch all the remaining light in a glimmer of gold. I rose too.

"'And of all this,' she went on mournfully, 'of all his promise, and of all his greatness, of his generous mind, of his noble heart, nothing remains—nothing but a memory. You and I——'

"'We shall always remember him,' I said hastily.

"'No!' she cried. 'It is impossible that all this should be lost—that such a life should be sacrificed to leave nothing—but sorrow. You know what vast plans he had. I knew of them too—I could not perhaps understand—but others knew of them. Something must remain. His words, at least, have not died.'

"'His words will remain,' I said.

"'And his example,' she whispered to herself. 'Men looked up to him—his goodness shone in every act. His example——'

"'True,' I said; 'his example too. Yes, his example. I forgot that.'

"'But I do not. I cannot—I cannot believe—not yet. I cannot believe that I shall never see him again, that nobody will see him again, never, never, never.'

"She put out her arms as if after a retreating figure, stretching them back and with clasped pale hands across the fading and narrow sheen of the window. Never see him! I saw him clearly enough then. I shall see this eloquent phantom as long as I live, and I shall see her too, a tragic and familiar Shade, resembling in this gesture another one, tragic also, and bedecked with powerless charms, stretching bare brown arms over the glitter of the infernal stream, the stream of darkness. She said suddenly very low, 'He died as he lived.'

"'His end,' said I, with dull anger stirring in me, 'was in every way worthy of his life.'

"'And I was not with him,' she murmured. My anger subsided before a feeling of infinite pity.

"'Everything that could be done——' I mumbled.

"'Ah, but I believed in him more than anyone on earth—more than his own mother, more than—himself. He needed me! Me! I would have treasured every sigh, every word, every sign, even glance.'

"I felt like a chill grip on my chest. 'Don't,' I said, in a muffled voice.

"'Forgive me. I—I—have mourned so long in silence—in silence. . . . You were with him—to the last? I think of his loneliness. Nobody near to understand him as I would have understood. Perhaps no one to hear . . .'

"'To the very end,' I said shakily. 'I heard his very last words. . . .' I stopped in a fright.

"'Repeat them,' she murmured in a heartbroken tone. 'I want—I want—something—something—to—to live with.'

"I was on the point of crying at her, 'Don't you hear them?' The dusk was repeating them in a persistent whisper all around us, in a whisper that seemed to swell menacingly like the first whisper of a rising wind. 'The horror! The horror!'

"'His last word—to live with,' she insisted. 'Don't you understand I loved him—I loved him—I loved him!'

"I pulled myself together and spoke slowly.

"'The last word he pronounced was—your name.'

"I heard a light sigh and then my heart stood still, stopped dead short by an exulting and terrible cry, by the cry of inconceivable triumph and of unspeakable pain. 'I knew it—I was sure!' . . . She knew. She was sure. I heard her weeping; she had hidden her face in her hands. It seemed to me that the house would collapse before I could escape, that the heavens would fall upon my head. But nothing happened. The heavens do not fall for such a trifle. Would they have fallen, I wonder, if I had rendered Kurtz that justice which was his due? Hadn't he said he wanted only justice? But I couldn't. I could not tell her. It would have been too dark—too dark altogether. . . ."

Marlow ceased, and sat apart, indistinct and silent, in the pose of a meditating Buddha. Nobody moved for a time. "We have lost the first of the ebb," said the Director suddenly. I raised my head. The offing was barred by a black bank of clouds, and the tranquil waterway leading to the uttermost ends of the earth flowed somber under an overcast sky—seemed to lead into the heart of an immense darkness.

Lord Jim

A ROMANCE

To
Mr. and Mrs. G.F.W. Hope
With Grateful Affection
After Many Years of Friendship

AUTHOR'S NOTE

When this novel first appeared in book form a notion got about that I had been bolted away with. Some reviewers maintained that the work starting as a short story had got beyond the writer's control. One or two discovered internal evidence of the fact, which seemed to amuse them. They pointed out the limitations of the narrative form. They argued that no man could have been expected to talk all that time, and other men to listen so long. It was not, they said, very credible.

After thinking it over for something like sixteen years, I am not so sure about that. Men have been known, both in the tropics and in the temperate zone, to sit up half the night "swapping yarns." This, however, is but one yarn, yet with interruptions affording some measure of relief; and in regard to the listeners' endurance, the postulate must be accepted that the story *was* interesting. It is the necessary preliminary assumption. If I hadn't believed that it *was* interesting I could never have begun to write it. As to the mere physical possibility, we all know that some speeches in Parliament have taken nearer six than three hours in delivery; whereas all that part of the book which is Marlow's narrative can be read through aloud, I should say, in less than three hours. Besides—though I have kept strictly all such insignificant details out of the tale—we may presume that there must have been refreshments on that night, a glass of mineral water of some sort to help the narrator on.

But, seriously, the truth of the matter is, that my first thought was of a short story, concerned only with the pilgrim ship episode; nothing more. And that was a legitimate conception. After writing a few pages, however, I became for some reason discontented and I laid them aside for a time. I didn't take them out of the drawer till the late Mr. William Blackwood suggested I should give something again to his magazine.

It was only then that I perceived that the pilgrim ship episode was a good starting point for a free and wandering tale; that it was an event, too, which could conceivably color the whole "sentiment of existence" in a simple and sensitive character. But all these preliminary moods and stirrings of spirit were rather obscure at the time, and they do not appear clearer to me now after the lapse of so many years.

The few pages I had laid aside were not without their weight in the choice of subject. But the whole was rewritten deliberately. When I sat down to it I knew it would be a long book, though I didn't foresee that it would spread itself over thirteen numbers of "Maga."

I have been asked at times whether this was not the book of mine I liked best. I am a great foe to favoritism in public life, in private life, and even in the delicate relationship of an author to his works. As a matter of principle I will have no favorites; but I don't go so far as to feel grieved and annoyed by the preference some people give to my *Lord Jim*. I won't even say that I "fail to understand . . ." No! But once I had occasion to be puzzled and surprised.

A friend of mine returning from Italy had talked with a lady there who did not like the book. I regretted that, of course, but what surprised me was the ground of her dislike. "You know," she said, "it is all so morbid."

The pronouncement gave me food for an hour's anxious thought. Finally I arrived at the conclusion that, making due allowances for the subject itself being rather foreign to women's normal sensibilities, the lady could not have been an Italian. I wonder whether she was European at all? In any case, no Latin temperament would have perceived anything morbid in the acute consciousness of lost honor. Such a consciousness may be wrong, or it may be right, or it may be condemned as artificial; and, perhaps, my Jim is not a type of wide commonness. But I can safely assure my readers that he is not the product of coldly perverted thinking. He is not a figure of Northern Mists either. One sunny morning in the commonplace surroundings of an Eastern roadstead, I saw his form pass by—appealing—significant—under a cloud—perfectly silent. Which is as it should be. It was for me, with all the sympathy of which I was capable, to seek fit words for his meaning. He was "one of us."

                                                                                                J.C.

June 1917

❧ 1 ❧

He was an inch, perhaps two, under six feet, powerfully built, and he advanced straight at you with a slight stoop of the shoulders, head forward, and a fixed from-under stare which made you think of a charging bull. His voice was deep, loud, and his manner displayed a kind of dogged self-assertion which had nothing aggressive in it. It seemed a necessity, and it was directed apparently as much at himself as at anybody else. He was spotlessly neat, appareled in immaculate white from shoes to hat, and in the various Eastern ports where he got his living as ship chandler's water-clerk he was very popular.

A water-clerk need not pass an examination in anything under the sun, but he must have Ability in the abstract and demonstrate it practically. His work consists in racing under sail, steam, or oars against other water-clerks for any ship about to anchor, greeting her captain cheerily, forcing upon him a card—the business card of the ship chandler—and on his first visit on shore piloting him firmly but without ostentation to a vast, cavern-like shop which is full of things that are eaten and drunk on board ship; where you can get everything to make her seaworthy and beautiful, from a set of chain-hooks for her cable to a book of gold leaf for the carvings of her stern; and where her commander is received like a brother by a ship chandler he has never seen before. There is a cool parlor, easy chairs, bottles, cigars, writing implements, a copy of harbor regulations, and a warmth of welcome that melts the salt of a three months' passage out of a seaman's heart. The connection thus begun is kept up, as long as the ship remains in harbor, by the daily visits of the water-clerk. To the captain he is faithful like a friend and attentive like a son, with the patience of Job, the unselfish devotion of a woman, and the jollity of a boon companion. Later on the bill is sent in. It is a beautiful and humane occupation. Therefore good water-clerks are scarce. When a water-clerk who possesses Ability in the abstract has also the advantage of having been brought up to the sea, he is worth to his employer a lot of money and some humoring. Jim had always good wages and as much humoring as would have bought the fidelity of a fiend. Nevertheless, with black ingratitude he would throw up the job suddenly and depart. To his employers the reasons he gave were

75

obviously inadequate. They said "Confounded fool!" as soon as his back was turned. This was their criticism on his exquisite sensibility.

To the white men in the waterside business and to the captains of ships he was just Jim—nothing more. He had, of course, another name, but he was anxious that it should not be pronounced. His incognito, which had as many holes as a sieve, was not meant to hide a personality but a fact. When the fact broke through the incognito he would leave suddenly the seaport where he happened to be at the time and go to another—generally farther east. He kept to seaports because he was a seaman in exile from the sea, and had Ability in the abstract, which is good for no other work but that of a water-clerk. He retreated in good order towards the rising sun, and the fact followed him casually but inevitably. Thus in the course of years he was known successively in Bombay, in Calcutta, in Rangoon, in Penang, in Batavia—and in each of these halting places was just Jim the water-clerk. Afterwards, when his keen perception of the Intolerable drove him away for good from seaports and white men, even into the virgin forest, the Malays of the jungle village, where he had elected to conceal his deplorable faculty, added a word to the monosyllable of his incognito. They called him Tuan Jim: as one might say— Lord Jim.

Originally he came from a parsonage. Many commanders of fine merchant ships come from these abodes of piety and peace. Jim's father possessed such certain knowledge of the Unknowable as made for the righteousness of people in cottages without disturbing the ease of mind of those whom an unerring Providence enables to live in mansions. The little church on a hill had the mossy grayness of a rock seen through a ragged screen of leaves. It had stood there for centuries, but the trees around probably remembered the laying of the first stone. Below, the red front of the rectory gleamed with a warm tint in the midst of grassplots, flowerbeds, and fir trees, with an orchard at the back, a paved stable yard to the left, and the sloping glass of greenhouses tacked along a wall of bricks. The living had belonged to the family for generations, but Jim was one of five sons, and when after a course of light holiday literature his vocation for the sea had declared itself, he was sent at once to a "training ship for officers of the mercantile marine."

He learned there a little trigonometry and how to cross topgallant yards. He was generally liked. He had the third place in navigation and pulled stroke in the first cutter. Having a steady head with an excellent physique, he was very smart aloft. His station was in the foretop, and often from there he looked down, with the contempt of a man destined to shine in the midst of dangers, at the peaceful multitude of roofs cut in two by the brown tide of the stream, while scattered on the outskirts of the surrounding plain the factory chimneys rose perpendicular against a grimy sky, each slender like a pencil, and belching out smoke like a volcano. He could see the big ships departing, the broad-beamed ferries constantly on the move, the little boats floating far below his feet, with the hazy splendor of the sea in the distance, and the hope of a stirring life in the world of adventure.

On the lower deck in the babel of two hundred voices he would forget himself, and beforehand live in his mind the sea-life of light literature. He saw himself saving people from sinking ships, cutting away masts in a hurricane, swimming through a surf with a line; or as a lonely castaway, barefooted and half naked, walking on uncovered reefs in search of shellfish to stave off starvation. He confronted savages on tropical shores, quelled mutinies on the high seas, and in a small boat upon the ocean kept up the hearts of despairing men—always an example of devotion to duty, and as unflinching as a hero in a book.

"Something's up. Come along."

He leaped to his feet. The boys were streaming up the ladders. Above could be heard a great scurrying about and shouting, and when he got through the hatchway he stood still—as if confounded.

It was the dusk of a winter's day. The gale had freshened since noon, stopping the traffic on the river, and now blew with the strength of a hurricane in fitful bursts that boomed like salvoes of great guns firing over the ocean. The rain slanted in sheets that flicked and subsided, and between whiles Jim had threatening glimpses of the tumbling tide, the small craft jumbled and tossing along the shore, the motionless buildings in the driving mist, the broad ferryboats pitching ponderously at anchor, the vast landing stages heaving up and down and smothered in sprays. The next gust seemed to blow all this away. The air was full of flying water. There was a fierce purpose in the gale, a furious earnestness in the screech of the wind, in the brutal tumult of earth and sky, that seemed directed at him, and made him hold his breath in awe. He stood still. It seemed to him he was whirled around.

He was jostled. "Man the cutter!" Boys rushed past him. A coaster running in for shelter had crashed through a schooner at anchor, and one of the ship's instructors had seen the accident. A mob of boys clambered on the rails, clustered round the davits. "Collision. Just ahead of us. Mr. Symons saw it." A push made him stagger against the mizzenmast, and he caught hold of a rope. The old training ship chained to her moorings quivered all over, bowing gently head to wind, and with her scanty rigging humming in a deep bass the breathless song of her youth at sea. "Lower away!" He saw the boat, manned, drop swiftly below the rail, and rushed after her. He heard a splash. "Let go; clear the falls!" He leaned over. The river alongside seethed in frothy streaks. The cutter could be seen in the falling darkness under the spell of tide and wind, that for a moment held her bound, and tossing abreast of the ship. A yelling voice in her reached him faintly:

"Keep stroke, you young whelps, if you want to save anybody! Keep stroke!" And suddenly she lifted high her bow, and, leaping with raised oars over a wave, broke the spell cast upon her by the wind and tide.

Jim felt his shoulder gripped firmly. "Too late youngster." The captain of the ship laid a restraining hand on that boy, who seemed on the point of leaping overboard, and Jim looked up with the pain of conscious defeat in his eyes. The captain smiled sympathetically. "Better luck next time. This will teach you to be smart."

A shrill cheer greeted the cutter. She came dancing back half full of water, and with two exhausted men washing about on her bottom boards. The tumult and the menace of wind and sea now appeared very contemptible to Jim, increasing the regret of his awe at their inefficient menace. Now he knew what to think of it. It seemed to him he cared nothing for the gale. He could affront greater perils. He would do so—better than anybody. Not a particle of fear was left. Nevertheless he brooded apart that evening while the bowman of the cutter—a boy with a face like a girl's and big gray eyes—was the hero of the lower deck. Eager questioners crowded round him. He narrated: "I just saw his head bobbing, and I dashed my boathook in the water. It caught in his breeches and I nearly went overboard, as I thought I would, only old Symons let go the tiller and grabbed my legs—the boat nearly swamped. Old Symons is a fine old chap. I don't mind a bit him being grumpy with us. He swore at me all the time he held my leg, but that was only his way of telling me to stick to the boathook. Old Symons is awfully excitable—isn't he? No—not the little fair chap—the other, the big one with a beard. When we pulled him in he groaned,'Oh, my leg! oh, my leg!' and turned up his eyes. Fancy such a big chap fainting like a girl. Would any of you fellows faint for a jab with a boathook? I wouldn't. It went into his leg so far." He showed the boathook, which he had carried below for the purpose, and produced a sensation. "No silly! It was not his flesh that held him—his breeches did. Lots of blood, of course."

Jim thought it a pitiful display of vanity. The gale had ministered to a heroism as spurious as its own pretense of terror. He felt angry with the brutal tumult of earth and sky for taking him unawares and checking unfairly a generous readiness for narrow escapes. Otherwise he was rather glad he had not gone into the cutter, since a lower achievement had served the turn. He had enlarged his knowledge more than those who had done the work. When all men flinched, then—he felt sure—he alone would know how to deal with the spurious menace of wind and seas. He knew what to think of it. Seen dispassionately, it seemed contemptible. He could detect no trace of emotion in himself, and the final effect of a staggering event was that, unnoticed and apart from the noisy crowd of boys, he exulted with fresh certitude in his avidity for adventure, and in a sense of many-sided courage.

❦ 2 ❦

After two years of training he went to sea, and entering the regions so well known to his imagination, found them strangely barren of adventure. He made many voyages. He knew the magic monotony of existence between sky and water: he had to bear the criticism of men, the exactions of the sea, and the prosaic severity of the daily task that gives bread—but whose only reward is in the perfect love of the work. This reward eluded him. Yet he could not go back, because there is nothing more enticing, disenchanting, and enslaving than the life at sea. Besides, his prospects were good. He was gentlemanly, steady, tractable, with a thorough knowledge of his duties; and in time, when yet very young, he became chief mate of a fine ship, without ever having been tested by those events of the sea that show in the light of day the inner worth of a man, the edge of his temper, and the fiber of his stuff; that reveal the quality of his resistance and the secret truth of his pretenses, not only to others but also to himself.

Only once in all that time he had again the glimpse of the earnestness in the anger of the sea. That truth is not so often made apparent as people might think. There are many shades in the danger of adventures and gales, and it is only now and then that there appears on the face of facts a sinister violence of intention—that indefinable something which forces it upon the mind and the heart of a man that this complication of accidents or these elemental furies are coming at him with a purpose of malice, with a strength beyond control, with an unbridled cruelty that means to tear out of him his hope and his fear, the pain of his fatigue and his longing for rest: which means to smash, to destroy, to annihilate all he had seen, known, loved, enjoyed, or hated; all that is priceless and necessary—the sunshine, the memories, the future—which means to sweep the whole precious world utterly away from his sight by the simple and appalling act of taking his life.

Jim, disabled by a falling spar at the beginning of a week of which his Scottish captain used to say afterwards, "Man! it's a pairfect meeracle to me how she lived through it!" spent many days stretched on his back, dazed, battered, hopeless, and tormented as if at the bottom of an abyss of unrest. He did not care what the end would be, and in his lucid moments overvalued his indifference. The danger, when not seen, has the imperfect vagueness of human thought. The fear grows shadowy;

and Imagination, the enemy of men, the father of all terrors, unstimulated, sinks to rest in the dullness of exhausted emotion. Jim saw nothing but the disorder of his tossed cabin. He lay there battened down in the midst of a small devastation, and felt secretly glad he had not to go on deck. But now and again an uncontrollable rush of anguish would grip him bodily, make him gasp and writhe under the blankets, and then the unintelligent brutality of an existence liable to the agony of such sensations filled him with a despairing desire to escape at any cost. Then fine weather returned, and he thought no more about it.

His lameness, however, persisted, and when the ship arrived at an Eastern port he had to go to the hospital. His recovery was slow, and he was left behind.

There were only two other patients in the white men's ward: the purser of a gunboat, who had broken his leg falling down a hatchway; and a kind of railway contractor from a neighboring province afflicted by some mysterious tropical disease, who held the doctor for an ass, and indulged in secret debaucheries of patent medicine which his Tamil servant used to smuggle in with unwearied devotion. They told each other the story of their lives, played cards a little, or, yawning and in pajamas, lounged through the day in easy chairs without saying a word. The hospital stood on a hill, and a gentle breeze entering through the windows, always flung wide open, brought into the bare room the softness of the sky, the languor of the earth, the bewitching breath of the Eastern waters. There were perfumes in it, suggestions of infinite repose, the gift of endless dreams. Jim looked every day over the thickets of gardens, beyond the roofs of the town, over the fronds of palms growing on the shore, at that roadstead which is a thoroughfare to the East—at the roadstead dotted by garlanded islets, lighted by festal sunshine, its ships like toys, its brilliant activity resembling a holiday pageant, with the eternal serenity of the Eastern sky overhead and the smiling peace of the Eastern seas possessing the space as far as the horizon.

Directly he could walk without a stick, he descended into the town to look for some opportunity to get home. Nothing offered just then, and, while waiting, he associated naturally with the men of his calling in the port. These were of two kinds. Some, very few and seen there but seldom, led mysterious lives, had preserved an undefaced energy with the temper of buccaneers and the eyes of dreamers. They appeared to live in a crazy maze of plans, hopes, dangers, enterprises, ahead of civilization, in the dark places of the sea; and their death was the only event of their fantastic existence that seemed to have a reasonable certitude of achievement. The majority were men who like himself, thrown there by some accident, had remained as officers of country ships. They had now a horror of the home service, with its harder conditions, severer view of duty, and the hazard of stormy oceans. They were attuned to the eternal peace of Eastern sky and sea. They loved short passages, good deck chairs, large native crews, and the distinction of being white. They shuddered at the thought of hard work, and led precariously easy lives, always on the verge of dismissal, always on the verge of engagement, serving Chinamen, Arabs, half-castes—would have served the devil himself had he made it easy enough. They talked everlastingly of turns of luck: how So-and-so got charge of a boat on the coast of China—a soft thing; how this one had an easy billet in Japan somewhere, and that one was doing well in the Siamese navy; and in all they said—in their actions, in their looks, in their persons—could be detected the soft spot, the place of decay, the determination to lounge safely through existence.

To Jim that gossiping crowd, viewed as seamen, seemed at first more unsubstantial than so many shadows. But at length he found a fascination in the sight of those men, in their appearance of doing so well on such a small allowance of danger and toil. In time, beside the original disdain, there grew up slowly another sentiment; and suddenly, giving up the idea of going home, he took a berth as chief mate of the *Patna*.

The *Patna* was a local steamer as old as the hills, lean like a greyhound, and eaten up with rust worse than a condemned water tank. She was owned by a Chinaman, chartered by an Arab, and commanded by a sort of renegade New South Wales German, very anxious to curse publicly his native country, but who, apparently on the strength of Bismarck's victorious policy, brutalized all those he was not afraid of, and wore a "blood-and-iron" air, combined with a purple nose and a red moustache. After she had been painted outside and whitewashed inside, eight hundred pilgrims (more or less) were driven on board of her as she lay with steam up alongside a wooden jetty.

They streamed aboard over three gangways, they streamed in urged by faith and the hope of paradise, they streamed in with a continuous tramp and shuffle of bare feet, without a word, a murmur, or a look back; and when clear of confining rails spread on all sides over the deck, flowed forward and aft, overflowed down the yawning hatchways, filled the inner recesses of the ship—like water filling a cistern, like water flowing into crevices and crannies, like water rising silently even with the rim. Eight hundred men and women with faith and hopes, with affections and memories, they had collected there, coming from north and south and from the outskirts of the East, after treading the jungle paths, descending the rivers, coasting in praus along the shallows, crossing in small canoes from island to island, passing through suffering, meeting strange sights, beset by strange fears, upheld by one desire. They came from solitary huts in the wilderness, from populous campongs, from villages by the sea. At the call of an idea they had left their forests, their clearings, the protection of their rulers, their prosperity, their poverty, the surroundings of their youth and the graves of their fathers. They came covered with dust, with sweat, with grime, with rags—the strong men at the head of family parties, the lean old men pressing forward without hope of return; young boys with fearless eyes glancing curiously, shy little girls with tumbled long hair; the timid women muffled up and clasping to their breasts, wrapped in loose ends of soiled head-cloths, their sleeping babies, the unconscious pilgrims of an exacting belief.

"Look at dese cattle," said the German skipper to his new chief mate.

An Arab, the leader of that pious voyage, came last. He walked slowly aboard, handsome and grave in his white gown and large turban. A string of servants followed, loaded with his luggage; the *Patna* cast off and backed away from the wharf.

She was headed between two small islets, crossed obliquely the anchoring-ground of sailing ships, swung through half a circle in the shadow of a hill, then ranged close to a ledge of foaming reefs. The Arab, standing up aft, recited aloud the prayer of travelers by sea. He invoked the favor of the Most High upon that journey, implored His blessing on men's toil and on the secret purposes of their hearts; the steamer pounded in the dusk the calm water of the Strait; and far astern of the pilgrim ship a screw-pile lighthouse, planted by unbelievers on a treacherous shoal, seemed to wink at her its eye of flame, as if in derision of her errand of faith.

She cleared the Straits, crossed the bay, continued on her way through the "One-degree" passage. She held on straight for the Red Sea under a serene sky, under a sky scorching and unclouded, enveloped in a fulgor of sunshine that killed all thought, oppressed the heart, withered all impulses of strength and energy. And under the sinister splendor of that sky the sea, blue and profound, remained still, without a stir, without a ripple, without a wrinkle—viscous, stagnant, dead. The *Patna*, with a slight hiss, passed over that plain luminous and smooth, unrolled a black ribbon of smoke across the sky, left behind her on the water a white ribbon of foam that vanished at once, like the phantom of a track drawn upon a lifeless sea by the phantom of a steamer.

Every morning the sun, as if keeping pace in his revolutions with the progress of the pilgrimage, emerged with a silent burst of light exactly at the same distance astern of the ship, caught up with her at noon, pouring the concentrated fire of his rays on the pious purposes of the men, glided past on his descent, and sank mysteriously into the sea evening after evening, preserving the same distance ahead of her advancing bows. The five whites on board lived amidships, isolated from the human cargo. The awnings covered the deck with a white roof from stem to stern, and a faint hum, a low murmur of sad voices, alone revealed the presence of a crowd of people upon the great blaze of the ocean. Such were the days, still, hot, heavy, disappearing one by one into the past, as if falling into an abyss forever open in the wake of the ship; and the ship, lonely under a wisp of smoke, held on her steadfast way black and smoldering in a luminous immensity, as if scorched by a flame flicked at her from a heaven without pity. The nights descended on her like a benediction.

❧ 3 ❧

A marvelous stillness pervaded the world, and the stars, together with the serenity of their rays, seemed to shed upon the earth the assurance of everlasting security. The young moon, recurved, and shining low in the west, was like a slender shaving thrown up from a bar of gold, and the Arabian Sea, smooth and cool to the eye like a sheet of ice, extended its perfect level to the perfect circle of a dark horizon. The propeller turned without a check, as though its beat had been part of the scheme of a safe universe; and on each side of the *Patna* two deep folds of water, permanent and somber on the unwrinkled shimmer, enclosed within their straight and diverging ridges a few white swirls of foam bursting in a low hiss, a few wavelets, a few ripples, a few undulations that, left behind, agitated the surface of the sea for an instant after the passage of the ship, subsided splashing gently, calmed down at last into the circular stillness of water and sky with the black speck of the moving hull remaining everlastingly in its center.

Jim on the bridge was penetrated by the great certitude of unbounded safety and peace that could be read on the silent aspect of nature like the certitude of fostering love upon the placid tenderness of a mother's face. Below the roof of awnings, surrendered to the wisdom of white men and to their courage, trusting the power of their unbelief and the iron shell of their fire ship, the pilgrims of an exacting faith slept on mats, on blankets, on bare planks, on every deck, in all the dark corners, wrapped in dyed cloths, muffled in soiled rags, with their heads resting on small bundles, with their faces pressed to bent forearms: the men, the women, the children; the old with the young, the decrepit with the lusty—all equal before sleep, death's brother.

A draught of air, fanned from forward by the speed of the ship, passed steadily through the long gloom between the high bulwarks, swept over the rows of prone bodies; a few dim flames in globe-lamps were hung short here and there under the ridge-poles, and in the blurred circles of light thrown down and trembling slightly to the unceasing vibration of the ship appeared a chin upturned, two closed eyelids, a dark hand with silver rings, a meager limb draped in a torn covering, a head bent back, a naked foot, a throat bared and stretched as if offering itself to the knife. The well-to-do had made for their families shelters with heavy boxes and dusty mats; the poor reposed side by side with all they had on earth tied up in a rag under their heads; the lone old men slept, with drawn-up legs, upon their prayer carpets, with their hands over their ear's and one elbow on each side of the face: a father, his shoulders up and his knees under his forehead, dozed dejectedly by a boy who slept on his back with tousled hair and one arm commandingly extended; a woman covered from head to foot, like a corpse, with a piece of white sheeting, had a naked child in the hollow of each arm; the Arab's belongings, piled right aft, made a heavy mound of broken outlines, with a cargo lamp swung above, and a great confusion of vague forms behind: gleams of paunchy brass pots, the footrest of a deck chair, blades of spears, the straight scabbard of an old sword leaning against a heap of pillows, the spout of a tin coffee pot. The patent log on the taffrail periodically rang a single tinkling stroke for every mile traversed on an errand of faith. Above the mass of sleepers a faint and patient sigh at times floated, the exhalation of a troubled dream; and short metallic clangs bursting out suddenly in the depths of the ship, the harsh scrape of a shovel, the violent slam of a furnace door, exploded brutally, as if the men handling the mysterious things below had their breasts full of fierce anger: while the slim high hull of the steamer went on evenly ahead, without a sway of her bare masts, cleaving continuously the great calm of the waters under the inaccessible serenity of the sky.

Jim paced athwart, and his footsteps in the vast silence were loud to his own ears, as if echoed by the watchful stars: his eyes, roaming about the line of the horizon, seemed to gaze hungrily into the unattainable, and did not see the shadow of the coming event. The only shadow on the sea was the shadow of the black smoke pouring heavily from the funnel its immense streamer, whose end was constantly dissolving in the air. Two Malays, silent and almost motionless, steered, one on each side of the wheel, whose brass rim shone fragmentarily in the oval of light thrown out by the binnacle. Now and then a hand, with black fingers alternately letting go and catching hold of revolving spokes, appeared in the illumined part; the links of wheel-chains ground heavily in the grooves of the barrel. Jim would glance at the compass, would glance around the unattainable horizon, would stretch himself till his joints cracked with a leisurely twist of the body in the very excess of well-being; and, as if made audacious by the invincible aspect of the peace, he felt he cared for nothing that could happen to him to the end of his days. From time to time he glanced idly at a chart pegged out with four drawing-pins on a low three-legged table abaft the steering-gear case. The sheet of paper portraying the depths of the sea presented a shiny surface under the light of a bull's-eye lamp lashed to a stanchion, a surface as level and smooth as the glimmering surface of the waters. Parallel rulers with a pair of dividers reposed on it; the ship's position at last noon was marked with a small black cross, and the

straight pencil-line drawn firmly as far as Perim figured the course of the ship—
the path of souls towards the holy place, the promise of salvation, the reward of
eternal life—while the pencil with its sharp end touching the Somali coast lay
round and still like a naked ship's spar floating in the pool of a sheltered dock.
"How steady she goes" thought Jim with wonder, with something like gratitude for
this high peace of sea and sky. At such times his thoughts would be full of valorous
deeds: he loved these dreams and the success of his imaginary achievements.
They were the best parts of life, its secret truth, its hidden reality. They had a gorgeous virility, the charm of vagueness, they passed before him with a heroic tread;
they carried his soul away with them and made it drunk with the divine philter of
an unbounded confidence in itself. There was nothing he could not face. He was
so pleased with the idea that he smiled, keeping perfunctorily his eyes ahead; and
when he happened to glance back he saw the white streak of the wake drawn as
straight by the ship's keel upon the sea as the black line drawn by the pencil upon
the chart.

The ash-buckets racketed, clanking up and down the stokehold ventilators, and
this tin-pot clatter warned him the end of his watch was near. He sighed with content, with regret as well, at having to part from that serenity which fostered the
adventurous freedom of his thoughts. He was a little sleepy too, and felt a pleasurable languor running through every limb as though all the blood in his body had
turned to warm milk. His skipper had come up noiselessly, in pajamas and with his
sleeping-jacket flung wide open. Red of face, only half awake, the left eye partly
closed, the right staring stupid and glassy, he hung his big head over the chart and
scratched his ribs sleepily. There was something obscene in the sight of his naked
flesh. His bared breast glistened soft and greasy, as though he had sweated out his
fat in his sleep. He pronounced a professional remark in a voice harsh and dead,
resembling the rasping sound of a wood-file on the edge of a plank; the fold of his
double chin hung like a bag triced up close under the hinge of his jaw. Jim started, and his answer was full of deference; but the odious and fleshy figure, as
though seen for the first time in a revealing moment, fixed itself in his memory
forever as the incarnation of everything vile and base that lurks in the world we
love: in our own hearts we trust for our salvation, in the men that surround us, in
the sights that fill our eyes, in the sounds that fill our ears, and in the air that fills
our lungs.

The thin gold shaving of the moon floating slowly downwards had lost itself on
the darkened surface of the waters, and the eternity beyond the sky seemed to
come down nearer to the earth, with the augmented glitter of the stars, with the
more profound somberness in the luster of the half-transparent dome covering the
flat disk of an opaque sea. The ship moved so smoothly that her onward motion
was imperceptible to the senses of men, as though she had been a crowded planet

speeding through the dark spaces of ether behind the swarm of suns, in the appalling and calm solitudes awaiting the breath of future creations. "Hot is no name for it down below," said a voice.

Jim smiled without looking round. The skipper presented an unmoved breadth of back: it was the renegade's trick to appear pointedly unaware of your existence unless it suited his purpose to turn at you with a devouring glare before he let loose a torrent of foamy, abusive jargon that came like a gush from a sewer. Now he emitted only a sulky grunt; the second engineer at the head of the bridge-ladder, kneading with damp palms a dirty sweat-rag, unabashed, continued the tale of his complaints. The sailors had a good time of it up here, and what was the use of them in the world he would be blowed if he could see. The poor devils of engineers had to get the ship along anyhow, and they could very well do the rest too; by gosh they——"Shut up!" growled the German, stolidly. "Oh yes! Shut up——and when anything goes wrong you fly to us, don't you?" went on the other. He was more than half cooked, he expected; but anyway, now, he did not mind how much he sinned, because these last three days he had passed through a fine course of training for the place where the bad boys go when they die—b'gosh, he had—besides being made jolly well deaf by the blasted racket below. The durned, compound, surface-condensing, rotten scrapheap rattled and banged down there like an old deck-winch, only more so; and what made him risk his life every night and day that God made amongst the refuse of a breaking-up yard flying round at fifty-seven revolutions, was more than *he* could tell. He must have been born reckless, b'gosh. He . . . "Where did you get drink?" inquired the German, very savage, but motionless in the light of the binnacle, like a clumsy effigy of a man cut out of a block of fat. Jim went on smiling at the retreating horizon; his heart was full of generous impulses, and his thought was contemplating his own superiority. "Drink!" repeated the engineer with amiable scorn: he was hanging on with both hands to the rail, a shadowy figure with flexible legs. "Not from you, captain. You're far too mean, b'gosh. You would let a good man die sooner than give him a drop of schnapps. That's what you Germans call economy. Penny wise, pound foolish." He became sentimental. The chief had given him a four-finger nip about ten o'clock—"only one, s'elp me!"—good old chief; but as to getting the old fraud out of his bunk—a five-ton crane couldn't do it. Not it. Not tonight anyhow. He was sleeping sweetly like a little child, with a bottle of prime brandy under his pillow. From the thick throat of the commander of the *Patna* came a low rumble, on which the sound of the word *schwein* fluttered high and low like a capricious feather in a faint stir of air. He and the chief engineer had been cronies for a good few years—serving the same jovial, crafty, old Chinaman, with horn-rimmed goggles and strings of red silk plaited into the venerable gray hairs of his pigtail. The quay-side opinion in the *Patna's* home port was that these two in the way of

brazen peculation "had done together pretty well everything you can think of."
Outwardly they were badly matched: one dull-eyed, malevolent, and of soft fleshy
curves; the other lean, all hollows, with a head long and bony like the head of an
old horse, with sunken cheeks, with sunken temples, with an indifferent glazed
glance of sunken eyes. He had been stranded out East somewhere—in Canton, in
Shanghai, or perhaps in Yokohama; he probably did not care to remember himself
the exact locality, nor yet the cause of his shipwreck. He had been, in mercy to his
youth, kicked quietly out of his ship twenty years ago or more, and it might have
been so much worse for him that the memory of the episode had in it hardly a
trace of misfortune. Then, steam navigation expanding in these seas, and men of
his craft being scarce at first, he had "got on" after a sort. He was eager to let
strangers know in a dismal mumble that he was "an old stager out here." When he
moved a skeleton seemed to sway loose in his clothes; his walk was mere wandering, and he was given to wander thus around the engine-room skylight, smoking,
without relish, doctored tobacco in a brass bowl at the end of a cherrywood stem
four feet long, with the imbecile gravity of a thinker evolving a system of philosophy from the hazy glimpse of a truth. He was usually anything but free with his private store of liquor; but on that night he had departed from his principles, so that
his second, a weak-headed child of Wapping, what with the unexpectedness of the
treat and the strength of the stuff, had become very happy, cheeky, and talkative.
The fury of the New South Wales German was extreme; he puffed like an exhaust
pipe, and Jim, faintly amused by the scene, was impatient for the time when he
could get below: the last ten minutes of the watch were irritating like a gun that
hangs fire; those men did not belong to the world of heroic adventure; they
weren't bad chaps, though. Even the skipper himself . . . His gorge rose at the
mass of panting flesh from which issued gurgling mutters, a cloudy trickle of filthy
expressions; but he was too pleasurably languid to dislike actively this or any
other thing. The quality of these men did not matter; he rubbed shoulders with
them, but they could not touch him; he shared the air they breathed, but he was
different . . . Would the skipper go for the engineer? . . . The life was easy and he
was too sure of himself—too sure of himself to . . . The line dividing his meditation
from a surreptitious doze on his feet was thinner than a thread in a spider's web.

The second engineer was coming by easy transitions to the consideration of his
finances and of his courage.

"Who's drunk? I? No, no, captain! That won't do. You ought to know by this time
the chief ain't free-hearted enough to make a sparrow drunk, b'gosh. I've never
been the worse for liquor in my life; the stuff ain't made yet that would make *me*
drunk. I could drink fire against your whiskey peg for peg, b'gosh, and keep as cool
as a cucumber. If I thought I was drunk I would jump overboard—do away with
myself, b'gosh. I would! Straight! And I won't go off the bridge. Where do you

expect me to take the air on a night like this, eh? On deck amongst that vermin down there? Likely—ain't it! And I am not afraid of anything you can do."

The German lifted two heavy fists to heaven and shook them a little without a word.

"I don't know what fear is," pursued the engineer, with the enthusiasm of sincere conviction. "I am not afraid of doing all the bloomin' work in this rotten hooker, b'gosh! And a jolly good thing for you that there are some of us about the world that aren't afraid of their lives, or where would you be—you and this old thing here with her plates like brown paper—brown paper, s'elp me? It's all very fine for you—you get a power of pieces out of her one way and another; but what about me—what do I get? A measely hundred and fifty dollars a month and find yourself. I wish to ask you respectfully—respectfully, mind—who wouldn't chuck a dratted job like this? 'Tain't safe, s'elp me, it ain't! Only I am one of them fearless fellows . . ."

He let go the rail and made ample gestures as if demonstrating in the air the shape and extent of his valor; his thin voice darted in prolonged squeaks upon the sea, he tiptoed back and forth for the better emphasis of utterance, and suddenly pitched down headfirst as though he had been clubbed from behind. He said "Damn!" as he tumbled; an instant of silence followed upon his screeching: Jim and the skipper staggered forward by common accord, and catching themselves up, stood very stiff and still gazing, amazed, at the undisturbed level of the sea. Then they looked upwards at the stars.

What had happened? The wheezy thump of the engines went on. Had the earth been checked in her course? They could not understand; and suddenly the calm sea, the sky without a cloud, appeared formidably insecure in their immobility, as it poised on the brow of yawning destruction. The engineer rebounded vertically full length and collapsed again into a vague heap. This heap said "What's that?" in the muffled accents of profound grief. A faint noise as of thunder, of thunder infinitely remote, less than a sound, hardly more than a vibration, passed slowly, and the ship quivered in response, as if the thunder had growled deep down in the water. The eyes of the two Malays at the wheel glittered towards the white men, but their dark hands remained closed on the spokes. The sharp hull driving on its way seemed to rise a few inches in succession through its whole length, as though it had become pliable, and settled down again rigidly to its work of cleaving the smooth surface of the sea. Its quivering stopped, and the faint noise of thunder ceased all at once, as though the ship had steamed across a narrow belt of vibrating water and of humming air.

❧ 4 ❧

A month or so afterwards, when Jim, in answer to pointed questions, tried to tell honestly the truth of this experience, he said, speaking of the ship: "She went over whatever it was as easy as a snake crawling over a stick." The illustration was good: the questions were aiming at facts, and the official Inquiry was being held in the police court of an Eastern port. He stood elevated in the witness box, with burning cheeks, in a cool, lofty room: the big framework of punkahs moved gently to and fro high above his head, and from below many eyes were looking at him out of dark faces, out of white faces, out of red faces, out of faces attentive, spellbound, as if all these people sitting in orderly rows upon narrow benches had been enslaved by the fascination of his voice. It was very loud, it rang startling in his own ears, it was the only sound audible in the world, for the terribly distinct questions that extorted his answers seemed to shape themselves in anguish and pain within his breast—came to him poignant and silent like the terrible questioning of one's conscience. Outside the court the sun blazed—within was the wind of great punkahs that made you shiver, the shame that made you burn, the attentive eyes whose glance stabbed. The face of the presiding magistrate, clean shaved and impassible, looked at him deadly pale between the red faces of the two nautical assessors. The light of a broad window under the ceiling fell from above on the heads and shoulders of the three men, and they were fiercely distinct in the half-light of the big courtroom where the audience seemed composed of staring shadows. They wanted facts. Facts! They demanded facts from him, as if facts could explain anything!

"After you had concluded you had collided with something floating awash, say a waterlogged wreck, you were ordered by your captain to go forward and ascertain if there was any damage done. Did you think it likely from the force of the blow?" asked the assessor sitting to the left. He had a thin horseshoe beard, salient cheekbones, and with both elbows on the desk clasped his rugged hands before his face, looking at Jim with thoughtful blue eyes; the other, a heavy, scornful man, thrown back in his seat, his left arm extended full length, drummed delicately with his fingertips on a blotting pad: in the middle the magistrate, upright in the roomy armchair, his head inclined slightly on the shoulder, had his arms crossed on his breast, and a few flowers in a glass vase by the side of his inkstand.

"I did not," said Jim. "I was told to call no one and to make no noise for fear of creating a panic. I thought the precaution reasonable. I took one of the lamps that were hung under the awnings and went forward. After opening the forepeak hatch I heard splashing in there. I lowered then the lamp the whole drift of its lanyard, and saw that the forepeak was more than half full of water already. I knew then there must be a big hole below the waterline." He paused.

"Yes," said the big assessor, with a dreamy smile at the blotting pad; his fingers played incessantly, touching the paper without noise.

"I did not think of danger just then. I might have been a little startled: all this happened in such a quiet way and so very suddenly. I knew there was no other bulkhead in the ship but the collision bulkhead separating the forepeak from the forehold. I went back to tell the captain. I came upon the second engineer getting up at the foot of the bridge-ladder: he seemed dazed, and told me he thought his left arm was broken; he had slipped on the top step when getting down while I was forward. He exclaimed, 'My God! That rotten bulkhead 'll give way in a minute, and the damned thing will go down under us like a lump of lead.' He pushed me away with his right arm and ran before me up the ladder, shouting as he climbed. His left arm hung by his side. I followed up in time to see the captain rush at him and knock him down flat on his back. He did not strike him again: he stood bending over him and speaking angrily but quite low. I fancy he was asking him why the devil he didn't go and stop the engines, instead of making a row about it on deck. I heard him say, 'Get up! Run, fly!' He swore also. The engineer slid down the starboard ladder and bolted round the skylight to the engine-room companion which was on the port side. He moaned as he ran . . ."

He spoke slowly; he remembered swiftly and with extreme vividness; he could have reproduced like an echo the moaning of the engineer for the better information of these men who wanted facts. After his first feeling of revolt he had come round to the view that only a meticulous precision of statement would bring out the true horror behind the appalling face of things. The facts those men were so eager to know had been visible, tangible, open to the senses, occupying their place in space and time, requiring for their existence a fourteen-hundred-ton steamer and twenty-seven minutes by the watch; they made a whole that had features, shades of expression, a complicated aspect that could be remembered by the eye, and something else besides, something invisible, a directing spirit of perdition that dwelt within, like a malevolent soul in a detestable body. He was anxious to make this clear. This had not been a common affair, everything in it had been of the utmost importance, and fortunately he remembered everything. He wanted to go on talking for truth's sake, perhaps for his own sake also; and while his utterance was deliberate, his mind positively flew round and round the serried circle of facts that had surged up all about him to cut him off from the rest of his kind: it was like a creature that, finding itself imprisoned within an enclo-sure of high stakes, dashes round and round, distracted in the night, trying to find a weak spot, a crevice, a place to scale, some opening through which it may squeeze itself and escape. This awful activity of mind made him hesitate at times in his speech. . . .

"The captain kept on moving here and there on the bridge; he seemed calm enough, only he stumbled several times; and once as I stood speaking to him he walked right into me as though he had been stone-blind. He made no definite answer to what I had to tell. He mumbled to himself; all I heard of it were a few words that sounded like 'confounded steam!' and 'infernal steam!'—something about steam. I thought . . ."

He was becoming irrelevant; a question to the point cut short his speech, like a pang of pain, and he felt extremely discouraged and weary. He was coming to that, he was coming to that—and now, checked brutally, he had to answer by yes or no. He answered truthfully by a curt "Yes, I did"; and fair of face, big of frame, with young, gloomy eyes, he held his shoulders upright above the box, while his soul writhed within him. He was made to answer another question so much to the point and so useless, then waited again. His mouth was tastelessly dry, as though he had been eating dust, then salt and bitter as after a drink of seawater. He wiped his damp forehead, passed his tongue over parched lips, felt a shiver run down his back. The big assessor had dropped his eyelids, and drummed on without a sound, careless and mournful; the eyes of the other above the sunburnt, clasped fingers seemed to glow with kindliness; the magistrate had swayed forward; his pale face hovered near the flowers, and then dropping sideways over the arm of his chair, he rested his temple in the palm of his hand. The wind of the punkahs eddied down on the heads, on the dark-faced natives wound about in voluminous draperies, on the Europeans sitting together very hot, and in drill suits that seemed to fit them as close as their skins, and holding their round pith hats on their knees; while gliding along the walls the court peons, buttoned tight in long white coats, flitted rapidly to and fro, running on bare toes, red-sashed, red turban on head, as noiseless as ghosts, and on the alert like so many retrievers.

Jim's eyes, wandering in the intervals of his answers, rested upon a white man who sat apart from the others, with his face worn and clouded, but with quiet eyes that glanced straight, interested, and clear. Jim answered another question, and was tempted to cry out, "What's the good of this, what's the good!" He tapped with his foot slightly, bit his lip, and looked away over the heads. He met the eyes of the white man. The glance directed at him was not the fascinated stare of the others. It was an act of intelligent volition. Jim between two questions forgot himself so far as to find leisure for a thought. This fellow—ran the thought—looks at me as though he could see somebody or something past my shoulder. He had come across that man before—in the street perhaps. He was positive he had never spoken to him. For days, for many days, he had spoken to no one, but had held silent, incoherent, and endless converse with himself, like a prisoner alone in his cell or like a wayfarer lost in a wilderness. At present he was answering questions that did not matter though they had a purpose, but he doubted whether he would ever again speak out as long as he lived. The sound of his own truthful statements confirmed his deliberate opinion that speech was of no use to him any longer. That man there seemed to be aware of his hopeless difficulty. Jim looked at him, then turned away resolutely, as after a final parting.

And later on, many times, in distant parts of the world, Marlow showed himself willing to remember Jim, to remember him at length, in detail and audibly.

Perhaps it would be after dinner, on a veranda draped in motionless foliage and crowned with flowers, in the deep dusk speckled by fiery cigar-ends. The elongated bulk of each cane chair harbored a silent listener. Now and then a small red glow would move abruptly, and expanding, light up the fingers of a languid hand, part of a face in profound repose, or flash a crimson gleam into a pair of pensive eyes overshadowed by a fragment of an unruffled forehead: and with the very first word uttered, Marlow's body, extended at rest in the seat, would become very still, as though his spirit had winged its way back into the lapse of time and were speaking through his lips from the past.

❦ 5 ❦

O h, yes. I attended the inquiry," he would say, "and to this day I haven't left off wondering why I went. I am willing to believe each of us has a guardian angel, if you fellows will concede to me that each of us has a familiar devil as well. I want you to own up, because I don't like to feel exceptional in any way, and I know I have him—the devil, I mean. I haven't seen him, of course, but I go upon circumstantial evidence. He is there right enough, and, being malicious, he lets me in for that kind of thing. What kind of thing, you ask? Why, the inquiry thing, the yellow-dog thing—you wouldn't think a mangy, native tyke would be allowed to trip up people in the veranda of a magistrate's court, would you?—the kind of thing that by devious, unexpected, truly diabolical ways causes me to run up against men with soft spots, with hard spots, with hidden plague spots by Jove! and loosens their tongues at the sight of me for their infernal confidences; as though, forsooth, I had no confidences to make to myself, as though—God help me!—I didn't have enough confidential information about myself to harrow my own soul till the end of my appointed time. And what I have done to be thus favored I want to know. I declare I am as full of my own concerns as the next man, and I have as much memory as the average pilgrim in this valley, so you see I am not particularly fit to be a receptacle of confessions. Then why? Can't tell—unless it be to make time pass away after dinner. Charley, my dear chap, your dinner was extremely good, and in consequence these men here look upon a quiet rubber as a tumultuous occupation. They wallow in your good chairs and think to themselves, 'Hang exertion. Let that Marlow talk.'

"Talk! So be it. And it's easy enough to talk of Master Jim, after a good spread, two hundred feet above the sea level, with a box of decent cigars handy, on a blessed evening of freshness and starlight that would make the best of us forget we are only on sufferance here and got to pick our way in cross lights, watching every precious minute and every irremediable step, trusting we shall manage yet to go out decently in the end—but not so sure of it after all—and with dashed little help to expect from those we touch elbows with right and left. Of course there are men here and there to whom the whole of life is like an after-dinner hour with a cigar; easy, pleasant, empty, perhaps enlivened by some fable of strife to be forgotten before the end is told—before the end is told—even if there happens to be any end to it.

"My eyes met his for the first time at that inquiry. You must know that everybody connected in any way with the sea was there, because the affair had been notorious for days, ever since that mysterious cable message came from Aden to start us all cackling. I say mysterious, because it was so in a sense though it contained a naked fact, about as naked and ugly as a fact can well be. The whole waterside talked of nothing else. First thing in the morning as I was dressing in my stateroom, I would hear through the bulkhead my Parsee Dubash jabbering about the *Patna* with the steward, while he drank a cup of tea, by favor, in the pantry. No sooner on shore I would meet some acquaintance, and the first remark would be, 'Did you ever hear of anything to beat this?' and according to his kind the man would smile cynically, or look sad, or let out a swear or two. Complete strangers would accost each other familiarly, just for the sake of easing their minds on the subject: every confounded loafer in the town came in for a harvest of drinks over this affair: you heard of it in the harbor office, at every shipbroker's, at your agent's, from whites, from natives, from half-castes, from the very boatmen squatting half-naked on the stone steps as you went up—by Jove! There was some indignation, not a few jokes, and no end of discussions as to what had become of them, you know. This went on for a couple of weeks or more, and the opinion that whatever was mysterious in this affair would turn out to be tragic as well, began to prevail, when one fine morning, as I was standing in the shade by the steps of the harbor office, I perceived four men walking towards me along the quay. I wondered for a while where that queer lot had sprung from, and suddenly, I may say, I shouted to myself, 'Here they are!'

"There they were, sure enough, three of them as large as life, and one much larger of girth than any living man has a right to be, just landed with a good breakfast inside of them from an outward bound Dale Line steamer that had come in about an hour after sunrise. There could be no mistake; I spotted the jolly skipper of the *Patna* at the first glance: the fattest man in the whole blessed tropical belt clear round that good old earth of ours. Moreover, nine months or so before, I had come across him in Samarang. His steamer was loading in the Roads, and he was abusing the tyrannical institutions of the German empire, and soaking himself in beer all day long and day after day in De Jongh's back-shop, till De Jongh, who charged a guilder for every bottle without as much as the quiver of an eyelid, would beckon me aside, and, with his little leathery face all puckered up, declare confidentially, 'Business is business, but this man, captain, he make me very sick. Tfui!'

"I was looking at him from the shade. He was hurrying on a little in advance, and the sunlight beating on him brought out his bulk in a startling way. He made me think of a trained baby elephant walking on hind legs. He was extravagantly gorgeous too—got up in a soiled sleeping suit, bright green and deep orange vertical stripes, with a pair of ragged straw slippers on his bare feet, and somebody's cast-off pith hat, very dirty and two sizes too small for him, tied up with a manilla rope-yarn on the top of his big head. You understand a man like that hasn't the ghost of a chance when it comes to borrowing clothes. Very well. On he came in hot haste, without a look right or left, passed within three feet of me, and in the innocence of his heart went on pelting upstairs into the harbor office to make his deposition, or report, or whatever you like to call it.

"It appears he addressed himself in the first instance to the principal shipping-master. Archie Ruthvel had just come in, and, as his story goes, was about to begin his arduous day by giving a dressing-down to his chief clerk. Some of you might have known him—an obliging little Portuguese half-caste with a miserably skinny neck, and always on the hop to get something from the shipmasters in the way of eatables—a piece of salt pork, a bag of biscuits, a few potatoes, or what not. One voyage, I recollect, I tipped him a live sheep out of the remnant of my sea-stock: not that I wanted him to do anything for me—he couldn't you know—but because his childlike belief in the sacred right to perquisites quite touched my heart. It was so strong as to be almost beautiful. The race—the two races rather—and the climate . . . However, nevermind. I know where I have a friend for life.

"Well, Ruthvel says he was giving him a severe lecture—on official morality, I suppose—when he heard a kind of subdued commotion at his back, and turning his head he saw, in his own words, something round and enormous, resembling a sixteen-hundred-weight sugar hogshead wrapped in striped flannelette, up-ended in the middle of the large floor space in the office. He declares he was so taken aback that for quite an appreciable time he did not realize the thing was alive, and sat still wondering for what purpose and by what means that object had been transported in front of his desk. The archway from the anteroom was crowded with punkah-pullers, sweepers, police peons, the coxswain and crew of the harbor steam launch, all craning their necks and almost climbing on each other's backs. Quite a riot. By that time the fellow had managed to tug and jerk his hat clear of his head, and advanced with slight bows at Ruthvel, who told me the sight was so discomposing that for some time he listened, quite unable to make out what that apparition wanted. It spoke in a voice harsh and lugubrious but intrepid, and little by little it dawned upon Archie that this was a development of the *Patna* case. He says that as soon as he understood who it was before him he felt quite unwell—Archie is so sympathetic and easily upset—but pulled himself together and shouted 'Stop! I can't listen to you. You must go to the Master Attendant. I can't possibly listen to you. Captain Elliot is the man you want to see. This way, this way.' He jumped up, ran round that long counter, pulled, shoved: the other let him, surprised but obedient at first, and only at the door of the private office some sort of animal instinct made him hang back and snort like a frightened bullock. 'Look here! what's up? Let go! Look here!' Archie flung open the door without knocking. 'The master of the *Patna*, sir,' he shouts. 'Go in, captain.' He saw the old man lift his head from some writing so sharp that his nose-nippers fell off, banged the door to, and fled to his desk, where he had some papers waiting for his signature: but he says the row that burst out in there was so awful that he couldn't collect his senses sufficiently to remember the spelling of his own name. Archie's the most sensitive shipping-master in the two hemispheres. He declares he felt as though he had thrown a man to a hungry lion. No doubt the noise was great. I heard it down below, and I have every reason to believe it was heard clear across the Esplanade as far as the bandstand. Old father Elliot had a great stock of words and could shout—and didn't mind who he shouted at either. He would have shouted at the Viceroy himself. As he used to tell me: 'I am as high as I can get; my pension is safe. I've a few pounds laid and if they don't like my notions of duty, I would just as soon go home as not. I am an old man, and I have always spoken my mind. All I care for now is to see my girls married before I die.' He was a little crazy on that point. His three daughters were awfully nice, though they resembled him amazingly, and on the mornings he woke up with a gloomy view of their matrimonial prospects the office would read it in his eye and tremble, because, they said, he was sure to have somebody for breakfast. However, that morning he did not eat the renegade, but, if I may be allowed to carry on the metaphor, chewed him up very small, so to speak, and—ah! ejected him again.

"Thus in a very few moments I saw his monstrous bulk descend in haste and stand still on the outer steps. He had stopped close to me for the purpose of profound meditation: his large purple cheeks quivered. He was biting his thumb, and after a while noticed me with a sidelong vexed look. The other three chaps that had landed with him made a little group waiting at some distance. There was a sallow-faced, mean little chap with his arm in a sling, and a long individual in a blue flannel coat, as dry as a chip and no stouter than a broomstick, with drooping gray moustaches, who looked about him with an air of jaunty imbecility. The third was an upstanding, broad-shouldered youth, with his hands in his pockets, turning his back on the other two who appeared to be talking together earnestly. He stared across the empty Esplanade. A ramshackle gharry, all dust and venetian blinds, pulled up short opposite the group, and the driver, throwing up his right foot over his knee, gave himself up to the critical examination of his toes. The young chap, making no movement, not even stirring his head, just stared into the sunshine. This was my first view of Jim. He looked as unconcerned and unapproachable as only the young can look. There he stood, clean-limbed, clean-faced, firm on his feet, as promising a boy as the sun ever shone on; and, looking at him, knowing all he knew and a little more too, I was as angry as though I had detected him trying to get something out of me by false pretenses. He had no business to look so sound. I thought to myself—well, if this sort can go wrong like that . . . and I felt as though I could fling down my hat and dance on it from sheer mortification, as I once saw the skipper of an Italian bark do because his duffer of a mate got into a mess with his anchors when making a flying moor in a roadstead full of ships. I asked myself, seeing him there apparently so much at ease—is he silly? is he callous? He seemed ready to start whistling a tune. And note, I did not care a rap about the behavior of the other two. Their persons somehow fitted the tale that was public property, and was going to be the subject of an official inquiry. 'That old mad rogue upstairs called me a hound,' said the captain of the *Patna.* I can't tell whether he recognized me—I rather think he did; but at any rate our glances met. He glared—I smiled; hound was the very mildest epithet that had reached me through the open window. 'Did he?' I said from some strange inability to hold my tongue. He nodded, bit his thumb again, swore under his breath: then lifting his head and looking at me with sullen and passionate impudence—'Bah! the Pacific is big, my friendt. You damned Englishmen can do your worst; I know where there's plenty room for a man like me: I am well aguaindt in Apia, in Honolulu, in . . .' He paused reflectively, while without effort I could depict to myself the sort of people he was 'aguaindt' with in those places. I won't make a secret of it that I had been 'aguaindt' with not a few of that sort myself. There are times when a man must act as though life were equally sweet in any company. I've known such a time, and what's more, I shan't now pretend to pull a long face over my necessity, because a good many of that bad company from want of moral—moral—what shall I say?—posture, or from some other equally profound cause, were twice as instructive and twenty times more amusing than the usual respectable thief of commerce you fellows ask to sit at your table without any real necessity—from habit, from cowardice, from good nature, from a hundred sneaking and inadequate reasons.

"'You Englishmen are all rogues,' went on my patriotic Flensborg or Stettin Australian. I really don't recollect now what decent little port on the shores of the Baltic was defiled by being the nest of that precious bird. 'What are you to shout? Eh? You tell me? You no better than other people, and that old rogue he make Gottam fuss with me.' His thick carcass trembled on its legs that were like a pair of pillars; it trembled from head to foot. 'That's what you English always make—make a tam' fuss—for any little thing, because I was not born in your tam' country. Take away my certificate. Take it. I don't want the certificate. A man like me don't want your verfluchte certificate. I shpit on it.' He spat. 'I vill an Amerigan citizen begome,' he cried, fretting and fuming and shuffling his feet as if to free his ankles from some invisible and mysterious grasp that would not let him get away from that spot. He made himself so warm that the top of his bullet head positively smoked. Nothing mysterious prevented me from going away: curiosity is the most obvious of sentiments, and it held me there to see the effect of a full information upon that young fellow who, hands in pockets, and turning his back upon the sidewalk, gazed across the grassplots of the Esplanade at the yellow portico of the Malabar Hotel with the air of a man about to go for a walk as soon as his friend is ready. That's how he looked, and it was odious. I waited to see him overwhelmed, confounded, pierced through and through, squirming like an impaled beetle—and I was half-afraid to see it too—if you understand what I mean. Nothing more awful than to watch a man who has been found out, not in a crime but in a more than criminal weakness. The commonest sort of fortitude prevents us from becoming criminals in a legal sense; it is from weakness unknown, but perhaps suspected, as in some parts of the world you suspect a deadly snake in every bush—from weakness that may lie hidden, watched or unwatched, prayed against or manfully scorned, repressed or maybe ignored more than half a lifetime, not one of us is safe. We are snared into doing things for which we get called names, and things for which we get hanged, and yet the spirit may well survive—survive the condemnation, survive the halter, by Jove! And there are things—they look small enough sometimes too—by which some of us are totally and completely undone. I watched the youngster there. I liked his appearance; I knew his appearance; he came from the right place; he was one of us. He stood there for all the parentage of his kind, for men and women by no means clever or amusing, but whose very existence is based upon honest faith, and upon the instinct of courage.

I don't mean military courage, or civil courage, or any special kind of courage. I mean just that inborn ability to look temptations straight in the face—a readiness unintellectual enough, goodness knows, but without a pose—a power of resistance, don't you see, ungracious if you like, but priceless—an unthinking and blessed stiffness before the outward and inward terrors, before the might of nature and the seductive corruption of men—backed by a faith invulnerable to the strength of facts, to the contagion of example, to the solicitation of ideas. Hang ideas! They are tramps, vagabonds, knocking at the backdoor of your mind, each taking a little of your substance, each carrying away some crumb of that belief in a few simple notions you must cling to if you want to live decently and would like to die easy!

"This has nothing to do with Jim, directly; only he was outwardly so typical of that good stupid kind we like to feel marching right and left of us in life, of the kind that is not disturbed by the vagaries of intelligence and the perversions of— of nerves, let us say. He was the kind of fellow you would, on the strength of his looks, leave in charge of the deck—figuratively and professionally speaking. I say I would, and I ought to know. Haven't I turned out youngsters enough in my time, for the service of the Red Rag, to the craft of the sea, to the craft whose whole secret could be expressed in one short sentence, and yet must be driven afresh every day into young heads till it becomes the component part of every waking thought—till it is present in every dream of their young sleep! The sea has been good to me, but when I remember all these boys that passed through my hands, some grown up now and some drowned by this time, but all good stuff for the sea, I don't think I have done badly by it either. Were I to go home tomorrow, I bet that before two days passed over my head some sunburnt young chief mate would overtake me at some dock gateway or other, and a fresh deep voice speaking above my hat would ask: 'Don't you remember me, sir? Why! little So-and-so. Such and such a ship. It was my first voyage.' And I would remember a bewildered little shaver, no higher than the back of this chair, with a mother and perhaps a big sister on the quay, very quiet but too upset to wave their handkerchiefs at the ship that glides out gently between the pier heads: or perhaps some decent middle-aged father who had come early with his boy to see him off, and stays all the morning, because he is interested in the windlass apparently, and stays too long, and has got to scramble ashore at last with no time at all to say goodbye. The mud pilot on the poop sings out to me in a drawl, 'Hold her with the check line for a moment, Mister Mate. There's a gentleman wants to get ashore. . . . Up with you, sir. Nearly got carried off to Talcahuano, didn't you? Now's your time; easy does it. . . . All right. Slack away again forward there.' The tugs, smoking like the pit of perdition, get hold and churn the old river into fury; the gentleman ashore is dusting his knees—the benevolent steward has shied his umbrella after him. All very proper.

He has offered his bit of sacrifice to the sea, and now he may go home pretending he thinks nothing of it; and the little willing victim shall be very seasick before next morning. By and by, when he has learned all the little mysteries and the one great secret of the craft, he shall be fit to live or die as the sea may decree; and the man who had taken a hand in this fool game, in which the sea wins every toss, will be pleased to have his back slapped by a heavy young hand, and to hear a cheery sea-puppy voice: 'Do you remember me, sir? The little So-and-so.'

"I tell you this is good; it tells you that once in your life at least you had gone the right way to work. I have been thus slapped, and I have winced, for the slap was heavy, and I have glowed all day long and gone to bed feeling less lonely in the world by virtue of that hearty thump. Don't I remember the little So-and-so's! I tell you I ought to know the right kind of looks. I would have trusted the deck to that youngster on the strength of a single glance, and gone to sleep with both eyes— and, by Jove! it wouldn't have been safe. There are depths of horror in that thought. He looked as genuine as a new sovereign, but there was some infernal alloy in his metal. How much? The least thing—the least drop of something rare and accursed; the least drop!—but he made you—standing there with his don't-care-hang air—he made you wonder whether perchance he were nothing more rare than brass.

"I couldn't believe it. I tell you I wanted to see him squirm for the honor of the craft. The other two no-account chaps spotted their captain, and began to move slowly towards us. They chatted together as they strolled, and I did not care any more than if they had not been visible to the naked eye. They grinned at each other—might have been exchanging jokes, for all I know. I saw that with one of them it was a case of a broken arm; and as to the long individual with gray moustaches he was the chief engineer, and in various ways a pretty notorious personality. They were nobodies. They approached. The skipper gazed in an inanimate way between his feet: he seemed to be swollen to an unnatural size by some awful disease, by the mysterious action of an unknown poison. He lifted his head, saw the two before him waiting, opened his mouth with an extraordinary, sneering contortion of his puffed face—to speak to them, I suppose—and then a thought seemed to strike him. His thick, purplish lips came together without a sound, he went off in a resolute waddle to the gharry and began to jerk at the door handle with such a blind brutality of impatience that I expected to see the whole concern overturned on its side, pony and all. The driver, shaken out of his meditation over the sole of his foot, displayed at once all the signs of intense terror, and held with both hands, looking round from his box at this vast carcass forcing its way into his conveyance. The little machine shook and rocked tumultuously, and the crimson nape of that lowered neck, the size of these straining thighs, the immense heaving of that dingy, striped green-and-orange back, the whole burrowing effort of that gaudy and sordid mass, troubled one's sense of probability with a droll and fear-some effect, like one of those grotesque and distinct visions that scare and fasci-nate one in a fever. He disappeared. I half expected the roof to split in two, the lit-tle box on wheels to burst open in the manner of a ripe cotton-pod—but it only sank with a click of flattened springs, and suddenly one venetian blind rattled down. His shoulders reappeared, jammed in the small opening; his head hung out, distended and tossing like a captive balloon, perspiring, furious, spluttering. He reached for the gharry-wallah with vicious flourishes of a fist as dumpy and red as a lump of raw meat. He roared at him to be off, to go on. Where? Into the Pacific, perhaps. The driver lashed; the pony snorted, reared once, and darted off at a gal-lop. Where? To Apia? to Honolulu? He had six thousand miles of tropical belt to disport himself in, and I did not hear the precise address. A snorting pony snatched him into 'ewigkeit' in the twinkling of an eye, and I never saw him again; and, what's more, I don't know of anybody that ever had a glimpse of him after he departed from my knowledge sitting inside a ramshackle little gharry that fled round the corner in a white smother of dust. He departed, disappeared, vanished, absconded; and absurdly enough it looked as though he had taken that gharry with him, for never again did I come across a sorrel pony with a slit ear and a lack-adaisical Tamil driver afflicted by a sore foot. The Pacific is indeed big; but whether he found a place for a display of his talents in it or not, the fact remains he had flown into space like a witch on a broomstick. The little chap with his arm in a sling started to run after the carriage, bleating, 'Captain! I say, Captain! I sa-a-ay!'—but after a few steps stopped short, hung his head, and walked back slowly. At the sharp rattle of the wheels, the young fellow spun round where he stood. He made no other movement, no gesture, no sign, and remained facing in the new direction after the gharry had swung out of sight.

"All this happened in much less time than it takes to tell, since I am trying to interpret for you into slow speech the instantaneous effect of visual impressions. Next moment the half-caste clerk, sent by Archie to look a little after the poor castaways of the *Patna,* came upon the scene. He ran out eager and bareheaded, looking right and left, and very full of his mission. It was doomed to be a failure as far as the principal person was concerned, but he approached the others with fussy importance, and, almost immediately, found himself involved in a violent altercation with the chap that carried his arm in a sling, and who turned out to be extremely anxious for a row. He wasn't going to be ordered about—'not he, b'gosh.' He wouldn't be terrified with a pack of lies by a cocky half-bred little quill-driver. He was not going to be bullied by 'no object of that sort,' if the story were true 'ever so'! He bawled his wish, his desire, his determination to go to bed. 'If you weren't a Godforsaken Portuguee,' I heard him yell, 'you would know that the hospital is the right place for me.' He pushed the fist of his sound arm under the other's nose; a crowd began to collect; the half-caste, flustered, but doing his best to appear dignified, tried to explain his intentions. I went away without waiting to see the end.

"But it so happened that I had a man in the hospital at the time, and going there to see about him the day before the opening of the Inquiry, I saw in the white men's ward that little chap tossing on his back, with his arm in splints, and quite light-headed. To my great surprise the other one, the long individual with drooping white moustache, had also found his way there. I remembered I had seen him slinking away during the quarrel, in a half prance, half shuffle, and try-ing very hard not to look scared. He was no stranger to the port, it seems, and in his distress was able to make tracks straight for Mariani's billiard-room and grog-shop near the bazaar. That unspeakable vagabond, Mariani, who had known the man and had ministered to his vices in one or two other places, kissed the ground, in a manner of speaking, before him, and shut him up with a supply of bottles in an upstairs room of his infamous hovel. It appears he was under some hazy apprehension as to his personal safety, and wished to be concealed. However, Mariani told me a long time after (when he came on board one day to dun my steward for the price of some cigars) that he would have done more for him without asking any questions, from gratitude for some unholy favor received very many years ago—as far as I could make out. He thumped twice his brawny chest, rolled enormous black and white eyes glistening with tears: 'Antonio never forget—Antonio never forget!' What was the precise nature of the immoral obligation I never learned, but be it what it may, he had every facility given him to remain under lock and key, with a chair, a table, a mattress in a corner, and a litter of fallen plaster on the floor, in an irrational state of funk, and keeping up his pecker with such tonics as Mariani dispensed. This lasted till the evening of the third day, when, after letting out a few horrible screams, he found himself compelled to seek safety in flight from a legion of centipedes. He burst the door open, made one leap for dear life down the crazy little stairway, landed bodily on Mariani's stomach, picked himself up, and bolted like a rabbit into the streets. The police plucked him off a garbage heap in the early morning. At first he had a notion they were carrying him off to be hanged, and fought for liberty like a hero, but when I sat down by his bed he had been very quiet for two days. His lean bronzed head, with white moustaches, looked fine and calm on the pillow, like the head of a war-worn soldier with a childlike soul, had it not been for a hint of spectral alarm that lurked in the blank glitter of his glance, resembling a nonde-script form of a terror crouching silently behind a pane of glass. He was so extremely calm that I began to indulge in the eccentric hope of hearing some-thing explanatory of the famous affair from his point of view. Why I longed to go grubbing into the deplorable details of an occurrence which, after all, concerned me no more than as a member of an obscure body of men held together by a community of inglorious toil and by fidelity to a certain standard of conduct, I can't explain. You may call it an unhealthy curiosity if you like; but I have a distinct notion I wished to find something. Perhaps, unconsciously, I hoped I would find that something, some profound and redeeming cause, some merciful explanation, some convincing shadow of an excuse. I see well enough now that I hoped for the impossible—for the laying of what is the most obstinate ghost of man's creation, of the uneasy doubt uprising like a mist, secret and gnawing like a worm, and more chilling than the certitude of death—the doubt of the sovereign power enthroned in a fixed standard of conduct. It is the hardest thing to stumble against; it is the thing that breeds yelling panics and good little quiet villainies; it's the true shadow of calamity. Did I believe in a miracle? and why did I desire it so ardently? Was it for my own sake that I wished to find some shadow of an excuse for that young fellow whom I had never seen before, but whose appearance alone added a touch of personal concern to the thoughts suggested by the knowledge of his weakness—made it a thing of mystery and terror—like a hint of a destructive fate ready for us all whose youth—in its day—had resembled his youth? I fear that such was the secret motive of my prying. I was, and no mistake, looking for a miracle. The only thing that at this distance of time strikes me as miraculous is the extent of my imbecility. I positively hoped to obtain from that battered and shady invalid some exorcism against the ghost of doubt. I must have been pretty desperate too, for, without loss of time, after a few indifferent and friendly sentences which he answered with languid readiness, just as any decent sick man would do, I produced the word *Patna* wrapped up in a delicate question as in a wisp of floss silk. I was delicate selfishly; I did not want to startle him; I had no solicitude for him; I was not furious with him and sorry for him: his experience was of no importance, his redemption would have had no point for me. He had grown old in minor iniquities, and could no longer inspire aversion or pity. He repeated *Patna?* interrogatively, seemed to make a short effort of memory, and said: 'Quite right. I am an old stager out here. I saw her go down.' I made ready to vent my indignation at such a stupid lie, when he added smoothly, 'She was full of reptiles.'

"This made me pause. What did he mean? The unsteady phantom of terror behind his glassy eyes seemed to stand still and look into mine wistfully. 'They turned me out of my bunk in the middle watch to look at her sinking,' he pursued in a reflective tone. His voice sounded alarmingly strong all at once. I was sorry for my folly. There was no snowy-winged coiff of a nursing sister to be seen flitting in the perspective of the ward; but away in the middle of a long row of empty iron bedsteads an accident case from some ship in the Roads sat up brown and gaunt with a white bandage set rakishly on the forehead. Suddenly my interesting invalid shot out an arm thin like a tentacle and clawed my shoulder. 'Only my eyes were good enough to see. I am famous for my eyesight. That's why they called me, I expect. None of them was quick enough to see her go, but they saw that she was gone right enough, and sang out together—like this.' . . . A wolfish howl searched the very recesses of my soul. 'Oh! make'im dry up,' whined the accident case irritably. 'You don't believe me, I suppose,' went on the other, with an air of ineffable conceit. 'I tell you there are no such eyes as mine this side of the Persian Gulf. Look under the bed.'

"Of course I stooped instantly. I defy anybody not to have done so. 'What can you see?' he asked. 'Nothing,' I said, feeling awfully ashamed of myself. He scrutinized my face with wild and withering contempt. 'Just so,' he said, 'but if I were to look I could see—there's no eyes like mine, I tell you.' Again he clawed, pulling at me downwards in his eagerness to relieve himself by a confidential communication. 'Millions of pink toads. There's no eyes like mine. Millions of pink toads. It's worse than seeing a ship sink. I could look at sinking ships and smoke my pipe all day long. Why don't they give me back my pipe? I would get a smoke while I watched these toads. The ship was full of them. They've got to be watched, you know.' He winked facetiously. The perspiration dripped on him off my head, my drill coat clung to my wet back: the afternoon breeze swept impetuously over the row of bedsteads, the stiff folds of curtains stirred perpendicularly, rattling on brass rods, the covers of empty beds blew about noiselessly near the bare floor all along the line, and I shivered to the very marrow. The soft wind of the tropics played in that naked ward as bleak as a winter's gale in an old barn at home. 'Don't you let him start his hollering, mister,' hailed from afar the accident case in a distressed angry shout that came ringing between the walls like a quavering call down a tunnel. The clawing hand hauled at my shoulders; he leered at me knowingly. 'The ship was full of them, you know, and we had to clear out on the strict Q.T.,' he whispered with extreme rapidity. 'All pink. All pink—as big as mastiffs, with an eye on the top of the head and claws all round their ugly mouths. Ough! Ough!' Quick jerks as of galvanic shocks disclosed under the flat coverlet the outlines of meager and agitated legs; he let go my shoulder and reached after something in the air; his body trembled tensely like a released harpstring; and while I looked down, the spectral horror in him broke through his glassy gaze. Instantly his face of an old soldier, with its noble and calm outlines, became decomposed before my eyes by the corruption of stealthy cunning, of an abominable caution and of desperate fear. He restrained a cry—'Ssh; what are they doing now down there?' he asked, pointing to the floor with fantastic precautions of voice and gesture, whose meaning, borne upon my mind in a lurid flash, made me very sick of my cleverness. 'They are all asleep,' I answered, watching him narrowly. That was it. That's what he wanted to hear; these were the exact words that could calm him. He drew a long breath. 'Ssh! Quiet, steady. I am an old stager out here. I know them brutes. Bash-in the head of the first that stirs. There's too many of them, and she won't swim more than ten minutes.' He panted again. 'Hurry up,' he yelled suddenly, and went on in a steady scream: 'They are all awake—millions of them. They are trampling on me! Wait! Oh, wait! I'll smash them in heaps like flies. Wait for me! Help! H-e-elp!' An interminable and sustained howl completed my discomfiture. I saw in the distance the accident case raise deplorably both his hands to his bandaged head; a dresser, aproned to the chin, showed himself in the vista of the ward, as if seen in the small end of a telescope. I confessed myself fairly routed, and without more ado, stepping out through one of the long windows, escaped into the outside gallery. The howl pursued me like a vengeance. I turned into a deserted landing, and suddenly all became very still and quiet around me, and I descended the bare and shiny staircase in a silence that enabled me to compose my distracted thoughts. Down below I met one of the resident surgeons who was crossing the courtyard and stopped me. 'Been to see your man, Captain? I think we may let him go tomorrow. These fools have no notion of taking care of themselves, though. I say, we've got the chief engineer of that pilgrim ship here. A curious case. D.T.'s of the worst kind. He has been drinking hard in that Greek's or Italian's grog-shop for three days. What can you expect? Four bottles of that kind of brandy a day, I am told. Wonderful, if true. Sheeted with boiler-iron inside, I should think. The head, ah! the head, of course, gone, but the curious part is there's some sort of method in his raving. I am trying to find out. Most unusual— that thread of logic in such a delirium. Traditionally he ought to see snakes, but he doesn't. Good old tradition's at a discount nowadays. Eh! His—er—visions are batrachian. Ha! ha! No, seriously, I never remember being so interested in a case of jim-jams before. He ought to be dead, don't you know, after such a festive experiment. Oh! he is a tough object. Four-and-twenty years of the tropics too. You ought really to take a peep at him. Noble-looking old boozer. Most extraordinary man I ever met—medically, of course. Won't you?'

"I had been all along exhibiting the usual polite signs of interest, but now, assuming an air of regret, I murmured of want of time, and shook hands in a hurry. 'I say,' he cried after me, 'he can't attend that inquiry. Is his evidence material, you think?'

"'Not in the least,' I called back from the gateway."

❧ 6 ❧

The authorities were evidently of the same opinion. The inquiry was not adjourned. It was held on the appointed day to satisfy the law, and it was well attended because of its human interest, no doubt. There was no incertitude as to facts—as to the one material fact, I mean. How the *Patna* came by her hurt it was impossible to find out; the court did not expect to find out; and in the whole audience there was not a man who cared. Yet, as I've told you, all the sailors in the port attended, and the waterside business was fully represented. Whether they knew it or not, the interest that drew them there was purely psychological—the expectation of some essential disclosure as to the strength, the power, the horror, of human emotions. Naturally nothing of the kind could be disclosed. The examination of the only man able and willing to face it was beating futilely round the well-known fact, and the play of questions upon it was as instructive as the tapping with a hammer on an iron box, were the object to find out what's inside. However, an official inquiry could not be any other thing. Its object was not the fundamental why, but the superficial how, of this affair.

"The young chap could have told them, and, though that very thing was the thing that interested the audience, the questions put to him necessarily led him away from what to me, for instance, would have been the only truth worth knowing. You can't expect the constituted authorities to inquire into the state of a man's soul—or is it only of his liver? Their business was to come down upon the consequences, and frankly, a casual police magistrate and two nautical assessors are not much good for anything else. I don't mean to imply these fellows were stupid. The magistrate was very patient. One of the assessors was a sailing-ship skipper with a reddish beard, and of a pious disposition. Brierly was the other. Big Brierly. Some of you must have heard of Big Brierly—the captain of the crack ship of the Blue Star line. That's the man.

"He seemed consumedly bored by the honor thrust upon him. He had never in his life made a mistake, never had an accident, never a mishap, never a check in his steady rise, and he seemed to be one of these lucky fellows who know nothing of indecision, much less of self-mistrust. At thirty-two he had one of the best commands going in the Eastern trade—and, what's more, he thought a lot of what he had. There was nothing like it in the world, and I suppose if you had asked him point-blank he would have confessed that in his opinion there was not such another commander. The choice had fallen upon the right man. The rest of mankind that did not command the sixteen-knot steel steamer *Ossa* were rather poor creatures. He had saved lives at sea, had rescued ships in distress, had a gold chronometer presented to him by the underwriters, and a pair of binoculars with a suitable inscription from some foreign Government, in commemoration of these services. He was acutely aware of his merits and of his rewards. I liked him well enough, though some I know—meek, friendly men at that—couldn't stand him at any price. I haven't the slightest doubt he considered himself vastly my superior—indeed, had you been Emperor of East and West you could not have ignored your inferiority in his presence—but I couldn't get up any real sentiment of offense. He did not despise me for anything I could help, for anything I was— don't you know? I was a negligible quantity simply because I was not *the* fortunate man of the earth, not Montague Brierly in command of the *Ossa,* not the owner of an inscribed gold chronometer and of silver-mounted binoculars testifying to the excellence of my seamanship and to my indomitable pluck; not possessed of an acute sense of my merits and of my rewards, besides the love and worship of a black retriever, the most wonderful of its kind—for never was such a man loved thus by such a dog. No doubt, to have all this forced upon you was exasperating enough; but when I reflected that I was associated in these fatal disadvantages with twelve hundred millions of other more or less human beings, I found I could bear my share of his good-natured and contemptuous pity for the sake of something indefinite and attractive in the man. I have never defined to myself this attraction, but there were moments when I envied him. The sting of life could do no more to his complacent soul than the scratch of a pin to the smooth face of a rock. This was enviable. As I looked at him, flanking on one side the unassuming pale-faced magistrate who presided at the inquiry, his self-satisfaction presented to me and to the world a surface as hard as granite. He committed suicide very soon after.

"No wonder Jim's case bored him, and while I thought with something akin to fear of the immensity of his contempt for the young man under examination, he was probably holding silent inquiry into his own case. The verdict must have been of unmitigated guilt, and he took the secret of the evidence with him in that leap into the sea. If I understand anything of men, the matter was no doubt of the gravest import—one of those trifles that awaken ideas, start into life some thought with which a man unused to such a companionship finds it impossible to live. I am in a position to know that it wasn't money, and it wasn't drink, and it wasn't woman. He jumped overboard at sea barely a week after the end of the inquiry, and less than three days after leaving port on his outward passage; as though on that exact spot in the midst of waters he had suddenly perceived the gates of the other world flung open wide for his reception.

"Yet it was not a sudden impulse. His gray-headed mate, a first-rate sailor and a nice old chap with strangers, but in his relations with his commander the surliest chief officer I've ever seen, would tell the story with tears in his eyes. It appears that when he came on deck in the morning Brierly had been writing in the chart room. 'It was ten minutes to four,' he said, and the middle watch was not relieved yet, of course. He heard my voice on the bridge speaking to the second mate, and called me in. I was loath to go, and that's the truth, Captain Marlow—I couldn't stand poor Captain Brierly, I tell you with shame; we never know what a man is made of. He had been promoted over too many heads, not counting my own, and he had a damnable trick of making you feel small, nothing but by the way he said "Good morning." I never addressed him, sir, but on matters of duty, and then it was as much as I could do to keep a civil tongue in my head.' (He flattered himself there. I often wondered how Brierly could put up with his manners for more than half a voyage.) 'I've a wife and children' he went on, 'and I had been ten years in the Company, always expecting the next command—more fool I. Says he, just like this: "Come in here, Mr. Jones," in that swagger voice of his—"Come in here, Mr. Jones." In I went. "We'll lay down her position," says he, stooping over the chart, a pair of dividers in hand. By the standing orders the officer going off duty would have done that at the end of his watch. However, I said nothing, and looked on while he marked off the ship's position with a tiny cross and wrote the date and the time. I can see him this moment writing his neat figures: seventeen, eight, four A.M. The year would be written in red ink at the top of the chart. He never used his charts more than a year, Captain Brierly didn't. I've the chart now. When he had done he stands looking down at the mark he had made and smiling to himself, then looks up at me. "Thirty-two miles more as she goes" says he, "and then we shall be clear, and you may alter the course twenty degrees to the southward."

"'We were passing to the north of the Hector Bank that voyage. I said, "All right, sir," wondering what he was fussing about, since I had to call him before altering the course anyhow. Just then eight bells were struck: we came out on the bridge, and the second mate before going off mentions in the usual way—"Seventy-one on the log." Captain Brierly looks at the compass and then all round. It was dark and clear, and all the stars were out as plain as on a frosty night in high latitudes. Suddenly he says with a sort of a little sigh: "I am going aft, and shall set the log at zero for you myself, so that there can be no mistake. Thirty-two miles more on this course and then you are safe. Let's see—the correction on the log is six per cent additive; say, then, thirty by the dial to run, and you may come twenty degrees to starboard at once. No use losing any distance—is there?" I had never heard him talk so much at a stretch, and to no purpose as it seemed to me. I said nothing. He went down the ladder, and the dog, that was always at his heels whenever he moved, night or day, followed, sliding nose first, after him. I heard his boot heels tap, tap on the afterdeck, then he stopped and spoke to the dog—"Go back, Rover. On the bridge, boy! Go on—get?" Then he calls out to me from the dark, "Shut that dog up in the chart room, Mr. Jones—will you?"

"'This was the last time I heard his voice, Captain Marlow. These are the last words he spoke in the hearing of any living human being, sir.' At this point the old chap's voice got quite unsteady. 'He was afraid the poor brute would jump after him, don't you see?' he pursued with a quaver. 'Yes, Captain Marlow. He set the log for me; he—would you believe it?—he put a drop of oil in it too. There was the oil-feeder where he left it near by. The boatswain's mate got the hose along aft to wash down at half-past five; by and by he knocks off and runs up on the bridge— "Will you please come aft, Mr. Jones," he says. "There's a funny thing. I don't like to touch it." It was Captain Brierly's gold chronometer watch carefully hung under the rail by its chain.

"'As soon as my eyes fell on it something struck me, and I knew, sir. My legs got soft under me. It was as if I had seen him go over; and I could tell how far behind he was left too. The taffrail-log marked eighteen miles and three-quarters, and four iron belaying-pins were missing round the mainmast. Put them in his pockets to help him down, I suppose; but, Lord! what's four iron pins to a powerful man like Captain Brierly. Maybe his confidence in himself was just shook a bit at the last. That's the only sign of fluster he gave in his whole life, I should think; but I am ready to answer for him, that once over he did not try to swim a stroke, the same as he would have had pluck enough to keep up all day long on the bare chance had he fallen overboard accidentally. Yes, sir. He was second to none—if he said so himself, as I heard him once. He had written two letters in the middle watch, one to the Company and the other to me. He gave me a lot of instructions as to the passage—I had been in the trade before he was out of his time—and no end of hints as to my conduct with our people in Shanghai, so that I should keep the command of the *Ossa*. He wrote like a father would to a favorite son, Captain Marlow, and I was five-and-twenty years his senior and had tasted salt water before he was fairly breeched. In his letter to the owners—it was left open for me to see—he said that he had always done his duty by them—up to that moment—and even now he was not betraying their confidence, since he was leaving the ship to as competent a seaman as could be found meaning me, sir, meaning me! He told them that if the last act of his life didn't take away all his credit with them, they would give weight to my faithful service and to his warm recommendation, when about to fill the vacancy made by his death. And much more like this, sir. I couldn't believe my eyes. It made me feel queer all over,' went on the old chap, in great perturbation, and squashing something in the corner of his eye with the end of a thumb as broad as a spatula. 'You would think, sir, he had jumped overboard only to give an unlucky man a last show to get on. What with the shock of him going in this awful rash way, and thinking myself a made man by that chance, I was nearly off my chump for a week. But no fear. The captain of the *Pelion* was shifted into the *Ossa*—came aboard in Shanghai—a little popinjay, sir, in a gray check suit, with his hair parted in the middle. "Aw—I am—aw—your new captain, Mister—Mister—aw—Jones." He was drowned in scent—fairly stunk with it, Captain Marlow. I daresay it was the look I gave him that made him stammer. He mumbled something about my natural disappointment—I had bet-ter know at once that his chief officer got the promotion to the *Pelion*—he had nothing to do with it, of course—suppose the office knew best—sorry. . . . Says I, "Don't you mind old Jones, sir; dam' his soul, he's used to it." I could see directly I had shocked his delicate ear, and while we sat at our first tiffin together he began to find fault in a nasty manner with this and that in the ship. I never heard such a voice out of a Punch and Judy show. I set my teeth hard, and glued my eyes to my plate, and held my peace as long as I could; but at last I had to say something: up he jumps tiptoeing, ruffling all his pretty plumes, like a little fighting cock. "You'll find you have a different person to deal with than the late Captain Brierly." "I've found it," says I, very glum, but pretending to be mighty busy with my steak. "You are an old ruffian, Mr.—aw—Jones; and what's more, you are known for an old ruffian in the employ," he squeaks at me. The damned bottle-washers stood about listening with their mouths stretched from ear to ear. "I may be a hard case," answers I, "but I ain't so far gone as to put up with the sight of you sitting in Captain Brierly's chair." With that I lay down my knife and fork. "You would like to sit in it yourself—that's where the shoe pinches," he sneers. I left the saloon, got my rags together, and was on the quay with all my dunnage about my feet before the stevedores had turned to again. Yes. Adrift—on shore—after ten years' service—and with a poor woman and four children six thousand miles off depending on my half-pay for every mouthful they ate. Yes, sir! I chucked it rather than hear Captain Brierly abused. He left me his night-glasses—here they are; and he wished me to take care of the dog—here he is. Halloo, Rover, poor boy. Where's the captain, Rover?' The dog looked up at us with mournful yellow eyes, gave one desolate bark, and crept under the table.

"All this was taking place, more than two years afterward, on board that nauti-cal ruin the *Fire-Queen* this Jones had got charge of—quite by a funny accident, too—from Matherson—mad Matherson they generally called him—the same who used to hand out in Haï-phong, you know, before the occupation days. The old chap snuffled on—

"'Ay, sir, Captain Brierly will be remembered here, if there's no other place on earth. I wrote fully to his father and did not get a word in reply—neither Thank you, nor Go to the devil!—nothing! Perhaps they did not want to know.'

"The sight of that watery-eyed old Jones mopping his bald head with a red cotton handkerchief, the sorrowing yelp of the dog, the squalor of that fly-blown cuddy which was the only shrine of his memory, threw a veil of inexpressible mean pathos over Brierly's remembered figure, the posthumous revenge of fate for that belief in his own splendor which had almost cheated his life of its legitimate terrors. Almost! Perhaps wholly. Who can tell what flattering view he had induced himself to take of his own suicide.

"'Why did he commit the rash act, Captain Marlow—can you think?' asked Jones, pressing his palms together. 'Why? It beats me! Why?' He slapped his low and wrinkled forehead. 'If he had been poor and old and in debt—and never a show—or else mad. But he wasn't of the kind that goes mad, not he. You trust me. What a mate don't know about his skipper isn't worth knowing. Young, healthy, well off, no cares. . . . I sit here sometimes thinking, thinking, till my head fairly begins to buzz. There was some reason.'

"'You may depend upon it, Captain Jones,' said I, 'it wasn't anything that would have disturbed much either of us two,' I said; and then, as if a light had been flashed into the muddle of his brain, poor old Jones found a last word of amazing profundity. He blew his nose, nodding at me dolefully: 'Ay, ay! neither you nor I, sir, had ever thought so much of ourselves.'

"Of course the recollection of my last conversation with Brierly is tinged with the knowledge of his end that followed so close upon it. I spoke with him for the last time during the progress of the inquiry. It was after the first adjournment, and he came up with me in the street. He was in a state of irritation, which I noticed with surprise, his usual behavior when he condescended to converse being perfectly cool, with a trace of amused tolerance, as if the existence of his interlocutor had been a rather good joke. 'They caught me for that inquiry, you see,' he began, and for a while enlarged complainingly upon the inconveniences of daily attendance in court. 'And goodness knows how long it will last. Three days, I suppose.' I heard him out in silence; in my then opinion it was a way as good as another of putting on side. 'What's the use of it? It is the stupidest set out you can imagine,' he pursued hotly. I remarked that there was no option. He interrupted me with a sort of pent-up violence. 'I feel like a fool all the time.' I looked up at him. This was going very far—for Brierly—when talking of Brierly. He stopped short, and seizing the lapel of my coat, gave it a slight tug. 'Why are we tormenting that young chap?' he asked. This question chimed in so well to the tolling of a certain thought of mine that, with the image of the absconding renegade in my eye, I answered at once, 'Hanged if I know, unless it be that he lets you.' I was astonished to see him fall into line, so to speak, with that utterance, which ought to have been tolerably cryptic. He said angrily, 'Why, yes. Can't he see that wretched skipper of his has cleared out? What does he expect to happen? Nothing can save him. He's done for.' We walked on in silence a few steps. 'Why eat all that dirt?' he exclaimed, with an oriental energy of expression—about the only sort of energy you can find a trace of east of the fiftieth meridian. I wondered greatly at the direction of his thoughts, but now I strongly suspect it was strictly in character: at bottom poor Brierly must have been thinking of himself. I pointed out to him that the skipper of the *Patna* was known to have feathered his nest pretty well, and could procure almost anywhere the means of getting away. With Jim it was otherwise: the Government was keeping him in the Sailors' Home for the time being, and probably he hadn't a penny in his pocket to bless himself with. It costs some money to run away. 'Does it? Not always,' he said, with a bitter laugh, and to some further remark of mine—'Well, then, let him creep twenty feet underground and stay there! By heavens! I would.' I don't know why his tone provoked me, and I said, 'There is a kind of courage in facing it out as he does, knowing very well that if he went away nobody would trouble to run after him.' 'Courage be hanged!' growled Brierly. 'That sort of courage is of no use to keep a man straight, and I don't care a snap for such courage. If you were to say it was a kind of cowardice now—of softness. I tell you what, I will put up two hundred rupees if you put up another hundred and undertake to make the beggar clear out early tomorrow morning. The fellow's a gentleman if he ain't fit to be touched—he will understand. He must! This infernal publicity is too shocking: there he sits while all these confounded natives, serangs, lascars, quartermasters, are giving evidence that's enough to burn a man to ashes with shame. This is abominable. Why, Marlow, don't you think, don't you feel, that this is abominable; don't you now—come—as a seaman? If he went away all this would stop at once.' Brierly said these words with a most unusual animation, and made as if to reach after his pocketbook. I restrained him, and declared coldly that the cowardice of these four men did not seem to me a matter of such great importance. 'And you call yourself a seaman, I suppose,' he pronounced angrily. I said that's what I called myself, and I hoped I was too. He heard me out, and made a gesture with his big arm that seemed to deprive me of my individuality, to push me away into the crowd. 'The worst of it,' he said, 'is that all you fellows have no sense of dignity; you don't think enough of what you are supposed to be.'

"We had been walking slowly meantime, and now stopped opposite the harbor office, in sight of the very spot from which the immense captain of the *Patna* had vanished as utterly as a tiny feather blown away in a hurricane. I smiled. Brierly went on: 'This is a disgrace. We've got all kinds amongst us—some anointed scoundrels in the lot; but, hang it, we must preserve professional decency or we become no better than so many tinkers going about loose. We are trusted. Do you understand?—trusted! Frankly, I don't care a snap for all the pilgrims that ever came out of Asia, but a decent man would not have behaved like this to a full cargo of old rags in bales. We aren't an organized body of men, and the only thing that holds us together is just the name for that kind of decency. Such an affair destroys one's confidence. A man may go pretty near through his whole sea-life without any call to show a stiff upper lip. But when the call comes. . . . Aha! . . . If I . . .'

"He broke off, and in a changed tone, 'I'll give you two hundred rupees now, Marlow, and you just talk to that chap. Confound him! I wish he had never come out here. Fact is, I rather think some of my people know his. The old man's a parson, and I remember now I met him once when staying with my cousin in Essex last year. If I am not mistaken, the old chap seemed rather to fancy his sailor son. Horrible. I can't do it myself—but you. . . .'

"Thus, apropos of Jim, I had a glimpse of the real Brierly a few days before he committed his reality and his sham together to the keeping of the sea. Of course I declined to meddle. The tone of this last 'but you' (poor Brierly couldn't help it), that seemed to imply I was no more noticeable than an insect, caused me to look at the proposal with indignation, and on account of that provocation, or for some other reason, I became positive in my mind that the inquiry was a severe punishment to that Jim, and that his facing it—practically of his own freewill—was a redeeming feature in his abominable case. I hadn't been so sure of it before. Brierly went off in a huff. At the time his state of mind was more of a mystery to me than it is now.

"Next day, coming into court late, I sat by myself. Of course I could not forget the conversation I had with Brierly, and now I had them both under my eyes. The demeanor of one suggested gloomy impudence and of the other a contemptuous boredom; yet one attitude might not have been truer than the other, and I was aware that one was not true. Brierly was not bored—he was exasperated; and if so, then Jim might not have been impudent. According to my theory he was not. I imagined he was hopeless. Then it was that our glances met. They met, and the look he gave me was discouraging of any intention I might have had to speak to him. Upon either hypothesis—insolence or despair—I felt I could be of no use to him. This was the second day of the proceedings. Very soon after that exchange of glances the inquiry was adjourned again to the next day. The white men began to troop out at once. Jim had been told to stand down some time before, and was able to leave amongst the first. I saw his broad shoulders and his head outlined in the light of the door, and while I made my way slowly out talking with someone— some stranger who had addressed me casually—I could see him from within the courtroom resting both elbows on the balustrade of the veranda and turning his

back on the small stream of people trickling down the few steps. There was a murmur of voices and a shuffle of boots.

"The next case was that of assault and battery committed upon a moneylender,
I believe; and the defendant—a venerable villager with a straight white beard—
sat on a mat just outside the door with his sons, daughters, sons-in-law, their
wives, and, I should think, half the population of his village besides, squatting or
standing around him. A slim dark woman, with part of her back and one black
shoulder bared, and with a thin gold ring in her nose, suddenly began to talk in a
high-pitched, shrewish tone. The man with me instinctively looked up at her. We
were then just through the door, passing behind Jim's burly back.

"Whether those villagers had brought the yellow dog with them, I don't know.
Anyhow, a dog was there, weaving himself in and out amongst people's legs in that
mute, stealthy way native dogs have, and my companion stumbled over him. The
dog leaped away without a sound; the man, raising his voice a little, said with a
slow laugh, 'Look at that wretched cur,' and directly afterwards we became separated by a lot of people pushing in. I stood back for a moment against the wall
while the stranger managed to get down the steps and disappeared. I saw Jim spin
round. He made a step forward and barred my way. We were alone; he glared at me
with an air of stubborn resolution. I became aware I was being held up, so to
speak, as if in a wood. The veranda was empty by then, the noise and movement in
court had ceased: a great silence fell upon the building, in which, somewhere far
within, an oriental voice began to whine abjectly. The dog, in the very act of trying
to sneak in at the door, sat down hurriedly to hunt for fleas.

"'Did you speak to me?' asked Jim very low, and bending forward, not so much
towards me but at me, if you know what I mean. I said 'No' at once. Something in
the sound of that quiet tone of his warned me to be on my defense. I watched him.
It was very much like a meeting in a wood, only more uncertain in its issue, since
he could possibly want neither my money nor my life—nothing that I could simply
give up or defend with a clear conscience. 'You say you didn't,' he said, very
somber. 'But I heard.' 'Some mistake,' I protested, utterly at a loss, and never taking my eyes off him. To watch his face was like watching a darkening sky before a
clap of thunder, shade upon shade imperceptibly coming on, the gloom growing
mysteriously intense in the calm of maturing violence.

"'As far as I know, I haven't opened my lips in your hearing,' I affirmed with
perfect truth. I was getting a little angry, too, at the absurdity of this encounter.
It strikes me now I have never in my life been so near a beating—I mean it literally; a beating with fists. I suppose I had some hazy prescience of that eventuality being in the air. Not that he was actively threatening me. On the contrary, he
was strangely passive—don't you know?—but he was lowering, and, though not
exceptionally big, he looked generally fit to demolish a wall. The most reassuring

symptom I noticed was a kind of slow and ponderous hesitation, which I took as a tribute to the evident sincerity of my manner and of my tone. We faced each other. In the court the assault case was proceeding. I caught the words: 'Well—buffalo—stick—in the greatness of my fear. . . .'

"'What did you mean by staring at me all the morning?' said Jim at last. He looked up and looked down again. 'Did you expect us all to sit with downcast eyes out of regard for your susceptibilities?' I retorted sharply. I was not going to submit meekly to any of his nonsense. He raised his eyes again, and this time continued to look me straight in the face. 'No. That's all right,' he pronounced with an air of deliberating with himself upon the truth of this statement—'that's all right. I am going through with that. Only'—and there he spoke a little faster—'I won't let any man call me names outside this court. There was a fellow with you. You spoke to him—oh, yes—I know; 'tis all very fine. You spoke to him, but you meant me to hear. . . .'

"I assured him he was under some extraordinary delusion. I had no conception how it came about. 'You thought I would be afraid to resent this,' he said, with just a faint tinge of bitterness. I was interested enough to discern the slightest shades of expression, but I was not in the least enlightened; yet I don't know what in these words, or perhaps just the intonation of that phrase, induced me suddenly to make all possible allowances for him. I ceased to be annoyed at my unexpected predicament. It was some mistake on his part; he was blundering, and I had an intuition that the blunder was of an odious, of an unfortunate nature. I was anxious to end this scene on grounds of decency, just as one is anxious to cut short some unprovoked and abominable confidence. The funniest part was, that in the midst of all these considerations of the higher order I was conscious of a certain trepidation as to the possibility—nay, likelihood—of this encounter ending in some disreputable brawl which could not possibly be explained, and would make me ridiculous. I did not hanker after a three days' celebrity as the man who got a black eye or something of the sort from the mate of the *Patna*. He in all probability did not care what he did, or at any rate would be fully justified in his own eyes. It took no magician to see he was amazingly angry about something, for all his quiet and even torpid demeanor. I don't deny I was extremely desirous to pacify him at all costs, had I only known what to do. But I didn't know, as you may well imagine. It was a blackness without a single gleam. We confronted each other in silence. He hung fire for about fifteen seconds, then made a step nearer, and I made ready to ward off a blow, though I don't think I moved a muscle. 'If you were as big as two men and as strong as six,' he said very softly, 'I would tell you what I think of you. You . . .' 'Stop!' I exclaimed. This checked him for a second. 'Before you tell me what you think of me,' I went on quickly, 'will you kindly tell me what it is I've said or done?' During

the pause that ensued he surveyed me with indignation, while I made supernatural efforts of memory, in which I was hindered by the oriental voice within the
courtroom expostulating with impassioned volubility against a charge of falsehood. Then we spoke almost together. 'I will soon show you I am not,' he said, in a
tone suggestive of a crisis. 'I declare I don't know,' I protested earnestly at the
same time. He tried to crush me by the scorn of his glance. 'Now that you see I
am not afraid you try to crawl out of it,' he said. 'Who's a cur now—hey?' Then, at
last, I understood.

"He had been scanning my features as though looking for a place where he
would plant his fist. 'I will allow no man,' . . . he mumbled threateningly. It was,
indeed, a hideous mistake; he had given himself away utterly. I can't give you an
idea how shocked I was. I suppose he saw some reflection of my feelings in my
face, because his expression changed just a little. 'Good God!' I stammered, 'you
don't think I . . .' 'But I am sure I've heard,' he persisted, raising his voice for the
first time since the beginning of this deplorable scene. Then with a shade of disdain he added, 'It wasn't you, then? Very well; I'll find the other.' 'Don't be a fool,' I
cried in exasperation; 'it wasn't that at all.' 'I've heard,' he said again, with an
unshaken and somber perseverance.

"There may be those who could have laughed at his pertinacity. I didn't. Oh, I
didn't! There had never been a man so mercilessly shown up by his own natural
impulse. A single word had stripped him of his discretion—of that discretion
which is more necessary to the decencies of our inner being than clothing is to
the decorum of our body. 'Don't be a fool,' I repeated. 'But the other man said it,
you don't deny that?' he pronounced distinctly, and looked in my face without
flinching. 'No, I don't deny,' said I, returning his gaze. At last his eyes followed
downwards the direction of my pointing finger. He appeared at first uncomprehending, then confounded, and at last amazed and scared, as though a dog had
been a monster, and he had never seen a dog before. 'Nobody dreamt of insulting
you,' I said.

"He contemplated the wretched animal, that moved no more than an effigy: it
sat with ears pricked and its sharp muzzle pointed into the doorway, and suddenly
snapped at a fly like a piece of mechanism.

"I looked at him. The red of his fair sunburnt complexion deepened suddenly
under the down of his cheeks, invaded his forehead, spread to the roots of his
curly hair. His ears became intensely crimson, and even the clear blue of his eyes
was darkened many shades by the rush of blood to his head. His lips pouted a little, trembling as though he had been on the point of bursting into tears. I perceived he was incapable of pronouncing a word from the excess of his humiliation.
From disappointment too—who knows? Perhaps he looked forward to that ham-
mering he was going to give me for rehabilitation, for appeasement? Who can tell

what relief he expected from this chance of a row? He was naive enough to expect anything; but he had given himself away for nothing in this case. He had been frank with himself—let alone with me—in the wild hope of arriving in that way at some effective refutation, and the stars had been ironically unpropitious. He made an inarticulate noise in his throat like a man imperfectly stunned by a blow on the head. It was pitiful.

"I didn't catch up again with him till well outside the gate. I had even to trot a bit at the last, but when, out of breath at his elbow, I taxed him with running away, he said, 'Never!' and at once turned at bay. I explained I never meant to say he was running away from *me*. 'From no man—from not a single man on earth,' he affirmed with a stubborn mien. I forbore to point out the one obvious exception which would hold good for the bravest of us; I thought he would find out by himself very soon. He looked at me patiently while I was thinking of something to say, but I could find nothing on the spur of the moment, and he began to walk on. I kept up, and anxious not to lose him, I said hurriedly that I couldn't think of leaving him under a false impression of my—of my—I stammered. The stupidity of the phrase appalled me while I was trying to finish it, but the power of sentences has nothing to do with their sense or the logic of their construction. My idiotic mumble seemed to please him. He cut it short by saying, with courteous placidity that argued an immense power of self-control or else a wonderful elasticity of spirits—'Altogether my mistake.' I marveled greatly at this expression: he might have been alluding to some trifling occurrence. Hadn't he understood its deplorable meaning? 'You may well forgive me,' he continued, and went on a little moodily, 'All these staring people in court seemed such fools that—that it might have been as I supposed.'

"This opened suddenly a new view of him to my wonder. I looked at him curiously, and met his unabashed and impenetrable eyes. 'I can't put up with this kind of thing,' he said, very simply, 'and I don't mean to. In court it's different; I've got to stand that—and I can do it too.'

"I don't pretend I understood him. The views he let me have of himself were like those glimpses through the shifting rents in a thick fog—bits of vivid and vanishing detail, giving no connected idea of the general aspect of a country. They fed one's curiosity without satisfying it; they were no good for purposes of orientation. Upon the whole he was misleading. That's how I summed him up to myself after he left me late in the evening. I had been staying at the Malabar House for a few days, and on my pressing invitation he dined with me there."

❖ 7 ❖

An outward-bound mail boat had come in that afternoon, and the big dining room of the hotel was more than half full of people with a hundred pounds round-the-world tickets in their pockets. There were married couples looking domesticated and bored with each other in the midst of their travels; there were small parties and large parties, and lone individuals dining solemnly or feasting boisterously, but all thinking, conversing, joking, or scowling as was their wont at home; and just as intelligently receptive of new impressions as their trunks upstairs. Henceforth they would be labeled as having passed through this and that place, and so would be their luggage. They would cherish this distinction of their persons, and preserve the gummed tickets on their portmanteaus as documentary evidence, as the only permanent trace of their improving enterprise. The dark-faced servants tripped without noise over the vast and polished floor; now and then a girl's laugh would be heard, as innocent and empty as her mind, or, in a sudden hush of crockery, a few words in an affected drawl from some wit embroidering for the benefit of a grinning tableful the last funny story of shipboard scandal. Two nomadic old maids, dressed up to kill, worked acrimoniously through the bill of fare, whispering to each other with faded lips, wooden-faced and bizarre, like two sumptuous scarecrows. A little wine opened Jim's heart and loosened his tongue. His appetite was good, too, I noticed. He seemed to have buried somewhere the opening episode of our acquaintance. It was like a thing of which there would be no more question in this world. And all the time I had before me these blue, boyish eyes looking straight into mine, this young face, these capable shoulders, the open bronzed forehead with a white line under the roots of clustering fair hair, this appearance appealing at sight to all my sympathies: this frank aspect, the artless smile, the youthful seriousness. He was of the right sort; he was one of us. He talked soberly, with a sort of composed unreserve, and with a quiet bearing that might have been the outcome of manly self-control, of impudence, of callousness, of a colossal unconsciousness, of a gigantic deception. Who can tell! From our tone we might have been discussing a third person, a football match, last year's weather. My mind floated in a sea of conjectures till the turn of the conversation enabled me, without being offensive, to remark that, upon the whole, this inquiry must have been pretty trying to him. He darted his arm across the tablecloth, and, clutching my hand by the side of my plate, glared fixedly. I *was* startled. 'It must be awfully hard,' I stammered, confused by this display of speechless feeling. 'It is—hell,' he burst out in a muffled voice.

"This movement and these words caused two well-groomed male globetrotters at a neighboring table to look up in alarm from their iced pudding. I rose, and we passed into the front gallery for coffee and cigars.

"On little octagon tables candles burned in glass globes; clumps of stiff-leaved plants separated sets of cozy wicker chairs; and between the pairs of columns, whose reddish shafts caught in a long row the sheen from the tall windows, the night, glittering and somber, seemed to hang like a splendid drapery. The riding-lights of the ships winked afar like setting stars, and the hills across the roadstead resembled rounded black masses of arrested thunderclouds.

"'I couldn't clear out,' Jim began. 'The skipper did—that's all very well for him. I couldn't and I wouldn't. They all got out of it in one way or another, but it wouldn't do for me.'

"I listened with concentrated attention, not daring to stir in my chair; I wanted to know—and to this day I don't know, I can only guess. He would be confident and depressed all in the same breath, as if some conviction of innate blamelessness had checked the truth writhing within him at every turn. He began by saying, in the tone in which a man would admit his inability to jump a twenty-foot wall, that he could never go home now; and this declaration recalled to my mind what Brierly had said, 'that the old parson in Essex seemed to fancy his sailor son not a little.'

"I can't tell you whether Jim knew he was especially 'fancied,' but the tone of his references to 'my Dad' was calculated to give me a notion that the good old rural dean was about the finest man that ever had been worried by the cares of a large family since the beginning of the world. This, though never stated, was implied with an anxiety that there should be no mistake about it, which was really very true and charming, but added a poignant sense of lives far off to the other elements of the story. 'He has seen it all in the home papers by this time,' said Jim. 'I can never face the poor old chap.' I did not dare to lift my eyes at this till I heard him add, 'I could never explain. He wouldn't understand.' Then I looked up. He was smoking reflectively, and after a moment, rousing himself, began to talk again. He discovered at once a desire that I should not confound him with his partners in—in crime, let us call it. He was not one of them; he was altogether of another sort. I gave no sign of dissent. I had no intention, for the sake of barren truth, to rob him of the smallest particle of any saving grace that would come in his way. I didn't know how much of it he believed himself. I didn't know what he was playing up to—if he was playing up to anything at all—and I suspect he did not know either; for it is my belief no man ever understands quite his own artful dodges to escape from the grim shadow of self-knowledge. I made no sound all the time he was wondering what he had better do after 'that stupid inquiry was over.'

"'Apparently he shared Brierly's contemptuous opinion of these proceedings ordained by law. He would not know where to turn, he confessed, clearly thinking aloud rather than talking to me. Certificate gone, career broken, no money to get away, no work that he could obtain as far as he could see. At home he could per-haps get something; but it meant going to his people for help, and that he would not do. He saw nothing for it but ship before the mast—could get perhaps a quar-termaster's billet in some steamer. Would do for a quartermaster. . . . 'Do you think you would?' I asked pitilessly. He jumped up, and going to the stone balustrade looked out into the night. In a moment he was back, towering above my chair with his youthful face clouded yet by the pain of a conquered emotion. He had under-stood very well I did not doubt his ability to steer a ship. In a voice that quavered a bit he asked me, 'Why did I say that? I had been "no end kind" to him. I had not even laughed at him when'—here he began to mumble—'that mistake, you know—made a confounded ass of myself.' I broke in by saying rather warmly that for me such a mistake was not a matter to laugh at. He sat down and drank delib-erately some coffee, emptying the small cup to the last drop. 'That does not mean I admit for a moment the cap fitted,' he declared distinctly. 'No?' I said. 'No,' he affirmed with quiet decision. 'Do you know what *you* would have done? Do you? And you don't think yourself' . . . he gulped something . . . 'you don't think yourself a—a—cur?'

"And with this—upon my honor!—he looked up at me inquisitively. It was a question it appears—a *bona fide* question! However, he didn't wait for an answer. Before I could recover he went on, with his eyes straight before him, as if reading off something written on the body of the night. 'It is all in being ready. I wasn't; not—not then. I don't want to excuse myself; but I would like to explain—I would like somebody to understand—somebody—one person at least! You! Why not you?'

"It was solemn, and a little ridiculous too, as they always are, those struggles of an individual trying to save from the fire his idea of what his moral identity should be, this precious notion of a convention, only one of the rules of the game, nothing more, but all the same so terribly effective by its assumption of unlimited power over natural instincts, by the awful penalties of its failure. He began his story qui-etly enough. On board that Dale Line steamer that had picked up these four float-ing in a boat upon the discreet sunset glow of the sea, they had been after the first day looked askance upon. The fat skipper told some story, the others had been silent, and at first it had been accepted. You don't cross-examine poor castaways you had the good luck to save, if not from cruel death, then at least from cruel suf-fering. Afterwards, with time to think it over, it might have struck the officers of the *Avondale* that there was 'something fishy' in the affair; but of course they would keep their doubts to themselves. They had picked up the captain, the mate, and two engineers of the steamer *Patna* sunk at sea, and that, very properly, was enough for them. I did not ask Jim about the nature of his feelings during the ten days he spent on board. From the way he narrated that part I was at liberty to infer he was partly stunned by the discovery he had made—the discovery about himself—and no doubt was at work trying to explain it away to the only man who was capable of appreciating all its tremendous magnitude. You must understand he did not try to minimize its importance. Of that I am sure; and therein lies his distinction. As to what sensations he experienced when he got ashore and heard the unforeseen conclusion of the tale in which he had taken such a pitiful part, he told me nothing of them, and it is difficult to imagine. I wonder whether he felt the ground cut from under his feet? I wonder? But no doubt he managed to get a fresh foothold very soon. He was ashore a whole fortnight waiting in the Sailors' Home, and as there were six or seven men staying there at the time, I had heard of him a little. Their languid opinion seemed to be that, in addition to his other shortcomings, he was a sulky brute. He had passed these days on the veranda, buried in a long chair, and coming out of his place of sepulture only at mealtimes or late at night, when he wandered on the quays all by himself, detached from his surroundings, irresolute and silent, like a ghost without a home to haunt. 'I don't think I've spoken three words to a living soul in all that time,' he said, making me very sorry for him; and directly he added, 'One of these fellows would have been sure to blurt out something I had made up my mind not to put up with, and I didn't want a row. No! Not then. I was too—too . . . I had no heart for it.' 'So that bulkhead held out after all,' I remarked cheerfully. 'Yes,' he murmured, 'it held. And yet I swear to you I felt it bulge under my hand.' 'It's extraordinary what strains old iron will stand sometimes,' I said. Thrown back in his seat, his legs stiffly out and arms hanging down, he nodded slightly several times. You could not conceive a sadder spectacle. Suddenly he lifted his head; he sat up; he slapped his thigh. 'Ah! what a chance missed! My God! what a chance missed!' he blazed out, but the ring of the last 'missed' resembled a cry wrung out by pain.

"He was silent again with a still, faraway look of fierce yearning after that missed distinction, with his nostrils for an instant dilated, sniffing the intoxicating breath of that wasted opportunity. If you think I was either surprised or shocked you do me an injustice in more ways than one! Ah, he was an imaginative beggar! He would give himself away; he would give himself up. I could see in his glance darted into the night all his inner being carried on, projected headlong into the fanciful realm of recklessly heroic aspirations. He had no leisure to regret what he had lost, he was so wholly and naturally concerned for what he had failed to obtain. He was very far away from me who watched him across three feet of space.

With every instant he was penetrating deeper into the impossible world of romantic achievements. He got to the heart of it at last! A strange look of beatitude overspread his features, his eyes sparkled in the light of the candle burning between
us; he positively smiled! He had penetrated to the very heart—to the very heart. It
was an ecstatic smile that your faces—or mine either—will never wear, my dear
boys. I whisked him back by saying, 'If you had stuck to the ship, you mean!'

"He turned upon me, his eyes suddenly amazed and full of pain, with a bewildered, startled, suffering face, as though he had tumbled down from a star.
Neither you nor I will ever look like this on any man. He shuddered profoundly, as
if a cold fingertip had touched his heart. Last of all he sighed.

"I was not in a merciful mood. He provoked one by his contradictory indiscretions. 'It is unfortunate you didn't know beforehand!' I said with every unkind
intention; but the perfidious shaft fell harmless—dropped at his feet like a spent
arrow, as it were, and he did not think of picking it up. Perhaps he had not even
seen it. Presently, lolling at ease, he said, 'Dash it all! I tell you it bulged. I was
holding up my lamp along the angle-iron in the lower deck when a flake of rust as
big as the palm of my hand fell off the plate, all of itself.' He passed his hand over
his forehead. 'The thing stirred and jumped off like something alive while I was
looking at it.' 'That made you feel pretty bad,' I observed casually. 'Do you suppose,' he said, 'that I was thinking of myself, with a hundred and sixty people at
my back, all fast asleep in that fore-'tween-deck alone—and more of them aft;
more on the deck—sleeping—knowing nothing about it—three times as many as
there were boats for, even if there had been time? I expected to see the iron open
out as I stood there and the rush of water going over them as they lay. . . . What
could I do—what?'

"I can easily picture him to myself in the peopled gloom of the cavernous place,
with the light of the globe-lamp falling on a small portion of the bulkhead that had
the weight of the ocean on the other side, and the breathing of unconscious sleepers in his ears. I can see him glaring at the iron, startled by the falling rust, over-
burdened by the knowledge of an imminent death. This, I gathered, was the second time he had been sent forward by that skipper of his, who, I rather think,
wanted to keep him away from the bridge. He told me that his first impulse was to
shout and straightaway make all those people leap out of sleep into terror; but
such an overwhelming sense of his helplessness came over him that he was not
able to produce a sound. This is, I suppose, what people mean by the tongue cleaving to the roof of the mouth. 'Too dry,' was the concise expression he used in reference to this state. Without a sound, then, he scrambled out on deck through the
number one hatch. A wind-sail rigged down there swung against him accidentally,
and he remembered that the light touch of the canvas on his face nearly knocked
him off the hatchway ladder.

"He confessed that his knees wobbled a good deal as he stood on the foredeck looking at another sleeping crowd. The engines having been stopped by that time, the steam was blowing off. Its deep rumble made the whole night vibrate like a bass string. The ship trembled to it.

"He saw here and there a head lifted off a mat, a vague form uprise in a sitting posture, listen sleepily for a moment, sink down again into the billowy confusion of boxes, steam-winches, ventilators. He was aware all these people did not know enough to take intelligent notice of that strange noise. The ship of iron, the men with white faces, all the sights, all the sounds, everything on board to that ignorant and pious multitude was strange alike, and as trustworthy as it would forever remain incomprehensible. It occurred to him that the fact was unfortunate. The idea of it was simply terrible.

"You must remember he believed, as any other man would have done in his place, that the ship would go down at any moment; the bulging, rust-eaten plates that kept back the ocean, fatally must give way, all at once like an undermined dam, and let in a sudden and overwhelming flood. He stood still looking at these recumbent bodies, a doomed man aware of his fate, surveying the silent company of the dead. They *were* dead! Nothing could save them! There were boats enough for half of them perhaps, but there was no time. No time! No time! It did not seem worthwhile to open his lips, to stir hand or foot. Before he could shout three words, or make three steps, he would be floundering in a sea whitened awfully by the desperate struggles of human beings, clamorous with the distress of cries for help. There was no help. He imagined what would happen perfectly; he went through it all motionless by the hatchway with the lamp in his hand—he went through it to the very last harrowing detail. I think he went through it again while he was telling me these things he could not tell the court.

"'I saw as clearly as I see you now that there was nothing I could do. It seemed to take all life out of my limbs. I thought I might just as well stand where I was and wait. I did not think I had many seconds. . . .' Suddenly the steam ceased blowing off. The noise, he remarked, had been distracting, but the silence at once became intolerably oppressive.

"'I thought I would choke before I got drowned,' he said.

"He protested he did not think of saving himself. The only distinct thought formed, vanishing, and re-forming in his brain, was: eight hundred people and seven boats; eight hundred people and seven boats.

"'Somebody was speaking aloud inside my head,' he said a little wildly. 'Eight hundred people and seven boats—and no time! Just think of it.' He leaned towards me across the little table, and I tried to avoid his stare. 'Do you think I was afraid of death?' he asked in a voice very fierce and low. He brought down his open hand with a bang that made the coffee cups dance. 'I am ready to swear I was not—I was not. . . . By God—no!' He hitched himself upright and crossed his arms; his chin fell on his breast.

"The soft clashes of crockery reached us faintly through the high windows. There was a burst of voices, and several men came out in high good-humor into the gallery. They were exchanging jocular reminiscences of the donkeys in Cairo. A pale anxious youth stepping softly on long legs was being chaffed by a strutting and rubicund globetrotter about his purchases in the bazaar. 'No, really—do you think I've been done to that extent?' he inquired very earnest and deliberate. The band moved away, dropping into chairs as they went; matches flared, illuminating for a second faces without the ghost of an expression and the flat glaze of white shirtfronts; the hum of many conversations animated with the ardor of feasting sounded to me absurd and infinitely remote.

"'Some of the crew were sleeping on the number one hatch within reach of my arm,' began Jim again.

"You must know that they kept Kalashee watch in that ship, all hands sleeping through the night, and only the reliefs of quartermasters and lookout men being called. He was tempted to grip and shake the shoulder of the nearest lascar, but he didn't. Something held his arm down along his sides. He was not afraid—oh, no! only he just couldn't—that's all. He was not afraid of death perhaps, but I'll tell you what, he was afraid of the emergency. His confounded imagination had evoked for him all the horrors of panic, the trampling rush, the pitiful screams, boats swamped—all the appalling incidents of a disaster at sea he had ever heard of. He might have been resigned to die; but I suspect he wanted to die without added terrors, quietly, in a sort of peaceful trance. A certain readiness to perish is not so very rare, but it is seldom that you meet men whose souls, steeled in the impenetrable armor of resolution, are ready to fight a losing battle to the last: the desire of peace waxes stronger as hope declines, till at last it conquers the very desire of life. Which of us here has not observed this, or maybe experienced something of that feeling in his own person—this extreme weariness of emotions, the vanity of effort, the yearning for rest? Those striving with unreasonable forces know it well—the shipwrecked castaways in boats, wanderers lost in a desert, men battling against the unthinking might of nature or the stupid brutality of crowds."

❧ 8 ❧

How long he stood stock-still by the hatch expecting every moment to feel the ship dip under his feet and the rush of water take him at the back and toss him like a chip, I cannot say. Not very long—two minutes perhaps. A couple of men he could not make out began to converse drowsily, and also, he could not tell where, he detected a curious noise of shuffling feet. Above these faint sounds there was that awful stillness preceding a catastrophe, that trying silence of the moment before the crash; then it came into his head that perhaps he would have time to rush along and cut all the lanyards of the gripes, so that the boats would float off as the ship went down.

"The *Patna* had a long bridge, and all the boats were up there, four on one side and three on the other—the smallest of them on the port side and nearly abreast of the steering-gear. He assured me, with evident anxiety to be believed, that he had been most careful to keep them ready for instant service. He knew his duty. I daresay he was a good enough mate as far as that went. 'I always believed in being prepared for the worst,' he continued, staring anxiously in my face. I nodded my approval of the sound principle, averting my eyes before the subtle unsoundness of the man.

"He started unsteadily to run. He had to step over legs, avoid stumbling against the heads. Suddenly someone caught hold of his coat from below, and a distressed voice spoke under his elbow. The light of the lamp he carried in his right hand fell upon an upturned dark face whose eyes entreated him together with the voice. He had picked up enough of the language to understand the word water, repeated several times in a tone of insistence, of prayer, almost of despair. He gave a jerk to get away, and felt an arm embrace his leg.

"'The beggar clung to me like a drowning man,' he said impressively. 'Water, water! What water did he mean What did he know? As calmly as I could I ordered him to let go. He was stopping me, time was pressing, other men began to stir; I wanted time—time to cut the boats adrift. He got hold of my hand now, and I felt that he would begin to shout. It flashed upon me it was enough to start a panic, and I hauled off with my free arm and slung the lamp in his face. The glass jingled, the light went out, but the blow made him let go, and I ran off—I wanted to get at the boats; I wanted to get at the boats. He leaped after me from behind. I turned on him. He would not keep quiet; he tried to shout; I had half throttled him before I made out what he wanted. He wanted some water—water to drink; they were on strict allowance, you know, and he had with him a young boy I had noticed several times. His child was sick—and thirsty. He had caught sight of me as I passed by, and was begging for a little water. That's all. We were under the bridge, in the dark. He kept on snatching at my wrists; there was no getting rid of him. I dashed into my berth, grabbed my water-bottle, and thrust it into his hands. He vanished. I didn't find out till then how much I was in want of a drink myself.' He leaned on one elbow with a hand over his eyes.

"I felt a creepy sensation all down my backbone; there was something peculiar in all this. The fingers of the hand that shaded his brow trembled slightly. He broke the short silence.

"'These things happen only once to a man and . . . Ah! well! When I got on the bridge at last the beggars were getting one of the boats off the chocks. A boat! I was running up the ladder when a heavy blow fell on my shoulder, just missing my head. It didn't stop me, and the chief engineer—they had got him out of his bunk by then—raised the boat-stretcher again. Somehow I had no mind to be surprised at anything. All this seemed natural—and awful—and awful. I dodged that miserable maniac, lifted him off the deck as though he had been a little child, and he started whispering in my arms: "Don't! don't! I thought you were one of them niggers." I flung him away, he skidded along the bridge and knocked the legs from under the little chap—the second. The skipper, busy about the boat, looked round and came at me head down, growling like a wild beast. I flinched no more than a stone. I was as solid standing there as this,' he tapped lightly with his knuckles the wall beside his chair. 'It was as though I had heard it all, seen it all, gone through it all twenty times already. I wasn't afraid of them. I drew back my fist, and he stopped short, muttering-

"'"Ah! it's you. Lend a hand quick."

"'That's what he said. Quick! As if anybody could be quick enough. Aren't you going to do something?' I asked. "Yes. Clear out," he snarled over his shoulder.

"'I don't think I understood then what he meant. The other two had picked themselves up by that time, and they rushed together to the boat. They tramped, they wheezed, they shoved, they cursed the boat, the ship, each other— cursed me. All in mutters. I didn't move, I didn't speak. I watched the slant of the ship. She was as still as if landed on the blocks in a dry dock—only she was like this.' He held up his hand, palm under, the tips of the fingers inclined downwards. 'Like this,' he repeated. 'I could see the line of the horizon before me, as clear as a bell, above her stem-head; I could see the water far off there black and sparkling, and still—still as a pond, deadly still, more still than ever sea was before—more still than I could bear to look at. Have you watched a ship floating head down, checked in sinking by a sheet of old iron too rotten to stand being shored up? Have you? Oh, yes, shored up? I thought of that—I thought of every mortal thing; but can you shore up a bulkhead in five minutes—or in fifty for that matter? Where was I going to get men that would go down below? And the timber—the timber! Would you have had the courage to swing the maul for the first blow if you had seen that bulkhead? Don't say you would: you had not seen it; nobody would. Hang it—to do a thing like that you must believe there is a chance, one in a thousand at least, some ghost of a chance; and you would not have believed. Nobody would have believed. You think me a cur for standing there, but what would you have done? What! You can't tell—nobody can tell. One must have time to turn round. What would you have me do? Where was the kindness in making crazy with fright all those people I could not save single-handed—that nothing could save? Look here! As true as I sit on this chair before you . . .'

"He drew quick breaths at every few words and shot quick glances at my face, as though in his anguish he were watchful of the effect. He was not speaking to me, he was only speaking before me, in a dispute with an invisible personality, an antagonistic and inseparable partner of his existence—another possessor of his soul. These were issues beyond the competency of a court of inquiry: it was a subtle and momentous quarrel as to the true essence of life, and did not want a judge. He wanted an ally, a helper, an accomplice. I felt the risk I ran of being circumvented, blinded, decoyed, bullied perhaps, into taking a definite part in a dispute impossible of decision if one had to be fair to all the phantoms in possession—to the reputable that had its claims and to the disreputable that had its exigencies. I can't explain to you who haven't seen him and who hear his words only at second hand the mixed nature of my feelings. It seemed to me I was being made to comprehend the Inconceivable—and I know of nothing to compare with the discomfort of such a sensation. I was made to look at the convention that lurks in all truth and on the essential sincerity of falsehood. He appealed to all sides at once—to the side turned perpetually to the light of day, and to that side of us which, like the other hemisphere of the moon, exists stealthily in perpetual darkness, with only a fearful ashy light falling at times on the edge. He swayed me. I own to it, I own up. The occasion was obscure, insignificant—what you will: a lost youngster, one in a million—but then he was one of us; an incident as completely devoid of importance as the flooding of an ant-heap, and yet the mystery of his attitude got hold of me as though he had been an individual in the forefront of his kind, as if the obscure truth involved were momentous enough to affect mankind's conception of itself. . . ."

Marlow paused to put new life into his expiring cheroot, seemed to forget all about the story, and abruptly began again.

"My fault, of course. One has no business really to get interested. It's a weakness of mine. His was of another kind. My weakness consists in not having a discriminating eye for the incidental—for the externals—no eye for the hod of the ragpicker or the fine linen of the next man. Next man—that's it. I have met so many men," he pursued, with momentary sadness—"met them too with a certain—certain—impact, let us say; like this fellow, for instance—and in each case all I could see was merely the human being. A confounded democratic quality of vision which may be better than total blindness, but has been of no advantage to me—I can assure you. Men expect one to take into account their fine linen. But I never could get up any enthusiasm about these things. Oh! it's a failing; it's a failing; and then comes a soft evening; a lot of men too indolent for whist—and a story. . . ."

He paused again to wait for an encouraging remark, perhaps, but nobody spoke; only the host, as if reluctantly performing a duty, murmured—

"You are so subtle, Marlow."

"Who? I?" said Marlow in a low voice. "Oh, no! But he was; and try as I may for the success of this yarn I am missing innumerable shades—they were so fine, so difficult to render in colorless words. Because he complicated matters by being so simple, too—the simplest poor devil! . . . By Jove! he was amazing. There he sat telling me that just as I saw him before my eyes he wouldn't be afraid to face anything—and believing in it too. I tell you it was fabulously innocent and it was enormous, enormous! I watched him covertly, just as though I had suspected him of an intention to take a jolly good rise out of me. He was confident that, on the square, 'on the square, mind!' there was nothing he couldn't meet. Ever since he had been 'so high'—'quite a little chap,' he had been preparing himself for all the difficulties that can beset one on land and water. He confessed proudly to this kind of foresight. He had been elaborating dangers and defenses, expecting the worst, rehearsing his best. He must have led a most exalted existence. Can you fancy it? A succession of adventures, so much glory, such a victorious progress! and the deep sense of his sagacity crowning every day of his inner life. He forgot himself; his eyes shone; and with every word my heart, searched by the light of his absurdity, was growing heavier in my breast. I had no mind to laugh, and lest I should smile I made for myself a stolid face. He gave signs of irritation.

"'It is always the unexpected that happens,' I said a propitiatory tone. My obtuseness provoked him into contemptuous 'Pshaw!' I suppose he meant that the unexpected couldn't touch him; nothing less than the unconceivable itself could get over his perfect state of preparation. He had been taken unawares—and he whispered to himself a malediction upon the waters and the firmament, upon the ship, upon the men. Everything had betrayed him! He had been tricked into that sort of high-minded resignation which prevented him lifting as much as his little finger, while these others who had a very clear perception of the actual necessity were tumbling against each other and sweating desperately over that boat business. Something had gone wrong there at the last moment. It appears that in their flurry they had contrived in some mysterious way to get the sliding bolt of the foremost boat-chock jammed tight, and forthwith had gone out of the remnants of their minds over the deadly nature of that accident. It must have been a pretty sight, the fierce industry of these beggars toiling on a motionless ship that floated quietly in the silence of a world asleep, fighting against time for the freeing of that boat, groveling on all fours, standing up in despair, tugging, pushing, snarling at each other venomously, ready to kill, ready to weep, and only kept from flying at each other's throats by the fear of death that stood silent behind them like an inflexible and cold-eyed taskmaster. Oh, yes! It must have been a pretty sight. He saw it all, he could talk about it with scorn and bitterness; he had a minute knowledge of it by means of some sixth sense, I conclude, because he swore to me he had remained apart without a glance at them and at the boat—without one single glance. And I believe him. I should think he was too busy watching the threatening slant of the ship, the suspended menace discovered in the midst of the most perfect security—fascinated by the sword hanging by a hair over his imaginative head.

"Nothing in the world moved before his eyes, and he could depict to himself without hindrance the sudden swing upwards of the dark skyline, the sudden tilt-up of the vast plain of the sea, the swift, still rise, the brutal fling, the grasp of the abyss, the struggle without hope, the starlight closing over his head forever like the vault of a tomb—the revolt of his young life—the black end. He could! By Jove! who couldn't? And you must remember he was a finished artist in that peculiar way, he was a gifted poor devil with the faculty of swift and forestalling vision. The sights it showed him had turned him into cold stone from the soles of his feet to the nape of his neck; but there was a hot dance of thoughts in his head, a dance of lame, blind, mute thoughts—a whirl of awful cripples. Didn't I tell you he confessed himself before me as though I had the power to bind and to loose. He burrowed deep, deep, in the hope of my absolution, which would have been of no good to him. This was one of these cases which no solemn deception can palliate, where no man can help; where his very Maker seems to abandon a sinner to his own devices.

"He stood on the starboard side of the bridge, as far as he could get from the struggle for the boat, which went on with the agitation of madness and the stealthiness of a conspiracy. The two Malays had meantime remained holding to the wheel. Just picture to yourselves the actors in that, thank God! unique episode of the sea, four beside themselves with fierce and secret exertions, and three looking on in complete immobility, above the awnings covering the profound ignorance of hundreds of human beings, with their weariness, with their dreams, with their hopes, arrested, held by an invisible hand on the brink of annihilation. For that they were so, makes no doubt to me: given the state of the ship, this was the deadliest possible description of accident that could happen. These beggars by the boat had every reason to go distracted with funk. Frankly, had I been there, I would not have given as much as a counterfeit farthing for the ship's chance to keep above water to the end of each successive second. And still she floated! These sleeping pilgrims were destined to accomplish their whole pilgrimage to the bitterness of some other end. It was as if the Omnipotence whose mercy they confessed had needed their humble testimony on earth for a while longer, and had looked down to make a sign, 'Thou shalt not!' to the ocean. Their escape would trouble me as a prodigiously inexplicable event, did I not know how tough old iron can be—as tough sometimes as the spirit of some men we meet now and then, worn to a shadow and breasting the weight of life. Not the least wonder of these twenty minutes, to my mind, is the behavior of the two helmsmen. They were amongst the native batch of all sorts brought over from Aden to give evidence at the inquiry. One of them, laboring under intense bashfulness, was very young, and with his smooth, yellow, cheery countenance looked even younger than he was. I remember perfectly Brierly asking him, through the interpreter, what he thought of it at the time, and the interpreter, after a short colloquy, turning to the court with an important air—

"'He says he thought nothing.'

"The other, with patient blinking eyes, a blue cotton handkerchief, faded with much washing, bound with a smart twist over a lot of gray wisps, his face shrunken into grim hollows, his brown skin made darker by a mesh of wrinkles, explained that he had a knowledge of some evil thing befalling the ship, but there had been no order; he could not remember an order; why should he leave the helm? To some further questions he jerked back his spare shoulders, and declared it never came into his mind then that the white men were about to leave the ship through fear of death. He did not believe it now. There might have been secret reasons. He wagged his old chin knowingly. Aha! secret reasons. He was a man of great experience, and he wanted *that* white Tuan to know—he turned towards Brierly, who didn't raise his head—that he had acquired a knowledge of many things by serving white men on the sea for a great number of years—and, suddenly, with shaky excitement he poured upon our spellbound attention a lot of queer sounding names, names of dead-and-gone skippers, names of forgotten country ships, names of familiar and distorted sound, as if the hand of dumb time had been at work on them for ages. They stopped him at last. A silence fell upon the court—a silence that remained unbroken for at least a minute, and passed gently into a deep murmur. This episode was *the* sensation of the second day's proceedings—affecting all the audience, affecting everybody except Jim, who was sitting moodily at the end of the first bench, and never looked up at this extraordinary and damning witness that seemed possessed of some mysterious theory of defense.

"So these two lascars stuck to the helm of that ship without steerageway, where death would have found them if such had been their destiny. The whites did not give them half a glance, had probably forgotten their existence. Assuredly Jim did not remember it. He remembered he could do nothing; he could do nothing, now he was alone. There was nothing to do but to sink with the ship. No use making a disturbance about it. Was there? He waited upstanding, without a sound, stiffened in the idea of some sort of heroic discretion. The first engineer ran cautiously across the bridge to tug at his sleeve.

"'Come and help! For God's sake, come and help!'

"He ran back to the boat on the points of his toes, and returned directly to worry at his sleeve, begging and cursing at the same time.

"'I believe he would have kissed my hands,' said Jim, savagely, 'and, next moment, he starts foaming and whispering in my face, "If I had the time I would like to crack your skull for you." I pushed him away. Suddenly he caught hold of me round the neck. Damn him! I hit him. I hit out without looking. "Won't you save your own life—you infernal coward," he sobs. Coward! He called me an infernal coward! Ha! ha! ha! ha! He called me—ha! ha! ha! . . .'

"He had thrown himself back and was shaking with laughter. I had never in my life heard anything so bitter as that noise. It fell like a blight on all the merriment about donkeys, pyramids, bazaars, or what not. Along the whole dim length of the gallery the voices dropped, the pale blotches of faces turned our way with one accord, and the silence became so profound that the clear tinkle of a teaspoon falling on the tessellated floor of the veranda rang out like a tiny and silvery scream.

"'You mustn't laugh like this, with all these people about,' I remonstrated. 'It isn't nice for them, you know.'

"He gave no sign of having heard at first, but after a while, with a stare that, missing me altogether, seemed to probe the heart of some awful vision, he muttered carelessly—'Oh! they'll think I am drunk.'

"And after that you would have thought from his appearance he would never make a sound again. But—no fear! He could no more stop telling now than he could have stopped living by the mere exertion of his will."

❧ 9 ❧

I was saying to myself, "Sink—curse you! Sink!" These were the words with which he began again. He wanted it over. He was severely left alone, and he formulated in his head this address to the ship in a tone of imprecation, while at the same time he enjoyed the privilege of witnessing scenes—as far as I can judge—of low comedy. They were still at that bolt. The skipper was ordering. 'Get under and try to lift'; and the others naturally shirked. You understand that to be squeezed flat under the keel of a boat wasn't a desirable position to be caught in if the ship went down suddenly. 'Why don't you—you the strongest?' whined the little engineer. 'Gott-for-dam! I am too thick,' spluttered the skipper in despair. It was funny enough to make angels weep. They stood idle for a moment, and suddenly the chief engineer rushed again at Jim.

"'Come and help, man! Are you mad to throw your only chance away? Come and help, man! Man! Look there—look!'

"And at last Jim looked astern where the other pointed with maniacal insistence. He saw a silent black squall which had eaten up already one-third of the sky. You know how these squalls come up there about that time of the year. First you see a darkening of the horizon—no more; then a cloud rises opaque like a wall. A straight edge of vapor lined with sickly whitish gleams flies up from the southwest, swallowing the stars in whole constellations; its shadow flies over the waters, and confounds sea and sky into one abyss of obscurity. And all is still. No thunder, no wind, no sound; not a flicker of lightning. Then in the tenebrous immensity a livid arch appears; a swell or two like undulations of the very darkness run past, and suddenly, wind and rain strike together with a peculiar impetuosity as if they had burst through something solid. Such a cloud had come up while they weren't looking. They had just noticed it, and were perfectly justified in surmising that if in absolute stillness there was some chance for the ship to keep afloat a few minutes longer, the least disturbance of the sea would make an end of her instantly. Her first nod to the swell that precedes the burst of such a squall would be also her last, would become a plunge, would, so to speak, be prolonged into a long dive, down, down to the bottom. Hence, these new capers of their fright, these new antics in which they displayed their aversion to die.

"'It was black, black,' pursued Jim with moody steadiness. 'It had sneaked upon us from behind. The infernal thing! I suppose there had been at the back of my head some hope yet. I don't know. But that was all over anyhow. It maddened me to see myself caught like this. I was angry, as though I had been trapped. I *was* trapped! The night was hot, too, I remember. Not a breath of air.'

"He remembered so well that, gasping in the chair, he seemed to sweat and choke before my eyes. No doubt it maddened him; it knocked him over afresh—in a manner of speaking—but it made him also remember that important purpose which had sent him rushing on that bridge only to slip clean out of his mind. He had intended to cut the lifeboats clear of the ship. He whipped out his knife and went to work slashing as though he had seen nothing, had heard nothing, had known of no one on board. They thought him hopelessly wrongheaded and crazy, but dared not protest noisily against this useless loss of time. When he had done he returned to the very same spot from which he had started. The chief was there, ready with a clutch at him to whisper close to his head, scathingly, as though he wanted to bite his ear—

"'You silly fool! do you think you'll get the ghost of a show when all that lot of brutes is in the water? Why, they will batter your head for you from these boats.'

"He wrung his hands, ignored, at Jim's elbow. The skipper kept up a nervous shuffle in one place and mumbled, 'Hammer! hammer! Mein Gott! Get a hammer.'

"The little engineer whimpered like a child, but, broken arm and all, he turned out the least craven of the lot as it seems, and, actually, mustered enough pluck to run an errand to the engine room. No trifle, it must be owned in fairness to him. Jim told me he darted desperate looks like a cornered man, gave one low wail, and dashed off. He was back instantly, clambering, hammer in hand, and without a pause flung himself at the bolt. The others gave up Jim at once and ran off to assist. He heard the tap, tap, of the hammer, the sound of the released chock falling over. The boat was clear. Only then he turned to look—only then. But he kept his distance—he kept his distance. He wanted me to know he had kept his distance; that there was nothing in common between him and these men—who had the hammer. Nothing whatever. It is more than probable he thought himself cut off from them by a space that could not be traversed, by an obstacle that could not be overcome, by a chasm without bottom. He was as far as he could get from them—the whole breadth of the ship.

"His feet were glued to that remote spot and his eyes to their indistinct group bowed together and swaying strangely in the common torment of fear. A hand lamp lashed to a stanchion above a little table rigged up on the bridge—the *Patna* had no chart-room amidships—threw a light on their laboring shoulders, on their arched and bobbing backs. They pushed at the bow of the boat; they pushed out into the night; they pushed, and would no more look back at him. They had given him up as if indeed he had been too far, too hopelessly separated from themselves, to be worth an appealing word, a glance, or a sign. They had no leisure to look back upon his passive heroism, to feel the sting of his abstention. The boat was heavy; they pushed at the bow with no breath to spare for an encouraging word: but the turmoil of terror that had scattered their self-command like chaff before the wind, converted their desperate exertions into a bit of fooling, upon my word, fit for knockabout clowns in a farce. They pushed with their hands, with their heads, they pushed for dear life with all the weight of their bodies, they pushed with all the might of their souls—only no sooner had they succeeded in canting the stem clear of the davit than they would leave off like one man and start a wild scramble into her. As a natural consequence the boat would swing in abruptly, driving them back, helpless and jostling against each other. They would stand nonplussed for a while, exchanging in fierce whispers all the infamous names they could call to mind, and go at it again. Three times this occurred. He described it to me with morose thoughtfulness. He hadn't lost a single movement of that comic business. 'I loathed them. I hated them. I had to look at all that,' he said without emphasis, turning upon me a somberly watchful glance. 'Was ever there anyone so shamefully tried!'

"He took his head in his hands for a moment, like a man driven to distraction by some unspeakable outrage. These were things he could not explain to the court—and not even to me; but I would have been little fitted for the reception of his confidences had I not been able at times to understand the pauses between the words. In this assault upon his fortitude there was the jeering intention of a spiteful and vile vengeance; there was an element of burlesque in his ordeal—a degradation of funny grimaces in the approach of death or dishonor.

"He related facts which I have not forgotten, but at this distance of time I couldn't recall his very words: I only remember that he managed wonderfully to convey the brooding rancor of his mind into the bare recital of events. Twice, he told me, he shut his eyes in the certitude that the end was upon him already, and twice he had to open them again. Each time he noted the darkening of the great stillness. The shadow of the silent cloud had fallen upon the ship from the zenith, and seemed to have extinguished every sound of her teeming life. He could no longer hear the voices under the awnings. He told me that each time he closed his eyes a flash of thought showed him that crowd of bodies, laid out for death, as plain as daylight. When he opened them, it was to see the dim struggle of four men fighting like mad with a stubborn boat. 'They would fall back before it time after time, stand swearing at each other, and suddenly make another rush in a bunch. . . . Enough to make you die laughing,' he commented with downcast eyes; then raising them for a moment to my face with a dismal smile, 'I ought to have a merry life of it, by God! for I shall see that funny sight a good many times yet before I die.' His eyes fell again. 'See and hear . . . See and hear,' he repeated twice, at long intervals, filled by vacant staring.

"He roused himself.

"'I made up my mind to keep my eyes shut,' he said, 'and I couldn't. I couldn't, and I don't care who knows it. Let them go through that kind of thing before they talk. Just let them—and do better—that's all. The second time my eyelids flew open and my mouth too. I had felt the ship move. She just dipped her bows—and lifted them gently—and slow! everlastingly slow; and ever so little. She hadn't done that much for days. The cloud had raced ahead, and this first swell seemed to travel upon a sea of lead. There was no life in that stir. It managed, though, to knock over something in my head. What would you have done? You are sure of yourself—aren't you? What would you do if you felt now—this minute—the house here move, just move a little under your chair. Leap! By heavens! you would take one spring from where you sit and land in that clump of bushes yonder.

"He flung his arm out at the night beyond the stone balustrade. I held my peace. He looked at me very steadily, very severe. There could be no mistake: I was being bullied now, and it behoved me to make no sign lest by a gesture or a word I should be drawn into a fatal admission about myself which would have some bearing on the case. I was not disposed to take any risk of that sort. Don't forget I had him before me, and really he was too much like one of us not to be dangerous. But if you want to know, I don't mind telling you that I did, with a rapid glance, estimate the distance to the mass of denser blackness in the middle of the grass plot before the veranda. He exaggerated. I would have landed short by several feet—and that's the only thing of which I am fairly certain.

"The last moment had come, as he thought, and he did not move. His feet remained glued to the planks, if his thoughts were knocking about loose in his head. It was at this moment too that he saw one of the men around the boat step backwards suddenly, clutch at the air with raised arms, totter and collapse. He didn't exactly fall, he only slid gently into a sitting posture, all bunched up, and with his shoulders propped against the side of the engine-room skylight. 'That was the donkey-man. A haggard, white-faced chap with a ragged moustache. Acted third engineer,' he explained.

"'Dead,' I said. We had heard something of that in court.

"'So they say,' he pronounced with somber indifference. 'Of course I never knew. Weak heart. The man had been complaining of being out of sorts for some time before. Excitement. Overexertion. Devil only knows. Ha! ha! ha! it was easy to see he did not want to die either. Droll, isn't it? May I be shot if he hadn't been fooled into killing himself! Fooled—neither more or less. Fooled into it, by heavens! just as I . . . Ah! If he had only kept still; if he had only told them to go to the devil when they came to rush him out of his bunk because the ship was sinking! If he had only stood by with his hands in his pockets and called them names!'

"He got up, shook his fist, glared at me, and sat down.

"'A chance missed, eh?' I murmured.

"'Why don't you laugh?' he said. 'A joke hatched in hell. Weak heart! . . . I wish sometimes mine had been.'

"This irritated me. 'Do you?' I exclaimed with deep-rooted irony. 'Yes! Can't *you* understand?' he cried. 'I don't know what more you could wish for,' I said angrily. He gave me an utterly uncomprehending glance. This shaft had also gone wide of the mark, and he was not the man to bother about stray arrows. Upon my word, he was too unsuspecting; he was not fair game. I was glad that my missile had been thrown away—that he had not even heard the twang of the bow.

"Of course he could not know at the time the man was dead. The next minute—his last on board—was crowded with a tumult of events and sensations which beat about him like the sea upon a rock. I use the simile advisedly, because from his relation I am forced to believe he had preserved through it all a strange illusion of passiveness, as though he had not acted but had suffered himself to be handled by the infernal powers who had selected him for the victim of their practical joke. The first thing that came to him was the grinding surge of the heavy davits swinging out at last—a jar which seemed to enter his body from the deck through the soles of his feet, and travel up his spine to the crown of his head. Then, the squall being very near now, another and a heavier swell lifted the passive hull in a threatening heave that checked his breath, while his brain and his heart together were pierced as with daggers by panic-stricken screams. 'Let go! For God's sake, let go! Let go! She's going.' Following upon that the boat-falls ripped through the blocks, and a lot of men began to talk in startled tones under the awnings. 'When these beggars did break out, their yelps were enough to wake the dead,' he said. Next, after the splashing shock of the boat literally dropped in the water, came the hollow noises of stamping and tumbling in her, mingled with confused shouts: 'Unhook! Unhook! Shove! Unhook! Shove for your life! Here's the squall down on us . . . .' He heard, high above his head, the faint muttering of the wind; he heard below his feet a cry of pain. A lost voice alongside started cursing a swivel-hook. The ship began to buzz fore and aft like a disturbed hive, and, as quietly as he was telling me of all this—because just then he was very quiet in attitude, in face, in voice—he went on to say without the slightest warning as it were, 'I stumbled over his legs.'

"This was the first I heard of his having moved at all. I could not restrain a grunt of surprise. Something had started him off at last, but of the exact moment, of the cause that tore him out of his immobility, he knew no more than the uprooted tree knows of the wind that laid it low. All this had come to him: the sounds, the sights, the legs of the dead man—by Jove! The infernal joke was being crammed devilishly down his throat, but—look you—he was not going to admit of any sort of swallowing motion in his gullet. It's extraordinary how he could cast upon you the spirit of his illusion. I listened as if to a tale of black magic at work upon a corpse.

"'He went over sideways, very gently, and this is the last thing I remember seeing on board,' he continued. 'I did not care what he did. It looked as though he were picking himself up. I thought he was picking himself up of course: I expected him to bolt past me over the rail and drop into the boat after the others. I could hear them knocking about down there, and a voice as if crying up a shaft called out "George." Then three voices together raised a yell. They came to me separately: one bleated, another screamed, one howled. Ough!'

"He shivered a little, and I beheld him rise slowly as if a steady hand from above had been pulling him out of the chair by his hair. Up, slowly—to his full height, and when his knees had locked stiff the hand let him go, and he swayed a little on his feet. There was a suggestion of awful stillness in his face, in his movements, in his very voice when he said 'They shouted'—and involuntarily I pricked up my ears for the ghost of that shout that would be heard directly through the false effect of silence. 'There were eight hundred people in that ship,' he said, impaling me to the back of my seat with an awful blank stare. 'Eight hundred living people, and they were yelling after the one dead man to come down and be saved. "Jump, George! Jump! Oh, jump!" I stood by with my hand on the davit. I was very quiet. It had come over pitch dark. You could see neither sky nor sea. I heard the boat alongside go bump, bump, and not another sound down there for a while, but the ship under me was full of talking noises. Suddenly the skipper howled, "Mein Gott! The squall! The squall! Shove off! "With the first hiss of rain, and the first gust of wind, they screamed, "Jump, George! We'll catch you! Jump!" The ship began a slow plunge; the rain swept over her like a broken sea; my cap flew off my head; my breath was driven back into my throat. I heard as if I had been on the top of a tower another wild screech, "Geo-o-o-rge! Oh, jump!" She was going down, down, head first under me. . . .'

"He raised his hand deliberately to his face, and made picking motions with his fingers as though he had been bothered with cobwebs, and afterwards he looked into the open palm for quite half a second before he blurted out—

"'I had jumped . . .' He checked himself, averted his gaze. . . . 'It seems,' he added.

"His clear blue eyes turned to me with a piteous stare, and looking at him standing before me, dumfounded and hurt, I was oppressed by a sad sense of resigned wisdom, mingled with the amused and profound pity of an old man helpless before a childish disaster.

"'Looks like it,' I muttered.

"'I knew nothing about it till I looked up,' he explained hastily. And that's possible too. You had to listen to him as you would to a small boy in trouble. He didn't know. It had happened somehow. It would never happen again. He had landed partly on somebody and fallen across a thwart. He felt as though all his ribs on his left side must be broken; then he rolled over, and saw vaguely the ship he had deserted uprising above him, with the red sidelight glowing large in the rain like a fire on the brow of a hill seen through a mist. 'She seemed higher than a wall; she loomed like a cliff over the boat, . . . I wished I could die,' he cried. 'There was no going back. It was as if I had jumped into a well—into an everlasting deep hole. . . .'"

❧ 10 ❧

He locked his fingers together and tore them apart. Nothing could be more true: he had indeed jumped into an everlasting deep hole. He had tumbled from a height he could never scale again. By that time the boat had gone driving forward past the bows. It was too dark just then for them to see each other, and, moreover, they were blinded and half drowned with rain. He told me it was like being swept by a flood through a cavern. They turned their backs to the squall; the skipper, it seems, got an oar over the stern to keep the boat before it, and for two or three minutes the end of the world had come through the deluge in a pitchy blackness. The sea hissed 'like twenty thousand kettles.' That's his simile, not mine. I fancy there was not much wind after the first gust; and he himself had admitted at the inquiry that the sea never got up that night to any extent. He crouched down in the bows and stole a furtive glance back. He saw just one yellow gleam of the masthead light high up and blurred like a last star ready to dissolve. 'It terrified me to see it still there,' he said. That's what he said. What terrified him was the thought that the drowning was not over yet. No doubt he wanted to be done with the abomination as quickly as possible. Nobody in the boat made a sound. In the dark she seemed to fly, but of course she could not have had much way. Then the shower swept ahead, and the great, distracting, hissing noise followed the rain into distance and died out. There was nothing to be heard then but the slight wash about the boat's sides. Somebody's teeth were chattering violently. A hand touched his back. A faint voice said, 'You there?' Another cried out shakily, 'She's gone!' and they all stood up together to look astern. They saw no lights. All was black. A thin cold drizzle was driving into their faces. The boat lurched slightly. The teeth chattered faster, stopped, and began again twice before the man could master his shiver sufficiently to say, 'Ju-ju-st in ti-ti-me. . . . Brrrr.' He recognized the voice of the chief engineer saying surlily, 'I saw her go down. I happened to turn my head.' The wind had dropped almost completely.

"They watched in the dark with their heads half turned to windward as if expecting to hear cries. At first he was thankful the night had covered up the scene before his eyes and then to know of it and yet to have seen and heard nothing appeared somehow the culminating point of an awful misfortune. 'Strange, isn't it?' he murmured, interrupting himself in his disjointed narrative.

"It did not seem so strange to me. He must have had an unconscious conviction that the reality could not be half as bad, not half as anguishing, appalling, and vengeful as the created terror of his imagination. I believe that, in this first moment, his heart was wrung with all the suffering, that his soul knew the accumulated savor of all the fear, all the horror, all the despair of eight hundred human beings pounced upon in the night by a sudden and violent death, else why should he have said, 'It seemed to me that I must jump out of that accursed boat and swim back to see—half a mile—more—any distance—to the very spot . . .'? Why this impulse? Do you see the significance? Why back to the very spot? Why not drown alongside—if he meant drowning—why back to the very spot, to see—as if his imagination had to be soothed by the assurance that all was over before death could bring relief? I defy any one of you to offer another explanation. It was one of those bizarre and exciting glimpses through the fog. It was an extraordinary disclosure. He let it out as the most natural thing one could say. He fought down that impulse and then he became conscious of the silence. He mentioned this to me. A silence of the sea, of the sky, merged into one indefinite immensity still as death around these saved, palpitating lives. 'You might have heard a pin drop in the boat,' he said with a queer contraction of his lips, like a man trying to master his sensibilities while relating some extremely moving fact. A silence! God alone, who had willed him as he was, knows what he made of it in his heart. 'I didn't think any spot on earth could be so still,' he said. 'You couldn't distinguish the sea from the sky; there was nothing to see and nothing to hear. Not a glimmer, not a shape, not a sound. You could have believed that every bit of dry land had gone to the bottom; that every man on earth but I and these beggars in the boat had got drowned.' He leaned over the table with his knuckles propped amongst coffee cups, liqueur glasses, cigar ends. 'I seemed to believe it. Everything was gone and—all was over' . . . he fetched a deep sigh . . . 'with me.'"

Marlow sat up abruptly and flung away his cheroot with force. It made a darting red trail like a toy rocket fired through the drapery of the creepers. Nobody stirred.

"Hey, what do you think of it?" he cried with sudden animation. "Wasn't he true to himself, wasn't he? His saved life was over for want of ground under his feet, for want of sights for his eyes, for want of voices in his ears. Annihilation—hey! And all the time it was only a clouded sky, a sea that did not break, the air that did not stir. Only a night; only a silence.

"It lasted for a while, and then they were suddenly and unanimously moved to make a noise over their escape. 'I knew from the first she would go.' 'Not a minute too soon.' 'A narrow squeak, b'gosh!' He said nothing, but the breeze that had dropped came back, a gentle draught freshened steadily, and the sea joined its murmuring voice to this talkative reaction succeeding the dumb moments of awe. She was gone! She was gone! Not a doubt of it. Nobody could have helped. They repeated the same words over and over again as though they couldn't stop themselves. Never doubted she would go. The lights were gone. No mistake. The lights were gone. Couldn't expect anything else. She had to go . . . . He noticed that they talked as though they had left behind them nothing but an empty ship. They concluded she would not have been long when she once started. It seemed to cause them some sort of satisfaction. They assured each other that she couldn't have been long about it—'Just shot down like a flatiron.' The chief engineer declared that the masthead light at the moment of sinking seemed to drop 'like a lighted match you throw down.' At this the second laughed hysterically. 'I am g-g-glad, I am gla-a-a-d.' His teeth went on 'like an electric rattle,' said Jim, 'and all at once he began to cry. He wept and blubbered like a child, catching his breath and sobbing, "Oh dear! oh dear! oh dear!" He would be quiet for a while and start suddenly, "Oh, my poor arm! oh, my poor a-a-a-arm!" I felt I could knock him down. Some of them sat in the stern-sheets. I could just make out their shapes. Voices came to me, mumble, mumble, grunt, grunt. All this seemed very hard to bear. I was cold too. And could do nothing. I thought that if I moved I would to go over the side and . . .'

"His hand groped stealthily, came in contact with a liqueur glass, and was withdrawn suddenly as if it had touched a red-hot coal. I pushed the bottle slightly. 'Won't you have some more?' I asked. He looked at me angrily. 'Don't you think I can tell you what there is to tell without screwing myself up?' he asked. The squad of globetrotters had gone to bed. We were alone but for a vague white form erect in the shadow, that, being looked at, cringed forward, hesitated, backed away silently. It was getting late, but I did not hurry my guest.

"In the midst of his forlorn state he heard his companions begin to abuse someone. 'What kept you from jumping, you lunatic?' said a scolding voice. The chief engineer left the stern-sheets, and could be heard clambering forward as if with hostile intentions against 'the greatest idiot that ever was.' The skipper shouted with rasping effort offensive epithets from where he sat at the oar. He lifted his head at that uproar, and heard the name 'George,' while a hand in the dark struck him on the breast. 'What have you got to say for yourself, you fool?'

queried somebody, with a sort of virtuous fury. 'They were after me,' he said. 'They were abusing me—abusing me . . . by the name of George.'

"He paused to stare, tried to smile, turned his eyes away and went on. 'That little second puts his head right under my nose, "Why, it's that blasted mate!" "What!" howls the skipper from the other end of the boat. "No!" shrieks the chief. And he too stooped to look at my face.'

"The wind had left the boat suddenly. The rain began to fall again, and the soft, uninterrupted, a little mysterious sound with which the sea receives a shower arose on all sides in the night. 'They were too taken aback to say anything more at first,' he narrated steadily, 'and what could I have to say to them?' He faltered for a moment, and made an effort to go on. 'They called me horrible names.' His voice, sinking to a whisper, now and then would leap up suddenly, hardened by the passion of scorn, as though he had been talking of secret abomination. 'Never mind what they called me,' he said grimly. 'I could hear hate in their voices. A good thing too. They could not forgive me for being in that boat. They hated it. It made them mad . . . .' He laughed short. . . . 'But it kept me from—Look! I was sitting with my arms crossed on the gunwale! . . .' He perched himself smartly on the edge of the table and crossed his arms. . . . 'Like this—see? One little tilt backwards and I would have been gone—after the others. One little tilt—the least bit—the least bit.' He frowned, and tapping his forehead with the tip of his middle finger, 'It was there all the time,' he said impressively. 'All the time—that notion. And the rain—cold, thick, cold as melted snow—colder—on my thin cotton clothes—I'll never be so cold again in my life, I know. And the sky was black too—all black. Not a star, not a light anywhere. Nothing outside that confounded boat and those two yapping before me like a couple of mean mongrels at a tree'd thief. Yap! yap! What you doing here? You're a fine sort! Too much of a bloomin' gentleman to put his hand to it. Come out of your trance, did you? To sneak in? Did you? Yap! yap! You ain't fit to live! Yap! yap! Two of them together trying to outbark each other. The other would bay from the stern through the rain—couldn't see him—couldn't make out—some of his filthy jargon. Yap! yap! Bow-ow-ow-ow-ow! Yap! yap! It was sweet to hear them; it kept me alive—I tell you. It has saved my life. At it they went, as if trying to drive me overboard with the noise! . . . I wonder you had pluck enough to jump. You ain't wanted here. If I had known who it was, I would have tipped you over—you skunk. What have you done with the other? Where did you get the pluck to jump—you coward? What's to prevent us three from firing you overboard? . . . They were out of breath; the shower passed away upon the sea. Then nothing. There was nothing round the boat, not even a sound. Wanted to see me overboard, did they? Upon my soul! I think they would have had their wish if they had only kept quiet. Fire me overboard! Would they? "Try," I said. "I would for twopence?" "Too good for you," they screeched together.

It was so dark that it was only when one or the other of them moved that I was quite sure of seeing him. By heavens! I only wish they had tried.'

"I couldn't help exclaiming, 'What an extraordinary affair!'

"'Not bad—eh?' he said, as if in some sort astounded. 'They pretended to think I had done away with that donkey-man for some reason or other. Why should I? And how the devil was I to know? Didn't I get somehow into that boat? into that boat—I . . .' The muscles round his lips contracted into an unconscious grimace that tore through the mask of his usual expression—something violent, short-lived, and illuminating like a twist of lightning that admits the eye for an instant into the secret convolutions of a cloud. 'I did. I was plainly there with them—wasn't I? Isn't it awful a man should be driven to do a thing like that—and be responsible? What did I know about their George they were howling after? I remembered I had seen him curled up on the deck. "Murdering coward!" the chief kept on calling me. He didn't seem able to remember any other two words. I didn't care, only his noise began to worry me. "Shut up," I said. At that he collected himself for a confounded screech. "You killed him! You killed him!" "No!" I shouted, "but I will kill you directly." I jumped up and he fell backwards over a thwart with an awful loud thump. I don't know why. Too dark. Tried to step back, I suppose. I stood still facing aft, and the wretched little second began to whine, "You ain't going to hit a chap with a broken arm—and you call yourself a gentleman, too." I heard a heavy tramp—one—two—and wheezy grunting. The other beast was coming at me, clattering his oar over the stern. I saw him moving, big, big—as you see a man in a mist, in a dream. "Come on," I cried. I would have tumbled him over like a bale of shakings. He stopped, muttered to himself, and went back. Perhaps he had heard the wind. I didn't. It was the last heavy gust we had. He went back to his oar. I was sorry. I would have tried to—to . . .'

"He opened and closed his curved fingers, and his hands had an eager and cruel flutter. 'Steady, steady,' I murmured.

"'Eh? What? I am not excited,' he remonstrated, awfully hurt, and with a convulsive jerk of his elbow knocked over the cognac bottle. I started forward, scraping my chair. He bounced off the table as if a mine had been exploded behind his back, and half turned before he alighted, crouching on his feet to show me a startled pair of eyes and a face white about the nostrils. A look of intense annoyance succeeded. 'Awfully sorry. How clumsy of me!' he mumbled, very vexed, while the pungent odor of spilt alcohol enveloped us suddenly with an atmosphere of a low drinking-bout in the cool, pure darkness of the night. The lights had been put out in the dining hall; our candle glimmered solitary in the long gallery, and the columns had turned black from pediment to capital. On the vivid stars the high corner of the Harbor Office stood out distinct across the Esplanade, as though the somber pile had glided nearer to see and hear.

"He assumed an air of indifference.

"'I daresay I am less calm now than I was then. I was ready for anything. These were trifles . . . .'

"'You had a lively time of it in that boat,' I remarked.

"'I was ready,' he repeated. 'After the ship's lights had gone, anything might have happened in that boat—anything in the world—and the world no wiser. I felt this, and I was pleased. It was just dark enough, too. We were like men walled up quick in a roomy grave. No concern with anything on earth. Nobody to pass an opinion. Nothing mattered.' For the third time during this conversation he laughed harshly, but there was no one about to suspect him of being only drunk. 'No fear, no law, no sounds, no eyes—not even our own, till—till sunrise at least.'

"I was struck by the suggestive truth of his words. There is something peculiar in a small boat upon the wide sea. Over the lives borne from under the shadow of death there seems to fall the shadow of madness. When your ship fails you, your whole world seems to fail you; the world that made you, restrained you, taken care of you. It is as if the souls of men floating on an abyss and in touch with immensity had been set free for any excess of heroism, absurdity, or abomination. Of course, as with belief, thought, love, hate, conviction, or even the visual aspect of material things, there are as many shipwrecks as there are men, and in this one there was something abject which made the isolation more complete—there was a villainy of circumstances that cut these men off more completely from the rest of mankind, whose ideal of conduct had never undergone the trial of a fiendish and appalling joke. They were exasperated with him for being a half-hearted shirker: he focused on them his hate of the whole thing; he would have liked to take a signal revenge for the abhorrent opportunity they had put in his way. Trust a boat on the high seas to bring out the Irrational that lurks at the bottom of every thought, sentiment, sensation, emotion. It was part of the burlesque meanness pervading that particular disaster at sea that they did not come to blows. It was all threats, all a terribly effective feint, a sham from beginning to end, planned by the tremendous disdain of the Dark Powers whose real terrors, always on the verge of triumph, are perpetually foiled by the steadfastness of men. I asked, after waiting for a while, 'Well, what happened?' A futile question. I knew too much already to hope for the grace of a single uplifting touch, for the favor of hinted madness, of shadowed horror. 'Nothing,' he said. 'I meant business, but they meant noise only. Nothing happened.'

"And the rising sun found him just as he had jumped up first in the bows of the boat. What a persistence of readiness! He had been holding the tiller in his hand, too, all the night. They had dropped the rudder overboard while attempting to ship it, and I suppose the tiller got kicked forward somehow while they were rushing up and down that boat trying to do all sorts of things at once so as to get clear of the side. It was a long, heavy piece of hard wood, and apparently he had been clutching it for six hours or so. If you don't call that being ready! Can you imagine him, silent and on his feet half the night, his face to the gusts of rain, staring at somber forms, watchful of vague movements, straining his ears to catch rare low murmurs in the stern-sheets! Firmness of courage or effort of fear? What do you think? And the endurance is undeniable, too. Six hours more or less on the defensive; six hours of alert immobility while the boat drove slowly or floated arrested, according to the caprice of the wind; while the sea, calmed, slept at last; while the clouds passed above his head; while the sky from an immensity, lusterless and black, diminished to a somber and lustrous vault, scintillated with a greater brilliance, faded to the east, paled at the zenith; while the dark shapes blotting the low stars astern got outlines, relief; became shoulders, heads, faces, features— confronted him with dreary stares, had disheveled hair, torn clothes, blinked red eyelids at the white dawn. 'They looked as though they had been knocking about drunk in gutters for a week,' he described graphically; and then he muttered something about the sunrise being of a kind that foretells a calm day. You know that sailor habit of referring to the weather in every connection. And on my side his few mumbled words were enough to make me see the lower limb of the sun clearing the line of the horizon, the tremble of a vast ripple running over all the visible expanse of the sea, as if the waters had shuddered, giving birth to the globe of light, while the last puff of the breeze would stir the air in a sigh of relief.

"'They sat in the stern shoulder to shoulder, with the skipper in the middle, like three dirty owls, and stared at me,' I heard him say with an intention of hate that distilled a corrosive virtue into the commonplace words like a drop of powerful poison falling into a glass of water; but my thoughts dwelt upon that sunrise. I could imagine under the pellucid emptiness of the sky these four men imprisoned in the solitude of the sea, the lonely sun, regardless of the speck of life, ascending the clear curve of the heaven as if to gaze ardently from a greater height at his own splendor reflected in the still ocean. 'They called out to me from aft,' said Jim, 'as though we had been chums together. I heard them. They were begging me to be sensible and drop that "blooming piece of wood." Why *would* I carry on so? They hadn't done me any harm—had they? There had been no harm . . . . No harm!'

"His face crimsoned as though he could not get rid of the air in his lungs.

"'No harm!' he burst out. 'I leave it to you. You can understand. Can't you? You see it—don't you? No harm! Good God! What more could they have done? Oh, yes, I know very well—I jumped. Certainly. I jumped! I told you I jumped; but I tell you they were too much for any man. It was their doing as plainly as if they had reached up with a boathook and pulled me over. Can't you see it? You must see it. Come. Speak—straight out.'

"His uneasy eyes fastened upon mine, questioned, begged, challenged, entreated. For the life of me I couldn't help murmuring, 'You've been tried.' 'More than is fair,' he caught up swiftly. 'I wasn't given half a chance—with a gang like that. And now they were friendly—oh, so damnably friendly! Chums, shipmates. All in the same boat. Make the best of it. They hadn't meant anything. They didn't care a hang for George. George had gone back to his berth for something at the last moment and got caught. The man was a manifest fool. Very sad, of course. . . . Their eyes looked at me; their lips moved; they wagged their heads at the other end of the boat—three of them; they beckoned—to me. Why not? Hadn't I jumped? I said nothing. There are no words for the sort of things I wanted to say. If I had opened my lips just then I would have simply howled like an animal. I was asking myself when I would wake up. They urged me aloud to come aft and hear quietly what the skipper had to say. We were sure to be picked up before the evening—right in the track of all the Canal traffic; there was smoke to the northwest now.

"'It gave me an awful shock to see this faint, faint blur, this low trail of brown mist through which you could see the boundary of sea and sky. I called out to them that I could hear very well where I was. The skipper started swearing, as hoarse as a crow. He wasn't going to talk at the top of his voice for *my* accommodation. "Are you afraid they will hear you on shore?" I asked. He glared as if he would have liked to claw me to pieces. The chief engineer advised him to humor me. He said I wasn't right in my head yet. The other rose astern, like a thick pillar of flesh—and talked—talked. . . .'

"Jim remained thoughtful. 'Well?' I said. 'What did I care what story they agreed to make up?' he cried recklessly. 'They could tell what they jolly well liked. It was their business. I knew the story. Nothing they could make people believe could alter it for me. I let him talk, argue—talk, argue. He went on and on and on. Suddenly I felt my legs give way under me. I was sick, tired—tired to death. I let fall the tiller, turned my back on them, and sat down on the foremost thwart. I had enough. They called to me to know if I understood—wasn't it true, every word of it? It was true, by God! after their fashion. I did not turn my head. I heard them palavering together. "The silly ass won't say anything." "Oh, he understands well enough." "Let him be; he will be all right." "What can he do?" What could I do! Weren't we all in the same boat. I tried to be deaf. The smoke had disappeared to the northward. It was a dead calm. They had a drink from the water-breaker, and I drank too. Afterwards they made a great business of spreading the boat-sail over the gunwales. Would I keep a lookout? They crept under, out of my sight, thank God! I felt weary, weary, done up, as if I hadn't had one hour's sleep since the day I was born. I couldn't see the water for the glitter of the sunshine. From time to time one of them would creep out, stand up to take a look all round, and get under again. I could hear spells of snoring below the sail. Some of them could sleep. One of them at least. I couldn't! All was light, light, and the boat seemed to be falling through it. Now and then I would feel quite surprised to find myself sitting on a thwart. . . .'

"He began to walk with measured steps to and fro before my chair, one hand in his trousers-pocket, his head bent thoughtfully, and his right arm at long intervals raised for a gesture that seemed to put out of his way an invisible intruder.

"'I suppose you think I was going mad,' he began in a changed tone. 'And well you may, if you remember I had lost my cap. The sun crept all the way from east to west over my bare head, but that day I could not come to any harm, I suppose. The sun could not make me mad. . . .' His right arm put aside the idea of madness. . . . 'Neither could it kill me. . . .' Again his arm repulsed a shadow. . . . *'That* rested with me.'

"'Did it?' I said, inexpressibly amazed at this new turn, and I looked at him with the same sort of feeling I might be fairly conceived to experience had he, after spinning round on his heel, presented an altogether new face.

"'I didn't get brain fever, I did not drop dead either,' he went on. 'I didn't bother myself at all about the sun over my head. I was thinking as coolly as any man that ever sat thinking in the shade. That greasy beast of a skipper poked his big cropped head from under the canvas and screwed his fishy eyes up at me. "Donnerwetter! you will die," he growled, and drew in like a turtle. I had seen him. I had heard him. He didn't interrupt me. I was thinking just then that I wouldn't.'

"He tried to sound my thought with an attentive glance dropped on me in passing. 'Do you mean to say you had been deliberating with yourself whether you would die?' I asked in as impenetrable a tone as I could command. He nodded without stopping. 'Yes, it had come to that as I sat there alone,' he said. He passed on a few steps to the imaginary end of his beat, and when he flung round to come back both his hands were thrust deep into his pockets. He stopped short in front of my chair and looked down. 'Don't you believe it?' he inquired with tense curiosity. I was moved to make a solemn declaration of my readiness to believe implicitly anything he thought fit to tell me."

❧ 11 ❧

He heard me out with his head on one side, and I had another glimpse through a rent in the mist in which he moved and had his being. The dim candle spluttered within the ball of glass, and that was all I had to see him by; at his back was the dark night with the clear stars, whose distant glitter disposed in retreating planes lured the eye into the depths of a greater darkness; and yet a mysterious light seemed to show me his boyish head, as if in that moment the youth within him had, for a moment, gleamed and expired. 'You are an awful good sort to listen like this,' he said. 'It does me good. You don't know what it is to me. You don't' . . . words seemed to fail him. It was a distinct glimpse. He was a youngster of the sort you like to see about you; of the sort you like to imagine yourself to have been; of the sort whose appearance claims the fellowship of these illusions you had thought gone out, extinct, cold, and which, as if rekindled at the approach of another flame, give a flutter deep, deep down somewhere, give a flutter of light . . . of heat! . . . Yes; I had a glimpse of him then, . . . and it was not the last of that kind . . . . 'You don't know what it is for a fellow in my position to be believed—make a clean breast of it to an elder man. It is so difficult—so awfully unfair—so hard to understand.'

"The mists were closing again. I don't know how old I appeared to him—and how much wise? Not half as old as I felt just then; not half as uselessly wise as I knew myself to be. Surely in no other craft as in that of the sea do the hearts of those already launched to sink or swim go out so much to the youth on the brink, looking with shining eyes upon that glitter of the vast surface which is only a reflection of his own glances full of fire. There is such magnificent vagueness in the expectations that had driven each of us to sea, such a glorious indefiniteness, such a beautiful greed of adventures that are their own and only reward! What we get—well, we won't talk of that; but can one of us restrain a smile? In no other kind of life is the illusion more wide of reality—in no other is the beginning *all* illusion—the disenchantment more swift—the subjugation more complete. Hadn't we all commenced with the same desire, ended with the same knowledge, carried the memory of the same cherished glamour through the sordid days of imprecation? What wonder that when some heavy prod gets home the bond is found to be close; that besides the fellowship of the craft there is felt the strength

146

of a wider feeling—the feeling that binds a man to a child. He was there before me, believing that age and wisdom can find a remedy against the pain of truth, giving me a glimpse of himself as a young fellow in a scrape that is the very devil of a scrape, the sort of scrape graybeards wag at solemnly while they hide a smile. And he had been deliberating upon death—confound him! He had found *that* to meditate about because he thought he had saved his life, while all its glamour had gone with the ship in the night. What more natural! It was tragic enough and funny enough in all conscience to call aloud for compassion, and in what was I better than the rest of us to refuse him my pity. And even as I looked at him the mists rolled into the rent, and his voice spoke:

"'I was so lost, you know. It was the sort of thing one does not expect to happen to one. It was not like a fight, for instance.'

"'It was not,' I admitted. He appeared changed, as if he had suddenly matured.

"'One couldn't be sure,' he muttered.

"'Ah! You were not sure,' I said, and was placated by the sound of a faint sigh that passed between us like the flight of a bird in the night.

"'Well, I wasn't,' he said courageously. 'It was something like that wretched story they made up. It was not a lie—but it wasn't truth all the same. It was some-thing. . . . One knows a downright lie. There was not the thickness of a sheet of paper between the right and the wrong of this affair.'

"'How much more did you want?' I asked; but I think I spoke so low that he did not catch what I said. He had advanced his argument as though life had been a network of paths separated by chasms. His voice sounded reasonable.

"'Suppose I had not—I mean to say, suppose I had stuck to the ship? Well. How much longer? Say a minute—half a minute. Come. In thirty seconds, as it seemed certain then, I would have been overboard; and do you think I would not have laid hold of the first thing that came in my way—oar, life buoy, grating—anything. Wouldn't you?'

"'And be saved,' I interjected.

"'I would have meant to be,' he retorted. 'And that's more than I meant when I' . . . he shivered as if to swallow some nauseous drug . . . 'jumped,' he pronounced with a convulsive effort, whose stress, as if propagated by the waves of the air, made my body stir a little in the chair. He fixed me with lowering eyes. 'Don't you believe me?' he cried. 'I swear! . . . Confound it! You got me here to talk, and . . . You must! . . . You said you would believe.' 'Of course I do,' I protested in a matter-of-fact tone which produced a calming effect, 'Forgive me,' he said. 'Of course I wouldn't have talked to you about all this if you had not been a gentleman. I ought to have known . . . I am—I am—a gentleman too. . . .' 'Yes,' I said hastily. He was looking me squarely in the face, and withdrew his gaze slowly. 'Now you understand why I didn't after all . . . didn't go out in that way. I wasn't going to be frightened at what I had done. And, anyhow, if I had stuck to the ship I would have done my best to be saved. Men have been known to float for hours—in the open sea—and be picked up not much the worse for it. I might have lasted it out better than many others. There's nothing the matter with *my* heart.' He withdrew his right fist from his pocket, and the blow he struck on his chest resounded like a muffled detonation in the night.

"'No,' I said. He meditated, with his legs slightly apart and his chin sunk. 'A hair's-breadth,' he muttered. 'Not the breadth of a hair between this and that. And at the time . . .'

"'It is difficult to see a hair at midnight,' I put in, a little viciously, I fear. Don't you see what I mean by the solidarity of the craft? I was aggrieved against him, as though he had cheated me—me!—of a splendid opportunity to keep up the illusion of my beginnings, as though he had robbed our common life of the last spark of its glamour. 'And so you cleared out—at once.'

"'Jumped,' he corrected me incisively. 'Jumped—mind!' he repeated, and I wondered at the evident but obscure intention. 'Well, yes! Perhaps I could not see then. But I had plenty of time and any amount of light in that boat. And I could think too. Nobody would know, of course, but this did not make it any easier for me. You've got to believe that too. I did not want all this talk . . . . No . . . Yes . . . I won't lie . . . I wanted it: it is the very thing I wanted—there. Do you think you or anybody could have made me if I . . . I am—I am not afraid to tell. And I wasn't afraid to think either. I looked it in the face. I wasn't going to run away. At first—at night, if it hadn't been for these fellows I might have . . . No! by heavens! I was not going to give them that satisfaction. They had done enough. They made up a story, and believed it for all I know. But I knew the truth, and I would live it down—alone, with myself. I wasn't going to give in to such a beastly unfair thing. What did it prove after all? I was confoundedly cut up. Sick of life—to tell you the truth; but what would have been the good to shirk it—in—in—that way? That was not the way. I believe—I believe it would have—it would have ended—nothing.'

"He had been walking up and down, but with the last word he turned short at me.

"'What do *you* believe?' he asked with violence. A pause ensued, and suddenly I felt myself overcome by a profound and hopeless fatigue, as though his voice had startled me out of a dream of wandering through empty spaces whose immensity had harassed my soul and exhausted my body.

"'. . . Would have ended nothing,' he muttered over me obstinately, after a little while. 'No! the proper thing was to face it out—alone before myself—wait for another chance—find out . . .'"

❧ 12 ❧

All around everything was still as far as the ear could reach. 'The mist of his feelings shifted between us, as if, disturbed by his struggles, and in the rifts of the immaterial veil, he would appear to my staring eyes distinct of form and pregnant with vague appeal like a symbolic figure in a picture. The chill air of the night seemed to lie on my limbs as heavy as a slab of marble.

"'I see,' I murmured, more to prove to myself that I could break my state of numbness than for any other reason.

"'The *Avondale* picked us up just before sunset,' he remarked moodily. 'Steamed right straight for us. We had only to sit and wait.'

"After a long interval, he said, 'They told their story.' And again there was that oppressive silence. 'Then only I knew what it was I had made up my mind to,' he added.

"'You said nothing,' I whispered.

"'What could I say?' he asked, in the same low tone. . . 'Shock slight. Stopped the ship. Ascertain the damage. Took measures to get the boats out without creating a panic. As the first boat was lowered ship went down in a squall. Sank like lead. . . . What could be more clear' . . . he hung his head . . 'and more awful?' His lips quivered while he looked straight into my eyes. 'I had jumped—hadn't I?' he asked, dismayed. 'That's what I had to live down. The story didn't matter.' . . . He clasped his hands for an instant, glanced right and left into the gloom: 'It was like cheating the dead,' he stammered.

"'And there were no dead,' I said.

"He went away from me at this. That is the only way I can describe it. In a moment I saw his back close to the balustrade. He stood there for some time, as if admiring the purity and the peace of the night. Some flowering shrub in the garden below spread its powerful scent through the damp air. He returned to me with hasty steps.

"'And that did not matter,' he said, as stubbornly as you please.

"'Perhaps not,' I admitted. I began to have a notion he was too much for me. After all, what did I know?

"'Dead or not dead, I could not get clear,' he said. 'I had to live; hadn't I?'

"'Well, yes—if you take it in that way,' I mumbled.

"'I was glad of course,' he threw out carelessly, with his mind fixed on something else. 'The exposure,' he pronounced slowly, and lifted his head. 'Do you know what was my first thought when I heard? I was relieved. I was relieved to learn that those shouts—did I tell you I had heard shouts? No? Well, I did. Shouts for help, . . . blown along with the drizzle. Imagination, I suppose. And yet I can hardly . . . How stupid. . . . The others did not. I asked them afterwards. They all said No. No? And I was hearing them even then! I might have known—but I didn't think—I only listened. Very faint screams—day after day. Then that little half-caste chap here came up and spoke to me. "The *Patna* . . . French gunboat . . . towed successfully to Aden . . . Investigation . . . Marine Office . . . Sailors' Home . . . arrangements made for your board and lodging!' I walked along with him, and I enjoyed the silence. So there had been no shouting. Imagination. I had to believe him. I could hear nothing anymore. I wonder how long I could have stood it. It was getting worse, too . . . I mean—louder.'

"He fell into thought.

"'And I had heard nothing! Well—so be it. But the lights! The lights did go! We did not see them. They were not there. If they had been, I would have swam back—I would have gone back and shouted alongside—I would have begged them to take me on board. . . . I would have had my chance. . . . You doubt me? . . . How do you know how I felt? . . . What right have you to doubt? . . . I very nearly did it as it was—do you understand?' His voice fell. 'There was not a glimmer—not a glimmer,' he protested mournfully. 'Don't you understand that if there had been, you would not have seen me here? You see me—and you doubt.'

"I shook my head negatively. This question of the lights being lost sight of when the boat could not have been more than a quarter of a mile from the ship was a matter for much discussion. Jim stuck to it that there was nothing to be seen after the first shower had cleared away; and the others had affirmed the same thing to the officers of the *Avondale*. Of course people shook their heads and smiled. One old skipper who sat near me in court tickled my ear with his white beard to murmur, 'Of course they would lie.' As a matter of fact nobody lied; not even the chief engineer with his story of the masthead light dropping like a match you throw down. Not consciously, at least. A man with his liver in such a state might very well have seen a floating spark in the corner of his eye when stealing a hurried glance over his shoulder. They had seen no light of any sort though they were well within range, and they could only explain this in one way: the ship had gone down. It was obvious and comforting. The foreseen fact coming so swiftly had justified their haste. No wonder they did not cast about for any other explanation. Yet the true one was very simple, and as soon as Brierly suggested it the court ceased to bother about the question. If you remember, the ship had been stopped, and was lying with her head on the course steered through the night, with her stern canted high and her bows brought low down in the water through the filling of the fore com-partment. Being thus out of trim, when the squall struck her a little on the quar-ter, she swung head to wind as sharply as though she had been at anchor. By this change in her position all her lights were in a very few moments shut off from the boat to leeward. It may very well be that, had they been seen, they would have had the effect of a mute appeal—that their glimmer lost in the darkness of the cloud would have had the mysterious power of the human glance that can awaken the feelings of remorse and pity. It would have said, 'I am here—still here,' . . . and what more can the eye of the most forsaken of human beings say? But she turned her back on them as if in disdain of their fate: she had swung round, burdened, to glare stubbornly at the new danger of the open sea which she so strangely sur-vived to end her days in a breaking-up yard, as if it had been her recorded fate to die obscurely under the blows of many hammers. What were the various ends their destiny provided for the pilgrims I am unable to say; but the immediate future brought, at about nine o'clock next morning, a French gunboat homeward bound from Réunion. The report of her commander was public property. He had swept a little out of his course to ascertain what was the matter with that steamer floating dangerously by the head upon a still and hazy sea. There was an ensign, union down, flying at her main gaff (the serang had the sense to make a signal of dis-tress at daylight); but the cooks were preparing the food in the cooking-boxes for-ward, as usual. The decks were packed as close as a sheep-pen; there were people perched all along the rails, jammed on the bridge in a solid mass; hundreds of eyes stared, and not a sound was heard when the gunboat ranged abreast, as if all that multitude of lips had been sealed by a spell.

"The Frenchman hailed, could get no intelligible reply, and after ascertaining through his binoculars that the crowd on deck did not look plague-stricken, decid-ed to send a boat. Two officers came on board, listened to the serang, tried to talk with the Arab, couldn't make head or tail of it: but of course the nature of the emergency was obvious enough. They were also very much struck by discovering a white man, dead and curled up peacefully on the bridge. '*Fort intrigués par ce cadavre,*' as I was informed a long time after by an elderly French lieutenant whom I came across one afternoon in Sydney, by the merest chance, in a sort of café and who remembered the affair perfectly. Indeed this affair, I may notice in passing, had an extraordinary power of defying the shortness of memories and the length of time: it seemed to live, with a sort of uncanny vitality, in the minds of men, on the tips of their tongues. I've had the questionable pleasure of meeting it often, years afterwards, thousands of miles away, emerging from the remotest pos-sible talk, coming to the surface of the most distant allusions. Has it not turned up tonight between us? And I am the only seaman here. I am the only one to whom it is a memory. And yet it has made its way out! But if two men who, unknown to each other, knew of this affair met accidentally on any spot of this earth, the thing would pop up between them as sure as fate, before they parted. I had never seen that Frenchman before, and at the end of an hour we had done with each other for life: he did not seem particularly talkative either; he was a quiet, massive chap in a creased uniform, sitting drowsily over a tumbler half full of some dark liquid. His shoulder straps were a bit tarnished, his clean-shaved cheeks were large and sallow; he looked like a man who would be given to taking snuff—don't you know? I won't say he did; but the habit would have fitted that kind of man. It all began by his handing me a number of 'Home News,' which I didn't want, across the marble table. I said 'Merci.' We exchanged a few apparently innocent remarks, and suddenly, before I knew how it had come about, we were in the midst of it, and he was telling me how much they had been 'intrigued by that corpse.' It turned out he had been one of the boarding officers.

"In the establishment where we sat one could get a variety of foreign drinks which were kept for the visiting naval officers, and he took a sip of the dark medical-looking stuff, which probably was nothing more nasty than *cassis à l'eau*, and glancing with one eye into the tumbler, shook his head slightly. '*Impossible de comprendre—vous concevez*,' he said, with a curious mixture of unconcern and thoughtfulness. I could very easily conceive how impossible it had been for them to understand. Nobody in the gunboat knew enough English to get hold of the story as told by the serang. There was a good deal of noise, too, round the two officers. 'They crowded upon us. There was a circle round that dead man (*autour de ce mort*),' he described. 'One had to attend to the most pressing. These people were beginning to agitate themselves—*Parbleu!* A mob like that—don't you see?' he interjected with philosophic indulgence. As to the bulkhead, he had advised his commander that the safest thing was to leave it alone, it was so villainous to look at. They got two hawsers on board promptly (*en toute hâte*) and took the *Patna* in tow—stern foremost at that—which, under the circumstances, was not so foolish, since the rudder was too much out of the water to be of any great use for steering, and this maneuver eased the strain on the bulkhead, whose state, he expounded with stolid glibness, demanded the greatest care (*éxigeait les plus grands ménagements*). I could not help thinking that my new acquaintance must have had a voice in most of these arrangements: he looked a reliable officer, no longer very active, and he was seamanlike too, in a way, though, as he sat there, with his thick fingers clasped lightly on his stomach, he reminded you of one of those snuffy, quiet village priests, into whose ears are poured the sins, the sufferings, the remorse of peasant generations, on whose faces the placid and simple expression is like a veil thrown over the mystery of pain and distress. He ought to have had a threadbare black *soutane* buttoned smoothly up to his ample chin, instead of a frock coat with shoulder straps and brass buttons. His broad bosom heaved regularly while he went on telling me that it had been the very devil of a job, as doubtless (*sans doute*) I could figure to myself in my quality of a seaman (*en votre qualité de marin*). At the end of the period he inclined his body slightly towards me, and, pursing his shaved lips, allowed the air to escape with a gentle hiss. 'Luckily,' he continued, 'the sea was level like this table, and there was no more wind than there is here.' . . . The place struck me as indeed intolerably stuffy and very hot; my face burned as though I had been young enough to be embarrassed and blushing. They had directed their course, he pursued, to the nearest English port '*naturellement*,' where their responsibility ceased, '*Dieu merci*.'. . . He blew out his flat cheeks a little. . . . 'Because, mind you (*notez bien*), all the time of towing we had two quartermasters stationed with axes by the hawsers, to cut us clear of our tow in case she . . .' He fluttered downwards his heavy eyelids, making his meaning as plain as possible . . . . 'What would you! One does what one can (*on fait ce qu'on peut*),' and for a moment he managed to invest his ponderous immobility with an air of resignation. 'Two quartermasters—thirty hours— always there. Two!' he repeated, lifting up his right hand a little, and exhibiting two fingers. This was absolutely the first gesture I saw him make. It gave me the opportunity to 'note' a starred scar on the back of his hand—effect of a gunshot clearly; and, as if my sight had been made more acute by this discovery, I perceived also the seam of an old wound, beginning a little below the temple and going out of sight under the short gray hair at the side of his head—the graze of a spear or the cut of a saber. He clasped his hands on his stomach again. 'I remained on board that, that—my memory is going (*s'en va*). Ah! *Patt-nà. C'est bien ça. Patt-nà. Merci.* It is droll how one forgets. I stayed on that ship thirty hours. . . .'

"'You did!' I exclaimed. Still gazing at his hands, he pursed his lips a little, but this time made no hissing sound. 'It was judged proper,' he said, lifting his eyebrows dispassionately, 'that one of the officers should remain to keep an eye open (*pour ouvrir l'oeil*)'. . . he sighed idly . . . 'and for communicating by signals with the towing ship—do you see—and so on. For the rest, it was my opinion too. We made our boats ready to drop over—and I also on that ship took measures. . . . *Enfin!* One has done one's possible. It was a delicate position. Thirty hours. They prepared me some food. As for the wine—go and whistle for it—not a drop.' In some extraordinary way, without any marked change in his inert attitude and in the placid expression of his face, he managed to convey the idea of profound disgust. 'I—you know—when it comes to eating without my glass of wine—I am nowhere.'

"I was afraid he would enlarge upon the grievance, for though he didn't stir a limb or twitch a feature, he made one aware how much he was irritated by the recollection. But he seemed to forget all about it. They delivered their charge to the 'port authorities,' as he expressed it. He was struck by the calmness with which it had been received. 'One might have thought they had such a droll find (*drôle de trouvaille*) brought them every day. You are extraordinary—you others,' he commented, with his back propped against the wall, and looking himself as incapable of an emotional display as a sack of meal. There happened to be a man-of-war and an Indian Marine steamer in the harbor at the time, and he did not conceal his admiration of the efficient manner in which the boats of these two ships cleared the *Patna* of her passengers. Indeed his torpid demeanor concealed nothing: it had that mysterious, almost miraculous, power of producing striking effects by means impossible of detection which is the last word of the highest art. 'Twenty-five minutes—watch in hand—twenty-five, no more.' . . . He unclasped and clasped again his fingers without removing his hands from his stomach, and made it infinitely more effective than if he had thrown up his arms to heaven in amazement. . . . 'All that lot (*tout ce monde*) on shore—with their little affairs—nobody left but a guard of seamen (*marins de l'État*) and that interesting corpse (*cet intéréssant cadavre*). Twenty-five minutes.' . . . With downcast eyes and his head tilted slightly on one side, he seemed to roll knowingly on his tongue the savor of a smart bit of work. He persuaded one, without any further demonstration, that his approval was eminently worth having, and resuming his hardly interrupted immobility, he went on to inform me that, being under orders to make the best of their way to Toulon, they left in two hours' time, 'so that (*de sorte que*) there are many things in this incident of my life (*dans cet épisode de ma vie*) which have remained obscure.'"

❧ 13 ❧

After these words, and without a change of attitude, he, so to speak, submitted himself passively to a state of silence. I kept him company; and suddenly, but not abruptly, as if the appointed time had arrived for his moderate and husky voice to come out of his immobility, he pronounced, '*Mon Dieu!* how the time passes!' Nothing could have been more commonplace than this remark; but its utterance coincided for me with a moment of vision. It's extraordinary how we go through life with eyes half shut, with dull ears, with dormant thoughts. Perhaps it's just as well; and it may be that it is this very dullness that makes life to the incalculable majority so supportable and so welcome. Nevertheless, there can be but few of us who have never known one of these rare moments of awakening when we see, hear, understand ever so much—everything—in a flash—before we fall back again into our agreeable somnolence. I raised my eyes when he spoke, and I saw him as though I had never seen him before. I saw his chin sunk on his breast, the clumsy folds of his coat, his clasped hands, his motionless pose, so curiously suggestive of his having been simply left there. Time had passed indeed: it had overtaken him and gone ahead. It had left him hopelessly behind with a few poor gifts: the iron-gray hair, the heavy fatigue of the tanned face, two scars, a pair of tarnished shoulder straps; one of those steady, reliable men, who are the raw material of great reputations, one of those uncounted lives that are buried without drums and trumpets under the foundations of monumental successes. 'I am now third lieutenant of *Victorieuse*' (she was the flagship of the French Pacific squadron at the time), he said, detaching his shoulders from the wall a couple of inches to introduce himself. I bowed slightly on my side of the table, and told him I commanded a merchant vessel at present anchored in Rushcutters' Bay. He had 'remarked' her—a pretty little craft. He was very civil about it in his impassive way. I even fancy he went the length of tilting his head in compliment as he repeated, breathing visibly the while, 'Ah, yes. A little craft painted black—very pretty—very pretty (*très coquet*).' After a time he twisted his body slowly to face the glass door on our right. 'A dull town (*Triste ville*),' he observed, staring into the street. It was a brilliant day; a southerly buster was raging, and we could see the passersby, men and women, buffeted by the wind on the sidewalks, the sunlit fronts of the houses across the road blurred by the tall whirls of dust. 'I descended on shore,' he said, 'to stretch my legs a little, but . . .' He didn't finish, and sank into the depths of his repose. 'Pray—tell me,' he began, coming up ponderously, 'what was there at the bottom of this affair precisely (*au juste*)? It is curious. That dead man, for instance—and so on.'

"'There were living men too,' I said; 'much more curious.'

"'No doubt, no doubt,' he agreed half inaudibly, then, as if, after mature consideration, murmured, 'Evidently.' I made no difficulty in communicating to him what had interested me most in this affair. It seemed as though he had a right to know: hadn't he spent thirty hours on board the *Patna*—had he not taken the succession, so to speak, had he not done 'his possible'? He listened to me, looking more priest-like than ever, and with what probably—on account of his downcast eyes—had the appearance of devout concentration. Once or twice he elevated his eyebrows (but without raising his eyelids) as one would say 'The devil!' Once he calmly exclaimed, 'Ah, bah!' under his breath, and when I had finished he pursed his lips in a deliberate way and emitted a sort of sorrowful whistle.

"In anyone else it might have been an evidence of boredom, a sign of indifference; but he, in his occult way, managed to make his immobility appear profoundly responsive, and as full of valuable thoughts as an egg is of meat. What he said at last was nothing more than a 'very interesting,' pronounced politely, and not much above a whisper. Before I got over my disappointment he added, but as if speaking to himself, 'That's it. That *is* it.' His chin seemed to sink lower on his breast, his body to weigh heavier on his seat. I was about to ask him what he meant when a sort of preparatory tremor passed over his whole person, as a faint ripple may be seen upon stagnant water even before the wind is felt. 'And so that poor young man ran away along with the others,' he said, with grave tranquility.

"I don't know what made me smile: it is the only genuine smile of mine I can remember in connection with Jim's affair. But somehow this simple statement of the matter sounded funny in French . . . . *S'est enfui avec les autres,*' had said the lieutenant. And suddenly I began to admire the discrimination of the man. He had made out the point at once: he did get hold of the only thing I cared about. I felt as though I were taking professional opinion on the case. His imperturbable and mature calmness was that of an expert in possession of the facts, and to whom one's perplexities are mere child's play. 'Ah! The young, the young,' he said indulgently. 'And after all, one does not die of it.' 'Die of what?' I asked swiftly. 'Of being afraid.' He elucidated his meaning and sipped his drink.

"I perceived that the three last fingers of his wounded hand were stiff and could not move independently of each other, so that he took up his tumbler with an ungainly clutch. 'One is always afraid. One may talk, but . . .' He put down the glass awkwardly. . . . 'The fear, the fear—look you—it is always there.' . . . He touched his breast near a brass button, on the very spot where Jim had given a thump to his own when protesting that there was nothing the matter with his heart. I suppose I made some sign of dissent, because he insisted, 'Yes! yes! One talks, one talks; this is all very fine; but at the end of the reckoning one is no cleverer than the next man—and no more brave. Brave! This is always to be seen. I have rolled my hump (*roulé ma bosse*),' he said, using the slang expression with imperturbable seriousness, 'in all parts of the world; I have known brave men—famous ones! *Allez!*' . . . He drank carelessly . . . . 'Brave—you conceive—in the Service—one has got to be—the trade demands it (*le métier veux ça*). Is it not so?' he appealed to me reasonably. '*Eh bien!* Each of them—I say each of them, if he were an honest man—*bien entendu*—would confess that there is a point—there is a point—for the best of us—there is somewhere a point when you let go everything (*vous lachez tout*). And you have got to live with that truth—do you see? Given a certain combination of circumstances, fear is sure to come. Abominable funk (*un trac épouvantable*). And even for those who do not believe this truth there is fear all the same—the fear of themselves. Absolutely so. Trust me. Yes. Yes. . . . At my age one knows what one is talking about—*que diable!*'. . . He had delivered himself of all this as immovably as though he had been the mouthpiece of abstract wisdom, but at this point he heightened the effect of detachment by beginning to twirl his thumbs slowly. 'It's evident—*parbleu!*' he continued; 'for, make up your mind as much as you like, even a simple headache or a fit of indigestion (*un dérangement d'estomac*) is enough to . . . Take me, for instance—I have made my proofs. *Eh bien!* I, who am speaking to you, once . . .'

"He drained his glass and returned to his twirling. 'No, no; one does not die of it,' he pronounced finally, and when I found he did not mean to proceed with the personal anecdote, I was extremely disappointed; the more so as it was not the sort of story, you know, one could very well press him for. I sat silent, and he, too, as if nothing could please him better. Even his thumbs were still now. Suddenly his lips began to move. 'That is so,' he resumed placidly. 'Man is born a coward (*L'homme est né poltron*). It is a difficulty—*parbleu!* It would be too easy otherwise. But habit—habit—necessity—do you see?—the eye of others—*voilà*. One puts up with it. And then the example of others who are no better than yourself, and yet make good countenance . . .'

"His voice ceased.

"'That young man—you will observe—had none of these inducements—at least at the moment,' I remarked.

"He raised his eyebrows forgivingly: 'I don't say; I don't say. The young man in question might have had the best dispositions—the best dispositions,' he repeated, wheezing a little.

"'I am glad to see you taking a lenient view,' I said. 'His own feeling in the matter was—ah!—hopeful, and . . .'

"The shuffle of his feet under the table interrupted me. He drew up his heavy eyelids. Drew up, I say—no other expression can describe the steady deliberation of the act—and at last was disclosed completely to me. I was confronted by two narrow gray circlets, like two tiny steel rings, around the profound blackness of the pupils. The sharp glance, coming from that massive body, gave a notion of extreme efficiency, like a razor-edge on a battle-axe. 'Pardon,' he said punctiliously. His right hand went up, and he swayed forward. 'Allow me . . . I contended that one may get on knowing very well that one's courage does not come of itself (*ne vient pas tout seul*). There's nothing much in that to get upset about. One truth the more ought not to make life impossible. . . . But the honor—the honor, monsieur! . . . The honor . . . that is real—that is! And what life may be worth when' . . . he got on his feet with a ponderous impetuosity, as a startled ox might scramble up from the grass . . . 'when the honor is gone—*ah ça! par exemple*—I can offer no opinion. I can offer no opinion—because—monsieur—I know nothing of it.'

"I had risen too, and, trying to throw infinite politeness into our attitudes, we faced each other mutely, like two china dogs on a mantelpiece. Hang the fellow! he had pricked the bubble. The blight of futility that lies in wait for men's speeches had fallen upon our conversation, and made it a thing of empty sounds. 'Very well,' I said, with a disconcerted smile; 'but couldn't it reduce itself to not being found out?' He made as if to retort readily, but when he spoke he had changed his mind. 'This, monsieur, is too fine for me—much above me—I don't think about it.' He bowed heavily over his cap, which he held before him by the peak, between the thumb and the forefinger of his wounded hand. I bowed too. We bowed together: we scraped our feet at each other with much ceremony, while a dirty specimen of a waiter looked on critically, as though he had paid for the performance. 'Serviteur,' said the Frenchman. Another scrape. 'Monsieur' . . . 'Monsieur.' . . . The glass door swung behind his burly back. I saw the southerly buster get hold of him and drive him down wind with his hand to his head, his shoulders braced, and the tails of his coat blown hard against his legs.

"I sat down again, alone and discouraged—discouraged about Jim's case. If you wonder that after more than three years it had preserved its actuality, you must know that I had seen him only very lately. I had come straight from Samarang, where I had loaded a cargo for Sydney: an utterly uninteresting bit of business—what Charley here would call one of my rational transactions and in Samarang I had seen something of Jim. He was then working for De Jongh, on my recommendation. Water-clerk. 'My representative afloat,' as De Jongh called him. You can't imagine a mode of life more barren of consolation, less capable of being invested with a spark of glamour—unless it be the business of an insurance canvasser. Little Bob Stanton—Charley here knew him well—had gone through that experience. The same who got drowned afterwards trying to save a lady's maid in the *Sephora* disaster. A case of collision on a hazy morning off the Spanish coast—you may remember. All the passengers had been packed tidily into the boats and shoved clear of the ship, when Bob sheered alongside again and scrambled back on deck to fetch that girl. How she had been left behind I can't make out; anyhow, she had gone completely crazy—wouldn't leave the ship—held to the rail like grim death. The wrestling match could be seen plainly from the boats; but poor Bob was the shortest chief mate in the merchant service, and the woman stood five feet ten in her shoes and was as strong as a horse, I've been told. So it went on, pull devil, pull baker, the wretched girl screaming all the time, and Bob letting out a yell now and then to warn his boat to keep well clear of the ship. One of the hands told me, hiding a smile at the recollection, 'It was for all the world, sir, like a naughty youngster fighting with his mother.' The same old chap said that 'At the last we could see that Mr. Stanton had given up hauling at the gal, and just stood by looking at her, watchful like. We thought afterwards he must've been reckoning that, maybe, the rush of water would tear her away from the rail by and by and give him a show to save her. We daren't come alongside for our life; and after a bit the old ship went down all on a sudden with a lurch to starboard—plop. The suck-in was something awful. We never saw anything alive or dead come up.' Poor Bob's spell of shore life had been one of the complications of a love affair, I believe. He fondly hoped he had done with the sea forever, and made sure he had got hold of all the bliss on earth, but it came to canvassing in the end. Some cousin of his in Liverpool put him up to it. He used to tell of his experiences in that line. He made us laugh till we cried, and, not altogether displeased at the effect, undersized and bearded to the waist like a gnome, he would tiptoe amongst us and say, 'It's all very well for you beggars to laugh, but my immortal soul was shriveled down to the size of a parched pea after a week of that work.' I don't know how Jim's soul accommodated itself to the new conditions of his life—I was kept too busy in getting him something to do that would keep body and soul together—but I am pretty certain his adventurous fancy was suffering all the pangs of starvation. It had certainly nothing to feed upon in this new calling. It was distressing to see him at it, though he tackled it with a stubborn serenity for which I must give him full credit. I kept my eye on his shabby plodding with a sort of notion that it was a punishment for the heroics of his fancy—an expiation for his craving after more glamour than he could carry. He had loved too well to imagine himself a glorious racehorse, and now he was condemned to toil without honor like a costermonger's donkey. He did it very well. He shut himself in, put his head down, said never a word. Very well; very well indeed—except for certain fantastic and violent outbreaks, on the deplorable occasions when the irrepressible *Patna* case cropped up. Unfortunately that scandal of the Eastern seas would not die out. And this is the reason why I could never feel I had done with Jim for good.

"I sat thinking of him after the French lieutenant had left, not, however, in connection with De Jongh's cool and gloomy back-shop, where we had hurriedly shaken hands not very long ago, but as I had seen him years before in the last flickers of the candle, alone with me in the long gallery of the Malabar House, with the chill and the darkness of the night at his back. The respectable sword of his country's law was suspended over his head. Tomorrow—or was it today? (midnight had slipped by long before we parted)—the marble-faced police magistrate, after distributing fines and terms of imprisonment in the assault-and-battery case, would take up the awful weapon and smite his bowed neck. Our communion in the night was uncommonly like a last vigil with a condemned man. He was guilty, too. He was guilty—as I had told myself repeatedly, guilty and done for; nevertheless, I wished to spare him the mere detail of a formal execution. I don't pretend to explain the reasons of my desire—I don't think I could; but if you haven't got a sort of notion by this time, then I must have been very obscure in my narrative, or you too sleepy to seize upon the sense of my words. I don't defend my morality. There was no morality in the impulse which induced me to lay before him Brierly's plan of evasion—I may call it—in all its primitive simplicity. There were the rupees—absolutely ready in my pocket and very much at his service. Oh! a loan; a loan, of course—and if an introduction to a man (in Rangoon) who could put some work in his way. . . . Why! with the greatest pleasure. I had pen, ink, and paper in my room on the first floor. And even while I was speaking I was impatient to begin the letter: day, month, year, 2:30 A.M. . . . for the sake of our old friendship I ask you to put some work in the way of Mr. James So-and-so, in whom, &c., &c. . . . I was even ready to write in that strain about him. If he had not enlisted my sympathies he had done better for himself—he had gone to the very fount and origin of that sentiment, he had reached the secret sensibility of my egoism. I am concealing nothing from you, because were I to do so my action would appear more unintelligible than any man's action has the right to be, and—in the second place—tomorrow you shall forget my sincerity along with the other lessons of the past. In this transaction, to speak grossly and precisely, I was the irreproachable man; but the subtle intentions of my immorality were defeated by the moral simplicity of the criminal. No doubt he was selfish, too, but his selfishness had a higher origin, a more lofty aim. I discovered that, say what I would, he was eager to go through the ceremony of execution; and I didn't say much, for I felt that in argument his youth would tell against me heavily: he believed where I had already ceased to doubt. There was something fine in the wildness of his unexpressed, hardly formulated hope. 'Clear out! Couldn't think of it,' he said, with a shake of the head. 'I make you an offer for which I neither demand nor expect any sort of gratitude,' I said; 'you shall repay me the money when convenient, and . . .' 'Awfully good of you,' he muttered, without looking up. I watched him narrowly; the future must have appeared horribly uncertain to him; but he did not falter, as though indeed there had been nothing wrong with his heart. I felt angry—not for the first time that night. 'The whole wretched business,' I said, 'is bitter enough, I should think, for a man of your kind. . . .' 'It is, it is,' he whispered twice, with his eyes fixed on the floor. It was heartrending. He towered above the light, and I could see the down on his cheek, the color mantling warm under the smooth skin of his face. Believe me or not, I say it was outrageously heartrending. It provoked me to brutality. 'Yes,' I said; 'and allow me to confess that I am totally unable to imagine what advantage you can expect from this licking of the dregs.' 'Advantage!' he murmured out of his stillness. 'I am dashed if I do,' I said, enraged. 'I've been trying to tell you all there is in it,' he went on slowly, as if meditating something unanswerable. 'But after all, it is *my* trouble.' I opened my mouth to retort, and discovered suddenly that I'd lost all confidence in myself; and it was as if he too had given me up, for he mumbled like a man thinking half aloud. 'Went away . . . went into hospitals . . . . Not one of them would face it. . . . They! . . .' He moved his hand slightly to imply disdain. 'But I've got to get over this thing, and I mustn't shirk any of it or . . . I won't shirk any of it.' He was silent. He gazed as though he had been haunted. His unconscious face reflected the passing expressions of scorn, of despair, of resolution—reflected them in turn, as a magic mirror would reflect the gliding passage of unearthly shapes. He lived surrounded by deceitful ghosts, by austere shades. 'Oh! nonsense, my dear fellow,' I began. He had a movement of impatience. 'You don't seem to understand,' he said incisively; then looking at me without a wink, 'I may have jumped, but I don't run away.' 'I meant no offense,' I said; and added stupidly, 'Better men than you have found it expedient to run, at times.' He colored all over, while in my confusion I half-choked myself with my own tongue. 'Perhaps so,' he said at last; 'I am not good enough; I can't afford it. I am bound to fight this thing down—I am fighting it *now*.' I got out of my chair and felt stiff all over. The silence was embarrassing, and to put an end to it I imagined nothing better but to remark, 'I had no idea it was so late,' in an airy tone. . . . 'I daresay you have had enough of this,' he said bruskly: 'and to tell you the truth'—he began to look round for his hat—'so have I.'

"Well! he had refused this unique offer. He had struck aside my helping hand; he was ready to go now, and beyond the balustrade the night seemed to wait for him very still, as though he had been marked down for its prey. I heard his voice. 'Ah! here it is.' He had found his hat. For a few seconds we hung in the wind. 'What will you do after—after . . .' I asked very low. 'Go to the dogs as likely as not,' he answered in a gruff mutter. I had recovered my wits in a measure, and judged best to take it lightly. 'Pray remember,' I said, 'that I should like very much to see you again before you go.' 'I don't know what's to prevent you. The damned thing won't make me invisible,' he said with intense bitterness,—'no such luck.' And then at the moment of taking leave he treated me to a ghastly muddle of dubious stammers and movements, to an awful display of hesitations. God forgive him—me! He had taken it into his fanciful head that I was likely to make some difficulty as to shaking hands. It was too awful for words. I believe I shouted suddenly at him as you would bellow to a man you saw about to walk over a cliff; I remember our voices being raised, the appearance of a miserable grin on his face, a crushing clutch on my hand, a nervous laugh. The candle spluttered out, and the thing was over at last, with a groan that floated up to me in the dark. He got himself away somehow. The night swallowed his form. He was a horrible bungler. Horrible. I heard the quick crunch-crunch of the gravel under his boots. He was running. Absolutely running, with nowhere to go to. And he was not yet four-and-twenty."

❧ 14 ❧

I slept little, hurried over my breakfast, and after a slight hesitation gave up my early morning visit to my ship. It was really very wrong of me, because, though my chief mate was an excellent man all round, he was the victim of such black imaginings that if he did not get a letter from his wife at the expected time he would go quite distracted with rage and jealousy, lose all grip on the work, quarrel with all hands, and either weep in his cabin or develop such a ferocity of temper as all but drove the crew to the verge of mutiny. The thing had always seemed inexplicable to me: they had been married thirteen years; I had a glimpse of her once, and honestly, I couldn't conceive a man abandoned enough to plunge into sin for the sake of such an unattractive person. I don't know whether I have not done wrong by refraining from putting that view before poor Selvin: the man made a little hell on earth for himself, and I also suffered indirectly; but some sort of, no doubt, false delicacy, prevented me. The marital relations of seamen would make an interesting subject, and I could tell you instances. . . . However, this is not the place, nor the time, and we are concerned with Jim—who was unmarried. If his imaginative conscience or his pride; if all the extravagant ghosts and austere shades that were the disastrous familiars of his youth, would not let him run away from the block, I, who of course can't be suspected of such familiars, was irresistibly impelled to go and see his head roll off. I wended my way towards the court. I didn't hope to be very much impressed or edified, or interested, or even frightened—though, as long as there is any life before one, a jolly good fright now and then is a salutary discipline. But neither did I expect to be so awfully depressed. The bitterness of his punishment was in its chill and mean atmosphere. The real significance of crime is in its being a breach of faith with the community of mankind, and from that point of view he was no mean traitor, but his execution was a hole-and-corner affair. There was no high scaffolding, no scarlet cloth (did they have scarlet cloth on Tower Hill? They should have had), no awe-stricken multitude to be horrified at his guilt and be moved to tears at his fate—no air of somber retribution. There was, as I walked along, the clear sunshine, a brilliance too passionate to be consoling, the streets full of jumbled bits of color like a damaged kaleidoscope: yellow, green, blue, dazzling white, the brown nudity of an undraped shoulder, a bullock-cart with a red canopy, a company of native infantry in a drab body with dark heads marching in dusty laced boots, a native policeman in a somber uniform of scanty cut and belted in patent leather, who looked up at me with orientally pitiful eyes as though his migrating spirit were suffering exceedingly from that unforeseen—what d'ye call'em?—avatar—incarnation. Under the shade of a lonely tree in the courtyard, the villagers connected with the assault case sat in a picturesque group, looking like a chromolithograph of a camp in a book of Eastern travel. One missed the obligatory thread of smoke in the foreground and the pack-animals grazing. A blank yellow wall rose behind, overtopping the tree, reflecting the glare. The courtroom was somber, seemed more vast. High up in the dim space the punkahs were swaying short to and fro, to and fro. Here and there a draped figure, dwarfed by the bare walls, remained without stirring amongst the rows of empty benches, as if absorbed in pious meditation. The plaintiff, who had been beaten, an obese chocolate-colored man with shaved head, one fat breast bare and bright yellow caste-mark above the bridge of his nose, sat in pompous immobility: only his eyes glittered, rolling in the gloom, and the nostrils dilated and collapsed violently as he breathed. Brierly dropped into his seat looking done up, as though he had spent the night in sprinting on a cinder-track. The pious sailing-ship skipper appeared excited and made uneasy movements, as if restraining with difficulty an impulse to stand up and exhort us earnestly to prayer and repentance. The head of the magistrate, delicately pale under the neatly arranged hair, resembled the head of a hopeless invalid after he had been washed and brushed and propped up in bed. He moved aside the vase of flowers—a bunch of purple with a few pink blossoms on long stalks—and seizing in both hands a long sheet of bluish paper, ran his eye over it, propped his forearms on the edge of the desk, and began to read aloud in an even, distinct, and careless voice.

"By Jove! For all my foolishness about scaffolds and heads rolling off—I assure you it was infinitely worse than a beheading. A heavy sense of finality brooded over all this, unrelieved by the hope of rest and safety following the fall of the axe. These proceedings had all the cold vengefulness of a death sentence, and the cruelty of a sentence of exile. This is how I looked at it that morning—and even now I seem to see an undeniable vestige of truth in that exaggerated view of a common occurrence. You may imagine how strongly I felt this at the time. Perhaps it is for that reason that I could not bring myself to admit the finality. The thing was always with me, I was always eager to take opinion on it, as though it had not been practically settled: individual opinion—international opinion—by Jove! That Frenchman's, for instance. His own country's pronouncement was uttered in the passionless and definite phraseology a machine would use, if machines could speak. The head of the magistrate was half hidden by the paper, his brow was like alabaster.

"There were several questions before the Court. The first as to whether the ship was in every respect fit and seaworthy for the voyage. The Court found she was not. The next point, I remember, was, whether up to the time of the accident the ship had been navigated with proper and seamanlike care. They said Yes to that, goodness knows why, and then they declared that there was no evidence to show the exact cause of the accident. A floating derelict probably. I myself remember that a Norwegian bark bound out with a cargo of pitch pine had been given up as missing about that time, and it was just the sort of craft that would capsize in a squall and float bottom up for months—a kind of maritime ghoul on the prowl to kill ships in the dark. Such wandering corpses are common enough in the North Atlantic, which is haunted by all the terrors of the sea—fogs, icebergs, dead ships bent upon mischief, and long sinister gales that fasten upon one like a vampire till all the strength and the spirit and even hope are gone, and one feels like the empty shell of a man. But there—in those seas—the incident was rare enough to resemble a special arrangement of a malevolent providence, which, unless it had for its object the killing of a donkey-man and the bringing of worse than death upon Jim, appeared an utterly aimless piece of deviltry. This view occurring to me took off my attention. For a time I was aware of the magistrate's voice as a sound merely; but in a moment it shaped itself into distinct words . . . 'in utter disregard of their plain duty,' it said. The next sentence escaped me somehow, and then . . . 'abandoning in the moment of danger the lives and property confided to their charge' . . . went on the voice evenly, and stopped. A pair of eyes under the white forehead shot darkly a glance above the edge of the paper. I looked for Jim hurriedly, as though I had expected him to disappear. He was very still—but he was there. He sat pink and fair and extremely attentive. 'Therefore, . . .' began the voice emphatically. He stared with parted lips, hanging upon the words of the man behind the desk. These came out into the stillness wafted on the wind made by the punkahs, and I, watching for their effect upon him, caught only the fragments of official language. . . . 'The Court . . . Gustav So-and-so, master . . . native of Germany, . . . James So-and-so . . . mate . . . certificates canceled.' A silence fell. The magistrate had dropped the paper, and leaning sideways on the arm of his chair, began to talk with Brierly easily. People started to move out; others were pushing in, and I also made for the door. Outside I stood still, and when Jim passed me on his way to the gate, I caught at his arm and detained him. The look he gave discomposed me as though I had been responsible for his state: he looked at me as if I had been the embodied evil of life. 'It's all over,' I stammered. 'Yes,' he said thickly. 'And now let no man' . . . He jerked his arm out of my grasp. I watched his back as he went away. It was a long street, and he remained in sight for some time. He walked rather slow, and straddling his legs a little, as if he had found it difficult to keep a straight line. Just before I lost him I fancied he staggered a bit.

"'Man overboard,' said a deep voice behind me. Turning round, I saw a fellow I

knew slightly, a West Australian; Chester was his name. He, too, had been looking
after Jim. He was a man with an immense girth of chest, a rugged, clean-shaved
face of mahogany color, and two blunt tufts of iron-gray, thick, wiry hairs on his
upper lip. He had been pearler, wrecker, trader, whaler too, I believe; in his own
words—anything and everything a man may be at sea, but a pirate. The Pacific,
north and south, was his proper hunting ground; but he had wandered so far afield
looking for a cheap steamer to buy. Lately he had discovered—so he said—a
guano island somewhere, but its approaches were dangerous, and the anchorage,
such as it was, could not be considered safe, to say the least of it. 'As good as a
gold mine,' he would exclaim. 'Right bang in the middle of the Walpole Reefs, and
if it's true enough that you can get no holding-ground anywhere in less than forty
fathom, then what of that? There are the hurricanes, too. But it's a first-rate thing.
As good as a gold mine—better! Yet there's not a fool of them that will see it. I
can't get a skipper or a shipowner to go near the place. So I made up my mind to
cart the blessed stuff myself.'. . . This was what he required a steamer for, and I
knew he was just then negotiating enthusiastically with a Parsee firm for an old,
brig-rigged, sea anachronism of ninety horsepower. We had met and spoken
together several times. He looked knowingly after Jim. 'Takes it to heart?' he
asked scornfully. 'Very much,' I said. 'Then he's no good,' he opined. 'What's all the
to-do about? A bit of ass's skin. That never yet made a man. You must see things
exactly as they are—if you don't you may just as well give in at once. You will
never do anything in this world. Look at me. I made it a practice never to take
anything to heart.' 'Yes,' I said, 'you see things as they are.' 'I wish I could see my
partner coming along, that's what I wish to see,' he said. 'Know my partner? Old
Robinson. Yes; *the* Robinson. Don't *you* know? The notorious Robinson. The man
who smuggled more opium and bagged more seals in his time than any loose
Johnny now alive. They say he used to board the sealing-schooners up Alaska way
when the fog was so thick that the Lord God, He alone, could tell one man from
another. Holy Terror Robinson. That's the man. He is with me in that guano thing.
The best chance he ever came across in his life.' He put his lips to my ear.
'Cannibal?—well, they used to give him the name years and years ago. You
remember the story? A shipwreck on the west side of Stewart Island; that's right;
seven of them got ashore, and it seems they did not get on very well together.
Some men are too cantankerous for anything—don't know how to make the best
of a bad job—don't see things as they are—as they *are*, my boy! And then what's
the consequence? Obvious! Trouble, trouble; as likely as not a knock on the head;
and serve 'em right too. That sort is the most useful when it's dead. The story goes
that a boat of Her Majesty's ship *Wolverine* found him kneeling on the kelp, naked
as the day he was born, and chanting some psalm-tune or other; light snow was
falling at the time. He waited till the boat was an oar's length from the shore, and

then up and away. They chased him for an hour up and down the boulders, till a marine flung a stone that took him behind the ear providentially and knocked him senseless. Alone? Of course. But that's like that tale of sealing-schooners; the Lord God knows the right and the wrong of that story. The cutter did not investigate much. They wrapped him in a boat-cloak and took him off as quick as they could, with a dark night coming on, the weather threatening, and the ship firing recall guns every five minutes. Three weeks afterwards he was as well as ever. He didn't allow any fuss that was made on shore to upset him; he just shut his lips tight, and let people screech. It was bad enough to have lost his ship, and all he was worth besides, without paying attention to the hard names they called him. That's the man for me.' He lifted his arm for a signal to someone down the street. 'He's got a little money, so I had to let him into my thing. Had to! It would have been sinful to throw away such a find, and I was cleaned out myself. It cut me to the quick, but I could see the matter just as it was, and if I *must* share—thinks I—with any man, then give me Robinson. I left him at breakfast in the hotel to come to court, because I've an idea . . . Ah! Good morning, Captain Robinson. . . . Friend of mine, Captain Robinson.'

"An emaciated patriarch in a suit of white drill, a solah topi with a green-lined rim on a head trembling with age, joined us after crossing the street in a trotting shuffle, and stood propped with both hands on the handle of an umbrella. A white beard with amber streaks hung lumpily down to his waist. He blinked his creased eyelids at me in a bewildered way. 'How do you do? how do you do?' he piped amiably, and tottered. 'A little deaf,' said Chester aside. 'Did you drag him over six thousand miles to get a cheap steamer?' I asked. 'I would have taken him twice round the world as soon as look at him,' said Chester with immense energy. 'The steamer will be the making of us, my lad. Is it my fault that every skipper and shipowner in the whole of blessed Australasia turns out a blamed fool? Once I talked for three hours to a man in Auckland. "Send a ship," I said, "send a ship. I'll give you half of the first cargo for yourself, free gratis for nothing—just to make a good start." Says he, "I wouldn't do it if there was no other place on earth to send a ship to." Perfect ass, of course. Rocks, currents, no anchorage, sheer cliff to lay to, no insurance company would take the risk, didn't see how he could get loaded under three years. Ass! I nearly went on my knees to him. "But look at the thing as it is," says I. "Damn rocks and hurricanes. Look at it as it is. There's guano there, Queensland sugar planters would fight for—fight for on the quay, I tell you." . . . What can you do with a fool?. . . "That's one of your little jokes, Chester," he says. . . . Joke! I could have wept. Ask Captain Robinson here. . . . And there was another shipowning fellow—a fat chap in a white waistcoat in Wellington, who seemed to think I was up to some swindle or other. "I don't know what sort of fool you're looking for," he says, "but I am busy just now. Good morning." I longed to take him in my two hands and smash him through the window of his own office. But I didn't. I was as mild as a curate. "Think of it," says I. "*Do* think it over. I'll call tomorrow." He grunted something about being "out all day." On the stairs I felt ready to beat my head against the wall from vexation. Captain Robinson here can tell you. It was awful to think of all that lovely stuff lying waste under the sun—stuff that would send the sugar cane shooting sky-high. The making of Queensland! The making of Queensland. And in Brisbane, where I went to have a last try, they gave me the name of a lunatic. Idiots! The only sensible man I came across was the cabman who drove me about. A broken-down swell he was, I fancy. Hey! Captain Robinson? You remember I told you about my cabby in Brisbane—don't you? The chap had a wonderful eye for things. He saw it all in a jiffy. It was a real pleasure to talk with him. One evening after a devil of a day amongst ship owners I felt so bad that, says I, "I must get drunk. Come along; I must get drunk, or I'll go mad." "I am your man," he says; "go ahead." I don't know what I would have done without him. Hey! Captain Robinson.'

"He poked the ribs of his partner. 'He! he! he!' laughed the Ancient, looked aimlessly down the street, then peered at me doubtfully with sad, dim pupils. . . . 'He! he! he!'. . . He leaned heavier on the umbrella, and dropped his gaze on the ground. I needn't tell you I had tried to get away several times, but Chester had foiled every attempt by simply catching hold of my coat. 'One minute. I've a notion.' 'What's your infernal notion?' I exploded at last. 'If you think I am going in with you . . .' 'No, no, my boy. Too late, if you wanted ever so much. We've got a steamer.' 'You've got the ghost of a steamer,' I said. 'Good enough for a start—there's no superior nonsense about us. Is there, Captain Robinson?' 'No! no! no!' croaked the old man without lifting his eyes, and the senile tremble of his head became almost fierce with determination. 'I understand you know that young chap,' said Chester, with a nod at the street from which Jim had disappeared long ago. 'He's been having grub with you in the Malabar last night—so I was told.'

"I said that was true; and after remarking that he too liked to live well and in style, only that, for the present, he had to be saving of every penny—'none too many for the business! Isn't that so, Captain Robinson?'—he squared his shoulders and stroked his dumpy moustache, while the notorious Robinson, coughing at his side, clung more than ever to the handle of the umbrella, and seemed ready to subside passively into a heap of old bones. 'You see the old chap has all the money,' whispered Chester confidentially. 'I've been cleaned out trying to engineer the dratted thing. But wait a bit, wait a bit. The good time is coming.'. . . He seemed suddenly astonished at the signs of impatience I gave. 'Oh, crakee!' he cried; 'I am telling you of the biggest thing that ever was, and you . . .' 'I have an appointment,' I pleaded mildly. 'What of that?' he asked with genuine surprise; 'let it wait.' 'That's exactly what I am doing now,' I remarked; 'hadn't you better tell me what it is you want?' 'Buy twenty hotels like that,' he growled to himself; 'and every joker boarding in them too—twenty times over.' He lifted his head smartly. 'I want that young chap.' 'I don't understand,' I said. 'He's no good, is he?' said Chester, crisply. 'I know nothing about it,' I protested. 'Why, you told me yourself he was taking it to heart,' argued Chester. 'Well, in my opinion a chap who . . . Anyhow, he can't be much good; but then you see I am on the lookout for somebody, and I've just got a thing that will suit him. I'll give him a job on my island.' He nodded significantly. 'I'm going to dump forty coolies there if I've to steal 'em. Somebody must work the stuff. Oh! I mean to act square: wooden shed, corrugated iron roof—I know a man in Hobart who will take my bill at six months for the materials. I do. Honor bright. Then there's the water supply. I'll have to fly round and get somebody to trust me for half-a-dozen secondhand iron tanks. Catch rainwater, hey? Let him take charge. Make him supreme boss over the coolies. Good idea, isn't it? What do you say?' 'There are whole years when not a drop of rain falls on Walpole,' I said, too amazed to laugh. He bit his lip and seemed bothered. 'Oh, well, I will fix up something for them—or land a supply. Hang it all! That's not the question.'

"I said nothing. I had a rapid vision of Jim perched on a shadowless rock, up to his knees in guano, with the screams of sea birds in his ears, the incandescent ball of the sun above his head; the empty sky and the empty ocean all a-quiver, simmering together in the heat as far as the eye could reach. 'I wouldn't advise my worst enemy . . .' I began. 'What's the matter with you?' cried Chester; 'I mean to give him a good screw—that is, as soon as the thing is set going, of course. It's as easy as falling off a log. Simply nothing to do; two six-shooters in his belt . . . Surely he wouldn't be afraid of anything forty coolies could do—with two six-shooters and he the only armed man too! It's much better than it looks. I want you to help me to talk him over.' 'No!' I shouted. Old Robinson lifted his bleared eyes dismally for a moment; Chester looked at me with infinite contempt. 'So you wouldn't advise him?' he uttered slowly. 'Certainly not,' I answered, as indignant as though he had requested me to help murder somebody; 'moreover, I am sure he wouldn't. He is badly cut up, but he isn't mad as far as I know.' 'He is no earthly good for anything,' Chester mused aloud. 'He would just have done for me. If you only could see a thing as it is, you would see it's the very thing for him. And besides . . . Why! it's the most splendid, sure chance . . .' He got angry suddenly. 'I must have a man. There! . . .' He stamped his foot and smiled unpleasantly. 'Anyhow, I could guarantee the island wouldn't sink under him—and I believe he is a bit particular on that point.' 'Good morning,' I said curtly. He looked at me as though I had been an incomprehensible fool. . . . 'Must be moving, Captain Robinson,' he yelled suddenly into the old man's ear. 'These Parsee Johnnies are waiting for us to clinch the bargain.' He took his partner under the arm with a firm grip, swung him round, and, unexpectedly, leered at me over his shoulder. 'I was trying to do him a kindness,' he asserted, with an air and tone that made my blood boil. 'Thank you for nothing—in his name,' I rejoined. 'Oh! you are devilish smart,' he sneered; 'but you are like the rest of them. Too much in the clouds. See what *you* will do with him.' 'I don't know that I want to do anything with him.' 'Don't you?' he spluttered; his gray moustache bristled with anger, and by his side the notorious Robinson, propped on the umbrella, stood with his back to me, as patient and still as a worn-out cab-horse. 'I haven't found a guano island,' I said. 'It's my belief you wouldn't know one if you were led right up to it by the hand,' he riposted quickly; 'and in this world you've got to see a thing first, before you can make use of it. Got to see it through and through at that, neither more nor less.' 'And get others to see it too,' I insinuated, with a glance at the bowed back by his side. Chester snorted at me. 'His eyes are right enough—don't you worry. He ain't a puppy.' 'Oh dear, no!' I said. 'Come along, Captain Robinson,' he shouted, with a sort of bullying deference under the rim of the old man's hat; the Holy Terror gave a submissive little jump. The ghost of a steamer was waiting for them, Fortune on that fair isle! They made a curious pair of Argonauts. Chester strode on leisurely, well set up, portly, and of conquering mien; the other, long, wasted, drooping, and hooked to his arm, shuffled his withered shanks with desperate haste."

❧ 15 ❧

I did not start in search of Jim at once, only because I had really an appointment which I could not neglect. Then, as ill luck would have it, in my agent's office I was fastened upon by a fellow fresh from Madagascar with a little scheme for a wonderful piece of business. It had something to do with cattle and cartridges and a Prince Ravonalo something; but the pivot of the whole affair was the stupidity of some admiral—Admiral Pierre, I think. Everything turned on that, and the chap couldn't find words strong enough to express his confidence. He had globular eyes starting out of his head with a fishy glitter, bumps on his forehead, and wore his long hair brushed back without a parting. He had a favorite phrase which he kept on repeating triumphantly, 'The minimum of risk with the maximum of profit is my motto. What?' He made my head ache, spoiled my tiffin, but got his own out of me all right; and as soon as I had shaken him off, I made straight for the waterside. I caught sight of Jim leaning over the parapet of the quay. Three native boatmen quarreling over five annas were making an awful

row at his elbow. He didn't hear me come up, but spun round as if the slight contact of my finger had released a catch. 'I was looking,' he stammered. I don't
remember what I said, not much anyhow, but he made no difficulty in following
me to the hotel.

"He followed me as manageable as a little child, with an obedient air, with no
sort of manifestation, rather as though he had been waiting for me there to come
along and carry him off. I need not have been so surprised as I was at his
tractability. On all the round earth, which to some seems so big and that others
affect to consider as rather smaller than a mustard seed, he had no place where
he could—what shall I say?—where he could withdraw. That's it! Withdraw—be
alone with his loneliness. He walked by my side very calm, glancing here and
there, and once turned his head to look after a Sidiboy fireman in a cutaway coat
and yellowish trousers, whose black face had silky gleams like a lump of
anthracite coal. I doubt, however, whether he saw anything, or even remained all
the time aware of my companionship, because if I had not edged him to the left
here, or pulled him to the right there, I believe he would have gone straight before
him in any direction till stopped by a wall or some other obstacle. I steered him
into my bedroom, and sat down at once to write letters. This was the only place in
the world (unless, perhaps, the Walpole Reef—but that was not so handy) where
he could have it out with himself without being bothered by the rest of the universe. The damned thing—as he had expressed it—had not made him invisible,
but I behaved exactly as though he were. No sooner in my chair I bent over my
writing desk like a medieval scribe, and, but for the movement of the hand holding the pen, remained anxiously quiet. I can't say I was frightened; but I certainly
kept as still as if there had been something dangerous in the room, that at the
first hint of a movement on my part would be provoked to pounce upon me. There
was not much in the room—you know how these bedrooms are—a sort of four-
poster bedstead under a mosquito net, two or three chairs, the table I was writing
at, a bare floor. A glass door opened on an upstairs veranda, and he stood with his
face to it, having a hard time with all possible privacy. Dusk fell; I lit a candle with
the greatest economy of movement and as much prudence as though it were an
illegal proceeding. There is no doubt that he had a very hard time of it, and so had
I, even to the point, I must own, of wishing him to the devil, or on Walpole Reef, at
least. It occurred to me once or twice that, after all, Chester was, perhaps, the
man to deal effectively with such a disaster. That strange idealist had found a
practical use for it at once, unerringly—as it were. It was enough to make one
suspect that, maybe, he really could see the true aspect of things that appeared
mysterious or utterly hopeless to less imaginative persons. I wrote and wrote; I
liquidated all the arrears of my correspondence, and then went on writing to people who had no reason whatever to expect from me a gossipy letter about nothing

at all. At times I stole a sidelong glance. He was rooted to the spot, but convulsive shudders ran down his back; his shoulders would heave suddenly. He was fighting, he was fighting—mostly for his breath, as it seemed. The massive shadows, cast all one way from the straight flame of the candle, seemed possessed of gloomy consciousness; the immobility of the furniture had to my furtive eye an air of attention. I was becoming fanciful in the midst of my industrious scribbling; and though, when the scratching of my pen stopped for a moment, there was complete silence and stillness in the room, I suffered from that profound disturbance and confusion of thought which is caused by a violent and menacing uproar—of a heavy gale at sea, for instance. Some of you may know what I mean, that mingled anxiety, distress, and irritation with a sort of craven feeling creeping in—not pleasant to acknowledge, but which gives a quite special merit to one's endurance. I don't claim any merit for standing the stress of Jim's emotions; I could take refuge in the letters; I could have written to strangers if necessary. Suddenly, as I was taking up a fresh sheet of notepaper, I heard a low sound, the first sound that, since we had been shut up together, had come to my ears in the dim stillness of the room. I remained with my head down, with my hand arrested. Those who have kept vigil by a sickbed have heard such faint sounds in the stillness of the night watches, sounds wrung from a racked body, from a weary soul. He pushed the glass door with such force that all the panes rang: he stepped out, and I held my breath, straining my ears without knowing what else I expected to hear. He was really taking too much to heart an empty formality which to Chester's rigorous criticism seemed unworthy the notice of a man who could see things as they were. An empty formality; a piece of parchment. Well, well. As to an inaccessible guano deposit, that was another story altogether. One could intelligibly break one's heart over that. A feeble burst of many voices mingled with the tinkle of silver and glass floated up from the dining room below; through the open door the outer edge of the light from my candle fell on his back faintly; beyond all was black; he stood on the brink of a vast obscurity, like a lonely figure by the shore of a somber and hopeless ocean. There was the Walpole Reef in it—to be sure—a speck in the dark void, a straw for the drowning man. My compassion for him took the shape of the thought that I wouldn't have liked his people to see him at that moment. I found it trying myself. His back was no longer shaken by his gasps; he stood straight as an arrow, faintly visible and still; and the meaning of this stillness sank to the bottom of my soul like lead into the water, and made it so heavy that for a second I wished heartily that the only course left open for me were to pay for his funeral. Even the law had done with him. To bury him would have been such an easy kindness! It would have been so much in accordance with the wisdom of life, which consists in putting out of sight all the reminders of our folly, of our weakness, of our mortality; all that makes against our efficiency—the memory of our failures, the hints of our undying fears, the bodies of our dead friends. Perhaps he did take it too much to heart. And if so then—Chester's offer. . . . At this point I took up a fresh sheet and began to write resolutely. There was nothing but myself between him and the dark ocean. I had a sense of responsibility. If I spoke, would that motionless and suffering youth leap into the obscurity—clutch at the straw? I found out how difficult it may be sometimes to make a sound. There is a weird power in a spoken word. And why the devil not? I was asking myself persistently while I drove on with my writing. All at once, on the blank page, under the very point of the pen, the two figures of Chester and his antique partner, very distinct and complete, would dodge into view with stride and gestures, as if reproduced in the field of some optical toy. I would watch them for a while. No! They were too phantasmal and extravagant to enter into anyone's fate. And a word carries far—very far—deals destruction through time as the bullets go flying through space. I said nothing; and he, out there with his back to the light, as if bound and gagged by all the invisible foes of man, made no stir and made no sound."

❦ 16 ❦

The time was coming when I should see him loved, trusted, admired, with a legend of strength and prowess forming round his name as though he had been the stuff of a hero. It's true—I assure you; as true as I'm sitting here talking about him in vain. He, on his side, had that faculty of beholding at a hint the face of his desire and the shape of his dream, without which the earth would know no lover and no adventurer. He captured much honor and an Arcadian happiness (I won't say anything about innocence) in the bush, and it was as good to him as the honor and the Arcadian happiness of the streets to another man. Felicity, felicity—how shall I say it?—is quaffed out of a golden cup in every latitude: the flavor is with you—with you alone, and you can make it as intoxicating as you please. He was of the sort that would drink deep, as you may guess from what went before. I found him, if not exactly intoxicated, then at least flushed with the elixir at his lips. He had not obtained it at once. There had been, as you know, a period of probation amongst infernal ship chandlers, during which he had suffered and I had worried about—about—my trust—you may call it. I don't know that I am completely reassured now, after beholding him in all his brilliance. That was my last view of him—in a strong light, dominating, and yet in complete accord with his surroundings—with the life of the forests and with the life of men. I own that I was impressed, but I must admit to myself that after all this is not the lasting impression. He was protected by his isolation, alone of his own superior kind, in close touch with nature, that keeps faith on such easy terms with her lovers. But I cannot fix before my eye the image of his safety. I shall always remember him as seen through the open door of my room, taking, perhaps, too much to heart the mere consequences of his failure. I am pleased, of course, that some good—and even some splendor—came out of my endeavors; but at times it seems to me it would have been better for my peace of mind if I had not stood between him and Chester's confoundedly generous offer. I wonder what his exuberant imagination would have made of Walpole islet—that most hopelessly forsaken crumb of dry land on the face of the waters. It is not likely I would ever have heard, for, I must tell you, that Chester, after calling at some Australian port to patch up his brig-rigged sea-anachronism, steamed out into the Pacific with a crew of twenty-two hands all told, and the only news having a possible bearing upon the mystery of his fate was the news of a hurricane which is supposed to have swept in its course over the Walpole shoals, a month or so afterwards. Not a vestige of the Argonauts ever turned up; not a sound came out of the waste. Finis! The Pacific is the most discreet of live, hot-tempered oceans: the chilly Antarctic can keep a secret too, but more in the manner of a grave.

"And there is a sense of blessed finality in such discretion, which is what we all more or less sincerely are ready to admit—for what else is it that makes the idea of death supportable? End! Finis! the potent word that exorcises from the house of life the haunting shadow of fate. This is what—notwithstanding the testimony of my eyes and his own earnest assurances—I miss when I look back upon Jim's success. While there's life there is hope, truly; but there is fear, too. I don't mean to say that I regret my action, nor will I pretend that I can't sleep o' nights in consequence; still the idea obtrudes itself that he made so much of his disgrace while it is the guilt alone that matters. He was not—if I may say so—clear to me. He was not clear. And there is a suspicion he was not clear to himself either. There were his fine sensibilities, his fine feelings, his fine longings—a sort of sublimated, idealized selfishness. He was—if you allow me to say so—very fine; very fine—and very unfortunate. A little coarser nature would not have borne the strain; it would have had to come to terms with itself—with a sigh, with a grunt, or even with a guffaw; a still coarser one would have remained invulnerably ignorant and completely uninteresting.

"But he was too interesting or too unfortunate to be thrown to the dogs, or even to Chester. I felt this while I sat with my face over the paper and he fought and gasped, struggling for his breath in that terribly stealthy way, in my room; I felt it when he rushed out on the veranda as if to fling himself over—and didn't; I felt it more and more all the time he remained outside, faintly lighted on the background of night, as if standing on the shore of a somber and hopeless sea.

"An abrupt heavy rumble made me lift my head. The noise seemed to roll away, and suddenly a searching and violent glare fell on the blind face of the night. The sustained and dazzling flickers seemed to last for an unconscionable time. The growl of the thunder increased steadily while I looked at him, distinct and black, planted solidly upon the shores of a sea of light. At the moment of greatest brilliance the darkness leaped back with a culminating crash, and he vanished before my dazzled eyes as utterly as though he had been blown to atoms. A blustering sigh passed; furious hands seemed to tear at the shrubs, shake the tops of the trees below, slam doors, break windowpanes all along the front of the building. He stepped in, closing the door behind him, and found me bending over the table: my sudden anxiety as to what he would say was very great, and akin to a fright. 'May I have a cigarette?' he asked. I gave a push to the box without raising my head. 'I want—want—tobacco,' he muttered. I became extremely buoyant. 'Just a moment,' I grunted pleasantly. He took a few steps here and there. 'That's over,' I heard him say. A single distant clap of thunder came from the sea like a gun of distress. 'The monsoon breaks up early this year,' he remarked conversationally, somewhere behind me. This encouraged me to turn round, which I did as soon as I had finished addressing the last envelope. He was smoking greedily in the middle of the room, and though he heard the stir I made, he remained with his back to me for a time.

"'Come—I carried it off pretty well,' he said, wheeling suddenly. 'Something's paid off—not much. I wonder what's to come.' His face did not show any emotion, only it appeared a little darkened and swollen, as though he had been holding his breath. He smiled reluctantly, as it were, and went on while I gazed up at him mutely. . . . 'Thank you, though—your room—jolly convenient—for a chap—badly hipped.'. . . The rain pattered and swished in the garden; a water pipe (it must have had a hole in it) performed just outside the window a parody of blubbering woe with funny sobs and gurgling lamentations, interrupted by jerky spasms of silence. . . . 'A bit of shelter,' he mumbled, and ceased.

"A flash of faded lightning darted in through the black framework of the windows and ebbed out without any noise. I was thinking how I had best approach him (I did not want to be flung off again) when he gave a little laugh. 'No better than a vagabond now' . . . the end of the cigarette smoldered between his fingers . . . 'without a single—single,' he pronounced slowly; 'and yet . . .' He paused; the rain fell with redoubled violence. 'Someday one's bound to come upon some sort of chance to get it all back again. Must!' he whispered distinctly, glaring at my boots.

"I did not even know what it was he wished so much to regain, what it was he had so terribly missed. It might have been so much that it was impossible to say. A piece of ass's skin, according to Chester. . . . He looked up at me inquisitively. 'Perhaps. If life's long enough,' I muttered through my teeth with unreasonable animosity. 'Don't reckon too much on it.'

"'Jove! I feel as if nothing could ever touch me,' he said in a tone of somber conviction. 'If this business couldn't knock me over, then there's no fear of there being not enough time to—climb out, and . . .' He looked upwards.

"It struck me that it is from such as he that the great army of waifs and strays is recruited, the army that marches down, down into all the gutters of the earth. As soon as he left my room, that 'bit of shelter,' he would take his place in the ranks, and begin the journey towards the bottomless pit. I at least had no illusions; but it was I, too, who a moment ago had been so sure of the power of words, and now was afraid to speak, in the same way one dares not move for fear of losing a slippery hold. It is when we try to grapple with another man's intimate need that we perceive how incomprehensible, wavering, and misty are the beings that share with us the sight of the stars and the warmth of the sun. It is as if loneliness were a hard and absolute condition of existence; the envelope of flesh and blood on which our eyes are fixed melts before the outstretched hand, and there remains only the capricious, inconsolable, and elusive spirit that no eye can follow, no hand can grasp. It was the fear of losing him that kept me silent, for it was borne upon me suddenly and with unaccountable force that should I let him slip away into the darkness I would never forgive myself.

"'Well. Thanks—once more. You've been—er—uncommonly—really there's no word to . . . Uncommonly! I don't know why, I am sure. I am afraid I don't feel as grateful as I would if the whole thing hadn't been so brutally sprung on me. Because at bottom . . . you, yourself . . .' He stuttered.

"'Possibly,' I struck in. He frowned.

"'All the same, one is responsible.' He watched me like a hawk.

"'And that's true, too,' I said.

"'Well. I've gone with it to the end, and I don't intend to let any man cast it in my teeth without—without—resenting it.' He clenched his fist.

"'There's yourself,' I said with a smile—mirthless enough, God knows—but he looked at me menacingly. 'That's my business,' he said. An air of indomitable resolution came and went upon his face like a vain and passing shadow. Next moment he looked a dear good boy in trouble, as before. He flung away the cigarette. 'Goodbye,' he said, with the sudden haste of a man who had lingered too long in view of a pressing bit of work waiting for him; and then for a second or so he made not the slightest movement. The downpour fell with the heavy uninterrupted rush of a sweeping flood, with a sound of unchecked, overwhelming fury that called to one's mind the images of collapsing bridges, of uprooted trees, of undermined mountains. No man could breast the colossal and headlong stream that seemed to break and swirl against the dim stillness in which we were precariously sheltered as if on an island. The perforated pipe gurgled, choked, spat, and splashed in odious ridicule of a swimmer fighting for his life. 'It is raining,' I remonstrated, 'and I . . .' 'Rain or shine,' he began bruskly, checked himself, and walked to the window. 'Perfect deluge,' he muttered after a while: he leaned his forehead on the glass. 'It's dark, too.'

"'Yes, it is very dark,' I said.

"He pivoted on his heels, crossed the room, and had actually opened the door leading into the corridor before I leaped up from my chair. 'Wait,' I cried, 'I want you to . . .' 'I can't dine with you again tonight,' he flung at me, with one leg out of the room already. 'I haven't the slightest intention to ask you,' I shouted. At this he drew back his foot, but remained mistrustfully in the very doorway. I lost no time in entreating him earnestly not to be absurd; to come in and shut the door."

❧ 17 ❧

He came in at last; but I believe it was mostly the rain that did it; it was falling just then with a devastating violence which quieted down gradually while we talked. His manner was very sober and set; his bearing was that of a naturally taciturn man possessed by an idea. My talk was of the material aspect of his position; it had the sole aim of saving him from the degradation, ruin, and despair that out there close so swiftly upon a friendless, homeless man; I pleaded with him to accept my help; I argued reasonably: and every time I looked up at that absorbed smooth face, so grave and youthful, I had a disturbing sense of being no help, but rather an obstacle, to some mysterious, inexplicable, impalpable striving of his wounded spirit.

"'I suppose you intend to eat and drink and to sleep under shelter in the usual way,' I remember saying with irritation. 'You say you won't touch the money that is due to you. . . .' He came as near as his sort can to making a gesture of horror. (There were three weeks and five days' pay owing him as mate of the *Patna*.) 'Well, that's too little to matter anyhow; but what will you do tomorrow? Where will you turn? You must live . . .' 'That isn't the thing,' was the comment that escaped him under his breath. I ignored it, and went on combating what I assumed to be the scruples of an exaggerated delicacy. 'On every conceivable ground,' I concluded, 'you must let me help you.' 'You can't,' he said very simply and gently, and holding fast to some deep idea which I could detect shimmering like a pool of water in the dark, but which I despaired of ever approaching near enough to fathom. I surveyed his well-proportioned bulk. 'At any rate,' I said, 'I am able to help what I can see of you. I don't pretend to do more.' He shook his head skeptically without looking at me. I got very warm. 'But I can,' I insisted. 'I can do even more. I *am* doing more. I am trusting you . . .' 'The money . . .' he began. 'Upon my word you deserve being told to go to the devil,' I cried, forcing the note of indignation. He was startled, smiled, and I pressed my attack home. 'It isn't a question of money at all. You are too superficial,' I said (and at the same time I was thinking to myself: Well, here goes! And perhaps he is, after all). 'Look at the letter I want you to take. I am writing to a man of whom I've never asked a favor, and I am writing about you in terms that one only ventures to use when speaking of an intimate friend. I make myself unreservedly responsible for you. That's what I am doing. And really if you will only reflect a little what that means . . .'

"He lifted his head. The rain had passed away; only the water pipe went on shedding tears with an absurd drip, drip outside the window. It was very quiet in the room, whose shadows huddled together in corners, away from the still flame of the candle flaring upright in the shape of a dagger; his face after a while seemed suffused by a reflection of a soft light as if the dawn had broken already.

"'Jove!' he gasped out. 'It is noble of you!'

"Had he suddenly put out his tongue at me in derision, I could not have felt more humiliated. I thought to myself—serve me right for a sneaking humbug. . . . His eyes shone straight into my face, but I perceived it was not a mocking brightness. All at once he sprang into jerky agitation, like one of these flat wooden figures that are worked by a string. His arms went up, then came down with a slap. He became another man altogether. 'And I had never seen,' he shouted; then suddenly bit his lip and frowned. 'What a bally ass I've been,' he said very slow in an awed tone. . . . 'You are a brick,' he cried next, in a muffled voice. He snatched my hand as though he had just then seen it for the first time, and dropped it at once. 'Why! this is what I—you—I . . .' he stammered, and then with a return of his old stolid, I may say mulish, manner, he began heavily, 'I would be a brute now if I . . .' and then his voice seemed to break. 'That's all right,' I said. I was almost alarmed by this display of feeling, through which pierced a strange elation. I had pulled the string accidentally, as it were; I did not fully understand the working of the toy. 'I must go now,' he said. 'Jove! You *have* helped me. Can't sit still. The very thing . . .' He looked at me with puzzled admiration. 'The very thing . . .'

"Of course it was the thing. It was ten to one that I had saved him from starvation—of that peculiar sort that is almost invariably associated with drink. This was all. I had not a single illusion on that score, but looking at him, I allowed myself to wonder at the nature of the one he had, within the last three minutes, so evidently taken unto his bosom. I had forced into his hand the means to carry on decently the serious business of life, to get food, drink, and shelter of the customary kind, while his wounded spirit, like a bird with a broken wing, might hop and flutter into some hole, to die quietly of inanition there. This is what I had thrust upon him: a definitely small thing; and—behold!—by the manner of its reception it loomed in the dim light of the candle like a big, indistinct, perhaps a dangerous, shadow. 'You don't mind me not saying anything appropriate,' he burst out. 'There isn't anything one could say. Last night already you have done me no end of good. Listening to me—you know. I give you my word I've thought more than once the top of my head would fly off . . .' He darted—positively darted—here and there, rammed his hands into his pockets, jerked them out again, flung his cap on his head. I had no idea it was in him to be so airily brisk. I thought of a dry leaf imprisoned in an eddy of wind, while a mysterious apprehension, a load of indefinite doubt, weighed me down in my chair. He stood stock-still, as if struck motionless by a discovery. 'You have given me confidence,' he declared soberly. 'Oh! for God's sake, my dear fellow—don't!' I entreated, as though he had hurt me. 'All right. I'll shut up now and henceforth. Can't prevent me thinking, though. . . . Nevermind! . . . I'll show yet . . .' He went to the door in a hurry, paused with his head down, and came back, stepping deliberately. 'I always thought that if a fellow could begin with a clean slate . . . And now you . . . in a measure . . . yes . . . clean slate.' I waved my hand, and he marched out without looking back; the sound of his footfalls died out gradually behind the closed door—the unhesitating tread of a man walking in broad daylight.

"But as to me, left alone with the solitary candle, I remained strangely unenlightened. I was no longer young enough to behold at every turn the magnificence that besets our insignificant footsteps in good and in evil. I smiled to think that, after all, it was yet he, of us two, who had the light. And I felt sad. A clean slate—did he say? As if the initial word of each our destiny were not graven in imperishable characters upon the face of a rock."

❦ 18 ❦

Six months afterwards my friend (he was a cynical, more than middle-aged bachelor, with a reputation for eccentricity, and owned a rice mill) wrote to me, and judging, from the warmth of my recommendation, that I would like to hear, enlarged a little upon Jim's perfections. These were apparently of a quiet and effective sort. 'Not having been able so far to find more in my heart than a resigned toleration for any individual of my kind, I have lived till now alone in a house that even in this steaming climate could be considered as too big for one man. I have had him to live with me for some time past. It seems I haven't made a mistake.' It seemed to me on reading this letter that my friend had found in his heart more than tolerance for Jim—that there were the beginnings of active liking. Of course he stated his grounds in a characteristic way. For one thing, Jim kept his freshness in the climate. Had he been a girl—my friend wrote—one could have said he was blooming—blooming modestly—like a violet, not like some of these blatant tropical flowers. He had been in the house for six weeks, and had not as yet attempted to slap him on the back, or address him as 'old boy,' or try to make him feel a superannuated fossil. He had nothing of the exasperating young man's chatter. He was good-tempered, had not much to say for himself, was not clever by any means, thank goodness—wrote my friend. It appeared, however, that Jim was clever enough to be quietly appreciative of his wit; while, on the other hand, he amused him by his naiveness. 'The dew is yet on him, and since I had the bright idea of giving him a room in the house and having him at meals I feel less withered myself. The other day he took it into his head to cross the room with no other purpose but to open a door for me; and I felt more in touch with mankind than I had been for years. Ridiculous, isn't it? Of course I guess there is something—some awful little scrape—which you know all about—but if I am sure that it is terribly heinous, I fancy one could manage to forgive it. For my part, I declare I am unable to imagine him guilty of anything much worse than robbing an orchard. *Is it* much worse? Perhaps you ought to have told me; but it is such a long time since we both turned saints that you may have forgotten we too had sinned in our time? It may be that some day I shall have to ask you, and then I shall expect to be told. I don't care to question him myself till I have some idea what it is. Moreover, it's too soon as yet. Let him open the door a few times more for me. . . .' Thus my friend. I was trebly pleased—at Jim's shaping so well, at the tone of the letter, at my own cleverness. Evidently I had known what I was doing. I had read characters aright, and so on. And what if something unexpected and wonderful were to come of it? That evening, reposing in a deck chair under the shade of my own poop-awning (it was in Hong Kong harbor), I laid on Jim's behalf the first stone of a castle in Spain.

"I made a trip to the northward, and when I returned I found another letter from my friend waiting for me. It was the first envelope I tore open. 'There are no spoons missing, as far as I know,' ran the first line; 'I haven't been interested enough to inquire. He is gone, leaving on the breakfast table a formal little note of apology, which is either silly or heartless. Probably both—and it's all one to me. Allow me to say, lest you should have some more mysterious young men in reserve, that I have shut up shop, definitely and forever. This is the last eccentricity I shall be guilty of. Do not imagine for a moment that I care a hang; but he is very much regretted at tennis parties, and for my own sake I've told a plausible lie at the club. . . .' I flung the letter aside and started looking through the batch on my table, till I came upon Jim's handwriting. Would you believe it? One chance in a hundred! But it is always that hundredth chance! That little second engineer of the *Patna* had turned up in a more or less destitute state and got a temporary job of looking after the machinery of the mill. 'I couldn't stand the familiarity of the little beast,' Jim wrote from a seaport seven hundred miles south of the place where he should have been in clover. 'I am now for the time with Egström & Blake, ship chandlers, as their—well—runner, to call the thing by its right name. For reference I gave them your name, which they know of course, and if you could write a word in my favor it would be a permanent employment.' I was utterly crushed under the ruins of my castle, but of course I wrote as desired. Before the end of the year my new charter took me that way, and I had an opportunity of seeing him.

"He was still with Egström & Blake, and we met in what they called 'our parlor,' opening out of the store. He had that moment come in from boarding a ship, and confronted me, head down, ready for a tussle. 'What have you got to say for yourself?' I began as soon as we had shaken hands. 'What I wrote you—nothing more,' he said stubbornly. 'Did the fellow blab—or what?' I asked. He looked up at me with a troubled smile. 'Oh, no! He didn't. He made it a kind of confidential business between us. He was most damnably mysterious whenever I came over to the mill; he would wink at me in a respectful manner—as much as to say, We know what we know. Infernally fawning and familiar—and that sort of thing . . .' He threw himself into a chair and stared down his legs. 'One day we happened to be alone and the fellow had the cheek to say, "Well, Mr. James"—I was called Mr. James there as if I had been the son—"here we are together once more. This is better than the old ship—ain't it?" . . . Wasn't it appalling, eh? I looked at him, and he put on a knowing air. "Don't you be uneasy, sir," he says. "I know a gentleman when I see one, and I know how a gentleman feels. I hope, though, you will be keeping me on this job. I had a hard time of it too, along of that rotten old *Patna* racket." Jove! It was awful. I don't know what I should have said or done if I had not just then heard Mr. Denver calling me in the passage. It was tiffin-time, and we walked together across the yard and through the garden to the bungalow. He began to chaff me in his kindly way . . . I believe he liked me . . .'

"Jim was silent for a while.

"'I know he liked me. That's what made it so hard. Such a splendid man! . . . That morning he slipped his hand under my arm . . . . He, too, was familiar with me.' He burst into a short laugh, and dropped his chin on his breast. 'Pah! When I remembered how that mean little beast had been talking to me,' he began suddenly in a vibrating voice, 'I couldn't bear to think of myself . . . I suppose you know. . .' I nodded . . . . 'More like a father,' he cried; his voice sank. 'I would have had to tell him. I couldn't let it go on—could I?' 'Well?' I murmured, after waiting a while. 'I preferred to go,' he said slowly; 'this thing must be buried.'

"We could hear in the shop Blake upbraiding Egström in an abusive, strained voice. They had been associated for many years, and every day from the moment the doors were opened to the last minute before closing, Blake, a little man with sleek, jetty hair and unhappy, beady eyes, could be heard rowing his partner incessantly with a sort of scathing and plaintive fury. The sound of that everlasting scolding was part of the place like the other fixtures; even strangers would very soon come to disregard it completely unless it be perhaps to mutter 'Nuisance,' or to get up suddenly and shut the door of the 'parlor.' Egström himself, a raw-boned, heavy Scandinavian, with a busy manner and immense blonde whiskers, went on directing his people, checking parcels, making out bills or writing letters at a stand-up desk in the shop, and comported himself in that clatter exactly as though he had been stone-deaf. Now and again he would emit a bothered perfunctory 'Sssh,' which neither produced, nor was expected to produce, the slightest effect. 'They are very decent to me here,' said Jim. 'Blake's a little cad, but Egström's all right.' He stood up quickly, and walking with measured steps to a tripod telescope standing in the window and pointed at the roadstead, he applied his eye to it. 'There's that ship which had been becalmed outside all the morning has got a breeze now and is coming in,' he remarked patiently; 'I must go and board.' We shook hands in silence, and he turned to go. 'Jim!' I cried. He looked round with his hand on the lock. 'You—you have thrown away something like a fortune.' He came back to me all the way from the door. 'Such a splendid old chap,' he said. 'How could I? How could I?' His lips twitched. '*Here* it does not matter.' 'Oh! you—you—' I began, and had to cast about for a suitable word, but before I became aware that there was no name that would just do, he was gone. I heard outside Egström's deep gentle voice saying cheerily, 'That's the *Sarah W. Granger*, Jimmy. You must manage to be first aboard;' and directly Blake struck in, screaming after the manner of an outraged cockatoo, 'Tell the captain we've got some of his mail here. That'll fetch him. D'ye hear, Mister What's-your-name?' And there was Jim answering Egström with something boyish in his tone. 'All right. I'll make a race of it.' He seemed to take refuge in the boat-sailing part of that sorry business.

"I did not see him again that trip, but on my next (I had a six months' charter) I went up to the store. Ten yards away from the door Blake's scolding met my ears, and when I came in he gave me a glance of utter wretchedness; Egström, all smiles, advanced, extending a large bony hand. 'Glad to see you, captain. . . . Sssh. . . . Been thinking you were about due back here. What did you say, sir? . . . Sssh. . . . Oh! him! He has left us. Come into the parlor.'. . . After the slam of the door Blake's strained voice became faint, as the voice of one scolding desperately in a wilderness. . . . 'Put us to a great inconvenience, too. Used us badly—I must say . . .' 'Where's he gone to? Do you know?' I asked. 'No. It's no use asking either,' said Egström, standing bewhiskered and obliging before me with his arms hanging down his sides clumsily, and a thin silver watch chain looped very low on a rucked-up blue serge waistcoat. 'A man like that don't go anywhere in particular.' I was too concerned at the news to ask for the explanation of that pronouncement, and he went on. 'He left—let's see—the very day a steamer with returning pilgrims from the Red Sea put in here with two blades of her propeller gone. Three weeks ago now.' 'Wasn't there something said about the *Patna* case?' I asked, fearing the worst. He gave a start and looked at me as if I had been a sorcerer. 'Why, yes! How do you know? Some of them were talking about it here. There was a captain or two, the manager of Vanlo's engineering shop at the harbor, two or three others, and myself. Jim was in here too, having a sandwich and a glass of beer; when we are busy—you see, captain—there's no time for a proper tiffin. He was standing by this table eating sandwiches, and the rest of us were round the telescope watching that steamer come in; and by and by Vanlo's manager began to talk about the chief of the *Patna*; he had done some repairs for him once, and from that he went on to tell us what an old ruin she was, and the money that had been made out of her. He came to mention her last voyage, and then we all struck in. Some said one thing, and some another—not much—what you or any other man might say; and there was some laughing. Captain O'Brien of the *Sarah W. Granger*, a large, noisy, old man with a stick—he was sitting listening to us in this armchair here—he let drive suddenly with his stick at the floor, and roars out, "Skunks!". . . Made us all jump. Vanlo's manager winks at us and asks, "What's the matter, Captain O'Brien?" "Matter! matter!" the old man began to shout; "what are you Injuns laughing at? It's no laughing matter. It's a disgrace to human natur'—that's what it is. I would despise being seen in the same room with one of those men. Yes, sir!" He seemed to catch my eye like, and I had to speak out of civility. "Skunks!" says I, "of course, Captain O'Brien, and I wouldn't care to have them here myself, so you're quite safe in this room, Captain O'Brien. Have a little something cool to drink." "Dam' your drink, Egström," says he, with a twinkle in his eye; "when I want a drink I will shout for it. I am going to quit. It stinks here now." At this all the others burst out laughing, and out they go after the old man. And then, sir, that blasted Jim he puts down the sandwich he had in his hand and walks around the table to me; there was his glass of beer poured out quite full. "I am off," he says—just like this. "It isn't half-past one yet," says I; "you might snatch a smoke first." I thought he meant it was time for him to go down to his work. When I understood what he was up to, my arms fell—so! Can't get a man like that every day, you know, sir; a regular devil for sailing a boat; ready to go out miles to sea to meet ships in any sort of weather. More than once a captain would come in here full of it, and the first thing he would say would be, "That's a reckless sort of a lunatic you've got for a water-clerk, Egström. I was feeling my way in at daylight under short canvas when there comes flying out of the mist right under my forefoot a boat half under water, sprays going over the masthead, two frightened niggers on the bottom boards, a yelling fiend at the tiller. Hey! hey! Ship ahoy! ahoy! Captain! Hey! hey! Egström & Blake's man first to speak to you! Hey! hey! Egström & Blake! Hallo! hey! whoop! Kick the niggers—out reefs—a squall—on at the time—shoots ahead whooping and yelling to me to make sail and he would give me a lead in—more like a demon than a man. Never saw a boat handled like that in all my life. Couldn't have been drunk—was he? Such a quiet, soft-spoken chap too—blush like a girl when he came on board. . . ." I tell you, Captain Marlow, nobody had a chance against us with a strange ship when Jim was out. The other ship chandlers just kept their old customers, and . . .'

"Egström appeared overcome with emotion.

"'Why, sir—it seemed as though he wouldn't mind going a hundred miles out to sea in an old shoe to nab a ship for the firm. If the business had been his own and all to make yet, he couldn't have done more in that way. And now . . . all at once . . . like this! Thinks I to myself: "Oho! a rise in the screw—that's the trouble—is it? All right," says I, "no need of all that fuss with me, Jimmy. Just mention your figure. Anything in reason." He looks at me as if he wanted to swallow something that stuck in his throat. "I can't stop with you." "What's that blooming joke?" I asks. He shakes his head, and I could see in his eye he was as good as gone already, sir. So I turned to him and slanged him till all was blue. "What is it you're running away from?" I asks. "Who has been getting at you? What scared you? You haven't as much sense as a rat; they don't clear out from a good ship. Where do you expect to get a better berth?—you this and you that." I made him look sick, I can tell you. "This business ain't going to sink," says I. He gave a big jump. "Goodbye," he says, nodding at me like a lord; "you ain't half a bad chap, Egström. I give you my word that if you knew my reasons you wouldn't care to keep me." "That's the biggest lie you ever told in your life," says I; "I know my own mind." He made me so mad that I had to laugh. "Can't you really stop long enough to drink this glass of beer here, you funny beggar, you?" I don't know what came over him; he didn't seem able to find the door, something comical, I can tell you, captain. I drank the beer myself. "Well, if you're in such a hurry, here's luck to you in your own drink," says I, "only, you mark my words, if you keep up this game you'll very soon find that the earth ain't big enough to hold you—that's all." He gave me one black look, and out he rushed with a face fit to scare little children.'

"Egström snorted bitterly, and combed one auburn whisker with knotty fingers. 'Haven't been able to get a man that was any good since. It's nothing but worry, worry, worry in business. And where might you have come across him, captain, if it's fair to ask?'

"'He was the mate of the *Patna* that voyage,' I said, feeling that I owed some explanation. For a time Egström remained very still, with his fingers plunged in his hair at the side of his face, and then exploded. 'And who the devil cares about that?' 'I daresay no one,' I began. . . . 'And what the devil is he—anyhow—for to go on like this?' He stuffed suddenly his left whisker into his mouth and stood amazed. 'Jee!' he exclaimed, 'I told him the earth wouldn't be big enough to hold his caper.'"

❧ 19 ❧

I have told you these two episodes at length to show his manner of dealing with himself under the new conditions of his life. There were many others of the sort, more than I could count on the fingers of my two hands. They were all equally tinged by a high-minded absurdity of intention which made their futility profound and touching. To fling away your daily bread so as to get your hands free for a grapple with a ghost may be an act of prosaic heroism. Men had done it before (though we who have lived know full well that it is not the haunted soul but the hungry body that makes an outcast), and men who had eaten and meant to eat every day had applauded the creditable folly. He was indeed unfortunate, for all his recklessness could not carry him out from under the shadow. There was always a doubt of his courage. The truth seems to be that it is impossible to lay the ghost of a fact. You can face it or shirk it—and I have come across a man or two who could wink at their familiar shades. Obviously Jim was not of the winking sort; but what I could never make up my mind about was whether his line of conduct amounted to shirking his ghost or to facing him out.

"I strained my mental eyesight only to discover that, as with the complexion of all our actions, the shade of difference was so delicate that it was impossible to say. It might have been flight and it might have been a mode of combat. To the common mind he became known as a rolling stone, because this was the funniest part: he did after a time become perfectly known, and even notorious, within the circle of his wanderings (which had a diameter of, say, three thousand miles), in the same way as an eccentric character is known to a whole countryside. For instance, in Bangkok, where he found employment with Yucker Brothers, charterers and teak merchants, it was almost pathetic to see him go about in sunshine hugging his secret, which was known to the very upcountry logs on the river. Schomberg, the keeper of the hotel where he boarded, a hirsute Alsatian of manly bearing and an irrepressible retailer of all the scandalous gossip of the place, would, with both elbows on the table, impart an adorned version of the story to any guest who cared to imbibe knowledge along with the more costly liquors. 'And, mind you, the nicest fellow you could meet,' would be his generous conclusion; 'quite superior.' It says a lot for the casual crowd that frequented Schomberg's establishment that Jim managed to hang out in Bangkok for a whole six months. I remarked that people, perfect strangers, took to him as one takes to a nice child. His manner was reserved, but it was as though his personal appearance, his hair, his eyes, his smile, made friends for him wherever he went. And, of course, he was no fool. I heard Siegmund Yucker (native of Switzerland), a gentle creature ravaged by a cruel dyspepsia, and so frightfully lame that his head swung through a quarter of a circle at every step he took, declare appreciatively that for one so young he was 'of great gabasidy,' as though it had been a mere question of cubic contents. 'Why not send him upcountry?' I suggested anxiously. (Yucker Brothers had concessions and teak forests in the interior.) 'If he has capacity, as you say, he will soon get hold of the work. And physically he is very fit. His health is always excellent.' 'Ach! It's a great ting in dis goundry to be vree vrom tispepshia,' sighed poor Yucker enviously, casting a stealthy glance at the pit of his ruined stomach. I left him drumming pensively on his desk and muttering, 'Es ist ein idee. Es ist ein idee.' Unfortunately, that very evening an unpleasant affair took place in the hotel.

"I don't know that I blame Jim very much, but it was a truly regrettable incident. It belonged to the lamentable species of barroom scuffles, and the other party to it was a cross-eyed Dane of sorts whose visiting card recited under his misbegotten name: first lieutenant in the Royal Siamese Navy. The fellow of course was utterly hopeless at billiards, but did not like to be beaten, I suppose. He had had enough to drink to turn nasty after the sixth game, and make some scornful remark at Jim's expense. Most of the people there didn't hear what was said, and those who had heard seemed to have had all precise recollection scared out of them by the appalling nature of the consequences that immediately ensued. It was very lucky for the Dane that he could swim, because the room opened on a veranda and the Menam flowed below very wide and black. A boatload of Chinamen, bound, as likely as not, on some thieving expedition, fished out the officer of the King of Siam, and Jim turned up at about midnight on board my ship without a hat. 'Everybody in the room seemed to know,' he said, gasping yet from the contest, as it were. He was rather sorry, on general principles, for what had happened, though in this case there had been, he said, 'no option.' But what dismayed him was to find the nature of his burden as well known to everybody as though he had gone about all that time carrying it on his shoulders. Naturally after this he couldn't remain in the place. He was universally condemned for the brutal violence, so unbecoming a man in his delicate position; some maintained he had been disgracefully drunk at the time; others criticized his want of tact. Even Schomberg was very much annoyed. 'He is a very nice young man,' he said argumentatively to me, 'but the lieutenant is a first-rate fellow too. He dines every night at my *table d'hôte,* you know. And there's a billiard cue broken. I can't allow that. First thing this morning I went over with my apologies to the lieutenant, and I think I've made it all right for myself; but only think, captain, if everybody started such games! Why, the man might have been drowned! And here I can't run out into the next street and buy a new cue. I've got to write to Europe for them. No, no! A temper like that won't do!'. . . He was extremely sore on the subject.

"This was the worst incident of all in his—his retreat. Nobody could deplore it more than myself; for if, as somebody said hearing him mentioned, 'Oh yes! I know. He has knocked about a good deal out here,' yet he had somehow avoided being battered and chipped in the process. This last affair, however, made me seriously uneasy, because if his exquisite sensibilities were to go the length of involving him in pothouse shindies, he would lose his name of an inoffensive, if aggravating, fool, and acquire that of a common loafer. For all my confidence in him I could not help reflecting that in such cases from the name to the thing itself is but a step. I suppose you will understand that by that time I could not think of washing my hands of him. I took him away from Bangkok in my ship, and we had a longish passage. It was pitiful to see how he shrank within himself. A seaman, even if a mere passenger, takes an interest in a ship, and looks at the sea-life around him with the critical enjoyment of a painter, for instance, looking at another man's work. In every sense of the expression he is 'on deck'; but my Jim, for the most part, skulked down below as though he had been a stowaway. He infected me so that I avoided speaking on professional matters, such as would suggest themselves naturally to two sailors during a passage. For whole days we did not exchange a word; I felt extremely unwilling to give orders to my officers in his presence. Often, when alone with him on deck or in the cabin, we didn't know what to do with our eyes.

"I placed him with De Jongh, as you know, glad enough to dispose of him in any way, yet persuaded that his position was now growing intolerable. He had lost some of that elasticity which had enabled him to rebound back into his uncompromising position after every overthrow. One day, coming ashore, I saw him standing on the quay; the water of the roadstead and the sea in the offing made one smooth ascending plane, and the outermost ships at anchor seemed to ride motionless in the sky. He was waiting for his boat, which was being loaded at our feet with packages of small stores for some vessel ready to leave. After exchanging greetings, we remained silent—side by side. 'Jove!' he said suddenly, 'this is killing work.'

"He smiled at me; I must say he generally could manage a smile. I made no reply. I knew very well he was not alluding to his duties; he had an easy time of it with De Jongh. Nevertheless, as soon as he had spoken I became completely convinced that the work was killing. I did not even look at him. 'Would you like,' said I, 'to leave this part of the world altogether; try California or the West Coast? I'll see what I can do . . .' He interrupted me a little scornfully. 'What difference would it make? . . .' I felt at once convinced that he was right. It would make no difference; it was not relief he wanted; I seemed to perceive dimly that what he wanted, what he was, as it were, waiting for, was something not easy to define—something in the nature of an opportunity. I had given him many opportunities, but they had been merely opportunities to earn his bread. Yet what more could any man do? The position struck me as hopeless, and poor Brierly's saying recurred to me, 'Let him creep twenty feet underground and stay there.' Better that, I thought, than this waiting above ground for the impossible. Yet one could not be sure even of that. There and then, before his boat was three oars' lengths away from the quay, I had made up my mind to go and consult Stein in the evening.

"This Stein was a wealthy and respected merchant. His 'house' (because it was a house, Stein & Co., and there was some sort of partner who, as Stein said, 'looked after the Moluccas') had a large inter-island business, with a lot of trading posts established in the most out-of-the-way places for collecting the produce. His wealth and his respectability were not exactly the reasons why I was anxious to seek his advice. I desired to confide my difficulty to him because he was one of the most trustworthy men I had ever known. The gentle light of a simple, unwearied, as it were, and intelligent good nature illumined his long hairless face. It had deep downward folds, and was pale as of a man who had always led a sedentary life— which was indeed very far from being the case. His hair was thin, and brushed back from a massive and lofty forehead. One fancied that at twenty he must have looked very much like he was now at threescore. It was a student's face; only the eyebrows nearly all white, thick and bushy, together with the resolute searching glance that came from under them, were not in accord with his, I may say, learned appearance. He was tall and loose-jointed; his slight stoop, together with an innocent smile, made him appear benevolently ready to lend you his ear; his long arms with pale big hands had rare deliberate gestures of a pointing out, demonstrating kind. I speak of him at length, because under this exterior, and in conjunction with an upright and indulgent nature, this man possessed an intrepidity of spirit and a physical courage that could have been called reckless had it not been like a natural function of the body—say good digestion, for instance—completely unconscious of itself. It is sometimes said of a man that he carries his life in his hand. Such a saying would have been inadequate if applied to him; during the early part of his existence in the East he had been playing ball with it. All this was in the past, but I knew the story of his life and the origin of his fortune. He was also a naturalist of some distinction, or perhaps I should say a learned collector. Entomology was his special study. His collection of *Buprestidae* and *Longicorns*—beetles all—horrible miniature monsters, looking malevolent in death and immobility, and this cabinet of butterflies, beautiful, and hovering under the glass of cases on lifeless wings, had spread his fame far over the earth. The name of this merchant, adventurer, sometime adviser of a Malay sultan (to whom he never alluded otherwise than as 'my poor Mohammed Bonso'), had, on account of a few bushels of dead insects, become known to learned persons in Europe, who could have had no conception, and certainly would not have cared to know anything, of his life and character. I, who knew, considered him an eminently suitable person to receive my confidences about Jim's difficulties as well as my own."

❧ 20 ❧

Late in the evening I entered his study, after traversing an imposing but empty dining room very dimly lit. The house was silent. I was preceded by an elderly grim Javanese servant in a sort of livery of white jacket and yellow sarong, who, after throwing the door open, exclaimed low, 'O master!' and stepping aside, vanished in a mysterious way as though he had been a ghost only momentarily embodied for that particular service. Stein turned round with the chair, and in the same movement his spectacles seemed to get pushed up on his forehead. He welcomed me in his quiet and humorous voice. Only one corner of the vast room, the corner in which stood his writing-desk, was strongly lighted by a shaded reading lamp, and the rest of the spacious apartment melted into shapeless gloom like a cavern. Narrow shelves filled with dark boxes of uniform shape and color ran round the walls, not from floor to ceiling, but in a somber belt about four feet broad. Catacombs of beetles. Wooden tablets were hung above at irregular intervals. The light reached one of them, and the word *Coleoptera* written in gold letters glittered mysteriously upon a vast dimness. The glass cases containing the collection of butterflies were ranged in three long rows upon slender-legged little tables. One of these cases had been removed from its place and stood on the desk, which was bestrewn with oblong slips of paper blackened with minute handwriting.

"'So you see me—so,' he said. His hand hovered over the case where a butterfly in solitary grandeur spread out dark bronze wings, seven inches or more across, with exquisite white veinings and a gorgeous border of yellow spots. 'Only one specimen like this they have in *your* London, and then—no more. To my small native town this, my collection, I shall bequeath. Something of me. The best.'

"He bent forward in the chair and gazed intently, his chin over the front of the case. I stood at his back. 'Marvelous,' he whispered, and seemed to forget my presence. His history was curious. He had been born in Bavaria, and when a youth of twenty-two had taken an active part in the revolutionary movement of 1848. Heavily compromised, he managed to make his escape, and at first found a refuge with a poor republican watchmaker in Trieste. From there he made his way to Tripoli with a stock of cheap watches to hawk about—not a very great opening truly, but it turned out lucky enough, because it was there he came upon a Dutch traveler—a rather famous man, I believe, but I don't remember his name. It was that naturalist who, engaging him as a sort of assistant, took him to the East. They traveled in the Archipelago together and separately, collecting insects and birds, for four years or more. Then the naturalist went home, and Stein, having no home to go to, remained with an old trader he had come across in his journeys in the interior of Celebes—if Celebes may be said to have an interior. This old Scotsman, the only white man allowed to reside in the country at the time, was a privileged friend of the chief ruler of Wajo States, who was a woman. I often heard Stein relate how that chap, who was slightly paralyzed on one side, had introduced him to the native court a short time before another stroke carried him off. He was a heavy man with a patriarchal white beard, and of imposing stature. He came into the council hall where all the rajahs, pangerans, and headmen were assembled, with the queen, a fat, wrinkled woman (very free in her speech, Stein said), reclining on a high couch under a canopy. He dragged his leg, thumping with his stick, and grasped Stein's arm, leading him right up to the couch. 'Look, queen, and you rajahs, this is my son,' he proclaimed in a stentorian voice. 'I have traded with your fathers, and when I die he shall trade with you and your sons.'

"By means of this simple formality Stein inherited the Scotsman's privileged position and all his stock-in-trade, together with a fortified house on the banks of the only navigable river in the country. Shortly afterwards the old queen, who was so free in her speech, died, and the country became disturbed by various pretenders to the throne. Stein joined the party of a younger son, the one of whom thirty years later he never spoke otherwise but as 'my poor Mohammed Bonso.' They both became the heroes of innumerable exploits; they had wonderful adventures, and once stood a siege in the Scotsman's house for a month, with only a score of followers against a whole army. I believe the natives talk of that war to this day. Meantime, it seems, Stein never failed to annex on his own account every butterfly or beetle he could lay hands on. After some eight years of war, negotiations, false truces, sudden outbreaks, reconciliation, treachery, and so on, and just as peace seemed at last permanently established, his 'poor Mohammed Bonso' was assassinated at the gate of his own royal residence while dismounting in the highest spirits on his return from a successful deerhunt. This event rendered Stein's position extremely insecure, but he would have stayed perhaps had it not been that a short time afterwards he lost Mohammed's sister ('my dear wife the princess,' he used to say solemnly), by whom he had had a daughter—mother and child both dying within three days of each other from some infectious fever. He left the country, which this cruel loss had made unbearable to him. Thus ended the first and adventurous part of his existence. What followed was so different that, but for the reality of sorrow which remained with him, this strange past must have resembled a dream. He had a little money; he started life afresh, and in the course of years acquired a considerable fortune. At first he had traveled a good deal amongst the islands, but age had stolen upon him, and of late he seldom left his spacious house three miles out of town, with an extensive garden, and surrounded by stables, offices, and bamboo cottages for his servants and dependents, of whom he had many. He drove in his buggy every morning to town, where he had an office with white and Chinese clerks. He owned a small fleet of schooners and native craft, and dealt in island produce on a large scale. For the rest he lived solitary, but not misanthropic, with his books and his collection, classing and arranging specimens, corresponding with entomologists in Europe, writing up a descriptive catalogue of his treasures. Such was the history of the man whom I had come to consult upon Jim's case without any definite hope. Simply to hear what he would have to say would have been a relief. I was very anxious, but I respected the intense, almost passionate, absorption with which he looked at a butterfly, as though on the bronze sheen of these frail wings, in the white tracings, in the gorgeous markings, he could see other things, an image of something as perishable and defying destruction as these delicate and lifeless tissues displaying a splendor unmarred by death.

"'Marvelous!' he repeated, looking up at me. 'Look! The beauty—but that is nothing—look at the accuracy, the harmony. And so fragile! And so strong! And so exact! This is Nature—the balance of colossal forces. Every star is so—and every blade of grass stands *so*—and the mighty Kosmos in perfect equilibrium produces—this. This wonder; this masterpiece of Nature—the great artist.'

"'Never heard an entomologist go on like this,' I observed cheerfully. 'Masterpiece! And what of man?'

"'Man is amazing, but he is not a masterpiece,' he said, keeping his eyes fixed on the glass case. 'Perhaps the artist was a little mad. Eh? What do you think? Sometimes it seems to me that man is come where he is not wanted, where there is no place for him; for if not, why should he want all the place? Why should he run about here and there making a great noise about himself, talking about the stars, disturbing the blades of grass? . . .'

"'Catching butterflies,' I chimed in.

"He smiled, threw himself back in his chair, and stretched his legs. 'Sit down,' he said. 'I captured this rare specimen myself one very fine morning. And I had a very big emotion. You don't know what it is for a collector to capture such a rare specimen. You can't know.'

"I smiled at my ease in a rocking chair. His eyes seemed to look far beyond the wall at which they stared; and he narrated how, one night, a messenger arrived from his 'poor Mohammed,' requiring his presence at the 'residenz'—as he called it—which was distant some nine or ten miles by a bridle path over a cultivated plain, with patches of forest here and there. Early in the morning he started from his fortified house, after embracing his little Emma, and leaving the 'princess,' his wife, in command. He described how she came with him as far as the gate, walking with one hand on the neck of his horse; she had on a white jacket, gold pins in her hair, and a brown leather belt over her left shoulder with a revolver in it. 'She talked as women will talk,' he said, 'telling me to be careful, and to try to get back before dark, and what a great wickedness it was for me to go alone. We were at war, and the country was not safe; my men were putting up bulletproof shutters to the house and loading their rifles, and she begged me to have no fear for her. She could defend the house against anybody till I returned. And I laughed with pleasure a little. I liked to see her so brave and young and strong. I too was young then. At the gate she caught hold of my hand and gave it one squeeze and fell back. I made my horse stand still outside till I heard the bars of the gate put up behind me. There was a great enemy of mine, a great noble—and a great rascal too—roaming with a band in the neighborhood. I cantered for four or five miles; there had been rain in the night, but the mists had gone up, up—and the face of the earth was clean; it lay smiling to me, so fresh and innocent—like a little child. Suddenly somebody fires a volley—twenty shots at least it seemed to me. I hear bullets sing in my ear, and my hat jumps to the back of my head. It was a little intrigue, you understand. They got my poor Mohammed to send for me and then laid that ambush. I see it all in a minute, and I think—This wants a little management. My pony snort, jump, and stand, and I fall slowly forward with my head on his mane. He begins to walk, and with one eye I could see over his neck a faint cloud of smoke hanging in front of a clump of bamboos to my left. I think—Aha! my friends, why you not wait long enough before you shoot? This is not yet *gelungen*. Oh, no! I get hold of my revolver with my right hand—quiet—quiet. After all, there were only seven of these rascals. They get up from the grass and start running with their sarongs tucked up, waving spears above their heads, and yelling to each other to look out and catch the horse, because I was dead. I let them come as close as the door here, and then bang, bang, bang—take aim each time too. One more shot I fire at a man's back, but I miss. Too far already. And then I sit alone on my horse with the clean earth smiling at me, and there are the bodies of three men lying on the ground. One was curled up like a dog, another on his back had an arm over his eyes as if to keep off the sun, and the third man he draws up his leg very slowly and makes it with one kick straight again. I watch him very carefully from my horse, but there is no more—*bleibt ganz ruhig*—keep still, so. And as I looked at his face for some sign of life I observed something like a faint shadow pass over his forehead. It was the shadow of this butterfly. Look at the form of the wing. This species fly high with a strong flight. I raised my eyes and I saw him fluttering away. I think—Can it be possible? And then I lost him. I dismounted and went on very slow, leading my horse and holding my revolver with one hand and my eyes darting up and down and right and left, everywhere! At last I saw him sitting on a small heap of dirt ten feet away. At once my heart began to beat quick. I let go my horse, keep my revolver in one hand, and with the other snatch my soft felt hat off my head. One step. Steady. Another step. Flop! I got him! When I got up I shook like a leaf with excitement, and when I opened these beautiful wings and made sure what a rare and so extraordinary perfect specimen I had, my head went round and my legs became so weak with emotion that I had to sit on the ground. I had greatly desired to possess myself of a specimen of that species when collecting for the professor. I took long journeys and underwent great privations; I had dreamed of him in my sleep, and here suddenly I had him in my fingers—for myself! In the words of the poet' (he pronounced it 'boet')—

> So halt' ich's endlich denn in meinen Händen,
> Und nenn' es in gewissem Sinne mein.

He gave to the last word the emphasis of a suddenly lowered voice, and withdrew his eyes slowly from my face. He began to charge a long-stemmed pipe busily and in silence, then, pausing with his thumb on the orifice of the bowl, looked again at me significantly.

"'Yes, my good friend. On that day I had nothing to desire; I had greatly annoyed my principal enemy; I was young, strong; I had friendship; I had the love' (he said 'lof') 'of woman, a child I had, to make my heart very full—and even what I had once dreamed in my sleep had come into my hand too!'

"He struck a match, which flared violently. His thoughtful placid face twitched once.

"'Friend, wife, child,' he said slowly, gazing at the small flame—'phoo!' The match was blown out. He sighed and turned again to the glass case. The frail and beautiful wings quivered faintly, as if his breath had for an instant called back to life that gorgeous object of his dreams.

"'The work,' he began suddenly, pointing to the scattered slips, and in his usual gentle and cheery tone, 'is making great progress. I have been this rare specimen describing. . . . Na! And what is your good news?'

"'To tell you the truth, Stein,' I said with an effort that surprised me, 'I came here to describe a specimen. . . .'

"'Butterfly?' he asked, with an unbelieving and humorous eagerness.

"'Nothing so perfect,' I answered, feeling suddenly dispirited with all sorts of doubts. 'A man!'

"'Ach so!' he murmured, and his smiling countenance, turned to me, became grave. Then after looking at me for a while he said slowly, 'Well—I am a man too.'

"Here you have him as he was; he knew how to be so generously encouraging as to make a scrupulous man hesitate on the brink of confidence; but if I did hesitate it was not for long.

"He heard me out, sitting with crossed legs. Sometimes his head would disappear completely in a great eruption of smoke, and a sympathetic growl would come out from the cloud. When I finished he uncrossed his legs, laid down his pipe, leaned forward towards me earnestly with his elbows on the arms of his chair, the tips of his fingers together.

"'I understand very well. He is romantic.'

"He had diagnosed the case for me, and at first I was quite startled to find how simple it was; and indeed our conference resembled so much a medical consultation—Stein, of learned aspect sitting in an armchair before his desk; I, anxious, in another, facing him, but a little to one side—that it seemed natural to ask—

"'What's good for it?'

"He lifted up a long forefinger.

"'There is only one remedy! One thing alone can us from being ourselves cure!' The finger came down on the desk with a smart rap. The case which he had made to look so simple before became if possible still simpler—and altogether hopeless. There was a pause. 'Yes,' said I, 'strictly speaking, the question is not how to get cured, but how to live?'

"He approved with his head, a little sadly as it seemed. *'Ja! ja!* In general, adapting the words of your great poet: That is the question. . . .' He went on nodding sympathetically. . . . 'How to be! *Ach!* How to be.'

"He stood up with the tips of his fingers resting on the desk.

"'We want in so many different ways to be,' he began again. 'This magnificent butterfly finds a little heap of dirt and sits still on it; but man he will never on his heap of mud keep still. He want to be so, and again he want to be so. . . .' He moved his hand up, then down. . . . 'He wants to be a saint, and he wants to be a devil—and every time he shuts his eyes he sees himself as a very fine fellow—so fine as he can never be. . . . In a dream. . . .'

"He lowered the glass lid, the automatic lock clicked sharply, and taking up the case in both hands he bore it religiously away to its place, passing out of the bright circle of the lamp into the ring of fainter light—into shapeless dusk at last.

It had an odd effect—as if these few steps had carried him out of this concrete and perplexed world. His tall form, as though robbed of its substance, hovered noiselessly over invisible things with stooping and indefinite movements; his voice, heard in that remoteness where he could be glimpsed mysteriously busy with immaterial cares, was no longer incisive, seemed to roll voluminous and grave—mellowed by distance.

"'And because you not always can keep your eyes shut there comes the real trouble—the heart pain—the world pain. I tell you, my friend, it is not good for you to find you cannot make your dream come true, for the reason that you not strong enough are, or not clever enough. *Ja!* . . . And all the time you are such a fine fellow too! *Wie? Was? Gott in Himmel!* How can that be? Ha! ha!'

"The shadow prowling amongst the graves of butterflies laughed boisterously.

"'Yes! Very funny this terrible thing is. A man that is born falls into a dream like a man who falls into the sea. If he tries to climb out into the air as inexperienced people endeavor to do, he drowns—*nicht war?* . . . No! I tell you! The way is to the destructive element submit yourself, and with the exertions of your hands and feet in the water make the deep, deep sea keep you up. So if you ask me—how to be?'

"His voice leaped up extraordinarily strong, as though away there in the dusk he had been inspired by some whisper of knowledge. 'I will tell you! For that too there is only one way.'

"With a hasty swish-swish of his slippers he loomed up in the ring of faint light, and suddenly appeared in the bright circle of the lamp. His extended hand aimed at my breast like a pistol; his deep-set eyes seemed to pierce through me, but his twitching lips uttered no word, and the austere exaltation of a certitude seen in the dusk vanished from his face. The hand that had been pointing at my breast fell, and by and by, coming a step nearer, he laid it gently on my shoulder. There were things, he said mournfully, that perhaps could never be told, only he had lived so much alone that sometimes he forgot—he forgot. The light had destroyed the assurance which had inspired him in the distant shadows. He sat down and, with both elbows on the desk, rubbed his forehead. 'And yet it is true—it is true. In the destructive element immerse. . . .' He spoke in a subdued tone, without looking at me, one hand on each side of his face. 'That was the way. To follow the dream, and again to follow the dream—and so—*ewig—usque ad finem*. . . .' The whisper of his conviction seemed to open before me a vast and uncertain expanse, as of a crepuscular horizon on a plain at dawn—or was it, perchance, at the coming of the night? One had not the courage to decide; but it was a charming and deceptive light, throwing the impalpable poetry of its dimness over pitfalls—over graves. His life had begun in sacrifice, in enthusiasm for generous ideas; he had traveled very far, on various ways, on strange paths, and whatever he followed it had been without faltering, and therefore without shame and without regret. In so far he was right. That was the way, no doubt. Yet for all that the great plain on which men wander amongst graves and pitfalls remained very desolate under the impalpable poesy of its crepuscular light, overshadowed in the center, circled with a bright edge as if surrounded by an abyss full of flames. When at last I broke the silence it was to express the opinion that no one could be more romantic than himself.

"He shook his head slowly, and afterwards looked at me with a patient and inquiring glance. It was a shame, he said. There we were sitting and talking like two boys, instead of putting our heads together to find something practical—a practical remedy—for the evil—for the great evil—he repeated, with a humorous and indulgent smile. For all that, our talk did not grow more practical. We avoided pronouncing Jim's name as though we had tried to keep flesh and blood out of our discussion, or he were nothing but an erring spirit, a suffering and nameless shade. 'Na!' said Stein, rising. 'Tonight you sleep here, and in the morning we shall do something practical—practical. . . .' He lit a two-branched candlestick and led the way. We passed through empty dark rooms, escorted by gleams from the lights Stein carried. They glided along the waxed floors, sweeping here and there over the polished surface of a table, leaped upon a fragmentary curve of a piece of fur- niture, or flashed perpendicularly in and out of distant mirrors, while the forms of two men and the flicker of two flames could be seen for a moment stealing silently across the depths of a crystalline void. He walked slowly a pace in advance with stooping courtesy; there was a profound, as it were a listening, quietude on his face; the long flaxen locks mixed with white threads were scattered thinly upon his slightly bowed neck.

"'He is romantic—romantic,' he repeated. 'And that is very bad—very bad. . . . Very good, too,' he added.

"'But *is he*?' I queried.

"'*Gewiss*,' he said, and stood holding up the candelabrum, but without looking at me. 'Evident! What is it that by inward pain makes him—know himself? What is it that for you and me makes him—exist?'

"At that moment it was difficult to believe in Jim's existence—starting from a country parsonage, blurred by crowds of men as by clouds of dust, silenced by the clashing claims of life and death in a material world—but his imperishable reality came to me with a convincing, with an irresistible force! I saw it vividly, as though in our progress through the lofty silent rooms amongst fleeting gleams of light and the sudden revelations of human figures stealing with flickering flames within unfathomable and pellucid depths, we had approached nearer to absolute Truth, which, like Beauty itself, floats elusive, obscure, half submerged, in the silent still waters of mystery. 'Perhaps he is,' I admitted with a slight laugh, whose unexpect- edly loud reverberation made me lower my voice directly; 'but I am sure you are.'

With his head dropping on his breast and the light held high he began to walk again. 'Well—I exist, too,' he said.

"He preceded me. My eyes followed his movements, but what I did see was not the head of the firm, the welcome guest at afternoon receptions, the correspondent of learned societies, the entertainer of stray naturalists; I saw only the reality of his destiny, which he had known how to follow with unfaltering footsteps, that life begun in humble surroundings, rich in generous enthusiasms, in friendship, love, war—in all the exalted elements of romance. At the door of my room he faced me. 'Yes,' I said, as though carrying on a discussion, 'and amongst other things you dreamed foolishly of a certain butterfly; but when one fine morning your dream came in your way you did not let the splendid opportunity escape. Did you? Whereas he . . .' Stein lifted his hand. 'And do you know how many opportunities I let escape; how many dreams I had lost that had come in my way?' He shook his head regretfully. 'It seems to me that some would have been very fine—if I had made them come true. Do you know how many? Perhaps I myself don't know.' 'Whether his were fine or not,' I said,'he knows of one which he certainly did not catch.' 'Everybody knows of one or two like that,' said Stein; 'and that is the trouble—the great trouble. . . .'

"He shook hands on the threshold, peered into my room under his raised arm. 'Sleep well. And tomorrow we must do something practical—practical. . . .'

"Though his own room was beyond mine I saw him return the way he came. He was going back to his butterflies."

❧ 21 ❧

I don't suppose any of you had ever heard of Patusan?" Marlow resumed, after a silence occupied in the careful lighting of a cigar. "It does not matter; there's many a heavenly body in the lot crowding upon us of a night that mankind had never heard of, it being outside the sphere of its activities and of no earthly importance to anybody but to the astronomers who are paid to talk learnedly about its composition, weight, path—the irregularities of its conduct, the aberrations of its light—a sort of scientific scandal-mongering. Thus with Patusan. It was referred to knowingly in the inner government circles in Batavia, especially as to its irregularities and aberrations, and it was known by name to some few, very few, in the mercantile world. Nobody, however, had been there, and I suspect no one desired to go there in person, just as an astronomer, I should fancy, would strongly object to being transported into a distant heavenly body, where, parted from his earthly emoluments, he would be bewildered by the view of an unfamiliar heavens. However, neither heavenly bodies nor astronomers have anything to do with Patusan. It was Jim who went there. I only meant you to understand that had Stein arranged to send him into a star of the fifth magnitude the change could not have been greater. He left his earthly failings behind him and that sort of reputation he had, and there was a totally new set of conditions for his imaginative faculty to work upon. Entirely new, entirely remarkable. And he got hold of them in a remarkable way.

"Stein was the man who knew more about Patusan than anybody else. More than was known in the government circles, I suspect. I have no doubt he had been there, either in his butterfly-hunting days or later on, when he tried in his incorrigible way to season with a pinch of romance the fattening dishes of his commercial kitchen. There were very few places in the Archipelago he had not seen in the original dusk of their being, before light (and even electric light) had been carried into them for the sake of better morality and—and—well—the greater profit too. It was at breakfast of the morning following our talk about Jim that he mentioned the place, after I had quoted poor Brierly's remark: 'Let him creep twenty feet underground and stay there.' He looked up at me with interested attention, as though I had been a rare insect. 'This could be done too,' he remarked, sipping his coffee. 'Bury him in some sort,' I explained. 'One doesn't like to do it of course, but it would be the best thing, seeing what he is.' 'Yes; he is young,' Stein mused. 'The youngest human being now in existence,' I affirmed. '*Schön.* There's Patusan,' he went on in the same tone. . . . 'And the woman is dead now,' he added incomprehensibly.

"Of course I don't know that story; I can only guess that once before Patusan had been used as a grave for some sin, transgression, or misfortune. It is impossible to suspect Stein. The only woman that had ever existed for him was the Malay girl he called 'My wife the princess,' or, more rarely, in moments of expansion, 'the mother of my Emma.' Who was the woman he had mentioned in connection with Patusan I can't say; but from his allusions I understand she had been an educated and very good-looking Dutch-Malay girl, with a tragic, or perhaps only a pitiful, history, whose most painful part no doubt was her marriage with a Malacca Portuguese who had been clerk in some commercial house in the Dutch colonies. I gathered from Stein that this man was an unsatisfactory person in more ways than one, all being more or less indefinite and offensive. It was solely for his wife's sake that Stein had appointed him manager of Stein & Company's trading post in Patusan; but commercially the arrangement was not a success, at any rate for the firm, and now the woman had died, Stein was disposed to try another agent there. The Portuguese, whose name was Cornelius, considered himself a very deserving but ill-used person, entitled by his abilities to a better position. This man Jim would have to relieve. 'But I don't think he will go away from the place,' remarked Stein. 'That has nothing to do with me. It was only for the sake of the woman that I . . . But as I think there is a daughter left, I shall let him, if he likes to stay, keep the old house.'

"Patusan is a remote district of a native-ruled state, and the chief settlement bears the same name. At a point on the river about forty miles from the sea, where the first houses come into view, there can be seen rising above the level of the forests the summits of two steep hills very close together, and separated by what looks like a deep fissure, the cleavage of some mighty stroke. As a matter of fact the valley between is nothing but a narrow ravine; the appearance from the settlement is of one irregularly conical hill split in two, and with the two halves leaning slightly apart. On the third day after the full, the moon, as seen from the open space in front of Jim's house (he had a very fine house in the native style when I visited him), rose exactly behind these hills, its diffused light at first throwing the two masses into intensely black relief, and then the nearly perfect disk, glowing ruddily, appeared, gliding upwards between the sides of the chasm, till it floated away above the summits, as if escaping from a yawning grave in gentle triumph. 'Wonderful effect,' said Jim by my side. 'Worth seeing. Is it not?'

"And this question was put with a note of personal pride that made me smile, as though he had had a hand in regulating that unique spectacle. He had regulated so many things in Patusan! Things that would have appeared as much beyond his control as the motions of the moon and the stars.

"It was inconceivable. That was the distinctive quality of the part into which Stein and I had tumbled him unwittingly, with no other notion than to get him out of the way; out of his own way, be it understood. That was our main purpose, though, I own, I might have had another motive which had influenced me a little. I was about to go home for a time; and it may be I desired, more than I was aware of myself, to dispose of him—to dispose of him, you understand—before I left. I was going home, and he had come to me from there, with his miserable trouble and his shadowy claim, like a man panting under a burden in a mist. I cannot say I had ever seen him distinctly—not even to this day, after I had my last view of him; but it seemed to me that the less I understood the more I was bound to him in the name of that doubt which is the inseparable part of our knowledge. I did not know so much more about myself. And then, I repeat, I was going home—to that home distant enough for all its hearthstones to be like one hearthstone, by which the humblest of us has the right to sit. We wander in our thousands over the face of the earth, the illustrious and the obscure, earning beyond the seas our fame, our money, or only a crust of bread; but; it seems to me that for each of us going home must be like going to render an account. We return to face our superiors, our kindred, our friends—those whom we obey, and those whom we love; but even they who have neither, the most free, lonely, irresponsible, and bereft of ties—even those for whom home holds no dear face, no familiar voice—even they have to meet the spirit that dwells within the land, under its sky, in its air, in its valleys, and on its rises, in its fields, in its waters and its trees—a mute friend, judge, and inspirer. Say what you like, to get its joy, to breathe its peace, to face its truth, one must return with a clear conscience. All this may seem to you sheer sentimentalism; and indeed very few of us have the will or the capacity to look consciously under the surface of familiar emotions. There are the girls we love, the men we look up to, the tenderness, the friendships, the opportunities, the pleasures! But the fact remains that you must touch your reward with clean hands, lest it turn to dead leaves, to thorns, in your grasp. I think it is the lonely, without a fireside or an affection they may call their own, those who return not to a dwelling but to the land itself, to meet its disembodied, eternal, and unchangeable spirit—it is those who understand best its severity, its saving power, the grace of its secular right to our fidelity, to our obedience. Yes! few of us understand, but we all feel it though, and I say *all* without exception, because those who do not feel do not count. Each blade of grass has its spot on earth whence it draws its life, its strength; and so is man rooted to the land from which he draws his faith together with his life. I don't know how much Jim understood; but I know he felt, he felt confusedly but powerfully, the demand of some such truth or some such illusion—I don't care how you call it, there is so little difference, and the difference means so little. The thing is that in virtue of his feeling he mattered. He would never go home now. Not he. Never. Had he been capable of picturesque manifestations he would have shuddered at the thought and made you shudder too. But he was not of that sort, though he was expressive enough in his way. Before the idea of going home he would grow desperately stiff and immovable, with lowered chin and pouted lips, and with those candid blue eyes of his glowering darkly under a frown, as if before something unbearable, as if before something revolting. There was imagination in that hard skull of his, over which the thick clustering hair fitted like a cap. As to me, I have no imagination (I would be more certain about him today, if I had), and I do not mean to imply that I figured to myself the spirit of the land uprising above the white cliffs of Dover, to ask me what I—returning with no bones broken, so to speak—had done with my very young brother. I could not make such a mistake. I knew very well he was of those about whom there is no inquiry; I had seen better men go out, disappear, vanish utterly without provoking a sound of curiosity or sorrow. The spirit of the land, as becomes the ruler of great enterprises, is careless of innumerable lives. Woe to the stragglers! We exist only in so far as we hang together. He had straggled in a way; he had not hung on; but he was aware of it with an intensity that made him touching, just as a man's more intense life makes his death more touching than the death of a tree. I happened to be handy, and I happened to be touched. That's all there is to it. I was concerned as to the way he would go out. It would have hurt me if, for instance, he had taken to drink. The earth is so small that I was afraid of, some day, being waylaid by a blear-eyed, swollen-faced, besmirched loafer, with no soles to his canvas shoes, and with a flutter of rags about the elbows, who, on the strength of old acquaintance, would ask for a loan of five dollars. You know the awful jaunty bearing of these scarecrows coming to you from a decent past, the rasping, careless voice, the half-averted impudent glances—those meetings more trying to a man who believes in the solidarity of our lives than the sight of an impenitent deathbed to a priest. That, to tell you the truth, was the only danger I could see for him and for me; but I also mistrusted my want of imagination. It might even come to something worse, in some way it was beyond my powers of fancy to foresee. He wouldn't let me forget how imaginative he was, and your imaginative people swing farther in any direction, as if given a longer scope of cable in the uneasy anchorage of life. They do. They take to drink, too. It may be I was belittling him by such a fear. How could I tell? Even Stein could say no more than that he was romantic. I only knew he was one of us. And what business had he to be romantic? I am telling you so much about my own instinctive feelings and bemused reflections because there remains so little to be told of him. He existed for me, and after all it is only through me that he exists for you. I've led him out by the hand; I have paraded him before you. Were my commonplace fears unjust? I won't say—not even now. You may be able to tell better, since the proverb has it that the onlookers see most of the game. At any rate, they were superfluous. He did not go out, not at all; on the contrary, he came on wonderfully, came on straight as a die and in excellent form, which showed that he could stay as well as spurt. I ought to be delighted, for it is a victory in which I had taken my part; but I am not so pleased as I would have expected to be. I ask myself whether his rush had really carried him out of that mist in which he loomed interesting if not very big, with floating outlines—a straggler yearning inconsolably for his humble place in the ranks. And besides, the last word is not said—probably shall never be said. Are not our lives too short for that full utterance which through all our stammerings is of course our only and abiding intention? I have given up expecting those last words, whose ring, if they could only be pronounced, would shake both heaven and earth. There is never time to say our last word—the last word of our love, of our desire, faith, remorse, submission, revolt. The heaven and the earth must not be shaken, I suppose—at least, not by us who know so many truths about either. My last words about Jim shall be few. I affirm he had achieved greatness; but the thing would be dwarfed in the telling, or rather in the hearing. Frankly, it is not my words that I mistrust, but your minds. I could be eloquent were I not afraid you fellows had starved your imaginations to feed your bodies. I do not mean to be offensive; it is respectable to have no illusions—and safe—and profitable—and dull. Yet you too in your time must have known the intensity of life, that light of glamour created in the shock of trifles, as amazing as the glow of sparks struck from a cold stone—and as short-lived, alas!"

❧ 22 ❧

The conquest of love, honor, men's confidence—the pride of it, the power of it, are fit materials for a heroic tale; only our minds are struck by the externals of such a success, and to Jim's successes there were no externals. Thirty miles of forest shut it off from the sight of an indifferent world, and the noise of the white surf along the coast overpowered the voice of fame. The stream of civilization, as if divided on a headland a hundred miles north of Patusan, branches east and southeast, leaving its plains and valleys, its old trees and its old mankind, neglected and isolated, such as an insignificant and crumbling islet between the two branches of a mighty, devouring stream. You find the name of the country pretty often in collections of old voyages. The seventeenth-century traders went there for pepper, because the passion for pepper seemed to burn like a flame of love in the breast of Dutch and English adventurers about the time of James the First. Where wouldn't they go for pepper! For a bag of pepper they would cut each other's throats without hesitation, and would forswear their souls, of which they were so careful otherwise: the bizarre obstinacy of that desire made them defy death in a thousand shapes; the unknown seas, the loathsome and strange diseases; wounds, captivity, hunger, pestilence, and despair. It made them great! By heavens! it made them heroic; and it made them pathetic, too, in their craving for trade with the inflexible death levying its toll on young and old. It seems impossible to believe that mere greed could hold men to such a steadfastness of purpose, to such a blind persistence in endeavor and sacrifice. And indeed those who adventured their persons and lives risked all they had for a slender reward. They left their bones to lie bleaching on distant shores, so that wealth might flow to the living at home. To us, their less tried successors, they appear magnified, not as agents of trade, but as instruments of a recorded destiny, pushing out into the unknown in obedience to an inward voice, to an impulse beating in the blood, to a dream of the future. They were wonderful; and it must be owned they were ready for the wonderful. They recorded it complacently in their sufferings, in the aspect of the seas, in the customs of strange nations, in the glory of splendid rulers.

"In Patusan they had found lots of pepper, and had been impressed by the magnificence and the wisdom of the Sultan; but somehow, after a century of checkered intercourse, the country seems to drop gradually out of the trade. Perhaps the pepper had given out. Be it as it may, nobody cares for it now; the glory has departed, the Sultan is an imbecile youth with two thumbs on his left hand and an uncertain and beggarly revenue extorted from a miserable population and stolen from him by his many uncles.

"This of course I have from Stein. He gave me their names and a short sketch of life and character of each. He was as full of information about native States as an official report, but infinitely more amusing. He *had* to know. He traded in so many, and in some districts—as in Patusan, for instance—his firm was the only one to have an agency by special permit from the Dutch authorities. The Government trusted his discretion, and it was understood that he took all the risks. The men he employed understood that too, but he made it worth their while apparently. He was perfectly frank with me over the breakfast table in the morning. As far as he was aware (the last news were thirteen months old, he stated precisely), utter insecurity for life and property was the normal condition. There were in Patusan antagonistic forces, and one of them was Rajah Allang, the worst of the Sultan's uncles, the governor of the river, who did the extorting and the stealing, and ground down to the point of extinction the country-born Malays, who, utterly defenseless, had not even the resource of emigrating—'for indeed,' as Stein remarked, 'where could they go, and how could they get away?' No doubt they did not even desire to get away. The world (which is circumscribed by lofty impassable mountains) has been given into the hand of the high-born, and *this* Rajah they knew: he was of their own royal house. I had the pleasure of meeting the gentleman later on. He was a dirty little used-up old man with evil eyes and a weak mouth, who swallowed an opium pill every two hours, and in defiance of common decency wore his hair uncovered and falling in wild stringy locks about his wizened, grimy face. When giving audience he would clamber upon a sort of narrow stage erected in a hall like a ruinous barn with a rotten bamboo floor, through the cracks of which you could see twelve or fifteen feet below the heaps of refuse and garbage of all kinds lying under the house. That is where and how he received us when, accompanied by Jim, I paid him a visit of ceremony. There were about forty people in the room, and perhaps three times as many in the great courtyard below. There was constant movement, coming and going, pushing and murmuring, at our backs. A few youths in gay silks glared from the distance; the majority, slaves and humble dependents, were half naked, in ragged sarongs, dirty with ashes and mud-stains. I had never seen Jim look so grave, so self-possessed, in an impenetrable, impressive way. In the midst of these dark-faced men, his stalwart figure in white apparel, the gleaming clusters of his fair hair, seemed to catch all the sunshine that trickled through the cracks in the closed shutters of that dim hall, with its walls of mats and a roof of thatch. He appeared like a creature not only of another kind, but of another essence. Had they not seen him come up in a canoe they might have thought he had descended upon them from the clouds. He did, however, come in a crazy dugout, sitting (very still and with his knees together, for fear of overturning the thing)—sitting on a tin box—which I had lent him—nursing on his lap a revolver of the navy pattern—presented by me on parting which, through the interposition of Providence, or through some wrongheaded notion, that was just like him, or less from sheer instinctive sagacity, he had decided to carry unloaded. That's how he ascended the Patusan river. Nothing could have been more prosaic and more unsafe, more extravagantly casual, more lonely. Strange, this fatality that would cast the complexion of a flight upon all his acts, of impulsive unreflecting desertion—of a jump into the unknown.

"It is precisely the casualness of it that strikes me most. Neither Stein nor I had a clear conception of what might be on the other side when we, metaphorically speaking, took him up and hove him over the wall with scant ceremony. At the moment I merely wished to achieve his disappearance; Stein characteristically enough had a sentimental motive. He had a notion of paying off (in kind, I suppose) the old debt he had never forgotten. Indeed he had been all his life especially friendly to anybody from the British Isles. His late benefactor, it is true, was a Scot—even to the length of being called Alexander M'Neil—and Jim came from a long way south of the Tweed; but at the distance of six or seven thousand miles Great Britain, though never diminished, looks foreshortened enough even to its own children to rob such details of their importance. Stein was excusable, and his hinted intentions were so generous that I begged him most earnestly to keep them secret for a time. I felt that no consideration of personal advantage should be allowed to influence Jim; that not even the risk of such influence should be run. We had to deal with another sort of reality. He wanted a refuge, and a refuge at the cost of danger should be offered him—nothing more.

"Upon every other point I was perfectly frank with him, and I even (as I believed at the time) exaggerated the danger of the undertaking. As a matter of fact I did not do it justice; his first day in Patusan was nearly his last—would have been his last if he had not been so reckless or so hard on himself and had condescended to load that revolver. I remember, as I unfolded our precious scheme for his retreat, how his stubborn but weary resignation was gradually replaced by surprise, interest, wonder, and by boyish eagerness. This was a chance he had been dreaming of. He couldn't think how he merited that I . . . He would be shot if he could see to what he owed . . . And it was Stein, Stein the merchant, who . . . but of course it was me he had to . . . I cut him short. He was not articulate, and his gratitude caused me inexplicable pain. I told him that if he owed this chance to anyone especially, it was to an old Scot of whom he had never heard, who had died many years ago, of whom little was remembered besides a roaring voice and a rough sort of honesty. There was really no one to receive his thanks. Stein was passing on to a young man the help he had received in his own young days, and I had done no more than to mention his name. Upon this he colored, and, twisting a bit of paper in his fingers, he remarked bashfully that I had always trusted him.

"I admitted that such was the case, and added after a pause that I wished he had been able to follow my example. 'You think I don't?' he asked uneasily, and remarked in a mutter that one had to get some sort of show first; then brightening up, and in a loud voice he protested he would give me no occasion to regret my confidence, which—which . . .

"'Do not misapprehend,' I interrupted. 'It is not in your power to make me regret anything.' There would be no regrets; but if there were, it would be altogether my own affair: on the other hand, I wished him to understand clearly that this arrangement, this—this—experiment, was his own doing; he was responsible for it, and no one else. 'Why? Why!' he stammered, 'this is the very thing that I' . . . I begged him not to be dense, and he looked more puzzled than ever. He was in a fair way to make life intolerable to himself. . . . 'Do you think so?' he asked, disturbed; but in a moment added confidently, 'I was going on, though. Was I not?' It was impossible to be angry with him: I could not help a smile, and told him that in the old days people who went on like this were on the way of becoming hermits in a wilderness. 'Hermits be hanged!' he commented with engaging impulsiveness. Of course he didn't mind a wilderness. . . . 'I was glad of it,' I said. That was where he would be going to. He would find it lively enough, I ventured to promise. 'Yes, yes,' he said keenly. He had shown a desire, I continued inflexibly, to go out and shut the door after him. . . . 'Did I?' he interrupted in a strange access of gloom that seemed to envelop him from head to foot like the shadow of a passing cloud. He was wonderfully expressive after all. Wonderfully! 'Did I?' he repeated bitterly. 'You can't say I made much noise about it. And I can keep it up, too—only, confound it! you show me a door.'. . . 'Very well. Pass on,' I struck in. I could make him a solemn promise that it would be shut behind him with a vengeance. His fate, whatever it was, would be ignored, because the country, for all its rotten state, was not judged ripe for interference. Once he got in, it would be for the outside world as though he had never existed. He would have nothing but the soles of his two feet to stand upon, and he would have first to find his ground at that. 'Never existed—that's it, by Jove,' he murmured to himself. His

eyes, fastened upon my lips, sparkled. If he had thoroughly understood the conditions, I concluded, he had better jump into the first gharry he could see and drive
on to Stein's house for his final instructions. He flung out of the room before I had
fairly finished speaking."

❦ 23 ❦

He did not return till next morning. He had been kept to dinner and for
the night. There never had been such a wonderful man as Mr. Stein. He
had in his pocket a letter for Cornelius ('the Johnnie who's going to get
the sack,' he explained with a momentary drop in his elation), and he exhibited
with glee a silver ring, such as natives use, worn down very thin and showing faint
traces of chasing.

"This was his introduction to an old chap called Doramin—one of the principal
men out there—a big pot—who had been Mr. Stein's friend in that country where
he had all these adventures. Mr. Stein called him 'war-comrade.' War-comrade was
good. Wasn't it? And didn't Mr. Stein speak English wonderfully well? Said he had
learned it in Celebes—of all places! That was awfully funny. Was it not? He did
speak with an accent—a twang—did I notice? That chap Doramin had given him
the ring. They had exchanged presents when they parted for the last time. Sort of
promising eternal friendship. He called it fine—did I not? They had to make a
dash for dear life out of the country when that Mohammed—Mohammed—
What's-his-name had been killed. I knew the story, of course. Seemed a beastly
shame, didn't it? . . .

"He ran on like this, forgetting his plate, with a knife and fork in hand (he had
found me at tiffin), slightly flushed, and with his eyes darkened many shades,
which was with him a sign of excitement. The ring was a sort of credential. ('It's
like something you read of in books,' he threw in appreciatively), and Doramin
would do his best for him. Mr. Stein had been the means of saving that chap's life
on some occasion; purely by accident, Mr. Stein had said, but he—Jim—had his
own opinion about that. Mr. Stein was just the man to look out for such accidents.
No matter. Accident or purpose, this would serve his turn immensely. Hoped to
goodness the jolly old beggar had not gone off the hooks meantime. Mr. Stein
could not tell. There had been no news for more than a year; they were kicking
up no end of an all-fired row amongst themselves, and the river was closed. Jolly
awkward, this; but, no fear; he would manage to find a crack to get in.

"He impressed, almost frightened, me with his elated rattle. He was voluble like a youngster on the eve of a long holiday with the prospect of delightful scrapes, and such an attitude of mind in a grown man and in this connection had in it something phenomenal, a little mad, dangerous, unsafe. I was on the point of entreating him to take things seriously when he dropped his knife and fork (he had begun eating, or rather swallowing food, as it were, unconsciously), and began a search all round his plate. The ring! The ring! Where the devil . . . Ah! Here it was . . . He closed his big hand on it, and tried all his pockets one after another. Jove! wouldn't do to lose the thing. He meditated gravely over his fist. Had it? Would hang the bally affair round his neck! And he proceeded to do this immediately, producing a string (which looked like a bit of a cotton shoelace) for the purpose. There! That would do the trick! It would be the deuce if . . . He seemed to catch sight of my face for the first time, and it steadied him a little. I probably didn't realize, he said with a naive gravity, how much importance he attached to that token. It meant a friend; and it is a good thing to have a friend. He knew something about that. He nodded at me expressively, but before my disclaiming gesture he leaned his head on his hand and for a while sat silent, playing thoughtfully with the breadcrumbs on the cloth . . . 'Slam the door—that was jolly well put,' he cried, and jumping up, began to pace the room, reminding me by the set of the shoulders, the turn of his head, the headlong and uneven stride, of that night when he had paced thus, confessing, explaining—what you will—but, in the last instance, living—living before me, under his own little cloud, with all his unconscious subtlety which could draw consolation from the very source of sorrow. It was the same mood, the same and different, like a fickle companion that, today guiding you on the true path, with the same eyes, the same step, the same impulse, tomorrow will lead you hopelessly astray. His tread was assured, his straying, darkened eyes seemed to search the room for something. One of his footfalls somehow sounded loader than the other—the fault of his boots probably—and gave a curious impression of an invisible halt in his gait. One of his hands was rammed deep into his trousers' pocket, the other waved suddenly above his head. 'Slam the door!' he shouted. 'I've been waiting for that. I'll show yet . . . I'll . . . I'm ready for any confounded thing . . . I've been dreaming of it . . . Jove! Get out of this. Jove! This is luck at last . . . You wait. I'll . . .'

"He tossed his head fearlessly, and I confess that for the first and last time in our acquaintance I perceived myself unexpectedly to be thoroughly sick of him. Why these vaporings? He was stumping about the room flourishing his arm absurdly, and now and then feeling on his breast for the ring under his clothes. Where was the sense of such exaltation in a man appointed to be a trading-clerk, and in a place where there was no trade—at that? Why hurl defiance at the universe? This was not a proper frame of mind to approach any undertaking; an improper frame of mind not only for him, I said, but for any man. He stood still, over me. Did I think so? he asked, by no means subdued, and with a smile in which I seemed to detect suddenly something insolent. But then I am twenty years his senior. Youth *is* insolent; it is its right—its necessity; it has got to assert itself, and all assertion in this world of doubts is a defiance, is an insolence. He went off into a far corner, and coming back, he, figuratively speaking, turned to rend me. I spoke like that because I—even I, who had been no end kind to him—even I remembered—remembered—against him—what—what had happened. And what about others—the—the—world. Where's the wonder he wanted to get out, meant to get out, meant to stay out—by heavens! And I talked about proper frames of mind!

"'It is not I or the world who remember,' I shouted. 'It is you—you, who remember.'

"He did not flinch, and went on with heat, 'Forget everything, everybody, everybody.' . . . His voice fell . . . 'But you,' he added.

"'Yes—me too—if it would help,' I said, also in a low tone. After this we remained silent and languid for a time as if exhausted. Then he began again, composedly, and told me that Mr. Stein had instructed him to wait for a month or so, to see whether it was possible for him to remain, before he began building a new house for himself, so as to avoid 'vain expense.' He did make use of funny expressions—Stein did. 'Vain expense' was good. . . . Remain? Why! of course. He would hang on. Let him only get in—that's all; he would answer for it he would remain. Never get out. It was easy enough to remain.

"'Don't be foolhardy,' I said, rendered uneasy by his threatening tone. 'If you only live long enough you will want to come back.'

"'Come back to what?' he asked absently, with his eyes fixed upon the face of a clock on the wall.

"I was silent for a while. 'Is it to be never, then?' I said. 'Never,' he repeated dreamily without looking at me, and then flew into sudden activity. 'Jove! Two o'clock, and I sail at four?'

"It was true. A brigantine of Stein's was leaving for the westward that afternoon, and he had been instructed to take his passage in her, only no orders to delay the sailing had been given. I suppose Stein forgot. He made a rush to get his things while I went aboard my ship, where he promised to call on his way to the outer roadstead. He turned up accordingly in a great hurry and with a small leather valise in his hand. This wouldn't do, and I offered him an old tin trunk of mine supposed to be watertight, or at least damp-tight. He effected the transfer by the simple process of shooting out the contents of his valise as you would empty a sack of wheat. I saw three books in the tumble; two small, in dark covers, and a thick green-and-gold volume—a half-crown complete Shakespeare. 'You read this?' I asked. 'Yes. Best thing to cheer up a fellow,' he said hastily. I was struck by this appreciation, but there was no time for Shakespearian talk. A heavy revolver and two small boxes of cartridges were lying on the cuddy-table. 'Pray take this,' I said. 'It may help you to remain.' No sooner were these words out of my mouth than I perceived what grim meaning they could bear. 'May help you to get in,' I corrected myself remorsefully. He however was not troubled by obscure meanings; he thanked me effusively and bolted out, calling goodbye over his shoulder. I heard his voice through the ship's side urging his boatmen to give way, and looking out of the stern-port I saw the boat rounding under the counter. He sat in her, leaning forward, exciting his men with voice and gestures; and as he had kept the revolver in his hand and seemed to be presenting it at their heads, I shall never forget the scared faces of the four Javanese, and the frantic swing of their stroke which snatched that vision from under my eyes. Then turning away, the first thing I saw were the two boxes of cartridges on the cuddy-table. He had forgotten to take them.

"I ordered my gig manned at once, but Jim's rowers, under the impression that their lives hung on a thread while they had that madman in the boat, made such excellent time that before I had traversed half the distance between the two vessels I caught sight of him clambering over the rail, and of his box being passed up. All the brigantine's canvas was loose, her mainsail was set, and the windlass was just beginning to clink as I stepped upon her deck: her master, a dapper little half-caste of forty or so, in a blue flannel suit, with lively eyes, his round face the color of lemon peel, and with a thin little black moustache drooping on each side of his thick, dark lips, came forward smirking. He turned out, notwithstanding his self-satisfied and cheery exterior, to be of a careworn temperament. In answer to a remark of mine (while Jim had gone below for a moment) he said, 'Oh, yes. Patusan.' He was going to carry the gentleman to the mouth of the river, but would 'never ascend.' His flowing English seemed to be derived from a dictionary compiled by a lunatic. Had Mr. Stein desired him to 'ascend,' he would have 'reverentially'—(I think he wanted to say respectfully—but devil only knows)—'reverentially made objects for the safety of properties.' If disregarded, he would have presented 'resignation to quit.' Twelve months ago he had made his last voyage there, and though Mr. Cornelius 'propitiated many offertories' to Mr. Rajah Allang and the 'principal populations,' on conditions which made the trade 'a snare and ashes in the mouth,' yet his ship had been fired upon from the woods by 'irresponsive parties' all the way down the river; which causing his crew 'from exposure to limb to remain silent in hidings' the brigantine was nearly stranded on a sandbank at the bar, where she 'would have been perishable beyond the act of man.' The angry disgust at the recollection, the pride of his fluency, to which he turned an attentive ear, struggled for the possession of his broad, simple face. He scowled and beamed at me, and watched with satisfaction the undeniable effect of his phraseology. Dark frowns ran swiftly over the placid sea, and the brigantine, with her fore-topsail to the mast and her main-boom amidships, seemed bewildered amongst the cat's-paws. He told me further, gnashing his teeth, that the Rajah was a 'laughable hyena' (can't imagine how he got hold of hyenas); while somebody else was many times falser than the 'weapons of a crocodile.' Keeping one eye on the movements of his crew forward, he let loose his volubility—comparing the place to a 'cage of beasts made ravenous by long impenitence.' I fancy he meant impunity. He had no intention, he cried, to 'exhibit himself to be made attached purposefully to robbery.' The long-drawn wails, giving the time for the pull of the men carting the anchor, came to an end, and he lowered his voice. 'Plenty too much enough of Patusan,' he concluded, with energy.

"I heard afterwards he had been so indiscreet as to get himself tied up by the neck with a rattan halter to a post planted in the middle of a mudhole before the Rajah's house. He spent the best part of a day and a whole night in that unwholesome situation, but there is every reason to believe the thing had been meant as a sort of joke. He brooded for a while over that horrid memory, I suppose, and then addressed in a quarrelsome tone the man coming aft to the helm. When he turned to me again it was to speak judicially, without passion. He would take the gentleman to the mouth of the river at Batu Kring (Patusan town 'being situated internally,' he remarked, 'thirty miles'). But in his eyes, he continued—a tone of bored, weary conviction replacing his previous voluble delivery—the gentleman was already 'in the similitude of a corpse.' 'What? What do you say?' I asked. He assumed a startlingly ferocious demeanor, and imitated to perfection the act of stabbing from behind. 'Already like the body of one deported,' he explained, with the insufferably conceited air of his kind after what they imagine a display of cleverness. Behind him I perceived Jim smiling silently at me, and with a raised hand checking the exclamation on my lips.

"Then, while the half-caste, bursting with importance, shouted his orders, while the yards swung creaking and the heavy boom came surging over, Jim and I, alone as it were, to leeward of the mainsail, clasped each other's hands and exchanged the last hurried words. My heart was freed from that dull resentment which had existed side by side with interest in his fate. The absurd chatter of the half-caste had given more reality to the miserable dangers of his path than Stein's careful statements. On that occasion the sort of formality that had been always present in our intercourse vanished from our speech. I believe I called him 'dear boy,' and he tacked on the words 'old man' to some half-uttered expression of gratitude, as though his risk set off against my years had made us more equal in age and in feeling. There was a moment of real and profound intimacy, unexpected and short-lived like a glimpse of some everlasting, of some saving truth. He exerted himself to soothe me as though he had been the more mature of the two. 'All right, all right,' he said rapidly and with feeling. 'I promise to take care of myself. Yes; I won't take any risks. Not a single blessed risk. Of course not. I mean to hang out. Don't you worry; Jove! I feel as if nothing could touch me. Why! this is luck from the word Go. I wouldn't spoil such a magnificent chance!' . . . A magnificent chance! Well, it *was* magnificent, but chances are what men make them, and how was I to know. As he had said, even I—even I remembered—his—his misfortune against him. It was true. And the best thing for him was to go.

"My gig had dropped in the wake of the brigantine, and I saw him aft detached upon the light of the westering sun, raising his cap high above his head. I heard an indistinct shout, 'You—shall—hear—of—me.' Of me, or from me, I don't know which. I think it must have been *of* me. My eyes were too dazzled by the glitter of the sea below his feet to see him clearly; I am fated never to see him clearly; but I can assure you no man could have appeared less 'in the similitude of a corpse,' as that half-caste croaker had put it. I could see the little wretch's face, the shape and color of a ripe pumpkin, poked out somewhere under Jim's elbow. He too raised his arm as if for a downward thrust. *Absit omen!*"

❧ 24 ❧

The coast of Patusan (I saw it nearly two years afterwards) is straight and somber, and faces a misty ocean, Red trails are seen like cataracts of rust streaming under the dark green foliage of bushes and creepers clothing the low cliffs. Swampy plains open out at the mouth of rivers, with a view of jagged blue peaks beyond the vast forests. In the offing a chain of islands, dark, crumbling shapes, stand out in the everlasting sunlit haze like the remnants of a wall breached by the sea.

"There is a village of fisher-folk at the mouth of the Batu Kring branch of the estuary. The river, which had been closed so long, was open then, and Stein's little schooner, in which I had my passage, worked her way up in three tides without being exposed to a fusillade from 'irresponsive parties.' Such a state of affairs belonged already to ancient history, if I could believe the elderly headman of the fishing village, who came on board to act as a sort of pilot. He talked to me (the second white man he had ever seen) with confidence, and most of his talk was about the first white man he had ever seen. He called him Tuan Jim, and the tone of his references was made remarkable by a strange mixture of familiarity and awe. They, in the village, were under that lord's special protection, which showed that Jim bore no grudge. If he had warned me that I would hear of him it was perfectly true. I was hearing of him. There was already a story that the tide had turned two hours before its time to help him on his journey up the river. The talkative old man himself had steered the canoe and had marveled at the phenomenon. Moreover, all the glory was in his family. His son and his son-in-law had paddled; but they were only youths without experience, who did not notice the speed of the canoe till he pointed out to them the amazing fact.

"Jim's coming to that fishing village was a blessing; but to them, as to many of us, the blessing came heralded by terrors. So many generations had been released since the last white man had visited the river that the very tradition had been lost. The appearance of the being that descended upon them and demanded inflexibly to be taken up to Patusan was discomposing; his insistence was alarming; his generosity more than suspicious. It was an unheard-of request. There was no precedent. What would the Rajah say to this? What would he do to them? The best part of the night was spent in consultation; but the immediate risk from the anger of that strange man seemed so great that at last a cranky dugout was got ready. The women shrieked with grief as it put off. A fearless old hag cursed the stranger.

"He sat in it, as I've told you, on his tin box, nursing the unloaded revolver on his lap. He sat with precaution—than which there is nothing more fatiguing—and thus entered the land he was destined to fill with the fame of his virtues, from the blue peaks inland to the white ribbon of surf on the coast. At the first bend he lost sight of the sea with its laboring waves forever rising, sinking, and vanishing to rise again—the very image of struggling mankind—and faced the immovable forests rooted deep in the soil, soaring towards the sunshine, everlasting in the shadowy might of their tradition, like life itself. And his opportunity sat veiled by his side like an Eastern bride waiting to be uncovered by the hand of the master. He too was the heir of a shadowy and mighty tradition! He told me, however, that he had never in his life felt so depressed and tired as in that canoe. All the movement he dared to allow himself was to reach, as it were by stealth, after the shell of half a coconut floating between his shoes, and bale some of the water out with a carefully restrained action. He discovered how hard the lid of a block-tin case was to sit upon. He had heroic health; but several times during that journey he experienced fits of giddiness, and between whiles he speculated hazily as to the size of the blister the sun was raising on his back. For amusement he tried by looking ahead to decide whether the muddy object he saw lying on the water's edge was a log of wood or an alligator. Only very soon he had to give that up. No fun in it. Always alligator. One of them flopped into the river and all but capsized the canoe. But this excitement was over directly. Then in a long empty reach he was very grateful to a troop of monkeys who came right down on the bank and made an insulting hullabaloo on his passage. Such was the way in which he was approaching greatness as genuine as any man ever achieved. Principally, he longed for sunset; and meantime his three paddlers were preparing to put into execution their plan of delivering him up to the Rajah.

"'I suppose I must have been stupid with fatigue, or perhaps I did doze off for a time,' he said. The first thing he knew was his canoe coming to the bank. He became instantaneously aware of the forest having been left behind, of the first houses being visible higher up, of a stockade on his left, and of his boatmen leaping out together upon a low point of land and taking to their heels. Instinctively he leaped out after them. At first he thought himself deserted for some inconceivable reason, but he heard excited shouts, a gate swung open, and a lot of people poured out, making towards him. At the same time a boat full of armed men appeared on the river and came alongside his empty canoe, thus shutting off his retreat.

"'I was too startled to be quite cool—don't you know? and if that revolver had been loaded I would have shot somebody—perhaps two, three bodies, and that would have been the end of me. But it wasn't . . .' 'Why not?' I asked. 'Well, I couldn't fight the whole population, and I wasn't coming to them as if I were afraid of my life,' he said, with just a faint hint of his stubborn sulkiness in the glance he gave me. I refrained from pointing out to him that they could not have known the chambers were actually empty. He had to satisfy himself in his own way. . . . 'Anyhow it wasn't,' he repeated good-humoredly, 'and so I just stood still and asked them what was the matter. That seemed to strike them dumb. I saw some of these thieves going off with my box. That long-legged old scoundrel Kassim (I'll show him to you tomorrow) ran out fussing to me about the Rajah wanting to see me. I said, "All right"; I too wanted to see the Rajah, and I simply walked in through the gate and—and—here I am.' He laughed, and then with unexpected emphasis, 'And do you know what's the best in it?' he asked. 'I'll tell you. It's the knowledge that had I been wiped out it is this place that would have been the loser.'

"He spoke thus to me before his house on that evening I've mentioned—after we had watched the moon float away above the chasm between the hills like an ascending spirit out of a grave; its sheen descended, cold and pale, like the ghost of dead sunlight. There is something haunting in the light of the moon; it has all the dispassionateness of a disembodied soul, and something of its inconceivable mystery. It is to our sunshine which—say what you like—is all we have to live by, what the echo is to the sound: misleading and confusing whether the note be mocking or sad. It robs all forms of matter—which, after all, is our domain—of their substance, and gives a sinister reality to shadows alone. And the shadows were very real around us, but Jim by my side looked very stalwart, as though noth-ing—not even the occult power of moonlight—could rob him of his reality in my eyes. Perhaps, indeed, nothing could touch him since he had survived the assault of the dark powers. All was silent, all was still; even on the river the moonbeams slept as on a pool. It was the moment of high water, a moment of immobility that accentuated the utter isolation of this lost corner of the earth. The houses crowd-ing along the wide shining sweep without ripple or glitter, stepping into the water in a line of jostling, vague, gray, silvery forms mingled with black masses of shad-ow, were like a spectral herd of shapeless creatures pressing forward to drink in a spectral and lifeless stream. Here and there a red gleam twinkled within the bam-boo walls, warm, like a living spark, significant of human affections, of shelter, of repose.

"He confessed to me that he often watched these tiny warm gleams go out one by one, that he loved to see people go to sleep under his eyes, confident in the security of tomorrow. 'Peaceful here, hey?' he asked. He was not eloquent, but there was a deep meaning in the words that followed. 'Look at these houses; there's not one where I am not trusted. Jove! I told you I would hang on. Ask any man, woman, or child . . .' He paused. 'Well, I am all right anyhow.'

"I observed quickly that he had found that out in the end. I had been sure of it, I added. He shook his head. 'Were you?' He pressed my arm lightly above the elbow. 'Well, then—you were right.'

"There was elation and pride, there was awe almost, in that low exclamation. 'Jove!' he cried, 'only think what it is to me.' Again he pressed my arm. 'And you asked me whether I thought of leaving. Good God! I! want to leave! Especially now after what you told me of Mr. Stein's . . . Leave! Why! That's what I was afraid of. It would have been—it would have been harder than dying. No—on my word. Don't laugh. I must feel—every day, every time I open my eyes—that I am trust-ed—that nobody has a right—don't you know? Leave! For where? What for? To get what?'

"I had told him (indeed it was the main object of my visit) that it was Stein's intention to present him at once with the house and the stock of trading goods, on certain easy conditions which would make the transaction perfectly regular and valid. He began to snort and plunge at first. 'Confound your delicacy!' I shouted. 'It isn't Stein at all. It's giving you what you had made for yourself. And in any case keep your remarks for M'Neil—when you meet him in the other world. I hope it won't happen soon. . . .' He had to give in to my arguments, because all his con-quests, the trust, the fame, the friendships, the love—all these things that made him master had made him a captive too. He looked with an owner's eye at the peace of the evening, at the river, at the houses, at the everlasting life of the forests, at the life of the old mankind, at the secrets of the land, at the pride of his own heart; but it was they that possessed him and made him their own to the innermost thought, to the slightest stir of blood, to his last breath.

"It was something to be proud of. I too was proud—for him, if not so certain of the fabulous value of the bargain. It was wonderful. It was not so much of his fearlessness that I thought. It is strange how little account I took of it: as if it had been something too conventional to be at the root of the matter. No. I was more struck by the other gifts he had displayed. He had proved his grasp of the unfamiliar situation, his intellectual alertness in that field of thought. There was his readiness too! Amazing. And all this had come to him in a manner like keen scent to a well-bred hound. He was not eloquent, but there was a dignity in this constitutional reticence, there was a high seriousness in his stammerings. He had still his old trick of stubborn blushing. Now and then, though, a word, a sentence, would escape him that showed how deeply, how solemnly, he felt about that work which had given him the certitude of rehabilitation. That is why he seemed to love the land and the people with a sort of fierce egoism, with a contemptuous tenderness."

❧ 25 ❧

This is where I was prisoner for three days,' he murmured to me (it was on the occasion of our visit to the Rajah), while we were making our way slowly through a kind of awestruck riot of dependents across Tunku Allang's courtyard. 'Filthy place, isn't it? And I couldn't get anything to eat, either, unless I made a row about it, and then it was only a small plate of rice and a fried fish not much bigger than a stickleback—confound them! Jove! *I've* been hungry prowling inside this stinking enclosure with some of these vagabonds shoving their mugs right under my nose. I had given up that famous revolver of yours at the first demand. Glad to get rid of the bally thing. Look like a fool walking about with an empty shooting-iron in my hand.' At that moment we came into the presence, and he became unflinchingly grave and complimentary with his late captor. Oh! magnificent! I want to laugh when I think of it. But I was impressed, too. The old, disreputable Tunku Allang could not help showing his fear (he was no hero, for all the tales of his hot youth he was fond of telling), and at the same time there was a wistful confidence in his manner towards his late prisoner. Note! Even where he would be most hated he was still trusted. Jim—as far as I could follow the conversation—was improving the occasion by the delivery of a lecture. Some poor villagers had been waylaid and robbed while on their way to Doramin's house with a few pieces of gum or beeswax which they wished to exchange for rice. 'It was Doramin who was a thief,' burst out the Rajah. A shaking fury seemed to enter that old frail body. He writhed weirdly on his mat, gesticulating with his hands and feet, tossing the tangled strings of his mop—an impotent incarnation of rage. There were staring eyes and dropping jaws all around us. Jim began to speak. Resolutely, coolly, and for some time he enlarged upon the text that no man should be prevented from getting his food and his children's food honestly. The other sat like a tailor at his board, one palm on each knee, his head low, and fixing Jim through the gray hair that fell over his very eyes. When Jim had done there was a great stillness. Nobody seemed to breathe even; no one made a sound till the old Rajah sighed faintly, and looking up, with a toss of his head, said quickly, 'You hear, my people! No more of these little games.' This decree was received in profound silence. A rather heavy man, evidently in a position of confidence, with intelligent eyes, a bony, broad, very dark face, and a cheerily officious manner (I learned later on he was the executioner), presented to us two cups of coffee on a brass tray, which he took from the hands of an inferior attendant. 'You needn't drink,' muttered Jim very rapidly. I didn't perceive the meaning at first, and only looked at him. He took a good sip and sat composedly, holding the saucer in his left hand. In a moment I felt excessively annoyed. 'Why the devil,' I whispered, smiling at him amiably, 'do you expose me to such a stupid risk?' I drank, of course, there was nothing for it, while he gave no sign, and almost immediately afterwards we took our leave. While we were going down the courtyard to our boat, escorted by the intelligent and cheery executioner, Jim said he was very sorry. It was the barest chance, of course. Personally, he thought nothing of poison. The remotest chance. He was—he assured me—considered to be infinitely more useful than dangerous, and so . . . 'But the Rajah is afraid of you abominably. Anybody can see that,' I argued with, I own, a certain peevishness, and all the time watching anxiously for the first twist of some sort of ghastly colic. I was awfully disgusted. 'If I am to do any good here and preserve my position,' he said, taking his seat by my side in the boat, 'I must stand the risk: I take it once every month, at least. Many people trust me to do that—for them. Afraid of me. That's just it. Most likely he is afraid of me because I am not afraid of his coffee.' Then showing me a place on the north front of the stockade where the pointed tops of several stakes were broken, 'This is where I leaped over on my third day in Patusan. They haven't put new stakes there yet. Good leap, eh?' A moment later we passed the mouth of a muddy creek. 'This is my second leap. I had a bit of a run and took this one flying, but fell short. Thought I would leave my skin there. Lost my shoes struggling. And all the time I was thinking to myself how beastly it would be to get a jab with a bally long spear while sticking in the mud like this. I remember how sick I felt wriggling in that slime. I mean really sick—as if I had bitten something rotten.'

"That's how it was—and the opportunity ran by his side, leaped over the gap, floundered in the mud . . . still veiled. The unexpectedness of his coming was the only thing, you understand, that saved him from being at once despatched with krises and flung into the river. They had him, but it was like getting hold of an apparition, a wraith, a portent. What did it mean? What to do with it? Was it too late to conciliate him? Hadn't he better be killed without more delay? But what would happen then? Wretched old Allang went nearly mad with apprehension and through the difficulty of making up his mind. Several times the council was broken up, and the advisers made a break helter-skelter for the door and out on to the veranda. One—it is said—even jumped down to the ground—fifteen feet, I should—judge and broke his leg. The royal governor of Patusan had bizarre mannerisms, and one of them was to introduce boastful rhapsodies into every arduous discussion, when, getting gradually excited, he would end by flying off his perch with a kris in his hand. But, barring such interruptions, the deliberations upon Jim's fate went on night and day.

"Meanwhile he wandered about the courtyard, shunned by some, glared at by others, but watched by all, and practically at the mercy of the first casual ragamuffin with a chopper, in there. He took possession of a small tumbledown shed to sleep in; the effluvia of filth and rotten matter incommoded him greatly: it seems he had not lost his appetite though, because—he told me—he had been hungry all the blessed time. Now and again 'some fussy ass' deputed from the council room would come out running to him, and in honeyed tones would administer amazing interrogatories. 'Were the Dutch coming to take the country? Would the white man like to go back down the river? What was the object of coming to such a miserable country? The Rajah wanted to know whether the white man could repair a watch?' They did actually bring out to him a nickel clock of New England make, and out of sheer unbearable boredom he busied himself in trying to get the alarum to work. It was apparently when thus occupied in his shed that the true perception of his extreme peril dawned upon him. He dropped the thing—he says—'like a hot potato,' and walked out hastily, without the slightest idea of what he would, or indeed could, do. He only knew that the position was intolerable. He strolled aimlessly beyond a sort of ramshackle little granary on posts, and his eyes fell on the broken stakes of the palisade; and then—he says—at once, without any mental process as it were, without any stir of emotion, he set about his escape as if executing a plan matured for a month. He walked off carelessly to give himself a good run, and when he faced about there was some dignitary with two spearmen in attendance close at his elbow ready with a question. He started off 'from under his very nose,' went over 'like a bird,' and landed on the other side with a fall that jarred all his bones and seemed to split his head. He picked himself instantly. He never thought of anything at the time; all he could remember—he said—was a great yell; the first houses of Patusan were before him four hundred yards away; he saw the creek, and as it were, mechanically put on more pace. The earth seemed fairly to fly backwards under his feet. He took off from the last dry spot, felt himself flying through the air, felt himself, without any shock, planted upright in an extremely soft and sticky mudbank, It was only when he tried to move his legs and found he couldn't, that, in his own words, 'he came to himself.' He began to think of the 'bally long spears.' As a matter of fact, considering that the people inside the stockade had to run to the gate, then get down to the landing place, get into boats, and pull round a point of land, he had more advance than he imagined. Besides, it being low water, the creek was without water—you couldn't call it dry—and practically he was safe for a time from everything but a very long shot perhaps. The higher firm ground was about six feet in front of him. 'I thought I would have to die there all the same,' he said. He reached and grabbed desperately with his hands, and only succeeded in gathering a horrible, cold, shiny heap of slime against his breast—up to his very chin. It seemed to him he was burying himself alive, and then he struck out madly, scattering the mud with his fists. It fell on his head, on his face, over his eyes, into his mouth. He told me that he remembered suddenly the courtyard, as you remember a place where you had been very happy years ago. He longed—so he said—to be back there again, mending the clock. Mending the clock—that as the idea. He made efforts, tremendous sobbing, gasping efforts, efforts that seemed to burst his eyeballs in their sockets and make him blind, and culminating into one mighty supreme effort in the darkness to crack the earth asunder, to throw it off his limbs—and he felt himself creeping feebly up the bank. He lay full length on the firm ground and saw the light, the sky. Then, as a sort of happy thought, the notion came to him that he would go to sleep. He will have it that he *did* actually go to sleep; that he slept—perhaps for a minute, perhaps for twenty seconds, or only for one second, but he recollects distinctly the violent convulsive start of awakening. He remained lying still for a while and then he arose muddy from head to foot and stood there, thinking he was alone of his kind for hundreds of miles, alone, with no help, no sympathy, no pity to expect from anyone, like a hunted animal. The first houses were not more than twenty yards from him; and it was the desperate screaming of a frightened woman trying to carry off a child that started him again. He pelted straight on in his socks, beplastered with filth out of all semblance to a human being. He traversed more than half the length of the settlement. The nimbler women fled right and left, the slower men just dropped whatever they had in their hands, and remained petrified with dropping jaws. He was a flying terror. He says he noticed the little children trying to run for life, falling on their little stomachs and kicking. He swerved between two houses up a slope, clambered in desperation over a barricade of felled trees (there wasn't a week without some fight in Patusan at that time), burst through a fence into a maize-patch, where a scared boy flung a stick at him, blundered upon a path, and ran all at once into the arms of several startled men. He just had breath enough to gasp out, 'Doramin! Doramin!' He remembers being half-carried, half-rushed to the top of the slope, and in a vast enclosure with palms and fruit trees being run up to a large man sitting massively in a chair in the midst of the greatest possible commotion and excitement. He fumbled in mud and clothes to produce the ring, and, finding himself suddenly on his back, wondered who had knocked him down. They had simply let him go—don't you know?—but he couldn't stand. At the foot of the slope random shots were fired, and above the roofs of the settlement there rose a dull roar of amazement. But he was safe. Doramin's people were barricad-ing the gate and pouring water down his throat; Doramin's old wife, full of busi-ness and commiseration, was issuing shrill orders to her girls. 'The old woman,' he said softly, 'made a to-do over me as if I had been her own son. They put me into an immense bed—her state bed—and she ran in and out wiping her eyes to give me pats on the back. I must have been a pitiful object. I just lay there like a log for I don't know how long.'

"He seemed to have a great liking for Doramin's old wife. She, on her side, had taken a motherly fancy to him. She had a round, nut-brown, soft face, all fine wrin-kles, large, bright red lips (she chewed betel assiduously), and screwed-up, wink-ing, benevolent eyes. She was constantly in movement, scolding busily and order-ing unceasingly a troop of young women with clear brown faces and big grave eyes, her daughters, her servants, her slave girls. You know how it is in these house-holds: it's generally impossible to tell the difference. She was very spare, and even her ample outer garment, fastened in front with jewelled clasps, had somehow a skimpy effect. Her dark bare feet were thrust into yellow straw slippers of Chinese make. I have seen her myself flitting about with her extremely thick, long, gray hair falling about her shoulders. She uttered homely shrewd sayings, was of noble birth, and was eccentric and arbitrary. In the afternoon she would sit in a very roomy armchair, opposite her husband, gazing steadily through a wide opening in the wall which gave an extensive view of the settlement and the river.

"She invariably tucked up her feet under her, but old Doramin sat squarely, sat imposingly as a mountain sits on a plain. He was only of the *nakhoda*, or mer-chant, class, but the respect shown to him and the dignity of his bearing were very striking. He was the chief of the second power in Patusan. The immigrants from Celebes (about sixty families that, with dependents and so on could muster some two hundred men 'wearing the kris') had elected him years ago for their head. The men of that race are intelligent, enterprising, revengeful, but with a more frank courage than the other Malays, and restless under oppression. They formed the party opposed to the Rajah. Of course, the quarrels were for trade. This was the primary cause of faction fights, of the sudden outbreaks that would fill this or that part of the settlement with smoke, flame, the noise of shots, and shrieks. Villages were burnt, men were dragged into the Rajah's stockade to be killed or tortured for the crime of trading with anybody else but himself. Only a day or two before Jim's arrival several heads of households in the very fishing village that was afterwards taken under his especial protection had been driven over the cliffs by a party of the Rajah's spearmen, on suspicion of having been collecting edible birds' nests for a Celebes trader. Rajah Allang pretended to be the only trader in his country, and the penalty for the breach of the monopoly was death; but his idea of trading was indistinguishable from the commonest forms of robbery. His cruelty and rapacity had no other bounds than his cowardice, and he was afraid of the organized power of the Celebes men, only—till Jim came—he was not afraid enough to keep quiet. He struck at them through his subjects, and thought himself pathetically in the right. The situation was complicated by a wandering stranger, an Arab half-breed, who, I believe, on purely religious grounds, had incited the tribes in the interior (the bush-folk, as Jim himself called them) to rise, and had established himself in a fortified camp on the summit of one of the twin hills. He hung over the town of Patusan like a hawk over a poultry yard, but he devastated the open country. Whole villages, deserted, rotted on their blackened posts over the banks of clear streams, dropping piecemeal into the water the grass of their walls, the leaves of their roofs, with a curious effect of natural decay as if they had been a form of vegetation stricken by a blight at its very root. The two parties in Patusan were not sure which one this partisan most desired to plunder. The Rajah intrigued with him feebly. Some of the Bugis settlers, weary with endless insecurity, were half inclined to call him in. The younger spirits amongst them, chaffing, advised to 'get Sherif Ali with his wild men and drive the Rajah Allang out of the country.' Doramin restrained them with difficulty. He was growing old, and though his influence had not diminished, the situation was getting beyond him. This was the state of affairs when Jim, bolting from the Rajah's stockade, appeared before the chief of the Bugis, produced the ring, and was received, in a manner of speaking, into the heart of the community."

❦ 26 ❦

Doramin was one of the most remarkable men of his race I had ever seen. His bulk for a Malay was immense, but he did not look merely fat; he looked imposing, monumental. This motionless body clad in rich stuffs, colored silks, gold embroideries; this huge head, enfolded in a red-and-gold headkerchief; the flat, big, round face, wrinkled, furrowed, with two semicircular heavy folds starting on each side of wide, fierce nostrils, and enclosing a thick-lipped mouth; the throat like a bull; the vast corrugated brow overhanging the staring proud eyes—made a whole that, once seen, can never be forgotten. His impassive repose (he seldom stirred a limb when once he sat down) was like a display of dignity. He was never known to raise his voice. It was a hoarse and powerful murmur, slightly veiled as if heard from a distance. When he walked, two short, sturdy young fellows, naked to the waist, in white sarongs and with black skullcaps on the backs of their heads, sustained his elbows: they would ease him down and stand behind his chair till he wanted to rise, when he would turn his head slowly, as if with difficulty, to the right and to the left, and then they would catch him under his armpits and help him up. For all that, there was nothing of a cripple about him: on the contrary, all his ponderous movements were like manifestations of a mighty deliberate force. It was generally believed he consulted his wife as to public affairs; but nobody, as far as I know, had ever heard them exchange a single word. When they sat in state by the wide opening it was in silence. They could see below them in the declining light the vast expanse of the forest country, a dark sleeping sea of somber green undulating as far as the violet and purple range of mountains; the shining sinuosity of the river like an immense letter S of beaten silver; the brown ribbon of houses following the sweep of both banks, overtopped by the twin-hills uprising above the nearer treetops. They were wonderfully contrasted: she, light, delicate, spare, quick, a little witch-like, with a touch of motherly fussiness in her repose; he, facing her, immense and heavy, like a figure of a man roughly fashioned of stone, with something magnanimous and ruthless in his immobility. The son of these old people was a most distinguished youth.

"They had him late in life. Perhaps he was not really so young as he looked. Four- or five-and-twenty is not so young when a man is already father of a family at eighteen. When he entered the large room, lined and carpeted with fine mats, and with a high ceiling of white sheeting, where the couple sat in state surrounded by a most deferential retinue, he would make his way straight to Doramin, to kiss his hand—which the other abandoned to him, majestically—and then would step across to stand by his mother's chair. I suppose I may say they idolized him, but I never caught them giving him an overt glance. Those, it is true, were public functions. The room was generally thronged. The solemn formality of greetings and leave-takings, the profound respect expressed in gestures, on the faces, in the low whispers, is simply indescribable. 'It's well worth seeing,' Jim had assured me while we were crossing the river, on our way back. 'They are like people in a book, aren't they?' he said triumphantly. 'And Dain Waris—their son—is the best friend (barring you) I ever had. What Mr. Stein would call a good "war-comrade." I was in luck. Jove! I was in luck when I tumbled amongst them at my last gasp.' He meditated with bowed head, then rousing himself he added—

"'Of course I didn't go to sleep over it, but . . .' He paused again. 'It seemed to come to me,' he murmured. 'All at once I saw what I had to do . . .'

"There was no doubt that it had come to him; and it had come through war, too, as is natural, since this power that came to him was the power to make peace. It is in this sense alone that might so often *is* right. You must not think he had seen his way at once. When he arrived the Bugis community was in a most critical position. 'They were all afraid,' he said to me—'each man afraid for himself; while I could see as plain as possible that they must do something at once if they did not want to go under one after another, what between the Rajah and that vagabond Sherif.' But to see that was nothing. When he got his idea he had to drive it into reluctant minds, through the bulwarks of fear, of selfishness. He drove it in at last. And that was nothing. He had to devise the means. He devised them—an audacious plan; and his task was only half done. He had to inspire with his own confidence a lot of people who had hidden and absurd reasons to hang back; he had to conciliate imbecile jealousies, and argue away all sorts of senseless mistrusts. Without the weight of Doramin's authority and his son's fiery enthusiasm he would have failed. Dain Waris, the distinguished youth, was the first to believe in him; theirs was one of these strange, profound, rare friendships between brown and white, in which the very difference of race seems to draw two human beings closer by some mystic element of sympathy. Of Dain Waris, his own people said with pride that he knew how to fight like a white man. This was true; he had that sort of courage—the courage in the open, I may say—but he had also a European mind. You meet them sometimes like that, and are surprised to discover unexpectedly a familiar turn of thought, an unobscured vision, a tenacity of purpose, a touch of altruism. Of small stature, but admirably well proportioned, Dain Waris had a proud carriage, a polished, easy bearing, a temperament like a clear flame. His dusky face, with big black eyes, was in action expressive, and in repose, thoughtful. He was of a silent disposition; a firm glance, an ironic smile, a courte-ous deliberation of manner seemed to hint at great reserves of intelligence and power. Such beings open to the Western eye, so often concerned with mere sur-faces, the hidden possibilities of races and lands over which hangs the mystery of unrecorded ages. He not only trusted Jim, he understood him, I firmly believe. I speak of him because he had captivated me. His—if I may say so—his caustic placidity, and, at the same time, his intelligent sympathy with Jim's aspirations, appealed to me. I seemed to behold the very origin of friendship. If Jim took the lead, the other had captivated his leader. In fact, Jim the leader was a captive in every sense. The land, the people, the friendship, the love, were like the jealous guardians of his body. Every day added a link to the fetters of that strange free-dom. I felt convinced of it, as from day to day I learned more of the story.

"The story! Haven't I heard the story? I've heard it on the march, in camp (he made me scour the country after invisible game); I've listened to a good part of it on one of the twin-summits, after climbing the last hundred feet or so on my hands and knees. Our escort (we had volunteer followers from village to village) had camped meantime on a bit of level ground half-way up the slope, and in the still breathless evening the smell of wood-smoke reached our nostrils from below with the penetrating delicacy of some choice scent. Voices also ascended, won-derful in their distinct and immaterial clearness. Jim sat on the trunk of a felled tree, and pulling out his pipe began to smoke. A new growth of grass and bushes was springing up; there were traces of an earthwork under a mass of thorny twigs. 'It all started from here,' he said, after a long and meditative silence. On the other hill, two hundred yards across a somber precipice, I saw a line of high, blackened stakes, showing here and there ruinously—the remnants of Sherif Ali's impregnable camp.

"But it had been taken, though. That had been his idea. He had mounted Doramin's old ordnance on the top of that hill; two rusty iron seven-pounders, a lot of small brass cannon—currency cannon. But if the brass guns represent wealth, they can also, when crammed recklessly to the muzzle, send a solid shot to some little distance. The thing was to get them up there. He showed me where he had fastened the cables, explained how he had improvised a rude capstan out of a hollowed log turning upon a pointed stake, indicated with the bowl of his pipe the outline of the earthwork. The last hundred feet of the ascent had been the most difficult. He had made himself responsible for success on his own head. He had induced the war party to work hard all night. Big fires lighted at intervals blazed all down the slope, 'but up here,' he explained, 'the hoisting gang had to fly around in the dark.' From the top he saw men moving on the hillside like ants at work. He himself on that night had kept on rushing down and climbing up like a squirrel, directing, encouraging, watching all along the line. Old Doramin had himself carried up the hill in his armchair. They put him down on the level place upon the slope, and he sat there in the light of one of the big fires 'amazing old chap—real old chieftain,' said Jim, 'with his little fierce eyes—a pair of immense flintlock pistols on his knees. Magnificent things, ebony, silver-mounted, with beautiful locks and a caliber like an old blunderbuss. A present from Stein, it seems—in exchange for that ring, you know. Used to belong to good old M'Neil. God only knows how *he* came by them. There he sat, moving neither hand nor foot, a flame of dry brushwood behind him, and lots of people rushing about, shouting and pulling round him—the most solemn, imposing old chap you can imagine. *He* wouldn't have had much chance if Sherif Ali had let his infernal crew loose at us and stampeded my lot. Eh? Anyhow, he had come up there to die if anything went wrong. No mistake! Jove! It thrilled me to see him there—like a rock. But the Sherif must have thought us mad, and never troubled to come and see how we got on. Nobody believed it could be done. Why! I think the very chaps who pulled and shoved and sweated over it did not believe it could be done! Upon my word I don't think they did . . .'

"He stood erect, the smoldering brierwood in his clutch, with a smile on his lips and a sparkle in his boyish eyes. I sat on the stump of a tree at his feet, and below us stretched the land, the great expanse of the forests, somber under the sunshine, rolling like a sea, with glints of winding rivers, the gray spots of villages, and here and there a clearing, like an islet of light amongst the dark waves of continuous treetops. A brooding gloom lay over this vast and monotonous landscape; the light fell on it as if into an abyss. The land devoured the sunshine; only far off, along the coast, the empty ocean, smooth and polished within the faint haze, seemed to rise up to the sky in a wall of steel.

"And there I was with him, high in the sunshine on the top of that historic hill of his. He dominated the forest, the secular gloom, the old mankind. He was like a figure set up on a pedestal, to represent in his persistent youth the power, and perhaps the virtues, of races that never grow old, that have emerged from the gloom. I don't know why he should always have appeared to me symbolic. Perhaps this is the real cause of my interest in his fate. I don't know whether it was exactly fair to him to remember the incident which had given a new direction to his life, but at that very moment I remembered very distinctly. It was like a shadow in the light."

❧ 27 ❧

Already the legend had gifted him with supernatural powers. Yes, it was said, there had been many ropes cunningly disposed, and a strange contrivance that turned by the efforts of many men, and each gun went up tearing slowly through the bushes, like a wild pig rooting its way in the undergrowth, but, . . . and the wisest shook their heads. There was something occult in all this, no doubt; for what is the strength of ropes and of men's arms? There is a rebellious soul in things which must be overcome by powerful charms and incantations. Thus old Sura—a very respectable householder of Patusan—with whom I had a quiet chat one evening. However, Sura was a professional sorcerer also, who attended all the rice sowings and reapings for miles around for the purpose of subduing the stubborn soul of things. This occupation he seemed to think a most arduous one, and perhaps the souls of things are more stubborn than the souls of men. As to the simple folk of outlying villages, they believed and said (as the most natural thing in the world) that Jim had carried the guns up the hill on his back—two at a time.

"This would make Jim stamp his foot in vexation and exclaim with an exasperated little laugh, 'What can you do with such silly beggars? They will sit up half the night talking bally rot, and the greater the lie the more they seem to like it.' You could trace the subtle influence of his surroundings in this irritation. It was part of his captivity. The earnestness of his denials was amusing, and at last I said, 'My dear fellow, you don't suppose I believe this.' He looked at me quite startled. 'Well, no! I suppose not,' he said, and burst into a Homeric peal of laughter. 'Well, anyhow the guns were there, and went off all together at sunrise. Jove! You should have seen the splinters fly,' he cried. By his side Dain Waris, listening with a quiet smile, dropped his eyelids and shuffled his feet a little. It appears that the success in mounting the guns had given Jim's people such a feeling of confidence that he ventured to leave the battery under charge of two elderly Bugis who had seen some fighting in their day, and went to join Dain Waris and the storming-party who were concealed in the ravine. In the small hours they began creeping up, and when two-thirds of the way up, lay in the wet grass waiting for the appearance of the sun, which was the agreed signal. He told me with what impatient anguishing emotion he watched the swift coming of the dawn; how, heated with the work and the climbing, he felt the cold dew chilling his very bones; how afraid he was he would begin to shiver and shake like a leaf before the time came for the advance. 'It was the slowest half-hour in my life,' he declared. Gradually the silent stockade came out on the sky above him. Men scattered all down the slope were crouching amongst the dark stones and dripping bushes. Dain Waris was lying flattened by his side. 'We looked at each other,' Jim said, resting a gentle hand on his friend's shoulder. 'He smiled at me as cheery as you please, and I dared not stir my lips for fear I would break out into a shivering fit. 'Pon my word, it's true! I had been streaming with perspiration when we took cover—so you may imagine . . .' He declared, and I believe him, that he had no fears as to the result. He was only anxious as to his ability to repress these shivers. He didn't bother about the result. He was bound to get to the top of that hill and stay there, whatever might happen. There could be no going back for him. Those people had trusted him implicitly. Him alone! His bare word. . . .

"I remember how, at this point, he paused with his eyes fixed upon me. 'As far as he knew, they never had an occasion to regret it yet,' he said. 'Never. He hoped to God they never would. Meantime—worse luck!—they had got into the habit of taking his word for anything and everything. I could have no idea! Why? Only the other day an old fool he had never seen in his life came from some village miles away to find out if he should divorce his wife. Fact. Solemn word. That's the sort of thing . . . He wouldn't have believed it. Would I? Squatted on the veranda chewing betel nut, sighing and spitting all over the place for more than an hour, and as glum as an undertaker before he came out with that dashed conundrum. That's the kind of thing that isn't so funny as it looks. What was a fellow to say?—Good wife?—Yes. Good wife—old, though; started a confounded long story about some brass pots. Been living together for fifteen years—twenty years—could not tell. A long, long time. Good wife. Beat her a little—not much—just a little, when she was young. Had to—for the sake of his honor. Suddenly in her old age she goes and lends three brass pots to her sister's son's wife, and begins to abuse him every day in a loud voice. His enemies jeered at him; his face was utterly blackened. Pots totally lost. Awfully cut up about it. Impossible to fathom a story like that; told him to go home, and promised to come along myself and settle it all. It's all very well to grin, but it was the dashedest nuisance! A day's journey through the forest, another day lost in coaxing a lot of silly villagers to get at the rights of the affair. There was the making of a sanguinary shindy in the thing. Every bally idiot took sides with one family or the other, and one-half of the village was ready to go for the other half with anything that came handy. Honor bright! No joke! . . . Instead of attending to their bally crops. Got him the infernal pots back of course—and pacified all hands. No trouble to settle it. Of course not. Could settle the deadliest quarrel in the country by crooking his little finger. The trouble was to get at the truth of anything. Was not sure to this day whether he had been fair to all the parties. It worried him. And the talk! Jove! There didn't seem to be any head or tail to it. Rather storm a twenty-foot-high old stockade any day. Much! Child's play to that other job. Wouldn't take so long, either. Well, yes; a funny set out, upon the whole—the fool looked old enough to be his grandfather. But from another point of view it was no joke. His word decided everything—ever since the smashing of Sherif Ali. An awful responsibility,' he repeated. 'No, really—joking apart, had it been three lives instead of three rotten brass pots it would have been the same. . . .'

"Thus he illustrated the moral effect of his victory in war. It was in truth immense. It had led him from strife to peace, and through death into the inner-most life of the people; but the gloom of the land spread out under the sunshine preserved its appearance of inscrutable, of secular repose. The sound of his fresh young voice (it's extraordinary how very few signs of wear he showed) floated lightly, and passed away over the unchanged face of the forests like the sound of the big guns on that cold dewy morning when he had no other concern on earth but the proper control of the chills in his body. With the first slant of sunrays along these immovable treetops the summit of one hill wreathed itself, with heavy reports, in white clouds of smoke, and the other burst into an amazing noise of yells, war cries, shouts of anger, of surprise, of dismay. Jim and Dain Waris were the first to lay their hands on the stakes. The popular story has it that Jim with a touch of one finger had thrown down the gate. He was, of course, anxious to dis-claim this achievement. The whole stockade—he would insist on explaining to you—was a poor affair (Sherif Ali trusted mainly to the inaccessible position); and, anyway, the thing had been already knocked to pieces and only hung together by a miracle. He put his shoulder to it like a little fool and went in head over heels. Jove! If it hadn't been for Dain Waris, a pockmarked tattooed vagabond would have pinned him with his spear to a balk of timber like one of Stein's bee-tles. The third man in, it seems, had been Tamb' Itam, Jim's own servant. This was a Malay from the north, a stranger who had wandered into Patusan, and had been forcibly detained by Rajah Allang as paddler of one of the state boats. He had made a bolt of it at the first opportunity, and finding a precarious refuge (but very little to eat) amongst the Bugis settlers, had attached himself to Jim's person. His complexion was very dark, his face flat, his eyes prominent and injected with bile. There was something excessive, almost fanatical, in his devotion to his 'white lord.' He was inseparable from Jim, like a morose shadow. On state occasions he would tread on his master's heels, one hand on the haft of his kris, keeping com-mon people at a distance by his truculent brooding glances. Jim had made him the headman of his establishment, and all Patusan respected and courted him as a person of much influence. At the taking of the stockade he had distinguished himself greatly by the methodical ferocity of his fighting. The storming-party had come on so quick—Jim said—that notwithstanding the panic of the garrison, there was a hot "five minutes" hand-to-hand inside that stockade, till some bally ass set fire to the shelters of boughs and dry grass, and we all had to clear out for dear life.'

"The rout, it seems, had been complete. Doramin waiting immovably in his chair on the hillside, with the smoke of the guns spreading slowly above his big head, received the news with a deep grunt. When informed that his son was safe and leading the pursuit he, without another sound, made a mighty effort to rise; his attendants hurried to his help, and, held up reverently, he shuffled with great dignity into a bit of shade, where he laid himself down to sleep covered entirely with a piece of white sheeting. In Patusan the excitement was intense. Jim told me that from the hill, turning his back on the stockade with its embers, black ashes, and half-consumed corpses, he could see time after time the open spaces between the houses on both sides of the stream fill suddenly with a seething rush of people and get empty in a moment. His ears caught feebly from below the tremendous din of gongs and drums; the wild shouts of the crowd reached him in bursts of faint roaring. A lot of streamers made a flutter as of little white, red, yellow birds amongst the brown ridges of roofs. 'You must have enjoyed it,' I murmured, feeling the stir of sympathetic emotion.

"'It was . . . it was immense! Immense!' he cried aloud, flinging his arms open. The sudden movement startled me as though I had seen him bare the secrets of his breast to the sunshine, to the brooding forests, to the steely sea. Below us the town reposed in easy curves upon the banks of a stream whose current seemed to sleep. 'Immense!' he repeated for a third time, speaking in a whisper, for himself alone.

"Immense! No doubt it was immense; the seal of success upon his words, the conquered ground for the soles of his feet, the blind trust of men, the belief in himself snatched from the fire, the solitude of his achievement. All this, as I've warned you, gets dwarfed in the telling. I can't with mere words convey to you the impression of his total and utter isolation. I know, of course, he was in every sense alone of his kind there, but the unsuspected qualities of his nature had brought him in such close touch with his surroundings that this isolation seemed only the effect of his power. His loneliness added to his stature. There was nothing within sight to compare him with, as though he had been one of these exceptional men who can be only measured by the greatness of their fame; and his fame, remember, was the greatest thing around for many a day's journey. You would have to paddle, pole, or track a long weary way through the jungle before you passed beyond the reach of its voice. Its voice was not the trumpeting of the disreputable goddess we all know—not blatant—not brazen. It took its tone from the stillness and gloom of the land without a past, where his word was the one truth of every passing day. It shared something of the nature of that silence through which it accompanied you into unexplored depths, heard continuously by your side, penetrating, far-reaching—tinged with wonder and mystery on the lips of whispering men."

❧ 28 ❧

The defeated Sherif Ali fled the country without making another stand, and when the miserable hunted villagers began to crawl out of the jungle back to their rotting houses, it was Jim who, in consultation with Dain Waris, appointed the headmen. Thus he became the virtual ruler of the land. As to old Tunku Allang, his fears at first had known no bounds. It is said that at the intelligence of the successful storming of the hill he flung himself, face down, on the bamboo floor of his audience-hall, and lay motionless for a whole night and a whole day, uttering stifled sounds of such an appalling nature that no man dared approach his prostrate form nearer than a spear's length. Already he could see himself driven ignominiously out of Patusan, wandering, abandoned, stripped, without opium, without his women, without followers, a fair game for the first comer to kill. After Sherif Ali his turn would come, and who could resist an attack led by such a devil? And indeed he owed his life, and such authority as he still possessed at the time of my visit, to Jim's idea of what was fair alone. The Bugis had been extremely anxious to pay off old scores, and the impassive old Doramin cherished the hope of yet seeing his son ruler of Patusan. During one of our interviews he deliberately allowed me to get a glimpse of this secret ambition. Nothing could be finer in its way than the dignified wariness of his approaches. He himself—he began by declaring—had used his strength in his young days, but now he had grown old and tired. . . . With his imposing bulk and haughty little eyes darting sagacious, inquisitive glances, he reminded one irresistibly of a cunning old elephant; the slow rise and fall of his vast breast went on powerful and regular, like the heave of a calm sea. He, too, as he protested, had an unbounded confidence in Tuan Jim's wisdom. If he could only obtain a promise! One word would be enough! . . . His breathing silences, the low rumblings of his voice, recalled the last efforts of a spent thunderstorm.

"I tried to put the subject aside. It was difficult, for there could be no question that Jim had the power; in his new sphere there did not seem to be anything that was not his to hold or to give. But that, I repeat, was nothing in comparison with the notion which occurred to me, while I listened with a show of attention, that he seemed to have come very near at last to mastering his fate. Doramin was anxious about the future of the country, and I was struck by the turn he gave to the argument. The land remains where God had put it, but white men—he said—they come to us and in a little while they go. They go away. Those they leave behind do not know when to look for their return. They go to their own land, to their people, and so this white man, too, would. . . . I don't know what induced me to commit myself at this point by a vigorous 'No, no.' The whole extent of this indiscretion became apparent when Doramin, turning full upon me his face, whose expression, fixed in rugged deep folds, remained unalterable, like a huge brown mask, said that this was good news indeed, reflectively; and then wanted to know why.

"His little, motherly witch of a wife sat on my other hand with her head covered and her feet tucked up, gazing through the great shutter-hole. I could only see a straying lock of gray hair, a high cheekbone, the slight masticating motion of the sharp chin. Without removing her eyes from the vast prospect of forests stretching as far as the hills, she asked me in a pitying voice why was it that he so young had wandered from his home, coming so far, through so many dangers? Had he no household there, no kinsmen in his own country? Had he no old mother, who would always remember his face? . . .

"I was completely unprepared for this. I could only mutter and shake my head vaguely. Afterwards I am perfectly aware I cut a very poor figure trying to extricate myself out of this difficulty. From that moment, however, the old *nakhoda* became taciturn. He was not very pleased, I fear, and evidently I had given him food for thought. Strangely enough, on the evening of that very day (which was my last in Patusan) I was once more confronted with the same question, with the unanswerable why of Jim's fate. And this brings me to the story of his love.

"I suppose you think it is a story that you can imagine for yourselves. We have heard so many such stories, and the majority of us don't believe them to be stories of love at all. For the most part we look upon them as stories of opportunities: episodes of passion at best, or perhaps only of youth and temptation, doomed to forgetfulness in the end, even if they pass through the reality of tenderness and regret. This view mostly is right, and perhaps in this case too. . . . Yet I don't know. To tell this story is by no means so easy as it should be—were the ordinary standpoint adequate. Apparently, it is a story very much like the others: for me, however, there is visible in its background the melancholy figure of a woman, the shadow of a cruel wisdom buried in a lonely grave, looking on wistfully, helplessly, with sealed lips. The grave itself, as I came upon it during an early morning stroll, was a rather shapeless brown mound, with an inlaid neat border of white lumps, of coral at the base, and enclosed within a circular fence made of split saplings, with the bark left on. A garland of leaves and flowers was woven about the heads of the slender posts—and the flowers were fresh.

"Thus, whether the shadow is of my imagination or not, I can at all events point out the significant fact of an unforgotten grave. When I tell you besides that Jim with his own hands had worked at the rustic fence, you will perceive directly the difference, the individual side of the story. There is in his espousal of memory and affection belonging to another human being something characteristic of his seriousness. He had a conscience, and it was a romantic conscience. Through her whole life the wife of the unspeakable Cornelius had no other companion, confidant, and friend but her daughter. How the poor woman had come to marry the awful little Malacca Portuguese—after the separation from the father of her girl—and how that separation had been brought about, whether by death, which can be sometimes merciful, or by the merciless pressure of conventions, is a mystery to me. From the little which Stein (who knew so many stories) had let drop in my hearing, I am convinced that she was no ordinary woman. Her own father had been a white; a high official; one of the brilliantly endowed men who are not dull enough to nurse a success, and whose careers so often end under a cloud. I suppose she too must have lacked the saving dullness—and her career ended in Patusan. Our common fate . . . for where is the man—I mean a real sentient man—who does not remember vaguely having been deserted in the fullness of possession by someone or something more precious than life? . . . our common fate fastens upon the women with a peculiar cruelty. It does not punish like a master, but inflicts lingering torment, as if to gratify a secret, unappeasable spite. One would think that, appointed to rule on earth, it seeks to revenge itself upon the beings that come nearest to rising above the trammels of earthly caution; for it is only women who manage to put at times into their love an element just palpable enough to give one a fright—an extraterrestrial touch. I ask myself with wonder—how the world can look to them—whether it has the shape and substance *we* know, the air *we* breathe! Sometimes I fancy it must be a region of unreasonable sublimities seething with the excitement of their adventurous souls, lighted by the glory of all possible risks and renunciations. However, I suspect there are very few women in the world, though of course I am aware of the multitudes of mankind and of the equality of sexes in point of numbers—that is. But I am sure that the mother was as much of a woman as the daughter seemed to be. I cannot help picturing to myself these two, at first the young woman and the child, then the old woman and the young girl, the awful sameness and the swift passage of time, the barrier of forest, the solitude and the turmoil round these two lonely lives, and every word spoken between them penetrated with sad meaning. There must have been confidences, not so much of fact, I suppose, as of innermost feeling—regrets—fears—warnings, no doubt: warnings that the younger did not fully

understand till the elder was dead—and Jim came along. Then I am sure she
understood much—not everything—the fear mostly, it seems. Jim called her by a
word that means precious, in the sense of a precious gem—jewel. Pretty, isn't it?
But he was capable of anything. He was equal to his fortune, as he—after all—
must have been equal to his misfortune. Jewel he called her; and he would say
this as he might have said 'Jane,' don't you know with a marital, homelike, peaceful effect. I heard the name for the first time ten minutes after I had landed in his
courtyard, when, after nearly shaking my arm off, he darted up the steps and
began to make a joyous, boyish disturbance at the door under the heavy eaves.
'Jewel! O! Jewel. Quick! Here's a friend come,'. . . and suddenly peering at me in
the dim veranda, he mumbled earnestly, 'You know—this—no confounded nonsense about it—can't tell you how much I owe to her—and so—you understand—I—exactly as if . . .' His hurried, anxious whispers were cut short by the
flitting of a white form within the house, a faint exclamation, and a childlike but
energetic little face with delicate features and a profound attentive glance peeped
out of the inner gloom, like a bird out of the recess of a nest. I was struck by the
name, of course; but it was not till later on that I connected it with an astonishing
rumor that had met me on my journey, at a little place on the coast about 230
miles south of Patusan river. Stein's schooner, in which I had my passage, put in
there, to collect some produce, and going ashore, I found to my great surprise that
the wretched locality could boast of a third-class deputy-assistant resident, a big,
fat, greasy, blinking fellow of mixed descent, with turned-out, shiny lips. I found
him lying extended on his back in a cane chair, odiously unbuttoned, with a large
green leaf of some sort on the top of his steaming head, and another in his hand
which he used lazily as a fan. . . . Going to Patusan? Oh, yes. Stein's Trading
Company. He knew. Had a permission. No business of his. It was not so bad there
now, he remarked negligently, and he went on drawling, 'there's some sort of
white vagabond had got in there, I hear. . . . Eh? What you say? Friend of yours?
So! . . . Then it was true there was one of these *vordamte*—What was he up to?
Found his way in, the rascal. Eh? I had not been sure. Patusan—they cut throats
there—no business of ours.' He interrupted himself to groan. 'Phoo! Almighty! The
heat! The heat! Well, then, there might be something in the story, too, after all,
and . . .' He shut one of his beastly glassy eyes (the eyelid went on quivering),
while he leered at me atrociously with the other. 'Look here,' says he mysteriously,
'if—do you understand?—if he has really got hold of something fairly good—none
of your bits of green glass—understand?—I am a government official—you tell
the rascal . . . Eh? What? Friend of yours?'. . . He continued wallowing calmly in
the chair . . . 'You said so; that's just it; and I am pleased to give you the hint. I
suppose you too would like to get something out of it? Don't interrupt. You just tell
him I've heard the tale, but to my government I have made no report. Not yet.

See? Why, make a report? Eh? Tell him to come to me if they let him get alive out of the country. He had better look out for himself. Eh? I promise to ask no questions. On the quiet—you understand? You too—you shall get something from me. Small commission for the trouble. Don't interrupt. I am a government official, and make no report. That's business. Understand? I know some good people that will buy anything worth having, and can give him more money than the scoundrel ever saw in his life. I know his sort.' He fixed me steadfastly with both his eyes open, while I stood over him utterly amazed, and asking myself whether he was mad or drunk. He perspired, puffed, moaning feebly, and scratching himself with such horrible composure that I could not bear the sight long enough to find out. Next day, talking casually with the people of the little native court of the place, I discovered that a story was traveling slowly down the coast about a mysterious white man in Patusan who had got hold of an extraordinary gem—namely, an emerald of an enormous size, and altogether priceless. The emerald seems to appeal more to the Eastern imagination than any other precious stone. The white man had obtained it, I was told, partly by the exercise of his wonderful strength and partly by cunning, from the ruler of a distant country, whence he had fled instantly, arriving in Patusan in utmost distress, but frightening the people by his extreme ferocity, which nothing seemed able to subdue. Most of my informants were of the opinion that the stone was probably unlucky—like the famous stone of the Sultan of Succadana, which in the old times had brought wars and untold calamities upon that country. Perhaps it was the same stone—one couldn't say. Indeed the story of a fabulously large emerald is as old as the arrival of the first white men in the Archipelago; and the belief in it is so persistent that less than forty years ago there had been an official Dutch inquiry into the truth of it. Such a jewel—it was explained to me by the old fellow from whom I heard most of this amazing Jim-myth—a sort of scribe to the wretched little Rajah of the place—such a jewel, he said, cocking his poor purblind eyes up at me (he was sitting on the cabin floor out of respect), is best preserved by being concealed about the person of a woman. Yet it is not every woman that would do. She must be young—he sighed deeply—and insensible to the seductions of love. He shook his head skeptically. But such a woman seemed to be actually in existence. He had been told of a tall girl, whom the white man treated with great respect and care, and who never went forth from the house unattended. People said the white man could be seen with her almost any day; they walked side by side, openly, he holding her arm under his—pressed to his side—thus—in a most extraordinary way. This might be a lie, he conceded, for it was indeed a strange thing for anyone to do: on the other hand, there could be no doubt she wore the white man's jewel concealed upon her bosom."

❧ 29 ❧

This was the theory of Jim's marital evening walks. I made a third on more than one occasion, unpleasantly aware every time of Cornelius, who nursed the aggrieved sense of his legal paternity, slinking in the neighborhood with that peculiar twist of his mouth as if he were perpetually on the point of gnashing his teeth. But do you notice how, three hundred miles beyond the end of telegraph cables and mailboat lines, the haggard utilitarian lies of our civilization wither and die, to be replaced by pure exercises of imagination, that have the futility, often the charm, and sometimes the deep hidden truthfulness, of works of art? Romance had singled Jim for its own—and that was the true part of the story, which otherwise was all wrong. He did not hide his jewel. In fact, he was extremely proud of it.

"It comes to me now that I had, on the whole, seen very little of her. What I remember best is the even, olive pallor of her complexion, and the intense blue-black gleams of her hair, flowing abundantly from under a small crimson cap she wore far back on her shapely head. Her movements were free, assured, and she blushed a dusky red. While Jim and I were talking, she would come and go with rapid glances at us, leaving on her passage an impression of grace and charm and a distinct suggestion of watchfulness. Her manner presented a curious combination of shyness and audacity. Every pretty smile was succeeded swiftly by a look of silent, repressed anxiety, as if put to flight by the recollection of some abiding danger. At times she would sit down with us and, with her soft cheek dimpled by the knuckles of her little hand, she would listen to our talk; her big clear eyes would remain fastened on our lips, as though each pronounced word had a visible shape. Her mother had taught her to read and write; she had learned a good bit of English from Jim, and she spoke it most amusingly, with his own clipping, boyish intonation. Her tenderness hovered over him like a flutter of wings. She lived so completely in his contemplation that she had acquired something of his outward aspect, something that recalled him in her movements, in the way she stretched her arm, turned her head, directed her glanced. Her vigilant affection had an intensity that made it almost perceptible to the senses; it seemed actually to exist in the ambient matter of space, to envelop him like a peculiar fragrance, to dwell in the sunshine like a tremulous, subdued, and impassioned note. I suppose you think that I too am romantic, but it is a mistake. I am relating to you the sober impressions of a bit of youth, of a strange uneasy romance that had come in my way. I observed with interest the work of his—well—good fortune. He was jealously loved, but why she should be jealous, and of what, I could not tell. The land, the people, the forests were her accomplices, guarding him with vigilant accord, with an air of seclusion, of mystery, of invincible possession. There was no appeal, as it were; he was imprisoned within the very freedom of his power, and she, though ready to make a footstool of her head for his feet, guarded her conquest inflexibly—as though he were hard to keep. The very Tamb' Itam, marching on our journeys upon the heels of his white lord, with his head thrown back, truculent and be-weaponed like a janissary, with kris, chopper, and lance (besides carrying Jim's gun); even Tamb' Itam allowed himself to put on the airs of uncompromising guardianship, like a surly, devoted jailer ready to lay down his life for his captive. On the evenings when we sat up late his silent, indistinct form would pass and repass under the veranda, with noiseless footsteps, or lifting my head I would unexpectedly make him out standing rigidly erect in the shadow. As a general rule he would vanish after a time, without a sound; but when we rose he would spring up close to us as if from the ground, ready for any orders Jim might wish to give. The girl, too, I believe, never went to sleep till we had separated for the night. More than once I saw her and Jim through the window of my room come out together quietly and lean on the rough balustrade—two white forms very close, his arm about her waist, her head on his shoulder. Their soft murmurs reached me, penetrating, tender, with a calm, sad note in the stillness of the night, like a self-communion of one being carried on in two tones. Later on, tossing on my bed under the mosquito net, I was sure to hear slight creakings, faint breathing, a throat cleared cautiously—and I would know that Tamb' Itam was still on the prowl. Though he had (by the favor of the white lord) a house in the compound, had 'taken wife,' and had lately been blessed with a child, I believe that, during my stay at all events, he slept on the veranda every night. It was very difficult to make this faithful and grim retainer talk. Even Jim himself was answered in jerky short sentences, under protest, as it were. Talking, he seemed to imply, was no business of his. The longest speech I heard him volunteer was one morning when, suddenly extending his hand towards the courtyard, he pointed at Cornelius, and said, 'Here comes the Nazarene.' I don't think he was addressing me, though I stood at his side; his object seemed rather to awaken the indignant attention of the universe. Some muttered allusions which followed, to dogs and the smell of roast meat, struck me as singularly felicitous. The courtyard, a large square space, was one torrid blaze of sunshine, and, bathed in intense light, Cornelius was creeping across in full view with an inexpressible effect of stealthiness, of dark and secret slinking. He reminded one of everything that is unsavory. His slow, laborious walk resembled the creeping of a repulsive beetle, the legs alone moving with horrid industry while the body glided evenly. I suppose he made straight enough for the place where he wanted to get to, but his progress with one shoulder carried forward seemed oblique. He was often seen circling slowly amongst the sheds as if following a scent; passing before the veranda with upward stealthy glances; disappearing without haste round the corner of some hut. That he seemed free of the place demonstrated Jim's absurd carelessness or else his infinite disdain, for Cornelius had played a very dubious part (to say the least of it) in a certain episode which might have ended fatally for Jim. As a matter of fact, it had redounded to his glory. But everything redounded to his glory; and it was the irony of his good fortune that he, who had been too careful of it once, seemed to bear a charmed life.

"You must know he had left Doramin's place very soon after his arrival—much too soon, in fact, for his safety, and of course a long time before the war. In this he was actuated by a sense of duty; he had to look after Stein's business, he said. Hadn't he? To that end, with an utter disregard of his personal safety, he crossed the river and took up his quarters with Cornelius. How the latter had managed to exist through the troubled times I can't say. As Stein's agent, after all, he must have had Doramin's protection in a measure; and in one way or another he had managed to wriggle through all the deadly complications, while I have no doubt that his conduct, whatever line he was forced to take, was marked by that abjectness which was like the stamp of the man. That was his characteristic; he was fundamentally and outwardly abject, as other men are markedly of a generous, distinguished, or venerable appearance. It was the element of his nature which permeated all his acts and passions and emotions; he raged abjectly, smiled abjectly, was abjectly sad; his civilities and his indignations were alike abject. I am sure his love would have been the most abject of his sentiments, but can one imagine a loathsome insect in love. And his loathsomeness too was abject, so that a simply disgusting person would have appeared noble by his side. He has his place neither in the background nor in the foreground of the story; he is simply seen skulking on its outskirts, enigmatical and unclean, tainting the fragrance of its youth and of its naiveness.

"His position, in any case, could not have been other than extremely miserable, yet it may very well be that he found some advantages in it. Jim told me he had been received at first with an abject display of the most amicable sentiments. 'The fellow apparently couldn't contain himself for joy,' said Jim with disgust. 'He flew at me every morning to shake both my hands—confound him! but I could never tell whether there would be any breakfast. If I got three meals in two days I considered myself jolly lucky, and he made me sign a chit for ten dollars every week. Said he was sure Mr. Stein did not mean him to keep me for nothing. Well—he

kept me on nothing as near as possible. Put it down to the unsettled state of the
country, and made as if to tear his hair out, begging my pardon twenty times a day,
so that I had at last to entreat him not to worry. It made me sick. Half the roof of
his house had fallen in, and the whole place had a mangy look, with wisps of dry
grass sticking out and the corners of broken mats flapping on every wall. He did
his best to make out that Mr. Stein owed him money on the last three years' trading, but his books were all torn, and some were missing. He tried to hint it was his
late wife's fault. Disgusting scoundrel! At last I had to forbid him to mention his
late wife at all. It made Jewel cry. I couldn't discover what had become of all the
trade-goods; there was nothing in the store but rats, having a high old time
amongst a litter of brown paper and old sacking. I was assured on every hand that
he had a lot of money buried somewhere, but of course could get nothing out of
him. It was the most miserable existence I led there in that wretched house. I
tried to do my duty by Stein, but I had also other matters to think of. When I
escaped to Doramin old Tunku Allang got frightened and returned all my things. It
was done in a roundabout way, and with no end of mystery, through a Chinaman
who keeps a small shop here; but as soon as I left the Bugis quarter and went to
live with Cornelius it began to be said openly that the Rajah had made up his
mind to have me killed before long. Pleasant, wasn't it? And I couldn't see what
was there to prevent him if he really *had* made up his mind. The worst of it was I
couldn't help feeling I wasn't doing any good either for Stein or for myself. Oh! it
was beastly—the whole six weeks of it.'"

❧ 30 ❧

He told me further that he didn't know what made him hang on—but of
course we may guess. He sympathized deeply with the defenseless girl,
at the mercy of that 'mean, cowardly scoundrel.' It appears Cornelius
led her an awful life, stopping only short of actual ill-usage, for which he had not
the pluck, I suppose. He insisted upon her calling him father—'and with respect
too—with respect,' he would scream, shaking a little yellow fist in her face. 'I am
a respectable man, and what are you? Tell me—what are you? You think I am
going to bring up somebody else's child and not be treated with respect? You
ought to be glad I let you. Come—say Yes, father. . . . No? . . . You wait a bit.'
Thereupon he would begin to abuse the dead woman, till the girl would run off
with her hands to her head. He pursued her, dashing in and out 'and round the

house and amongst the sheds, would drive her into some corner, where she would fall on her knees stopping her ears, and then he would stand at a distance and declaim filthy denunciations at her back for half an hour at a stretch. 'Your mother was a devil, a deceitful devil—and you too are a devil,' he would shriek in a final outburst, pick up a bit of dry earth or a handful of mud, (there was plenty of mud around the house), and fling it into her hair. Sometimes, though, she would hold out full of scorn, confronting him in silence, her face somber and contracted, and only now and then uttering a word or two that would make the other jump and writhe with the sting. Jim told me these scenes were terrible. It was indeed a strange thing to come upon in a wilderness. The endlessness of such a subtly cruel situation was appalling—if you think of it. The respectable Cornelius (Inchi 'Nelyus, the Malays called him, with a grimace that meant many things) was a much-disappointed man. I don't know what he had expected would be done for him in consideration of his marriage; but evidently the liberty to steal, and embezzle, and appropriate to himself for many years and in any way that suited him best, the goods of Stein's Trading Company (Stein kept the supply up unfalteringly as long as he could get his skippers to take it there) did not seem to him a fair equivalent for the sacrifice of his honorable name. Jim would have enjoyed exceedingly thrashing Cornelius within an inch of his life; on the other hand, the scenes were of so painful a character, so abominable, that his impulse would be to get out of earshot, in order to spare the girl's feelings. They left her agitated, speechless, clutching her bosom now and then with a stony, desperate face, and then Jim would lounge up and say unhappily, 'Now—come—really—what's the use—you must try to eat a bit,' or give some such mark of sympathy. Cornelius would keep on slinking through the doorways, across the veranda and back again, as mute as a fish, and with malevolent, mistrustful, underhand glances. 'I can stop his game,' Jim said to her once. 'Just say the word.' And do you know what she answered? She said—Jim told me impressively—that if she had not been sure he was intensely wretched himself, she would have found the courage to kill him with her own hands. 'Just. fancy that! The poor devil of a girl, almost a child, being driven to talk like that,' he exclaimed in horror. It seemed impossible to save her, not only from that mean rascal, but even from herself! It wasn't that he pitied her so much, he affirmed; it was more than pity; it was as if he had something on his conscience while that life went on. To leave the house would have appeared a base desertion. He had understood at last that there was nothing to expect from a longer stay, neither accounts nor money, nor truth of any sort, but he stayed on, exasperating Cornelius to the verge, I won't say of insanity, but almost of courage. Meantime, he felt all sorts of dangers gathering obscurely about him. Doramin had sent over twice a trusty servant to tell him seriously that he could do nothing for his safety unless he would recross the river again and live amongst the Bugis, as at first. People of every condition used to call, often in the dead of night, in order to disclose to him plots for his assassination. He was to be poisoned. He was to be stabbed in the bathhouse. Arrangements were being made to have him shot from a boat on the river. Each of these informants professed himself to be his very good friend. It was enough—he told me—to spoil a fellow's rest forever. Something of the kind was extremely possible—nay, probable—but the lying warnings gave him only the sense of deadly scheming going on all around him, on all sides, in the dark. Nothing more calculated to shake the best of nerve. Finally, one night, Cornelius himself, with a great apparatus of alarm and secrecy, unfolded in solemn wheedling tones a little plan wherein, for one hundred dollars—or even for eighty; let's say eighty—he, Cornelius, would procure a trustworthy man to smuggle Jim out of the river, all safe. There was nothing else for it now—if Jim cared a pin for his life. What's eighty dollars? A trifle. An insignificant sum. While he, Cornelius, who had to remain behind, was absolutely courting death by this proof of devotion to Mr. Stein's young friend. The sight of his abject grimacing was—Jim told me—very hard to bear: he clutched at his hair, beat his breast, rocked himself to and fro with his hands pressed to his stomach, and actually pretended to shed tears. 'Your blood be on your own head,' he squeaked at last, and rushed out. It is a curious question how far Cornelius was sincere in that performance. Jim confessed to me that he did not sleep a wink after the fellow had gone. He lay on his back on a thin mat spread over the bamboo flooring, trying idly to make out the bare rafters, and listening to the rustlings in the torn thatch. A star suddenly twinkled through a hole in the roof. His brain was in a whirl; but nevertheless, it was on that very night that he matured his plan for overcoming Sherif Ali. It had been the thought of all the moments he could spare from the hopeless investigation into Stein's affairs, but the notion—he says—came to him then all at once. He could see, as it were, the guns mounted on the top of the hill. He got very hot and excited lying there; sleep was out of the question more than ever. He jumped up, and went out barefooted on the veranda. Walking silently, he came upon the girl, motionless against the wall, as if on the watch. In his then state of mind it did not surprise him to see her up, nor yet to hear her ask in an anxious whisper where Cornelius could be. He simply said he did not know. She moaned a little, and peered into the *campong*. Everything was very quiet. He was possessed by his new idea, and so full of it that he could not help telling the girl all about it at once. She listened, clapped her hands lightly, whispered softly her admiration, but was evidently on the alert all the time. It seems he had been used to make a confidant of her all along—and that she, on her part, could and did give him a lot of useful hints as to Patusan affairs there is no doubt. He assured me more than once that he had never found himself the worse for her advice. At any rate, he was proceeding to explain his plan fully to her there and then, when she pressed his arm once, and vanished from his side. Then Cornelius appeared from somewhere, and perceiving Jim, ducked sideways, as though he had been shot at, and afterwards stood very still in the dusk. At last he came forward prudently, like a suspicious cat. 'There were some fishermen there—with fish,' he said in a shaky voice. 'To sell fish—you understand.'. . . It must have been then two o'clock in the morning—a likely time for anybody to hawk fish about!

"Jim, however, let the statement pass, and did not give it a single thought. Other matters occupied his mind, and besides, he had neither seen nor heard anything. He contented himself by saying, 'Oh!' absently, got a drink of water out of a pitcher standing there, and leaving Cornelius a prey to some inexplicable emotion—that made him embrace with both arms the worm-eaten rail of the veranda as if his legs had failed—went in again and lay down on his mat to think. By and by he heard stealthy footsteps. They stopped. A voice whispered tremulously through the wall, 'Are you asleep?' 'No! What is it?' he answered briskly, and there was an abrupt movement outside, and then all was still, as if the whisperer had been startled. Extremely annoyed at this, Jim came out impetuously, and Cornelius, with a faint shriek, fled along the veranda as far as the steps, where he hung on to the broken banister. Very puzzled, Jim called out to him from the distance to know what the devil he meant. 'Have you given your consideration to what I spoke to you about?' asked Cornelius, pronouncing the words with difficulty, like a man in the cold fit of a fever. 'No!' shouted Jim in a passion. 'I did not, and I don't intend to. I am going to live here, in Patusan.' 'You shall d-d-die h-h-here,' answered Cornelius, still shaking violently, and in a sort of expiring voice. The whole performance was so absurd and provoking that Jim didn't know whether he ought to be amused or angry. 'Not till I had seen you tucked away, you bet,' he called out, exasperated, yet ready to laugh. Half seriously (being excited with his own thoughts, you know) he went on shouting, 'Nothing can touch me! You can do your damnedest.' Somehow, the shadowy Cornelius far off there seemed to be the hateful embodiment of all the annoyances and difficulties he had found in his path. He let himself go—his nerves had been overwrought for days and called him many pretty names—swindler, liar, sorry rascal: in fact, carried on in an extraordinary way. He admits he passed all bounds, that he was quite beside himself—defied all Patusan to scare him away—declared he would make them all dance to his own tune yet, and so on, in a menacing, boasting strain. Perfectly bombastic and ridiculous, he said. His ears burned at the bare recollection. Must have been off his chump in some way. . . . The girl, who was sitting with us, nodded her little head at me quickly, frowned faintly, and said, 'I heard him,' with childlike solemnity. He laughed and blushed. What stopped him at last, he said, was the silence, the complete deathlike silence, of the indistinct figure far over there, that seemed to hang collapsed, doubled over the rail in a weird immobility. He came to his senses, and ceasing suddenly, wondered greatly at himself. He watched for a while. Not a stir, not a sound. 'Exactly as if the chap had died while I had been making all that noise,' he said. He was so ashamed of himself that he went indoors in a hurry without another word, and flung himself down again. The row seemed to have done him good, though, because he went to sleep for the rest of the night like a baby. Hadn't slept like that for weeks. 'But *I* didn't sleep,' struck in the girl, one elbow on the table and nursing her cheek. 'I watched.' Her big eyes flashed, rolling a little, and then she fixed them on my face intently."

❖ 31 ❖

Y ou may imagine with what interest I listened. All these details were perceived to have some significance twenty-four hours later. In the morning Cornelius made no allusion to the events of the night. 'I suppose you will come back to my poor house,' he muttered surlily, slinking up just as Jim was entering the canoe to go over to Doramin's *campong*. Jim only nodded, without looking at him. 'You find it good fun, no doubt,' muttered the other in a sour tone. Jim spent the day with the old *nakhoda*, preaching the necessity of vigorous action to the principal men of the Bugis community, who had been summoned for a big talk. He remembered with pleasure how very eloquent and persuasive he had been. 'I managed to put some backbone into them that time, and no mistake,' he said. Sherif Ali's last raid had swept the outskirts of the settlement, and some women belonging to the town had been carried off to the stockade. Sherif Ali's emissaries had been seen in the marketplace the day before, strutting about haughtily in white cloaks, and boasting of the Rajah's friendship for their master. One of them stood forward in the shade of a tree, and, leaning on the long barrel of a rifle, exhorted the people to prayer and repentance, advising them to kill all the strangers in their midst, some of whom, he said, were infidels and others even worse—children of Satan in the guise of Moslems. It was reported that several of the Rajah's people amongst the listeners had loudly expressed their approbation. The terror amongst the common people was intense. Jim, immensely pleased with his day's work, crossed the river again before sunset.

"As he had got the Bugis irretrievably committed to action, and had made himself responsible for success on his own head, he was so elated that in the lightness of his heart he absolutely tried to be civil with Cornelius. But Cornelius became wildly jovial in response, and it was almost more than he could stand, he says, to hear his little squeaks of false laughter, to see him wriggle and blink, and suddenly catch hold of his chin and crouch low over the table with a distracted stare. The girl did not show herself, and Jim retired early. When he rose to say goodnight, Cornelius jumped up, knocking his chair over, and ducked out of sight as if to pick up something he had dropped. His goodnight came huskily from under the table. Jim was amazed to see him emerge out with a dropping jaw, and staring, stupidly frightened eyes. He clutched the edge of the table. 'What's the matter? Are you unwell?' asked Jim. 'Yes, yes, yes. A great colic in my stomach,' says the other; and it is Jim's opinion that it was perfectly true. If so, it was, in view of his contemplated action, an abject sign of a still imperfect callousness for which he must be given all due credit.

"Be it as it may, Jim's slumbers were disturbed by a dream of heavens like brass resounding with a great voice, which called upon him to Awake! Awake! so loud that, notwithstanding his desperate determination to sleep on, he did wake up in reality. The glare of a red spluttering conflagration going on in midair fell on his eyes. Coils of black thick smoke curved round the head of some apparition, some unearthly being, all in white, with a severe, drawn, anxious face. After a second or so he recognized the girl. She was holding a dammar torch at arm's length aloft, and in a persistent, urgent monotone she was repeating, 'Get up! Get up! Get up!'

"Suddenly he leaped to his feet; at once she put into his hand a revolver, his own revolver, which had been hanging on a nail, but loaded this time. He gripped it in silence, bewildered, blinking in the light. He wondered what he could do for her.

"She asked rapidly and very low, 'Can you face four men with this?' He laughed while narrating this part at the recollection of his polite alacrity. It seems he made a great display of it. 'Certainly—of course—certainly—command me.' He was not properly awake, and had a notion of being very civil in these extraordinary circumstances, of showing his unquestioning, devoted readiness. She left the room, and he followed her; in the passage they disturbed an old hag who did the casual cooking of the household, though she was so decrepit as to be hardly able to understand human speech. She got up and hobbled behind them, mumbling toothlessly. On the veranda a hammock of sailcloth, belonging to Cornelius, swayed lightly to the touch of Jim's elbow. It was empty.

"The Patusan establishment, like all the posts of Stein's Trading Company, had originally consisted of four buildings. Two of them were represented by two heaps of sticks, broken bamboos, rotten thatch, over which the four corner-posts of hardwood leaned sadly at different angles: the principal storeroom, however, stood yet, facing the agent's house. It was an oblong hut, built of mud and clay: it had at one end a wide door of stout planking, which so far had not come off the hinges, and in one of the side walls there was a square aperture, a sort of window, with three wooden bars. Before descending the few steps the girl turned her face over her shoulder and said quickly, 'You were to be set upon while you slept.' Jim tells me he experienced a sense of deception. It was the old story. He was weary of these attempts upon his life. He had had his fill of these alarms. He was sick of them. He assured me he was angry with the girl for deceiving him. He had followed her under the impression that it was she who wanted his help, and now he had half a mind to turn on his heel and go back in disgust. 'Do you how,' he commented profoundly, 'I rather think I was not quite myself for whole weeks on end about that time?' 'Oh, yes. You were, though,' I couldn't help contradicting.

"But she moved on swiftly, and he followed her into the courtyard. All its fences had fallen in a long time ago; the neighbors' buffaloes would pace in the morning across the open space, snorting profoundly, without haste; the very jungle was invading it already. Jim and the girl stopped in the rank grass. The light in which they stood made a dense blackness all round, and only above their heads there was an opulent glitter of stars. He told me it was a beautiful night— quite cool, with a little stir of breeze from the river. It seems he noticed its friendly beauty. Remember this is a love story I am telling you now. A lovely night that seemed to breathe on them a soft caress. The flame of the torch streamed now and then with a fluttering noise like a flag, and for a time this was the only sound. 'They are in the storeroom waiting,' whispered the girl; 'they are waiting for the signal.' 'Who's to give it?' he asked. She shook the torch, which blazed up after a shower of sparks. 'Only you have been sleeping so restlessly,' she continued in a murmur. 'I watched your sleep too.' 'You!' he exclaimed, craning his neck to look about him. 'You think I watched on this night only!' she said, with a sort of despairing indignation.

"He says it was as if he had received a blow on the chest. He gasped. He thought he had been an awful brute somehow, and he felt remorseful, touched, happy, elated. This, let me remind you again, is a love story; you can see it by the imbecility, not a repulsive imbecility, the exalted imbecility of these proceedings, this station in torchlight, as if they had come there on purpose to have it out for the edification of concealed murderers. If Sherif Ali's emissaries had been possessed—as Jim remarked—of a pennyworth of spunk, this was the time to make a rush. His heart was thumping—not with fear—but he seemed to hear the grass rustle, and he stepped smartly out of the light. Something dark, imperfectly seen, flitted rapidly out of sight. He called out in a strong voice, 'Cornelius! O Cornelius!' A profound silence succeeded: his voice did not seem to have carried twenty feet. Again the girl was by his side. 'Fly!' she said. The old woman was coming up; her broken figure hovered in crippled little jumps on the edge of the light; they heard her mumbling, and a light, moaning sigh. 'Fly!' repeated the girl excitedly. 'They are frightened now—this light—the voices. They know you are awake now—they know you are big, strong, fearless . . .' 'If I am all that,' he began, but she inter-rupted him. 'Yes—tonight! But what of tomorrow night? Of the next night? Of the night after—of all the many, many nights? Can I be always watching?' A sobbing catch of her breath affected him beyond the power of words.

"He told me that he had never felt so small, so powerless and as to courage, what was the good of it, he thought. He was so helpless that even flight seemed of no use; and though she kept on whispering, 'Go to Doramin, go to Doramin,' with feverish insistence, he realized that for him there was no refuge from that loneli-ness which centupled all his dangers except—in her. 'I thought,' he said to me, 'that if I went away from her it would be the end of everything, somehow.' Only as they couldn't stop there forever in the middle of that courtyard, he made up his mind to go and look into the storehouse. He let her follow him without thinking of any protest, as if they had been indissolubly united. 'I am fearless—am I?' he mut-tered through his teeth. She restrained his arm. 'Wait till you hear my voice,' she said, and, torch in hand, ran lightly round the corner. He remained alone in the darkness, his face to the door: not a sound, not a breath came from the other side. The old hag let out a dreary groan somewhere behind his back. He heard a high-pitched, almost screaming, call from the girl. 'Now! Push!' He pushed violently; the door swung with a creak and a clatter, disclosing to his intense astonishment the low dungeon-like interior illuminated by a lurid, wavering glare. A turmoil of smoke eddied down upon an empty wooden crate in the middle of the floor, a lit-ter of rags and straw tried to soar, but only stirred feebly in the draught. She had thrust the light through the bars of the window. He saw her bare round arm, extended and rigid, holding up the torch with the steadiness of an iron bracket. A conical ragged heap of old mats cumbered a distant corner almost to the ceiling, and that was all.

"He explained to me that he was bitterly disappointed at this. His fortitude had been tried by so many warnings, he had been for weeks surrounded by so many hints of danger, that he wanted the relief of some reality, of something tangible that he could meet. 'It would have cleared the air for a couple of hours at least, if you know what I mean,' he said to me. 'Jove! I had been living for days with a stone on my chest.' Now at last he had thought he would get hold of something, and—nothing! Not a trace, not a sign of anybody. He had raised his weapon as the door flew open, but now his arm fell. 'Fire! Defend yourself,' the girl outside cried in an agonizing voice. She, being in the dark and with her arm thrust in to the shoulder through the small hole, couldn't see what was going on, and she dared not withdraw the torch now to run round. 'There's nobody here!' yelled Jim, con-temptuously, but his impulse to burst into a resentful exasperated laugh died without a sound: he had perceived in the very act of turning away that he was exchanging glances with a pair of eyes in the heap of mats. He saw a shifting gleam of whites. 'Come out!' he cried in a fury, a little doubtful, and a dark-faced head, a head without a body, shaped itself in the rubbish, a strangely detached head, that looked at him with a steady scowl. Next moment the whole mound stirred, and with a low grunt a man emerged swiftly, and bounded towards Jim. Behind him the mats, as it were, jumped and flew, his right arm was raised with a crooked elbow, and the dull blade of a *kris* protruded from his fist, held off a little above his head. A cloth wound tight round his loins seemed dazzlingly white on his bronze skin; his naked body glistened as if wet.

"Jim noted all this. He told me he was experiencing a feeling of unutterable relief, of vengeful elation. He held his shot he says, deliberately. He held it for the tenth part of a second, for three strides of the man—an unconscionable time. He held it for the pleasure of saying to himself, That's a dead man! He was absolutely positive and certain. He let him come on because it did not matter. A dead man, anyhow. He noticed the dilated nostrils, the wide eyes, the intent, eager stillness of the face, and then he fired.

"The explosion in that confined space was stunning. He stepped back a pace. He saw the man jerk his head up, fling his arms forward, and drop the *kris*. He ascertained afterwards that he had shot him through the mouth, a little upwards, the bullet coming out high at the back of the skull. With the impetus of his rush the man drove straight on, his face suddenly gaping disfigured, with his hands open before him gropingly, as though blinded, and landed with terrific violence on his forehead, just short of Jim's bare toes. Jim says he didn't lose the smallest detail of all this. He found himself calm, appeased, without rancor, without uneasiness, as if the death of that man had atoned for everything. The place was getting very full of sooty smoke from the torch, in which the unswaying flame burned blood-red without a flicker. He walked in resolutely, striding over the dead body, and covered with his revolver another naked figure outlined vaguely at the other end. As he was about to pull the trigger, the man threw away with force a short, heavy spear, and squatted submissively on his hams, his back to the wall and his clasped hands between his legs. 'You want your life?' Jim said. The other made no sound. 'How many more of you?' asked Jim again. 'Two more, Tuan,' said the man very softly, looking with big fascinated eyes into the muzzle of the revolver. Accordingly, two more crawled from under the mats, holding out ostentatiously their empty hands."

❦ 32 ❦

Jim took up an advantageous position and shepherded them out in a bunch through the doorway: all that time the torch had remained vertical in the grip of a little hand, without so much as a tremble. The three men obeyed him, perfectly mute, moving automatically. He ranged them in a row. 'Link arms!' he ordered. They did so. 'The first who withdraws his arm or turns his head is a dead man,' he said. 'March!' They stepped out together rigidly; he followed, and at the side the girl, in a trailing white gown, her black hair falling as low as her waist, bore the light. Erect and swaying, she seemed to glide without touching the earth; the only sound was the silky swish and rustle of the long grass. 'Stop!' cried Jim.

"The riverbank was steep; a great freshness ascended, the light fell on the edge of smooth, dark water frothing without a ripple; right and left the shapes of the houses ran together below the sharp outlines of the roofs. 'Take my greetings to Sherif Ali—till I come myself,' said Jim. Not one head of the three budged. 'Jump!' he thundered. The three splashes made one splash, a shower flew up, black heads bobbed convulsively, and disappeared; but a great blowing and spluttering went on, growing faint, for they were diving industriously, in great fear of a parting shot. Jim turned to the girl, who had been a silent and attentive observer. His heart seemed suddenly to grow too big for his breast and choke him in the hollow of his throat. This probably made him speechless for so long, and after returning his gaze she flung the burning torch with a wide sweep of the arm into the river. The ruddy fiery glare, taking a long flight through the night, sank with a vicious hiss, and the calm soft starlight descended upon them, unchecked.

"He did not tell me what it was he said when at last he recovered his voice. I don't suppose he could be very eloquent. The world was still, the night breathed on them, one of those nights that seem created for the sheltering of tenderness, and there are moments when our souls, as if freed from their dark envelope, glow with an exquisite sensibility that makes certain silences more lucid than speeches. As to the girl, he told me, 'She broke down a bit. Excitement—don't you know. Reaction. Deucedly tired she must have been—and all that kind of thing. And—and—hang it all—she was fond of me, don't you see. . . . I too . . . didn't know, of course . . . never entered my head . . .'

"There he got up and began to walk about in some agitation. 'I—I love her dearly. More than I could tell. Of course one cannot tell. You take a different view of your actions when you come to understand, when you are *made* to understand every day that your existence is necessary—you see, absolutely necessary—to another person. I am made to feel that. Wonderful. But only try to think what her life had been. It is too extravagantly awful! Isn't it? And me finding her here like this—as you may go out for a stroll and come suddenly upon somebody drowning in a lonely, dark place. Jove! No time to lose. Well, it is a trust too. . . . I believe I am equal to it. . . .'

"I must tell you the girl had left us to ourselves some time before. He slapped his chest. 'Yes! I feel that, but I believe I am equal to all my luck!' He had the gift of finding a special meaning in everything that happened to him. This was the view he took of his love affair; it was idyllic, a little solemn, and also true, since his belief had all the unshakable seriousness of youth. Some time after, on another occasion, he said to me, 'I've been only two years here, and now, upon my word, I can't conceive being able to live anywhere else. The very thought of the world outside is enough to give me a fright; because, don't you see,' he continued, with downcast eyes watching the action of his boot busied in squashing thoroughly a tiny bit of dried mud (we were strolling on the riverbank)—'Because I have not forgotten why I came here. Not yet!'

"I refrained from looking at him, but I think I heard a short sigh; we took a turn or two in silence. 'Upon my soul and conscience,' he began again, 'if such a thing can be forgotten, then I think I have a right to dismiss it from my mind. Ask any man here' . . . his voice changed. 'Is it not strange,' he went on in a gentle, almost yearning tone, 'that all these people, all these people who would do anything for me, can never be made to understand? Never! If you disbelieved me I could not call them up. It seems hard, somehow. I am stupid, am I not? What more can I want? If you ask them who is brave—who is true—who is just—who is it they would trust with their lives?—they would say, Tuan Jim. And yet they can never know the real, real truth . . .'

"That's what he said to me on my last day with him. I did not let a murmur escape me: I felt he was going to say more, and come no nearer to the root of the matter. The sun, whose concentrated glare dwarfs the earth into a restless mote of dust, had sunk behind the forest, and the diffused light from an opal sky seemed to cast upon a world without shadows and without brilliance the illusion of a calm and pensive greatness. I don't know why, listening to him, I should have noted so distinctly the gradual darkening of the river, of the air; the irresistible slow work of the night settling silently on all the visible forms, effacing the outlines, burying the shapes deeper and deeper, like a steady fall of impalpable black dust.

"'Jove!' he began abruptly, 'there are days when a fellow is too absurd for anything; only I know I can tell you what I like. I talk about being done with it—with the bally thing at the back of my head . . . Forgetting . . . Hang me if I know! I can think of it quietly. After all, what has it proved? Nothing. I suppose you don't think so . . .'

"I made a protesting murmur.

"'No matter,' he said. 'I am satisfied . . . nearly. I've got to look only at the face of the first man that comes along, to regain my confidence. They can't be made to understand what is going on in me. What of that? Come I haven't done so badly.'

"'Not so badly,' I said.

"'But all the same, you wouldn't like to have me aboard your own ship—hey?'

"'Confound you!' I cried. 'Stop this.'

"'Aha! You see,' he said, crowing, as it were, over me placidly. 'Only,' he went on, 'you just try to tell this to any of them here. They would think you a fool, a liar, or worse. And so I can stand it. I've done a thing or two for them, but this is what they have done for me.'

"'My dear chap,' I cried, 'you shall always remain for them an insoluble mystery.' Thereupon we were silent.

"'Mystery,' he repeated, before looking up. 'Well, then, let me always remain here.'

"After the sun had set, the darkness seemed to drive upon us, borne in every faint puff of the breeze. In the middle of a hedged path I saw the arrested, gaunt, watchful, and apparently one-legged silhouette of Tamb' Itam; and across the dusky space my eye detected something white moving to and fro behind the supports of the roof. As soon as Jim, with Tamb' Itam at his heels, had started upon his evening rounds, I went up to the house alone, and unexpectedly found myself waylaid by the girl, who had been clearly waiting for this opportunity.

"It is hard to tell you what it was precisely she wanted to wrest from me. Obviously, it would be something very simple—the simplest impossibility in the world; as, for instance, the exact description of the form of a cloud. She wanted an assurance, a statement, a promise, an explanation—I don't know how to call it: the thing has no name. It was dark under the projecting roof, and all I could see were the flowing lines of her gown, the pale small oval of her face, with the white flash of her teeth, and, turned towards me, the big somber orbits of her eyes, where there seemed to be a faint stir, such as you may fancy you can detect when you plunge your gaze to the bottom of an immensely deep well. What is it that moves there? you ask yourself. Is it a blind monster, or only a lost gleam from the universe? It occurred to me—don't laugh—that all things being dissimilar, she was more inscrutable in her childish ignorance than the sphinx propounding childish riddles to wayfarers. She had been carried off to Patusan before her eyes were open. She had grown up there; she had seen nothing, she had known nothing, she had no conception of anything. I ask myself whether she were sure that anything else existed. What notions she may have formed of the outside world is to me inconceivable: all that she knew of its inhabitants were a betrayed woman and a sinister pantaloon. Her lover also came to her from there, gifted with irresistible seductions; but what would become of her if he should return to these inconceivable regions that seemed always to claim back their own! Her mother had warned her of this with tears, before she died . . .

"She had caught hold of my arm firmly, and as soon as I had stopped she had withdrawn her hand in haste. She was audacious and shrinking. She feared nothing, but she was checked by the profound incertitude and the extreme strangeness—a brave person groping in the dark. I belonged to this Unknown that might claim Jim for its own at any moment. I was, as it were, in the secret of its nature and of its intentions—the confidant of a threatening mystery—armed with its power, perhaps! I believe she supposed I could with a word whisk Jim away out of her very arms: it is my sober conviction she went through agonies of apprehension during my long talks with Jim; through a real and intolerable anguish that might have conceivably driven her into plotting my murder, had the fierceness of her soul been equal to the tremendous situation it had created. This is my impression, and it is all I can give you: the whole thing dawned gradually upon me, and as it got clearer and clearer I was overwhelmed by a slow, incredulous amazement. She made me believe her, but there is no word that on my lips could render the effect of the headlong and vehement whisper, of the soft, passionate tones, of the sudden breathless pause and the appealing movement of the white arms extended swiftly. They fell; the ghostly figure swayed like a slender tree in the wind, the pale oval of the face drooped; it was impossible to distinguish her features, the darkness of the eyes was unfathomable; two wide sleeves uprose in the dark like unfolding wings, and she stood silent, holding her head in her hands."

❦ 33 ❦

I was immensely touched: her youth, her ignorance, her pretty beauty, which had the simple charm and the delicate vigor of a wildflower, her pathetic pleading, her helplessness, appealed to me with almost the strength of her own unreasonable and natural fear. She feared the unknown as we all do, and her ignorance made the unknown infinitely vast. I stood for it, for myself, for you fellows, for all the world that neither cared for Jim nor needed him in the least. I would have been ready enough to answer for the indifference of the teeming earth but for the reflection that he too belonged to this mysterious unknown of her fears, and that, however much I stood for, I did not stand for him. This made me hesitate. A murmur of hopeless pain unsealed my lips. I began by protesting that I at least had come with no intention to take Jim away.

"Why did I come, then? After a slight movement she was as still as a marble statue in the night. I tried to explain briefly: friendship, business; if I had any wish in the matter it was rather to see him stay. . . . 'They always leave us,' she murmured. The breath of sad wisdom from the grave which her piety wreathed with flowers seemed to pass in a faint sigh. . . . Nothing, said I, could separate Jim from her.

"It is my firm conviction now; it was my conviction at the time; it was the only possible conclusion from the facts of the case. It was not made more certain by her whispering in a tone in which one speaks to oneself, 'He swore this to me.' 'Did you ask him?' I said.

"She made a step nearer. 'No. Never!' She had asked him only to go away. It was that night on the riverbank, after he had killed the man—after, she had flung the torch into the water because he was looking at her so. There was too much light, and the danger was over then—for a little time—for a little time. He said then he would not abandon her to Cornelius. She had insisted. She wanted him to leave her. He said that he could not— that it was impossible. He trembled while he said this. She had felt him tremble. . . . One does not require much imagination to see the scene, almost to hear their whispers. She was afraid for him too. I believe that then she saw in him only a predestined victim of dangers which she understood better than himself. Though by nothing but his mere presence he had mastered her heart, had filled all her thoughts, and had possessed himself of all her affections, she underestimated his chances of success. It is obvious that at about that time everybody was inclined to underestimate his chances. Strictly speaking, he didn't seem to have any. I know this was Cornelius's view. He confessed that much to me in extenuation of the shady part he had played in Sherif Ali's plot to do away with the infidel. Even Sherif Ali himself, as it seems certain now, had nothing but contempt for the white man. Jim was to be murdered mainly on religious grounds, I believe. A simple act of piety (and so far infinitely meritorious), but otherwise without much importance. In the last part of this opinion Cornelius concurred. 'Honorable sir,' he argued abjectly on the only occasion he managed to have me to himself—'Honorable sir, how was I to know? Who was he? What could he do to make people believe him? What did Mr. Stein mean sending a boy like that to talk to an old servant? I was ready to save him for eighty dollars. Only eighty dollars. Why didn't the fool go? Was I to get stabbed myself for the sake of a stranger?' He groveled in spirit before me, with his body doubled up insinuatingly and his hands hovering about my knees, as though he were ready to embrace my legs. 'What's eighty dollars? An insignificant sum to give to a defenseless old man ruined for life by a deceased she-devil.' Here he wept. But I anticipate. I didn't that night chance upon Cornelius till I had had it out with the girl.

"She was unselfish when she urged Jim to leave her, and even to leave the country. It was his danger that was foremost in her thoughts—even if she wanted to save herself too—perhaps unconsciously: but then look at the warning she had, look at the lesson that could be drawn from every moment of the recently ended life in which all her memories were centered. She fell at his feet—she told me so—there by the river, in the discreet light of stars which showed nothing except great masses of silent shadows, indefinite open spaces, and trembling faintly upon the broad stream made it appear as wide as the sea. He had lifted her up. He lifted her up, and then she would struggle no more. Of course not. Strong arms, a tender voice, a stalwart shoulder to rest her poor lonely little head upon. The need—the infinite need—of all this for the aching heart, for the bewildered mind—the promptings of youth—the necessity of the moment. What would you have? One understands—unless one is incapable of understanding anything under the sun. And so she was content to be lifted up—and held. 'You know—Jove! this is serious—no nonsense in it!' as Jim had whispered hurriedly with a troubled, concerned face on the threshold of his house. I don't know so much about nonsense, but there was nothing lighthearted in their romance: they came together under the shadow of a life's disaster, like knight and maiden meeting to exchange vows amongst haunted ruins. The starlight was good enough for that story, a light so faint and remote that it cannot resolve shadows into shapes, and show the other shore of a stream. I did look upon the stream that night and from the very place; it rolled silent and as black as Styx: the next day I went away, but I am not likely to forget what it was she wanted to be saved from when she entreated him to leave her while there was time. She told me what it was, calmed—she was now too passionately interested for mere excitement—in a voice as quiet in the obscurity as her white, half-lost figure. She told me, 'I didn't want to die weeping.' I thought I had not heard aright.

"'You did not want to die weeping?' I repeated after her. 'Like my mother,' she added readily. The outlines of her white shape did not stir in the least. 'My mother had wept bitterly before she died,' she explained. An inconceivable calmness seemed to have risen from the ground around us, imperceptibly, like the still rise of a flood in the night, obliterating the familiar landmarks of emotions. There came upon me, as though I had felt myself losing my footing in the midst of waters, a sudden dread—the dread of the unknown depths. She went on explaining that, during the last moments, being alone with her mother, she had to leave the side of the couch to go and set her back against the door, in order to keep Cornelius out. He desired to get in, and kept on drumming with both fists, only desisting now and again to shout huskily, 'Let me in! Let me in! Let me in!' In a far corner upon a few mats the moribund woman, already speechless and unable to lift her arm, rolled her head over, and with a feeble movement of her hand seemed to command—No! No! and the obedient daughter, setting her shoulders with all her strength against the door, was looking on. 'The tears fell from her eyes—and then she died,' concluded the girl in an imperturbable monotone, which more than anything else, more than the white statuesque immobility of her person, more than mere words could do, troubled my mind profoundly with the passive, irremediable horror of the scene. It had the power to drive me out of my conception of existence, out of that shelter each of us makes for himself to creep under in moments of danger, as a tortoise withdraws within its shell. For a moment I had a view of a world that seemed to wear a vast and dismal aspect of disorder, while, in truth, thanks to our unwearied efforts, it is as sunny an arrangement of small conveniences as the mind of man can conceive. But still—it was only a moment: I went back into my shell directly. One *must*—don't you know?—though I seemed to have lost all my words in the chaos of dark thoughts I had contemplated for a second or two beyond the pale. These came back too, very soon, for words also belong to the sheltering conception of light and the order which is our refuge. I had them ready at my disposal before she whispered softly, 'He swore he would never leave me, when we stood there alone! He swore to me!'. . . 'And is it possible that you—you! do not believe him?' I asked, sincerely reproachful, genuinely shocked. Why couldn't she believe? Wherefore this craving for incertitude, this clinging to fear, as if incertitude and fear had been the safeguards of her love. It was monstrous. She should have made for herself a shelter of inexpugnable peace out of that honest affection. She had not the knowledge—not the skill, perhaps. The night had come on apace; it had grown pitch-dark where we were, so that without stirrings she had faded like the intangible form of a wistful and perverse spirit. And suddenly I heard her quiet whisper again, 'Other men had sworn the same thing.' It was like a meditative comment on some thoughts full of sadness, of awe. And she added, still lower if possible, 'My father did.' She paused the time to draw an inaudible breath. 'Her father too.'. . . These were the things she knew! At once I said, 'Ah! but he is not like that.' This, it seemed, she did not intend to dispute; but after a time the strange still whisper, wandering dreamily in the air, stole into my ears. 'Why is he different? Is he better? Is he . . .' 'Upon my word of honor,' I broke in, 'I believe he is.' We subdued our tones to a mysterious pitch. Amongst the huts of Jim's workmen (they were mostly liberated slaves from the Sherif's stockade) somebody started a shrill, drawling song. Across the river a big fire (at Doramin's, I think) made a glowing ball, completely isolated in the night. 'Is he more true?' she murmured. 'Yes,' I said.

"'More true than any other man,' she repeated, in lingering accents. 'Nobody here,' I said, 'would dream of doubting his word—nobody would dare—except you.'

"I think she made a movement at this. 'More brave,' she went on in a changed tone. 'Fear shall never drive him away from you,' I said a little nervously. The song stopped short on a shrill note, and was succeeded by several voices talking in the distance. Jim's voice, too. I was struck by her silence. 'What has he been telling you? He had been telling you something?' I asked. There was no answer. 'What is it he told you?' I insisted.

"'Do you think I can tell you? How am I to know? How am I to understand?' she cried at last. There was a stir. I believe she was wringing her hands. 'There is something he can never forget.'

"'So much the better for you,' I said gloomily.

"'What is it? What is it?' She put an extraordinary force of appeal into her supplicating tone. 'He says he had been afraid. How can I believe this! Am I a mad woman to believe this? You all remember something! You all go back to it. What is it? You tell me! What is this thing? Is it alive?—is it dead? I hate it. It is cruel. Has it got a face and a voice—this calamity? Will he see it—will he hear it? In his sleep, perhaps, when he cannot see me—and then arise and go. Ah! I shall never forgive him. My mother had forgiven—but I, never! Will it be a sign—a call . . .'

"It was a wonderful experience. She mistrusted his very slumbers—and she seemed to think I could tell her why! Thus a poor mortal seduced by the charm of an apparition might have tried to wring from another ghost the tremendous secret of the claim the other world holds over a disembodied soul astray amongst the passions of this earth. The very ground on which I stood seemed to melt under my feet. And it was so simple, too; but if the spirits evoked by our fears and our unrest have ever to vouch for each other's constancy before the forlorn magicians that we are, then I—I alone of us dwellers in the flesh—have shuddered in the hopeless chill of such a task. A sign, a call! How telling in its expression was her ignorance. A few words! How she came to know them, how she came to pronounce them, I can't imagine. Women find their inspiration in the stress of moments that for us are merely awful, absurd, or futile. To discover that she had a voice at all was enough to strike awe into the heart. Had a spurned stone cried out in pain it could not have appeared a greater and more pitiful miracle. These few sounds wandering in the dark had made their two benighted lives tragic to my mind. It was impossible to make her understand. I chafed silently at my impotence. And Jim, too—poor devil! Who would need him? Who would remember him? He had what he wanted. His very existence probably had been forgotten by this time. They had mastered their fates. They were tragic.

"Her immobility before me was clearly expectant, and my part was to speak for my brother from the realm of forgetful shades. I was deeply moved at my responsibility and at her distress. I would have given anything for the power to soothe her frail soul, tormenting itself in its invincible ignorance like a small bird beating about the cruel wires of a cage. Nothing easier than to say, Have no fear! Nothing more difficult. How does one kill fear, I wonder? How do you shoot a specter through the heart, slash off its spectral head, take it by its spectral throat? It is an enterprise you rush into while you dream, and are glad to make your escape with wet hair and every limb shaking. The bullet is not run, the blade not forged, the man not born; even the winged words of truth drop at your feet like lumps of lead. You require for such a desperate encounter an enchanted and poisoned shaft dipped in a lie too subtle to be found on earth. An enterprise for a dream, my masters!

"I began my exorcism with a heavy heart, with a sort of sullen anger in it too. Jim's voice, suddenly raised with a stern intonation, carried across the courtyard reproving the carelessness of some dumb sinner by the riverside. Nothing—I said, speaking in a distinct murmur—there could be nothing in that unknown world she fancied so eager to rob her of her happiness, there was nothing, neither living nor dead, there was no face, no voice, no power, that could tear Jim from her side. I drew breath and she whispered softly, 'He told me so.' 'He told you the truth,' I said. 'Nothing,' she sighed out, and abruptly turned upon me with a barely audible intensity of tone. 'Why did you come to us from out there? He speaks of you too often. You make me afraid. Do you—do you want him?' A sort of stealthy fierceness had crept into our hurried mutters. 'I shall never come again,' I said bitterly. 'And I don't want him. No one wants him.' 'No one,' she repeated in a tone of doubt. 'No one,' I affirmed, feeling myself swayed by some strange excitement. 'You think him strong, wise, courageous, great—why not believe him to be true, too? I shall go tomorrow—and that is the end. You shall never be troubled by a voice from there again. This world you don't know is too big to miss him. You understand? Too big. You've got his heart in your hand. You must feel that. You must know that.' 'Yes, I know that,' she breathed out, hard and still as a statue might whisper.

"I felt I had done nothing. And what is it that I had wished to do? I am not sure now. At the time I was animated by an inexplicable ardor, as if before some great and necessary task—the influence of the moment upon my mental and emotional state. There are in all our lives such moments, such influences, coming from the outside, as it were, irresistible, incomprehensible—as if brought about by the mysterious conjunctions of the planets. She owned, as I had put it to her, his heart. She had that and everything else—if she could only believe it. What I had to tell her was that in the whole world there was no one who ever would need his heart, his mind, his hand. It was a common fate, and yet it seemed an awful thing to say of any man. She listened without a word, and her stillness now was like the protest of an invincible unbelief. What need she care for the world beyond the forests? I asked. From all the multitudes that peopled the vastness of that unknown there would come, I assured her, as long as he lived, neither a call nor a sign for him. Never. I was carried away. Never! Never! I remember with wonder the sort of dogged fierceness I displayed. I had the illusion of having got the specter by the throat at last. Indeed, the whole real thing has left behind the detailed and amazing impression of a dream. Why should she fear? She knew him to be strong, true, wise, brave. He was all that. Certainly. He was more. He was great—invincible—and the world did not want him, it had forgotten him, it would not even know him.

"I stopped; the silence over Patusan was profound, and the feeble dry sound of a paddle striking the side of a canoe somewhere in the middle of the river seemed to make it infinite. 'Why? ' she murmured. I felt that sort of rage one feels during a hard tussle. The specter was trying to slip out of my grasp. 'Why?' she repeated louder; 'tell me!' And as I remained confounded, she stamped with her foot like a spoilt child. 'Why? Speak.' 'You want to know,' I asked in a fury. 'Yes!' she cried. 'Because he is not good enough,' I said brutally. During the moment's pause I noticed the fire on the other shore blaze up, dilating the circle of its glow like an amazed stare, and contract suddenly to a red pinpoint. I only knew how close to me she had been when I felt the clutch of her fingers on my forearm. Without raising her voice, she threw into it an infinity of scathing contempt, bitterness, and despair.

"'This is the very thing he said. . . . You lie!'

"The last two words she cried at me in the native dialect. 'Hear me out!' I entreated; she caught her breath tremulously, flung my arm away. 'Nobody, nobody is good enough,' I began with the greatest earnestness. I could hear the sobbing labor of her breath frightfully quickened. I hung my head. What was the use? Footsteps were approaching; I slipped away without another word. . . ."

❧ 34 ❧

Marlow swung his legs out, got up quickly, and staggered a little, as though he had been set down after a rush through space. He leaned his back against the balustrade and faced a disordered array of long cane chairs. The bodies prone in them seemed startled out of their torpor by his movement. One or two sat up as if alarmed; here and there a cigar glowed yet; Marlow looked at them all with the eyes of a man returning from the excessive remoteness of a dream. A throat was cleared; a calm voice encouraged negligently, "Well?"

"Nothing," said Marlow with a slight start. "He had told her—that's all. She did not believe him—nothing more. As to myself, I do not know whether it be just, proper, decent for me to rejoice or to be sorry. For my part, I cannot say what I believed—indeed I don't know to this day, and never shall probably. But what did the poor devil believe himself? Truth shall prevail—don't you know. *Magna est veritas et* . . . Yes, when it gets a chance. There is a law, no doubt—and likewise a law regulates your luck in the throwing of dice. It is not Justice the servant of men, but accident, hazard, Fortune—the ally of patient Time—that holds an even and scrupulous balance. Both of us had said the very same thing. Did we both speak the truth—or one of us did—or neither?"

Marlow paused, crossed his arms on his breast, and in a changed tone—

"She said we lied. Poor soul. Well—let's leave it to chance, whose ally is Time, that cannot be hurried, and whose enemy is Death, that will not wait. I had retreated—a little cowed, I must own. I had tried a fall with fear itself and got thrown—of course. I had only succeeded in adding to her anguish the hint of some mysterious collusion, of an inexplicable and incomprehensible conspiracy to keep her forever in the dark. And it had come easily, naturally, unavoidably, by his act, by her own act! It was as though I had been shown the working of the implacable destiny of which we are the victims—and the tools. It was appalling to think of the girl whom I had left standing there motionless; Jim's footsteps had a fateful sound as he tramped by, without seeing me, in his heavy laced boots. 'What? No lights!' he said in a loud, surprised voice. 'What are you doing in the dark—you two.' Next moment he caught sight of her, I suppose. 'Hallo, girl!' he cried cheerily. 'Hallo, boy!' she answered at once, with amazing pluck.

"This was their usual greeting to each other, and the bit of swagger she would put into her rather high but sweet voice was very droll, pretty, and childlike. It delighted Jim greatly. This was the last occasion on which I heard them exchange this familiar hail, and it struck a chill into my heart. There was the high sweet voice, the pretty effort, the swagger; but it all seemed to die out prematurely, and the playful call sounded like a moan. It was too confoundedly awful. 'What have you done with Marlow?' Jim was asking; and then, 'Gone down—has he? Funny I didn't meet him. . . . You there, Marlow?'

"I didn't answer. I wasn't going in—not yet, at any rate. I really couldn't. While he was calling me I was engaged in making my escape through a little gate leading out upon a stretch of newly cleared ground. No; I couldn't face them yet. I walked hastily with lowered head along a trodden path. The ground rose gently, the few big trees had been felled, the undergrowth had been cut down and the grass fired. He had a mind to try a coffee plantation there. The big hill, rearing its double summit coal-black in the clear yellow glow of the rising moon, seemed to cast its shadow upon the ground prepared for that experiment. He was going to try ever so many experiments; I had admired his energy, his enterprise, and his shrewdness. Nothing on earth seemed less real now than his plans, his energy, and his enthusiasm; and raising my eyes, I saw part of the moon glittering through the bushes at the bottom of the chasm. For a moment it looked as though the smooth disk, falling from its place in the sky upon the earth, had rolled to the bottom of that precipice: its ascending movement was like a leisurely rebound; it disengaged itself from the tangle of twigs; the bare contorted limb of some tree, growing on the slope, made a black crack right across its face. It threw its level rays afar as if from a cavern, and in this mournful eclipse-like light the stumps of felled trees uprose very dark, the heavy shadows fell at my feet on all sides, my own moving shadow, and across my path the shadow of the solitary grave perpetually garlanded with flowers. In the darkened moonlight the interlaced blossoms took on shapes foreign to one's memory and colors indefinable to the eye, as though they had been special flowers gathered by no man, grown not in this world, and destined for the use of the dead alone. Their powerful scent hung in the warm air, making it thick and heavy like the fumes of incense. The lumps of white coral shone round the dark mound like a chaplet of bleached skulls, and everything around was so quiet that when I stood still all sound and all movement in the world seemed to come to an end.

"It was a great peace, as if the earth had been one grave, and for a time I stood there thinking mostly of the living who, buried in remote places out of the knowledge of mankind, still are fated to share in its tragic or grotesque miseries. In its noble struggles, too—who knows? The human heart is vast enough to contain all the world. It is valiant enough to bear the burden, but where is the courage that would cast it off?

"I suppose I must have fallen into a sentimental mood; I only know that I stood there long enough for the sense of utter solitude to get hold of me so completely that all I had lately seen, all I had heard, and the very human speech itself, seemed to have passed away out of existence, living only for a while longer in my memory, as though I had been the last of mankind. It was a strange and melancholy illusion, evolved half-consciously like all our illusions, which I suspect only to be visions of remote unattainable truth, seen dimly. This was, indeed, one of the lost, forgotten, unknown places of the earth; I had looked under its obscure surface; and I felt that when tomorrow I had left it forever, it would slip out of existence, to live only in my memory till I myself passed into oblivion. I have that feeling about me now; perhaps it is that feeling which has incited me to tell you the story, to try to hand over to you, as it were, its very existence, its reality—the truth disclosed in a moment of illusion.

"Cornelius broke upon it. He bolted out, vermin-like, from the long grass growing in a depression of the ground. I believe his house was rotting somewhere near by, though I've never seen it, not having been far enough in that direction. He ran towards me upon the path; his feet, shod in dirty white shoes, twinkled on the dark earth; he pulled himself up, and began to whine and cringe under a tall stovepipe hat. His dried-up little carcass was swallowed up, totally lost, in a suit of black broadcloth. That was his costume for holidays and ceremonies, and it reminded me that this was the fourth Sunday I had spent in Patusan. All the time of my stay I had been vaguely aware of his desire to confide in me, if he only could get me all to himself. He hung about with an eager craving look on his sour yellow little face; but his timidity had kept him back as much as my natural reluctance to have anything to do with such an unsavory creature. He would have succeeded, nevertheless, had he not been so ready to slink off as soon as you looked at him. He would slink off before Jim's severe gaze, before my own, which I tried to make indifferent, even before Tamb' Itam's surly, superior glance. He was perpetually slinking away; whenever seen he was seen moving off deviously, his face over his shoulder, with either a mistrustful snarl or a woebegone, piteous, mute aspect; but no assumed expression could conceal this innate irremediable abjectness of his nature, any more than an arrangement of clothing can conceal some monstrous deformity of the body.

"I don't know whether it was the demoralization of my utter defeat in my encounter with a specter of fear less than an hour ago, but I let him capture me without even a show of resistance. I was doomed to be the recipient of confidences, and to be confounded with unanswerable questions. It was trying; but the contempt, the unreasoned contempt, the man's appearance provoked, made it easier to bear. He couldn't possibly matter. Nothing mattered, since I had made up my mind that Jim, for whom alone I cared, had at last mastered his fate. He had told me he was satisfied . . . nearly. This is going further than most of us dare. I—who have the right to think myself good enough. . . . dare not. Neither does any of you here, I suppose? . . ."

Marlow paused, as if expecting an answer. Nobody spoke.

"Quite right" he began again. "Let no soul know, since the truth can be wrung out of us only by some cruel, little, awful catastrophe. But he is one of us, and he could say he was satisfied . . . nearly. Just fancy this! Nearly satisfied. One could almost envy him his catastrophe. Nearly satisfied. After this nothing could matter. It did not matter who suspected him, who trusted him, who loved him, who hated him—especially as it was Cornelius who hated him.

"Yet after all this was a kind of recognition. You shall judge of a man by his foes as well as by his friends, and this enemy of Jim was such as no decent man would be ashamed to own, without, however, making too much of him. This was the view Jim took, and in which I shared; but Jim disregarded him on general grounds. 'My dear Marlow,' he said, 'I feel that if I go straight nothing can touch me. Indeed I do. Now you have been long enough here to have a good look round—and, frankly, don't you think I am pretty safe? It all depends upon me, and, by Jove! I have lots of confidence in myself. The worst thing he could do would be to kill me, I suppose. I don't think for a moment he would. He couldn't, you know—not if, I were myself to hand him a loaded rifle for the purpose, and then turn my back on him. That's the sort of thing he is. And suppose he would—suppose he could? Well— what of that? I didn't come here flying for my life—did I? I came here to set my back against the wall, and I am going to stay here . . .'

"'Till you are *quite* satisfied,' I struck in.

"We were sitting at the time under the roof in the stern of his boat; twenty paddles flashed like one, ten on a side, striking the water with a single splash, while behind our backs Tamb' Itam dipped silently right and left, and stared right down the river, attentive to keep the long canoe in the greatest strength of the current. Jim bowed his head, and our last talk seemed to flicker out for good. He was seeing me off as far as the mouth of the river. The schooner had left the day before, working down and drifting on the ebb, while I had prolonged my stay overnight. And now he was seeing me off.

"Jim had been a little angry with me for mentioning Cornelius at all. I had not, in truth, said much. The man was too insignificant to be dangerous, though he was as full of hate as he could hold. He had called me 'honorable sir' at every second sentence, and had whined at my elbow as he followed me from the grave of his 'late wife' to the gate of Jim's compound. He declared himself the most unhappy of men, a victim, crushed like a worm; he entreated me to look at him. I wouldn't turn my head to do so; but I could see out of the corner of my eye his obsequious shadow gliding after mine, while the moon, suspended on our right hand, seemed to gloat serenely upon the spectacle. He tried to explain—as I've told you—his share in the events of the memorable night. It was a matter of expediency. How could he know who was going to get the upper hand? 'I would have saved him, honorable sir! I would have saved him for eighty dollars,' he protested, in dulcet tones, keeping a pace behind me. 'He has saved himself,' I said, 'and he has forgiven you.' I heard a sort of tittering, and turned upon him; at once he appeared ready to take to his heels. 'What are you laughing at?' I asked, standing still. 'Don't be deceived, honorable sir!' he shrieked, seemingly losing all control over his feelings. '*He* save himself! He knows nothing, honorable sir—nothing whatever. Who is he? What does he want here—the big thief? What does he want here? He throws dust into everybody's eyes; he throws dust into your eyes, honorable sir; but he can't throw dust into my eyes. He is a big fool, honorable sir.' I laughed contemptuously, and, turning on my heel, began to walk on again. He ran up to my elbow and whispered forcibly, 'He's no more than a little child here—like a little child—a little child.' Of course, I didn't take the slightest notice, and seeing the time pressed, because we were approaching the bamboo fence that glittered over the blackened ground of the clearing, he came to the point. He commenced by being abjectly lachrymose. His great misfortunes had affected his head. He hoped I would kindly forget what nothing but his troubles made him say. He didn't mean anything by it; only the honorable sir did not know what it was to be ruined, broken down, trampled upon. After this introduction he approached the matter near his heart, but in such a rambling, ejaculatory, craven fashion, that for a long time I couldn't make out what he was driving at. He wanted me to intercede with Jim in his favor. It seemed, too, to be some sort of money affair. I heard time and again the words, 'Moderate provision—suitable present.' He seemed to be claiming value for something, and he even went the length of saying with some warmth that life was not worth having if a man were to be robbed of everything. I did not breathe a word, of course, but neither did I stop my ears. The gist of the affair, which became clear to me gradually, was in this, that he regarded himself as entitled to some money in exchange for the girl. He had brought her up. Somebody else's child. Great trouble and pains—old man now—suitable present. If the honorable sir would say a word. . . . I stood still to look at him with curiosity, and fearful lest I should think him extortionate, I suppose, he hastily brought himself to make a concession. In consideration of a 'suitable present' given at once, he would, he declared, be willing to undertake the charge of the girl, 'without any other provision—when the time came for the gentleman to go home.' His little yellow face, all crumpled as though it had been squeezed together, expressed the most anxious, eager avarice. His voice whined coaxingly, 'No more trouble—natural guardian—a sum of money . . .'

"I stood there and marveled. That kind of thing, with him, was evidently a vocation. I discovered suddenly in his cringing attitude a sort of assurance, as though he had been all his life dealing in certitudes. He must have thought I was dispassionately considering his proposal, because he became as sweet as honey. 'Every gentleman made a provision when the time came to go home,' he began insinuatingly. I slammed the little gate. 'In this case, Mr. Cornelius,' I said, 'the time shall never come.' He took a few seconds to gather this in. 'What!' he fairly squealed. 'Why,' I continued from my side of the gate, 'haven't you heard him say so himself? He will never go home.' 'Oh! this is too much,' he shouted. He would not address me as 'honorable sir' anymore. He was very still for a time, and then, without a trace of humility, began very low. 'Never go—ah! He—he—he comes here devil knows from where—comes here—devil knows why—to trample on me till I die—ah—trample' (he stamped softly with both feet), 'trample like this—nobody knows why—till I die. . . .' His voice became quite extinct; he was bothered by a little cough; he came up close to the fence and told me, dropping into a confidential and piteous tone, that he would *not* be trampled upon. 'Patience—patience,' he muttered, striking his breast. I had done laughing at him, but unexpectedly he treated me to a wild cracked burst of it. 'Ha! ha! ha! We shall see! We shall see! What? Steal from me? Steal from me everything. Everything! Everything!' His head drooped on one shoulder, his hands were hanging before him lightly clasped. One would have thought he had cherished the girl with surpassing love, that his spirit had been crushed and his heart broken by the most cruel of spoliations. Suddenly he lifted his head and shot out an infamous word. 'Like her mother—she is like her deceitful mother. Exactly. In her face, too. In her face. The devil!' He leaned his forehead against the fence, and in that position uttered threats and horrible blasphemies in Portuguese in very weak ejaculations, mingled with miserable plaints and groans, coming out with a heave of the shoulders as though he had been overtaken by a deadly fit of sickness. It was an inexpressibly grotesque and vile performance, and I hastened away. He tried to shout something after me. Some disparagement of Jim, I believe—not too loud, though, we were too near the house. All I heard distinctly was, 'No more than a little child—a little child.'"

❧ 35 ❧

But next morning, at the first bend of the river shutting off the houses of Patusan, all this dropped out of my sight bodily, with its color, its design, and its meaning, like a picture created by fancy on a canvas, upon which, after long contemplation, you turn your back for the last time. It remains in the memory motionless, unfaded, with its life arrested, in an unchanging light. There are the ambitions, the fears, the hate, the hopes, and they remain in my mind just as I had seen them—intense and as if forever suspended in their expression. I had turned away from the picture and was going back to the world where events move, men change, light flickers, life flows in a clear stream, no matter whether over mud or over stones. I wasn't going to dive into it; I would have enough to do to keep my head above the surface. But as to what I was leaving behind, I cannot imagine any alteration. The immense and magnanimous Doramin and his little motherly witch of a wife, gazing together upon the land and nursing secretly their dreams of parental ambition; Tunku Allang, wizened and greatly perplexed; Dain Waris, intelligent and brave, with his faith in Jim, with his firm glance and his ironic friendliness; the girl, absorbed in her frightened, suspicious adoration; Tamb' Itam, surly and faithful; Cornelius, leaning his forehead against the fence under the moonlight—I am certain of them. They exist as if under an enchanter's wand. But the figure round which all these are grouped—that one lives, and I am not certain of him. No magician's wand can immobilize him under my eyes. He is one of us.

"Jim, as I've told you, accompanied me on the first stage of my journey back to the world he had renounced, and the way at times seemed to lead through the very heart of untouched wilderness. The empty reaches sparkled under the high sun; between the high walls of vegetation the heat drowsed upon the water, and the boat, impelled vigorously, cut her way through the air that seemed to have settled dense and warm under the shelter of lofty trees.

"The shadow of the impending separation had already put an immense space between us, and when we spoke it was with an effort, as if to force our low voices across a vast and increasing distance. The boat fairly flew; we sweltered side by side in the stagnant superheated air; the smell of mud, of marsh, the primeval smell of fecund earth, seemed to sting our faces, till suddenly at a bend it was as if a great hand far away had lifted a heavy curtain, had flung open an immense portal. The light itself seemed to stir, the sky above our heads widened, a far-off murmur reached our ears, a freshness enveloped us, filled our lungs, quickened our thoughts, our blood, our regrets—and, straight ahead, the forests sank down against the dark-blue ridge of the sea.

"I breathed deeply, I reveled in the vastness of the opened horizon, in the different atmosphere that seemed to vibrate with the toil of life, with the energy of an impeccable world. This sky and this sea were open to me. The girl was right—there was a sign, a call in them—something to which I responded with every fiber of my being. I let my eyes roam through space, like a man released from bonds who stretches his cramped limbs, runs, leaps, responds to the inspiring elation of freedom. 'This is glorious!' I cried, and then I looked at the sinner by my side. He sat with his head sunk on his breast and said 'Yes' without raising his eyes, as if afraid to see writ large on the clear sky of the offing the reproach of his romantic conscience.

"I remember the smallest details of that afternoon. We landed on a bit of white beach. It was backed by a low cliff wooded on the brow, draped in creepers to the very foot. Below us the plain of the sea, of a serene and intense blue, stretched with a slight upward tilt to the thread-line of the horizon drawn at the height of our eyes. Great waves of glitter blew lightly along the pitted dark surface, as swift as feathers chased by the breeze. A chain of islands sat broken and massive, facing the wide estuary, displayed in a sheet of pale glassy water reflecting faithfully the contour of the shore. High in the colorless sunshine a solitary bird, all black, hovered, dropping and soaring above the same spot with a slight rocking motion of the wings. A ragged, sooty bunch of flimsy mat-hovels was perched over its own inverted image upon a crooked multitude of high piles the color of ebony. A tiny black canoe put off from amongst them with two tiny men, all black, who toiled exceedingly, striking down at the pale water; and the canoe seemed to slide painfully on a mirror. This bunch of miserable hovels was the fishing village that boasted of the white lord's especial protection, and the two men crossing over were the old headman and his son-in-law. They landed and walked up to us on the white sand, lean, dark-brown, as if dried in smoke, with ashy patches on the skin of their naked shoulders and breasts. Their heads were bound in dirty but careful-ly folded headkerchiefs, and the old man began at once to state a complaint, volu-ble, stretching a lank arm, screwing up at Jim his old bleared eyes confidently. The Rajah's people would not leave them alone; there had been some trouble about a lot of turtles' eggs his people had collected on the islets there—and lean-ing at arm's-length upon his paddle, he pointed with a brown skinny hand over the sea. Jim listened for a time without looking up, and at last told him gently to wait. He would hear him by and by. They withdrew obediently to some little distance, and sat on their heels, with their paddles lying before them on the sand; the sil-very gleams in their eyes followed our movements patiently; and the immensity of the outspread sea, the stillness of the coast, passing north and south beyond the limits of my vision, made up one colossal Presence watching us four dwarfs isolat-ed on a strip of glistening sand.

"'The trouble is,' remarked Jim moodily, 'that for generations these beggars of fishermen in that village there had been considered as the Rajah's personal slaves—and the old rip can't get it into his head that . . .'

"He paused. 'That you have changed all that,' I said.

"'Yes. I've changed all that,' he muttered in a gloomy voice.

"'You have had your opportunity,' I pursued.

"'Had I? ' he said. 'Well, yes. I suppose so. Yes. I have got back my confidence in myself—a good name—yet sometimes I wish . . . No! I shall hold what I've got. Can't expect anything more.' He flung his arm out towards the sea. 'Not out there, anyhow.' He stamped his foot upon the sand. 'This is my limit, because nothing less will do.'

"We continued pacing the beach. 'Yes, I've changed all that,' he went on, with a sidelong glance at the two patient squatting fishermen; 'but only try to think what it would be if I went away. Jove! can't you see it? Hell loose. No! Tomorrow I shall go and take my chance of drinking that silly old Tunku Allang's coffee and I shall make no end of fuss over these rotten turtles' eggs. No. I can't say—enough. Never. I must go on, go on forever holding up my end, to feel sure that nothing can touch me. I must stick to their belief in me to feel safe and to—to'. . . He cast about for a word, seemed to look for it on the sea . . . 'to keep in touch with'. . . His voice sank suddenly to a murmur . . . 'with those whom, perhaps, I shall never see anymore. With—with—you, for instance.'

"I was profoundly humbled by his words. 'For God's sake,' I said, 'don't set me up, my dear fellow; just look to yourself.' I felt a gratitude, an affection, for that straggler whose eyes had singled me out, keeping my place in the ranks of an insignificant multitude. How little that was to boast of, after all! I turned my burning face away; under the low sun, glowing, darkened, and crimson, like an ember snatched from the fire, the sea lay outspread, offering all its immense stillness to the approach of the fiery orb. Twice he was going to speak, but checked himself; at last, as if he had found a formula—

"'I shall be faithful,' he said quietly. 'I shall be faithful,' he repeated, without looking at me, but for the first time letting his eyes wander upon the waters, whose blueness had changed to a gloomy purple under the fires of sunset. Ah! he was romantic, romantic. I recalled some words of Stein's. . . . 'In the destructive element immerse! . . . To follow the dream and again to follow the dream—and so—always—*usque ad fineto* . . .' He was romantic, but nonetheless true. Who could tell what forms, what visions, what faces, what forgiveness he could see in the glow of the west! . . . A small boat, leaving the schooner, moved slowly, with a regular beat of two oars, towards the sandbank to take me off. 'And then there's Jewel,' he said, out of the great silence of earth, sky, and sea, which had mastered my very thoughts so that his voice made me start. 'There's Jewel.' 'Yes,' I murmured. 'I need not tell you what she is to me,' he pursued. 'You've seen. In time she will come to understand. . . .' 'I hope so,' I interrupted. 'She trusts me, too,' he mused, and then changed his tone. 'When shall we meet next, I wonder?' he said.

"'Never—unless you come out,' I answered, avoiding his glance. He didn't seem to be surprised; he kept very quiet for a while.

"'Goodbye, then,' he said, after a pause. 'Perhaps it's just as well.'

"We shook hands, and I walked to the boat, which waited with her nose on the beach. The schooner, her mainsail set and jib-sheet to windward, curveted on the purple sea; there was a rosy tinge on her sails. 'Will you be going home again soon?' asked Jim, just as I swung my leg over the gunwale. 'In a year or so, if I live,' I said. The forefoot grated on the sand, the boat floated, the wet oars flashed and dipped once, twice. Jim, at the water's edge, raised his voice. 'Tell them . . .' he began. I signed to the men to cease rowing, and waited in wonder. Tell who? The half-submerged sun faced him; I could see its red gleam in his eyes that looked dumbly at me. . . . 'No—nothing,' he said, and with a slight wave of his hand motioned the boat away. I did not look again at the shore till I had clambered on board the schooner.

"By that time the sun had set. The twilight lay over the east, and the coast, turned black, extended infinitely its somber wall that seemed the very stronghold of the night; the western horizon was one great blaze of gold and crimson in which a big detached cloud floated dark and still, casting a slaty shadow on the water beneath, and I saw Jim on the beach watching the schooner fall off and gather headway.

"The two half-naked fishermen had arisen as soon as I had gone; they were no doubt pouring the plaint of their trifling, miserable, oppressed lives into the ears of the white lord, and no doubt he was listening to it, making it his own, for was it not a part of his luck—the luck 'from the word Go'—the luck to which he had assured me he was so completely equal. They too, I should think, were in luck, and I was sure their pertinacity would be equal to it. Their dark-skinned bodies vanished on the dark background long before I had lost sight of their protector. He was white from head to foot, and remained persistently visible with the stronghold of the night at his back, the sea at his feet, the opportunity by his side—still veiled. What do you say? Was it still veiled? I don't know. For me that white figure in the stillness of coast and sea seemed to stand at the heart of a vast enigma. The twilight was ebbing fast from the sky above his head, the strip of sand had sunk already under his feet, he himself appeared no bigger than a child—then only a speck, a tiny white speck, that seemed to catch all the light left in a darkened world. . . . And, suddenly, I lost him. . . ."

❧ 36 ❧

With these words Marlow had ended his narrative, and his audience had broken up forthwith, under his abstract, pensive gaze. Men drifted off the veranda in pairs or alone without loss of time, without offering a remark, as if the last image of that incomplete story, its incompleteness itself, and the very tone of the speaker, had made discussion vain and comment impossible. Each of them seemed to carry away his own impression, to carry it away with him like a secret; but there was only one man of all these listeners who was ever to hear the last word of the story. It came to him at home, more than two years later, and it came contained in a thick packet addressed in Marlow's upright and angular handwriting.

The privileged man opened the packet, looked in, then, laying it down, went to the window. His rooms were in the highest flat of a lofty building, and his glance could travel afar beyond the clear panes of glass, as though he were looking out of the lantern of a lighthouse. The slopes of the roofs glistened, the dark broken ridges succeeded each other without end like somber, uncrested waves, and from the depths of the town under his feet ascended a confused and unceasing mutter.

The spires of churches, numerous, scattered haphazard, uprose like beacons on a maze of shoals without a channel; the driving rain mingled with the falling dusk of a winter's evening; and the booming of a big clock on a tower striking the hour, rolled past in voluminous, austere bursts of sound, with a shrill vibrating cry at the core. He drew the heavy curtains.

The light of his shaded reading lamp slept like a sheltered pool, his footfalls made no sound on the carpet, his wandering days were over. No more horizons as boundless as hope, no more twilights within the forests as solemn as temples, in the hot quest for the Ever-undiscovered Country over the hill, across the stream, beyond the wave. The hour was striking! No more! No more!—but the opened packet under the lamp brought back the sounds, the visions, the very savor of the past—a multitude of fading faces, a tumult of low voices, dying away upon the shores of distant seas under a passionate and unconsoling sunshine. He sighed and sat down to read.

At first he saw three distinct enclosures. A good many pages closely blackened and pinned together; a loose, square sheet of grayish paper with a few words traced in a handwriting he had never seen before, and an explanatory letter from Marlow. From this last fell another letter, yellowed by time and frayed on the folds. He picked it up and, laying it aside, turned to Marlow's message, ran swiftly over the opening lines, and, checking himself, thereafter read on deliberately, like one approaching with slow feet and alert eyes the glimpse of an undiscovered country.

". . . I don't suppose you've forgotten," went on the letter. "You alone have showed an interest in him that survived the telling of his story, though I remember well you would not admit he had mastered his fate. You prophesied for him the disaster of weariness and of disgust with acquired honor, with the self-appointed task, with the love sprung from pity and youth. You had said you knew so well 'that kind of thing,' its illusory satisfaction, its unavoidable deception. You said also—I call to mind—that 'giving your life up to them' (*them* meaning all of mankind with skins brown, yellow, or black in color) 'was like selling your soul to a brute.' You contended that 'that kind of thing' was only endurable and enduring when based on a firm conviction in the truth of ideas racially our own, in whose name are established the order, the morality of an ethical progress. 'We want its strength at our backs,' you had said. 'We want a belief in its necessity and its justice, to make a worthy and conscious sacrifice of our lives. Without it the sacrifice is only forgetfulness, the way of offering is no better than the way to perdition.' In other words, you maintained that we must fight in the ranks or our lives don't count. Possibly! You ought to know—be it said without malice—you who have rushed into one or two places single-handed and come out cleverly, without singeing your wings. The point, however, is that, of all mankind, Jim had no dealings but with himself, and the question is whether at the last he had not confessed to a faith mightier than the laws of order and progress.

"I affirm nothing. Perhaps you may pronounce—after you've read. There is much truth—after all—in the common expression 'under a cloud.' It is impossible to see him clearly—especially as it is through the eyes of others that we take our last look at him. I have no hesitation in imparting to you all I know of the last episode that, as he used to say, had 'come to him.' One wonders whether this was perhaps that supreme opportunity, that last and satisfying test for which I had always suspected him to be waiting, before he could frame a message to the impeccable world. You remember that when I was leaving him for the last time he had asked whether I would be going home soon, and suddenly cried after me, 'Tell them!'. . . I had waited—curious, I'll own, and hopeful, too—only to hear him shout, 'No—nothing.' That was all then—and there shall be nothing more; there shall be no message, unless such as each of us can interpret for himself from the language of facts, that are so often more enigmatic than the craftiest arrangement of words. He made, it is true, one more attempt to deliver himself; but that too failed, as you may perceive if you look at the sheet of grayish foolscap enclosed here. He had tried to write; do you notice the commonplace hand? It is headed 'The Fort, Patusan.' I suppose he had carried out his intention of making out of his house a place of defense. It was an excellent plan: a deep ditch, an earth-wall topped by a palisade, and at the angles guns mounted on platforms to sweep each side of the square. Doramin had agreed to furnish him the guns; and so each man of his party would know there was a place of safety, upon which every faithful partisan could rally in case of some sudden danger. All this showed his judicious foresight, his faith in the future. What he called 'my own people'—the liberated captives of the Sherif— were to make a distinct quarter of Patusan, with their huts and little plots of ground under the walls of the stronghold. Within, he would be an invincible host in himself. 'The Fort, Patusan.' No date, as you observe. What is a number and a name to a day of days? It is also impossible to say whom he had in his mind when he seized the pen: Stein—myself—the world at large—or was this only the aimless, startled cry of a solitary man confronted by his fate? 'An awful thing has happened,' he wrote before he flung the pen down for the first time; look at the ink blot resembling the head of an arrow under these words. After a while he had tried again, scrawling heavily, as if with a hand of lead, another line. 'I must now at once . . .' The pen had spluttered, and that time he gave it up. There's nothing more; he had seen a broad gulf that neither eye nor voice could span. I can understand this. He was overwhelmed by the inexplicable; he was overwhelmed by his own personality—the gift of that destiny which he had done his best to master.

"I send you also an old letter—a very old letter. It was found carefully preserved in his writing case. It is from his father, and by the date you can see he
must have received it a few days before he joined the *Patna*. Thus it must be the
last letter he ever had from home. He had treasured it all these years. The good
old parson fancied his sailor-son. I've looked in at a sentence here and there.
There is nothing in it except just affection. He tells his 'dear James' that the last
long letter from him was very 'honest and entertaining.' He would not have him
'judge men harshly or hastily.' There are four pages of it, easy morality and family
news. Tom had 'taken orders.' Carrie's husband had 'money losses.' The old chap
goes on equally trusting Providence and the established order of the universe, but
alive to its small dangers and its small mercies. One can almost see him, gray-
haired and serene, in the inviolable shelter of his book-lined, faded, and comfortable study, where for forty years he had conscientiously gone over and over
again the round of his little thoughts, about faith and virtue, about the conduct of
life and the only proper manner of dying; where he had written so many sermons,
where he sits talking to his boy, over there, on the other side of the earth. But
what of the distance. Virtue is one all over the world, and there is only one faith,
one conceivable conduct of life, one manner of dying. He hopes his 'dear James'
will never forget that 'who once gives way to temptation, in the very instant hazards his total depravity and everlasting ruin. Therefore resolve fixedly, never,
through any possible motives, to do anything which you believe to be wrong.'
There is also some news of a favorite dog; and a pony, 'which all you boys used to
ride,' had gone blind from old age and had to be shot. The old chap invokes
Heaven's blessing; the mother and all the girls then at home send their love. . . .
No, there is nothing much in that yellow frayed letter fluttering out of his cherishing grasp after so many years. It was never answered, but who can say what converse he may have held with all these placid, colorless forms of men and women
peopling that quiet corner of the world as free of danger or strife as a tomb, and
breathing equably the air of undisturbed rectitude. It seems amazing that he
should belong to it, he to whom so many things 'had come.' Nothing ever came to
them; they would never be taken unawares, and never be called upon to grapple
with fate. Here they all are, evoked by the mild gossip of the father, all these
brothers and sisters, bone of his bone and flesh of his flesh, gazing with clear,
unconscious eyes, while I seem to see him, returned at last, no longer a mere
white speck at the heart of an immense mystery, but of full stature, standing disregarded amongst their untroubled shapes, with a stern and romantic aspect, but
always mute, dark—under a cloud.

"The story of the last events you shall find in the few pages enclosed here. You
must admit that it is romantic beyond the wildest dreams of his boyhood, and yet
there is to my mind a sort of profound and terrifying logic in it, as if it were our

imagination alone that could set loose upon us the might of an overwhelming destiny. The imprudence of our thoughts recoils upon our heads; who toys with the sword shall perish by the sword. This astounding adventure, of which the most astounding part is that it is true, comes on as an unavoidable necessity. Something of the sort had to happen. You repeat this to yourself while you marvel that such a thing could happen in the year of grace before last. But it has happened—and there is no disputing its logic.

"I relate it for you as though I had been an eyewitness. My information was fragmentary, but I put the pieces together, and there is enough of them to make an intelligible picture. I wonder how he would have related it himself. He has confided so much in me that at times it seems as though he must come in presently and tell the story in his own words, in his careless yet feeling voice, with his off-hand manner, a little puzzled, a little bothered, a little hurt, but now and then by a word or a phrase giving one of these glimpses of his very own self that were never any good for purposes of orientation. It's difficult to believe he will never come. I shall never hear his voice again, nor shall I see his smooth tan-and-pink face with a white line on the forehead, and the youthful eyes darkened by excitement to a profound, unfathomable blue."

❧ 37 ❧

It all begins with a remarkable exploit of a man called Brown, who stole with complete success a Spanish schooner out of a small bay near Zamboanga. Till I discovered the fellow my information was incomplete; but most unexpectedly I did come upon him a few hours before he gave up his arrogant ghost. Fortunately, he was willing and able to talk between the choking fits of asthma, and his racked body writhed with malicious exultation at the bare thought of Jim. He exulted thus at the idea that he had 'paid out the stuck-up beggar, after all.' He gloated over his action. I had to bear the sunken glare of his fierce crowfoot eyes if I wanted to know; and so I bore it, reflecting how much certain forms of evil are akin to madness, derived from intense egoism, inflamed by resistance, tearing the soul to pieces, and giving factitious rigor to the body. The story also reveals unsuspected depths of cunning in the wretched Cornelius, whose abject and intense hate acts like a subtle inspiration, pointing out an unerring way towards revenge.

"'I could see directly I set my eyes on him what sort of a fool he was,' gasped the dying Brown. 'He a man! Hell! He was a hollow sham. As if he couldn't have said straight out, "Hands off my plunder!" blast him! That would have been like a man! Rot his superior soul! He had me there—but he hadn't devil enough in him to make an end of me. Not he! A thing like that letting me off as if I wasn't worth a kick! . . . ' Brown struggled desperately for breath. . . . 'Fraud. . . . Letting me off. . . . And so I did make an end of him, after all. . . .' He choked again. . . . 'I expect this thing'll kill me, but I shall die easy now. You . . . you here. . . . I don't know your name—I would give you a five-pound note if—if I had it—for the news—or my name's not Brown. . . .' He grinned horribly. . . .'Gentleman Brown.'

"He said all these things in profound gasps, staring at me with his yellow eyes out of a long, ravaged, brown face; he jerked his left arm; a pepper-and-salt matted beard hung almost into his lap; a dirty, ragged blanket covered his legs. I had found him out in Bangkok through that busybody Schomberg, the hotel-keeper, who had, confidentially, directed me where to look. It appears that a sort of loafing, fuddled vagabond—a white man living amongst the natives with a Siamese woman—had considered it a great privilege to give a shelter to the last days of the famous Gentleman Brown. While he was talking to me in the wretched hovel, and, as it were, fighting for every minute of his life, the Siamese woman, with big bare legs and a stupid coarse face, sat in a dark corner chewing betel stolidly. Now and then she would get up for the purpose of shooing a chicken away from the door. The whole hut shook when she walked. An ugly yellow child, naked and pot-bellied like a little heathen god, stood at the foot of the couch, finger in mouth, lost in a profound and calm contemplation of the dying man.

"He talked feverishly, with a gleeful ferocity and a savage, unforgiving contempt for poor Jim; but in the middle of a word, perhaps, an invisible hand would take him by the throat, and he would look at me dumbly with a heaving breast and an expression of doubt and anguish. You could see his coarse lips turn blue behind the drooping, wiry hairs. He seemed to fear that I would get tired of waiting for the end of the choking fit and go away, leaving him with his tale untold, with his exultation unexpressed Nothing was farther from my thoughts; I was only afraid that death, hovering over him, would swoop down suddenly and baffle my desire to know. He died during the night, I believe, but by that time I had nothing more to learn.

"I knew the story before, of course; he had only cleared up an obscure point, though the profound blackness of the act cannot be dispelled.

"So much as to Brown, for the present.

"Eight months before this, coming into Samarang, I went as usual to see Stein. On the garden side of the house a Malay on the veranda greeted me shyly, and I remembered that I had seen him in Patusan, in Jim's house, amongst other Bugis men who used to come in the evening to talk interminably over their war reminiscences and to discuss State affairs. Jim had pointed him out to me once as a respectable petty trader owning a small seagoing native craft, who had showed himself 'one of the best at the taking of the stockade.' I was not very surprised to see him, since any Patusan trader venturing as far as Samarang would naturally find his way to Stein's house. I returned his greeting and passed on. At the door of Stein's room I came upon another Malay in whom I recognized Tamb' Itam.

"I asked him at once what he was doing there; it occurred to me that Jim might have come on a visit. I own I was pleased and excited at the thought. Tamb' Itam looked as if he did not know what to say. 'Is Tuan Jim inside?' I asked impatiently. 'No,' he mumbled, hanging his head for a moment, and then with sudden earnestness, 'He would not fight. He would not fight,' he repeated twice. As he seemed unable to say anything else, I pushed him aside and went in.

"Stein, tall and stooping, stood alone in the middle of the room, between the rows of butterfly cases. 'Ach! is it you, my friend?' he said sadly, peering through his glasses. A drab sack-coat of alpaca hung, unbuttoned, down to his knees. He had a Panama hat on his head, and there were deep furrows on his pale cheeks. 'What's the matter now?' I asked nervously. 'There's Tamb' Itam there. . . . ' 'Come and see the girl. Come and see the girl. She is here,' he said, with a half-hearted show of activity. I tried to detain him, but with gentle obstinacy he would take no notice of my eager questions. 'She is here, she is here,' he repeated in great perturbation. 'They came here two days ago. An old man like me, a stranger—*sehen sie*—cannot do much. . . . Come this way. . . . Young hearts are forgiving. . . .' I could see he was in utmost distress. . . . 'The strength of life in them, the cruel strength of life. . . .' He mumbled, leading me round the house; I followed him, lost in dismal and angry conjectures. At the door of the drawing room he barred my way. 'He loved her very much,' he said interrogatively, and I only nodded, feeling so bitterly disappointed that I would not trust myself to speak. 'Very frightful,' he murmured. 'She can't understand me. I am only a strange old man. Perhaps you . . . she knows you. Talk to her. We can't leave it like this. Tell her to forgive him. It was very frightful.' 'No doubt,' I said, exasperated at being in the dark; 'but have *you* forgiven him?' He looked at me dark; queerly. 'You shall hear,' he said, and opening the door, absolutely pushed me in.

"You know Stein's big house and the two immense reception rooms, uninhabited and uninhabitable, clean, full of solitude and of shining things that look as if never beheld by the eye of man? They are cool on the hottest days, and you enter them as you would a scrubbed cave underground. I passed through one, and in the other I saw the girl sitting at the end of a big mahogany table, on which she rested her head, the face hidden in her arms. The waxed floor reflected her dimly as though it had been a sheet of frozen water. The rattan screens were down, and through the strange greenish gloom made by the foliage of the trees outside a strong wind blew in gusts, swaying the long draperies of windows and doorways. Her white figure seemed shaped in snow; the pendent crystals of a great chandelier clicked above her head like glittering icicles. She looked up and watched my approach. I was chilled as if these vast apartments had been the cold abode of despair.

"She recognized me at once, and as soon as I had stopped looking down at her: 'He has left me,' she said quietly; 'you always leave us—for your own ends.' Her face was set. All the heat of life seemed withdrawn within some inaccessible spot in her breast. 'It would have been easy to die with him,' she went on, and made a slight weary gesture as if giving up the incomprehensible. 'He would not! It was like a blindness—and it was I who was speaking to him; it was I who stood before his eyes; it was at me that he looked all the time! Ah! you are hard, treacherous, without truth, without compassion. What makes you so wicked? Or is it that you are all mad?'

"I took her hand; it was inert, and when I dropped it it hung down to the floor. That indifference, more awful than tears, cries, and reproaches, seemed to defy time and consolation. You felt that it would never exhaust itself, and that nothing you could say would reach the seat of the still and benumbing pain.

"Stein had told me, 'You shall hear.'. . . I did hear. I heard it all, listening with amazement, with awe, to the tones of her inflexible weariness. She could not grasp the real sense of what she was telling me, and her resentment filled me with pity for her—for him, too. I stood rooted to the spot after she had finished. Leaning on her arm, she stared with hard eyes, and the wind passed in gusts, the crystals kept on clicking in the greenish gloom. She went on whispering to herself: 'And yet he was looking at me! He could see my face, hear my voice, hear my grief! When I used to sit at his feet, with my cheek against his knee and his hand on my head, the curse of cruelty and madness was already within him, waiting for the day. The day came! . . . and before the sun had set he could not see me anymore—he was made blind and deaf and without pity, as you all are. He shall have no tears from me. Never, never. Not one tear. I will not! He went away from me as if I had been worse than death. He fled as if driven by some accursed thing he had heard or seen in his sleep. . . .'

"Her steady eyes seemed to strain after the shape of a man torn out of her arms by the strength of a dream. She made no sign to my silent bow. I was glad to escape.

"I saw her once again, the same afternoon. On leaving her I had gone in search of Stein, whom I could not find indoors; and I wandered out, pursued by distressful thoughts, into the gardens, these famous gardens of Stein, in which you can find every plant and tree of tropical lowlands. I followed the course of the canalized stream, and sat for a long time on a shaded bench near the ornamental pond, where some waterfowl with clipped wings were diving and splashing noisily. The branches of casuarina trees behind me swayed slightly, incessantly, reminding me of the soughing of the fir trees at home.

"This mournful and restless sound was a fit accompaniment to my meditations. She had said he had been driven away from her by a dream, and there was no answer one could make her—there seemed to be no forgiveness for such a transgression. And yet is not mankind itself, pushing on its blind way, driven by a dream of its greatness and its power upon the dark paths of excessive cruelty and excessive devotion? And what is the pursuit of truth—after all?

"When I rose to get back to the house I caught sight of Stein's drab coat through a gap in the foliage, and very soon at a turn of the path I came upon him walking with the girl. Her little hand rested on his forearm, and under the broad, flat rim of his Panama hat he bent over her, gray-haired, paternal, with compassionate and chivalrous deference. I stood aside, but they stopped, facing me. His gaze was bent on the ground at his feet; the girl, erect and slight on his arm, stared somberly beyond my shoulder with big, clear, motionless eyes. '*Schrecklich*,' he murmured. 'Terrible! Terrible! What can one do? ' He seemed to be appealing to me, but her youth, the length of days suspended over her head, appealed to me more; and suddenly, even as I realized that nothing could be said, I found myself pleading his cause for her sake. 'You must forgive him,' I concluded, and my own voice seemed to me muffled, lost in an irresponsive deaf immensity. 'We all want to be forgiven,' I added, after a while.

"'What have I done?' she asked with her lips only.

"'You always mistrusted him,' I said.

"'He was like the others,' she pronounced slowly.

"'Not like the others,' I protested, but she continued evenly, without any feeling—

"'He was false.' And suddenly Stein broke in. 'No! no! no! My poor child! . . .' He patted her hand lying passively on his sleeve. 'No! no! Not false! True! true! true!' He tried to look into her stony face. 'You don't understand. Ach! Why you do not understand? . . . Terrible,' he said to me. 'Some day she *shall* understand.'

"'Will *you* explain?' I asked, looking hard at him. They moved on.

"I watched them. Her gown trailed on the path, her black hair fell loose. She walked upright and light by the side of the tall man, whose long, shapeless coat hung in perpendicular folds from the stooping shoulders, whose feet moved slowly. They disappeared beyond that spinney (you may remember) where sixteen different kinds of bamboo grow together, all distinguishable to the learned eye. For my part, I was fascinated by the exquisite grace and beauty of that fluted grove, crowned with pointed leaves and feathery heads, the lightness, the rigor, the charm as distinct as a voice of that unperplexed luxuriating life. I remember staying to look at it for a long time, as one would linger within reach of a consoling whisper. The sky was pearly gray. It was one of these overcast days so rare in the tropics, in which memories crowd upon one, memories of other shores, of other faces.

"I drove back to town the same afternoon, taking with me Tamb' Itam and the other Malay, in whose seagoing craft they had escaped in the bewilderment, fear, and gloom of the disaster. The shock of it seemed to have changed their natures. It had turned her passion into stone, and it made the surly, taciturn Tamb' Itam almost loquacious. His surliness, too, was subdued into puzzled humility, as though he had seen the failure of a potent charm in a supreme moment. The Bugis trader, a shy, hesitating man, was very clear in the little he had to say. Both were evidently overawed by a sense of deep, inexpressible wonder, by the touch of an inscrutable mystery."

There with Marlow's signature the letter proper ended. The privileged reader screwed up his lamp, and solitary above the billowy roofs of the town, like a lighthouse keeper above the sea, he turned to the pages of the story.

❦ 38 ❦

It all begins, as I've told you, with the man called Brown," ran the opening sentence of Marlow's narrative. "You who have knocked about in the Western Pacific must have heard of him. He was the show ruffian on the Australian coast, not that he was often to be seen there, but because he was always trotted out in the stories of lawless life a visitor from home is treated to; and the mildest of these stories which were told about him from Cape York to Eden Bay was more than enough to hang a man if told in the right place. They never failed to tell you he was supposed to be the son of a baronet. Be it as it may, it is certain he had deserted from a home ship in the early gold-digging days, and in a few years became talked about as the terror of this or that group of islands in Polynesia. He would kidnap natives, he would strip some lonely white trader to the very pajamas he stood in, and after he had robbed the poor devil, he would as likely as not invite him to fight a duel with shotguns on the beach, which would have been fair enough as these things go, if the other man hadn't been by that time already half-dead with fright. Brown was a latter-day buccaneer, sorry enough, like his more celebrated prototypes; but what distinguished him from his contemporary brother ruffians, like Bully Hayes or the mellifluous Pease, or that perfumed, Dundreary-whiskered, dandified scoundrel known as Dirty Dick, was the arrogant temper of his misdeeds and a vehement scorn for mankind at large and for his victims in particular. The others were merely vulgar and greedy brutes, but he seemed moved by some complex intention. He would rob a man as if only to demonstrate his poor opinion of the creature, and he would bring to the shooting or maiming of some quiet, unoffending stranger a savage and vengeful earnestness fit to terrify the most reckless of desperadoes. In the days of his greatest glory he owned an armed bark, manned by a mixed crew of Kanakas and runaway whalers, and boasted, I don't know with what truth, of being financed on the quiet by a most respectable firm of copra merchants. Later on he ran off—it was reported— with the wife of a missionary, a very young girl from Clapham way, who had married the mild, flatfooted fellow in a moment of enthusiasm, and suddenly transplanted to Melanesia, lost her bearings, somehow. It was a dark story. She was ill at the time he carried her off, and died on board his ship. It is said—as the most wonderful part of the tale—that over her body he gave way to an outburst of somber and violent grief. His luck left him, too, very soon after. He lost his ship on some rocks off Malaita, and disappeared for a time as though he had gone down with her. He is heard of next at Nuka-Hiva, where he bought an old French schooner out of Government service. What creditable enterprise he might have had in view when he made that purchase I can't say, but it is evident that what with High Commissioners, consuls, men-of-war, and international control, the South Seas were getting too hot to hold gentlemen of his kidney. Clearly, he must have shifted the scene of his operations farther west; because a year later he plays an incredibly audacious, but not a very profitable part, in a serio-comic business in Manila Bay, in which a peculating governor and an absconding treasurer are the principal figures; thereafter he seems to have hung around the Philippines in his rotten schooner, battling with an adverse fortune, till at last, running his appointed course, he sails into Jim's history, a blind accomplice of the Dark Powers.

"His tale goes that when a Spanish patrol-cutter captured him he was simply trying to run a few guns for the insurgents. If so, then I can't understand what he was doing off the south coast of Mindanao. My belief, however, is that he was blackmailing the native villages along the coast. The principal thing is that the cutter, throwing a guard on board, made him sail in company towards Zamboanga. On the way, for some reason or other, both vessels had to come-to off one of these new Spanish settlements—which never came to anything in the end—where there was not only a civil official in charge on shore, but a good stout coasting schooner lying at anchor in the little bay; and this craft, in every way much better than his own, Brown made up his mind to steal.

"He was down on his luck—as he told me himself. The world he had bullied for twenty years with fierce, aggressive disdain, had yielded him nothing in the way of material advantage except a small bag of silver dollars, which was concealed in his cabin so that 'the devil himself couldn't smell it out.' And that was all— absolutely all. He was tired of his life, and not afraid of death. But this man, who would stake his existence on a whim, with a bitter and jeering recklessness, was mortally afraid of a prison. He had an unreasoning cold-sweat, nerve-shaking, blood-to-water-turning sort of horror at the bare possibility of being locked up— the sort of fear a superstitious man would feel at the thought of being embraced by a specter. Therefore, the civil official who came on board to make a preliminary investigation into the capture, investigated arduously all day long, and only went ashore after dark, muffled up in a cloak, and taking great care not to let Brown's dollars clink in their bag. Afterwards, being a man of his word, he contrived, the very next evening, to send off the Government cutter on some urgent bit of special service. As her commander could not spare a prize crew, he contented himself by taking away before he left all the sails of Brown's schooner to the very, last rag, and towed his two boats on to the beach a couple of miles off.

"But in Brown's crew there was a Solomon Islander, kidnapped in his youth and devoted to Brown, who was the best man of the whole gang. That fellow swam off to the coaster—five hundred yards or so—with the end of a warp made up of all the running gear unrove for the purpose. The water was smooth, and the bay dark, 'like the inside of a cow,' as Brown described it. The Solomon Islander clambered over the bulwarks with the end of the rope in his teeth. The crew of the coaster— all Tagals—were ashore having a jollification in the native village. The two ship- keepers left on board woke up and saw the devil. It had glittering eyes and leaped quick as lightning about the deck. They fell on their knees, paralyzed with fear, crossing themselves and mumbling prayers. With a knife he found in the caboose the Solomon Islander, without interrupting their orisons, stabbed first one, then the other; with the same knife he set to sawing patiently at the coir cable till sud- denly it parted under the blade with a splash. Then, in the silence of the bay, he let out a cautious shout, and Brown's gang, who meantime had been peering and straining their hopeful ears in the darkness, began to pull gently at their end of the warp. In less than five minutes the two schooners came together with a slight shock and a creak of spars.

"Brown's crowd transferred themselves without losing an instant, taking with them their firearms and a large supply of ammunition. They were sixteen in all: two runaway blue-jackets, a lanky deserter from a Yankee man-of-war, a couple of simple, blond Scandinavians, a mulatto of sorts, one bland Chinaman who cooked—and the rest of the nondescript spawn of the South Seas. None of them cared; Brown bent them to his will, and Brown, indifferent to the gallows, was running away from the specter of a Spanish prison. He didn't give them the time to trans-ship enough provisions; the weather was calm, the air was charged with dew, and when they cast off the ropes and set sail to a faint offshore draught there was no flutter in the damp canvas; their old schooner seemed to detach itself gently from the stolen craft and slip away silently, together with the black mass of the coast, into the night.

"They got clear away. Brown related to me in detail their passage down the Straits of Macassar. It is a harrowing and desperate story. They were short of food and water; they boarded several native craft and got a little from each. With a stolen ship Brown did not dare to put into any port, of course. He had no money to buy anything, no papers to show, and no lie plausible enough to get him out again. An Arab bark, under the Dutch flag, surprised one night at anchor off Poulo Laut, yielded a little dirty rice, a bunch of bananas, and a cask of water; three days of squally, misty weather from the northeast shot the schooner across the Java Sea. The yellow, muddy waves drenched that collection of hungry ruffians. They sighted mailboats moving on their appointed routes; passed well-found home ships with rusty iron sides anchored in the shallow sea waiting for a change of weather or the turn of the tide; an English gunboat, white and trim, with two slim masts, crossed their bows one day in the distance; and on another occasion a Dutch corvette, black and heavily sparred, loomed up on their quarter, steaming dead slow in the mist. They slipped through unseen or disregarded, a wan, sallow-faced band of utter outcasts, enraged with hunger and hunted by fear. Brown's idea was to make for Madagascar, where he expected, on grounds not altogether illusory, to sell the schooner in Tamatave, and no questions asked, or perhaps obtain some more or less forged papers for her. Yet before he could face the long passage across the Indian Ocean food was wanted—water too.

"Perhaps he had heard of Patusan—or perhaps he just only happened to see the name written in small letters on the chart—probably that of a largish village up a river in a native state, perfectly defenseless, far from the beaten tracks of the sea and from the ends of submarine cables. He had done that kind of thing before—in the way of business; and this now was an absolute necessity, a question of life and death—or rather of liberty. Of liberty! He was sure to get provisions—bullocks—rice—sweet potatoes. The sorry gang licked their chops. A cargo of produce for the schooner perhaps could be extorted—and, who knows—some real, ringing, coined money! Some of these chiefs and village headmen can be made to part freely. He told me he would have roasted them rather than be balked. I believe him. His men believed him, too. They didn't cheer aloud, being a dumb pack, but made ready wolfishly.

"Luck served him as to weather. A few days of calm would have brought unmentionable horrors on board that schooner, but with the help of land and sea breezes, in less than a week after clearing the Sunda Straits, he anchored off the

Batu Kring mouth within a pistol shot of the fishing village.

"Fourteen of them packed into the schooner's longboat (which was big, having been used for cargo work) and started up the river, while two remained in charge of the schooner with food enough to keep starvation off for ten days. The tide and wind helped, and early one afternoon the big white boat under a ragged sail shouldered its way before the sea breeze into Patusan Reach, manned by fourteen assorted scarecrows glaring hungrily ahead, and fingering the breech-blocks of cheap rifles. Brown calculated upon the terrifying surprise of his appearance. They sailed in with the last of the flood; the Rajah's stockade gave no sign; the first houses on both sides of the stream seemed deserted. A few canoes were seen up the reach in full flight. Brown was astonished at the size of the place. A profound silence reigned. The wind dropped between the houses; two oars were got out and the boat held on upstream, the idea being to effect a lodgment in the center of the town before the inhabitants could think of resistance.

"It seems, however, that the headman of the fishing village at Batu Kring had managed to send off a timely warning. When the longboat came abreast of the mosque (which Doramin had built: a structure with gables and roof finials of carved coral) the open space before it was full of people. A shout went up, and was followed by a clash of gongs all up the river. From a point above two little brass six-pounders were discharged, and the round shot came skipping down the empty reach, spitting glittering jets of water in the sunshine. In front of the mosque a shouting lot of men began firing in volleys that whipped athwart the current of the river; an irregular, rolling fusillade was opened on the boat from both banks, and Brown's men replied with a wild, rapid fire. The oars had been got in.

"The turn of the tide at high water comes on very quick in that river, and the boat in midstream, nearly hidden in smoke, began to drift back, stern foremost. Along both shores the smoke thickened also, lying below the roofs in a level streak as you may see a long cloud cutting the slope of a mountain. A tumult of war cries, the vibrating clang of gongs, the deep snoring of drums, yells of rage, crashes of volley-firing, made an awful din, in which Brown sat confounded but steady at the tiller, working himself into a fury of hate and rage against those people who dared to defend themselves. Two of his men had been wounded, and he saw his retreat cut off below the town by some boats that had put off from Tunku Allang's stockade. There were six of them full of men. While he was thus beset he perceived the entrance of the narrow creek (the same which Jim had jumped at low water). It was then brim full. Steering the longboat in, they landed, and to make a long story short, they established themselves on a little knoll about nine hundred yards from the stockade, which, in fact, they commanded from that position. The slopes of the knoll were bare, but there were a few trees on the summit. They went to work cutting these down for a breastwork, and were fairly entrenched before dark; meantime the Rajah's boats remained in the river with curious neutrality. When the sun set the glare of many brushwood blazes lighted on the riverfront, and between the double line of houses on the land side threw into black relief the roofs, the groups of slender palms, the heavy clumps of fruit trees. Brown ordered the grass round his position to be fired; a low ring of thin flames under the slow ascending smoke wriggled rapidly down the slopes of the knoll; here and there a dry bush caught with a tall, vicious roar. The conflagration made a clear zone of fire for the rifles of the small party, and expired smoldering on the edge of the forests and along the muddy bank of the creek. A strip of jungle luxuriating in a damp hollow between the knoll and the Rajah's stockade stopped it on that side with a great crackling and detonations of bursting bamboo stems. The sky was somber, velvety, and swarming with stars. The blackened ground smoked quietly with low, creeping wisps, till a little breeze came on and blew everything away. Brown expected an attack to be delivered as soon as the tide had flowed enough again to enable the war-boats which had cut off his retreat to enter the creek. At any rate, he was sure there would be an attempt to carry off his longboat, which lay below the hill, a dark, high lump on the feeble sheen of a wet mudflat. But no move of any sort was made by the boats in the river. Over the stockade and the Rajah's buildings Brown saw their lights on the water. They seemed to be anchored across the stream. Other lights afloat were moving in the reach, crossing and recrossing from side to side. There were also lights twinkling motionless upon the long walls of houses up the reach, as far as the bend, and more still beyond, others isolated inland. The loom of the big fires disclosed buildings, roofs, black piles as far as he could see. It was an immense place. The fourteen desperate invaders lying flat behind the felled trees raised their chins to look over at the stir of that town that seemed to extend up river for miles and swarm with thousands of angry men. They did not speak to each other. Now and then they would hear a loud yell, or a single shot rang out, fired very far somewhere. But round their position everything was still, dark, silent. They seemed to be forgotten, as if the excitement keeping awake all the population had nothing to do with them, as if they had been dead already."

❧ 39 ❧

All the events of that night have a great importance, since they brought about a situation which remained unchanged till Jim's return. Jim had been away in the interior for more than a week, and it was Dain Waris who had directed the first repulse. That brave and intelligent youth ('who knew how to fight after the manner of white men') wished to settle the business off-hand, but his people were too much for him. He had not Jim's racial prestige and the reputation of invincible, supernatural power. He was not the visible, tangible incarnation of unfailing truth and of unfailing victory. Beloved, trusted, and admired as he was, he was still one of *them*, while Jim was one of *us*. Moreover, the white man, a tower of strength in himself, was invulnerable, while Dain Waris could be killed. Those unexpressed thoughts guided the opinions of the chief men of the town who elected to assemble in Jim's fort for deliberation upon the emergency as if to draw strength from the spirit of the absent white man. Their temper was unforgiving. The Bugis especially were exasperated. The shooting of Brown's ruffians was so far good and lucky that there had been half-a-dozen casualties amongst the defenders. The wounded were lying on the veranda tended by their women-folk. The women and children from the lower part of the town had been sent into the fort at the first alarm. There Jewel was in command, very efficient and high-spirited, obeyed by Jim's 'own people,' who, quitting in a body their little settlement under the stockade, had gone in to form the garrison. The refugees crowded round her; and through the whole affair, to the very disastrous last, she showed an extraordinary martial ardor. It was to her that Dain Waris had gone at once at the first intelligence of danger, for you must know that Jim was the only one in Patusan who possessed a store of gunpowder. Stein, with whom he had kept up intimate relations by letters, had obtained from the Dutch Government a special authorization to export five hundred kegs of it to Patusan. The powder magazine was a small hut of rough logs covered entirely with earth, and in Jim's absence the girl had the key. In the council held at eleven o'clock in the evening in Jim's dining room, she backed up Waris's advice for immediate and vigorous action. I am told that she stood up by the side of Jim's empty chair at the head of the long table and made a warlike, impassioned speech, which for the moment extorted murmurs of approbation from the assembled headmen. Old Doramin, who had not showed himself outside his own gate for more than a year, had been brought across with great difficulty. He was, of course, the chief man there. The temper of the council was very unforgiving, and the old man's word would have been decisive; but it is my opinion that, well aware of his son's fiery courage, he dared not pronounce the word. More dilatory counsels prevailed. A certain Haji Saman pointed out at great length that 'these tyrannical and ferocious men had delivered themselves to a certain death in any case. They would stand fast on their hill and starve, or they would try to regain their boat and be shot from ambushes across the creek, or they would break and fly into the forest and perish singly there.' He argued that by the use of proper stratagems these evil-minded strangers could be destroyed without the risk of a battle, and his words had a great weight, especially with the Patusan men proper. What unsettled the minds of the town-folk was the failure of the Rajah's boats to act at the decisive moment. It was the diplomatic Kassim who represented the Rajah at the council. He spoke very little, listened smilingly, very friendly and impenetrable. During the sitting messengers kept arriving every few minutes almost, with reports of the invaders' proceedings. Wild and exaggerated rumors were flying: there was a large ship at the mouth of the river with big guns and many more men—some white, others savages with black skins and of bloodthirsty appearance. They were coming with many more boats to exterminate every living thing. A sense of near incomprehensible danger affected the common folk. At one moment there was a panic in the courtyard amongst the women; shrieking; a rush; children crying—Haji Saman went out to quiet them. Then a fort sentry fired at something moving on the river, and nearly killed a villager bringing in his women-folk in a canoe together with the best of his domestic utensils and a dozen fowls. This caused more confusion. Meantime, the palaver inside Jim's house went on in the presence of the girl. Doramin sat fierce-faced, heavy, looking at the speakers in turn, and breathing slow like a bull. He didn't speak till the last, after Kassim had declared that the Rajah's boats would be called in because the men were required to defend his master's stockade. Dain Waris in his father's presence would offer no opinion, though the girl entreated him in Jim's name to speak out. She offered him Jim's own men, in her anxiety, to have these intruders driven out at once. He only shook his head after a glance or two at Doramin. Finally, when the council broke up, it had been decided that the houses nearest the creek should be strongly occupied to obtain the command of the enemy's boat. The boat itself was not to be interfered with openly, so that the robbers on the hill should be tempted to embark, when a well-directed fire would kill most of them, no doubt. To cut the escape of those who might survive, and to prevent more of them coming up, Dain Waris was ordered by Doramin to take an armed party of Bugis down the river to a certain spot fifteen miles below Patusan, and there form a camp on the shore and blockade the stream with the canoes. I don't believe for a moment that Doramin feared the arrival of fresh forces. My opinion is that his conduct was guided solely by his wish to keep his son out of harm's way. To prevent a rush being made into the town the construction of a stockade was to be commenced at daylight at the end of the street on the left bank. The old *nakhoda* declared his intention to command there himself. A distribution of powder, bullets, and percussion caps was made immediately under the girl's supervision. Several messengers were to be dispatched in different directions after Jim, whose exact whereabouts were unknown. These men started at dawn, but before that time Kassim had managed to open communications with the besieged Brown.

"That accomplished diplomatist and confidant of the Rajah, on leaving the fort to go back to his master, took into his boat Cornelius, whom he found slinking mutely amongst the people in the courtyard. Kassim had a little plan of his own and wanted him for an interpreter. Thus it came about that towards morning Brown, reflecting upon the desperate nature of his position, heard from the marshy overgrown hollow an amicable, quavering, strained voice crying—in English—for permission to come up, under a promise of personal safely and on a very important errand. He was overjoyed. If he was spoken to he was no longer a hunted wild beast. These friendly sounds took off at once the awful stress of vigilant watchfulness as of so many blind men not knowing whence the deathblow might come. He pretended a great reluctance. The voice declared itself 'a white man. A poor, ruined, old man who had been living here for years.' A mist, wet and chilly, lay on the slopes of the hill, and after some more shouting from one to the other, Brown called out, 'Come on, then, but alone, mind!' As a matter of fact—he told me, writhing with rage at the recollection of his helplessness—it made no difference. They couldn't see more than a few yards before them, and no treachery could make their position worse. By and by Cornelius, in his weekday attire of a ragged dirty shirt and pants, barefooted, with a broken-rimmed pith hat on his head, was made out vaguely, sidling up to the defenses, hesitating, stopping to listen in a peering posture. 'Come along! You are safe,' yelled Brown, while his men stared. All their hopes of life became suddenly centered in that dilapidated, mean newcomer, who in profound silence clambered clumsily over a felled tree trunk, and shivering, with his sour, mistrustful face, looked about at the knot of bearded, anxious, sleepless desperadoes.

"Half an hour's confidential talk with Cornelius opened Brown's eyes as to the home affairs of Patusan. He was on the alert at once. There were possibilities; immense possibilities; but before he would talk over Cornelius's proposals he demanded that some food should be sent up the hill as a guarantee of good faith. Cornelius went off, creeping sluggishly down the hill on the side of the Rajah's palace, and after some delay a few of Tunku Allang's men came up, bringing a scanty supply of rice, chilies, and dried fish. This was immeasurably better than nothing. Later on Cornelius returned, accompanying Kassim, who stepped out with an air of perfect good-humored trustfulness, in sandals, and muffled up from neck to ankles in white sheeting. He shook hands with Brown discreetly, and the three drew aside for a conference. Brown's men, recovering their confidence, were slapping each other on the back, and cast knowing glances at their captain while they busied themselves with preparations for cooking.

"Kassim disliked Doramin and his Bugis very much, but he hated the new order of things still more. It had occurred to him that these whites, together with the Rajah's followers, could attack and defeat the Bugis before Jim's return. Then he reasoned general defection was sure to follow, and the reign of the white man who protected poor people would be over. Afterwards, the new allies could be dealt with. They would have no friends. The fellow was perfectly able to perceive the difference of character, and had seen enough of white men to know that these newcomers were outcasts, men without country. Brown preserved a stern and inscrutable demeanor. When he first heard Cornelius's voice demanding admittance it brought merely the hope of a loophole for escape. In less than an hour other thoughts were seething in his head. Urged by an extreme necessity, he had come there to steal food, a few tons of rubber or gum maybe, perhaps a handful of dollars, and had found himself enmeshed by deadly dangers. Now, in consequence of these overtures from Kassim, he began to think of stealing the whole country. Some confounded fellow had apparently accomplished something of the kind— single-handed at that. Couldn't have done it very well, though. Perhaps they could work together—squeeze everything dry, and then go out quietly. In the course of his negotiations with Kassim he became aware that he was supposed to have a big ship with plenty of men outside. Kassim begged him earnestly to have this big ship with his many guns and men brought up the river without delay for the Rajah's service. Brown professed himself willing, and on this basis the negotiation was carried on with mutual distrust. Three times in the course of the morning the courteous and active Kassim went down to consult the Rajah, and came up busily with his long stride. Brown, while bargaining, had a sort of grim enjoyment in thinking of his wretched schooner with nothing but a heap of dirt in her hold, that stood for an armed ship, and a Chinaman and a lame ex-beachcomber of Levuka on board, who represented all his many men. In the afternoon he obtained further doles of food, a promise of some money, and supply of mats for his men to make shelters for themselves. They lay down and snored, protected from the burning sunshine; but Brown, sitting fully exposed on one of the felled trees, feasted his eyes upon the view of the town and the river. There was much loot there. Cornelius, who made himself at home in the camp, talked at his elbow, pointing out the localities, imparting advice, giving his own version of Jim's character and commenting in his own fashion upon the events of the last three years. Brown, who, apparently indifferent and gazing away, listened with attention to every word, could not make out clearly what sort of man this Jim could be. 'What's his name? Jim! Jim! That's not enough for a man's name.' 'They call him,' said Cornelius scornfully, 'Tuan Jim here. As you may say, Lord Jim.' 'What is he? Where does he come from?' inquired Brown. 'What sort of man is he? Is he an Englishman?' 'Yes, yes, he's an Englishman. I am an Englishman too. From Malacca. He is a fool. All you have to do is to kill him and then you are king here. Everything belongs to him,' explained Cornelius. 'It strikes me he may be made to share with somebody before very long,' commented Brown half-aloud. 'No, no. The proper way is to kill him the first chance you get, and then you can do what you like,' Cornelius would insist earnestly. 'I have lived for many years here, and I am giving you a friend's advice.'

"In such converse and in gloating over the view of Patusan, which he had determined in his mind should become his prey, Brown whiled away most of the afternoon while his men rested. On that day Dain Waris's fleet of canoes, stealing one by one under the shore farthest from the creek, went down to close the river against his retreat. Of this Brown was not aware, and Kassim, who came up the knoll an hour before sunset, took good care not to enlighten him. He wanted the white man's ship to come up the river, and this news, he feared, would be discouraging. He was very pressing with Brown to send the 'order,' offering, at the same time, a trusty messenger, who for greater secrecy (as he explained) would make his way by land to the mouth of the river and deliver the 'order' on board. After some reflection Brown judged it expedient to tear a page out of his pocket-book, on which he simply wrote, 'We are getting on. Big job. Detain the man.' The stolid youth selected by Kassim for that service performed it faithfully, and was rewarded by being suddenly tipped, head first, into the schooner's empty hold by the ex-beachcomber and the Chinaman, who thereupon hastened to put on the hatches. What became of him afterwards Brown did not say."

❧ 40 ❧

Brown's object was to gain time by fooling with Kassim's diplomacy. For doing a real stroke of business he could not help thinking the white man, was the person to work with. He could not imagine such a chap (who must be confoundedly clever, after all, to get hold of the natives like that) refusing a help that would do away with the necessity for slow, cautious, risky cheating, that imposed itself as the only possible line of conduct for a single-handed man. He, Brown, would offer him the power. No man could hesitate. Everything was in coming to a clear understanding. Of course they would share. The idea of there being a fort—all ready to his hand—a real fort, with artillery (he knew this from Cornelius), excited him. Let him only once get in and . . . He would impose modest conditions. Not too low, though. The man was no fool, it seemed. They would work like brothers till . . . till the time came for a quarrel and a shot that would settle all accounts. With grim impatience of plunder he wished himself to be talking with the man now. The land already seemed to be his to tear to pieces, squeeze, and throw away. Meantime, Kassim had to be fooled for the sake of food first— and for a second string. But the principal thing was to get something to eat from day to day. Besides, he was not averse to begin fighting on that Rajah's account, and teach a lesson to those people who had received him with shots. The lust of battle was upon him.

"I am sorry that I can't give you this part of the story, which of course I have mainly from Brown, in Brown's own words. There was in the broken, violent speech of that man, unveiling before me his thoughts with the very hand of Death upon his throat, an undisguised ruthlessness of purpose, a strange vengeful attitude towards his own past, and a blind belief in the righteousness of his will as against all mankind, something of that feeling which could induce the leader of a horde of wandering cutthroats to call himself proudly the Scourge of God. No doubt the natural senseless ferocity which is the basis of such a character was exasperated by failure, ill-luck, and the recent privations, as well as by the desperate position in which he found himself; but what was most remarkable of all was this, that while he planned treacherous alliances, had already settled in his mind the fate of the white man, and intrigued in an overbearing, offhand manner with Kassim, one could perceive that what he really desired,

284

almost in spite of himself, was to play havoc with that jungle town which had defied him, to see it strewn over with corpses and enveloped in flames. Listening to his pitiless, panting voice, I could imagine how he must have looked at it from the hillock, peopling it with images of murder and rapine. The part nearest to the creek wore an abandoned aspect, though as a matter of fact every house concealed a few armed men on the alert. Suddenly, far over the stretch of waste ground, interspersed with small patches of low, dense bush, excavation, heaps of rubbish, with trodden paths between, a man, solitary and looking very small, strolled out into the deserted opening of the street between the shut-up, dark, lifeless buildings at the end. Perhaps one of the inhabitants, who had fled to the other bank of the river, coming back for some object of domestic use. Evidently, he supposed himself quite safe at that distance from the hill on the other side of the creek. A light stockade, set up hastily, was just round the turn of the street, full of his friends. He moved leisurely. Brown saw him, and instantly called to his side the Yankee deserter, who acted as a sort of second in command. This lanky, loose-jointed fellow came forward, wooden-faced, trailing his rifle lazily. When he understood what was wanted from him, a homicidal and conceited smile uncovered his teeth, making two deep folds down his sallow, leathery cheeks. He prided himself on being a dead shot. He dropped on one knee, and taking aim from a steady rest through the unlopped branches of a felled tree, fired, and at once stood up to look. The man, far away, turned his head to the report, made another step forward, seemed to hesitate, and abruptly got down on his hands and knees. In the silence that fell upon the sharp crack of the rifle, the dead shot, keeping his eyes fixed upon the quarry, guessed that 'this there coon's health would never be a source of anxiety to his friends any more.' The man's limbs were seen to move rapidly under his body in an endeavor to run on all fours. In that empty space arose a multitudinous shout of dismay and surprise. The man sank flat, face down, and moved no more. 'That showed them what we could do,' said Brown to me. 'Struck the fear of sudden death into them. That was what we wanted. They were two hundred to one, and this gave them something to think over for the night. Not one of them had an idea of such a long shot before. That beggar belonging to the Rajah scouted downhill with his eyes hanging out of his head.'

"As he was telling me this he tried with a shaking hand to wipe the thin foam from his blue, writhing lips. 'Two hundred to one. Two hundred to one . . . strike terror, . . . terror, terror, I tell you. . . .' His own eyes were starting out of their sockets. He fell back, clawing the air with skinny, earthy fingers, sat up again, bowed and hairy, glared at me sideways like some man-beast of folklore, with open mouth in his miserable and awful agony before he got his speech back after that fit. There are sights one never forgets.

"Furthermore, to draw the enemy's fire and locate such parties as might have been hiding in the bushes along the creek, Brown ordered the Solomon Islander to go down to the boat and bring an oar, as you send a spaniel after a stick into the water. This failed, and the fellow came back without a single shot having been fired at him from anywhere. 'There's nobody,' opined some of the men. It is 'onnatural,' remarked the Yankee. Kassim, indeed, had gone, very much impressed, pleased too, and also uneasy. Pursuing his tortuous policy, he had despatched a message to Dain Waris warning him to look out for the white men's ship, which, he had had information, was about to come up the river. He minimized its strength and exhorted him to oppose its passage. This double-dealing answered his purpose, which was to keep the Bugis forces divided and to weaken them by fighting. On the other hand, he had in the course of that day sent word to the assembled Bugis chiefs in town assuring them that he was trying to induce the invaders to retire; his messages to the fort asked earnestly for powder for the Rajah's men. It was a long time since Tunku Allang had had ammunition for the score or so of old muskets rusting in their arm-racks in the audience hall. The open intercourse between the hill and the palace unsettled all the minds. It was already time for men to take sides, it began to be said. There would soon be much bloodshed, and thereafter great trouble for many people. The social fabric of orderly, peaceful life, when every man was sure of tomorrow, the edifice raised by Jim's hands, seemed on that evening ready to collapse into a ruin reeking with blood. The poorer folk were already taking to the bush or flying up the river. A good many of the upper class judged it necessary to go and pay their court to the Rajah. The Rajah's youths jostled them rudely. Old Tunku Allang, almost out of his mind with fear and indecision, either kept a sullen silence or abused them violently for daring to come with empty hands; they departed very much frightened; only old Doramin kept his countrymen together and pursued his tactics inflexibly. Enthroned in a big chair behind the improvised stockade, he issued his orders in a deeply veiled rumble, unmoved, like a deaf man, in the flying rumors.

"Dusk fell, hiding first the body of the dead man, which had been left lying with arms outstretched as if nailed to the ground, and then the revolving sphere of the night rolled smoothly over Patusan and came to a rest, showering the glitter of countless worlds upon the earth. Again, in the exposed part of the town, big fires blazed along the only street, revealing from distance to distance upon their glares the falling straight lines of roofs, the fragments of wattled walls jumbled in confusion, here and there a whole hut elevated in the glow upon the vertical black stripes of a group of high piles; and all this line of dwellings, revealed in patches by the swaying flames, seemed to flicker tortuously away up river into the gloom at the heart of the land. A great silence, in which the looms of successive fires played without noise, extended into the darkness at the foot of the hill; but the other bank of the river, all dark save for a solitary bonfire at the river front before the fort, sent out into the air an increasing tremor that might have been the stamping of a multitude of feet, the hum of many voices, or the fall of an immensely distant waterfall. It was then, Brown confessed to me, while, turning his back on his men, he sat looking at it all, that notwithstanding his disdain, his ruthless faith in himself, a feeling came over him that at last he had run his head against a stone wall. Had his boat been afloat at the time, he believed he would have tried to steal away, taking his chances of a long chase down the river and of starvation at sea. It is very doubtful whether he would have succeeded in getting away. However, he didn't try this. For another moment he had a passing thought of trying to rush the town, but he perceived very well that in the end he would find himself in the lighted street, where they would be shot down like dogs from the houses. They were two hundred to one—he thought, while his men, huddling round two heaps of smoldering embers, munched the last of the bananas and roasted the few yams they owed to Kassim's diplomacy. Cornelius sat amongst them dozing sulkily.

"Then one of the whites remembered that some tobacco had been left in the boat, and, encouraged by the impunity of the Solomon Islander, said he would go to fetch it. At this all the others shook off their despondency. Brown, applied to, said, 'Go, and be damned to you,' scornfully. He didn't think there was any danger in going to the creek in the dark. The man threw a leg over the tree trunk and disappeared. A moment later he was heard clambering into the boat and then clambering out. 'I've got it,' he cried. A flash and a report at the very foot of the hill followed. 'I am hit' yelled the man. 'Look out, look out—I am hit,' and instantly all the rifles went off. The hill squirted fire and noise into the night like a little volcano, and when Brown and the Yankee, with curses and cuffs, stopped the panic-stricken firing, a profound, weary groan floated up from the creek, succeeded by a plaint whose heartrending sadness was like some poison turning the blood cold in the veins. Then a strong voice pronounced several distinct incomprehensible words somewhere beyond the creek. 'Let no one fire,' shouted Brown. 'What does it mean?'. . . 'Do you hear on the hill? Do you hear? Do you hear?' repeated the voice three times. Cornelius translated, and then prompted the answer. 'Speak,' cried Brown, 'we hear.' Then the voice, declaiming in the sonorous inflated tone of a herald, and shifting continually on the edge of the vague wasteland, proclaimed that between the men of the Bugis nation living in Patusan and the white men on the hill and those with them, there would be no faith, no compassion, no speech, no peace. A bush rustled; a haphazard volley rang out. 'Dam' foolishness,' muttered the Yankee, vexedly grounding the butt. Cornelius translated. The wounded man below the hill, after crying out twice, 'Take me up! take me up!' went on complaining in moans. While he had kept on the blackened earth of the slope, and afterwards crouching in the boat, he had been safe enough. It seems that in his joy at finding the tobacco he forgot himself and jumped out on her offside, as it were. The white boat, lying high and dry, showed him up; the creek was no more than seven yards wide in that place, and there happened to be a man crouching in the bush on the other bank.

"He was a Bugis of Tondano only lately come to Patusan, and a relation of the man shot in the afternoon. That famous long shot had indeed appalled the beholders. The man, in utter security, had been struck down, in full view of his friends, dropping with a joke on his lips, and they seemed to see in the act an atrocity which had stirred a bitter rage. That relation of his, Si-Lapa by name, was then with Doramin in the stockade only a few feet away. You who know these chaps must admit that the fellow showed an unusual pluck by volunteering to carry the message, alone, in the dark. Creeping across the open ground, he had deviated to the left and found himself opposite the boat. He was startled when Brown's man shouted. He came to a sitting position with his gun to his shoulder, and when the other jumped out, exposing himself, he pulled the trigger and lodged three jagged slugs pointblank into the poor wretch's stomach. Then, lying flat on his face, he gave himself up for dead, while a thin hail of lead chopped and swished the bushes close on his right hand; afterwards he delivered his speech shouting, bent double, dodging all the time in cover. With the last word he leaped sideways, lay close for a while, and afterwards got back to the houses unharmed, having achieved on that night such a renown as his children will not willingly allow to die.

"And on the hill the forlorn band let the two little heaps of embers go out under their bowed heads. They sat dejected on the ground with compressed lips and downcast eyes, listening to their comrade below. He was a strong man and died hard, with moans now loud, now sinking to a strange confidential note of pain. Sometimes he shrieked, and again, after a period of silence, he could be heard muttering deliriously a long and unintelligible complaint. Never for a moment did he cease.

"'What's the good?' Brown had said, unmoved once, seeing the Yankee, who had been swearing under his breath, prepare to go down. 'That's so,' assented the deserter, reluctantly desisting. 'There's no encouragement for wounded men here. Only his noise is calculated to make all the others think too much of the hereafter, cap'n.' 'Water!' cried the wounded man in an extraordinary clear, vigorous voice, and then went off moaning feebly. 'Ay, water. Water will do it,' muttered the other to himself resignedly. 'Plenty by and by. The tide is flowing.'

"At last the tide flowed, silencing the plaint and the cries of pain, and the dawn was near when Brown, sitting with his chin in the palm of his hand before Patusan, as one might stare at the unscalable side of a mountain, heard the brief ringing bark of a brass six-pounder far away in town somewhere. 'What's this?' he asked of Cornelius, who hung about him. Cornelius listened. A muffled roaring shout rolled down river over the town; a big drum began to throb, and others responded, pulsating and droning. Tiny scattered lights began to twinkle in the dark half of the town, while the part lighted by the loom of fires hummed with a deep and prolonged murmur. 'He has come,' said Cornelius. 'What? Already? Are you sure?' Brown asked. 'Yes! yes! Sure. Listen to the noise.' 'What are they making that row about?' pursued Brown. 'For joy,' snorted Cornelius; 'he is a very great man, but all the same, he knows no more than a child, and so they make a great noise to please him, because they know no better.' 'Look here,' said Brown, 'how is one to get at him?' 'He shall come to talk to you,' Cornelius declared. 'What do you mean? Come down here strolling, as it were?' Cornelius nodded vigorously in the dark. 'Yes. He will come straight here and talk to you. He is just like a fool. You shall see what a fool he is.' Brown was incredulous. 'You shall see; you shall see,' repeated Cornelius. 'He is not afraid—not afraid of anything. He will come and order you to leave his people alone. Everybody must leave his people alone. He is like a little child. He will come to you straight.' Alas! he knew Jim well—that 'mean little skunk,' as Brown called him to me. 'Yes, certainly,' he pursued with ardor, 'and then, captain, you tell that tall man with a gun to shoot him. Just you kill him, and you shall frighten everybody so much that you can do anything you like with them afterwards—get what you like—go away when you like. Ha! ha! ha! Fine . . .' He almost danced with impatience and eagerness, and Brown, looking over his shoulder at him, could see, shown up by the pitiless dawn, his men drenched with dew, sitting amongst the cold ashes and the litter of the camp, haggard, cowed, and in rags."

❧ 41 ❧

To the very last moment, till the full day came upon them with a spring, the fires on the west bank blazed bright and clear; and then Brown saw in a knot of colored figures motionless between the advanced houses a man in European clothes, in a helmet, all white. 'That's him; look! look!' Cornelius said excitedly. All Brown's men had sprung up and crowded at his back with lusterless eyes. The group of vivid colors and dark faces with the white figure in their midst were observing the knoll. Brown could see naked arms being raised to shade the eyes and other brown arms pointing. What should he do? He looked around, and the forests that faced him on all sides walled the cockpit of an unequal contest. He looked once more at his men. A contempt, a weariness, the desire of life, the wish to try for one more chance—for some other grave—struggled in his breast. From the outline the figure presented it seemed to him that the white man there, backed up by all the power of the land, was examining his position through binoculars. Brown jumped up on the log, throwing his arms up, the palms outwards. The colored group closed round the white man, and fell back twice before he got clear of them, walking slowly alone. Brown remained standing on the log till Jim, appearing and disappearing between the patches of thorny scrub, had nearly reached the creek; then Brown jumped off and went down to meet him on his side.

"They met, I should think, not very far from the place, perhaps on the very spot, where Jim took the second desperate leap of his life—the leap that landed him into the life of Patusan, into the trust, the love, the confidence of the people. They faced each other across the creek, and with steady eyes tried to understand each other before they opened their lips. Their antagonism must have been expressed in their glances; I know that Brown hated Jim at first sight. Whatever hopes he might have had vanished at once. This was not the man he had expected to see. He hated him for this—and in a checked flannel shirt with sleeves cut off at the elbows, gray-bearded, with a sunken, sun-blackened face—he cursed in his heart the other's youth and assurance, his clear eyes, and his untroubled bearing. That fellow had got in a long way before him! He did not look like a man who would be willing to give anything for assistance. He had all the advantages on his side—possession, security, power; he was on the side of an overwhelming force! He was not hungry and desperate, and he did not seem in the least afraid. And there was something in the very neatness of Jim's clothes, from the white helmet to the canvas leggings and the pipeclayed shoes, which in Brown's somber, irritated eyes seemed to belong to things he had in the very shaping of his life condemned and flouted.

"'Who are you?' asked Jim at last, speaking in his usual voice. 'My name's Brown,' answered the other loudly. 'Captain Brown. What's yours?' and Jim, after a little pause, went on quietly, as if he had not heard: 'What made you come here?' 'You want to know,' said Brown, bitterly. 'It's easy to tell. Hunger. And what made you?'

"'The fellow started at this,' said Brown, relating to me the opening of this strange conversation between those two men, separated only by the muddy bed of a creek, but standing on the opposite poles of that conception of life which includes all mankind—'The fellow started at this and got very red in the face. Too big to be questioned, I suppose. I told him that if he looked upon me as a dead man with whom you may take liberties, he himself was not a whit better off really. I had a fellow up there who had a bead drawn on him all the time, and only waited for a sign from me. There was nothing to be shocked at in this. He had come down of his own free will. "Let us agree," said I, "that we are both dead men, and let us talk on that basis, as equals. We are all equals before death," I said. I admitted I was there like a rat in a trap, but we had been driven to it, and even a trapped rat can give a bite. He caught me up in a moment. "Not if you don't go near the trap till the rat is dead." I told him that sort of game was good enough for these native friends of his, but I would have thought him too white to serve even a rat so. Yes, I had wanted to talk with him. Not to beg for my life, though. My fellows were—well—what they were—men like himself, anyhow. All we wanted from him was to come on in the devil's name and have it out. "God damn it," said I, while he stood there as still as a wooden post, "you don't want to come out here every day with your glasses to count how many of us are left on our feet. Come. Either bring your infernal crowd along or let us go out and starve in the open sea, by God! You have been white once, for all your tall talk of this being your own people and you being one with them. Are you? And what the devil do you get for it; what is it you've found here that is so damned precious? Hey? You don't want us to come down here, perhaps—do you? You are two hundred to one. You don't want us to come down into the open. Ah! I promise you we shall give you some sport before you've done. You talk about me making a cowardly set upon unoffending people. What's that to me that they are unoffending when I am starving for next to no offense? But I am not a coward. Don't you be one. Bring them along, or, by all the fiends, we shall yet manage to send half of your unoffending town to heaven with us in smoke!'"

"He was terrible—relating this to me—this tortured skeleton of a man drawn up together with his face over his knees, upon a miserable bed in that wretched hovel, and lifting his head to look at me with malignant triumph.

"'That's what I told him—I knew what to say,' he began again, feebly at first, but working himself up with incredible speed into a fiery utterance of his scorn. 'We aren't going into the forest to wander like a string of living skeletons dropping one after another for ants to go to work upon us before we are fairly dead. Oh, no! . . . "You don't deserve a better fate," he said. "And what do you deserve," I shouted at him, "you that I find skulking here with your mouth full of your responsibility, of innocent lives, of your infernal duty? What do you know more of me than I know of you? I came here for food. D'ye hear?—food to fill our bellies. And what did *you* come for? What did you ask for when you came here? We don't ask you for anything but to give us a fight or a clear road to go back whence we came. . . ." "I would fight with you now," says he, pulling at his little moustache. "And I would let you shoot me, and welcome," I said. "This is as good a jumping-off place for me as another. I am sick of my infernal luck. But it would be too easy. There are my men in the same boat—and, by God, I am not the sort to jump out of trouble and leave them in a damned lurch," I said. He stood thinking for a while and then wanted to know what I had done ("out there," he says, tossing his head down stream) to be hazed about so. "Have we met to tell each other the story of our lives?" I asked him. "Suppose you begin. No? Well, I am sure I don't want to hear. Keep it to yourself. I know it is no better than mine. I've lived—and so did you, though you talk as if you were one of those people that should have wings so as to go about without touching the dirty earth. Well—it is dirty. I haven't got any wings. I am here because I was afraid once in my life. Want to know what of? Of a prison. That scares me, and you may know it—if it's any good to you. I won't ask you what scared you into this infernal hole, where you seem to have found pretty pickings. That's your luck and this is mine—the privilege to beg for the favor of being shot quickly, or else kicked out to go free and starve in my own way.". . .'

"His debilitated body shook with an exultation so vehement, so assured, and so malicious that it seemed to have driven off the death waiting for him in that hut. The corpse of his mad self-love uprose from rags and destitution as from the dark horrors of a tomb. It is impossible to say how much he lied to Jim then, how much he lied to me now—and to himself always. Vanity plays lurid tricks with our memory, and the truth of every passion wants some pretense to make it live. Standing at the gate of the other world in the guise of a beggar, he had slapped this world's face, he had spat on it, he had thrown upon it an immensity of scorn and revolt at the bottom of his misdeeds. He had overcome them all—men, women, savages, traders, ruffians, missionaries—and Jim—that beefy-faced beggar. I did not begrudge him this triumph *in articulo mortis*, this almost posthumous illusion of having trampled all the earth under his feet. While he was boasting to me, in his sordid and repulsive agony, I couldn't help thinking of the chuckling talk relating to the time of his greatest splendor, when, during a year or more, Gentleman Brown's ship was to be seen, for many days on end, hovering down Erromanga way, off an islet befringed with green upon azure, with the dark dot of the mission-house on a white beach; while Gentleman Brown, ashore, was casting the spell of his fame over a romantic girl for whom Melanesia had been too much, and giving hopes of a remarkable conversion to her husband. The poor man, some time or other, had been heard to express the hope of winning 'Captain Brown to a better way of life.'. . 'Bag Gentleman Brown for Glory'—as a leery-eyed loafer expressed it once—'just to let them see up above what a Western Pacific trading skipper looks like.' And this was the man, too, who had run off with a dying woman, and had shed tears over her body. 'Carried on like a big baby,' his then mate was never tired of telling, 'and where the fun came in may I be kicked to death by diseased Kanakas if *I* know. Why, gents! She was too far gone when he brought her aboard to know him; she just lay there on her back in his bunk staring at the beam with awful shining eyes—and then she died. Dam' bad sort of fever, I guess . . . .' I remembered all these stories while, wiping his matted lump of a beard with a livid, bony hand, he was telling me from his noisome couch how he got round, got in, got home, on that confounded, immaculate, don't-you-touch-me sort of fellow. He admitted that he couldn't be scared, but there was a way, 'as broad as a turnpike, to get in and shake his twopenny soul around and inside out and upside down—by God!'"

❧ 42 ❧

I don't think he could do more than perhaps look upon that straight path. He seemed to have been puzzled by what he saw, for he interrupted himself in his narrative more than once to exclaim, 'He nearly slipped from me there. I could not make him out. Who was he?' And after glaring at me wildly he would go on, jubilating and sneering. To me the conversation of these two across the creek appears now as the deadliest kind of duel on which Fate looked on with her cold-eyed knowledge of the end. No, he didn't turn Jim's soul inside out, but I am much mistaken if the spirit so utterly out of his reach had not been made to taste to the full the bitterness of that contest. These were the emissaries with whom the world he had renounced was pursuing him in his retreat. White men from 'out there,' where he did not think himself good enough to live. This was all that came to him—a menace, a shock, a danger to his work. I suppose it is this sad, half-resentful, half-resigned feeling, piercing through the few words Jim said now and then that puzzled Brown so much in the reading of his character. Some great men owe most of their greatness to the ability of detecting in those they destine for their tools the exact quality of strength that matters for their work; and Brown, as though he had been really great, had a satanic gift of finding out the best and the weakest spot in his victims. He admitted to me that Jim wasn't of the sort that can be got over by truckling, and accordingly he took care to show himself as a man confronting without dismay ill-luck, censure, and disaster. The smuggling of a few guns was no great crime, he pointed out. As to coming to Patusan, who had the right to say he hadn't come to beg? The infernal people here let loose at him from both banks without staying to ask questions. He made the point brazenly, for, in truth, Dain Waris's energetic action had prevented the greatest calamities; because Brown told me distinctly that, perceiving the size of the place, he had resolved instantly in his mind that as soon as he had gained a footing he would set fire right and left, and begin by shooting down everything living in sight, in order to cow and terrify the population. The disproportion of forces was so great that this was the only way giving him the slightest chance of attaining his ends—he argued in a fit of coughing. But he didn't tell Jim this. As to the hardships and starvation they had gone through, these had been very real; it was enough to look at his band. He made, at the sound of a shrill whistle, all his men appear standing in a row on the logs in full view, so that Jim could see them. For the killing of the man, it had been done—well, it had—but was not this war, bloody war—in a corner? and the fellow had been killed cleanly, shot through the chest, not like that poor devil of his lying now in the creek. They had to listen to him dying for six hours, with his entrails torn with slugs. At any rate, this was a life for a life. . . . And all this was said with the weariness, with the recklessness of a man spurred on and on by ill-luck till he cares not where he runs. Not a gleam of light, not a break in the mischance. When he asked Jim, with a sort of brusk, despairing frankness, whether he himself—straight now—didn't understand that when 'it came to saving one's life in the dark, one didn't care who else went—three, thirty, three hundred people'—it was as if a demon had been whispering advice in his ear. 'I made him wince,' boasted Brown to me. 'He very soon left off coming the righteous over me. He just stood there with nothing to say, and looking as black as thunder—not at me—on the ground.' He asked Jim whether he had nothing fishy in his life to remember that he was so damnedly hard upon a man trying to get out of a deadly hole by the first means that came to hand—and so on, and so on. And there ran through the rough talk a vein of subtle reference to their common blood, an assumption of common experience; a sickening suggestion of common guilt, of a secret knowledge that was like a bond to their minds and their hearts.

"At last Brown threw himself down full length and watched Jim out of the corners of his eyes. Jim, on his side of the creek, stood thinking and switching his leg. The houses in view were silent as if a pestilence had swept them clean of every breath of life; but many invisible eyes watched from within the two men with the creek between them, a stranded white boat, and the body of the third man half sunk in the mud. On the river canoes were moving again, for Patusan was recovering its belief in the stability of earthly institutions since the return of the white lord. The right bank, the platforms of the houses, the rafts moored along the shores, even the roofs of bathing-huts, were covered with people that, far away out of earshot and almost out of sight, were straining their eyes towards the knoll beyond the Rajah's stockade. Within the wide irregular ring of forests, broken in two places by the sheen of the river, there was a silence. 'Will you promise to leave the coast?' Jim asked. Brown lifted and let fall his arm, giving everything up, as it were—accepting the inevitable. 'And surrender your arms?' Jim went on. Brown sat up and glared across. 'Surrender our arms! Not till you come to take them out of our stiff hands. You think I am gone crazy with funk? Oh, no! That and the rags I stand in are all I have got in the world, besides a few more breechloaders on .

board; and I expect to sell the lot in Madagascar, if I ever get so far—begging my way from ship to ship.'

"Jim said nothing to this. At last, throwing away the switch he held in his hand, he said, as if speaking to himself, 'I don't know whether I have the power. . . .' 'You don't know! And you wanted me just now to give up my arms! That's good, too,' cried Brown. 'Suppose they say one thing to you, and do the other thing to me.' He calmed down markedly. 'I daresay you have the power, or what's the meaning of all this talk?' he continued. 'What did you come down here for? To pass the time of day?'

"'Very well,' said Jim, lifting his head suddenly after a long silence. 'You shall have a clear road or a clear fight.' He turned on his heel and walked away.

"Brown got up at once, but he did not go up the hill till he had seen Jim disappear between the first houses. He never set his eyes on him again. On his way back he met Cornelius slouching down with his head between his shoulders. He stopped before Brown. 'Why didn't you kill him?' he demanded in a sour, discontented voice. 'Because I could do better than that,' Brown said, with an amused smile. 'Never! never!' protested Cornelius, with energy. 'Couldn't. I have lived here for many years.' Brown looked up at him curiously. There were many sides to the life of that place in arms against him; things he would never find out. Cornelius slunk past dejectedly in the direction of the river. He was now leaving his new friends; he accepted the disappointing course of events with a sulky obstinacy which seemed to draw more together his little, yellow, old face; and as he went down he glanced askant here and there, never giving up his fixed idea.

"'Henceforth events move fast without a check, flowing from the very hearts of men like a stream from a dark source, and we see Jim amongst them, mostly through Tamb' Itam's eyes. The girl's eyes had watched him, too, but her life is too much entwined with his: there is her passion, her wonder, her anger, and, before all, her fear and her unforgiving love. Of the faithful servant, uncomprehending as the rest of them, it is the fidelity alone that comes into play; a fidelity and a belief in his lord so strong that even amazement is subdued to a sort of saddened acceptance of a mysterious failure. He had eyes only for one figure, and through all the mazes of bewilderment he preserves his air of guardianship, of obedience, of care.

"His master came back from his talk with the white men, walking slowly towards the stockade in the street. Everybody was rejoiced to see him return, for while he was away every man was afraid, not only of him being killed, but also of what would come after. Jim went into one of the houses where old Doramin had retired, and remained alone for a long time with the head of the Bugis settlers. No doubt he discussed the course to follow with him then, but no man was present at the conversation. Only Tamb' Itam, keeping as close to the door as he could, heard his master say, 'Yes. I shall let all the people know that such is my wish; but I spoke to you, O Doramin, before all the others, and alone; for you know my heart as well as I know yours, and its greatest desire. But you know well also that I have no thought but for the people's good.' Then his master, lifting the sheeting in the doorway, went out, and he, Tamb' Itam, had a glimpse of old Doramin within, sitting in the chair with his hands on his knees, and looking between his feet. Afterwards he followed his master to the fort, where all the principal Bugis and Patusan inhabitants had been summoned for a talk. Tamb' Itam himself hoped there would be some fighting. 'What was it but the taking of another hill?' he exclaimed mournfully. However, in the town many hoped that the rapacious strangers would be induced, by the sight of so many brave men making ready to fight, to go away. It would be a good thing if they went away. Since Jim's arrival had been made known before daylight by the gun fired from the fort and the beating of the big drum there, the fear that had hung over Patusan had broken and subsided like a wave on a rock, leaving the seething foam of excitement, curiosity, and endless speculation. Half of the population had been ousted out of their homes for purposes of defense and were living in the street on the left side of the river, crowding round the fort, and in momentary expectation of seeing their abandoned dwellings on the threatened bank burst into flames. The general anxiety was to see the matter settled quickly. Food, through Jewel's care, had been served out to the refugees. Nobody knew what their white man would do. Some remarked that it was worse than in Sherif Ali's war. Then many people did not care; now everybody had something to lose. The movements of canoes passing to and fro between the two parts of the town were watched with interest. A couple of Bugis war-boats lay anchored in the middle of the stream to protect the river, and a thread of smoke stood at the bow of each; the men in them were cooking their midday rice when Jim, after his interviews with Brown and Doramin, crossed the river and entered by the water gate of his fort. The people inside crowded round him so that he could hardly make his way to the house. They had not seen him before, because on his arrival during the night he had only exchanged a few words with the girl, who had come down to the landing-stage for the purpose, and had then gone on at once to join the chiefs and the fighting men on the other bank. People shouted greetings after him. One old woman raised a laugh by pushing her way to the front madly, and enjoining him in a scolding voice to see to it that her two sons, who were with Doramin, did not come to harm at the hands of the robbers. Several of the bystanders tried to pull her away, but she struggled and cried, 'Let me go. What is this, O Muslims? This laughter is unseemly. Are they not cruel, bloodthirsty robbers bent on killing?' 'Let her be,' said Jim, and as a silence fell suddenly, he said slowly, 'Everybody shall be safe.' He entered the house before the great sigh and the loud murmurs of satisfaction had died out.

"There's no doubt his mind was made up that Brown should have his way clear back to the sea. His fate, revolted, was forcing his hand. He had for the first time to affirm his will in the face of outspoken opposition. 'There was much talk, and at first my master was silent,' Tamb' Itam said. 'Darkness came, and then I lit the candles on the long table. The chiefs sat on each side, and the lady remained by my master's right hand.'

"When he began to speak the unaccustomed difficulty seemed only to fix his resolve more immovably. The white men were now waiting for his answer on the hill. Their chief had spoken to him in the language of his own people, making clear many things difficult to explain in any other speech. They were erring men whom suffering had made blind to right and wrong. It is true that lives had been lost already, but why lose more? He declared to his hearers, the assembled heads of the people, that their welfare was his welfare, their losses his losses, their mourning his mourning. He looked round at the grave listening faces and told them to remember that they had fought and worked side by side. They knew his courage . . . Here a murmur interrupted him . . . And that he had never deceived them. For many years they had dwelt together. He loved the land and the people living in it with a very great love. He was ready to answer with his life for any harm that should come to them if the white men with beards were allowed to retire. They were evildoers, but their destiny had been evil too. Had he ever advised them ill? Had his words ever brought suffering to the people? he asked. He believed that it would be best to let these whites and their followers go with their lives. It would be a small gift. 'I whom you have tried and found always true ask you to let them go.' He turned to Doramin. The old *nakhoda* made no movement. 'Then,' said Jim, 'call in Dain Waris, your son, my friend, for in this business I shall not lead.'"

❧ 43 ❧

Tamb' Itam behind his chair was thunderstruck. The declaration produced an immense sensation. 'Let them go, because this is best, in my knowledge, which has never deceived you,' said Jim. There was a silence. In the darkness of the courtyard there could be heard the subdued whispering, shuffling noise of many people. Doramin raised his heavy head and said that there was no more reading of hearts than touching the sky with the hand, but—he consented. The others gave their opinion in turn. 'It is best,' 'Let them go,' and so on. But most of them simply said that they 'believed Tuan Jim.'

"In this simple form of assent to his will lies the whole gist of the situation; their creed, his truth; and the testimony to that faithfulness which made him in his own eyes the equal of the impeccable men who never fall out of the ranks. Stein's words, 'Romantic!—romantic!' seem to ring over those distances that will never give him up now to a world indifferent to his failing and his virtues, and to that ardent and clinging affection that refuses him the dole of tears in the bewilderment of a great grief and of eternal separation. From the moment the sheer truthfulness of his last three years of life carries the day against the ignorance, the fear, and the anger of men, he appears no longer to me as I saw him last—a white speck catching all the dim light left upon a somber coast and the darkened sea—but greater and more pitiful in the loneliness of his soul, that remains even for her who loved him best a cruel and insoluble mystery.

"It is evident that he did not mistrust Brown; there was no reason to doubt the story, whose truth seemed warranted by the rough frankness, by a sort of virile sincerity in accepting the morality and the consequences of his acts. But Jim did not know the almost inconceivable egotism of the man which made him, when resisted and foiled in his will, mad with the indignant and revengeful rage of a thwarted autocrat. But if Jim did not mistrust Brown, he was evidently anxious that some misunderstanding should not occur, ending perhaps in collision and bloodshed. It was for this reason that directly the Malay chiefs had gone he asked Jewel to get him something to eat, as he was going out of the fort to take command in the town. On her remonstrating against this on the score of his fatigue, he said that something might happen for which he would never forgive himself. 'I am responsible for every life in the land,' he said. He was moody at first; she served him with her own hands, taking the plates and dishes (of the dinner service presented him by Stein) from Tamb' Itam. He brightened up after a while; told her she would be again in command for another night. 'There's no sleep for us, old girl,' he said, 'while our people are in danger.' Later on he said jokingly that she was the best man of them all. 'If you and Dain Waris had done what you wanted, not one of these poor devils would be alive today.' 'Are they very bad?' she asked, leaning over his chair. 'Men act badly sometimes without being much worse than others,' he said, after some hesitation.

"Tamb' Itam followed his master to the landing-stage outside the fort. The night was clear but without a moon, and the middle of the river was dark, while the water under each bank reflected the light of many fires 'as on a night of Ramadan,' Tamb' Itam said. War-boats drifted silently in the dark lane or, anchored, floated motionless with a loud ripple. That night there was much paddling in a canoe and walking at his master's heels for Tamb' Itam: up and down the street they tramped, where the fires were burning, inland on the outskirts of the town where small parties of men kept guard in the fields. Tuan Jim gave his orders, and was obeyed. Last of all they went to the Rajah's stockade, which a detachment of Jim's people manned on that night. The old Rajah had fled early in the morning with most of his women to a small house he had near a jungle village on a tributary stream. Kassim, left behind, had attended the council with his air of diligent activity to explain away the diplomacy of the day before. He was considerably cold-shouldered, but managed to preserve his smiling, quiet alertness, and professed himself highly delighted when Jim told him sternly that he proposed to occupy the stockade on that night with his own men. After the council broke up he was heard outside accosting this and that departing chief, and speaking in a loud, gratified tone of the Rajah's property being protected in the Rajah's absence.

"About ten or so of Jim's men marched in. The stockade commanded the mouth of the creek, and Jim meant to remain there till Brown had passed below. A small fire was lit on the flat, grassy point outside the wall of stakes, and Tamb' Itam placed a little folding stool for his master. Jim told him to try and sleep. Tamb' Itam got a mat and lay down a little way off; but he could not sleep, though he knew he had to go on an important journey before the night was out. His master walked to and fro before the fire with bowed head and with his hands behind his back. His face was sad. Whenever his master approached him Tamb' Itam pretended to sleep, not wishing his master to know he had been watched. At last his master stood still, looking down on him as he lay, and said softly, 'It is time.'

"Tamb' Itam arose directly and made his preparations. His mission was to go down the river, preceding Brown's boat by an hour or more, to tell Dain Waris, finally and formally, that the whites were to be allowed to pass out unmolested. Jim would not trust anybody else with that service. Before starting, Tamb' Itam, more as a matter of form (since his position about Jim made him perfectly known), asked for a token. 'Because, Tuan,' he said, 'the message is important, and these are thy very words I carry.' His master first put his hand into one pocket, then into another, and finally took off his forefinger Stein's silver ring, which he habitually wore, and gave it to Tamb' Itam. When Tamb' Itam left on his mission, Brown's camp on the knoll was dark but for a single small glow shining through the branches of one of the trees the white men had cut down.

"Early in the evening Brown had received from Jim a folded piece of paper on which was written, 'You get the clear road. Start as soon as your boat floats on the morning tide. Let your men be careful. The bushes on both sides of the creek and the stockade at the mouth are full of well-armed men. You would have no chance, but I don't believe you want bloodshed.' Brown read it, tore the paper into small pieces, and, turning to Cornelius, who had brought it, said jeeringly, 'Goodbye, my excellent friend.' Cornelius had been in the fort, and had been sneaking around Jim's house during the afternoon. Jim chose him to carry the note because he could speak English, was known to Brown, and was not likely to be shot by some nervous mistake of one of the men, as a Malay approaching in the dusk, perhaps, might have been.

"Cornelius didn't go away after delivering the paper. Brown was sitting up over a tiny fire; all the others were lying down. 'I could tell you something you would like to know,' Cornelius mumbled crossly. Brown paid no attention. 'You did not kill him,' went on the other, 'and what do you get for it? You might have had money from the Rajah, besides the loot of all the Bugis houses, and now you get nothing.' 'You had better clear out from here,' growled Brown, without even look-ing at him. But Cornelius let himself drop by his side and began to whisper very fast, touching his elbow from time to time. What he had to say made Brown sit up at first, with a curse. He had simply informed him of Dain Waris's armed party down the river. At first Brown saw himself completely sold and betrayed, but a moment's reflection convinced him that there could be no treachery intended. He said nothing, and after a while Cornelius remarked, in a tone of complete indiffer-ence, that there was another way out of the river which he knew very well. 'A good thing to know, too,' said Brown, pricking up his ears; and Cornelius began to talk of what went on in town and repeated all that had been said in council, gossiping in an even undertone at Brown's ear as you talk amongst sleeping men you do not wish to wake. 'He thinks he has made me harmless, does he?' mumbled Brown very low . . . 'Yes. He is a fool. A little child. He came here and robbed me,' droned on Cornelius, 'and he made all the people believe him. But if something happened that they did not believe him anymore, where would he be? And the Bugis Dain who is waiting for you down the river there, captain, is the very man who chased you up here when you first came.' Brown observed nonchalantly that it would be just as well to avoid him, and with the same detached, musing air Cornelius declared himself acquainted with a backwater broad enough to take Brown's boat past Waris's camp. 'You will have to be quiet,' he said, as an afterthought, 'for in one place we pass close behind his camp. Very close. They are camped ashore with their boats hauled up.' 'Oh, we know how to be as quiet as mice. Never fear,' said Brown. Cornelius stipulated that in case he were to pilot Brown out, his canoe should be towed. 'I'll have to get back quick,' he explained.

"It was two hours before the dawn when word was passed to the stockade from outlying watchers that the white robbers were coming down to their boat. In a very short time every armed man from one end of Patusan to the other was on the alert, yet the banks of the river remained so silent that but for the fires burning with sudden blurred flares the town might have been asleep as if in peacetime. A heavy mist lay very low on the Water, making a sort of illusive gray light that showed nothing. When Brown's longboat glided out of the creek into the river, Jim was standing on the low point of land before the Rajah's stockade—on the very spot where for the first time he put his foot on Patusan shore. A shadow loomed up, moving in the grayness, solitary, very bulky, and yet constantly eluding the eye. A murmur of low talking came out of it. Brown at the tiller heard Jim speak calmly: 'A clear road. You had better trust to the current while it's so thick; but this will lift presently.' 'Yes, presently we shall see clear,' replied Brown.

"The thirty or forty men standing with muskets at ready outside the stockade held their breath. The Bugis owner of the prau, whom I saw on Stein's veranda, and who was amongst them, told me that the boat, shaving the low point close, seemed for a moment to grow big and hang over it like a mountain. 'If you think it worth your while to wait a day outside,' called out Jim, 'I'll try to send you down something—a bullock, some yams—what I can.' The high shadow went on moving. 'Yes. Do,' said a voice, blank and muffled, out of the fog. Not one of the many attentive listeners understood what the words meant; and then Brown and his men in their boat floated away, fading spectrally without the slightest sound.

"Thus Brown, invisible in the mist, goes out of Patusan elbow to elbow with Cornelius in the stern-sheets of the longboat. 'Perhaps you shall get a small bullock,' said Cornelius. 'Oh, yes. Bullock. Yam. You'll get it if *he* said so. He always speaks the truth. He stole everything I had. I suppose you like a small bullock better than the loot of many houses.' 'I would advise you to hold your tongue, or somebody here may fling you overboard into this damned fog,' said Brown. The boat seemed to be standing still; nothing could be seen, not even the river alongside, only the water-dust flew and trickled, condensed, down their beards and faces. It was weird, Brown told me. Every individual man of them felt as though he were adrift alone in a boat, haunted by an almost imperceptible suspicion of sighing, muttering ghosts. 'Throw me out, would you? But I would know where I was,' mumbled Cornelius, surlily. 'I've lived many years here.' 'Not long enough to see through a fog like this,' Brown said, lolling back with his arm swinging to and fro on the useless tiller. 'Yes. Long enough for that,' snarled Cornelius. 'That's very useful,' commented Brown. 'Am I to believe you could find that backway you spoke of blindfold, like this?' Cornelius grunted. 'Are you too tired to row?' he asked, after a silence. 'No, by God!' shouted Brown, suddenly. 'Out with your oars there.' There was a great knocking in the fog, which after a while settled into a regular grind of invisible sweeps against invisible thole-pins. Otherwise, nothing was changed, and but for the slight splash of a dipped blade it was like rowing a balloon-car in a cloud, said Brown. Thereafter Cornelius did not open his lips except to ask querulously for somebody to bale out his canoe, which was towing behind the longboat. Gradually the fog whitened and became luminous ahead. To the left Brown saw a darkness as though he had been looking at the back of the departing night. All at once a big bough covered with leaves appeared above his head, and ends of twigs, dripping and still curved slenderly, close alongside. Cornelius, without a word, took the tiller from his hand."

❧ 44 ❧

I don't think they spoke together again. The boat entered a narrow by-channel, where it was pushed by the oar blades set into crumbling banks, and there was a gloom as if enormous black wings had been outspread above the mist that filled its depth to the summits of the trees. The branches overhead showered big drops through the gloomy fog. At a mutter from Cornelius, Brown ordered his men to load. 'I'll give you a chance to get even with them before we're done, you dismal cripples, you,' he said to his gang. 'Mind you don't throw it away—you hounds.' Low growls answered that speech. Cornelius showed much fussy concern for the safety of his canoe.

"Meantime Tamb' Itam had reached the end of his journey. The fog had delayed him a little, but he had paddled steadily, keeping in touch with the south bank. By and by daylight came like a glow in a ground glass globe. The shores made on each side of the river a dark smudge, in which one could detect hints of columnar forms and shadows of twisted branches high up. The mist was still thick on the water, but a good watch was being kept, for as Tamb' Itam approached the camp the figures of two men emerged out of the white vapor, and voices spoke to him boisterously. He answered, and presently a canoe lay alongside of his dugout, and he exchanged news with the paddlers. All was well. The trouble was over. Then the men in the canoe let go their grip on the side of his dugout and incontinently fell out of sight. He pursued his way till he heard voices coming to him quietly over the water, and saw now, under the lifting, swirling mist, the glow of many little fires burning on a sandy stretch, backed by lofty thin timber and bushes. There again a lookout was kept, for he was challenged. He shouted his name as the two last sweeps of his paddle ran his canoe up on the strand. It was a big camp. Men crouched in many little knots under a steady murmur of early morning talk. Many thin threads of smoke curled slowly on the white mist. Little shelters, elevated above the ground, had been built for the chiefs. Muskets were stacked in small pyramids, and long spears were stuck singly into the sand near the fires.

"Tamb' Itam, assuming an air of importance, demanded to be led to Dain Waris. He found the friend of his white lord lying on a raised couch made of bamboo, and sheltered by a sort of shed of sticks covered with mats. Dain Waris was awake, and a bright fire was burning before his sleeping-place, which resembled a rude

shrine. The only son of Nakhoda Doramin answered his greeting kindly. Tamb'
Itam began by handing him the ring which vouched for the truth of the messenger's words. Dain Waris, reclining on his elbow, bade him speak and tell all the
news. Beginning with the consecrated formula, 'The news is good,' Tamb' Itam
delivered Jim's own words. The white men, departing with the consent of all the
chiefs, were to be allowed to pass down the river. In answer to a question or two,
Tamb' Itam then reported the proceedings of the last council. Dain Waris listened
attentively to the end, toying with the ring which ultimately he slipped on the
forefinger of his right hand. After hearing all he had to say he dismissed Tamb'
Itam to have food and rest. Orders for the return in the afternoon were given
immediately. Afterwards Dain Waris lay down again, open-eyed, while his personal
attendants were preparing his food at the fire by which Tamb' Itam also sat talking to the men who lounged up to hear the latest intelligence from the town. The
sun was eating up the mist. A good watch was kept upon the reach of the main
stream where the boat of the whites was expected to appear every moment.

"It was then that Brown took his revenge upon the world which, after twenty
years of contemptuous and reckless bullying, refused him the tribute of a common
robber's success. It was an act of cold-blooded ferocity, and it consoled him on his
deathbed like a memory of an indomitable defiance. Stealthily he landed his men
on the other side of the island opposite to the Bugis camp, and led them across.
After a short but quite silent scuffle Cornelius, who had tried to slink away at the
moment of landing, resigned himself to show the way where the undergrowth was
most sparse. Brown held both his skinny hands together behind his back in the
grip of one vast fist, and now and then impelled him forward with a fierce push.
Cornelius remained as mute as a fish, abject but faithful to his purpose, whose
accomplishment loomed before him dimly. At the edge of the patch of forest
Brown's men spread themselves out in cover and waited. The camp was plain from
end to end before their eyes, and no one looked their way. Nobody even dreamed
that the white men could have any knowledge of the narrow channel at the back
of the island. Both its entrances were so narrow and overgrown that the very
natives passing in canoes had to look for them carefully. Brown yelled, 'Let them
have it,' and fourteen shots rang out like one.

"Tamb' Itam told me the surprise was so great that, except for those who fell
dead or wounded, not a soul of them moved for quite an appreciable time after the
first discharge. Then a man screamed, and after that scream a great yell of amazement and fear went up from all the throats. A blind panic drove these men in a
surging, swaying mob to and fro along the shore like a herd of cattle afraid of the
water. Some few jumped into the river then, but most of them did so only after the
third discharge. Three times Brown's men fired into the ruck, Brown, the only one
in view, cursing and yelling, 'Aim low! aim low!'

"Tamb' Itam says that, as for him, he understood at the first volley what had happened. Though untouched, he fell down and lay as if dead, but with his eyes open. At the sound of the first shots Dain Waris, reclining on the couch, jumped up and ran out upon the open shore, just in time to receive a bullet in his forehead at the second discharge. Tamb' Itam saw him fling his arms wide open before he fell. Then, he says, a great fear came upon him—not before. The white men retired as they had come—unseen.

"Thus Brown balanced his account with the evil fortune. Notice that even in this awful outbreak there is a superiority as of a man who carries right—the abstract thing—within the envelope of his common desires. It was not a vulgar and treacherous massacre; it was a lesson, a retribution—a demonstration of some obscure and awful attribute of our nature which, I am afraid, is not so very far under the surface as we like to think.

"Afterwards the whites depart unseen by Tamb' Itam, and seem to vanish from before men's eyes altogether; and the schooner, too, vanishes after the manner of stolen goods. But a story is told of a white longboat picked up a month later in the Indian Ocean by a cargo steamer. Two parched, yellow, glassy-eyed, whispering skeletons in her recognized the authority of a third, who declared that his name was Brown. His schooner, he reported, bound south with a cargo of Java sugar, had sprung a bad leak and sank under his feet. He and his companions were the survivors of a crew of six. The two died on board the steamer which rescued them. No matter. Brown lived to be seen by me, and I can testify that he had played his part to the last.

"It seems, however, that in going away they had neglected to cast off Cornelius's canoe. Cornelius himself Brown had let go at the beginning of the shooting, with a kick for a parting benediction. Tamb' Itam, after arising from amongst the dead, saw the Nazarene running about up and down the shore amongst the corpses and the expiring fires. He uttered little cries. Suddenly he rushed to the water, and made frantic efforts to get one of the Bugis' boats into the water. 'Afterwards, till he had seen me,' related Tamb' Itam, 'he stood looking at the heavy canoe and scratching his head.' 'What became of him?' I asked. Tamb' Itam, staring hard at me, made an expressive gesture with his right arm. 'Twice I struck, Tuan,' he said. 'When he beheld me approaching he cast himself violently on the ground and made a great outcry, kicking. Twice I gave a blow. He screeched like a frightened hen till he felt the point; then he was still, and lay staring at me while his life went out of his eyes.'

"This done, Tamb' Itam did not tarry. He understood the importance of being the first with the awful news at the fort. There were, of course, many survivors of Dain Waris's party; but in the extremity of panic some had swam across the river, others had bolted into the bush. The fact is that they did not know really who struck that blow—whether more white robbers were not coming, whether they had not already got hold of the whole land. They imagined themselves to be the victims of a vast treachery, and utterly doomed to destruction. It is said that some small parties did not come in till three days afterwards. However, a few tried to make their way back to Patusan at once, and one of the canoes that were patrolling the river that morning was in sight of the camp at the very moment of the attack. It is true that at first the men in her leaped overboard and swam to the opposite bank, but afterwards they returned to their boat and started hesitatingly up stream. Of these Tamb' Itam had an hour's advance."

❧ 45 ❧

When Tamb' Itam, paddling madly, came into the town-reach, the women, thronging the platforms before the houses, were looking out for the return of Dain Waris's little fleet of boats. The town had a festive air; here and there men, still with spears or guns in their hands, could be seen moving or standing on the shore in groups. Chinamen's shops had been opened early; but the marketplace was empty, and a sentry, still posted at the corner of the fort, made out Tamb' Itam, and shouted to those within. The gate was wide open. Tamb' Itam jumped ashore and ran in headlong. The first person he met was the girl coming down from the house.

"Tamb' Itam, disordered, panting, with trembling lips and wild eyes, stood for a time before her as if a sudden spell had been laid on him. Then he broke out very quickly: 'They have killed Dain Waris and many more.' She clapped her hands, and her first words were, 'Shut the gates.' Most of the fort-men had gone back to their houses, but Tamb' Itam hurried on the few who remained for their turn of duty within. The girl stood in the middle of the courtyard while the others ran about. 'Doramin,' she cried fearfully, as Tamb' Itam passed her. Next time he went by he answered her thought rapidly, 'Yes. But we have all the powder in Patusan.' She caught him by the arm, and, pointing at the house, 'Call him out,' she whispered, trembling.

"Tamb' Itam ran up the steps. His master was sleeping. 'It is I, Tamb' Itam,' he cried at the door, 'with tidings that cannot wait.' He saw Jim turn over on the pillow and open his eyes, and he burst out at once. 'This, Tuan, is a day of evil, an accursed day.' His master raised himself on his elbow to listen—just as Dain Waris had done. And then Tamb' Itam began his tale, trying to relate the story in order, calling Dain Waris Panglima, and saying, 'The Panglima then called out to the chief of his own boatmen, "Give Tamb' Itam something to eat"'—when his master put his feet to the ground and looked at him with such a discomposed face that the words remained in his throat.

"'Speak out,' said Jim. 'Is he dead?' 'May you live long,' cried Tamb' Itam. 'It was a most cruel treachery. He ran out at the first shots and fell.'. . . His master walked to the window and with his fist struck at the shutter. The room was made light; and then in a steady voice, but speaking fast, he began to give him orders to assemble a fleet of boats for immediate pursuit, go to this man, to the other— send messengers; and as he talked he sat down on the bed, stooping to lace his boots hurriedly, and suddenly looked up. 'Why do you stand here?' he asked, very red-faced. 'Waste no time.' Tamb' Itam did not move. 'Forgive me, Tuan, but . . . but,' he began to stammer. 'What?' cried his master aloud, looking terrible, lean-ing forward with his hands gripping the edge of the bed. 'It is not safe for thy ser-vant to go out amongst the people,' said Tamb' Itam, after hesitating a moment.

"Then Jim understood. He had retreated from one world, for a small matter of an impulsive jump, and now the other, the work of his own hands, had fallen in ruins upon his head. It was not safe for his servant to go out amongst his own peo-ple! I believe that in that very moment he had decided to defy the disaster in the only way it occurred to him such a disaster could be defied; but all I know is that without a word he came out of his room and sat before the long table, at the head of which he was accustomed to regulate the affairs of his world, proclaiming daily the truth that surely lived in his heart. But he was romantic—romantic—and, nevertheless, true. The dark powers should not rob him twice of his peace. He sat like a stone figure. Tamb' Itam, deferential, hinted at preparations for defense. The girl he loved came in and spoke to him, but he made a sign with his hand, and she was awed by the dumb appeal for silence in it. She went out on the veranda and sat on the threshold, as if to guard him with her body from dangers outside.

"What thoughts passed through his head—what memories? Who can tell. Everything was gone, and he who had been once unfaithful to his trust had lost again all men's confidence. It was then, I believe, he tried to write—to some-body—and gave it up. Loneliness was closing on him. People had trusted him with their lives—only for that; and yet they could never, as he had said, never be made to understand him. Those without did not hear him make a sound. Later, towards the evening, he came to the door and called for Tamb' Itam. 'Well,' he asked. 'There is much weeping. Much anger, too,' said Tamb' Itam. Jim looked up at him. 'You know,' he murmured. 'Yes, Tuan,' said Tamb' Itam. 'Thy servant does know, and the gates are closed. We shall have to fight.' 'Fight! What for?' he asked. 'For our lives.' 'I have no life,' he said. Tamb' Itam heard a cry from the girl at the door. 'Who knows?' said Tamb' Itam. 'By audacity and cunning we may even escape.

There is much fear in men's hearts, too.' He went out, thinking vaguely of boats and of open sea, leaving Jim and the girl together.

"I haven't the heart to set down here such glimpses as she had given me of the hour or more she had passed in there wrestling with him for the possession of her happiness. Whether he had any hope—what he expected, what he imagined—it is impossible to say. He was inflexible, and with the growing loneliness of his obstinacy his spirit seemed to rise above the ruins of his existence. She cried 'Fight!' into his ears. She did not understand. There was nothing to fight for. He was going to prove his power in another way and conquer the fatal destiny itself. He came out into the courtyard, and behind him, with streaming hair, wild of face, breathless, she staggered out, and leaned on the side of the doorway. 'Open the gates,' he ordered. Afterwards turning to those of his men who were inside, he gave them leave to depart to their homes. 'For how long, Tuan?' asked one of them timidly. 'For all life,' he said, in a somber tone.

"A hush had fallen upon the town after the outburst of wailing and lamentation that had swept over the river like a gust of wind from the opened abode of sorrow. But rumors flew in whispers, filling the hearts with consternation and horrible doubts. The robbers were coming back, bringing many others with them, in a great ship, and there would be no refuge in the land for anyone. A sense of utter insecurity, as during an earthquake, pervaded the minds of men who whispered their suspicions, looking at each other as if in the presence of some awful portent.

"The sun was sinking towards the forests when Dain Waris's body was brought into Doramin's *campong*. Four men carried it in, covered decently with a white sheet which the old mother had sent out down to the gate to meet her son on his return. They laid him at Doramin's feet, and the old man sat still for a long time, one hand on each knee, looking down. The fronds of palms swayed gently and the foliage of fruit trees stirred above his head. Every single man of his people was there, fully armed, when the old *nakhoda* at last raised his eyes. He moved them slowly over the crowd, as if seeking for a missing face. Again his chin sank on his breast. The whispers of many men mingled with the slight rustling of the leaves.

"The Malay who had brought Tamb' Itam and the girl to Samarang was there too. 'Not so angry as many,' he said to me, but struck with a great awe and wonder at the 'suddenness of men's fate, which hangs over their heads like a cloud charged with thunder.' He told me that when Dain Waris's body was uncovered at a sign of Doramin's, he whom they often called the white lord's friend was disclosed lying unchanged with his eyelids a little open as if about to wake. Doramin leaned forward a little more like one looking for something fallen on the ground. His eyes searched the body from its feet to its head, for the wound maybe. It was in the forehead, and small; and there was no word spoken while one of the bystanders, stooping over the body, took off the silver ring from the cold, stiff hand. In silence he held it up before Doramin. A murmur of dismay and horror ran through the crowd at the sight of that familiar token. The old *nakhoda* stared at it, and suddenly let out one great fierce cry, deep from the chest, a roar of pain and fury, as mighty as the bellow of a wounded bull, bringing great fear into men's hearts by the magnitude of his anger and his sorrow that could be plainly discerned without words. There was a great stillness afterwards for a space, while the body was being borne aside by four men. They laid it down under a tree, and on the instant, with one long shriek, all the women of the household began to wail together; they mourned with shrill cries; the sun was setting, and in the intervals of screamed lamentations the high sing-song voices of two old men intoning the Koran chanted alone.

"About this time Jim, leaning on a gun-carriage, looked at the river, and turned his back on the house; and the girl, in the doorway, panting as if she had run herself to a standstill, was looking at him across the yard. Tamb' Itam stood not far from his master, waiting patiently for what might happen. All at once, Jim, who seemed to be lost in quiet thought, turned to him and said, 'Time to finish this.'

"'Tuan?' said Tamb' Itam, with alacrity. He did not know what his master meant, but as soon as Jim made a movement the girl started too and walked down into the open space. It seems that no one else of the people of the house was in sight. She tottered slightly, and about halfway down called out to Jim, who had apparently resumed his peaceful contemplation of the river. He turned round, setting his back against the gun. 'Will you fight?' she cried. 'There is nothing to fight for,' he said; 'nothing is lost.' Saying this, he made a step towards her. 'Will you fly?' she cried again. 'There is no escape,' he said, stopping short, and she stood still also, silent, devouring him with her eyes. 'And you shall go?' she said slowly. He bent his head. 'Ah!' she exclaimed, peering at him as it were, 'you are mad or false. Do you remember the night I prayed you to go away, and you said that you could not? That it was impossible! Impossible! Do you remember you said you would never leave me? Why? I asked for no promise. You promised unasked—remember.' 'Enough, poor girl,' he said. 'I should not be worth having.'

"Tamb' Itam said that while they were talking she would laugh loud and senselessly like one under the visitation of God. His master put his hands to his head. He was fully dressed as for every day, but without a hat. She stopped laughing suddenly. 'For the last time,' she cried menacingly, 'will you defend yourself?' 'Nothing can touch me,' he said, in a last flicker of superb egoism. Tamb' Itam saw her lean forward where she stood, open her arms, and run at him swiftly. She flung herself upon his breast and clasped him round the neck.

"'Ah! but I shall hold thee thus,' she cried. . . . 'Thou art mine!'

"She sobbed violently. The sky over Patusan was blood-red, immense, streaming like an open vein. An enormous sun nestled crimson amongst the treetops, and the forest below had a black and forbidding face.

"Tamb' Itam tells me that on that evening the aspect of the heavens was angry and frightful. I may well believe it, for I know that on that very day a cyclone passed within sixty miles of the coast, but there was hardly more than a languid stir of the air in the place.

"Suddenly Tamb' Itam saw Jim catch her arms, trying to unclasp her hands. She hung on them with her head fallen back; her hair touched the ground. 'Come here!' his master called, and Tamb' Itam helped to ease her down. It was difficult to separate her fingers. Jim, bending over her, looked long at her face, and all at once ran to the landing-stage. Tamb' Itam followed him, but turning his head, he saw that she had struggled up to her feet. She ran after them a few steps, then fell down heavily on her knees. 'Tuan! Tuan!' called Tamb' Itam, 'Look back'; but Jim was already in a canoe, standing up, paddle in hand. He did not look back. Tamb' Itam had just time to scramble in after him when the canoe floated clear. The girl was then on her knees, with clasped hands, at the watergate. She remained thus for a time in a supplicating attitude before she sprang up. 'You are false!' she screamed out after Jim. 'Forgive me,' he cried. 'Never! Never!' she called back.

"Tamb' Itam took the paddle from Jim's hands, it being unseemly that he should sit while his lord paddled. When they reached the other shore his master forbade him to come any farther; but Tamb' Itam did follow him at a distance, walking up the slope to Doramin's *campong*.

"It was beginning to grow dark. Torches twinkled here and there. Those they met stood aside hastily to let Jim pass. The wailing of women came from above. The courtyard was full of armed Bugis with their followers, and of Patusan people.

"I do not know what this gathering really meant. Were these preparations for war, or for vengeance, or to repulse a threatened invasion? Many days elapsed before the people had ceased to look out, quaking, for the return of the white men with long beards and in rags, whose exact relation to their own white man they could never understand. Even for those simple minds poor Jim remains under a cloud.

"Doramin, alone, immense and desolate, sat in his armchair with the pair of flintlock pistols on his knees, faced by an armed throng. When Jim appeared, at somebody's exclamation, all the heads turned round together, and then the mass opened right and left, and he walked up a lane of averted glances. Whispers followed him; murmurs: 'He has worked all the evil.' 'He hath a charm.'. . . He heard them—perhaps!

"When he came up into the light of torches the wailing of the women ceased suddenly. Doramin did not lift his head, and Jim stood silent before him for a time. Then he looked to the left, and moved in that direction with measured steps.

Dain Waris's mother crouched at the head of the body, and the gray disheveled hair concealed her face. Jim came up slowly, looked at his dead friend, lifting the sheet, then dropped it without a word. Slowly he walked back.

"'He came! He came,' was running from lip to lip, making a murmur to which he moved. 'He hath taken it upon his own head,' a voice said aloud. He heard this and turned to the crowd. 'Yes. Upon my head.' A few people recoiled. Jim waited a while before Doramin, and then said gently, 'I am come in sorrow.' He waited again. 'I am come, ready and unarmed,' he repeated.

"The unwieldy old man, lowering his big forehead like an ox under a yoke, made an effort to rise, clutching at the flintlock pistols on his knees. From his throat came gurgling, choking, inhuman sounds, and his two attendants helped him from behind. People remarked that the ring which he had dropped on his lap fell and rolled against the foot of the white man, and that poor Jim glanced down at the talisman that had opened for him the door of fame, love, and success within the wall of forests fringed with white foam, within the coast that under the western sun looks like the very stronghold of the night. Doramin, struggling to keep his feet, made with his two supporters a swaying, tottering group; his little eyes stared with an expression of mad pain, of rage, with a ferocious glitter, which the bystanders noticed, and then, while Jim stood—stiffened and with bared head in the light of torches looking him straight in the face—he clung heavily with his left arm round the neck of a bowed youth, and lifting deliberately his right, shot his son's friend through the chest.

"The crowd, which had fallen apart behind Jim as soon as Doramin had raised his hand, rushed tumultuously forward after the shot. They say that the white man sent right and left at all those faces a proud and unflinching glance. Then, with his hand over his lips, he fell forward, dead.

"And that's the end. He passes away under a cloud, inscrutable at heart, forgotten, unforgiven, and excessively romantic. Not in the wildest days of his boyish visions could he have seen the alluring shape of such an extraordinary success! For it may very well be that in the short moment of his last proud and unflinching glance, he had beheld the face of that opportunity which, like an Eastern bride, had come veiled to his side?

"But we can see him, an obscure conqueror of fame, tearing himself out of the arms of a jealous love at the sign, at the call of his exalted egoism. He goes away from a living woman to celebrate his pitiless wedding with a shadowy ideal of conduct. Is he satisfied—quite, now, I wonder? We ought to know. He is one of us—and have I not stood up once, like an evoked ghost, to answer for his eternal constancy? Was I so very wrong, after all? Now he is no more, there are days when the reality of his existence comes to me with an immense, with an overwhelming force; and yet, upon my honor, there are moments, too, when I believe him to have been only a disembodied spirit astray amongst the passions of this earth—surrendering himself faithfully to the claim of his own world of shades.

"Who knows? He is gone, inscrutable at heart, and the poor girl is leading a sort of soundless, inert life in Stein's home. Stein has aged greatly of late. He feels it himself, and says often that he is 'preparing to leave all this; preparing to leave, . . .' while he waves his hand sadly at his butterflies."

THE END

THE
SECRET AGENT

A SIMPLE TALE

To
H.G. Wells
The chronicler of Mr. Lewisham's love
the biographer of Kipps and the
historian of the ages to come
this simple tale of the nineteenth century
is affectionately offered

❧ 1 ❧

Mr. Verloc, going out in the morning, left his shop nominally in charge of his brother-in-law. It could be done, because there was very little business at any time, and practically none at all before the evening. Mr. Verloc cared but little about his ostensible business. And, moreover, his wife was in charge of his brother-in-law.

The shop was small, and so was the house. It was one of those grimy brick houses which existed in large quantities before the era of reconstruction dawned upon London. The shop was a square box of a place, with the front glazed in small panes. In the daytime the door remained closed; in the evening it stood discreetly but suspiciously ajar.

The window contained photographs of more or less undressed dancing girls; nondescript packages in wrappers like patent medicines; closed yellow paper envelopes, very flimsy, and marked two-and-six in heavy black figures; a few numbers of ancient French comic publications hung across a string as if to dry; a dingy blue china bowl, a casket of black wood, bottles of marking ink, and rubber stamps; a few books, with titles hinting at impropriety; a few apparently old copies of obscure newspapers, badly printed, with titles like *The Torch, The Gong*—rousing titles. And the two gas jets inside the panes were always turned low, either for economy's sake or for the sake of the customers.

These customers were either very young men, who hung about the window for a time before slipping in suddenly; or men of a more mature age, but looking generally as if they were not in funds. Some of that last kind had the collars of their overcoats turned right up to their moustaches, and traces of mud on the bottom of their nether garments, which had the appearance of being much worn and not very valuable. And the legs inside them did not, as a general rule, seem of much account either. With their hands plunged deep in the side pockets of their coats, they dodged in sideways, one shoulder first, as if afraid to start the bell going.

The bell, hung on the door by means of a curved ribbon of steel, was difficult to circumvent. It was hopelessly cracked; but of an evening, at the slightest provocation, it clattered behind the customer with impudent virulence.

It clattered; and at that signal, through the dusty glass door behind the painted deal counter, Mr. Verloc would issue hastily from the parlor at the back. His eyes were naturally heavy; he had an air of having wallowed, fully dressed, all day on an unmade bed. Another man would have felt such an appearance a distinct disadvantage. In a commercial transaction of the retail order much depends on the seller's engaging and amiable aspect. But Mr. Verloc knew his business, and remained undisturbed by any sort of aesthetic doubt about his appearance. With a firm, steady-eyed impudence, which seemed to hold back the threat of some abominable menace, he would proceed to sell over the counter some object looking obviously and scandalously not worth the money which passed in the transaction: a small cardboard box with apparently nothing inside, for instance, or one of those carefully closed yellow flimsy envelopes, or a soiled volume in paper covers with a promising title. Now and then it happened that one of the faded, yellow dancing girls would get sold to an amateur, as though she had been alive and young.

Sometimes it was Mrs. Verloc who would appear at the call of the cracked bell. Winnie Verloc was a young woman with a full bust, in a tight bodice, and with broad hips. Her hair was very tidy. Steady-eyed like her husband, she preserved an air of unfathomable indifference behind the rampart of the counter. Then the customer of comparatively tender years would get suddenly disconcerted at having to deal with a woman, and with rage in his heart would proffer a request for a bottle of marking ink, retail value sixpence (price in Verloc's shop one-and-sixpence), which, once outside, he would drop stealthily into the gutter.

The evening visitors—the men with collars turned up and soft hats rammed down—nodded familiarly to Mrs. Verloc, and with a muttered greeting, lifted up the flap at the end of the counter in order to pass into the back parlor, which gave access to a passage and to a steep flight of stairs. The door of the shop was the only means of entrance to the house in which Mr. Verloc carried on his business of a seller of shady wares, exercised his vocation of a protector of society, and cultivated his domestic virtues. These last were pronounced. He was thoroughly domesticated. Neither his spiritual, nor his mental, nor his physical needs were of the kind to take him much abroad. He found at home the ease of his body and the peace of his conscience, together with Mrs. Verloc's wifely attentions and Mrs. Verloc's mother's deferential regard.

Winnie's mother was a stout, wheezy woman, with a large brown face. She wore a black wig under a white cap. Her swollen legs rendered her inactive. She considered herself to be of French descent, which might have been true; and after a good many years of married life with a licensed victualler of the more common sort, she provided for the years of widowhood by letting furnished apartments for gentlemen near Vauxhall Bridge Road in a square once of some splendor and still included in the district of Belgravia. This topographical fact was of some advantage in advertising her rooms; but the patrons of the worthy widow were not exactly of the fashionable kind. Such as they were, her daughter Winnie helped to look after them. Traces of the French descent which the widow boasted of were apparent in Winnie, too. They were apparent in the extremely neat and artistic arrangement of her glossy dark hair. Winnie had also other charms: her youth; her full, rounded form; her clear complexion; the provocation of her unfathomable reserve, which never went so far as to prevent conversation, carried on on the lodger's part with animation, and on hers with an equable amiability. It must be that Mr. Verloc was susceptible to these fascinations. Mr. Verloc was an intermittent patron. He came and went without any very apparent reason. He generally arrived in London (like the influenza) from the Continent, only he arrived unheralded by the Press; and his visitations set in with great severity. He breakfasted in bed, and remained wallowing there with an air of quiet enjoyment till noon every day—and sometimes even to a later hour. But when he went out he seemed to experience a great difficulty in finding his way back to his temporary home in the Belgravian square. He left it late, and returned to it early—as early as three or four in the morning; and on waking up at ten addressed Winnie, bringing in the breakfast tray, with jocular, exhausted civility, in the hoarse, failing tones of a man who had been talking vehemently for many hours together. His prominent, heavy-lidded eyes rolled sideways amorously and languidly, the bedclothes were pulled up to his chin, and his dark smooth moustache covered his thick lips capable of much honeyed banter.

In Winnie's mother's opinion Mr. Verloc was a very nice gentleman. From her life's experience gathered in various "business houses" the good woman had taken into her retirement an ideal of gentlemanliness as exhibited by the patrons of private saloon bars. Mr. Verloc approached that ideal; he attained it, in fact.

"Of course, we'll take over your furniture, mother," Winnie had remarked.

The lodging house was to be given up. It seems it would not answer to carry it on. It would have been too much trouble for Mr. Verloc. It would not have been convenient for his other business. What his business was he did not say; but after his engagement to Winnie he took the trouble to get up before noon, and descending the basement stairs, make himself pleasant to Winnie's mother in the break-fast room downstairs where she had her motionless being. He stroked the cat, poked the fire, had his lunch served to him there. He left its slightly stuffy coziness with evident reluctance, but, all the same, remained out till the night was far advanced. He never offered to take Winnie to theaters, as such a nice gentleman ought to have done. His evenings were occupied. His work was in a way political, he told Winnie once. She would have, he warned her, to be very nice to his political friends. And with her straight, unfathomable glance she answered that she would be so, of course.

How much more he told her as to his occupation it was impossible for Winnie's mother to discover. The married couple took her over with the furniture. The mean aspect of the shop surprised her. The change from the Belgravian square to the narrow street in Soho affected her legs adversely. They became of an enormous size. On the other hand, she experienced a complete relief from material cares. Her son-in-law's heavy good nature inspired her with a sense of absolute safety. Her daughter's future was obviously assured, and even as to her son Stevie she need have no anxiety. She had not been able to conceal from herself that he was a terrible encumbrance, that poor Stevie. But in view of Winnie's fondness for her delicate brother, and of Mr. Verloc's kind and generous disposition, she felt that the poor boy was pretty safe in this rough world. And in her heart of hearts she was not perhaps displeased that the Verlocs had no children. As that circumstance seemed perfectly indifferent to Mr. Verloc, and as Winnie found an object of quasi-maternal affection in her brother, perhaps this was just as well for poor Stevie.

For he was difficult to dispose of, that boy. He was delicate and, in a frail way, good-looking, too, except for the vacant droop of his lower lip. Under our excellent system of compulsory education he had learned to read and write, notwithstanding the unfavorable aspect of the lower lip. But as errand boy he did not turn out a great success. He forgot his messages; he was easily diverted from the straight path of duty by the attractions of stray cats and dogs, which he followed down narrow alleys into unsavory courts; by the comedies of the streets, which he contemplated open-mouthed, to the detriment of his employer's interests; or by the dramas of fallen horses, whose pathos and violence induced him sometimes to shriek piercingly in a crowd, which disliked to be disturbed by sounds of distress in its quiet enjoyment of the national spectacle. When led away by a grave and protecting policeman, it would often become apparent that poor Stevie had forgotten his address—at least for a time. A brusk question caused him to stutter to the point of suffocation. When startled by anything perplexing he used to squint horribly. However, he never had any fits (which was encouraging); and before the natural outbursts of impatience on the part of his father he could always, in his childhood's days, run for protection behind the short skirts of his sister Winnie. On the other hand, he might have been suspected of hiding a fund of reckless naughtiness. When he had reached the age of fourteen a friend of his late father, an agent for a foreign preserved milk firm, having given him an opening as office boy, he was discovered one foggy afternoon, in his chief's absence, busy letting off fireworks on the staircase. He touched off in quick succession a set of fierce rockets, angry catherine wheels, loudly exploding squibs—and the matter might have turned out very serious. An awful panic spread through the whole building. Wild-eyed, choking clerks stampeded through the passages full of smoke, silk hats and elderly businessmen could be seen rolling independently down the stairs. Stevie did not seem to derive any personal gratification from what he had done.

His motives for this stroke of originality were difficult to discover. It was only later on that Winnie obtained from him a misty and confused confession. It seems that two other office boys in the building had worked upon his feelings by tales of injustice and oppression till they had wrought his compassion to the pitch of that frenzy. But his father's friend, of course, dismissed him summarily as likely to ruin his business. After that altruistic exploit Stevie was put to help wash the dishes in the basement kitchen, and to black the boots of the gentlemen patronizing the Belgravian mansion. There was obviously no future in such work. The gentlemen tipped him a shilling now and then. Mr. Verloc showed himself the most generous of lodgers. But altogether all that did not amount to much either in the way of gain or prospects; so that when Winnie announced her engagement to Mr. Verloc her mother could not help wondering, with a sigh and a glance towards the scullery, what would become of poor Stephen now.

It appeared that Mr. Verloc was ready to take him over together with his wife's mother and with the furniture, which was the whole visible fortune of the family. Mr. Verloc gathered everything as it came to his broad, good-natured breast. The furniture was disposed to the best advantage all over the house, but Mrs. Verloc mother was confined to two back rooms on the first floor. The luckless Stevie slept in one of them. By this time a growth of thin fluffy hair had come to blur, like a golden mist, the sharp line of his small lower jaw. He helped his sister with blind love and docility in her household duties. Mr. Verloc thought that some occupation would be good for him. His spare time he occupied by drawing circles with compass and pencil on a piece of paper. He applied himself to that pastime with great industry, with his elbows spread out and bowed low over the kitchen table. Through the open door of the parlor at the back of the shop Winnie, his sister, glanced at him from time to time with maternal vigilance.

2

Such was the house, the household, and the business Mr. Verloc left behind him on his way westward at the hour of half-past ten in the morning. It was unusually early for him; his whole person exhaled the charm of almost dewy freshness; he wore his blue cloth overcoat unbuttoned; his boots were shiny; his cheeks, freshly shaven, had a sort of gloss; and even his heavy-lidded eyes, refreshed by a night of peaceful slumber, sent out glances of comparative alertness. Through the park railings these glances beheld men and women riding in the Row, couples cantering past harmoniously, others advancing sedately at a walk, loitering groups of three or four, solitary horsemen looking unsociable, and solitary women followed at a long distance by a groom with a cockade to his hat and a leather belt over his tightfitting coat. Carriages went bowling by, mostly two-horse broughams, with here and there a victoria with the skin of some wild beast inside and a woman's face and hat emerging above the folded hood. And a peculiarly London sun—against which nothing could be said except that it looked bloodshot—glorified all this by its stare. It hung at a moderate elevation above Hyde Park Corner with an air of punctual and benign vigilance. The very pavement under Mr. Verloc's feet had an old-gold tinge in that diffused light, in which neither wall, nor tree, nor beast, nor man cast a shadow. Mr. Verloc was going westward through a town without shadows in an atmosphere of powdered old gold. There were red, coppery gleams on the roofs of houses, on the corners of walls, on the panels of carriages, on the very coats of the horses, and on the broad back of Mr. Verloc's overcoat, where they produced a dull effect of rustiness. But Mr. Verloc was not in the least conscious of having got rusty. He surveyed through the park railings the evidences of the town's opulence and luxury with an approving eye. All these people had to be protected. Protection is the first necessity of opulence and luxury. They had to be protected; and their horses, carriages, houses, servants had to be protected; and the source of their wealth had to be protected in the heart of the city and the heart of the country; the whole social order favorable to their hygienic idleness had to be protected against the shallow enviousness of unhygienic labor. It had to—and Mr. Verloc would have rubbed his hands with satisfaction had he not been constitutionally averse from every superfluous exertion. His idleness was not hygienic, but it suited him very well. He was in a manner devoted to it with a sort of inert fanaticism, or perhaps rather with a fanatical inertness. Born of industrious parents for a life of toil, he had embraced indolence from an impulse as profound, as inexplicable and as imperious as the impulse which directs a man's preference for one particular woman in a given thousand. He was too lazy even for a mere demagogue, for a workman orator, for a leader of labor. It was too much trouble. He required a more perfect form of ease; or it might have been that he was the victim of a philosophical unbelief in the effectiveness of every human effort. Such a form of indolence requires, implies, a certain amount of intelligence. Mr. Verloc was not devoid of intelligence—and at the notion of a menaced social order he would perhaps have winked to himself if there had not been an effort to make in that sign of skepticism. His big, prominent eyes were not well adapted to winking. They were rather of the sort that closes solemnly in slumber with majestic effect.

Undemonstrative and burly in a fat-pig style, Mr. Verloc, without either rubbing his hands with satisfaction or winking skeptically at his thoughts, proceeded on his way. He trod the pavement heavily with his shiny boots, and his general get-up was that of a well-to-do mechanic in business for himself. He might have been anything from a picture-frame maker to a locksmith; an employer of labor in a small way. But there was also about him an indescribable air which no mechanic could have acquired in the practice of his handicraft however dishonestly exercised: the air common to men who live on the vices, the follies, or the baser fears of mankind; the air of moral nihilism common to keepers of gambling hells and disorderly houses; to private detectives and inquiry agents; to drink sellers and, I should say, to the sellers of invigorating electric belts and to the inventors of patent medicines. But of that last I am not sure, not having carried my investigations so far into the depths. For all I know, the expression of these last may be perfectly diabolic. I shouldn't be surprised. What I want to affirm is that Mr. Verloc's expression was by no means diabolic.

Before reaching Knightsbridge, Mr. Verloc took a turn to the left out of the busy main thoroughfare, uproarious with the traffic of swaying omnibuses and trotting vans, in the almost silent, swift flow of hansoms. Under his hat, worn with a slight backward tilt, his hair had been carefully brushed into respectful sleekness; for his business was with an Embassy. And Mr. Verloc, steady like a rock—a soft kind of rock—marched now along a street which could with every propriety be described as private. In its breadth, emptiness, and extent it had the majesty of inorganic nature, of matter that never dies. The only reminder of mortality was a doctor's brougham arrested in august solitude close to the curbstone. The polished knockers of the doors gleamed as far as the eye could reach, the clean windows shone with a dark opaque luster. And all was still. But a milk cart rattled noisily across the distant perspective; a butcher boy, driving with the noble recklessness of a charioteer at Olympic Games, dashed round the corner sitting high above a pair of red wheels. A guilty-looking cat issuing from under the stones ran for a while in front of Mr. Verloc, then dived into another basement; and a thick police constable, looking a stranger to every emotion, as if he, too, were part of inorganic nature, surging apparently out of a lamppost, took not the slightest notice of Mr. Verloc. With a turn to the left Mr. Verloc pursued his way along a narrow street by the side of a yellow wall which, for some inscrutable reason, had No. 1 Chesham Square written on it in black letters. Chesham Square was at least sixty yards away, and Mr. Verloc, cosmopolitan enough not to be deceived by London's topographical mysteries, held on steadily, without a sign of surprise or indignation. At last, with businesslike persistency, he reached the Square, and made diagonally for the number 10. This belonged to an imposing carriage gate in a high, clean wall between two houses, of which one rationally enough bore the number 9 and the other was numbered 37; but the fact that this last belonged to Porthill Street, a street well known in the neighborhood, was proclaimed by an inscription placed above the ground-floor windows by whatever highly efficient authority is charged with the duty of keeping track of London's strayed houses. Why powers are not asked of Parliament (a short act would do) for compelling those edifices to return where they belong is one of the mysteries of municipal administration. Mr. Verloc did not trouble his head about it, his mission in life being the protection of the social mechanism, not its perfectionment or even its criticism.

It was so early that the porter of the Embassy issued hurriedly out of his lodge still struggling with the left sleeve of his livery coat. His waistcoat was red, and he wore knee breeches, but his aspect was flustered. Mr. Verloc, aware of the rush on his flank, drove it off by simply holding out an envelope stamped with the arms of the Embassy, and passed on. He produced the same talisman also to the footman who opened the door, and stood back to let him enter the hall.

A clear fire burned in a tall fireplace, and an elderly man standing with his back to it, in evening dress and with a chain round his neck, glanced up from the newspaper he was holding spread out in both hands before his calm and severe face. He didn't move; but another lackey, in brown trousers and clawhammer coat edged with thin yellow cord, approaching Mr. Verloc listened to the murmur of his name, and turning round on his heel in silence, began to walk, without looking back once. Mr. Verloc, thus led along a ground-floor passage to the left of the great carpeted staircase, was suddenly motioned to enter a quite small room furnished with a heavy writing table and a few chairs. The servant shut the door, and Mr. Verloc remained alone. He did not take a seat. With his hat and stick held in one hand he glanced about, passing his other pudgy hand over his uncovered sleek head.

Another door opened noiselessly, and Mr. Verloc immobilizing his glance in that direction saw at first only black clothes, the bald top of a head, and a drooping dark gray whisker on each side of a pair of wrinkled hands. The person who had entered was holding a batch of papers before his eyes and walked up to the table with a rather mincing step, turning the papers over the while. Privy Councillor Wurmt, Chancelier d'Ambassade, was rather shortsighted. This meritorious official, laying the papers on the table, disclosed a face of pasty complexion and of melancholy ugliness surrounded by a lot of fine, long dark gray hairs, barred heavily by thick and bushy eyebrows. He put on a black-framed pince-nez upon a blunt and shapeless nose, and seemed struck by Mr. Verloc's appearance. Under the enormous eyebrows his weak eyes blinked pathetically through the glasses.

He made no sign of greeting; neither did Mr. Verloc who certainly knew his place; but a subtle change about the general outlines of his shoulders and back suggested a slight bending of Mr. Verloc's spine under the vast surface of his overcoat. The effect was of unobtrusive deference.

"I have here some of your reports," said the bureaucrat in an unexpectedly soft and weary voice, and pressing the tip of his forefinger on the papers with force. He paused; and Mr. Verloc, who had recognized his own handwriting very well, waited in an almost breathless silence. "We are not very satisfied with the attitude of the police here," the other continued, with every appearance of mental fatigue.

The shoulders of Mr. Verloc, without actually moving, suggested a shrug. And for the first time since he left his home that morning his lips opened.

"Every country has its police," he said, philosophically. But as the official of the Embassy went on blinking at him steadily he felt constrained to add: "Allow me to observe that I have no means of action upon the police here."

"What is desired," said the man of papers, "is the occurrence of something definite which should stimulate their vigilance. That is within your province—is it not so?"

Mr. Verloc made no answer except by a sigh, which escaped him involuntarily, for instantly he tried to give his face a cheerful expression. The official blinked doubtfully, as if affected by the dim light of the room. He repeated vaguely:

"The vigilance of the police—and the severity of the magistrates. The general leniency of the judicial procedure here, and the utter absence of all repressive measures, are a scandal to Europe. What is wished for just now is the accentuation of the unrest—of the fermentation which undoubtedly exists—"

"Undoubtedly, undoubtedly," broke in Mr. Verloc in a deep, deferential bass of an oratorical quality, so utterly different from the tone in which he had spoken before that his interlocutor remained profoundly surprised. "It exists to a dangerous degree. My reports for the last twelve months make it sufficiently clear."

"Your reports for the last twelve months," State Councillor Wurmt began in his gentle and dispassionate tone, "have been read by me. I failed to discover why you wrote them at all."

A sad silence reigned for a time. Mr. Verloc seemed to have swallowed his tongue, and the other gazed at the papers on the table fixedly. At last he gave them a slight push.

"The state of affairs you expose there is assumed to exist as the first condition of your employment. What is required at present is not writing, but the bringing to light of a distinct, significant fact—I would almost say of an alarming fact."

"I need not say that all my endeavors shall be directed to that end," Mr. Verloc said, with convinced modulations in his conversational husky tone. But the sense of being blinked at watchfully behind the blind glitter of these eyeglasses on the other side of the table disconcerted him. He stopped short with a gesture of absolute devotion. The useful hardworking, if obscure member of the Embassy had an air of being impressed by some newly-born thought.

"You are very corpulent," he said.

This observation, really of a psychological nature, and advanced with the modest hesitation of an office-man more familiar with ink and paper than with the requirements of active life, stung Mr. Verloc in the manner of a rude personal remark. He stepped back a pace.

"Eh? What were you pleased to say?" he exclaimed, with husky resentment.

The Chancelier d'Ambassade, entrusted with the conduct of this interview, seemed to find it too much for him.

"I think," he said, "that you had better see Mr. Vladimir. Yes, decidedly I think you ought to see Mr. Vladimir. Be good enough to wait here," he added, and went out with mincing steps.

At once Mr. Verloc passed his hand over his hair. A slight perspiration had broken out on his forehead. He let the air escape from his pursed-up lips like a man blowing at a spoonful of hot soup. But when the servant in brown appeared at the door silently, Mr. Verloc had not moved an inch from the place he had occupied throughout the interview. He had remained motionless, as if feeling himself surrounded by pitfalls.

He walked along a passage lighted by a lonely gas jet, then up a flight of winding stairs, and through a glazed and cheerful corridor on the first floor. The footman threw open a door, and stood aside. The feet of Mr. Verloc felt a thick carpet. The room was large, with three windows; and a young man with a shaven, big face, sitting in a roomy armchair before a vast mahogany writing table, said in French to the Chancelier d'Ambassade, who was going out with the papers in his hand:

"You are quite right, mon cher. He's fat—the animal." Mr. Vladimir, First Secretary, had a drawing-room reputation as an agreeable and entertaining man. He was something of a favorite in society. His wit consisted in discovering droll connections between incongruous ideas; and when talking in that strain he sat well forward on his seat, with his left hand raised, as if exhibiting his funny demonstrations between the thumb and forefinger, while his round and clean-shaven face wore an expression of merry perplexity.

But there was no trace of merriment or perplexity in the way he looked at Mr. Verloc. Lying far back in the deep armchair, with squarely spread elbows, and throwing one leg over a thick knee, he had with his smooth and rosy countenance the air of a preternaturally thriving baby that will not stand nonsense from anybody. "You understand French, I suppose?" he said.

Mr. Verloc stated huskily that he did. His whole vast bulk had a forward inclination. He stood on the carpet in the middle of the room, clutching his hat and stick in one hand; the other hung lifelessly by his side. He muttered unobtrusively somewhere deep down in his throat something about having done his military service in the French artillery. At once, with contemptuous perversity, Mr. Vladimir changed the language, and began to speak idiomatic English without the slightest trace of a foreign accent.

"Ah! Yes. Of course. Let's see. How much did you get for obtaining the design of the improved breechblock of their new field gun?"

"Five years' rigorous confinement in a fortress," Mr. Verloc answered, unexpectedly, but without any sign of feeling.

"You got off easily," was Mr. Vladimir's comment. "And, anyhow, it served you right for letting yourself get caught. What made you go in for that sort of thing—eh?"

Mr. Verloc's husky conversational voice was heard speaking of youth, of a fatal infatuation for an unworthy—

"Aha! Cherchez la femme," Mr. Vladimir deigned to interrupt, unbending, but without affability; there was, on the contrary, a touch of grimness in his condescension. "How long have you been employed by the Embassy here?" he asked.

"Ever since the time of the late Baron Stott-Wartenheim," Mr. Verloc answered in subdued tones, and protruding his lips sadly, in sign of sorrow for the deceased diplomat. The First Secretary observed this play of physiognomy steadily.

"Ah! ever since. . . . Well! What have you got to say for yourself?" he asked, sharply.

Mr. Verloc answered with some surprise that he was not aware of having anything special to say. He had been summoned by a letter—And he plunged his hand busily into the side pocket of his overcoat, but before the mocking, cynical watchfulness of Mr. Vladimir, concluded to leave it there.

"Bah!" said the latter. "What do you mean by getting out of condition like this? You haven't got even the physique of your profession. You—a member of a starving proletariat—never! You—a desperate socialist or anarchist—which is it?"

"Anarchist," stated Mr. Verloc in a deadened tone.

"Bosh!" went on Mr. Vladimir, without raising his voice. "You startled old Wurmt himself. You wouldn't deceive an idiot. They all are that by-the-by, but you seem to me simply impossible. So you began your connection with us by stealing the French gun designs. And you got yourself caught. That must have been very disagreeable to our Government. You don't seem to be very smart."

Mr. Verloc tried to exculpate himself huskily.

"As I've had occasion to observe before, a fatal infatuation for an unworthy—"

Mr. Vladimir raised a large, white, plump hand.

"Ah, yes. The unlucky attachment—of your youth. She got hold of the money and then sold you to the police—eh?"

The doleful change in Mr. Verloc's physiognomy, the momentary drooping of his whole person, confessed that such was the regrettable case. Mr. Vladimir's hand clasped the ankle reposing on his knee. The sock was of dark blue silk.

"You see, that was not very clever of you. Perhaps you are too susceptible."

Mr. Verloc intimated in a throaty, veiled murmur that he was no longer young.

"Oh! That's a failing which age does not cure," Mr. Vladimir remarked, with sinister familiarity. "But no! You are too fat for that. You could not have come to look like this if you had been at all susceptible. I'll tell you what I think is the matter: you are a lazy fellow. How long have you been drawing pay from this Embassy?"

"Eleven years," was the answer, after a moment of sulky hesitation. "I've been charged with several missions to London while His Excellency Baron Stott-Wartenheim was still Ambassador in Paris. Then by his Excellency's instructions I settled down in London. I am English."

"You are! Are you? Eh?"

"A natural-born British subject," Mr. Verloc said, stolidly. "But my father was French, and so—"

"Never mind explaining," interrupted the other. "I daresay you could have been legally a Marshal of France and a Member of Parliament in England—and then, indeed, you would have been of some use to our Embassy."

This flight of fancy provoked something like a faint smile on Mr. Verloc's face. Mr. Vladimir retained an imperturbable gravity.

"But, as I've said, you are a lazy fellow; you don't use your opportunities. In the time of Baron Stott-Wartenheim we had a lot of soft-headed people running this Embassy. They caused fellows of your sort to form a false conception of the nature of a secret service fund. It is my business to correct this misapprehension by telling you what the secret service is not. It is not a philanthropic institution. I've had you called here on purpose to tell you this."

Mr. Vladimir observed the forced expression of bewilderment on Verloc's face, and smiled sarcastically.

"I see that you understand me perfectly. I daresay you are intelligent enough for your work. What we want now is activity—activity."

On repeating this last word Mr. Vladimir laid a long white forefinger on the edge of the desk. Every trace of huskiness disappeared from Verloc's voice. The nape of his gross neck became crimson above the velvet collar of his overcoat. His lips quivered before they came widely open.

"If you'll only be good enough to look up my record," he boomed out in his great, clear, oratorical bass, "you'll see I gave a warning only three months ago on the occasion of the Grand Duke Romuald's visit to Paris, which was telegraphed from here to the French police, and—"

"Tut, tut!" broke out Mr. Vladimir, with a frowning grimace. "The French police had no use for your warning. Don't roar like this. What the devil do you mean?"

With a note of proud humility Mr. Verloc apologized for forgetting himself. His voice, famous for years at open-air meetings and at workmen's assemblies in large halls, had contributed, he said, to his reputation of a good and trustworthy comrade. It was, therefore, a part of his usefulness. It had inspired confidence in his principles. "I was always put up to speak by the leaders at a critical moment," Mr. Verloc declared, with obvious satisfaction. There was no uproar above which he could not make himself heard, he added; and suddenly he made a demonstration.

"Allow me," he said. With lowered forehead, without looking up, swiftly and ponderously, he crossed the room to one of the French windows. As if giving way to an uncontrollable impulse, he opened it a little. Mr. Vladimir, jumping up amazed from the depths of the armchair, looked over his shoulder; and below, across the courtyard of the Embassy, well beyond the open gate, could be seen the broad back of a policeman watching idly the gorgeous perambulator of a wealthy baby being wheeled in state across the Square.

"Constable!" said Mr. Verloc, with no more effort than if he were whispering; and Mr. Vladimir burst into a laugh on seeing the policeman spin round as if prodded by a sharp instrument. Mr. Verloc shut the window quietly, and returned to the middle of the room.

"With a voice like that," he said, putting on the husky conversational pedal, "I was naturally trusted. And I knew what to say, too."

Mr. Vladimir, arranging his cravat, observed him in the glass over the mantelpiece.

"I daresay you have the social revolutionary jargon by heart well enough," he said, contemptuously. "Vox et. . . . You haven't ever studied Latin—have you?"

"No," growled Mr. Verloc. "You did not expect me to know it. I belong to the million. Who knows Latin? Only a few hundred imbeciles who aren't fit to take care of themselves."

For some thirty seconds longer Mr. Vladimir studied in the mirror the fleshy profile, the gross bulk, of the man behind him. And at the same time he had the advantage of seeing his own face, clean-shaved and round, rosy about the gills, and with the thin, sensitive lips formed exactly for the utterance of those delicate witticisms which had made him such a favorite in the very highest society. Then he turned, and advanced into the room with such determination that the very ends of his quaintly old-fashioned bow necktie seemed to bristle with unspeakable menaces. The movement was so swift and fierce that Mr. Verloc, casting an oblique glance, quailed inwardly.

"Aha! You dare be impudent," Mr. Vladimir began, with an amazingly guttural intonation not only utterly un-English, but absolutely un-European, and startling even to Mr. Verloc experience of cosmopolitan slums. "You dare! Well, I am going to speak plain English to you. Voice won't do. We have no use for your voice. We don't want a voice. We want facts—startling facts—damn you," he added, with a sort of ferocious discretion, right into Mr. Verloc's face.

"Don't you try to come over me with your Hyperborean manners," Mr. Verloc defended himself, huskily, looking at the carpet. At this his interlocutor, smiling mockingly above the bristling bow of his necktie, switched the conversation into French.

"You give yourself for an 'agent provocateur.' The proper business of an 'agent provocateur' is to provoke. As far as I can judge from your record kept here, you have done nothing to earn your money for the last three years."

"Nothing!" exclaimed Verloc, stirring not a limb, and not raising his eyes, but with the note of sincere feeling in his tone. "I have several times prevented what might have been—"

"There is a proverb in this country which says prevention is better than cure," interrupted Mr. Vladimir, throwing himself into the armchair. "It is stupid in a general way. There is no end to prevention. But it is characteristic. They dislike finality in this country. Don't you be too English. And in this particular instance, don't be absurd. The evil is already here. We don't want prevention—we want cure."

He paused, turned to the desk, and turning over some papers lying there, spoke in a changed, businesslike tone, without looking at Mr. Verloc.

"You know, of course, of the International Conference assembled in Milan?"

Mr. Verloc intimated hoarsely that he was in the habit of reading the daily papers. To a further question his answer was that, of course, he understood what he read. At this Mr. Vladimir, smiling faintly at the documents he was still scanning one after another, murmured "As long as it is not written in Latin, I suppose."

"Or Chinese," added Mr. Verloc, stolidly.

"H'm. Some of your revolutionary friends' effusions are written in a *charabia* every bit as incomprehensible as Chinese—" Mr. Vladimir let fall disdainfully a gray sheet of printed matter. "What are all these leaflets headed F.P., with a hammer, pen, and torch crossed? What does it mean, this F.P.?" Mr. Verloc approached the imposing writing table.

"The Future of the Proletariat. It's a society," he explained, standing ponderously by the side of the armchair, "not anarchist in principle, but open to all shades of revolutionary opinion."

"Are you in it?"

"One of the Vice-Presidents," Mr. Verloc breathed out heavily; and the First Secretary of the Embassy raised his head to look at him.

"Then you ought to be ashamed of yourself," he said, incisively. "Isn't your society capable of anything else but printing this prophetic bosh in blunt type on this filthy paper—eh? Why don't you do something? Look here. I've this matter in hand now, and I tell you plainly that you will have to earn your money. The good old Stott-Wartenheim times are over. No work, no pay."

Mr. Verloc felt a queer sensation of faintness in his stout legs. He stepped back one pace, and blew his nose loudly.

He was, in truth, startled and alarmed. The rusty London sunshine struggling clear of the London mist shed a lukewarm brightness into the First Secretary's private room: and in the silence Mr. Verloc heard against a windowpane the faint buzzing of a fly—his first fly of the year—heralding better than any number of swallows the approach of spring. The useless fussing of that tiny, energetic organism affected unpleasantly this big man threatened in his indolence.

In the pause Mr. Vladimir formulated in his mind a series of disparaging remarks concerning Mr. Verloc's face and figure. The fellow was unexpectedly vulgar, heavy, and impudently unintelligent. He looked uncommonly like a master plumber come to present his bill. The First Secretary of the Embassy, from his occasional excursions into the field of American humor, had formed a special notion of that class of mechanic as the embodiment of fraudulent laziness and incompetency.

This was then the famous and trusty secret agent, so secret that he was never designated otherwise but by the symbol Δ in the late Baron Stott-Wartenheim's official, semi-official, and confidential correspondence; the celebrated agent Δ whose warnings had the power to change the schemes and the dates of royal, imperial, grand-ducal journeys, and sometimes cause them to be put off altogether! This fellow! And Mr. Vladimir indulged mentally in an enormous and derisive fit of merriment, partly at his own astonishment, which he judged naive, but mostly at the expense of the universally regretted Baron Stott-Wartenheim. His late Excellency, whom the august favor of his Imperial master had imposed as Ambassador upon several reluctant Ministers of Foreign Affairs, had enjoyed in his lifetime a fame for an owlish, pessimistic gullibility. His Excellency had the social revolution on the brain. He imagined himself to be a diplomatist set apart by a special dispensation to watch the end of diplomacy, and pretty nearly the end of the world, in a horrid, democratic upheaval. His prophetic and doleful dispatches had been for years the joke of Foreign Offices. He was said to have exclaimed on his deathbed (visited by his Imperial friend and master): "Unhappy Europe! Thou shalt perish by the moral insanity of thy children!" He was fated to be the victim of the first humbugging rascal that came along, thought Mr. Vladimir, smiling vaguely at Mr. Verloc.

"You ought to venerate the memory of Baron Stott-Wartenheim," he exclaimed, suddenly.

The lowered physiognomy of Mr. Verloc expressed a somber and weary annoyance.

"Permit me to observe to you," he said, "that I came here because I was summoned by a peremptory letter. I have been here only twice before in the last eleven years, and certainly never at eleven in the morning. It isn't very wise to call me up like this. There is just a chance of being seen. And that would be no joke for me."

Mr. Vladimir shrugged his shoulders.

"It would destroy my usefulness," continued the other hotly.

"That's your affair," murmured Mr. Vladimir, with soft brutality. "When you cease to be useful you shall cease to be employed. Yes. Right off. Cut short. You shall——" Mr. Vladimir, frowning, paused, at a loss for a sufficiently idiomatic expression, and instantly brightened up, with a grin of beautifully white teeth. "You shall be chucked," he brought out, ferociously.

Once more Mr. Verloc had to react with all the force of his will against that sensation of faintness running down one's legs which once upon a time had inspired some poor devil with the felicitous expression: "My heart went down into my boots." Mr. Verloc, aware of the sensation, raised his head bravely.

Mr. Vladimir bore the look of heavy inquiry with perfect serenity.

"What we want is to administer a tonic to the Conference in Milan," he said, airily. "Its deliberations upon international action for the suppression of political crime don't seem to get anywhere. England lags. This country is absurd with its sentimental regard for individual liberty. It's intolerable to think that all your friends have got only to come over to——"

"In that way I have them all under my eye," Mr. Verloc interrupted, huskily.

"It would be much more to the point to have them all under lock and key. England must be brought into line. The imbecile bourgeoisie of this country make themselves the accomplices of the very people whose aim is to drive them out of their houses to starve in ditches. And they have the political power still, if they only had the sense to use it for their preservation. I suppose you agree that the middle classes are stupid?"

Mr. Verloc agreed hoarsely.

"They are."

"They have no imagination. They are blinded by an idiotic vanity. What they want just now is a jolly good scare. This is the psychological moment to set your friends to work. I have had you called here to develop to you my idea."

And Mr. Vladimir developed his idea from on high, with scorn and condescension, displaying at the same time an amount of ignorance as to the real aims, thoughts, and methods of the revolutionary world which filled the silent Mr. Verloc with inward consternation. He confounded causes with effects more than was excusable; the most distinguished propagandists with impulsive bomb throwers; assumed organization where in the nature of things it could not exist; spoke of the social revolutionary party one moment as of a perfectly disciplined army where the word of chiefs was supreme, and at another as if it had been the loosest association of desperate brigands that ever camped in a mountain gorge. Once Mr. Verloc had opened his mouth for a protest, but the raising of a shapely, large white hand arrested him. Very soon he became too appalled to even try to protest. He listened in a stillness of dread which resembled the immobility of profound attention.

"A series of outrages," Mr. Vladimir continued, calmly "executed here in this country; not only *planned* here—that would not do—they would not mind. Your friends could set half the Continent on fire without influencing the public opinion here in favor of a universal repressive legislation. They will not look outside their backyard here."

Mr. Verloc cleared his throat, but his heart failed him, and he said nothing.

"These outrages need not be especially sanguinary," Mr. Vladimir went on, as if delivering a scientific lecture, "but they must be sufficiently startling—effective. Let them be directed against buildings, for instance. What is the fetish of the hour that all the bourgeoisie recognize—eh, Mr. Verloc?"

Mr. Verloc opened his hands and shrugged his shoulders slightly.

"You are too lazy to think," was Mr. Vladimir's comment upon that gesture. "Pay attention to what I say. The fetish of today is neither royalty nor religion. Therefore the palace and the church should be left alone. You understand what I mean, Mr. Verloc?"

The dismay and the scorn of Mr. Verloc found vent in an attempt at levity.

"Perfectly. But what of the Embassies? A series of attacks on the various Embassies," he began; but he could not withstand the cold, watchful stare of the First Secretary.

"You can be facetious, I see," the latter observed, carelessly. "That's all right. It may enliven your oratory at socialistic congresses. But this room is no place for it. It would be infinitely safer for you to follow carefully what I am saying. As you are being called upon to furnish facts instead of cock-and-bull stories, you had better try to make your profit off what I am taking the trouble to explain to you. The sacrosanct fetish of today is science. Why don't you get some of your friends to go for that wooden-faced panjandrum—eh? Is it not part of these institutions which must be swept away before the F.P. comes along?"

Mr. Verloc said nothing. He was afraid to open his lips lest a groan should escape him.

"This is what you should try for. An attempt upon a crowned head or on a president is sensational enough in a way, but not so much as it used to be. It has entered into the general conception of the existence of all chiefs of state. It's almost conventional—especially since so many presidents have been assassinated. Now let us take an outrage upon—say a church. Horrible enough at first sight, no doubt, and yet not so effective as a person of an ordinary mind might think. No matter how revolutionary and anarchist in inception, there would be fools enough to give such an outrage the character of a religious manifestation. And that would detract from the especial alarming significance we wish to give to the act. A murderous attempt on a restaurant or a theater would suffer in the same way from the suggestion of nonpolitical passion; the exasperation of a hungry man, an act of social revenge. All this is used up; it is no longer instructive as an object lesson in revolutionary anarchism. Every newspaper has ready-made phrases to explain such manifestations away. I am about to give you the philosophy of bomb throwing from my point of view; from the point of view you pretend to have been serving for the last eleven years. I will try not to talk above your head. The sensibilities of the class you are attacking are soon blunted. Property seems to them an indestructible thing. You can't count upon their emotions either of pity or fear for very long. A bomb outrage to have any influence on public opinion now must go beyond the intention of vengeance or terrorism. It must be purely destructive. It must be that, and only that, beyond the faintest suspicion of any other object. You anarchists should make it clear that you are perfectly determined to make a clean sweep of the whole social creation. But how to get that appallingly absurd notion into the heads of the middle classes so that there should be no mistake? That's the question. By directing your blows at something outside the ordinary passions of humanity is the answer. Of course, there is art. A bomb in the National Gallery would make some noise. But it would not be serious enough. Art has never been their fetish. It's like breaking a few back windows in a man's house; whereas, if you want to make him really sit up, you must try at least to raise the roof. There would be some screaming of course, but from whom? Artists—art critics and such like—people of no account. Nobody minds what they say. But there is learning—science. Any imbecile that has got an income believes in that. He does not know why, but he believes it matters somehow. It is the sacrosanct fetish. All the damned professors are radicals at heart. Let them know that their great panjandrum has got to go, too, to make room for the Future of the Proletariat. A howl from all these intellectual idiots is bound to help forward the labors of the Milan Conference. They will be writing to the papers. Their indignation would be above suspicion, no material interests being openly at stake, and it will alarm every selfishness of the class which should be impressed. They believe that in some mysterious way science is at the source of their material prosperity. They do. And the absurd ferocity of such a demonstration will affect them more profoundly than the mangling of a whole street—or theater—full of their own kind. To that last they can always say: 'Oh! it's mere class hate.' But what is one to say to an act of destructive ferocity so absurd as to be incomprehensible, inexplicable, almost unthinkable; in fact, mad? Madness alone is truly terrifying, inasmuch as you cannot placate it either by threats, persuasion, or bribes. Moreover, I am a civilized man. I would never dream of directing you to organize a mere butchery, even if I expected the best results from it. But I wouldn't expect from a butchery the result

I want. Murder is always with us. It is almost an institution. The demonstration must be against learning—science. But not every science will do. The attack must have all the shocking senselessness of gratuitous blasphemy. Since bombs are your means of expression, it would be really telling if one could throw a bomb into pure mathematics. But that is impossible. I have been trying to educate you; I have expounded to you the higher philosophy of your usefulness, and suggested to you some serviceable arguments. The practical application of my teaching interests *you* mostly. But from the moment I have undertaken to interview you I have also given some attention to the practical aspect of the question. What do you think of having a go at astronomy?"

For some time already Mr. Verloc's immobility by the side of the armchair resembled a state of collapsed coma—a sort of passive insensibility interrupted by slight convulsive starts, such as may be observed in the domestic dog having a nightmare on the hearth-rug. And it was in an uneasy, doglike growl that he repeated the word:

"Astronomy."

He had not recovered thoroughly as yet from the state of bewilderment brought about by the effort to follow Mr. Vladimir's rapid, incisive utterance. It had overcome his power of assimilation. It had made him angry. This anger was complicated by incredulity. And suddenly it dawned upon him that all this was an elaborate joke. Mr. Vladimir exhibited his white teeth in a smile, with dimples on his round, full face posed with a complacent inclination above the bristling bow of his necktie. The favorite of intelligent society women had assumed his drawing room attitude accompanying the delivery of delicate witticisms. Sitting well forward, his white hand upraised, he seemed to hold delicately between his thumb and forefinger the subtlety of his suggestion.

"There could be nothing better. Such an outrage combines the greatest possible regard for humanity with the most alarming display of ferocious imbecility. I defy the ingenuity of journalists to persuade their public that any given member of the proletariat can have a personal grievance against astronomy. Starvation itself could hardly be dragged in there—eh? And there are other advantages. The whole civilized world has heard of Greenwich. The very bootblacks in the basement of Charing Cross Station know something of it. See?"

The features of Mr. Vladimir, so well known in the best society by their humorous urbanity, beamed with cynical self-satisfaction, which would have astonished the intelligent women his wit entertained so exquisitely. "Yes," he continued, with a contemptuous smile, "the blowing up of the first meridian is bound to raise a howl of execration."

"A difficult business," Mr. Verloc mumbled, feeling that this was the only safe thing to say.

"What is the matter? Haven't you the whole gang under your hand? The very pick of the basket? That old terrorist Yundt is here. I see him walking about Piccadilly in his green havelock almost every day. And Michaelis, the ticket-of-leave apostle—you don't mean to say you don't know where he is? Because if you don't, I can tell you," Mr. Vladimir went on menacingly. "If you imagine that you are the only one on the secret fund list, you are mistaken."

This perfectly gratuitous suggestion caused Mr. Verloc to shuffle his feet slightly.

"And the whole Lausanne lot—eh? Haven't they been flocking over here at the first hint of the Milan Conference? This is an absurd country."

"It will cost money," Mr. Verloc said, by a sort of instinct.

"That cock won't fight," Mr. Vladimir retorted, with an amazingly genuine English accent. "You'll get your screw every month, and no more till something happens. And if nothing happens very soon you won't get even that. What's your ostensible occupation? What are you supposed to live by?"

"I keep a shop," answered Mr. Verloc.

"A shop! What sort of shop?"

"Stationery, newspapers. My wife—"

"Your what?" interrupted Mr. Vladimir in his guttural Central Asian tones.

"My wife." Mr. Verloc raised his husky voice slightly. "I am married."

"That be damned for a yarn," exclaimed the other in unfeigned astonishment. "Married! And you a professed anarchist, too! What is this confounded nonsense? But I suppose it's merely a manner of speaking. Anarchists don't marry. It's well known. They can't. It would be apostasy."

"My wife isn't one," Mr. Verloc mumbled, sulkily. "Moreover, it's no concern of yours."

"Oh, yes, it is," snapped Mr. Vladimir. "I am beginning to be convinced that you are not at all the man for the work you've been employed on. Why you must have discredited yourself completely in your own world by your marriage. Couldn't you have managed without? This is your virtuous attachment—eh? What with one sort of attachment and another you are doing away with your usefulness."

Mr. Verloc, puffing out his cheeks, let the air escape violently, and that was all. He had armed himself with patience. It was not to be tried much longer. The First Secretary became suddenly very curt, detached, final.

"You may go now," he said. "A dynamite outrage must be provoked. I give you a month. The sittings of the Conference are suspended. Before it reassembles again something must have happened here, or your connection with us ceases."

He changed the note once more with an unprincipled versatility.

"Think over my philosophy, Mr.—Mr.—Verloc," he said, with a sort of charting condescension, waving his hand towards the door. "Go for the first meridian. You don't know the middle classes as well as I do. Their sensibilities are jaded. The first meridian. Nothing better, and nothing easier, I should think."

He had got up, and with his thin sensitive lips twitching humorously, watched in the glass over the mantelpiece Mr. Verloc backing out of the room heavily, hat and stick in hand. The door closed.

The footman in trousers, appearing suddenly in the corridor, let Mr. Verloc another way out and through a small door in the corner of the courtyard. The porter standing at the gate ignored his exit completely; and Mr. Verloc retraced the path of his morning's pilgrimage as if in a dream—an angry dream. This detachment from the material world was so complete that, though the mortal envelope of Mr. Verloc had not hastened unduly along the streets, that part of him to which it would be unwarrantably rude to refuse immortality found itself at the shop door all at once, as borne from west to east on the wings of a great wind. He walked straight behind the counter, and sat down on a wooden chair that stood there. No one appeared to disturb his solitude. Stevie, put into a green baize apron, was now sweeping and dusting upstairs, intent and conscientious, as though he were playing at it; and Mrs. Verloc, warned in the kitchen by the clatter of the cracked bell, had merely come to the glazed door of the parlor, and putting the curtain aside a little, had peered into the dim shop. Seeing her husband sitting there shadowy and bulky, with his hat tilted far back on his head, she had at once returned to her stove. An hour or more later she took the green baize apron off her brother Stevie, and instructed him to wash his hands and face in the peremptory tone she had used in that connection for fifteen years or so—ever since she had, in fact, ceased to attend to the boy's hands and face herself. She spared presently a glance away from her dishing-up for the inspection of that face and those hands which Stevie, approaching the kitchen table, offered for her approval with an air of self-assurance hiding a perpetual residue of anxiety. Formerly the anger of the father was the supremely effective sanction of these rites, but Mr. Verloc's placidity in domestic life would have made all mention of anger incredible—even to poor Stevie's nervousness. The theory was that Mr. Verloc would have been inexpressibly pained and shocked by any deficiency of cleanliness at meal times. Winnie after the death of her father found considerable consolation in the feeling that she need no longer tremble for poor Stevie. She could not bear to see the boy hurt. It maddened her. As a little girl she had often faced with blazing eyes the irascible licensed victualler in defense of her brother. Nothing now in Mrs. Verloc's appearance could lead one to suppose that she was capable of a passionate demonstration.

She finished her dishing-up. The table was laid in the parlor. Going to the foot of the stairs she screamed out "Mother!" Then opening the glazed door leading to the shop, she said quietly "Adolf!" Mr. Verloc had not changed his position; he had not apparently stirred a limb for an hour and a half. He got up heavily, and came to his dinner in his overcoat and with his hat on, without uttering a word. His silence in itself had nothing startlingly unusual in this household, hidden in the shades of the sordid street seldom touched by the sun, behind the dim shop with its wares of disreputable rubbish. Only that day Mr. Verloc's taciturnity was so obviously thoughtful that the two women were impressed by it. They sat silent themselves, keeping a watchful eye on poor Stevie, lest he should break out into one of his fits of loquacity. He faced Mr. Verloc across the table, and remained very good and quiet, staring vacantly. The endeavor to keep him from making himself objectionable in any way to the master of the house put no inconsiderable anxiety into these two women's lives. "That boy," as they alluded to him softly between themselves, had been a source of that sort of anxiety almost from the very day of his birth. The late licensed victualler's humiliation at having such a very peculiar boy for a son manifested itself by a propensity to brutal treatment; for he was a person of fine sensibilities, and his sufferings as a man and a father were perfectly genuine. Afterwards Stevie had to be kept from making himself a nuisance to the single gentlemen lodgers, who are themselves a queer lot, and are easily aggriev- ed. And there was always the anxiety of his mere existence to face. Visions of a workhouse infirmary for her child had haunted the old woman in the basement breakfast room of the decayed Belgravian house. "If you had not found such a good husband, my dear," she used to say to her daughter, "I don't know what would have become of that poor boy."

Mr. Verloc extended as much recognition to Stevie as a man not particularly fond of animals may give to his wife's beloved cat; and this recognition, benevo- lent and perfunctory, was essentially of the same quality. Both women admitted to themselves that not much more could be reasonably expected. It was enough to earn for Mr. Verloc the old woman's reverential gratitude. In the early days, made skeptical by the trials of friendless life, she used sometimes to ask anxiously: "You don't think, my dear, that Mr. Verloc is getting tired of seeing Stevie about?" To this Winnie replied habitually by a slight toss of her head. Once, however, she retorted, with a rather grim pertness: "He'll have to get tired of me first." A long silence ensued. The mother, with her feet propped up on a stool, seemed to be try- ing to get to the bottom of that answer, whose feminine profundity had struck her all of a heap. She had never really understood why Winnie had married Mr. Verloc. It was very sensible of her, and evidently had turned out for the best, but her girl might have naturally hoped to find somebody of a more suitable age. There had been a steady young fellow, only son of a butcher in the next street, helping his father in business, with whom Winnie had been walking out with obvious gusto. He was dependent on his father, it is true; but the business was good, and his prospects excellent. He took her girl to the theater on several evenings. Then just as she began to dread to hear of their engagement (for what could she have done with that big house alone, with Stevie on her hands), that romance came to an abrupt end, and Winnie went about looking very dull. But Mr. Verloc, turning up providentially to occupy the first-floor front bedroom, there had been no more question of the young butcher. It was clearly providential.

❧ 3 ❧

". . . All idealization makes life poorer. To beautify it is to take away its character of complexity—it is to destroy it. Leave that to the moralists, my boy. History is made by men, but they do not make it in their heads. The ideas that are born in their consciousness play an insignificant part in the march of events. History is dominated and determined by the tool and the production— by force of economic conditions. Capitalism has made socialism, and the laws made by capitalism for the protection of property are responsible for anarchism. No one can tell what form the social organization may take in the future. Then why indulge in prophetic fantasies? At best they can only interpret the mind of the prophet, and can have no objective value. Leave that pastime to the moralists, my boy."

Michaelis, the ticket-of-leave apostle, was speaking in an even voice, a voice that wheezed as if deadened and oppressed by the layer of fat on his chest. He had come out of a highly hygienic prison round like a tub, with an enormous stomach and distended cheeks of a pale, semi-transparent complexion, as though for fifteen years the servants of an outraged society had made a point of stuffing him with fattening foods in a damp and lightless cellar. And ever since he had never managed to get his weight down as much as an ounce.

It was said that for three seasons running a very wealthy old lady had sent him for a cure to Marienbad—where he was about to share the public curiosity once with a crowned head—but the police on that occasion ordered him to leave within twelve hours. His martyrdom was continued by forbidding him all access to the healing waters. But he was resigned now.

With his elbow presenting no appearance of a joint, but more like a bend in a dummy's limb, thrown over the back of a chair, he leaned forward slightly over his short and enormous thighs to spit into the grate.

"Yes! I had the time to think things out a little," he added without emphasis. "Society has given me plenty of time for meditation."

On the other side of the fireplace, in the horsehair armchair where Mrs. Verloc's mother was generally privileged to sit, Karl Yundt giggled grimly, with a faint black grimace of a toothless mouth. The terrorist, as he called himself, was old and bald, with a narrow, snow-white wisp of a goatee hanging limply from his chin. An extraordinary expression of underhand malevolence survived in his extinguished eyes. When he rose painfully the thrusting forward of a skinny groping hand deformed by gouty swellings suggested the effort of a moribund murderer summoning all his remaining strength for a last stab. He leaned on a thick stick, which trembled under his other hand.

"I have always dreamed,' he mouthed, fiercely, "of a band of men absolute in their resolve to discard all scruples in the choice of means, strong enough to give themselves frankly the name of destroyers, and free from the taint of that resigned pessimism which rots the world. No pity for anything on earth, including themselves, and death enlisted for good and all in the service of humanity—that's what I would have liked to see."

His little bald head quivered, imparting a comical vibration to the wisp of white goatee. His enunciation would have been almost totally unintelligible to a stranger. His worn-out passion, resembling in its impotent fierceness the excitement of a senile sensualist, was badly served by a dried throat and toothless gums which seemed to catch the tip of his tongue. Mr. Verloc, established in the corner of the sofa at the other end of the room, emitted two hearty grunts of assent.

The old terrorist turned slowly his head on his skinny neck from side to side.

"And I could never get as many as three such men together. So much for your rotten pessimism," he snarled at Michaelis, who uncrossed his thick legs similar to bolsters, and slid his feet abruptly under his chair in sign of exasperation.

He a pessimist! Preposterous! He cried out that the charge was outrageous. He was so far from pessimism that he saw already the end of all private property coming along logically, unavoidably, by the mere development of its inherent viciousness. The possessors of property had not only to face the awakened proletariat, but they had also to fight amongst themselves. Yes. Struggle, warfare, was the condition of private ownership. It was fatal. Ah! he did not depend upon emotional excitement to keep up his belief, no declamations, no anger, no visions of blood-red flags waving, or metaphorical lurid suns of vengeance rising above the horizon of a doomed society. Not he! Cold reason, he boasted, was the basis of his optimism. Yes, optimism—

His laborious wheezing stopped, then, after a gasp or two, he added:

"Don't you think that, if I had not been the optimist I am, I could not have found in fifteen years some means to cut my throat? And, in the last instance, there were always the walls of my cell to dash my head against."

The shortness of breath took all fire, all animation out of his voice; his great, pale cheeks hung like filled pouches, motionless, without a quiver; but in his blue eyes, narrowed as if peering, there was the same look of confident shrewdness, a little crazy in its fixity, they must have had while the indomitable optimist sat thinking at night in his cell. Before him, Karl Yundt remained standing, one wing of his faded greenish havelock thrown back cavalierly over his shoulder. Seated in front of the fireplace, Comrade Ossipon, ex-medical student, the principal writer of the F.P. leaflets, stretched out his robust legs, keeping the soles of his boots turned up to the glow in the grate. A bush of crinkly yellow hair topped his red, freckled face, with a flattened nose and prominent mouth cast in the rough mold of the negro type. His almond-shaped eyes leered languidly over the high cheekbones. He wore a gray flannel shirt, the loose ends of a black silk tie hung down the buttoned breast of his serge coat; and his head resting on the back of his chair, his throat largely exposed, he raised to his lips a cigarette in a long wooden tube, puffing jets of smoke straight up at the ceiling.

Michaelis pursued his idea—*the* idea of his solitary reclusion—the thought vouchsafed to his captivity and growing like a faith revealed in visions. He talked to himself, indifferent to the sympathy or hostility of his hearers, indifferent indeed to their presence, from the habit he had acquired of thinking aloud hopefully in the solitude of the four whitewashed walls of his cell, in the sepulchral silence of the great blind pile of bricks near a river, sinister and ugly like a colossal mortuary for the socially drowned.

He was no good in discussion, not because any amount of argument could shake his faith, but because the mere fact of hearing another voice disconcerted him painfully, confusing his thoughts at once—these thoughts that for so many years, in a mental solitude more barren than a waterless desert, no living voice had ever combated, commented, or approved.

No one interrupted him now, and he made again the confession of his faith, mastering him irresistible and complete like an act of grace: the secret of fate discovered in the material side of life; the economic condition of the world responsible for the past and shaping the future; the source of all history, of all ideas, guiding the mental development of mankind and the very impulses of their passion—

A harsh laugh from Comrade Ossipon cut the tirade dead short in a sudden faltering of the tongue and a bewildered unsteadiness of the apostle's mildly exalted eyes. He closed them slowly for a moment, as if to collect his routed thoughts. A silence fell; but what with the two gas jets over the table and the glowing grate the little parlor behind Mr. Verloc's shop had become frightfully hot. Mr. Verloc, getting off the sofa with ponderous reluctance, opened the door leading into the kitchen to get more air, and thus disclosed the innocent Stevie, seated very good and quiet at a deal table, drawing circles, circles, circles; innumerable circles, concentric, eccentric; a coruscating whirl of circles that by their tangled multitude of repeated curves, uniformity of form, and confusion of intersecting lines suggested a rendering of cosmic chaos, the symbolism of a mad art attempting the inconceivable. The artist never turned his head; and in all his soul's application to the task his back quivered, his thin neck, sunk into a deep hollow at the base of the skull, seemed ready to snap.

Mr. Verloc, after a grunt of disapproving surprise, returned to the sofa. Alexander Ossipon got up, tall in his threadbare blue serge suit under the low ceiling, shook off the stiffness of long immobility, and strolled away into the kitchen (down two steps) to look over Stevie's shoulder. He came back, pronouncing oracularly: "Very good. Very characteristic, perfectly typical."

"What's very good?" grunted, inquiringly, Mr. Verloc, settled again in the corner of the sofa. The other explained his meaning negligently, with a shade of condescension and a toss of his head towards the kitchen:

"Typical of this form of degeneracy—these drawings, I mean."

"You would call that lad a degenerate, would you?" mumbled Mr. Verloc.

Comrade Alexander Ossipon—nicknamed the Doctor, ex-medical student without a degree; afterwards wandering lecturer to workingmen's associations upon the socialistic aspects of hygiene; author of a popular quasi-medical study (in the form of a cheap pamphlet seized promptly by the police) entitled "The Corroding Vices of the Middle Classes"; special delegate of the more or less mysterious Red Committee, together with Karl Yundt and Michaelis for the work of literary propaganda—turned upon the obscure familiar of at least two Embassies that glance of insufferable, hopelessly dense sufficiency which nothing but the frequentation of science can give to the dullness of common mortals.

"That's what he may be called scientifically. Very good type, too, altogether, of that sort of degenerate. It's enough to glance at the lobes of his ears. If you read Lombroso—"

Mr. Verloc, moody and spread largely on the sofa, continued to look down the row of his waistcoat buttons; but his cheeks became tinged by a faint blush. Of late even the merest derivative of the word science (a term in itself inoffensive and of indefinite meaning) had the curious power of evoking a definitely offensive mental vision of Mr. Vladimir, in his body as he lived, with an almost supernatural clearness. And this phenomenon, deserving justly to be classed amongst the marvels of science, induced in Mr. Verloc an emotional state of dread and exasperation tending to express itself in violent swearing. But he said nothing. It was Karl Yundt who was heard, implacable to his last breath.

"Lombroso is an ass."

Comrade Ossipon met the shock of this blasphemy by an awful, vacant stare. And the other, his extinguished eyes without gleams blackening the deep shadows under the great, bony forehead, mumbled, catching the tip of his tongue between his lips at every second word as though he were chewing it angrily:

"Did you ever see such an idiot? For him the criminal is the prisoner. Simple, is it not? What about those who shut him up there—forced him in there? Exactly. Forced him in there. And what is crime? Does he know that, this imbecile who has made his way in this world of gorged fools by looking at the ears and teeth of a lot of poor, luckless devils? Teeth and ears mark the criminal? Do they? And what about the law that marks him still better—the pretty branding instrument invented by the overfed to protect themselves against the hungry? Red-hot applications on their vile skins—hey? Can't you smell and hear from here the thick hide of the people burn and sizzle? That's how criminals are made for your Lombrosos to write their silly stuff about."

The knob of his stick and his legs shook together with passion, whilst the trunk, draped in the wings of the havelock, preserved his historic attitude of defiance. He seemed to sniff the tainted air of social cruelty, to strain his ear for its atrocious sounds. There was an extraordinary force of suggestion in this posturing. The all but moribund veteran of dynamite wars had been a great actor in his time—actor on platforms, in secret assemblies, in private interviews. The famous terrorist had never in his life raised personally as much as his little finger against the social edifice. He was no man of action; he was not even an orator of torrential eloquence, sweeping the masses along in the rushing noise and foam of a great enthusiasm. With a more subtle intention, he took the part of an insolent and venomous evoker of sinister impulses which lurk in the blind envy and exasperated vanity of ignorance, in the suffering and misery of poverty, in all the hopeful and noble illusions of righteous anger, pity, and revolt. The shadow of his evil gift clung to him yet like the smell of a deadly drug in an old vial of poison, emptied now, useless, ready to be thrown away upon the rubbish heap of things that had served their time.

Michaelis, the ticket-of-leave apostle, smiled vaguely with his glued lips; his pasty moon face drooped under the weight of melancholy assent. He had been a prisoner himself. His own skin had sizzled under the red-hot brand, he murmured softly. But Comrade Ossipon, nicknamed the Doctor, had got over the shock by that time.

"You don't understand," he began, disdainfully, but stopped short, intimidated by the dead blackness of the cavernous eyes in the face turned slowly towards him with a blind stare, as if guided only by the sound. He gave the discussion up, with a slight shrug of the shoulders.

Stevie, accustomed to move about disregarded, had got up from the kitchen table, carrying off his drawing to bed with him. He had reached the parlor door in time to receive in full the shock of Karl Yundt's eloquent imagery. The sheet of paper covered with circles dropped out of his fingers, and he remained staring at the old terrorist, as if rooted suddenly to the spot by his morbid horror and dread of physical pain. Stevie knew very well that hot iron applied to one's skin hurt very much. His scared eyes blazed with indignation: it would hurt terribly. His mouth dropped open.

Michaelis by staring unwinkingly at the fire had regained that sentiment of isolation necessary for the continuity of his thought. His optimism had begun to flow from his lips. He saw Capitalism doomed in its cradle, born with the poison of the principle of competition in its system. The great capitalists devouring the little capitalists, concentrating the power and the tools of production in great masses, perfecting industrial processes, and in the madness of self-aggrandizement only preparing, organizing, enriching, making ready the lawful inheritance of the suffering proletariat. Michaelis pronounced the great word "Patience"—and his clear blue glance, raised to the low ceiling of Mr. Verloc's parlor, had a character of seraphic trustfulness. In the doorway Stevie, calmed, seemed sunk in hebetude.

Comrade Ossipon's face twitched with exasperation.

"Then it's no use doing anything—no use whatever."

"I don't say that," protested Michaelis, gently. His vision of truth had grown so intense that the sound of a strange voice failed to rout it this time. He continued to look down at the red coals. Preparation for the future was necessary, and he was willing to admit that the great change would perhaps come in the upheaval of a revolution. But he argued that revolutionary propaganda was a delicate work of high conscience. It was the education of the masters of the world. It should be as careful as the education given to kings. He would have it advance its tenets cautiously, even timidly, in our ignorance of the effect that may be produced by any given economic change upon the happiness, the morals, the intellect, the history of mankind. For history is made with tools, not with ideas; and everything is changed by economic conditions—art, philosophy, love, virtue—truth itself!

The coals in the grate settled down with a slight crash; and Michaelis, the hermit of visions in the desert of a penitentiary, got up impetuously. Round like a distended balloon, he opened his short, thick arms, as if in a pathetically hopeless attempt to embrace and hug to his breast a self-regenerated universe. He gasped with ardor.

"The future is as certain as the past—slavery, feudalism, individualism, collectivism. This is the statement of a law, not an empty prophecy."

The disdainful pout of Comrade Ossipon's thick lips accentuated the negro type of his face.

"Nonsense," he said, calmly enough. "There is no law and no certainty. The teaching propaganda be hanged. What the people knows does not matter, were its knowledge ever so accurate. The only thing that matters to us is the emotional state of the masses. Without emotion there is no action."

He paused, then added with modest firmness:

"I am speaking now to you scientifically—scientifically—Eh? What did you say, Verloc?"

"Nothing," growled from the sofa Mr. Verloc, who, provoked by the abhorrent sound, had merely muttered a "Damn."

The venomous spluttering of the old terrorist without teeth was heard.

"Do you know how I would call the nature of the present economic conditions? I would call it cannibalistic. That's what it is! They are nourishing their greed on the quivering flesh and the warm blood of the people—nothing else."

Stevie swallowed the terrifying statement with an audible gulp, and at once, as though it had been swift poison, sank limply in a sitting posture on the steps of the kitchen door.

Michaelis gave no signs of having heard anything. His lips seemed glued together for good; not a quiver passed over his heavy cheeks. With troubled eyes he looked for his round, hard hat, and put it on his round head. His round and obese body seemed to float low between the chairs under the sharp elbow of Karl Yundt. The old terrorist, raising an uncertain and claw-like hand, gave a swaggering tilt to a black felt sombrero shading the hollows and ridges of his wasted face. He got in motion slowly, striking the floor with his stick at every step. It was rather an affair to get him out of the house because, now and then, he would stop, as if to think, and did not offer to move again till impelled forward by Michaelis. The gentle apostle grasped his arm with brotherly care; and behind them, his hands in his pockets, the robust Ossipon yawned vaguely. A blue cap with a patent leather peak set well at the back of his yellow bush of hair gave him the aspect of a Norwegian sailor bored with the world after a thundering spree. Mr. Verloc saw his guests off the premises, attending them bareheaded, his heavy overcoat hanging open, his eyes on the ground.

He closed the door behind their backs with restrained violence, turned the key, shot the bolt. He was not satisfied with his friends. In the light of Mr. Vladimir's philosophy of bomb throwing they appeared hopelessly futile. The part of Mr. Verloc in revolutionary politics having been to observe, he could not all at once, either in his own home or in larger assemblies, take the initiative of action. He had to be cautious. Moved by the just indignation of a man well over forty, menaced in what is dearest to him—his repose and his security—he asked himself scornfully what else could have been expected from such a lot, this Karl Yundt, this Michaelis—this Ossipon.

Pausing in his intention to turn off the gas burning in the middle of the shop, Mr. Verloc descended into the abyss of moral reflections. With the insight of a kindred temperament he pronounced his verdict. A lazy lot—this Karl Yundt, nursed by a blear-eyed old woman, a woman he had years ago enticed away from a friend, and afterwards had tried more than once to shake off into the gutter. Jolly lucky for Yundt that she had persisted in coming up time after time, or else there would have been no one now to help him out of the 'bus by the Green Park railings, where that specter took its constitutional crawl every fine morning. When that indomitable snarling old witch died the swaggering specter would have to vanish, too—there would be an end to fiery Karl Yundt. And Mr. Verloc's morality was offended also by the optimism of Michaelis, annexed by his wealthy old lady, who had taken lately to sending him to a cottage she had in the country. The ex-prisoner could moon about the shady lanes for days together in a delicious and humanitarian idleness. As to Ossipon, that beggar was sure to want for nothing as long as there were silly girls with savings-bank books in the world. And Mr. Verloc, temperamentally identical with his associates, drew fine distinctions in his mind on the strength of insignificant differences. He drew them with a certain complacency, because the instinct of conventional respectability was strong within him, being only overcome by his dislike of all kinds of recognized labor—a temperamental defect which he shared with a large proportion of revolutionary reformers of a given social state. For obviously one does not revolt against the advantages and opportunities of that state, but against the price which must be paid for the same in the coin of accepted morality, self-restraint, and toil. The majority of revolutionists are the enemies of discipline and fatigue mostly. There are natures, too, to whose sense of justice the price exacted looms up monstrously enormous, odious, oppressive, worrying, humiliating, extortionate, intolerable. Those are the fanatics. The remaining portion of social rebels is accounted for by vanity, the mother of all noble and vile illusions, the companion of poets, reformers, charlatans, prophets, and incendiaries.

Lost for a whole minute in the abyss of meditation, Mr. Verloc did not reach the depth of these abstract considerations. Perhaps he was not able. In any case he had not the time. He was pulled up painfully by the sudden recollection of Mr. Vladimir, another of his associates, whom in virtue of subtle moral affinities he was capable of judging correctly. He considered him as dangerous. A shade of envy crept into his thoughts. Loafing was all very well for these fellows, who knew not Mr. Vladimir, and had women to fall back upon; whereas he had a woman to provide for—

At this point, by a simple association of ideas, Mr. Verloc was brought face to face with the necessity of going to bed some time or other that evening. Then why not go now—at once? He sighed. The necessity was not so normally pleasurable as it ought to have been for a man of his age and temperament. He dreaded the demon of sleeplessness, which he felt had marked him for its own. He raised his arm, and turned off the flaring gas jet above his head.

A bright band of light fell through the parlor door into the part of the shop behind the counter. It enabled Mr. Verloc to ascertain at a glance the number of silver coins in the till. These were but few; and for the first time since he opened his shop he took a commercial survey of its value. This survey was unfavorable. He had gone into trade for no commercial reasons. He had been guided in the selection of this peculiar line of business by an instinctive leaning towards shady transactions, where money is picked up easily. Moreover, it did not take him out of his own sphere—the sphere which is watched by the police. On the contrary, it gave him a publicly confessed standing in that sphere, and as Mr. Verloc had unconfessed relations which made him familiar with yet careless of the police, there was a distinct advantage in such a situation. But as a means of livelihood it was by itself insufficient.

He took the cash-box out of the drawer, and turning to leave the shop, became aware that Stevie was still downstairs.

What on earth is he doing there? Mr. Verloc asked himself. What's the meaning of these antics? He looked dubiously at his brother-in-law, but he did not ask him for information. Mr. Verloc's intercourse with Stevie was limited to the casual mutter of a morning, after breakfast, "My boots," and even that was more a communication at large of a need than a direct order or request. Mr. Verloc perceived with some surprise that he did not know really what to say to Stevie. He stood still in the middle of the parlor, and looked into the kitchen in silence. Nor yet did he know what would happen if he did say anything. And this appeared very queer to Mr. Verloc in view of the fact, borne upon him suddenly, that he had to provide for this fellow, too. He had never given a moment's thought till then to that aspect of Stevie's existence.

Positively he did not know how to speak to the lad. He watched him gesticulating and murmuring in the kitchen. Stevie prowled round the table like an excited animal in a cage. A tentative "Hadn't you better go to bed now?" produced no effect whatever; and Mr. Verloc, abandoning the stony contemplation of his brother-in-law's behavior, crossed the parlor wearily, cash-box in hand. The cause of the general lassitude he felt while climbing the stairs being purely mental, he became alarmed by its inexplicable character. He hoped he was not sickening for anything. He stopped on the dark landing to examine his sensations. But a slight and continuous sound of snoring pervading the obscurity interfered with their clearness. The sound came from his mother-in-law's room. Another one to provide for, he thought—and on this thought walked into the bedroom.

Mrs. Verloc had fallen asleep with the lamp (no gas was laid upstairs) turned up full on the table by the side of the bed. The light thrown down by the shade fell dazzlingly on the white pillow sunk by the weight of her head reposing with closed eyes and dark hair done up in several plaits for the night. She woke up with the sound of her name in her ears, and saw her husband standing over her.

"Winnie! Winnie!"

At first she did not stir, lying very quiet and looking at the cash-box in Mr. Verloc's hand. But when she understood that her brother was "capering all over the place downstairs" she swung out in one sudden movement on to the edge of the bed. Her bare feet, as if poked through the bottom of an unadorned, sleeved calico sack buttoned tightly at neck and wrists, felt over the rug for the slippers while she looked upward into her husband's face.

"I don't know how to manage him," Mr. Verloc explained, peevishly. "Won't do to leave him downstairs alone with the lights."

She said nothing, glided across the room swiftly, and the door closed upon her white form.

Mr. Verloc deposited the cash-box on the night table, and began the operation of undressing by flinging his overcoat on to a distant chair. His coat and waistcoat followed. He walked about the room in his stockinged feet, and his burly figure, with the hands worrying nervously at his throat, passed and repassed across the long strip of looking glass in the door of his wife's wardrobe. Then after slipping his braces off his shoulders he pulled up violently the venetian blind, and leaned his forehead against the cold windowpane—a fragile film of glass stretched between him and the enormity of cold, black, wet, muddy, inhospitable accumulation of bricks, slates, and stones, things in themselves unlovely and unfriendly to man.

Mr. Verloc felt the latent unfriendliness of all out of doors with a force approaching to positive bodily anguish. There is no occupation that fails a man more completely than that of a secret agent of police. It's like your horse suddenly falling dead under you in the midst of an uninhabited and thirsty plain. The comparison occurred to Mr. Verloc because he had sat astride various army horses in his time, and had now the sensation of an incipient fall. The prospect was as black as the windowpane against which he was leaning his forehead. And suddenly the face of Mr. Vladimir, clean-shaved and witty, appeared enhaloed in the glow of its rosy complexion like a sort of pink seal impressed on the fatal darkness.

This luminous and mutilated vision was so ghastly physically that Mr. Verloc started away from the window, letting down the venetian blind with a great rattle. Discomposed and speechless with the apprehension of more such visions, he beheld his wife re-enter the room and get into bed in a calm, businesslike manner which made him feel hopelessly lonely in the world. Mrs. Verloc expressed her surprise at seeing him up yet.

"I don't feel very well," he muttered, passing his hands over his moist brow.

"Giddiness?"

"Yes. Not at all well."

Mrs. Verloc, with all the placidity of an experienced wife, expressed a confident opinion as to the cause, and suggested the usual remedies; but her husband, rooted in the middle of the room, shook his lowered head sadly.

"You'll catch cold standing there," she observed.

Mr. Verloc made an effort, finished undressing, and got into bed. Down below in the quiet, narrow street measured footsteps approached the house, then died away, unhurried and firm, as if the passerby had started to pace out all eternity, from gas-lamp to gas-lamp in a night without end; and the drowsy ticking of the old clock on the landing became distinctly audible in the bedroom.

Mrs. Verloc, on her back, and staring at the ceiling, made a remark.

"Takings very small today."

Mr. Verloc, in the same position, cleared his throat as if for an important statement, but merely inquired:

"Did you turn off the gas downstairs?"

"Yes; I did," answered Mrs. Verloc, conscientiously. "That poor boy is in a very excited state tonight," she murmured, after a pause which lasted for three ticks of the clock.

Mr. Verloc cared nothing for Stevie's excitement, but he felt horribly wakeful, and dreaded facing the darkness and silence that would follow the extinguishing of the lamp. This dread led him to make the remark that Stevie had disregarded his suggestion to go to bed. Mrs. Verloc, falling into the trap, started to demonstrate at length to her husband that this was not "impudence" of any sort, but simply "excitement." There was no young man of his age in London more willing and docile than Stephen, she affirmed; none more affectionate and ready to please, and even useful, as long as people did not upset his poor head. Mrs. Verloc, turning towards her recumbent husband, raised herself on her elbow, and hung over him in her anxiety that he should believe Stevie to be a useful member of the family. That ardor of protecting compassion exalted morbidly in her childhood by the misery of another child tinged her sallow cheeks with a faint dusky blush, made her big eyes gleam under the dark lids. Mrs. Verloc then looked younger; she looked as young as Winnie used to look, and much more animated than the Winnie of the Belgravian mansion days had ever allowed herself to appear to gentlemen lodgers. Mr. Verloc's anxieties had prevented him from attaching any sense to what his wife was saying. It was as if her voice was talking on the other side of a very thick wall. It was her aspect that recalled him to himself.

He appreciated this woman, and the sentiment of this appreciation, stirred by a display of something resembling emotion, only added another pang to his mental anguish. When her voice ceased he moved uneasily, and said:

"I haven't been feeling well for the last few days."

He might have meant this as an opening to a complete confidence; but Mrs. Verloc laid her head on the pillow again, and staring upward, went on:

"That boy hears too much of what is talked about here. If I had known they were coming tonight I would have seen to it that he went to bed at the same time

I did. He was out of his mind with something he overheard about eating people's flesh and drinking blood. What's the good of talking like that?"

There was a note of indignant scorn in her voice. Mr. Verloc was fully responsive now.

"Ask Karl Yundt," he growled, savagely.

Mrs. Verloc, with great decision, pronounced Karl Yundt "a disgusting old man." She declared openly her affection for Michaelis. Of the robust Ossipon, in whose presence she always felt uneasy behind an attitude of stony reserve, she said nothing whatever. And continuing to talk of that brother, who had been for so many years an object of care and fears:

"He isn't fit to hear what's said here. He believes it's all true. He knows no better. He gets into his passions over it."

Mr. Verloc made no comment.

"He glared at me, as if he didn't know who I was, when I went downstairs. His heart was going like a hammer. He can't help being excitable. I woke mother up, and asked her to sit with him till he went to sleep. It isn't his fault. He's no trouble when he's left alone."

Mr. Verloc made no comment.

"I wish he had never been to school," Mrs. Verloc began again, bruskly. "He's always taking away those newspapers from the window to read. He gets a red face poring over them. We don't get rid of a dozen numbers in a month. They only take up room in the front window. And Mr. Ossipon brings every week a pile of these F.P. tracts to sell at a halfpenny each. I wouldn't give a halfpenny for the whole lot. It's silly reading—that's what it is. There's no sale for it. The other day Stevie got hold of one, and there was a story in it of a German soldier officer tearing half-off the ear of a recruit, and nothing was done to him for it. The brute! I couldn't do anything with Stevie that afternoon. The story was enough, too, to make one's blood boil. But what's the use of printing things like that? We aren't German slaves here, thank God. It's not our business—is it?"

Mr. Verloc made no reply.

"I had to take the carving knife from the boy," Mrs. Verloc continued, a little sleepily now. "He was shouting and stamping and sobbing. He can't stand the notion of any cruelty. He would have stuck that officer like a pig if he had seen him then. It's true, too! Some people don't deserve much mercy." Mrs. Verloc's voice ceased, and the expression of her motionless eyes became more and more contemplative and veiled during the long pause. "Comfortable, dear?" she asked in a faint, far-away voice. "Shall I put out the light now?"

The dreary conviction that there was no sleep for him held Mr. Verloc mute and hopelessly inert in his fear of darkness. He made a great effort.

"Yes. Put it out," he said at last in a hollow tone.

❧ 4 ❧

Most of the thirty or so little tables covered by red cloths with a white design stood ranged at right angles to the deep brown wainscoting of the underground hall. Bronze chandeliers with many globes depended from the low, slightly vaulted ceiling, and the fresco paintings ran flat and dull all round the walls without windows, representing scenes of the chase and of outdoor revelry in medieval costumes. Varlets in green jerkins brandished hunting knives and raised on high tankards of foaming beer.

"Unless I am very much mistaken, you are the man who would know the inside of this confounded affair," said the robust Ossipon, leaning over, his elbows far out on the table and his feet tucked back completely under his chair. His eyes stared with wild eagerness.

An upright semi-grand piano near the door, flanked by two palms in pots, executed suddenly all by itself a valse tune with aggressive virtuosity. The din it raised was deafening. When it ceased, as abruptly as it had started, the bespectacled, dingy little man who faced Ossipon behind a heavy glass mug full of beer emitted calmly what had the sound of a general proposition.

"In principle what one of us may or may not know as to any given fact can't be a matter for inquiry to the others."

"Certainly not," Comrade Ossipon agreed in a quiet undertone. "In principle."

With his big florid face held between his hands he continued to stare hard, while the dingy little man in spectacles coolly took a drink of beer and stood the glass mug back on the table. His flat, large ears departed widely from the sides of his skull, which looked frail enough for Ossipon to crush between thumb and forefinger; the dome of the forehead seemed to rest on the rim of the spectacles; the flat cheeks, of a greasy, unhealthy complexion, were merely smudged by the miserable poverty of a thin dark whisker. The lamentable inferiority of the whole physique was made ludicrous by the supremely self-confident bearing of the individual. His speech was curt, and he had a particularly impressive manner of keeping silent.

Ossipon spoke again from between his hands in a mutter.

"Have you been out much today?"

"No. I stayed in bed all the morning," answered the other. "Why?"

"Oh! Nothing," said Ossipon, gazing earnestly and quivering inwardly with the desire to find out something, but obviously intimidated by the little man's overwhelming air of unconcern. When talking with this comrade—which happened but rarely—the big Ossipon suffered from a sense of moral and even physical insignificance. However, he ventured another question. "Did you walk down here?"

"No; omnibus," the little man answered, readily enough. He lived far away in Islington, in a small house down a shabby street, littered with straw and dirty paper, where out of school hours a troop of assorted children ran and squabbled with a shrill, joyless, rowdy clamor. His single back room, remarkable for having an extremely large cupboard, he rented furnished from two elderly spinsters, dressmakers in a humble way with a clientele of servant girls mostly. He had a heavy padlock put on the cupboard, but otherwise he was a model lodger, giving no trouble, and requiring practically no attendance. His oddities were that he insisted on being present when his room was being swept, and that when he went out he locked his door, and took the key away with him.

Ossipon had a vision of these round black-rimmed spectacles progressing along the streets on the top of an omnibus, their self-confident glitter falling here and there on the walls of houses or lowered upon the heads of the unconscious stream of people on the pavements. The ghost of a sickly smile altered the set of Ossipon's thick lips at the thought of the walls nodding, of people running for life at the sight of those spectacles. If they had only known! What a panic! He murmured interrogatively: "Been sitting long here?"

"An hour or more," answered the other, negligently, and took a pull at the dark beer. All his movements—the way he grasped the mug, the act of drinking, the way he set the heavy glass down and folded his arms—had a firmness, an assured precision which made the big and muscular Ossipon, leaning forward with staring eyes and protruding lips, look the picture of eager indecision.

"An hour," he said. "Then it may be you haven't heard yet the news I've heard just now—in the street. Have you?"

The little man shook his head negatively the least bit. But as he gave no indication of curiosity Ossipon ventured to add that he had heard it just outside the place. A newspaper boy had yelled the thing under his very nose, and not being prepared for anything of that sort, he was very much startled and upset. He had to come in there with a dry mouth. "I never thought of finding you here," he added, murmuring steadily, with his elbows planted on the table.

"I come here sometimes," said the other, preserving his provoking coolness of demeanor.

"It's wonderful that you of all people should have heard nothing of it," the big Ossipon continued. His eyelids snapped nervously upon the shining eyes. "You of all people," he repeated, tentatively. This obvious restraint argued an incredible and inexplicable timidity of the big fellow before the calm little man, who again lifted the glass mug, drank, and put it down with brusk and assured movements. And that was all.

Ossipon, after waiting for something, word or sign, that did not come, made an effort to assume a sort of indifference.

"Do you," he said, deadening his voice still more, "give your stuff to anybody who's up to asking you for it?"

"My absolute rule is never to refuse anybody—as long as I have a pinch by me," answered the little man with decision.

"That's a principle?" commented Ossipon.

"It's a principle."

"And you think it's sound?"

The large round spectacles, which gave a look of staring self-confidence to the sallow face, confronted Ossipon like sleepless, unwinking orbs flashing a cold fire.

"Perfectly. Always. Under every circumstance. What could stop me? Why should I not? Why should I think twice about it?"

Ossipon gasped, as it were, discreetly.

"Do you mean to say you would hand it over to a "tec" if one came to ask you for your wares?"

The other smiled faintly.

"Let them come and try it on, and you will see," he said. "They know me, but I know also every one of them. They won't come near me—not they."

His thin, livid lips snapped together firmly. Ossipon began to argue.

"But they could send someone—rig a plant on you. Don't you see? Get the stuff from you in that way, and then arrest you with the proof in their hands."

"Proof of what? Dealing in explosives without a license perhaps." This was meant for a contemptuous jeer, though the expression of the thin, sickly face remained unchanged, and the utterance was negligent. "I don't think there's one of them anxious to make that arrest. I don't think they could get one of them to apply for a warrant. I mean one of the best. Not one."

"Why?" Ossipon asked.

"Because they know very well I take care never to part with the last handful of my wares. I've it always by me." He touched the breast of his coat lightly. "In a thick glass flask," he added.

"So I have been told," said Ossipon, with a shade of wonder in his voice. "But I didn't know if—"

"They know," interrupted the little man, crisply, leaning against the straight chair back, which rose higher than his fragile head. "I shall never be arrested. The game isn't good enough for any policeman of them all. To deal with a man like me you require sheer, naked, inglorious heroism."

Again his lips closed with a self-confident snap. Ossipon repressed a movement of impatience.

"Or recklessness—or simply ignorance," he retorted. "They've only to get somebody for the job who does not know you carry enough stuff in your pocket to blow yourself and everything within sixty yards of you to pieces."

"I never affirmed I could not be eliminated," rejoined the other. "But that wouldn't be an arrest. Moreover, it's not so easy as it looks."

"Bah!" Ossipon contradicted. "Don't be too sure of that. What's to prevent half-a-dozen of them jumping upon you from behind in the street? With your arms pinned to your sides you could do nothing—could you?"

"Yes; I could. I am seldom out in the streets after dark," said the little man, impassively, "and never very late. I walk always with my right hand closed round the india-rubber ball which I have in my trouser pocket. The pressing of this ball actuates a detonator inside the flask I carry in my pocket. It's the principle of the pneumatic instantaneous shutter for a camera lens. The tube leads up—"

With a swift, disclosing gesture he gave Ossipon a glimpse of an india-rubber tube, resembling a slender brown worm, issuing from the armhole of his waistcoat and plunging into the inner breast pocket of his jacket. His clothes, of a nondescript brown mixture, were threadbare and marked with stains, dusty in the folds, with ragged buttonholes. "The detonator is partly mechanical, partly chemical," he explained, with casual condescension.

"It is instantaneous, of course?" murmured Ossipon, with a slight shudder.

"Far from it," confessed the other, with a reluctance which seemed to twist his mouth dolorously. "A full twenty seconds must elapse from the moment I press the ball till the explosion takes place."

"Phew!" whistled Ossipon, completely appalled. "Twenty seconds! Horrors! You mean to say that you could face that? I should go crazy—"

"Wouldn't matter if you did. Of course, it's the weak point of this special system, which is only for my own use. The worst is that the manner of exploding is always the weak point with us. I am trying to invent a detonator that would adjust itself to all conditions of action, and even to unexpected changes of conditions. A variable and yet perfectly precise mechanism. A really intelligent detonator."

"Twenty seconds," muttered Ossipon again. "Ough! And then—"

With a slight turn of the head the glitter of the spectacles seemed to gauge the size of the beer saloon in the basement of the renowned Silenus Restaurant.

"Nobody in this room could hope to escape," was the verdict of that survey. "Nor yet this couple going up the stairs now."

The piano at the foot of the staircase clanged through a mazurka with brazen impetuosity, as though a vulgar and impudent ghost were showing off. The keys sank and rose mysteriously. Then all became still. For a moment

Ossipon imagined the overlighted place changed into a dreadful black hole belching horrible fumes choked with ghastly rubbish of smashed brickwork and mutilated corpses. He had such a distinct perception of ruin and death that he shuddered again. The other observed, with an air of calm sufficiency:

"In the last instance it is character alone that makes for one's safety. There are very few people in the world whose character is as well established as mine."

"I wonder how you managed it," growled Ossipon. "Force of personality," said the other, without raising his voice; and coming from the mouth of that obviously miserable organism the assertion caused the robust Ossipon to bite his lower lip. "Force of personality," he repeated, with ostentatious calm.

"I have the means to make myself deadly, but that by itself, you understand, is absolutely nothing in the way of protection. What is effective is the belief those people have in my will to use the means. That's their impression. It is absolute. Therefore I am deadly."

"There are individuals of character amongst that lot, too," muttered Ossipon ominously.

"Possibly. But it is a matter of degree obviously, since, for instance, I am not impressed by them. Therefore they are inferior. They cannot be otherwise. Their character is built upon conventional morality. It leans on the social order. Mine stands free from everything artificial. They are bound in all sorts of conventions. They depend on life, which, in this connection, is a historical fact surrounded by all sorts of restraints and considerations, a complex, organized fact open to attack at every point; whereas I depend on death, which knows no restraint and cannot be attacked. My superiority is evident."

"This is a transcendental way of putting it," said Ossipon, watching the cold glitter of the round spectacles. "I've heard Karl Yundt say much the same thing not very long ago."

"Karl Yundt," mumbled the other, contemptuously, "the delegate of the International Red Committee, has been a posturing shadow all his life. There are three of you delegates, aren't there? I won't define the other two, as you are one of them. But what you say means nothing. You are the worthy delegates for revolutionary propaganda, but the trouble is not only that you are as unable to think independently as any respectable grocer or journalist of them all, but that you have no character whatever."

Ossipon could not restrain a start of indignation.

"But what do you want from us?" he exclaimed in a deadened voice. "What is it you are after yourself?"

"A perfect detonator," was the peremptory answer. "What are you making that face for? You see, you can't even bear the mention of something conclusive."

"I am not making a face," growled the annoyed Ossipon, bearishly.

"You revolutionists," the other continued, with leisurely self-confidence, "are the slaves of the social convention, which is afraid of you; slaves of it as much as the very police that stands up in the defense of that convention. Clearly you are, since you want to revolutionize it. It governs your thought, of course, and your action, too, and thus neither your thought nor your action can ever be conclusive." He paused, tranquil, with that air of close, endless silence, then almost immediately went on: "You are not a bit better than the forces arrayed against you—than the police, for instance. The other day I came suddenly upon Chief Inspector Heat at the corner of Tottenham Court Road. He looked at me very steadily. But I did not look at him. Why should I give him more than a glance? He was thinking of many things—of his superiors, of his reputation, of the law courts, of his salary, of newspapers—of a hundred things. But I was thinking of my perfect detonator only. He meant nothing to me. He was as insignificant as—I can't call to mind anything insignificant enough to compare him with—except Karl Yundt perhaps. Like to like. The terrorist and the policeman both come from the same basket. Revolution, legality—countermoves in the same game; forms of idleness at bottom identical. He plays his little game—so do you propagandists. But I don't play; I work fourteen hours a day, and go hungry sometimes. My experiments cost money now and again, and then I must do without food for a day or two. You're looking at my beer. Yes. I have had two glasses already, and shall have another presently. This is a little holiday, and I celebrate it alone. Why not? I've the grit to work alone, quite alone, absolutely alone. I've worked alone for years."

Ossipon's face had turned dusky red.

"At the perfect detonator—eh?" he sneered, very low.

"Yes," retorted the other. "It is a good definition. You couldn't find anything half so precise to define the nature of your activity with all your committees and delegations. It is I who am the true propagandist."

"We won't discuss that point," said Ossipon, with an air of rising above personal considerations. "I am afraid I'll have to spoil your holiday for you, though. There's a man blown up in Greenwich Park this morning."

"How do you know?"

"They have been yelling the news in the streets since two o'clock. I bought the paper, and just ran in here. Then I saw you sitting at this table. I've got it in my pocket now."

He pulled the newspaper out. It was a good-sized, rosy sheet, as if flushed by the warmth of its own convictions, which were optimistic. He scanned the pages rapidly.

"Ah! Here it is. Bomb in Greenwich Park. There isn't much so far. Half-past eleven. Foggy morning. Effects of explosion felt as far as Romney Road and Park Place. Enormous hole in the ground under a tree filled with smashed roots and broken branches. All round fragments of a man's body blown to pieces. That's all. The rest's mere newspaper gup. No doubt a wicked attempt to blow up the Observatory, they say. H'm. That's hardly credible."

He looked at the paper for a while longer in silence then passed it to the other, who after gazing abstractedly at the print laid it down without comment.

It was Ossipon who spoke first—still resentful.

"The fragments of only *one* man, you note. Ergo: blew *himself* up. That spoils your day off for you—don't it? Were you expecting that sort of move? I hadn't the slightest idea—not the ghost of a notion of anything of the sort being planned to come off here—in this country. Under the present circumstances it's nothing short of criminal."

The little man lifted his thin black eyebrows with dispassionate scorn.

"Criminal! What is that? What *is* crime? What can be the meaning of such an assertion?"

"How am I to express myself? One must use the current words," said Ossipon, impatiently. "The meaning of this assertion is that this business may affect our position very adversely in this country. Isn't that crime enough for you? I am convinced you have been giving away some of your stuff lately."

Ossipon stared hard. The other, without flinching, lowered and raised his head slowly.

"You have!" burst out the editor of the F.P. leaflets in an intense whisper. "No! And are you really handing it over at large like this, for the asking, to the first fool that comes along?"

"Just so! The condemned social order has not been built up on paper and ink, and I don't fancy that a combination of paper and ink will ever put an end to it, what ever you may think. Yes, I would give the stuff with both hands to every man, woman, or fool that likes to come along. I know what you are thinking about. But I am not taking my cue from the Red Committee. I would see you all hounded out of here, or arrested—or beheaded for that matter—without turning a hair. What happens to us as individuals is not of the least consequence."

He spoke carelessly, without heat, almost without feeling, and Ossipon, secretly much affected, tried to copy this detachment.

"If the police here knew their business they would shoot you full of holes with revolvers, or else try to sandbag you from behind in broad daylight."

The little man seemed already to have considered that point of view in his dispassionate, self-confident manner.

"Yes," he assented with the utmost readiness. "But for that they would have to face their own institutions. Do you see? That requires uncommon grit. Grit of a special kind."

Ossipon blinked.

"I fancy that's exactly what would happen to you if you were to set up your laboratory in the States. They don't stand on ceremony with their institutions there."

"I am not likely to go and see. Otherwise your remark is just," admitted the other. "They have more character over there, and their character is essentially anarchistic. Fertile ground for us, the States—very good ground. The great Republic has the root of the destructive matter in her. The collective temperament is lawless. Excellent. They may shoot us down, but—"

"You are too transcendental for me," growled Ossipon, with moody concern.

"Logical," protested the other. "There are several kinds of logic. This is the enlightened kind. America is all right. It is this country that is dangerous, with her idealistic conception of legality. The social spirit of this people is wrapped up in scrupulous prejudices, and that is fatal to our work. You talk of England being our only refuge! So much the worse. Capua! What do we want with refuges? Here you talk, print, plot, and do nothing. I daresay it's very convenient for such Karl Yundts."

He shrugged his shoulders slightly, then added with the same leisurely assurance: "To break up the superstition and worship of legality should be our aim. Nothing would please me more than to see Inspector Heat and his likes take to shooting us down in broad daylight with the approval of the public. Half our battle would be won then; the disintegration of the old morality would have set in in its very temple. That is what you ought to aim at. But you revolutionists will never understand that. You plan the future, you lose yourselves in reveries of economical systems derived from what is; whereas what's wanted is a clean sweep and a clear start for a new conception of life. That sort of future will take care of itself if you will only make room for it. Therefore I would shovel my stuff in heaps at the corners of the streets if I had enough for that; and as I haven't, I do my best by perfecting a really dependable detonator."

Ossipon, who had been mentally swimming in deep waters, seized upon the last word as if it were a saving plank.

"Yes. Your detonators. I shouldn't wonder if it weren't one of your detonators that made a clean sweep of the man in the park."

A shade of vexation darkened the determined, sallow face confronting Ossipon.

"My difficulty consists precisely in experimenting practically with the various kinds. They must be tried, after all. Besides—"

Ossipon interrupted.

"Who could that fellow be? I assure you that we in London had no knowledge— Couldn't you describe the person you gave the stuff to?"

The other turned his spectacles upon Ossipon like a pair of searchlights.

"Describe him," he repeated, slowly. "I don't think there can be the slightest objection now. I will describe him to you in one word—Verloc."

Ossipon, whom curiosity had lifted a few inches off his seat, dropped back, as if hit in the face.

"Verloc! Impossible."

The self-possessed little man nodded slightly once.

"Yes. He's the person. You can't say that in this case I was giving my stuff to the first fool that came along. He was a prominent member of the group as far as I understand."

"Yes," said Ossipon. "Prominent. No, not exactly. He was the center for general intelligence, and—usually received comrades coming over here. More useful than important. Man of no ideas. Years ago he used to speak at meetings—in France, I believe. Not very well, though. He was trusted by such men as Latorre, Moser, and all that old lot. The only talent he showed really was his ability to elude the attentions of the police somehow. Here, for instance, he did not seem to be looked after very closely. He was regularly married, you know. I suppose it's with her money that he staffed that shop. Seemed to make it pay, too."

Ossipon paused abruptly, muttered to himself "I wonder what that woman will do now?" and fell into thought.

The other waited with ostentatious indifference. His parentage was obscure, and he was generally known only by his nickname of Professor. His title to that designation consisted in his having been once assistant demonstrator in chemistry at some technical institute. He quarreled with the authorities upon a question of unfair treatment. Afterwards he obtained a post in the laboratory of a manufactory of dyes. There, too, he had been treated with revolting injustice. His struggles, his privations, his hard work to raise himself in the social scale, had filled him with such an exalted conviction of his merits that it was extremely difficult for the world to treat him with justice—the standard of that notion depending so much upon the patience of the individual. The Professor had genius, but lacked the great social virtue of resignation.

"Intellectually a nonentity," Ossipon pronounced aloud, abandoning suddenly the inward contemplation of Mrs. Verloc's bereaved person and business. "Quite an ordinary personality. You are wrong in not keeping more in touch with the comrades, Professor," he added in a reproving tone. "Did he say anything to you—give you some idea of his intentions? I hadn't seen him for a month. It seems impossible that he should be gone."

"He told me it was going to be a demonstration against a building," said the Professor. "I had to know that much to prepare the missile. I pointed out to him that I had hardly a sufficient quantity for a completely destructive result, but he pressed me very earnestly to do my best. As he wanted something that could be carried openly in the hand, I proposed to make use of an old one-gallon copal varnish can I happened to have by me. He was pleased at the idea. It gave me some trouble, because I had to cut out the bottom first and solder it on after-wards. When prepared for use, the can enclosed a wide-mouthed, well-corked jar of thick glass packed around with some wet clay and containing sixteen ounces of X2 green powder. The detonator was connected with the screw top of the can. It was ingenious—a combination of time and shock. I explained the system to him. It was a thin tube of tin enclosing a—"

Ossipon's attention had wandered.

"What do you think has happened?" he interrupted.

"Can't tell. Screwed the top on tight, which would make the connection, and then forgot the time. It was set for twenty minutes. On the other hand, the time contact being made, a sharp shock would bring about the explosion at once. He either ran the time too close, or simply let the thing fall. The contact was made all right—that's clear to me at any rate. The system's worked perfectly. And yet you would think that a common fool in a hurry would be much more likely to forget to make the contact altogether. I was worrying myself about that sort of failure most-ly. But there are more kinds of fools than one can guard against. You can't expect a detonator to be absolutely foolproof."

He beckoned to a waiter. Ossipon sat rigid, with the abstracted gaze of mental travail. After the man had gone away with the money he roused himself, with an air of profound dissatisfaction.

"It's extremely unpleasant for me," he mused. "Karl has been in bed with bron-chitis for a week. There's an even chance that he will never get up again. Michaelis is luxuriating in the country somewhere. A fashionable publisher has offered him five hundred pounds for a book. It will be a ghastly failure. He has lost the habit of consecutive thinking in prison, you know."

The Professor on his feet, now buttoning his coat, looked about him with per-fect indifference.

"What are you going to do?" asked Ossipon, wearily. He dreaded the blame of the Central Red Committee, a body which had no permanent place of abode, and of whose membership he was not exactly informed. If this affair eventuated in the stoppage of the modest subsidy allotted to the publication of the F.P. pamphlets, then indeed he would have to regret Verloc's inexplicable folly.

"Solidarity with the extremest form of action is one thing, and silly reckless-ness is another," he said, with a sort of moody brutality. "I don't know what came to Verloc. There's some mystery there. However, he's gone. You may take it as you like, but under the circumstances the only policy for the militant revolutionary group is to disclaim all connection with this damned freak of yours. How to make the disclaimer convincing enough is what bothers me."

The little man on his feet, buttoned up and ready to go, was no taller than the seated Ossipon. He leveled his spectacles at the latter's face point-blank.

"You might ask the police for a testimonial of good conduct. They know where every one of you slept last night. Perhaps if you asked them they would consent to publish some sort of official statement."

"No doubt they are aware well enough that we had nothing to do with this," mumbled Ossipon, bitterly. "What they will say is another thing." He remained thoughtful, disregarding the short, owlish, shabby figure standing by his side. "I must lay hands on Michaelis at once, and get him to speak from his heart at one of our gatherings. The public has a sort of sentimental regard for that fellow. His name is known. And I am in touch with a few reporters on the big dailies. What he would say would be utter bosh, but he has a turn of talk that makes it go down all the same."

"Like treacle," interjected the Professor, rather low, keeping an impassive expression.

The perplexed Ossipon went on communing with himself half audibly, after the manner of a man reflecting in perfect solitude.

"Confounded ass! To leave such an imbecile business on my hands. And I don't even know if—"

He sat with compressed lips. The idea of going for news straight to the shop lacked charm. His notion was that Verloc's shop might have been turned already into a police trap. They will be bound to make some arrests, he thought, with something resembling virtuous indignation, for the even tenor of his revolutionary life was menaced by no fault of his. And yet unless he went there he ran the risk of remaining in ignorance of what perhaps it would be very material for him to know. Then he reflected that, if the man in the park had been so very much blown to pieces as the evening papers said, he could not have been identified. And if so, the police could have no special reason for watching Verloc's shop more closely than any other place known to be frequented by marked anarchists—no more reason, in fact, than for watching the doors of the Silenus. There would be a lot of watching all round, no matter where he went. Still—

"I wonder what I had better do now?" he muttered, taking counsel with himself.

A rasping voice at his elbow said, with sedate scorn:

"Fasten yourself upon the woman for all she's worth."

After uttering these words the Professor walked away from the table. Ossipon, whom that piece of insight had taken unawares, gave one ineffectual start, and remained still, with a helpless gaze, as though nailed fast to the seat of his chair. The lonely piano, without as much as a music stool to help it, struck a few chords courageously, and beginning a selection of national airs, played him out at last to the tune of "Blue Bells of Scotland." The painfully detached notes grew faint behind his back while he went slowly upstairs, across the hall, and into the street.

In front of the great doorway a dismal row of newspaper sellers standing clear of the pavement dealt out their wares from the gutter. It was a raw, gloomy day of the early spring; and the grimy sky, the mud of the streets, the rags of the dirty men harmonized excellently with the eruption of the damp, rubbishy sheets of paper soiled with printers' ink. The posters, maculated with filth, garnished like tapestry the sweep of the curbstone. The trade in afternoon papers was brisk, yet, in comparison with the swift, constant march of foot traffic, the effect was of indifference, of a disregarded distribution. Ossipon looked hurriedly both ways before stepping out into the crosscurrents, but the Professor was already out of sight.

❧ 5 ❧

The Professor had turned into a street to the left, and walked along, with his head carried rigidly erect, in a crowd whose every individual almost overtopped his stunted stature. It was vain to pretend to himself that he was not disappointed. But that was mere feeling; the stoicism of his thought could not be disturbed by this or any other failure. Next time, or the time after next, a telling stroke would be delivered—something really startling—a blow fit to open the first crack in the imposing front of the great edifice of legal conceptions sheltering the atrocious injustice of society. Of humble origin, and with an appearance really so mean as to stand in the way of his considerable natural abilities, his imagination had been fired early by the tales of men rising from the depths of poverty to positions of authority and affluence. The extreme, almost ascetic purity of his thought, combined with an astounding ignorance of worldly conditions, had set before him a goal of power and prestige to be attained without the medium of arts, graces, tact, wealth—by sheer weight of merit alone. On that view he considered himself entitled to undisputed success. His father, a delicate dark enthusiast with a sloping forehead, had been an itinerant and rousing preacher of some obscure but rigid Christian sect—a man supremely confident in the privileges of his righteousness. In the son, individualist by temperament, once the science of colleges had replaced thoroughly the faith of conventicles, this moral attitude translated itself into a frenzied puritanism of ambition. He nursed it as something secularly holy. To see it thwarted opened his eyes to the true nature of the world, whose morality was artificial, corrupt, and blasphemous. The way of even the most justifiable revolutions is prepared by personal impulses disguised into creeds. The

Professor's indignation found in itself a final cause that absolved him from the sin of turning to destruction as the agent of his ambition. To destroy public faith in legality was the imperfect formula of his pedantic fanaticism; but the subconscious conviction that the framework of an established social order cannot be effectually shattered except by some form of collective or individual violence was precise and correct. He was a moral agent—that was settled in his mind. By exercising his agency with ruthless defiance he procured for himself the appearances of power and personal prestige. That was undeniable to his vengeful bitterness. It pacified its unrest; and in their own way the most ardent of revolutionaries are perhaps doing no more but seeking for peace in common with the rest of mankind—the peace of soothed vanity, of satisfied appetites, or perhaps of appeased conscience.

Lost in the crowd, miserable and undersized, he meditated confidently on his power, keeping his hand in the left pocket of his trousers, grasping lightly the india-rubber ball, the supreme guarantee of his sinister freedom; but after a while he became disagreeably affected by the sight of the roadway thronged with vehicles and of the pavement crowded with men and women. He was in a long, straight street, peopled by a mere fraction of an immense multitude; but all round him, on and on, even to the limits of the horizon hidden by the enormous piles of bricks, he felt the mass of mankind mighty in its numbers. They swarmed numerous like locusts, industrious like ants, thoughtless like a natural force, pushing on blind and orderly and absorbed, impervious to sentiment, to logic, to terror, too, perhaps.

That was the form of doubt he feared most. Impervious to fear! Often while walking abroad, when he happened also to come out of himself, he had such moments of dreadful and sane mistrust of mankind. What if nothing could move them? Such moments come to all men whose ambition aims at a direct grasp upon humanity—to artists, politicians, thinkers, reformers, or saints. A despicable emotional state this, against which solitude fortifies a superior character; and with severe exultation the Professor thought of the refuge of his room, with its padlocked cupboard, lost in a wilderness of poor houses, the hermitage of the perfect anarchist. In order to reach sooner the point where he could take his omnibus, he turned bruskly out of the populous street into a narrow and dusky alley paved with flagstones. On one side the low brick houses had in their dusty windows the sightless, moribund look of incurable decay—empty shells awaiting demolition. From the other side life had not departed wholly as yet. Facing the only gas-lamp yawned the cavern of a secondhand furniture dealer, where, deep in the gloom of a sort of narrow avenue winding through a bizarre forest of wardrobes, with an undergrowth tangle of table legs, a tall pier-glass glimmered like a pool of water in a wood. An unhappy, homeless couch, accompanied by two unrelated chairs, stood in the open. The only human being making use of the alley besides the Professor, coming stalwart and erect from the opposite direction, checked his swinging pace suddenly.

"Hallo!" he said, and stood a little on one side watchfully.

The Professor had already stopped, with a ready half turn which brought his shoulders very near the other wall. His right hand fell lightly on the back of the outcast couch, the left remained purposefully plunged deep in the trousers pocket, and the roundness of the heavy rimmed spectacles imparted an owlish character to his moody, unperturbed face.

It was like a meeting in a side corridor of a mansion full of life. The stalwart man was buttoned up in a dark overcoat, and carried an umbrella. His hat, tilted back, uncovered a good deal of forehead, which appeared very white in the dusk. In the dark patches of the orbits the eyeballs glimmered piercingly. Long, drooping moustaches, the color of ripe corn, flamed with their points the square block of his shaved chin.

"I am not looking for you," he said, curtly.

The Professor did not stir an inch. The blended noises of the enormous town sank down to an inarticulate low murmur. Chief Inspector Heat of the Special Crimes Department changed his tone.

"Not in a hurry to get home?" he asked, with mocking simplicity.

The unwholesome-looking little moral agent of destruction exulted silently in the possession of personal prestige, keeping in check this man armed with the defensive mandate of a menaced society. More fortunate than Caligula, who wished that the Roman Senate had only one head for the better satisfaction of his cruel lust, he beheld in that one man all the forces he had set at defiance: the force of law, property, oppression, and injustice. He beheld all his enemies and fearlessly confronted them all in a supreme satisfaction of his vanity. They stood perplexed before him as if before a dreadful portent. He gloated inwardly over the chance of this meeting affirming his superiority over all the multitude of mankind.

It was in reality a chance meeting. Chief Inspector Heat had had a disagreeably busy day since his department received the first telegram from Greenwich a little before eleven in the morning. First of all, the fact of the outrage being attempted less than a week after he had assured a high official that no outbreak of anarchist activity was to be apprehended was sufficiently annoying. If he ever thought himself safe in making a statement, it was then. He had made that statement with infinite satisfaction to himself, because it was clear that the high official desired greatly to hear that very thing. He had affirmed that nothing of the sort could even be thought of without the department being aware of it within twenty-four hours; and he had spoken thus in his consciousness of being the great expert of his department. He had gone even so far as to utter words which true wisdom would have kept back. But Chief Inspector Heat was not very wise—at least not truly so. True wisdom, which is not certain of anything in this world of contradictions, would have prevented him from attaining his present position. It would have alarmed his superiors, and done away with his chances of promotion. His promotion had been very rapid.

"There isn't one of them, sir, that we couldn't lay our hands on at any time of night and day. We know what each of them is doing hour by hour," he had declared. And the high official had deigned to smile. This was so obviously the right thing to say for an officer of Chief Inspector Heat's reputation that it was perfectly delightful. The high official believed the declaration, which chimed in with his idea of the fitness of things. His wisdom was of an official kind, or else he might have reflected upon a matter not of theory but of experience that in the close-woven stuff of relations between conspirator and police there occur unexpected solutions of continuity, sudden holes in space and time. A given anarchist may be watched inch by inch and minute by minute, but a moment always comes when somehow all sight and touch of him are lost for a few hours, during which something (generally an explosion) more or less deplorable does happen. But the high official, carried away by his sense of the fitness of things, had smiled, and now the recollection of that smile was very annoying to Chief Inspector Heat, principal expert in anarchist procedure.

This was not the only circumstance whose recollection depressed the usual serenity of the eminent specialist. There was another dating back only to that very morning. The thought that when called urgently to his Assistant Commissioner's private room he had been unable to conceal his astonishment was distinctly vexing. His instinct of a successful man had taught him long ago that, as a general rule, a reputation is built on manner as much as on achievement. And he felt that his manner when confronted with the telegram had not been impressive. He had opened his eyes widely, and had exclaimed "Impossible!" exposing himself thereby to the unanswerable retort of a fingertip laid forcibly on the telegram which the Assistant Commissioner, after reading it aloud, had flung on the desk. To be crushed, as it were, under the tip of a forefinger was an unpleasant experience. Very damaging, too! Furthermore, Chief Inspector Heat was conscious of not having mended matters by allowing himself to express a conviction.

"One thing I can tell you at once: none of our lot had anything to do with this."

He was strong in his integrity of a good detective, but he saw now that an impenetrably attentive reserve towards this incident would have served his reputation better. On the other hand, he admitted to himself that it was difficult to preserve one's reputation if rank outsiders were going to take a hand in the business. Outsiders are the bane of the police as of other professions. The tone of the Assistant Commissioner's remarks had been sour enough to set one's teeth on edge.

And since breakfast Chief Inspector Heat had not managed to get anything to eat.

Starting immediately to begin his investigation on the spot, he had swallowed a good deal of raw, unwholesome fog in the park. Then he had walked over to the hospital; and when the investigation in Greenwich was concluded at last he had lost his inclination for food. Not accustomed, as the doctors are, to examine closely the mangled remains of human beings, he had been shocked by the sight disclosed to his view when a waterproof sheet had been lifted off a table in a certain apartment of the hospital.

Another waterproof sheet was spread over that table in the manner of a tablecloth, with the corners turned up over a sort of mound—a heap of rags, scorched and bloodstained, half concealing what might have been an accumulation of raw material for a cannibal feast. It required considerable firmness of mind not to recoil before that sight. Chief Inspector Heat, an efficient officer of his department, stood his ground, but for a whole minute he did not advance. A local constable in uniform cast a sidelong glance, and said with stolid simplicity:

"He's all there. Every bit of him. It was a job."

He had been the first man on the spot after the explosion. He mentioned the fact again. He had seen something like a heavy flash of lightning in the fog. At that time he was standing at the door of the King William Street Lodge talking to the keeper. The concussion made him tingle all over. He ran between the trees towards the Observatory. "As fast as my legs would carry me," he repeated twice.

Chief Inspector Heat, bending forward over the table in a gingerly and horrified manner, let him run on. The hospital porter and another man turned down the corners of the cloth, and stepped aside. The Chief Inspector's eyes searched the gruesome detail of that heap of mixed things, which seemed to have been collected in shambles and rag shops.

"You used a shovel," he remarked, observing a sprinkling of small gravel, tiny brown bits of bark, and particles of splintered wood as fine as needles.

"Had to in one place," said the stolid constable. "I sent a keeper to fetch a spade. When he heard me scraping the ground with it he leaned his forehead against a tree, and was as sick as a dog."

The Chief Inspector, stooping guardedly over the table, fought down the unpleasant sensation in his throat. The shattering violence of destruction which had made of that body a heap of nameless fragments affected his feelings with a sense of ruthless cruelty, though his reason told him the effect must have been as swift as a flash of lightning. The man, whoever he was, had died instantaneously; and yet it seemed impossible to believe that a human body could have reached that state of disintegration without passing through the pangs of inconceivable agony. No physiologist, and still less of a metaphysician,

Chief Inspector Heat rose by the force of sympathy, which is a form of fear, above the vulgar conception of time. Instantaneous! He remembered all he had ever read in popular publications of long and terrifying dreams dreamed in the instant of waking; of the whole past life lived with frightful intensity by a drowning man as his doomed head bobs up, streaming, for the last time. The inexplicable mysteries of conscious existence beset Chief Inspector Heat till he evolved a horrible notion that ages of atrocious pain and mental torture could be contained between two successive winks of an eye. And meantime the Chief Inspector went on peering at the table with a calm face and the slightly anxious attention of an indigent customer bending over what may be called the by-products of a butcher's shop with a view to an inexpensive Sunday dinner. All the time his trained faculties of an excellent investigator, who scorns no chance of information, followed the self-satisfied, disjointed loquacity of the constable.

"A fair-haired fellow," the last observed in a placid tone, and paused. "The old woman who spoke to the sergeant noticed a fair-haired fellow coming out of Maze Hill Station." He paused. "And he was a fair-haired fellow. She noticed two men coming out of the station after the uptrain had gone on," he continued, slowly. "She couldn't tell if they were together. She took no particular notice of the big one, but the other was a fair, slight chap, carrying a tin varnish can in one hand." The constable ceased.

"Know the woman?" muttered the Chief Inspector, with his eyes fixed on the table, and a vague notion in his mind of an inquest to be held presently upon a person likely to remain forever unknown.

"Yes. She's housekeeper to a retired publican, and attends the chapel in Park Place sometimes," the constable uttered weightily, and paused, with another oblique glance at the table. Then suddenly: "Well, here he is—all of him I could see. Fair. Slight—slight enough. Look at that foot there. I picked up the legs first, one after another. He was that scattered you didn't know where to begin."

The constable paused; the least flicker of an innocent, self-laudatory smile invested his round face with an infantile expression.

"Stumbled," he announced, positively. "I stumbled once myself, and pitched on my head, too, while running up. Them roots do stick out all about the place. Stumbled against the root of a tree and fell, and that thing he was carrying must have gone off right under his chest, I expect."

The echo of the words "Person unknown" repeating itself in his inner consciousness bothered the Chief Inspector considerably. He would have liked to trace this affair back to its mysterious origin for his own information. He was professionally curious. Before the public he would have liked to vindicate the efficiency of his department by establishing the identity of that man. He was a loyal servant. That, however, appeared impossible. The first term of the problem was unreadable—lacked all suggestion but that of atrocious cruelty.

Overcoming his physical repugnance, Chief Inspector Heat stretched out his hand without conviction for the salving of his conscience, and took up the least soiled of the rags. It was a narrow strip of velvet with a larger triangular piece of dark blue cloth hanging from it. He held it up to his eyes; and the police constable spoke.

"Velvet collar. Funny the old woman should have noticed the velvet collar. Dark blue overcoat with a velvet collar, she has told us. He was the chap she saw, and no mistake. And here he is all complete, velvet collar and all. I don't think I missed a single piece as big as a postage stamp."

At this point the trained faculties of the Chief Inspector ceased to hear the voice of the constable. He moved to one of the windows for better light. His face, averted from the room, expressed a startled, intense interest while he examined closely the triangular piece of broadcloth. By a sudden jerk he detached it, and only after stuffing it into his pocket turned round to the room, and flung the velvet collar back on the table.

"Cover up," he directed the attendants, curtly, without another look, and, saluted by the constable, carried off his spoil hastily.

A convenient train whirled him up to town, alone and pondering deeply, in a third-class compartment. That singed piece of cloth was incredibly valuable, and he could not defend himself from astonishment at the casual manner it had come into his possession. It was as if Fate had thrust that clue into his hands. And after the manner of the average man, whose ambition is to command events, he began to mistrust such a gratuitous and accidental success—just because it seemed forced upon him. The practical value of success depends not a little on the way you look at it. But Fate looks at nothing. It has no discretion. He no longer considered it eminently desirable all round to establish publicly the identity of the man who had blown himself up that morning with such horrible completeness. But he was not certain of the view his department would take. A department is to those it employs a complex personality with ideas and even fads of its own. It depends on the loyal devotion of its servants, and the devoted loyalty of trusted servants is associated with a certain amount of affectionate contempt, which keeps it sweet, as it were. By a benevolent provision of Nature no man is a hero to his valet, or else the heroes would have to brush their own clothes. Likewise no department appears perfectly wise to the intimacy of its workers. A department does not know so much as some of its servants. Being a dispassionate organism, it can never be perfectly informed. It would not be good for its efficiency to know too much. Chief Inspector Heat got out of the train in a state of thoughtfulness entirely untainted with disloyalty, but not quite free of that jealous mistrust which so often springs on the ground of perfect devotion, whether to women or to institutions.

It was in this mental disposition, physically very empty, but still nauseated by what he had seen, that he had come upon the Professor. Under these conditions which make for irascibility in a sound, normal man, this meeting was specially unwelcome to Chief Inspector Heat. He had not been thinking of the Professor; he had not been thinking of any individual anarchist at all. The complexion of that case had somehow forced upon him the general idea of the absurdity of things human, which in the abstract is sufficiently annoying to an unphilosophical temperament, and in concrete instances becomes exasperating beyond endurance. At the beginning of his career Chief Inspector Heat had been concerned with the more energetic forms of thieving. He had gained his spurs in that sphere, and naturally enough had kept for it, after his promotion to another department, a feeling not very far removed from affection. Thieving was not a sheer absurdity. It was a form of human industry, perverse indeed, but still an industry exercised in an industrious world; it was work undertaken for the same reason as the work in potteries, in coal mines, in fields, in tool-grinding shops. It was labor, whose practical difference from the other forms of labor consisted in the nature of its risk, which did not lie in ankylosis, or lead poisoning, or fire damp, or gritty dust, but in what may be briefly defined in its own special phraseology as "Seven years hard." Chief Inspector Heat was, of course, not insensible to the gravity of moral differences. But neither were the thieves he had been looking after. They submitted to the severe sanctions of a morality familiar to Chief Inspector Heat with a certain resignation. They were his fellow-citizens gone wrong because of imperfect education, Chief Inspector Heat believed; but allowing for that difference, he could understand the mind of a burglar, because, as a matter of fact, the mind and the instincts of a burglar are of the same kind as the mind and the instincts of a police officer. Both recognize the same conventions, and have a working knowledge of each other's methods and of the routine of their respective trades. They understand each other, which is advantageous to both, and establishes a sort of amenity in their relations. Products of the same machine, one classed as useful and the other as noxious, they take the machine for granted in different ways, but with a seriousness essentially the same. The mind of Chief Inspector Heat was inaccessible to ideas of revolt. But his thieves were not rebels. His bodily vigor, his cool, inflexible manner, his courage, and his fairness, had secured for him much respect and some adulation in the sphere of his early successes. He had felt himself revered and admired. And Chief Inspector Heat, arrested within six paces of the anarchist nicknamed the Professor, gave a thought of regret to the world of thieves—sane, without morbid ideals, working by routine, respectful of constituted authorities, free from all taint of hate and despair.

After paying this tribute to what is normal in the constitution of society (for the idea of thieving appeared to his instinct as normal as the idea of property), Chief Inspector Heat felt very angry with himself for having stopped, for having spoken, for having taken that way at all on the ground of it being a short cut from the station to the headquarters. And he spoke again in his big, authoritative voice, which, being moderated, had a threatening character.

"You are not wanted, I tell you," he repeated.

The anarchist did not stir. An inward laugh of derision uncovered not only his teeth but his gums as well, shook him all over, without the slightest sound. Chief Inspector Heat was led to add, against his better judgment:

"Not yet. When I want you I will know where to find you."

Those were perfectly proper words, within the tradition and suitable to his character of a police officer addressing one of his special flock. But the reception they got departed from tradition and propriety. It was outrageous. The stunted, weakly figure before him spoke at last.

"I've no doubt the papers would give you an obituary notice then. You know best what that would be worth to you. I should think you can imagine easily the sort of stuff that would be printed. But you may be exposed to the unpleasantness of being buried together with me, though I suppose your friends would make an effort to sort us out as much as possible."

With all his healthy contempt for the spirit dictating such speeches, the atrocious allusiveness of the words had its effect on Chief Inspector Heat. He had too much insight, and too much exact information as well, to dismiss them as rot. The dusk of this narrow lane took on a sinister tint from the dark, frail little figure, its back to the wall, and speaking with a weak, self-confident voice. To the vigorous, tenacious vitality of the Chief Inspector, the physical wretchedness of that being, so obviously not fit to live, was ominous; for it seemed to him that if he had the misfortune to be such a miserable object he would not have cared how soon he died. Life had such a strong hold upon him that a fresh wave of nausea broke out in slight perspiration upon his brow. The murmur of town life, the subdued rumble of wheels in the two invisible streets to the right and left, came through the curve of the sordid lane to his ears with a precious familiarity and an appealing sweetness. He was human. But Chief Inspector Heat was also a man, and he could not let such words pass.

"All this is good to frighten children with," he said. "I'll have you yet."

It was very well said, without scorn, with an almost austere quietness.

"Doubtless," was the answer; "but there's no time like the present, believe me. For a man of real convictions this is a fine opportunity of self-sacrifice. You may not find another so favorable, so humane. There isn't even a cat near us, and these condemned old houses would make a good heap of bricks where you stand. You'll never get me at so little cost to life and property, which you are paid to protect."

"You don't know who you're speaking to," said Chief Inspector Heat, firmly. "If I were to lay my hands on you now I would be no better than yourself."

"Ah! The game!"

"You may be sure our side will win in the end. It may yet be necessary to make people believe that some of you ought to be shot at sight like mad dogs. Then that will be the game. But I'll be damned if I know what yours is. I don't believe you know yourselves. You'll never get anything by it."

"Meantime, it's you who get something from it—so far. And you get it easily, too. I won't speak of your salary, but haven't you made your name simply by not understanding what we are after?"

"What are you after, then?" asked Chief Inspector Heat, with scornful haste, like a man in a hurry who perceives he is wasting his time.

The perfect anarchist answered by a smile which did not part his thin, colorless lips; and the celebrated Chief Inspector felt a sense of superiority which induced him to raise a warning finger.

"Give it up—whatever it is," he said in an admonishing tone, but not so kindly as if he were condescending to give good advice to a cracksman of repute. "Give it up. You'll find we are too many for you."

The fixed smile on the Professor's lips wavered, as if the mocking spirit within had lost its assurance. Chief Inspector Heat went on:

"Don't you believe me—eh? Well, you've only got to look about you. We are. And anyway, you're not doing it well. You're always making a mess of it. Why, if the thieves didn't know their work better they would starve."

The hint of an invincible multitude behind that man's back roused a somber indignation in the breast of the Professor. He smiled no longer his enigmatic and mocking smile. The resisting power of numbers, the unattackable stolidity of a great multitude, was the haunting fear of his sinister loneliness. His lips trembled for some time before he managed to say in a strangled voice:

"I am doing my work better than you're doing yours."

"That'll do now," interrupted Chief Inspector Heat, hurriedly; and the Professor laughed right out this time. While still laughing he moved on; but he did not laugh long. It was a sad-faced, miserable little man who emerged from the narrow passage into the bustle of the broad thoroughfare. He walked with the nerveless gait of a tramp going on, still going on, indifferent to rain or sun in a sinister detachment from the aspects of sky and earth. Chief Inspector Heat, on the other hand, after watching him for a while, stepped out with the purposeful briskness of a man disregarding indeed the inclemencies of the weather, but conscious of having an authorized mission on this earth and the moral support of his kind. All the inhabitants of the immense town, the population of the whole country, and even the teeming millions struggling upon the planet, were with him— down to the very thieves and mendicants. Yes, the thieves themselves were sure to be with him in his present work. The consciousness of universal support in his general activity heartened him to grapple with the particular problem.

The problem immediately before the Chief Inspector was that of managing the Assistant Commissioner of his department, his immediate superior. This is the perennial problem of trusty and loyal servants; anarchism gave it its particular complexion, but nothing more. Truth to say, Chief Inspector Heat thought but little of anarchism. He did not attach undue importance to it, and could never bring himself to consider it seriously. It had more the character of disorderly conduct; disorderly without the human excuse of drunkenness, which at any rate implies good feeling and an amiable leaning towards festivity. As criminals, anarchists were distinctly no class—no class at all. And recalling the Professor, Chief Inspector Heat, without checking his swinging pace, muttered through his teeth:

"Lunatic."

Catching thieves was another matter altogether. It had that quality of seriousness belonging to every form of open sport where the best man wins under perfectly comprehensible rules. There were no rules for dealing with anarchists. And that was distasteful to the Chief Inspector. It was all foolishness, but that foolishness excited the public mind, affected persons in high places, and touched upon international relations. A hard, merciless contempt settled rigidly on the Chief Inspector's face as he walked on. His mind ran over all the anarchists of his flock. Not one of them had half the spunk of this or that burglar he had known. Not half—not one tenth.

At headquarters the Chief Inspector was admitted at once to the Assistant Commissioner's private room. He found him, pen in hand, bent over a great table bestrewn with papers, as if worshipping an enormous double inkstand of bronze and crystal. Speaking tubes resembling snakes were tied by the heads to the back of the Assistant Commissioner's wooden armchair, and their gaping mouths seemed ready to bite his elbows. And in this attitude he raised only his eyes, whose lids were darker than his face and very much creased. The reports had come in: every anarchist had been exactly accounted for.

After saying this he lowered his eyes, signed rapidly two single sheets of paper, and only then laid down his pen, and sat well back, directing an inquiring gaze at his renowned subordinate. The Chief Inspector stood it well, deferential but inscrutable.

"I daresay you were right," said the Assistant Commissioner, "in telling me at first that the London anarchists had nothing to do with this. I quite appreciate the excellent watch kept on them by your men. On the other hand, this, for the public, does not amount to more than a confession of ignorance."

The Assistant Commissioner's delivery was leisurely, as it were cautious. His thought seemed to rest poised on a word before passing to another, as though words had been the steppingstones for his intellect picking its way across the waters of error. "Unless you have brought something useful from Greenwich," he added.

The Chief Inspector began at once the account of his investigation in a clear, matter-of-fact manner. His superior turning his chair a little, and crossing his thin legs, leaned sideways on his elbow, with one hand shading his eyes. His listening attitude had a sort of angular and sorrowful grace. Gleams as of highly burnished silver played on the sides of his ebony black head when he inclined it slowly at the end.

Chief Inspector Heat waited with the appearance of turning over in his mind all he had just said, but, as a matter of fact, considering the advisability of saying something more. The Assistant Commissioner cut his hesitation short.

"You believe there were two men?" he asked, without uncovering his eyes.

The Chief Inspector thought it more than probable. In his opinion, the two men had parted from each other within a hundred yards from the Observatory walls. He explained also how the other man could have got out of the park speedily without being observed. The fog, though not very dense, was in his favor. He seemed to have escorted the other to the spot, and then to have left him there to do the job single-handed. Taking the time those two were seen coming out of Maze Hill Station by the old woman, and the time when the explosion was heard, the Chief Inspector thought that the other man might have been actually at the Greenwich Park Station, ready to catch the next train up, at the moment his comrade was destroying himself so thoroughly.

"Very thoroughly—eh?" murmured the Assistant Commissioner from under the shadow of his hand.

The Chief Inspector in a few vigorous words described the aspect of the remains. "The coroner's jury will have a treat," he added, grimly.

The Assistant Commissioner uncovered his eyes.

"We shall have nothing to tell them," he remarked, languidly.

He looked up, and for a time watched the markedly non-committal attitude of his Chief Inspector. His nature was one that is not easily accessible to illusions. He knew that a department is at the mercy of its subordinate officers, who have their own conceptions of loyalty. His career had begun in a tropical colony. He had liked his work there. It was police work. He had been very successful in tracking and breaking up certain nefarious secret societies amongst the natives. Then he took his long leave, and got married rather impulsively. It was a good match from a worldly point of view, but his wife formed an unfavorable opinion of the colonial climate on hearsay evidence. On the other hand, she had influential connections. It was an excellent match. But he did not like the work he had to do now. He felt himself dependent on too many subordinates and too many masters. The near presence of that strange emotional phenomenon called public opinion weighed upon his spirits, and alarmed him by its irrational nature. No doubt that from ignorance he exaggerated to himself its power for good and evil—especially for evil; and the rough east winds of the English spring (which agreed with his wife) augmented his general mistrust of men's motives and of the efficiency of their organization. The futility of office work especially appalled him on those days so trying to his sensitive liver.

He got up, unfolding himself to his full height, and with a heaviness of step remarkable in so slender a man, moved across the room to the window. The panes streamed with rain, and the short street he looked down into lay wet and empty, as if swept clear suddenly by a great flood. It was a very trying day, choked in raw fog to begin with, and now drowned in cold rain. The flickering, blurred flames of gas-lamps seemed to be dissolving in a watery atmosphere. And the lofty pretensions of a mankind oppressed by the miserable indignities of the weather appeared as a colossal and hopeless vanity deserving of scorn, wonder, and compassion.

"Horrible, horrible!" thought the Assistant Commissioner to himself, with his face near the windowpane. "We have been having this sort of thing now for ten days; no, a fortnight—a fortnight." He ceased to think completely for a time. That utter stillness of his brain lasted about three seconds. Then he said, perfunctorily: "You have set inquiries on foot for tracing that other man up and down the line?"

He had no doubt that everything needful had been done. Chief Inspector Heat knew, of course, thoroughly the business of manhunting. And these were the routine steps, too, that would be taken as a matter of course by the merest beginner. A few inquiries amongst the ticket collectors and the porters of the two small railway stations would give additional details as to the appearance of the two men; the inspection of the collected tickets would show at once where they came from that morning. It was elementary, and could not have been neglected. Accordingly, the Chief Inspector answered that all this had been done directly the old woman had come forward with her deposition. And he mentioned the name of a station. "That's where they came from, sir," he went on. "The porter who took the tickets at Maze Hill remembers two chaps answering to the description passing the barrier. They seemed to him two respectable workingmen of a superior sort—sign painters or house decorators. The big man got out of a third-class compartment backward, with a bright tin can in his hand. On the platform he gave it to carry to the fair young fellow who followed him. All this agrees exactly with what the old woman told the police sergeant in Greenwich."

The Assistant Commissioner, still with his face turned to the window, expressed his doubt as to these two men having had anything to do with the outrage. All this theory rested upon the utterances of an old charwoman who had been nearly knocked down by a man in a hurry. Not a very substantial authority indeed, unless on the ground of sudden inspiration, which was hardly tenable.

"Frankly now, could she have been really inspired?" he queried, with grave irony, keeping his back to the room, as if entranced by the contemplation of the town's colossal forms half lost in the night. He did not even look round when he heard the mutter of the word "Providential" from the principal subordinate of his department, whose name, printed sometimes in the papers, was familiar to the great public as that of one of its zealous and hardworking protectors. Chief Inspector Heat raised his voice a little.

"Strips and bits of bright tin were quite visible to me," he said. "That's a pretty good corroboration."

"And these men came from that little country station," the Assistant Commissioner mused aloud, wondering. He was told that such was the name on two tickets out of three given up out of that train at Maze Hill. The third person who got out was a hawker from Gravesend well known to the porters. The Chief Inspector imparted that information in a tone of finality with some ill humor, as loyal servants will do in the consciousness of their fidelity and with the sense of the value of their loyal exertions. And still the Assistant Commissioner did not turn away from the darkness outside, as vast as a sea.

"Two foreign anarchists coming from that place," he said, apparently to the windowpane. "It's rather unaccountable."

"Yes, sir. But it would be still more unaccountable if that Michaelis weren't staying in a cottage in the neighborhood."

At the sound of that name, falling unexpectedly into this annoying affair, the Assistant Commissioner dismissed bruskly the vague remembrance of his daily whist party at his club. It was the most comforting habit of his life, in a mainly successful display of his skill without the assistance of any subordinate. He entered his club to play from five to seven, before going home to dinner, forgetting for those two hours whatever was distasteful in his life, as though the game were a beneficent drug for allaying the pangs of moral discontent. His partners were the gloomily humorous editor of a celebrated magazine; a silent, elderly barrister with malicious little eyes; and a highly martial, simpleminded old Colonel with nervous brown hands. They were his club acquaintances merely. He never met them elsewhere except at the card table. But they all seemed to approach the game in the spirit of co-sufferers, as if it were indeed a drug against the secret ills of existence; and every day as the sun declined over the countless roofs of the town, a mellow, pleasurable impatience, resembling the impulse of a sure and profound friendship, lightened his professional labors. And now this pleasurable sensation went out of him with something resembling a physical shock, and was replaced by a special kind of interest in his work of social protection—an improper sort of interest, which may be defined best as a sudden and alert mistrust of the weapon in his hand.

❧ 6 ❧

The lady patroness of Michaelis, the ticket-of-leave apostle of humanitarian hopes, was one of the most influential and distinguished connections of the Assistant Commissioner's wife, whom she called Annie, and treated still rather as a not very wise and utterly inexperienced young girl. But she had consented to accept him on a friendly footing, which was by no means the case with all of his wife's influential connections. Married young and splendidly at some remote epoch of the past, she had had for a time a close view of great affairs and even of some great men. She herself was a great lady. Old now in the number of her years, she had that sort of exceptional temperament which defies time with scornful disregard, as if it were a rather vulgar convention submitted to by the mass of inferior mankind. Many other conventions easier to set aside, alas! failed to obtain her recognition, also on temperamental grounds—either because they bored her, or else because they stood in the way of her scorns and sympathies. Admiration was a sentiment unknown to her (it was one of the secret griefs of her most noble husband against her)—first, as always more or less tainted with mediocrity, and next as being in a way an admission of inferiority. And both were frankly inconceivable to her nature. To be fearlessly outspoken in her opinions came easily to her, since she judged solely from the standpoint of her social position. She was equally untrammeled in her actions; and as her tactfulness proceeded from genuine humanity, her bodily vigor remained remarkable and her superiority was serene and cordial, three generations had admired her infinitely, and the last she was likely to see had pronounced her a wonderful woman. Meantime, intelligent, with a sort of lofty simplicity, and curious at heart, but not like many women merely of social gossip, she amused her age by attracting within her ken through the power of her great, almost historical, social prestige everything that rose above the dead level of mankind, lawfully or unlawfully, by position, wit, audacity, fortune or misfortune. Royal Highnesses, artists, men of science, young statesmen, and charlatans of all ages and conditions, who, unsubstantial and light, bobbing up like corks, show best the direction of the surface currents, had been welcomed in that house, listened to, penetrated, understood, appraised, for her own edification. In her own words, she liked to watch what the world was coming to. And as she had a practical mind her judgment of men and things, though based on special prejudices, was seldom totally wrong, and almost never wrongheaded. Her drawing room was probably the only place in the wide world where an Assistant Commissioner of Police could meet a convict liberated on a ticket-of-leave on other than professional and official ground. Who had brought Michaelis there one afternoon the Assistant Commissioner did not remember very well. He had a notion it must have been a certain Member of Parliament of illustrious parentage and unconventional sympathies, which were the standing joke of the comic papers. The notabilities and even the simple notorieties of the day brought each other freely to that temple of an old woman's not ignoble curiosity. You never could guess whom you were likely to come upon being received in semi-privacy within the faded blue silk and gilt frame screen, making a cozy nook for a couch and a few armchairs in the great drawing room, with its hum of voices and the groups of people seated or standing in the light of six tall windows.

Michaelis had been the object of a revulsion of popular sentiment, the same sentiment which years ago had applauded the ferocity of the life sentence passed upon him for complicity in a rather mad attempt to rescue some prisoners from a police van. The plan of the conspirators had been to shoot down the horses and overpower the escort. Unfortunately, one of the police constables got shot, too. He left a wife and three small children, and the death of that man aroused through the length and breadth of a realm for whose defense, welfare, and glory men die every day as matter of duty, an outburst of furious indignation, of a raging, implacable pity for the victim. Three ringleaders got hanged. Michaelis, young and slim, locksmith by trade, and great frequenter of evening schools, did not even know that anybody had been killed, his part with a few others being to force open the door at the back of the special conveyance. When arrested he had a bunch of skeleton keys in one pocket, a heavy chisel in another, and a short crowbar in his hand: neither more nor less than a burglar. But no burglar would have received such a heavy sentence. The death of the constable had made him miserable at heart, but the failure of the plot also. He did not conceal either of these sentiments from his empaneled countrymen, and that sort of compunction appeared shockingly imperfect to the crammed court. The judge on passing sentence commented feelingly upon the depravity and callousness of the young prisoner.

That made the groundless fame of his condemnation; the fame of his release was made for him on no better grounds by people who wished to exploit the sentimental aspect of his imprisonment either for purposes of their own or for no intelligible purpose. He let them do so in the innocence of his heart and the simplicity of his mind. Nothing that happened to him individually had any importance. He was like those saintly men whose personality is lost in the contemplation of their faith. His ideas were not in the nature of convictions. They were inaccessible to reasoning. They formed in all their contradictions and obscurities an invincible and humanitarian creed, which he confessed rather than preached, with an obstinate gentleness, a smile of pacific assurance on his lips, and his candid blue eyes cast down because the sight of faces troubled his inspiration developed in solitude. In that characteristic attitude, pathetic in his grotesque and incurable obesity which he had to drag like a galley slave's bullet to the end of his days, the Assistant Commissioner of Police beheld the ticket-of-leave apostle filling a privileged armchair within the screen. He sat there by the head of the old lady's couch, mild-voiced and quiet, with no more self-consciousness than a very small child, and with something of a child's charm—the appealing charm of trustfulness. Confident of the future, whose secret ways had been revealed to him within the four walls of a well-known penitentiary, he had no reason to look with suspicion upon anybody. If he could not give the great and curious lady a very definite idea as to what the world was coming to, he had managed without effort to impress her by his unembittered faith, by the sterling quality of his optimism.

A certain simplicity of thought is common to serene souls at both ends of the social scale. The great lady was simple in her own way. His views and beliefs had nothing in them to shock or startle her, since she judged them from the standpoint of her lofty position. Indeed, her sympathies were easily accessible to a man of that sort. She was not an exploiting capitalist herself; she was, as it were, above the play of economic conditions. And she had a great capacity of pity for the more obvious forms of common human miseries, precisely because she was such a complete stranger to them that she had to translate her conception into terms of mental suffering before she could grasp the notion of their cruelty. The Assistant Commissioner remembered very well the conversation between these two. He had listened in silence. It was something as exciting in a way, and even touching in its foredoomed futility, as the efforts at moral intercourse between the inhabitants of remote planets. But this grotesque incarnation of humanitarian passion appealed, somehow, to one's imagination. At last Michaelis rose, and taking the great lady's extended hand, shook it, retained it for a moment in his great cushioned palm with unembarrassed friendliness, and turned upon the semiprivate nook of the drawing room his back, vast and square, and as if distended under the short tweed jacket. Glancing about in serene benevolence, he waddled along to the distant door between the knots of other visitors. The murmur of conversations paused on his passage. He smiled innocently at a tall, brilliant girl, whose eyes met his accidentally, and went out unconscious of the glances following him across the room. Michaelis' first appearance in the world was a success—a success of esteem unmarred by a single murmur of derision. The interrupted conversations were resumed in their proper tone, grave or light. Only a well-setup, long-limbed, active-looking man of forty talking with two ladies near a window remarked aloud, with an unexpected depth of feeling: "Eighteen stone, I should say, and not five foot six. Poor fellow! It's terrible—terrible."

The lady of the house, gazing absently at the Assistant Commissioner, left alone with her on the private side of the screen, seemed to be rearranging her mental impressions behind her thoughtful immobility of a handsome old face. Men with gray moustaches and full, healthy, vaguely smiling countenances approached, circling round the screen; two mature women with a matronly air of gracious resolution; a clean-shaved individual with sunken cheeks, and dangling a gold-mounted eyeglass on a broad black ribbon with an old-world, dandified effect. A silence deferential, but full of reserves, reigned for a moment, and then the great lady exclaimed, not with resentment, but with a sort of protesting indignation:

"And that officially is supposed to be a revolutionist! What nonsense." She looked hard at the Assistant Commissioner, who murmured, apologetically:

"Not a dangerous one perhaps."

"Not dangerous—I should think not indeed. He is a mere believer. It's the temperament of a saint," declared the great lady in a firm tone. "And they kept him shut up for twenty years. One shudders at the stupidity of it. And now they have let him out everybody belonging to him is gone away somewhere or dead. His parents are dead; the girl he was to marry has died while he was in prison; he has lost the skill necessary for his manual occupation. He told me all this himself with the sweetest patience; but then, he said, he had had plenty of time to think out things for himself. A pretty compensation! If that's the stuff revolutionists are made of some of us may well go on their knees to them," she continued in a slightly bantering voice, while the banal society smiles hardened on the worldly faces turned towards her with conventional deference. "The poor creature is obviously no longer in a position to take care of himself. Somebody will have to look after him a little."

"He should be recommended to follow a treatment of some sort," the soldierly voice of the active-looking man was heard advising earnestly from a distance. He was in the pink of condition for his age, and even the texture of his long frock coat had a character of elastic soundness, as if it were a living tissue. "The man is virtually a cripple," he added with unmistakable feeling.

Other voices, as if glad of the opening, murmured hasty compassion. "Quite startling," "Monstrous," "Most painful to see." The lank man, with the eyeglass on a broad ribbon, pronounced mincingly the word "Grotesque," whose justness was appreciated by those standing near him. They smiled at each other.

The Assistant Commissioner had expressed no opinion either then or later, his position making it impossible for him to ventilate any independent view of a ticket-of-leave convict. But, in truth, he shared the view of his wife's friend and patron that Michaelis was a humanitarian sentimentalist, a little mad, but upon the whole incapable of hurting a fly intentionally. So when that name cropped up suddenly in this vexing bomb affair he realized all the danger of it for the ticket-of-leave apostle, and his mind reverted at once to the old lady's well-established infatuation. Her arbitrary kindness would not brook patiently any interference with Michaelis' freedom. It was a deep, calm, convinced infatuation. She had not only felt him to be inoffensive, but she had said so, which last by a confusion of her absolutist mind became a sort of incontrovertible demonstration. It was as if the monstrosity of the man, with his candid infant's eyes and a fat angelic smile, had fascinated her. She had come to believe almost his theory of the future, since it was not repugnant to her prejudices. She disliked the new element of plutocracy in the social compound, and industrialism as a method of human development appeared to her singularly repulsive in its mechanical and unfeeling character. The humanitarian hopes of the mild Michaelis tended not towards utter destruction, but merely towards the complete economic ruin of the system. And she did not really see where was the moral harm of it. It would do away with all the multitude of the "parvenus," whom she disliked and mistrusted, not because they had arrived anywhere (she denied that), but because of their profound unintelligence of the world, which was the primary cause of the crudity of their perceptions and the aridity of their hearts. With the annihilation of all capital they would vanish, too; but universal ruin (providing it was universal, as it was revealed to Michaelis) would leave the social values untouched. The disappearance of the last piece of money could not affect people of position. She could not conceive how it could affect her position, for instance. She had developed these discoveries to the Assistant Commissioner with all the serene fearlessness of an old woman who had escaped the blight of indifference. He had made for himself the rule to receive everything of that sort in a silence which he took care from policy and inclination not to make offensive. He had an affection for the aged disciple of Michaelis, a complex sentiment depending a little on her prestige, on her personality, but most of all on the instinct of flattered gratitude. He felt himself really liked in her house. She was kindness personified. And she was practically wise, too, after the manner of experienced women. She made his married life much easier than it would have been without her generously full recognition of his rights as Annie's husband. Her influence upon his wife, a woman devoured by all sorts of small selfishnesses, small envies, small jealousies, was excellent. Unfortunately, both her kindness and her wisdom were of unreasonable complexion, distinctly feminine, and difficult to deal with. She remained a perfect woman all along her full tale of years, and not as some of them do become—a sort of slippery, pestilential old man in petticoats. And it was as of a woman that he thought of her—the specially choice incarnation of the feminine, wherein is recruited the tender, ingenuous, and fierce bodyguard for all sorts of men who talk under the influence of an emotion, true or fraudulent; for preachers, seers, prophets, or reformers.

Appreciating the distinguished and good friend of his wife, and himself, in that way, the Assistant Commissioner became alarmed at the convict Michaelis' possible fate. Once arrested on suspicion of being in some way, however remote, a party to this outrage, the man could hardly escape being sent back to finish his sentence at least. And that would kill him; he would never come out alive. The Assistant Commissioner made a reflection extremely unbecoming his official position without being really creditable to his humanity.

"If the fellow is laid hold of again," he thought, "she will never forgive me."

The frankness of such a secretly outspoken thought could not go without some derisive self-criticism. No man engaged in a work he does not like can preserve many saving illusions about himself. The distaste, the absence of glamour, extend from the occupation to the personality. It is only when our appointed activities seem by a lucky accident to obey the particular earnestness of our temperament that we can taste the comfort of complete self-deception. The Assistant Commissioner did not like his work at home. The police work he had been engaged on in a distant part of the globe had the saving character of an irregular sort of warfare or at least the risk and excitement of open-air sport. His real abilities, which were mainly of an administrative order, were combined with an adventurous disposition. Chained to a desk in the thick of four millions of men, he considered himself the victim of an ironic fate—the same, no doubt, which had brought about his marriage with a woman exceptionally sensitive in the matter of colonial climate, besides other limitations testifying to the delicacy of her nature—and her tastes. Though he judged his alarm sardonically he did not dismiss the improper thought from his mind. The instinct of self-preservation was strong within him. On the contrary, he repeated it mentally with profane emphasis and a fuller precision: "Damn it! If that infernal Heat has his way the fellow'll die in prison smothered in his fat, and she'll never forgive me."

His black, narrow figure, with the white band of the collar under the silvery gleams on the close-cropped hair at the back of the head, remained motionless. The silence had lasted such a long time that Chief Inspector Heat ventured to clear his throat. This noise produced its effect. The zealous and intelligent officer was asked by his superior, whose back remained turned to him immovably:

"You connect Michaelis with this affair?"

Chief Inspector Heat was very positive, but cautious.

"Well, sir," he said, "we have enough to go upon. A man like that has no business to be at large, anyhow."

"You will want some conclusive evidence," came the observation in a murmur.

Chief Inspector Heat raised his eyebrows at the black, narrow back, which remained obstinately presented to his intelligence and his zeal.

"There will be no difficulty in getting up sufficient evidence against *him*," he said, with virtuous complacency. "You may trust me for that, sir," he added, quite unnecessarily, out of the fullness of his heart; for it seemed to him an excellent thing to have that man in hand to be thrown down to the public should it think fit to roar with any special indignation in this case. It was impossible to say yet whether it would roar or not. That in the last instance depended, of course, on the newspaper press. But in any case, Chief Inspector Heat, purveyor of prisons by trade, and a man of legal instincts, did logically believe that incarceration was the proper fate for every declared enemy of the law. In the strength of that conviction he committed a fault of tact. He allowed himself a little conceited laugh, and repeated:

"Trust me for that, sir."

This was too much for the forced calmness under which the Assistant Commissioner had for upwards of eighteen months concealed his irritation with the system and the subordinates of his office. A square peg forced into a round hole, he had felt like a daily outrage that long-established smooth roundness into which a man of less sharply angular shape would have fitted himself, with voluptuous acquiescence, after a shrug or two. What he resented most was just the necessity of taking so much on trust. At the little laugh of Chief Inspector Heat's he spun swiftly on his heels, as if whirled away from the windowpane by an electric shock. He caught on the latter's face not only the complacency proper to the occasion lurking under the moustache, but the vestiges of experimental watchfulness in the round eyes, which had been, no doubt, fastened on his back, and now met his glance for a second before the intent character of their stare had the time to change to a merely startled appearance.

The Assistant Commissioner of Police had really some qualifications for his post. Suddenly his suspicion was awakened. It is but fair to say that his suspicions of the police methods (unless the police happened to be a semi-military body organized by himself) was not difficult to arouse. If it ever slumbered from sheer weariness, it was but lightly; and his appreciation of Chief Inspector Heat's zeal and ability, moderate in itself, excluded all notion of moral confidence. "He's up to something," he exclaimed, mentally, and at once became angry. Crossing over to his desk with headlong strides, he sat down violently. "Here I am stuck in a litter of paper," he reflected, with unreasonable resentment, "supposed to hold all the threads in my hands, and yet I can but hold what is put in my hand, and nothing else. And they can fasten the other ends of the threads where they please."

He raised his head, and turned towards his subordinate a long, meager face with the accentuated features of an energetic Don Quixote.

"Now what is it you've got up your sleeve?"

The other stared. He stared without winking in a perfect immobility of his round eyes, as he was used to stare at the various members of the criminal class when, after being duly cautioned, they made their statements in the tones of injured innocence, or false simplicity, or sullen resignation. But behind that professional and stony fixity there was some surprise, too, for in such a tone, combining nicely the note of contempt and impatience, Chief Inspector Heat, the right-hand man of the department, was not used to be addressed. He began in a procrastinating manner, like a man taken unawares by a new and unexpected experience.

"What I've got against that man Michaelis you mean, sir?"

The Assistant Commissioner watched the bullet head; the points of that Norse rover's moustache, falling below the line of the heavy jaw; the whole full and pale physiognomy, whose determined character was marred by too much flesh; at the cunning wrinkles radiating from the outer corners of the eyes—and in that purposeful contemplation of the valuable and trusted officer he drew a conviction so sudden that it moved him like an inspiration.

"I have reason to think that when you came into this room," he said in measured tones, "it was not Michaelis who was in your mind; not principally—perhaps not at all."

"You have reason to think, sir?" muttered Chief Inspector Heat, with every appearance of astonishment, which up to a certain point was genuine enough. He had discovered in this affair a delicate and perplexing side, forcing upon the discoverer a certain amount of insincerity—that sort of insincerity which, under the names of skill, prudence, discretion, turns up at one point or another in most human affairs. He felt at the moment like a tightrope artist might feel if suddenly, in the middle of the performance, the manager of the Music Hall were to rush out of the proper managerial seclusion and begin to shake the rope. Indignation, the sense of moral insecurity engendered by such a treacherous proceeding joined to the immediate apprehension of a broken neck, would, in the colloquial phrase, put him in a state. And there would be also some scandalized concern for his art, too, since a man must identify himself with something more tangible than his own personality, and establish his pride somewhere, either in his social position, or in the quality of the work he is obliged to do, or simply in the superiority of the idleness he may be fortunate enough to enjoy.

"Yes," said the Assistant Commissioner; "I have. I do not mean to say that you have not thought of Michaelis at all. But you are giving the fact you've mentioned a prominence which strikes me as not quite candid, Inspector Heat. If that is really the track of discovery, why haven't you followed it up at once, either personally or by sending one of your men to that village?"

"Do you think, sir, I have failed in my duty there?" the Chief Inspector asked, in a tone which he sought to make simply reflective. Forced unexpectedly to concentrate his faculties upon the task of preserving his balance, he had seized upon that point, and exposed himself to a rebuke; for the Assistant Commissioner, frowning slightly, observed that this was a very improper remark to make.

"But since you've made it," he continued, coldly, "I'll tell you that this is not my meaning."

He paused, with a straight glance of his sunken eyes which was a full equivalent of the unspoken termination "and you know it." The head of the so-called Special Crimes Department, debarred by his position from going out of doors personally in quest of secrets locked up in guilty breasts, had a propensity to exercise his considerable gifts for the detection of incriminating truth upon his own subordinates. That peculiar instinct could hardly be called a weakness. It was natural. He was a born detective. It had unconsciously governed his choice of a career, and if it ever failed him in life it was perhaps in the one exceptional circumstance of his marriage—which was also natural. It fed, since it could not roam abroad, upon the human material which was brought to it in its official seclusion. We can never cease to be ourselves.

His elbow on the desk, his thin legs crossed and nursing his cheek in the palm of his meager hand, the Assistant Commissioner in charge of the Special Crimes branch was getting hold of the case with growing interest. His Chief Inspector, if not an absolutely worthy foeman of his penetration, was at any rate the most worthy of all within his reach. A mistrust of established reputations was strictly in character with the Assistant Commissioner's ability as detector. His memory evoked a certain old fat and wealthy native chief in the distant colony whom it was a tradition for the successive Colonial Governors to trust and make much of as a firm friend and supporter of the order and legality established by white men; whereas, when examined skeptically, he was found out to be principally his own good friend, and nobody else's. Not precisely a traitor, but still a man of many dangerous reservations in his fidelity, caused by a due regard for his own advantage, comfort, and safety. A fellow of some innocence in his naive duplicity, but nonetheless dangerous. He took some finding out. He was physically a big man, too, and (allowing for the difference of color, of course) Chief Inspector Heat's appearance recalled him to the memory of his superior. It was not the eyes nor yet the lips exactly. It was bizarre. But does not Alfred Wallace relate in his famous book on the Malay Archipelago how, amongst the Aru Islanders, he discovered in an old and naked savage with a sooty skin a peculiar resemblance to a dear friend at home?

For the first time since he took up his appointment the Assistant Commissioner felt as if he were going to do some real work for his salary. And that was a pleasurable sensation. "I'll turn him inside out like an old glove," thought the Assistant Commissioner, with his eyes resting pensively upon Chief Inspector Heat.

"No, that was not my thought," he began again. "There is no doubt about you knowing your business—no doubt at all; and that's precisely why I—" He stopped short, and changing his tone: "What could you bring up against Michaelis of a definite nature? I mean apart from the fact that the two men under suspicion—you're certain there were two of them—came last from a railway station within three miles of the village where Michaelis is living now."

"This by itself is enough for us to go upon, sir, with that sort of man," said the Chief Inspector, with returning composure. The slight, approving movement of the Assistant Commissioner's head went far to pacify the resentful astonishment of the renowned officer. For Chief Inspector Heat was a kind man, an excellent husband, a devoted father; and the public and departmental confidence he enjoyed, acting favorably upon an amiable nature, disposed him to feel friendly towards the successive Assistant Commissioners he had seen pass through that very room. There had been three in his time. The first one, a soldierly, abrupt, red-faced person, with white eyebrows and an explosive temper, could be managed with a silken thread. He left on reaching the age limit. The second, a perfect gentleman, knowing his own and everybody else's place to a nicety, on resigning to take up a higher appointment out of England got decorated for (really) Inspector Heat's services. To work with him had been a pride and a pleasure. The third, a bit of a dark horse from the first, was at the end of eighteen months something of a dark horse still to the department. Upon the whole Chief Inspector Heat believed him to be in the main harmless—odd-looking, but harmless. He was speaking now, and the Chief Inspector listened with outward deference (which means nothing, being a matter of duty) and inwardly with benevolent toleration.

"Michaelis reported himself before leaving London for the country?"

"Yes, sir. He did."

"And what may he be doing there?" continued the Assistant Commissioner, who was perfectly informed on that point. Fitted with painful tightness into an old wooden armchair, before a worm-eaten oak table in an upstairs room of a four-roomed cottage with a roof of moss-grown tiles, Michaelis was writing night and day in a shaky, slanting hand that "Autobiography of a Prisoner" which was to be like a book of Revelation in the history of mankind. The conditions of confined space, seclusion, and solitude in a small four-roomed cottage were favorable to his inspiration. It was like being in prison, except that one was never disturbed for the odious purpose of taking exercise according to the tyrannical regulations of his old home in the penitentiary. He could not tell whether the sun still shone on the earth or not. The perspiration of the literary labor dropped from his brow. A delightful enthusiasm urged him on. It was the liberation of his inner life, the letting out of his soul into the wide world. And the zeal of his guileless vanity (first awakened by the offer of five hundred pounds from a publisher) seemed something predestined and holy.

"It would be, of course, most desirable to be informed exactly," insisted the Assistant Commissioner, uncandidly.

Chief Inspector Heat, conscious of renewed irritation at this display of scrupulousness, said that the county police had been notified from the first of Michaelis' arrival, and that a full report could be obtained in a few hours. A wire to the superintendent—

Thus he spoke, rather slowly, while his mind seemed already to be weighing the consequences. A slight knitting of the brow was the outward sign of this. But he was interrupted by a question.

"You've sent that wire already?"

"No, sir," he answered, as if surprised.

The Assistant Commissioner uncrossed his legs suddenly. The briskness of that movement contrasted with the casual way in which he threw out a suggestion.

"Would you think that Michaelis had anything to do with the preparation of that bomb, for instance?"

The Chief Inspector assumed a reflective manner.

"I wouldn't say so. There's no necessity to say anything at present. He associates with men who are classed as dangerous. He was made a delegate of the Red Committee less than a year after his release on license. A sort of compliment, I suppose."

And the Chief Inspector laughed a little angrily, a little scornfully. With a man of that sort scrupulousness was a misplaced and even an illegal sentiment. The celebrity bestowed upon Michaelis on his release two years ago by some emotional journalists in want of special copy had rankled ever since in his breast. It was perfectly legal to arrest that man on the barest suspicion. It was legal and expedient on the face of it. His two former chiefs would have seen the point at once; whereas this one, without saying either yes or no, sat there, as if lost in a dream. Moreover, besides being legal and expedient, the arrest of Michaelis solved a little personal difficulty which worried Chief Inspector Heat somewhat. This difficulty had its bearing upon his reputation, upon his comfort, and even upon the efficient performance of his duties. For, if Michaelis no doubt knew something about this outrage, the Chief Inspector was fairly certain that he did not know too much. This was just as well. He knew much less—the Chief Inspector was positive—than certain other individuals he had in his mind, but whose arrest seemed to him inexpedient, besides being a more complicated matter, on account of the rules of the game. The rules of the game did not protect so much Michaelis, who was an ex-convict. It would be stupid not to take advantage of legal facilities, and the journalists who had written him up with emotional gush would be ready to write him down with emotional indignation.

This prospect, viewed with confidence, had the attraction of a personal triumph for Chief Inspector Heat. And deep down in his blameless bosom of an average married citizen, almost unconscious but potent nevertheless, the dislike of being compelled by events to meddle with the desperate ferocity of the Professor had its say. This dislike had been strengthened by the chance meeting in the lane. The encounter did not leave behind with Chief Inspector Heat that satisfactory sense of superiority the members of the police force get from the unofficial but intimate side of their intercourse with the criminal classes, by which the vanity of power is soothed, and the vulgar love of domination over our fellow-creatures is flattered as worthily as it deserves.

The perfect anarchist was not recognized as a fellow-creature by Chief Inspector Heat. He was impossible—a mad dog to be left alone. Not that the Chief Inspector was afraid of him; on the contrary, he meant to have him some day. But not yet: he meant to get hold of him in his own time, properly and effectively, according to the rules of the game. The present was not the right time for attempting that feat, not the right time for many reasons, personal and of public service. This being the strong feeling of Inspector Heat, it appeared to him just and proper that this affair should be shunted off its obscure and inconvenient track, leading goodness knows where, into a quiet (and lawful) siding called Michaelis. And he repeated, as if reconsidering the suggestion conscientiously:

"The bomb. No, I would not say that exactly. We may never find that out. But it's clear that he is connected with this in some way, which we can find out without much trouble."

His countenance had that look of grave, overbearing indifference once well known and much dreaded by the better sort of thieves. Chief Inspector Heat, though what is called a man, was not a smiling animal. But his inward state was that of satisfaction at the passively receptive attitude of the Assistant Commissioner, who murmured gently:

"And you really think that the investigation should be made in that direction?"

"I do, sir."

"Quite convinced?"

"I am, sir. That's the true line for us to take."

The Assistant Commissioner withdrew the support of his hand from his reclining head with a suddenness that, considering his languid attitude, seemed to menace his whole person with collapse. But, on the contrary, he sat up, extremely alert, behind the great writing table on which his hand had fallen with the sound of a sharp blow.

"What I want to know is what put it out of your head till now."

"Put it out of my head," repeated the Chief Inspector very slowly.

"Yes. Till you were called into this room—you know." .

The Chief Inspector felt as if the air between his clothing and his skin had become unpleasantly hot. It was the sensation of an unprecedented and incredible experience.

"Of course," he said, exaggerating the deliberation of his utterance to the utmost limits of possibility, "if there is a reason, of which I know nothing, for not interfering with the convict Michaelis, perhaps it's just as well I didn't start the county police after him."

This took such a long time to say that the unflagging attention of the Assistant Commissioner seemed a wonderful feat of endurance. His retort came without delay.

"No reason whatever that I know of. Come, Chief Inspector, this finessing with me is highly improper on your part—highly improper. And it's also unfair, you know. You shouldn't leave me to puzzle things out for myself like this. Really, I am surprised."

He paused, then added smoothly: "I need scarcely tell you that this conversation is altogether unofficial."

These words were far from pacifying the Chief Inspector. The indignation of a betrayed tightrope performer was strong within him. In his pride of a trusted servant he was affected by the assurance that the rope was not shaken for the purpose of breaking his neck, as by an exhibition of impudence. As if anybody were afraid! Assistant Commissioners come and go, but a valuable Chief Inspector is not an ephemeral office phenomenon. He was not afraid of getting a broken neck. To have his performance spoiled was more than enough to account for the glow of honest indignation. And as thought is no respecter of persons, the thought of Chief Inspector Heat took a threatening and prophetic shape. "You, my boy," he said to himself, keeping his round and habitually roving eyes fastened upon the Assistant Commissioner's face—"you, my boy, you don't know your place, and your place won't know you very long either, I bet."

As if in provoking answer to that thought, something like the ghost of an amiable smile passed on the lips of the Assistant Commissioner. His manner was easy and businesslike while he persisted in administering another shake to the tightrope.

"Let us come now to what you have discovered on the spot, Chief Inspector," he said.

"A fool and his job are soon parted," went on the train of prophetic thought in Chief Inspector Heat's head. But it was immediately followed by the reflection that a higher official, even when "fired out" (this was the precise image), has still the time as he flies through the door to launch a nasty kick at the shinbones of a subordinate. Without softening very much the basilisk nature of his stare, he said, impassively:

"We are coming to that part of my investigation, sir,"

"That's right. Well, what have you brought away from it?"

The Chief Inspector, who had made up his mind to jump off the rope, came to the ground with gloomy frankness.

"I've brought away an address," he said, pulling out of his pocket without haste a singed rag of dark blue cloth. "This belongs to the overcoat the fellow who got himself blown to pieces was wearing. Of course, the overcoat may not have been his, and may even have been stolen. But that's not at all probable if you look at this."

The Chief Inspector, stepping up to the table, smoothed out carefully the rag of blue cloth. He had picked it up from the repulsive heap in the mortuary, because a tailor's name is found sometimes under the collar. It is not often of much use, but still—He only half expected to find anything useful, but certainly he did not expect to find—not under the collar at all, but stitched carefully on the under side of the lapel—a square piece of calico with an address written on it in marking ink.

The Chief Inspector removed his smoothing hand.

"I carried it off with me without anybody taking notice," he said. "I thought it best. It can always be produced if required."

The Assistant Commissioner, rising a little in his chair, pulled the cloth over to his side of the table. He sat looking at it in silence. Only the number 32 and the name of Brett Street were written in marking ink on a piece of calico slightly larger than an ordinary cigarette paper. He was genuinely surprised.

"Can't understand why he should have gone about labeled like this," he said, looking up at Chief Inspector Heat. "It's a most extraordinary thing."

"I met once in the smoking room of a hotel an old gentleman who went about with his name and address sewn on in all his coats in case of an accident or sudden illness," said the Chief Inspector. "He professed to be eighty-four years old, but he didn't look his age. He told me he was also afraid of losing his memory suddenly, like those people he had been reading of in the papers."

A question from the Assistant Commissioner, who wanted to know what was No. 32 Brett Street, interrupted that reminiscence abruptly. The Chief Inspector, driven down to the ground by unfair artifices, had elected to walk the path of unreserved openness. If he believed firmly that to know too much was not good for the department, the judicious holding back of knowledge was as far as his loyalty dared to go for the good of the service. If the Assistant Commissioner wanted to mismanage this affair nothing, of course, could prevent him. But, on his own part, he now saw no reason for a display of alacrity. So he answered concisely:

"It's a shop, sir."

The Assistant Commissioner, with his eyes lowered on the rag of blue cloth, waited for more information. As that did not come he proceeded to obtain it by a series of questions propounded with gentle patience. Thus he acquired an idea of the nature of Mr. Verloc's commerce, of his personal appearance, and heard at last his name. In a pause the Assistant Commissioner raised his eyes, and discovered some animation on the Chief Inspector's face. They looked at each other in silence.

"Of course," said the latter, "the department has no record of that man."

"Did any of my predecessors have any knowledge of what you have told me now?" asked the Assistant Commissioner, putting his elbows on the table and raising his joined hands before his face, as if about to offer prayer, only that his eyes had not a pious expression.

"No, sir; certainly not. What would have been the object? That sort of man could never be produced publicly to any good purpose. It was sufficient for me to know who he was, and to make use of him in a way that could be used publicly."

"And do you think that sort of private knowledge consistent with the official position you occupy?"

"Perfectly, sir. I think it's quite proper. I will take the liberty to tell you, sir, that it makes me what I am—and I am looked upon as a man who knows his work. It's a private affair of my own. A personal friend of mine in the French police gave me the hint that the fellow was an Embassy spy. Private friendship, private information, private use of it—that's how I look upon it."

The Assistant Commissioner, after remarking to himself that the mental state of the renowned Chief Inspector seemed to affect the outline of his lower jaw, as if the lively sense of his high professional distinction had been located in that part of his anatomy, dismissed the point for the moment with a calm "I see." Then leaning his cheek on his joined hands:

"Well, then—speaking privately if you like—how long have you been in private touch with this Embassy spy?"

To this inquiry the private answer of the Chief Inspector, so private that it was never shaped into audible words, was:

"Long before you were even thought of for your place here."

The so-to-speak public utterance was much more precise.

"I saw him for the first time in my life a little more than seven years ago, when two Imperial Highnesses and the Imperial Chancellor were on a visit here. I was put in charge of all the arrangements for looking after them. Baron Stott-Wartenheim was Ambassador then. He was a very nervous old gentleman. One evening, three days before the Guildhall Banquet, he sent word that he wanted to see me for a moment. I was downstairs, and the carriages were at the door to take the Imperial Highnesses and the Chancellor to the opera. I went up at once. I found the Baron walking up and down his bedroom in a pitiable state of distress, squeezing his hands together. He assured me he had the fullest confidence in our police and in my abilities, but he had there a man just come over from Paris whose information could be trusted implicitly. He wanted me to hear what that man had to say. He took me at once into a dressing room next door, where I saw a big fellow in a heavy overcoat sitting all alone on a chair, and holding his hat and stick in one hand. The Baron said to him in French 'Speak, my friend.' The light in that room was not very good. I talked with him for some five minutes perhaps. He certainly gave me a piece of very startling news. Then the Baron took me aside nervously to praise him up to me, and when I turned round again I discovered that the fellow had vanished like a ghost. Got up and sneaked out down some back stairs, I suppose. There was no time to run after him, as I had to hurry off after the Ambassador down the great staircase, and see the party started safe for the opera. However, I acted upon the information that very night. Whether it was perfectly correct or not, it did look serious enough. Very likely it saved us from an ugly trouble on the day of the Imperial visit to the City.

"Some time later, a month or so after my promotion to Chief Inspector, my attention was attracted to a big burly man, I thought I had seen somewhere before, coming out in a hurry from a jeweler's shop in the Strand. I went after him, as it was on my way towards Charing Cross, and there seeing one of our detectives across the road, I beckoned him over, and pointed out the fellow to him, with instructions to watch his movements for a couple of days, and then report to me. No later than next afternoon my man turned up to tell me that the fellow had married his landlady's daughter at a registrar's office that very day at 11:30 A.M., and had gone off with her to Margate for a week. Our man had seen the luggage being put on the cab. There were some old Paris labels on one of the bags. Somehow I couldn't get the fellow out of my head, and the very next time I had to go to Paris on service I spoke about him to that friend of mine in the Paris police. My friend said: 'From what you tell me I think you must mean a rather well-known hanger-on and emissary of the Revolutionary Red Committee. He says he is an Englishman by birth. We have an idea that he has been for a good few years now a secret agent of one of the foreign Embassies in London." This woke up my memory completely. He was the vanishing fellow I saw sitting on a chair in

Baron Stott-Wartenheim's bathroom. I told my friend that he was quite right. The fellow was a secret agent to my certain knowledge. Afterwards my friend took the trouble to ferret out the complete record of that man for me. I thought I had better know all there was to know; but I don't suppose you want to hear his history now, sir?"

The Assistant Commissioner shook his supported head. "The history of your relations with that useful personage is the only thing that matters just now," he said, closing slowly his weary, deep-set eyes, and then opening them swiftly with a greatly refreshed glance.

"There's nothing official about them," said the Chief Inspector, bitterly. "I went into his shop one evening, told him who I was, and reminded him of our first meeting. He didn't as much as twitch an eyebrow. He said that he was married and settled now, and that all he wanted was not to be interfered with in his little business. I took it upon myself to promise him that, as long as he didn't go in for anything obviously outrageous, he would be left alone by the police. That was worth something to him, because a word from us to the Custom House people would have been enough to get some of these packages he gets from Paris and Brussels opened in Dover, with confiscation to follow for certain, and perhaps a prosecution as well at the end of it."

"That's a very precarious trade," murmured the Assistant Commissioner. "Why did he go in for that?"

The Chief Inspector raised scornful eyebrows dispassionately.

"Most likely got a connection—friends on the Continent—amongst people who deal in such wares. They would be just the sort he would consort with. He's a lazy dog, too—like the rest of them."

"What do you get from him in exchange for your protection?"

The Chief Inspector was not inclined to enlarge on the value of Mr. Verloc's services.

"He would not be much good to anybody but myself. One has got to know a good deal beforehand to make use of a man like that. I can understand the sort of hint he can give. And when I want a hint he can generally furnish it to me."

The Chief Inspector lost himself suddenly in a discreet reflective mood; and the Assistant Commissioner repressed a smile at the fleeting thought that the reputation of Chief Inspector Heat might possibly have been made in a great part by the Secret Agent Verloc.

"In a more general way of being of use, all our men of the Special Crimes section on duty at Charing Cross and Victoria have orders to take careful notice of anybody they may see with him. He meets the new arrivals frequently, and afterwards keeps track of them. He seems to have been told off for that sort of duty. When I want an address in a hurry, I can always get it from him. Of course, I know how to manage our relations. I haven't seen him to speak to three times in the last two years. I drop him a line, unsigned, and he answers me in the same way at my private address."

From time to time the Assistant Commissioner gave an almost imperceptible nod. The Chief Inspector added that he did not suppose Mr. Verloc to be deep in the confidence of the prominent members of the Revolutionary International Council, but that he was generally trusted of that there could be no doubt. "Whenever I've had reason to think there was something in the wind," he concluded, "I've always found he could tell me something worth knowing."

The Assistant Commissioner made a significant remark.

"He failed you this time."

"Neither had I wind of anything in any other way," retorted Chief Inspector Heat. "I asked him nothing so he could tell me nothing. He isn't one of our men. It isn't as if he were in our pay."

"No," muttered the Assistant Commissioner. "He's a spy in the pay of a foreign government. We could never confess to him."

"I must do my work in my own way," declared the Chief Inspector. "When it comes to that I would deal with the devil himself, and take the consequences. There are things not fit for everybody to know."

"Your idea of secrecy seems to consist in keeping the chief of your department in the dark. That's stretching it perhaps a little too far, isn't it? He lives over his shop?"

"Who—Verloc? Oh, yes. He lives over his shop. The wife's mother, I fancy, lives with them."

"Is the house watched?"

"Oh, dear, no. It wouldn't do. Certain people who come there are watched. My opinion is that he knows nothing of this affair."

"How do you account for this?" The Assistant Commissioner nodded at the cloth rag lying before him on the table.

"I don't account for it at all, sir. It's simply unaccountable. It can't be explained by what I know." The Chief Inspector made those admissions with the frankness of a man whose reputation is established as if on a rock. "At any rate not at this present moment. I think that the man who had most to do with it will turn out to be Michaelis."

"You do?"

"Yes, sir; because I can answer for all the others."

"What about that other man supposed to have escaped from the park?"

"I should think he's far away by this time," opined the Chief Inspector.

The Assistant Commissioner looked hard at him, and rose suddenly, as though having made up his mind to some course of action. As a matter of fact, he had that very moment succumbed to a fascinating temptation. The Chief Inspector heard himself dismissed with instructions to meet his superior early next morning for further consultation upon the case. He listened with an impenetrable face, and walked out of the room with measured steps.

Whatever might have been the plans of the Assistant Commissioner they had nothing to do with that desk work, which was the bane of his existence because of its confined nature and apparent lack of reality. It could not have had, or else the general air of alacrity that came upon the Assistant Commissioner would have been inexplicable. As soon as he was left alone he looked for his hat impulsively, and put it on his head. Having done that, he sat down again to reconsider the whole matter. But as his mind was already made up, this did not take long. And before Chief Inspector Heat had gone very far on the way home, he also left the building.

❧ 7 ❧

The Assistant Commissioner walked along a short and narrow street like a wet, muddy trench, then crossing a very broad thoroughfare entered a public edifice, and sought speech with a young private secretary (unpaid) of a great personage.

This fair, smooth-faced young man, whose symmetrically arranged hair gave him the air of a large and neat schoolboy, met the Assistant Commissioner's request with a doubtful look, and spoke with bated breath.

"Would he see you? I don't know about that. He has walked over from the House an hour ago to talk with the permanent Under-Secretary, and now he's ready to walk back again. He might have sent for him; but he does it for the sake of a little exercise, I suppose. It's all the exercise he can find time for while this session lasts. I don't complain; I rather enjoy these little strolls. He leans on my arm, and doesn't open his lips. But, I say, he's very tired, and—well—not in the sweetest of tempers just now."

"It's in connection with that Greenwich affair."

"Oh! I say! He's very bitter against you people. But I will go and see, if you insist."

"Do. That's a good fellow," said the Assistant Commissioner.

The unpaid secretary admired this pluck. Composing for himself an innocent face, he opened a door, and went in with the assurance of a nice and privileged child. And presently he reappeared, with a nod to the Assistant Commissioner, who passing through the same door left open for him, found himself with the great personage in a large room.

Vast in bulk and stature, with a long white face, which, broadened at the base by a big double chin, appeared egg-shaped in the fringe of thin grayish whisker, the great personage seemed an expanding man. Unfortunate from a tailoring point of view, the cross-folds in the middle of a buttoned black coat added to the impression, as if the fastenings of the garment were tried to the utmost. From the head, set upward on a thick neck, the eyes, with puffy lower lids, stared with a haughty droop on each side of a hooked, aggressive nose, nobly salient in the vast pale circumference of the face. A shiny silk hat and a pair of worn gloves lying ready on the end of a long table looked expanded, too, enormous.

He stood on the hearth-rug in big, roomy boots, and uttered no word of greeting.

"I would like to know if this is the beginning of another dynamite campaign," he asked at once in a deep, very smooth voice. "Don't go into details. I have no time for that."

The Assistant Commissioner's figure before this big and rustic Presence had the frail slenderness of a reed addressing an oak. And indeed the unbroken record of that man's descent surpassed in the number of centuries the age of the oldest oak in the country.

"No. As far as one can be positive about anything I can assure you that it is not."

"Yes. But your idea of assurances over there," said the great man, with a contemptuous wave of his hand towards a window giving on the broad thoroughfare, "seems to consist mainly in making the Secretary of State look a fool. I have been told positively in this very room less than a month ago that nothing of the sort was even possible."

The Assistant Commissioner glanced in the direction of the window calmly.

"You will allow me to remark, Sir Ethelred, that so far I have had no opportunity to give you assurances of any kind."

The haughty droop of the eyes was focused now upon the Assistant Commissioner.

"True," confessed the deep, smooth voice. "I sent for Heat. You are still rather a novice in your new berth. And how are you getting on over there?"

"I believe I am learning something every day."

"Of course, of course. I hope you will get on."

"Thank you, Sir Ethelred. I've learned something today, and even within the last hour or so. There is much in this affair of a kind that does not meet the eye in a usual anarchist outrage, even if one looked into it as deep as can be. That's why I am here."

The great man put his arms akimbo, the backs of his big hands resting on his hips.

"Very well. Go on. Only no details, pray. Spare me the details."

"You shall not be troubled with them, Sir Ethelred," the Assistant Commissioner began, with a calm and untroubled assurance. While he was speaking the hands on the face of the clock behind the great man's back—a heavy, glistening affair of massive scrolls in the same dark marble as the mantelpiece, and with a ghostly, evanescent tick—had moved through the space of seven minutes. He spoke with a studious fidelity to a parenthetical manner, into which every little fact—that is, every detail—fitted with delightful ease. Not a murmur nor even a movement hinted at interruption. The great Personage might have been the statue of one of his own princely ancestors stripped of a crusader's war harness, and put into an ill-fitting frock coat. The Assistant Commissioner felt as though he were at liberty to talk for an hour. But he kept his head, and at the end of the time mentioned above he broke off with a sudden conclusion, which, reproducing the opening statement, pleasantly surprised Sir Ethelred by its apparent swiftness and force.

"The kind of thing which meets us under the surface of this affair, otherwise without gravity, is unusual—in this precise form at least—and requires special treatment."

The tone of Sir Ethelred was deepened, full of conviction.

"I should think so—involving the Ambassador of a foreign power!"

"Oh! The Ambassador!" protested the other, erect and slender, allowing himself a mere half smile. "It would be stupid of me to advance anything of the kind. And it is absolutely unnecessary, because if I am right in my surmises, whether ambassador or hall porter it's a mere detail."

Sir Ethelred opened a wide mouth, like a cavern, into which the hooked nose seemed anxious to peer; there came from it a subdued rolling sound, as from a distant organ with the scornful indignation stop.

"No! These people are too impossible. What do they mean by importing their methods of Crim-Tartary here? A Turk would have more decency."

"You forget, Sir Ethelred, that strictly speaking we know nothing positively—as yet."

"No! But how would you define it? Shortly?"

"Barefaced audacity amounting to childishness of a peculiar sort."

"We can't put up with the innocence of nasty little children," said the great and expanded personage, expanding a little more, as it were. The haughty, drooping glance struck crushingly the carpet at the Assistant Commissioner's feet. "They'll have to get a hard rap on the knuckles over this affair. We must be in a position to—What is your general idea, stated shortly? No need to go into details."

"No, Sir Ethelred. In principle, I should lay it down that the existence of secret agents should not be tolerated, as tending to augment the positive dangers of the evil against which they are used. That the spy will fabricate his information is a mere commonplace. But in the sphere of political and revolutionary action, relying partly on violence, the professional spy has every facility to fabricate the very facts themselves, and will spread the double evil of emulation in one direction, and of panic, hasty legislation, unreflecting hate, on the other. However, this is an imperfect world—"

The deep-voiced Presence on the hearth-rug, motionless, with big elbows stuck out, said hastily:

"Be lucid, please."

"Yes, Sir Ethelred—An imperfect world. Therefore directly the character of this affair suggested itself to me, I thought it should be dealt with with special secrecy, and ventured to come over here."

"That's right," approved the great Personage, glancing down complacently over his double chin. "I am glad there's somebody over at your shop who thinks that the Secretary of State may be trusted now and then."

The Assistant Commissioner had an amused smile.

"I was really thinking that it might be better at this stage for Heat to be replaced by—"

"What! Heat? An ass—eh?" exclaimed the great man, with distinct animosity.

"Not at all. Pray, Sir Ethelred, don't put that unjust interpretation on my remarks."

"Then what? Too clever by half?"

"Neither—at least not as a rule. All the grounds of my surmises I have from him. The only thing I've discovered by myself is that he has been making use of that man privately. Who could blame him? He's an old police hand. He told me virtually that he must have tools to work with. It occurred to me that this tool should be surrendered to the Special Crimes division as a whole, instead of remaining the private property of Chief Inspector Heat. I extended my conception of our departmental duties to the suppression of the secret agent. But Chief Inspector Heat is an old departmental hand. He would accuse me of perverting its morality and attacking its efficiency. He would define it bitterly as protection extended to the criminal class of revolutionists. It would mean just that to him.'

"Yes. But what do you mean?"

"I mean to say, first, that there's but poor comfort in being able to declare that any given act of violence—damaging property or destroying life—is not the work of anarchism at all, but of something else altogether—some species of authorized scoundrelism. This, I fancy, is much more frequent than we suppose. Next, it's obvious that the existence of these people in the pay of foreign governments destroys in a measure the efficiency of our supervision. A spy of that sort can afford to be more reckless than the most reckless of conspirators. His occupation is free from all restraint. He's without as much faith as is necessary for complete negation, and without that much law as is implied in lawlessness. Thirdly, the existence of these spies amongst the revolutionary groups, which we are reproached for harboring here, does away with all certitude. You have received a reassuring statement from Chief Inspector Heat some time ago. It was by no means groundless—and yet this episode happens. I call it an episode, because this affair, I make bold to say is episodic; it is no part of any general scheme, however wild. The very peculiarities which surprise and perplex Chief Inspector Heat establish its character in my eyes. I am keeping clear of details, Sir Ethelred."

The Personage on the hearth-rug had been listening with profound attention.

"Just so. Be as concise as you can."

The Assistant Commissioner intimated by an earnest, deferential gesture that he was anxious to be concise.

"There is a peculiar stupidity and feebleness in the conduct of this affair which gives me excellent hopes of getting behind it and finding there something else than an individual freak of fanaticism. For it is a planned thing, undoubtedly. The actual perpetrator seems to have been led by the hand to the spot, and then abandoned hurriedly to his own devices. The inference is that he was imported from abroad for the purpose of committing this outrage. At the same time one is forced to the conclusion that he did not know enough English to ask his way, unless one were to accept the fantastic theory that he was a deaf mute. I wonder now—But this is idle. He has destroyed himself by an accident, obviously. Not an extraordinary accident. But an extraordinary little fact remains: the address on his clothing discovered by the merest accident, too. It is an incredible little fact, so incredible that the explanation which will account for it is bound to touch the bottom of this affair. Instead of instructing Heat to go on with this case, my intention is to seek this explanation personally—by myself, I mean—where it may be picked up. That is in a certain shop in Brett Street, and on the lips of a certain secret agent once upon a time the confidential and trusted spy of the late Baron Stott-Wartenheim, Ambassador of a Great Power to the Court of St. James."

The Assistant Commissioner paused, then added: "Those fellows are a perfect pest." In order to raise his drooping glance to the speaker's face, the Personage on the hearth-rug had gradually tilted his head farther back, which gave him an aspect of extraordinary haughtiness.

"Why not leave it to Heat?"

"Because he is an old departmental hand. They have their own morality. My line of inquiry would appear to him an awful perversion of duty. For him the plain duty is to fasten the guilt upon as many prominent anarchists as he can on some slight indications he had picked up in the course of his investigation on the spot; whereas I, he would say, am bent upon vindicating their innocence. I am trying to be as lucid as I can in presenting this obscure matter to you without details."

"He would, would he?" muttered the proud head of Sir Ethelred from its lofty elevation.

"I am afraid so—with an indignation and disgust of which you or I can have no idea. He's an excellent servant. We must not put an undue strain on his loyalty. That's always a mistake. Besides, I want a free hand—a freer hand than it would be perhaps advisable to give Chief Inspector Heat. I haven't the slightest wish to spare this man Verloc. He will, I imagine, be extremely startled to find his connection with this affair, whatever it may be, brought home to him so quickly. Frightening him will not be very difficult. But our true objective lies behind him somewhere. I want your authority to give him such assurances of personal safety as I may think proper."

"Certainly," said the Personage on the hearth-rug. "Find out as much as you can; find it out in your own way."

"I must set about it without loss of time, this very evening," said the Assistant Commissioner.

Sir Ethelred shifted one hand under his coat tails, and tilting back his head, looked at him steadily.

"We'll have a late sitting tonight," he said. "Come to the House with your discoveries if we are not gone home. I'll warn Toodles to look out for you. He'll take you into my room."

The numerous family and the wide connections of the youthful-looking Private Secretary cherished for him the hope of an austere and exalted destiny. Meantime, the social sphere he adorned in his hours of idleness chose to pet him under the above nickname. And Sir Ethelred, hearing it on the lips of his wife and girls every day (mostly at breakfast time), had conferred upon it the dignity of unsmiling adoption.

The Assistant Commissioner was surprised and gratified extremely.

"I shall certainly bring my discoveries to the House on the chance of you having the time to—"

"I won't have the time," interrupted the great Personage. "But I will see you. I haven't the time now—And you are going yourself?"

"Yes, Sir Ethelred. I think it the best way."

The Personage had tilted his head so far back that, in order to keep the Assistant Commissioner under his observation, he had to nearly close his eyes.

"H'm. Ha! And how do you propose—Will you assume a disguise?"

"Hardly a disguise! I'll change my clothes, of course."

"Of course," repeated the great man, with a sort of absent-minded loftiness. He turned his big head slowly, and over his shoulder gave a haughty, oblique stare to the ponderous marble timepiece with the sly, feeble tick. The gilt hands had taken the opportunity to steal through no less than five and twenty minutes behind his back.

The Assistant Commissioner, who could not see them, grew a little nervous in the interval. But the great man presented to him a calm and undismayed face.

"Very well," he said, and paused, as if in deliberate contempt of the official clock. "But what first put you in motion in this direction?"

"I have been always of opinion," began the Assistant Commissioner.

"Ah. Yes! Opinion. That's of course. But the immediate motive?"

"What shall I say, Sir Ethelred? A new man's antagonism to old methods. A desire to know something at first hand. Some impatience. It's my old work, but the harness is different. It has been chafing me a little in one or two tender places."

"I hope you'll get on over there," said the great man, kindly, extending his hand, soft to the touch, but broad and powerful like the hand of a glorified farmer. The Assistant Commissioner shook it, and withdrew.

In the outer room Toodles, who had been waiting perched on the edge of a table, advanced to meet him, subduing his natural buoyancy.

"Well? Satisfactory?" he asked, with airy importance.

"Perfectly. You've earned my undying gratitude," answered the Assistant Commissioner, whose long face looked wooden in contrast with the peculiar character of the other's gravity, which seemed perpetually ready to break into ripples and chuckles.

"That's all right. But, seriously, you can't imagine how irritated he is by the attacks on his Bill for the Nationalization of Fisheries. They call it the beginning of social revolution. Of course, it is a revolutionary measure. But these fellows have no decency. The personal attacks—"

"I read the papers," remarked the Assistant Commissioner.

"Odious? Eh? And you have no notion what a mass of work he has got to get through every day. He does it all himself. Seems unable to trust anyone with these Fisheries."

"And yet he's given a whole half hour to the consideration of my very small sprat," interjected the Assistant Commissioner.

"Small! Is it? I'm glad to hear that. But it's a pity you didn't keep away, then. This fight takes it out of him frightfully. The man's getting exhausted. I feel it by the way he leans on my arm as we walk over. And, I say, is he safe in the streets? Mullins has been marching his men up here this afternoon. There's a constable stuck by every lamppost, and every second person we meet between this and Palace Yard is an obvious 'tec.' It will get on his nerves presently. I say, these foreign scoundrels aren't likely to throw something at him—are they? It would be a national calamity. The country can't spare him."

"Not to mention yourself. He leans on your arm," suggested the Assistant Commissioner, soberly. "You would both go."

"It would be an easy way for a young man to go down into history? Not so many British Ministers have been assassinated as to make it a minor incident. But seriously now—"

"I am afraid that if you want to go down into history you'll have to do something for it. Seriously, there's no danger whatever for both of you but from overwork."

The sympathetic Toodles welcomed this opening for a chuckle.

"The Fisheries won't kill me. I am used to late hours," he declared, with ingenuous levity. But, feeling an instant compunction, he began to assume an air of statesmanlike moodiness, as one draws on a glove. "His massive intellect will stand any amount of work. It's his nerves that I am afraid of. The reactionary gang, with that abusive brute Cheeseman at their head, insult him every night."

"If he will insist on beginning a revolution!" murmured the Assistant Commissioner.

"The time has come, and he is the only man great enough for the work," protested the revolutionary Toodles, flaring up under the calm, speculative gaze of the Assistant Commissioner. Somewhere in a corridor a distant bell tinkled urgently, and with devoted vigilance the young man pricked up his ears at the sound. "He's ready to go now," he exclaimed in a whisper, snatched up his hat, and vanished from the room.

The Assistant Commissioner went out by another door in a less elastic manner. Again he crossed the wide thoroughfare, walked along a narrow street, and re-entered hastily his own departmental buildings. He kept up this accelerated pace to the door of his private room. Before he had closed it fairly his eyes sought his desk. He stood still for a moment, then walked up, looked all round on the floor, sat down in his chair, rang a bell, and waited.

"Chief Inspector Heat gone yet?"

"Yes, sir. Went away half-an-hour ago."

He nodded. "That will do." And sitting still, with his hat pushed off his forehead, he thought that it was just like Heat's confounded cheek to carry off quietly the only piece of material evidence. But he thought this without animosity. Old and valued servants will take liberties. The piece of overcoat with the address sewn on was certainly not a thing to leave about. Dismissing from his mind this manifestation of Chief Inspector Heat's mistrust, he wrote and dispatched a note to his wife, charging her to make his apologies to Michaelis' great lady, with whom they were engaged to dine that evening.

The short jacket and the low, round hat he assumed in a sort of curtained alcove containing a washstand, a row of wooden pegs and a shelf, brought out wonderfully the length of his grave, brown face. He stepped back into the full light of the room, looking like the vision of a cool, reflective Don Quixote, with the sunken eyes of a dark enthusiast and a very deliberate manner. He left the scene of his daily labors quickly like an unobtrusive shadow. His descent into the street was like the descent into a slimy aquarium from which the water had been run off. A murky, gloomy dampness enveloped him. The walls of the houses were wet, the mud of the roadway glistened with an effect of phosphorescence, and when he emerged into the Strand out of a narrow street by the side of Charing Cross Station the genius of the locality assimilated him. He might have been but one more of the queer foreign fish that can be seen of an evening about there flitting round the dark corners.

He came to a stand on the very edge of the pavement, and waited. His exercised eyes had made out in the confused movements of lights and shadows thronging the roadway the crawling approach of a hansom. He gave no sign; but when the low step gliding along the curbstone came to his feet he dodged in skillfully in front of the big turning wheel, and spoke up through the little trap door almost before the man gazing supinely ahead from his perch was aware of having been boarded by a fare.

It was not a long drive. It ended by signal abruptly, nowhere in particular, between two lampposts before a large drapery establishment—a long range of shops already lapped up in sheets of corrugated iron for the night. Tendering a coin through the trap door the fare slipped out and away, leaving an effect of uncanny, eccentric ghostliness upon the driver's mind. But the size of the coin was satisfactory to his touch, and his education not being literary, he remained untroubled by the fear of finding it presently turned to a dead leaf in his pocket. Raised above the world of fares by the nature of his calling, he contemplated their action with a limited interest. The sharp pulling of his horse right round expressed his philosophy.

Meantime, the Assistant Commissioner was already giving his order to a waiter in a little Italian restaurant round the corner—one of those traps for the hungry, long and narrow, baited with a perspective of mirrors and white napery; without air, but with an atmosphere of their own—an atmosphere of fraudulent cookery mocking an abject mankind in the most pressing of its miserable necessities. In this immoral atmosphere the Assistant Commissioner, reflecting upon his enterprise, seemed to lose some more of his identity. He had a sense of loneliness, of evil freedom. It was rather pleasant. When, after paying for his short meal, he stood up and waited for his change, he saw himself in the sheet of glass, and was struck by his foreign appearance. He contemplated his own image with a melancholy and inquisitive gaze, then by sudden inspiration raised the collar of his jacket. This arrangement appeared to him commendable, and he completed it by giving an upward twist to the ends of his black moustache. He was satisfied by the subtle modification of his personal aspect caused by these small changes. "That'll do very well," he thought. "I'll get a little wet, a little splashed—"

He became aware of the waiter at his elbow and of a small pile of silver coins on the edge of the table before him. The waiter kept one eye on it, while his other eye followed the long back of a tall, not very young girl, who passed up to a distant table looking perfectly sightless and altogether unapproachable. She seemed to be an habitual customer.

On going out the Assistant Commissioner made to himself the observation that the patrons of the place had lost in the frequentation of fraudulent cookery all their national and private characteristics. And this was strange, since the Italian restaurant is such a peculiarly British institution. But these people were as denationalized as the dishes set before them with every circumstance of unstamped respectability. Neither was their personality stamped in any way, professionally, socially, or racially. They seemed created for the Italian restaurant, unless the Italian restaurant had been perchance created for them. But that last hypothesis was unthinkable, since one could not place them anywhere outside those special establishments. One never met these enigmatical persons elsewhere. It was impossible to form a precise idea what occupations they followed by day and where they went to bed at night. And he himself had become unplaced. It would have been impossible for anybody to guess his occupation. As to going to bed, there was a doubt even in his own mind. Not indeed in regard to his domicile itself, but very much so in respect of the time when he would be able to return there. A pleasurable feeling of independence possessed him when he heard the glass doors swing to behind his back with a sort of imperfect baffled thud. He advanced at once into an immensity of greasy slime and damp plaster interspersed with lamps, and enveloped, oppressed, penetrated, choked, and suffocated by the blackness of a wet London night, which is composed of soot and drops of water.

Brett Street was not very far away. It branched off, narrow, from the side of an open triangular space surrounded by dark and mysterious houses, temples of petty commerce emptied of traders for the night. Only a fruiterer's stall at the corner made a violent blaze of light and color. Beyond all was black, and the few people passing in that direction vanished at one stride beyond the glowing heaps of oranges and lemons. No footsteps echoed. They would never be heard of again. The adventurous head of the Special Crimes Department watched these disappearances from a distance with an interested eye. He felt lighthearted, as though he had been ambushed all alone in a jungle many thousands of miles away from departmental desks and official inkstands. This joyousness and dispersion of thought before a task of some importance seems to prove that this world of ours is not such a very serious affair after all. For the Assistant Commissioner was not constitutionally inclined to levity.

The policeman on the beat projected his somber and moving form against the luminous glory of oranges and lemons, and entered Brett Street without haste. The Assistant Commissioner, as though he were a member of the criminal classes, lingered out of sight, awaiting his return. But this constable seemed to be lost forever to the force. He never returned: must have gone out at the other end of Brett Street.

The Assistant Commissioner, reaching this conclusion, entered the street in his turn, and came upon a large van arrested in front of the dimly lit windowpanes of a carters' eating-house. The man was refreshing himself inside, and the horses, their big heads lowered to the ground, fed out of nose bags steadily. Farther on, on the opposite side of the street, another suspect patch of dim light issued from Mr. Verloc's shop front, hung with papers, heaving with vague piles of cardboard boxes and the shapes of books. The Assistant Commissioner stood observing it across the roadway. There could be no mistake. By the side of the front window, encumbered by the shadows of nondescript things, the door, standing ajar, let escape on the pavement a narrow, clear streak of gaslight within.

Behind the Assistant Commissioner the van and horses, merged into one mass, seemed something alive—a square-backed black monster blocking half the street, with sudden iron-shod stampings, fierce jingles, and heavy, blowing sighs. The harshly festive, ill-omened glare of a large and prosperous public house faced the other end of Brett Street across a wide road. This barrier of blazing lights, opposing the shadows gathered about the humble abode of Mr. Verloc's domestic happiness, seemed to drive the obscurity of the street back upon itself, make it more sullen, brooding, and sinister.

❧ 8 ❧

Having infused by persistent importunities some sort of heat into the chilly interest of several licensed victuallers (the acquaintances once upon a time of her late unlucky husband), Mrs. Verloc's mother had at last secured her admission to certain almshouses founded by a wealthy innkeeper for the destitute widows of the trade.

This end, conceived in the astuteness of her uneasy heart, the old woman had pursued with secrecy and determination. That was the time when her daughter Winnie could not help passing a remark to Mr. Verloc that "mother has been spending half-crowns and five shillings almost every day this last week in cab fares." But the remark was not made grudgingly. Winnie respected her mother's infirmities. She was only a little surprised at this sudden mania for locomotion. Mr. Verloc, who was sufficiently magnificent in his way, had grunted the remark impatiently aside as interfering with his meditations. These were frequent, deep, and prolonged; they bore upon a matter more important than five shillings. Distinctly more important, and beyond all comparison more difficult to consider in all its aspects with philosophical serenity.

Her object attained in astute secrecy, the heroic old woman had made a clean breast of it to Mrs. Verloc. Her soul was triumphant and her heart tremulous. Inwardly she quaked, because she dreaded and admired the calm, self-contained character of her daughter Winnie, whose displeasure was made redoubtable by a diversity of dreadful silences. But she did not allow her inward apprehensions to rob her of the advantage of venerable placidity conferred upon her outward person by her triple chin, the floating ampleness of her ancient form, and the impotent condition of her legs.

The shock of the information was so unexpected that Mrs. Verloc, against her usual practice when addressed, interrupted the domestic occupation she was engaged upon. It was the dusting of the furniture in the parlor behind the shop. She turned her head towards her mother.

"Whatever did you want to do that for?" she exclaimed, in scandalized astonishment.

The shock must have been severe to make her depart from that distant and uninquiring acceptance of facts which was her force and her safeguard in life.

"Weren't you made comfortable enough here?"

She had lapsed into these inquiries, but next moment she saved the consistency of her conduct by resuming her dusting, while the old woman sat scared and dumb under her dingy white cap and lusterless dark wig.

Winnie finished the chair, and ran the duster along the mahogany at the back of the horsehair sofa on which Mr. Verloc loved to take his ease in hat and overcoat. She was intent on her work, but presently she permitted herself another question.

"How in the world did you manage it, mother?"

As not affecting the inwardness of things, which it was Mrs. Verloc's principle to ignore, this curiosity was excusable. It bore merely on the methods. The old woman welcomed it eagerly as bringing forward something that could be talked about with much sincerity.

She favored her daughter by an exhaustive answer full of names and enriched by side comments upon the ravages of time as observed in the alteration of human countenances. The names were principally the names of licensed victuallers—"poor daddy's friends, my dear." She enlarged with special appreciation on the kindness and condescension of a large brewer, a Baronet and an M.P., the Chairman of the Governors of the Charity. She expressed herself thus warmly because she had been allowed to interview by appointment his Private Secretary—"a very polite gentleman, all in black, with a gentle, sad voice, but so very, very thin and quiet. He was like a shadow, my dear."

Winnie, prolonging her dusting operations till the tale was told to the end, walked out of the parlor into the kitchen (down two steps) in her usual manner, without the slightest comment.

Shedding a few tears in sign of rejoicing at her daughter's mansuetude in this terrible affair, Mrs. Verloc's mother gave play to her astuteness in the direction of her furniture, because it was her own; and sometimes she wished it hadn't been. Heroism is all very well, but there are circumstances when the disposal of a few tables and chairs, brass bedsteads, and so on, may be big with remote and disastrous consequences. She required a few pieces herself, the Foundation which, after many importunities, had gathered her to its charitable breast, giving nothing but bare planks and cheaply papered bricks to the objects of its solicitude. The delicacy guiding her choice to the least valuable and most dilapidated articles passed unacknowledged, because Winnie's philosophy consisted in not taking notice of the inside of facts; she assumed that mother took what suited her best. As to Mr. Verloc, his intense meditation, like a sort of Chinese wall, isolated him completely from the phenomena of this world of vain effort and illusory appearances.

Her selection made, the disposal of the rest became a perplexing question in a particular way. She was leaving it in Brett Street, of course. But she had two children. Winnie was provided for by her sensible union with that excellent husband, Mr. Verloc. Stevie was destitute—and a little peculiar. His position had to be considered before the claims of legal justice and even the promptings of partiality. The possession of the furniture would not be in any sense a provision. He ought to have it—the poor boy. But to give it to him would be like tampering with his position of complete dependence. It was a sort of claim which she feared to weaken. Moreover, the susceptibilities of Mr. Verloc would perhaps not brook being beholden to his brother-in-law for the chairs he sat on. In a long experience of gentlemen lodgers, Mrs. Verloc's mother had acquired a dismal but resigned notion of the fantastic side of human nature. What if Mr. Verloc suddenly took it into his head to tell Stevie to take his blessed sticks somewhere out of that? A division, on the other hand, however carefully made, might give some cause of offense to Winnie. No. Stevie must remain destitute and dependent. And at the moment of leaving Brett Street she had said to her daughter: "No use waiting till I am dead, is there? Everything I leave here is altogether your own now, my dear."

Winnie, with her hat on, silent behind her mother's back, went on arranging the collar of the old woman's cloak. She got her handbag, an umbrella, with an impassive face. The time had come for the expenditure of the sum of three-and-sixpence on what might well be supposed the last cab drive of Mrs. Verloc's mother's life. They went out at the shop door.

The conveyance awaiting them would have illustrated the proverb that "truth can be more cruel than caricature," if such a proverb existed. Crawling behind an infirm horse, a metropolitan hackney carriage drew up on wobbly wheels and with a maimed driver on the box. This last peculiarity caused some embarrassment. Catching sight of a hooked iron contrivance protruding from the left sleeve of the man's coat, Mrs. Verloc's mother lost suddenly the heroic courage of these days. She really couldn't trust herself. "What do you think, Winnie?" She hung back. The passionate expostulations of the big-faced cabman seemed to be squeezed out of a blocked throat. Leaning over from his box, he whispered with mysterious indignation. What was the matter now? Was it possible to treat a man so? His enormous and unwashed countenance flamed red in the muddy stretch of the street. Was it likely they would have given him a license, he inquired desperately, if—

The police constable of the locality quieted him by a friendly glance; then addressing himself to the two women without marked consideration, said:

"He's been driving a cab for twenty years. I never knew him to have an accident."

"Accident!" shouted the driver in a scornful whisper.

The policeman's testimony settled it. The modest assemblage of seven people, mostly under age, dispersed. Winnie followed her mother into the cab. Stevie climbed on the box. His vacant mouth and distressed eyes depicted the state of his mind in regard to the transactions which were taking place. In the narrow streets the progress of the journey was made sensible to those within by the near fronts of the houses gliding past slowly and shakily, with a great rattle and jingling of glass, as if about to collapse behind the cab; and the infirm horse, with the harness hung over his sharp backbone flapping very loose about his thighs, appeared to be dancing mincingly on his toes with infinite patience. Later on, in the wider space of Whitehall, all visual evidences of motion became imperceptible. The rattle and jingle of glass went on indefinitely in front of the long Treasury building— and time itself seemed to stand still.

At last Winnie observed: "This isn't a very good horse."

Her eyes gleamed in the shadow of the cab straight ahead, immovable. On the box, Stevie shut his vacant mouth first, in order to ejaculate earnestly: "Don't."

The driver, holding high the reins twisted around the hook, took no notice. Perhaps he had not heard. Stevie's breast heaved.

"Don't whip."

The man turned slowly his bloated and sodden face of many colors bristling with white hairs. His little red eyes glistened with moisture. His big lips had a violet tint. They remained closed. With the dirty back of his whip-hand he rubbed the stubble sprouting on his enormous chin.

"You mustn't," stammered out Stevie, violently, "it hurts."

"Mustn't whip," queried the other in a thoughtful whisper, and immediately whipped. He did this, not because his soul was cruel and his heart evil, but because he had to earn his fare. And for a time the walls of St. Stephen's, with its towers and pinnacles, contemplated in immobility and silence a cab that jingled. It rolled, too, however. But on the bridge there was a commotion. Stevie suddenly proceeded to get down from the box. There were shouts on the pavement, people ran forward, the driver pulled up, whispering curses of indignation and astonishment. Winnie lowered the window, and put her head out, white as a ghost. In the depths of the cab, her mother was exclaiming, in tones of anguish: "Is that boy hurt? Is that boy hurt?"

Stevie was not hurt, he had not even fallen, but excitement as usual had robbed him of the power of connected speech. He could do no more than stammer at the window: "Too heavy. Too heavy." Winnie put out her hand on to his shoulder.

"Stevie! Get up on the box directly, and don't try to get down again."

"No. No. Walk. Must walk."

In trying to state the nature of that necessity he stammered himself into utter incoherence. No physical impossibility stood in the way of his whim. Stevie could have managed easily to keep pace with the infirm, dancing horse without getting out of breath. But his sister withheld her consent decisively. "The idea! Who ever heard of such a thing! Run after a cab!" Her mother, frightened and helpless in the depths of the conveyance, entreated:

"Oh, don't let him, Winnie. He'll get lost. Don't let him."

"Certainly not. What next! Mr. Verloc will be sorry to hear of this nonsense, Stevie—I can tell you. He won't be happy at all."

The idea of Mr. Verloc's grief and unhappiness acting as usual powerfully upon Stevie's fundamentally docile disposition, he abandoned all resistance, and climbed up again on the box, with a face of despair.

The cabby turned at him his enormous and inflamed countenance truculently. "Don't you go for trying this silly game again, young fellow."

After delivering himself thus in a stern whisper, strained almost to extinction, he drove on, ruminating solemnly. To his mind the incident remained somewhat obscure. But his intellect, though it had lost its pristine vivacity in the benumbing years of sedentary exposure to the weather, lacked not independence or sanity. Gravely he dismissed the hypothesis of Stevie being a drunken young nipper.

Inside the cab the spell of silence, in which the two women had endured shoulder to shoulder the jolting, rattling, and jingling of the journey, had been broken by Stevie's outbreak. Winnie raised her voice.

"You've done what you wanted, mother. You'll have only yourself to thank for it if you aren't happy afterwards. And I don't think you'll be. That I don't. Weren't you comfortable enough in the house? Whatever people'll think of us—you throwing yourself like this on a Charity?"

"My dear," screamed the old woman earnestly above the noise, "you've been the best of daughters to me. As to Mr. Verloc—there—"

Words failing her on the subject of Mr. Verloc's excellence, she turned her old tearful eyes to the roof of the cab. Then she averted her head on the pretense of looking out of the window, as if to judge of their progress. It was insignificant, and went on close to the curbstone. Night, the early dirty night, the sinister, noisy, hopeless, and rowdy night of South London, had overtaken her on her last cab drive. In the gaslight of the low-fronted shops her big cheeks glowed with an orange hue under a black and mauve bonnet.

Mrs. Verloc's mother's complexion had become yellow by the effect of age and from a natural predisposition to biliousness, favored by the trials of a difficult and worried existence, first as wife, then as widow. It was a complexion that under the influence of a blush would take on an orange tint. And this woman, modest indeed but hardened in the fires of adversity, of an age, moreover, when blushes are not expected, had positively blushed before her daughter. In the privacy of a four-wheeler, on her way to a charity cottage (one of a row) which by the exiguity of its dimensions and the simplicity of its accommodation, might well have been devised in kindness as a place of training for the still more straitened circumstances of the grave, she was forced to hide from her own child a blush of remorse and shame.

Whatever people will think? She knew very well what they did think, the people Winnie had in her mind—the old friends of her husband, and others too, whose interest she had solicited with such flattering success. She had not known before what a good beggar she could be. But she guessed very well what inference was drawn from her application. On account of that shrinking delicacy, which exists side by side with aggressive brutality in masculine nature, the inquiries into her circumstances had not been pushed very far. She had checked them by a visible compression of the lips and some display of an emotion determined to be eloquently silent. And the men would become suddenly incurious, after the manner of their kind. She congratulated herself more than once on having nothing to do with women, who being naturally more callous and avid of details, would have been anxious to be exactly informed by what sort of unkind conduct her daughter and son-in-law had driven her to that sad extremity. It was only before the Secretary of the great brewer M.P. and Chairman of the Charity, who, acting for his principal, felt bound to be conscientiously inquisitive as to the real circumstances of the applicant, that she had burst into tears outright and aloud, as a cornered woman will weep. The thin and polite gentleman, after contemplating her with an air of being "struck all of a heap," abandoned his position under the cover of soothing remarks. She must not distress herself. The deed of the Charity did not absolutely specify "childless widows." In fact, it did not by any means disqualify her. But the discretion of the Committee must be an informed discretion. One could understand very well her unwillingness to be a burden, etc., etc. Thereupon, to his profound disappointment, Mrs. Verloc's mother wept some more with an augmented vehemence.

The tears of that large female in a dark, dusty wig, and ancient silk dress festooned with dingy white cotton lace, were the tears of genuine distress. She had wept because she was heroic and unscrupulous and full of love for both her children. Girls frequently get sacrificed to the welfare of the boys. In this case she was sacrificing Winnie. By the suppression of truth she was slandering her. Of course, Winnie was independent, and need not care for the opinion of people that she would never see and who would never see her; whereas poor Stevie had nothing in the world he could call his own except his mother's heroism and unscrupulousness.

The first sense of security following on Winnie's marriage wore off in time (for nothing lasts), and Mrs. Verloc's mother, in the seclusion of the back bedroom, had recalled the teaching of that experience which the world impresses upon a widowed woman. But she had recalled it without vain bitterness; her store of resignation amounted almost to dignity. She reflected stoically that everything decays, wears out, in this world; that the way of kindness should be made easy to the well disposed; that her daughter Winnie was a most devoted sister, and a very self-confident wife indeed. As regards Winnie's sisterly devotion, her stoicism flinched. She excepted that sentiment from the rule of decay affecting all things human and some things divine. She could not help it; not to do so would have frightened her too much. But in considering the conditions of her daughter's married state, she rejected firmly all flattering illusions. She took the cold and reasonable view that the less strain put on Mr. Verloc's kindness the longer its effects were likely to last. That excellent man loved his wife, of course, but he would, no doubt, prefer to keep as few of her relations as was consistent with the proper display of that sentiment. It would be better if its whole effect were concentrated on poor Stevie. And the heroic old woman resolved on going away from her children as an act of devotion and as a move of deep policy.

The "virtue" of this policy consisted in this (Mrs. Verloc's mother was subtle in her way), that Stevie's moral claim would be strengthened. The poor boy—a good, useful boy, if a little peculiar—had not a sufficient standing. He had been taken over with his mother, somewhat in the same way as the furniture of the Belgravian mansion had been taken over, as if on the ground of belonging to her exclusively. What will happen, she asked herself (for Mrs. Verloc's mother was in a measure imaginative), when I die? And when she asked herself that question it was with dread. It was also terrible to think that she would not then have the means of knowing what happened to the poor boy. But by making him over to his sister, by going thus away, she gave him the advantage of a directly dependent position. This was the more subtle sanction of Mrs. Verloc's mother's heroism and unscrupulousness. Her act of abandonment was really an arrangement for settling her son permanently in life. Other people made material sacrifices for such an object, she in that way. It was the only way. Moreover, she would be able to see how it worked. Ill or well she would avoid the horrible incertitude on the deathbed. But it was hard, hard, cruelly hard.

The cab rattled, jingled, jolted; in fact, the last was quite extraordinary. By its disproportionate violence and magnitude it obliterated every sensation of onward movement; and the effect was of being shaken in a stationary apparatus like a medieval device for the punishment of crime, or some very newfangled invention for the cure of a sluggish liver. It was extremely distressing; and the raising of Mrs. Verloc's mother's voice sounded like a wail of pain.

"I know, my dear, you'll come to see me as often as you can spare the time. Won't you?"

"Of course," answered Winnie, shortly, staring straight before her.

And the cab jolted in front of a steamy, greasy shop in a blaze of gas and in the smell of fried fish. The old woman raised a wail again.

"And, my dear, I must see that poor boy every Sunday. He won't mind spending the day with his old mother—"

Winnie screamed out stolidly:

"Mind! I should think not. That poor boy will miss you something cruel. I wish you had thought a little of that, mother."

Not think of it! The heroic woman swallowed a playful and inconvenient object like a billiard ball, which had tried to jump out of her throat. Winnie sat mute for a while, pouting at the front of the cab, then snapped out, which was an unusual tone with her:

"I expect I'll have a job with him at first, he'll be that restless—"

"Whatever you do, don't let him worry your husband, my dear."

Thus they discussed on familiar lines the bearings of a new situation. And the cab jolted. Mrs. Verloc's mother expressed some misgivings. Could Stevie be trusted to come all that way alone? Winnie maintained that he was much less "absent-minded" now. They agreed as to that. It could not be denied. Much less—hardly at all. They shouted at each other in the jingle with comparative cheerfulness. But suddenly the maternal anxiety broke out afresh. There were two omnibuses to take, and a short walk between. It was too difficult! The old woman gave way to grief and consternation.

Winnie stared forward.

"Don't you upset yourself like this, mother. You must see him, of course."

"No, my dear. I'll try not to."

She mopped her streaming eyes.

"But you can't spare the time to come with him, and if he should forget himself and lose his way and somebody spoke to him sharply, his name and address may slip his memory, and he'll remain lost for days and days—"

The vision of a workhouse infirmary for poor Stevie—if only during inquiries— wrung her heart. For she was a proud woman. Winnie's stare had grown hard, intent, inventive.

"I can't bring him to you myself every week," she cried. "But don't you worry, mother. I'll see to it that he don't get lost for long."

They felt a peculiar bump; a vision of brick pillars lingered before the rattling windows of the cab; a sudden cessation of atrocious jolting and uproarious jingling dazed the two women. What had happened? They sat motionless and scared in the profound stillness, till the door came open, and a rough, strained whispering was heard:

"'Ere you are!"

A range of gabled little houses, each with one dim yellow window, on the ground floor, surrounded the dark open space of a grassplot planted with shrubs and railed off from the patchwork of lights and shadows in the wide road, resounding with the dull rumble of traffic. Before the door of one of these tiny houses—one without a light in the little downstairs window—the cab had come to a standstill. Mrs. Verloc's mother got out first, backwards, with a key in her hand. Winnie lingered on the flagstone path to pay the cabman. Stevie, after help-ing to carry inside a lot of small parcels, came out and stood under the light of a gas-lamp belonging to the Charity. The cabman looked at the pieces of silver, which, appearing very minute in his big, grimy palm, symbolized the insignificant results which reward the ambitious courage and toil of a mankind whose day is short on this earth of evil.

He had been paid decently—four one-shilling pieces—and he contemplated them in perfect stillness, as if they had been the surprising terms of a melan-choly problem. The slow transfer of that treasure to an inner pocket demanded much laborious groping in the depths of decayed clothing. His form was squat and without flexibility. Stevie, slender, his shoulders a little up, and his hands thrust deep in the side pockets of his warm overcoat, stood at the edge of the path, pouting.

The cabman, pausing in his deliberate movements, seemed struck by some misty recollection.

"Oh! 'Ere you are, young fellow," he whispered. "You'll know him again— won't you?"

Stevie was staring at the horse, whose hind quarters appeared unduly elevated by the effect of emancipation. The little stiff tail seemed to have been fitted in for a heartless joke; and at the other end the thin, flat neck, like a plank covered with old horsehide, drooped to the ground under the weight of an enormous bony head. The ears hung at different angles, negligently; and the macabre figure of that mute dweller on the earth steamed straight up from ribs and backbone in the muggy stillness of the air.

The cabman struck lightly Stevie's breast with the iron hook protruding from a ragged, greasy sleeve.

"Look 'ere, young feller. 'Ow'd *you* like to sit behind this 'oss up to two o'clock in the morning p'raps?"

Stevie looked vacantly into the fierce little eyes with red-edged lids.

"He ain't lame," pursued the other, whispering with energy. "He ain't got no sore places on 'im. 'Ere he is. 'Ow would *you* like—"

His strained, extinct voice invested his utterance with a character of vehement secrecy. Stevie's vacant gaze was changing slowly into dread.

"You may well look! Till three and four o'clock in the morning. Cold and 'ungry. Looking for fares. Drunks."

His jovial purple cheeks bristled with white hairs; and like Virgil's Silenus, who, his face smeared with the juice of berries, discoursed of Olympian Gods to the innocent shepherds of Sicily, he talked to Stevie of domestic matters and the affairs of men whose sufferings are great and immortality by no means assured.

"I am a night cabby, I am," he whispered, with a sort of boastful exasperation. "I've got to take out what they will blooming well give me at the yard. I've got my missus and four kids at 'ome."

The monstrous nature of that declaration of paternity seemed to strike the world dumb. A silence reigned, during which the flanks of the old horse, the steed of apocalyptic misery, smoked upwards in the light of the charitable gas-lamp.

The cabman grunted, then added in his mysterious whisper:

"This ain't an easy world."

Stevie's face had been twitching for some time and at last his feelings burst out in their usual concise form.

"Bad! Bad!"

His gaze remained fixed on the ribs of the horse, self-conscious and somber, as though he were afraid to look about him at the badness of the world. And his slenderness, his rosy lips and pale, clear complexion, gave him the aspect of a delicate boy, notwithstanding the fluffy growth of golden hair on his cheeks. He pouted in a scared way like a child. The cabman, short and broad, eyed him with his fierce little eyes that seemed to smart in a clear and corroding liquid.

"Ard on 'osses, but dam' sight 'arder on poor chaps like me," he wheezed just audibly.

"Poor! Poor!" stammered out Stevie, pushing his hands deeper into his pocket with convulsive sympathy. He could say nothing; for the tenderness to all pain and all misery, the desire to make the horse happy and the cabman happy, had reached the point of a bizarre longing to take them to bed with him. And that, he knew, was impossible. For Stevie was not mad. It was, as it were, a symbolic longing; and at the same time it was very distinct, because springing from experience, the mother of wisdom. Thus when as a child he cowered in a dark corner scared, wretched, sore, and miserable with the black, black misery of the soul, his sister Winnie used to come along, and carry him off to bed with her, as into a heaven of consoling peace. Stevie, though apt to forget mere facts, such as his name and address for instance, had a faithful memory of sensations. To be taken into a bed of compassion was the supreme remedy, with the only one disadvantage of being difficult of application on a large scale. And looking at the cabman, Stevie perceived this clearly, because he was reasonable.

The cabman went on with his leisurely preparations as if Stevie had not existed. He made as if to hoist himself on the box, but at the last moment, from some obscure motive, perhaps merely from disgust with carriage exercise, desisted. He approached instead the motionless partner of his labors, and stooping to seize the bridle, lifted up the big, weary head to the height of his shoulder with one effort of his right arm, like a feat of strength.

"Come on," he whispered, secretly.

Limping, he led the cab away. There was an air of austerity in this departure, the scrunched gravel of the drive crying out under the slowly turning wheels, the horse's lean thighs moving with ascetic deliberation away from the light into the obscurity of the open space bordered dimly by the pointed roofs and the feebly shining windows of the little almshouses. The plaint of the gravel traveled slowly all round the drive. Between the lamps of the charitable gateway the slow cortège reappeared, lighted up for a moment, the short, thick man limping busily, with the horse's head held aloft in his fist, the lank animal walking in stiff and forlorn dignity, the dark, low box on wheels rolling behind comically with an air of waddling. They turned to the left. There was a pub down the street, within fifty yards of the gate.

Stevie left alone beside the private lamppost of the Charity, his hands thrust deep into his pockets, glared with vacant sulkiness. At the bottom of his pockets his incapable, weak hands were clinched hard into a pair of angry fists. In the face of anything which affected directly or indirectly his morbid dread of pain, Stevie ended by turning vicious. A magnanimous indignation swelled his frail chest to bursting, and caused his candid eyes to squint. Supremely wise in knowing his own powerlessness, Stevie was not wise enough to restrain his passions. The tenderness of his universal charity had two phases as indissolubly joined and connected as the reverse and obverse sides of a medal. The anguish of immoderate compassion was succeeded by the pain of an innocent but pitiless rage. Those two states expressing themselves outwardly by the same signs of futile bodily agitation, his sister Winnie soothed his excitement without ever fathoming its twofold character. Mrs. Verloc wasted no portion of this transient life in seeking for fundamental information. This is a sort of economy having all the appearances and some of the advantages of prudence. Obviously it may be good for one not to know too much. And such a view accords very well with constitutional indolence.

On that evening on which it may be said that Mrs. Verloc's mother having parted for good from her children had also departed this life, Winnie Verloc did not investigate her brother's psychology. The poor boy was excited, of course. After once more assuring the old woman on the threshold that she would know how to guard against the risk of Stevie losing himself for very long on his pilgrimages of filial piety, she took her brother's arm to walk away. Stevie did not even mutter to himself, but with the special sense of sisterly devotion developed in her earliest infancy, she felt that the boy was very much excited indeed. Holding tight to his arm, under the appearance of leaning on it, she thought of some words suitable to the occasion.

"Now, Stevie, you must look well after me at the crossings, and get first into the 'bus, like a good brother."

This appeal to manly protection was received by Stevie with his usual docility. It flattered him. He raised his head and threw out his chest.

"Don't be nervous, Winnie. Mustn't be nervous! 'Bus all right," he answered in a brusk, slurring stammer partaking of the timorousness of a child and the resolution of a man. He advanced fearlessly with the woman on his arm, but his lower lip dropped. Nevertheless, on the pavement of the squalid and wide thoroughfare, whose poverty in all the amenities of life stood foolishly exposed by a mad profusion of gaslights, their resemblance to each other was so pronounced as to strike the casual passersby.

Before the doors of the public house at the corner, where the profusion of gaslight reached the height of positive wickedness, a four-wheeled cab standing by the curbstone, with no one on the box, seemed cast out into the gutter on account of irremediable decay. Mrs. Verloc recognized the conveyance. Its aspect was so profoundly lamentable, with such a perfection of grotesque misery and weirdness of macabre detail, as if it were the Cab of Death itself, that Mrs. Verloc, with that ready compassion of a woman for a horse (when she is not sitting behind him), exclaimed vaguely:

"Poor brute."

Hanging back suddenly, Stevie inflicted an arresting jerk upon his sister.

"Poor! Poor!" he ejaculated, appreciatively. "Cabman poor, too. He told me himself."

The contemplation of the infirm and lonely steed overcame him. Jostled, but obstinate, he would remain there, trying to express the view newly opened to his sympathies of the human and equine misery in close association. But it was very difficult. "Poor brute, poor people!" was all he could repeat. It did not seem forcible enough, and he came to a stop with an angry splutter: "Shame!" Stevie was no master of phrases, and perhaps for that very reason his thoughts lacked clearness and precision. But he felt with greater completeness and some profundity. That little word contained all his sense of indignation and horror at one sort of wretchedness having to feed upon the anguish of the other—at the poor cabman beating the poor horse in the name, as it were, of his poor kids at home. And Stevie knew what it was to be beaten. He knew it from experience. It was a bad world. Bad! Bad!

Mrs. Verloc, his only sister, guardian, and protector, could not pretend to such depths of insight. Moreover, she had not experienced the magic of the cabman's eloquence. She was in the dark as to the inwardness of the word "Shame." And she said placidly:

"Come along, Stevie. You can't help that."

The docile Stevie went along; but now he went along without pride, shamblingly, and muttering half words, and even words that would have been whole if they had not been made up of halves that did not belong to each other. It was as though he had been trying to fit all the words he could remember to his sentiments in order to get some sort of corresponding idea. And, as a matter of fact, he got it at last. He hung back to utter it at once.

"Bad world for poor people."

Directly he had expressed that thought he became aware that it was familiar to him already in all its consequences. This circumstance strengthened his conviction immensely, but also augmented his indignation. Somebody, he felt, ought to be punished for it—punished with great severity. Being no skeptic, but a moral creature, he was in a manner at the mercy of his righteous passions.

"Beastly!" he added, concisely.

It was clear to Mrs. Verloc that he was greatly excited.

"Nobody can help that," she said. "Do come along. Is that the way you're taking care of me?"

Stevie mended his pace obediently. He prided himself on being a good brother. His morality, which was very complete, demanded that from him. Yet he was pained at the information imparted by his sister Winnie who was good. Nobody could help that! He came along gloomily, but presently he brightened up. Like the rest of mankind, perplexed by the mystery of the universe, he had his moments of consoling trust in the organized powers of the earth.

"Police," he suggested, confidently.

"The police aren't for that," observed Mrs. Verloc, cursorily, hurrying on her way.

Stevie's face lengthened considerably. He was thinking. The more intense his thinking, the slacker was the droop of his lower jaw. And it was with an aspect of hopeless vacancy that he gave up his intellectual enterprise.

"Not for that?" he mumbled, resigned but surprised. "Not for that?" He had formed for himself an ideal conception of the metropolitan police as a sort of benevolent institution for the suppression of evil. The notion of benevolence especially was very closely associated with his sense of the power of the men in blue. He had liked all police constables tenderly, with a guileless trustfulness. And he was pained. He was irritated, too, by a suspicion of duplicity in the members of the force. For Stevie was frank and as open as the day himself. What did they mean by pretending then? Unlike his sister, who put her trust in face values, he wished to go to the bottom of the matter. He carried on his inquiry by means of an angry challenge.

"What are they for then, Winn? What are they for? Tell me."

Winnie disliked controversy. But fearing most a fit of black depression consequent on Stevie missing his mother very much at first, she did not altogether decline the discussion. Guiltless of all irony, she answered yet in a form which was not perhaps unnatural in the wife of Mr. Verloc, Delegate of the Central Red Committee, personal friend of certain anarchists, and a votary of social revolution.

"Don't you know what the police are for, Stevie? They are there so that them as have nothing shouldn't take anything away from them who have."

She avoided using the verb "to steal," because it always made her brother uncomfortable. For Stevie was delicately honest. Certain simple principles had been instilled into him so anxiously (on account of his "queerness") that the mere names of certain transgressions filled him with horror. He had been always easily impressed by speeches. He was impressed and startled now, and his intelligence was very alert.

"What?" he asked at once, anxiously. "Not even if they were hungry? Mustn't they?"

The two had paused in their walk.

"Not if they were ever so," said Mrs. Verloc, with the equanimity of a person untroubled by the problem of the distribution of wealth, and exploring the perspective of the roadway for an omnibus of the right color. "Certainly not. But what's the use of talking about all that? You aren't ever hungry."

She cast a swift glance at the boy, like a young man, by her side. She saw him amiable, attractive, affectionate, and only a little, a very little peculiar. And she could not see him otherwise, for he was connected with what there was of the salt of passion in her tasteless life—the passion of indignation, of courage, of pity, and even of self-sacrifice. She did not add: "And you aren't likely ever to be as long as I live." But she might very well have done so, since she had taken effectual steps to that end. Mr. Verloc was a very good husband. It was her honest impression that nobody could help liking the boy. She cried out suddenly:

"Quick, Stevie. Stop that green 'bus."

And Stevie, tremulous and important with his sister Winnie on his arm, flung up the other high above his head at the approaching 'bus, with complete success.

An hour afterwards Mr. Verloc raised his eyes from a newspaper he was reading, or at any rate looking at, behind the counter, and in the expiring clatter of the doorbell beheld Winnie, his wife, enter and cross the shop on her way upstairs, followed by Stevie, his brother-in-law. The sight of his wife was agreeable to Mr. Verloc. It was his idiosyncrasy. The figure of his brother-in-law remained imperceptible to him because of the morose thoughtfulness that lately had fallen like a veil between Mr. Verloc and the appearances of the world of senses. He looked after his wife fixedly, without a word, as though she had been a phantom. His voice for home use was husky and placid, but now it was heard not at all. It was not heard at supper, to which he was called by his wife in the usual brief manner: "Adolf." He sat down to consume it without conviction, wearing his hat pushed far back on his head. It was not devotion to an outdoor life, but the frequentation of foreign cares which was responsible for that habit, investing with a character of unceremonious impermanency Mr. Verloc's steady fidelity to his own fireside. Twice at the clatter of the cracked bell he arose without a word, disappeared into the shop, and came back silently. During these absences Mrs. Verloc, becoming acutely aware of the vacant place at her right hand, missed her mother very much, and stared stonily; while Stevie, from the same reason, kept on shuffling his feet, as though the floor under the table were uncomfortably hot. When Mr. Verloc returned to sit in his place, like the very embodiment of silence, the character of Mrs. Verloc's stare underwent a subtle change, and Stevie ceased to fidget with his feet, because of his great and awed regard for his sister's husband. He directed at him glances of respectful compassion. Mr. Verloc was sorry. His sister Winnie had impressed upon him (in the omnibus) that Mr.

Verloc would be found at home in a state of sorrow, and must not be worried. His father's anger, the irritability of gentlemen lodgers, and Mr. Verloc's predisposition to immoderate grief, had been the main sanctions of Stevie's self-restraint. Of these sentiments, all easily provoked, but not always easy to understand, the last had the greatest moral efficiency—because Mr. Verloc was *good*. His mother and his sister had established that ethical fact on an unshakable foundation. They had established, erected, consecrated it behind Mr. Verloc's back, for reasons that had nothing to do with abstract morality. And Mr. Verloc was not aware of it. It is but bare justice to him to say that he had no notion of appearing good to Stevie. Yet so it was. He was even the only man so qualified in Stevie's knowledge, because the gentlemen lodgers had been too transient and too remote to have anything very distinct about them but perhaps their boots; and as regards the disciplinary measures of his father, the desolation of his mother and sister shrank from setting up a theory of goodness before the victim. It would have been too cruel. And it was even possible that Stevie would not have believed them. As far as Mr. Verloc was concerned, nothing could stand in the way of Stevie's belief. Mr. Verloc was obviously yet mysteriously *good*. And the grief of a good man is august.

Stevie gave glances of reverential compassion to his brother-in-law. Mr. Verloc was sorry. The brother of Winnie had never before felt himself in such close communion with the mystery of that man's goodness. It was an understandable sorrow. And Stevie himself was sorry. He was very sorry. The same sort of sorrow. And his attention being drawn to this unpleasant state, Stevie shuffled his feet. His feelings were habitually manifested by the agitation of his limbs.

"Keep your feet quiet, dear," said Mrs. Verloc, with authority and tenderness; then turning towards her husband in an indifferent voice, the masterly achievement of instinctive tact: "Are you going out tonight?" she asked.

The mere suggestion seemed repugnant to Mr. Verloc. He shook his head moodily, and then sat still with downcast eyes, looking at the piece of cheese on his plate for a whole minute. At the end of that time he got up, and went out— went right out in the clatter of the shop doorbell. He acted thus inconsistently, not from any desire to make himself unpleasant, but because of an unconquerable restlessness. It was no earthly good going out. He could not find anywhere in London what he wanted. But he went out. He led a cortège of dismal thoughts along dark streets, through lighted streets, in and out of two flash bars, as if in a half-hearted attempt to make a night of it, and finally back again to his menaced home, where he sat down fatigued behind the counter, and they crowded urgently round him, like a pack of hungry black hounds. After locking up the house and putting out the gas he took them upstairs with him—a dreadful escort for a man going to bed. His wife had preceded him some time before, and with her ample form defined vaguely under the counterpane, her head on the pillow, and a hand under the cheek, offered to his distraction the view of early drowsiness arguing the possession of an equable soul. Her big eyes stared wide open, inert and dark against the snowy whiteness of the linen. She did not move.

She had an equable soul. She felt profoundly that things do not stand much looking into. She made her force and her wisdom of that instinct. But the taciturnity of Mr. Verloc had been lying heavily upon her for a good many days. It was, as a matter of fact, affecting her nerves. Recumbent and motionless, she said placidly:

"You'll catch cold walking about in your socks like this."

This speech, becoming the solicitude of the wife and the prudence of the woman, took Mr. Verloc unawares. He had left his boots downstairs, but he had forgotten to put on his slippers, and he had been turning about the bedroom on noiseless pads like a bear in a cage. At the sound of his wife's voice he stopped and stared at her with a somnambulistic, expressionless gaze so long that Mrs. Verloc moved her limbs slightly under the bedclothes. But she did not move her black head sunk in the white pillow, one hand under her cheek and the big, dark, unwinking eyes.

Under her husband's expressionless stare, and remembering her mother's empty room across the landing, she felt an acute pang of loneliness. She had never been parted from her mother before. They had stood by each other. She felt that they had, and she said to herself that now mother was gone—gone for good. Mrs. Verloc had no illusions. Stevie remained, however. And she said:

"Mother's done what she wanted to do. There's no sense in it that I can see. I'm sure she couldn't have thought you had enough of her. It's perfectly wicked, leaving us like that."

Mr. Verloc was not a well-read person; his range of allusive phrases was limited, but there was a peculiar aptness in circumstances which made him think of rats leaving a doomed ship. He very nearly said so. He had grown suspicious and embittered. Could it be that the old woman had such an excellent nose? But the unreasonableness of such a suspicion was patent, and Mr. Verloc held his tongue. Not altogether, however. He muttered, heavily:

"Perhaps it's just as well."

He began to undress. Mrs. Verloc kept very still, perfectly still, with her eyes fixed in a dreamy, quiet stare. And her heart for the fraction of a second seemed to stand still, too. That night she was "not quite herself," as the saying is, and it was borne upon her with some force that a simple sentence may hold several diverse meanings—mostly disagreeable. How was it just as well? And why? But she did not allow herself to fall into the idleness of barren speculation. She was rather confirmed in her belief that things did not stand being looked into. Practical and subtle in her way, she brought Stevie to the front without loss of time, because in her the singleness of purpose had the unerring nature and the force of an instinct.

"What I am going to do to cheer up that boy for the first few days I'm sure I don't know. He'll be worrying himself from morning till night before he gets used to mother being away. And he's such a good boy. I couldn't do without him."

Mr. Verloc went on divesting himself of his clothing with the unnoticing inward concentration of a man undressing in the solitude of a vast and hopeless desert. For thus inhospitably did this fair earth, our common inheritance, present itself to the mental vision of Mr. Verloc. All was so still without and within that the lonely ticking of the clock on the landing stole into the room as if for the sake of company.

Mr. Verloc, getting into bed on his own side, remained prone and mute behind Mrs. Verloc's back. His thick arms rested abandoned on the outside of the counterpane like dropped weapons, like discarded tools. At that moment he was within a hair's breadth of making a clean breast of it all to his wife. The moment seemed propitious. Looking out of the corners of his eyes, he saw her ample shoulders draped in white, the back of her head, with the hair done for the night in three plaits tied up with black tapes at the ends. And he forbore. Mr. Verloc loved his wife as a wife should be loved—that is, maritally, with the regard one has for one's chief possession. This head arranged for the night, those ample shoulders, had an aspect of familiar sacredness—the sacredness of domestic peace. She moved not, massive and shapeless like a recumbent statue in the rough; he remembered her wide-open eyes looking into the empty room. She was mysterious, with the mysteriousness of living beings. The far-famed secret agent Δ of the late Baron Stott-Wartenheim's alarmist dispatches was not the man to break into such mysteries. He was easily intimidated. And he was also indolent, with the indolence which is so often the secret of good nature. He forbore touching that mystery out of love, timidity, and indolence. There would be always time enough. For several minutes he bore his sufferings silently in the drowsy silence of the room. And then he disturbed it by a resolute declaration.

"I am going on the Continent tomorrow."

His wife might have fallen asleep already. He could not tell. As a matter of fact, Mrs. Verloc had heard him. Her eyes remained very wide open, and she lay very still, confirmed in her instinctive conviction that things don't bear looking into very much. And yet it was nothing very unusual for Mr. Verloc to take such a trip. He renewed his stock from Paris and Brussels. Often he went over to make his purchases personally. A little select connection of amateurs was forming around the shop in Brett Street, a secret connection eminently proper for any business undertaken by Mr. Verloc, who, by a mystic accord of temperament and necessity, had been set apart to be a secret agent all his life.

He waited for a while, then added: "I'll be away a week or perhaps a fortnight. Get Mrs. Neale to come for the day."

Mrs. Neale was the charwoman of Brett Street. Victim of her marriage with a debauched joiner, she was oppressed by the needs of many infant children. Red-armed, and aproned in coarse sacking up to the armpits, she exhaled the anguish of the poor in a breath of soapsuds and rum, in the uproar of scrubbing, in the clatter of tin pails.

Mrs. Verloc, full of deep purpose, spoke in the tone of the shallowest indifference.

"There is no need to have the woman here all day. I shall do very well with Stevie."

She let the lonely clock on the landing count off fifteen ticks into the abyss of eternity, and asked:

"Shall I put the light out?"

Mr. Verloc snapped at his wife huskily.

"Put it out."

❦ 9 ❦

Mr. Verloc, returning from the Continent at the end of ten days, brought back a mind evidently unrefreshed by the wonders of foreign travel and a countenance unlighted by the joys of homecoming. He entered in the clatter of the shop-bell with an air of somber and vexed exhaustion. His bag in hand, his head lowered, he strode straight behind the counter, and let himself fall into the chair, as though he had tramped all the way from Dover. It was early morning. Stevie, dusting various objects displayed in the front windows, turned to gape at him with reverence and awe.

"Here!" said Mr. Verloc, giving a slight kick to the gladstone bag on the floor; and Stevie flung himself upon it, seized it, bore it off with triumphant devotion. He was so prompt that Mr. Verloc was distinctly surprised.

Already at the clatter of the shop-bell Mrs. Neale, blackleading the parlor grate, had looked through the door, and rising from her knees had gone, aproned, and grimy with everlasting toil, to tell Mrs. Verloc in the kitchen that "there was the master come back."

Winnie came no farther than the inner shop door.

"You'll want some breakfast," she said from a distance.

Mr. Verloc moved his hands slightly, as if overcome by an impossible suggestion. But once enticed into the parlor he did not reject the food set before him. He ate as if in a public place, his hat pushed off his forehead, the skirts of his heavy overcoat hanging in a triangle on each side of the chair. And across the length of the table covered with brown oilcloth Winnie, his wife, talked evenly at him the wifely talk, as artfully adapted, no doubt, to the circumstances of this return as the talk of Penelope to the return of the wandering Odysseus. Mrs. Verloc, however, had done no weaving during her husband's absence. But she had had all the upstairs room cleaned thoroughly, had sold some wares, had seen Mr. Michaelis several times. He had told her the last time that he was going away to live in a cottage in the country, somewhere on the London, Chatham, and Dover line. Karl Yundt had come, too, once, led under the arm by that "wicked old housekeeper of his." He was "a disgusting old man." Of Comrade Ossipon, whom she had received curtly, entrenched behind the counter with a stony face and a far-away gaze, she said nothing, her mental reference to the robust anarchist being marked by a short pause, with the faintest possible blush. And bringing her brother Stevie as soon as she could into the current of domestic events, she mentioned that the boy had moped a good deal.

"It's all along of mother leaving us like this."

Mr. Verloc neither said "Damn!" nor yet "Stevie be hanged!" And Mrs. Verloc, not let into the secret of his thoughts, failed to appreciate the generosity of this restraint.

"It isn't that he doesn't work as well as ever," she continued. "He's been making himself very useful. You'd think he couldn't do enough for us."

Mr. Verloc directed a casual and somnolent glance at Stevie, who sat on his right, delicate, pale-faced, his rosy mouth open vacantly. It was not a critical glance. It had no intention. And if Mr. Verloc thought for a moment that his wife's brother looked uncommonly useless, it was only a dull and fleeting thought, devoid of that force and durability which enables sometimes a thought to move the world. Leaning back, Mr. Verloc uncovered his head. Before his extended arm could put down the hat Stevie pounced upon it, and bore it off reverently into the kitchen. And again Mr. Verloc was surprised.

"You could do anything with that boy, Adolf," Mrs. Verloc said, with her best air of inflexible calmness. "He would go through fire for you. He—"

She paused attentive, her ear turned towards the door of the kitchen.

There Mrs. Neale was scrubbing the floor. At Stevie's appearance she groaned lamentably, having observed that he could be induced easily to bestow for the benefit of her infant children the shilling his sister Winnie presented him with from time to time. On all fours amongst the puddles, wet and begrimed, like a sort of amphibious and domestic animal living in ash bins and dirty water, she uttered the usual exordium: "It's all very well for you, kept doing nothing like a gentle-man." And she followed it with the everlasting plaint of the poor, pathetically mendacious, miserably authenticated by the horrible breath of cheap rum and soap suds. She scrubbed hard, snuffling all the time, and talking volubly. And she was sincere. And on each side of her thin red nose her bleared, misty eyes swam in tears, because she felt really the want of some sort of stimulant in the morning.

In the parlor Mrs. Verloc observed, with knowledge:

"There's Mrs. Neale at it again with her harrowing tales about her little chil-dren. They can't be all so little as she makes them out. Some of them must be big enough by now to try to do something for themselves. It only makes Stevie angry."

These words were confirmed by a thud as of a fist striking the kitchen table. In the normal evolution of his sympathy Stevie had become angry on discovering that he had no shilling in his pocket. In his inability to relieve at once Mrs. Neale's "little 'uns" privations, he felt that somebody should be made to suffer for it. Mrs. Verloc rose, and went into the kitchen to "stop that nonsense." And she did it firmly but gently. She was well aware that directly Mrs. Neale received her money she went round the corner to drink ardent spirits in a mean and musty public house—the unavoidable station on the *via dolorosa* of her life. Mrs. Verloc's comment upon this practice had an unexpected profundity, as com-ing from a person disinclined to look under the surface of things. "Of course, what is she to do to keep up? If I were like Mrs. Neale I expect I wouldn't act any different."

In the afternoon of the same day, as Mr. Verloc, coming with a start out of the last of a long series of dozes before the parlor fire, declared his intention of going out for a walk, Winnie said from the shop:

"I wish you would take that boy out with you, Adolf."

For the third time that day Mr. Verloc was surprised. He stared stupidly at his wife. She continued in her steady manner. The boy, whenever he was not doing anything, moped in the house. It made her uneasy; it made her nervous, she con-fessed. And that from the calm Winnie sounded like exaggeration. But, in truth, Stevie moped in the striking fashion of an unhappy domestic animal. He would go up on the dark landing, to sit on the floor at the foot of the tall clock, with his knees drawn up and his head in his hands. To come upon his pallid face, with its big eyes gleaming in the dusk, was discomposing; to think of him up there was uncomfortable.

Mr. Verloc got used to the startling novelty of the idea. He was fond of his wife as a man should be—that is, generously. But a weighty objection presented itself to his mind, and he formulated it.

"He'll lose sight of me perhaps, and get lost in the street," he said.

Mrs. Verloc shook her head competently.

"He won't. You don't know him. That boy just worships you. But if you should miss him—"

Mrs. Verloc paused for a moment, but only for a moment.

"You just go on, and have your walk out. Don't worry. He'll be all right. He's sure to turn up safe here before very long."

This optimism procured for Mr. Verloc his fourth surprise of the day.

"Is he?" he grunted, doubtfully. But perhaps his brother-in-law was not such an idiot as he looked. His wife would know best. He turned away his heavy eyes, saying huskily: "Well, let him come along, then," and relapsed into the clutches of black care, that perhaps prefers to sit behind a horseman, but knows also how to tread close on the heels of people not sufficiently well off to keep horses—like Mr. Verloc, for instance.

Winnie, at the shop door, did not see this fatal attendant upon Mr. Verloc's walks. She watched the two figures down the squalid street, one tall and burly, the other slight and short, with a thin neck, and the peaked shoulders raised slightly under the large semi-transparent ears. The material of their overcoats was the same, their hats were black and round in shape. Inspired by the similarity of wearing apparel, Mrs. Verloc gave rein to her fancy.

"Might be father and son," she said to herself. She thought also that Mr. Verloc was as much of a father as poor Stevie ever had in his life. She was aware also that it was her work. And with peaceful pride she congratulated herself on a certain resolution she had taken a few years before. It had cost her some effort, and even a few tears.

She congratulated herself still more on observing in the course of days that Mr. Verloc seemed to be taking kindly to Stevie's companionship. Now, when ready to go out for his walk, Mr. Verloc called aloud to the boy, in the spirit, no doubt, in which a man invites the attendance of the household dog, though, of course, in a different manner. In the house Mr. Verloc could be detected staring curiously at Stevie a good deal. His own demeanor had changed. Taciturn still, he was not so listless. Mrs. Verloc thought that he was rather jumpy at times. It might have been regarded as an improvement. As to Stevie, he moped no longer at the foot of the clock, but muttered to himself in corners instead in a threatening tone. When asked "What is it you're saying, Stevie?" he merely opened his mouth, and squinted at his sister. At odd times he clenched his fists without apparent cause, and when discovered in solitude would be scowling at the wall, with the sheet of paper and the pencil given him for drawing circles lying blank and idle on the kitchen table. This was a change, but it was no improvement. Mrs. Verloc, including all these vagaries under the general definition of excitement, began to fear that Stevie was hearing more than was good for him of her husband's conversations with his friends. During his "walks" Mr. Verloc, of course, met and conversed with various persons. It could hardly be otherwise. His walks were an integral part of his outdoor activities, which his wife had never looked deeply into. Mrs. Verloc felt that the position was delicate, but she faced it with the same impenetrable calmness which impressed and even astonished the customers of the shop and made the other visitors keep their distance a little wonderingly. No! She feared that there were things not good for Stevie to hear of, she told her husband. It only excited the poor boy, because he could not help them being so. Nobody could.

It was in the shop. Mr. Verloc made no comment. He made no retort, and yet the retort was obvious. But he refrained from pointing out to his wife that the idea of making Stevie the companion of his walks was her own, and nobody else's. At that moment, to an impartial observer, Mr. Verloc would have appeared more than human in his magnanimity. He took down a small cardboard box from a shelf, peeped in to see that the contents were all right, and put it down gently on the counter. Not till that was done did he break the silence, to the effect that most likely Stevie would profit greatly by being sent out of town for a while; only he supposed his wife could not get on without him.

"Could not get on without him!" repeated Mrs. Verloc, slowly. "I couldn't get on without him if it were for his good! The idea! Of course, I can get on without him. But there's nowhere for him to go."

Mr. Verloc got out some brown paper and a ball of string; and meanwhile he muttered that Michaelis was living in a little cottage in the country. Michaelis wouldn't mind giving Stevie a room to sleep in. There were no visitors and no talk there. Michaelis was writing a book.

Mrs. Verloc declared her affection for Michaelis; mentioned her abhorrence of Karl Yundt, "nasty old man"; and of Ossipon she said nothing. As to Stevie, he could be no other than very pleased. Mr. Michaelis was always so nice and kind to him. He seemed to like the boy. Well, the boy was a good boy.

"You, too, seem to have grown quite fond of him of late," she added, after a pause, with her inflexible assurance.

Mr. Verloc, tying up the cardboard box into a parcel for the post, broke the string by an injudicious jerk, and muttered several swear words confidentially to himself. Then raising his tone to the usual husky mutter, he announced his willingness to take Stevie into the country himself, and leave him all safe with Michaelis.

He carried out this scheme on the very next day. Stevie offered no objection. He seemed rather eager, in a bewildered sort of way. He turned his candid gaze inquisitively to Mr. Verloc's heavy countenance at frequent intervals, especially when his sister was not looking at him. His expression was proud, apprehensive, and concentrated, like that of a small child entrusted for the first time with a box of matches and the permission to strike a light. But Mrs. Verloc, gratified by her brother's docility, recommended him not to dirty his clothes unduly in the country. At this Stevie gave his sister, guardian, and protector a look, which for the first time in his life seemed to lack the quality of perfect childlike trustfulness. It was haughtily gloomy. Mrs. Verloc smiled.

"Goodness me! You needn't be offended. You know you do get yourself very untidy when you get a chance, Stevie."

Mr. Verloc was already gone some way down the street.

Thus in consequence of her mother's heroic proceedings, and of her brother's absence on this villegiature, Mrs. Verloc found herself oftener than usual all alone not only in the shop, but in the house. For Mr. Verloc had to take his walks. She was alone longer than usual on the day of the attempted bomb outrage in Greenwich Park, because Mr. Verloc went out very early that morning and did not come back till nearly dusk. She did not mind being alone. She had no desire to go out. The weather was too bad, and the shop was cozier than the streets. Sitting behind the counter with some sewing, she did not raise her eyes from her work when Mr. Verloc entered in the aggressive clatter of the bell. She had recognized his step on the pavement outside.

She did not raise her eyes, but as Mr. Verloc, silent, and with his hat rammed down upon his forehead, made straight for the parlor door, she said, serenely:

"What a wretched day. You've been perhaps to see Stevie?"

"No! I haven't," said Mr. Verloc, softly, and slammed the glazed parlor door behind him with unexpected energy.

For some time Mrs. Verloc remained quiescent, with her work dropped in her lap, before she put it away under the counter and got up to light the gas. This done, she went into the parlor on her way to the kitchen. Mr. Verloc would want his tea presently. Confident of the power of her charms, Winnie did not expect from her husband in the daily intercourse of their married life a ceremonious amenity of address and courtliness of manner; vain and antiquated forms at best, probably never very exactly observed, discarded nowadays even in the highest spheres, and always foreign to the standards of her class. She did not look for courtesies from him. But he was a good husband, and she had a loyal respect for his rights.

Mrs. Verloc would have gone through the parlor and on to her domestic duties in the kitchen with the perfect serenity of a woman sure of the power of her charms. But a slight, very slight, and rapid rattling sound grew upon her hearing. Bizarre and incomprehensible, it arrested Mrs. Verloc's attention. Then as its character became plain to the ear she stopped short, amazed and concerned. Striking a match on the box she held in her hand, she turned on and lighted, above the parlor table, one of the two gas-burners, which being defective, first whistled as if astonished, and then went on purring comfortably like a cat.

Mr. Verloc, against his usual practice, had thrown off his overcoat. It was lying on the sofa. His hat, which he must also have thrown off, rested overturned under the edge of the sofa. He had dragged a chair in front of the fireplace, and his feet planted inside the fender, his head held between his hands, he was hanging low over the glowing grate. His teeth rattled with an ungovernable violence, causing his whole enormous back to tremble at the same rate. Mrs. Verloc was startled.

"You've been getting wet," she said.

"Not very," Mr. Verloc managed to falter out, in a profound shudder. By a great effort he suppressed the rattling of his teeth.

"I'll have you laid up on my hands," she said, with genuine uneasiness.

"I don't think so," remarked Mr. Verloc, snuffling huskily.

He had certainly contrived somehow to catch an abominable cold between seven in the morning and five in the afternoon. Mrs. Verloc looked at his bowed back.

"Where have you been today?" she asked.

"Nowhere," answered Mr. Verloc in a low, choked nasal tone. His attitude suggested aggrieved sulks or a severe headache. The unsufficiency and uncandidness of his answer became painfully apparent in the dead silence of the room. He snuffled apologetically, and added: "I've been to the bank."

Mrs. Verloc became attentive.

"You have!" she said, dispassionately. "What for?"

Mr. Verloc mumbled, with his nose over the grate, and with marked unwillingness: "Draw the money out!"

"What do you mean? All of it?"

"Yes. All of it."

Mrs. Verloc spread out with care the scanty tablecloth, got two knives and two forks out of the table drawer, and suddenly stopped in her methodical proceedings.

"What did you do that for?"

"May want it soon," snuffled vaguely Mr. Verloc, who was coming to the end of his calculated indiscretions.

"I don't know what you mean," remarked his wife in a tone perfectly casual, but standing stock still between the table and the cupboard.

"You know you can trust me," Mr. Verloc remarked to the grate, with hoarse feeling.

Mrs. Verloc turned slowly towards the cupboard, saying with deliberation:

"Oh, yes. I can trust you."

And she went on with her methodical proceedings. She laid two plates, got the bread, the butter, going to and fro quietly between the table and the cupboard in the peace and silence of her home. On the point of taking out the jam, she reflected practically: "He will be feeling hungry, having been away all day," and she returned to the cupboard once more to get the cold beef. She set it under the purring gas-jet, and with a passing glance at her motionless husband hugging the fire, she went (down two steps) into the kitchen. It was only when coming back, carving knife and fork in hand, that she spoke again.

"If I hadn't trusted you I wouldn't have married you."

Bowed under the overmantel, Mr. Verloc, holding his head in both hands, seemed to have gone to sleep. Winnie made the tea, and called out in an undertone:

"Adolf."

Mr. Verloc got up at once, and staggered a little before he sat down at the table. His wife, examining the sharp edge of the carving knife, placed it on the dish, and called his attention to the cold beef. He remained insensible to the suggestion, with his chin on his breast.

"You should feed your cold," Mrs. Verloc said, dogmatically.

He looked up, and shook his head. His eyes were bloodshot and his face red. His fingers had ruffled his hair into a dissipated untidiness. Altogether he had a disreputable aspect, expressive of the discomfort, the irritation, and the gloom following a heavy debauch. But Mr. Verloc was not a debauched man. In his conduct he was respectable. His appearance might have been the effect of a feverish cold. He drank three cups of tea, but abstained from food entirely. He recoiled from it with somber aversion when urged by Mrs. Verloc, who said at last:

"Aren't your feet wet? You had better put on your slippers. You aren't going out anymore this evening."

Mr. Verloc intimated by morose grunts and signs that his feet were not wet, and that anyhow he did not care. The proposal as to slippers was disregarded as beneath his notice. But the question of going out in the evening received an unexpected development. It was not of going out in the evening that Mr. Verloc was thinking. His thoughts embraced a vaster scheme. From moody and incomplete phrases it became apparent that Mr. Verloc had been considering the expediency of emigrating. It was not very clear whether he had in his mind France or California.

The utter unexpectedness, improbability, and inconceivableness of such an event robbed this vague declaration of all its effect. Mrs. Verloc, as placidly as if her husband had been threatening her with the end of the world, said:

"The idea!"

Mr. Verloc declared himself sick and tired of everything, and besides—She interrupted him.

"You've a bad cold."

It was indeed obvious that Mr. Verloc was not in his usual state, physically and even mentally. A somber irresolution held him silent for a while. Then he murmured a few ominous generalities on the theme of necessity.

"Will have to," repeated Winnie, sitting calmly back, with folded arms, opposite her husband. "I should like to know who's to make you. You ain't a slave. No one need be a slave in this country—and don't you make yourself one." She paused, and with invincible and steady candor: "The business isn't so bad," she went on. "You've a comfortable home."

She glanced all round the parlor, from the corner cupboard to the good fire in the grate. Ensconced cozily behind the shop of doubtful wares, with the mysteriously dim window, and its door suspiciously ajar in the obscure and narrow street, it was in all essentials of domestic propriety and domestic comfort a respectable home. Her devoted affection missed out of it her brother Stevie, now enjoying a damp villegiature in the Kentish lanes under the care of Mr. Michaelis. She missed him poignantly, with all the force of her protecting passion. This was the boy's home, too—the roof, the cupboard, the stoked grate. On this thought Mrs. Verloc rose, and walking to the other end of the table, said in the fullness of her heart:

"And you are not tired of me."

Mr. Verloc made no sound. Winnie leaned on his shoulder from behind, and pressed her lips to his forehead. Thus she lingered. Not a whisper reached them from the outside world. The sound of footsteps on the pavement died out in the discreet dimness of the shop. Only the gas jet above the table went on purring equably in the brooding silence of the parlor.

During the contact of that unexpected and lingering kiss Mr. Verloc, gripping with both hands the edges of his chair, preserved a hieratic immobility. When the pressure was removed he let go the chair, rose, and went to stand before the fireplace. He turned no longer his back to the room. With his features swollen and an air of being drugged, he followed his wife's movements with his eyes.

Mrs. Verloc went about serenely, clearing up the table. Her tranquil voice commented on the idea thrown out in a reasonable and domestic tone. It wouldn't stand examination. She condemned it from every point of view. But her only real concern was Stevie's welfare. He appeared to her thought in that connection as sufficiently "peculiar" not to be taken rashly abroad. And that was all. But talking round that vital point, she approached absolute vehemence in her delivery. Meanwhile, with brusk movements, she arrayed herself in an apron for the washing up of cups. And as if excited by the sound of her uncontradicted voice, she went so far as to say in a tone almost tart:

"If you go abroad you'll have to go without me."

"You know I wouldn't," said Mr. Verloc, huskily, and the unresonant voice of his private life trembled with an enigmatical emotion.

Already Mrs. Verloc was regretting her words. They had sounded more unkind than she meant them to be. They had also the unwisdom of unnecessary things.

In fact, she had not meant them at all. It was a sort of phrase that is suggested by the demon of perverse inspiration. But she knew a way to make it as if it had not been.

She turned her head over her shoulder and gave that man planted heavily in front of the fireplace a glance, half arch, half cruel, out of her large eyes—a glance of which the Winnie of the Belgravian mansion days would have been incapable, because of her respectability and her ignorance. But the man was her husband now, and she was no longer ignorant. She kept it on him for a whole second, with her grave face motionless like a mask, while she said playfully:

"You couldn't. You would miss me too much."

Mr. Verloc started forward.

"Exactly," he said in a louder tone, throwing his arms out and making a step towards her. Something wild and doubtful in his expression made it appear uncertain whether he meant to strangle or to embrace his wife. But Mrs. Verloc's attention was called away from that manifestation by the clatter of the shop-bell.

"Shop, Adolf. You go."

He stopped, his arms came down slowly.

"You go," repeated Mrs. Verloc. "I've got my apron on."

Mr. Verloc obeyed woodenly, stony-eyed, and like an automaton whose face had been painted red. And this resemblance to a mechanical figure went so far that he had an automaton's absurd air of being aware of the machinery inside of him.

He closed the parlor door, and Mrs. Verloc, moving briskly, carried the tray into the kitchen. She washed the cups and some other things before she stopped in her work to listen. No sound reached her. The customer was a long time in the shop. It was a customer, because if he had not been Mr. Verloc would have taken him inside. Undoing the strings of her apron with a jerk, she threw it on a chair, and walked back to the parlor slowly.

At that precise moment Mr. Verloc entered from the shop.

He had gone in red. He came out a strange papery white. His face, losing its drugged, feverish stupor, had in that short time acquired a bewildered and harassed expression. He walked straight to the sofa, and stood looking down at his overcoat lying there, as though he were afraid to touch it.

"What's the matter?" asked Mrs. Verloc in a subdued voice. Through the door left ajar she could see that the customer was not gone yet.

"I find I'll have to go out this evening," said Mr. Verloc. He did not attempt to pick up his outer garment.

Without a word Winnie made for the shop, and shutting the door after her, walked in behind the counter. She did not look overtly at the customer till she had established herself comfortably on the chair. But by that time she had noted that he was tall and thin, and wore his moustaches twisted up. In fact, he gave the sharp points a twist just then. His long, bony face rose out of a turned-up collar. He was a little splashed, a little wet. A dark man, with the ridge of the cheekbone well defined under the slightly hollow temple. A complete stranger. Not a customer, either.

Mrs. Verloc looked at him placidly

"You came over from the Continent?" she said after a time.

The long, thin stranger, without exactly looking at Mrs. Verloc, answered only by a faint and peculiar smile. Mrs. Verloc's steady, incurious gaze rested on him.

"You understand English, don't you?"

"Oh, yes. I understand English."

There was nothing foreign in his accent, except that he seemed in his slow enunciation to be taking pains with it. And Mrs. Verloc, in her varied experience, had come to the conclusion that some foreigners could speak better English than the natives. She said, looking at the door of the parlor fixedly:

"You don't think perhaps of staying in England for good?"

The stranger gave her again a silent smile. He had a kindly mouth and probing eyes. And he shook his head a little sadly, it seemed.

"My husband will see you through all right. Meantime, for a few days you couldn't do better than take lodgings with Mr. Guigliani. Continental Hotel it's called. Private. It's quiet. My husband will take you there."

"A good idea," said the thin, dark man, whose glance had hardened suddenly.

"You knew Mr. Verloc before—didn't you? Perhaps in France?"

"I have heard of him," admitted the visitor in his slow, painstaking tone, which yet had a certain curtness of intention.

There was a pause. Then he spoke again, in a far less elaborate manner.

"Your husband has not gone out to wait for me in the street by chance?"

"In the street!" repeated Mrs. Verloc, surprised. "He couldn't. There's no other door to the house."

For a moment she sat impassive, then left her seat to go and peep through the glazed door. Suddenly she opened it, and disappeared into the parlor.

Mr. Verloc had done no more than put on his overcoat. But why he should remain afterwards leaning over the table propped up on his two arms as though he were feeling giddy or sick, she could not understand. "Adolf," she called out half aloud; and when he had raised himself:

"Do you know that man?" she asked, rapidly.

"I've heard of him," whispered uneasily Mr. Verloc, darting a wild glance at the door.

Mrs. Verloc's fine, incurious eyes lighted up with a flash of abhorrence.

"One of Karl Yundt's friends—beastly old man."

"No! No!" protested Mr. Verloc, busy fishing for his hat. But when he got it from under the sofa he held it as if he did not know the use of a hat.

"Well—he's waiting for you," said Mrs. Verloc at last. "I say, Adolf, he ain't one of them Embassy people you have been bothered with of late?"

"Bothered with Embassy people," repeated Mr. Verloc, with a heavy start of surprise and fear. "Who's been talking to you of the Embassy people?"

"Yourself."

"I! I! Talked of the Embassy to you!"

Mr. Verloc seemed scared and bewildered beyond measure. His wife explained:

"You've been talking a little in your sleep of late, Adolf."

"What—what did I say? What do you know?"

"Nothing much. It seemed mostly nonsense. Enough to let me guess that something worried you."

Mr. Verloc rammed his hat on his head. A crimson flood of anger ran over his face.

"Nonsense—eh? The Embassy people! I would cut their hearts out one after another. But let them look out. I've got a tongue in my head."

He fumed, pacing up and down between the table and the sofa, his open overcoat catching against the angles. The red flood of anger ebbed out, and left his face all white, with quivering nostrils. Mrs. Verloc, for the purposes of practical existence, put down these appearances to the cold.

"Well," she said, "get rid of the man whoever he is, as soon as you can, and come back home to me. You want looking after for a day or two."

Mr. Verloc calmed down, and, with resolution imprinted on his pale face, had already opened the door, when his wife called him back in a whisper:

"Adolf! Adolf!" He came back, startled. "What about that money you drew out?" she asked. "You've got it in your pocket? Hadn't you better—"

Mr. Verloc gazed stupidly into the palm of his wife's extended hand for some time before he slapped his brow.

"Money! Yes! Yes! I didn't know what you meant."

He drew out of his breast pocket a new pigskin pocketbook. Mrs. Verloc received it without another word, and stood still till the bell, clattering after Mr. Verloc and Mr. Verloc's visitor, had quieted down. Only then she peeped in at the amount, drawing the notes out for the purpose. After this inspection she looked round thoughtfully, with an air of mistrust in the silence and solitude of the house. This abode of her married life appeared to her as lonely and unsafe as though it had been situated in the midst of a forest. No receptacle she could think of amongst the solid, heavy furniture seemed other but flimsy and particularly tempting to her conception of a housebreaker. It was an ideal conception, endowed with sublime faculties and a miraculous insight. The till was not to be thought of. It was the first spot a thief would make for. Mrs. Verloc, unfastening hastily a couple of hooks, slipped the pocketbook under the bodice of her dress. Having thus disposed of her husband's capital, she was rather glad to hear the clatter of the doorbell, announcing an arrival. Assuming the fixed, unabashed stare and the stony expression reserved for the casual customer, she walked in behind the counter.

A man standing in the middle of the shop was inspecting it with a swift, cool, all-round glance. His eyes ran over the walls, took in the ceiling, noted the floor— all in a moment. The points of a long fair moustache fell below the line of the jaw. He smiled the smile of an old if distant acquaintance, and Mrs. Verloc remembered having seen him before. Not a customer. She softened her "customer stare" to mere indifference, and faced him across the counter.

He approached, on his side, confidentially, but not too markedly so.

"Husband at home, Mrs. Verloc?" he asked in an easy, full tone.

"No. He's gone out."

"I am sorry for that. I've called to get from him a little private information."

This was the exact truth. Chief Inspector Heat had been all the way home and had even gone so far as to think of getting into his slippers, since practically he was, he told himself, chucked out of that case. He indulged in some scornful and in a few angry thoughts, and found the occupation so unsatisfactory that he resolved to seek relief out of doors. Nothing prevented him paying a friendly call on Mr. Verloc, casually as it were. It was in the character of a private citizen that walking out privately he made use of his customary conveyances. Their general direction was towards Mr. Verloc's home. Chief Inspector Heat respected his own private character so consistently that he took especial pains to avoid all the police constables on point and patrol duty in the vicinity of Brett Street. This precaution was much more necessary for a man of his standing than for an obscure Assistant Commissioner. Private Citizen Heat entered the street, maneuvering in a way which in a member of the criminal classes would have been stigmatized as slinking. The piece of cloth picked up in Greenwich was in his pocket. Not that he had the slightest intention of producing it in his private capacity. On the contrary, he wanted to know just what Mr. Verloc would be disposed to say voluntarily. He hoped Mr. Verloc's talk would be of a nature to incriminate Michaelis. It was a conscientiously professional hope in the main, but not without its moral value. For Chief Inspector Heat was a servant of justice. Finding Mr. Verloc from home, he felt disappointed.

"I would wait for him a little if I were sure he wouldn't be long," he said.

Mrs. Verloc volunteered no assurance of any kind.

"The information I need is quite private," he repeated. "You understand what I mean? I wonder if you could give me a notion where he's gone to?"

Mrs. Verloc shook her head.

"Can't say."

She turned away to range some boxes on the shelves behind the counter. Chief Inspector Heat looked at her thoughtfully for a time.

"I suppose you know who I am?" he said.

Mrs. Verloc glanced over her shoulder. Chief Inspector Heat was amazed at her coolness.

"Come! You know I am in the police," he said, sharply.

"I don't trouble my head much about it," Mrs. Verloc remarked, returning to the ranging of her boxes.

"My name is Heat. Chief Inspector Heat of the Special Crimes section."

Mrs. Verloc adjusted nicely in its place a small cardboard box, and turning round, faced him again, heavy-eyed, with idle hands hanging down. A silence reigned for a time.

"So your husband went out a quarter of an hour ago! And he didn't say when he would be back?"

"He didn't go out alone," Mrs. Verloc let fall negligently.

"A friend?"

Mrs. Verloc touched the back of her hair. It was in perfect order.

"A stranger who called."

"I see. What sort of man was that stranger? Would you mind telling me?"

Mrs. Verloc did not mind. And when Chief Inspector Heat heard of a man dark, thin, with a long face and turned-up moustaches, he gave signs of perturbation, and exclaimed:

"Dash me if I didn't think so! He hasn't lost any time."

He was intensely disgusted in the secrecy of his heart at the unofficial conduct of his immediate chief. But he was not quixotic. He lost all desire to await Mr. Verloc's return. What they had gone out for he did not know, but he imagined it possible that they would return together. The case is not followed properly, it's being tampered with, he thought, bitterly.

"I am afraid I haven't time to wait for your husband," he said.

Mrs. Verloc received this declaration listlessly. Her detachment had impressed Chief Inspector Heat all along. At this precise moment it whetted his curiosity. Chief Inspector Heat hung in the wind, swayed by his passions like the most private of citizens.

"I think," he said, looking at her steadily, "that you could give me a pretty good notion of what's going on if you liked."

Forcing her fine, inert eyes to return his gaze, Mrs. Verloc murmured:

"Going on! What *is* going on?"

"Why, the affair I came to talk about a little with your husband."

That day Mrs. Verloc had glanced at a morning paper as usual. But she had not stirred out of doors. The newsboys never invaded Brett Street. It was not a street for their business. And the echo of their cries, drifting along the populous thoroughfares, expired between the dirty brick walls without reaching the threshold of the shop. Her husband had not brought an evening paper home. At any rate she had not seen it. Mrs. Verloc knew nothing whatever of any affair. And she said so, with a genuine note of wonder in her quiet voice.

Chief Inspector Heat did not believe for a moment in so much ignorance. Curtly, without amiability, he stated the bare fact.

Mrs. Verloc turned away her eyes.

"I call it silly," she pronounced, slowly. She paused. "We ain't downtrodden slaves here."

The Chief Inspector waited watchfully. Nothing more came.

"And your husband didn't mention anything to you when he came home?"

Mrs. Verloc simply turned her face from right to left in sign of negation. A languid, baffling silence reigned in the shop. Chief Inspector Heat felt provoked beyond endurance.

"There was another small matter," he began in a detached tone, "which I wanted to speak to your husband about. There came into our hands a—a—what we believe is—a stolen overcoat."

Mrs. Verloc, with her mind specially aware of thieves that evening, touched lightly the bosom of her dress.

"We have lost no overcoat," she said, calmly.

"That's funny," continued Private Citizen Heat. "I see you keep a lot of marking ink here—"

He took up a small bottle, and looked at it against the gas jet in the middle of the shop.

"Purple—isn't it?" he remarked, setting it down again. "As I said, it's strange. Because the overcoat has got a label sewn on the inside with your address written in marking ink."

Mrs. Verloc leaned over the counter with a low exclamation.

"That's my brother's, then."

"Where's your brother? Can I see him?" asked the Chief Inspector, briskly. Mrs. Verloc leaned a little more over the counter.

"No. He isn't here. I wrote that label myself."

"Where's your brother now?"

"He's been away living with—a friend—in the country."

"The overcoat comes from the country. And what's the name of the friend?"

"Michaelis," confessed Mrs. Verloc in an awed whisper.

The Chief Inspector let out a whistle. His eyes snapped.

"Just so. Capital. And your brother now, what's he like—a sturdy, darkish chap—eh?"

"Oh, no," exclaimed Mrs. Verloc, fervently. "That must be the thief. Stevie's slight and fair."

"Good," said the Chief Inspector in an approving tone. And while Mrs. Verloc, wavering between alarm and wonder, stared at him, he sought for information. Why have the address sewn like this inside the coat? And he heard that the mangled remains he had inspected that morning with extreme repugnance were those of a youth, nervous, absentminded, peculiar, and also that the woman who was speaking to him had had the charge of that boy since he was a baby.

"Easily excitable?" he suggested.

"Oh, yes. He is. But how did he come to lose his coat—"

Chief Inspector Heat suddenly pulled out a pink newspaper he had bought less than half-an-hour ago. He was interested in horses. Forced by his calling into an attitude of doubt and suspicion towards his fellow citizens, Chief Inspector Heat relieved the instinct of credulity implanted in the human breast by putting unbounded faith in the sporting prophets of that particular evening publication. Dropping the extra special on to the counter, he plunged his hand again into his pocket, and pulling out the piece of cloth fate had presented him with out of a heap of things that seemed to have been collected in shambles and rag shops, he offered it to Mrs. Verloc for inspection.

"I suppose you recognize this?"

She took it mechanically in both her hands. Her eyes seemed to grow bigger as she looked.

"Yes," she whispered, then raised her head, and staggered backward a little.

"Whatever for is it torn out like this?"

The Chief Inspector snatched across the counter the cloth out of her hands, and she sat heavily on the chair. He thought: identification's perfect. And in that moment he had a glimpse into the whole amazing truth. Verloc was the "other man."

"Mrs. Verloc," he said, "it strikes me that you know more of this bomb affair than even you yourself are aware of."

Mrs. Verloc sat still, amazed, lost in boundless astonishment. What was the connection? And she became so rigid all over that she was not able to turn her head at the clatter of the bell, which caused the private investigator Heat to spin round on his heel. Mr. Verloc had shut the door, and for a moment the two men looked at each other.

Mr. Verloc, without looking at his wife, walked up to the Chief Inspector, who was relieved to see him return alone.

"You here!" muttered Mr. Verloc, heavily. "Who are you after?"

"No one," said Chief Inspector Heat in a low tone. "Look here, I would like a word or two with you."

Mr. Verloc, still pale, had brought an air of resolution with him. Still he didn't look at his wife. He said:

"Come in here, then." And he led the way into the parlor.

The door was hardly shut when Mrs. Verloc, jumping up from the chair, ran to it as if to fling it open, but instead of doing so fell on her knees, with her ear to the keyhole. The two men must have stopped directly they were through, because she heard plainly the Chief Inspector's voice, though she could not see his finger pressed against her husband's breast emphatically.

"You are the other man, Verloc. Two men were seen entering the park."

And the voice of Mr. Verloc said:

"Well, take me now. What's to prevent you? You have the right."

"Oh, no! I know too well who you have been giving yourself away to. He'll have to manage this little affair all by himself. But don't you make a mistake, it's I who found you out."

Then she heard only muttering. Inspector Heat must have been showing to Mr. Verloc the piece of Stevie's overcoat, because Stevie's sister, guardian, and protector heard her husband a little louder.

"I never noticed that she had hit upon that dodge."

Again for a time Mrs. Verloc heard nothing but murmurs, whose mysteriousness was less nightmarish to her brain than the horrible suggestions of shaped words. Then Chief Inspector Heat, on the other side of the door, raised his voice:

"You must have been mad."

And Mr. Verloc's voice answered, with a sort of gloomy fury:

"I have been mad for a month or more, but I am not mad now. It's all over. It shall all come out of my head, and hang the consequences."

There was a silence, and then Private Citizen Heat murmured:

"What's coming out?"

"Everything," exclaimed the voice of Mr. Verloc, and then sank very low.

After a while it rose again.

"You have known me for several years now, and you've found me useful, too. You know I was a straight man. Yes, straight."

This appeal to old acquaintance must have been extremely distasteful to the Chief Inspector.

His voice took on a warning note.

"Don't you trust so much to what you have been promised. If I were you I would clear out. I don't think we will run after you."

Mr. Verloc was heard to laugh a little.

"Oh, yes; you hope the others will get rid of me for you—don't you? No, no; you don't shake me off now. I have been a straight man to those people too long, and now everything must come out."

"Let it come out, then," the indifferent voice of Chief Inspector Heat assented. "But tell me now how did you get away?"

"I was making for Chesterfield Walk," Mrs. Verloc heard her husband's voice, "when I heard the bang. I started running then. Fog. I saw no one till I was past the end of George Street. Don't think I met anyone till then."

"So easy as that!" marveled the voice of Chief Inspector Heat. "The bang startled you, eh?"

"Yes; it came too soon," confessed the gloomy, husky voice of Mr. Verloc.

Mrs. Verloc pressed her ear to the keyhole; her lips were blue, her hands cold as ice, and her pale face, in which the two eyes seemed like two black holes, felt to her as if it were enveloped in flames.

On the other side of the door the voices sank very low. She caught words now and then, sometimes in her husband's voice, sometimes in the smooth tones of the Chief Inspector. She heard this last say:

"We believe he stumbled against the root of a tree?"

There was a husky, voluble murmur, which lasted for some time, and then the Chief Inspector, as if answering some inquiry, spoke emphatically:

"Of course. Blown to small bits: limbs, gravel, clothing, bones, splinters—all mixed up together. I tell you they had to fetch a shovel to gather him up with."

Mrs. Verloc sprang up suddenly from her crouching position, and stopping her ears, reeled to and fro between the counter and the shelves on the wall towards the chair. Her crazed eyes noted the sporting sheet left by the Chief Inspector, and as she knocked herself against the counter she snatched it up, fell into the chair, tore the optimistic, rosy sheet right across in trying to open it, then flung it on the floor. On the other side of the door, Chief Inspector Heat was saying to Mr. Verloc, the secret agent:

"So your defense will be practically a full confession?"

"It will. I am going to tell the whole story."

"You won't be believed as much as you fancy you will."

And the Chief Inspector remained thoughtful. The turn this affair was taking meant the disclosure of many things—the laying waste of fields of knowledge, which, cultivated by a capable man, had a distinct value for the individual and for the society. It was sorry, sorry meddling. It would leave Michaelis unscathed; it would drag to light the Professor's home industry; disorganize the whole system of supervision; make no end of a row in the papers, which, from that point of view, appeared to him by a sudden illumination as invariably written by fools for the reading of imbeciles. Mentally he agreed with the words Mr. Verloc let fall at last in answer to his last remark.

"Perhaps not. But it will upset many things. I have been a straight man, and I shall keep straight in this—"

"If they let you," said the Chief Inspector, cynically. "You will be preached to, no doubt, before they put you into the dock. And in the end you may yet get let in for a sentence that will surprise you. I wouldn't trust too much the gentleman who's been talking to you."

Mr. Verloc listened, frowning.

"My advice to you is to clear out while you may. I have no instructions. There are some of them," continued Chief Inspector Heat, laying a peculiar stress on the word "them," "who think you are already out of the world."

"Indeed!" Mr. Verloc was moved to say. Though since his return from Greenwich he had spent most of his time sitting in the taproom of an obscure little public house, he could hardly have hoped for such favorable news.

"That's the impression about you." The Chief Inspector nodded at him. "Vanish. Clear out."

"Where to?" snarled Mr. Verloc. He raised his head, and gazing at the closed door of the parlor, muttered feelingly: "I only wish you would take me away tonight. I would go quietly."

"I daresay," assented sardonically the Chief Inspector, following the direction of his glance.

The brow of Mr. Verloc broke into slight moisture. He lowered his husky voice confidentially before the unmoved Chief Inspector.

"The lad was half-witted, irresponsible. Any court would have seen that at once. Only fit for the asylum. And that was the worst that would've happened to him if—"

The Chief Inspector, his hand on the door handle, whispered into Mr. Verloc's face:

"He may've been half-witted, but you must have been crazy. What drove you off your head like this?"

Mr. Verloc, thinking of Mr. Vladimir, did not hesitate in the choice of words.

"A Hyperborean swine," he hissed, forcibly. "A what you might call a—a gentleman."

The Chief Inspector, steady-eyed, nodded briefly his comprehension, and opened the door. Mrs. Verloc, behind the counter, might have heard but did not see his departure, pursued by the aggressive clatter of the bell. She sat at her post of duty behind the counter. She sat rigidly erect in the chair with two dirty pink pieces of paper lying spread out at her feet. The palms of her hands were pressed convulsively to her face, with the tips of the fingers contracted against the forehead, as though the skin had been a mask which she was ready to tear off violently. The perfect immobility of her pose expressed the agitation of rage and despair, all the potential violence of tragic passions, better than any shallow display of shrieks, with the beating of a distracted head against the walls, could have done. Chief Inspector Heat, crossing the shop at his busy, swinging pace, gave her only a cursory glance. And when the cracked bell ceased to tremble on its curved ribbon of steel nothing stirred near Mrs. Verloc, as if her attitude had the locking power of a spell. Even the butterfly-shaped gas flames posed on the ends of the suspended T-bracket burned without a quiver. In that shop of shady wares fitted with deal shelves painted a dull brown, which seemed to devour the sheen of the light, the gold circlet of the wedding ring on Mrs. Verloc's left hand glittered exceedingly with the untarnished glory of a piece from some splendid treasure of jewels, dropped in a dustbin.

❧ 10 ❧

The Assistant Commissioner, driven rapidly in a hansom from the neighborhood of Soho in the direction of Westminster, got out at the very center of the Empire on which the sun never sets. Some stalwart constables, who did not seem particularly impressed by the duty of watching the august spot, saluted him. Penetrating through a portal by no means lofty into the precincts of the House which is *the* House, *par excellence,* in the minds of many millions of men, he was met at last by the volatile and revolutionary Toodles.

That neat and nice young man concealed his astonishment at the early appearance of the Assistant Commissioner, whom he had been told to look out for some time about midnight. His turning up so early he concluded to be the sign that things, whatever they were, had gone wrong. With an extremely ready sympathy, which in nice youngsters goes often with a joyous temperament, he felt sorry for the great Presence he called "The Chief," and also for the Assistant Commissioner, whose face appeared to him more ominously wooden than ever before, and quite wonderfully long. "What a queer, foreign-looking chap he is," he thought to himself, smiling from a distance with friendly buoyancy. And directly they came together he began to talk with the kind intention of burying the awkwardness of failure under a heap of words. It looked as if the great assault threatened for that night were going to fizzle out. An inferior henchman of "that brute Cheeseman" was up boring mercilessly a very thin House with some shamelessly cooked statistics. He, Toodles, hoped he would bore them into a count out every minute. But then he might be only marking time to let that guzzling Cheeseman dine at his leisure. Anyway, the Chief could not be persuaded to go home.

"He will see you at once, I think. He's sitting all alone in his room thinking of all the fishes of the sea," concluded Toodles, airily "Come along."

Notwithstanding the kindness of his disposition, the young private secretary (unpaid) was accessible to the common failings of humanity. He did not wish to harrow the feelings of the Assistant Commissioner, who looked to him uncommonly like a man who has made a mess of his job. But his curiosity was too strong to be restrained by mere compassion. He could not help, as they went along, to throw over his shoulder lightly:

"And your sprat?"

"Got him," answered the Assistant Commissioner with a concision which did not mean to be repellent in the least.

"Good. You've no idea how these great men dislike to be disappointed in small things."

After this profound observation the experienced Toodles seemed to reflect. At any rate he said nothing for quite two seconds. Then:

"I'm glad. But—I say—is it really such a very small thing as you make it out?"

"Do you know what may be done with a sprat?" the Assistant Commissioner asked in his turn.

"He's sometimes put into a sardine box," chuckled Toodles, whose erudition on the subject of the fishing industry was fresh and, in comparison with his ignorance of all other industrial matters, immense. "There are sardine canneries on the Spanish coast which—"

The Assistant Commissioner interrupted the apprentice statesman.

"Yes. Yes. But a sprat is also thrown away sometimes in order to catch a whale."

"A whale. Phew!" exclaimed Toodles, with bated breath. "You're after a whale, then?"

"Not exactly. What I am after is more like a dogfish. You don't know perhaps what a dogfish is like."

"Yes; I do. We're buried in special books up to our necks—whole shelves full of them—with plates. . . . It's a noxious, rascally-looking, altogether detestable beast, with a sort of smooth face and moustaches."

"Described to a T," commended the Assistant Commissioner. "Only mine is clean-shaven altogether. You've seen him. It's a witty fish."

"I have seen him!" said Toodles, incredulously. "I can't conceive where I could have seen him."

"At the Explorers', I should say," dropped the Assistant Commissioner, calmly. At the name of that extremely exclusive club Toodles looked scared, and stopped short.

"Nonsense," he protested, but in an awestruck tone. "What do you mean? A member?"

"Honorary," muttered the Assistant Commissioner through his teeth.

"Heavens!"

Toodles looked so thunderstruck that the Assistant Commissioner smiled faintly.

"That's between ourselves strictly," he said.

"That's the beastliest thing I've ever heard in my life," declared Toodles, feebly, as if astonishment had robbed him of all his buoyant strength in a second.

The Assistant Commissioner gave him an unsmiling glance. Till they came to the door of the great man's room, Toodles preserved a scandalized and solemn silence, as though he were offended with the Assistant Commissioner for exposing such an unsavory and disturbing fact. It revolutionized his idea of the Explorers' Club's extreme selectness, of its social purity. Toodles was revolutionary only in politics; his social beliefs and personal feelings he wished to preserve unchanged through all the years allotted to him on this earth which, upon the whole, he believed to be a nice place to live on.

He stood aside.

"Go in without knocking," he said.

Shades of green silk fitted low over all the lights imparted to the room something of a forest's deep gloom. The haughty eyes were physically the great man's weak point. This point was wrapped up in secrecy. When an opportunity offered, he rested them conscientiously. The Assistant Commissioner entering saw at first only a big pale hand supporting a big head, and concealing the upper part of a big pale face. An open dispatch-box stood on the writing table near a few oblong sheets of paper and a scattered handful of quill pens. There was absolutely nothing else on the large flat surface except a little bronze statuette draped in a toga, mysteriously watchful in its shadowy immobility. The Assistant Commissioner, invited to take a chair, sat down. In the dim light, the salient points of his personality, the long face, the black hair, his lankness, made him look more foreign than ever.

The great man manifested no surprise, no eagerness, no sentiment whatever. The attitude in which he rested his menaced eyes was profoundly meditative. He did not alter it the least bit. But his tone was not dreamy.

"Well! What is it that you've found out already? You came upon something unexpected on the first step."

"Not exactly unexpected, Sir Ethelred. What I mainly came upon was a psychological state."

The Great Presence made a slight movement.

"You must be lucid, please."

"Yes, Sir Ethelred. You know no doubt that most criminals at some time or other feel an irresistible need of confessing—of making a clean breast of it to somebody to anybody. And they do it often to the police. In that Verloc whom Heat wished so much to screen I've found a man in that particular psychological state. The man, figuratively speaking, flung himself on my breast. It was enough on my part to whisper to him who I was and to add "I know that you are at the bottom of this affair." It must have seemed miraculous to him that we should know already, but he took it all in the stride. The wonderfulness of it never checked him for a moment. There remained for me only to put to him the two questions: Who put you up to it? and Who was the man who did it? He answered the first with remarkable emphasis. As to the second question, I gather that the fellow with the bomb was his brother-in-law—quite a lad—a weak-minded creature. . . . It is rather a curious affair—too long perhaps to state fully just now."

"What then have you learned?" asked the great man.

"First, I've learned that the ex-convict Michaelis had nothing to do with it, though indeed the lad had been living with him temporarily in the country up to eight o'clock this morning. It is more than likely that Michaelis knows nothing of it to this moment."

"You are positive as to that?" asked the great man.

"Quite certain, Sir Ethelred. This fellow Verloc went there this morning, and took away the lad on the pretense of going out for a walk in the lanes. As it was not the first time that he did this, Michaelis could not have the slightest suspicion of anything unusual. For the rest, Sir Ethelred, the indignation of this man Verloc had left nothing in doubt—nothing whatever. He had been driven out of his mind almost by an extraordinary performance, which for you or me it would be difficult to take as seriously meant, but which produced a great impression obviously on him."

The Assistant Commissioner then imparted briefly to the great man, who sat still, resting his eyes under the screen of his hand, Mr. Verloc's appreciation of Mr. Vladimir's proceedings and character. The Assistant Commissioner did not seem to refuse it a certain amount of competency. But the great personage remarked: "All this seems very fantastic."

"Doesn't it? One would think a ferocious joke. But our man took it seriously, it appears. He felt himself threatened. Formerly, you know, he was in direct communication with old Stott-Wartenheim himself, and had come to regard his services as indispensable. It was an extremely rude awakening. I imagine that he lost his head. He became angry and frightened. Upon my word, my impression is that he thought these Embassy people quite capable not only to throw him out but to give him away, too, in some manner or other—"

"How long were you with him?" interrupted the Presence from behind his big hand.

"Some forty minutes, Sir Ethelred, in a house of bad repute called Continental Hotel, closeted in a room which by-the-by I took for the night. I found him under the influence of that reaction which follows the effort of crime. The man cannot be defined as a hardened criminal. It is obvious that he did not plan the death of that wretched lad—his brother-in-law. That was a shock to him—I could see that. Perhaps he is a man of strong sensibilities. Perhaps he was even fond of the lad— who knows? He might have hoped that the fellow would get clear away; in which case it would have been almost impossible to bring this thing home to anyone. At any rate, he risked consciously nothing more but arrest for him."

The Assistant Commissioner paused in his speculations to reflect for a moment.

"Though how, in that last case, he could hope to have his own share in the business concealed is more than I can tell," he continued, in his ignorance of poor Stevie's devotion to Mr. Verloc (who was *good*), and of his truly peculiar dumbness, which in the old affair of fireworks on the stairs had for many years resisted entreaties, coaxing, anger, and other means of investigation used by his beloved sister. For Stevie was loyal. . . . "No, I can't imagine. It's possible that he never thought of that at all. It sounds an extravagant way of putting it, Sir Ethelred, but his state of dismay suggested to me an impulsive man who, after committing suicide with the notion that it would end all his troubles, had discovered that it did nothing of the kind."

The Assistant Commissioner gave this definition in an apologetic voice. But in truth there is a sort of lucidity proper to extravagant language, and the great man was not offended. A slight jerky movement of the big body half lost in the gloom of the green silk shades, of the big head leaning on the big hand, accompanied an intermittent stifled but powerful sound. The great man had laughed.

"What have you done with him?"

The Assistant Commissioner answered very readily:

"As he seemed very anxious to get back to his wife in the shop I let him go, Sir Ethelred."

"You did? But the fellow will disappear."

"Pardon me. I don't think so. Where could he go to? Moreover, you must remember that he has got to think of the danger from his comrades, too. He's there at his post. How could he explain leaving it? But even if there were no obstacles to his freedom of action he would do nothing. At present he hasn't enough moral energy to take a resolution of any sort. Permit me also to point out that if I had detained him we would have been committed to a course of action on which I wished to know your precise intentions first."

The great personage rose heavily, an imposing, shadowy form in the greenish gloom of the room.

"I'll see the Attorney General tonight, and will send for you tomorrow morning. Is there anything more you'd wish to tell me now?"

The Assistant Commissioner had stood up also, slender and flexible.

"I think not, Sir Ethelred, unless I were to enter into details which—"

"No. No details, please."

The great shadowy form seemed to shrink away as if in physical dread of details; then came forward, expanded, enormous, and weighty, offering a large hand. "And you say that this man has got a wife?"

"Yes, Sir Ethelred," said the Assistant Commissioner, pressing deferentially the extended hand. "A genuine wife and a genuinely, respectably, marital relation. He told me that after his interview at the Embassy he would have thrown everything up, would have tried to sell his shop, and leave the country, only he felt certain that his wife would not even hear of going abroad. Nothing could be more characteristic of the respectable bond than that," went on, with a touch of grimness, the Assistant Commissioner, whose own wife, too, had refused to hear of going abroad. "Yes, a genuine wife. And the victim was a genuine brother-in-law. From a certain point of view we are here in the presence of a domestic drama."

The Assistant Commissioner laughed a little; but the great man's thoughts seemed to have wandered far away, perhaps to the questions of his country's domestic policy, the battleground of his crusading valor against the paynim Cheeseman. The Assistant Commissioner withdrew quietly, unnoticed, as if already forgotten.

He had his own crusading instincts. This affair, which, in one way or another, disgusted Chief Inspector Heat, seemed to him a providentially given starting point for a crusade. He had it much at heart to begin. He walked slowly home, meditating that enterprise on the way, and thinking over Mr. Verloc's psychology in a composite mood of repugnance and satisfaction. He walked all the way home. Finding the drawing room dark, he went upstairs, and spent some time between the bedroom and the dressing room, changing his clothes, going to and fro with the air of a thoughtful somnambulist. But he shook it off before going out again to join his wife at the house of the great lady patroness of Michaelis.

He knew he would be welcome there. On entering the smaller of the two drawing rooms he saw his wife in a small group near the piano. A youngish composer in pass of becoming famous was discoursing from a music stool to two thick men whose backs looked old, and three slender women whose backs looked young. Behind the screen the great lady had only two persons with her: a man and a woman, who sat side by side on armchairs at the foot of her couch. She extended her hand to the Assistant Commissioner.

"I never hoped to see you here tonight. Annie told me—"

"Yes. I had no idea myself that my work would be over so soon."

The Assistant Commissioner added in a low tone: "I am glad to tell you that Michaelis is altogether clear of this—"

The patroness of the ex-convict received this assurance indignantly.

"Why? Were your people stupid enough to connect him with—"

"Not stupid," interrupted the Assistant Commissioner, contradicting deferentially. "Clever enough—quite clever enough for that."

A silence fell. The man at the foot of the couch had stopped speaking to the lady, and looked on with a faint smile.

"I don't know whether you ever met before," said the great lady.

Mr. Vladimir and the Assistant Commissioner, introduced, acknowledged each other's existence with punctilious and guarded courtesy.

"He's been frightening me," declared suddenly the lady who sat by the side of Mr. Vladimir, with an inclination of the head towards that gentleman. The Assistant Commissioner knew the lady.

"You do not look frightened," he pronounced, after surveying her conscientiously with his tired and equable gaze. He was thinking meantime to himself that in this house one met everybody sooner or later. Mr. Vladimir's rosy countenance was wreathed in smiles, because he was witty, but his eyes remained serious, like the eyes of convinced man.

"Well, he tried to at least," amended the lady.

"Force of habit perhaps," said the Assistant Commissioner, moved by an irresistible inspiration.

"He has been threatening society with all sorts of horrors," continued the lady, whose enunciation was caressing and slow, "apropos of this explosion in Greenwich Park. It appears we all ought to quake in our shoes at what's coming if those people are not suppressed all over the world. I had no idea this was such a grave affair."

Mr. Vladimir, affecting not to listen, leaned towards the couch, talking amiably in subdued tones, but he heard the Assistant Commissioner say:

"I've no doubt that Mr. Vladimir has a very precise notion of the true importance of this affair."

Mr. Vladimir asked himself what that confounded and intrusive policeman was driving at. Descended from generations victimized by the instruments of an arbitrary power, he was racially, nationally, and individually afraid of the police. It was an inherited weakness, altogether independent of his judgment, of his reason, of his experience. He was born to it. But that sentiment, which resembled the irrational horror some people have of cats, did not stand in the way of his immense contempt for the English police. He finished the sentence addressed to the great lady, and turned slightly in his chair.

"You mean that we have a great experience of these people. Yes; indeed, we suffer greatly from their activity, while you"—Mr. Vladimir hesitated for a moment, in smiling perplexity—"While you suffer their presence gladly in your midst," he finished, displaying a dimple in each clean-shaven cheek. Then he added more gravely: "I may even say—because you do."

When Mr. Vladimir ceased speaking the Assistant Commissioner lowered his glance, and the conversation dropped. Almost immediately afterwards Mr. Vladimir took leave. Directly his back was turned on the couch the Assistant Commissioner rose, too.

"I thought you were going to stay and take Annie home," said the lady patroness of Michaelis.

"I find that I've yet a little work to do tonight."

"In connection—?"

"Well, yes—in a way."

"Tell me, what is it really—this horror?"

"It's difficult to say what it is, but it may yet be a *cause célèbre*," said the Assistant Commissioner.

He left the drawing room hurriedly, and found Mr. Vladimir still in the hall, wrapping up his throat carefully in a large silk handkerchief. Behind him a footman waited, holding his overcoat. Another stood ready to open the door. The Assistant Commissioner was duly helped into his coat, and let out at once. After descending the front steps he stopped, as if to consider the way he should take. On seeing this through the door held open, Mr. Vladimir lingered in the hall to get out a cigar and asked for a light. It was furnished to him by an elderly man out of livery with an air of calm solicitude. But the match went out; the footman then closed the door, and Mr. Vladimir lighted his large Havana with leisurely care. When at last he got out of the house, he saw with disgust the "confounded policeman" still standing on the pavement.

"Can he be waiting for me?" thought Mr. Vladimir, looking up and down for some signs of a hansom. He saw none. A couple of carriages waited by the curbstone, their lamps blazing steadily, the horses standing perfectly still, as if carved in stone, the coachmen sitting motionless under the big fur capes, without as much as a quiver stirring the white thongs of their big whips. Mr. Vladimir walked on, and the "confounded policeman" fell into step at his elbow. He said nothing. At the end of the fourth stride Mr. Vladimir felt infuriated and uneasy. This could not last.

"Rotten weather," he growled, savagely.

"Mild," said the Assistant Commissioner without passion. He remained silent for a little while. "We've got hold of a man called Verloc," he announced, casually.

Mr. Vladimir did not stumble, did not stagger back, did not change his stride. But he could not prevent himself from exclaiming: "What?" The Assistant

Commissioner did not repeat his statement. "You know him," he went on in the same tone.

Mr. Vladimir stopped, and became guttural.

"What makes you say that?"

"I don't. It's Verloc who says that."

"A lying dog of some sort," said Mr. Vladimir in somewhat Oriental phraseology. But in his heart he was almost awed by the miraculous cleverness of the English police. The change of his opinion on the subject was so violent that it made him for a moment feel slightly sick. He threw away his cigar, and moved on.

"What pleased me most in this affair," the Assistant Commissioner went on, talking slowly, "is that it makes such an excellent starting point for a piece of work which I've felt must be taken in hand—that is, the clearing out of this country of all the foreign political spies, police, and that sort of—of—dogs. In my opinion they are a ghastly nuisance; also an element of danger. But we can't very well seek them out individually. The only way is to make their employment unpleasant to their employers. The thing's becoming indecent. And dangerous, too, for us, here."

Mr. Vladimir stopped again for a moment.

"What do you mean?"

"The prosecution of this Verloc will demonstrate to the public both the danger and the indecency."

"Nobody will believe what a man of that sort says," said Mr. Vladimir, contemptuously.

"The wealth and precision of detail will carry conviction to the great mass of the public," advanced the Assistant Commissioner gently.

"So that is seriously what you mean to do."

"We've got the man; we have no choice."

"You will be only feeding up the lying spirit of these revolutionary scoundrels," Mr. Vladimir protested. "What do you want to make a scandal for?—from morality —or what?"

Mr. Vladimir's anxiety was obvious. The Assistant Commissioner, having ascertained in this way that there must be some truth in the summary statements of Mr. Verloc, said indifferently:

"There's a practical side, too. We have really enough to do to look after the genuine article. You can't say we are not effective. But we don't intend to let ourselves be bothered by shams under any pretext whatever."

Mr. Vladimir's tone became lofty.

"For my part, I can't share your view. It is selfish. My sentiments for my own country cannot be doubted; but I've always felt that we ought to be good Europeans besides—I mean governments and men."

"Yes," said the Assistant Commissioner simply. "Only you look at Europe from its other end. But," he went on in a good-natured tone, "the foreign governments cannot complain of the inefficiency of our police. Look at this outrage; a case specially difficult to trace inasmuch as it was a sham. In less than twelve hours we have established the identity of a man literally blown to shreds, have found the organizer of the attempt, and have had a glimpse of the inciter behind him. And we could have gone further; only we stopped at the limits of our territory."

"So this instructive crime was planned abroad," Mr. Vladimir said, quickly. "You admit it was planned abroad?"

"Theoretically. Theoretically only, on foreign territory; abroad only by a fiction," said the Assistant Commissioner, alluding to the character of Embassies which are supposed to be part and parcel of the country to which they belong. "But that's a detail. I talked to you of this business because it's your government that grumbles most at our police. You see that we are not so bad. I wanted particularly to tell you of our success."

"I'm sure I'm very grateful," muttered Mr. Vladimir through his teeth.

"We can put our finger on every anarchist here," went on the Assistant Commissioner, as though he were quoting Chief Inspector Heat. "All that's wanted now is to do away with the agent provocateur to make everything safe."

Mr. Vladimir held up his hand to a passing hansom.

"You're not going in here," remarked the Assistant Commissioner, looking at a building of noble proportions and hospitable aspect, with the light of a great hall falling through its glass doors on a broad flight of steps.

But Mr. Vladimir, sitting, stony-eyed, inside the hansom, drove off without a word.

The Assistant Commissioner himself did not turn into the noble building. It was the Explorers' Club. The thought passed through his mind that Mr. Vladimir, honorary member, would not be seen very often there in the future. He looked at his watch. It was only half-past ten. He had had a very full evening.

❧ 11 ❧

After Chief Inspector Heat had left him Mr. Verloc moved about the parlor. From time to time he eyed his wife through the open door. "She knows all about it now," he thought to himself with commiseration for her sorrow and with some satisfaction as regarded himself. Mr. Verloc's soul, if lacking greatness perhaps, was capable of tender sentiments. The prospect of having to break the news to her had put him into a fever. Chief Inspector Heat had relieved him of the task. That was good as far as it went. It remained for him now to face her grief.

Mr. Verloc had never expected to have to face it on account of death, whose catastrophic character cannot be argued away by sophisticated reasoning or persuasive eloquence. Mr. Verloc never meant Stevie to perish with such abrupt violence. He did not mean him to perish at all. Stevie dead was a much greater nuisance than ever he had been when alive. Mr. Verloc had augured a favorable issue to his enterprise, basing himself not on Stevie's intelligence, which sometimes plays queer tricks with a man, but on the blind docility and on the blind devotion of the boy. Though not much of a psychologist, Mr. Verloc had gauged the depth of Stevie's fanaticism. He dared cherish the hope of Stevie walking away from the walls of the Observatory as he had been instructed to do, taking the way shown to him several times previously, and rejoining his brother-in-law, the wise and good Mr. Verloc, outside the precincts of the park. Fifteen minutes ought to have been enough for the veriest fool to deposit the engine and walk away. And the Professor had guaranteed more than fifteen minutes. But Stevie had stumbled within five minutes of being left to himself. And Mr. Verloc was shaken morally to pieces. He had foreseen everything but that. He had foreseen Stevie distracted and lost— sought for—found in some police station or provincial workhouse in the end. He had foreseen Stevie arrested, and was not afraid, because Mr. Verloc had a great opinion of Stevie's loyalty, which had been carefully indoctrinated with the necessity of silence in the course of many walks. Like a peripatetic philosopher, Mr. Verloc, strolling along the streets of London, had modified Stevie's view of the police by conversations full of subtle reasonings. Never had a sage a more attentive and admiring disciple. The submission and worship were so apparent that Mr. Verloc had come to feel something like a liking for the boy. In any case, he had not

449

foreseen the swift bringing home of his connection. That his wife should hit upon the precaution of sewing the boy's address inside his overcoat was the last thing Mr. Verloc would have thought of. One can't think of everything. That was what she meant when she said that he need not worry if he lost Stevie during their walks. She had assured him that the boy would turn up all right. Well, he had turned up with a vengeance!

"Well, well," muttered Mr. Verloc in his wonder. What did she mean by it? Spare him the trouble of keeping an anxious eye on Stevie? Most likely she had meant well. Only she ought to have told him of the precaution she had taken.

Mr. Verloc walked behind the counter of the shop. His intention was not to overwhelm his wife with bitter reproaches. Mr. Verloc felt no bitterness. The unexpected march of events had converted him to the doctrine of fatalism. Nothing could be helped now. He said:

"I didn't mean any harm to come to the boy."

Mrs. Verloc shuddered at the sound of her husband's voice. She did not uncover her face. The trusted secret agent of the late Baron Stott-Wartenheim looked at her for a time with a heavy, persistent, undiscerning glance. The torn evening paper was lying at her feet. It could not have told her much. Mr. Verloc felt the need of talking to his wife.

"It's that damned Heat—eh?" he said. "He upset you. He's a brute, blurting it out like this to a woman. I made myself ill thinking how to break it to you. I sat for hours in the little parlor of Cheshire Cheese thinking over the best way. You understand I never meant any harm to come to that boy."

Mr. Verloc, the Secret Agent, was speaking the truth. It was his marital affection that had received the greatest shock from the premature explosion. He added:

"I didn't feel particularly gay sitting there and thinking of you."

He observed another slight shudder of his wife, which affected his sensibility. As she persisted in hiding her face in her hands, he thought he had better leave her alone for a while. On this delicate impulse Mr. Verloc withdrew into the parlor again, where the gas-jet purred like a contented cat. Mrs. Verloc's wifely forethought had left the cold beef on the table with carving knife and fork and half a loaf of bread for Mr. Verloc's supper. He noticed all these things now for the first time, and cutting himself a piece of bread and meat, began to eat.

His appetite did not proceed from callousness. Mr. Verloc had not eaten any breakfast that day. He had left his home fasting. Not being an energetic man, he found his resolution in nervous excitement, which seemed to hold him mainly by the throat. He could not have swallowed anything solid. Michaelis' cottage was as destitute of provisions as the cell of a prisoner. The ticket-of-leave apostle lived on a little milk and crusts of stale bread. Moreover, when Mr. Verloc arrived he had already gone upstairs after his frugal meal. Absorbed in the toil and delight of literary composition, he had not even answered Mr. Verloc's shout up the little staircase.

"I am taking this young fellow home for a day or two."

And, in truth, Mr. Verloc did not wait for an answer, but had marched out of the cottage at once, followed by the obedient Stevie.

Now that all action was over and his fate taken out of his hands with unexpected swiftness, Mr. Verloc felt terribly empty physically. He carved the meat, cut the bread, and devoured his supper standing by the table, and now and then casting a glance towards his wife. Her prolonged immobility disturbed the comfort of his refection. He walked again into the shop, and came up very close to her. This sorrow with a veiled face made Mr. Verloc uneasy. He expected, of course, his wife to be very much upset, but he wanted her to pull herself together. He needed all her assistance and all her loyalty in these new conjunctures his fatalism had already accepted.

"Can't be helped," he said in a tone of gloomy sympathy. "Come, Winnie, we've got to think of tomorrow. You'll want all your wits about you after I am taken away."

He paused. Mrs. Verloc's breast heaved convulsively. This was not reassuring to Mr. Verloc, in whose view the newly created situation required from the two people most concerned in it calmness, decision, and other qualities incompatible with the mental disorder of passionate sorrow. Mr. Verloc was a humane man; he had come home prepared to allow every latitude to his wife's affection for her brother. Only he did not understand either the nature or the whole extent of that sentiment. And in this he was excusable, since it was impossible for him to understand it without ceasing to be himself. He was startled and disappointed, and his speech conveyed it by a certain roughness of tone.

"You might look at a fellow," he observed after waiting a while.

As if forced through the hands covering Mrs. Verloc's face the answer came, deadened, almost pitiful.

"I don't want to look at you as long as I live."

"Eh? What!" Mr. Verloc was merely startled by the superficial and literal meaning of this declaration. It was obviously unreasonable, the mere cry of exaggerated grief. He threw over it the mantle of his marital indulgence. The mind of Mr. Verloc lacked profundity. Under the mistaken impression that the value of individuals consists in what they are in themselves, he could not possibly comprehend the value of Stevie in the eyes of Mrs. Verloc. She was taking it confoundedly hard, he thought to himself. It was all the fault of that damned Heat. What did he want to upset the woman for? But she mustn't be allowed, for her own good, to carry on so till she got quite beside herself.

"Look here! You can't sit like this in the shop," he said with affected severity, in which there was some real annoyance; for urgent practical matters must be talked over if they had to sit up all night. "Somebody might come in at any minute," he added, and waited again. No effect was produced, and the idea of the finality of death occurred to Mr. Verloc during the pause. He changed his tone. "Come. This won't bring him back," he said, gently, feeling ready to take her in his arms and press her to his breast, where impatience and compassion dwelt side by side. But except for a short shudder Mrs. Verloc remained apparently unaffected by the force of that terrible truism. It was Mr. Verloc himself who was moved. He was moved in his simplicity to urge moderation by asserting the claims of his own personality.

"Do be reasonable, Winnie. What would it have been if you had lost me?"

He had vaguely expected to hear her cry out. But she did not budge. She leaned back a little, quieted down to a complete, unreadable stillness. Mr. Verloc's heart began to beat faster with exasperation and something resembling alarm. He laid his hand on her shoulder, saying:

"Don't be a fool, Winnie."

She gave no sign. It was impossible to talk to any purpose with a woman whose face one cannot see. Mr. Verloc caught hold of his wife's wrists. But her hands seemed glued fast. She swayed forward bodily to his tug, and nearly went off the chair. Startled to feel her so helplessly limp, he was trying to put her back on the chair when she stiffened suddenly all over, tore herself out of his hands, ran out of the shop, across the parlor, and into the kitchen. This was very swift. He had just a glimpse of her face and that much of her eyes that he knew she had not looked at him.

It all had the appearance of a struggle for the possession of a chair, because Mr. Verloc instantly took his wife's place in it. Mr. Verloc did not cover his face with his hands, but a somber thoughtfulness veiled his features. A term of imprisonment could not be avoided. He did not wish now to avoid it. A prison was a place as safe from certain unlawful vengeances as the grave, with this advantage, that in a prison there is room for hope. What he saw before him was a term of imprisonment, an early release, and then life abroad somewhere, such as he had contemplated already, in case of failure. Well, it was a failure, if not exactly the sort of failure he had feared. It had been so near success that he could have positively terrified Mr. Vladimir out of his ferocious scoffing with this proof of occult efficiency. So at least it seemed now to Mr. Verloc. His prestige with the Embassy would have been immense if—if his wife had not had the unlucky notion of sewing on the address inside Stevie's overcoat. Mr. Verloc, who was no fool, had soon perceived the extraordinary character of the influence he had over Stevie, though he did not understand exactly its origin—the doctrine of his supreme wisdom and goodness inculcated by two anxious women. In all the eventualities he had fore-seen Mr. Verloc had calculated with correct insight on Stevie's instinctive loyalty and blind discretion. The eventuality he had not foreseen had appalled him as a humane man and a fond husband. From every other point of view it was rather advantageous. Nothing can equal the everlasting discretion of death. Mr. Verloc, sitting perplexed and frightened in the small parlor of the Cheshire Cheese, could not help acknowledging that to himself, because his sensibility did not stand in the way of his judgment. Stevie's violent disintegration, however disturbing to think about, only assured the success; for, of course, the knocking down of a wall was not the aim of Mr. Vladimir's menaces, but the production of a moral effect. With much trouble and distress on Mr. Verloc's part the effect might be said to have been produced. When, however, most unexpectedly, it came home to roost in Brett Street, Mr. Verloc, who had been straggling like a man in a nightmare for the preservation of his position, accepted the blow in the spirit of a convinced fatalist. The position was gone through no one's fault really. A small, tiny fact had done it. It was like slipping on a bit of orange peel in the dark and breaking your leg.

Mr. Verloc drew a weary breath. He nourished no resentment against his wife. He thought: She will have to look after the shop while they keep me locked up. And thinking also how cruelly she would miss Stevie at first, he felt greatly con-cerned about her health and spirits. How would she stand her solitude—absolute-ly alone in that house? It would not do for her to break down while he was locked up. What would become of the shop then? The shop was an asset. Though Mr. Verloc's fatalism accepted his undoing as a secret agent, he had no mind to be utterly ruined, mostly, it must be owned, from regard for his wife.

Silent, and out of his line of sight in the kitchen, she frightened him. If only she had her mother with her. But that silly old woman—An angry dismay possessed Mr. Verloc. He must talk with his wife. He could tell her certainly that a man does get desperate under certain circumstances. But he did not go incontinently to impart to her that information. First of all, it was clear to him that this evening was no time for business. He got up to close the street door and put the gas out in the shop.

Having thus assured a solitude around his hearthstone Mr. Verloc walked into the parlor, and glanced down into the kitchen. Mrs. Verloc was sitting in the place where poor Stevie usually established himself of an evening with paper and pencil for the pastime of drawing these coruscations of innumerable circles suggesting chaos and eternity. Her arms were folded on the table, and her head was lying on her arms. Mr. Verloc contemplated her back and the arrangement of her hair for a time, then walked away from the kitchen door. Mrs. Verloc's philosophical, almost disdainful incuriosity, the foundation of their accord in domestic life, made it extremely difficult to get into contact with her, now this tragic necessity had arisen. Mr. Verloc felt this difficulty acutely. He turned around the table in the parlor with his usual air of a large animal in a cage.

Curiosity being one of the forms of self-revelation, a systematically incurious person remains always partly mysterious. Every time he passed near the door Mr. Verloc glanced at his wife uneasily. It was not that he was afraid of her. Mr. Verloc imagined himself loved by that woman. But she had not accustomed him to make confidences. And the confidence he had to make was of a profound psychological order. How with his want of practice could he tell her what he himself felt but vaguely: that there are conspiracies of fatal destiny, that a notion grows in a mind sometimes till it acquires an outward existence, an independent power of its own, and even a suggestive voice? He could not inform her that a man may be haunted by a fat, witty, clean-shaved face till the wildest expedient to get rid of it appears a child of wisdom.

On this mental reference to a First Secretary of a great Embassy, Mr. Verloc stopped in the doorway, and looking down into the kitchen with an angry face and clenched fists, addressed his wife.

"You don't know what a brute I had to deal with."

He started off to make another perambulation of the table; then when he had come to the door again he stopped, glaring in from the height of two steps.

"A silly, jeering, dangerous brute, with no more sense than—After all these years! A man like me! And I have been playing my head at that game. You didn't know. Quite right, too. What was the good of telling you that I stood the risk of having a knife stuck into me any time these seven years we've been married? I am not a chap to worry a woman that's fond of me. You had no business to know."

Mr. Verloc took another turn round the parlor, fuming.

"A venomous beast," he began again from the doorway. "Drive me out into a ditch to starve for a joke. I could see he thought it was a damned good joke. A man like me! Look here! Some of the highest in the world got to thank me for walking on their two legs to this day. That's the man you've got married to, my girl!"

He perceived that his wife had sat up. Mrs. Verloc's arms remained lying stretched on the table. Mr. Verloc watched her back as if he could read there the effect of his words.

"There isn't a murdering plot for the last eleven years that I hadn't my finger in at the risk of my life. There's scores of these revolutionists I've sent off, with their bombs in their blamed pockets, to get themselves caught on the frontier. The old Baron knew what I was worth to his country. And here suddenly a swine comes along—an ignorant, overbearing swine."

Mr. Verloc, stepping slowly down two steps, entered the kitchen, took a tumbler off the dresser, and holding it in his hand, approached the sink, without looking at his wife.

"It wasn't the old Baron who would have had the wicked folly of getting me to call on him at eleven in the morning. There are two or three in this town that, if they had seen me going in, would have made no bones about knocking me on the head sooner or later. It was a silly, murderous trick to expose for nothing a man—like me."

Mr. Verloc, turning on the tap above the sink, poured three glasses of water, one after another, down his throat to quench the fires of his indignation. Mr. Vladimir's conduct was like a hot brand which set his internal economy in a blaze. He could not get over the disloyalty of it. This man, who would not work at the usual hard tasks which society sets to its humbler members, had exercised his secret industry with an indefatigable devotion. There was in Mr. Verloc a fund of loyalty. He had been loyal to his employers, to the cause of social stability—and to his affections, too—as became apparent when, after standing the tumbler in the sink, he turned about, saying:

"If I hadn't thought of you I would have taken the bullying brute by the throat and rammed his head into the fireplace. I'd have been more than a match for that pink-faced, smooth-shaved—"

Mr. Verloc neglected to finish the sentence, as if there could be no doubt of the terminal word. For the first time in his life he was taking that incurious woman into his confidence. The singularity of the event, the force and importance of the personal feelings aroused in the course of this confession, drove Stevie's fate clean out of Mr. Verloc's mind. The boy's stuttering existence of fears and indignations, together with the violence of his end, had passed out of Mr. Verloc's mental sight for a time. For that reason, when he looked up he was startled by the inappropriate character of his wife's stare. It was not a wild stare, and it was not inattentive, but its attention was peculiar and not satisfactory, inasmuch that it seemed concentrated upon some point beyond Mr. Verloc's person. The impression was so strong that Mr. Verloc glanced over his shoulder. There was nothing behind him: there was just the whitewashed wall. The excellent husband of Winnie Verloc saw no writing on the wall. He turned to his wife again, repeating, with some emphasis:

"I would have taken him by the throat. As true as I stand here, if I hadn't thought of you then I would have half choked the life out of the brute before I let him get up. And don't you think he would have been anxious to call the police—either. He wouldn't have dared. You understand why—don't you?"

He blinked at his wife knowingly.

"No," said Mrs. Verloc in an unresonant voice, and without looking at him at all. "What are you talking about?"

A great discouragement, the result of fatigue, came upon Mr. Verloc. He had had a very full day, and his nerves had been tried to the utmost. After a month of maddening worry, ending in an unexpected catastrophe, the storm-tossed spirit of Mr. Verloc longed for repose. His career as a secret agent had come to an end in a way no one could have foreseen; only, now, perhaps he could manage to get a night's sleep at last. But looking at his wife, he doubted it. She was taking it very hard—not at all like herself, he thought. He made an effort to speak.

"You'll have to pull yourself together, my girl," he said, sympathetically. "What's done can't be undone."

Mrs. Verloc gave a slight start, though not a muscle of her white face moved in the least. Mr. Verloc, who was not looking at her, continued ponderously:

"You go to bed now. What you want is a good cry."

This opinion had nothing to recommend it but the general consent of mankind. It is universally understood that, as if it were nothing more substantial than vapor floating in the sky, every emotion of a woman is bound to end in a shower. And it is very probable that had Stevie died in his bed under her despairing gaze, in her protecting arms, Mrs. Verloc's grief would have found relief in a flood of bitter and pure tears. Mrs. Verloc, in common with other human beings, was provided with a fund of unconscious resignation sufficient to meet the normal manifestation of human destiny. Without "troubling her head about it," she was aware that it "did not stand looking into very much." But the lamentable circumstances of Stevie's end, which to Mr. Verloc's mind had only an episodic character, as part of a greater disaster, dried her tears at their very source. It was the effect of a white-hot iron drawn across her eyes; at the same time her heart, hardened and chilled into a lump of ice, kept her body in an inward shudder, set her features into a frozen, contemplative immobility addressed to a whitewashed wall with no writing on it. The exigencies of Mrs. Verloc's temperament, which, when stripped of its philosophical reserve, was maternal and violent, forced her to roll a series of thoughts in her motionless head. These thoughts were rather imagined than expressed. Mrs. Verloc was a woman of singularly few words, either for public or private use. With the rage and dismay of a betrayed woman, she reviewed the tenor of her life in visions concerned mostly with Stevie's difficult existence from its earliest days. It was a life of single purpose and of a noble unity of inspiration, like those rare lives that have left their mark on the thoughts and feelings of mankind. But the visions of Mrs. Verloc lacked nobility and magnificence. She saw herself putting the boy to bed by the light of a single candle on the deserted top floor of a "business house," dark under the roof and scintillating exceedingly with lights and cut glass at the level of the street like a fairy palace. That meretricious splendor was the only one to be met in Mrs. Verloc's visions. She remembered brushing the boy's hair and tying his pinafores—herself in a pinafore still; the consolations administered to a small and badly scared creature by another creature nearly as small but not quite so badly scared; she had the vision of the blows intercepted (often with her own head), of a door held desperately shut against a man's rage (not for very long); of a poker flung once (not very far), which stilled that particular storm into the dumb and awful silence which follows a thunder-clap. And all these scenes of violence came and went accompanied by the unrefined noise of deep vociferations proceeding from a man wounded in his paternal pride, declaring himself obviously accursed since one of his kids was a "slobbering idjut and the other a wicked she-devil." It was of her that this had been said many years ago.

Mrs. Verloc heard the words again in a ghostly fashion, and then the dreary shadow of the Belgravian mansion descended upon her shoulders. It was a crushing memory, an exhausting vision of countless breakfast trays carried up and down innumerable stairs, of endless haggling over pence, of the endless drudgery of sweeping, dusting, cleaning, from basement to attics; while the impotent mother, staggering on swollen legs, cooked in a grimy kitchen, and poor Stevie, the unconscious presiding genius of all their toil, blacked the gentlemen's boots in the scullery. But this vision had a breath of a hot London summer in it, and for a central figure a young man wearing his Sunday best, with a straw hat on his dark head and a wooden pipe in his mouth. Affectionate and jolly, he was a fascinating companion for a voyage down the sparkling stream of life; only his boat was very small. There was room in it for a girl-partner at the oar, but no accommodation for passengers. He was allowed to drift away from the threshold of the Belgravian mansion while Winnie averted her tearful eyes. He was not a lodger. The lodger was Mr. Verloc, indolent and keeping late hours, sleepily jocular of a morning from under his bedclothes, but with gleams of infatuation in his heavy-lidded eyes, and always with some money in his pockets. There was no sparkle of any kind on the lazy stream of his life. It flowed through secret places. But his bark seemed a roomy craft, and his taciturn magnanimity accepted as a matter of course the presence of passengers.

Mrs. Verloc pursued the visions of seven years' security for Stevie loyally paid for on her part; of security growing into confidence, into a domestic feeling, stagnant and deep like a placid pool, whose guarded surface hardly shuddered on the occasional passage of Comrade Ossipon, the robust anarchist with shamelessly inviting eyes, whose glance had a corrupt clearness sufficient to enlighten any woman not absolutely imbecile.

A few seconds only had elapsed since the last word had been uttered aloud in the kitchen, and Mrs. Verloc was staring already at the vision of an episode not more than a fortnight old. With eyes whose pupils were extremely dilated she stared at the vision of her husband and poor Stevie walking up Brett Street side by side away from the shop. It was the last scene of an existence created by Mrs. Verloc's genius; an existence foreign to all grace and charm, without beauty and almost without decency, but admirable in the continuity of feeling and tenacity of purpose. And this last vision had such plastic relief, such nearness of form, such a fidelity of suggestive detail, that it wrung from Mrs. Verloc an anguished and faint murmur, reproducing the supreme illusion of her life, an appalled murmur that died out on her blanched lips.

"Might have been father and son."

Mr. Verloc stopped, and raised a careworn face. "Eh? What did you say?" he asked. Receiving no reply, he resumed his sinister tramping. Then with a menacing flourish of a thick, fleshy fist, he burst out:

"Yes. The Embassy people. A pretty lot, ain't they! Before a week's out I'll make some of them wish themselves twenty feet under ground. Eh? What?"

He glanced sideways, with his head down. Mrs. Verloc gazed at the whitewashed wall. A blank wall—perfectly blank. A blankness to run at and dash your head against. Mrs. Verloc remained immovably seated. She kept still as the population of half the globe would keep still in astonishment and despair, were the sun suddenly put out in the summer sky by the perfidy of a trusted providence.

"The Embassy," Mr. Verloc began again, after a preliminary grimace which bared his teeth wolfishly. "I wish I could get loose in there with a cudgel for half-an-hour. I would keep on hitting till there wasn't a single unbroken bone left amongst the whole lot. But never mind, I'll teach them yet what it means trying to throw out a man like me to rot in the streets. I've a tongue in my head. All the world shall know what I've done for them. I am not afraid. I don't care. Everything'll come out. Every damned thing. Let them look out!"

In these terms did Mr. Verloc declare his thirst for revenge. It was a very appropriate revenge. It was in harmony with the promptings of Mr. Verloc's genius. It had also the advantage of being within the range of his powers and of adjusting itself easily to the practice of his life, which had consisted precisely in betraying the secret and unlawful proceedings of his fellow-men. Anarchists or diplomats were all one to him. Mr. Verloc was temperamentally no respecter of persons. His scorn was equally distributed over the whole field of his operations. But as a member of a revolutionary proletariat—which he undoubtedly was—he nourished a rather inimical sentiment against social distinction.

"Nothing on earth can stop me now," he added, and paused, looking fixedly at his wife, who was looking fixedly at a blank wall.

The silence in the kitchen was prolonged, and Mr. Verloc felt disappointed. He had expected his wife to say something. But Mrs. Verloc's lips, composed in their usual form, preserved a statuesque immobility like the rest of her face. And Mr. Verloc was disappointed. Yet the occasion did not, he recognized, demand speech from her. She was a woman of very few words. For reasons involved in the very foundation of his psychology, Mr. Verloc was inclined to put his trust in any woman who had given herself to him. Therefore he trusted his wife. Their accord was perfect, but it was not precise. It was a tacit accord, congenial to Mrs. Verloc's incuriosity and to Mr. Verloc's habits of mind, which were indolent and secret. They refrained from going to the bottom of facts and motives.

This reserve, expressing, in a way, their profound confidence in each other, introduced at the same time a certain element of vagueness into their intimacy. No system of conjugal relations is perfect. Mr. Verloc presumed that his wife had understood him but he would have been glad to hear her say what she thought at the moment. It would have been a comfort.

There were several reasons why this comfort was denied him. There was a physical obstacle: Mrs. Verloc had not sufficient command over her voice. She did not see any alternative between screaming and silence, and instinctively she chose the silence. Winnie Verloc was temperamentally a silent person. And there was the paralyzing atrocity of the thought which occupied her. Her cheeks were blanched, her lips ashy, her immobility amazing. And she thought without looking at Mr. Verloc: "This man took the boy away to murder him. He took the boy away from his home to murder him. He took the boy away from me to murder him!"

Mrs. Verloc's whole being was racked by that inconclusive and maddening thought. It was in her veins, in her bones, in the roots of her hair. Mentally she assumed the biblical attitude of mourning—the covered face, the rent garments; the sound of wailing and lamentation filled her head. But her teeth were violently clenched, and her tearless eyes were hot with rage, because she was not a submissive creature. The protection she had extended over her brother had been in its origin of a fierce and indignant complexion. She had to love him with a militant love. She had battled for him—even against herself. His loss had the bitterness of defeat, with the anguish of a baffled passion. It was not an ordinary stroke of death. Moreover, it was not death that took Stevie from her. It was Mr. Verloc who took him away. She had seen him. She had watched him, without raising a hand, take the boy away. And she had let him go, like—like a fool—a blind fool. Then after he had murdered the boy he came home to her. Just came home like any other man would come home to his wife. . . .

Through her set teeth Mrs. Verloc muttered at the wall:

"And I thought he had caught a cold."

Mr. Verloc heard these words and appropriated them.

"It was nothing," he said, moodily. "I was upset. I was upset on your account."

Mrs. Verloc, turning her head slowly, transferred her stare from the wall to her husband's person. Mr. Verloc, with the tips of his fingers between his lips, was looking on the ground.

"Can't be helped," he mumbled, letting his hand fall. "You must pull yourself together. You'll want all your wits about you. It is you who brought the police about our ears. Never mind, I won't say anything more about it," continued Mr. Verloc, magnanimously. "You couldn't know."

"I couldn't," breathed out Mrs. Verloc. It was as if a corpse had spoken. Mr. Verloc took up the thread of his discourse.

"I don't blame you. I'll make them sit up. Once under lock and key it will be safe enough for me to talk—you understand. You must reckon on me being two years away from you," he continued, in a tone of sincere concern. "It will be easier for you than for me. You'll have something to do, while I—Look here, Winnie, what you must do is to keep this business going for two years. You know enough for that. You've a good head on you. I'll send you word when it's time to go about trying to sell. You'll have to be extra careful. The comrades will be keeping an eye on you all the time. You'll have to be as artful as you know how, and as close as the grave. No one must know what you are going to do. I have no mind to get a knock on the head or a stab in the back directly I am let out."

Thus spoke Mr. Verloc, applying his mind with ingenuity and forethought to the problems of the future. His voice was somber, because he had a correct sentiment of the situation. Everything which he did not wish to pass had come to pass. The future had become precarious. His judgment, perhaps, had been momentarily obscured by his dread of Mr. Vladimir's truculent folly. A man somewhat over forty may be excusably thrown into considerable disorder by the prospect of losing his employment, especially if the man is a secret agent of political police, dwelling secure in the consciousness of his high value and in the esteem of high person-ages. He was excusable.

Now the thing had ended in a crash. Mr. Verloc was cool; but he was not cheer-ful. A secret agent who throws his secrecy to the winds from desire of vengeance, and flaunts his achievements before the public eye, becomes the mark for desper-ate and bloodthirsty indignations. Without unduly exaggerating the danger, Mr. Verloc tried to bring it clearly before his wife's mind. He repeated that he had no intention of letting the revolutionists do away with him.

He looked straight into his wife's eyes. The enlarged pupils of the woman received his stare into their unfathomable depths.

"I am too fond of you for that," he said, with a little nervous laugh.

A faint flush colored Mrs. Verloc's ghastly and motionless face. Having done with the visions of the past, she had not only heard, but had also understood the words uttered by her husband. By their extreme disaccord with her mental condi-tion these words produced on her a slightly suffocating effect. Mrs. Verloc's men-tal condition had the merit of simplicity; but it was not sound. It was governed too much by a fixed idea. Every nook and cranny of her brain was filled with the thought that this man, with whom she had lived without distaste for seven years, had taken the "poor boy" away from her in order to kill him—the man to whom she had grown accustomed in body and mind; the man whom she had trusted, took the boy away to kill him! In its form, in its substance, in its effect, which was universal, altering even the aspect of inanimate things, it was a thought to sit still and marvel at forever and ever. Mrs. Verloc sat still. And across that thought (not across the kitchen) the form of Mr. Verloc went to and fro, familiarly in hat and overcoat, stamping with his boots upon her brain. He was probably talking, too; but Mrs. Verloc's thought for the most part covered the voice.

Now and then, however, the voice would make itself heard. Several connected words emerged at times. Their purport was generally hopeful. On each of these occasions Mrs. Verloc's dilated pupils, losing their far-off fixity, followed her husband's movements with the effect of black care and impenetrable attention. Well informed upon all matters relating to his secret calling, Mr. Verloc augured well for the success of his plans and combinations. He really believed that it would be upon the whole easy for him to escape the knife of infuriated revolutionists. He had exaggerated the strength of their fury and the length of their arm (for professional purposes) too often to have many illusions one way or the other. For to exaggerate with judgment one must begin by measuring with nicety. He knew also how much virtue and how much infamy is forgotten in two years—two long years. His first really confidential discourse to his wife was optimistic from conviction. He also thought it good policy to display all the assurance he could muster. It would put heart into the poor woman. On his liberation, which, harmonizing with the whole tenor of his life, would be secret, of course, they would vanish together without loss of time. As to covering up the tracks, he begged his wife to trust him for that. He knew how it was to be done so that the devil himself—

He waved his hand. He seemed to boast. He wished only to put heart into her. It was a benevolent intention, but Mr. Verloc had the misfortune not to be in accord with his audience.

The self-confident tone grew upon Mrs. Verloc's ear which let most of the words go by; for what were words to her now? What could words do to her for good or evil in the face of her fixed idea? Her black glance followed that man who was asserting his impunity—the man who had taken poor Stevie from home to kill him somewhere. Mrs. Verloc could not remember exactly where, but her heart began to beat very perceptibly

Mr. Verloc, in a soft and conjugal tone, was now expressing his firm belief that there were yet a good few years of quiet life before them both. He did not go into the question of means. A quiet life it must be and, as it were, nestling in the shade, concealed among men whose flesh is grass; modest, like the life of violets. The words used by Mr. Verloc were: "Lie low for a bit." And far from England, of course. It was not clear whether Mr. Verloc had in his mind Spain or South America; but at any rate somewhere abroad.

This last word, falling into Mrs. Verloc's ear, produced a definite impression. This man was talking of going abroad. The impression was completely disconnected; and such is the force of mental habit that Mrs. Verloc at once and automatically asked herself: "And what of Stevie?"

It was a sort of forgetfulness; but instantly she became aware that there was no longer any occasion for anxiety on that score. There would never be any occasion anymore. The poor boy had been taken out and killed. The poor boy was dead.

This shaking piece of forgetfulness stimulated Mrs. Verloc's intelligence. She began to perceive certain consequences which would have surprised Mr. Verloc. There was no need for her now to stay there, in that kitchen, in that house, with that man—since the boy was gone forever. No need whatever. And on that Mrs. Verloc rose as if raised by a spring. But neither could she see what there was to keep her in the world at all. And this inability arrested her. Mr. Verloc watched her with marital solicitude.

"You're looking more like yourself," he said, uneasily. Something peculiar in the blackness of his wife's eyes disturbed his optimism. At that precise moment Mrs. Verloc began to look upon herself as released from all earthly ties. She had her freedom. Her contract with existence, as represented by that man standing over there, was at an end. She was a free woman. Had this view become in some way perceptible to Mr. Verloc he would have been extremely shocked. In his affairs of the heart Mr. Verloc had been always carelessly generous, yet always with no other idea than that of being loved for himself. Upon this matter, his ethical notions being in agreement with his vanity, he was completely incorrigible. That this should be so in the case of his virtuous and legal connection he was perfectly certain. He had grown older, fatter, heavier, in the belief that he lacked no fascination for being loved for his own sake. When he saw Mrs. Verloc starting to walk out of the kitchen without a word he was disappointed.

"Where are you going to?" he called out rather sharply. "Upstairs?"

Mrs. Verloc in the doorway turned at the voice. An instinct of prudence born of fear, the excessive fear of being approached and touched by that man, induced her to nod at him slightly (from the height of two steps), with a stir of the lips which the conjugal optimism of Mr. Verloc took for a wan and uncertain smile.

"That's right," he encouraged her gruffly. "Rest and quiet's what you want. Go on. It won't be long before I am with you."

Mrs. Verloc, the free woman who had had really no idea where she was going to, obeyed the suggestion with rigid steadiness.

Mr. Verloc watched her. She disappeared up the stairs. He was disappointed. There was that within him which would have been more satisfied if she had been moved to throw herself upon his breast. But he was generous and indulgent. Winnie was always undemonstrative and silent. Neither was Mr. Verloc himself prodigal of endearments and words as a rule. But this was not an ordinary evening. It was an occasion when a man wants to be fortified and strengthened by open proofs of sympathy and affection. Mr. Verloc sighed, and put out the gas in the kitchen. Mr. Verloc's sympathy with his wife was genuine and intense. It almost brought tears into his eyes as he stood in the parlor reflecting on the loneliness hanging over her head. In this mood Mr. Verloc missed Stevie very much out of a difficult world. He thought mournfully of his end. If only that lad had not stupidly destroyed himself!

The sensation of unappeasable hunger, not unknown after the strain of a hazardous enterprise to adventurers of tougher fiber than Mr. Verloc, overcame him again. The piece of roast beef, laid out in the likeness of funereal baked meats for Stevie's obsequies, offered itself largely to his notice. And Mr. Verloc again partook. He partook ravenously, without restraint and decency, cutting thick slices with the sharp carving knife, and swallowing them without bread. In the course of that refection it occurred to Mr. Verloc that he was not hearing his wife move about the bedroom as he should have done. The thought of finding her perhaps sitting on the bed in the dark not only cut Mr. Verloc's appetite, but also took from him the inclination to follow her upstairs just yet. Laying down the carving knife, Mr. Verloc listened with careworn attention.

He was comforted by hearing her move at last. She walked suddenly across the room, and threw the window up. After a period of stillness up there, during which he figured her to himself with her head out, he heard the sash being lowered slowly. Then she made a few steps, and sat down. Every resonance of his house was familiar to Mr. Verloc, who was thoroughly domesticated. When next he heard his wife's footsteps overhead he knew, as well as if he had seen her doing it, that she had been putting on her walking shoes. Mr. Verloc wriggled his shoulders slightly at this ominous symptom, and moving away from the table, stood with his back to the fireplace, his head on one side, and gnawing perplexedly at the tips of his fingers. He kept track of her movements by the sound. She walked here and there violently, with abrupt stoppages, now before the chest of drawers, then in front of the wardrobe. An immense load of weariness, the harvest of a day of shocks and surprises, weighed Mr. Verloc's energies to the ground.

He did not raise his eyes till he heard his wife descending the stairs. It was as he had guessed, she was dressed for going out.

Mrs. Verloc was a free woman. She had thrown open the window of the bedroom either with the intention of screaming Murder! Help! or of throwing herself out. For she did not exactly know what use to make of her freedom. Her personality seemed to have been torn into two pieces, whose mental operations did not adjust themselves very well to each other. The street, silent and deserted from end to end, repelled her by taking sides with that man who was so certain of his impunity. She was afraid to shout lest no one should come. Obviously no one would come. Her instinct of self-preservation recoiled from the depth of the fall into that sort of slimy, deep trench. Mrs. Verloc closed the window, and dressed herself to go out into the street by another way. She was a free woman. She had dressed herself thoroughly, down to the tying of a black veil over her face. As she appeared before him in the light of the parlor, Mr. Verloc observed that she had even her little handbag hanging from her left wrist. . . . Flying off to her mother, of course.

The thought that women were wearisome creatures after all presented itself to his fatigued brain. But he was too generous to harbor it for more than an instant. This man, hurt cruelly in his vanity, remained magnanimous in his conduct, allowing himself no satisfaction of a bitter smile or of a contemptuous gesture. With true greatness of soul, he only glanced at the wooden clock on the wall, and said in a perfectly calm but forcible manner:

"Five and twenty minutes past eight, Winnie. There's no sense in going over there so late. You will never manage to get back tonight."

Before his extended hand Mrs. Verloc had stopped short. He added, heavily: "Your mother will be gone to bed before you get there. This is the sort of news that can wait."

Nothing was further from Mrs. Verloc's thoughts than going to her mother. She recoiled at the mere idea, and feeling a chair behind her, she obeyed the suggestion of the touch, and sat down. Her intention had been simply to get outside the door forever. And if this feeling was correct, its mental form took an unrefined shape corresponding to her origin and station. "I would rather walk the streets all the days of my life," she thought. But this creature, whose moral nature had been subjected to a shock of which, in the physical order, the most violent earthquake of history could only be a faint and languid rendering, was at the mercy of mere trifles, of casual contacts. She sat down. With her hat and veil she had the air of a visitor, of having looked in on Mr. Verloc for a moment. Her instant docility encouraged him, whilst her aspect of only temporary and silent acquiescence provoked him a little.

"Let me tell you, Winnie," he said with authority, "that your place is here this evening. Hang it all! you brought the damned police high and low about my ears. I don't blame you—but it's your doing all the same. You'd better take this confounded hat off. I can't let you go out, old girl," he added in a softened voice.

Mrs. Verloc's mind got hold of that declaration with morbid tenacity. The man who had taken Stevie out from under her very eyes to murder him in a locality whose name was at the moment not present to her memory would not allow her to go out. Of course he wouldn't. Now he had murdered Stevie he would never let her go. He would want to keep her for nothing. And on this characteristic reasoning, having all the force of insane logic, Mrs. Verloc's disconnected wits went to work practically. She could slip by him, open the door, run out. But he would dash out after her, seize her round the body, drag her back into the shop. She could scratch, kick, and bite—and stab, too; but for stabbing she wanted a knife. Mrs. Verloc sat still under her black veil, in her own house, like a masked and mysterious visitor of impenetrable intentions.

Mr. Verloc's magnanimity was not more than human. She had exasperated him at last. "Can't you say something? You have your own dodges for vexing a man. Oh, yes! I know your deaf-and-dumb trick. I've seen you at it before today. But just now it won't do. And to begin with, take this damned thing off. One can't tell whether one is talking to a dummy or to a live woman."

He advanced, and stretching out his hand, dragged the veil off, unmasking a still unreadable face, against which his nervous exasperation was shattered like a glass bubble flung against a rock. "That's better," he said, to cover his momentary uneasiness, and retreated back to his old station by the mantelpiece. It never entered his head that his wife could give him up. He felt a little ashamed of himself, for he was fond and generous. What could he do? Everything had been said already. He protested vehemently.

"By heavens! You know that I hunted high and low. I ran the risk of giving myself away to find somebody for that accursed job. And I tell you again I couldn't find anyone crazy enough or hungry enough. What do you take me for—a murderer, or what? The boy is gone. Do you think I wanted him to blow himself up? He's gone. His troubles are over. Ours are just going to begin, I tell you, precisely because he did blow himself up. I don't blame you. But just try to understand that it was a pure accident; as much an accident as if he had been run over by a 'bus while crossing the street."

His generosity was not infinite, because he was a human being—and not a monster, as Mrs. Verloc believed him to be. He paused, and a snarl lifting his moustaches above a gleam of white teeth gave him the expression of a reflective beast, not very dangerous—a slow beast with a sleek head, gloomier than a seal, and with a husky voice.

"And when it comes to that, it's as much your doing as mine. That's so. You may glare as much as you like. I know what you can do in that way. Strike me dead if I ever would have thought of the lad for that purpose. It was you who kept on shoving him in my way when I was half distracted with the worry of keeping the lot of us out of trouble. What the devil made you? One would think you were doing it on purpose. And I am damned if I know that you didn't. There's no saying how much of what's going on you have got hold of on the sly with your infernal don't-care-a-damn way of looking nowhere in particular, and saying nothing at all. . . ."

His husky, domestic voice ceased for a while. Mrs. Verloc made no reply. Before that silence he felt ashamed of what he had said. But as often happens to peaceful men in domestic tiffs, being ashamed he pushed another point.

"You have a devilish way of holding your tongue sometimes," he began again, without raising his voice. "Enough to make some men go mad. It's lucky for you that I am not so easily put out as some of them would be by your deaf-and-dumb sulks. I am fond of you. But don't you go too far. This isn't the time for it. We ought to be thinking of what we've got to do. And I can't let you go out tonight, galloping off to your mother with some crazy tale or other about me. I won't have it. Don't you make any mistake about it: if you will have it that I killed the boy, then you've killed him as much as I."

In sincerity of feeling and openness of statement, these words went far beyond anything that had ever been said in this home, kept up on the wages of a secret industry eked out by the sale of more or less secret wares: the poor expedients devised by a mediocre mankind for preserving an imperfect society from the dangers of moral and physical corruption, both secret, too, of their kind. They were spoken because Mr. Verloc had felt himself really outraged; but the reticent decencies of this home life, nestling in a shady street behind a shop where the sun never shone, remained apparently undisturbed. Mrs. Verloc heard him out with perfect propriety, and then rose from her chair in her hat and jacket like a visitor at the end of a call. She advanced towards her husband, one arm extended as if for a silent leave-taking. Her net veil dangling down by one end of the left side of her face gave an air of disorderly formality to her restrained movements. But when she arrived as far as the hearth-rug, Mr. Verloc was no longer standing there. He had moved off in the direction of the sofa, without raising his eyes to watch the effect of his tirade. He was tired, resigned in a truly marital spirit. But he felt hurt in the tender spot of his secret weakness. If she would go on sulking in that dreadful overcharged silence—why then she must. She was a master in that domestic art. Mr. Verloc flung himself heavily upon the sofa, disregarding as usual the fate of his hat, which, as if accustomed to take care of itself, made for a safe shelter under the table.

He was tired. The last particle of his nervous force had been expended in the wonders and agonies of this day full of surprising failures coming at the end of a harassing month of scheming and insomnia. He was tired. A man isn't made of stone. Hang everything! Mr. Verloc reposed characteristically, clad in his outdoor garments. One side of his open overcoat was lying partly on the ground. Mr. Verloc wallowed on his back. But he longed for a more perfect rest—for sleep—for a few hours of delicious forgetfulness. That would come later. Provisionally he rested. And he thought: "I wish she would give over this damned nonsense. It's exasperating."

There must have been something imperfect in Mrs. Verloc's sentiment of regained freedom. Instead of taking the way of the door she leaned back, with her shoulders against the tablet of the mantelpiece, as a wayfarer rests against a fence. A tinge of wildness in her aspect was derived from the black veil hanging like a rag against her cheek, and from the fixity of her black gaze where the light of the room was absorbed and lost without the trace of a single gleam. This woman, capable of a bargain the mere suspicion of which would have been infinitely shocking to Mr. Verloc's idea of love, remained irresolute, as if scrupulously aware of something wanting on her part for the formal closing of the transaction.

On the sofa Mr. Verloc wriggled his shoulders into perfect comfort, and from the fullness of his heart emitted a wish which was certainly as pious as anything likely to come from such a source.

"I wish to goodness," he growled, huskily, "I had never seen Greenwich Park or anything belonging to it."

The veiled sound filled the small room with its moderate volume, well adapted to the modest nature of the wish. The waves of air of the proper length, propagated in accordance with correct mathematical formulas, flowed around all the inanimate things in the room, lapped against Mrs. Verloc's head as if it had been a head of stone. And incredible as it may appear, the eyes of Mrs. Verloc seemed to grow still larger. The audible wish of Mr. Verloc's overflowing heart flowed into an empty place in his wife's memory. Greenwich Park. A park! That's where the boy was killed. A park—smashed branches, torn leaves, gravel, bits of brotherly flesh and bone, all spouting up together in the manner of a firework. She remembered now what she had heard, and she remembered it pictorially. They had to gather him up with the shovel. Trembling all over with irrepressible shudders, she saw before her the very implement with its ghastly load scraped up from the ground. Mrs. Verloc closed her eyes desperately, throwing upon that vision the night of her eyelids, where after a rainlike fall of mangled limbs the decapitated head of Stevie lingered suspended alone, and fading out slowly like the last star of a pyrotechnic display. Mrs. Verloc opened her eyes.

Her face was no longer stony. Anybody could have noted the subtle change on her features, in the stare of her eyes, giving her a new and startling expression; an expression seldom observed by competent persons under the conditions of leisure and security demanded for thorough analysis, but whose meaning could not he mistaken at a glance. Mrs. Verloc's doubts as to the end of the bargain no longer existed; her wits, no longer disconnected, were working under the control of her will. But Mr. Verloc observed nothing. He was reposing in that pathetic condition of optimism induced by excess of fatigue. He did not want any more trouble—with his wife, too—of all people in the world. He had been unanswerable in his vindication. He was loved for himself. The present phase of her silence he interpreted favorably. This was the time to make it up with her. The silence had lasted long enough. He broke it by calling to her in an undertone:

"Winnie."

"Yes," answered obediently Mrs. Verloc the free woman. She commanded her wits now, her vocal organs; she felt herself to be in an almost preternaturally perfect control of every fiber of her body It was all her own, because the bargain was at an end. She was clear sighted. She had become cunning. She chose to answer him so readily for a purpose. She did not wish that man to change his position on the sofa which was very suitable to the circumstances. She succeeded. The man did not stir. But after answering him she remained leaning negligently against the mantelpiece in the attitude of a resting wayfarer. She was unhurried. Her brow was smooth. The head and shoulders of Mr. Verloc were hidden from her by the high side of the sofa. She kept her eyes fixed on his feet.

She remained thus mysteriously still and suddenly collected till Mr. Verloc was heard with an accent of marital authority, and moving slightly to make room for her to sit on the edge of the sofa.

"Come here," he said in a peculiar tone, which might have been the tone of brutality, but was intimately known to Mrs. Verloc as the note of wooing.

She started forward at once, as if she were still a loyal woman bound to that man by an unbroken contract. Her right hand skimmed slightly the end of the table, and when she had passed on towards the sofa the carving knife had vanished without the slightest sound from the side of the dish. Mr. Verloc heard the creaky plank in the floor, and was content. He waited. Mrs. Verloc was coming. As if the homeless soul of Stevie had flown for shelter straight to the breast of his sister, guardian, and protector, the resemblance of her face with that of her brother grew at every step, even to the droop of the lower lip, even to the slight divergence of the eyes. But Mr. Verloc did not see that. He was lying on his back and staring upwards. He saw partly on the ceiling and partly on the wall the moving shadow of an arm with a clenched hand holding a carving knife. It flickered up and down. Its movements were leisurely. They were leisurely enough for Mr. Verloc to recognize the limb and the weapon.

They were leisurely enough for him to take in the full meaning of the portent, and to taste the flavor of death rising in his gorge. His wife had gone raving mad—murdering mad. They were leisurely enough for the first paralyzing effect of this discovery to pass away before a resolute determination to come out victorious from the ghastly struggle with that armed lunatic. They were leisurely enough for Mr. Verloc to elaborate a plan of defense involving a dash behind the table, and the felling of the woman to the ground with a heavy wooden chair. But they were not leisurely enough to allow Mr. Verloc the time to move either hand or foot. The knife was already planted in his breast. It met no resistance on its way. Hazard has such accuracies. Into that plunging blow, delivered over the side of the couch, Mrs. Verloc had put all the inheritance of her immemorial and obscure descent, the simple ferocity of the age of caverns, and the unbalanced nervous fury of the age of barrooms. Mr. Verloc, the Secret Agent, turning slightly on his side with the force of the blow, expired without stirring a limb, in the muttered sound of the word "Don't" by way of protest.

Mrs. Verloc had let go the knife, and her extraordinary resemblance to her late brother had faded, had become very ordinary now. She drew a deep breath, the first easy breath since Chief Inspector Heat had exhibited to her the labeled piece of Stevie's overcoat. She leaned forward on her folded arms over the side of the sofa. She adopted that easy attitude not in order to watch or gloat over the body of Mr. Verloc, but because of the undulatory and swinging movements of the parlor, which for some time behaved as though it were at sea in a tempest. She was giddy but calm. She had become a free woman with a perfection of freedom which left her nothing to desire and absolutely nothing to do, since Stevie's urgent claim on her devotion no longer existed. Mrs. Verloc, who thought in images, was not troubled now by visions, because she did not think at all. And she did not move. She was a woman enjoying her complete irresponsibility and endless leisure, almost in the manner of a corpse. She did not move, she did not think. Neither did the mortal envelope of the late Mr. Verloc reposing on the sofa. Except for the fact that Mrs. Verloc breathed these two would have been perfectly in accord: that accord of prudent reserve without superfluous words, and sparing of signs, which had been the foundation of their respectable home life. For it had been respectable, covering by a decent reticence the problems that may arise in the practice of a secret profession and the commerce of shady wares. To the last its decorum had remained undisturbed by unseemly shrieks and other misplaced sincerities of conduct. And after the striking of the blow, this respectability was continued in immobility and silence.

Nothing moved in the parlor till Mrs. Verloc raised her head slowly and looked at the clock with inquiring mistrust. She had become aware of a ticking sound in the room. It grew upon her ear, while she remembered clearly that the clock on the wall was silent, had no audible tick. What did it mean by beginning to tick so loudly all of a sudden? Its face indicated ten minutes to nine. Mrs. Verloc cared nothing for time, and the ticking went on. She concluded it could not be the clock, and her sullen gaze moved along the walls, wavered, and became vague, while she strained her hearing to locate the sound. Tic, tic, tic.

After listening for some time Mrs. Verloc lowered her gaze deliberately on her husband's body. Its attitude of repose was so homelike and familiar that she could do so without feeling embarrassed by any pronounced novelty in the phenomena of her home life. Mr. Verloc was taking his habitual ease. He looked comfortable.

By the position of the body the face of Mr. Verloc was not visible to Mrs. Verloc, his widow. Her fine, sleepy eyes, traveling downward on the track of the sound, became contemplative on meeting a flat object of bone which protruded a little beyond the edge of the sofa. It was the handle of the domestic carving knife with nothing strange about it but its position at right angles to Mr. Verloc's waistcoat and the fact that something dripped from it. Dark drops fell on the floorcloth one after another, with a sound of ticking growing fast and furious like the pulse of an insane clock. At its highest speed this ticking changed into a continuous sound of trickling. Mrs. Verloc watched that transformation with shadows of anxiety coming and going on her face. It was a trickle, dark, swift, thin. . . . Blood!

At this unforeseen circumstance Mrs. Verloc abandoned her pose of idleness and irresponsibility.

With a sudden snatch at her skirts and a faint shriek she ran to the door, as if the trickle had been the first sign of a destroying flood. Finding the table in her way she gave it a push with both hands as though it had been alive, with such force that it went for some distance on its four legs, making a loud, scraping racket, whilst the big dish with the joint crashed heavily on the floor.

Then all became still. Mrs. Verloc on reaching the door had stopped. A round hat disclosed in the middle of the floor by the moving of the table rocked slightly on its crown in the wind of her flight.

❧ 12 ❧

Winnie Verloc, the widow of Mr. Verloc, the sister of the late faithful Stevie (blown to fragments in a state of innocence and in the conviction of being engaged in a humanitarian enterprise), did not run beyond the door of the parlor. She had indeed run away so far from a mere trickle of blood, but that was a movement of instinctive repulsion. And there she had paused, with staring eyes and lowered head. As though she had run through long years in her flight across the small parlor, Mrs. Verloc by the door was quite a different person from the woman who had been leaning over the sofa, a little swimmy in her head, but otherwise free to enjoy the profound calm of idleness and irresponsibility. Mrs. Verloc was no longer giddy. Her head was steady. On the other hand, she was no longer calm. She was afraid.

If she avoided looking in the direction of her reposing husband it was not because she was afraid of him. Mr. Verloc was not frightful to behold. He looked comfortable. Moreover, he was dead. Mrs. Verloc entertained no vain delusions on the subject of the dead. Nothing brings them back, neither love nor hate. They can do nothing to you. They are as nothing. Her mental state was tinged by a sort of austere contempt for that man who had let himself be killed so easily. He had been the master of a house, the husband of a woman, and the murderer of her Stevie. And now he was of no account in every respect. He was of less practical account than the clothing on his body, than his overcoat, than his boots—than that hat lying on the floor. He was nothing. He was not worth looking at. He was even no longer the murderer of poor Stevie. The only murderer that would be found in the room when people came to look for Mr. Verloc would be—herself!

Her hands shook so that she failed twice in the task of refastening her veil. Mrs. Verloc was no longer a person of leisure and irresponsibility. She was afraid. The stabbing of Mr. Verloc had been only a blow. It had relieved the pent-up agony of shrieks strangled in her throat, of tears dried up in her hot eyes, of the maddening and indignant rage at the atrocious part played by that man, who was less than nothing now, in robbing her of the boy. It had been an obscurely prompted blow. The blood trickling on the floor off the handle of the knife had turned it into an extremely plain case of murder. Mrs. Verloc, who always refrained from looking deep into things, was compelled to look into the very bottom of this thing. She saw there no haunting face, no reproachful shade, no vision of remorse, no sort of ideal conception. She saw there an object. That object was the gallows. Mrs. Verloc was afraid of the gallows.

She was terrified of them ideally. Having never set eyes on that last argument of men's justice except in illustrative woodcuts to a certain type of tales, she first saw them erect against a black and stormy background, festooned with chains and human bones, circled about by birds that peck at dead men's eyes. This was frightful enough, but Mrs. Verloc, though not a well-informed woman, had a sufficient knowledge of the institutions of her country to know that gallows are no longer erected romantically on the banks of dismal rivers or on windswept headlands, but in the yards of jails. There within four high walls, as if into a pit, at dawn of day, the murderer was brought out to be executed, with a horrible quietness and, as the reports in the newspapers always said, "in the presence of the authorities." With her eyes staring on the floor, her nostrils quivering with anguish and shame, she imagined herself all alone amongst a lot of strange gentlemen in silk hats who were calmly proceeding about the business of hanging her by the neck. That— never! Never! And how was it done? The impossibility of imagining the details of such quiet execution added something maddening to her abstract terror. The newspapers never gave any details except one, but that one with some affectation was always there at the end of a meager report. Mrs. Verloc remembered its nature. It came with a cruel burning pain into her head, as if the words "The drop given was fourteen feet" had been scratched on her brain with a hot needle. "The drop given was fourteen feet."

These words affected her physically, too. Her throat became convulsed in waves to resist strangulation; and the apprehension of the jerk was so vivid that she seized her head in both hands as if to save it from being torn off her shoulders. "The drop given was fourteen feet." No! that must never be. She could not stand *that*. The thought of it even was not bearable. She could not stand thinking of it. Therefore Mrs. Verloc formed the resolution to go at once and throw herself into the river off one of the bridges.

This time she managed to refasten her veil. With her face as if masked, all black from head to foot except for some flowers in her hat, she looked up mechanically at the clock. She thought it must have stopped. She could not believe that only two minutes had passed since she had looked at it last. Of course not. It had been stopped all the time. As a matter of fact, only three minutes had elapsed from the moment she had drawn the first deep, easy breath after the blow, to this moment when Mrs. Verloc formed the resolution to drown herself in the Thames. But Mrs. Verloc could not believe that. She seemed to have heard or read that clocks and watches always stopped at the moment of murder for the undoing of the murderer. She did not care. "To the bridge—and over I go.". . . But her movements were slow.

She dragged herself painfully across the shop, and had to hold on to the handle of the door before she found the necessary fortitude to open it. The street frightened her, since it led either to the gallows or to the river. She floundered over the doorstep head forward, arms thrown out, like a person falling over the parapet of a bridge. This entrance into the open air had a foretaste of drowning; a slimy dampness enveloped her, entered her nostrils, clung to her hair. It was not actually raining, but each gas-lamp had a rusty little halo of mist. The van and horses were gone, and in the black street the curtained window of the carters' eating-house made a square patch of soiled blood-red light glowing faintly very near the level of the pavement. Mrs. Verloc, dragging herself slowly towards it, thought that she was a very friendless woman. It was true. It was so true that, in a sudden longing to see some friendly face, she could think of no one else but of Mrs. Neale, the charwoman. She had no acquaintances of her own. Nobody would miss her in a social way. It must not be imagined that the Widow Verloc had forgotten her mother. This was not so. Winnie had been a good daughter because she had been a devoted sister. Her mother had always leaned on her for support. No consolation or advice could be expected there. Now that Stevie was dead the bond seemed to be broken. She could not face the old woman with the horrible tale. Moreover, it was too far. The river was her present destination. Mrs. Verloc tried to forget her mother.

Each step cost her an effort of will which seemed the last possible. Mrs. Verloc had dragged herself past the red glow of the eating-house window. "To the bridge—and over I go," she repeated to herself with fierce obstinacy. She put out her hand just in time to steady herself against a lamppost. "I'll never get there before morning," she thought. The fear of death paralyzed her efforts to escape the gallows. It seemed to her she had been staggering in that street for hours. "I'll never get there," she thought. "They'll find me knocking about the streets. It's too far." She held on, panting under her black veil.

"The drop given was fourteen feet."

She pushed the lamppost away from her violently, and found herself walking. But another wave of faintness overtook her like a great sea, washing away her heart clean out of her breast. "I will never get there," she muttered, suddenly arrested, swaying lightly where she stood. "Never."

And perceiving the utter impossibility of walking as far as the nearest bridge, Mrs. Verloc thought of a flight abroad.

It came to her suddenly. Murderers escaped. They escaped abroad. Spain or California. Mere names. The vast world created for the glory of man was only a vast blank to Mrs. Verloc. She did not know which way to turn. Murderers had friends, relations, helpers—they had knowledge. She had nothing. She was the most lonely of murderers that ever struck a mortal blow. She was alone in London: and the whole town of marvels and mud, with its maze of streets and its mass of lights, was sunk in a hopeless night, rested at the bottom of a black abyss from which no unaided woman could hope to scramble out.

She swayed forward, and made a fresh start blindly, with an awful dread of falling down; but at the end of a few steps, unexpectedly, she found a sensation of support, of security. Raising her head, she saw a man's face peering closely at her veil. Comrade Ossipon was not afraid of strange women, and no feeling of false delicacy could prevent him from striking an acquaintance with a woman apparently very much intoxicated. Comrade Ossipon was interested in women. He held up this one between his two large palms, peering at her in a businesslike way till he heard her say faintly "Mr. Ossipon!" and then he very nearly let her drop to the ground.

"Mrs. Verloc!" he exclaimed. "You here!"

It seemed impossible to him that she should have been drinking. But one never knows. He did not go into that question, but attentive not to discourage kind fate surrendering to him the widow of Comrade Verloc, he tried to draw her to his breast. To his astonishment she came quite easily, and even rested on his arm for a moment before she attempted to disengage herself. Comrade Ossipon would not be brusk with kind fate. He withdrew his arm in a natural way.

"You recognized me," she faltered out, standing before him, fairly steady on her legs.

"Of course I did," said Ossipon with perfect readiness. "I was afraid you were going to fall. I've thought of you too often lately not to recognize you anywhere, at any time. I've always thought of you—ever since I first set eyes on you."

Mrs. Verloc seemed not to hear. "You were coming to the shop?" she said, nervously.

"Yes; at once," answered Ossipon. "Directly I read the paper."

In fact, Comrade Ossipon had been skulking for a good two hours in the neighborhood of Brett Street, unable to make up his mind for a bold move. The robust anarchist was not exactly a bold conqueror. He remembered that Mrs. Verloc had never responded to his glances by the slightest sign of encouragement. Besides, he thought the shop might be watched by the police, and Comrade Ossipon did not wish the police to form an exaggerated notion of his revolutionary sympathies. Even now he did not know precisely what to do. In comparison with his usual amatory speculations this was a big and serious undertaking. He ignored how much there was in it and how far he would have to go in order to get hold of what there was to get—supposing there was a chance at all. These perplexities checking his elation imparted to his tone a soberness well in keeping with the circumstances.

"May I ask you where you were going?" he inquired in a subdued voice.

"Don't ask me!" cried Mrs. Verloc with a shuddering, repressed violence. All her strong vitality recoiled from the idea of death. "Never mind where I was going. . . ."

Ossipon concluded that she was very much excited but perfectly sober. She remained silent by his side for a moment, then all at once she did something which he did not expect. She slipped her hand under his arm. He was startled by the act itself certainly, and quite as much, too, by the palpably resolute character of this movement. But this being a delicate affair, Comrade Ossipon behaved with delicacy. He contented himself by pressing the hand slightly against his robust ribs. At the same time he felt himself being impelled forward, and yielded to the impulse. At the end of Brett Street he became aware of being directed to the left. He submitted.

The fruiterer at the corner had put out the blazing glory of his oranges and lemons, and Brett Place was all darkness, interspersed with the misty halos of the few lamps defining its triangular shape, with a cluster of three lights on one stand in the middle. The dark forms of the man and woman glided slowly arm in arm along the walls with a loverlike and homeless aspect in the miserable night.

"What would you say if I were to tell you that I was going to find you?" Mrs. Verloc asked, gripping his arm with force.

"I would say that you couldn't find anyone more ready to help you in your trouble," answered Ossipon, with a notion of making tremendous headway. In fact, the progress of this delicate affair was almost taking his breath away.

"In my trouble!" Mrs. Verloc repeated, slowly.

"Yes."

"And do you know what my trouble is?" she whispered with strange intensity.

"Ten minutes after seeing the evening paper," explained Ossipon with ardor, "I met a fellow whom you may have seen once or twice at the shop perhaps, and I had a talk with him which left no doubt whatever in my mind. Then I started for here, wondering whether you—I've been fond of you beyond words ever since I set eyes on your face," he cried, as if unable to command his feelings.

Comrade Ossipon assumed correctly that no woman was capable of wholly disbelieving such a statement. But he did not know that Mrs. Verloc accepted it with all the fierceness the instinct of self-preservation imparts to the grip of a drowning person. To the widow of Mr. Verloc the robust anarchist was like a radiant messenger of life.

They walked slowly, in step. "I thought so," Mrs. Verloc murmured, faintly.

"You've read it in my eyes," suggested Ossipon with great assurance.

"Yes," she breathed out into his inclined ear.

"A love like mine could not be concealed from a woman like you," he went on, trying to detach his mind from material considerations such as the business value of the shop, and the amount of money Mr. Verloc might have left in the bank. He applied himself to the sentimental side of the affair. In his heart of hearts he was a little shocked at his success. Verloc had been a good fellow, and certainly a very decent husband as far as one could see. However, Comrade Ossipon was not going to quarrel with his luck for the sake of a dead man. Resolutely he suppressed his sympathy for the ghost of Comrade Verloc, and went on:

"I could not conceal it. I was too full of you. I daresay you could not help seeing it in my eyes. But I could not guess it. You were always so distant. . . ."

"What else did you expect?" burst out Mrs. Verloc. "I was a respectable woman—"

She paused, then added, as if speaking to herself, in sinister resentment: "Till he made me what I am."

Ossipon let that pass, and took up his running.

"He never did seem to me to be quite worthy of you," he began, throwing loyalty to the winds. "You were worthy of a better fate."

Mrs. Verloc interrupted bitterly:

"Better fate! He cheated me out of seven years of life."

"You seemed to live so happily with him." Ossipon tried to exculpate the luke-warmness of his past conduct. "It's that what's made me timid. You seemed to love him. I was surprised—and jealous," he added.

"Love him!" Mrs. Verloc cried out in a whisper full of scorn and rage. "Love him! I was a good wife to him. I am a respectable woman. You thought I loved him! You did! Look here, Tom—"

The sound of this name thrilled Comrade Ossipon with pride. For his name was Alexander, and he was called Tom by arrangement with the most familiar of his intimates. It was a name of friendship—of moments of expansion. He had no idea that she had ever heard it used by anybody. It was apparent that she had not only caught it, but had treasured it in her memory—perhaps in her heart.

"Look here, Tom! I was a young girl. I was done up. I was tired. I had two people depending on what I could do, and it did seem as if I couldn't do any more. Two people—mother and the boy. He was much more mine than mother's. I sat up nights and nights with him on my lap, all alone upstairs, when I wasn't more than eight years old myself. And then—He was mine, I tell you. . . . You can't under-stand that. No man can understand it. What was I to do? There was a young fel-low—"

The memory of the early romance with the young butcher survived, tenacious, like the image of a glimpsed ideal in that heart quailing before the fear of the gal-lows and full of revolt against death.

"That was the man I loved then," went on the widow of Mr. Verloc. "I suppose he could see it in my eyes, too. Five and twenty shillings a week, and his father threatened to kick him out of the business if he made such a fool of himself as to marry a girl with a crippled mother and a crazy idiot of a boy on her hands. But he would hang about me, till one evening I found the courage to slam the door in his face. I had to do it. I loved him dearly. Five and twenty shillings a week! There was that other man—a good lodger. What is a girl to do? Could I've gone on the streets? He seemed kind. He wanted me, anyhow. What was I to do with mother and that poor boy? Eh? I said yes. He seemed good-natured, he was freehanded, he had money, he never said anything. Seven years—seven years a good wife to him, the kind, the good, the generous, the—And he loved me. Oh, yes. He loved me till I sometimes wished myself—Seven years. Seven years a wife to him. And do you know what he was, that dear friend of yours? Do you know what he was? . . . He was a devil!"

The superhuman vehemence of that whispered statement completely stunned Comrade Ossipon. Winnie Verloc turning about held him by both arms, facing him under the falling mist in the darkness and solitude of Brett Place, in which all sounds of life seemed lost as if in a triangular well of asphalt and bricks, of blind houses and unfeeling stones.

"No; I didn't know," he declared, with a sort of flabby stupidity, whose comical aspect was lost upon a woman haunted by the fear of the gallows, "but I do now. I—I understand," he floundered on, his mind speculating as to what sort of atrocities Verloc could have practiced under the sleepy, placid appearances of his married estate. It was positively awful. "I understand," he repeated, and then by a sudden inspiration uttered an "Unhappy woman!" of lofty commiseration instead of the more familiar "Poor darling!" of his usual practice. This was no usual case. He felt conscious of something abnormal going on, while he never lost sight of the greatness of the stake. "Unhappy, brave woman!"

He was glad to have discovered that variation; but he could discover nothing else. "Ah, but he is dead now," was the best he could do. And he put a remarkable amount of animosity into his guarded exclamation. Mrs. Verloc caught at his arm with a sort of frenzy. "You guessed then he was dead," she murmured, as if beside herself. "You! You guessed what I had to do. Had to!"

There were suggestions of triumph, relief, gratitude in the indefinable tone of these words. It engrossed the whole attention of Ossipon to the detriment of mere literal sense. He wondered what was up with her, why she had worked herself into this state of wild excitement. He even began to wonder whether the hidden causes of that Greenwich Park affair did not lie deep in the unhappy circumstances of the Verlocs' married life. He went so far as to suspect Mr. Verloc of having selected that extraordinary manner of committing suicide. By Jove! that would account for the utter inanity and wrongheadedness of the thing. No anarchist manifestation was required by the circumstances. Quite the contrary; and Verloc was as well aware of that as any other revolutionist of his standing. What an immense joke if Verloc had simply made fools of the whole of Europe, of the revolutionary world, of the police, of the press, and of the cocksure Professor as well. Indeed, thought Ossipon, in astonishment, it seemed almost certain that he did! Poor beggar! It struck him as very possible that of that household of two it wasn't precisely the man who was the devil.

Alexander Ossipon, nicknamed the Doctor, was naturally inclined to think indulgently of his men friends. He eyed Mrs. Verloc hanging on his arm. Of his women friends he thought in a specially practical way. Why Mrs. Verloc should exclaim at his knowledge of Mr. Verloc's death, which was no guess at all, did not disturb him beyond measure. Women often talked like lunatics. But he was curious to know how she had been informed. The papers could tell her nothing beyond the mere fact: the man blown to pieces in Greenwich Park not having been identified. It was inconceivable on any theory that Verloc should have given her an inkling of his intention—whatever it was. This problem interested Comrade Ossipon immensely. He stopped short. They had gone then along the three sides of Brett Place, and were near the end of Brett Street again.

"How did you first come to hear of it?" he asked in a tone he tried to render appropriate to the character of the revelations which had been made to him by the woman at his side.

She shook violently for a while before she answered in a listless voice:

"From the police. A chief inspector came. Chief Inspector Heat he said he was. He showed me—"

Mrs. Verloc choked. "Oh, Tom, they had to gather him up with a shovel."

Her breast heaved with dry sobs. In a moment Ossipon found his tongue.

"The police! Do you mean to say the police came already? That Chief Inspector Heat himself actually came to tell you?"

"Yes," she confirmed in the same listless tone. "He came. Just like this. He came. I didn't know. He showed me a piece of overcoat, and—Just like that. Do you know this? he says."

"Heat! Heat! And what did he do?"

Mrs. Verloc's head dropped. "Nothing. He did nothing. He went away. The police were on that man's side," she murmured, tragically. "Another one came, too."

"Another—another inspector, do you mean?" asked Ossipon, in great excitement, and very much in the tone of a scared child.

"I don't know. He came. He looked like a foreigner. He may have been one of them Embassy people."

Comrade Ossipon nearly collapsed under this new shock.

"Embassy! Are you aware what you are saying? What Embassy? What on earth do you mean by Embassy?"

"It's that place in Chesham Square. The people he cursed so. I don't know. What does it matter!"

"And that fellow, what did he do or say to you?"

"I don't remember. . . . Nothing. . . . I don't care. Don't ask me," she pleaded in a weary voice.

"All right. I won't," assented Ossipon, tenderly. And he meant it, too, not because he was touched by the pathos of the pleading voice, but because he felt himself losing his footing in the depths of this tenebrous affair. Police! Embassy! Phew! For fear of adventuring his intelligence into ways where its natural lights might fail to guide it safely he dismissed resolutely all suppositions, surmises, and theories out of his mind. He had the woman there, absolutely flinging herself at him, and that was the principal consideration. But after what he had heard nothing could astonish him anymore. And when Mrs. Verloc, as if startled suddenly out of a dream of safety, began to urge upon him wildly the necessity of an immediate flight on the Continent, he did not exclaim in the least. He simply said with unaffected regret that there was no train till the morning, and stood looking thoughtfully at her face, veiled in black net, in the light of a gas-lamp veiled in a gauze of mist.

Near him, her black form merged in the night, like a figure half chiseled out of a block of black stone. It was impossible to say what she knew, how deep she was involved with policemen and Embassies. But if she wanted to get away, it was not for him to object. He was anxious to be off himself. He felt that the business, the shop so strangely familiar to chief inspectors and members of foreign Embassies, was not the place for him. That must be dropped. But there was the rest. These savings. The money!

"You must hide me till the morning somewhere," she said in a dismayed voice.

"Fact is, my dear, I can't take you where I live. I share the room with a friend."

He was somewhat dismayed himself. In the morning the blessed 'tecs will be out in all the stations, no doubt. And if they once got hold of her, for one reason or another she would be lost to him indeed.

"But you must. Don't you care for me at all—at all? What are you thinking of?"

She said this violently, but she let her clasped hands fall in discouragement. There was a silence, while the mist fell, and darkness reigned undisturbed over Brett Place. Not a soul, not even the vagabond, lawless, and amorous soul of a cat, came near the man and the woman facing each other.

"It would be possible perhaps to find a safe lodging somewhere," Ossipon spoke at last. "But the truth is, my dear, I have not enough money to go and try with— only a few pence. We revolutionists are not rich."

He had fifteen shillings in his pocket. He added:

"And there's the journey before us, too—first thing in the morning at that."

She did not move, made no sound, and Comrade Ossipon's heart sank a little. Apparently she had no suggestion to offer. Suddenly she clutched at her breast, as if she had felt a sharp pain there.

"But I have," she gasped. "I have the money. I have enough money. Tom! Let us go from here."

"How much have you got?" he inquired, without stirring to her tug; for he was a cautious man.

"I have the money, I tell you. All the money."

"What do you mean by it? All the money there was in the bank, or what?" he asked, incredulously, but ready not to be surprised at anything in the way of luck.

"Yes, yes!" she said, nervously. "All there was. I've it all."

"How on earth did you manage to get hold of it already?" he marveled.

"He gave it to me," she murmured, suddenly subdued and trembling. Comrade Ossipon put down his rising surprise with a firm hand.

"Why, then—we are saved," he uttered, slowly.

She leaned forward, and sank against his breast. He welcomed her there. She had all the money. Her hat was in the way of very marked effusion; her veil, too. He was adequate in his manifestations, but no more. She received them without resistance and without abandonment, passively, as if only half-sensible. She freed herself from his lax embrace without difficulty.

"You will save me, Tom," she broke out, recoiling, but still keeping her hold on him by the two lapels of his damp coat. "Save me. Hide me. Don't let them have me. You must kill me first. I couldn't do it myself—I couldn't, I couldn't—not even for what I am afraid of."

She was confoundedly bizarre, he thought. She was beginning to inspire him with an indefinite uneasiness. He said surlily, for he was busy with important thoughts:

"What the devil *are* you afraid of?"

"Haven't you guessed what I was driven to do!" cried the woman. Distracted by the vividness of her dreadful apprehensions, her head ringing with forceful words, that kept the horror of her position before her mind, she had imagined her incoherence to be clearness itself. She had no conscience of how little she had audibly said in the disjointed phrases completed only in her thought. She had felt the relief of a full confession, and she gave a special meaning to every sentence spoken by Comrade Ossipon, whose knowledge did not in the least resemble her own. "Haven't you guessed what I was driven to do!" Her voice fell. "You needn't be long in guessing then what I am afraid of," she continued, in a bitter and somber murmur. "I won't have it. I won't. I won't. I won't. You must promise to kill me first!" She shook the lapels of his coat. "It must never be!"

He assured her curtly that no promises on his part were necessary, but he took good care not to contradict her in set terms, because he had had much to do with excited women, and he was inclined in general to let his experience guide his conduct in preference to applying his sagacity to each special case. His sagacity in this case was busy in other directions. Women's words fell into water, but the shortcomings of timetables remained. The insular nature of Great Britain obtruded itself upon his notice in an odious form. "Might just as well be put under lock and key every night," he thought irritably, as nonplussed as though he had a wall to scale with the woman on his back. Suddenly he slapped his forehead. He had by dint of cudgeling his brains just thought of the Southampton—St. Malo service. The boat left about midnight. There was a train at 10:30. He became cheery and ready to act.

"From Waterloo. Plenty of time. We are all right after all . . . What's the matter now? This isn't the way," he protested.

Mrs. Verloc, having hooked her arm into his, was trying to drag him into Brett Street again.

"I've forgotten to shut the shop door as I went out," she whispered, terribly agitated.

The shop and all that was in it had ceased to interest Comrade Ossipon. He knew how to limit his desires. He was on the point of saying "What of that? Let it be," but he refrained. He disliked argument about trifles. He even mended his pace considerably on the thought that she might have left the money in the drawer. But his willingness lagged behind her feverish impatience.

The shop seemed to be quite dark at first. The door stood ajar. Mrs. Verloc, leaning against the front, grasped out:

"Nobody has been in. Look! The light—the light in the parlor."

Ossipon, stretching his head forward, saw a faint gleam in the darkness of the shop.

"There is," he said.

"I forgot it." Mrs. Verloc's voice came from behind her veil faintly. And as he stood waiting for her to enter first, she said louder: "Go in and put it out—or I'll go mad."

He made no immediate objection to this proposal, so strangely motived. "Where's all that money?" he asked.

"On me! Go, Tom. Quick! Put it out. . . . Go in!" she cried, seizing him by both shoulders from behind.

Not prepared for a display of physical force, Comrade Ossipon stumbled far into the shop before her push. He was astonished at the strength of the woman and scandalized by her proceedings. But he did not retrace his steps in order to remonstrate with her severely in the street. He was beginning to be disagreeably impressed by her fantastic behavior. Moreover, this or never was the time to humor the woman. Comrade Ossipon avoided easily the end of the counter, and approached calmly the glazed door of the parlor. The curtain over the panes being drawn back a little he, by a very natural impulse, looked in, just as he made ready to turn the handle. He looked in without a thought, without intention, without curiosity of any sort. He looked in because he could not help looking in. He looked in, and discovered Mr. Verloc reposing quietly on the sofa.

A yell coming from the innermost depths of his chest died out unheard and transformed into a sort of greasy, sickly taste on his lips. At the same time the mental personality of Comrade Ossipon executed a frantic leap backwards. But his body, left thus without intellectual guidance, held on to the door handle with the unthinking force of an instinct. The robust anarchist did not even totter. And he stared, his face close to the glass, his eyes protruding out of his head. He would have given anything to get away, but his returning reason informed him that it would not do to let go the door handle. What was it—madness, a nightmare, or a trap into which he had been decoyed with fiendish artfulness? Why—what for? He did not know. Without any sense of guilt in his breast, in the full peace of his conscience as far as these people were concerned, the idea that he would be murdered for mysterious reasons by the couple Verloc passed not so much across his mind as across the pit of his stomach, and went out, leaving behind a trail of sickly faintness—an indisposition. Comrade Ossipon did not feel very well in a very special way for a moment—a long moment. And he stared. Mr. Verloc lay very still meanwhile, simulating sleep for reasons of his own, while that savage woman of his was guarding the door—invisible and silent in the dark and deserted street. Was all this some sort of terrifying arrangement invented by the police for his especial benefit? His modesty shrank from that explanation.

But the true sense of the scene he was beholding came to Ossipon through the contemplation of the hat. It seemed an extraordinary thing, an ominous object, a sign. Black, and rim upward, it lay on the floor before the couch as if prepared to receive the contributions of pence from people who would come presently to behold Mr. Verloc in the fullness of his domestic ease reposing on a sofa. From the hat the eyes of the robust anarchist wandered to the displaced table, gazed at the broken dish for a time, received a kind of optical shock from observing a white gleam under the imperfectly closed eyelids of the man on the couch. Mr. Verloc did not seem so much asleep now as lying down with a bent head and looking insistently at his left breast. And when Comrade Ossipon had made out the handle of the knife he turned away from the glazed door, and retched violently.

The crash of the street door flung to made his very soul leap in a panic. This house with its harmless tenant could still be made a trap of—a trap of a terrible kind. Comrade Ossipon had no settled conception now of what was happening to him. Catching his thigh against the end of the counter, he spun round, staggered with a cry of pain, felt in the distracting clatter of the bell his arms pinned to his sides by a convulsive hug, while the cold lips of a woman moved creepily on his very ear to form the words:

"Policeman! He has seen me!"

He ceased to struggle; she never let him go. Her hands had locked themselves with an inseparable twist of fingers on his robust back. While the footsteps approached, they breathed quickly, breast to breast, with hard, labored breaths, as if theirs had been the attitude of a deadly struggle, while, in fact, it was the attitude of deadly fear. And the time was long.

The constable on the beat had in truth seen something of Mrs. Verloc; only coming from the lighted thoroughfare at the other end of Brett Street, she had been no more to him than a flutter in the darkness. And he was not even quite sure that there had been a flutter. He had no reason to hurry up. On coming abreast of the shop he observed that it had been closed early. There was nothing very unusual in that. The men on duty had special instructions about that shop: what went on about there was not to be meddled with unless absolutely disorderly, but any observations made were to be reported. There were no observations to make; but from a sense of duty and for the peace of his conscience, owing also to that doubtful flutter of the darkness, the constable crossed the road, and tried the door. The spring latch, whose key was reposing forever off duty in the late Mr. Verloc's waistcoat pocket, held as well as usual. While the conscientious officer was shaking the handle, Ossipon felt the cold lips of the woman stirring again creepily against his very ear:

"If he comes in kill me—kill me, Tom."

The constable moved away, flashing as he passed the light of his dark lantern, merely for form's sake, at the shop window. For a moment longer the man and the woman inside stood motionless, panting, breast to breast; then her fingers came unlocked, her arms fell by her sides slowly. Ossipon leaned against the counter. The robust anarchist wanted support badly. This was awful. He was almost too disgusted for speech. Yet he managed to utter a plaintive thought, showing at least that he realized his position.

"Only a couple of minutes later and you'd have made me blunder against the fellow poking about here with his damned dark lantern."

The widow of Mr. Verloc, motionless in the middle of the shop, said insistently:

"Go in and put that light out, Tom. It will drive me crazy."

She saw vaguely his vehement gesture of refusal. Nothing in the world would have induced Ossipon to go into the parlor. He was not superstitious, but there was too much blood on the floor; a beastly pool of it all round the hat. He judged he had been already too near that corpse for his peace of mind—for the safety of his neck, perhaps!

"At the meter then! There. Look. In that corner."

The robust form of Comrade Ossipon, striding brusk and shadowy across the shop, squatted in a corner obediently; but this obedience was without grace. He fumbled nervously—and suddenly in the sound of a muttered curse the light behind the glazed door flicked out to a gasping, hysterical sigh of a woman. Night, the inevitable reward of men's faithful labors on this earth, night had fallen on Mr. Verloc, the tried revolutionist—"one of the old lot"—the humble guardian of society; the invaluable Secret Agent Δ of Baron Stott-Wartenheim's dispatches; a servant of law and order, faithful, trusted, accurate, admirable, with perhaps one single amiable weakness: the idealistic belief in being loved for himself.

Ossipon groped his way back through the stuffy atmosphere, as black as ink now, to the counter. The voice of Mrs. Verloc, standing in the middle of the shop, vibrated after him in that blackness with a desperate protest.

"I will not be hanged, Tom. I will not—"

She broke off. Ossipon from the counter issued a warning: "Don't shout like this," then seemed to reflect profoundly. "You did this thing quite by yourself?" he inquired in a hollow voice, but with an appearance of masterful calmness which filled Mrs. Verloc's heart with grateful confidence in his protecting strength. "Yes," she whispered, invisible.

"I wouldn't have believed it possible," he muttered. "Nobody would." She heard him move about and the snapping of a lock in the parlor door. Comrade Ossipon had turned the key on Mr. Verloc's repose; and this he did not from reverence for its eternal nature or any other obscurely sentimental consideration, but for the precise reason that he was not at all sure that there was not someone else hiding somewhere in the house. He did not believe the woman, or rather he was incapable by now of judging what could be true, possible, or even probable on this astounding universe. He was terrified out of all capacity for belief or disbelief in regard to this extraordinary affair, which began with police inspectors and Embassies and would end goodness knows where—on the scaffold for someone. He was terrified at the thought that he could not prove the use he made of his time ever since seven o'clock, for he had been skulking about Brett Street. He was terrified at this savage woman who had brought him in there, and would probably saddle him with complicity, at least if he were not careful. He was terrified at the rapidity with which he had been involved in such danger—decoyed into it. It was some twenty minutes since he had met her—not more.

The voice of Mrs. Verloc rose subdued, pleading piteously: "Don't let them hang me, Tom! Take me out of the country. I'll work for you. I'll slave for you. I'll love you. I've no one in the world. . . . Who would look at me if you don't!" She ceased for a moment; then in the depths of the loneliness made round her by an insignificant thread of blood trickling off the handle of a knife, she found a dreadful inspiration to her—who had been the respectable girl of the Belgravian mansion, the loyal, respectable wife of Mr. Verloc. "I won't ask you to marry me," she breathed out in shamefaced accents.

She moved a step forward in the darkness. He was terrified at her. He would not have been surprised if she had suddenly produced another knife destined for his breast. He certainly would have made no resistance. He had really not enough fortitude in him just then to tell her to keep back. But he inquired in a cavernous, strange tone: "Was he asleep?"

"No," she cried, and went on rapidly: "He wasn't. Not he. He had been telling me that nothing could touch him. After taking the boy away from under my very eyes to kill him—the loving, innocent, harmless lad. My own, I tell you. He was lying on the couch quite easy—after killing the boy—my boy. I would have gone on the streets to get out of his sight. And he says to me like this: 'Come here,' after telling me I had helped to kill the boy. You hear, Tom? He says like this: 'Come here,' after taking my very heart out of me along with the boy to smash in the dirt."

She ceased, then dreamily repeated twice: "Blood and dirt. Blood and dirt." A great light broke upon Comrade Ossipon. It was that half-witted lad then who had perished in the park. And the fooling of everybody all round appeared more complete than ever—colossal. He exclaimed scientifically, in the extremity of his astonishment: "The degenerate—by heavens!"

"Come here." The voice of Mrs. Verloc rose again. "What did he think I was made of? Tell me, Tom. Come here! Me! Like this! I had been looking at the knife, and I thought I would come then if he wanted me so much. Oh, yes! I came—for the last time. . . . With the knife."

He was excessively terrified at her—the sister of the degenerate—a degenerate herself of a murdering type . . . or else of the lying type. Comrade Ossipon might have been said to be terrified scientifically in addition to all other kinds of fear. It was an immeasurable and composite funk, which from its very excess gave him in the dark a false appearance of calm and thoughtful deliberation. For he moved and spoke with difficulty, being as if half frozen in his will and mind—and no one could see his ghastly face. He felt half dead.

He leaped a foot high. Unexpectedly Mrs. Verloc had desecrated the unbroken, reserved decency of her home by a shrill and terrible shriek.

"Help, Tom! Save me. I won't be hanged!"

He rushed forward, groping for her mouth with a silencing hand, and the shriek died out. But in his rush he had knocked her over. He felt her now clinging round his legs, and his terror reached its culminating point, became a sort of intoxication, entertained delusions, acquired the characteristics of delirium tremens. He positively saw snakes now. He saw the woman twined round him like a snake, not to be shaken off. She was not deadly. She was death itself—the companion of life.

Mrs. Verloc, as if relieved by the outburst, was very far from behaving noisily now. She was pitiful.

"Tom, you can't throw me off now," she murmured from the floor. "Not unless you crush my head under your heel. I won't leave you."

"Get up," said Ossipon.

His face was so pale as to be quite visible in the profound black darkness of the shop; while Mrs. Verloc, veiled, had no face, almost no discernible form. The trembling of something small and white, a flower in her hat, marked her place, her movements.

It rose in the blackness. She had got up from the floor, and Ossipon regretted not having run out at once into the street. But he perceived easily that it would not do. It would not do. She would run after him. She would pursue him shrieking till she sent every policeman within hearing in chase. And then goodness only knew what she would say of him. He was so frightened that for a moment the insane notion of strangling her in the dark passed through his mind. And he became more frightened than ever! She had him. He saw himself living in abject terror in some obscure hamlet in Spain or Italy; till some fine morning they found him dead, too, with a knife in his breast—like Mr. Verloc. He sighed deeply. He dared not move. And Mrs. Verloc waited in silence the good pleasure of her savior, deriving comfort from his reflective silence.

Suddenly he spoke up in an almost natural voice. His reflections had come to an end.

"Let's get out, or we will lose the train."

"Where are we going to, Tom?" she asked, timidly. Mrs. Verloc was no longer a free woman.

"Let's get to Paris first, the best way we can. . . . Go out first, and see if the way's clear."

She obeyed. Her voice came subdued through the cautiously opened door.

"It's all right."

Ossipon came out. Notwithstanding his endeavors to be gentle, the cracked bell clattered behind the closed door in the empty shop, as if trying in vain to warn the reposing Mr. Verloc of the final departure of his wife—accompanied by his friend.

In the hansom they presently picked up, the robust anarchist became explanatory. He was still awfully pale, with eyes that seemed to have sunk a whole half-inch into his tense face. But he seemed to have thought of everything with extraordinary method.

"When we arrive," he discoursed in a queer, monotonous tone, "you must go into the station ahead of me, as if we did not know each other. I will take the tickets, and slip yours into your hand as I pass you. Then you will go into the first-class ladies' waiting room, and sit there till ten minutes before the train starts. Then you come out. I will be outside. You go in first on the platform, as if you did not know me. There may be eyes watching there that know what's what. Alone you are only a woman going off by train. I am known. With me, you may be guessed at as Mrs. Verloc running away. Do you understand, my dear?" he added, with an effort.

"Yes," said Mrs. Verloc, sitting there against him in the hansom all rigid with the dread of the gallows and the fear of death. "Yes, Tom." And she added to herself, like an awful refrain: "The drop given was fourteen feet."

Ossipon, not looking at her, and with a face like a fresh plaster cast of himself after a wasting illness, said: "By-the-by, I ought to have the money for the tickets now."

Mrs. Verloc, undoing some hooks of her bodice, while she went on staring ahead beyond the splashboard, handed over to him the new pigskin pocketbook. He received it without a word, and seemed to plunge it deep somewhere into his very breast. Then he slapped his coat on the outside.

All this was done without the exchange of a single glance; they were like two people looking out for the first sight of a desired goal. It was not till the hansom swung round a corner and towards the bridge that Ossipon opened his lips again.

"Do you know how much money there is in that thing?" he asked, as if addressing slowly some hobgoblin sitting between the ears of the horse.

"No," said Mrs. Verloc. "He gave it to me. I didn't count. I thought nothing of it at the time. Afterwards—"

She moved her right hand a little. It was so expressive, that little movement of that right hand which had struck the deadly blow into a man's heart less than an hour before, that Ossipon could not repress a shudder. He exaggerated it then purposely, and muttered:

"I am cold. I got chilled through."

Mrs. Verloc looked straight ahead at the perspective of her escape. Now and then, like a sable streamer blown across a road, the words "The drop given was fourteen feet" got in the way of her tense stare. Through her black veil the whites of her big eyes gleamed lustrously like the eyes of a masked woman.

Ossipon's rigidity had something businesslike, a queer official expression. He was heard again all of a sudden, as though he had released a catch in order to speak.

"Look here! Do you know whether your—whether he kept his account at the bank in his own name or in some other name?"

Mrs. Verloc turned upon him her masked face and the big white gleam of her eyes.

"Other name?" she said, thoughtfully.

"Be exact in what you say," Ossipon lectured in the swift motion of the hansom. "It's extremely important. I will explain to you. The bank has the numbers of these notes. If they were paid to him in his own name, then when his—his death becomes known, the notes may serve to track us since we have no other money. You have no other money on you?"

She shook her head negatively.

"None whatever?" he insisted.

"A few coppers."

"It would be dangerous in that case. The money would have then to be dealt specially with. Very specially. We'd have perhaps to lose more than half the amount in order to get these notes changed in a certain safe place I know of in Paris. In the other case—I mean if he had his account and got paid out under some other name—say Smith, for instance—the money is perfectly safe to use. You understand? The bank has no means of knowing that Mr. Verloc and, say, Smith are one and the same person. Do you see how important it is that you should make no mistake in answering me? Can you answer that query at all? Perhaps not. Eh?"

She said composedly:

"I remember now! He didn't bank in his own name. He told me once that it was on deposit in the name of Prozor."

"You are sure?"

"Certain."

"You don't think the bank had any knowledge of his real name? Or anybody in the bank or—"

She shrugged her shoulders.

"How can I know? Is it likely, Tom?"

"No. I suppose it's not likely. It would have been more comfortable to know. . . . Here we are. Get out first, and walk straight in. Move smartly."

He remained behind, and paid the cabman out of his own loose silver. The program traced by his minute foresight was carried out. When Mrs. Verloc, with her ticket for St. Malo in her hand, entered the ladies' waiting room, Comrade Ossipon walked into the bar, and in seven minutes absorbed three goes of hot brandy and water.

"Trying to drive out a cold," he explained to the barmaid, with a friendly nod and a grimacing smile. Then he came out, bringing out from that festive interlude the face of a man who had drunk at the very Fountain of Sorrow. He raised his eyes to the clock. It was time. He waited.

Punctual, Mrs. Verloc came out, with her veil down, and all black—black as commonplace death itself, crowned with a few cheap and pale flowers. She passed close to a little group of men who were laughing, but whose laughter could have been struck dead by a single word. Her walk was indolent, but her back was straight, and Comrade Ossipon looked after it in terror before making a start himself.

The train was drawn up, with hardly anybody about its row of open doors. Owing to the time of the year and to the abominable weather there were but few passengers. Mrs. Verloc walked slowly along the line of empty compartments till Ossipon touched her elbow from behind.

"In here."

She got in, and he remained on the platform looking about. She bent forward, and in a whisper:

"What is it, Tom? Is there any danger?"

"Wait a moment. There's the guard."

She saw him accost the man in uniform. They talked for a while. She heard the guard say "Very well, sir," and saw him touch his cap. Then Ossipon came back, saying: "I told him not to let anybody get into our compartment."

She was leaning forward on her seat. "You think of everything. . . . You'll get me off, Tom?" she asked in a gust of anguish, lifting her veil bruskly to look at her savior.

She had uncovered a face like adamant. And out of this face the eyes looked on, big, dry, enlarged, lightless, burnt out like two black holes in the white, shining globes.

"There is no danger," he said, gazing into them with an earnestness almost rapt, which to Mrs. Verloc, flying from the gallows, seemed to be full of force and tenderness. This devotion deeply moved her—and the adamantine face lost the stern rigidity of its terror. Comrade Ossipon gazed at it as no lover ever gazed at his mistress's face. Alexander Ossipon, anarchist, nicknamed the Doctor, author of a medical (and improper) pamphlet, late lecturer on the social aspects of hygiene to working men's clubs, was free from the trammels of conventional morality—but he submitted to the rule of science. He was scientific, and he gazed scientifically at that woman, the sister of a degenerate, a degenerate herself—of a murdering type. He gazed at her, and invoked Lombroso, as an Italian peasant recommends himself to his favorite saint. He gazed scientifically. He gazed at her cheeks, at her nose, at her eyes, at her ears. . . . Bad! . . . Fatal! Mrs. Verloc's pale lips parting, slightly relaxed under his passionately attentive gaze, he gazed also at her teeth. . . . Not a doubt remained . . . a murdering type. . . . If Comrade Ossipon did not recommend his terrified soul to Lombroso, it was only because on scientific grounds he could not believe that he carried about him such a thing as a soul. But he had in him the scientific spirit, which moved him to testify on the platform of a railway station in nervous, jerky phrases.

"He was an extraordinary lad, that brother of yours. Most interesting to study. A perfect type in a way. Perfect!"

He spoke scientifically in his secret fear. And Mrs. Verloc, hearing these words of commendation vouchsafed to her beloved dead, swayed forward with a flicker of light in her somber eyes, like a ray of sunshine heralding a tempest of rain.

"He was that indeed," she whispered, softly, with quivering lips. "You took a lot of notice of him, Tom. I loved you for it."

"It's almost incredible the resemblance there was between you two," pursued Ossipon, giving a voice to his abiding dread, and trying to conceal his nervous, sickening impatience for the train to start. "Yes, he resembled you. "

These words were not especially touching or sympathetic. But the fact of that resemblance insisted upon was enough in itself to act upon her emotions powerfully. With a little faint cry, and throwing her arms out, Mrs. Verloc burst into tears at last.

Ossipon entered the carriage, hastily closed the door and looked out to see the time by the station clock. Eight minutes more. For the first three of these Mrs. Verloc wept violently and helplessly without pause or interruption. Then she recovered somewhat, and sobbed gently in an abundant fall of tears. She tried to talk to her savior, to the man who was the messenger of life.

"Oh, Tom! How could I fear to die after he was taken away from me so cruelly! How could I! How could I be such a coward!"

She lamented aloud her love of life, that life without grace or charm, and almost without decency, but of an exalted faithfulness of purpose, even unto murder. And, as often happens in the lament of poor humanity rich in suffering but indigent in words, the truth—the very cry of truth—was found in a worn and artificial shape picked up somewhere among the phrases of sham sentiment.

"How could I be so afraid of death! Tom, I tried. But I am afraid. I tried to do away with myself. And I couldn't. Am I hard? I suppose the cup of horrors was not full enough for such as me. Then when you came. . . ."

She paused. Then in a gust of confidence and gratitude, "I will live all my days for you, Tom!" she sobbed out.

"Go over into the other corner of the carriage, away from the platform," said Ossipon, solicitously. She let her savior settle her comfortably, and he watched the coming on of another crisis of weeping, still more violent than the first. He watched the symptoms with a sort of medical air, as if counting seconds. He heard the guard's whistle at last. An involuntary contraction of the upper lip bared his teeth with all the aspect of savage resolution as he felt the train beginning to move. Mrs. Verloc heard and felt nothing, and Ossipon, her savior, stood still. He felt the train roll quicker, rumbling heavily to the sound of the woman's loud sobs, and then crossing the carriage in two long strides he opened the door deliberately, and leaped out.

He had leaped out at the very end of the platform; and such was his determination in sticking to his desperate plan that he managed by a sort of miracle, performed almost in the air, to slam to the door of the carriage. Only then did he find himself rolling head over heels like a shot rabbit. He was bruised, shaken, pale as death, and out of breath when he got up. But he was calm, and perfectly able to meet the excited crowd of railway men who had gathered round him in a moment. He explained, in gentle and convincing tones, that his wife had started at a moment's notice for Brittany to her dying mother; that, of course, she was greatly upset, and he considerably concerned at her state; that he was trying to cheer her up, and had absolutely failed to notice at first that the train was moving out. To the general exclamation "Why didn't you go on to Southampton, then, sir?" he objected the inexperience of a young sister-in-law left alone in the house with three small children, and her alarm at his absence, the telegraph offices being closed. He had acted on impulse. "But I don't think I'll ever try that again," he concluded; smiled all round; distributed some small change, and marched without a limp out of the station.

Outside, Comrade Ossipon, flush of safe banknotes as never before in his life, refused the offer of a cab.

"I can walk," he said, with a little friendly laugh to the civil driver.

He could walk. He walked. He crossed the bridge. Later on the towers of the Abbey saw in their massive immobility the yellow bush of his hair passing under the lamps. The lights of Victoria saw him, too, and Sloane Square, and the railings of the park. And Comrade Ossipon once more found himself on a bridge. The river, a sinister marvel of still shadows and flowing gleams mingling below in a black silence, arrested his attention. He stood looking over the parapet for a long time. The clock tower boomed a brazen blast above his drooping head. He looked up at the dial. . . . Half-past twelve of a wild night in the Channel.

And again Comrade Ossipon walked. His robust form was seen that night in distant parts of the enormous town slumbering monstrously on a carpet of mud under a veil of raw mist. It was seen crossing the streets without life and sound, or diminishing in the interminable straight perspectives of shadowy houses bordering empty roadways lined by strings of gas-lamps. He walked through Squares, Places, Ovals, Commons, through monotonous streets with unknown names where the dust of humanity settles inert and hopeless out of the stream of life. He walked. And suddenly turning into a strip of a front garden with a mangy grass-plot, he let himself into a small grimy house with a latchkey he took out of his pocket.

He threw himself down on his bed all dressed, and lay still for a whole quarter of an hour. Then he sat up suddenly, drawing up his knees, and clasping his legs. The first dawn found him open-eyed, in that same posture. This man who could walk so long, so far, so aimlessly, without showing a sign of fatigue, could also remain sitting still for hours without stirring a limb or an eyelid. But when the late sun sent its rays into the room he unclasped his hands, and fell back on the pillow. His eyes stared at the ceiling. And suddenly they closed. Comrade Ossipon slept in the sunlight.

❧ 13 ❧

The enormous iron padlock on the doors of the wall cupboard was the only object in the room on which the eye could rest without becoming afflicted by the miserable unloveliness of forms and the poverty of material. Unsaleable in the ordinary course of business on account of its noble proportions, it had been ceded to the Professor for a few pence by a marine dealer in the east of London. The room was large, clean, respectable, and poor with that poverty suggesting the starvation of every human need except mere bread. There was nothing on the walls but the paper, an expanse of arsenical green, soiled with indelible smudges here and there, and with stains resembling faded maps of uninhabited continents.

At a deal table near a window sat Comrade Ossipon, holding his head between his fists. The Professor, dressed in his only suit of shoddy tweeds, but flapping to and fro on the bare boards a pair of incredibly dilapidated slippers, had thrust his hands deep into the overstrained pockets of his jacket. He was relating to his robust guest a visit he had lately been paying to the Apostle Michaelis. The Perfect Anarchist had even been unbending a little.

"The fellow didn't know anything of Verloc's death. Of course! He never looks at the newspapers. They make him too sad, he says. But never mind. I walked into his cottage. Not a soul anywhere. I had to shout half-a-dozen times before he answered me. I thought he was fast asleep yet, in bed. But not at all. He had been writing his book for four hours already. He sat in that tiny cage in a litter of manuscript. There was a half-eaten raw carrot on the table near him. His breakfast. He lives on a diet of raw carrots and a little milk now."

"How does he look on it?" asked Comrade Ossipon, listlessly.

"Angelic. . . . I picked up a handful of his pages from the floor. The poverty of reasoning is astonishing. He has no logic. He can't think consecutively. But that's nothing. He has divided his biography into three parts, entitled—'Faith, Hope, Charity.' He is elaborating now the idea of a world planned out like an immense and nice hospital, with gardens and flowers, in which the strong are to devote themselves to the nursing of the weak."

The Professor paused.

"Conceive you this folly, Ossipon? The weak! The source of all evil on this earth!" he continued with his grim assurance. "I told him that I dreamt of a world like shambles, where the weak would be taken in hand for utter extermination.

"Do you understand, Ossipon? The source of all evil! They are our sinister masters—the weak, the flabby, the silly, the cowardly, the faint of heart, and the slavish of mind. They have power. They are the multitude. Theirs is the kingdom of the earth. Exterminate, exterminate! That is the only way of progress. It is! Follow me, Ossipon. First the great multitude of the weak must go, then the only relatively strong. You see? First the blind, then the deaf and the dumb, then the halt and the lame—and so on. Every taint, every vice, every prejudice, every convention must meet its doom."

"And what remains?" asked Ossipon in a stifled voice.

"I remain—if I am strong enough," asserted the sallow little Professor, whose large ears, thin like membranes, and standing far out from the sides of his frail skull, took on suddenly a deep red tint.

"Haven't I suffered enough from this oppression of the weak?" he continued, forcibly. Then tapping the breast-pocket of his jacket: "And yet *I am* the force," he went on. "But the time! The time! Give me time! Ah! that multitude, too stupid to feel either pity or fear. Sometimes I think they have everything on their side. Everything—even death—my own weapon."

"Come and drink some beer with me at the Silenus," said the robust Ossipon after an interval of silence pervaded by the rapid flap, flap of the slippers on the feet of the Perfect Anarchist. This last accepted. He was jovial that day in his own peculiar way. He slapped Ossipon's shoulder.

"Beer! So be it! Let us drink and be merry, for we are strong, and tomorrow we die."

He busied himself with putting on his boots, and talked meanwhile in his curt, resolute tones.

"What's the matter with you, Ossipon? You look glum and seek even my company. I hear that you are seen constantly in places where men utter foolish things over glasses of liquor. Why? Have you abandoned your collection of women? They are the weak who feed the strong—eh?"

He stamped one foot, and picked up his other laced boot, heavy, thick-soled, unblacked, mended many times. He smiled to himself grimly.

"Tell me, Ossipon, terrible man, has ever one of your victims killed herself for you—or are your triumphs so far incomplete—for blood alone puts a seal on greatness? Blood. Death. Look at history."

"You be damned," said Ossipon, without turning his head.

"Why? Let that be the hope of the weak, whose theology has invented hell for the strong. Ossipon, my feeling for you is amicable contempt. You couldn't kill a fly."

But rolling to the feast on the top of the omnibus the Professor lost his high spirits. The contemplation of the multitudes thronging the pavements extinguished his assurance under a load of doubt and uneasiness which he could shake off after a period of seclusion in the room with the large cupboard closed by an enormous padlock.

"And so," said over his shoulder Comrade Ossipon, who sat on the seat behind. "And so Michaelis dreams of a world like a beautiful and cheery hospital."

"Just so. An immense charity for the healing of the weak," assented the Professor, sardonically.

"That's silly," admitted Ossipon. "You can't heal weakness. But after all Michaelis may not be so far wrong. In two hundred years doctors will rule the world. Science reigns already. It reigns in the shade maybe—but it reigns. And all science must culminate at last in the science of healing—not the weak, but the strong. Mankind wants to live—to live."

"Mankind," asserted the Professor with a self-confident glitter of his iron-rimmed spectacles, "does not know what it wants."

"But you do," growled Ossipon. "Just now you've been crying for time—time. Well, the doctors will serve you out your time—if you are good. You profess yourself to be one of the strong—because you carry in your pocket enough stuff to send yourself and, say, twenty other people into eternity. But eternity is a damned hole. It's time that you need. You—if you met a man who could give you for certain ten years of time, you would call him your master."

"My device is: No God! No master," said the Professor, sententiously, as he rose to get off the 'bus.

Ossipon followed. "Wait till you are lying flat on your back at the end of your time," he retorted, jumping off the footboard after the other. "Your scurvy, shabby, mangy little bit of time," he continued across the street, and hopping on to the curbstone.

"Ossipon, I think that you are a humbug," the Professor said, opening masterfully the doors of the renowned Silenus. And when they had established themselves at a little table he developed further this gracious thought. "You are not even a doctor. But you are funny. Your notion of a humanity universally putting out the tongue and taking the pill from pole to pole at the bidding of a few solemn jokers is worthy of the prophet. Prophecy! What's the good of thinking of what will be!" He raised his glass. "To the destruction of what is," he said, calmly.

He drank and relapsed into his peculiarly close manner of silence. The thought of a mankind as numerous as the sands of the seashore, as indestructible, as difficult to handle, oppressed him. The sound of exploding bombs was lost in their immensity of passive grains without an echo. For instance, this Verloc affair. Who thought of it now?

Ossipon, as if suddenly compelled by some mysterious force, pulled a much-folded newspaper out of his pocket. The Professor raised his head at the rustle.

"What's that paper? Anything in it?" he asked.

Ossipon started like a scared somnambulist.

"Nothing. Nothing whatever. The thing's ten days old. I forgot it in my pocket, I suppose."

But he did not throw the old thing away. Before returning it to his pocket he stole a glance at the last lines of a paragraph. They ran thus: "*An impenetrable mystery seems destined to hang forever over this act of madness or despair.*"

Such were the end words of an item of news headed:

"Suicide of Lady Passenger from a cross-Channel Boat." Comrade Ossipon was familiar with the beauties of its journalistic style. "*An impenetrable mystery seems destined to hang forever. . . .*" He knew every word by heart. "*An impene-*

trable mystery. . . ." And the robust anarchist, hanging his head on his breast, fell into a long reverie.

He was menaced by this thing in the very sources of his existence. He could not issue forth to meet his various conquests, those that he courted on benches in Kensington Gardens, and those he met near area railings, without the dread of beginning to talk to them of an impenetrable mystery destined. . . . He was becoming scientifically afraid of insanity lying in wait for him amongst these lines. *"To hang forever over."* It was an obsession, a torture. He had lately failed to keep several of these appointments, whose note used to be an unbounded trustfulness in the language of sentiment and manly tenderness. The confiding disposition of various classes of women satisfied the needs of his self-love, and put some material means into his hand. He needed it to live. It was there. But if he could no longer make use of it, he ran the risk of starving his ideals and his body . . . *"This act of madness or despair."*

"An impenetrable mystery" was sure "to hang forever" as far as all mankind was concerned. But what of that if he alone of all men could never get rid of the cursed knowledge? And Comrade Ossipon's knowledge was as precise as the newspaper man could make it—up to the very threshold of the *"mystery destined to hang forever.* . . ."

Comrade Ossipon was well informed. He knew what the gangway man of the steamer had seen: "A lady in a black dress and a black veil, wandering at midnight alongside, on the quay. "Are you going by the boat, ma'am?" he had asked her, encouragingly. "This way." She seemed not to know what to do. He helped her on board. She seemed weak."

And Ossipon knew also what the stewardess had seen: A lady in black with a white face standing in the middle of the empty ladies' cabin. The stewardess induced her to lie down there. The lady seemed quite unwilling to speak, and as if she were in some awful trouble. The next the stewardess knew she was gone from the ladies' cabin. The stewardess then went on deck to look for her, and Comrade Ossipon was informed that the good woman found the unhappy lady lying down in one of the hooded seats. Her eyes were open, but she would not answer anything that was said to her. She seemed very ill. The stewardess fetched the chief steward, and those two people stood by the side of the hooded seat consulting over their extraordinary and tragic passenger. They talked in audible whispers (for she seemed past hearing) of St. Malo and the Consul there, of communicating with her people in England. Then they went away to arrange for her removal down below, for indeed by what they could see of her face she seemed to them to be dying. But Comrade Ossipon knew that behind that white mask of despair there was struggling against terror and despair a vigor of vitality, a love of life that could resist the furious anguish which drives to murder and the fear, the blind, mad fear of the gallows. He knew. But the stewardess and the chief steward knew nothing, except that when they came back for her in less than five minutes the lady in black was no longer in the hooded seat. She was nowhere. She was gone. It was then five o'clock in the morning, and it was no accident either. An hour afterwards one of the steamer's hands found a wedding ring left lying on the seat. It had stuck to the wood in a bit of wet, and its glitter caught the man's eye. There was a date, 24th June, 1879, engraved inside. *"An impenetrable mystery is destined to hang forever...."*

And Comrade Ossipon raised his bowed head, beloved of various humble women of these isles, Apollo-like in the sunniness of its bush of hair.

The Professor had grown restless meantime. He rose.

"Stay," said Ossipon, hurriedly. "Here, what do you know of madness and despair?"

The Professor passed the tip of his tongue on his dry, thin lips, and said doctorally:

"There are no such things. All passion is lost now. The world is mediocre, limp, without force. And madness and despair are a force. And force is a crime in the eyes of the fools, the weak and the silly who rule the roost. You are mediocre. Verloc, whose affair the police has managed to smother so nicely, was mediocre. And the police murdered him. He was mediocre. Everybody is mediocre. Madness and despair! Give me that for a lever, and I'll move the world. Ossipon, you have my cordial scorn. You are incapable of conceiving even what the fat-fed citizen would call a crime. You have no force." He paused, smiling sardonically under the fierce glitter of his thick glasses.

"And let me tell you that this little legacy they say you've come into has not improved your intelligence. You sit at your beer like a dummy. Goodbye."

"Will you have it?" said Ossipon, looking up with an idiotic grin.

"Have what?"

"The legacy. All of it."

The incorruptible Professor only smiled. His clothes were all but falling off him, his boots, shapeless with repairs, heavy like lead, let water in at every step. He said:

"I will send you by-and-by a small bill for certain chemicals which I shall order tomorrow. I need them badly. Understood—eh?"

Ossipon lowered his head slowly. He was alone. *"An impenetrable mystery...."* It seemed to him that suspended in the air before him he saw his own brain pulsating to the rhythm of an impenetrable mystery. It was diseased clearly.... *"This act of madness or despair."*

The mechanical piano near the door played through a valse cheekily, then fell silent all at once, as if gone grumpy.

Comrade Ossipon, nicknamed the Doctor, went out of the Silenus beer hall. At the door he hesitated, blinking at a not too splendid sunlight—and the paper with the report of the suicide of a lady was in his pocket. His heart was beating against it. The suicide of a lady—*this act of madness or despair*.

He walked along the street without looking where he put his feet; and he walked in a direction which would not bring him to the place of appointment with another lady (an elderly nursery governess putting her trust in an Apollo-like ambrosial head). He was walking away from it. He could face no woman. It was ruin. He could neither think, work, sleep, nor eat. But he was beginning to drink with pleasure, with anticipation, with hope. It was ruin. His revolutionary career, sustained by the sentiment and trustfulness of many women, was menaced by an impenetrable mystery—the mystery of a human brain pulsating wrongfully to the rhythm of journalistic phrases. ". . . *Will hang forever over this act. . . .* It was inclining towards the gutter . . . *of madness or despair. . . .*"

"I am seriously ill," he muttered to himself with scientific insight. Already his robust form, with an Embassy's secret-service money (inherited from Mr. Verloc) in his pockets, was marching in the gutter as if in training for the task of an inevitable future. Already he bowed his broad shoulders, his head of ambrosial locks, as if ready to receive the leather yoke of the sandwich board. As on that night, more than a week ago, Comrade Ossipon walked without looking where he put his feet, feeling no fatigue, feeling nothing, seeing nothing, hearing not a sound. "*An impenetrable mystery. . . .*" He walked disregarded. . . . "*This act of madness or despair.*"

And the incorruptible Professor walked, too, averting his eyes from the odious multitude of mankind. He had no future. He disdained it. He was a force. His thoughts caressed the images of ruin and destruction. He walked frail, insignificant, shabby, miserable—and terrible in the simplicity of his idea calling madness and despair to the regeneration of the world. Nobody looked at him. He passed on unsuspected and deadly, like a pest in the street full of men.

THE END

UNDER WESTERN EYES

PART FIRST

To begin with, I wish to disclaim the possession of those high gifts of imagination and expression which would have enabled my pen to create for the reader the personality of the man who called himself, after the Russian custom, Cyril son of Isidor—Kirylo Sidorovitch—Razumov.

If I have ever had these gifts in any sort of living form they have been smothered out of existence a long time ago under a wilderness of words. Words, as is well known, are the great foes of reality. I have been for many years a teacher of languages. It is an occupation which at length becomes fatal to whatever share of imagination, observation, and insight an ordinary person may be heir to. To a teacher of languages there comes a time when the world is but a place of many words, and man appears a mere talking animal not much more wonderful than a parrot.

This being so, I could not have observed Mr. Razumov or guessed at his reality by the force of insight, much less have imagined him as he was. Even to invent the mere bald facts of his life would have been utterly beyond my powers. But I think that without this declaration the readers of these pages will be able to detect in the story the marks of documentary evidence. And that is perfectly correct. It is based on a document; all I have brought to it is my knowledge of the Russian language, which is sufficient for what is attempted here. The document, of course, is something in the nature of a journal, a diary, yet not exactly that in its actual form. For instance, most of it was not written up from day to day, though all the entries are dated. Some of these entries cover months of time and extend over dozens of pages. All the earlier part is a retrospect, in a narrative form, relating to an event which took place about a year before.

I must mention that I have lived for a long time in Geneva. A whole quarter of that town, on account of many Russians residing there, is called La Petite Russie—Little Russia. I had a rather extensive connection in Little Russia at that time. Yet I confess that I have no comprehension of the Russian character. The illogicality of their attitude, the arbitrariness of their conclusions, the frequency of the exceptional, should present no difficulty to a student of many grammars; but there must be something else in the way, some special human trait—one of those subtle differences that are beyond the ken of mere professors. What must remain striking to a teacher of languages is the Russians' extraordinary love of words. They gather them up; they cherish them, but they don't hoard them in their breasts; on the contrary, they are always ready to pour them out by the hour or by the night with an enthusiasm, a sweeping abundance, with such an aptness of application sometimes that, as in the case of very accomplished parrots, one can't defend oneself from the suspicion that they really understand what they say. There is a generosity in their ardor of speech which removes it as far as possible from common loquacity; and it is ever too disconnected to be classed as elo-quence. . . . But I must apologize for this digression.

It would be idle to inquire why Mr. Razumov has left this record behind him. It is inconceivable that he should have wished any human eye to see it. A mysterious impulse of human nature comes into play here. Putting aside Samuel Pepys, who has forced in this way the door of immortality, innumerable people, criminals, saints, philosophers, young girls, statesmen, and simple imbeciles, have kept self-revealing records from vanity no doubt, but also from other more inscrutable motives. There must be a wonderful soothing power in mere words since so many men have used them for self-communion. Being myself a quiet individual, I take it that what all men are really after is some form, or perhaps only some formula, of peace. Certainly they are crying loud enough for it at the present day. What sort of peace Kirylo Sidorovitch Razumov expected to find in the writing up of his record it passeth my understanding to guess.

The fact remains that he has written it.

Mr. Razumov was a tall, well-proportioned young man, quite unusually dark for a Russian from the Central Provinces. His good looks would have been unques-tionable if it had not been for a peculiar lack of fineness in the features. It was as if a face modeled vigorously in wax (with some approach even to a classical cor-rectness of type) had been held close to a fire till all sharpness of line had been lost in the softening of the material. But even thus he was sufficiently good-look-ing. His manner, too, was good. In discussion he was easily swayed by argument and authority. With his younger compatriots he took the attitude of an inscrutable listener, a listener of the kind that hears you out intelligently and then—just changes the subject.

This sort of trick, which may arise either from intellectual insufficiency or from an imperfect trust in one's own convictions, procured for Mr. Razumov a rep-utation of profundity. Amongst a lot of exuberant talkers, in the habit of exhaust-ing themselves daily by ardent discussion, a comparatively taciturn personality is naturally credited with reserve power. By his comrades at the St. Petersburg University, Kirylo Sidorovitch Razumov, third year's student in philosophy, was looked upon as a strong nature—an altogether trustworthy man. This, in a country where an opinion may be a legal crime visited by death or sometimes by a fate worse than mere death, meant that he was worthy of being trusted with forbidden opinions. He was liked also for his amiability and for his quiet readiness to oblige his comrades even at the cost of personal inconvenience.

Mr. Razumov was supposed to be the son of an archpriest and to be protected by a distinguished nobleman—perhaps of his own distant province. But his outward appearance accorded badly with such humble origin. Such a descent was not credible. It was, indeed, suggested that Mr. Razumov was the son of an archpriest's pretty daughter—which, of course, would put a different complexion on the matter. This theory also rendered intelligible the protection of the distinguished nobleman. All this, however, had never been investigated, maliciously or otherwise. No one knew or cared who the nobleman in question was. Razumov received a modest but very sufficient allowance from the hands of an obscure attorney, who seemed to act as his guardian in some measure. Now and then he appeared at some professor's informal reception. Apart from that, Razumov was not known to have any social relations in the town. He attended the obligatory lectures regularly, and was considered by the authorities as a very promising student. He worked at home in the manner of a man who means to get on, but did not shut himself up severely for that purpose. He was always accessible, and there was nothing secret or reserved in his life.

I

The origin of Mr. Razumov's record is connected with an event characteristic of modern Russia in the actual fact: the assassination of a prominent statesman— and still more characteristic of the moral corruption of an oppressed society where the noblest aspirations of humanity, the desire of freedom, an ardent patriotism, the love of justice, the sense of pity, and even the fidelity of simple minds are prostituted to the lusts of hate and fear, the inseparable companions of an uneasy despotism.

The fact alluded to above is the successful attempt on the life of Mr. de P——, the President of the notorious Repressive Commission of some years ago, the Minister of State invested with extraordinary powers. The newspapers made noise enough about that fanatical, narrow-chested figure in gold-laced uniform, with a face of crumpled parchment, insipid, bespectacled eyes, and the cross of the

Order of St. Procopius hung under the skinny throat. For a time, it may be remembered, not a month passed without his portrait appearing in some one of the illustrated papers of Europe. He served the monarchy by imprisoning, exiling, or sending to the gallows men and women, young and old, with an equable, unwearied industry. In his mystic acceptance of the principle of autocracy he was bent on extirpating from the land every vestige of anything that resembled freedom in public institutions; and in his ruthless persecution of the rising generation he seemed to aim at the destruction of the very hope of liberty itself.

It is said that this execrated personality had not enough imagination to be aware of the hate he inspired. It is hardly credible; but it is a fact that he took very few precautions for his safety. In the preamble of a certain famous State paper he had declared once that "the thought of liberty has never existed in the Act of the Creator. From the multitude of men's counsel nothing could come but revolt and disorder; and revolt and disorder in a world created for obedience and stability is sin. It was not Reason but Authority which expressed the Divine Intention. God was the Autocrat of the Universe. . . ." It may be that the man who made this declaration believed that heaven itself was bound to protect him in his remorseless defense of autocracy on this earth.

No doubt the vigilance of the police saved him many times; but, as a matter of fact, when his appointed fate overtook him, the competent authorities could not have given him any warning. They had no knowledge of any conspiracy against the Minister's life, had no hint of any plot through their usual channels of information, had seen no signs, were aware of no suspicious movements or dangerous persons.

Mr. de P—— was being driven towards the railway station in a two-horse uncovered sleigh with footman and coachman on the box. Snow had been falling all night, making the roadway, uncleared as yet at this early hour, very heavy for the horses. It was still falling thickly. But the sleigh must have been observed and marked down. As it drew over to the left before taking a turn, the footman noticed a peasant walking slowly on the edge of the pavement with his hands in the pockets of his sheepskin coat and his shoulders hunched up to his ears under the falling snow. On being overtaken this peasant suddenly faced about and swung his arm. In an instant there was a terrible shock, a detonation muffled in the multitude of snowflakes; both horses lay dead and mangled on the ground, and the coachman, with a shrill cry, had fallen off the box mortally wounded. The footman (who survived) had no time to see the face of the man in the sheepskin coat. After throwing the bomb this last got away, but it is supposed that, seeing a lot of people surging up on all sides of him in the falling snow, and all running towards the scene of the explosion, he thought it safer to turn back with them.

In an incredibly short time an excited crowd assembled round the sledge. The Minister-President, getting out unhurt into the deep snow, stood near the groaning coachman and addressed the people repeatedly in his weak, colorless voice: "I beg of you to keep off. For the love of God, I beg of you good people to keep off."

It was then that a tall young man who had remained standing perfectly still within a carriage gateway, two houses lower down, stepped out into the street and walking up rapidly flung another bomb over the heads of the crowd. It actually struck the Minister-President on the shoulder as he stooped over his dying servant, then falling between his feet exploded with a terrific concentrated violence, striking him dead to the ground, finishing the wounded man and practically annihilating the empty sledge in the twinkling of an eye. With a yell of horror the crowd broke up and fled in all directions, except for those who fell dead or dying where they stood nearest to the Minister-President, and one or two others who did not fall till they had run a little way.

The first explosion had brought together a crowd as if by enchantment, the second made as swiftly a solitude in the street for hundreds of yards in each direction. Through the falling snow people looked from afar at the small heap of dead bodies lying upon each other near the carcasses of the two horses. Nobody dared to approach till some Cossacks of a street-patrol galloped up and, dismounting, began to turn over the dead. Amongst the innocent victims of the second explosion laid out on the pavement there was a body dressed in a peasant's sheepskin coat; but the face was unrecognizable, there was absolutely nothing found in the pockets of its poor clothing, and it was the only one whose identity was never established.

That day Mr. Razumov got up at his usual hour and spent the morning within the university buildings listening to the lectures and working for some time in the library. He heard the first vague rumor of something in the way of bomb-throwing at the table of the students' ordinary, where he was accustomed to eat his two o'clock dinner. But this rumor was made up of mere whispers, and this was Russia, where it was not always safe, for a student especially, to appear too much interested in certain kinds of whispers. Razumov was one of those men who, living in a period of mental and political unrest, keep an instinctive hold on normal, practical, everyday life. He was aware of the emotional tension of his time; he even responded to it in an indefinite way. But his main concern was with his work, his studies, and with his own future.

Officially and in fact without a family (for the daughter of the archpriest had long been dead), no home influences had shaped his opinions or his feelings. He was as lonely in the world as a man swimming in the deep sea. The word Razumov was the mere label of a solitary individuality. There were no Razumovs belonging to him anywhere. His closest parentage was defined in the statement that he was a Russian. Whatever good he expected from life would be given to or withheld from his hopes by that connection alone. This immense parentage suffered from the throes of internal dissensions, and he shrank mentally from the fray as a good-natured man may shrink from taking definite sides in a violent family quarrel.

Razumov, going home, reflected that having prepared all the matters of the forthcoming examination, he could now devote his time to the subject of the prize essay. He hankered after the silver medal. The prize was offered by the Ministry of Education; the names of the competitors would be submitted to the Minister himself. The mere fact of trying would be considered meritorious in the higher quarters; and the possessor of the prize would have a claim to an administrative appointment of the better sort after he had taken his degree. The student Razumov in an access of elation forgot the dangers menacing the stability of the institutions which give rewards and appointments. But, remembering the medalist of the year before, Razumov, the young man of no parentage, was sobered. He and some others happened to be assembled in their comrade's rooms at the very time when that last received the official advice of his success. He was a quiet, unassuming young man: "Forgive me," he had said, with a faint apologetic smile and taking up his cap, "I am going out to order up some wine. But I must first send a telegram to my folk at home. I say! Won't the old people make it a festive time for the neighbors for twenty miles around our place?"

Razumov thought there was nothing of that sort for him in the world. His success would matter to no one. But he felt no bitterness against the nobleman his protector, who was not a provincial magnate as was generally supposed. He was in fact nobody less than Prince K——, once a great and splendid figure in the world, and now, his day being over, a senator and a gouty invalid, living in a still splendid but more domestic manner. He had some young children, and a wife as aristocratic and proud as himself.

In all his life Razumov was allowed only once to come into personal contact with the prince.

It had the air of a chance meeting in the little attorney's office. One day Razumov, coming in by appointment, found a stranger standing there—a tall, aristocratic-looking personage with silky gray side whiskers. The baldheaded, sly little lawyer-fellow called out, "Come in—come in, Mr. Razumov," with a sort of ironic heartiness. Then turning deferentially to the stranger with the grand air, "A ward of mine, your Excellency. One of the most promising students of his faculty in the St. Petersburg University."

To his intense surprise Razumov saw a white shapely hand extended to him. He took it in great confusion (it was soft and passive) and heard at the same time a condescending murmur in which he caught only the words "Satisfactory" and "Persevere." But the most amazing thing of all was to feel suddenly a distinct pressure of the white shapely hand just before it was withdrawn: a light pressure like a secret sign. The emotion of it was terrible. Razumov's heart seemed to leap into his throat. When he raised his eyes the aristocratic personage, motioning the little lawyer aside, had opened the door and was going out.

The attorney rummaged amongst the papers on his desk for a time. "Do you know who that was?" he asked suddenly.

Razumov, whose heart was thumping hard yet, shook his head in silence.

"That was Prince K——. You wonder what he could be doing in the hole of a poor legal rat like myself—eh? These awfully great people have their sentimental curiosities like common sinners. But if I were you, Kirylo Sidorovitch," he continued, leering and laying a peculiar emphasis on the patronymic, "I wouldn't boast at large of the introduction. It would not be prudent, Kirylo Sidorovitch. Oh dear, no! It would be, in fact, dangerous for your future."

The young man's ears burned like fire; his sight was dim. "That man!" Razumov was saying to himself. "He!"

Henceforth it was by this monosyllable that Mr. Razumov got into the habit of referring mentally to the stranger with gray silky side whiskers. From that time too, when walking in the more fashionable quarters, he noted with interest the magnificent horses and carriages with Prince K——'s liveries on the box. Once he saw the princess get out—she was shopping—followed by two girls, of which one was nearly a head taller than the other. Their fair hair hung loose down their backs in the English style; they had merry eyes; their coats, muffs, and little fur caps were exactly alike; and their cheeks and noses were tinged a cheerful pink by the frost. They crossed the pavement in front of him, and Razumov went on his way smiling shyly to himself. "His" daughters. They resembled "Him." The young man felt a glow of warm friendliness towards these girls who would never know of his existence. Presently they would marry generals or Kammerherrs and have girls and boys of their own, who perhaps would be aware of him as a celebrated old professor, decorated, possibly a Privy Councillor, one of the glories of Russia—nothing more!

But a celebrated professor was a somebody. Distinction would convert the label Razumov into an honored name. There was nothing strange in the student Razumov's wish for distinction. A man's real life is that accorded to him in the thoughts of other men by reason of respect or natural love. Returning home on the day of the attempt on Mr. de P——'s life, Razumov resolved to have a good try for the silver medal.

Climbing slowly the four flights of the dark, dirty staircase in the house where he had his lodgings, he felt confident of success. The winner's name would be published in the papers on New Year's Day. And at the thought that "He" would most probably read it there, Razumov stopped short on the stairs for an instant, then went on smiling faintly at his own emotion. "This is but a shadow," he said to himself, "but the medal is a solid beginning."

With those ideas of industry in his head the warmth of his room was agreeable and encouraging. "I shall put in four hours of good work," he thought. But no sooner had he closed the door than he was horribly startled. All black against the usual tall stove of white tiles gleaming in the dusk, stood a strange figure, wearing a skirted, closefitting, brown cloth coat strapped round the waist, in long boots, and with a little Astrakhan cap on its head. It loomed lithe and martial. Razumov was utterly confounded. It was only when the figure, advancing two paces, asked in an untroubled, grave voice if the outer door was closed, that he regained his power of speech.

"Haldin! . . . Victor Victorovitch! . . . Is that you? . . . Yes. The outer door is shut all right. But this is indeed unexpected."

Victor Haldin, a student older than most of his contemporaries at the university, was not one of the industrious set. He was hardly ever seen at lectures; the authorities had marked him as "restless" and "unsound"—very bad notes. But he had a great personal prestige with his comrades and influenced their thoughts. Razumov had never been intimate with him. They had met from time to time at gatherings in other students' houses. They had even had a discussion together—one of those discussions on first principles dear to the sanguine minds of youth.

Razumov wished the man had chosen some other time to come for a chat. He felt in good trim to tackle the prize essay. But as Haldin could not be slightingly dismissed, Razumov adopted the tone of hospitality, asking him to sit down and smoke.

"Kirylo Sidorovitch," said the other, flinging off his cap, "we are not perhaps in exactly the same camp. Your judgment is more philosophical. You are a man of few words, but I haven't met anybody who dared to doubt the generosity of your sentiments. There is a solidity about your character which cannot exist without courage."

Razumov felt flattered and began to murmur shyly something about being very glad of his good opinion, when Haldin raised his hand.

"That is what I was saying to myself," he continued, "as I dodged in the wood-yard down by the riverside. 'He has a strong character, this young man,' I said to myself. 'He does not throw his soul to the winds.' Your reserve has always fascinated me, Kirylo Sidorovitch. So I tried to remember your address. But look here—it was a piece of luck. Your dvornik was away from the gate talking to a sleigh-driver on the other side of the street. I met no one on the stairs, not a soul. As I came up to your floor I caught sight of your landlady coming out of your rooms. But she did not see me. She crossed the landing to her own side, and then I slipped in. I have been here two hours expecting you to come in every moment."

Razumov had listened in astonishment; but before he could open his mouth Haldin added, speaking deliberately, "It was I who removed de P—— this morning."

Razumov kept down a cry of dismay. The sentiment of his life being utterly ruined by this contact with such a crime, expressed itself quaintly by a sort of half-derisive mental exclamation, "There goes my silver medal!"

Haldin continued after waiting a while:

"You say nothing, Kirylo Sidorovitch! I understand your silence. To be sure, I cannot expect you with your frigid English manner to embrace me. But never mind your manners. You have enough heart to have heard the sound of weeping and gnashing of teeth this man raised in the land. That would be enough to get over any philosophical hopes. He was uprooting the tender plant. He had to be stopped. He was a dangerous man—a convinced man. Three more years of his work would have put us back fifty years into bondage—and look at all the lives wasted, at all the souls lost in that time."

His curt, self-confident voice suddenly lost its ring and it was in a dull tone that he added, "Yes, brother, I have killed him. It's weary work."

Razumov had sunk into a chair. Every moment he expected a crowd of policemen to rush in. There must have been thousands of them out looking for that man walking up and down in his room. Haldin was talking again in a restrained, steady voice. Now and then he flourished an arm, slowly, without excitement.

He told Razumov how he had brooded for a year; how he had not slept properly for weeks. He and "Another" had a warning of the Minister's movements from "a certain person" late the evening before. He and that "Another" prepared their "engines" and resolved to have no sleep till "the deed" was done. They walked the streets under the falling snow with the "engines" on them, exchanging not a word the livelong night. When they happened to meet a police patrol they took each other by the arm and pretended to be a couple of peasants on the spree. They reeled and talked in drunken hoarse voices. Except for these strange outbreaks they kept silence, moving on ceaselessly. Their plans had been previously arranged. At daybreak they made their way to the spot which they knew the sledge must pass. When it appeared in sight they exchanged a muttered goodbye and separated. The "other" remained at the corner, Haldin took up a position a little farther up the street. . . .

After throwing his "engine" he ran off and in a moment was overtaken by the panic-struck people flying away from the spot after the second explosion. They were wild with terror. He was jostled once or twice. He slowed down for the rush to pass him and then turned to the left into a narrow street. There he was alone.

He marveled at this immediate escape. The work was done. He could hardly believe it. He fought with an almost irresistible longing to lie down on the pavement and sleep. But this sort of faintness—a drowsy faintness—passed off quickly. He walked faster, making his way to one of the poorer parts of the town in order to look up Ziemianitch.

This Ziemianitch, Razumov understood, was a sort of town-peasant who had got on; owner of a small number of sledges and horses for hire. Haldin paused in his narrative to exclaim:

"A bright spirit! A hardy soul! The best driver in St. Petersburg. He has a team of three horses there. . . . Ah! He's a fellow!"

This man had declared himself willing to take out safely, at any time, one or two persons to the second or third railway station on one of the southern lines. But there had been no time to warn him the night before. His usual haunt seemed to be a low-class eating-house on the outskirts of the town. When Haldin got there the man was not to be found. He was not expected to turn up again till the evening. Haldin wandered away restlessly.

He saw the gate of a wood-yard open and went in to get out of the wind which swept the bleak, broad thoroughfare. The great rectangular piles of cut wood loaded with snow resembled the huts of a village. At first the watchman who discovered him crouching amongst them talked in a friendly manner. He was a dried-up old man wearing two ragged army coats one over the other; his wizened little face, tied up under the jaw and over the ears in a dirty red handkerchief, looked comical. Presently he grew sulky, and then all at once without rhyme or reason began to shout furiously:

"Aren't you ever going to clear out of this, you loafer? We know all about factory hands of your sort. A big, strong, young chap! You aren't even drunk. What do you want here? You don't frighten us. Take yourself and your ugly eyes away."

Haldin stopped before the sitting Razumov. His supple figure, with the white forehead above which the fair hair stood straight up, had an aspect of lofty daring.

"He did not like my eyes," he said. "And so . . . here I am."

Razumov made an effort to speak calmly. "But pardon me, Victor Victorovitch. We know each other so little . . . . I don't see why you . . . "

"Confidence," said Haldin.

This word sealed Razumov's lips as if a hand had been clapped on his mouth. His brain seethed with arguments.

"And so—here you are," he muttered through his teeth.

The other did not detect the tone of anger. Never suspected it.

"Yes. And nobody knows I am here. You are the last person that could be suspected—should I get caught. That's an advantage, you see. And then—speaking to a superior mind like yours I can well say all the truth. It occurred to me that you—you have no one belonging to you—no ties, no one to suffer for it if this came out by some means. There have been enough ruined Russian homes as it is. But I don't see how my passage through your rooms can be ever known. If I should be got hold of, I'll know how to keep silent—no matter what they may be pleased to do to me," he added grimly.

He began to walk again while Razumov sat still appalled.

"You thought that——" he faltered out, almost sick with indignation.

"Yes, Razumov. Yes, brother. Some day you shall help to build. You suppose that I am a terrorist, now—a destructor of what is. But consider that the true destroyers are they who destroy the spirit of progress and truth, not the avengers who merely kill the bodies of the persecutors of human dignity. Men like me are necessary to make room for self-contained, thinking men like you. Well, we have made the sacrifice of our lives, but all the same I want to escape if it can be done. It is not my life I want to save, but my power to do. I won't live idle. Oh no! Don't make any mistake, Razumov. Men like me are rare. And, besides, an example like this is more awful to oppressors when the perpetrator vanishes without a trace. They sit in their offices and palaces and quake. All I want you to do is to help me to vanish. No great matter that. Only to go by-and-by and see Ziemianitch for me at that place where I went this morning. Just tell him, 'He whom you know wants a well-horsed sledge to pull up half an hour after midnight at the seventh lamppost on the left counting from the upper end of Karabelnaya. If nobody gets in, the sledge is to run round a block or two, so as to come back past the same spot in ten minutes' time.'"

Razumov wondered why he had not cut short that talk and told this man to go away long before. Was it weakness or what?

He concluded that it was a sound instinct. Haldin must have been seen. It was impossible that some people should not have noticed the face and appearance of the man who threw the second bomb. Haldin was a noticeable person. The police in their thousands must have had his description within the hour. With every moment the danger grew. Sent out to wander in the streets he could not escape being caught in the end.

The police would very soon find out all about him. They would set about discovering a conspiracy. Everybody Haldin had ever known would be in the greatest danger. Unguarded expressions, little facts in themselves innocent would be counted for crimes. Razumov remembered certain words he said, the speeches he had listened to, the harmless gatherings he had attended—it was almost impossible for a student to keep out of that sort of thing, without becoming suspect to his comrades.

Razumov saw himself shut up in a fortress, worried, badgered, perhaps ill-used. He saw himself deported by an administrative order, his life broken, ruined, and robbed of all hope. He saw himself—at best—leading a miserable existence under police supervision, in some small far-away provincial town, without friend to assist his necessities or even take any steps to alleviate his lot—as others had. Others had fathers, mothers, brothers, relations, connections, to move heaven and earth on their behalf—he had no one. The very officials that sentenced him some morning would forget his existence before sunset.

He saw his youth pass away from him in misery and half-starvation—his strength give way, his mind become an abject thing. He saw himself creeping, broken down and shabby, about the streets—dying unattended in some filthy hole of a room, or on the sordid bed of a Government hospital.

He shuddered. Then the peace of bitter calmness came over him. It was best to keep this man out of the streets till he could be got rid of with some chance of escaping. That was the best that could be done. Razumov, of course, felt the safety of his lonely existence to be permanently endangered. This evening's doings could turn up against him at any time as long as this man lived and the present institutions endured. They appeared to him rational and indestructible at that moment. They had a force of harmony—in contrast with the horrible discord of this man's presence. He hated the man. He said quietly:

"Yes, of course, I will go. You must give me precise directions, and for the rest—depend on me."

"Ah! You are a fellow! Collected—cool as a cucumber. A regular Englishman. Where did you get your soul from? There aren't many like you. Look here, brother! Men like me leave no posterity, but their souls are not lost. No man's soul is ever lost. It works for itself—or else where would be the sense of self-sacrifice, of martyrdom, of conviction, of faith—the labors of the soul? What will become of my soul when I die in the way I must die—soon—very soon perhaps? It shall not perish. Don't make a mistake, Razumov. This is not murder—it is war, war. My spirit shall go on warring in some Russian body till all falsehood is swept out of the world. The modern civilization is false, but a new revelation shall come out of Russia. Ha! you say nothing. You are a skeptic. I respect your philosophical skepticism, Razumov, but don't touch the soul—the Russian soul that lives in all of us. It has a future. It has a mission, I tell you, or else why should I have been moved to do this—reckless—like a butcher—in the middle of all these innocent people— scattering death? I! I! . . . I wouldn't hurt a fly!"

"Not so loud," warned Razumov harshly.

Haldin sat down abruptly, and leaning his head on his folded arms burst into tears. He wept for a long time. The dusk had deepened in the room. Razumov, motionless in somber wonder, listened to the sobs.

The other raised his head, got up and with an effort mastered his voice.

"Yes. Men like me leave no posterity," he repeated in a subdued tone. "I have a sister though. She's with my old mother—I persuaded them to go abroad this year—thank God. Not a bad little girl my sister. She has the most trustful eyes of any human being that ever walked this earth. She will marry well, I hope. She may have children—sons perhaps. Look at me. My father was a

Government official in the provinces. He had a little land too. A simple servant of God—a true Russian in his way. His was the soul of obedience. But I am not like him. They say I resemble my mother's eldest brother, an officer. They shot him in '28. Under Nicholas, you know. Haven't I told you that this is war, war? . . . But, God of Justice! this is weary work."

Razumov, in his chair, leaning his head on his hand, spoke as if from the bottom of an abyss.

"You believe in God, Haldin?"

"There you go catching at words that are wrung from one. What does it matter? What was it the Englishman said: 'There is a divine soul in things . . .'? Devil take him—I don't remember now. But he spoke the truth. When the day of you thinkers comes don't you forget what's divine in the Russian soul—and that's resignation. Respect that in your intellectual restlessness and don't let your arrogant wisdom spoil its message to the world. I am speaking to you now like a man with a rope round his neck. What do you imagine I am? A being in revolt? No. It's you thinkers who are in everlasting revolt. I am one of the resigned. When the necessity of this heavy work came to me and I understood that it had to be done—what did I do? Did I exult? Did I take pride in my purpose? Did I try to weigh its worth and consequences? No! I was resigned. I thought, 'God's will be done.'"

He threw himself full length on Razumov's bed, and putting the backs of his hands over his eyes remained perfectly motionless and silent. Not even the sound of his breathing could be heard. The dead stillness of the room remained undisturbed till in the darkness Razumov said gloomily:

"Haldin."

"Yes," answered the other readily, quite invisible now on the bed and without the slightest stir.

"Isn't it time for me to start?"

"Yes, brother." The other was heard, lying still in the darkness as though he were talking in his sleep. "The time has come to put fate to the test."

He paused, then gave a few lucid directions in the quiet impersonal voice of a man in a trance. Razumov made ready without a word of answer. As he was leaving the room the voice on the bed said after him:

"Go with God, thou silent soul."

On the landing, moving softly, Razumov locked the door and put the key in his pocket.

II

The words and events of that evening must have been graven as if with a steel tool on Mr. Razumov's brain, since he was able to write his relation with such fullness and precision a good many months afterwards.

The record of the thoughts which assailed him in the street is even more minute and abundant. They seem to have rushed upon him with the greater freedom because his thinking powers were no longer crushed by Haldin's presence—the appalling presence of a great crime and the stunning force of a great fanaticism. On looking through the pages of Mr. Razumov's diary I own that a "rush of thoughts" is not an adequate image.

The more adequate description would be a tumult of thoughts—the faithful reflection of the state of his feelings. The thoughts in themselves were not numerous—they were like the thoughts of most human beings, few and simple—but they cannot be reproduced here in all their exclamatory repetitions which went on in an endless and weary turmoil—for the walk was long.

If to the Western reader they appear shocking, inappropriate, or even improper, it must be remembered that as to the first this may be the effect of my crude statement. For the rest I will only remark here that this is not a story of the West of Europe.

Nations it may be have fashioned their Governments, but the Governments have paid them back in the same coin. It is unthinkable that any young Englishman should find himself in Razumov's situation. This being so, it would be a vain enterprise to imagine what he would think. The only safe surmise to make is that he would not think as Mr. Razumov thought at this crisis of his fate. He would not have a hereditary and personal knowledge of the means by which a historical autocracy represses ideas, guards its power, and defends its existence. By an act of mental extravagance he might imagine himself arbitrarily thrown into prison, but it would never occur to him unless he were delirious (and perhaps not even then) that he could be beaten with whips as a practical measure either of investigation or of punishment.

This is but a crude and obvious example of the different conditions of Western thought. I don't know that this danger occurred specially to Mr. Razumov. No doubt it entered unconsciously into the general dread and the general appallingness of this crisis. Razumov, as has been seen, was aware of more subtle ways in which an individual may be undone by the proceedings of a despotic Government. A simple expulsion from the university (the very least that could happen to him), with an impossibility to continue his studies anywhere, was enough to ruin utterly a young man depending entirely upon the development of his natural abilities for his place in the world. He was a Russian: and for him to be implicated meant simply sinking into the lowest social depths amongst the hopeless and the destitute—the night-birds of the city.

The peculiar circumstances of Razumov's parentage, or rather of his lack of parentage, should be taken into the account of his thoughts. And he remembered them too. He had been lately reminded of them in a peculiarly atrocious way by this fatal Haldin. "Because I haven't that, must everything else be taken away from me?" he thought.

He nerved himself for another effort to go on. Along the roadway sledges glided phantom-like and jingling through a fluttering whiteness on the black face of the night. "For it is a crime," he was saying to himself. "A murder is a murder. Though, of course, some sort of liberal institutions . . ."

A feeling of horrible sickness came over him. "I must be courageous," he exhorted himself mentally. All his strength was suddenly gone as if taken out by a hand. Then by a mighty effort of will it came back because he was afraid of fainting in the street and being picked up by the police with the key of his lodgings in his pocket. They would find Haldin there, and then, indeed, he would be undone.

Strangely enough it was this fear which seems to have kept him up to the end. The passersby were rare. They came upon him suddenly, looming up black in the snowflakes close by, then vanishing all at once—without footfalls.

It was the quarter of the very poor. Razumov noticed an elderly woman tied up in ragged shawls. Under the street lamp she seemed a beggar off duty. She walked leisurely in the blizzard as though she had no home to hurry to, she hugged under one arm a round loaf of black bread with an air of guarding a priceless booty; and Razumov, averting his glance, envied her the peace of her mind and the serenity of her fate.

To one reading Mr. Razumov's narrative it is really a wonder how he managed to keep going as he did along one interminable street after another on pavements that were gradually becoming blocked with snow. It was the thought of Haldin locked up in his rooms and the desperate desire to get rid of his presence which drove him forward. No rational determination had any part in his exertions. Thus, when on arriving at the low eating-house he heard that the man of horses, Ziemianitch, was not there, he could only stare stupidly.

The waiter, a wild-haired youth in tarred boots and a pink shirt, exclaimed, uncovering his pale gums in a silly grin, that Ziemianitch had got his skinful early in the afternoon and had gone away with a bottle under each arm to keep it up amongst the horses—he supposed.

The owner of the vile den, a bony short man in a dirty cloth caftan coming down to his heels, stood by, his hands tucked into his belt, and nodded confirmation.

The reek of spirits, the greasy, rancid steam of food, got Razumov by the throat. He struck a table with his clenched hand and shouted violently:

"You lie."

Bleary unwashed faces were turned to his direction. A mild-eyed ragged tramp drinking tea at the next table moved farther away. A murmur of wonder arose with an undertone of uneasiness. A laugh was heard too, and an exclamation, "There! there!" jeeringly soothing. The waiter looked all round and announced to the room:

"The gentleman won't believe that Ziemianitch is drunk."

From a distant corner a hoarse voice belonging to a horrible, nondescript, shaggy being with a black face like the muzzle of a bear grunted angrily:

"The cursed driver of thieves. What do we want with his gentlemen here? We are all honest folk in this place."

Razumov, biting his lip till blood came to keep himself from bursting into imprecations, followed the owner of the den, who, whispering "Come along, little father," led him into a tiny hole of a place behind the wooden counter, whence proceeded a sound of splashing. A wet and bedraggled creature, a sort of sexless and shivering scarecrow, washed glasses in there, bending over a wooden tub by the light of a tallow dip.

"Yes, little father," the man in the long caftan said plaintively. He had a brown, cunning little face, a thin grayish beard. Trying to light a tin lantern he hugged it to his breast and talked garrulously the while.

He would show Ziemianitch to the gentleman to prove there were no lies told. And he would show him drunk. His woman, it seems, ran away from him last night. "Such a hag she was! Thin! Pfui!" He spat. They were always running away from that driver of the devil—and he sixty years old too; could never get used to it. But each heart knows sorrow after its own kind, and Ziemianitch was a born fool all his days. And then he would fly to the bottle. "'Who could bear life in our land without the bottle?' he says. A proper Russian man—the little pig. . . . Be pleased to follow me."

Razumov crossed a quadrangle of deep snow enclosed between high walls with innumerable windows. Here and there a dim yellow light hung within the four-square mass of darkness. The house was an enormous slum, a hive of human vermin, a monumental abode of misery towering on the verge of starvation and despair.

In a corner the ground sloped sharply down, and Razumov followed the light of the lantern through a small doorway into a long cavernous place like a neglected subterranean byre. Deep within, three shaggy little horses tied up to rings hung their heads together, motionless and shadowy in the dim light of the lantern. It must have been the famous team of Haldin's escape. Razumov peered fearfully into the gloom. His guide pawed in the straw with his foot.

"Here he is. Ah! the little pigeon. A true Russian man. 'No heavy hearts for me,' he says. 'Bring out the bottle and take your ugly mug out of my sight.' Ha, ha, ha! That's the fellow he is."

He held the lantern over a prone form of a man, apparently fully dressed for outdoors. His head was lost in a pointed cloth hood. On the other side of a heap of straw protruded a pair of feet in monstrous thick boots.

"Always ready to drive," commented the keeper of the eating-house. "A proper Russian driver that. Saint or devil, night or day is all one to Ziemianitch when his heart is free from sorrow. 'I don't ask who you are, but where you want to go,' he says. He would drive Satan himself to his own abode and come back chirruping to his horses. Many a one he has driven who is clanking his chains in the Nertchinsk mines by this time."

Razumov shuddered.

"Call him, wake him up," he faltered out.

The other set down his light, stepped back and launched a kick at the prostrate sleeper. The man shook at the impact but did not move. At the third kick he grunted but remained inert as before.

The eating-house keeper desisted and fetched a deep sigh.

"You see for yourself how it is. We have done what we can for you."

He picked up the lantern. The intense black spokes of shadow swung about in the circle of light. A terrible fury—the blind rage of self-preservation—possessed Razumov.

"Ah! The vile beast," he bellowed out in an unearthly tone which made the lantern jump and tremble! "I shall wake you! Give me . . . Give me . . ."

He looked round wildly, seized the handle of a stable-fork and rushing forward struck at the prostrate body with inarticulate cries. After a time his cries ceased, and the rain of blows fell in the stillness and shadows of the cellar-like stable. Razumov belabored Ziemianitch with an insatiable fury, in great volleys of sounding thwacks. Except for the violent movements of Razumov nothing stirred, neither the beaten man nor the spoke-like shadows on the walls. And only the sound of blows was heard. It was a weird scene.

Suddenly there was a sharp crack. The stick broke and half of it flew far away into the gloom beyond the light. At the same time Ziemianitch sat up. At this Razumov became as motionless as the man with the lantern—only his breast heaved for air as if ready to burst.

Some dull sensation of pain must have penetrated at last the consoling night of drunkenness enwrapping the "bright Russian soul" of Haldin's enthusiastic praise. But Ziemianitch evidently saw nothing. His eyeballs blinked all white in the light once, twice—then the gleam went out. For a moment he sat in the straw with closed eyes with a strange air of weary meditation, then fell over slowly on his side without making the slightest sound. Only the straw rustled a little. Razumov stared wildly, fighting for his breath. After a second or two he heard a light snore.

He flung from him the piece of stick remaining in his grasp, and went off with great hasty strides without looking back once.

After going heedlessly for some fifty yards along the street he walked into a snowdrift and was up to his knees before he stopped.

This recalled him to himself; and glancing about he discovered he had been going in the wrong direction. He retraced his steps, but now at a more moderate pace. When passing before the house he had just left he flourished his fist at the somber refuge of misery and crime rearing its sinister bulk on the white ground. It had an air of brooding. He let his arm fall by his side—discouraged.

Ziemianitch's passionate surrender to sorrow and consolation had baffled him. That was the people. A true Russian man! Razumov was glad he had beaten that brute—the "bright soul" of the other. Here they were: the people and the enthusiast.

Between the two he was done for: between the drunkenness of the peasant incapable of action and the dream-intoxication of the idealist incapable of perceiving the reason of things, and the true character of men. It was a sort of terrible childishness. But children had their masters. "Ah! the stick, the stick, the stern hand," thought Razumov, longing for power to hurt and destroy.

He was glad he had thrashed that brute. The physical exertion had left his body in a comfortable glow. His mental agitation, too, was clarified as if all the feverishness had gone out of him in a fit of outward violence. Together with the persisting sense of terrible danger he was conscious now of a tranquil, unquenchable hate.

He walked slower and slower. And indeed, considering the guest he had in his rooms, it was no wonder he lingered on the way. It was like harboring a pestilential disease that would not perhaps take your life, but would take from you all that made life worth living—a subtle pest that would convert earth into a hell.

What was he doing now? Lying on the bed as if dead, with the back of his hands over his eyes? Razumov had a morbidly vivid vision of Haldin on his bed—the white pillow hollowed by the head, the legs in long boots, the upturned feet. And in his abhorrence he said to himself, "I'll kill him when I get home." But he knew very well that that was of no use. The corpse hanging round his neck would be nearly as fatal as the living man. Nothing short of complete annihilation would do. And that was impossible. What then? Must one kill oneself to escape this visitation?

Razumov's despair was too profoundly tinged with hate to accept that issue.

And yet it was despair—nothing less—at the thought of having to live with Haldin for an indefinite number of days in mortal alarm at every sound. But perhaps when he heard that this "bright soul" of Ziemianitch suffered from a drunken eclipse the fellow would take his infernal resignation somewhere else. And that was not likely on the face of it.

Razumov thought: "I am being crushed—and I can't even run away." Other men had somewhere a corner of the earth—some little house in the provinces where they had a right to take their troubles. A material refuge. He had nothing. He had not even a moral refuge—the refuge of confidence. To whom could he go with this tale—in all this great, great land?

Razumov stamped his foot—and under the soft carpet of snow felt the hard ground of Russia, inanimate, cold, inert, like a sullen and tragic mother hiding her face under a winding sheet—his native soil!—his very own—without a fireside, without a heart!

He cast his eyes upwards and stood amazed. The snow had ceased to fall, and now, as if by a miracle, he saw above his head the clear black sky of the northern winter, decorated with the sumptuous fires of the stars. It was a canopy fit for the resplendent purity of the snows.

Razumov received an almost physical impression of endless space and of countless millions.

He responded to it with the readiness of a Russian who is born to an inheritance of space and numbers. Under the sumptuous immensity of the sky, the snow covered the endless forests, the frozen rivers, the plains of an immense country, obliterating the landmarks, the accidents of the ground, leveling everything under its uniform whiteness, like a monstrous blank page awaiting the record of an inconceivable history. It covered the passive land with its lives of countless people like Ziemianitch and its handful of agitators like this Haldin—murdering foolishly.

It was a sort of sacred inertia. Razumov felt a respect for it. A voice seemed to cry within him, "Don't touch it." It was a guarantee of duration, of safety, while the travail of maturing destiny went on—a work not of revolutions, with their passionate levity of action and their shifting impulses, but of peace. What it needed was not the conflicting aspirations of a people, but a will strong and one: it wanted not the babble of many voices, but a man—strong and one!

Razumov stood on the point of conversion. He was fascinated by its approach, by its overpowering logic. For a train of thought is never false. The falsehood lies deep in the necessities of existence, in secret fears and half-formed ambitions, in the secret confidence combined with a secret mistrust of ourselves, in the love of hope and the dread of uncertain days.

In Russia, the land of spectral ideas and disembodied aspirations, many brave minds have turned away at last from the vain and endless conflict to the one great historical fact of the land. They turned to autocracy for the peace of their patriotic conscience as a weary unbeliever, touched by grace, turns to the faith of his fathers for the blessing of spiritual rest. Like other Russians before him, Razumov, in conflict with himself, felt the touch of grace upon his forehead.

"Haldin means disruption," he thought to himself, beginning to walk again. "What is he with his indignation, with his talk of bondage—with his talk of God's justice? All that means disruption. Better that thousands should suffer than that a people should become a disintegrated mass, helpless like dust in the wind. Obscurantism is better than the light of incendiary torches. The seed germinates in the night. Out of the dark soil springs the perfect plant. But a volcanic eruption is sterile, the ruin of the fertile ground. And am I, who love my country—who have nothing but that to love and put my faith in—am I to have my future, perhaps my usefulness, ruined by this sanguinary fanatic?"

The grace entered into Razumov. He believed now in the man who would come at the appointed time.

What is a throne? A few pieces of wood upholstered in velvet. But a throne is a seat of power too. The form of government is the shape of a tool—an instrument. But twenty thousand bladders inflated by the noblest sentiments and jostling against each other in the air are a miserable encumbrance of space, holding no power, possessing no will, having nothing to give.

He went on thus, heedless of the way, holding a discourse with himself with extraordinary abundance and facility. Generally his phrases came to him slowly, after a conscious and painstaking wooing. Some superior power had inspired him with a flow of masterly argument as certain converted sinners become overwhelmingly loquacious.

He felt an austere exultation.

"What are the luridly smoky lucubrations of that fellow to the clear grasp of my intellect?" he thought. "Is not this my country? Have I not got forty million brothers?" he asked himself, unanswerably victorious in the silence of his breast. And the fearful thrashing he had given the inanimate Ziemianitch seemed to him a sign of intimate union, a pathetically severe necessity of brotherly love. "No! If I must suffer let me at least suffer for my convictions, not for a crime my reason—my cool superior reason—rejects."

He ceased to think for a moment. The silence in his breast was complete. But he felt a suspicious uneasiness, such as we may experience when we enter an unlighted strange place—the irrational feeling that something may jump upon us in the dark—the absurd dread of the unseen.

Of course he was far from being a moss-grown reactionary. Everything was not for the best. Despotic bureaucracy . . . abuses . . . corruption . . . and so on. Capable men were wanted. Enlightened intelligences. Devoted hearts. But absolute power should be preserved—the tool ready for the man—for the great autocrat of the future. Razumov believed in him. The logic of history made him unavoidable. The state of the people demanded him. "What else?" he asked himself ardently, "could move all that mass in one direction? Nothing could. Nothing but a single will."

He was persuaded that he was sacrificing his personal longings of liberalism—rejecting the attractive error for the stern Russian truth. "That's patriotism," he observed mentally, and added, "There's no stopping midway on that road," and then remarked to himself, "I am not a coward."

And again there was a dead silence in Razumov's breast. He walked with lowered head, making room for no one. He walked slowly and his thoughts returning spoke within him with solemn slowness:

"What is this Haldin? And what am I? Only two grains of sand. But a great mountain is made up of just such insignificant grains. And the death of a man or of many men is an insignificant thing. Yet we combat a contagious pestilence. Do I want his death? No! I would save him if I could—but no one can do that—he is the withered member which must be cut off. If I must perish through him, let me at least not perish with him, and associated against my will with his somber folly that understands nothing either of men or things. Why should I leave a false memory?"

It passed through his mind that there was no one in the world who cared what sort of memory he left behind him. He exclaimed to himself instantly, "Perish vainly for a falsehood! . . . What a miserable fate!"

He was now in a more animated part of the town. He did not remark the crash of two colliding sledges close to the curb. The driver of one bellowed tearfully at his fellow:

"Oh, thou vile wretch!"

This hoarse yell, let out nearly in his ear, disturbed Razumov. He shook his head impatiently and went on looking straight before him. Suddenly on the snow, stretched on his back right across his path, he saw Haldin, solid, distinct, real, with his inverted hands over his eyes, clad in a brown closefitting coat and long boots. He was lying out of the way a little, as though he had selected that place on purpose. The snow round him was untrodden.

This hallucination had such a solidity of aspect that the first movement of Razumov was to reach for his pocket to assure himself that the key of his rooms was there. But he checked the impulse with a disdainful curve of his lips. He understood. His thought, concentrated intensely on the figure left lying on his bed, had culminated in this extraordinary illusion of the sight. Razumov tackled the phenomenon calmly. With a stern face, without a check and gazing far beyond the vision, he walked on, experiencing nothing but a slight tightening of the chest. After passing he turned his head for a glance, and saw only the unbroken track of his footsteps over the place where the breast of the phantom had been lying.

Razumov walked on and after a little time whispered his wonder to himself:

"Exactly as if alive! Seemed to breathe! And right in my way too! I have had an extraordinary experience."

He made a few steps and muttered through his set teeth:

"I shall give him up."

Then for some twenty yards or more all was blank. He wrapped his cloak closer round him. He pulled his cap well forward over his eyes.

"Betray. A great word. What is betrayal? They talk of a man betraying his country, his friends, his sweetheart. There must be a moral bond first. All a man can betray is his conscience. And how is my conscience engaged here; by what bond of common faith, of common conviction, am I obliged to let that fanatical idiot drag me down with him? On the contrary—every obligation of true courage is the other way."

Razumov looked round from under his cap.

"What can the prejudice of the world reproach me with? Have I provoked his confidence? No! Have I by a single word, look, or gesture given him reason to suppose that I accepted his trust in me? No! It is true that I consented to go and see his Ziemianitch. Well, I have been to see him. And I broke a stick on his back too—the brute."

Something seemed to turn over in his head, bringing uppermost a singularly hard, clear facet of his brain.

"It would be better, however," he reflected, with a quite different mental accent, "to keep that circumstance altogether to myself."

He had passed beyond the turn leading to his lodgings, and had reached a wide and fashionable street. Some shops were still open, and all the restaurants. Lights fell on the pavement where men in expensive fur coats, with here and there the elegant figure of a woman, walked with an air of leisure. Razumov looked at them with the contempt of an austere believer for the frivolous crowd. It was the world—those officers, dignitaries, men of fashion, officials, members of the Yacht Club. The event of the morning affected them all. What would they say if they knew what this student in a cloak was going to do?

"Not one of them is capable of feeling and thinking as deeply as I can. How many of them could accomplish an act of conscience?"

Razumov lingered in the well-lighted street. He was firmly decided. Indeed, it could hardly be called a decision. He had simply discovered what he had meant to do all along. And yet he felt the need of some other mind's sanction.

With something resembling anguish he said to himself:

"I want to be understood." The universal aspiration with all its profound and melancholy meaning assailed heavily Razumov, who, amongst eighty millions of his kith and kin, had no heart to which he could open himself.

The attorney was not to be thought of. He despised the little agent of chicane too much. One could not go and lay one's conscience before the policeman at the corner. Neither was Razumov anxious to go to the chief of his district's police—a common-looking person whom he used to see sometimes in the street in a shabby uniform and with a smoldering cigarette stuck to his lower lip. "He would begin by locking me up most probably. At any rate, he is certain to get excited and create an awful commotion," thought Razumov practically.

An act of conscience must be done with outward dignity.

Razumov longed desperately for a word of advice, for moral support. Who knows what true loneliness is—not the conventional word, but the naked terror? To the lonely themselves it wears a mask. The most miserable outcast hugs some memory or some illusion. Now and then a fatal conjunction of events may lift the veil for an instant. For an instant only. No human being could bear a steady view of moral solitude without going mad.

Razumov had reached that point of vision. To escape from it he embraced for a whole minute the delirious purpose of rushing to his lodgings and flinging himself on his knees by the side of the bed with the dark figure stretched on it; to pour out a full confession in passionate words that would stir the whole being of that man to its innermost depths; that would end in embraces and tears; in an incredible fellowship of souls—such as the world had never seen. It was sublime!

Inwardly he wept and trembled already. But to the casual eyes that were cast upon him he was aware that he appeared as a tranquil student in a cloak, out for a leisurely stroll. He noted, too, the sidelong, brilliant glance of a pretty woman— with a delicate head, and covered in the hairy skins of wild beasts down to her feet, like a frail and beautiful savage—which rested for a moment with a sort of mocking tenderness on the deep abstraction of that good-looking young man.

Suddenly Razumov stood still. The glimpse of a passing gray whisker, caught and lost in the same instant, had evoked the complete image of Prince K——, the man who once had pressed his hand as no other man had pressed it—a faint but lingering pressure like a secret sign, like a half-unwilling caress.

And Razumov marveled at himself. Why did he not think of him before?

"A senator, a dignitary, a great personage, the very man—He!"

A strange softening emotion came over Razumov—made his knees shake a little. He repressed it with a newborn austerity. All that sentiment was pernicious nonsense. He couldn't be quick enough; and when he got into a sledge he shouted to the driver:

"To the K—— Palace. Get on—you! Fly!"

The startled moujik, bearded up to the very whites of his eyes, answered obsequiously:

"I hear, your high Nobility."

It was lucky for Razumov that Prince K—— was not a man of timid character. On the day of Mr. de P——'s murder an extreme alarm and despondency prevailed in the high official spheres.

Prince K——, sitting sadly alone in his study, was told by his alarmed servants that a mysterious young man had forced his way into the hall, refused to tell his name and the nature of his business, and would not move from there till he had seen His Excellency in private. Instead of locking himself up and telephoning for the police, as nine out of ten high personages would have done that evening, the prince gave way to curiosity and came quietly to the door of his study.

In the hall, the front door standing wide open, he recognized at once Razumov, pale as death, his eyes blazing, and surrounded by perplexed lackeys.

The prince was vexed beyond measure, and even indignant. But his humane instincts and a subtle sense of self-respect could not allow him to let this young man be thrown out into the street by base menials. He retreated unseen into his room, and after a little rang his bell. Razumov heard in the hall an ominously raised harsh voice saying somewhere far away:

"Show the gentleman in here."

Razumov walked in without a tremor. He felt himself invulnerable—raised far above the shallowness of common judgment. Though he saw the prince looking at him with black displeasure, the lucidity of his mind, of which he was very conscious, gave him an extraordinary assurance. He was not asked to sit down.

Half an hour later they appeared in the hall together. The lackeys stood up, and the prince, moving with difficulty on his gouty feet, was helped into his furs. The carriage had been ordered before. When the great double door was flung open with a crash, Razumov, who had been standing silent with a lost gaze but with every faculty intensely on the alert, heard the prince's voice:

"Your arm, young man."

The mobile, superficial mind of the ex-Guards' officer, man of showy missions, experienced in nothing but the arts of gallant intrigue and worldly success, had been equally impressed by the more obvious difficulties of such a situation and by Razumov's quiet dignity in stating them.

He had said, "No. Upon the whole I can't condemn the step you ventured to take by coming to me with your story. It is not an affair for police under-strappers. The greatest importance is attached to . . . Set your mind at rest. I shall see you through this most extraordinary and difficult situation."

Then the prince rose to ring the bell, and Razumov, making a short bow, had said with deference:

"I have trusted my instinct. A young man having no claim upon anybody in the world has in an hour of trial involving his deepest political convictions turned to an illustrious Russian—that's all."

The prince had exclaimed hastily:

"You have done well."

In the carriage—it was a small brougham on sleigh runners—Razumov broke the silence in a voice that trembled slightly.

"My gratitude surpasses the greatness of my presumption."

He gasped, feeling unexpectedly in the dark a momentary pressure on his arm.

"You have done well," repeated the prince.

When the carriage stopped the prince murmured to Razumov, who had never ventured a single question:

"The house of General T——"

In the middle of the snow-covered roadway blazed a great bonfire. Some Cossacks, the bridles of their horses over the arm, were warming themselves around it. Two sentries stood at the door, several gendarmes lounged under the great carriage gateway, and on the first floor landing two orderlies rose and stood at attention. Razumov walked at the prince's elbow.

A surprising quantity of hothouse plants in pots cumbered the floor of the ante-room. Servants came forward. A young man in civilian clothes arrived hurriedly, was whispered to, bowed low, and exclaiming zealously, "Certainly—this minute," fled within somewhere. The prince signed to Razumov.

They passed through a suite of reception rooms all barely lit and one of them prepared for dancing. The wife of the general had put off her party. An atmosphere of consternation pervaded the place. But the general's own room, with heavy somber hangings, two massive desks, and deep armchairs, had all the lights turned on. The footman shut the door behind them and they waited.

There was a coal fire in an English grate; Razumov had never before seen such a fire; and the silence of the room was like the silence of the grave; perfect, measureless, for even the clock on the mantelpiece made no sound. Filling a corner, on a black pedestal, stood a quarter-life-size smooth-limbed bronze of an adolescent figure, running. The prince observed in an undertone:

"Spontini's 'Flight of Youth.' Exquisite."

"Admirable," assented Razumov faintly.

They said nothing more after this, the prince silent with his grand air, Razumov staring at the statue. He was worried by a sensation resembling the gnawing of hunger.

He did not turn when he heard an inner door fly open, and a quick footstep muffled on the carpet.

The prince's voice immediately exclaimed, thick with excitement:

"We have got him—*ce misérable*. A worthy young man came to me——No! It's incredible. . . ."

Razumov held his breath before the bronze as if expecting a crash. Behind his back a voice he had never heard before insisted politely:

"*Asseyez-vous donc.*"

The prince almost shrieked, "*Mais comprenez-vous, mon cher! L'assassin!* the murderer—we have got him. . . ."

Razumov spun round. The general's smooth big cheeks rested on the stiff collar of his uniform. He must have been already looking at Razumov, because that last saw the pale blue eyes fastened on him coldly.

The prince from a chair waved an impressive hand.

"This is a most honorable young man whom Providence itself . . . Mr. Razumov."

The general acknowledged the introduction by frowning at Razumov, who did not make the slightest movement.

Sitting down before his desk the general listened with compressed lips. It was impossible to detect any sign of emotion on his face.

Razumov watched the immobility of the fleshy profile. But it lasted only a moment, till the prince had finished; and when the general turned to the providential young man, his florid complexion, the blue, unbelieving eyes and the bright white flash of an automatic smile had an air of jovial, careless cruelty. He expressed no wonder at the extraordinary story—no pleasure or excitement—no incredulity either. He betrayed no sentiment whatever. Only with a politeness almost deferential suggested that "the bird might have flown while Mr.—Mr. Razumov was running about the streets."

Razumov advanced to the middle of the room and said, "The door is locked and I have the key in my pocket."

His loathing for the man was intense. It had come upon him so unawares that he felt he had not kept it out of his voice. The general looked up at him thoughtfully, and Razumov grinned.

All this went over the head of Prince K—— seated in a deep armchair, very tired and impatient.

"A student called Haldin," said the general thoughtfully.

Razumov ceased to grin.

"That is his name," he said unnecessarily loud. "Victor Victorovitch Haldin—a student."

The general shifted his position a little.

"How is he dressed? Would you have the goodness to tell me?"

Razumov angrily described Haldin's clothing in a few jerky words. The general stared all the time, then addressing the prince:

"We were not without some indications," he said in French. "A good woman who was in the street described to us somebody wearing a dress of the sort as the thrower of the second bomb. We have detained her at the Secretariat, and everyone in a Tcherkess coat we could lay our hands on has been brought to her to look at. She kept on crossing herself and shaking her head at them. It was exasperating. . . ."

He turned to Razumov, and in Russian, with friendly reproach:

"Take a chair, Mr. Razumov—do. Why are you standing?"

Razumov sat down carelessly and looked at the general.

"This goggle-eyed imbecile understands nothing," he thought.

The prince began to speak loftily.

"Mr. Razumov is a young man of conspicuous abilities. I have it at heart that his future should not . . ."

"Certainly," interrupted the general, with a movement of the hand. "Has he any weapons on him, do you think, Mr. Razumov?"

The general employed a gentle musical voice. Razumov answered with suppressed irritation:

"No. But my razors are lying about—you understand."

The general lowered his head approvingly.

"Precisely."

Then to the prince, explaining courteously:

"We want that bird alive. It will be the devil if we can't make him sing a little before we are done with him."

The grave-like silence of the room with its mute clock fell upon the polite modulations of this terrible phrase. The prince, hidden in the chair, made no sound.

The general unexpectedly developed a thought.

"Fidelity to menaced institutions on which depend the safety of a throne and of a people is no child's play. We know that, *mon Prince*, and—*tenez*——" he went on with a sort of flattering harshness, "Mr. Razumov here begins to understand that too."

His eyes, which he turned upon Razumov, seemed to be starting out of his head. This grotesqueness of aspect no longer shocked Razumov. He said with gloomy conviction:

"Haldin will never speak."

"That remains to be seen," muttered the general.

"I am certain," insisted Razumov. "A man like this never speaks. . . . Do you imagine that I am here from fear?" he added violently. He felt ready to stand by his opinion of Haldin to the last extremity.

"Certainly not," protested the general, with great simplicity of tone. "And I don't mind telling you, Mr. Razumov, that if he had not come with his tale to such a staunch and loyal Russian as you, he would have disappeared like a stone in the water . . . which would have had a detestable effect," he added, with a bright, cruel smile under his stony stare. "So you see, there can be no suspicion of any fear here."

The prince intervened, looking at Razumov round the back of the armchair.

"Nobody doubts the moral soundness of your action. Be at ease in that respect, pray."

He turned to the general uneasily.

"That's why I am here. You may be surprised why I should . . ."

The general hastened to interrupt:

"Not at all. Extremely natural. You saw the importance . . ."

"Yes," broke in the prince. "And I venture to ask insistently that mine and Mr. Razumov's intervention should not become public. He is a young man of promise—of remarkable aptitudes."

"I haven't a doubt of it," murmured the general. "He inspires confidence."

"All sorts of pernicious views are so widespread nowadays—they taint such unexpected quarters—that, monstrous as it seems, he might suffer. . . . His studies . . . His . . ."

The general, with his elbows on the desk, took his head between his hands.

"Yes. Yes. I am thinking it out. . . . How long is it since you left him at your rooms, Mr. Razumov?"

Razumov mentioned the hour which nearly corresponded with the time of his distracted flight from the big slum house. He had made up his mind to keep Ziemianitch out of the affair completely. To mention him at all would mean imprisonment for the "bright soul," perhaps cruel floggings, and in the end a journey to Siberia in chains. Razumov, who had beaten Ziemianitch, felt for him now a vague, remorseful tenderness.

The general, giving way for the first time to his secret sentiments, exclaimed contemptuously:

"And you say he came in to make you this confidence like this—for nothing—*à propos des bottes*."

Razumov felt danger in the air. The merciless suspicion of despotism had spoken openly at last. Sudden fear sealed Razumov's lips. The silence of the room resembled now the silence of a deep dungeon, where time does not count, and a suspect person is sometimes forgotten forever. But the prince came to the rescue.

"Providence itself has led the wretch in a moment of mental aberration to seek Mr. Razumov on the strength of some old, utterly misinterpreted exchange of ideas—some sort of idle speculative conversation—months ago—I am told—and completely forgotten till now by Mr. Razumov."

"Mr. Razumov," queried the general meditatively, after a short silence, "do you often indulge in speculative conversation?"

"Half an hour after midnight. Till then we have to depend on you, Mr. Razumov. You don't think he is likely to change his purpose?"

"How can I tell?" said Razumov. "Those men are not of the sort that ever change their purpose."

"What men do you mean?"

"Fanatical lovers of liberty in general. Liberty with a capital L, Excellency. Liberty that means nothing precise. Liberty in whose name crimes are committed."

The general murmured:

"I detest rebels of every kind. I can't help it. It's my nature!"

He clenched a fist and shook it, drawing back his arm. "They shall be destroyed, then."

"They have made a sacrifice of their lives beforehand," said Razumov with malicious pleasure and looking the general straight in the face. "If Haldin does change his purpose tonight, you may depend on it that it will not be to save his life by flight in some other way. He would have thought then of something else to attempt. But that is not likely."

The general repeated as if to himself, "They shall be destroyed."

Razumov assumed an impenetrable expression. The prince exclaimed: "What a terrible necessity!"

The general's arm was lowered slowly.

"One comfort there is. That brood leaves no posterity. I've always said it; one effort, pitiless, persistent, steady—and we are done with them forever."

Razumov thought to himself that this man entrusted with so much arbitrary power must have believed what he said or else he could not have gone on bearing the responsibility.

The general repeated again with extreme animosity:

"I detest rebels. These subversive minds! These intellectual debauchees! My existence has been built on fidelity. It's a feeling. To defend it I am ready to lay down my life—and even my honor—if that were needed. But pray tell me what honor can there be as against rebels—against people that deny God Himself—perfect unbelievers? Brutes! It is horrible to think of."

During this tirade Razumov, facing the general, had nodded slightly twice. Prince K——, standing on one side with his grand air, murmured, casting up his eyes:

"*Hélas!*"

Then lowering his glance and with great decision declared:

"This young man, General, is perfectly fit to apprehend the bearing of your memorable words."

The general's whole expression changed from dull resentment to perfect urbanity.

"No, Excellency," answered Razumov coolly, in a sudden access of
dence. "I am a man of deep convictions. Crude opinions are in the air.
not always worth combating. But even the silent contempt of a serious n
be misinterpreted by headlong Utopists."

The general stared from between his hands. Prince K—— murmured:

"A serious young man. *Un esprit supérieur.*"

"I see that, *mon cher Prince*," said the general. "Mr. Razumov is quit
with me. I am interested in him. He has, it seems, the great and useful q
of inspiring confidence. What I was wondering at is why the other sh
mention anything at all—I mean even the bare fact alone—if his object
only to obtain temporary shelter for a few hours. For, after all, nothing
easier than to say nothing about it unless, indeed, he were trying, unde
crazy misapprehension of your true sentiments, to enlist your assistance—
Mr. Razumov?"

It seemed to Razumov that the floor was moving slightly. This grotesque man i
a tight uniform was terrible. It was right that he should be terrible.

"I can see what your Excellency has in your mind. But I can only answer that I
don't know why."

"I have nothing in my mind," murmured the general, with gentle surprise.

"I am his prey—his helpless prey," thought Razumov. The fatigues and the dis-
gusts of that afternoon, the need to forget, the fear which he could not keep off,
reawakened his hate for Haldin.

"Then I can't help your Excellency. I don't know what he meant. I only know
there was a moment when I wished to kill him. There was also a moment when I
wished myself dead. I said nothing. I was overcome. I provoked no confidence—I
asked for no explanations——"

Razumov seemed beside himself; but his mind was lucid. It was really a calculated outburst.

"It is rather a pity," the general said, "that you did not. Don't you know at al
what he means to do?"

Razumov calmed down and saw an opening there.

"He told me he was in hopes that a sledge would meet him about half an hou
after midnight at the seventh lamppost on the left from the upper end
Karabelnaya. At any rate, he meant to be there at that time. He did not even a
me for a change of clothes."

"*Ah voilà!*" said the general, turning to Prince K—— with an air of satisf
tion. "There is a way to keep your protégé, Mr. Razumov, quite clear of any conr
tion with the actual arrest. We shall be ready for that gentleman in Karabelnay

The prince expressed his gratitude. There was real emotion in his vo
Razumov, motionless, silent, sat staring at the carpet. The general turned to h

"I would ask now Mr. Razumov," he said, "to return to his home. Note that I don't ask Mr. Razumov whether he has justified his absence to his guest. No doubt he did this sufficiently. But I don't ask. Mr. Razumov inspires confidence. It is a great gift. I only suggest that a more prolonged absence might awaken the criminal's suspicions and induce him perhaps to change his plans."

He rose and with a scrupulous courtesy escorted his visitors to the anteroom encumbered with flowerpots.

Razumov parted with the prince at the corner of a street. In the carriage he had listened to speeches where natural sentiment struggled with caution. Evidently the prince was afraid of encouraging any hopes of future intercourse. But there was a touch of tenderness in the voice uttering in the dark the guarded general phrases of goodwill. And the prince, too, said:

"I have perfect confidence in you, Mr. Razumov."

"They all, it seems, have confidence in me," thought Razumov dully. He had an indulgent contempt for the man sitting shoulder to shoulder with him in the confined space. Probably he was afraid of scenes with his wife. She was said to be proud and violent.

It seemed to him bizarre that secrecy should play such a large part in the comfort and safety of lives. But he wanted to put the prince's mind at ease; and with a proper amount of emphasis he said that, being conscious of some small abilities and confident in his power of work, he trusted his future to his own exertions. He expressed his gratitude for the helping hand. Such dangerous situations did not occur twice in the course of one life—he added.

"And you have met this one with a firmness of mind and correctness of feeling which give me a high idea of your worth," the prince said solemnly. "You have now only to persevere—to persevere."

On getting out on the pavement Razumov saw an ungloved hand extended to him through the lowered window of the brougham. It detained his own in its grasp for a moment, while the light of a street lamp fell upon the prince's long face and old-fashioned gray whiskers.

"I hope you are perfectly reassured now as to the consequences. . . ."

"After what your Excellency has condescended to do for me, I can only rely on my conscience."

"Adieu," said the whiskered head with feeling.

Razumov bowed. The brougham glided away with a slight swish in the snow— he was alone on the edge of the pavement.

He said to himself that there was nothing to think about, and began walking towards his home.

He walked quietly. It was a common experience to walk thus home to bed after an evening spent somewhere with his fellows or in the cheaper seats of a theater.

After he had gone a little way the familiarity of things got hold of him. Nothing was changed. There was the familiar corner; and when he turned it he saw the familiar dim light of the provision shop kept by a German woman. There were loaves of stale bread, bunches of onions, and strings of sausages behind the small windowpanes. They were closing it. The sickly lame fellow whom he knew so well by sight staggered out into the snow embracing a large shutter.

Nothing would change. There was the familiar gateway yawning black with feeble glimmers marking the arches of the different staircases.

The sense of life's continuity depended on trifling bodily impressions. The trivialities of daily existence were an armor for the soul. And this thought reinforced the inward quietness of Razumov as he began to climb the stairs familiar to his feet in the dark, with his hand on the familiar clammy banister. The exceptional could not prevail against the material contacts which make one day resemble another. Tomorrow would be like yesterday.

It was only on the stage that the unusual was outwardly acknowledged.

"I suppose," thought Razumov, "that if I had made up my mind to blow out my brains on the landing I would be going up these stairs as quietly as I am doing it now. What's a man to do? What must be must be. Extraordinary things do happen. But when they have happened they are done with. Thus, too, when the mind is made up. That question is done with. And the daily concerns, the familiarities of our thought swallow it up—and the life goes on as before with its mysterious and secret sides quite out of sight, as they should be. Life is a public thing."

Razumov unlocked his door and took the key out; entered very quietly and bolted the door behind him carefully.

He thought, "He hears me," and after bolting the door he stood still, holding his breath. There was not a sound. He crossed the bare outer room, stepping deliberately in the darkness. Entering the other, he felt all over his table for the matchbox. The silence, but for the groping of his hand, was profound. Could the fellow be sleeping so soundly?

He struck a light and looked at the bed. Haldin was lying on his back as before, only both his hands were under his head. His eyes were open. He stared at the ceiling.

Razumov held the match up. He saw the clearcut features, the firm chin, the white forehead, and the topknot of fair hair against the white pillow. There he was, lying flat on his back. Razumov thought suddenly, "I have walked over his chest."

He continued to stare till the match burnt itself out; then struck another and lit the lamp in silence without looking towards the bed anymore. He had turned his back on it and was hanging his coat on a peg when he heard Haldin sigh profoundly, then ask in a tired voice:

"Well! And what have you arranged?"

The emotion was so great that Razumov was glad to put his hands against the wall. A diabolical impulse to say, "I have given you up to the police," frightened him exceedingly. But he did not say that. He said, without turning round, in a muffled voice:

"It's done."

Again he heard Haldin sigh. He walked to the table, sat down with the lamp before him, and only then looked towards the bed.

In the distant corner of the large room far away from the lamp, which was small and provided with a very thick china shade, Haldin appeared like a dark and elongated shape—rigid with the immobility of death. This body seemed to have less substance than its own phantom walked over by Razumov in the street white with snow. It was more alarming in its shadowy, persistent reality than the distinct but vanishing illusion.

Haldin was heard again.

"You must have had a walk—such a walk . . ." he murmured deprecatingly. "This weather . . ."

Razumov answered with energy:

"Horrible walk. . . . A nightmare of a walk."

He shuddered audibly. Haldin sighed once more, then:

"And so you have seen Ziemianitch—brother?"

"I've seen him."

Razumov, remembering the time he had spent with the prince, thought it prudent to add, "I had to wait some time."

"A character—eh? It's extraordinary what a sense of the necessity of freedom there is in that man. And he has sayings too—simple, to the point, such as only the people can invent in their rough sagacity. A character that . . ."

"I, you understand, haven't had much opportunity . . ." Razumov muttered through his teeth.

Haldin continued to stare at the ceiling.

"You see, brother, I have been a good deal in that house of late. I used to take there books—leaflets. Not a few of the poor people who live there can read. And, you see, the guests for the feast of freedom must be sought for in byways and hedges. The truth is, I have almost lived in that house of late. I slept sometimes in the stable. There is a stable . . ."

"That's where I had my interview with Ziemianitch," interrupted Razumov gently. A mocking spirit entered into him and he added, "It was satisfactory in a sense. I came away from it much relieved."

"Ah! he's a fellow," went on Haldin, talking slowly at the ceiling. "I came to know him in that way, you see. For some weeks now, ever since I resigned myself to do what had to be done, I tried to isolate myself. I gave up my rooms. What was the good of exposing a decent widow woman to the risk of being worried out of her mind by the police? I gave up seeing any of our comrades . . ."

Razumov drew to himself a half sheet of paper and began to trace lines on it with a pencil.

"Upon my word," he thought angrily, "he seems to have thought of everybody's safety but mine."

Haldin was talking on:

"This morning—ah! this morning—that was different. How can I explain to you? Before the deed was done I wandered at night and lay hid in the day, thinking it out, and I felt restful. Sleepless but restful. What was there for me to torment myself about? But this morning—after! Then it was that I became restless. I could not have stopped in that big house full of misery. The miserable of this world can't give you peace. Then when that silly caretaker began to shout, I said to myself, 'There is a young man in this town head and shoulders above common prejudices.'"

"Is he laughing at me?" Razumov asked himself, going on with his aimless drawing of triangles and squares. And suddenly he thought: "My behavior must appear to him strange. Should he take fright at my manner and rush off somewhere I shall be undone completely. That infernal general . . ."

He dropped the pencil and turned abruptly towards the bed with the shadowy figure extended full length on it so much more indistinct than the one over whose breast he had walked without filtering. Was this, too, a phantom?

The silence had lasted a long time. "He is no longer here," was the thought against which Razumov struggled desperately, quite frightened at its absurdity. "He is already gone and this . . . only . . ."

He could resist no longer. He sprang to his feet, saying aloud, "I am intolerably anxious," and in a few headlong strides stood by the side of the bed. His hand fell lightly on Haldin's shoulder, and directly he felt its reality he was beset by an insane temptation to grip that exposed throat and squeeze the breath out of that body lest it should escape his custody, leaving only a phantom behind.

Haldin did not stir a limb, but his overshadowed eyes moving a little gazed upwards at Razumov with wistful gratitude for this manifestation of feeling.

Razumov turned away and strode up and down the room. "It would have been possibly a kindness," he muttered to himself, and was appalled by the nature of that apology for a murderous intention his mind had found somewhere within him. And all the same he could not give it up. He became lucid about it. "What can he expect?" he thought. "The halter—in the end. And . . ."

This argument was interrupted by Haldin's voice.

"Why be anxious for me? They can kill my body, but they cannot exile my soul from this world. I tell you what—I believe in this world so much that I cannot conceive eternity otherwise than as a very long life. That is perhaps the reason I am so ready to die."

"H'm," muttered Razumov, and biting his lower lip he continued to walk up and down and to carry on his strange argument.

Yes, to a man in such a situation—of course it would be an act of kindness. The question, however, was not how to be kind, but how to be firm. He was a slippery customer...

"I too, Victor Victorovitch, believe in this world of ours," he said with force. "I too, while I live. . . . But you seem determined to haunt it. You can't seriously mean..."

The voice of the motionless Haldin began:

"Haunt it! Truly, the oppressors of thought which quickens the world, the destroyers of souls which aspire to perfection of human dignity, they shall be haunted. As to the destroyers of my mere body, I have forgiven them beforehand."

Razumov had stopped apparently to listen, but at the same time he was observing his own sensations. He was vexed with himself for attaching so much importance to what Haldin said.

"The fellow's mad," he thought firmly, but this opinion did not mollify him towards Haldin. It was a particularly impudent form of lunacy—and when it got loose in the sphere of public life of a country, it was obviously the duty of every good citizen...

This train of thought broke off short there and was succeeded by a paroxysm of silent hatred towards Haldin, so intense that Razumov hastened to speak at random.

"Yes. Eternity, of course. I, too, can't very well represent it to myself. . . . I imagine it, however, as something quiet and dull. There would be nothing unexpected—don't you see? The element of time would be wanting."

He pulled out his watch and gazed at it. Haldin turned over on his side and looked on intently.

Razumov got frightened at this movement. A slippery customer this fellow with a phantom. It was not midnight yet. He hastened on:

"And unfathomable mysteries! Can you conceive secret places in Eternity? Impossible. Whereas life is full of them. There are secrets of birth, for instance. One carries them on to the grave. There is something comical . . . but never mind. And there are secret motives of conduct. A man's most open actions have a secret side to them. That is interesting and so unfathomable! For instance, a man goes out of a room for a walk. Nothing more trivial in appearance. And yet it may be momentous. He comes back—he has seen perhaps a drunken brute, taken particular notice of the snow on the ground—and behold he is no longer the same man. The most unlikely things have a secret power over one's thoughts—the gray whiskers of a particular person—the goggle eyes of another."

Razumov's forehead was moist. He took a turn or two in the room, his head low, and smiling to himself viciously.

"Have you ever reflected on the power of goggle eyes and gray whiskers? Excuse me. You seem to think I must be crazy to talk in this vein at such a time. But I am not talking lightly. I have seen instances. It has happened to me once to be talking to a man whose fate was affected by physical facts of that kind. And the man did not know it. Of course, it was a case of conscience, but the material facts such as these brought about the solution. . . . And you tell me, Victor Victorovitch, not to be anxious! Why! I am responsible for you," Razumov almost shrieked.

He avoided with difficulty a burst of Mephistophelian laughter. Haldin, very pale, raised himself on his elbow.

"And the surprises of life," went on Razumov, after glancing at the other uneasily. "Just consider their astonishing nature. A mysterious impulse induces you to come here. I don't say you have done wrong. Indeed, from a certain point of view you could not have done better. You might have gone to a man with affections and family ties. You have such ties yourself. As to me, you know I have been brought up in an educational institute where they did not give us enough to eat. To talk of affection in such a connection—you perceive yourself . . . As to ties, the only ties I have in the world are social. I must get acknowledged in some way before I can act at all. I sit here working . . . And don't you think I am working for progress too? I've got to find my own ideas of the true way. . . . Pardon me," continued Razumov, after drawing breath and with a short, throaty laugh, "but I haven't inherited a revolutionary inspiration together with a resemblance from an uncle."

He looked again at his watch and noticed with sickening disgust that there were yet a good many minutes to midnight. He tore watch and chain off his waistcoat and laid them on the table well in the circle of bright lamplight. Haldin, reclining on his elbow, did not stir. Razumov was made uneasy by this attitude. "What move is he meditating over so quietly?" he thought. "He must be prevented. I must keep on talking to him."

He raised his voice.

"You are a son, a brother, a nephew, a cousin—I don't know what—to no end of people. I am just a man. Here I stand before you. A man with a mind. Did it ever occur to you how a man who had never heard a word of warm affection or praise in his life would think on matters on which you would think first with or against your class, your domestic tradition—your fireside prejudices? . . . Did you ever consider how a man like that would feel? I have no domestic tradition. I have nothing to think against. My tradition is historical. What have I to look back to but that national past from which you gentlemen want to wrench away your future? Am I to let my intelligence, my aspirations towards a better lot, be robbed of the only thing it has to go upon at the will of violent enthusiasts? You come from your province, but all this land is mine—or I have nothing. No doubt you shall be looked upon as a martyr some day—a sort of hero—a political saint. But I beg to be excused. I am content in fitting myself to be a worker. And what can you people do by scattering a few drops of blood on the snow? On this Immensity. On this unhappy Immensity! I tell you," he cried, in a vibrating subdued voice, and advancing one step nearer the bed, "that what it needs is not a lot of haunting phantoms that I could walk through—but a man!"

Haldin threw his arms forward as if to keep him off in horror.

"I understand it all now," he exclaimed with awestruck dismay. "I understand—at last."

Razumov staggered back against the table. His forehead broke out in perspiration while a cold shudder ran down his spine.

"What have I been saying?" he asked himself. "Have I let him slip through my fingers after all?"

He felt his lips go stiff like buckram, and instead of a reassuring smile only achieved an uncertain grimace.

"What will you have?" he began in a conciliating voice which got steady after the first trembling word or two. "What will you have? Consider—a man of studious, retired habits—and suddenly like this . . . I am not practiced in talking delicately. But . . ."

He felt anger, a wicked anger, get hold of him again.

"What were we to do together till midnight? Sit here opposite each other and think of your—your—shambles?"

Haldin had a subdued, heartbroken attitude. He bowed his head; his hands hung between his knees. His voice was low and pained but calm.

"I see now how it is, Razumov—brother. You are a magnanimous soul, but my action is abhorrent to you—alas! . . ."

Razumov stared. From fright he had set his teeth so hard that his whole face ached. It was impossible for him to make a sound.

"And even my person, too, is loathsome to you perhaps," Haldin added mournfully, after a short pause, looking up for a moment, then fixing his gaze on the floor. "For indeed, unless one . . ."

He broke off, evidently waiting for a word. Razumov remained silent. Haldin nodded his head dejectedly twice.

"Of course. Of course," he murmured. . . . "Ah! weary work!"

He remained perfectly still for a moment, then made Razumov's leaden heart strike a ponderous blow by springing up briskly.

"So be it," he cried sadly in a low, distinct tone. "Farewell then."

Razumov started forward, but the sight of Haldin's raised hand checked him before he could get away from the table. He leaned on it heavily, listening to the faint sounds of some town clock tolling the hour. Haldin, already at the door, tall and straight as an arrow, with his pale face and a hand raised attentively, might have posed for the statue of a daring youth listening to an inner voice. Razumov mechanically glanced down at his watch. When he looked towards the door again Haldin had vanished. There was a faint rustling in the outer room, the feeble click of a bolt drawn back lightly. He was gone—almost as noiseless as a vision.

Razumov ran forward unsteadily, with parted, voiceless lips. The outer door stood open. Staggering out on the landing, he leaned far over the banister. Gazing down into the deep black shaft with a tiny glimmering flame at the bottom, he traced by ear the rapid spiral descent of somebody running down the stairs on tip-toe. It was a light, swift, pattering sound, which sank away from him into the depths; a fleeting shadow passed over the glimmer—a wink of the tiny flame. Then stillness.

Razumov hung over, breathing the cold raw air tainted by the evil smells of the unclean staircase. All quiet.

He went back into his room slowly, shutting the doors after him. The peaceful steady light of his reading lamp shone on the watch. Razumov stood looking down at the little white dial. It wanted yet three minutes to midnight. He took the watch into his hand fumblingly.

"Slow," he muttered, and a strange fit of nervelessness came over him. His knees shook, the watch and chain slipped through his fingers in an instant and fell on the floor. He was so startled that he nearly fell himself. When at last he regained enough confidence in his limbs to stoop for it he held it to his ear at once. After a while he growled:

"Stopped," and paused for quite a long time before he muttered sourly:

"It's done. . . . And now to work."

He sat down, reached haphazard for a book, opened it in the middle and began to read; but after going conscientiously over two lines he lost his hold on the print completely and did not try to regain it. He thought:

"There was to a certainty a police agent of some sort watching the house across the street."

He imagined him lurking in a dark gateway, goggle-eyed, muffled up in a cloak to the nose and with a general's plumed, cocked hat on his head. This absurdity made him start in the chair convulsively. He literally had to shake his head violently to get rid of it. The man would be disguised perhaps as a peasant . . . a beggar. . . . Perhaps he would be just buttoned up in a dark overcoat and carrying a loaded stick—a shifty-eyed rascal, smelling of raw onions and spirits.

This evocation brought on positive nausea. "Why do I want to bother about this?" thought Razumov with disgust. "Am I a gendarme? Moreover, it is done."

He got up in great agitation. It was not done. Not yet. Not till half-past twelve. And the watch had stopped. This reduced him to despair. Impossible to know the time! The landlady and all the people across the landing were asleep. How could he go and . . . God knows what they would imagine, or how much they would guess. He dared not go into the streets to find out. "I am a suspect now. There's no use shirking that fact," he said to himself bitterly. If Haldin from some cause or another gave them the slip and failed to turn up in the Karabelnaya the police would be invading his lodging. And if he were not in he could never clear himself. Never. Razumov looked wildly about as if for some means of seizing upon time which seemed to have escaped him altogether. He had never, as far as he could remember, heard the striking of that town clock in his rooms before this night. And he was not even sure now whether he had heard it really on this night.

He went to the window and stood there with slightly bent head on the watch for the faint sound. "I will stay here till I hear something," he said to himself. He stood still, his ear turned to the panes. An atrocious aching numbness with shooting pains in his back and legs tortured him. He did not budge. His mind hovered on the borders of delirium. He heard himself suddenly saying, "I confess," as a person might do on the rack. "I am on the rack," he thought. He felt ready to swoon. The faint deep boom of the distant clock seemed to explode in his head—he heard it so clearly. . . One!

If Haldin had not turned up, the police would have been already here ransacking the house. No sound reached him. This time it was done.

He dragged himself painfully to the table and dropped into the chair. He flung the book away and took a square sheet of paper. It was like the pile of sheets covered with his neat minute handwriting, only blank. He took a pen bruskly and dipped it with a vague notion of going on with the writing of his essay—but his pen remained poised over the sheet. It hung there for some time before it came down and formed long scrawly letters.

Still-faced and his lips set hard, Razumov began to write. When he wrote a large hand his neat writing lost its character altogether—became unsteady, almost childish. He wrote five lines one under the other.

> History not Theory.
> Patriotism not Internationalism.
> Evolution not Revolution.
> Direction not Destruction.
> Unity not Disruption.

He gazed at them dully. Then his eyes strayed to the bed and remained fixed there for a good many minutes, while his right hand groped all over the table for the penknife.

He rose at last, and walking up with measured steps stabbed the paper with the penknife to the lath and plaster wall at the head of the bed. This done, he stepped back a pace and flourished his hand with a glance round the room.

After that he never looked again at the bed. He took his big cloak down from its peg and, wrapping himself up closely, went to lie down on the hard horsehair sofa at the other side of his room. A leaden sleep closed his eyelids at once. Several times that night he woke up shivering from a dream of walking through drifts of snow in a Russia where he was as completely alone as any betrayed autocrat could be; an immense, wintry Russia which, somehow, his view could embrace in all its enormous expanse as if it were a map. But after each shuddering start his heavy eyelids fell over his glazed eyes and he slept again.

III

Approaching this part of Mr. Razumov's story, my mind, the decent mind of an old teacher of languages, feels more and more the difficulty of the task.

The task is not, in truth, the writing in the narrative form a précis of a strange human document, but the rendering—I perceive it now clearly—of the moral conditions ruling over a large portion of this earth's surface: conditions not easily to be understood, much less discovered in the limits of a story, till some keyword is found; a word that could stand at the back of all the words covering the pages; a word which, if not truth itself, may perchance hold truth enough to help the moral discovery which should be the object of every tale.

I turn over for the hundredth time the leaves of Mr. Razumov's record, I lay it aside, I take up the pen—and the pen being ready for its office of setting down black on white I hesitate. For the word that persists in creeping under its point is no other word than "cynicism."

For that is the mark of Russian autocracy and of Russian revolt. In its pride of numbers, in its strange pretensions of sanctity, and in the secret readiness to abase itself in suffering, the spirit of Russia is the spirit of cynicism. It informs the declarations of her statesmen, the theories of her revolutionists, and the mystic vaticinations of prophets to the point of making freedom look like a form of debauch, and the Christian virtues themselves appear actually indecent. . . . But I must apologize for the digression. It proceeds from the consideration of the course taken by the story of Mr. Razumov after his conservative convictions, diluted in a vague liberalism natural to the ardor of his age, had become crystallized by the shock of his contact with Haldin.

Razumov woke up for the tenth time perhaps with a heavy shiver. Seeing the light of day in his window, he resisted the inclination to lay himself down again. He did not remember anything, but he did not think it strange to find himself on the sofa in his cloak and chilled to the bone. The light coming through the window seemed strangely cheerless, containing no promise as the light of each new day should for a young man. It was the awakening of a man mortally ill, or of a man ninety years old. He looked at the lamp, which had burnt itself out. It stood there, the extinguished beacon of his labors, a cold object of brass and porcelain, amongst the scattered pages of his notes and small piles of books—a mere litter of blackened paper—dead matter—without significance or interest.

He got on his feet, and divesting himself of his cloak hung it on the peg, going through all the motions mechanically. An incredible dullness, a ditch-water stagnation was sensible to his perceptions, as though life had withdrawn itself from all things and even from his own thoughts. There was not a sound in the house.

Turning away from the peg, he thought in that same lifeless manner that it must be very early yet; but when he looked at the watch on his table he saw both hands arrested at twelve o'clock.

"Ah, yes," he mumbled to himself, and as if beginning to get roused a little he took a survey of his room. The paper stabbed to the wall arrested his attention. He eyed it from the distance without approval or perplexity; but when he heard the servant-girl beginning to bustle about in the outer room with the samovar for his morning tea, he walked up to it and took it down with an air of profound indifference.

While doing this he glanced down at the bed on which he had not slept that night. The hollow in the pillow made by the weight of Haldin's head was very noticeable.

Even his anger at this sign of the man's passage was dull. He did not try to nurse it into life. He did nothing all that day; he neglected even to brush his hair. The idea of going out never occurred to him—and if he did not start a connected train of thought it was not because he was unable to think. It was because he was not interested enough.

He yawned frequently. He drank large quantities of tea, he walked about aimlessly, and when he sat down he did not budge for a long time. He spent some time drumming on the window with his fingertips quietly. In his listless wanderings round about the table he caught sight of his own face in the looking glass and that arrested him. The eyes which returned his stare were the most unhappy eyes he had ever seen. And this was the first thing which disturbed the mental stagnation of that day.

He was not affected personally. He merely thought that life without happiness is impossible. What was happiness? He yawned and went on shuffling about and about between the walls of his room. Looking forward was happiness—that's all—nothing more. To look forward to the gratification of some desire, to the gratification of some passion, love, ambition, hate—hate, too, indubitably. Love and hate. And to escape the dangers of existence, to live without fear, was also happiness. There was nothing else. Absence of fear—looking forward. "Oh! the miserable lot of humanity!" he exclaimed mentally; and added at once in his thought, "I ought to be happy enough as far as that goes." But he was not excited by that assurance. On the contrary, he yawned again as he had been yawning all day. He was mildly surprised to discover himself being overtaken by night. The room grew dark swiftly though time had seemed to stand still. How was it that he had not noticed the passing of that day? Of course, it was the watch being stopped. . . .

He did not light his lamp, but went over to the bed and threw himself on it without any hesitation. Lying on his back, he put his hands under his head and stared upward. After a moment he thought, "I am lying here like that man. I wonder if he slept while I was struggling with the blizzard in the streets. No, he did not sleep. But why should I not sleep?" and he felt the silence of the night press upon all his limbs like a weight.

In the calm of the hard frost outside, the clearcut strokes of the town clock counting off midnight penetrated the quietness of his suspended animation.

Again he began to think. It was twenty-four hours since that man left his room. Razumov had a distinct feeling that Haldin in the fortress was sleeping that night. It was a certitude which made him angry because he did not want to think of Haldin, but he justified it to himself by physiological and psychological reasons. The fellow had hardly slept for weeks on his own confession, and now every incertitude was at an end for him. No doubt he was looking forward to the consummation of his martyrdom. A man who resigns himself to kill need not go very far for resignation to die. Haldin slept perhaps more soundly than General T——, whose task—weary work too—was not done, and over whose head hung the sword of revolutionary vengeance.

Razumov, remembering the thickset man with his heavy jowl resting on the collar of his uniform, the champion of autocracy, who had let no sign of surprise, incredulity, or joy escape him, but whose goggle eyes could express a mortal hatred of all rebellion—Razumov moved uneasily on the bed.

"He suspected me," he thought. "I suppose he must suspect everybody. He would be capable of suspecting his own wife, if Haldin had gone to her boudoir with his confession."

Razumov sat up in anguish. Was he to remain a political suspect all his days? Was he to go through life as a man not wholly to be trusted—with a bad secret police note tacked on to his record? What sort of future could he look forward to?

"I am now a suspect," he thought again; but the habit of reflection and that desire of safety, of an ordered life, which was so strong in him came to his assistance as the night wore on. His quiet, steady, and laborious existence would vouch at length for his loyalty. There were many permitted ways to serve one's country. There was an activity that made for progress without being revolutionary. The field of influence was great and infinitely varied—once one had conquered a name.

His thought, like a circling bird, reverted after four-and-twenty hours to the silver medal, and as it were poised itself there.

When the day broke he had not slept, not for a moment, but he got up not very tired and quite sufficiently self-possessed for all practical purposes.

He went out and attended three lectures in the morning. But the work in the library was a mere dumb show of research. He sat with many volumes open before him trying to make notes and extracts. His new tranquility was like a flimsy garment, and seemed to float at the mercy of a casual word. Betrayal! Why! the fellow had done all that was necessary to betray himself. Precious little had been needed to deceive him.

"I have said no word to him that was not strictly true. Not one word," Razumov argued with himself.

Once engaged on this line of thought there could be no question of doing useful work. The same ideas went on passing through his mind, and pronounced mentally the same words over and over again. He shut up all the books and rammed all his papers into his pocket with convulsive movements, raging inwardly against Haldin.

As he was leaving the library, a long bony student in a threadbare overcoat joined him, stepping moodily by his side. Razumov answered his mumbled greeting without looking at him at all.

"What does he want with me?" he thought, with a strange dread of the unexpected which he tried to shake off lest it should fasten itself upon his life for good and all. And the other, muttering cautiously with downcast eyes, supposed that his comrade had seen the news of de P——'s executioner—that was the expression he used—having been arrested the night before last. . . .

"I've been ill—shut up in my rooms," Razumov mumbled through his teeth.

The tall student, raising his shoulders, shoved his hands deep into his pockets. He had a hairless, square, tallowy chin which trembled slightly as he spoke, and his nose nipped bright red by the sharp air looked like a false nose of painted cardboard between the sallow cheeks. His whole appearance was stamped with the mark of cold and hunger. He stalked deliberately at Razumov's elbow with his eyes on the ground.

"It's an official statement," he continued in the same cautious mutter. "It may be a lie. But there was somebody arrested between midnight and one in the morning on Tuesday. This is certain."

And talking rapidly under the cover of his downcast air, he told Razumov that this was known through an inferior Government clerk employed at the Central Secretariat. That man belonged to one of the revolutionary circles. "The same, in fact, I am affiliated to," remarked the student.

They were crossing a wide quadrangle. An infinite distress possessed Razumov, annihilated his energy, and before his eyes everything appeared confused and as if evanescent. He dared not leave the fellow there. "He may be affiliated to the police," was the thought that passed through his mind. "Who could tell?" But eyeing the miserable frost-nipped, famine-struck figure of his companion he perceived the absurdity of his suspicion.

"But I—you know—I don't belong to any circle."

He dared not say any more. Neither dared he mend his pace. The other, raising and setting down his lamentably shod feet with exact deliberation, protested in a low tone that it was not necessary for everybody to belong to an organization. The most valuable personalities remained outside. Some of the best work was done outside the organization. Then very fast, with whispering, feverish lips:

"The man arrested in the street was Haldin."

And accepting Razumov's dismayed silence as natural enough, he assured him that there was no mistake. That Government clerk was on night duty at the Secretariat. Hearing a great noise of footsteps in the hall and aware that political prisoners were brought over sometimes at night from the fortress, he opened the door of the room in which he was working, suddenly. Before the gendarme on duty could push him back and slam the door in his face, he had seen a prisoner being partly carried, partly dragged along the hall by a lot of policemen. He was being used very brutally. And the clerk had recognized Haldin perfectly. Less than half an hour afterwards General T—— arrived at the Secretariat to examine that prisoner personally.

"Aren't you astonished?" concluded the gaunt student.

"No," said Razumov roughly—and at once regretted his answer.

"Everybody supposed Haldin was in the provinces—with his people. Didn't you?"

The student turned his big hollow eyes upon Razumov, who said unguardedly:

"His people are abroad."

He could have bitten his tongue out with vexation. The student pronounced in a tone of profound meaning:

"So! You alone were aware . . ." and stopped.

"They have sworn my ruin," thought Razumov. "Have you spoken of this to anyone else?" he asked with bitter curiosity.

The other shook his head.

"No, only to you. Our circle thought that as Haldin had been often heard expressing a warm appreciation of your character . . ."

Razumov could not restrain a gesture of angry despair which the other must have misunderstood in some way, because he ceased speaking and turned away his black, lackluster eyes.

They moved side by side in silence. Then the gaunt student began to whisper again, with averted gaze:

"As we have at present no one affiliated inside the fortress so as to make it possible to furnish him with a packet of poison, we have considered already some sort of retaliatory action—to follow very soon . . ."

Razumov trudging on interrupted:

"Were you acquainted with Haldin? Did he know where you live?"

"I had the happiness to hear him speak twice," his companion answered in the feverish whisper contrasting with the gloomy apathy of his face and bearing. "He did not know where I live. . . . I am lodging poorly . . . with an artisan family. . . . I have just a corner in a room. It is not very practicable to see me there, but if you should need me for anything I am ready. . . ."

Razumov trembled with rage and fear. He was beside himself, but kept his voice low.

"You are not to come near me. You are not to speak to me. Never address a single word to me. I forbid you."

"Very well," said the other submissively, showing no surprise whatever at this abrupt prohibition. "You don't wish for secret reasons . . . perfectly . . . I understand."

He edged away at once, not looking up even; and Razumov saw his gaunt, shabby, famine-stricken figure cross the street obliquely with lowered head and that peculiar exact motion of the feet.

He watched him as one would watch a vision out of a nightmare, then he continued on his way, trying not to think. On his landing the landlady seemed to be waiting for him. She was a short, thick, shapeless woman with a large yellow face wrapped up everlastingly in a black woolen shawl. When she saw him come up the last flight of stairs she flung both her arms up excitedly, then clasped her hands before her face.

"Kirylo Sidorovitch—little father—what have you been doing? And such a quiet young man, too! The police have just gone this moment after searching your rooms."

Razumov gazed down at her with silent, scrutinizing attention. Her puffy yellow countenance was working with emotion. She screwed up her eyes at him entreatingly.

"Such a sensible young man! Anybody can see you are sensible. And now—like this—all at once. . . . What is the good of mixing yourself up with these Nihilists? Do give over, little father. They are unlucky people."

Razumov moved his shoulders slightly.

"Or is it that some secret enemy has been calumniating you, Kirylo Sidorovitch? The world is full of black hearts and false denunciations nowadays. There is much fear about."

"Have you heard that I have been denounced by someone?" asked Razumov, without taking his eyes off her quivering face.

But she had not heard anything. She had tried to find out by asking the police captain while his men were turning the room upside down. The police captain of the district had known her for the last eleven years and was a humane person. But he said to her on the landing, looking very black and vexed:

"My good woman, do not ask questions. I don't know anything myself. The order comes from higher quarters."

And indeed there had appeared, shortly after the arrival of the policeman of the district, a very superior gentleman in a fur coat and a shiny hat, who sat down in the room and looked through all the papers himself. He came alone and went away by himself, taking nothing with him. She had been trying to put things straight a little since they left.

Razumov turned away bruskly and entered his rooms.

All his books had been shaken and thrown on the floor. His landlady followed him, and stooping painfully began to pick them up into her apron. His papers and notes, which were kept always neatly sorted (they all related to his studies), had been shuffled up and heaped together into a ragged pile in the middle of the table.

This disorder affected him profoundly, unreasonably. He sat down and stared. He had a distinct sensation of his very existence being undermined in some mysterious manner, of his moral supports falling away from him one by one. He even experienced a slight physical giddiness and made a movement as if to reach for something to steady himself with.

The old woman, rising to her feet with a low groan, shot all the books she had collected in her apron on to the sofa and left the room muttering and sighing.

It was only then that he noticed that the sheet of paper which for one night had remained stabbed to the wall above his empty bed was lying on top of the pile.

When he had taken it down the day before, he had folded it in four, absent-mindedly, before dropping it on the table. And now he saw it lying uppermost, spread out, smoothed out even and covering all the confused pile of pages, the record of his intellectual life for the last three years. It had not been flung there. It had been placed there—smoothed out, too! He guessed in that an intention of profound meaning—or perhaps some inexplicable mockéry.

He sat staring at the piece of paper till his eyes began to smart. He did not attempt to put his papers in order, either that evening or the next day—which he spent at home in a state of peculiar irresolution. This irresolution bore upon the question whether he should continue to live—neither more nor less. But its nature was very far removed from the hesitation of a man contemplating suicide. The idea of laying violent hands upon his body did not occur to Razumov. The unrelated organism bearing that label, walking, breathing, wearing these clothes, was of no importance to anyone, unless maybe to the landlady. The true Razumov had his being in the willed, in the determined future—in that future menaced by the lawlessness of autocracy—for autocracy knows no law—and the lawlessness of revolution. The feeling that his moral personality was at the mercy of these lawless forces was so strong that he asked himself seriously if it were worthwhile to go on accomplishing the mental functions of that existence which seemed no longer his own.

"What is the good of exerting my intelligence, of pursuing the systematic development of my faculties and all my plans of work?" he asked himself. "I want to guide my conduct by reasonable convictions, but what security have I against something—some destructive horror—walking in upon me as I sit here? . . ."

Razumov looked apprehensively towards the door of the outer room as if expecting some shape of evil to turn the handle and appear before him silently.

"A common thief," he said to himself, "finds more guarantees in the law he is breaking, and even a brute like Ziemianitch has his consolation." Razumov envied the materialism of the thief and the passion of the incorrigible lover. The consequences of their actions were always clear and their lives remained their own.

But he slept as soundly that night as though he had been consoling himself in the manner of Ziemianitch. He dropped off suddenly, lay like a log, remembered no dream on waking. But it was as if his soul had gone out in the night to gather the flowers of wrathful wisdom. He got up in a mood of grim determination and as if with a new knowledge of his own nature. He looked mockingly on the heap of papers on his table; and left his room to attend the lectures, muttering to himself, "We shall see."

He was in no humor to talk to anybody or hear himself questioned as to his absence from lectures the day before. But it was difficult to repulse rudely a very good comrade with a smooth pink face and fair hair, bearing the nickname amongst his fellow-students of "Madcap Kostia." He was the idolized only son of a very wealthy and illiterate Government contractor, and attended the lectures only during the periodical fits of contrition following upon tearful paternal remon-

strances. Noisily blundering like a retriever puppy, his elated voice and great gestures filled the bare academy corridors with the joy of thoughtless animal life, provoking indulgent smiles at a great distance. His usual discourses treated of trotting horses, wine parties in expensive restaurants, and the merits of persons of
easy virtue, with a disarming artlessness of outlook. He pounced upon Razumov
about midday, somewhat less uproariously than his habit was, and led him aside.

"Just a moment, Kirylo Sidorovitch. A few words here in this quiet corner."

He felt Razumov's reluctance, and insinuated his hand under his arm.

"No—pray do. I don't want to talk to you about any of my silly scrapes. What
are my scrapes? Absolutely nothing. Mere childishness. The other night I flung a
fellow out of a certain place where I was having a fairly good time. A tyrannical little beast of a quill-driver from the Treasury department. . . . He was bullying the
people of the house. I rebuked him. 'You are not behaving humanely to God's creatures that are a jolly sight more estimable than yourself,' I said. I can't bear to see
any tyranny, Kirylo Sidorovitch. Upon my word I can't. He didn't take it in good
part at all. 'Who's that impudent puppy?' he begins to shout. I was in excellent
form as it happened, and he went through the closed window very suddenly. He
flew quite a long way into the yard. I raged like—like a—minotaur. The women
clung to me and screamed, the fiddlers got under the table. . . . Such fun! My dad
had to put his hand pretty deep into his pocket, I can tell you."

He chuckled.

"My dad is a very useful man. Jolly good thing it is for me, too. I do get into
unholy scrapes."

His elation fell. That was just it. What was his life? Insignificant; no good to
anyone; a mere festivity. It would end some fine day in his getting his skull split
with a champagne bottle in a drunken brawl. At such times, too, when men were
sacrificing themselves to ideas. But he could never get any ideas into his head. His
head wasn't worth anything better than to be split by a champagne bottle.

Razumov, protesting that he had no time, made an attempt to get away. The
other's tone changed to confidential earnestness.

"For God's sake, Kirylo, my dear soul, let me make some sort of sacrifice. It
would not be a sacrifice really. I have my rich dad behind me. There's positively no
getting to the bottom of his pocket."

And rejecting indignantly Razumov's suggestion that this was drunken raving,
he offered to lend him some money to escape abroad with. He could always get
money from his dad. He had only to say that he had lost it at cards or something of
that sort, and at the same time promise solemnly not to miss a single lecture for
three months on end. That would fetch the old man; and he, Kostia, was quite
equal to the sacrifice. Though he really did not see what was the good for him to
attend the lectures. It was perfectly hopeless.

"Won't you let me be of some use?" he pleaded to the silent Razumov, who, with his eyes on the ground and utterly unable to penetrate the real drift of the other's intention, felt a strange reluctance to clear up the point.

"What makes you think I want to go abroad?" he asked at last very quietly.

Kostia lowered his voice.

"You had the police in your rooms yesterday. There are three or four of us who have heard of that. Never mind how we know. It is sufficient that we do. So we have been consulting together."

"Ah! You got to know that so soon," muttered Razumov negligently.

"Yes. We did. And it struck us that a man like you . . ."

"What sort of a man do you take me to be?" Razumov interrupted him.

"A man of ideas—and a man of action too. But you are very deep, Kirylo. There's no getting to the bottom of your mind. Not for fellows like me. But we all agreed that you must be preserved for our country. Of that we have no doubt whatever—I mean all of us who have heard Haldin speak of you on certain occasions. A man doesn't get the police ransacking his rooms without there being some devilry hanging over his head. . . . And so if you think that it would be better for you to bolt at once."

Razumov tore himself away and walked down the corridor, leaving the other motionless with his mouth open. But almost at once he returned and stood before the amazed Kostia, who shut his mouth slowly. Razumov looked him straight in the eyes, before saying with marked deliberation and separating his words:

"I thank—you—very—much."

He went away again rapidly. Kostia, recovering from his surprise at these maneuvers, ran up behind him pressingly.

"No! Wait! Listen. I really mean it. It would be like giving your compassion to a starving fellow. Do you hear, Kirylo? And any disguise you may think of, that too I could procure from a costumier, a Jew I know. Let a fool be made serviceable according to his folly. Perhaps also a false beard or something of that kind may be needed."

Razumov turned at bay.

"There are no false beards needed in this business, Kostia—you good-hearted lunatic, you. What do you know of my ideas? My ideas may be poison to you."

The other began to shake his head in energetic protest.

"What have you got to do with ideas? Some of them would make an end of your dad's moneybags. Leave off meddling with what you don't understand. Go back to your trotting horses and your girls, and then you'll be sure at least of doing no harm to anybody, and hardly any to yourself."

The enthusiastic youth was overcome by this disdain.

"You're sending me back to my pig's trough, Kirylo. That settles it. I am an unlucky beast—and I shall die like a beast too. But mind—it's your contempt that has done for me."

Razumov went off with long strides. That this simple and grossly festive soul should have fallen too under the revolutionary curse affected him as an ominous symptom of the time. He reproached himself for feeling troubled. Personally he ought to have felt reassured. There was an obvious advantage in this conspiracy of mistaken judgment taking him for what he was not. But was it not strange?

Again he experienced that sensation of his conduct being taken out of his hands by Haldin's revolutionary tyranny. His solitary and laborious existence had been destroyed—the only thing he could call his own on this earth. By what right? he asked himself furiously. In what name?

What infuriated him most was to feel that the "thinkers" of the university were evidently connecting him with Haldin—as a sort of confidant in the background apparently. A mysterious connection! Ha, ha! . . . He had been made a personage without knowing anything about it. How that wretch Haldin must have talked about him! Yet it was likely that Haldin had said very little. The fellow's casual utterances were caught up and treasured and pondered over by all these imbeciles. And was not all secret revolutionary action based upon folly, self-deception, and lies?

"Impossible to think of anything else," muttered Razumov to himself. "I'll become an idiot if this goes on. The scoundrels and the fools are murdering my intelligence."

He lost all hope of saving his future, which depended on the free use of his intelligence.

He reached the doorway of his house in a state of mental discouragement which enabled him to receive with apparent indifference an official-looking envelope from the dirty hand of the dvornik.

"A gendarme brought it," said the man. "He asked if you were at home. I told him, 'No, he's not at home.' So he left it. 'Give it into his own hand,' says he. Now you've got it—eh?"

He went back to his sweeping, and Razumov climbed his stairs, envelope in hand. Once in his room he did not hasten to open it. Of course this official missive was from the superior direction of the police. A suspect! A suspect!

He stared in dreary astonishment at the absurdity of his position. He thought with a sort of dry, unemotional melancholy; three years of good work gone, the course of forty more perhaps jeopardized—turned from hope to terror, because events started by human folly link themselves into a sequence which no sagacity can foresee and no courage can break through. Fatality enters your rooms while your landlady's back is turned; you come home and find it in possession bearing a man's name, clothed in flesh—wearing a brown cloth coat and long boots—

lounging against the stove. It asks you, "Is the outer door closed?"—and you don't know enough to take it by the throat and fling it downstairs. You don't know. You welcome the crazy fate. "Sit down," you say. And it is all over. You cannot shake it off anymore. It will cling to you forever. Neither halter nor bullet can give you back the freedom of your life and the sanity of your thought. . . . It was enough to dash one's head against a wall.

Razumov looked slowly all round the walls as if to select a spot to dash his head against. Then he opened the letter. It directed the student Kirylo Sidorovitch Razumov to present himself without delay at the General Secretariat.

Razumov had a vision of General T——'s goggle eyes waiting for him—the embodied power of autocracy, grotesque and terrible. He embodied the whole power of autocracy because he was its guardian. He was the incarnate suspicion, the incarnate anger, the incarnate ruthlessness of a political and social regime on its defense. He loathed rebellion by instinct. And Razumov reflected that the man was simply unable to understand a reasonable adherence to the doctrine of absolutism.

"What can he want with me precisely—I wonder?" he asked himself.

As if that mental question had evoked the familiar phantom, Haldin stood suddenly before him in the room with an extraordinary completeness of detail. Though the short winter day had passed already into the sinister twilight of a land buried in snow, Razumov saw plainly the narrow leather strap round the Tcherkess coat. The illusion of that hateful presence was so perfect that he half expected it to ask, "Is the outer door closed?" He looked at it with hatred and contempt. Souls do not take a shape of clothing. Moreover, Haldin could not be dead yet. Razumov stepped forward menacingly; the vision vanished—and turning short on his heel he walked out of his room with infinite disdain.

But after going down the first flight of stairs it occurred to him that perhaps the superior authorities of police meant to confront him with Haldin in the flesh. This thought struck him like a bullet, and had he not clung with both hands to the banister he would have rolled down to the next landing most likely. His legs were of no use for a considerable time. . . . But why? For what conceivable reason? To what end?

There could be no rational answer to these questions; but Razumov remembered the promise made by the general to Prince K——. His action was to remain unknown.

He got down to the bottom of the stairs, lowering himself as it were from step to step, by the banister. Under the gate he regained much of his firmness of thought and limb. He went out into the street without staggering visibly. Every moment he felt steadier mentally. And yet he was saying to himself that General T—— was perfectly capable of shutting him up in the fortress for an indefinite time. His temperament fitted his remorseless task, and his omnipotence made him inaccessible to reasonable argument.

But when Razumov arrived at the Secretariat he discovered that he would have nothing to do with General T——. It is evident from Mr. Razumov's diary that this dreaded personality was to remain in the background. A civilian of superior rank received him in a private room after a period of waiting in outer offices where a lot of scribbling went on at many tables in a heated and stuffy atmosphere.

The clerk in uniform who conducted him said in the corridor:

"You are going before Gregory Matvieitch Mikulin."

There was nothing formidable about the man bearing that name. His mild, expectant glance was turned on the door already when Razumov entered. At once, with the penholder he was holding in his hand, he pointed to a deep sofa between two windows. He followed Razumov with his eyes while that last crossed the room and sat down. The mild gaze rested on him, not curious, not inquisitive—certainly not suspicious—almost without expression. In its passionless persistence there was something resembling sympathy.

Razumov, who had prepared his will and his intelligence to encounter General T—— himself, was profoundly troubled. All the moral bracing up against the possible excesses of power and passion went for nothing before this sallow man, who wore a full unclipped beard. It was fair, thin, and very fine. The light fell in coppery gleams on the protuberances of a high, rugged forehead. And the aspect of the broad, soft physiognomy was so homely and rustic that the careful middle parting of the hair seemed a pretentious affectation.

The diary of Mr. Razumov testifies to some irritation on his part. I may remark here that the diary proper, consisting of the more or less daily entries, seems to have been begun on that very evening after Mr. Razumov had returned home.

Mr. Razumov, then, was irritated. His strung-up individuality had gone to pieces within him very suddenly.

"I must be very prudent with him," he warned himself in the silence during which they sat gazing at each other. It lasted some little time, and was characterized (for silences have their character) by a sort of sadness imparted to it perhaps by the mild and thoughtful manner of the bearded official. Razumov learned later that he was the chief of a department in the General Secretariat, with a rank in the Civil Service equivalent to that of a colonel in the Army.

Razumov's mistrust became acute. The main point was, not to be drawn into saying too much. He had been called there for some reason. What reason? To be given to understand that he was a suspect—and also no doubt to be pumped. As to what precisely? There was nothing. Or perhaps Haldin had been telling lies. . . . Every alarming uncertainty beset Razumov. He could bear the silence no longer, and cursing himself for his weakness spoke first, though he had promised himself not to do so on any account.

"I haven't lost a moment's time," he began in a hoarse, provoking tone; and then the faculty of speech seemed to leave him and enter the body of Councillor Mikulin, who chimed in approvingly:

"Very proper. Very proper. Though as a matter of fact . . ."

But the spell was broken, and Razumov interrupted him boldly, under a sudden conviction that this was the safest attitude to take. With a great flow of words he complained of being totally misunderstood. Even as he talked with a perception of his own audacity he thought that the word "misunderstood" was better than the word "mistrusted," and he repeated it again with insistence. Suddenly he ceased, being seized with fright before the attentive immobility of the official. "What am I talking about?" he thought, eyeing him with a vague gaze. Mistrusted—not misunderstood—was the right symbol for these people. Misunderstood was the other kind of curse. Both had been brought on his head by that fellow Haldin. And his head ached terribly. He passed his hand over his brow—an involuntary gesture of suffering, which he was too careless to restrain. At that moment Razumov beheld his own brain suffering on the rack—a long, pale figure drawn asunder horizontally with terrific force in the darkness of a vault, whose face he failed to see. It was as though he had dreamed for an infinitesimal fraction of time of some dark print of the Inquisition. . . .

It is not to be seriously supposed that Razumov had actually dozed off and had dreamed in the presence of Councillor Mikulin, of an old print of the Inquisition. He was indeed extremely exhausted, and he records a remarkably dreamlike experience of anguish at the circumstance that there was no one whatever near the pale and extended figure. The solitude of the racked victim was particularly horrible to behold. The mysterious impossibility to see the face, he also notes, inspired a sort of terror. All these characteristics of an ugly dream were present. Yet he is certain that he never lost the consciousness of himself on the sofa, leaning forward with his hands between his knees and turning his cap round and round in his fingers. But everything vanished at the voice of Councillor Mikulin. Razumov felt profoundly grateful for the even simplicity of its tone.

"Yes. I have listened with interest. I comprehend in a measure your . . . But, indeed, you are mistaken in what you . . ." Councillor Mikulin uttered a series of broken sentences. Instead of finishing them he glanced down his beard. It was a deliberate curtailment which somehow made the phrases more impressive. But he could talk fluently enough, as became apparent when changing his tone to persuasiveness he went on: "By listening to you as I did, I think I have proved that I do not regard our intercourse as strictly official. In fact, I don't want it to have that character at all. . . . Oh yes! I admit that the request for your presence here had an official form. But I put it to you whether it was a form which would have been used to secure the attendance of a . . ."

"Suspect," exclaimed Razumov, looking straight into the official's eyes. They were big with heavy eyelids, and met his boldness with a dim, steadfast gaze. "A suspect." The open repetition of that word which had been haunting all his waking hours gave Razumov a strange sort of satisfaction. Councillor Mikulin shook his head slightly. "Surely you do know that I've had my rooms searched by the police?"

"I was about to say a 'misunderstood person,' when you interrupted me," insinuated quietly Councillor Mikulin.

Razumov smiled without bitterness. The renewed sense of his intellectual superiority sustained him in the hour of danger. He said a little disdainfully:

"I know I am but a reed. But I beg you to allow me the superiority of the thinking reed over the unthinking forces that are about to crush him out of existence. Practical thinking in the last instance is but criticism. I may perhaps be allowed to express my wonder at this action of the police being delayed for two full days during which, of course, I could have annihilated everything compromising by burning it—let us say—and getting rid of the very ashes, for that matter."

"You are angry," remarked the official, with an unutterable simplicity of tone and manner. "Is that reasonable?"

Razumov felt himself coloring with annoyance.

"I am reasonable. I am even—permit me to say—a thinker, though, to be sure, this name nowadays seems to be the monopoly of hawkers of revolutionary wares, the slaves of some French or German thought—devil knows what foreign notions. But I am not an intellectual mongrel. I think like a Russian. I think faithfully— and I take the liberty to call myself a thinker. It is not a forbidden word, as far as I know."

"No. Why should it be a forbidden word?" Councillor Mikulin turned in his seat with crossed legs, and resting his elbow on the table propped his head on the knuckles of a half-closed hand. Razumov noticed a thick forefinger clasped by a massive gold band set with a blood-red stone—a signet ring that, looking as if it could weigh half a pound, was an appropriate ornament for that ponderous man with the accurate middle-parting of glossy hair above a rugged Socratic forehead.

"Could it be a wig?" Razumov detected himself wondering with an unexpected detachment. His self-confidence was much shaken. He resolved to chatter no more. Reserve! Reserve! All he had to do was to keep the Ziemianitch episode secret with absolute determination, when the question came. Keep Ziemianitch strictly out of all the answers.

Councillor Mikulin looked at him dimly. Razumov's self-confidence abandoned him completely. It seemed impossible to keep Ziemianitch out. Every question would lead to that, because, of course, there was nothing else. He made an effort to brace himself up. It was a failure. But Councillor Mikulin was surprisingly detached too.

"Why should it be forbidden?" he repeated. "I too consider myself a thinking man, I assure you. The principal condition is to think correctly. I admit it is difficult sometimes at first for a young man abandoned to himself—with his generous impulses undisciplined, so to speak—at the mercy of every wild wind that blows. Religious belief, of course, is a great . . ."

Councillor Mikulin glanced down his beard, and Razumov, whose tension was relaxed by that unexpected and discursive turn, murmured with gloomy discontent:

"That man, Haldin, believed in God."

"Ah! You are aware," breathed out Councillor Mikulin, making the point softly, as if with discretion, but making it nevertheless plainly enough, as if he too were put off his guard by Razumov's remark. The young man preserved an impassive, moody countenance, though he reproached himself bitterly for a pernicious fool, to have given thus an utterly false impression of intimacy. He kept his eyes on the floor. "I must positively hold my tongue unless I am obliged to speak," he admonished himself. And at once against his will the question, "Hadn't I better tell him everything?" presented itself with such force that he had to bite his lower lip. Councillor Mikulin could not, however, have nourished any hope of confession. He went on:

"You tell me more than his judges were able to get out of him. He was judged by a commission of three. He would tell them absolutely nothing. I have the report of the interrogatories here, by me. After every question there stands 'Refuses to answer—refuses to answer.' It's like that, page after page. You see, I have been entrusted with some further investigations around and about this affair. He has left me nothing to begin my investigations on. A hardened miscreant. And so, you say, he believed in . . ."

Again Councillor Mikulin glanced down his beard with a faint grimace; but he did not pause for long. Remarking with a shade of scorn that blasphemers also had that sort of belief, he concluded by supposing that Mr. Razumov had conversed frequently with Haldin on the subject.

"No," said Razumov loudly, without looking up. "He talked and I listened. That is not a conversation."

"Listening is a great art," observed Mikulin parenthetically.

"And getting people to talk is another," mumbled Razumov.

"Well, no—that is not very difficult," Mikulin said innocently, "except, of course, in special cases. For instance, this Haldin. Nothing could induce him to talk. He was brought four times before the delegated judges. Four secret interrogatories—and even during the last, when your personality was put forward ..."

"My personality put forward?" repeated Razumov, raising his head bruskly. "I don't understand."

Councillor Mikulin turned squarely to the table, and taking up some sheets of gray foolscap dropped them one after another, retaining only the last in his hand. He held it before his eyes while speaking.

"It was—you see—judged necessary. In a case of that gravity no means of action upon the culprit should be neglected. You understand that yourself, I am certain."

Razumov stared with enormous wide eyes at the side view of Councillor Mikulin, who now was not looking at him at all.

"So it was decided (I was consulted by General T——) that a certain question should be put to the accused. But in deference to the earnest wishes of Prince K—— your name has been kept out of the documents and even from the very knowledge of the judges themselves. Prince K—— recognized the propriety, the necessity of what we proposed to do, but he was concerned for your safety. Things do leak out—that we can't deny. One cannot always answer for the discretion of inferior officials. There was, of course, the secretary of the special tribunal—one or two gendarmes in the room. Moreover, as I have said, in deference to Prince K—— even the judges themselves were to be left in ignorance. The question ready framed was sent to them by General T—— (I wrote it out with my own hand) with instructions to put it to the prisoner the very last of all. Here it is."

Councillor Mikulin threw back his head into proper focus and went on reading monotonously: "Question—Was the man well known to you, in whose rooms you remained for several hours on Monday and on whose information you have been arrested—has he had any previous knowledge of your intention to commit a political murder? ... Prisoner refuses to reply.

"Question repeated. Prisoner preserves the same stubborn silence.

"The venerable Chaplain of the Fortress being then admitted and exhorting the prisoner to repentance, entreating him also to atone for his crime by an unreserved and full confession which should help to liberate from the sin of rebellion against the Divine laws and the sacred Majesty of the Ruler of our Christ-loving land—the prisoner opens his lips for the first time during this morning's audience and in a loud, clear voice rejects the venerable Chaplain's ministrations.

"At eleven o'clock the Court pronounces in summary form the death sentence.

"The execution is fixed for four o'clock in the afternoon, subject to further instructions from superior authorities."

Councillor Mikulin dropped the page of foolscap, glanced down his beard, and turning to Razumov, added in an easy, explanatory tone:

"We saw no object in delaying the execution. The order to carry out the sentence was sent telegraph at noon. I wrote out the telegram myself. He was hanged at four o'clock this afternoon."

The definite information of Haldin's death gave Razumov the feeling of general lassitude which follows a great exertion or a great excitement. He kept very still on the sofa, but a murmur escaped him:

"He had a belief in a future existence."

Councillor Mikulin shrugged his shoulders slightly, and Razumov got up with an effort. There was nothing now to stay for in that room. Haldin had been hanged at four o'clock. There could be no doubt of that. He had, it seemed, entered upon his future existence, long boots, Astrakhan fur cap and all, down to the very leather strap round his waist. A flickering, vanishing sort of existence. It was not his soul, it was his mere phantom he had left behind on this earth—thought Razumov, smiling caustically to himself while he crossed the room, utterly forgetful of where he was and of Councillor Mikulin's existence. The official could have set a lot of bells ringing all over the building without leaving his chair. He let Razumov go quite up to the door before he spoke:

"Come, Kirylo Sidorovitch—what are you doing?"

Razumov turned his head and looked at him in silence. He was not in the least disconcerted. Councillor Mikulin's arms were stretched out on the table before him and his body leaned forward a little with an effort of his dim gaze.

"Was I actually going to clear out like this?" Razumov wondered at himself with an impassive countenance. And he was aware of this impassiveness concealing a lucid astonishment.

"Evidently I was going out if he had not spoken," he thought. "What would he have done then? I must end this affair one way or another. I must make him show his hand."

For a moment longer he reflected behind the mask as it were, then let go the door handle and came back to the middle of the room.

"I'll tell you what you think," he said explosively, but not raising his voice. "You think that you are dealing with a secret accomplice of that unhappy man. No, I do not know that he was unhappy. He did not tell me. He was a wretch from my point of view, because to keep alive a false idea is a greater crime than to kill a man. I suppose you will not deny that? I hated him! Visionaries work everlasting evil on earth. Their Utopias inspire in the mass of mediocre minds a disgust of reality and a contempt for the secular logic of human development."

Razumov shrugged his shoulders and stared. "What a tirade!" he thought. The silence and immobility of Councillor Mikulin impressed him. The bearded bureaucrat sat at his post, mysteriously self-possessed like an idol with dim, unreadable eyes. Razumov's voice changed involuntarily.

"If you were to ask me where is the necessity of my hate for such as Haldin, I would answer you—there is nothing sentimental in it. I did not hate him because he had committed the crime of murder. Abhorrence is not hate. I hated him simply because I am sane. It is in that character that he outraged me. His death . . ."

Razumov felt his voice growing thick in his throat. The dimness of Councillor Mikulin's eyes seemed to spread all over his face and made it indistinct to Razumov's sight. He tried to disregard these phenomena.

"Indeed," he pursued, pronouncing each word carefully, "what is his death to me? If he were lying here on the floor I could walk over his. . . . The fellow is a mere phantom. . . ."

Razumov's voice died out very much against his will. Mikulin behind the table did not allow himself the slightest movement. The silence lasted for some little time before Razumov could go on again.

"He went about talking of me. . . . Those intellectual fellows sit in each other's rooms and get drunk on foreign ideas in the same way young Guards' officers treat each other with foreign wines. Merest debauchery. . . . Upon my word,"—Razumov, enraged by a sudden recollection of Ziemianitch, lowered his voice forcibly—"upon my word, we Russians are a drunken lot. Intoxication of some sort we must have: to get ourselves wild with sorrow or maudlin with resignation; to lie inert like a log or set fire to the house. What is a sober man to do, I should like to know? To cut oneself entirely from one's kind is impossible. To live in a desert one must be a saint. But if a drunken man runs out of the grog-shop, falls on your neck and kisses you on both cheeks because something about your appearance has taken his fancy, what then—kindly tell me? You may break, perhaps, a cudgel on his back and yet not succeed in beating him off. . . ."

Councillor Mikulin raised his hand and passed it down his face deliberately.

"That's . . . of course," he said in an undertone.

The quiet gravity of that gesture made Razumov pause. It was so unexpected too. What did it mean? It had an alarming aloofness. Razumov remembered his intention of making him show his hand.

"I have said all this to Prince K——," he began, with assumed indifference, but lost it on seeing Councillor Mikulin's slow nod of assent. "You know it? You've heard . . . Then why should I be called here to be told of Haldin's execution? Did you want to confront me with his silence now that the man is dead? What is his silence to me? This is incomprehensible. You want in some way to shake my moral balance."

"No. Not that," murmured Councillor Mikulin, just audibly. "The service you have rendered is appreciated . . ."

"Is it?" interrupted Razumov ironically.

". . . and your position too." Councillor Mikulin did not raise his voice. "But only think! You fall into Prince K——'s study as if from the sky with your startling information. . . . You are studying yet, Mr. Razumov, but we are serving already—don't forget that. . . . And naturally some curiosity was bound to . . ."

Councillor Mikulin looked down his beard. Razumov's lips trembled.

"An occurrence of that sort marks a man," the homely murmur went on. "I admit I was curious to see you. General T—— thought it would be useful too. . . . Don't think I am incapable of understanding your sentiments. When I was young like you I studied . . ."

"Yes—you wished to see me," said Razumov in a tone of profound distaste. "Naturally you have the right—I mean the power. It all amounts to the same thing. But it is perfectly useless, if you were to look at me and listen to me for a year. I begin to think there is something about me which people don't seem able to make out. It's unfortunate. I imagine, however, that Prince K—— understands. He seems to."

Councillor Mikulin moved slightly and spoke. "Prince K—— is aware of everything that is being done, and I don't mind informing you that he approved my intention of becoming personally acquainted with you."

Razumov concealed an immense disappointment under the accents of railing surprise.

"So he is curious too! . . . Well—after all, Prince K—— knows me very little. It is really very unfortunate for me, but—it is not exactly my fault."

Councillor Mikulin raised a hasty deprecatory hand and inclined his head slightly over his shoulder.

"Now, Mr. Razumov—is it necessary to take it in that way? Everybody I am sure can . . ."

He glanced rapidly down his beard, and when he looked up again there was for a moment an interested expression in his misty gaze. Razumov discouraged it with a cold, repellent smile.

"No. That's of no importance, to be sure—except that in respect of all this curiosity being aroused by a very simple matter. . . . What is to be done with it? It is unappeasable. I mean to say there is nothing to appease it with. I happen to have been born a Russian with patriotic instincts—whether inherited or not I am not in a position to say."

Razumov spoke consciously with elaborate steadiness.

"Yes, patriotic instincts developed by a faculty of independent thinking—of detached thinking. In that respect I am more free than any social democratic revolution could make me. It is more than probable that I don't think exactly as you are thinking. Indeed, how could it be? You would think most likely at this moment that I am elaborately lying to cover up the track of my repentance."

Razumov stopped. His heart had grown too big for his breast. Councillor Mikulin did not flinch.

"Why so?" he said simply. "I assisted personally at the search of your rooms. I looked through all the papers myself. I have been greatly impressed by a sort of political confession of faith. A very remarkable document. Now may I ask for what purpose . . ."

"To deceive the police naturally," said Razumov savagely. . . . "What is all this mockery? Of course, you can send me straight from this room to Siberia. That would be intelligible. To what is intelligible I can submit. But I protest against this comedy of persecution. The whole affair is becoming too comical altogether for my taste. A comedy of errors, phantoms, and suspicions. It's positively indecent . . ."

Councillor Mikulin turned an attentive ear.

"Did you say phantoms?" he murmured.

"I could walk over dozens of them." Razumov, with an impatient wave of his hand, went on headlong, "But, really, I must claim the right to be done once for all with that man. And in order to accomplish this I shall take the liberty . . ."

Razumov on his side of the table bowed slightly to the seated bureaucrat.

". . . To retire—simply to retire," he finished with great resolution.

He walked to the door, thinking, "Now he must show his hand. He must ring and have me arrested before I am out of the building, or he must let me go. And either way . . ."

An unhurried voice said:

"Kirylo Sidorovitch."

Razumov at the door turned his head.

"To retire," he repeated.

"Where to?" asked Councillor Mikulin softly.

PART SECOND

I

In the conduct of an invented story there are, no doubt, certain proprieties to be observed for the sake of clearness and effect. A man of imagination, however inexperienced in the art of narrative, has his instinct to guide him in the choice of his words, and in the development of the action. A grain of talent excuses many mistakes. But this is not a work of imagination; I have no talent; my excuse for this undertaking lies not in its art, but in its artlessness. Aware of my limitations and strong in the sincerity of my purpose, I would not try (were I able) to invent anything. I push my scruples so far that I would not even invent a transition.

Dropping then Mr. Razumov's record at the point where Councillor Mikulin's question, "Where to?" comes in with the force of an insoluble problem, I shall simply say that I made the acquaintance of these ladies about six months before that time. By "these ladies" I mean, of course, the mother and the sister of the unfortunate Haldin.

By what arguments he had induced his mother to sell their little property and go abroad for an indefinite time, I cannot tell precisely. I have an idea that Mrs. Haldin, at her son's wish, would have set fire to her house and emigrated to the moon without any sign of surprise or apprehension; and that Miss Haldin—Nathalie, caressingly Natalia—would have given her assent to the scheme.

Their proud devotion to that young man became clear to me in a very short time. Following his directions they went straight to Switzerland—to Zurich—where they remained the best part of a year. From Zurich, which they did not like, they came to Geneva. A friend of mine in Lausanne, a lecturer in history at the university (he had married a Russian lady, a distant connection of Mrs. Haldin's), wrote to me suggesting I should call on these ladies. It was a very kindly meant business suggestion. Miss Haldin wished to go through a course of reading the best English authors with a competent teacher.

Mrs. Haldin received me very kindly. Her bad French, of which she was smilingly conscious, did away with the formality of the first interview. She was a tall woman in a black silk dress. A wide brow, regular features, and delicately cut lips testified to her past beauty. She sat upright in an easy chair, and in a rather weak, gentle voice told me that her Natalia simply thirsted after knowledge. Her thin hands were lying on her lap, her facial immobility had in it something monachal. "In Russia," she went on, "all knowledge was tainted with falsehood. Not chemistry and all that, but education generally," she explained. The Government corrupted the teaching for its own purposes. Both her children felt that. Her Natalia had obtained a diploma of a superior school for women, and her son was a student at the St. Petersburg University. He had a brilliant intellect, a most noble unselfish nature, and he was the oracle of his comrades. Early next year, she hoped, he would join them and they would then go to Italy together. In any other country but their own she would have been certain of a great future for a man with the extraordinary abilities and the lofty character of her son—but in Russia . . .

The young lady sitting by the window turned her head and said:

"Come, mother. Even with us things change with years."

Her voice was deep, almost harsh, and yet caressing in its harshness. She had a dark complexion, with red lips and a full figure. She gave the impression of strong vitality. The old lady sighed.

"You are both young—you two. It is easy for you to hope. But I, too, am not hopeless. Indeed, how could I be with a son like this?"

I addressed Miss Haldin, asking her what authors she wished to read. She directed upon me her gray eyes shaded by black eyelashes, and I became aware, notwithstanding my years, how attractive physically her personality could be to a man capable of appreciating in a woman something else than the mere grace of femininity. Her glance was as direct and trustful as that of a young man yet unspoiled by the world's wise lessons. And it was intrepid, but in this intrepidity there was nothing aggressive. A naive yet thoughtful assurance is a better definition. She had reflected already (in Russia the young begin to think early), but she had never known deception as yet, because obviously she had never yet fallen under the sway of passion. She was—to look at her was enough—very capable of being roused by an idea or simply by a person. At least, so I judged with I believe an unbiased mind; for clearly my person could not be the person—and as to my ideas! . . .

We became excellent friends in the course of our reading. It was very pleasant. Without fear of provoking a smile, I will confess that I became very much attached to that young girl. At the end of four months I told her that now she could very well go on reading English by herself. It was time for the teacher to depart. My pupil looked unpleasantly surprised.

Mrs. Haldin, with her immobility of feature and kindly expression of the eyes, uttered from her armchair in her uncertain French, *"Mais l'ami reviendra."* And so it was settled. I returned—not four times a week as before, but pretty frequently. In the autumn we made some short excursions together in company with other Russians. My friendship with these ladies gave me a standing in the Russian colony which otherwise I could not have had.

The day I saw in the papers the news of Mr. de P——'s assassination—it was a Sunday—I met the two ladies in the street and walked with them for some distance. Mrs. Haldin wore a heavy gray cloak, I remember, over her black silk dress, and her fine eyes met mine with a very quiet expression.

"We have been to the late service," she said. "Natalia came with me. Her girl-friends, the students here, of course don't. . . . With us in Russia the Church is so identified with oppression, that it seems almost necessary when one wishes to be free in this life, to give up all hope of a future existence. But I cannot give up praying for my son."

She added with a sort of stony grimness, coloring slightly, and in French, *"Ce n'est peut-être qu'une habitude."* ("It may be only habit.")

Miss Haldin was carrying the prayer book. She did not glance at her mother.

"You and Victor are both profound believers," she said.

I communicated to them the news from their country which I had just read in a café. For a whole minute we walked together fairly briskly in silence. Then Mrs. Haldin murmured:

"There will be more trouble, more persecutions for this. They may be even closing the university. There is neither peace nor rest in Russia for one but in the grave."

"Yes. The way is hard," came from the daughter, looking straight before her at the Chain of Jura covered with snow, like a white wall closing the end of the street. "But concord is not so very far off."

"That is what my children think," observed Mrs. Haldin to me.

I did not conceal my feeling that these were strange times to talk of concord. Nathalie Haldin surprised me by saying, as if she had thought very much on the subject, that the Occidentals did not understand the situation. She was very calm and youthfully superior.

"You think it is a class conflict, or a conflict of interests, as social contests are with you in Europe. But it is not that at all. It is something quite different."

"It is quite possible that I don't understand," I admitted.

That propensity of lifting every problem from the plane of the understandable by means of some sort of mystic expression, is very Russian. I knew her well enough to have discovered her scorn for all the practical forms of political liberty known to the Western world. I suppose one must be a Russian to understand

Russian simplicity, a terrible corroding simplicity in which mystic phrases clothe a naive and hopeless cynicism. I think sometimes that the psychological secret of the profound difference of that people consists in this, that they detest life, the irremediable life of the earth as it is, whereas we Westerners cherish it with perhaps an equal exaggeration of its sentimental value. But this is a digression indeed. . . .

I helped these ladies into the tramcar, and they asked me to call in the afternoon. At least Mrs. Haldin asked me as she climbed up, and her Natalia smiled down at the dense Westerner indulgently from the rear platform of the moving car. The light of the clear wintry forenoon was softened in her gray eyes.

Mr. Razumov's record, like the open book of fate, revives for me the memory of that day as something startlingly pitiless in its freedom from all forebodings. Victor Haldin was still with the living, but with the living whose only contact with life is the expectation of death. He must have been already referring to the last of his earthly affections, the hours of that obstinate silence, which for him was to be prolonged into eternity. That afternoon the ladies entertained a good many of their compatriots—more than was usual for them to receive at one time; and the drawing room on the ground floor of a large house on the Boulevard des Philosophes was very much crowded.

I outstayed everybody; and when I rose Miss Haldin stood up too. I took her hand and was moved to revert to that morning's conversation in the street.

"Admitting that we Occidentals do not understand the character of your people . . ." I began.

It was as if she had been prepared for me by some mysterious foreknowledge. She checked me gently:

"Their impulses—their . . ." she sought the proper expression and found it, but in French . . . "their *mouvements d'âme*."

Her voice was not much above a whisper.

"Very well," I said. "But still we are looking at a conflict. You say it is not a conflict of classes and not a conflict of interests. Suppose I admitted that. Are antagonistic ideas then to be reconciled more easily—can they be cemented with blood and violence into that concord which you proclaim to be so near?"

She looked at me searchingly with her clear gray eyes, without answering my reasonable question—my obvious, my unanswerable question.

"It is inconceivable," I added, with something like annoyance.

"Everything is inconceivable," she said. "The whole world is inconceivable to the strict logic of ideas. And yet the world exists to our senses, and we exist in it. There must be a necessity superior to our conceptions. It is a very miserable and a very false thing to belong to the majority. We Russians shall find some better form of national freedom than an artificial conflict of parties—which is wrong because it is a conflict and contemptible because it is artificial. It is left for us Russians to discover a better way."

Mrs. Haldin had been looking out of the window. She turned upon me the almost lifeless beauty of her face, and the living benign glance of her big dark eyes.

"That's what my children think," she declared.

"I suppose," I addressed Miss Haldin, "that you will be shocked if I tell you that I haven't understood—I won't say a single word; I've understood all the words. . . . But what can be this era of disembodied concord you are looking forward to? Life is a thing of form. It has its plastic shape and a definite intellectual aspect. The most idealistic conceptions of love and forbearance must be clothed in flesh as it were before they can be made understandable."

I took my leave of Mrs. Haldin, whose beautiful lips never stirred. She smiled with her eyes only. Nathalie Haldin went with me as far as the door, very amiable.

"Mother imagines that I am the slavish echo of my brother Victor. It is not so. He understands me better than I can understand him. When he joins us and you come to know him you will see what an exceptional soul it is." She paused. "He is not a strong man in the conventional sense, you know," she added. "But his character is without a flaw."

"I believe that it will not be difficult for me to make friends with your brother Victor."

"Don't expect to understand him quite," she said, a little maliciously. "He is not at all—at all—Western at bottom."

And on this unnecessary warning I left the room with another bow in the doorway to Mrs. Haldin in her armchair by the window. The shadow of autocracy all unperceived by me had already fallen upon the Boulevard des Philosophes, in the free, independent, and democratic city of Geneva, where there is a quarter called "La Petite Russie." Whenever two Russians come together, the shadow of autocracy is with them, tingeing their thoughts, their views, their most intimate feelings, their private life, their public utterances—haunting the secret of their silences.

What struck me next in the course of a week or so was the silence of these ladies. I used to meet them walking in the public garden near the university. They greeted me with their usual friendliness, but I could not help noticing their taciturnity. By that time it was generally known that the assassin of Mr. de P—— had been caught, judged, and executed. So much had been declared officially to the news agencies. But for the world at large he remained anonymous. The official secrecy had withheld his name from the public. I really cannot imagine for what reason.

One day I saw Miss Haldin walking alone in the main valley of the Bastions under the naked trees.

"Mother is not very well," she explained.

As Mrs. Haldin had, it seemed, never had a day's illness in her life, this indisposition was disquieting. It was nothing definite, too.

"I think she is fretting because we have not heard from my brother for rather a long time."

"No news—good news," I said cheerfully, and we began to walk slowly side by side.

"Not in Russia," she breathed out so low that I only just caught the words. I looked at her with more attention.

"You too are anxious?"

She admitted after a moment of hesitation that she was.

"It is really such a long time since we heard . . ."

And before I could offer the usual banal suggestions she confided in me.

"Oh! But it is much worse than that. I wrote to a family we know in Petersburg. They had not seen him for more than a month. They thought he was already with us. They were even offended a little that he should have left Petersburg without calling on them. The husband of the lady went at once to his lodgings. Victor had left there and they did not know his address."

I remember her catching her breath rather pitifully. Her brother had not been seen at lectures for a very long time either. He only turned up now and then at the university gate to ask the porter for his letters. And the gentleman friend was told that the student Haldin did not come to claim the last two letters for him. But the police came to inquire if the student Haldin ever received any correspondence at the university and took them away. "My last two letters," she said.

We faced each other. A few snowflakes fluttered under the naked boughs. The sky was dark.

"What do you think could have happened?" I asked.

Her shoulders moved slightly.

"One can never tell—in Russia."

I saw then the shadow of autocracy lying upon Russian lives in their submission or their revolt. I saw it touch her handsome open face nestled in a fur collar and darken her clear eyes that shone upon me brilliantly gray in the murky light of a beclouded, inclement afternoon.

"Let us move on," she said. "It is cold standing—today."

She shuddered a little and stamped her little feet. We moved briskly to the end of the alley and back to the great gates of the garden.

"Have you told your mother?" I ventured to ask.

"No. Not yet. I came out to walk off the impression of this letter."

I heard a rustle of paper somewhere. It came from her muff. She had the letter with her in there.

"What is it that you are afraid of?" I asked.

To us Europeans of the West, all ideas of political plots and conspiracies seem childish, crude inventions for the theater or a novel. I did not like to be more definite in my inquiry.

"For us—for my mother specially, what I am afraid of is incertitude. People do disappear. Yes, they do disappear. I leave you to imagine what it is—the cruelty of the dumb weeks—months—years! This friend of ours has abandoned his inquiries when he heard of the police getting hold of the letters. I suppose he was afraid of compromising himself. He has a wife and children—and why should he, after all? . . . Moreover, he is without influential connections and not rich. What could he do? . . . Yes, I am afraid of silence—for my poor mother. She won't be able to bear it. For my brother I am afraid of . . ." she became almost indistinct, "of anything."

We were now near the gate opposite the theater. She raised her voice.

"But lost people do turn up even in Russia. Do you know what my last hope is? Perhaps the next thing we know, we shall see him walking into our rooms."

I raised my hat and she passed out of the gardens, graceful and strong, after a slight movement of the head to me, her hands in the muff, crumpling the cruel Petersburg letter.

On returning home I opened the newspaper I receive from London, and glancing down the correspondence from Russia—not the telegrams but the correspondence—the first thing that caught my eye was the name of Haldin. Mr. de P——'s death was no longer an actuality, but the enterprising correspondent was proud of having ferreted out some unofficial information about that fact of modern history. He had got hold of Haldin's name, and had picked up the story of the midnight arrest in the street. But the sensation from a journalistic point of view was already well in the past. He did not allot to it more than twenty lines out of a full column. It was quite enough to give me a sleepless night. I perceived that it would have been a sort of treason to let Miss Haldin come without preparation upon that journalistic discovery which would infallibly be reproduced on the morrow by French and Swiss newspapers. I had a very bad time of it till the morning, wakeful with nervous worry and nightmarish with the feeling of being mixed up with something theatrical and morbidly affected. The incongruity of such a complication in those two women's lives was sensible to me all night in the form of absolute anguish. It seemed due to their refined simplicity that it should remain concealed from them forever. Arriving at an unconscionably early hour at the door of their apartment, I felt as if I were about to commit an act of vandalism. . . .

The middle-aged servant-woman led me into the drawing room, where there was a duster on a chair and a broom leaning against the center table. The motes danced in the sunshine. I regretted I had not written a letter instead of coming myself, and was thankful for the brightness of the day. Miss Haldin, in a plain black dress, came lightly out of her mother's room with a fixed uncertain smile on her lips.

I pulled the paper out of my pocket. I did not imagine that a number of the *Standard* could have the effect of Medusa's head. Her face went stony in a moment—her eyes—her limbs. The most terrible thing was that being stony she remained alive. One was conscious of her palpitating heart. I hope she forgave me the delay of my clumsy circumlocution. It was not very prolonged; she could not have kept so still from head to foot for more than a second or two; and then I heard her draw a breath. As if the shock had paralyzed her moral resistance and affected the firmness of her muscles, the contours of her face seemed to have given way. She was frightfully altered. She looked aged—ruined. But only for a moment. She said with decision:

"I am going to tell my mother at once."

"Would that be safe in her state?" I objected.

"What can be worse than the state she has been in for the last month? We understand this in another way. The crime is not at his door. Don't imagine I am defending him before you."

She went to the bedroom door, then came back to ask me in a low murmur not to go till she returned. For twenty interminable minutes not a sound reached me. At last Miss Haldin came out and walked across the room with her quick light step. When she reached the armchair she dropped into it heavily as if completely exhausted.

Mrs. Haldin, she told me, had not shed a tear. She was sitting up in bed, and her immobility, her silence, were very alarming. At last she lay down gently and had motioned her daughter away.

"She will call me in presently," added Miss Haldin. "I left a bell near the bed."

I confess that my very real sympathy had no standpoint. The Western readers for whom this story is written will understand what I mean. It was, if I may say so, the want of experience. Death is a remorseless spoliator. The anguish of irreparable loss is familiar to us all. There is no life so lonely as to be safe against that experience. But the grief I had brought to these two ladies had gruesome associations. It had the associations of bombs and gallows—a lurid, Russian coloring which made the complexion of my sympathy uncertain.

I was grateful to Miss Haldin for not embarrassing me by an outward display of deep feeling. I admired her for that wonderful command over herself, even while I was a little frightened at it. It was the stillness of a great tension. What if it should suddenly snap? Even the door of Mrs. Haldin's room, with the old mother alone in there, had a rather awful aspect.

Nathalie Haldin murmured sadly:

"I suppose you are wondering what my feelings are?"

Essentially that was true. It was that very wonder which unsettled my sympathy of a dense Occidental. I could get hold of nothing but of some commonplace phrases, those futile phrases that give the measure of our impotence before each other's trials. I mumbled something to the effect that, for the young, life held its hopes and compensations. It held duties too—but of that I was certain it was not necessary to remind her.

She had a handkerchief in her hands and pulled at it nervously.

"I am not likely to forget my mother," she said. "We used to be three. Now we are two—two women. She's not so very old. She may live quite a long time yet. What have we to look for in the future? For what hope and what consolation?"

"You must take a wider view," I said resolutely, thinking that with this exceptional creature this was the right note to strike. She looked at me steadily for a moment, and then the tears she had been keeping down flowed unrestrained. She jumped up and stood in the window with her back to me.

I slipped away without attempting even to approach her. Next day I was told at the door that Mrs. Haldin was better. The middle-aged servant remarked that a lot of people—Russians—had called that day, but Miss Haldin had not seen anybody. A fortnight later, when making my daily call, I was asked in and found Mrs. Haldin sitting in her usual place by the window.

At first one would have thought that nothing was changed. I saw across the room the familiar profile, a little sharper in outline and overspread by a uniform pallor as might have been expected in an invalid. But no disease could have accounted for the change in her black eyes, smiling no longer with gentle irony. She raised them as she gave me her hand. I observed the three weeks' old number of the *Standard* folded with the correspondence from Russia uppermost, lying on a little table by the side of the armchair. Mrs. Haldin's voice was startlingly weak and colorless. Her first words to me framed a question:

"Has there been anything more in your newspapers?"

I released her long, emaciated hand, shook my head negatively, and sat down.

"The English Press is wonderful. Nothing can be kept secret from it, and all the world must hear. Only our Russian news is not always easy to understand. Not always easy. . . . But English mothers do not look for news like that . . ."

She laid her hand on the newspaper and took it away again. I said:

"We too have had tragic times in our history."

"A long time ago. A very long time ago."

"Yes."

"There are nations that have made their bargain with Fate," said Miss Haldin, who had approached us. "We need not envy them."

"Why this scorn?" I asked gently. "It may be that our bargain was not a very lofty one. But the terms men and nations obtain from Fate are hallowed by the price."

Mrs. Haldin turned her head away and looked out of the window for a time, with that new, somber, extinct gaze of her sunken eyes which so completely made another woman of her.

"That Englishman, this correspondent," she addressed me suddenly, "do you think it is possible that he knew my son?"

To this strange question I could only say that it was possible, of course. She saw my surprise.

"If one knew what sort of man he was one could perhaps write to him," she murmured.

"Mother thinks," explained Miss Haldin, standing between us, with one hand resting on the back of my chair, "that my poor brother perhaps did not try to save himself."

I looked up at Miss Haldin in sympathetic consternation, but Miss Haldin was looking down calmly at her mother. The latter said:

"We do not know the address of any of his friends. Indeed, we know nothing of his Petersburg comrades. He had a multitude of young friends, only he never spoke much of them. One could guess that they were his disciples and that they idolized him. But he was so modest. One would think that with so many devoted . . ."

She averted her head again and looked down the Boulevard des Philosophes, a singularly arid and dusty thoroughfare, where nothing could be seen at the moment but two dogs, a little girl in a pinafore hopping on one leg, and in the distance a workman wheeling a bicycle.

"Even amongst the Apostles of Christ there was found a Judas," she whispered as if to herself, but with the evident intention to be heard by me.

The Russian visitors assembled in little knots, conversed amongst themselves meantime, in low murmurs, and with brief glances in our direction. It was a great contrast to the usual loud volubility of these gatherings. Miss Haldin followed me into the anteroom.

"People will come," she said. "We cannot shut the door in their faces."

While I was putting on my overcoat she began to talk to me of her mother. Poor Mrs. Haldin was fretting after more news. She wanted to go on hearing about her unfortunate son. She could not make up her mind to abandon him quietly to the dumb unknown. She would persist in pursuing him in there through the long days of motionless silence face to face with the empty Boulevard des Philosophes. She could not understand why he had not escaped—as so many other revolutionists and conspirators had managed to escape in other instances of that kind. It was really inconceivable that the means of secret revolutionary organizations should have failed so inexcusably to preserve her son. But in reality the inconceivable that staggered her mind was nothing but the cruel audacity of Death passing over her head to strike at that young and precious heart.

Miss Haldin mechanically, with an absorbed look, handed me my hat. I understood from her that the poor woman was possessed by the somber and simple idea that her son must have perished because he did not want to be saved. It could not have been that he despaired of his country's future. That was impossible. Was it possible that his mother and sister had not known how to merit his confidence; and that, after having done what he was compelled to do, his spirit became crushed by an intolerable doubt, his mind distracted by a sudden mistrust?

I was very much shocked by this piece of ingenuity. "Our three lives were like that!" Miss Haldin twined the fingers of both her hands together in demonstration, then separated them slowly, looking straight into my face. "That's what poor mother found to torment herself and me with, for all the years to come," added the strange girl. At that moment her indefinable charm was revealed to me in the conjunction of passion and stoicism. I imagined what her life was likely to be by the side of Mrs. Haldin's terrible immobility, inhabited by that fixed idea. But my concern was reduced to silence by my ignorance of her modes of feeling. Difference of nationality is a terrible obstacle for our complex Western natures. But Miss Haldin probably was too simple to suspect my embarrassment. She did not wait for me to say anything, but as if reading my thoughts on my face she went on courageously:

"At first poor mother went numb, as our peasants say; then she began to think, and she will go on now thinking and thinking in that unfortunate strain. You see yourself how cruel that is. . . ."

I never spoke with greater sincerity than when I agreed with her that it would be deplorable in the highest degree. She took an anxious breath.

"But all these strange details in the English paper," she exclaimed suddenly. "What is the meaning of them? I suppose they are true? But is it not terrible that my poor brother should be caught wandering alone, as if in despair, about the streets at night? . . ."

We stood so close to each other in the dark anteroom that I could see her biting her lower lip to suppress a dry sob. After a short pause she said:

"I suggested to mother that he may have been betrayed by some false friend or simply by some cowardly creature. It may be easier for her to believe that."

I understood now the poor woman's whispered allusion to Judas.

"It may be easier," I admitted, admiring inwardly the directness and the subtlety of the girl's outlook. She was dealing with life as it was made for her by the political conditions of her country. She faced cruel realities, not morbid imaginings of her own making. I could not defend myself from a certain feeling of respect when she added simply:

"Time they say can soften every sort of bitterness. But I cannot believe that it has any power over remorse. It is better that mother should think some person guilty of Victor's death, than that she should connect it with a weakness of her son or a shortcoming of her own."

"But you, yourself, don't suppose that? . . ." I began.

She compressed her lips and shook her head. She harbored no evil thought against anyone, she declared—and perhaps nothing that happened was unnecessary. On these words, pronounced low and sounding mysterious in the half obscurity of the anteroom, we parted with an expressive and warm handshake. The grip of her strong, shapely hand had a seductive frankness, a sort of exquisite virility. I do not know why she should have felt so friendly to me. It may be that she thought I understood her much better than I was able to do. The most precise of her sayings seemed always to me to have enigmatical prolongations vanishing somewhere beyond my reach. I am reduced to suppose that she appreciated my attention and my silence. The attention she could see was quite sincere, so that the silence could not be suspected of coldness. It seemed to satisfy her. And it is to be noted that if she confided in me it was clearly not with the expectation of receiving advice, for which, indeed, she never asked.

II

Our daily relations were interrupted at this period for something like a fortnight. I had to absent myself unexpectedly from Geneva. On my return I lost no time in directing my steps up the Boulevard des Philosophes.

Through the open door of the drawing room I was annoyed to hear a visitor holding forth steadily in an unctuous deep voice.

Mrs. Haldin's armchair by the window stood empty. On the sofa, Nathalie Haldin raised her charming gray eyes in a glance of greeting accompanied by the merest hint of a welcoming smile. But she made no movement. With her strong white hands lying inverted in the lap of her mourning dress she faced a man who presented to me a robust back covered with black broadcloth, and well in keeping with the deep voice. He turned his head sharply over his shoulder, but only for a moment.

"Ah! your English friend. I know. I know. That's nothing."

He wore spectacles with smoked glasses, a tall silk hat stood on the floor by the side of his chair. Flourishing slightly a big soft hand he went on with his discourse, precipitating his delivery a little more.

"I have never changed the faith I held while wandering in the forests and bogs of Siberia. It sustained me then—it sustains me now. The Great Powers of Europe are bound to disappear—and the cause of their collapse will be very simple. They will exhaust themselves struggling against their proletariat. In Russia it is different. In Russia we have no classes to combat each other, one holding the power of wealth, and the other mighty with the strength of numbers. We have only an unclean bureaucracy in the face of a people as great and as incorruptible as the ocean. No, we have no classes. But we have the Russian woman. The admirable Russian woman! I receive most remarkable letters signed by women. So elevated in tone, so courageous, breathing such a noble ardor of service! The greatest part of our hopes rests on women. I behold their thirst for knowledge. It is admirable. Look how they absorb, how they are making it their own. It is miraculous. But what is knowledge? . . . I understand that you have not been studying anything especially—medicine, for instance. No? That's right. Had I been honored by being asked to advise you on the use of your time when you arrived here, I would have been strongly opposed to such a course. Knowledge in itself is mere dross."

He had one of those bearded Russian faces without shape, a mere appearance of flesh and hair with not a single feature having any sort of character. His eyes being hidden by the dark glasses, there was an utter absence of all expression. I knew him by sight. He was a Russian refugee of mark. All Geneva knew his burly, black-coated figure. At one time all Europe was aware of the story of his life written by himself and translated into seven or more languages. In his youth he had led an idle, dissolute life. Then a society girl he was about to marry died suddenly, and thereupon he abandoned the world of fashion and began to conspire in a spirit of repentance, and, after that, his native autocracy took good care that the usual things should happen to him. He was imprisoned in fortresses, beaten within an inch of his life, and condemned to work in mines with common criminals. The great success of his book, however, was the chain.

I do not remember now the details of the weight and length of the fetters riveted on his limbs by an "Administrative" order, but it was in the number of pounds and the thickness of links an appalling assertion of the divine right of autocracy. Appalling and futile too, because this big man managed to carry off that simple engine of government with him into the woods. The sensational clink of these fetters is heard all through the chapters describing his escape—a subject of wonder to two continents. He had begun by concealing himself successfully from his guard in a hole on a riverbank. It was the end of the day; with infinite labor he managed to free one of his legs. Meantime night fell. He was going to begin on his other leg when he was overtaken by a terrible misfortune. He dropped his file.

All this is precise yet symbolic; and the file had its pathetic history. It was given to him unexpectedly one evening, by a quiet, pale-faced girl. The poor creature had come out to the mines to join one of his fellow-convicts, a delicate young man, a mechanic and a social democrat, with broad cheekbones and large staring eyes. She had worked her way across half Russia and nearly the whole of Siberia to be near him, and, as it seems, with the hope of helping him to escape. But she arrived too late. Her lover had died only a week before.

Through that obscure episode, as he says, in the history of ideas in Russia, the file came into his hands, and inspired him with an ardent resolution to regain his liberty. When it slipped through his fingers it was as if it had gone straight into the earth. He could by no manner of means put his hand on it again in the dark. He groped systematically in the loose earth, in the mud, in the water; the night was passing meantime, the precious night on which he counted to get away into the forests, his only chance of escape. For a moment he was tempted by despair to give up; but recalling the quiet, sad face of the heroic girl, he felt profoundly ashamed of his weakness. She had selected him for the gift of liberty and he must show himself worthy of the favor conferred by her feminine, indomitable soul. It appeared to be a sacred trust. To fail would have been a sort of treason against the sacredness of self-sacrifice and womanly love.

There are in his book whole pages of self-analysis whence emerges like a white figure from a dark confused sea the conviction of woman's spiritual superiority— his new faith confessed since in several volumes. His first tribute to it, the great act of his conversion, was his extraordinary existence in the endless forests of the Okhotsk Province, with the loose end of the chain wound about his waist. A strip torn off his convict shirt secured the end firmly. Other strips fastened it at intervals up his left leg to deaden the clanking and to prevent the slack links from getting hooked in the bushes. He became very fierce. He developed an unsuspected genius for the arts of a wild and hunted existence. He learned to creep into villages without betraying his presence by anything more than an occasional faint jingle. He broke into outhouses with an axe he managed to purloin in a woodcutters' camp. In the deserted tracts of country he lived on wild berries and hunted for honey. His clothing dropped off him gradually. His naked, tawny figure, glimpsed vaguely through the bushes with a cloud of mosquitoes and flies hovering about the shaggy head, spread tales of terror through whole districts. His temper grew savage as the days went by, and he was glad to discover that there was so much of a brute in him. He had nothing else to put his trust in. For it was as though there had been two human beings indissolubly joined in that enterprise. The civilized man, the enthusiast of advanced humanitarian ideals thirsting for the triumph of spiritual love and political liberty; and the stealthy, primeval savage, pitilessly cunning in the preservation of his freedom from day to day, like a tracked wild beast.

The wild beast was making its way instinctively eastward to the Pacific coast, and the civilized humanitarian in fearful anxious dependence watched the proceedings with awe. Through all these weeks he could never make up his mind to appeal to human compassion. In the wary primeval savage this shyness might have been natural, but the other too, the civilized creature, the thinker, the escaping "political," had developed an absurd form of morbid pessimism, a form of temporary insanity, originating perhaps in the physical worry and discomfort of the chain. These links, he fancied, made him odious to the rest of mankind. It was a repugnant and suggestive load. Nobody could feel any pity at the disgusting sight of a man escaping with a broken chain. His imagination became affected by his fetters in a precise, matter-of-fact manner. It seemed to him impossible that people could resist the temptation of fastening the loose end to a staple in the wall while they went for the nearest police official. Crouching in holes or hidden in thickets, he had tried to read the faces of unsuspecting free settlers working in the clearings or passing along the paths within a foot or two of his eyes. His feeling was that no man on earth could be trusted with the temptation of the chain.

One day, however, he chanced to come upon a solitary woman. It was on an open slope of rough grass outside the forest. She sat on the bank of a narrow stream; she had a red handkerchief on her head and a small basket was lying on the ground near her hand. At a little distance could be seen a cluster of log cabins, with a water mill over a dammed pool shaded by birch trees and looking bright as glass in the twilight. He approached her silently, his hatchet stuck in his iron belt, a thick cudgel in his hand; there were leaves and bits of twig in his tangled hair, in his matted beard; bunches of rags he had wound round the links fluttered from his waist. A faint clink of his fetters made the woman turn her head. Too terrified by this savage apparition to jump up or even to scream, she was yet too stout-hearted to faint. . . . Expecting nothing less than to be murdered on the spot, she covered her eyes with her hands to avoid the sight of the descending axe. When at last she found courage to look again, she saw the shaggy wild man sitting on the bank six feet away from her. His thin, sinewy arms hugged his naked legs; the long beard covered the knees on which he rested his chin; all these clasped, folded limbs, the bare shoulders, the wild head with red staring eyes, shook and trembled violently while the bestial creature was making efforts to speak. It was six weeks since he had heard the sound of his own voice. It seemed as though he had lost the faculty of speech. He had become a dumb and despairing brute, till the woman's sudden, unexpected cry of profound pity, the insight of her feminine compassion discovering the complex misery of the man under the terrifying aspect of the monster, restored him to the ranks of humanity. This point of view is presented in his book with a very effective eloquence. She ended, he says, by shedding tears over him, sacred, redeeming tears, while he also wept with joy in the manner of a converted sinner. Directing him to hide in the bushes and wait patiently (a police patrol was expected in the Settlement) she went away towards the houses, promising to return at night.

As if providentially appointed to be the newly wedded wife of the village black-smith, the woman persuaded her husband to come out with her, bringing some tools of his trade, a hammer, a chisel, a small anvil. . . . . "My fetters"—the book says—"were struck off on the banks of the stream, in the starlight of a calm night by an athletic, taciturn young man of the people, kneeling at my feet, while the woman like a liberating genius stood by with clasped hands." Obviously a symbolic couple. At the same time they furnished his regained humanity with some decent clothing, and put heart into the new man by the information that the seacoast of the Pacific was only a very few miles away. It could be seen, in fact, from the top of the next ridge. . . .

The rest of his escape does not lend itself to mystic treatment and symbolic interpretation. He ended by finding his way to the West by the Suez Canal route in the usual manner. Reaching the shores of South Europe he sat down to write his autobiography—the great literary success of its year. This book was followed by other books written with the declared purpose of elevating humanity. In these works he preached generally the cult of the woman. For his own part he practiced it under the rites of special devotion to the transcendental merits of a certain Madame de S——, a lady of advanced views, no longer very young, once upon a time the intriguing wife of a now dead and forgotten diplomat. Her loud preten-sions to be one of the leaders of modern thought and of modern sentiment, she sheltered (like Voltaire and Madame de Staël) on the republican territory of Geneva. Driving through the streets in her big landau she exhibited to the indif-ference of the natives and the stares of the tourists a long-waisted, youthful figure of hieratic stiffness, with a pair of big gleaming eyes, rolling restlessly behind a short veil of black lace, which, coming down no farther than her vividly red lips, resembled a mask. Usually the "heroic fugitive" (this name was bestowed upon him in a review of the English edition of his book)—the "heroic fugitive" accom-panied her, sitting, portentously bearded and darkly bespectacled, not by her side, but opposite her, with his back to the horses. Thus, facing each other, with no one else in the roomy carriage, their airings suggested a conscious public manifesta-tion. Or it may have been unconscious. Russian simplicity often marches inno-cently on the edge of cynicism for some lofty purpose. But it is a vain enterprise for sophisticated Europe to try and understand these doings. Considering the air of gravity extending even to the physiognomy of the coachman and the action of the showy horses, this quaint display might have possessed a mystic significance, but to the corrupt frivolity of a Western mind, like my own, it seemed hardly decent.

However, it is not becoming for an obscure teacher of languages to criticize a "heroic fugitive" of worldwide celebrity. I was aware from hearsay that he was an industrious busybody, hunting up his compatriots in hotels, in private lodgings, and—I was told—conferring upon them the honor of his notice in public gardens when a suitable opening presented itself. I was under the impression that after a visit or two, several months before, he had given up the ladies Haldin—no doubt reluctantly, for there could be no question of his being a determined person. It was perhaps to be expected that he should reappear again on this terrible occasion, as a Russian and a revolutionist, to say the right thing, to strike the true, perhaps a comforting, note. But I did not like to see him sitting there. I trust that an unbecoming jealousy of my privileged position had nothing to do with it. I made no claim to a special standing for my silent friendship. Removed by the difference of age and nationality as if into the sphere of another existence, I produced, even upon myself, the effect of a dumb, helpless ghost, of an anxious immaterial thing that could only hover about without the power to protect or guide by as much as a whisper. Since Miss Haldin with her sure instinct had refrained from introducing me to the burly celebrity, I would have retired quietly and returned later on, had I not met a peculiar expression in her eyes which I interpreted as a request to stay, with the view, perhaps, of shortening an unwelcome visit.

He picked up his hat, but only to deposit it on his knees.

"We shall meet again, Natalia Victorovna. Today I have called only to mark those feelings towards your honored mother and yourself, the nature of which you cannot doubt. I needed no urging, but Eleanor—Madame de S—— herself has in a way sent me. She extends to you the hand of feminine fellowship. There is positively in all the range of human sentiments no joy and no sorrow that woman cannot understand, elevate, and spiritualize by her interpretation. That young man newly arrived from St. Petersburg, I have mentioned to you, is already under the charm."

At this point Miss Haldin got up abruptly. I was glad. He did not evidently expect anything so decisive, and, at first, throwing his head back, he tilted up his dark glasses with bland curiosity. At last, recollecting himself, he stood up hastily, seizing his hat off his knees with great adroitness.

"How is it, Natalia Victorovna, that you have kept aloof so long, from what after all is—let disparaging tongues say what they like—a unique center of intellectual freedom and of effort to shape a high conception of our future? In the case of your honored mother I understand in a measure. At her age new ideas—new faces—are not perhaps . . . But you! Was it mistrust—or indifference? You must come out of your reserve. We Russians have no right to be reserved with each other. In our circumstances it is almost a crime against humanity. The luxury of private grief is not for us. Nowadays the devil is not combated by prayers and fasting. And what is fasting, after all, but starvation? You must not starve yourself, Natalia Victorovna. Strength is what we want—spiritual strength, I mean. As to the other kind, what could withstand us Russians if we only put it forth? Sin is different in our day, and the way of salvation for pure souls is different too. It is no longer to be found in monasteries, but in the world, in the . . ."

The deep sound seemed to rise from under the floor, and one felt steeped in it to the lips. Miss Haldin's interruption resembled the effort of a drowning person to keep above water. She struck in with an accent of impatience:

"But, Peter Ivanovitch, I don't mean to retire into a monastery. Who would look for salvation there?"

"I spoke figuratively," he boomed.

"Well, then, I am speaking figuratively too. But sorrow is sorrow and pain is pain in the old way. They make their demands upon people. One has got to face them the best way one can. I know that the blow which has fallen upon us so unexpectedly is only an episode in the fate of a people. You may rest assured that I don't forget that. But just now I have to think of my mother. How can you expect me to leave her to herself? . . ."

"That is putting it in a very crude way," he protested in his great, effortless voice.

Miss Haldin did not wait for the vibration to die out.

"And run about visiting amongst a lot of strange people? The idea is distasteful for me; and I do not know what else you may mean."

He towered before her, enormous, deferential, cropped as close as a convict; and this big pinkish poll evoked for me the vision of a wild head with matted locks peering through parted bushes, glimpses of naked, tawny limbs slinking behind the masses of sodden foliage under a cloud of flies and mosquitoes. It was an involuntary tribute to the rigor of his writing. Nobody could doubt that he had wandered in Siberian forests, naked and girt with a chain. The black broadcloth coat invested his person with a character of austere decency—something recalling a missionary.

"Do you know what I want, Natalia Victorovna?" he uttered solemnly. "*I* want you to be a fanatic."

"A fanatic?"

"Yes. Faith alone won't do."

His voice dropped to a still lower tone. He raised for a moment one thick arm; the other remained hanging down against his thigh, with the fragile silk hat at the end.

"I shall tell you now something which I entreat you to ponder over carefully. Listen, we need a force that would move heaven and earth—nothing less."

The profound, subterranean note of this "nothing less" made one shudder, almost, like the deep muttering of wind in the pipes of an organ.

"And are we to find that force in the salon of Madame de S——? Excuse me, Peter Ivanovitch, if I permit myself to doubt it. Is not that lady a woman of the great world, an aristocrat?"

"Prejudice!" he cried. "You astonish me. And suppose she was all that! She is also a woman of flesh and blood. There is always something to weigh down the spiritual side in all of us. But to make of it a reproach is what I did not expect from you. No! I did not expect that. One would think you have listened to some malevolent scandal."

"I have heard no gossip, I assure you. In our province how could we? But the world speaks of her. What can there be in common in a lady of that sort and an obscure country girl like me?"

"She is a perpetual manifestation of a noble and peerless spirit," he broke in. "Her charm—no, I shall not speak of her charm. But, of course, everybody who approaches her falls under the spell. . . . Contradictions vanish, trouble falls away from one. . . . Unless I am mistaken—but I never make a mistake in spiritual matters—you are troubled in your soul, Natalia Victorovna."

Miss Haldin's clear eyes looked straight at his soft, enormous face; I received the impression that behind these dark spectacles of his he could be as impudent as he chose.

"Only the other evening walking back to town from Château Borel with our latest interesting arrival from Petersburg, I could notice the powerful soothing influence—I may say reconciling influence. . . . There he was, all these kilometers along the shores of the lake, silent, like a man who has been shown the way of peace. I could feel the leaven working in his soul, you understand. For one thing, he listened to me patiently. I myself was inspired that evening by the firm and exquisite genius of Eleanor—Madame de S——, you know. It was a full moon and I could observe his face. I cannot be deceived. . . ."

Miss Haldin, looking down, seemed to hesitate.

"Well! I will think of what you said, Peter Ivanovitch. I shall try to call as soon as I can leave mother for an hour or two safely."

Coldly as these words were said I was amazed at the concession. He snatched her right hand with such fervor that I thought he was going to press it to his lips or his breast. But he only held it by the fingertips in his great paw and shook it a little up and down while he delivered his last volley of words.

"That's right. That's right. I haven't obtained your full confidence as yet, Natalia Victorovna, but that will come. All in good time. The sister of Victor Haldin cannot be without importance. . . . It's simply impossible. And no woman can remain sitting on the steps. Flowers, tears, applause—that has had its time; it's a medieval conception. The arena, the arena itself is the place for women!"

He relinquished her hand with a flourish, as if giving it to her for a gift, and remained still, his head bowed in dignified submission before her femininity.

"The arena! . . . You must descend into the arena, Natalia."

He made one step backwards, inclined his enormous body, and was gone swiftly. The door fell to behind him. But immediately the powerful resonance of his voice was heard addressing in the anteroom the middle-aged servant-woman who was letting him out. Whether he exhorted her too to descend into the arena I cannot tell. The thing sounded like a lecture, and the slight crash of the outer door cut it short suddenly.

III

We remained looking at each other for a time.

"Do you know who he is?"

Miss Haldin, coming forward, put this question to me in English.

I took her offered hand.

"Everybody knows. He is a revolutionary feminist, a great writer, if you like, and—how shall I say it?—the—the familiar guest of Madame de S——'s mystic revolutionary salon."

Miss Haldin passed her hand over her forehead.

"You know, he was with me for more than an hour before you came in. I was so glad mother was lying down. She has many nights without sleep, and then sometimes in the middle of the day she gets a rest of several hours. It is sheer exhaustion—but still, I am thankful. . . . If it were not for these intervals . . ."

She looked at me and, with that extraordinary penetration which used to disconcert me, shook her head.

"No. She would not go mad."

"My dear young lady," I cried, by way of protest, the more shocked because in my heart I was far from thinking Mrs. Haldin quite sane.

"You don't know what a fine, lucid intellect mother had," continued Nathalie Haldin, with her calm, clear-eyed simplicity, which seemed to me always to have a quality of heroism.

"I am sure . . ." I murmured.

"I darkened mother's room and came out here. I've wanted for so long to think quietly."

She paused, then, without giving any sign of distress, added, "It's so difficult," and looked at me with a strange fixity, as if watching for a sign of dissent or surprise.

I gave neither. I was irresistibly impelled to say:

"The visit from that gentleman has not made it any easier, I fear."

Miss Haldin stood before me with a peculiar expression in her eyes.

"I don't pretend to understand Peter Ivanovitch completely. Some guide one must have, even if one does not wholly give up the direction of one's conduct to him. I am an inexperienced girl, but I am not slavish. There has been too much of that in Russia. Why should I not listen to him? There is no harm in having one's thoughts directed. But I don't mind confessing to you that I have not been completely candid with Peter Ivanovitch. I don't quite know what prevented me at the moment . . ."

She walked away suddenly from me to a distant part of the room; but it was only to open and shut a drawer in a bureau. She returned with a piece of paper in her hand. It was thin and blackened with close handwriting. It was obviously a letter.

"I wanted to read you the very words," she said. "This is one of my poor brother's letters. He never doubted. How could he doubt? They make only such a small handful, these miserable oppressors, before the unanimous will of our people."

"Your brother believed in the power of a people's will to achieve anything?"

"It was his religion," declared Miss Haldin.

I looked at her calm face and her animated eyes.

"Of course the will must be awakened, inspired, concentrated," she went on. "That is the true task of real agitators. One has got to give up one's life to it. The degradation of servitude, the absolutist lies must be uprooted and swept out. Reform is impossible. There is nothing to reform. There is no legality, there are no institutions. There are only arbitrary decrees. There is only a handful of cruel— perhaps blind—officials against a nation."

The letter rustled slightly in her hand. I glanced down at the flimsy blackened pages whose very handwriting seemed cabalistic, incomprehensible to the experience of Western Europe.

"Stated like this," I confessed, "the problem seems simple enough. But I fear I shall not see it solved. And if you go back to Russia I know that I shall not see you again. Yet once more I say: go back! Don't suppose that I am thinking of your preservation. No! I know that you will not be returning to personal safety. But I had much rather think of you in danger there than see you exposed to what may be met here."

"I tell you what," said Miss Haldin, after a moment of reflection. "I believe that you hate revolution; you fancy it's not quite honest. You belong to a people which has made a bargain with Fate and wouldn't like to be rude to it. But we have made no bargain. It was never offered to us—so much liberty for so much hard cash. You shrink from the idea of revolutionary action for those you think well of as if it were something—how shall I say it?—not quite decent."

I bowed my head.

"You are quite right," I said. "I think very highly of you."

"Don't suppose I do not know it," she began hurriedly. "Your friendship has been very valuable."

"I have done little else but look on."

She was a little flushed under the eyes.

"There is a way of looking on which is valuable. I have felt less lonely because of it. It's difficult to explain."

"Really? Well, I too have felt less lonely. That's easy to explain, though. But it won't go on much longer. The last thing I want to tell you is this: in a real revolution—not a simple dynastic change or a mere reform of institutions—in a real revolution the best characters do not come to the front. A violent revolution falls into the hands of narrow-minded fanatics and of tyrannical hypocrites at first. Afterwards comes the turn of all the pretentious intellectual failures of the time. Such are the chiefs and the leaders. You will notice that I have left out the mere rogues. The scrupulous and the just, the noble, humane, and devoted natures; the unselfish and the intelligent may begin a movement—but it passes away from them. They are not the leaders of a revolution. They are its victims: the victims of disgust, of disenchantment—often of remorse. Hopes grotesquely betrayed, ideals caricatured—that is the definition of revolutionary success. There have been in every revolution hearts broken by such successes. But enough of that. My meaning is that I don't want you to be a victim."

"If I could believe all you have said I still wouldn't think of myself," protested Miss Haldin. "I would take liberty from any hand as a hungry man would snatch at a piece of bread. The true progress must begin after. And for that the right men shall be found. They are already amongst us. One comes upon them in their obscurity, unknown, preparing themselves. . . ."

She spread out the letter she had kept in her hand all the time, and looking down at it:

"Yes! One comes upon such men!" she repeated, and then read out the words, "Unstained, lofty, and solitary existences."

Folding up the letter, while I looked at her interrogatively, she explained:

"These are the words which my brother applies to a young man he came to know in St. Petersburg. An intimate friend, I suppose. It must be. His is the only name my brother mentions in all his correspondence with me. Absolutely the only one, and—would you believe it?—the man is here. He arrived recently in Geneva."

"Have you seen him?" I inquired. "But, of course, you must have seen him."

"No! No! I haven't! I didn't know he was here. It's Peter Ivanovitch himself who told me. You have heard him yourself mentioning a new arrival from Petersburg. . . . Well, that is the man of 'unstained, lofty, and solitary existence.' My brother's friend!"

"Compromised politically, I suppose," I remarked.

"I don't know. Yes. It must be so. Who knows! Perhaps it was this very friendship with my brother which . . . But no! It is scarcely possible. Really, I know nothing except what Peter Ivanovitch told me of him. He has brought a letter of introduction from Father Zosim—you know, the priest-democrat; you have heard of Father Zosim?"

"Oh yes. The famous Father Zosim was staying here in Geneva for some two months about a year ago," I said. "When he left here he seems to have disappeared from the world."

"It appears that he is at work in Russia again. Somewhere in the center," Miss Haldin said, with animation. "But please don't mention that to anyone—don't let it slip from you, because if it got into the papers it would be dangerous for him."

"You are anxious, of course, to meet that friend of your brother?" I asked.

Miss Haldin put the letter into her pocket. Her eyes looked beyond my shoulder at the door of her mother's room.

"Not here," she murmured. "Not for the first time, at least."

After a moment of silence I said goodbye, but Miss Haldin followed me into the anteroom, closing the door behind us carefully.

"I suppose you guess where I mean to go tomorrow?"

"You have made up your mind to call on Madame de S——."

"Yes. I am going to the Château Borel. I must."

"What do you expect to hear there?" I asked, in a low voice.

I wondered if she were not deluding herself with some impossible hope. It was not that, however.

"Only think—such a friend. The only man mentioned in his letters. He would have something to give me, if nothing more than a few poor words. It may be something said and thought in those last days. Would you want me to turn my back on what is left of my poor brother—a friend?"

"Certainly not," I said. "I quite understand your pious curiosity."

"Unstained, lofty, and solitary existences," she murmured to herself. "There are! There are! Well, let me question one of them about the loved dead."

"How do you know, though, that you will meet him there? Is he staying in the château as a guest—do you suppose?"

"I can't really tell," she confessed. "He brought a written introduction from Father Zosim—who, it seems, is a friend of Madame de S—— too. She can't be such a worthless woman after all."

"There were all sorts of rumors afloat about Father Zosim himself," I observed.

She shrugged her shoulders.

"Calumny is a weapon of our government too. It's well known. Oh yes! It is a fact that Father Zosim had the protection of the Governor-General of a certain province. We talked on the subject with my brother two years ago, I remember. But his work was good. And now he is proscribed. What better proof can one require? But no matter what that priest was or is. All that cannot affect my brother's friend. If I don't meet him there I shall ask these people for his address. And, of course, mother must see him too, later on. There is no guessing what he may have to tell us. It would be a mercy if mamma could be soothed. You know what she imagines. Some explanation perhaps may be found, or—or even made up, perhaps. It would be no sin."

"Certainly," I said, "it would be no sin. It may be a mistake, though."

"I want her only to recover some of her old spirit. While she is like this I cannot think of anything calmly."

"Do you mean to invent some sort of pious fraud for your mother's sake?" I asked.

"Why fraud? Such a friend is sure to know something of my brother in these last days. He could tell us. . . . There is something in the facts which will not let me rest. I am certain he meant to join us abroad—that he had some plans—some great patriotic action in view; not only for himself, but for both of us. I trusted in that. I looked forward to the time, oh! with such hope and impatience. . . . I could have helped. And now suddenly this appearance of recklessness—as if he had not cared. . . ."

She remained silent for a time, then obstinately she concluded:

"I want to know . . ."

Thinking it over, later on, while I walked slowly away from the Boulevard des Philosophes, I asked myself critically, what precisely was it that she wanted to know? What I had heard of her history was enough to give me a clue. In the educational establishment for girls where Miss Haldin finished her studies she was looked upon rather unfavorably. She was suspected of holding independent views on matters settled by official teaching. Afterwards, when the two ladies returned to their country place, both mother and daughter, by speaking their minds openly on public events, had earned for themselves a reputation of liberalism. The three-horse trap of the district police captain began to be seen frequently in their village. "I must keep an eye on the peasants"—so he explained his visits up at the house. "Two lonely ladies must be looked after a little." He would inspect the walls as though he wanted to pierce them with his eyes, peer at the photographs, turn over the books in the drawing room negligently, and after the usual refreshments, would depart. But the old priest of the village came one evening in the greatest distress and agitation, to confess that he—the priest—had been ordered to watch and ascertain in other ways too (such as using his spiritual power with the servants) all that was going on in the house, and especially in respect of the visitors these ladies received, who they were, the length of their stay, whether any of them were strangers to that part of the country, and so on. The poor, simple old man was in an agony of humiliation and terror. "I came to warn you. Be cautious in your conduct, for the love of God. I am burning with shame, but there is no getting out from under the net. I shall have to tell them what I see, because if I did not there is my deacon. He would make the worst of things to curry favor. And then my son-in-law, the husband of my Parasha, who is a writer in the Government Domain office; they would soon kick him out—and maybe send him away somewhere." The old man lamented the necessities of the times— "when people do not agree somehow," and wiped his eyes. He did not wish to spend the evening of his days with a shaven head in the penitent's cell of some monastery—"and subjected to all the severities of ecclesiastical discipline; for they would show no mercy to an old man," he groaned. He became almost hysterical, and the two ladies, full of commiseration, soothed him the best they could before they let him go back to his cottage. But, as a matter of fact, they had very few visitors. The neighbors—some of them old friends—began to keep away; a few from timidity, others with marked disdain, being grand people that came only for the summer—Miss Haldin explained to me—aristocrats, reactionaries. It was a solitary existence for a young girl. Her relations with her mother were of the tenderest and most open kind; but Mrs. Haldin had seen the experiences of her own generation, its sufferings, its deceptions, its apostasies too. Her affection for her children was expressed by the suppression of all signs of anxiety. She maintained a heroic reserve. To Nathalie Haldin, her brother with his Petersburg existence, not enigmatical in the least (there could be no doubt of what he felt or thought) but conducted a little mysteriously, was the only visible representative of a proscribed liberty. All the significance of freedom, its indefinite promises, lived in their long discussions, which breathed the loftiest hope of action and faith in success. Then, suddenly, the action, the hopes, came to an end with the details ferreted out by the English journalist. The concrete fact, the fact of his death, remained; but it remained obscure in its deeper causes. She felt herself abandoned without explanation. But she did not suspect him. What she wanted was to learn almost at any cost how she could remain faithful to his departed spirit.

IV

Several days elapsed before I met Nathalie Haldin again. I was crossing the place in front of the theater when I made out her shapely figure in the very act of turning between the gate pillars of the unattractive public promenade of the Bastions. She walked away from me, but I knew we should meet as she returned down the main alley—unless, indeed, she were going home. In that case, I don't think I should have called on her yet. My desire to keep her away from these people was as strong as ever, but I had no illusions as to my power. I was but a Westerner, and it was clear that Miss Haldin would not, could not, listen to my wisdom; and as to my desire of listening to her voice, it were better, I thought, not to indulge overmuch in that pleasure. No, I should not have gone to the Boulevard des Philosophes; but when at about the middle of the principal alley I saw Miss Haldin coming towards me, I was too curious, and too honest, perhaps, to run away.

There was something of the spring harshness in the air. The blue sky was hard, but the young leaves clung like soft mist about the uninteresting range of trees; and the clear sun put little points of gold into the gray of Miss Haldin's frank eyes, turned to me with a friendly greeting.

I inquired after the health of her mother.

She had a slight movement of the shoulders and a little sad sigh.

"But, you see, I did come out for a walk . . . for exercise, as you English say."

I smiled approvingly, and she added an unexpected remark:

"It is a glorious day."

Her voice, slightly harsh, but fascinating with its masculine and bird-like quality, had the accent of spontaneous conviction. I was glad of it. It was as though she had become aware of her youth—for there was but little of spring-like glory in the rectangular railed space of grass and trees, framed visibly by the orderly roof-slopes of that town, comely without grace, and hospitable without sympathy. In the very air through which she moved there was but little warmth; and the sky, the sky of a land without horizons, swept and washed clean by the April showers, extended a cold, cruel blue, without elevation, narrowed suddenly by the ugly, dark wall of the Jura, where, here and there, lingered yet a few miserable trails and patches of snow. All the glory of the season must have been within herself— and I was glad this feeling had come into her life, if only for a little time.

"I am pleased to hear you say these words."

She gave me a quick look—quick, not stealthy. If there was one thing of which she was absolutely incapable, it was stealthiness. Her sincerity was expressed in the very rhythm of her walk. It was I who was looking at her covertly—if I may say so. I knew where she had been, but I did not know what she had seen and heard in that nest of aristocratic conspiracies. I use the word aristocratic for want of a better term. The Château Borel, embowered in the trees and thickets of its neglected grounds, had its fame in our day, like the residence of that other dangerous and exiled woman, Madame de Staël, in the Napoleonic era. Only the Napoleonic despotism, the booted heir of the Revolution, which counted that intellectual woman for an enemy worthy to be watched, was something quite unlike the autocracy in mystic vestments, engendered by the slavery of a Tartar conquest. And Madame de S—— was very far from resembling the gifted author of *Corinne*. She made a great noise about being persecuted. I don't know if she were regarded in certain circles as dangerous. As to being watched, I imagine that the Château Borel could be subjected only to a most distant observation. It was in its exclusiveness an ideal abode for hatching superior plots—whether serious or futile. But all this did not interest me. I wanted to know the effect its extraordinary inhabitants and its special atmosphere had produced on a girl like Miss Haldin, so true, so honest, but so dangerously inexperienced! Her unconsciously lofty ignorance of the baser instincts of mankind left her disarmed before her own impulses. And there was also that friend of her brother, the significant new arrival from Russia. . . . I wondered whether she had managed to meet him.

We walked for some time, slowly and in silence.

"You know," I attacked her suddenly, "if you don't intend to tell me anything, you must say so distinctly, and then, of course, it shall be final. But I won't play at delicacy. I ask you point-blank for all the details."

She smiled faintly at my threatening tone.

"You are as curious as a child."

"No. I am only an anxious old man," I replied earnestly.

She rested her glance on me as if to ascertain the degree of my anxiety or the number of my years. My physiognomy has never been expressive, I believe, and as to my years I am not ancient enough as yet to be strikingly decrepit. I have no long beard like the good hermit of a romantic ballad; my footsteps are not tottering, my aspect not that of a slow, venerable sage. Those picturesque advantages are not mine. I am old, alas! in a brisk, commonplace way. And it seemed to me as though there were some pity for me in Miss Haldin's prolonged glance. She stepped out a little quicker.

"You ask for all the details. Let me see. I ought to remember them. It was novel enough for a—a village girl like me."

After a moment of silence she began by saying that the Château Borel was almost as neglected inside as outside. It was nothing to wonder at. A Hamburg banker, I believe, retired from business, had it built to cheer his remaining days by the view of that lake whose precise, orderly, and well-to-do beauty must have been attractive to the unromantic imagination of a businessman. But he died soon. His wife departed too (but only to Italy), and this house of moneyed ease, presumably unsalable, had stood empty for several years. One went to it up a grav-el drive, round a large, coarse grassplot, with plenty of time to observe the degradation of its stuccoed front. Miss Haldin said that the impression was unpleasant. It grew more depressing as one came nearer.

She observed green stains of moss on the steps of the terrace. The front door stood wide open. There was no one about. She found herself in a wide, lofty, and absolutely empty hall, with a good many doors. These doors were all shut. A broad, bare stone staircase faced her, and the effect of the whole was of an untenanted house. She stood still, disconcerted by the solitude, but after a while she became aware of a voice speaking continuously somewhere.

"You were probably being observed all the time," I suggested. "There must have been eyes."

"I don't see how that could be," she retorted. "I haven't seen even a bird in the grounds. I don't remember hearing a single twitter in the trees. The whole place appeared utterly deserted except for the voice."

She could not make out the language—Russian, French, or German. No one seemed to answer it. It was as though the voice had been left behind by the departed inhabitants to talk to the bare walls. It went on volubly, with a pause now and then. It was lonely and sad. The time seemed very long to Miss Haldin. An invincible repugnance prevented her from opening one of the doors in the hall. It was so hopeless. No one would come, the voice would never stop. She confessed to me that she had to resist an impulse to turn round and go away unseen, as she had come.

"Really? You had that impulse?" I cried, full of regret. "What a pity you did not obey it."

She shook her head.

"What a strange memory it would have been for one. Those deserted grounds, that empty hall, that impersonal, voluble voice, and—nobody, nothing, not a soul."

The memory would have been unique and harmless. But she was not a girl to run away from an intimidating impression of solitude and mystery. "No, I did not run away," she said. "I stayed where I was—and I did see a soul. Such a strange soul."

As she was gazing up the broad staircase, and had concluded that the voice came from somewhere above, a rustle of a dress attracted her attention. She looked down and saw a woman crossing the hall, having issued apparently through one of the many doors. Her face was averted, so that at first she was not aware of Miss Haldin.

On turning her head and seeing a stranger, she appeared very much startled. From her slender figure Miss Haldin had taken her for a young girl; but if her face was almost childishly round, it was also sallow and wrinkled, with dark rings under the eyes. A thick crop of dusty brown hair was parted boyishly on the side with a lateral wave above the dry, furrowed forehead. After a moment of dumb blinking, she suddenly squatted down on the floor.

"What do you mean by squatted down?" I asked, astonished. "This is a very strange detail."

Miss Haldin explained the reason. This person when first seen was carrying a small bowl in her hand. She had squatted down to put it on the floor for the benefit of a large cat, which appeared then from behind her skirts, and hid its head into the bowl greedily. She got up, and approaching Miss Haldin asked with nervous bluntness:

"What do you want? Who are you?"

Miss Haldin mentioned her name and also the name of Peter Ivanovitch. The girlish, elderly woman nodded and puckered her face into a momentary expression of sympathy. Her black silk blouse was old and even frayed in places; the black serge skirt was short and shabby. She continued to blink at close quarters, and her eyelashes and eyebrows seemed shabby too. Miss Haldin, speaking gently to her, as if to an unhappy and sensitive person, explained how it was that her visit could not be an altogether unexpected event to Madame de S——.

"Ah! Peter Ivanovitch brought you an invitation. How was I to know? A *dame de compagnie* is not consulted, as you may imagine."

The shabby woman laughed a little. Her teeth, splendidly white and admirably even, looked absurdly out of place, like a string of pearls on the neck of a ragged tramp. "Peter Ivanovitch is the greatest genius of the century perhaps, but he is the most inconsiderate man living. So if you have an appointment with him you must not be surprised to hear that he is not here."

Miss Haldin explained that she had no appointment with Peter Ivanovitch. She became interested at once in that bizarre person.

"Why should he put himself out for you or any one else? Oh, these geniuses! If you only knew! Yes! And their books—I mean, of course, the books that the world admires, the inspired books. But you have not been behind the scenes. Wait till you have to sit at a table for half a day with a pen in your hand. He can walk up and down his rooms for hours and hours. I used to get so stiff and numb that I was afraid I would lose my balance and fall off the chair all at once."

She kept her hands folded in front of her, and her eyes, fixed on Miss Haldin's face, betrayed no animation whatever. Miss Haldin, gathering that the lady who called herself a *dame de compagnie* was proud of having acted as secretary to Peter Ivanovitch, made an amiable remark.

"You could not imagine a more trying experience," declared the lady. "There is an Anglo-American journalist interviewing Madame de S—— now, or I would take you up," she continued in a changed tone and glancing towards the staircase. "I act as master of ceremonies."

It appeared that Madame de S—— could not bear Swiss servants about her person; and, indeed, servants would not stay for very long in the Château Borel. There were always difficulties. Miss Haldin had already noticed that the hall was like a dusty barn of marble and stucco with cobwebs in the corners and faint tracks of mud on the black and white tessellated floor.

"I look also after this animal," continued the *dame de compagnie,* keeping her hands folded quietly in front of her; and she bent her worn gaze upon the cat. "I don't mind a bit. Animals have their rights; though, strictly speaking, I see no reason why they should not suffer as well as human beings. Do you? But of course they never suffer so much. That is impossible. Only, in their case it is more pitiful because they cannot make a revolution. I used to be a Republican. I suppose you are a Republican?"

Miss Haldin confessed to me that she did not know what to say. But she nodded slightly, and asked in her turn:

"And are you no longer a Republican?"

"After taking down Peter Ivanovitch from dictation for two years, it is difficult for me to be anything. First of all, you have to sit perfectly motionless. The slightest movement you make puts to flight the ideas of Peter Ivanovitch. You hardly dare to breathe. And as to coughing—God forbid! Peter Ivanovitch changed the position of the table to the wall because at first I could not help raising my eyes to look out of the window, while waiting for him to go on with his dictation. That was not allowed. He said I stared so stupidly. I was likewise not permitted to look at him over my shoulder. Instantly Peter Ivanovitch stamped his foot, and would roar, 'Look down on the paper!' It seems my expression, my face, put him off. Well, I know that I am not beautiful, and that my expression is not hopeful either. He said that my air of unintelligent expectation irritated him. These are his own words."

Miss Haldin was shocked, but admitted to me that she was not altogether surprised.

"Is it possible that Peter Ivanovitch could treat any woman so rudely?" she cried.

The *dame de compagnie* nodded several times with an air of discretion, then assured Miss Haldin that she did not mind in the least. The trying part of it was to have the secret of the composition laid bare before her; to see the great author of the revolutionary gospels grope for words as if he were in the dark as to what he meant to say.

"I am quite willing to be the blind instrument of higher ends. To give one's life for the cause is nothing. But to have one's illusions destroyed—that is really almost more than one can bear. I really don't exaggerate," she insisted. "It seemed to freeze my very beliefs in me—the more so that when we worked in winter, Peter Ivanovitch, walking up and down the room, required no artificial heat to keep himself warm. Even when we move to the South of France there are bitterly cold days, especially when you have to sit still for six hours at a stretch. The walls of these villas on the Riviera are so flimsy. Peter Ivanovitch did not seem to be aware of anything. It is true that I kept down my shivers from fear of putting him out. I used to set my teeth till my jaws felt absolutely locked. In the moments when Peter Ivanovitch interrupted his dictation, and sometimes these intervals were very long—often twenty minutes, no less, while he walked to and fro behind my back muttering to himself—I felt I was dying by inches, I assure you. Perhaps if I had let my teeth rattle Peter Ivanovitch might have noticed my distress, but I don't think it would have had any practical effect. He's very miserly in such matters."

The *dame de compagnie* glanced up the staircase. The big cat had finished the milk and was rubbing its whiskered cheek sinuously against her skirt. She dived to snatch it up from the floor.

"Miserliness is rather a quality than otherwise, you know," she continued, holding the cat in her folded arms. "With us it is misers who can spare money for worthy objects—not the so-called generous natures. But pray don't think I am a sybarite. My father was a clerk in the Ministry of Finances with no position at all. You may guess by this that our home was far from luxurious, though, of course, we did not actually suffer from cold. I ran away from my parents, you know, directly I began to think by myself. It is not very easy, such thinking. One has got to be put in the way of it—awakened to the truth. I am indebted for my salvation to an old apple-woman, who had her stall under the gateway of the house we lived in. She had a kind, wrinkled face, and the most friendly voice imaginable. One day, casually, we began to talk about a child, a ragged little girl we had seen begging from men in the streets at dusk; and from one thing to another my eyes began to open gradually to the horrors from which innocent people are made to suffer in this world, only in order that Governments might exist. After I once understood the crime of the upper classes, I could not go on living with my parents. Not a single charitable word was to be heard in our home from year's end to year's end; there was nothing but the talk of vile office intrigues, and of promotion and of salaries, and of courting the favor of the chiefs. The mere idea of marrying one day such another man as my father made me shudder. I, don't mean that there was anyone wanting to marry me. There was not the slightest prospect of anything of the kind. But was it not sin enough to live on a Government salary while half Russia was dying of hunger? The Ministry of Finances! What a grotesque horror it is! What does the starving, igno-rant people want with a Ministry of Finances? I kissed my old folks on both cheeks, and went away from them to live in cellars with the proletariat. I tried to make myself useful to the utterly hopeless. I suppose you understand what I mean? I mean the people who have nowhere to go and nothing to look forward to in this life. Do you understand how frightful that is—nothing to look forward to! Sometimes I think that it is only in Russia that there are such people and such a depth of misery can be reached. Well, I plunged into it, and—do you know?—there isn't much that one can do in there. No, indeed—at least as long as there are Ministries of Finances and such-like grotesque horrors to stand in the way. I suppose I would have gone mad there just trying to fight the vermin, if it had not been for a man. It was my old friend and teacher, the poor saintly apple-woman, who discovered him for me, quite accidentally. She came to fetch me late one evening in her quiet way. I followed her where she would lead; that part of my life was in her hands altogether, and without her my spirit would have perished miserably. The man was a young workman, a lithographer by trade, and he had got into trouble in connection with that affair of temperance tracts—you remember. There was a lot of people put in prison for that. The Ministry of Finances again! What would become of it if the poor folk ceased making beasts of themselves with drink? Upon my word, I would think that finances and all the rest of it are an invention of the devil—only that a belief in a supernatural source of evil is not necessary; men alone are quite capable of every wickedness. Finances indeed!"

Hatred and contempt hissed in her utterance of the word "finances," but at the very moment she gently stroked the cat reposing in her arms. She even raised them slightly, and inclining her head rubbed her cheek against the fur of the animal, which received this caress with the complete detachment so characteristic of its kind. Then looking at Miss Haldin she excused herself once more for not taking her upstairs to Madame S——. The interview could not be interrupted. Presently the journalist would be seen coming down the stairs. The best thing was to remain in the hall; and besides, all these rooms (she glanced all round at the many doors), all these rooms on the ground floor were unfurnished.

"Positively there is no chair down here to offer you," she continued. "But if you prefer your own thoughts to my chatter, I will sit down on the bottom step here and keep silent."

Miss Haldin hastened to assure her that, on the contrary, she was very much interested in the story of the journeyman lithographer. He was a revolutionist, of course.

"A martyr, a simple man," said the *dame de compagnie,* with a faint sigh, and gazing through the open front door dreamily. She turned her misty brown eyes on Miss Haldin.

"I lived with him for four months. It was like a nightmare."

As Miss Haldin looked at her inquisitively she began to describe the emaciated face of the man, his fleshless limbs, his destitution. The room into which the apple-woman had led her was a tiny garret, a miserable den under the roof of a sordid house. The plaster fallen off the walls covered the floor, and when the door was opened a horrible tapestry of black cobwebs waved in the draught. He had been liberated a few days before—flung out of prison into the streets. And Miss Haldin seemed to see for the first time a name and a face upon the body of that suffering people whose hard fate had been the subject of so many conversations, between her and her brother, in the garden of their country house.

He had been arrested with scores and scores of other people in that affair of the lithographed temperance tracts. Unluckily, having got hold of a great many suspected persons, the police thought they could extract from some of them other information relating to the revolutionist propaganda.

"They beat him so cruelly in the course of investigation," went on the *dame de compagnie*, "that they injured him internally. When they had done with him he was doomed. He could do nothing for himself. I beheld him lying on a wooden bedstead without any bedding, with his head on a bundle of dirty rags, lent to him out of charity by an old ragpicker who happened to live in the basement of the house. There he was, uncovered, burning with fever, and there was not even a jug in the room for the water to quench his thirst with. There was nothing whatever—just that bedstead and the bare floor."

"Was there no one in all that great town amongst the liberals and revolutionaries to extend a helping hand to a brother?" asked Miss Haldin indignantly.

"Yes. But you do not know the most terrible part of that man's misery. Listen. It seems that they ill-used him so atrociously that, at last, his firmness gave way, and he did let out some information. Poor soul, the flesh is weak, you know. What it was he did not tell me. There was a crushed spirit in that mangled body. Nothing I found to say could make him whole. When they let him out, he crept into that hole, and bore his remorse stoically. He would not go near any one he knew. I would have sought assistance for him, but, indeed, where could I have gone looking for it? Where was I to look for anyone who had anything to spare or any power to help? The people living round us were all starving and drunken. They were the victims of the Ministry of Finances. Don't ask me how we lived. I couldn't tell you. It was like a miracle of wretchedness. I had nothing to sell, and I assure you my clothes were in such a state that it was impossible for me to go out in the daytime. I was indecent. I had to wait till it was dark before I ventured into the streets to beg for a crust of bread, or whatever I could get, to keep him and me alive. Often I got nothing, and then I would crawl back and lie on the floor by the side of his couch. Oh yes, I can sleep quite soundly on bare boards. That is nothing, and I am only mentioning it to you so that you should not think I am a sybarite. It was infinitely less killing than the task of sitting for hours at a table in a cold study to take the books of Peter Ivanovitch from dictation. But you shall see yourself what that is like, so I needn't say any more about it."

"It is by no means certain that I will ever take Peter Ivanovitch from dictation," said Miss Haldin.

"No!" cried the other incredulously. "Not certain? You mean to say that you have not made up your mind?"

When Miss Haldin assured her that there never had been any question of that between her and Peter Ivanovitch, the woman with the cat compressed her lips tightly for a moment.

"Oh, you will find yourself settled at the table before you know that you have made up your mind. Don't make a mistake, it is disenchanting to hear Peter Ivanovitch dictate, but at the same time there is a fascination about it. He is a man of genius. Your face is certain not to irritate him; you may perhaps even help his inspiration, make it easier for him to deliver his message. As I look at you, I feel certain that you are the kind of woman who is not likely to check the flow of his inspiration."

Miss Haldin thought it useless to protest against all these assumptions.

"But this man—this workman—did he die under your care?" she said, after a short silence.

The *dame de compagnie,* listening up the stairs where now two voices were alternating with some animation, made no answer for a time. When the loud sounds of the discussion had sunk into an almost inaudible murmur, she turned to Miss Haldin.

"Yes, he died, but not, literally speaking, in my arms, as you might suppose. As a matter of fact, I was asleep when he breathed his last. So even now I cannot say I have seen anybody die. A few days before the end, some young men found us out in our extremity. They were revolutionists, as you might guess. He ought to have trusted in his political friends when he came out of prison. He had been liked and respected before, and nobody would have dreamed of reproaching him with his indiscretion before the police. Everybody knows how they go to work, and the strongest man has his moments of weakness before pain. Why, even hunger alone is enough to give one queer ideas as to what may be done. A doctor came, our lot was alleviated as far as physical comforts go, but otherwise he could not be con-soled—poor man. I assure you, Miss Haldin, that he was very lovable, but I had not the strength to weep. I was nearly dead myself. But there were kind hearts to take care of me. A dress was found to clothe my nakedness. I tell you, I was not decent—and after a time the revolutionists placed me with a Jewish family going abroad, as governess. Of course I could teach the children, I finished the sixth class of the Lyceum; but the real object was, that I should carry some important papers across the frontier. I was entrusted with a packet which I carried next my heart. The gendarmes at the station did not suspect the governess of a Jewish family, busy looking after three children. I don't suppose those Hebrews knew what I had on me, for I had been introduced to them in a very roundabout way by persons who did not belong to the revolutionary movement, and naturally I had been instructed to accept a very small salary. When we reached Germany I left that family and delivered my papers to a revolutionist in Stuttgart; after this I was employed in various ways. But you do not want to hear all that. I have never felt that I was very useful, but I live in hopes of seeing all the Ministries destroyed, finances and all. The greatest joy of my life has been to hear what your brother has done."

She directed her round eyes again to the sunshine outside, while the cat reposed within her folded arms in lordly beatitude and sphinx-like meditation.

"Yes, I rejoiced," she began again. "For me there is a heroic ring about the very name of Haldin. They must have been trembling with fear in their Ministries—all those men with fiendish hearts. Here I stand talking to you, and when I think of all the cruelties, oppressions, and injustices that are going on at this very moment, my head begins to swim. I have looked closely at what would seem inconceivable if one's own eyes had not to be trusted. I have looked at things that made me hate myself for my helplessness. I hated my hands that had no power, my voice that could not be heard, my very mind that would not become unhinged. Ah! I have seen things. And you?"

Miss Haldin was moved. She shook her head slightly.

"No, I have seen nothing for myself as yet," she murmured. "We have always lived in the country. It was my brother's wish."

"It is a curious meeting—this—between you and me," continued the other. "Do you believe in chance, Miss Haldin? How could I have expected to see you, his sister, with my own eyes? Do you know that when the news came the revolutionaries here were as much surprised as pleased, every bit? No one seemed to know anything about your brother. Peter Ivanovitch himself had not foreseen that such a blow was going to be struck. I suppose your brother was simply inspired. I myself think that such deeds should be done by inspiration. It is a great privilege to have the inspiration and the opportunity. Did he resemble you at all? Don't you rejoice, Miss Haldin?"

"You must not expect too much from me," said Miss Haldin, repressing an inclination to cry which came over her suddenly. She succeeded, then added calmly, "I am not a heroic person!"

"You think you couldn't have done such a thing yourself, perhaps?"

"I don't know. I must not even ask myself till I have lived a little longer, seen more . . ."

The other moved her head appreciatively. The purring of the cat had a loud complacency in the empty hall. No sound of voices came from upstairs. Miss Haldin broke the silence.

"What is it precisely that you heard people say about my brother? You said that they were surprised. Yes, I suppose they were. Did it not seem strange to them that my brother should have failed to save himself after the most difficult part— that is, getting away from the spot—was over? Conspirators should understand these things well. There are reasons why I am very anxious to know how it is he failed to escape."

The *dame de compagnie* had advanced to the open hall door. She glanced rapidly over her shoulder at Miss Haldin, who remained within the hall.

"Failed to escape," she repeated absently. "Didn't he make the sacrifice of his life? Wasn't he just simply inspired? Wasn't it an act of abnegation? Aren't you certain?"

"What I am certain of," said Miss Haldin, "is that it was not an act of despair. Have you not heard some opinion expressed here upon his miserable capture?"

The *dame de compagnie* mused for a while in the doorway.

"Did I hear? Of course, everything is discussed here. Has not all the world been speaking about your brother? For my part, the mere mention of his achievement plunges me into an envious ecstasy. Why should a man certain of immortality think of his life at all?"

She kept her back turned to Miss Haldin. Upstairs from behind a great, dingy, white-and-gold door, visible behind the balustrade of the first floor landing, a deep voice began to drone formally, as if reading over notes or something of the sort. It paused frequently, and then ceased altogether.

"I don't think I can stay any longer now," said Miss Haldin. "I may return another day."

She waited for the *dame de compagnie* to make room for her exit; but the woman appeared lost in the contemplation of sunshine and shadows, sharing between themselves the stillness of the deserted grounds. She concealed the view of the drive from Miss Haldin. Suddenly she said:

"It will not be necessary; here is Peter Ivanovitch himself coming up. But he is not alone. He is seldom alone now."

Hearing that Peter Ivanovitch was approaching, Miss Haldin was not so pleased as she might have been expected to be. Somehow she had lost the desire to see either the heroic captive or Madame de S——, and the reason of that shrinking which came upon her at the very last minute is accounted for by the feeling that those two people had not been treating the woman with the cat kindly.

"Would you please let me pass?" said Miss Haldin at last, touching lightly the shoulder of the *dame de compagnie*.

But the other, pressing the cat to her breast, did not budge.

"I know who is with him," she said, without even looking back.

More unaccountably than ever Miss Haldin felt a strong impulse to leave the house.

"Madame de S—— may be engaged for some time yet, and what I have got to say to Peter Ivanovitch is just a simple question which I might put to him when I meet him in the grounds on my way down. I really think I must go. I have been some time here, and I am anxious to get back to my mother. Will you let me pass, please?"

The *dame de compagnie* turned her head at last.

"I never supposed that you really wanted to see Madame de S——," she said, with unexpected insight. "Not for a moment." There was something confidential and mysterious in her tone. She passed through the door, with Miss Haldin following her, on to the terrace, and they descended side by side the moss-grown stone steps. There was no one to be seen on the part of the drive visible from the front of the house.

"They are hidden by the trees over there," explained Miss Haldin's new acquaintance, "but you shall see them directly. I don't know who that young man is to whom Peter Ivanovitch has taken such a fancy. He must be one of us, or he would not be admitted here when the others come. You know what I mean by the others. But I must say that he is not at all mystically inclined. I don't know that I have made him out yet. Naturally I am never for very long in the drawing room. There is always something for me to do, though the establishment here is not so extensive as the villa on the Riviera. But still there are plenty of opportunities for me to make myself useful."

To the left, passing by the ivy-grown end of the stables, appeared Peter Ivanovitch and his companion. They walked very slowly, conversing with some animation. They stopped for a moment, and Peter Ivanovitch was seen to gesticulate, while the young man listened motionless, with his arms hanging down and his head bowed a little. He was dressed in a dark brown suit and a black hat. The round eyes of the *dame de compagnie* remained fixed on the two figures, which had resumed their leisurely approach.

"An extremely polite young man," she said. "You shall see what a bow he will make; and it won't altogether be so exceptional either. He bows in the same way when he meets me alone in the hall."

She moved on a few steps, with Miss Haldin by her side, and things happened just as she had foretold. The young man took off his hat, bowed and fell back, while Peter Ivanovitch advanced quicker, his black, thick arms extended heartily, and seized hold of both Miss Haldin's hands, shook them, and peered at her through his dark glasses.

"That's right, that's right!" he exclaimed twice, approvingly. "And so you have been looked after by . . ." He frowned slightly at the *dame de compagnie,* who was still nursing the cat. "I conclude Eleanor—Madame de S—— is engaged. I know she expected somebody today. So the newspaper man did turn up, eh? She is engaged?"

For all answer the *dame de compagnie* turned away her head.

"It is very unfortunate—very unfortunate indeed. I very much regret that you should have been . . ." He lowered suddenly his voice. "But what is it—surely you are not departing, Natalia Victorovna? You got bored waiting, didn't you?"

"Not in the least," Miss Haldin protested. "Only I have been here some time, and I am anxious to get back to my mother."

"The time seemed long, eh? I am afraid our worthy friend here"—(Peter Ivanovitch suddenly jerked his head sideways towards his right shoulder and jerked it up again)—"our worthy friend here has not the art of shortening the moments of waiting. No, distinctly she has not the art; and in that respect good intentions alone count for nothing."

The *dame de compagnie* dropped her arms, and the cat found itself suddenly on the ground. It remained quite still after alighting, one hind leg stretched backwards. Miss Haldin was extremely indignant on behalf of the lady companion.

"Believe me, Peter Ivanovitch, that the moments I have passed in the hall of this house have been not a little interesting, and very instructive too. They are memorable. I do not regret the waiting, but I see that the object of my call here can be attained without taking up Madame de S——'s time."

At this point I interrupted Miss Haldin. The above relation is rounded on her narrative, which I have not so much dramatized as might be supposed. She had rendered, with extraordinary feeling and animation, the very accent almost of the disciple of the old apple-woman, the irreconcilable hater of Ministries, the voluntary servant of the poor. Miss Haldin's true and delicate humanity had been extremely shocked by the uncongenial fate of her new acquaintance, that lady companion, secretary, whatever she was. For my own part, I was pleased to discover in it one more obstacle to intimacy with Madame de S——. I had a positive abhorrence for the painted, bedizened, dead-faced, glassy-eyed Egeria of Peter Ivanovitch. I do not know what was her attitude to the unseen, but I know that in the affairs of this world she was avaricious, greedy, and unscrupulous. It was within my knowledge that she had been worsted in a sordid and desperate quarrel about money matters with the family of her late husband, the diplomatist. Some very august personages indeed (whom in her fury she had insisted upon scandalously involving in her affairs) had incurred her animosity. I find it perfectly easy to believe that she had come to within an ace of being spirited away, for reasons of State, into some discreet *maison de santé*—a madhouse of sorts, to be plain. It appears, however, that certain highplaced personages opposed it for reasons which . . .

But it is no use to go into details.

Wonder may be expressed at a man in the position of a teacher of languages knowing all this with such definiteness. A novelist says this and that of his personages, and if only he knows how to say it earnestly enough he may not be questioned upon the inventions of his brain in which his own belief is made sufficiently manifest by a telling phrase, a poetic image, the accent of emotion. Art is great? But I have no art, and not having invented Madame de S——, I feel bound to explain how I came to know so much about her.

My informant was the Russian wife of a friend of mine already mentioned, the professor of Lausanne University. It was from her that I learned the last fact of Madame de S——'s history, with which I intend to trouble my readers. She told me, speaking positively, as a person who trusts her sources, of the cause of Madame de S——'s flight from Russia, some years before. It was neither more nor less than this: that she became suspect to the police in connection with the assassination of the Emperor Alexander. The ground of this suspicion was either some unguarded expressions that escaped her in public, or some talk overheard in her salon—overheard, we must believe, by some guest, perhaps a friend, who hastened to play the informer, I suppose. At any rate, the overheard matter seemed to imply her foreknowledge of that event, and I think she was wise in not waiting for the investigation of such a charge. Some of my readers may remember a little book from her pen, published in Paris, a mystically bad-tempered, declamatory, and frightfully disconnected piece of writing, in which she all but admits the foreknowledge, more than hints at its supernatural origin, and plainly suggests in venomous innuendoes that the guilt of the act was not with the terrorists, but with a palace intrigue. When I observed to my friend, the professor's wife, that the life of Madame de S——, with its unofficial diplomacy, its intrigues, lawsuits, favors, disgrace, expulsions, its atmosphere of scandal, occultism, and charlatanism, was more fit for the eighteenth century than for the conditions of our own time, she assented with a smile, but a moment after went on in a reflective tone: "Charlatanism?—yes, in a certain measure. Still, times are changed. There are forces now which were nonexistent in the eighteenth century. I should not be surprised if she were more dangerous than an Englishman would be willing to believe. And what's more, she is looked upon as really dangerous by certain people—*chez nous*."

Chez nous in this connection meant Russia in general, and the Russian political police in particular. The object of my digression from the straight course of Miss Haldin's relation (in my own words) of her visit to the Château Borel, was to bring forward that statement of my friend, the professor's wife. I wanted to bring it forward simply to make what I have to say presently of Mr. Razumov's presence in Geneva a little more credible—for this is a Russian story for Western ears, which, as I have observed already, are not attuned to certain tones of cynicism and cruelty, of moral negation, and even of moral distress already silenced at our end of Europe. And this I state as my excuse for having left Miss Haldin standing, one of the little group of two women and two men who had come together below the terrace of the Château Borel.

The knowledge which I have just stated was in my mind when, as I have said, I interrupted Miss Haldin. I interrupted her with the cry of profound satisfaction:

"So you never saw Madame de S—— after all?"

Miss Haldin shook her head. It was very satisfactory to me. She had not seen Madame de S——! That was excellent, excellent! I welcomed the conviction that she would never know Madame de S—— now. I could not explain the reason of the conviction but by the knowledge that Miss Haldin was standing face to face with her brother's wonderful friend. I preferred him to Madame de S—— as the companion and guide of that young girl, abandoned to her inexperience by the miserable end of her brother. But, at any rate, that life now ended had been sincere, and perhaps its thoughts might have been lofty, its moral sufferings profound, its last act a true sacrifice. It is not for us, the staid lovers calmed by the possession of a conquered liberty, to condemn without appeal the fierceness of thwarted desire.

I am not ashamed of the warmth of my regard for Miss Haldin. It was, it must be admitted, an unselfish sentiment, being its own reward. The late Victor Haldin—in the light of that sentiment—appeared to me not as a sinister conspirator, but as a pure enthusiast. I did not wish indeed to judge him, but the very fact that he did not escape, that fact which brought so much trouble to both his mother and his sister, spoke to me in his favor. Meantime, in my fear of seeing the girl surrender to the influence of the Château Borel revolutionary feminism, I was more than willing to put my trust in that friend of the late Victor Haldin. He was nothing but a name, you will say. Exactly! A name! And what's more, the only name; the only name to be found in the correspondence between brother and sister. The young man had turned up; they had come face to face, and, fortunately, without the direct interference of Madame de S——. What will come of it? what will she tell me presently? I was asking myself.

It was only natural that my thought should turn to the young man, the bearer of the only name uttered in all the dream-talk of a future to be brought about by a revolution. And my thought took the shape of asking myself why this young man had not called upon these ladies. He had been in Geneva for some days before Miss Haldin heard of him first in my presence from Peter Ivanovitch. I regretted that last's presence at their meeting. I would rather have had it happen somewhere out of his spectacled sight. But I supposed that, having both these young people there, he introduced them to each other.

I broke the silence by beginning a question on that point:

"I suppose Peter Ivanovitch . . ."

Miss Haldin gave vent to her indignation. Peter Ivanovitch directly he had got his answer from her had turned upon the *dame de compagnie* in a shameful manner.

"Turned upon her?" I wondered. "What about? For what reason?"

"It was unheard of; it was shameful," Miss Haldin pursued, with angry eyes. "*Il lui a fait une scène*—like this, before strangers. And for what? You would never guess. For some eggs. . . . Oh!"

I was astonished. "Eggs, did you say?"

"For Madame de S——. That lady observes a special diet, or something of the sort. It seems she complained the day before to Peter Ivanovitch that the eggs were not rightly prepared. Peter Ivanovitch suddenly remembered this against the poor woman, and flew out at her. It was most astonishing. I stood as if rooted."

"Do you mean to say that the great feminist allowed himself to be abusive to a woman?" I asked.

"Oh, not that! It was something you have no conception of. It was an odious performance. Imagine, he raised his hat to begin with. He made his voice soft and deprecatory. 'Ah! you are not kind to us—you will not deign to remember . . .' This sort of phrases, that sort of tone. The poor creature was terribly upset. Her eyes ran full of tears. She did not know where to look. I shouldn't wonder if she would have preferred abuse, or even a blow."

I did not remark that very possibly she was familiar with both on occasions when no one was by. Miss Haldin walked by my side, her head up in scornful and angry silence.

"Great men have their surprising peculiarities," I observed inanely. "Exactly like men who are not great. But that sort of thing cannot be kept up forever. How did the great feminist wind up this very characteristic episode?"

Miss Haldin, without turning her face my way, told me that the end was brought about by the appearance of the interviewer, who had been closeted with Madame de S——.

He came up rapidly, unnoticed, lifted his hat slightly, and paused to say in French: "The Baroness has asked me, in case I met a lady on my way out, to desire her to come in at once."

After delivering this message, he hurried down the drive. The *dame de compagnie* flew towards the house, and Peter Ivanovitch followed her hastily, looking uneasy. In a moment Miss Haldin found herself alone with the young man, who undoubtedly must have been the new arrival from Russia. She wondered whether her brother's friend had not already guessed who she was.

I am in a position to say that, as a matter of fact, he had guessed. It is clear to me that Peter Ivanovitch, for some reason or other, had refrained from alluding to these ladies' presence in Geneva. But Razumov had guessed. The trustful girl! Every word uttered by Haldin lived in Razumov's memory. They were like haunting shapes; they could not be exorcised. The most vivid amongst them was the mention of the sister. The girl had existed for him ever since. But he did not recognize her at once. Coming up with Peter Ivanovitch, he did observe her; their eyes had met, even. He had responded, as no one could help responding, to the harmonious charm of her whole person, its strength, its grace, its tranquil frankness—and then he had turned his gaze away. He said to himself that all this was not for him; the beauty of women and the friendship of men were not for him. He accepted that feeling with a purposeful sternness, and tried to pass on. It was only her outstretched hand which brought about the recognition. It stands recorded in the pages of his self-confession, that it nearly suffocated him physically with an emotional reaction of hate and dismay, as though her appearance had been a piece of accomplished treachery.

He faced about. The considerable elevation of the terrace concealed them from anyone lingering in the doorway of the house; and even from the upstairs windows they could not have been seen. Through the thickets run wild, and the trees of the gently sloping grounds, he had cold, placid glimpses of the lake. A moment of perfect privacy had been vouchsafed to them at this juncture. I wondered to myself what use they had made of that fortunate circumstance.

"Did you have time for more than a few words?" I asked.

That animation with which she had related to me the incidents of her visit to the Château Borel had left her completely. Strolling by my side, she looked straight before her; but I noticed a little color on her cheek. She did not answer me.

After some little time I observed that they could not have hoped to remain forgotten for very long, unless the other two had discovered Madame de S—— swooning with fatigue, perhaps, or in a state of morbid exaltation after the long interview. Either would require their devoted ministrations. I could depict to myself Peter Ivanovitch rushing busily out of the house again, bareheaded, perhaps, and on across the terrace with his swinging gait, the black skirts of the frock coat floating clear of his stout light-gray legs. I confess to having looked upon these young people as the quarry of the "heroic fugitive." I had the notion that they would not be allowed to escape capture. But of that I said nothing to Miss Haldin, only as she still remained uncommunicative, I pressed her a little.

"Well—but you can tell me at least your impression."

She turned her head to look at me, and turned away again.

"Impression?" she repeated slowly, almost dreamily; then in a quicker tone:

"He seems to be a man who has suffered more from his thoughts than from evil fortune."

"From his thoughts, you say?"

"And that is natural enough in a Russian," she took me up. "In a young Russian; so many of them are unfit for action, and yet unable to rest."

"And you think he is that sort of man?"

"No, I do not judge him. How could I, so suddenly? You asked for my impression—I explain my impression. I—I—don't know the world, nor yet the people in it; I have been too solitary—I am too young to trust my own opinions."

"Trust your instinct," I advised her. "Most women trust to that, and make no worse mistakes than men. In this case you have your brother's letter to help you."

She drew a deep breath like a light sigh.

"'Unstained, lofty, and solitary existences,'" she quoted as if to herself. But I caught the wistful murmur distinctly.

"High praise," I whispered to her.

"The highest possible."

"So high that, like the award of happiness, it is more fit to come only at the end of a life. But still no common or altogether unworthy personality could have suggested such a confident exaggeration of praise and . . ."

"Ah!" She interrupted me ardently. "And if you had only known the heart from which that judgment has come!"

She ceased on that note, and for a space I reflected on the character of the words which I perceived very well must tip the scale of the girl's feelings in that young man's favor. They had not the sound of a casual utterance. Vague they were to my Western mind and to my Western sentiment, but I could not forget that, standing by Miss Haldin's side, I was like a traveler in a strange country. It had also become clear to me that Miss Haldin was unwilling to enter into the details of the only material part of their visit to the Château Borel. But I was not hurt. Somehow I didn't feel it to be a want of confidence. It was some other difficulty—a difficulty I could not resent. And it was without the slightest resentment that I said:

"Very well. But on that high ground, which I will not dispute, you, like anyone else in such circumstances, you must have made for yourself a representation of that exceptional friend, a mental image of him, and—please tell me—you were not disappointed?"

"What do you mean? His personal appearance?"

"I don't mean precisely his good looks, or otherwise."

We turned at the end of the alley and made a few steps without looking at each other.

"His appearance is not ordinary," said Miss Haldin at last.

"No, I should have thought not—from the little you've said of your first impression. After all, one has to fall back on that word. Impression! What I mean is that something indescribable which is likely to mark a 'not ordinary' person."

I perceived that she was not listening. There was no mistaking her expression; and once more I had the sense of being out of it—not because of my age, which at any rate could draw inferences—but altogether out of it, on another plane whence I could only watch her from afar. And so ceasing to speak I watched her stepping out by my side.

"No," she exclaimed suddenly, "I could not have been disappointed with a man of such strong feeling."

"Aha! Strong feeling," I muttered, thinking to myself censoriously: like this, at once, all in a moment!

"What did you say?" inquired Miss Haldin innocently.

"Oh, nothing. I beg your pardon. Strong feeling. I am not surprised."

"And you don't know how abruptly I behaved to him!" she cried remorsefully.

I suppose I must have appeared surprised, for, looking at me with a still more heightened color, she said she was ashamed to admit that she had not been sufficiently collected; she had failed to control her words and actions as the situation demanded. She lost the fortitude worthy of both the men, the dead and the living—the fortitude which should have been the note of the meeting of Victor Haldin's sister with Victor Haldin's only known friend. He was looking at her keenly, but said nothing, and she was—she confessed—painfully affected by his want of comprehension. All she could say was: "You are Mr. Razumov." A slight frown passed over his forehead. After a short, watchful pause, he made a little bow of assent, and waited.

At the thought that she had before her the man so highly regarded by her brother, the man who had known his value, spoken to him, understood him, had listened to his confidences, perhaps had encouraged him—her lips trembled, her eyes ran full of tears; she put out her hand, made a step towards him impulsively, saying with an effort to restrain her emotion, "Can't you guess who I am?" He did not take the proffered hand. He even recoiled a pace, and Miss Haldin imagined that he was unpleasantly affected. Miss Haldin excused him, directing her displeasure at herself. She had behaved unworthily, like an emotional French girl. A manifestation of that kind could not be welcomed by a man of stern, self-contained character.

He must have been stern indeed, or perhaps very timid with women, not to respond in a more human way to the advances of a girl like Nathalie Haldin—I thought to myself. Those "lofty and solitary existences" (I remembered the words suddenly) make a young man shy and an old man savage—often.

"Well?" I encouraged Miss Haldin to proceed.

She was still very dissatisfied with herself.

"I went from bad to worse," she said, with an air of discouragement very foreign to her. "I did everything foolish except actually bursting into tears. I am thankful to say I did not do that. But I was unable to speak for quite a long time."

She had stood before him, speechless, swallowing her sobs, and when she managed at last to utter something, it was only her brother's name—"Victor—Victor Haldin!" she gasped out, and again her voice failed her.

"Of course," she commented to me, "this distressed him. He was quite overcome. I have told you my opinion that he is a man of deep feeling—it is impossible to doubt it. You should have seen his face. He positively reeled. He leaned against the wall of the terrace. Their friendship must have been the very brotherhood of souls! I was grateful to him for that emotion, which made me feel less ashamed of my own lack of self-control. Of course I had regained the power of speech at once, almost. All this lasted not more than a few seconds. 'I am his sister,' I said. 'Maybe you have heard of me.'"

"And had he?" I interrupted.

"I don't know. How could it have been otherwise? And yet . . . But what does that matter? I stood there before him, near enough to be touched and surely not looking like an impostor. All I know is, that he put out both his hands then to me, I may say flung them out at me, with the greatest readiness and warmth, and that I seized and pressed them, feeling that I was finding again a little of what I thought was lost to me forever, with the loss of my brother—some of that hope, inspiration, and support which I used to get from my dear dead . . ."

I understood quite well what she meant. We strolled on slowly. I refrained from looking at her. And it was as if answering my own thoughts that I murmured:

"No doubt it was a great friendship—as you say. And that young man ended by welcoming your name, so to speak, with both hands. After that, of course, you would understand each other. Yes, you would understand each other quickly."

It was a moment before I heard her voice.

"Mr. Razumov seems to be a man of few words. A reserved man—even when he is strongly moved."

Unable to forget—or even to forgive—the bass-toned expansiveness of Peter Ivanovitch, the arch-patron of revolutionary parties, I said that I took this for a favorable trait of character. It was associated with sincerity—in my mind.

"And, besides, we had not much time," she added.

"No, you would not have, of course." My suspicion and even dread of the feminist and his Egeria was so ineradicable that I could not help asking with real anxiety, which I made smiling:

"But you escaped all right?"

She understood me, and smiled too, at my uneasiness.

"Oh yes! I escaped, if you like to call it that. I walked away quickly. There was no need to run. I am neither frightened nor yet fascinated, like that poor woman who received me so strangely."

"And Mr.—Mr. Razumov . . . ?"

"He remained there, of course. I suppose he went into the house after I left him. You remember that he came here strongly recommended to Peter Ivanovitch—possibly entrusted with important messages for him."

"Ah yes! From that priest who . . ."

"Father Zosim—yes. Or from others, perhaps."

"You left him, then. But have you seen him since, may I ask?"

For some time Miss Haldin made no answer to this very direct question, then:

"I have been expecting to see him here today," she said quietly.

"You have! Do you meet, then, in this garden? In that case I had better leave you at once."

"No; why leave me? And we don't meet in this garden. I have not seen Mr. Razumov since that first time. Not once. But I have been expecting him . . ."

She paused. I wondered to myself why that young revolutionist should show so little alacrity.

"Before we parted I told Mr. Razumov that I walked here for an hour every day at this time. I could not explain to him then why I did not ask him to come and see us at once. Mother must be prepared for such a visit. And then, you see, I do not know myself what Mr. Razumov has to tell us. He, too, must be told first how it is with poor mother. All these thoughts flashed through my mind at once. So I told him hurriedly that there was a reason why I could not ask him to see us at home, but that I was in the habit of walking here. . . . This is a public place, but there are never many people about at this hour. I thought it would be very well. And it is so near our apartments. I don't like to be very far away from mother. Our servant knows where I am in case I should be wanted suddenly."

"Yes. It is very convenient from that point of view," I agreed.

In fact, I thought the Bastions a very convenient place, since the girl did not think it prudent as yet to introduce that young man to her mother. It is here, then, I thought, looking round at that plot of ground of deplorable banality, that their acquaintance will begin and go on in the exchange of generous indignations and of extreme sentiments, too poignant, perhaps, for a non-Russian mind to conceive. I saw these two, escaped out of fourscore millions of human beings ground between the upper and nether millstone, walking under these trees, their young heads close together. Yes, an excellent place to stroll and talk in. It even occurred to me, while we turned once more away from the wide iron gates, that when tired they would have plenty of accommodation to rest themselves. There was a quantity of tables and chairs displayed between the restaurant chalet and the bandstand, a whole raft of painted deals spread out under the trees. In the very middle of it I observed a solitary Swiss couple, whose fate was made secure from the cradle to the grave by the perfected mechanism of democratic institutions in a republic that could almost be held in the palm of one's hand. The man, colorlessly uncouth, was drinking beer out of a glittering glass; the woman, rustic and placid, leaning back in the rough chair, gazed idly around.

There is little logic to be expected on this earth, not only in the matter of thought, but also of sentiment. I was surprised to discover myself displeased with that unknown young man. A week had gone by since they met. Was he callous, or shy, or very stupid? I could not make it out.

"Do you think," I asked Miss Haldin, after we had gone some distance up the great alley, "that Mr. Razumov understood your intention?"

"Understood what I meant?" she wondered. "He was greatly moved. That I know! In my own agitation I could see it. But I spoke distinctly. He heard me; he seemed, indeed, to hang on my words . . ."

Unconsciously she had hastened her pace. Her utterance, too, became quicker.

I waited a little before I observed thoughtfully:

"And yet he allowed all these days to pass."

"How can we tell what work he may have to do here? He is not an idler traveling for his pleasure. His time may not be his own—nor yet his thoughts, perhaps."

She slowed her pace suddenly, and in a lowered voice added:

"Or his very life"—then paused and stood still. "For all I know, he may have had to leave Geneva the very day he saw me."

"Without telling you!" I exclaimed incredulously.

"I did not give him time. I left him quite abruptly. I behaved emotionally to the end. I am sorry for it. Even if I had given him the opportunity he would have been justified in taking me for a person not to be trusted. An emotional, tearful girl is not a person to confide in. But even if he has left Geneva for a time, I am confident that we shall meet again."

"Ah! you are confident. . . . I dare say. But on what ground?"

"Because I've told him that I was in great need of someone, a fellow-countryman, a fellow-believer, to whom I could give my confidence in a certain matter."

"I see. I don't ask you what answer he made. I confess that this is good ground for your belief in Mr. Razumov's appearance before long. But he has not turned up today?"

"No," she said quietly, "not today"; and we stood for a time in silence, like people that have nothing more to say to each other and let their thoughts run widely asunder before their bodies go off their different ways. Miss Haldin glanced at the watch on her wrist and made a brusk movement. She had already overstayed her time, it seemed.

"I don't like to be away from mother," she murmured, shaking her head: "It is not that she is very ill now. But somehow when I am not with her I am more uneasy than ever."

Mrs. Haldin had not made the slightest allusion to her son for the last week or more. She sat, as usual, in the armchair by the window, looking out silently on that hopeless stretch of the Boulevard des Philosophes. When she spoke, a few lifeless words, it was of indifferent, trivial things.

"For anyone who knows what the poor soul is thinking of, that sort of talk is more painful than her silence. But that is bad too; I can hardly endure it, and I dare not break it."

Miss Haldin sighed, refastening a button of her glove which had come undone. I knew well enough what a hard time of it she must be having. The stress, its causes, its nature, would have undermined the health of an Occidental girl; but Russian natures have a singular power of resistance against the unfair strains of life. Straight and supple, with a short jacket open on her black dress, which made her figure appear more slender and her fresh but colorless face more pale, she compelled my wonder and admiration.

"I can't stay a moment longer. You ought to come soon to see mother. You know she calls you 'L'ami.' It is an excellent name, and she really means it. And now au revoir, I must run."

She glanced vaguely down the broad walk—the hand she put out to me eluded my grasp by an unexpected upward movement, and rested upon my shoulder. Her red lips were slightly parted, not in a smile, however, but expressing a sort of startled pleasure. She gazed towards the gates and said quickly, with a gasp:

"There! I knew it. Here he comes!"

I understood that she must mean Mr. Razumov. A young man was walking up the alley, without haste. His clothes were some dull shade of brown, and he carried a stick. When my eyes first fell on him, his head was hanging on his breast as if in deep thought. While I was looking at him he raised it sharply, and at once stopped. I am certain he did, but that pause was nothing more perceptible than a faltering check in his gait, instantaneously overcome. Then he continued his approach, looking at us steadily. Miss Haldin signed to me to remain, and advanced a step or two to meet him.

I turned my head away from that meeting, and did not look at them again till I heard Miss Haldin's voice uttering his name in the way of introduction. Mr. Razumov was informed, in a warm, low tone, that, besides being a wonderful teacher, I was a great support "in our sorrow and distress."

Of course I was described also as an Englishman. Miss Haldin spoke rapidly, faster than I have ever heard her speak, and that by contrast made the quietness of her eyes more expressive.

"I have given him my confidence," she added, looking all the time at Mr. Razumov. That young man did, indeed, rest his gaze on Miss Haldin, but certainly did not look into her eyes which were so ready for him. Afterwards he glanced backwards and forwards at us both, while the faint commencement of a forced smile, followed by the suspicion of a frown, vanished one after another; I detected them, though neither could have been noticed by a person less intensely bent upon divining him than myself. I don't know what Nathalie Haldin had observed, but my attention seized the very shades of these movements. The attempted smile was given up, the incipient frown was checked, and smoothed so that there should be no sign; but I imagined him exclaiming inwardly:

"Her confidence! To this elderly person—this foreigner!"

I imagined this because he looked foreign enough to me. I was upon the whole favorably impressed. He had an air of intelligence and even some distinction quite above the average of the students and other inhabitants of the *Petite Russie*. His features were more decided than in the generality of Russian faces; he had a line of the jaw, a clean-shaven, sallow cheek; his nose was a ridge, and not a mere protuberance. He wore the hat well down over his eyes, his dark hair curled low on the nape of his neck; in the ill-fitting brown clothes there were sturdy limbs; a slight stoop brought out a satisfactory breadth of shoulders. Upon the whole I was not disappointed. Studious—robust—shy. . . .

Before Miss Haldin had ceased speaking I felt the grip of his hand on mine, a muscular, firm grip, but unexpectedly hot and dry. Not a word or even a mutter assisted this short and arid handshake.

I intended to leave them to themselves, but Miss Haldin touched me lightly on the forearm with a significant contact, conveying a distinct wish. Let him smile who likes, but I was only too ready to stay near Nathalie Haldin, and I am not ashamed to say that it was no smiling matter to me. I stayed, not as a youth would have stayed, uplifted, as it were poised in the air, but soberly, with my feet on the ground and my mind trying to penetrate her intention. She had turned to Razumov.

"Well. This is the place. Yes, it is here that I meant you to come. I have been walking every day. . . . Don't excuse yourself—I understand. I am grateful to you for coming today, but all the same I cannot stay now. It is impossible. I must hurry off home. Yes, even with you standing before me, I must run off. I have been too long away. . . . You know how it is?"

These last words were addressed to me. I noticed that Mr. Razumov passed the tip of his tongue over his lips just as a parched, feverish man might do. He took her hand in its black glove, which closed on his, and held it—detained it quite visibly to me against a drawing-back movement.

"Thank you once more for—for understanding me," she went on warmly. He interrupted her with a certain effect of roughness. I didn't like him speaking to this frank creature so much from under the brim of his hat, as it were. And he produced a faint, rasping voice quite like a man with a parched throat.

"What is there to thank me for? Understand you? . . . How did I understand you? . . . You had better know that I understand nothing. I was aware that you wanted to see me in this garden. I could not come before. I was hindered. And even today, you see . . . late."

She still held his hand.

"I can, at any rate, thank you for not dismissing me from your mind as a weak, emotional girl. No doubt I want sustaining. I am very ignorant. But I can be trusted. Indeed I can!"

"You are ignorant," he repeated thoughtfully. He had raised his head, and was looking straight into her face now, while she held his hand. They stood like this for a long moment. She released his hand.

"Yes. You did come late. It was good of you to come on the chance of me having loitered beyond my time. I was talking with this good friend here. I was talking of you. Yes, Kirylo Sidorovitch, of you. He was with me when I first heard of your being here in Geneva. He can tell you what comfort it was to my bewildered spirit to hear that news. He knew I meant to seek you out. It was the only object of my accepting the invitation of Peter Ivanovitch . . ."

"Peter Ivanovitch talked to you of me?" he interrupted, in that wavering, hoarse voice which suggested a horribly dry throat.

"Very little. Just told me your name, and that you had arrived here. Why should I have asked for more? What could he have told me that I did not know already from my brother's letter? Three lines! And how much they meant to me! I will show them to you one day, Kirylo Sidorovitch. But now I must go. The first talk between us cannot be a matter of five minutes, so we had better not begin. . . ."

I had been standing a little aside, seeing them both in profile. At that moment it occurred to me that Mr. Razumov's face was older than his age.

"If mother"—the girl had turned suddenly to me—"were to wake up in my absence (so much longer than usual) she would perhaps question me. She seems to miss me more, you know, of late. She would want to know what delayed me—and, you see, it would be painful for me to dissemble before her."

I understood the point very well. For the same reason she checked what seemed to be on Mr. Razumov's part a movement to accompany her.

"No, no! I go alone, but meet me here as soon as possible." Then to me in a lower, significant tone:

"Mother may be sitting at the window at this moment, looking down the street. She must not know anything of Mr. Razumov's presence here till—till something is arranged." She paused before she added a little louder, but still speaking to me, "Mr. Razumov does not quite understand my difficulty, but you know what it is."

V

With a quick inclination of the head for us both, and an earnest, friendly glance at the young man, Miss Haldin left us covering our heads and looking after her straight, supple figure receding rapidly. Her walk was not that hybrid and uncertain gliding affected by some women, but a frank, strong, healthy movement forward. Rapidly she increased the distance—disappeared with suddenness at last. I discovered only then that Mr. Razumov, after ramming his hat well over his brow, was looking me over from head to foot. I dare say I was a very unexpected fact for that young Russian to stumble upon. I caught in his physiognomy, in his whole bearing, an expression compounded of curiosity and scorn, tempered by alarm— as though he had been holding his breath while I was not looking. But his eyes met mine with a gaze direct enough. I saw then for the first time that they were of a clear brown color and fringed with thick black eyelashes. They were the youngest feature of his face. Not at all unpleasant eyes. He swayed slightly, leaning on his stick and generally hung in the wind. It flashed upon me that in leaving us together Miss Haldin had an intention—that something was entrusted to me, since by a mere accident I had been found at hand. On this assumed ground I put all possible friendliness into my manner. I cast about for some right thing to say, and suddenly in Miss Haldin's last words I perceived the clue to the nature of my mission.

"No," I said gravely, if with a smile, "you cannot be expected to understand."

His clean-shaven lip quivered ever so little before he said, as if wickedly amused:

"But haven't you heard just now? I was thanked by that young lady for understanding so well."

I looked at him rather hard. Was there a hidden and inexplicable sneer in this retort? No. It was not that. It might have been resentment. Yes. But what had he to resent? He looked as though he had not slept very well of late. I could almost feel on me the weight of his unrefreshed, motionless stare, the stare of a man who lies unwinking in the dark, angrily passive in the toils of disastrous thoughts. Now, when I know how true it was, I can honestly affirm that this *was* the effect he produced on me. It was painful in a curiously indefinite way—for, of course, the definition comes to me now while I sit writing in the fullness of my knowledge. But this is what the effect was at that time of absolute ignorance. This new sort of uneasiness which he seemed to be forcing upon me I attempted to put down by assuming a conversational, easy familiarity.

"That extremely charming and essentially admirable young girl (I am—as you see—old enough to be frank in my expressions) was referring to her own feelings. Surely you must have understood that much?"

He made such a brusk movement that he even tottered a little.

"Must understand this! Not expected to understand that! I may have other things to do. And the girl is charming and admirable. Well—and if she is! I suppose I can see that for myself."

This sally would have been insulting if his voice had not been practically extinct, dried up in his throat; and the rustling effort of his speech too painful to give real offense.

I remained silent, checked between the obvious fact and the subtle impression. It was open to me to leave him there and then; but the sense of having been entrusted with a mission, the suggestion of Miss Haldin's last glance, was strong upon me. After a moment of reflection I said:

"Shall we walk together a little?"

He shrugged his shoulders so violently that he tottered again. I saw it out of the corner of my eye as I moved on, with him at my elbow. He had fallen back a little and was practically out of my sight, unless I turned my head to look at him. I did not wish to indispose him still further by an appearance of marked curiosity. It might have been distasteful to such a young and secret refugee from under the pestilential shadow hiding the true, kindly face of his land. And the shadow, the attendant of his countrymen, stretching across the middle of Europe, was lying on him too, darkening his figure to my mental vision. "Without doubt," I said to myself, "he seems a somber, even a desperate revolutionist; but he is young, he may be unselfish and humane, capable of compassion, of . . ."

I heard him clear gratingly his parched throat, and became all attention.

"This is beyond everything," were his first words. "It is beyond everything! I find you here, for no reason that I can understand, in possession of something I cannot be expected to understand! A confidant! A foreigner! Talking about an admirable Russian girl. Is the admirable girl a fool, I begin to wonder? What are you at? What is your object?"

He was barely audible, as if his throat had no more resonance than a dry rag, a piece of tinder. It was so pitiful that I found it extremely easy to control my indignation.

"When you have lived a little longer, Mr. Razumov, you will discover that no woman is an absolute fool. I am not a feminist, like that illustrious author, Peter Ivanovitch, who, to say the truth, is not a little suspect to me. . . ."

He interrupted me, in a surprising note of whispering astonishment:

"Suspect to you! Peter Ivanovitch suspect to you! To you! . . ."

"Yes, in a certain aspect he is," I said, dismissing my remark lightly. "As I was saying, Mr. Razumov, when you have lived long enough, you will learn to discriminate between the noble trustfulness of a nature foreign to every meanness and the flattered credulity of some women; though even the credulous, silly as they may be, unhappy as they are sure to be, are never absolute fools. It is my belief that no woman is ever completely deceived. Those that are lost leap into the abyss with their eyes open, if all the truth were known."

"Upon my word," he cried at my elbow, "what is it to me whether women are fools or lunatics? I really don't care what you think of them. I—I am not interested in them. I let them be. I am not a young man in a novel. How do you know that I want to learn anything about women? . . . What is the meaning of all this?"

"The object, you mean, of this conversation, which I admit I have forced upon you in a measure?"

"Forced! Object!" he repeated, still keeping half a pace or so behind me. "You wanted to talk about women apparently. That's a subject. But I don't care for it. I have never . . . In fact, I have had other subjects to think about."

"I am concerned here with one woman only—a young girl—the sister of your dead friend—Miss Haldin. Surely you can think a little of her. What I meant from the first was that there is a situation which you cannot be expected to understand."

I listened to his unsteady footfalls by my side for the space of several strides.

"I think that it may prepare the ground for your next interview with Miss Haldin if I tell you of it. I imagine that she might have had something of the kind in her mind when she left us together. I believe myself authorized to speak. The peculiar situation I have alluded to has arisen in the first grief and distress of Victor Haldin's execution. There was something peculiar in the circumstances of his arrest. You no doubt know the whole truth. . . ."

I felt my arm seized above the elbow, and next instant found myself swung so as to face Mr. Razumov.

"You spring up from the ground before me with this talk. Who the devil are you? This is not to be borne! Why? What for? What do you know what is or is not peculiar? What have you to do with any confounded circumstances, or with anything that happens in Russia, anyway?"

He leaned on his stick with his other hand heavily; and when he let go my arm, I was certain in my mind that he was hardly able to keep on his feet.

"Let us sit down at one of these vacant tables," I proposed, disregarding this display of unexpectedly profound emotion. It was not without its effect on me, I confess. I was sorry for him.

"What tables? What are you talking about? Oh—the empty tables. . . The tables there. Certainly. I will sit at one of the empty tables."

I led him away from the path to the very center of the raft of deals before the chalet. The Swiss couple were gone by that time. We were alone on the raft, so to speak. Mr. Razumov dropped into a chair, let fall his stick, and propped on his elbows, his head between his hands, stared at me persistently, openly, and continuously, while I signaled the waiter and ordered some beer. I could not quarrel with this silent inspection very well, because, truth to tell, I felt somewhat guilty of having been sprung on him with some abruptness—of having "sprung from the ground," as he expressed it.

While waiting to be served I mentioned that, born from parents settled in St. Petersburg, I had acquired the language as a child. The town I did not remember, having left it for good as a boy of nine, but in later years I had renewed my acquaintance with the language. He listened, without as much as moving his eyes the least little bit. He had to change his position when the beer came, and the instant draining of his glass revived him. He leaned back in his chair and, folding his arms across his chest, continued to stare at me squarely. It occurred to me that his clean-shaven, almost swarthy face was really of the very mobile sort, and that the absolute stillness of it was the acquired habit of a revolutionist, of a conspirator everlastingly on his guard against self-betrayal in a world of secret spies.

"But you are an Englishman—a teacher of English literature," he murmured, in a voice that was no longer issuing from a parched throat. "I have heard of you. People told me you have lived here for years."

"Quite true. More than twenty years. And I have been assisting Miss Haldin with her English studies."

"You have been reading English poetry with her," he said, immovable now, like another man altogether, a complete stranger to the man of the heavy and uncertain footfalls a little while ago—at my elbow.

"Yes, English poetry," I said. "But the trouble of which I speak was caused by an English newspaper."

He continued to stare at me: I don't think he was aware that the story of the midnight arrest had been ferreted out by an English journalist and given to the world. When I explained this to him he muttered contemptuously, "It may have been altogether a lie."

"I should think you are the best judge of that," I retorted, a little disconcerted. "I must confess that to me it looks to be true in the main."

"How can you tell truth from lies?" he queried in his new, immovable manner.

"I don't know how you do it in Russia," I began, rather nettled by his attitude. He interrupted me.

"In Russia, and in general everywhere—in a newspaper, for instance. The color of the ink and the shapes of the letters are the same."

"Well, there are other trifles one can go by. The character of the publication, the general verisimilitude of the news, the consideration of the motive, and so on. I don't trust blindly the accuracy of special correspondents—but why should this one have gone to the trouble of concocting a circumstantial falsehood on a matter of no importance to the world?"

"That's what it is," he grumbled. "What's going on with us is of no importance—a mere sensational story to amuse the readers of the papers—the superior contemptuous Europe. It is hateful to think of. But let them wait a bit!"

He broke off on this sort of threat addressed to the Western world. Disregarding the anger in his stare, I pointed out that whether the journalist was well- or ill-informed, the concern of the friends of these ladies was with the effect the few lines of print in question had produced—the effect alone. And surely he must be counted as one of the friends—if only for the sake of his late comrade and intimate fellow-revolutionist. At that point I thought he was going to speak vehemently; but he only astounded me by the convulsive start of his whole body. He restrained himself, folded his loosened arms tighter across his chest, and sat back with a smile in which there was a twitch of scorn and malice.

"Yes, a comrade and an intimate. . . . Very well," he said.

"I ventured to speak to you on that assumption. And I cannot be mistaken. I was present when Peter Ivanovitch announced your arrival here to Miss Haldin, and I saw her relief and thankfulness when your name was mentioned. Afterwards she showed me her brother's letter, and read out the few words in which he alludes to you. What else but a friend could you have been?"

"Obviously. That's perfectly well known. A friend. Quite correct. . . . Go on. You were talking of some effect."

I said to myself: "He puts on the callousness of a stern revolutionist, the insensibility to common emotions of a man devoted to a destructive idea. He is young, and his sincerity assumes a pose before a stranger, a foreigner, an old man. Youth must assert itself. . . ." As concisely as possible I exposed to him the state of mind poor Mrs. Haldin had been thrown into by the news of her son's untimely end.

He listened—I felt it—with profound attention. His level stare deflected gradually downwards, left my face, and rested at last on the ground at his feet.

"You can enter into the sister's feelings. As you said, I have only read a little English poetry with her, and I won't make myself ridiculous in your eyes by trying to speak of her. But you have seen her. She is one of those rare human beings that do not want explaining. At least I think so. They had only that son, that brother, for a link with the wider world, with the future. The very groundwork of active existence for Nathalie Haldin is gone with him. Can you wonder then that she turns with eagerness to the only man her brother mentions in his letters? Your name is a sort of legacy."

"What could he have written of me?" he cried, in a low, exasperated tone.

"Only a few words. It is not for me to repeat them to you, Mr. Razumov; but you may believe my assertion that these words are forcible enough to make both his mother and his sister believe implicitly in the worth of your judgment and in the truth of anything you may have to say to them. It's impossible for you now to pass them by like strangers."

I paused, and for a moment sat listening to the footsteps of the few people passing up and down the broad central walk. While I was speaking his head had sunk upon his breast above his folded arms. He raised it sharply.

"Must I go then and lie to that old woman?"

It was not anger; it was something else, something more poignant, and not so simple. I was aware of it sympathetically, while I was profoundly concerned at the nature of that exclamation.

"Dear me! Won't the truth do, then? I hoped you could have told them something consoling. I am thinking of the poor mother now. Your Russia *is* a cruel country."

He moved a little in his chair.

"Yes," I repeated. "I thought you would have had something authentic to tell."

The twitching of his lips before he spoke was curious.

"What if it is not worth telling?"

"Not worth? From what point of view? I don't understand."

"From every point of view."

I spoke with some asperity.

"I should think that anything which could explain the circumstances of that midnight arrest . . ."

"Reported by a journalist for the amusement of the civilized Europe," he broke in scornfully.

"Yes, reported. . . . But aren't they true? I can't make out your attitude in this. Either the man is a hero to you, or . . ."

He approached his face with fiercely distended nostrils close to mine so suddenly that I had the greatest difficulty in not starting back.

"You ask me! I suppose it amuses you, all this. Look here! I am a worker. I studied. Yes, I studied very hard. There is intelligence here." (He tapped his forehead with his fingertips.) "Don't you think a Russian may have sane ambitions? Yes—I had even prospects. Certainly! I had. And now you see me here, abroad, everything gone, lost, sacrificed. You see me here—and you ask! You see me, don't you?— sitting before you."

He threw himself back violently. I kept outwardly calm.

"Yes, I see you here; and I assume you are here on account of the Haldin affair?"

His manner changed.

"You call it the Haldin affair—do you?" he observed indifferently.

"I have no right to ask you anything," I said. "I wouldn't presume. But in that case the mother and the sister of him who must be a hero in your eyes cannot be indifferent to you. The girl is a frank and generous creature, having the noblest—well—illusions. You will tell her nothing—or you will tell her everything. But speaking now of the object with which I've approached you: first, we have to deal with the morbid state of the mother. Perhaps something could be invented under your authority as a cure for a distracted and suffering soul filled with maternal affection."

His air of weary indifference was accentuated, I could not help thinking, willfully.

"Oh yes. Something might," he mumbled carelessly.

He put his hand over his mouth to conceal a yawn. When he uncovered his lips they were smiling faintly.

"Pardon me. This has been a long conversation, and I have not had much sleep the last two nights."

This unexpected, somewhat insolent sort of apology had the merit of being perfectly true. He had had no nightly rest to speak of since that day when, in the grounds of the Château Borel, the sister of Victor Haldin had appeared before him. The perplexities and the complex terrors—I may say—of this sleeplessness are recorded in the document I was to see later—the document—which is the main source of this narrative. At the moment he looked to me convincingly tired, gone slack all over, like a man who has passed through some sort of crisis.

"I have had a lot of urgent writing to do," he added.

I rose from my chair at once, and he followed my example, without haste, a little heavily.

"I must apologize for detaining you so long," I said.

"Why apologize? One can't very well go to bed before night. And you did not detain me. I could have left you at any time."

I had not stayed with him to be offended.

"I am glad you have been sufficiently interested," I said calmly. "No merit of mine, though—the commonest sort of regard for the mother of your friend was enough. . . . As to Miss Haldin herself, she at one time was disposed to think that her brother had been betrayed to the police in some way."

To my great surprise Mr. Razumov sat down again suddenly. I stared at him, and I must say that he returned my stare without winking for quite a considerable time.

"In some way," he mumbled, as if he had not understood or could not believe his ears.

"Some unforeseen event, a sheer accident might have done that," I went on. "Or, as she characteristically put it to me, the folly or weakness of some unhappy fellow-revolutionist."

"Folly or weakness," he repeated bitterly.

"She is a very generous creature," I observed after a time. The man admired by Victor Haldin fixed his eyes on the ground. I turned away and moved off, apparently unnoticed by him. I nourished no resentment of the moody bruskness with which he had treated me. The sentiment I was carrying away from that conversation was that of hopelessness. Before I had got fairly clear of the raft of chairs and tables he had rejoined me.

"H'm, yes!" I heard him at my elbow again. "But what do you think?"

I did not even look round.

"I think that you people are under a curse."

He made no sound. It was only on the pavement outside the gate that I heard him again.

"I should like to walk with you a little."

After all, I preferred this enigmatical young man to his celebrated compatriot, the great Peter Ivanovitch. But I saw no reason for being particularly gracious.

"I am going now to the railway station, by the shortest way from here, to meet a friend from England," I said, for all answer to his unexpected proposal. I hoped that something informing could come of it. As we stood on the curbstone waiting for a tramcar to pass, he remarked gloomily:

"I like what you said just now."

"Do you?"

We stepped off the pavement together.

"The great problem," he went on, "is to understand thoroughly the nature of the curse."

"That's not very difficult, I think."

"I think so too," he agreed with me, and his readiness, strangely enough, did not make him less enigmatical in the least.

"A curse is an evil spell," I tried him again.

"And the important, the great, problem is to find the means to break it."

"Yes. To find the means."

That was also an assent, but he seemed to be thinking of something else. We had crossed diagonally the open space before the theater, and began to descend a broad, sparely frequented street in the direction of one of the smaller bridges. He kept on by my side without speaking for a long time.

"You are not thinking of leaving Geneva soon?" I asked.

He was silent for so long that I began to think I had been indiscreet, and should get no answer at all. Yet on looking at him I almost believed that my question had caused him something in the nature of positive anguish. I detected it mainly in the clasping of his hands, in which he put a great force stealthily. Once, however, he had overcome that sort of agonizing hesitation sufficiently to tell me that he had no such intention, he became rather communicative—at least relatively to the former offhand curtness of his speeches. The tone, too, was more amiable. He informed me that he intended to study and also to write. He went even so far as to tell me he had been to Stuttgart. Stuttgart, I was aware, was one of the revolutionary centers. The directing committee of one of the Russian parties (I can't tell now which) was located in that town. It was there that he got into touch with the active work of the revolutionists outside Russia.

"I have never been abroad before," he explained, in a rather inanimate voice now. Then, after a slight hesitation, altogether different from the agonizing irresolution my first simple question "whether he meant to stay in Geneva" had aroused, he made me an unexpected confidence:

"The fact is, I have received a sort of mission from them."

"Which will keep you here in Geneva?"

"Yes. Here. In this odious . . ."

I was satisfied with my faculty for putting two and two together when I drew the inference that the mission had something to do with the person of the great Peter Ivanovitch. But I kept that surmise to myself naturally, and Mr. Razumov said nothing more for some considerable time. It was only when we were nearly on the bridge we had been making for that he opened his lips again abruptly:

"Could I see that precious article anywhere?"

I had to think for a moment before I saw what he was referring to.

"It has been reproduced in parts by the Press here. There are files to be seen in various places. My copy of the English newspaper I left with Miss Haldin, I remember, on the day after it reached me. I was sufficiently worried by seeing it lying on a table by the side of the poor mother's chair for weeks. Then it disappeared. It was a relief, I assure you."

He had stopped short.

"I trust," I continued, "that you will find time to see these ladies fairly often— that you will make time."

He stared at me so queerly that I hardly knew how to define his aspect. I could not understand it in this connection at all. What ailed him? I asked myself. What strange thought had come into his head? What vision of all the horrors that can be seen in his hopeless country had come suddenly to haunt his brain? If it were anything connected with the fate of Victor Haldin, then I hoped earnestly he would keep it to himself forever. I was, to speak plainly, so shocked that I tried to conceal my impression by—Heaven forgive me—a smile and the assumption of a light manner.

"Surely," I exclaimed, "that needn't cost you a great effort."

He turned away from me and leaned over the parapet of the bridge. For a moment I waited, looking at his back. And yet, I assure you, I was not anxious just then to look at his face again. He did not move at all. He did not mean to move. I walked on slowly on my way towards the station, and at the end of the bridge I glanced over my shoulder. No, he had not moved. He hung well over the parapet, as if captivated by the smooth rush of the blue water under the arch. The current there is swift, extremely swift; it makes some people dizzy; I myself can never look at it for any length of time without experiencing a dread of being suddenly snatched away by its destructive force. Some brains cannot resist the suggestion of irresistible power and of headlong motion.

It apparently had a charm for Mr. Razumov. I left him hanging far over the parapet of the bridge. The way he had behaved to me could not be put down to mere boorishness. There was something else under his scorn and impatience. Perhaps, I thought, with sudden approach to hidden truth, it was the same thing which had kept him over a week, nearly ten days indeed, from coming near Miss Haldin. But what it was I could not tell.

PART THIRD

I

The water under the bridge ran violent and deep. Its slightly undulating rush seemed capable of scouring out a channel for itself through solid granite while you looked. But had it flowed through Razumov's breast, it could not have washed away the accumulated bitterness the wrecking of his life had deposited there.

"What is the meaning of all this?" he thought, staring downwards at the headlong flow so smooth and clean that only the passage of a faint air bubble, or a thin vanishing streak of foam like a white hair, disclosed its vertiginous rapidity, its terrible force. "Why has that meddlesome old Englishman blundered against me? And what is this silly tale of a crazy old woman?"

He was trying to think brutally on purpose, but he avoided any mental reference to the young girl. "A crazy old woman," he repeated to himself. "It is a fatality! Or ought I to despise all this as absurd? But no! I am wrong! I can't afford to despise anything. An absurdity may be the starting point of the most dangerous complications. How is one to guard against it? It puts to rout one's intelligence. The more intelligent one is, the less one suspects an absurdity."

A wave of wrath choked his thoughts for a moment. It even made his body leaning over the parapet quiver; then he resumed his silent thinking, like a secret dialogue with himself. And even in that privacy, his thought had some reservations of which he was vaguely conscious.

"After all, this is not absurd. It is insignificant. It is absolutely insignificant—absolutely. The craze of an old woman—the fussy officiousness of a blundering elderly Englishman. What devil put him in the way? Haven't I treated him cavalierly enough? Haven't I just? That's the way to treat these meddlesome persons. Is it possible that he still stands behind my back, waiting?"

Razumov felt a faint chill run down his spine. It was not fear. He was certain that it was not fear—not fear for himself—but it was, all the same, a sort of apprehension as if for another, for someone he knew without being able to put a name on the personality. But the recollection that the officious Englishman had a train to meet tranquilized him for a time. It was too stupid to suppose that he should be wasting his time in waiting. It was unnecessary to look round and make sure.

But what did the man mean by his extraordinary rigmarole about the newspaper, and that crazy old woman? he thought suddenly. It was a damnable presumption, anyhow, something that only an Englishman could be capable of. All this was a sort of sport for him—the sport of revolution—a game to look at from the height of his superiority. And what on earth did he mean by his exclamation, "Won't the truth do?"

Razumov pressed his folded arms to the stone coping over which he was leaning with force. "Won't the truth do? The truth for the crazy old mother of the——"

The young man shuddered again. Yes. The truth would do! Apparently it would do. Exactly. And receive thanks, he thought, formulating the unspoken words cynically. "Fall on my neck in gratitude, no doubt," he jeered mentally. But this mood abandoned him at once. He felt sad, as if his heart had become empty suddenly. "Well, I must be cautious," he concluded, coming to himself as though his brain had been awakened from a trance. "There is nothing, no one, too insignificant, too absurd to be disregarded," he thought wearily. "I must be cautious."

Razumov pushed himself with his hand away from the balustrade, and, retracing his steps along the bridge, walked straight to his lodgings, where, for a few days, he led a solitary and retired existence. He neglected Peter Ivanovitch, to whom he was accredited by the Stuttgart group; he never went near the refugee revolutionists, to whom he had been introduced on his arrival. He kept out of that world altogether. And he felt that such conduct, causing surprise and arousing suspicion, contained an element of danger for himself.

This is not to say that during these few days he never went out. I met him several times in the streets, but he gave me no recognition. Once, going home after an evening call on the ladies Haldin, I saw him crossing the dark roadway of the Boulevard des Philosophes. He had a broad-brimmed soft hat, and the collar of his coat turned up. I watched him make straight for the house, but, instead of going in, he stopped opposite the still lighted windows, and after a time went away down a side-street.

I knew that he had not been to see Mrs. Haldin yet. Miss Haldin told me he was reluctant; moreover, the mental condition of Mrs. Haldin had changed. She seemed to think now that her son was living, and she perhaps awaited his arrival. Her immobility in the great armchair in front of the window had an air of expectancy, even when the blind was down and the lamps lighted.

For my part, I was convinced that she had received her death-stroke; Miss Haldin, to whom, of course, I said nothing of my forebodings, thought that no good would come from introducing Mr. Razumov just then, an opinion which I shared fully. I knew that she met the young man on the Bastions. Once or twice I saw them strolling slowly up the main alley. They met every day for weeks. I avoided passing that way during the hour when Miss Haldin took her exercise there. One day, however, in a fit of absent-mindedness, I entered the gates and came upon her walking alone. I stopped to exchange a few words. Mr. Razumov failed to turn up, and we began to talk about him—naturally.

"Did he tell you anything definite about your brother's activities—his end?" I ventured to ask.

"No," admitted Miss Haldin, with some hesitation. "Nothing definite."

I understood well enough that all their conversations must have been referred mentally to that dead man who had brought them together. That was unavoidable. But it was in the living man that she was interested. That was unavoidable too, I suppose. And as I pushed my inquiries I discovered that he had disclosed himself to her as a by no means conventional revolutionist, contemptuous of catchwords, of theories, of men too. I was rather pleased at that—but I was a little puzzled.

"His mind goes forward, far ahead of the struggle," Miss Haldin explained. "Of course, he is an actual worker too," she added.

"And do you understand him?" I inquired point-blank.

She hesitated again. "Not altogether," she murmured.

I perceived that he had fascinated her by an assumption of mysterious reserve.

"Do you know what I think?" she went on, breaking through her reserved, almost reluctant attitude: "I think that he is observing, studying me, to discover whether I am worthy of his trust."

"And that pleases you?"

She kept mysteriously silent for a moment. Then with energy, but in a confidential tone:

"I am convinced," she declared, "that this extraordinary man is meditating some vast plan, some great undertaking; he is possessed by it—he suffers from it—and from being alone in the world."

"And so he's looking for helpers?" I commented, turning away my head.

Again there was a silence.

"Why not?" she said at last.

The dead brother, the dying mother, the foreign friend, had fallen into a distant background. But, at the same time, Peter Ivanovitch was absolutely nowhere now. And this thought consoled me. Yet I saw the gigantic shadow of Russian life deepening around her like the darkness of an advancing night. It would devour her presently. I inquired after Mrs. Haldin—that other victim of the deadly shade.

A remorseful uneasiness appeared in her frank eyes. Mother seemed no worse, but if I only knew what strange fancies she had sometimes! Then Miss Haldin, glancing at her watch, declared that she could not stay a moment longer, and with a hasty handshake ran off lightly.

Decidedly, Mr. Razumov was not to turn up that day. Incomprehensible youth! . . .

But less than an hour afterwards, while crossing the Place Mollard, I caught sight of him boarding a South Shore tramcar.

"He's going to the Château Borel," I thought.

•   •   •   •   •   •   •   •

After depositing Razumov at the gates of the Château Borel, some half a mile or so from the town, the car continued its journey between two straight lines of shady trees. Across the roadway in the sunshine a short wooden pier jutted into the shallow pale water, which farther out had an intense blue tint contrasting unpleasantly with the green orderly slopes on the opposite shore. The whole view, with the harbor jetties of white stone underlining lividly the dark front of the town to the left, and the expanding space of water to the right with jutting promontories of no particular character, had the uninspiring, glittering quality of a very fresh oleograph. Razumov turned his back on it with contempt. He thought it odious—oppressively odious—in its unsuggestive finish: the very perfection of mediocrity attained at last after centuries of toil and culture. And turning his back on it, he faced the entrance to the grounds of the Château Borel.

The bars of the central way and the wrought-iron arch between the dark weather-stained stone piers were very rusty; and, though fresh tracks of wheels ran under it, the gate looked as if it had not been opened for a very long time. But close against the lodge, built of the same gray stone as the piers (its windows were all boarded up), there was a small side entrance. The bars of that were rusty too; it stood ajar and looked as though it had not been closed for a long time. In fact, Razumov, trying to push it open a little wider, discovered it was immovable.

"Democratic virtue. There are no thieves here apparently," he muttered to himself, with displeasure. Before advancing into the grounds he looked back sourly at an idle working man lounging on a bench in the clean, broad avenue. The fellow had thrown his feet up; one of his arms hung over the low back of the public seat; he was taking a day off in lordly repose, as if everything in sight belonged to him.

"Elector! Eligible! Enlightened!" Razumov muttered to himself. "A brute, all the same."

Razumov entered the grounds and walked fast up the wide sweep of the drive, trying to think of nothing—to rest his head, to rest his emotions too. But arriving at the foot of the terrace before the house he faltered, affected physically by some invisible interference. The mysteriousness of his quickened heartbeats startled him. He stopped short and looked at the brick wall of the terrace, faced with shallow arches, meagerly clothed by a few unthriving creepers, with an ill-kept narrow flower bed along its foot.

"It is here!" he thought, with a sort of awe. "It is here—on this very spot . . ."

He was tempted to flight at the mere recollection of his first meeting with Nathalie Haldin. He confessed it to himself; but he did not move, and that not because he wished to resist an unworthy weakness, but because he knew that he had no place to fly to. Moreover, he could not leave Geneva. He recognized, even without thinking, that it was impossible. It would have been a fatal admission, an act of moral suicide. It would have been also physically dangerous. Slowly he ascended the stairs of the terrace, flanked by two stained greenish stone urns of funereal aspect.

Across the broad platform, where a few blades of grass sprouted on the discolored gravel, the door of the house, with its ground-floor windows shuttered, faced him, wide open. He believed that his approach had been noted, because, framed in the doorway, without his tall hat, Peter Ivanovitch seemed to be waiting for his approach.

The ceremonious black frock coat and the bared head of Europe's greatest feminist accentuated the dubiousness of his status in the house rented by Madame de S——, his Egeria. His aspect combined the formality of the caller with the freedom of the proprietor. Florid and bearded and masked by the dark blue glasses, he met the visitor, and at once took him familiarly under the arm.

Razumov suppressed every sign of repugnance by an effort which the constant necessity of prudence had rendered almost mechanical. And this necessity had settled his expression in a cast of austere, almost fanatical, aloofness. The "heroic fugitive," impressed afresh by the severe detachment of this new arrival from revolutionary Russia, took a conciliatory, even a confidential tone. Madame de S—— was resting after a bad night. She often had bad nights. He had left his hat upstairs on the landing and had come down to suggest to his young friend a stroll and a good openhearted talk in one of the shady alleys behind the house. After voicing this proposal, the great man glanced at the unmoved face by his side, and could not restrain himself from exclaiming:

"On my word, young man, you are an extraordinary person."

"I fancy you are mistaken, Peter Ivanovitch. If I were really an extraordinary person, I would not be here, walking with you in a garden in Switzerland, Canton of Geneva, Commune of—what's the name of the Commune this place belongs to? . . . Never mind—the heart of democracy, anyhow. A fit heart for it; no bigger than a parched pea and about as much value. I am no more extraordinary than the rest of us Russians wandering abroad."

But Peter Ivanovitch dissented emphatically:

"No, no! You are not ordinary. I have some experience of Russians who are—well—living abroad. You appear to me, and to others too, a marked personality."

"What does he mean by this?" Razumov asked himself, turning his eyes fully on his companion. The face of Peter Ivanovitch expressed a meditative seriousness.

"You don't suppose, Kirylo Sidorovitch, that I have not heard of you from various points where you made yourself known on your way here? I have had letters."

"Oh, we are great in talking about each other," interjected Razumov, who had listened with great attention. "Gossip, tales, suspicions, and all that sort of thing, we know how to deal in to perfection. Calumny, even."

In indulging in this sally, Razumov managed very well to conceal the feeling of anxiety which had come over him. At the same time he was saying to himself that there could be no earthly reason for anxiety. He was relieved by the evident sincerity of the protesting voice.

"Heavens!" cried Peter Ivanovitch. "What are you talking about? What reason can *you* have to . . . ?"

The great exile flung up his arms as if words had failed him in sober truth. Razumov was satisfied. Yet he was moved to continue in the same vein.

"I am talking of the poisonous plants which flourish in the world of conspirators, like evil mushrooms in a dark cellar."

"You are casting aspersions," remonstrated Peter Ivanovitch, "which as far as you are concerned——"

"No!" Razumov interrupted without heat. "Indeed, I don't want to cast aspersions, but it's just as well to have no illusions."

Peter Ivanovitch gave him an inscrutable glance of his dark spectacles, accompanied by a faint smile.

"The man who says that he has no illusions has at least that one," he said, in a very friendly tone. "But I see how it is, Kirylo Sidorovitch. You aim at stoicism."

"Stoicism! That's a pose of the Greeks and the Romans. Let's leave it to them. We are Russians, that is—children; that is—sincere; that is—cynical, if you like. But that's not a pose."

A long silence ensued. They strolled slowly under the lime trees. Peter Ivanovitch had put his hands behind his back. Razumov felt the ungraveled ground of the deeply shaded walk damp and as if slippery under his feet. He asked himself, with uneasiness, if he were saying the right things. The direction of the conversation ought to have been more under his control, he reflected. The great man appeared to be reflecting on his side too. He cleared his throat slightly, and Razumov felt at once a painful reawakening of scorn and fear.

"I am astonished," began Peter Ivanovitch gently. "Supposing you are right in your indictment, how can you raise any question of calumny or gossip, in your case? It is unreasonable. The fact is, Kirylo Sidorovitch, there is not enough

known of you to give hold to gossip or even calumny. Just now you are a man associated with a great deed, which had been hoped for, and tried for too, without success. People have perished for attempting that which you and Haldin have done at
last. You come to us out of Russia with that prestige. But you cannot deny that you
have not been communicative, Kirylo Sidorovitch. People you have met imparted
their impressions to me; one wrote this, another that, but I form my own opinions.
I waited to see you first. You are a man out of the common. That's positively so.
You are close, very close. This taciturnity, this severe brow, this something inflexible and secret in you, inspires hopes and a little wonder as to what you may mean.
There is something of a Brutus . . ."

"Pray spare me those classical allusions!" burst out Razumov nervously. "What
comes Junius Brutus to do here? It is ridiculous! Do you mean to say," he added
sarcastically, but lowering his voice, "that the Russian revolutionists are all patricians and that I am an aristocrat?"

Peter Ivanovitch, who had been helping himself with a few gestures, clasped
his hands again behind his back and made a few steps, pondering.

"Not *all* patricians," he muttered at last. "But you, at any rate, are one of *us*."

Razumov smiled bitterly.

"To be sure my name is not Gugenheimer," he said in a sneering tone. "I am not
a democratic Jew. How can I help it? Not everybody has such luck. I have no
name, I have no . . ."

The European celebrity showed a great concern. He stepped back a pace and
his arms flew in front of his person, extended, deprecatory, almost entreating. His
deep bass voice was full of pain.

"But, my dear young friend!" he cried. "My dear Kirylo Sidorovitch . . ."

Razumov shook his head.

"The very patronymic you are so civil as to use when addressing me I have no
legal right to—but what of that? I don't wish to claim it. I have no father. So much
the better. But I will tell you what: my mother's grandfather was a peasant—a
serf. See how much I am one of *you*. I don't want anyone to claim me. But Russia
can't disown me. She cannot!"

Razumov struck his breast with his fist. "I am *it!*"

Peter Ivanovitch walked on slowly, his head lowered. Razumov followed, vexed
with himself. That was not the right sort of talk. All sincerity was an imprudence.
Yet one could not renounce truth altogether, he thought, with despair. Peter
Ivanovitch, meditating behind his dark glasses, became to him suddenly so odious that if he had had a knife, he fancied he could have stabbed him not only
without compunction, but with a horrible, triumphant satisfaction. His imagination dwelt on that atrocity in spite of himself. It was as if he were becoming light-
headed. "It is not what is expected of me," he repeated to himself. "It is not what

is—I could get away by breaking the fastening on the little gate I see there in the back wall. It is a flimsy lock. Nobody in the house seems to know he is here with me. Oh yes. The hat! These women would discover presently the hat he has left on the landing. They would come upon him, lying dead in this damp, gloomy shade—but I would be gone and no one could ever . . . Lord! Am I going mad?" he asked himself in a fright.

The great man was heard—musing in an undertone.

"H'm, yes! That—no doubt—in a certain sense . . ." He raised his voice. "There is a deal of pride about you . . ."

The intonation of Peter Ivanovitch took on a homely, familiar ring, acknowledging, in a way, Razumov's claim to peasant descent.

"A great deal of pride, brother Kirylo. And I don't say that you have no justification for it. I have admitted you had. I have ventured to allude to the facts of your birth simply because I attach no mean importance to it. You are one of us—*un des nôtres*. I reflect on that with satisfaction."

"I attach some importance to it also," said Razumov quietly. "I won't even deny that it may have some importance for you too," he continued, after a slight pause and with a touch of grimness of which he was himself aware, with some annoyance. He hoped it had escaped the perception of Peter Ivanovitch. "But suppose we talk no more about it?"

"Well, we shall not—not after this one time, Kirylo Sidorovitch," persisted the noble archpriest of revolution. "This shall be the last occasion. You cannot believe for a moment that I had the slightest idea of wounding your feelings. You are clearly a superior nature—that's how I read you. Quite above the common—h'm—susceptibilities. But the fact is, Kirylo Sidorovitch, I don't know your susceptibilities. Nobody, out of Russia, knows much of you—as yet!"

"You have been watching me?" suggested Razumov.

"Yes."

The great man had spoken in a tone of perfect frankness, but as they turned their faces to each other Razumov felt baffled by the dark spectacles. Under their cover, Peter Ivanovitch hinted that he had felt for some time the need of meeting a man of energy and character, in view of a certain project. He said nothing more precise, however; and after some critical remarks upon the personalities of the various members of the committee of revolutionary action in Stuttgart, he let the conversation lapse for quite a long while. They paced the alley from end to end. Razumov, silent too, raised his eyes from time to time to cast a glance at the back of the house. It offered no sign of being inhabited. With its grimy, weather-stained walls and all the windows shuttered from top to bottom, it looked damp and gloomy and deserted. It might very well have been haunted in traditional style by some doleful, groaning, futile ghost of a middle-class order. The shades evoked, as worldly rumor had it, by Madame de S—— to meet statesmen, diplomatists, deputies of various European Parliaments, must have been of another sort. Razumov had never seen Madame de S—— but in the carriage.

Peter Ivanovitch came out of his abstraction.

"Two things I may say to you at once. I believe, first, that neither a leader nor any decisive action can come out of the dregs of a people. Now, if you ask me what are the dregs of a people—h'm—it would take too long to tell. You would be surprised at the variety of ingredients that for me go to the making up of these dregs—of that which ought, *must* remain at the bottom. Moreover, such a statement might be subject to discussion. But I can tell you what is *not* the dregs. On that it is impossible for us to disagree. The peasantry of a people is not the dregs; neither is its highest class—well—the nobility. Reflect on that, Kirylo Sidorovitch! I believe you are well fitted for reflection. Everything in a people that is not genuine, not its own by origin or development, is—well—dirt! Intelligence in the wrong place is that. Foreign-bred doctrines are that. Dirt! Dregs! The second thing I would offer to your meditation is this: that for us at this moment there yawns a chasm between the past and the future. It can never be bridged by foreign liberalism. All attempts at it are either folly or cheating. Bridged it can never be! It has to be filled up."

A sort of sinister jocularity had crept into the tones of the burly feminist. He seized Razumov's arm above the elbow, and gave it a slight shake.

"Do you understand, enigmatical young man? It has got to be just filled up."

Razumov kept an unmoved countenance.

"Don't you think that I have already gone beyond meditation on that subject?" he said, freeing his arm by a quiet movement which increased the distance a little between himself and Peter Ivanovitch, as they went on strolling abreast. And he added that surely whole cartloads of words and theories could never fill that chasm. No meditation was necessary. A sacrifice of many lives could alone—— He fell silent without finishing the phrase.

Peter Ivanovitch inclined his big hairy head slowly. After a moment he proposed that they should go and see if Madame de S—— was now visible.

"We shall get some tea," he said, turning out of the shaded gloomy walk with a brisker step.

The lady companion had been on the look out. Her dark skirt whisked into the doorway as the two men came in sight round the corner. She ran off somewhere altogether, and had disappeared when they entered the hall. In the crude light falling from the dusty glass skylight upon the black-and-white tessellated floor, covered with muddy tracks, their footsteps echoed faintly. The great feminist led the way up the stairs. On the balustrade of the first-floor landing a shiny tall hat reposed, rim upwards, opposite the double door of the drawing room, haunted, it

was said, by evoked ghosts, and frequented, it was to be supposed, by fugitive revolutionists. The cracked white paint of the panels, the tarnished gilt of the mold-
ings, permitted one to imagine nothing but dust and emptiness within. Before
turning the massive brass handle, Peter Ivanovitch gave his young companion a
sharp, partly critical, partly preparatory glance.

"No one is perfect," he murmured discreetly. Thus, the possessor of a rare jewel
might, before opening the casket, warn the profane that no gem perhaps is flaw-
less.

He remained with his hand on the door handle so long that Razumov assented
by a moody "No."

"Perfection itself would not produce that effect," pursued Peter Ivanovitch, "in
a world not meant for it. But you shall find there a mind—no!—the quintessence
of feminine intuition which will understand any perplexity you may be suffering
from by the irresistible, enlightening force of sympathy. Nothing can remain
obscure before that—that—inspired, yes, inspired penetration, this true light of
femininity."

The gaze of the dark spectacles in its glossy steadfastness gave his face an
air of absolute conviction. Razumov felt a momentary shrinking before that
closed door.

"Penetration? Light?" he stammered out. "Do you mean some sort of
thought-reading?"

Peter Ivanovitch seemed shocked.

"I mean something utterly different," he retorted, with a faint, pitying smile.

Razumov began to feel angry, very much against his wish.

"This is very mysterious," he muttered through his teeth.

"You don't object to being understood, to being guided?" queried the great
feminist.

Razumov exploded in a fierce whisper:

"In what sense? Be pleased to understand that I am a serious person. Who do
you take me for?"

They looked at each other very closely. Razumov's temper was cooled by the
impenetrable earnestness of the blue glasses meeting his stare. Peter Ivanovitch
turned the handle at last.

"You shall know directly," he said, pushing the door open.

A low-pitched grating voice was heard within the room:

"*Enfin. Vous voilà.*"

In the doorway, his black-coated bulk blocking the view, Peter Ivanovitch
boomed in a hearty tone with something boastful in it.

"Yes. Here I am!"

He glanced over his shoulder at Razumov, who waited for him to move on.

"And I am bringing you a proved conspirator—a real one this time. *Un vrai celui-là.*"

This pause in the doorway gave the "proved conspirator" time to make sure that his face did not betray his angry curiosity and his mental disgust.

These sentiments stand confessed in Mr. Razumov's memorandum of his first interview with Madame de S——. The very words I used in my narrative are written where their sincerity cannot be suspected. The record, which could not have been meant for anyone's eyes but his own, was not, I think, the outcome of that strange impulse of indiscretion common to men who lead secret lives, and accounting for the invariable existence of "compromising documents" in all the plots and conspiracies of history. Mr. Razumov looked at it, I suppose, as a man looks at himself in a mirror, with wonder, perhaps with anguish, with anger or despair. Yes, as a threatened man may look fearfully at his own face in the glass, formulating to himself reassuring excuses for his appearance marked by the taint of some insidious hereditary disease.

II

The Egeria of the "Russian Mazzini" produced, at first view, a strong effect by the death-like immobility of an obviously painted face. The eyes appeared extraordinarily brilliant. The figure, in a closefitting dress, admirably made, but by no means fresh, had an elegant stiffness. The rasping voice inviting him to sit down; the rigidity of the upright attitude with one arm extended along the back of the sofa, the white gleam of the big eyeballs setting off the black, fathomless stare of the enlarged pupils, impressed Razumov more than anything he had seen since his hasty and secret departure from St. Petersburg. A witch in Parisian clothes, he thought. A portent! He actually hesitated in his advance, and did not even comprehend, at first, what the rasping voice was saying.

"Sit down. Draw your chair nearer me. There——"

He sat down. At close quarters the rouged cheekbones, the wrinkles, the fine lines on each side of the vivid lips, astounded him. He was being received graciously, with a smile which made him think of a grinning skull.

"We have been hearing about you for some time."

He did not know what to say, and murmured some disconnected words. The grinning-skull effect vanished.

"And do you know that the general complaint is that you have shown yourself very reserved everywhere?"

Razumov remained silent for a time, thinking of his answer.

"I, don't you see, am a man of action," he said huskily, glancing upwards.

Peter Ivanovitch stood in portentous expectant silence by the side of his chair. A slight feeling of nausea came over Razumov. What could be the relations of these two people to each other? She like a galvanized corpse out of some Hoffmann's Tale; he the preacher of feminist gospel for all the world, and a super-revolutionist besides! This ancient, painted mummy with unfathomable eyes, and this burly, bull-necked, deferential . . . what was it? Witchcraft, fascination. . . . "It's for her money," he thought. "She has millions!"

The walls, the floor of the room were bare like a barn. The few pieces of furniture had been discovered in the garrets and dragged down into service without even having been properly dusted. It was the refuse the banker's widow had left behind her. The windows without curtains had an indigent, sleepless look. In two of them the dirty yellowy-white blinds had been pulled down. All this spoke, not of poverty, but of sordid penuriousness.

The hoarse voice on the sofa uttered angrily:

"You are looking round, Kirylo Sidorovitch. I have been shamefully robbed, positively ruined."

A rattling laugh, which seemed beyond her control, interrupted her for a moment.

"A slavish nature would find consolation in the fact that the principal robber was an exalted and almost a sacrosanct person—a Grand Duke, in fact. Do you understand, Mr. Razumov? A Grand Duke—No! You have no idea what thieves those people are! Downright thieves!"

Her bosom heaved, but her left arm remained rigidly extended along the back of the couch.

"You will only upset yourself," breathed out a deep voice, which, to Razumov's startled glance, seemed to proceed from under the steady spectacles of Peter Ivanovitch, rather than from his lips, which had hardly moved.

"What of that? I say thieves! *Voleurs! Voleurs!*"

Razumov was quite confounded by this unexpected clamor, which had in it something of wailing and croaking, and more than a suspicion of hysteria.

"*Voleurs! Voleurs! Vol . . .*"

"No power on earth can rob you of your genius," shouted Peter Ivanovitch in an overpowering bass, but without stirring, without a gesture of any kind. A profound silence fell.

Razumov remained outwardly impassive. "What is the meaning of this performance?" he was asking himself. But with a preliminary sound of bumping outside some door behind him, the lady companion, in a threadbare black skirt and frayed blouse, came in rapidly, walking on her heels, and carrying in both hands a big Russian samovar, obviously too heavy for her. Razumov made an instinctive movement to help, which startled her so much that she nearly dropped her hissing burden. She managed, however, to land it on the table, and looked so frightened that Razumov hastened to sit down. She produced then, from an adjacent room, four glass tumblers, a teapot, and a sugar-basin, on a black iron tray.

The rasping voice asked from the sofa abruptly:

"*Les gâteaux*? Have you remembered to bring the cakes?"

Peter Ivanovitch, without a word, marched out on to the landing and returned instantly with a parcel wrapped up in white glazed paper, which he must have extracted from the interior of his hat. With imperturbable gravity he undid the string and smoothed the paper open on a part of the table within reach of Madame de S——'s hand. The lady companion poured out the tea, then retired into a distant corner out of everybody's sight. From time to time Madame de S—— extended a clawlike hand, glittering with costly rings, towards the paper of cakes, took up one and devoured it, displaying her big false teeth ghoulishly. Meantime she talked in a hoarse tone of the political situation in the Balkans. She built great hopes on some complication in the peninsula for arousing a great movement of national indignation in Russia against "these thieves—thieves—thieves!"

"You will only upset yourself," Peter Ivanovitch interposed, raising his glassy gaze. He smoked cigarettes and drank tea in silence, continuously. When he had finished a glass, he flourished his hand above his shoulder. At that signal the lady companion, ensconced in her corner, with round eyes like a watchful animal, would dart out to the table and pour him out another tumblerful.

Razumov looked at her once or twice. She was anxious, tremulous, though neither Madame de S—— nor Peter Ivanovitch paid the slightest attention to her. "What have they done between them to that forlorn creature?" Razumov asked himself. "Have they terrified her out of her senses with ghosts, or simply have they only been beating her?" When she gave him his second glass of tea, he noticed that her lips trembled in the manner of a scared person about to burst into speech. But, of course, she said nothing, and retired into her corner, as if hugging to herself the smile of thanks he gave her.

"She may be worth cultivating," thought Razumov suddenly.

He was calming down, getting hold of the actuality into which he had been thrown—for the first time perhaps since Victor Haldin had entered his room . . . and had gone out again. He was distinctly aware of being the object of the famous—or notorious—Madame de S——'s ghastly graciousness.

Madame de S—— was pleased to discover that this young man was different from the other types of revolutionist members of committees, secret emissaries, vulgar and unmannerly fugitive professors, rough students, ex-cobblers with apostolic faces, consumptive and ragged enthusiasts, Hebrew youths, common fellows of all sorts that used to come and go around Peter Ivanovitch—fanatics, pedants, proletarians all. It was pleasant to talk to this young man of notably good appearance—for Madame de S—— was not always in a mystical state of mind. Razumov's taciturnity only excited her to a quicker, more voluble utterance. It still dealt with the Balkans. She knew all the statesmen of that region, Turks, Bulgarians, Montenegrins, Romanians, Greeks, Armenians, and nondescripts, young and old, the living and the dead. With some money an intrigue could be started which would set the peninsula in a blaze, and outrage the sentiment of the Russian people. A cry of abandoned brothers could be raised, and then, with the nation seething with indignation, a couple of regiments or so would be enough to begin a military revolution in St. Petersburg and make an end of these thieves. . . .

"Apparently I've got only to sit still and listen," the silent Razumov thought to himself. "As to that hairy and obscene brute" (in such terms did Mr. Razumov refer mentally to the popular expounder of a feministic conception of social state), "as to him, for all his cunning he too shall speak out some day."

Razumov ceased to think for a moment. Then a somber-toned reflection formulated itself in his mind, ironical and bitter. "I have the gift of inspiring confidence." He heard himself laughing aloud. It was like a goad to the painted, shiny-eyed harridan on the sofa.

"You may well laugh!" she cried hoarsely. "What else can one do? Perfect swindlers—and what base swindlers at that! Cheap Germans—Holstein-Gottorps! Though, indeed, it's hardly safe to say who and what they are. A family that counts a creature like Catherine the Great in its ancestry—you understand!"

"You are only upsetting yourself," said Peter Ivanovitch, patiently but in a firm tone. This admonition had its usual effect on the Egeria. She dropped her thick, discolored eyelids and changed her position on the sofa. All her angular and lifeless movements seemed completely automatic now that her eyes were closed. Presently she opened them very full. Peter Ivanovitch drank tea steadily, without haste.

"Well, I declare!" She addressed Razumov directly. "The people who have seen you on your way here are right. You are very reserved. You haven't said twenty words altogether since you came in. You let nothing of your thoughts be seen in your face either."

"I have been listening, Madame," said Razumov, using French for the first time hesitatingly, not being certain of his accent. But it seemed to produce an excellent impression. Madame de S—— looked meaningly into Peter Ivanovitch's spectacles, as if to convey her conviction of this young man's merit. She even nodded the least bit in his direction, and Razumov heard her murmur under her breath the words, "Later on in the diplomatic service," which could not but refer to the favorable impression he had made. The fantastic absurdity of it revolted him; because it seemed to outrage his ruined hopes with the vision of a mock-career. Peter Ivanovitch, impassive as though he were deaf, drank some more tea. Razumov felt that he must say something.

"Yes," he began deliberately, as if uttering a meditated opinion. "Clearly. Even in planning a purely military revolution the temper of the people should be taken into account."

"You have understood me perfectly. The discontent should be spiritualized. That is what the ordinary heads of revolutionary committees will not understand. They are incapable of it. For instance, Mordatiev was in Geneva last month. Peter Ivanovitch brought him here. You know Mordatiev? Well, yes—you have heard of him. They call him an eagle—a hero! He has never done half as much as you have. Never attempted—not half. . . ."

Madame de S—— agitated herself angularly on the sofa.

"We, of course, talked to him. And do you know what he said to me? 'What have we to do with Balkan intrigues? We must simply extirpate the scoundrels.' Extirpate is all very well—but what then? The imbecile! I screamed at him, 'But you must spiritualize—don't you understand?—spiritualize the discontent.'. . ."

She felt nervously in her pocket for a handkerchief; she pressed it to her lips.

"Spiritualize?" said Razumov interrogatively, watching her heaving breast. The long ends of an old black lace scarf she wore over her head slipped off her shoulders and hung down on each side of her ghastly rosy cheeks.

"An odious creature," she burst out again. "Imagine a man who takes five lumps of sugar in his tea. . . . Yes, I said spiritualize! How else can you make discontent effective and universal?"

"Listen to this, young man." Peter Ivanovitch made himself heard solemnly. "Effective and universal."

Razumov looked at him suspiciously.

"Some say hunger will do that," he remarked.

"Yes. I know. Our people are starving in heaps. But you can't make famine universal. And it is not despair that we want to create. There is no moral support to be got out of that. It is indignation . . ."

Madame de S—— let her thin, extended arm sink on her knees.

"I am not a Mordatiev," began Razumov.

"*Bien sûr!*" murmured Madame de S——.

"Though I too am ready to say extirpate, extirpate! But in my ignorance of political work, permit me to ask: A Balkan—well—intrigue, wouldn't that take a very long time?"

Peter Ivanovitch got up and moved off quietly, to stand with his face to the window. Razumov heard a door close; he turned his head and perceived that the lady companion had scuttled out of the room.

"In matters of politics I am a supernaturalist." Madame de S—— broke the silence harshly.

Peter Ivanovitch moved away from the window and struck Razumov lightly on the shoulder. This was a signal for leaving, but at the same time he addressed Madame de S—— in a peculiar reminding tone:

"Eleanor!"

Whatever it meant, she did not seem to hear him. She leaned back in the corner of the sofa like a wooden figure. The immovable peevishness of the face, framed in the limp, rusty lace, had a character of cruelty.

"As to extirpating," she croaked at the attentive Razumov, "there is only one class in Russia which must be extirpated. Only one. And that class consists of only one family. You understand me? That one family must be extirpated."

Her rigidity was frightful, like the rigor of a corpse galvanized into harsh speech and glittering stare by the force of murderous hate. The sight fascinated Razumov—yet he felt more self-possessed than at any other time since he had entered this weirdly bare room. He was interested. But the great feminist by his side again uttered his appeal:

"Eleanor!"

She disregarded it. Her carmine lips vaticinated with an extraordinary rapidity. The liberating spirit would use arms before which rivers would part like Jordan, and ramparts fall down like the walls of Jericho. The deliverance from bondage would be effected by plagues and by signs, by wonders and by war. The women . . .

"Eleanor!"

She ceased; she had heard him at last. She pressed her hand to her forehead.

"What is it? Ah yes! That girl—the sister of . . ."

It was Miss Haldin that she meant. That young girl and her mother had been leading a very retired life. They were provincial ladies—were they not? The mother had been very beautiful—traces were left yet. Peter Ivanovitch, when he called there for the first time, was greatly struck. . . . But the cold way they received him was really surprising.

"He is one of our national glories," Madame de S—— cried out, with sudden vehemence. "All the world listens to him."

"I don't know these ladies," said Razumov loudly, rising from his chair.

"What are you saying, Kirylo Sidorovitch? I understand that she was talking to you here, in the garden, the other day."

"Yes, in the garden," said Razumov gloomily. Then, with an effort, "She made herself known to me."

"And then ran away from us all," Madame de S—— continued, with ghastly vivacity. "After coming to the very door! What a peculiar proceeding! Well, I have been a shy little provincial girl at one time. Yes, Razumov" (she fell into this familiarity intentionally, with an appalling grimace of graciousness. Razumov gave a perceptible start), "yes, that's my origin. A simple provincial family."

"You are a marvel," Peter Ivanovitch uttered in his deepest voice.

But it was to Razumov that she gave her death's-head smile. Her tone was quite imperious.

"You must bring the wild young thing here. She is wanted. I reckon upon your success—mind!"

"She is not a wild young thing," muttered Razumov, in a surly voice.

"Well, then—that's all the same. She may be one of those young conceited democrats. Do you know what I think? I think she is very much like you in character. There is a smoldering fire of scorn in you. You are darkly self-sufficient, but I can see your very soul."

Her shiny eyes had a dry, intense stare, which, missing Razumov, gave him an absurd notion that she was looking at something which was visible to her behind him. He cursed himself for an impressionable fool, and asked with forced calmness:

"What is it you see? Anything resembling me?"

She moved her rigidly set face from left to right negatively.

"Some sort of phantom in my image?" pursued Razumov slowly. "For, I suppose, a soul when it is seen is just that. A vain thing. There are phantoms of the living as well as of the dead."

The tenseness of Madame de S——'s stare had relaxed, and now she looked at Razumov in a silence that became disconcerting.

"I myself have had an experience," he stammered out, as if compelled. "I've seen a phantom once."

The unnaturally red lips moved to frame a question harshly.

"Of a dead person?"

"No. Living."

"A friend?"

"No."

"An enemy?"

"I hated him."

"Ah! It was not a woman, then?"

"A woman!" repeated Razumov, his eyes looking straight into the eyes of Madame de S——. "Why should it have been a woman? And why this conclusion? Why should I not have been able to hate a woman?"

As a matter of fact, the idea of hating a woman was new to him. At that moment he hated Madame de S——. But it was not exactly hate. It was more like the abhorrence that may be caused by a wooden or plaster figure of a repulsive kind. She moved no more than if she were such a figure; even her eyes, whose unwinking stare plunged into his own, though shining, were lifeless, as though they were as artificial as her teeth. For the first time Razumov became aware of a faint perfume, but faint as it was it nauseated him exceedingly. Again Peter Ivanovitch tapped him slightly on the shoulder. Thereupon he bowed, and was about to turn away when he received the unexpected favor of a bony, inanimate hand extended to him, with the two words in hoarse French:

"Au revoir!"

He bowed over the skeleton hand and left the room, escorted by the great man, who made him go out first. The voice from the sofa cried after them:

"You remain here, Pierre."

"Certainly, *ma chère amie*."

But he left the room with Razumov, shutting the door behind him. The landing was prolonged into a bare corridor, right and left, desolate perspectives of white-and-gold decoration without a strip of carpet. The very light, pouring through a large window at the end, seemed dusty; and a solitary speck reposing on the balustrade of white marble—the silk top hat of the great feminist—asserted itself extremely, black and glossy in all that crude whiteness.

Peter Ivanovitch escorted the visitor without opening his lips. Even when they had reached the head of the stairs, Peter Ivanovitch did not break the silence. Razumov's impulse to continue down the flight and out of the house without as much as a nod abandoned him suddenly. He stopped on the first step and leaned his back against the wall. Below him the great hall with its checkered floor of black and white seemed absurdly large and like some public place where a great power of resonance awaits the provocation of footfalls and voices. As if afraid of awakening the loud echoes of that empty house, Razumov adopted a low tone.

"I really have no mind to turn into a dilettante spiritualist."

Peter Ivanovitch shook his head slightly, very serious.

"Or spend my time in spiritual ecstasies or sublime meditations upon the gospel of feminism," continued Razumov. "I made my way here for my share of action—action, most respected Peter Ivanovitch! It was not the great European writer who attracted me, here, to this odious town of liberty. It was somebody much greater. It was the idea of the chief which attracted me. There are starving young men in Russia who believe in you so much that it seems the only thing that keeps them alive in their misery. Think of that, Peter Ivanovitch! No! But only think of that!"

The great man, thus entreated, perfectly motionless and silent, was the very image of patient, placid respectability.

"Of course I don't speak of the people. They are brutes," added Razumov, in the same subdued but forcible tone. At this, a protesting murmur issued from the "heroic fugitive's" beard—a murmur of authority:

"Say—children."

"No! Brutes!" Razumov insisted bluntly.

"But they are sound, they are innocent," the great man pleaded in a whisper.

"As far as that goes, a brute is sound enough." Razumov raised his voice at last. "And you can't deny the natural innocence of a brute. But what's the use of disputing about names? You just try to give these children the power and stature of men and see what they will be like. You just give it to them and see. . . . But never mind. I tell you, Peter Ivanovitch, that half a dozen young men do not come together nowadays in a shabby student's room without your name being whispered, not as a leader of thought, but as a center of revolutionary energies—the center of action. What else has drawn me near you, do you think? It is not what all the world knows of you surely. It's precisely what the world at large does not know. I was irresistibly drawn—let us say impelled, yes, impelled; or, rather, compelled, driven—driven," repeated Razumov loudly, and ceased, as if startled by the hollow reverberation of the word "driven" along two bare corridors and in the great empty hall.

Peter Ivanovitch did not seem startled in the least. The young man could not control a dry, uneasy laugh. The great revolutionist remained unmoved with an effect of commonplace, homely superiority.

"Curse him," said Razumov to himself, "he is waiting behind his spectacles for me to give myself away." Then aloud, with a satanic enjoyment of the scorn prompting him to play with the greatness of the great man:

"Ah, Peter Ivanovitch, if you only knew the force which drew—no, which *drove* me towards you! The irresistible force."

He did not feel any desire to laugh now. This time Peter Ivanovitch moved his head sideways, knowingly, as much as to say, "Don't I?" This expressive movement was almost imperceptible. Razumov went on in secret derision:

"All these days you have been trying to read me, Peter Ivanovitch. That is natural. I have perceived it and I have been frank. Perhaps you may think I have not been very expansive? But with a man like you it was not needed; it would have looked like an impertinence, perhaps. And besides, we Russians are prone to talk too much, as a rule. I have always felt that. And yet, as a nation, we are dumb. I assure you that I am not likely to talk to you so much again—ha, ha!——"

Razumov, still keeping on the lower step, came a little nearer to the great man.

"You have been condescending enough. I quite understood it was to lead me on. You must render me the justice that I have not tried to please. I have been impelled, compelled, or rather sent—let us say sent—towards you for a work that no one but myself can do. You would call it a harmless delusion: a ridiculous delusion at which you don't even smile. It is absurd of me to talk like this, yet some day you will remember these words, I hope. Enough of this. Here I stand before you—confessed! But one thing more I must add to complete it: a mere blind tool I can never consent to be."

Whatever acknowledgment Razumov was prepared for, he was not prepared to have both his hands seized in the great man's grasp. The swiftness of the movement was aggressive enough to startle. The burly feminist could not have been quicker had his purpose been to jerk Razumov treacherously up on the landing and bundle him behind one of the numerous closed doors nearby. This idea actually occurred to Razumov; his hands being released after a darkly eloquent squeeze, he smiled, with a beating heart, straight at the beard and the spectacles hiding that impenetrable man.

He thought to himself (it stands confessed in his handwriting), "I won't move from here till he either speaks or turns away. This is a duel." Many seconds passed without a sign or sound.

"Yes, yes," the great man said hurriedly, in subdued tones, as if the whole thing had been a stolen, breathless interview. "Exactly. Come to see us here in a few days. This must be gone into deeply—deeply, between you and me. Quite to the bottom. To the . . . And, by-the-bye, you must bring along Natalia Victorovna—you know, the Haldin girl . . ."

"Am I to take this as my first instruction from you?" inquired Razumov stiffly.

Peter Ivanovitch seemed perplexed by this new attitude.

"Ah! h'm ! You are naturally the proper person—*la personne indiquée*. Everyone shall be wanted presently. Everyone."

He bent down from the landing over Razumov, who had lowered his eyes.

"The moment of action approaches," he murmured.

Razumov did not look up. He did not move till he heard the door of the drawing room close behind the greatest of feminists returning to his painted Egeria. Then he walked down slowly into the hall. The door stood open, and the shadow of the house was lying aslant over the greatest part of the terrace. While crossing it slowly, he lifted his hat and wiped his damp forehead, expelling his breath with force to get rid of the last vestiges of the air he had been breathing inside. He looked at the palms of his hands, and rubbed them gently against his thighs.

He felt, bizarre as it may seem, as though another self, an independent sharer of his mind, had been able to view his whole person very distinctly indeed. "This is curious," he thought. After a while he formulated his opinion of it in the mental ejaculation: "Beastly!" This disgust vanished before a marked uneasiness. "This is an effect of nervous exhaustion," he reflected with weary sagacity. "How am I to go on day after day if I have no more power of resistance—moral resistance?"

He followed the path at the foot of the terrace. "Moral resistance, moral resistance"; he kept on repeating these words mentally. Moral endurance. Yes, that was the necessity of the situation. An immense longing to make his way out of these grounds and to the other end of the town, of throwing himself on his bed and going to sleep for hours, swept everything clean out of his mind for a moment. "Is it possible that I am but a weak creature after all?" he asked himself, in sudden alarm. "Eh! What's that?"

He gave a start as if awakened from a dream. He even swayed a little before recovering himself.

"Ah! You stole away from us quietly to walk about here," he said.

The lady companion stood before him, but how she came there he had not the slightest idea. Her folded arms were closely cherishing the cat.

"I have been unconscious as I walked, it's a positive fact," said Razumov to himself in wonder. He raised his hat with marked civility.

The sallow woman blushed duskily. She had her invariably scared expression, as if somebody had just disclosed to her some terrible news. But she held her ground, Razumov noticed, without timidity. "She is incredibly shabby," he thought. In the sunlight her black costume looked greenish, with here and there threadbare patches where the stuff seemed decomposed by age into a velvety, black, furry state. Her very hair and eyebrows looked shabby. Razumov wondered whether she were sixty years old. Her figure, though, was young enough. He observed that she did not appear starved, but rather as if she had been fed on unwholesome scraps and leavings of plates.

Razumov smiled amiably and moved out of her way. She turned her head to keep her scared eyes on him.

"I know what you have been told in there," she affirmed, without preliminaries. Her tone, in contrast with her manner, had an unexpectedly assured character which put Razumov at his ease.

"Do you? You must have heard all sorts of talk on many occasions in there."

She varied her phrase, with the same incongruous effect of positiveness.

"I know to a certainty what you have been told to do."

"Really?" Razumov shrugged his shoulders a little. He was about to pass on with a bow, when a sudden thought struck him. "Yes. To be sure! In your confidential position you are aware of many things," he murmured, looking at the cat.

That animal got a momentary convulsive hug from the lady companion.

"Everything was disclosed to me a long time ago," she said.

"Everything," Razumov repeated absently.

"Peter Ivanovitch is an awful despot," she jerked out.

Razumov went on studying the stripes on the gray fur of the cat.

"An iron will is an integral part of such a temperament. How else could he be a leader? And I think that you are mistaken in——"

"There!" she cried. "You tell me that I am mistaken. But I tell you all the same that he cares for no one." She jerked her head up. "Don't you bring that girl here. That's what you have been told to do—to bring that girl here. Listen to me; you had better tie a stone round her neck and throw her into the lake."

Razumov had a sensation of chill and gloom, as if a heavy cloud had passed over the sun.

"The girl?" he said. "What have I to do with her?"

"But you have been told to bring Nathalie Haldin here. Am I not right? Of course I am right. I was not in the room, but I know. I know Peter Ivanovitch sufficiently well. He is a great man. Great men are horrible. Well, that's it. Have nothing to do with her. That's the best you can do, unless you want her to become like me—disillusioned! Disillusioned!"

"Like you," repeated Razumov, glaring at her face, as devoid of all comeliness of feature and complexion as the most miserable beggar is of money. He smiled, still feeling chilly—a peculiar sensation which annoyed him. "Disillusioned as to Peter Ivanovitch! Is that all you have lost?"

She declared, looking frightened, but with immense conviction, "Peter Ivanovitch stands for everything." Then she added, in another tone, "Keep the girl away from this house."

"And are you absolutely inciting me to disobey Peter Ivanovitch just because—because you are disillusioned?"

She began to blink.

"Directly I saw you for the first time I was comforted. You took your hat off to me. You looked as if one could trust you. Oh!"

She shrank before Razumov's savage snarl of, "I have heard something like this before."

She was so confounded that she could do nothing but blink for a long time.

"It was your humane manner," she explained plaintively. "I have been starving for, I won't say kindness, but just for a little civility, for I don't know how long. And now you are angry . . ."

"But no, on the contrary," he protested. "I am very glad you trust me. It's possible that later on I may . . ."

"Yes, if you were to get ill," she interrupted eagerly, "or meet some bitter trouble, you would find I am not a useless fool. You have only to let me know. I will come to you. I will indeed. And I will stick to you. Misery and I are old acquaintances—but this life here is worse than starving."

She paused anxiously, then in a voice for the first time sounding really timid, she added:

"Or if you were engaged in some dangerous work. Sometimes a humble companion—I would not want to know anything. I would follow you with joy. I could carry out orders. I have the courage."

Razumov looked attentively at the scared round eyes, at the withered, sallow, round cheeks. They were quivering about the corners of the mouth.

"She wants to escape from here," he thought.

"Suppose I were to tell you that I am engaged in dangerous work?" he uttered slowly.

She pressed the cat to her threadbare bosom with a breathless exclamation. "Ah!" Then not much above a whisper: "Under Peter Ivanovitch?"

"No, not under Peter Ivanovitch."

He read admiration in her eyes, and made an effort to smile.

"Then—alone?"

He held up his closed hand with the index raised.

"Like this finger," he said.

She was trembling slightly. But it occurred to Razumov that they might have been observed from the house, and he became anxious to be gone. She blinked, raising up to him her puckered face, and seemed to beg mutely to be told something more, to be given a word of encouragement for her starving, grotesque, and pathetic devotion.

"Can we be seen from the house?" asked Razumov confidentially.

She answered, without showing the slightest surprise at the question:

"No, we can't, on account of this end of the stables." And she added, with an acuteness which surprised Razumov, "But anybody looking out of an upstairs window would know that you have not passed through the gates yet."

"Who's likely to spy out of the window?" queried Razumov. "Peter Ivanovitch?"

She nodded.

"Why should he trouble his head?"

"He expects somebody this afternoon."

"You know the person?"

"There's more than one."

She had lowered her eyelids. Razumov looked at her curiously.

"Of course. You hear everything they say."

She murmured without any animosity:

"So do the tables and chairs."

He understood that the bitterness accumulated in the heart of that helpless creature had got into her veins, and, like some subtle poison, had decomposed her fidelity to that hateful pair. It was a great piece of luck for him, he reflected; because women are seldom venal after the manner of men, who can be bought for material considerations. She would be a good ally, though it was not likely that she was allowed to hear as much as the tables and chairs of the Château Borel. That could not be expected. But still . . . And, at any rate, she could be made to talk.

When she looked up, her eyes met the fixed stare of Razumov, who began to speak at once.

"Well, well, dear . . . but, upon my word, I haven't the pleasure of knowing your name yet. Isn't it strange?"

For the first time she made a movement of the shoulders.

"Is it strange? No one is told my name. No one cares. No one talks to me, no one writes to me. My parents don't even know if I'm alive. I have no use for a name, and I have almost forgotten it myself."

Razumov murmured gravely, "Yes, but still . . ."

She went on much slower, with indifference:

"You may call me Tekla, then. My poor Andrei called me so. I was devoted to him. He lived in wretchedness and suffering, and died in misery. That is the lot of all us Russians, nameless Russians. There is nothing else for us, and no hope anywhere, unless . . ."

"Unless what?"

"Unless all these people with names are done away with," she finished, blinking and pursing up her lips.

"It will be easier to call you Tekla, as you direct me," said Razumov, "if you consent to call me Kirylo, when we are talking like this—quietly—only you and me."

And he said to himself, "Here's a being who must be terribly afraid of the world, else she would have run away from this situation before." Then he reflected that the mere fact of leaving the great man abruptly would make her a suspect. She could expect no support or countenance from anyone. This revolutionist was not fit for an independent existence.

She moved with him a few steps, blinking and nursing the cat with a small balancing movement of her arms.

"Yes—only you and I. That's how I was with my poor Andrei, only he was dying, killed by these official brutes—while you! You are strong. You kill the monsters. You have done a great deed. Peter Ivanovitch himself must consider you. Well—don't forget me—especially if you are going back to work in Russia. I could follow you, carrying anything that was wanted—at a distance, you know. Or I could watch for hours at the corner of a street if necessary—in wet or snow—yes, I could—all day long. Or I could write for you dangerous documents, lists of names or instructions, so that in case of mischance the handwriting could not compromise you. And you need not be afraid if they were to catch me. I would know how to keep dumb. We women are not so easily daunted by pain. I heard Peter Ivanovitch say it is our blunt nerves or something. We can stand it better. And it's true; I would just as soon bite my tongue out and throw it at them as not. What's the good of speech to me? Who would ever want to hear what I could say? Ever since I closed the eyes of my poor Andrei I haven't met a man who seemed to care for the sound of my voice. I should never have spoken to you if the very first time you appeared here you had not taken notice of me so nicely. I could not help speaking of you to that charming dear girl. Oh, the sweet creature! And strong! One can see that at once. If you have a heart don't let her set her foot in here. Goodbye!"

Razumov caught her by the arm. Her emotion at being thus seized manifested itself by a short struggle, after which she stood still, not looking at him.

"But you can tell me," he spoke in her ear, "why they—those people in that house there—are so anxious to get hold of her?"

She freed herself to turn upon him, as if made angry by the question.

"Don't you understand that Peter Ivanovitch must direct, inspire, influence? It is the breath of his life. There can never be too many disciples. He can't bear thinking of anyone escaping him. And a woman, too! There is nothing to be done without women, he says. He has written it. He——"

The young man was staring at her passion when she broke off suddenly and ran away behind the stable.

III

Razumov, thus left to himself, took the direction of the gate. But on this day of many conversations, he discovered that very probably he could not leave the grounds without having to hold another one.

Stepping in view from beyond the lodge appeared the expected visitors of Peter Ivanovitch: a small party composed of two men and a woman. They noticed him too, immediately, and stopped short as if to consult. But in a moment the woman, moving aside, motioned with her arm to the two men, who, leaving the drive at once, struck across the large neglected lawn, or rather grassplot, and made directly for the house. The woman remained on the path waiting for Razumov's approach. She had recognized him. He, too, had recognized her at the first glance. He had been made known to her at Zurich, where he had broken his journey while on his way from Dresden. They had been much together for the two days of his stay.

She was wearing the very same costume in which he had seen her first. A blouse of crimson silk made her noticeable at a distance. With that she wore a short brown skirt and a leather belt. Her complexion was the color of coffee and milk, but very clear; her eyes black and glittering, her figure erect. A lot of thick hair, nearly white, was done up loosely under a dusty Tyrolese hat of dark cloth, which seemed to have lost some of its trimmings.

The expression of her face was grave, intent; so grave that Razumov, after approaching her close, felt obliged to smile. She greeted him with a manly handgrasp.

"What! Are you going away?" she exclaimed. "How is that, Razumov?"

"I am going away because I haven't been asked to stay," Razumov answered, returning the pressure of her hand with much less force than she had put into it.

She jerked her head sideways like one who understands. Meantime Razumov's eyes had strayed after the two men. They were crossing the grassplot obliquely, without haste. The shorter of the two was buttoned up in a narrow overcoat of some thin gray material, which came nearly to his heels. His companion, much taller and broader, wore a short, closefitting jacket and tight trousers tucked into shabby top boots.

The woman, who had sent them out of Razumov's way apparently, spoke in a businesslike voice:

"I had to come rushing from Zurich on purpose to meet the train and take these two along here to see Peter Ivanovitch. I've just managed it."

"Ah, indeed!" Razumov said perfunctorily, and very vexed at her staying behind to talk to him. "From Zurich—yes, of course. And these two, they come from . . ."

She interrupted, without emphasis:

"From quite another direction. From a distance, too. A considerable distance."

Razumov shrugged his shoulders. The two men from a distance, after having reached the wall of the terrace, disappeared suddenly at its foot as if the earth had opened to swallow them up.

"Oh, well, they have just come from America." The woman in the crimson blouse shrugged her shoulders too a little before making that statement. "The time is drawing near," she interjected, as if speaking to herself. "I did not tell them who you were. Yakovlitch would have wanted to embrace you."

"Is that he with the wisp of hair hanging from his chin, in the long coat?"

"You've guessed aright. That's Yakovlitch."

"And they could not find their way here from the station without you coming on purpose from Zurich to show it to them? Verily, without women we can do nothing. So it stands written, and apparently so it is."

He was conscious of an immense lassitude under his effort to be sarcastic. And he could see that she had detected it with those steady, brilliant black eyes.

"What is the matter with you?"

"I don't know. Nothing. I've had a devil of a day."

She waited, with her black eyes fixed on his face. Then:

"What of that? You men are so impressionable and self-conscious. One day is like another, hard, hard—and there's an end of it, till the great day comes. I came over for a very good reason. They wrote to warn Peter Ivanovitch of their arrival. But where from? Only from Cherbourg on a bit of ship's notepaper. Anybody could have done that. Yakovlitch has lived for years and years in America. I am the only one at hand who had known him well in the old days. I knew him very well indeed. So Peter Ivanovitch telegraphed, asking me to come. It's natural enough, is it not?"

"You came to vouch for his identity?" inquired Razumov.

"Yes. Something of the kind. Fifteen years of a life like his make changes in a man. Lonely, like a crow in a strange country. When I think of Yakovlitch before he went to America———"

The softness of the low tone caused Razumov to glance at her sideways. She sighed: her black eyes were looking away; she had plunged the fingers of her right hand deep into the mass of nearly white hair, and stirred them there absently. When she withdrew her hand the little hat perched on the top of her head remained slightly tilted, with a queer inquisitive effect, contrasting strongly with the reminiscent murmur that escaped her.

"We were not in our first youth even then. But a man is a child always."

Razumov thought suddenly, "They have been living together." Then aloud:

"Why didn't you follow him to America?" he asked point-blank.

She looked up at him with a perturbed air.

"Don't you remember what was going on fifteen years ago? It was a time of activity. The Revolution has its history by this time. You are in it and yet you don't seem to know it. Yakovlitch went away then on a mission; I went back to Russia. It had to be so. Afterwards there was nothing for him to come back to."

"Ah, indeed!" muttered Razumov, with affected surprise. "Nothing!"

"What are you trying to insinuate?" she exclaimed quickly. "Well, and what then if he did get discouraged a little? . . ."

"He looks like a Yankee, with that goatee hanging from his chin. A regular Uncle Sam," growled Razumov. "Well, and you? You who went to Russia? You did not get discouraged."

"Never mind. Yakovlitch is a man who cannot be doubted. He, at any rate, is the right sort."

Her black, penetrating gaze remained fixed upon Razumov while she spoke, and for a moment afterwards.

"Pardon me," Razumov inquired coldly, "but does it mean that you, for instance, think that I am not the right sort?"

She made no protest, gave no sign of having heard the question; she continued looking at him in a manner which he judged not to be absolutely unfriendly. In Zurich when he passed through she had taken him under her charge, in a way, and was with him from morning till night during his stay of two days. She took him round to see several people. At first she talked to him a great deal and rather unreservedly, but always avoiding all reference to herself; towards the middle of the second day she fell silent, attending him zealously as before, and even seeing him off at the railway station, where she pressed his hand firmly through the lowered carriage window, and, stepping back without a word, waited till the train moved. He had noticed that she was treated with quiet regard. He knew nothing of her parentage, nothing of her private history or political record; he judged her from his own private point of view, as being a distinct danger in his path. "Judged" is not perhaps the right word. It was more of a feeling, the summing up of slight impressions aided by the discovery that he could not despise her as he despised all the others. He had not expected to see her again so soon.

No, decidedly; her expression was not unfriendly. Yet he perceived an acceleration in the beat of his heart. The conversation could not be abandoned at that point. He went on in accents of scrupulous inquiry:

"Is it perhaps because I don't seem to accept blindly every development of the general doctrine—such, for instance, as the feminism of our great Peter Ivanovitch? If that is what makes me suspect, then I can only say I would scorn to be a slave even to an idea."

She had been looking at him all the time, not as a listener looks at one, but as if the words he chose to say were only of secondary interest. When he finished she slipped her hand, by a sudden and decided movement, under his arm and impelled him gently towards the gate of the grounds. He felt her firmness and obeyed the impulsion at once, just as the other two men had, a moment before, obeyed unquestioningly the wave of her hand.

They made a few steps like this.

"No, Razumov, your ideas are probably all right," she said. "You may be valuable—very valuable. What's the matter with you is that you don't like us."

She released him. He met her with a frosty smile.

"Am I expected, then, to have love as well as convictions?"

She shrugged her shoulders.

"You know very well what I mean. People have been thinking you not quite wholehearted. I have heard that opinion from one side and another. But I have understood you at the end of the first day . . ."

Razumov interrupted her, speaking steadily.

"I assure you that your perspicacity is at fault here."

"What phrases he uses!" she exclaimed parenthetically. "Ah! Kirylo Sidorovitch, you, like other men, are fastidious, full of self-love, and afraid of trifles. Moreover, you had no training. What you want is to be taken in hand by some woman. I am sorry I am not staying here a few days. I am going back to Zurich tomorrow, and shall take Yakovlitch with me most likely."

This information relieved Razumov.

"I am sorry too," he said. "But, all the same, I don't think you understand me."

He breathed more freely; she did not protest, but asked, "And how did you get on with Peter Ivanovitch? You have seen a good deal of each other. How is it between you two?"

Not knowing what answer to make, the young man inclined his head slowly.

Her lips had been parted in expectation. She pressed them together, and seemed to reflect.

"That's all right."

This had a sound of finality, but she did not leave him. It was impossible to guess what she had in her mind. Razumov muttered:

"It is not of me that you should have asked that question. In a moment you shall see Peter Ivanovitch himself, and the subject will come up naturally. He will be curious to know what has delayed you so long in this garden."

"No doubt Peter Ivanovitch will have something to say to me. Several things. He may even speak of you—question me. Peter Ivanovitch is inclined to trust me generally."

"Question you? That's very likely."

She smiled, half serious.

"Well—and what shall I say to him?"

"I don't know. You may tell him of your discovery."

"What's that?"

"Why—my lack of love for . . ."

"Oh! That's between ourselves," she interrupted, it was hard to say whether in jest or earnest.

"I see that you want to tell Peter Ivanovitch something in my favor," said Razumov, with grim playfulness. "Well, then, you can tell him that I am very much in earnest about my mission. I mean to succeed."

"You have been given a mission!" she exclaimed quickly.

"It amounts to that. I have been told to bring about a certain event."

She looked at him searchingly.

"A mission," she repeated, very grave and interested all at once. "What sort of mission?"

"Something in the nature of propaganda work."

"Ah! Far away from here?"

"No. Not very far," said Razumov, restraining a sudden desire to laugh, though he did not feel joyous in the least.

"So!" she said thoughtfully. "Well, I am not asking questions. It's sufficient that Peter Ivanovitch should know what each of us is doing. Everything is bound to come right in the end."

"You think so?"

"I don't think, young man. I just simply believe it."

"And is it to Peter Ivanovitch that you owe that faith?"

She did not answer the question, and they stood idle, silent, as if reluctant to part with each other.

"That's just like a man," she murmured at last. "As if it were possible to tell how a belief comes to one." Her thin Mephistophelian eyebrows moved a little. "Truly there are millions of people in Russia who would envy the life of dogs in this country. It is a horror and a shame to confess this even between ourselves. One must believe for very pity. This can't go on. No! It can't go on. For twenty years I have been coming and going, looking neither to the left nor to the right. . . . What are you smiling to yourself for? You are only at the beginning. You have begun well, but you just wait till you have trodden every particle of yourself under your feet in your comings and goings. For that is what it comes to. You've got to trample down every particle of your own feelings; for stop you cannot, you must not. I have been young, too—but perhaps you think that I am complaining—eh?"

"I don't think anything of the sort," protested Razumov indifferently.

"I dare say you don't, you dear superior creature. You don't care."

She plunged her fingers into the bunch of hair on the left side, and that brusk movement had the effect of setting the Tyrolese hat straight on her head. She frowned under it without animosity, in the manner of an investigator. Razumov averted his face carelessly.

"You men are all alike. You mistake luck for merit. You do it in good faith too! I would not be too hard on you. It's masculine nature. You men are ridiculously piti-ful in your aptitude to cherish childish illusions down to the very grave. There are a lot of us who have been at work for fifteen years—I mean constantly—trying one way after another, underground and above-ground, looking neither to the right nor to the left! I can talk about it. I have been one of those that never rested. . . . There! What's the use of talking? . . . Look at my gray hairs! And here two babies come along—I mean you and Haldin—you come along and manage to strike a blow at the very first try."

At the name of Haldin falling from the rapid and energetic lips of the woman revolutionist, Razumov had the usual brusk consciousness of the irrevocable. But in all the months which had passed over his head he had become hardened to the experience. The consciousness was no longer accompanied by the blank dismay and the blind anger of the early days. He had argued himself into new beliefs; and he had made for himself a mental atmosphere of gloomy and sardonic reverie, a sort of murky medium through which the event appeared like a featureless shad-ow having vaguely the shape of a man—a shape extremely familiar, yet utterly inexpressive, except for its air of discreet waiting in the dusk. It was not alarming.

"What was *he* like?" the woman revolutionist asked unexpectedly.

"What was he like?" echoed Razumov, making a painful effort not to turn upon her savagely. But he relieved himself by laughing a little while he stole a glance at her out of the corners of his eyes. This reception of her inquiry disturbed her.

"How like a woman," he went on. "What is the good of concerning yourself with his appearance? Whatever it was, he is removed beyond all feminine influences now."

A frown, making three folds at the root of her nose, accentuated the Mephistophelian slant of her eyebrows.

"You suffer, Razumov," she suggested, in her low, confident voice.

"What nonsense!" Razumov faced the woman fairly. "But now I think of it, I am not sure that he is beyond the influence of one woman at least; the one over there—Madame de S——, you know. Formerly the dead were allowed to rest, but now it seems they are at the beck and call of a crazy old harridan. We revolutionists make wonderful discoveries. It is true that they are not exactly our own. We have nothing of our own. But couldn't the friend of Peter Ivanovitch satisfy your feminine curiosity? Couldn't she conjure him up for you?"—he jested like a man in pain.

Her concentrated frowning expression relaxed, and she said, a little wearily, "Let us hope she will make an effort and conjure up some tea for us. But that is by no means certain. I am tired, Razumov."

"You tired! What a confession! Well, there has been tea up there. I had some. If you hurry on after Yakovlitch, instead of wasting your time with such an unsatisfactory skeptical person as myself, you may find the ghost of it—the cold ghost of it—still lingering in the temple. But as to you being tired I can hardly believe it. We are not supposed to be. We mustn't. We can't. The other day I read in some paper or other an alarmist article on the tireless activity of the revolutionary parties. It impresses the world. It's our prestige."

"He flings out continually these flouts and sneers"; the woman in the crimson blouse spoke as if appealing quietly to a third person, but her black eyes never left Razumov's face. "And what for, pray? Simply because some of his conventional notions are shocked, some of his petty masculine standards. You might think he was one of those nervous sensitives that come to a bad end. And yet," she went on, after a short, reflective pause and changing the mode of her address, "and yet I have just learned something which makes me think that you are a man of character, Kirylo Sidorovitch. Yes, indeed!—you are."

The mysterious positiveness of this assertion startled Razumov. Their eyes met. He looked away and, through the bars of the rusty gate, stared at the clean, wide road shaded by the leafy trees. An electric tramcar, quite empty, ran along the avenue with a metallic rustle. It seemed to him he would have given anything to be sitting inside all alone. He was inexpressibly weary, weary in every fiber of his body, but he had a reason for not being the first to break off the conversation. At any instant, in the visionary and criminal babble of revolutionists, some momentous words might fall on his ear; from her lips, from anybody's lips. As long as he managed to preserve a clear mind and to keep down his irritability there was nothing to fear. The only condition of success and safety was indomitable willpower, he reminded himself.

He longed to be on the other side of the bars, as though he were actually a prisoner within the grounds of this center of revolutionary plots, of this house of folly, of blindness, of villainy and crime. Silently he indulged his wounded spirit in a feeling of immense moral and mental remoteness. He did not even smile when he heard her repeat the words:

"Yes! A strong character."

He continued to gaze through the bars like a moody prisoner, not thinking of escape, but merely pondering upon the faded memories of freedom.

"If you don't look out," he mumbled, still looking away, "you will certainly miss seeing as much as the mere ghost of that tea."

She was not to be shaken off in such a way. As a matter of fact he had not expected to succeed.

"Never mind, it will be no great loss. I mean the missing of her tea and only the ghost of it at that. As to the lady, you must understand that she has her positive uses. See *that*, Razumov."

He turned his head at this imperative appeal and saw the woman revolutionist making the motions of counting money into the palm of her hand.

"That's what it is. You see?"

Razumov uttered a slow "I see," and returned to his prisoner-like gazing upon the neat and shady road.

"Material means must be obtained in some way, and this is easier than breaking into banks. More certain too. There! I am joking. . . . What is he muttering to himself now?" she cried under her breath.

"My admiration of Peter Ivanovitch's devoted self-sacrifice, that's all. It's enough to make one sick."

"Oh, you squeamish, masculine creature. Sick! Makes him sick! And what do you know of the truth of it? There's no looking into the secrets of the heart. Peter Ivanovitch knew her years ago, in his worldly days, when he was a young officer in the Guards. It is not for us to judge an inspired person. That's where you men have an advantage. You are inspired sometimes both in thought and action. I have always admitted that when you *are* inspired, when you manage to throw off your masculine cowardice and prudishness, you are not to be equaled by us. Only, how seldom . . . Whereas the silliest woman can always be made of use. And why? Because we have passion, unappeasable passion. . . . I should like to know what he is smiling at?"

"I am not smiling," protested Razumov gloomily.

"Well! How is one to call it? You made some sort of face. Yes, I know! You men can love here and hate there and desire something or other—and you make a great to-do about it, and you call it passion! Yes! While it lasts! But we women are in love with love, and with hate, with these very things I tell you, and with desire itself. That's why we can't be bribed off so easily as you men. In life, you see, there is not much choice. You have either to rot or to burn. And there is not one of us, painted or unpainted, that would not rather burn than rot."

She spoke with energy, but in a matter-of-fact tone. Razumov's attention had wandered away on a track of its own—outside the bars of the gate—but not out of earshot. He stuck his hands into the pockets of his coat.

"Rot or burn! Powerfully stated. Painted or unpainted. Very vigorous. Painted or . . . Do tell me—she would be infernally jealous of him, wouldn't she?"

"Who? What? The Baroness? Eleanor Maximovna? Jealous of Peter Ivanovitch? Heavens! Are these the questions the man's mind is running on? Such a thing is not to be thought of."

"Why? Can't a wealthy old woman be jealous? Or, are they all pure spirits together?"

"But what put it into your head to ask such a question?" she wondered.

"Nothing. I just asked. Masculine frivolity, if you like."

"I don't like," she retorted at once. "It is not the time to be frivolous. What are you flinging your very heart against? Or, perhaps, you are only playing a part."

Razumov had felt that woman's observation of him like a physical contact, like a hand resting lightly on his shoulder. At that moment he received the mysterious impression of her having made up her mind for a closer grip. He stiffened himself inwardly to bear it without betraying himself.

"Playing a part," he repeated, presenting to her an unmoved profile. "It must be done very badly since you see through the assumption."

She watched him, her forehead drawn into perpendicular folds, the thin black eyebrows diverging upwards like the antennae of an insect. He added hardly audibly:

"You are mistaken. I am doing it no more than the rest of us."

"Who is doing it?" she snapped out.

"Who? Everybody," he said impatiently. "You are a materialist, aren't you?"

"Eh! My dear soul, I have outlived all that nonsense."

"But you must remember the definition of Cabanis: 'Man is a digestive tube.' I imagine now . . ."

"I spit on him."

"What? On Cabanis? All right. But you can't ignore the importance of a good digestion. The joy of life—you know the joy of life?—depends on a sound stomach, whereas a bad digestion inclines one to skepticism, breeds black fancies and thoughts of death. These are facts ascertained by physiologists. Well, I assure you that ever since I came over from Russia I have been stuffed with indigestible foreign concoctions of the most nauseating kind—pah!"

"You are joking," she murmured incredulously. He assented in a detached way.

"Yes. It is all a joke. It's hardly worthwhile talking to a man like me. Yet for that very reason men have been known to take their own life."

"On the contrary, I think it *is* worthwhile talking to you."

He kept her in the corner of his eye. She seemed to be thinking out some scathing retort, but ended by only shrugging her shoulders slightly.

"Shallow talk! I suppose one must pardon this weakness in you," she said, putting a special accent on the last word. There was something anxious in her indulgent conclusion.

Razumov noted the slightest shades in this conversation, which he had not expected, for which he was not prepared. That was it. "I was not prepared," he said to himself. "It has taken me unawares." It seemed to him that if he only could allow himself to pant openly like a dog for a time this oppression would pass away. "I shall never be found prepared," he thought, with despair. He laughed a little, saying as lightly as he could:

"Thanks. I don't ask for mercy." Then affecting a playful uneasiness, "But aren't you afraid Peter Ivanovitch might suspect us of plotting something unauthorized together by the gates here?"

"No, I am not afraid. You are quite safe from suspicions while you are with me, my dear young man." The humorous gleam in her black eyes went out. "Peter Ivanovitch trusts me," she went on, quite austerely. "He takes my advice. I am his right hand, as it were, in certain most important things. . . . That amuses you— what? Do you think I am boasting?"

"God forbid. I was just only saying to myself that Peter Ivanovitch seems to have solved the woman question pretty completely."

Even as he spoke he reproached himself for his words, for his tone. All day long he had been saying the wrong things. It was folly, worse than folly. It was weakness; it was this disease of perversity overcoming his will. Was this the way to meet speeches which certainly contained the promise of future confidences from that woman who apparently had a great store of secret knowledge and so much influence? Why give her this puzzling impression? But she did not seem inimical. There was no anger in her voice. It was strangely speculative.

"One does not know what to think, Razumov. You must have bitten something bitter in your cradle."

Razumov gave her a sidelong glance.

"H'm! Something bitter? That's an explanation," he muttered. "Only it was much later. And don't you think, Sophia Antonovna, that you and I come from the same cradle?"

The woman, whose name he had forced himself at last to pronounce (he had experienced a strong repugnance in letting it pass his lips), the woman revolutionist murmured, after a pause:

"You mean—Russia?"

He disdained even to nod. She seemed softened, her black eyes very still, as though she were pursuing the simile in her thoughts to all its tender associations. But suddenly she knitted her brows in a Mephistophelian frown.

"Yes. Perhaps no wonder, then. Yes. One lies there lapped up in evils, watched over by beings that are worse than ogres, ghouls, and vampires. They must be driven away, destroyed utterly. In regard of that task nothing else matters if men and women are determined and faithful. That's how I came to feel in the end. The great thing is not to quarrel amongst ourselves about all sorts of conventional trifles. Remember that, Razumov."

Razumov was not listening. He had even lost the sense of being watched in a sort of heavy tranquility. His uneasiness, his exasperation, his scorn were blunted at last by all these trying hours. It seemed to him that now they were blunted forever. "I am a match for them all," he thought, with a conviction too firm to be exulting. The woman revolutionist had ceased speaking; he was not looking at her; there was no one passing along the road. He almost forgot that he was not alone. He heard her voice again, curt, businesslike, and yet betraying the hesitation which had been the real reason of her prolonged silence.

"I say, Razumov!"

Razumov, whose face was turned away from her, made a grimace like a man who hears a false note.

"Tell me: is it true that on the very morning of the deed you actually attended the lectures at the university?"

An appreciable fraction of a second elapsed before the real import of the question reached him, like a bullet which strikes some time after the flash of the fired shot. Luckily his disengaged hand was ready to grip a bar of the gate. He held it with a terrible force, but his presence of mind was gone. He could make only a sort of gurgling, grumpy sound.

"Come, Kirylo Sidorovitch!" she urged him. "I know you are not a boastful man. *That* one must say for you. You are a silent man. Too silent, perhaps. You are feeding on some bitterness of your own. You are not an enthusiast. You are, perhaps, all the stronger for that. But you might tell me. One would like to understand you a little more. I was so immensely struck . . . Have you really done it?"

He got his voice back. The shot had missed him. It had been fired at random, altogether, more like a signal for coming to close quarters. It was to be a plain struggle for self-preservation. And she was a dangerous adversary too. But he was ready for battle; he was so ready that when he turned towards her not a muscle of his face moved.

"Certainly," he said, without animation, secretly strung up but perfectly sure of himself. "Lectures—certainly. But what makes you ask?"

It was she who was animated.

"I had it in a letter, written by a young man in Petersburg; one of us, of course. You were seen—you were observed with your notebook, impassible, taking notes . . ."

He enveloped her with his fixed stare.

"What of that?"

"I call such coolness superb—that's all. It is a proof of uncommon strength of character. The young man writes that nobody could have guessed from your face and manner the part you had played only some two hours before—the great, momentous, glorious part . . ."

"Oh no. Nobody could have guessed," assented Razumov gravely, "because, don't you see, nobody at that time . . ."

"Yes, yes. But all the same you are a man of exceptional fortitude, it seems. You looked exactly as usual. It was remembered afterwards with wonder . . ."

"It cost me no effort," Razumov declared, with the same staring gravity.

"Then it's almost more wonderful still!" she exclaimed, and fell silent while Razumov asked himself whether he had not said there something utterly unnecessary—or even worse.

She raised her head eagerly.

"Your intention was to stay in Russia? You had planned . . ."

"No," interrupted Razumov without haste. "I had made no plans of any sort."

"You just simply walked away?" she struck in.

He bowed his head in slow assent. "Simply—yes." He had gradually released his hold on the bar of the gate, as though he had acquired the conviction that no random shot could knock him over now. And suddenly he was inspired to add, "The snow was coming down very thick, you know."

She had a slight appreciative movement of the head, like an expert in such enterprises, very interested, capable of taking every point professionally. Razumov remembered something he had heard.

"I turned into a narrow side street, you understand," he went on negligently, and paused as if it were not worth talking about. Then he remembered another detail and dropped it before her, like a disdainful dole to her curiosity.

"I felt inclined to lie down and go to sleep there."

She clicked her tongue at that symptom, very struck indeed. Then:

"But the notebook! The amazing notebook, man. You don't mean to say you had put it in your pocket beforehand!" she cried.

Razumov gave a start. It might have been a sign of impatience.

"I went home. Straight home to my rooms," he said distinctly.

"The coolness of the man! You dared?"

"Why not? I assure you I was perfectly calm. Ha! Calmer than I am now perhaps."

"I like you much better as you are now than when you indulge that bitter vein of yours, Razumov. And nobody in the house saw you return—eh? That might have appeared queer."

"No one," Razumov said firmly. "Dvornik, landlady, girl, all out of the way. I went up like a shadow. It was a murky morning. The stairs were dark. I glided up like a phantom. Fate? Luck? What do you think?"

"I just see it!" The eyes of the woman revolutionist snapped darkly. "Well—and then you considered . . ."

Razumov had it all ready in his head.

"No. I looked at my watch, since you want to know. There was just time. I took that notebook and ran down the stairs on tiptoe. Have you ever listened to the pit-pat of a man running round and round the shaft of a deep staircase? They have a gaslight at the bottom burning night and day. I suppose it's gleaming down there now . . . . The sound dies out—the flame winks . . ."

He noticed the vacillation of surprise passing over the steady curiosity of the black eyes fastened on his face as if the woman revolutionist received the sound of his voice into her pupils instead of her ears. He checked himself, passed his hand over his forehead, confused, like a man who has been dreaming aloud.

"Where could a student be running if not to his lectures in the morning? At night it's another matter. I did not care if all the house had been there to look at me. But I don't suppose there was anyone. It's best not to be seen or heard. Aha! The people that are neither seen nor heard are the lucky ones—in Russia. Don't you admire my luck?"

"Astonishing," she said. "If you have luck as well as determination, then indeed you are likely to turn out an invaluable acquisition for the work in hand."

Her tone was earnest; and it seemed to Razumov that it was speculative, even as though she were already apportioning him, in her mind, his share of the work. Her eyes were cast down. He waited, not very alert now, but with the grip of the ever-present danger giving him an air of attentive gravity. Who could have written about him in that letter from Petersburg? A fellow-student, surely—some imbecile victim of revolutionary propaganda, some foolish slave of foreign, subversive ideals. A long, famine-stricken, red-nosed figure presented itself to his mental search. That must have been the fellow!

He smiled inwardly at the absolute wrongheadedness of the whole thing, the self-deception of a criminal idealist shattering his existence like a thunderclap out of a clear sky, and re-echoing amongst the wreckage in the false assumptions of those other fools. Fancy that hungry and piteous imbecile furnishing to the curiosity of the revolutionist refugees this utterly fantastic detail! He appreciated it as by no means constituting a danger. On the contrary. As things stood it was for his advantage rather, a piece of sinister luck which had only to be accepted with proper caution.

"And yet, Razumov," he heard the musing voice of the woman, "you have not the face of a lucky man." She raised her eyes with renewed interest. "And so that was the way of it. After doing your work you simply walked off and made for your rooms. That sort of thing succeeds sometimes. I suppose it was agreed beforehand that, once the business was over, each of you would go his own way?"

Razumov preserved the seriousness of his expression and the deliberate, if cautious, manner of speaking.

"Was not that the best thing to do?" he asked, in a dispassionate tone. "And anyway," he added, after waiting a moment, "we did not give much thought to what would come after. We never discussed formally any line of conduct. It was understood, I think."

She approved his statement with slight nods.

"You, of course, wished to remain in Russia?"

"In St. Petersburg itself," emphasized Razumov. "It was the only safe course for me. And, moreover, I had nowhere else to go."

"Yes, yes! I know. Clearly. And the other—this wonderful Haldin appearing only to be regretted—you don't know what he intended?"

Razumov had foreseen that such a question would certainly come to meet him sooner or later. He raised his hands a little and let them fall helplessly by his side—nothing more.

It was the white-haired woman conspirator who was the first to break the silence.

"Very curious," she pronounced slowly. "And you did not think, Kirylo Sidorovitch, that he might perhaps wish to get in touch with you again?"

Razumov discovered that he could not suppress the trembling of his lips. But he thought that he owed it to himself to speak. A negative sign would not do again. Speak he must, if only to get at the bottom of what that St. Petersburg letter might have contained.

"I stayed at home next day," he said, bending down a little and plunging his glance into the black eyes of the woman so that she should not observe the trembling of his lips. "Yes, I stayed at home. As my actions are remembered and written about, then perhaps you are aware that I was *not* seen at the lectures next day. Eh? You didn't know? Well, I stopped at home—the livelong day."

As if moved by his agitated tone, she murmured a sympathetic "I see! It must have been trying enough."

"You seem to understand one's feelings," said Razumov steadily. "It was trying. It was horrible; it was an atrocious day. It was not the last."

"Yes, I understand. Afterwards, when you heard they had got him. Don't I know how one feels after losing a comrade in the good fight? One's ashamed of being left. And I can remember so many. Never mind. They shall be avenged before long. And what is death? At any rate, it is not a shameful thing like some kinds of life."

Razumov felt something stir in his breast, a sort of feeble and unpleasant tremor.

"Some kinds of life?" he repeated, looking at her searchingly.

"The subservient, submissive life. Life? No! Vegetation on the filthy heap of iniquity which the world is. Life, Razumov, not to be vile must be a revolt—a pitiless protest—all the time."

She calmed down, the gleam of suffused tears in her eyes dried out instantly by the heat of her passion, and it was in her capable, businesslike manner that she went on:

"You understand me, Razumov. You are not an enthusiast, but there is an immense force of revolt in you. I felt it from the first, directly I set my eyes on you—you remember—in Zurich. Oh! You are full of bitter revolt. That is good. Indignation flags sometimes, revenge itself may become a weariness, but that uncompromising sense of necessity and justice which armed your and Haldin's hands to strike down that fanatical brute . . . for it was that—nothing but that! I have been thinking it out. It could have been nothing else but that."

Razumov made a slight bow, the irony of which was concealed by an almost sinister immobility of feature.

"I can't speak for the dead. As for myself, I can assure you that my conduct was dictated by necessity and by the sense of—well—retributive justice."

"Good, that," he said to himself, while her eyes rested upon him, black and impenetrable like the mental caverns where revolutionary thought should sit plotting the violent way of its dream of changes. As if anything could be changed! In this world of men nothing can be changed—neither happiness nor misery. They can only be displaced at the cost of corrupted consciences and broken lives—a futile game for arrogant philosophers and sanguinary triflers. Those thoughts darted through Razumov's head while he stood facing the old revolutionary hand, the respected, trusted, and influential Sophia Antonovna, whose word had such a weight in the "active" section of every party. She was much more representative than the great Peter Ivanovitch. Stripped of rhetoric, mysticism, and theories, she was the true spirit of destructive revolution. And she was the personal adversary he had to meet. It gave him a feeling of triumphant pleasure to deceive her out of her own mouth. The epigrammatic saying that speech has been given to us for the purpose of concealing our thought came into his mind. Of that cynical theory this was a very subtle and a very scornful application, flouting in its own words the very spirit of ruthless revolution, embodied in that woman with her white hair and black eyebrows, like slightly sinuous lines of India ink, drawn together by the perpendicular folds of a thoughtful frown.

"That's it. Retributive. No pity!" was the conclusion of her silence. And this once broken, she went on impulsively in short, vibrating sentences:

"Listen to my story, Razumov! . . ." Her father was a clever but unlucky artisan. No joy had lighted up his laborious days. He died at fifty; all the years of his life he had panted under the thumb of masters whose rapacity exacted from him the price of the water, of the salt, of the very air he breathed—taxed the sweat of his brow and claimed the blood of his sons. No protection, no guidance! What had society to say to him? Be submissive and be honest. If you rebel I shall kill you. If you steal I shall imprison you. But if you suffer I have nothing for you—nothing except perhaps a beggarly dole of bread—but no consolation for your trouble, no respect for your manhood, no pity for the sorrows of your miserable life.

And so he labored, he suffered, and he died. He died in the hospital. Standing by the common grave she thought of his tormented existence—she saw it whole. She reckoned the simple joys of life, the birthright of the humblest, of which his gentle heart had been robbed by the crime of a society which nothing can absolve.

"Yes, Razumov," she continued, in an impressive, lowered voice, "it was like a lurid light in which I stood, still almost a child, and cursed not the toil, not the misery which had been his lot, but the great social iniquity of the system resting on unrequited toil and unpitied sufferings. From that moment I was a revolutionist."

Razumov, trying to raise himself above the dangerous weaknesses of contempt or compassion, had preserved an impassive countenance. She, with an unaffected touch of mere bitterness, the first he could notice since he had come in contact with the woman, went on:

"As I could not go to the Church where the priests of the system exhorted such unconsidered vermin as I to resignation, I went to the secret societies as soon as I knew how to find my way. I was sixteen years old—no more, Razumov! And—look at my white hair."

In these last words there was neither pride nor sadness. The bitterness, too, was gone.

"There is a lot of it. I had always magnificent hair, even as a chit of a girl. Only, at that time we were cutting it short and thinking that there was the first step towards crushing the social infamy. Crush the Infamy! A fine watchword! I would placard it on the walls of prisons and palaces, carve it on hard rocks, hang it out in letters of fire on that empty sky for a sign of hope and terror—a portent of the end . . ."

"You are eloquent, Sophia Antonovna," Razumov interrupted suddenly. "Only, so far you seem to have been writing it in water . . ."

She was checked but not offended. "Who knows? Very soon it may become a fact written all over that great land of ours," she hinted meaningly. "And then one would have lived long enough. White hair won't matter."

Razumov looked at her white hair: and this mark of so many uneasy years seemed nothing but a testimony to the invincible vigor of revolt. It threw out into an astonishing relief the unwrinkled face, the brilliant black glance, the upright compact figure, the simple, brisk self-possession of the mature personality—as though in her revolutionary pilgrimage she had discovered the secret, not of everlasting youth, but of everlasting endurance.

How un-Russian she looked, thought Razumov. Her mother might have been a Jewess or an Armenian or—devil knew what. He reflected that a revolutionist is seldom true to the settled type. All revolt is the expression of strong individualism—ran his thought vaguely. One can tell them a mile off in any society, in any surroundings. It was astonishing that the police . . .

"We shall not meet again very soon, I think," she was saying, "I am leaving tomorrow."

"For Zurich?" Razumov asked casually, but feeling relieved, not from any distinct apprehension, but from a feeling of stress as if after a wrestling match.

"Yes, Zurich—and farther on, perhaps, much farther. Another journey. When I think of all my journeys! The last must come some day. Never mind, Razumov. We had to have a good long talk. I would have certainly tried to see you if we had not met. Peter Ivanovitch knows where you live? Yes. I meant to have asked him—but it's better like this. You see, we expect two more men; and I had much rather wait here talking with you than up there at the house with . . ."

Having cast a glance beyond the gate, she interrupted herself. "Here they are," she said rapidly. "Well, Kirylo Sidorovitch, we shall have to say goodbye presently."

IV

In his incertitude of the ground on which he stood, Razumov felt perturbed. Turning his head quickly, he saw two men on the opposite side of the road. Seeing themselves noticed by Sophia Antonovna, they crossed over at once, and passed one after another through the little gate by the side of the empty lodge. They looked hard at the stranger, but without mistrust, the crimson blouse being a flaring safety signal. The first, great white hairless face, double chin, prominent stomach, which he seemed to carry forward consciously within a strongly distended overcoat, only nodded and averted his eyes peevishly; his companion—lean, flushed cheekbones, a military red moustache below a sharp, salient nose—at once approached Sophia Antonovna, greeting her warmly. His voice was very strong but inarticulate. It sounded like a deep buzzing. The woman revolutionist was quietly cordial . . . .

"This is Razumov," she announced in a clear voice.

The lean newcomer made an eager half-turn. "He will want to embrace me," thought our young man with a deep recoil of all his being, while his limbs seemed too heavy to move. But it was a groundless alarm. He had to do now with a generation of conspirators who did not kiss each other on both cheeks; and raising an arm that felt like lead he dropped his hand into a largely-outstretched palm, fleshless and hot as if dried up by fever, giving a bony pressure, expressive, seeming to say, "Between us there's no need of words."

The man had big, wide-open eyes. Razumov fancied he could see a smile behind their sadness.

"This is Razumov," Sophia Antonovna repeated loudly for the benefit of the fat man, who at some distance displayed the profile of his stomach.

No one moved. Everything, sounds, attitudes, movements, and immobility, seemed to be part of an experiment, the result of which was a thin voice piping with comic peevishness:

"Oh yes! Razumov. We have been hearing of nothing but Mr. Razumov for months. For my part, I confess I would rather have seen Haldin on this spot instead of Mr. Razumov."

The squeaky stress put on the name "Razumov—Mr. Razumov" pierced the ear ridiculously, like the falsetto of a circus clown beginning an elaborate joke. Astonishment was Razumov's first response, followed by sudden indignation.

"What's the meaning of this?" he asked in a stern tone.

"Tut! Silliness. He's always like that."

Sophia Antonovna was obviously vexed. But she dropped the information, "Necator," from her lips just loud enough to be heard by Razumov. The abrupt squeaks of the fat man seemed to proceed from that thing like a balloon he carried under his overcoat. The solidity of his attitude, the big feet, the lifeless, hanging hands, the enormous bloodless cheek, the thin wisps of hair straggling down the fat nape of the neck, fascinated Razumov into a stare on the verge of horror and laughter.

Nikita, surnamed Necator, with a sinister aptness of alliteration! Razumov had heard of him. He had heard so much since crossing the frontier of these celebrities of the militant revolution; the legends, the stories, the authentic chronicle which now and then peeps out before a half-incredulous world. Razumov had heard of him. He was supposed to have killed more gendarmes and police agents than any revolutionist living. He had been entrusted with executions.

The paper with the letters N.N., the very pseudonym of murder, found pinned on the stabbed breast of a certain notorious spy (this picturesque detail of a sensational murder case had got into the newspapers), was the mark of his handiwork. "By order of the Committee.—N.N." A corner of the curtain lifted to strike the imagination of the gaping world. He was said to have been innumerable times in and out of Russia, the Necator of bureaucrats or provincial governors, of obscure informers. He lived between whiles, Razumov had heard, on the shores of the Lake of Como, with a charming wife, devoted to the cause, and two young children. But how could that creature, so grotesque as to set town dogs barking at its mere sight, go about on those deadly errands and slip through the meshes of the police?

"What now? what now?" the voice squeaked. "I am only sincere. It's not denied that the other was the leading spirit. Well, it would have been better if he had been the one spared to us. More useful. I am not a sentimentalist. Say what I think . . . only natural."

Squeak, squeak, squeak, without a gesture, without a stir—the horrible squeaky burlesque of professional jealousy—this man of a sinister alliterative nickname, this executioner of revolutionary verdicts, the terrifying N.N. exasperated like a fashionable tenor by the attention attracted to the performance of an obscure amateur. Sophia Antonovna shrugged her shoulders. The comrade with the martial red moustache hurried towards Razumov full of conciliatory intentions in his strong, buzzing voice.

"Devil take it! And in this place, too, in the public street, so to speak. But you can see yourself how it is. One of his fantastic sallies. Absolutely of no consequence."

"Pray don't concern yourself," cried Razumov, going off into a long fit of laughter. "Don't mention it."

The other, his hectic flush like a pair of burns on his cheekbones, stared for a moment and burst out laughing too. Razumov, whose hilarity died out all at once, made a step forward.

"Enough of this," he began in a clear, incisive voice, though he could hardly control the trembling of his legs. "I will have no more of it. I shall not permit anyone. . . . I can see very well what you are at with those allusions. . . . Inquire, investigate! I defy you, but I will not be played with."

He had spoken such words before. He had been driven to cry them out in the face of other suspicions. It was an infernal cycle bringing round that protest like a fatal necessity of his existence. But it was no use. He would be always played with. Luckily life does not last forever.

"I won't have it!" he shouted, striking his fist into the palm of his other hand.

"Kirylo Sidorovitch—what has come to you?" The woman revolutionist interfered with authority. They were all looking at Razumov now; the slayer of spies and gendarmes had turned about, presenting his enormous stomach in full, like a shield.

"Don't shout. There are people passing." Sophia Antonovna was apprehensive of another outburst. A steam-launch from Monrepos had come to the landing-stage opposite the gate, its hoarse whistle and the churning noise alongside all unnoticed, had landed a small bunch of local passengers who were dispersing their several ways. Only a specimen of early tourist in knickerbockers, conspicuous by a brand-new yellow leather glass-case, hung about for a moment, scenting something unusual about these four people within the rusty iron gates of what looked like the grounds run wild of an unoccupied private house. Ah! If he had only known what the chance of commonplace traveling had suddenly put in his way! But he was a well-bred person; he averted his gaze and moved off with short steps along the avenue, on the watch for a tramcar.

A gesture from Sophia Antonovna, "Leave him to me," had sent the two men away—the buzzing of the inarticulate voice growing fainter and fainter, and the thin pipe of "What now? what's the matter?" reduced to the proportions of a squeaking toy by the distance. They had left him to her. So many things could be left safely to the experience of Sophia Antonovna. And at once, her black eyes turned to Razumov, her mind tried to get at the heart of that outburst. It had some meaning. No one is born an active revolutionist. The change comes disturbingly, with the force of a sudden vocation, bringing in its train agonizing doubts, assertive violences, an unstable state of the soul, till the final appeasement of the convert in the perfect fierceness of conviction. She had seen—often had only divined—scores of these young men and young women going through an emotional crisis. This young man looked like a moody egotist. And besides, it was a special—a unique case. She had never met an individuality which interested and puzzled her so much.

"Take care, Razumov, my good friend. If you carry on like this you will go mad. You are angry with everybody and bitter with yourself, and on the lookout for something to torment yourself with."

"It's intolerable!" Razumov could only speak in gasps. "You must admit that I can have no illusions on the attitude which . . . it isn't clear . . . or rather . . . only too clear."

He made a gesture of despair. It was not his courage that failed him. The choking fumes of falsehood had taken him by the throat—the thought of being condemned to struggle on and on in that tainted atmosphere without the hope of ever renewing his strength by a breath of fresh air.

"A glass of cold water is what you want." Sophia Antonovna glanced up the grounds at the house and shook her head, then out of the gate at the brimful placidity of the lake. With a half-comical shrug of the shoulders, she gave the remedy up in the face of that abundance.

"It is you, my dear soul, who are flinging yourself at something which does not exist. What is it? Self-reproach, or what? It's absurd. You couldn't have gone and given yourself up because your comrade was taken."

She remonstrated with him reasonably, at some length too. He had nothing to complain of in his reception. Every newcomer was discussed more or less. Everybody had to be thoroughly understood before being accepted. No one that she could remember had been shown from the first so much confidence. Soon, very soon, perhaps sooner than he expected, he would be given an opportunity of showing his devotion to the sacred task of crushing the Infamy.

Razumov, listening quietly, thought: "It may be that she is trying to lull my suspicions to sleep. On the other hand, it is obvious that most of them are fools." He moved aside a couple of paces, and, folding his arms on his breast, leaned back against the stone pillar of the gate.

"As to what remains obscure in the fate of that poor Haldin," Sophia Antonovna dropped into a slowness of utterance which was to Razumov like the falling of molten lead drop by drop; "as to that—though no one ever hinted that either from fear or neglect your conduct has not been what it should have been—well, I have a bit of intelligence . . ."

Razumov could not prevent himself from raising his head, and Sophia Antonovna nodded slightly.

"I have. You remember that letter from St. Petersburg I mentioned to you a moment ago?"

"The letter? Perfectly. Some busybody has been reporting my conduct on a certain day. It's rather sickening. I suppose our police are greatly edified when they open these interesting and—and—superfluous letters."

"Oh dear, no! The police do not get hold of our letters as easily as you imagine. The letter in question did not leave St. Petersburg till the ice broke up. It went by the first English steamer which left the Neva this spring. They have a fireman on board—one of us, in fact. It has reached me from Hull . . ."

She paused as if she were surprised at the sullen fixity of Razumov's gaze, but went on at once, and much faster.

"We have some of our people there who . . . but never mind. The writer of the letter relates an incident which he thinks may possibly be connected with Haldin's arrest. I was just going to tell you when those two men came along."

"That also was an incident," muttered Razumov, "of a very charming kind—for me."

"Leave off that!" cried Sophia Antonovna. "Nobody cares for Nikita's barking. There's no malice in him. Listen to what I have to say. You may be able to throw a light. There was in St. Petersburg a sort of town-peasant—a man who owned horses. He came to town years ago to work for some relation as a driver and ended by owning a cab or two."

She might have well spared herself the slight effort of the gesture: "Wait!" Razumov did not mean to speak; he could not have interrupted her now, not to save his life. The contraction of his facial muscles had been involuntary, a mere surface stir, leaving him sullenly attentive as before.

"He was not a quite ordinary man of his class—it seems," she went on. "The people of the house—my informant talked with many of them—you know, one of those enormous houses of shame and misery . . ."

Sophia Antonovna need not have enlarged on the character of the house. Razumov saw clearly, towering at her back, a dark mass of masonry veiled in snowflakes, with the long row of windows of the eating-shop shining greasily very near the ground. The ghost of that night pursued him. He stood up to it with rage and with weariness.

"Did the late Haldin ever by chance speak to you of that house?" Sophia Antonovna was anxious to know.

"Yes." Razumov, making that answer, wondered whether he were falling into a trap. It was so humiliating to lie to these people that he probably could not have said no. "He mentioned to me once," he added, as if making an effort of memory, "a house of that sort. He used to visit some workmen there."

"Exactly."

Sophia Antonovna triumphed. Her correspondent had discovered that fact quite accidentally from the talk of the people of the house, having made friends with a workman who occupied a room there. They described Haldin's appearance perfectly. He brought comforting words of hope into their misery. He came irregularly, but he came very often, and—her correspondent wrote—sometimes he spent a night in the house, sleeping, they thought, in a stable which opened upon the inner yard.

"Note that, Razumov! In a stable."

Razumov had listened with a sort of ferocious but amused acquiescence.

"Yes. In the straw. It was probably the cleanest spot in the whole house."

"No doubt," assented the woman with that deep frown which seemed to draw closer together her black eyes in a sinister fashion. No four-footed beast could stand the filth and wretchedness so many human beings were condemned to suffer from in Russia. The point of this discovery was that it proved Haldin to have been familiar with that horse-owning peasant—a reckless, independent, free-living fellow not much liked by the other inhabitants of the house. He was believed to have been the associate of a band of housebreakers. Some of these got captured. Not while he was driving them, however; but still there was a suspicion against the fellow of having given a hint to the police and . . .

The woman revolutionist checked herself suddenly.

"And you? Have you ever heard your friend refer to a certain Ziemianitch?"

Razumov was ready for the name. He had been looking out for the question. "When it comes I shall own up," he had said to himself. But he took his time.

"To be sure!" he began slowly. "Ziemianitch, a peasant owning a team of horses. Yes. On one occasion. Ziemianitch! Certainly! Ziemianitch of the horses. . . . How could it have slipped my memory like this? One of the last conversations we had together."

"That means"—Sophia Antonovna looked very grave—"that means, Razumov, it was very shortly before—eh?"

"Before what?" shouted Razumov, advancing at the woman, who looked astonished but stood her ground. "Before . . . Oh! Of course, it was before! How could it have been after? Only a few hours before."

"And he spoke of him favorably?"

"With enthusiasm! The horses of Ziemianitch! The free soul of Ziemianitch!"

Razumov took a savage delight in the loud utterance of that name, which had never before crossed his lips audibly. He fixed his blazing eyes on the woman till at last her fascinated expression recalled him to himself.

"The late Haldin," he said, holding himself in, with downcast eyes, "was inclined to take sudden fancies to people on—on—what shall I say?—insufficient grounds."

"There!" Sophia Antonovna clapped her hands. "That, to my mind, settles it. The suspicions of my correspondent were aroused . . ."

"Aha! Your correspondent," Razumov said in an almost openly mocking tone. "What suspicions? How aroused? By this Ziemianitch? Probably some drunken, gabbling, plausible . . ."

"You talk as if you had known him." Razumov looked up.

"No. But I knew Haldin."

Sophia Antonovna nodded gravely.

"I see. Every word you say confirms to my mind the suspicion communicated to me in that very interesting letter. This Ziemianitch was found one morning hanging from a hook in the stable—dead."

Razumov felt a profound trouble. It was visible, because Sophia Antonovna was moved to observe vivaciously:

"Aha! You begin to see."

He saw it clearly enough—in the light of a lantern casting spokes of shadow in a cellar-like stable, the body in a sheepskin coat and long boots hanging against the wall. A pointed hood, with the ends wound about up to the eyes, hid the face. "But that does not concern me," he reflected. "It does not affect my position at all. He never knew who had thrashed him. He could not have known." Razumov felt sorry for the old lover of the bottle and women.

"Yes. Some of them end like that," he muttered. "What is your idea, Sophia Antonovna?"

It was really the idea of her correspondent, but Sophia Antonovna had adopted it fully. She stated it in one word—"Remorse." Razumov opened his eyes very wide at that. Sophia Antonovna's informant, by listening to the talk of the house, by putting this and that together, had managed to come very near to the truth of Haldin's relation to Ziemianitch.

"It is I who can tell you what you were not certain of—that your friend had some plan for saving himself afterwards, for getting out of St. Petersburg, at any rate. Perhaps that and no more, trusting to luck for the rest. And that fellow's horses were part of the plan."

"They have actually got at the truth," Razumov marveled to himself, while he nodded judicially. "Yes, that's possible, very possible." But the woman revolutionist was very positive that it was so. First of all, a conversation about horses between Haldin and Ziemianitch had been partly overheard. Then there were the suspicions of the people in the house when their "young gentleman" (they did not know Haldin by his name) ceased to call at the house. Some of them used to charge Ziemianitch with knowing something of this absence. He denied it with exasperation; but the fact was that ever since Haldin's disappearance he was not himself, growing moody and thin. Finally, during a quarrel with some woman (to whom he was making up), in which most of the inmates of the house took part apparently, he was openly abused by his chief enemy, an athletic peddlar, for an informer, and for having driven "our young gentleman to Siberia, the same as you did those young fellows who broke into houses." In consequence of this there was a fight, and Ziemianitch got flung down a flight of stairs. Thereupon he drank and moped for a week, and then hanged himself.

Sophia Antonovna drew her conclusions from the tale. She charged Ziemianitch either with drunken indiscretion as to a driving job on a certain date, overheard by some spy in some low grog-shop—perhaps in the very eating-shop on the ground floor of the house—or, maybe, a downright denunciation, followed by remorse. A man like that would be capable of anything. People said he was a flighty old chap. And if he had been once before mixed up with the police—as seemed certain, though he always denied it—in connection with these thieves, he would be sure to be acquainted with some police underlings, always on the look out for something to report. Possibly at first his tale was not made anything of till the day that scoundrel de P—— got his deserts. Ah! But then every bit and scrap of hint and information would be acted on, and fatally they were bound to get Haldin.

Sophia Antonovna spread out her hands—"Fatally."

Fatality—chance! Razumov meditated in silent astonishment upon the queer verisimilitude of these inferences. They were obviously to his advantage.

"It is right now to make this conclusive evidence known generally." Sophia Antonovna was very calm and deliberate again. She had received the letter three days ago, but did not write at once to Peter Ivanovitch. She knew then that she would have the opportunity presently of meeting several men of action assembled for an important purpose.

"I thought it would be more effective if I could show the letter itself at large. I have it in my pocket now. You understand how pleased I was to come upon you."

Razumov was saying to himself, "She won't offer to show the letter to me. Not likely. Has she told me everything that correspondent of hers has found out?" He longed to see the letter, but he felt he must not ask.

"Tell me, please, was this an investigation ordered, as it were?"

"No, no," She protested. "There you are again with your sensitiveness. It makes you stupid. Don't you see, there was no starting-point for an investigation even if anyone had thought of it. A perfect blank! That's exactly what some people were pointing out as the reason for receiving you cautiously. It was all perfectly accidental, arising from my informant striking an acquaintance with an intelligent skin-dresser lodging in that particular slum-house. A wonderful coincidence!"

"A pious person," suggested Razumov, with a pale smile, "would say that the hand of God had done it all."

"My poor father would have said that." Sophia Antonovna did not smile. She dropped her eyes. "Not that his God ever helped him. It's a long time since God has done anything for the people. Anyway, it's done."

"All this would be quite final," said Razumov, with every appearance of reflective impartiality, "if there was any certitude that the 'our young gentleman' of these people was Victor Haldin. Have we got that?"

"Yes. There's no mistake. My correspondent was as familiar with Haldin's personal appearance as with your own," the woman affirmed decisively.

"It's the red-nosed fellow beyond a doubt," Razumov said to himself, with reawakened uneasiness. Had his own visit to that accursed house passed unnoticed? It was barely possible. Yet it was hardly probable. It was just the right sort of food for the popular gossip that gaunt busybody had been picking up. But the letter did not seem to contain any allusion to that. Unless she had suppressed it. And, if so, why? If it had really escaped the prying of that hunger-stricken democrat with a confounded genius for recognizing people from description, it could only be for a time. He would come upon it presently and hasten to write another letter—and then!

For all the envenomed recklessness of his temper, fed on hate and disdain, Razumov shuddered inwardly. It guarded him from common fear, but it could not defend him from disgust at being dealt with in any way by these people. It was a sort of superstitious dread. Now, since his position had been made more secure by their own folly at the cost of Ziemianitch, he felt the need of perfect safety, with its freedom from direct lying, with its power of moving amongst them silent, unquestioning, listening, impenetrable, like the very fate of their crimes and their folly. Was this advantage his already? Or not yet? Or never would be?

"Well, Sophia Antonovna," his air of reluctant concession was genuine in so far that he was really loath to part with her without testing her sincerity by a question it was impossible to bring about in any way; "well, Sophia Antonovna, if that is so, then——"

"The creature has done justice to himself," the woman observed, as if thinking aloud.

"What? Ah yes! Remorse," Razumov muttered, with equivocal contempt.

"Don't be harsh, Kirylo Sidorovitch, if you have lost a friend." There was no hint of softness in her tone, only the black glitter of her eyes seemed detached for an instant from vengeful visions. "He was a man of the people. The simple Russian soul is never wholly impenitent. It's something to know that."

"Consoling?" insinuated Razumov, in a tone of inquiry.

"Leave off railing," she checked him explosively. "Remember, Razumov, that women, children, and revolutionists hate irony, which is the negation of all saving instincts, of all faith, of all devotion, of all action. Don't rail! Leave off. . . . I don't know how it is, but there are moments when you are abhorrent to me. . . . "

She averted her face. A languid silence, as if all the electricity of the situation had been discharged in this flash of passion, lasted for some time. Razumov had not flinched. Suddenly she laid the tips of her fingers on his sleeve.

"Don't mind."

"I don't mind," he said very quietly.

He was proud to feel that she could read nothing on his face. He was really mollified, relieved, if only for a moment, from an obscure oppression. And suddenly he asked himself, "Why the devil did I go to that house? It was an imbecile thing to do."

A profound disgust came over him. Sophia Antonovna lingered, talking in a friendly manner with an evident conciliatory intention. And it was still about the famous letter, referring to various minute details given by her informant, who had never seen Ziemianitch. The "victim of remorse" had been buried several weeks before her correspondent began frequenting the house. It—the house—contained very good revolutionary material. The spirit of the heroic Haldin had passed through these dens of black wretchedness with a promise of universal redemption from all the miseries that oppress mankind. Razumov listened without hearing, gnawed by the newborn desire of safety with its independence from that degrading method of direct lying which at times he found it almost impossible to practice.

No. The point he wanted to hear about could never come into this conversation. There was no way of bringing it forward. He regretted not having composed a perfect story for use abroad, in which his fatal connection with the house might have been owned up to. But when he left Russia he did not know that Ziemianitch had hanged himself. And, anyway, who could have foreseen this woman's "informant" stumbling upon that particular slum, of all the slums awaiting destruction in the purifying flame of social revolution? Who could have foreseen? Nobody! "It's a perfect, diabolic surprise," thought Razumov, calm-faced in his attitude of inscrutable superiority, nodding assent to Sophia Antonovna's remarks upon the psychology of "the people." "Oh yes—certainly," rather coldly, but with a nervous longing in his fingers to tear some sort of confession out of her throat.

Then, at the very last, on the point of separating, the feeling of relaxed tension already upon him, he heard Sophia Antonovna allude to the subject of his uneasiness. How it came about he could only guess, his mind being absent at the moment, but it must have sprung from Sophia Antonovna's complaints of the illogical absurdity of the people. For instance—that Ziemianitch was notoriously irreligious, and yet, in the last weeks of his life, he suffered from the notion that he had been beaten by the devil.

"The devil," repeated Razumov, as though he had not heard aright.

"The actual devil. The devil in person. You may well look astonished, Kirylo Sidorovitch. Early on the very night poor Haldin was taken, a complete stranger turned up and gave Ziemianitch a most fearful thrashing while he was lying dead drunk in the stable. The wretched creature's body was one mass of bruises. He showed them to the people in the house."

"But you, Sophia Antonovna, you don't believe in the actual devil?"

"Do you?" retorted the woman curtly. "Not but that there are plenty of men worse than devils to make a hell of this earth," she muttered to herself.

Razumov watched her, vigorous and white-haired, with the deep fold between her thin eyebrows, and her black glance turned idly away. It was obvious that she did not make much of the story—unless, indeed, this was the perfection of duplicity. "A dark young man," she explained further. "Never seen there before, never seen afterwards. Why are you smiling, Razumov?"

"At the devil being still young after all these ages," he answered composedly. "But who was able to describe him, since the victim, you say, was dead-drunk at the time?"

"Oh! The eating-house keeper has described him. An overbearing, swarthy young man in a student's cloak, who came rushing in, demanded Ziemianitch, beat him furiously, and rushed away without a word, leaving the eating-house keeper paralyzed with astonishment."

"Does he, too, believe it was the devil?"

"That I can't say. I am told he's very reserved on the matter. Those sellers of spirits are great scoundrels generally. I should think he knows more of it than anybody."

"Well, and you, Sophia Antonovna, what's your theory?" asked Razumov, in a tone of great interest. "Yours and your informant's, who is on the spot."

"I agree with him. Some police-hound in disguise. Who else could beat a helpless man so unmercifully? As for the rest, if they were out that day on every trail, old and new, it is probable enough that they might have thought it just as well to have Ziemianitch at hand for more information, or for identification, or what not. Some scoundrelly detective was sent to fetch him along, and being vexed at finding him so drunk broke a stable fork over his ribs. Later on, after they had the big game safe in the net, they troubled their heads no more about that peasant."

Such were the last words of the woman revolutionist in this conversation, keeping so close to the truth, departing from it so far in the verisimilitude of thoughts and conclusions as to give one the notion of the invincible nature of human error, a glimpse into the utmost depths of self-deception. Razumov, after shaking hands with Sophia Antonovna, left the grounds, crossed the road, and walking out on the little steamboat pier, leaned over the rail.

His mind was at ease—ease such as he had not known for many days, ever since that night . . . the night. The conversation with the woman revolutionist had given him the view of his danger at the very moment this danger vanished, characteristically enough. "I ought to have foreseen the doubts that would arise in those people's minds," he thought. Then his attention being attracted by a stone of a peculiar shape, which he could see clearly lying at the bottom, he began to speculate as to the depth of water in that spot. But very soon, with a start of wonder at this extraordinary instance of ill-timed detachment, he returned to his train of thought. "I ought to have told very circumstantial lies from the first," he said to himself, with a mortal distaste of the mere idea which silenced his mental utterance for quite a perceptible interval. "Luckily, that's all right now," he reflected, and after a time spoke to himself, half aloud, "Thanks to the devil," and laughed a little.

The end of Ziemianitch then arrested his wandering thoughts. He was not exactly amused at the interpretation, but he could not help detecting in it a certain piquancy. He owned to himself that, had he known of that suicide before leaving Russia, he would have been incapable of making such excellent use of it for his own purposes. He ought to be infinitely obliged to the fellow with the red nose for his patience and ingenuity. "A wonderful psychologist apparently," he said to himself sarcastically. Remorse, indeed! It was a striking example of your true conspirator's blindness, of the stupid subtlety of people with one idea. This was a drama of love, not of conscience, Razumov continued to himself mockingly. A woman the old fellow was making up to! A robust peddlar, clearly a rival, throwing him down a flight of stairs. . . . And at sixty, for a lifelong lover, it was not an easy matter to get over. That was a feminist of a different stamp from Peter Ivanovitch. Even the comfort of the bottle might conceivably fail him in this supreme crisis. At such an age nothing but a halter could cure the pangs of an unquenchable passion. And, besides, there was the wild exasperation aroused by the unjust aspersions and the contumely of the house, with the maddening impossibility to account for that mysterious thrashing, added to these simple and bitter sorrows. "Devil, eh?" Razumov exclaimed, with mental excitement, as if he had made an interesting discovery. "Ziemianitch ended by falling into mysticism. So many of our true Russian souls end in that way! Very characteristic." He felt pity for Ziemianitch, a large, neutral pity, such as one may feel for an unconscious multitude, a great people seen from above—like a community of crawling ants working out its destiny. It was as if this Ziemianitch could not possibly have done anything else. And Sophia Antonovna's cocksure and contemptuous "some police-hound" was characteristically Russian in another way. But there was no tragedy there. This was a comedy of errors. It was as if the devil himself were playing a game with all of them in turn. First with him, then with Ziemianitch, then with those revolutionists. The devil's own game this. . . . He interrupted his earnest mental soliloquy with a jocular thought at his own expense. "Hullo! I am falling into mysticism too."

His mind was more at ease than ever. Turning about, he put his back against the rail comfortably. "All this fits with marvelous aptness," he continued to think. "The brilliance of my reputed exploit is no longer darkened by the fate of my supposed colleague. The mystic Ziemianitch accounts for that. An incredible chance has served me. No more need of lies. I shall have only to listen and to keep my scorn from getting the upper hand of my caution."

He sighed, folded his arms, his chin dropped on his breast, and it was a long time before he started forward from that pose, with the recollection that he had made up his mind to do something important that day. What it was he could not immediately recall, yet he made no effort of memory, for he was uneasily certain that he would remember presently.

He had not gone more than a hundred yards towards the town when he slowed down, almost faltered in his walk, at the sight of a figure walking in the contrary direction, draped in a cloak, under a soft, broad-brimmed hat, picturesque but diminutive, as if seen through the big end of an opera-glass. It was impossible to avoid that tiny man, for there was no issue for retreat.

"Another one going to that mysterious meeting," thought Razumov. He was right in his surmise, only *this* one, unlike the others who came from a distance, was known to him personally. Still, he hoped to pass on with a mere bow, but it was impossible to ignore the little thin hand with hairy wrist and knuckles protruded in a friendly wave from under the folds of the cloak, worn Spanish-wise, in disregard of a fairly warm day, a corner flung over the shoulder.

"And how is Herr Razumov?" sounded the greeting in German, by that alone made more odious to the object of the affable recognition. At closer quarters the diminutive personage looked like a reduction of an ordinary-sized man, with a lofty brow bared for a moment by the raising of the hat, the great pepper-and-salt full beard spread over the proportionally broad chest. A fine bold nose jutted over a thin mouth hidden in the mass of fine hair. All this, accented features, strong limbs in their relative smallness, appeared delicate without the slightest sign of debility. The eyes alone, almond-shaped and brown, were too big, with the whites slightly bloodshot by much pen labor under a lamp. The obscure celebrity of the tiny man was well known to Razumov. Polyglot, of unknown parentage, of indefinite nationality, anarchist, with a pedantic and ferocious temperament, and an amazingly inflammatory capacity for invective, he was a power in the background, this violent pamphleteer clamoring for revolutionary justice, this Julius Laspara, editor of the *Living Word,* confidant of conspirators, inditer of sanguinary menaces and manifestos, suspected of being in the secret of every plot. Laspara lived in the old town in a somber, narrow house presented to him by a naive middle-class admirer of his humanitarian eloquence. With him lived his two daughters, who overtopped him head and shoulders, and a pasty-faced, lean boy of six, languishing in the dark rooms in blue cotton overalls and clumsy boots, who might have belonged to either one of them or to neither. No stranger could tell. Julius Laspara no doubt knew which of his girls it was who, after casually vanishing for a few years, had as casually returned to him possessed of that child; but, with admirable pedantry, he had refrained from asking her for details—no, not so much as the name of the father, because maternity should be an anarchist function. Razumov had been admitted twice to that suite of several small dark rooms on the top floor: dusty windowpanes, litter of all sorts of sweepings all over the place, half-full glasses of tea forgotten on every table, the two Laspara daughters prowling about enigmatically silent, sleepy-eyed, corsetless, and generally, in their want of shape and the disorder of their rumpled attire, resembling old dolls; the great but obscure Julius, his feet twisted round his three-legged stool, always ready to receive the visitors, the pen instantly dropped, the body screwed round with a striking display of the lofty brow and of the great austere beard. When he got down from his stool it was as though he had descended from the heights of Olympus. He was dwarfed by his daughters, by the furniture, by any caller of ordinary stature. But he very seldom left it, and still more rarely was seen walking in broad daylight.

It must have been some matter of serious importance which had driven him out in that direction that afternoon. Evidently he wished to be amiable to that young man whose arrival had made some sensation in the world of political refugees. In Russian now, which he spoke, as he spoke and wrote four or five other European languages, without distinction and without force (other than that of invective), he inquired if Razumov had taken his inscriptions at the university as yet. And the young man shaking his head negatively:

"There's plenty of time for that. But, meantime, are you not going to write something for us?"

He could not understand how anyone could refrain from writing on anything, social, economic, historical—anything. Any subject could be treated in the right spirit, and for the ends of social revolution. And, as it happened, a friend of his in London had got in touch with a review of advanced ideas. "We must educate, educate everybody—develop the great thought of absolute liberty and of revolutionary justice."

Razumov muttered rather surlily that he did not even know English.

"Write in Russian. We'll have it translated. There can be no difficulty. Why, without seeking further, there is Miss Haldin. My daughters go to see her sometimes." He nodded significantly. "She does nothing, has never done anything in her life. She would be quite competent, with a little assistance. Only write. You know you must. And so goodbye for the present."

He raised his arm and went on. Razumov backed against the low wall, looked after him, spat violently, and went on his way with an angry mutter:

"Cursed Jew!"

He did not know anything about it. Julius Laspara might have been a Transylvanian, a Turk, an Andalusian, or a citizen of one of the Hanse towns for anything he could tell to the contrary. But this is not a story of the West, and this exclamation must be recorded, accompanied by the comment that it was merely an expression of hate and contempt, best adapted to the nature of the feelings Razumov suffered from at the time. He was boiling with rage, as though he had been grossly insulted. He walked as if blind, following instinctively the shore of the diminutive harbor along the quay, through a pretty, dull garden, where dull people sat on chairs under the trees, till, his fury abandoning him, he discovered himself in the middle of a long, broad bridge. He slowed down at once. To his right, beyond the toy-like jetties, he saw the green slopes framing the Petit Lac in all the marvelous banality of the picturesque made of painted cardboard, with the more distant stretch of water inanimate and shining like a piece of tin.

He turned his head away from that view for the tourists, and walked on slowly, his eyes fixed on the ground. One or two persons had to get out of his way, and then turned round to give a surprised stare at his profound absorption. The insistence of the celebrated subversive journalist rankled in his mind strangely. Write! Must write! He! Write! A sudden light flashed upon him. To write was the very thing he had made up his mind to do that day. He had made up his mind irrevocably to that step and then had forgotten all about it. That incorrigible tendency to escape from the grip of the situation was fraught with serious danger. He was ready to despise himself for it. What was it? Levity, or deep-seated weakness? Or an unconscious dread?

"Is it that I am shrinking? It can't be! It's impossible. To shrink now would be worse than moral suicide; it would be nothing less than moral damnation," he thought. "Is it possible that I have a conventional conscience?"

He rejected that hypothesis with scorn, and, checked on the edge of the pavement, made ready to cross the road and proceed up the wide street facing the head of the bridge; and that for no other reason except that it was there before him. But at the moment a couple of carriages and a slow-moving cart interposed, and suddenly he turned sharp to the left, following the quay again, but now away from the lake.

"It may be just my health," he thought, allowing himself a very unusual doubt of his soundness; for, with the exception of a childish ailment or two, he had never been ill in his life. But that was a danger too. Only, it seemed as though he were being looked after in a specially remarkable way. "If I believed in an active Providence," Razumov said to himself, amused grimly, "I would see here the working of an ironical finger. To have a Julius Laspara put in my way as if expressly to remind me of my purpose is—— Write, he had said. I must write—I must, indeed! I shall write—never fear. Certainly. That's why I am here. And for the future I shall have something to write about."

He was exciting himself by this mental soliloquy. But the idea of writing evoked the thought of a place to write in, of shelter, of privacy, and naturally of his lodgings, mingled with a distaste for the necessary exertion of getting there, with a mistrust as of some hostile influence awaiting him within those odious four walls.

"Suppose one of those revolutionists," he asked himself, "were to take a fancy to call on me while I am writing?" The mere prospect of such an interruption made him shudder. One could lock one's door, or ask the tobacconist downstairs (some sort of a refugee himself) to tell inquirers that one was not in. Not very good precautions these. The manner of his life, he felt, must be kept clear of every cause for suspicion or even occasion for wonder, down to such trifling occurrences as a delay in opening a locked door. "I wish I were in the middle of some field miles away from everywhere," he thought.

He had unconsciously turned to the left once more and now was aware of being on a bridge again. This one was much narrower than the other, and instead of being straight, made a sort of elbow or angle. At the point of that angle a short arm joined it to a hexagonal islet with a soil of gravel and its shores faced with dressed stone, a perfection of puerile neatness. A couple of tall poplars and a few other trees stood grouped on the clean, dark gravel, and under them a few garden benches and a bronzed effigy of Jean Jacques Rousseau seated on its pedestal.

On setting his foot on it Razumov became aware that, except for the woman in charge of the refreshment chalet, he would be alone on the island. There was something of naive, odious, and inane simplicity about that unfrequented tiny crumb of earth named after Jean Jacques Rousseau. Something pretentious and shabby too. He asked for a glass of milk, which he drank, standing, at one draught (nothing but tea had passed his lips since the morning), and was going away with a weary, lagging step when a thought stopped him short. He had found precisely what he needed. If solitude could ever be secured in the open air in the middle of a town, he would have it there on this absurd island, together with the faculty of watching the only approach.

He went back heavily to a garden seat, dropped into it. This was the place for making a beginning of that writing which had to be done. The materials he had on him. "I shall always come here," he said to himself, and afterwards sat for quite a long time motionless, without thought and sight and hearing, almost without life. He sat long enough for the declining sun to dip behind the roofs of the town at his back, and throw the shadow of the houses on the lake front over the islet, before he pulled out of his pocket a fountain pen, opened a small notebook on his knee, and began to write quickly, raising his eyes now and then at the connecting arm of the bridge. These glances were needless; the people crossing over in the distance seemed unwilling even to look at the islet where the exiled effigy of the author of the *Social Contract* sat enthroned above the bowed head of Razumov in the somber immobility of bronze. After finishing his scribbling, Razumov, with a sort of feverish haste, put away the pen, then rammed the notebook into his pocket, first tearing out the written pages with an almost convulsive bruskness. But the folding of the flimsy batch on his knee was executed with thoughtful nicety. That done, he leaned back in his seat and remained motionless, holding the papers in his left hand. The twilight had deepened. He got up and began to pace to and fro slowly under the trees.

"There can be no doubt that now I am safe," he thought. His fine ear could detect the faintly accentuated murmurs of the current breaking against the point of the island, and he forgot himself in listening to them with interest. But even to his acute sense of hearing the sound was too elusive.

"Extraordinary occupation I am giving myself up to," he murmured. And it occurred to him that this was about the only sound he could listen to innocently, and for his own pleasure, as it were. Yes, the sound of water, the voice of the wind—completely foreign to human passions. All the other sounds of this earth brought contamination to the solitude of a soul.

This was Mr. Razumov's feeling—the soul, of course, being his own, and the word being used not in the theological sense, but standing, as far as I can understand it, for that part of Mr. Razumov which was not his body, and more specially in danger from the fires of this earth. And it must be admitted that in Mr. Razumov's case the bitterness of solitude from which he suffered was not an altogether morbid phenomenon.

PART FOURTH

I

That I should, at the beginning of this retrospect, mention again that Mr. Razumov's youth had no one in the world, as literally no one as it can be honestly affirmed of any human being, is but a statement of fact from a man who believes in the psychological value of facts. There is also, perhaps, a desire of punctilious fairness. Unidentified with anyone in this narrative where the aspects of honor and shame are remote from the ideas of the Western world, and taking my stand on the ground of common humanity, it is for that very reason that I feel a strange reluctance to state baldly here what every reader has most likely already discovered himself. Such reluctance may appear absurd if it were not for the thought that because of the imperfection of language there is always something ungracious (and even disgraceful) in the exhibition of naked truth. But the time has come when Councillor of State Mikulin can no longer be ignored. His simple question, "Where to?" on which we left Mr. Razumov in St. Petersburg, throws a light on the general meaning of this individual case.

"Where to?" was the answer in the form of a gentle question to what we may call Mr. Razumov's declaration of independence. The question was not menacing in the least, and, indeed, had the ring of innocent inquiry. Had it been taken in a merely topographical sense, the only answer to it would have appeared sufficiently appalling to Mr. Razumov. Where to? Back to his rooms, where the Revolution had sought him out to put to a sudden test his dormant instincts, his half-conscious thoughts and almost wholly unconscious ambitions, by the touch as of some furious and dogmatic religion, with its call to frantic sacrifices, its tender resignations, its dreams and hopes uplifting the soul by the side of the most somber moods of despair. And Mr. Razumov had let go the door handle and had come back to the middle of the room, asking Councillor Mikulin angrily, "What do you mean by it?"

As far as I can tell, Councillor Mikulin did not answer that question. He drew Mr. Razumov into familiar conversation. It is the peculiarity of Russian natures that, however strongly engaged in the drama of action, they are still turning their ear to the murmur of abstract ideas. This conversation (and others later on) need not be recorded. Suffice it to say that it brought Mr. Razumov as we know him to the test of another faith. There was nothing official in its expression, and Mr. Razumov was led to defend his attitude of detachment. But Councillor Mikulin would have none of his arguments. "For a man like you," were his last weighty words in the discussion, "such a position is impossible. Don't forget that I have seen that interesting piece of paper. I understand your liberalism. I have an intellect of that kind myself. Reform for me is mainly a question of method. But the principle of revolt is a physical intoxication, a sort of hysteria which must be kept away from the masses. You agree to this without reserve, don't you? Because, you see, Kirylo Sidorovitch, abstention, reserve, in certain situations, come very near to political crime. The ancient Greeks understood that very well."

Mr. Razumov, listening with a faint smile, asked Councillor Mikulin point-blank if this meant that he was going to have him watched.

The high official took no offense at the cynical inquiry.

"No, Kirylo Sidorovitch," he answered gravely. "I don't mean to have you watched."

Razumov, suspecting a lie, affected yet the greatest liberty of mind during the short remainder of that interview. The older man expressed himself throughout in familiar terms, and with a sort of shrewd simplicity. Razumov concluded that to get to the bottom of that mind was an impossible feat. A great disquiet made his heart beat quicker. The high official, issuing from behind the desk, was actually offering to shake hands with him.

"Goodbye, Mr. Razumov. An understanding between intelligent men is always a satisfactory occurrence. Is it not? And, of course, these rebel gentlemen have not the monopoly of intelligence."

"I presume that I shall not be wanted anymore?" Razumov brought out that question while his hand was still being grasped. Councillor Mikulin released it slowly.

"That, Mr. Razumov," he said with great earnestness, "is as it may be. God alone knows the future. But you may rest assured that I never thought of having you watched. You are a young man of great independence. Yes. You are going away free as air, but you will end by coming back to us."

"I! I!" Razumov exclaimed, in an appalled murmur of protest. "What for?" he added feebly.

"Yes! You yourself, Kirylo Sidorovitch," the high police functionary insisted in a low, severe tone of conviction. "You will be coming back to us. Some of our greatest minds had to do that in the end."

"Our greatest minds?" repeated Razumov in a dazed voice.

"Yes, indeed! Our greatest minds . . . Goodbye."

Razumov, shown out of the room, walked away from the door. But before he got to the end of the passage he heard heavy footsteps, and a voice calling upon him to stop. He turned his head and was startled to see Councillor Mikulin pursuing him in person. The high functionary hurried up, very simple, slightly out of breath.

"One minute. As to what we were talking about just now, it shall be as God wills it. But I may have occasion to require you again. You look surprised, Kirylo Sidorovitch. Yes, again . . . to clear up any further point that may turn up."

"But I don't know anything," stammered out Razumov. "I couldn't possibly know anything."

"Who can tell? Things are ordered in a wonderful manner. Who can tell what *may* become disclosed to you before this day is out? You have been already the instrument of Providence. You smile, Kirylo Sidorovitch; you are an *esprit fort*." (Razumov was not conscious of having smiled.) "But I believe firmly in Providence. Such a confession on the lips of an old hardened official like me may sound to you funny. But you yourself yet some day will recognize . . . Or else what happened to you cannot be accounted for at all. Yes, decidedly I shall have occasion to see you again, but not here. This wouldn't be quite—h'm . . . Some convenient place shall be made known to you. And even the written communications between us in *that* respect or in any other had better pass through the intermediacy of our—if I may express myself so—common friend, Prince K——. Now I beg you, Kirylo Sidorovitch—don't! I am certain he'll consent. You must give me the credit of being aware of what I am saying. You have no better friend than Prince K——, and as to myself, it is a long time now since I've been honored by his . . ."

He glanced down his beard.

"I won't detain you any longer. We live in difficult times, in times of monstrous chimeras and evil dreams and criminal follies. We shall certainly meet once more. It may be some little time, though, before we do. Till then may Heaven send you fruitful reflections!"

Once in the street, Razumov started off rapidly, without caring for the direction. At first he thought of nothing; but in a little while the consciousness of his position presented itself to him as something so ugly, dangerous, and absurd, the difficulty of ever fleeing himself from the toils of that complication so insoluble, that the idea of going back and, as he termed it to himself, *confessing* to Councillor Mikulin, flashed through his mind.

Go back! What for? Confess! To what? "I have been speaking to him with the greatest openness," he said to himself with perfect truth. "What else could I tell him? That I have undertaken to carry a message to that brute Ziemianitch?

Establish a false complicity and destroy what chance of safety I have won for nothing—what folly!"

Yet he could not defend himself from fancying that Councillor Mikulin was, perhaps, the only man in the world able to understand his conduct. To be understood appeared extremely fascinating.

On the way home he had to stop several times; all his strength seemed to run out of his limbs; and in the movement of the busy streets, isolated as if in a desert, he remained suddenly motionless for a minute or so before he could proceed on his way. He reached his rooms at last.

Then came an illness, something in the nature of a low fever, which all at once removed him to a great distance from the perplexing actualities, from his very room, even. He never lost consciousness; he only seemed to himself to be existing languidly somewhere very far away from everything that had ever happened to him. He came out of this state slowly, with an effect, that is to say, of extreme slowness, though the actual number of days was not very great. And when he had got back into the middle of things they were all changed, subtly and provokingly, in their nature: inanimate objects, human faces, the landlady, the rustic servant-girl, the staircase, the streets, the very air. He tackled these changed conditions in a spirit of severity. He walked to and fro to the university, ascended stairs, paced the passages, listened to lectures, took notes, crossed courtyards in angry aloofness, his teeth set hard till his jaws ached.

He was perfectly aware of Madcap Kostia gazing like a young retriever from a distance, of the famished student with the red drooping nose, keeping scrupulously away as desired; of twenty others, perhaps, he knew well enough to speak to. And they all had an air of curiosity and concern as if they expected something to happen. "This can't last much longer," thought Razumov more than once. On certain days he was afraid that anyone addressing him suddenly in a certain way would make him scream out insanely a lot of filthy abuse. Often, after returning home, he would drop into a chair in his cap and cloak and remain still for hours holding some book he had got from the library in his hand; or he would pick up the little penknife and sit there scraping his nails endlessly and feeling furious all the time—simply furious. "This is impossible," he would mutter suddenly to the empty room.

Fact to be noted: this room might conceivably have become physically repugnant to him, emotionally intolerable, morally uninhabitable. But no. Nothing of the sort (and he had himself dreaded it at first), nothing of the sort happened. On the contrary, he liked his lodgings better than any other shelter he, who had never known a home, had ever hired before. He liked his lodgings so well that often, on that very account, he found a certain difficulty in making up his mind to go out. It resembled a physical seduction such as, for instance, makes a man reluctant to leave the neighborhood of a fire on a cold day.

For as, at that time, he seldom stirred except to go to the university (what else was there to do?) it followed that whenever he went abroad he felt himself at once closely involved in the moral consequences of his act. It was there that the dark prestige of the Haldin mystery fell on him, clung to him like a poisoned robe it was impossible to fling off. He suffered from it exceedingly, as well as from the conversational, commonplace, unavoidable intercourse with the other kind of students. "They must be wondering at the change in me," he reflected anxiously. He had an uneasy recollection of having savagely told one or two innocent, nice enough fellows to go to the devil. Once a married professor he used to call upon formerly addressed him in passing: "How is it we never see you at our Wednesdays now, Kirylo Sidorovitch?" Razumov was conscious of meeting this advance with odious, muttering boorishness. The professor was obviously too astonished to be offended. All this was bad. And all this was Haldin, always Haldin—nothing but Haldin—everywhere Haldin: a moral specter infinitely more effective than any visible apparition of the dead. It was only the room through which that man had blundered on his way from crime to death that his specter did not seem to be able to haunt. Not, to be exact, that he was ever completely absent from it, but that there he had no sort of power. There it was Razumov who had the upper hand, in a composed sense of his own superiority. A vanquished phantom—nothing more. Often in the evening, his repaired watch faintly ticking on the table by the side of the lighted lamp, Razumov would look up from his writing and stare at the bed with an expectant, dispassionate attention. Nothing was to be seen there. He never really supposed that anything ever could be seen there. After a while he would shrug his shoulders slightly and bend again over his work. For he had gone to work, and, at first, with some success. His unwillingness to leave that place where he was safe from Haldin grew so strong that at last he ceased to go out at all. From early morning till far into the night he wrote, he wrote for nearly a week; never looking at the time, and only throwing himself on the bed when he could keep his eyes open no longer. Then, one afternoon, quite casually, he happened to glance at his watch. He laid down his pen slowly.

"At this very hour," was his thought, "the fellow stole unseen into this room while I was out. And there he sat quiet as a mouse—perhaps in this very chair."

Razumov got up and began to pace the floor steadily, glancing at the watch now and then. "This is the time when I returned and found him standing against the stove," he observed to himself. When it grew dark he lit his lamp. Later on he interrupted his tramping once more, only to wave away angrily the girl who attempted to enter the room with tea and something to eat on a tray. And presently he noted the watch pointing at the hour of his own going forth into the falling snow on that terrible errand.

"Complicity," he muttered faintly, and resumed his pacing, keeping his eye on the hands as they crept on slowly to the time of his return.

"And, after all," he thought suddenly, "I might have been the chosen instrument of Providence. This is a manner of speaking, but there may be truth in every manner of speaking. What if that absurd saying were true in its essence?"

He meditated for a while, then sat down, his legs stretched out, with stony eyes, and with his arms hanging down on each side of the chair like a man totally abandoned by Providence—desolate.

He noted the time of Haldin's departure and continued to sit still for another half-hour; then muttering, "And now to work," drew up to the table, seized the pen and instantly dropped it under the influence of a profoundly disquieting reflection: "There's three weeks gone by and no word from Mikulin."

What did it mean? Was he forgotten? Possibly. Then why not remain forgotten—creep in somewhere? Hide. But where? How? With whom? In what hole? And was it to be forever, or what?

But a retreat was big with shadowy dangers. The eye of the social revolution was on him, and Razumov for a moment felt an unnamed and despairing dread, mingled with an odious sense of humiliation. Was it possible that he no longer belonged to himself? This was damnable. But why not simply keep on as before? Study. Advance. Work hard as if nothing had happened (and first of all win the Silver Medal), acquire distinction, become a great reforming servant of the greatest of States. Servant, too, of the mightiest homogeneous mass of mankind with a capability for logical, guided development in a brotherly solidarity of force and aim such as the world had never dreamt of . . . the Russian nation!

Calm, resolved, steady in his great purpose, he was stretching his hand towards the pen when he happened to glance towards the bed. He rushed at it, enraged, with a mental scream: "It's you, crazy fanatic, who stand in the way!" He flung the pillow on the floor violently, tore the blankets aside. . . . Nothing there. And, turning away, he caught for an instant in the air, like a vivid detail in a dissolving view of two heads, the eyes of General T—— and of Privy Councillor Mikulin side by side fixed upon him, quite different in character, but with the same unflinching and weary and yet purposeful expression . . . servants of the nation!

Razumov tottered to the washstand very alarmed about himself, drank some water and bathed his forehead. "This will pass and leave no trace," he thought confidently. "I am all right." But as to supposing that he had been forgotten it was perfect nonsense. He was a marked man on that side. And that was nothing.

It was what that miserable phantom stood for which had to be got out of the way. . . . "If one only could go and spit it all out at some of them—and take the consequences."

He imagined himself accosting the red-nosed student and suddenly shaking his fist in his face. "From that one, though," he reflected, "there's nothing to be got, because he has no mind of his own. He's living in a red democratic trance. Ah! you want to smash your way into universal happiness, my boy. I will give you universal happiness, you silly, hypnotized ghoul, you! And what about my own happiness, eh? Haven't I got any right to it, just because I can think for myself? . . ."

And again, but with a different mental accent, Razumov said to himself, "I am young. Everything can be lived down." At that moment he was crossing the room slowly, intending to sit down on the sofa and try to compose his thoughts. But before he had got so far everything abandoned him—hope, courage, belief in himself, trust in men. His heart had, as it were, suddenly emptied itself. It was no use struggling on. Rest, work, solitude, and the frankness of intercourse with his kind were alike forbidden to him. Everything was gone. His existence was a great cold blank, something like the enormous plain of the whole of Russia leveled with snow and fading gradually on all sides into shadows and mists.

He sat down, with swimming head, closed his eyes, and remained like that, sitting bolt upright on the sofa and perfectly awake for the rest of the night; till the girl bustling into the outer room with the samovar thumped with her fist on the door, calling out, "Kirylo Sidorovitch, please! It is time for you to get up!"

Then, pale like a corpse obeying the dread summons of judgment, Razumov opened his eyes and got up.

•   •   •   •   •   •   •   •   •

Nobody will be surprised to hear, I suppose, that when the summons came he went to see Councillor Mikulin. It came that very morning, while, looking white and shaky, like an invalid just out of bed, he was trying to shave himself. The envelope was addressed in the little attorney's handwriting. That envelope contained another, superscribed to Razumov, in Prince K——'s hand, with the request "Please forward under cover at once" in a corner. The note inside was an autograph of Councillor Mikulin. The writer stated candidly that nothing had arisen which needed clearing up, but nevertheless appointed a meeting with Mr. Razumov at a certain address in town which seemed to be that of an oculist.

Razumov read it, finished shaving, dressed, looked at the note again, and muttered gloomily, "Oculist." He pondered over it for a time, lit a match, and burned the two envelopes and the enclosure carefully. Afterwards he waited, sitting perfectly idle and not even looking at anything in particular till the appointed hour drew near—and then went out.

Whether, looking at the unofficial character of the summons, he might have refrained from attending to it is hard to say. Probably not. At any rate, he went; but, what's more, he went with a certain eagerness, which may appear incredible till it is remembered that Councillor Mikulin was the only person on earth with whom Razumov could talk, taking the Haldin adventure for granted. And Haldin, when once taken for granted, was no longer a haunting, falsehood-breeding specter. Whatever troubling power he exercised in all the other places of the earth, Razumov knew very well that at this oculist's address he would be merely the hanged murderer of Mr. de P—— and nothing more. For the dead can live only with the exact intensity and quality of the life imparted to them by the living. So Mr. Razumov, certain of relief, went to meet Councillor Mikulin with the eagerness of a pursued person welcoming any sort of shelter.

This much said, there is no need to tell anything more of that first interview and of the several others. To the morality of a Western reader an account of these meetings would wear perhaps the sinister character of old legendary tales where the Enemy of Mankind is represented holding subtly mendacious dialogues with some tempted soul. It is not my part to protest. Let me but remark that the Evil One, with his single passion of satanic pride for the only motive, is yet, on a larger, modern view, allowed to be not quite so black as he used to be painted. With what greater latitude, then, should we appraise the exact shade of mere mortal man, with his many passions and his miserable ingenuity in error, always dazzled by the base glitter of mixed motives, everlastingly betrayed by a shortsighted wisdom.

Councillor Mikulin was one of those powerful officials who, in a position not obscure, not occult, but simply inconspicuous, exercise a great influence over the methods rather than over the conduct of affairs. A devotion to Church and Throne is not in itself a criminal sentiment; to prefer the will of one to the will of many does not argue the possession of a black heart or prove congenital idiocy. Councillor Mikulin was not only a clever but also a faithful official. Privately he was a bachelor with a love of comfort, living alone in an apartment of five rooms luxuriously furnished; and was known by his intimates to be an enlightened patron of the art of female dancing. Later on the larger world first heard of him in the very hour of his downfall, during one of those State trials which astonish and puzzle the average plain man who reads the newspapers, by a glimpse of unsuspected intrigues. And in the stir of vaguely seen monstrosities, in that momentary, mysterious disturbance of muddy waters, Councillor Mikulin went under, dignified, with only a calm, emphatic protest of his innocence—nothing more. No disclosures damaging to a harassed autocracy, complete fidelity to the secrets of the miserable *arcana imperii* deposited in his patriotic breast, a display of bureaucratic stoicism in a Russian official's ineradicable, almost sublime contempt for truth; stoicism of silence understood only by the very few of the initiated, and not without a certain cynical grandeur of self-sacrifice on the part of a sybarite. For the terribly heavy sentence turned Councillor Mikulin civilly into a corpse, and actually into something very much like a common convict.

It seems that the savage autocracy, no more than the divine democracy, does not limit its diet exclusively to the bodies of its enemies. It devours its friends and servants as well. The downfall of His Excellency Gregory Gregorievitch Mikulin (which did not occur till some years later) completes all that is known of the man. But at the time of Mr. de P——'s murder (or execution) Councillor Mikulin, under the modest style of Head of Department at the General Secretariat, exercised a wide influence as the confidant and right-hand man of his former schoolfellow and lifelong friend, General T——. One can imagine them talking over the case of Mr. Razumov, with the full sense of their unbounded power over all the lives in Russia, with cursory disdain, like two Olympians glancing at a worm. The relationship with Prince K—— was enough to save Razumov from some carelessly arbitrary proceeding, and it is also very probable that after the interview at the Secretariat he would have been left alone. Councillor Mikulin would not have forgotten him (he forgot no one who ever fell under his observation), but would have simply dropped him forever. Councillor Mikulin was a good-natured man and wished no harm to anyone. Besides (with his own reforming tendencies) he was favorably impressed by that young student, the son of Prince K——, and apparently no fool.

But as fate would have it, while Mr. Razumov was finding that no way of life was possible to him, Councillor Mikulin's discreet abilities were rewarded by a very responsible post—nothing less than the direction of the general police supervision over Europe. And it was then, and then only, when taking in hand the perfecting of the service which watches the revolutionist activities abroad, that he thought again of Mr. Razumov. He saw great possibilities of special usefulness in that uncommon young man on whom he had a hold already, with his peculiar temperament, his unsettled mind and shaken conscience, struggling in the toils of a false position. . . . It was as if the revolutionists themselves had put into his hand that tool so much finer than the common base instruments, so perfectly fitted, if only vested with sufficient credit, to penetrate into places inaccessible to common informers. Providential! Providential! And Prince K——, taken into the secret, was ready enough to adopt that mystical view too. "It will be necessary, though, to make a career for him afterwards," he had stipulated anxiously. "Oh! absolutely. We shall make that our affair," Mikulin had agreed. Prince K——'s mysticism was of an artless kind; but Councillor Mikulin was astute enough for two.

Things and men have always a certain sense, a certain side by which they must be got hold of if one wants to obtain a solid grasp and a perfect command. The power of Councillor Mikulin consisted in the ability to seize upon that sense, that side in the men he used. It did not matter to him what it was—vanity, despair, love, hate, greed, intelligent pride or stupid conceit, it was all one to him as long as the man could be made to serve. The obscure, unrelated young student Razumov, in the moment of great moral loneliness, was allowed to feel that he was an object of interest to a small group of people of high position. Prince K—— was persuaded to intervene personally, and on a certain occasion gave way to a manly emotion which, all unexpected as it was, quite upset Mr. Razumov. The sudden embrace of that man, agitated by his loyalty to a throne and by suppressed paternal affection, was a revelation to Mr. Razumov of something within his own breast.

"So that was it!" he exclaimed to himself. A sort of contemptuous tenderness softened the young man's grim view of his position as he reflected upon that agitated interview with Prince K——. This simple-minded, worldly ex-Guardsman and senator whose soft gray official whiskers had brushed against his cheek, his aristocratic and convinced father, was he a whit less estimable or more absurd than that famine-stricken, fanatical revolutionist, the red-nosed student?

And there was some pressure, too, besides the persuasiveness. Mr. Razumov was always being made to feel that he had committed himself. There was no getting away from that feeling, from that soft, unanswerable "Where to?" of Councillor Mikulin. But no susceptibilities were ever hurt. It was to be a dangerous mission to Geneva for obtaining, at a critical moment, absolutely reliable information from a very inaccessible quarter of the inner revolutionary circle. There were indications that a very serious plot was being matured. . . . The repose indispensable to a great country was at stake. . . . A great scheme of orderly reforms would be endangered. . . . The highest personages in the land were patriotically uneasy, and so on. In short, Councillor Mikulin knew what to say. This skill is to be inferred clearly from the mental and psychological self-confession, self-analysis of Mr. Razumov's written journal—the pitiful resource of a young man who had near him no trusted intimacy, no natural affection to turn to.

How all this preliminary work was concealed from observation need not be recorded. The expedient of the oculist gives a sufficient instance. Councillor Mikulin was resourceful, and the task not very difficult. Any fellow-student, even the red-nosed one, was perfectly welcome to see Mr. Razumov entering a private house to consult an oculist. Ultimate success depended solely on the revolutionary self-delusion which credited Razumov with a mysterious complicity in the Haldin affair. To be compromised in it was credit enough—and it was their own doing. It was precisely *that* which stamped Mr. Razumov as a providential man, wide as poles apart from the usual type of agent for "European supervision."

And it was *that* which the Secretariat set itself the task to foster by a course of calculated and false indiscretions.

It came at last to this, that one evening Mr. Razumov was unexpectedly called upon by one of the "thinking" students whom formerly, before the Haldin affair, he used to meet at various private gatherings; a big fellow with a quiet, unassuming manner and a pleasant voice.

Recognizing his voice raised in the anteroom, "May one come in?" Razumov, lounging idly on his couch, jumped up. "Suppose he were coming to stab me?" he thought sardonically, and, assuming a green shade over his left eye, said in a severe tone, "Come in."

The other was embarrassed; hoped he was not intruding.

"You haven't been seen for several days, and I've wondered." He coughed a little. "Eye better?"

"Nearly well now."

"Good. I won't stop a minute; but you see I, that is, we—anyway, I have undertaken the duty to warn you, Kirylo Sidorovitch, that you are living in false security maybe."

Razumov sat still with his head leaning on his hand, which nearly concealed the unshaded eye.

"I have that idea too."

"That's all right, then. Everything seems quiet now, but those people are preparing some move of general repression. That's of course. But it isn't that I came to tell you." He hitched his chair closer, dropped his voice. "You will be arrested before long—we fear."

An obscure scribe in the Secretariat had overheard a few words of a certain conversation, and had caught a glimpse of a certain report. This intelligence was not to be neglected.

Razumov laughed a little, and his visitor became very anxious.

"Ah, Kirylo Sidorovitch, this is no laughing matter. They have left you alone for a while, but . . . ! Indeed, you had better try to leave the country, Kirylo Sidorovitch, while there's yet time."

Razumov jumped up and began to thank him for the advice with mocking effusiveness, so that the other, coloring up, took himself off with the notion that this mysterious Razumov was not a person to be warned or advised by inferior mortals.

Councillor Mikulin, informed the next day of the incident, expressed his satisfaction. "H'm. Ha! Exactly what was wanted to . . ." and glanced down his beard.

"I conclude," said Razumov, "that the moment has come for me to start on my mission."

"The psychological moment," Councillor Mikulin insisted softly—very gravely—as if awed.

All the arrangements to give verisimilitude to the appearance of a difficult escape were made. Councillor Mikulin did not expect to see Mr. Razumov again before his departure. These meetings were a risk, and there was nothing more to settle.

"We have said everything to each other by now, Kirylo Sidorovitch," said the high official feelingly, pressing Razumov's hand with that unreserved heartiness a Russian can convey in his manner. "There is nothing obscure between us. And I will tell you what! I consider myself fortunate in having—h'm—your . . ."

He glanced down his beard, and, after a moment of thoughtful silence, handed to Razumov a half-sheet of notepaper—an abbreviated note of matters already discussed, certain points of inquiry, the line of conduct agreed on, a few hints as to personalities, and so on. It was the only compromising document in the case, but, as Councillor Mikulin observed, "it could be easily destroyed. Mr. Razumov had better not see anyone now—till on the other side of the frontier, when, of course, it will be just that . . . See and hear and . . ."

He glanced down his beard; but when Razumov declared his intention to see one person at least before leaving St. Petersburg, Councillor Mikulin failed to conceal a sudden uneasiness. The young man's studious, solitary, and austere existence was well known to him. It was the greatest guarantee of fitness. He became deprecatory. Had his dear Kirylo Sidorovitch considered whether, in view of such a momentous enterprise, it wasn't really advisable to sacrifice every sentiment? . . .

Razumov interrupted the remonstrance scornfully. It was not a young woman, it was a young fool he wished to see for a certain purpose. Councillor Mikulin was relieved, but surprised.

"Ah! And what for—precisely?"

"For the sake of improving the aspect of verisimilitude," said Razumov curtly, in a desire to affirm his independence. "I must be trusted in what I do."

Councillor Mikulin gave way tactfully, murmuring, "Oh, certainly, certainly. Your judgment . . ."

And with another handshake they parted.

The fool of whom Mr. Razumov had thought was the rich and festive student known as Madcap Kostia. Feather-headed, loquacious, excitable, one could make certain of his utter and complete indiscretion. But that riotous youth, when reminded by Razumov of his offers of service some time ago, passed from his usual elation into boundless dismay.

"Oh, Kirylo Sidorovitch, my dearest friend—my savior—what shall I do? I've blown last night every ruble I had from my dad the other day. Can't you give me till Thursday? I shall rush round to all the usurers I know. . . . No, of course you can't! Don't look at me like that. What shall I do? No use asking the old man. I tell you he's given me a fistful of big notes three days ago. Miserable wretch that I am."

He wrung his hands in despair. Impossible to confide in the old man. "They" had given him a decoration, a cross on the neck only last year, and he had been cursing the modern tendencies ever since. Just then he would see all the intellectuals in Russia hanged in a row rather than part with a single ruble.

"Kirylo Sidorovitch, wait a moment. Don't despise me. I have it. I'll, yes—I'll do it—I'll break into his desk. There's no help for it. I know the drawer where he keeps his plunder, and I can buy a chisel on my way home. He will be terribly upset, but, you know, the dear old duffer really loves me. He'll have to get over it—and I, too. Kirylo, my dear soul, if you can only wait for a few hours—till this evening—I shall steal all the blessed lot I can lay my hands on! You doubt me! Why? You've only to say the word."

"Steal, by all means," said Razumov, fixing him stonily.

"To the devil with the Ten Commandments!" cried the other, with the greatest animation. "It's the new future now."

But when he entered Razumov's room late in the evening it was with an unaccustomed soberness of manner, almost solemnly.

"It's done," he said.

Razumov, sitting bowed, his clasped hands hanging between his knees, shuddered at the familiar sound of these words. Kostia deposited slowly in the circle of lamplight a small brown-paper parcel tied with a piece of string.

"As I've said—all I could lay my hands on. The old boy'll think the end of the world has come."

Razumov nodded from the couch, and contemplated the harebrained fellow's gravity with a feeling of malicious pleasure.

"I've made my little sacrifice," sighed mad Kostia. "And I've to thank you, Kirylo Sidorovitch, for the opportunity."

"It has cost you something?"

"Yes, it has. You see, the dear old duffer really loves me. He'll be hurt."

"And you believe all they tell you of the new future and the sacred will of the people?"

"Implicitly. I would give my life . . . Only, you see, I am like a pig at a trough. I am no good. It's my nature."

Razumov, lost in thought, had forgotten his existence till the youth's voice, entreating him to fly without loss of time, roused him unpleasantly.

"All right. Well—goodbye."

"I am not going to leave you till I've seen you out of St. Petersburg," declared Kostia unexpectedly, with calm determination. "You can't refuse me that now. For God's sake, Kirylo, my soul, the police may be here any moment, and when they get you they'll immure you somewhere for ages—till your hair turns gray. I have down there the best trotter of dad's stables and a light sledge. We shall do thirty miles before the moon sets, and find some roadside station . . ."

Razumov looked up amazed. The journey was decided—unavoidable. He had fixed the next day for his departure on the mission. And now he discovered suddenly that he had not believed in it. He had gone about listening, speaking, thinking, planning his simulated flight, with the growing conviction that all this was preposterous. As if anybody ever did such things! It was like a game of make-believe. And now he was amazed! Here was somebody who believed in it with desperate earnestness. "If I don't go now, at once," thought Razumov, with a start of fear, "I shall never go." He rose without a word, and the anxious Kostia thrust his cap on him, helped him into his cloak, or else he would have left the room bareheaded as he stood. He was walking out silently when a sharp cry arrested him.

"Kirylo!"

"What?" He turned reluctantly in the doorway. Upright, with a stiffly extended arm, Kostia, his face set and white, was pointing an eloquent forefinger at the brown little packet lying forgotten in the circle of bright light on the table. Razumov hesitated, came back for it under the severe eyes of his companion, at whom he tried to smile. But the boyish, mad youth was frowning. "It's a dream," thought Razumov, putting the little parcel into his pocket and descending the stairs; "nobody does such things." The other held him under the arm, whispering of dangers ahead, and of what he meant to do in certain contingencies. "Preposterous," murmured Razumov, as he was being tucked up in the sledge. He gave himself up to watching the development of the dream with extreme attention. It continued on foreseen lines, inexorably logical—the long drive, the wait at the small station sitting by a stove. They did not exchange half a dozen words altogether. Kostia, gloomy himself, did not care to break the silence. At parting they embraced twice—it had to be done; and then Kostia vanished out of the dream.

When dawn broke, Razumov, very still in a hot, stuffy railway car full of bedding and of sleeping people in all its dimly lighted length, rose quietly, lowered the glass a few inches, and flung out on the great plain of snow a small brown-paper parcel. Then he sat down again muffled up and motionless. "For the people," he thought, staring out of the window. The great white desert of frozen, hard earth glided past his eyes without a sign of human habitation.

That had been a waking act; and then the dream had him again: Prussia, Saxony, Würtemberg, faces, sights, words—all a dream, observed with an angry, compelled attention. Zurich, Geneva—still a dream, minutely followed, wearing one into harsh laughter, to fury, to death—with the fear of awakening at the end. . . .

II

"Perhaps life is just that," reflected Razumov, pacing to and fro under the trees of the little island, all alone with the bronze statue of Rousseau. "A dream and a fear." The dusk deepened. The pages written over and torn out of his notebook were the first fruit of his "mission." No dream that. They contained the assurance that he was on the eve of real discoveries. "I think there is no longer anything in the way of my being completely accepted."

He had resumed his impressions in those pages, some of the conversations. He even went so far as to write: "By-the-bye, I have discovered the personality of that terrible N.N. A horrible, paunchy brute. If I hear anything of his future movements I shall send a warning."

The futility of all this overcame him like a curse. Even then he could not believe in the reality of his mission. He looked round despairingly, as if for some way to redeem his existence from that unconquerable feeling. He crushed angrily in his hand the pages of the notebook. "This must be posted," he thought.

He gained the bridge and returned to the north shore, where he remembered having seen in one of the narrower streets a little obscure shop stocked with cheap wood carvings, its walls lined with extremely dirty cardboard-bound volumes of a small circulating library. They sold stationery there too. A morose, shabby old man dozed behind the counter. A thin woman in black, with a sickly face, produced the envelope he had asked for without even looking at him. Razumov thought that these people were safe to deal with because they no longer cared for anything in the world. He addressed the envelope on the counter with the German name of a certain person living in Vienna. But Razumov knew that this, his first communication for Councillor Mikulin, would find its way to the Embassy there, be copied in cipher by somebody trustworthy, and sent on to its destination, all safe, along with the diplomatic correspondence. That was the arrangement contrived to cover up the track of the information from all unfaithful eyes, from all indiscretions, from all mishaps and treacheries. It was to make him safe—absolutely safe.

He wandered out of the wretched shop and made for the post office. It was then that I saw him for the second time that day. He was crossing the Rue Mont Blanc with every appearance of an aimless stroller. He did not recognize me, but I made him out at some distance. He was very good-looking, I thought, this remarkable friend of Miss Haldin's brother. I watched him go up to the letter box and then retrace his steps. Again he passed me very close, but I am certain he did not see me that time, either. He carried his head well up, but he had the expression of a somnambulist struggling with the very dream which drives him forth to wander in dangerous places. My thoughts reverted to

Natalia Haldin, to her mother. He was all that was left to them of their son and brother.

The Westerner in me was discomposed. There was something shocking in the expression of that face. Had I been myself a conspirator, a Russian political refugee, I could have perhaps been able to draw some practical conclusion from this chance glimpse. As it was, it only discomposed me strongly, even to the extent of awakening an indefinite apprehension in regard to Natalia Haldin. All this is rather inexplicable, but such was the origin of the purpose I formed there and then to call on these ladies in the evening, after my solitary dinner. It was true that I had met Miss Haldin only a few hours before, but Mrs. Haldin herself I had not seen for some considerable time. The truth is, I had shirked calling of late.

Poor Mrs. Haldin! I confess she frightened me a little. She was one of those natures, rare enough, luckily, in which one cannot help being interested, because they provoke both terror and pity. One dreads their contact for oneself, and still more for those one cares for, so clear it is that they are born to suffer and to make others suffer too. It is strange to think that, I won't say liberty, but the mere liberalism of outlook which for us is a matter of words, of ambitions, of votes (and if of feeling at all, then of the sort of feeling which leaves our deepest affections untouched), may be for other beings very much like ourselves and living under the same sky, a heavy trial of fortitude, a matter of tears and anguish and blood. Mrs. Haldin had felt the pangs of her own generation. There was that enthusiast brother of hers—the officer they shot under Nicholas. A faintly ironic resignation is no armor for a vulnerable heart. Mrs. Haldin, struck at through her children, was bound to suffer afresh from the past, and to feel the anguish of the future. She was of those who do not know how to heal themselves, of those who are too much aware of their heart, who, neither cowardly nor selfish, look passionately at its wounds—and count the cost.

Such thoughts as these seasoned my modest, lonely bachelor's meal. If anybody wishes to remark that this was a roundabout way of thinking of Natalia Haldin, I can only retort that she was well worth some concern. She had all her life before her. Let it be admitted, then, that I was thinking of Natalia Haldin's life in terms of her mother's character, a manner of thinking about a girl permissible for an old man, not too old yet to have become a stranger to pity. There was almost all her youth before her—youth robbed arbitrarily of its natural lightness and joy, overshadowed by an un-European despotism; a terribly somber youth given over to the hazards of a furious strife between equally ferocious antagonisms.

I lingered over my thoughts more than I should have done. One felt so helpless, and even worse—so unrelated in a way. At the last moment I hesitated as to going there at all. What was the good?

The evening was already advanced when, turning into the Boulevard des Philosophes, I saw the light in the window at the corner. The blind was down, but I could imagine behind it Mrs. Haldin seated in the chair, in her usual attitude, looking out for someone, which had lately acquired the poignant quality of mad expectation.

I thought that I was sufficiently authorized by the light to knock at the door. The ladies had not retired as yet. I only hoped they would not have any visitors of their own nationality. A broken-down, retired Russian official was to be found there sometimes in the evening. He was infinitely forlorn and wearisome by his mere dismal presence. I think these ladies tolerated his frequent visits because of an ancient friendship with Mr. Haldin, the father, or something of that sort. I made up my mind that if I found him prosing away there in his feeble voice I should remain but a very few minutes.

The door surprised me by swinging open before I could ring the bell. I was confronted by Miss Haldin, in hat and jacket, obviously on the point of going out. At that hour! For the doctor, perhaps?

Her exclamation of welcome reassured me. It sounded as if I had been the very man she wanted to see. My curiosity was awakened. She drew me in, and the faithful Anna, the elderly German maid, closed the door, but did not go away afterwards. She remained near it as if in readiness to let me out presently. It appeared that Miss Haldin had been on the point of going out to find me.

She spoke in a hurried manner very unusual with her. She would have gone straight and rung at Mrs. Ziegler's door, late as it was, for Mrs. Ziegler's habits . . .

Mrs. Ziegler, the widow of a distinguished professor who was an intimate friend of mine, lets me have three rooms out of her very large and fine apartment, which she didn't give up after her husband's death; but I have my own entrance opening on the same landing. It was an arrangement of at least ten years' standing. I said that I was very glad that I had the idea to . . .

Miss Haldin made no motion to take off her outdoor things. I observed her heightened color, something pronouncedly resolute in her tone. Did I know where Mr. Razumov lived?

Where Mr. Razumov lived? Mr. Razumov? At this hour—so urgently? I threw my arms up in sign of utter ignorance. I had not the slightest idea where he lived. If I could have foreseen her question only three hours ago, I might have ventured to ask him on the pavement before the new post office building, and possibly he would have told me, but very possibly, too, he would have dismissed me rudely to mind my own business. And possibly, I thought, remembering that extraordinary hallucined, anguished, and absent expression, he might have fallen down in a fit from the shock of being spoken to. I said nothing of all this to Miss Haldin, not even mentioning that I had a glimpse of the young man so recently. The impression had been so extremely unpleasant that I would have been glad to forget it myself.

"I don't see where I could make inquiries," I murmured helplessly. I would have been glad to be of use in any way, and would have set off to fetch any man, young or old, for I had the greatest confidence in her common sense. "What made you think of coming to me for that information?" I asked.

"It wasn't exactly for that," she said, in a low voice. She had the air of someone confronted by an unpleasant task.

"Am I to understand that you must communicate with Mr. Razumov this evening?"

Natalia Haldin moved her head affirmatively; then, after a glance at the door of the drawing room, said in French:

"*C'est maman*," and remained perplexed for a moment. Always serious, not a girl to be put out by any imaginary difficulties, my curiosity was suspended on her lips, which remained closed for a moment. What was Mr. Razumov's connection with this mention of her mother? Mrs. Haldin had not been informed of her son's friend's arrival in Geneva.

"May I hope to see your mother this evening?" I inquired.

Miss Haldin extended her hand as if to bar the way.

"She is in a terrible state of agitation. Oh, you would not be able to detect . . . It's inward, but I who know mother, I am appalled. I haven't the courage to face it any longer. It's all my fault; I suppose I cannot play a part; I've never before hidden anything from mother. There has never been an occasion for anything of that sort between us. But you know yourself the reason why I refrained from telling her at once of Mr. Razumov's arrival here. You understand, don't you? Owing to her unhappy state. And—there——I am no actress. My own feelings being strongly engaged, I somehow . . . I don't know. She noticed something in my manner. She thought I was concealing something from her. She noticed my longer absences, and, in fact, as I have been meeting Mr. Razumov daily, I used to stay away longer than usual when I went out. Goodness knows what suspicions arose in her mind. You know that she has not been herself ever since. . . . So this evening she—who has been so awfully silent for weeks—began to talk all at once. She said that she did not want to reproach me; that I had my character as she had her own; that she did not want to pry into my affairs or even into my thoughts; for her part, she had never had anything to conceal from her children. . . . Cruel things to listen to. And all this in her quiet voice, with that poor, wasted face as calm as a stone. It was unbearable."

Miss Haldin talked in an undertone and more rapidly than I had ever heard her speak before. That in itself was disturbing. The anteroom being strongly lighted, I could see under the veil the heightened color of her face. She stood erect, her left hand was resting lightly on a small table. The other hung by her side without stirring. Now and then she caught her breath slightly.

"It was too startling. Just fancy! She thought that I was making preparations to leave her without saying anything. I knelt by the side of her chair and entreated her to think of what she was saying! She put her hand on my head, but she persists in her delusion all the same. She had always thought that she was worthy of her children's confidence, but apparently it was not so. Her son could not trust her love nor yet her understanding—and now I was planning to abandon her in the same cruel and unjust manner, and so on, and so on. Nothing I could say . . . It is morbid obstinacy. . . . She said that she felt there was something, some change in me. . . . If my convictions were calling me away, why this secrecy, as though she had been a coward or a weakling not safe to trust? 'As if my heart could play traitor to my children,' she said. . . . It was hardly to be borne. And she was smoothing my head all the time. . . . It was perfectly useless to protest. She is ill. Her very soul is . . ."

I did not venture to break the silence which fell between us. I looked into her eyes, glistening through the veil.

"I! Changed!" she exclaimed in the same low tone. "My convictions calling me away! It was cruel to hear this, because my trouble is that I am weak and cannot see what I ought to do. You know that. And to end it all I did a selfish thing. To remove her suspicions of myself I told her of Mr. Razumov. It was selfish of me. You know we were completely right in agreeing to keep the knowledge away from her. Perfectly right. Directly I told her of our poor Victor's friend being here I saw how right we have been. She ought to have been prepared; but in my distress I just blurted it out. Mother got terribly excited at once. How long has he been here? What did he know, and why did he not come to see us at once, this friend of her Victor? What did that mean? Was she not to be trusted even with such memories as there were left of her son? . . . Just think how I felt seeing her, white as a sheet, perfectly motionless, with her thin hands gripping the arms of the chair. I told her it was all my fault."

I could imagine the motionless dumb figure of the mother in her chair, there, behind the door, near which the daughter was talking to me. The silence in there seemed to call aloud for vengeance against an historical fact and the modern instances of its working. That view flashed through my mind, but I could not doubt that Miss Haldin had had an atrocious time of it. I quite understood when she said that she could not face the night upon the impression of that scene. Mrs. Haldin had given way to most awful imaginings, to most fantastic and cruel suspicions. All this had to be lulled at all costs and without loss of time. It was no shock to me to learn that Miss Haldin had said to her, "I will go and bring him here at once." There was nothing absurd in that cry, no exaggeration of sentiment. I was not even doubtful in my "Very well, but how?"

It was perfectly right that she should think of me, but what could I do in my ignorance of Mr. Razumov's quarters?

"And to think he may be living nearby, within a stone's-throw, perhaps!" she exclaimed.

I doubted it; but I would have gone off cheerfully to fetch him from the other end of Geneva. I suppose she was certain of my readiness, since her first thought was to come to me. But the service she meant to ask of me really was to accompany her to the Château Borel.

I had an unpleasant mental vision of the dark road, of the somber grounds, and the desolately suspicious aspect of that home of necromancy and intrigue and feminist adoration. I objected that Madame de S—— most likely would know nothing of what we wanted to find out. Neither did I think it likely that the young man would be found there. I remembered my glimpse of his face, and somehow gained the conviction that a man who looked worse than if he had seen the dead would want to shut himself up somewhere where he could be alone. I felt a strange certitude that Mr. Razumov was going home when I saw him.

"It is really of Peter Ivanovitch that I was thinking," said Miss Haldin quietly. Ah! He, of course, would know. I looked at my watch. It was twenty minutes past nine only. . . . Still."

"I would try his hotel, then," I advised. "He has rooms at the Cosmopolitan, somewhere on the top floor."

I did not offer to go by myself, simply from mistrust of the reception I should meet with. But I suggested the faithful Anna, with a note asking for the information.

Anna was still waiting by the door at the other end of the room, and we two discussed the matter in whispers. Miss Haldin thought she must go herself. Anna was timid and slow. Time would be lost in bringing back the answer, and from that point of view it was getting late, for it was by no means certain that Mr. Razumov lived nearby.

"If I go myself," Miss Haldin argued, "I can go straight to him from the hotel. And in any case I should have to go out, because I must explain to Mr. Razumov personally—prepare him in a way. You have no idea of mother's state of mind."

Her color came and went. She even thought that both for her mother's sake and for her own it was better that they should not be together for a little time. Anna, whom her mother liked, would be at hand.

"She could take her sewing into the room," Miss Haldin continued, leading the way to the door. Then, addressing in German the maid who opened it before us, "You may tell my mother that this gentleman called and is gone with me to find Mr. Razumov. She must not be uneasy if I am away for some length of time."

We passed out quickly into the street, and she took deep breaths of the cool night air. "I did not even ask you," she murmured.

"I should think not," I said, with a laugh. The manner of my reception by the great feminist could not be considered now. That he would be annoyed to see me, and probably treat me to some solemn insolence, I had no doubt, but I supposed that he would not absolutely dare to throw me out. And that was all I cared for. "Won't you take my arm?" I asked.

She did so in silence, and neither of us said anything worth recording till I let her go first into the great hall of the hotel. It was brilliantly lighted, and with a good many people lounging about.

"I could very well go up there without you," I suggested.

"I don't like to be left waiting in this place," she said in a low voice. "I will come too."

I led her straight to the lift then. At the top floor the attendant directed us to the right: "End of the corridor."

The walls were white, the carpet red, electric lights blazed in confusion, and the emptiness, the silence, the closed doors all alike and numbered, made me think of the perfect order of some severely luxurious model penitentiary on the solitary confinement principle. Up there under the roof of that enormous pile for housing travelers no sound of any kind reached us, the thick crimson felt muffled our footsteps completely. We hastened on, not looking at each other till we found ourselves before the very last door of that long passage. Then our eyes met, and we stood thus for a moment lending ear to a faint murmur of voices inside.

"I suppose this is it," I whispered unnecessarily. I saw Miss Haldin's lips move without a sound, and after my sharp knock the murmur of voices inside ceased. A profound stillness lasted for a few seconds, and then the door was bruskly opened by a short black-eyed woman in a red blouse, with a lot of nearly white hair, done up negligently in an untidy and unpicturesque manner. Her thin, jetty eyebrows were drawn together. I learned afterwards with interest that she was the famous—or the notorious—Sophia Antonovna, but I was struck then by the quaint Mephistophelian character of her inquiring glance, because it was so curiously evil-less, so I may say—un-devilish. It got softened still more as she looked up at Miss Haldin, who stated, in her rich, even voice, her wish to see Peter Ivanovitch for a moment.

"I am Miss Haldin," she added.

At this, with her brow completely smoothed out now, but without a word in answer, the woman in the red blouse walked away to a sofa and sat down, leaving the door wide open.

And from the sofa, her hands lying on her lap, she watched us enter, with her black, glittering eyes.

Miss Haldin advanced into the middle of the room; I, faithful to my part of mere attendant, remained by the door after closing it behind me. The room, quite a large one, but with a low ceiling, was scantily furnished, and an electric bulb with a porcelain shade pulled low down over a big table (with a very large map spread on it) left its distant parts in a dim, artificial twilight. Peter Ivanovitch was not to be seen, neither was Mr. Razumov present. But, on the sofa, near Sophia Antonovna, **a** bony-faced man with a goatee beard leaned forward with his hands on his knees, staring hard with a kindly expression. In a remote corner a broad, pale face and a bulky shape could be made out, uncouth, and as if insecure on the low seat on which it rested. The only person known to me was little Julius Laspara, who seemed to have been poring over the map, his feet twined tightly round the chair legs. He got down briskly and bowed to Miss Haldin, looking absurdly like a hooknosed boy with a beautiful false pepper-and-salt beard. He advanced, offering his seat, which Miss Haldin declined. She had only come in for a moment to say a few words to Peter Ivanovitch.

His high-pitched voice became painfully audible in the room.

"Strangely enough, I was thinking of you this very afternoon, Natalia Victorovna. I met Mr. Razumov. I asked him to write me an article on anything he liked. You could translate it into English—with such a teacher."

He nodded complimentarily in my direction. At the name of Razumov an indescribable sound, a sort of feeble squeak, as of some angry small animal, was heard in the corner occupied by the man who seemed much too large for the chair on which he sat. I did not hear what Miss Haldin said. Laspara spoke again.

"It's time to do something, Natalia Victorovna. But I suppose you have your own ideas. Why not write something yourself? Suppose you came to see us soon? We could talk it over. Any advice . . ."

Again I did not catch Miss Haldin's words. It was Laspara's voice once more.

"Peter Ivanovitch? He's retired for a moment into the other room. We are all waiting for him."

The great man, entering at that moment, looked bigger, taller, quite imposing in a long dressing gown of some dark stuff. It descended in straight lines down to his feet. He suggested a monk or a prophet, a robust figure of some desert-dweller—something Asiatic; and the dark glasses in conjunction with this costume made him more mysterious than ever in the subdued light.

Little Laspara went back to his chair to look at the map, the only brilliantly lit object in the room. Even from my distant position by the door I could make out, by the shape of the blue part representing the water, that it was a map of the Baltic provinces. Peter Ivanovitch exclaimed slightly, advancing towards Miss Haldin, checked himself on perceiving me, very vaguely no doubt, and peered with his dark, bespectacled stare. He must have recognized me by my gray hair, because, with a marked shrug of his broad shoulders, he turned to Miss Haldin in benevolent indulgence. He seized her hand in his thick cushioned palm, and put his other big paw over it like a lid.

While those two standing in the middle of the floor were exchanging a few inaudible phrases no one else moved in the room; Laspara, with his back to us, kneeling on the chair, his elbows propped on the big-scale map, the shadowy enormity in the corner, the frankly staring man with the goatee on the sofa, the woman in the red blouse by his side—not one of them stirred. I suppose that really they had no time, for Miss Haldin withdrew her hand immediately from Peter Ivanovitch and before I was ready for her was moving to the door. A disregarded Westerner, I threw it open hurriedly and followed her out, my last glance leaving them all motionless in their varied poses: Peter Ivanovitch alone standing up, with his dark glasses like an enormous blind teacher, and behind him the vivid patch of light on the colored map, pored over by the diminutive Laspara.

Later on, much later on, at the time of the newspaper rumors (they were vague and soon died out) of an abortive military conspiracy in Russia, I remembered the glimpse I had of that motionless group with its central figure. No details ever came out, but it was known that the revolutionary parties abroad had given their assistance, had sent emissaries in advance, that even money was found to dispatch a steamer with a cargo of arms and conspirators to invade the Baltic provinces. And while my eyes scanned the imperfect disclosures (in which the world was not much interested), I thought that the old, settled Europe had been given in my person attending that Russian girl something like a glimpse behind the scenes. A short, strange glimpse on the top floor of a great hotel of all places in the world: the great man himself; the motionless great bulk in the corner of the slayer of spies and gendarmes; Yakovlitch, the veteran of ancient terrorist campaigns; the woman, with her hair as white as mine and the lively black eyes, all in a mysterious half-light, with the strongly lighted map of Russia on the table. The woman I had the opportunity to see again. As we were waiting for the lift she came hurrying along the corridor, with her eyes fastened on Miss Haldin's face, and drew her aside as if for a confidential communication. It was not long. A few words only.

Going down in the lift, Natalia Haldin did not break the silence. It was only when out of the hotel and as we moved along the quay in the fresh darkness spangled by the quay lights, reflected in the black water of the little port on our left hand, and with lofty piles of hotels on our right, that she spoke.

"That was Sophia Antonovna—you know the woman?"

"Yes, I know—the famous . . ."

"The same. It appears that after we went out Peter Ivanovitch told them why I had come. That was the reason she ran out after us. She named herself to me, and then she said, 'You are the sister of a brave man who shall be remembered. You may see better times.' I told her I hoped to see the time when all this would be forgotten, even if the name of my brother were to be forgotten too. Something moved me to say that, but you understand?"

"Yes," I said. "You think of the era of concord and justice."

"Yes. There is too much hate and revenge in that work. It must be done. It is a sacrifice—and so let it be all the greater. Destruction is the work of anger. Let the tyrants and the slayers be forgotten together, and only the reconstructors be remembered."

"And did Sophia Antonovna agree with you?" I asked skeptically.

"She did not say anything except, 'It is good for you to believe in love.' I should think she understood me. Then she asked me if I hoped to see Mr. Razumov presently. I said I trusted I could manage to bring him to see my mother this evening, as my mother had learned of his being here and was morbidly impatient to learn if he could tell us something of Victor. He was the only friend of my brother we knew of, and a great intimate. She said, 'Oh! Your brother—yes. Please tell Mr. Razumov that I have made public the story which came to me from St. Petersburg. It concerns your brother's arrest,' she added. 'He was betrayed by a man of the people who has since hanged himself. Mr. Razumov will explain it all to you. I gave him the full information this afternoon. And please tell Mr. Razumov that Sophia Antonovna sends him her greetings. I am going away early in the morning—far away.'"

And Miss Haldin added, after a moment of silence:

"I was so moved by what I heard so unexpectedly that I simply could not speak to you before. . . . A man of the people! Oh, our poor people!"

She walked slowly, as if tired out suddenly. Her head drooped; from the windows of a building with terraces and balconies came the banal sound of hotel music; before the low mean portals of the Casino two red posters blazed under the electric lamps, with a cheap provincial effect—and the emptiness of the quays, the desert aspect of the streets, had an air of hypocritical respectability and of inexpressible dreariness.

I had taken for granted she had obtained the address, and let myself be guided by her. On the Mont Blanc bridge, where a few dark figures seemed lost in the wide and long perspective defined by the lights, she said:

"It isn't very far from our house. I somehow thought it couldn't be. The address is Rue de Carouge. I think it must be one of those big new houses for artisans."

She took my arm confidingly, familiarly, and accelerated her pace. There was something primitive in our proceedings. We did not think of the resources of civilization. A late tramcar overtook us; a row of fiacres stood by the railing of the gardens. It never entered our heads to make use of these conveyances. She was too hurried, perhaps, and as to myself—well, she had taken my arm confidingly. As we were ascending the easy incline of the Corraterie, all the shops shuttered and no light in any of the windows (as if all the mercenary population had fled at the end of the day), she said tentatively:

"I could run in for a moment to have a look at mother. It would not be much out of the way."

I dissuaded her. If Mrs. Haldin really expected to see Razumov that night it would have been unwise to show herself without him. The sooner we got hold of the young man and brought him along to calm her mother's agitation the better. She assented to my reasoning, and we crossed diagonally the Place de Théâtre, bluish gray with its floor of slabs of stone, under the electric light, and the lonely equestrian statue all black in the middle. In the Rue de Carouge we were in the poorer quarters and approaching the outskirts of the town. Vacant building plots alternated with high, new houses. At the corner of a side street the crude light of a whitewashed shop fell into the night, fanlike, through a wide doorway. One could see from a distance the inner wall with its scantily furnished shelves, and the deal counter painted brown. That was the house. Approaching it along the dark stretch of a fence of tarred planks, we saw the narrow pallid face of the cut angle, five single windows high, without a gleam in them, and crowned by the heavy shadow of a jutting roof slope.

"We must inquire in the shop," Miss Haldin directed me.

A sallow, thinly whiskered man, wearing a dingy white collar and a frayed tie, laid down a newspaper, and, leaning familiarly on both elbows far over the bare counter, answered that the person I was inquiring for was indeed his *locataire* on the third floor, but that for the moment he was out.

"For the moment," I repeated, after a glance at Miss Haldin. "Does this mean that you expect him back at once?"

He was very gentle, with ingratiating eyes and soft lips. He smiled faintly as though he knew all about everything. Mr. Razumov, after being absent all day, had returned early in the evening. He was very surprised about half an hour or a little more ago to see him come down again. Mr. Razumov left his key, and in the course of some words which passed between them had remarked that he was going out because he needed air.

From behind the bare counter he went on smiling at us, his head held between his hands. Air. Air. But whether that meant a long or a short absence it was difficult to say. The night was very close certainly.

After a pause, his ingratiating eyes turned to the door, he added:

"The storm will drive him in."

"There's going to be a storm?" I asked.

"Why, yes!"

As if to confirm his words we heard a very distant, deep rumbling noise.

Consulting Miss Haldin by a glance, I saw her so reluctant to give up her quest that I asked the shopkeeper, in case Mr. Razumov came home within half an hour, to beg him to remain downstairs in the shop. We would look in again presently.

For all answer he moved his head imperceptibly. The approval of Miss Haldin was expressed by her silence. We walked slowly down the street, away from the town; the low garden walls of the modest villas doomed to demolition were overhung by the boughs of trees and masses of foliage, lighted from below by gas lamps. The violent and monotonous noise of the icy waters of the Arve falling over a low dam swept towards us with a chilly draught of air across a great open space, where a double line of lamplights outlined a street as yet without houses. But on the other shore, overhung by the awful blackness of the thundercloud, a solitary dim light seemed to watch us with a weary stare. When we had strolled as far as the bridge, I said:

"We had better get back. . . ."

In the shop the sickly man was studying his smudgy newspaper, now spread out largely on the counter. He just raised his head when I looked in and shook it negatively, pursing up his lips. I rejoined Miss Haldin outside at once, and we moved off at a brisk pace. She remarked that she would send Anna with a note the first thing in the morning. I respected her taciturnity, silence being perhaps the best way to show my concern.

The semi-rural street we followed on our return changed gradually to the usual town thoroughfare, broad and deserted. We did not meet four people altogether, and the way seemed interminable, because my companion's natural anxiety had communicated itself sympathetically to me. At last we turned into the Boulevard des Philosophes, more wide, more empty, more dead—the very desolation of slumbering respectability. At the sight of the two lighted windows, very conspicuous from afar, I had the mental vision of Mrs. Haldin in her armchair keeping a dreadful, tormenting vigil under the evil spell of an arbitrary rule: a victim of tyranny and revolution, a sight at once cruel and absurd.

III

"You will come in for a moment?" said Natalia Haldin.

I demurred on account of the late hour. "You know mother likes you so much," she insisted.

"I will just come in to hear how your mother is."

She said, as if to herself, "I don't even know whether she will believe that I could not find Mr. Razumov, since she has taken it into her head that I am concealing something from her. You may be able to persuade her. . . . "

"Your mother may mistrust me too," I observed.

"You! Why? What could you have to conceal from her? You are not a Russian nor a conspirator."

I felt profoundly my European remoteness, and said nothing, but I made up my mind to play my part of helpless spectator to the end. The distant rolling of thunder in the valley of the Rhone was coming nearer to the sleeping town of prosaic virtues and universal hospitality. We crossed the street opposite the great dark gateway, and Miss Haldin rang at the door of the apartment. It was opened almost instantly, as if the elderly maid had been waiting in the anteroom for our return. Her flat physiognomy had an air of satisfaction. The gentleman was there, she declared, while closing the door.

Neither of us understood. Miss Haldin turned round bruskly to her. "Who?"

"Herr Razumov," she explained.

She had heard enough of our conversation before we left to know why her young mistress was going out. Therefore, when the gentleman gave his name at the door, she admitted him at once.

"No one could have foreseen that," Miss Haldin murmured, with her serious gray eyes fixed upon mine. And, remembering the expression of the young man's face seen not much more than four hours ago, the look of a haunted somnambulist, I wondered with a sort of awe.

"You asked my mother first?" Miss Haldin inquired of the maid.

"No. I announced the gentleman," she answered, surprised at our troubled faces.

"Still," I said in an undertone, "your mother was prepared."

"Yes. But he has no idea . . ."

It seemed to me she doubted his tact. To her question how long the gentleman had been with her mother, the maid told us that *der Herr* had been in the drawing room no more than a short quarter of an hour.

She waited a moment, then withdrew, looking a little scared. Miss Haldin gazed at me in silence.

"As things have turned out," I said, "you happen to know exactly what your brother's friend has to tell your mother. And surely after that . . ."

"Yes," said Natalia Haldin slowly. "I only wonder, as I was not here when he came, if it wouldn't be better not to interrupt now."

We remained silent, and I suppose we both strained our ears, but no sound reached us through the closed door. The features of Miss Haldin expressed a painful irresolution; she made a movement as if to go in, but checked herself. She had heard footsteps on the other side of the door. It came open, and Razumov, without pausing, stepped out into the anteroom. The fatigue of that day and the struggle with himself had changed him so much that I would have hesitated to recognize that face, which, only a few hours before, when he brushed against me in front of the post office, had been startling enough but quite different. It had been not so livid then, and its eyes not so somber. They certainly looked more sane now, but there was upon them the shadow of something consciously evil.

I speak of that, because, at first, their glance fell on me, though without any sort of recognition or even comprehension. I was simply in the line of his stare. I don't know if he had heard the bell or expected to see anybody. He was going out, I believe, and I do not think that he saw Miss Haldin till she advanced towards him a step or two. He disregarded the hand she put out.

"It's you, Natalia Victorovna. . . . Perhaps you are surprised . . . at this late hour. But, you see, I remembered our conversations in that garden. I thought really it was your wish that I should—without loss of time . . . so I came. No other reason. Simply to tell . . ."

He spoke with difficulty. I noticed that, and remembered his declaration to the man in the shop that he was going out because he "needed air." If that was his object, then it was clear that he had miserably failed. With downcast eyes and lowered head he made an effort to pick up the strangled phrase.

"To tell what I have heard myself only today—today . . ."

Through the door he had not closed I had a view of the drawing room. It was lighted only by a shaded lamp—Mrs. Haldin's eyes could not support either gas or electricity. It was a comparatively big room, and in contrast with the strongly lighted anteroom its length was lost in semi-transparent gloom backed by heavy shadows; and on that ground I saw the motionless figure of Mrs. Haldin, inclined slightly forward, with a pale hand resting on the arm of the chair.

She did not move. With the window before her she had no longer that attitude suggesting expectation. The blind was down; and outside there was only the night sky harboring a thundercloud, and the town indifferent and hospitable in its cold, almost scornful, toleration—a respectable town of refuge to which all these sorrows and hopes were nothing. Her white head was bowed.

The thought that the real drama of autocracy is not played on the great stage of politics came to me as, fated to be a spectator, I had this other glimpse behind the scenes, something more profound than the words and gestures of the public play. I had the certitude that this mother refused in her heart to give her son up after all. It was more than Rachel's inconsolable mourning, it was something deeper, more inaccessible in its frightful tranquility. Lost in the ill-defined mass of the high-backed chair, her white, inclined profile suggested the contemplation of something in her lap, as though a beloved head were resting there.

I had this glimpse behind the scenes, and then Miss Haldin, passing by the young man, shut the door. It was not done without hesitation. For a moment I thought that she would go to her mother, but she sent in only an anxious glance. Perhaps if Mrs. Haldin had moved . . . but no. There was in the immobility of that bloodless face the dreadful aloofness of suffering without remedy.

Meantime the young man kept his eyes fixed on the floor. The thought that he would have to repeat the story he had told already was intolerable to him. He had expected to find the two women together. And then, he had said to himself, it would be over for all time—for all time. "It's lucky I don't believe in another world," he had thought cynically.

Alone in his room after having posted his secret letter, he had regained a certain measure of composure by writing in his secret diary. He was aware of the danger of that strange self-indulgence. He alludes to it himself, but he could not refrain. It calmed him—it reconciled him to his existence. He sat there scribbling by the light of a solitary candle, till it occurred to him that having heard the explanation of Haldin's arrest, as put forward by Sophia Antonovna, it behooved him to tell these ladies himself. They were certain to hear the tale through some other channel, and then his abstention would look strange, not only to the mother and sister of Haldin, but to other people also. Having come to this conclusion, he did not discover in himself any marked reluctance to face the necessity, and very soon an anxiety to be done with it began to torment him. He looked at his watch. No; it was not absolutely too late.

The fifteen minutes with Mrs. Haldin were like the revenge of the unknown: that white face, that weak, distinct voice; that head, at first turned to him eagerly, then, after a while, bowed again and motionless—in the dim, still light of the room in which his words which he tried to subdue resounded so loudly—had troubled him like some strange discovery. And there seemed to be a secret obstinacy in that sorrow, something he could not understand; at any rate, something he had not expected. Was it hostile? But it did not matter. Nothing could touch him now; in the eyes of the revolutionists there was now no shadow on his past. The phantom of Haldin had been indeed walked over, was left behind lying powerless and passive on the pavement covered with snow. And this was the phantom's mother consumed with grief and white as a ghost. He had felt a pitying surprise. But that, of course, was of no importance. Mothers did not matter. He could not shake off the poignant impression of that silent, quiet, white-haired woman, but a sort of sternness crept into his thoughts. These were the consequences. Well, what of it? "Am I then on a bed of roses?" he had exclaimed to himself, sitting at some distance with his eyes fixed upon that figure of sorrow. He had said all he had to say to her, and when he had finished she had not uttered a word. She had turned away her head while he was speaking. The silence which had fallen on his last words had lasted for five minutes or more. What did it mean? Before its incomprehensible character he became conscious of anger in his stern mood, the old anger against Haldin reawakened by the contemplation of Haldin's mother. And was it not something like enviousness which gripped his heart, as if of a privilege denied to him alone of all the men that had ever passed through this world? It was the other who had attained to repose and yet continued to exist in the affection of that mourning old woman, in the thoughts of all these people posing for lovers of humanity. It was impossible to get rid of him. "It's myself whom I have given up to destruction," thought Razumov. "He has induced me to do it. I can't shake him off."

Alarmed by that discovery, he got up and strode out of the silent, dim room with its silent old woman in the chair, that mother! He never looked back. It was frankly a flight. But on opening the door he saw his retreat cut off. There was the sister. He had never forgotten the sister, only he had not expected to see her then—or ever anymore, perhaps. Her presence in the anteroom was as unforeseen as the apparition of her brother had been. Razumov gave a start as though he had discovered himself cleverly trapped. He tried to smile, but could not manage it, and lowered his eyes. "Must I repeat that silly story now?" he asked himself, and felt a sinking sensation. Nothing solid had passed his lips since the day before, but he was not in a state to analyze the origins of his weakness. He meant to take up his hat and depart with as few words as possible, but Miss Haldin's swift movement to shut the door took him by surprise. He half-turned after her, but without raising his eyes, passively, just as a feather might stir in the disturbed air. The next moment she was back in the place she had started from, with another half-turn on his part, so that they came again into the same relative positions.

"Yes, yes," she said hurriedly. "I am very grateful to you, Kirylo Sidorovitch, for coming at once—like this. . . . Only, I wish I had . . . Did mother tell you?"

"I wonder what she could have told me that I did not know before," he said, obviously to himself, but perfectly audible. "Because I always *did* know it," he added louder, as if in despair.

He hung his head. He had such a strong sense of Natalia Haldin's presence that to look at her he felt would be a relief. It was she who had been haunting him now. He had suffered that persecution ever since she had suddenly appeared before him in the garden of the Villa Borel with an extended hand and the name of her brother on her lips. . . . The anteroom had a row of hooks on the wall nearest to the outer door, while against the wall opposite there stood a small dark table and one chair. The paper, bearing a very faint design, was all but white. The light of an electric bulb high up under the ceiling searched that clear square box into its four bare corners, crudely, without shadows—a strange stage for an obscure drama. "What do you mean?" asked Miss Haldin. "What is it that you knew always?"

He raised his face, pale, full of unexpressed suffering. But that look in his eyes of dull, absent obstinacy, which struck and surprised everybody he was talking to, began to pass away. It was as though he were coming to himself in the awakened consciousness of that marvelous harmony of feature, of lines, of glances, of voice, which made of the girl before him a being so rare, outside, and, as it were, above the common notion of beauty. He looked at her so long that she colored slightly.

"What is it that you knew?" she repeated vaguely.

That time he managed to smile.

"Indeed, if it had not been for a word of greeting or two, I would doubt whether your mother was aware at all of my existence. You understand?"

Natalia Haldin nodded; her hands moved slightly by her side.

"Yes. Is it not heartbreaking? She has not shed a tear yet—not a single tear."

"Not a tear! And you, Natalia Victorovna? You have been able to cry?"

"I have. And then I am young enough, Kirylo Sidorovitch, to believe in the future. But when I see my mother so terribly distracted, I almost forget everything. I ask myself whether one should feel proud—or only resigned. We had such a lot of people coming to see us. There were utter strangers who wrote asking for permission to call to present their respects. It was impossible to keep our door shut forever. You know that Peter Ivanovitch himself . . . Oh yes, there was much sympathy, but there were persons who exulted openly at that death. Then, when I was left alone with poor mother, all this seemed so wrong in spirit, something not worth the price she is paying for it. But directly I heard you were here in Geneva, Kirylo Sidorovitch, I felt that you were the only person who could assist me . . ."

"In comforting a bereaved mother? Yes!" he broke in, in a manner which made her open her clear, unsuspecting eyes. "But there is a question of fitness. Has this occurred to you?"

There was a breathlessness in his utterance which contrasted with the monstrous hint of mockery in his intention.

"Why!" whispered Natalia Haldin with feeling. "Who more fit than you?"

He had a convulsive movement of exasperation, but controlled himself.

"Indeed! Directly you heard that I was in Geneva, before even seeing me? It is another proof of that confidence which . . ."

All at once his tone changed, became more incisive and more detached.

"Men are poor creatures, Natalia Victorovna. They have no intuition of senti-ment. In order to speak fittingly to a mother of her lost son one must have had some experience of the filial relation. It is not the case with me—if you must know the whole truth. Your hopes have to deal here with 'a breast unwarmed by any affection,' as the poet says. . . . That does not mean it is insensible," he added in a lower tone.

"I am certain your heart is not unfeeling," said Miss Haldin softly.

"No. It is not as hard as a stone," he went on in the same introspective voice, and looking as if his heart were lying as heavy as a stone in that unwarmed breast of which he spoke. "No, not so hard. But how to prove what you give me credit for—ah! that's another question. No one has ever expected such a thing from me before. No one whom my tenderness would have been of any use to. And now you come. You! Now! No, Natalia Victorovna. It's too late. You come too late. You must expect nothing from me."

She recoiled from him a little, though he had made no movement, as if she had seen some change in his face, charging his words with the significance of some hidden sentiment they shared together. To me, the silent spectator, they looked like two people becoming conscious of a spell which had been lying on them ever since they first set eyes on each other. Had either of them cast a glance then in my direction, I would have opened the door quietly and gone out. But neither did; and I remained, every fear of indiscretion lost in the sense of my enormous remote-ness from their captivity within the somber horizon of Russian problems, the boundary of their eyes, of their feelings—the prison of their souls.

Frank, courageous, Miss Haldin controlled her voice in the midst of her trouble.

"What can this mean?" she asked, as if speaking to herself.

"It may mean that you have given yourself up to vain imaginings while I have managed to remain amongst the truth of things and the realities of life—our Russian life—such as they are."

"They are cruel," she murmured.

"And ugly. Don't forget that—and ugly. Look where you like. Look near you, here abroad where you are, and then look back at home, whence you came."

"One must look beyond the present." Her tone had an ardent conviction.

"The blind can do that best. I have had the misfortune to be born clear-eyed. And if you only knew what strange things I have seen! What amazing and unex-pected apparitions! . . . But why talk of all this?"

"On the contrary, I want to talk of all this with you," she protested with earnest serenity. The somber humors of her brother's friend left her unaffected, as though that bitterness, that suppressed anger, were the signs of an indignant rectitude. She saw that he was not an ordinary person, and perhaps she did not want him to be other than he appeared to her trustful eyes. "Yes, with you especially," she insisted. "With you of all the Russian people in the world. . . . " A faint smile dwelt for a moment on her lips. "I am like poor mother in a way. I too seem unable to give up our beloved dead, who, don't forget, was all in all to us. I don't want to abuse your sympathy, but you must understand that it is in you that we can find all that is left of his generous soul."

I was looking at him; not a muscle of his face moved in the least. And yet, even at the time, I did not suspect him of insensibility. It was a sort of rapt thoughtfulness. Then he stirred slightly.

"You are going, Kirylo Sidorovitch?" she asked.

"I! Going? Where? Oh yes, but I must tell you first . . ." His voice was muffled and he forced himself to produce it with visible repugnance, as if speech were something disgusting or deadly. "That story, you know—the story I heard this afternoon . . ."

"I know the story already," she said sadly.

"You know it! Have you correspondents in St. Petersburg too?"

"No. It's Sophia Antonovna. I have seen her just now. She sends you her greetings. She is going away tomorrow."

He had lowered at last his fascinated glance; she too was looking down, and standing thus before each other in the glaring light, between the four bare walls, they seemed brought out from the confused immensity of the Eastern borders to be exposed cruelly to the observation of my Western eyes. And I observed them. There was nothing else to do. My existence seemed so utterly forgotten by these two that I dared not now make a movement. And I thought to myself that, of course, they had to come together, the sister and the friend of that dead man. The ideas, the hopes, the aspirations, the cause of Freedom, expressed in their common affection for Victor Haldin, the moral victim of autocracy—all this must draw them to each other fatally. Her very ignorance and his loneliness to which he had alluded so strangely must work to that end. And, indeed, I saw that the work was done already. Of course. It was manifest that they must have been thinking of each other for a long time before they met. She had the letter from that beloved brother kindling her imagination by the severe praise attached to that one name; and for him to see that exceptional girl was enough. The only cause for surprise was his gloomy aloofness before her clearly expressed welcome. But he was young, and however austere and devoted to his revolutionary ideals, he was not blind. The period of reserve was over; he was coming forward in his own way. I could not mistake the significance of this late visit, for in what he had to say there was nothing urgent. The true cause dawned upon me: he had discovered that he needed her—and she was moved by the same feeling. It was the second time that I saw them together, and I knew that next time they met I would not be there, either remembered or forgotten. I would have virtually ceased to exist for both these young people.

I made this discovery in a very few moments. Meantime, Natalia Haldin was telling Razumov briefly of our peregrinations from one end of Geneva to the other. While speaking she raised her hands above her head to untie her veil, and that movement displayed for an instant the seductive grace of her youthful figure, clad in the simplest of mourning. In the transparent shadow the hat rim threw on her face her gray eyes had an enticing luster. Her voice, with its unfeminine yet exquisite timbre, was steady, and she spoke quickly, frank, unembarrassed. As she justified her action by the mental state of her mother, a spasm of pain marred the generously confiding harmony of her features. I perceived that with his downcast eyes he had the air of a man who is listening to a strain of music rather than to articulated speech. And in the same way, after she had ceased, he seemed to listen yet, motionless, as if under the spell of suggestive sound. He came to himself, muttering:

"Yes, yes. She has not shed a tear. She did not seem to hear what I was saying. I might have told her anything. She looked as if no longer belonging to this world."

Miss Haldin gave signs of profound distress. Her voice faltered. "You don't know how bad it has come to be. She expects now to *see him*!" The veil dropped from her fingers and she clasped her hands in anguish. "It will end by her seeing him," she cried.

Razumov raised his head sharply and attached on her a prolonged, thoughtful glance.

"H'm. That's very possible," he muttered in a peculiar tone, as if giving his opinion on a matter of fact. "I wonder what . . ." He checked himself.

"That would be the end. Her mind will be gone then, and her spirit will follow."

Miss Haldin unclasped her hands and let them fall by her side.

"You think so?" he queried profoundly. Miss Haldin's lips were slightly parted. Something unexpected and unfathomable in that young man's character had fascinated her from the first. "No! There's neither truth nor consolation to be got from the phantoms of the dead," he added after a weighty pause. "I might have told her something true; for instance, that your brother meant to save his life—to escape. There can be no doubt of that. But I did not."

"You did not! But why?"

"I don't know. Other thoughts came into my head," he answered. He seemed to me to be watching himself inwardly, as though he were trying to count his own heartbeats, while his eyes never for a moment left the face of the girl. "You were not there," he continued. "I had made up my mind never to see you again."

This seemed to take her breath away for a moment.

"You . . . How is it possible?"

"You may well ask. . . . However. I think that I refrained from telling your mother from prudence. I might have assured her that in the last conversation he held as a free man he mentioned you both . . ."

"That last conversation was with you," she struck in, in her deep, moving voice. "Someday you must . . ."

"It was with me. Of you he said that you had trustful eyes. And why I have not been able to forget that phrase I don't know. It meant that there is in you no guile, no deception, no falsehood, no suspicion—nothing in your heart that could give you a conception of a living, acting, speaking lie, if ever it came in your way. That you are a predestined victim . . . Ha! what a devilish suggestion!"

The convulsive, uncontrolled tone of the last words disclosed the precarious hold he had over himself. He was like a man defying his own dizziness in high places and tottering suddenly on the very edge of the precipice. Miss Haldin pressed her hand to her breast. The dropped black veil lay on the floor between them. Her movement steadied him. He looked intently on that hand till it descended slowly, and then raised again his eyes to her face. But he did not give her time to speak.

"No? You don't understand? Very well." He had recovered his calm by a miracle of will. "So you talked with Sophia Antonovna?"

"Yes. Sophia Antonovna told me . . ." Miss Haldin stopped, wonder growing in her wide eyes.

"H'm. That's the respectable enemy," he muttered, as though he were alone.

"The tone of her references to you was extremely friendly," remarked Miss Haldin, after waiting for a while.

"Is that your impression? And she the most intelligent of the lot, too. Things then are going as well as possible. Everything conspires to . . . Ah! those conspirators," he said slowly, with an accent of scorn; "they would get hold of you in no time! You know, Natalia Victorovna, I have the greatest difficulty in saving myself from the superstition of an active Providence. It's irresistible. . . . The alternative, of course, would be the personal Devil of our simple ancestors. But, if so, he has overdone it altogether—the old Father of Lies—our national patron—our domestic god, whom we take with us when we go abroad. He has overdone it. It seems that I am not simple enough . . . That's it! I ought to have known . . . And I did know it," he added in a tone of poignant distress which overcame my astonishment.

"This man is deranged," I said to myself, very much frightened.

The next moment he gave me a very special impression beyond the range of commonplace definitions. It was as though he had stabbed himself outside and had come in there to show it; and more than that—as though he were turning the knife in the wound and watching the effect. That was the impression, rendered in physical terms. One could not defend oneself from a certain amount of pity. But it was for Miss Haldin, already so tried in her deepest affections, that I felt a serious concern. Her attitude, her face, expressed compassion struggling with doubt on the verge of terror.

"What is it, Kirylo Sidorovitch?" There was a hint of tenderness in that cry. He only stared at her in that complete surrender of all his faculties which in a happy lover would have had the name of ecstasy.

"Why are you looking at me like this, Kirylo Sidorovitch? I have approached you frankly. I need at this time to see clearly in myself . . ." She ceased for a moment as if to give him an opportunity to utter at last some word worthy of her exalted trust in her brother's friend. His silence became impressive, like a sign of a momentous resolution.

In the end Miss Haldin went on appealingly:

"I have waited for you anxiously. But now that you have been moved to come to us in your kindness, you alarm me. You speak obscurely. It seems as if you were keeping back something from me."

"Tell me, Natalia Victorovna," he was heard at last in a strange, unringing voice, "whom did you see in that place?"

She was startled, and as if deceived in her expectations.

"Where? In Peter Ivanovitch's rooms? There was Mr. Laspara and three other people."

"Ha! The vanguard—the forlorn hope of the great plot," he commented to himself. "Bearers of the spark to start an explosion which is meant to change fundamentally the lives of so many millions in order that Peter Ivanovitch should be the head of a State."

"You are teasing me," she said. "Our dear one told me once to remember that men serve always something greater than themselves—the idea."

"Our dear one," he repeated slowly. The effort he made to appear unmoved absorbed all the force of his soul. He stood before her like a being with hardly a breath of life. His eyes, even as under great physical suffering, had lost all their fire. "Ah! your brother . . . But on your lips, in your voice, it sounds . . . and indeed in you everything is divine. . . . I wish I could know the innermost depths of your thoughts, of your feelings."

"But why, Kirylo Sidorovitch?" she cried, alarmed by these words coming out of strangely lifeless lips.

"Have no fear. It is not to betray you. So you went there? . . . And Sophia Antonovna, what did she tell you, then?"

"She said very little, really. She knew that I should hear everything from you. She had no time for more than a few words." Miss Haldin's voice dropped and she became silent for a moment. "The man, it appears, has taken his life," she said sadly.

"Tell me, Natalia Victorovna," he asked after a pause, "do you believe in remorse?"

"What a question!"

"What can *you* know of it?" he muttered thickly. "It is not for such as you . . . What I meant to ask was whether you believed in the efficacy of remorse."

She hesitated as though she had not understood, then her face lighted up.

"Yes," she said firmly.

"So he is absolved. Moreover, that Ziemianitch was a brute, a drunken brute."

A shudder passed through Natalia Haldin.

"But a man of the people," Razumov went on, "to whom they, the revolutionists, tell a tale of sublime hopes. Well, the people must be forgiven. . . . And you must not believe all you've heard from that source, either," he added, with a sort of sinister reluctance.

"You are concealing something from me," she exclaimed.

"Do you, Natalia Victorovna, believe in the duty of revenge?"

"Listen, Kirylo Sidorovitch. I believe that the future will be merciful to us all. Revolutionist and reactionary, victim and executioner, betrayer and betrayed, they shall all be pitied together when the light breaks on our black sky at last. Pitied and forgotten; for without that there can be no union and no love."

"I hear. No revenge for you, then? Never? Not the least bit?" He smiled bitterly with his colorless lips. "You yourself are like the very spirit of that merciful future. Strange that it does not make it easier. . . . No! But suppose that the real betrayer of your brother—Ziemianitch had a part in it too, but insignificant and quite involuntary—suppose that he was a young man, educated, an intellectual worker, thoughtful, a man your brother might have trusted lightly, perhaps, but still—suppose . . . But there's a whole story there."

"And you know the story! But why, then——"

"I have heard it. There is a staircase in it, and even phantoms, but that does not matter if a man always serves something greater than himself—the idea. I wonder who is the greatest victim in that tale?"

"In that tale!" Miss Haldin repeated. She seemed turned into stone.

"Do you know why I came to you? It is simply because there is no one anywhere in the whole great world I could go to. Do you understand what I say? Not one to go to. Do you conceive the desolation of the thought—no one—to—go—to?"

Utterly misled by her own enthusiastic interpretation of two lines in the letter of a visionary, under the spell of her own dread of lonely days, in their overshadowed world of angry strife, she was unable to see the truth struggling on his lips. What she was conscious of was the obscure form of his suffering. She was on the point of extending her hand to him impulsively when he spoke again.

"An hour after I saw you first I knew how it would be. The terrors of remorse, revenge, confession, anger, hate, fear, are like nothing to the atrocious temptation which you put in my way the day you appeared before me with your voice, with your face, in the garden of that accursed villa."

She looked utterly bewildered for a moment; then, with a sort of despairing insight went straight to the point.

"The story, Kirylo Sidorovitch, the story!"

"There is no more to tell!" He made a movement forward, and she actually put her hand on his shoulder to push him away; but her strength failed her, and he kept his ground, though trembling in every limb. "It ends here—on this very spot." He pressed a denunciatory finger to his breast with force, and became perfectly still.

I ran forward, snatching up the chair, and was in time to catch hold of Miss Haldin and lower her down. As she sank into it she swung half round on my arm, and remained averted from us both, drooping over the back. He looked at her with an appalling expressionless tranquility. Incredulity, struggling with astonishment, anger, and disgust, deprived me for a time of the power of speech. Then I turned on him, whispering from very rage:

"This is monstrous. What are you staying for? Don't let her catch sight of you again. Go away! . . ." He did not budge. "Don't you understand that your presence is intolerable—even to me? If there's any sense of shame in you . . ."

Slowly his sullen eyes moved in my direction. "How did this old man come here?" he muttered, astounded.

Suddenly Miss Haldin sprang up from the chair, made a few steps, and tottered. Forgetting my indignation, and even the man himself, I hurried to her assistance. I took her by the arm, and she let me lead her into the drawing room. Away from the lamp, in the deeper dusk of the distant end, the profile of Mrs. Haldin, her hands, her whole figure had the stillness of a somber painting. Miss Haldin stopped, and pointed mournfully at the tragic immobility of her mother, who seemed to watch a beloved head lying in her lap.

That gesture had an unequaled force of expression, so far-reaching in its human distress that one could not believe that it pointed out merely the ruthless working of political institutions. After assisting Miss Haldin to the sofa, I turned round to go back and shut the door. Framed in the opening, in the searching glare of the white anteroom, my eyes fell on Razumov, still there, standing before the empty chair, as if rooted forever to the spot of his atrocious confession. A wonder came over me that the mysterious force which had torn it out of him had failed to destroy his life, to shatter his body. It was there unscathed. I stared at the broad line of his shoulders, his dark head, the amazing immobility of his limbs. At his feet the veil dropped by Miss Haldin looked intensely black in the white crudity of the light. He was gazing at it spellbound. Next moment, stooping with an incredible, savage swiftness, he snatched it up and pressed it to his face with both hands. Something, extreme astonishment perhaps, dimmed my eyes, so that he seemed to vanish before he moved.

The slamming of the outer door restored my sight, and I went on contemplating the empty chair in the empty anteroom. The meaning of what I had seen reached my mind with a staggering shock. I seized Natalia Haldin by the shoulder.

"That miserable wretch has carried off your veil!" I cried, in the scared, deadened voice of an awful discovery. "He . . ."

The rest remained unspoken. I stepped back and looked down at her in silent horror. Her hands were lying lifelessly, palms upwards, on her lap. She raised her gray eyes slowly. Shadows seemed to come and go in them as if the steady flame of her soul had been made to vacillate at last in the crosscurrents of poisoned air from the corrupted dark immensity claiming her for its own, where virtues themselves fester into crimes in the cynicism of oppression and revolt.

"It is impossible to be more unhappy. . . . " The languid whisper of her voice struck me with dismay. "It is impossible. . . . I feel my heart becoming like ice."

IV

Razumov walked straight home on the wet glistening pavement. A heavy shower passed over him; distant lightning played faintly against the fronts of the dumb houses with the shuttered shops all along the Rue de Carouge; and now and then, after the faint flash, there was a faint, sleepy rumble; but the main forces of the thunderstorm remained massed down the Rhône valley as if loath to attack the respectable and passionless abode of democratic liberty, the serious-minded town of dreary hotels, tendering the same indifferent hospitality to tourists of all nations and to international conspirators of every shade.

The owner of the shop was making ready to close when Razumov entered and without a word extended his hand for the key of his room. On reaching it for him, from a shelf, the man was about to pass a small joke as to taking the air in a thunderstorm, but, after looking at the face of his lodger, he only observed, just to say something:

"You've got very wet."

"Yes, I am washed clean," muttered Razumov, who was dripping from head to foot, and passed through the inner door towards the staircase leading to his room.

He did not change his clothes, but, after lighting the candle, took off his watch and chain, laid them on the table, and sat down at once to write. The book of his compromising record was kept in a locked drawer, which he pulled out violently, and did not even trouble to push back afterwards.

In this queer pedantism of a man who had read, thought, lived, pen in hand, there is the sincerity of the attempt to grapple by the same means with another profounder knowledge. After some passages which have been already made use of in the building up of this narrative, or add nothing new to the psychological side of this disclosure (there is even one more allusion to the silver medal in this last entry), comes a page and a half of incoherent writing where his expression is baffled by the novelty and the mysteriousness of that side of our emotional life to which his solitary existence had been a stranger. Then only he begins to address directly the reader he had in his mind, trying to express in broken sentences, full of wonder and awe, the sovereign (he uses that very word) power of her person over his imagination, in which lay the dormant seed of her brother's words.

". . . The most trustful eyes in the world—your brother said of you when he was as well as a dead man already. And when you stood before me with your hand extended, I remembered the very sound of his voice, and I looked into your eyes— and that was enough. I knew that something had happened, but I did not know then what. . . . But don't be deceived, Natalia Victorovna. I believed that I had in my breast nothing but an inexhaustible fund of anger and hate for you both. I remembered that he had looked to you for the perpetuation of his visionary soul. He, this man who had robbed me of my hardworking, purposeful existence. I, too, had my guiding idea; and remember that, amongst us, it is more difficult to lead a life of toil and self-denial than to go out in the street and kill from conviction. But enough of that. Hate or no hate, I felt at once that, while shunning the sight of you, I could never succeed in driving away your image. I would say, addressing that dead man, 'Is this the way you are going to haunt me?' It is only later on that I understood—only today, only a few hours ago. What could I have known of what was tearing me to pieces and dragging the secret forever to my lips? You were appointed to undo the evil by making me betray myself back into truth and peace. You! And you have done it in the same way, too, in which he ruined me: by forcing upon me your confidence. Only what I detested him for, in you ended by appearing noble and exalted. But, I repeat, be not deceived. I was given up to evil. I exulted in having induced that silly innocent fool to steal his father's money. He was a fool, but not a thief. I made him one. It was necessary. I had to confirm myself in my contempt and hate for what I betrayed. I have suffered from as many vipers in my heart as any social democrat of them all—vanity, ambitions, jealousies, shameful desires, evil passions of envy and revenge. I had my security stolen from me, years of good work, my best hopes. Listen—now comes the true confession. The other was nothing. To save me, your trustful eyes had to entice my thought to the very edge of the blackest treachery. I could see them constantly looking at me with the confidence of your pure heart which had not been touched by evil things. Victor Haldin had stolen the truth of my life from me, who had nothing else in the world, and he boasted of living on through you on this earth where I had no place to lay my head. She will marry someday, he had said—and your eyes were trustful. And do you know what I said to myself? I shall steal his sister's soul from her. When we met that first morning in the gardens, and you spoke to me confidingly in the generosity of your spirit, I was thinking, 'Yes, he himself by talking of her trustful eyes has delivered her into my hands!' If you could have looked then into my heart, you would have cried out aloud with terror and disgust.

"Perhaps no one will believe the baseness of such an intention to be possible. It's certain that, when we parted that morning, I gloated over it. I brooded upon the best way. The old man you introduced me to insisted on walking with me. I don't know who he is. He talked of you, of your lonely, helpless state, and every word of that friend of yours was egging me on to the unpardonable sin of stealing a soul. Could he have been the devil himself in the shape of an old Englishman? Natalia Victorovna, I was possessed! I returned to look at you every day, and drink in your presence the poison of my infamous intention. But I foresaw difficulties. Then Sophia Antonovna, of whom I was not thinking—I had forgotten her exis- tence—appears suddenly with that tale from St. Petersburg. . . . The only thing needed to make me safe—a trusted revolutionist forever.

"It was as if Ziemianitch had hanged himself to help me on to further crime. The strength of falsehood seemed irresistible. These people stood doomed by the folly and illusion that was in them—they being themselves the slaves of lies. Natalia Victorovna, I embraced the might of falsehood, I exulted in it—I gave myself up to it for a time. Who could have resisted! You yourself were the prize of it. I sat alone in my room, planning a life, the very thought of which makes me shudder now, like a believer who had been tempted to an atrocious sacrilege. But I brooded ardently over its images. The only thing was that there seemed to be no air in it. And also I was afraid of your mother. I never knew mine. I've never known any kind of love. There is something in the mere word . . . Of you I was not afraid—forgive me for telling you this. No, not of you. You were truth itself. You could not suspect me. As to your mother, you yourself feared already that her mind had given way from grief. Who could believe anything against me? Had not Ziemianitch hanged himself from remorse? I said to myself, 'Let's put it to the test, and be done with it once for all.' I trembled when I went in; but your mother hardly listened to what I was saying to her, and, in a little while, seemed to have forgotten my very existence. I sat looking at her. There was no longer anything between you and me. You were defenseless—and soon, very soon, you would be alone. . . . I thought of you. Defenseless. For days you have talked with me— opening your heart. I remembered the shadow of your eyelashes over your gray, trustful eyes. And your pure forehead! It is low like the forehead of statues—calm, unstained. It was as if your pure brow bore a light which fell on me, searched my heart and saved me from ignominy, from ultimate undoing. And it saved you too. Pardon my presumption. But there was that in your glances which seemed to tell me that you . . . Your light! your truth! I felt that I must tell you that I had ended by loving you. And to tell you that I must first confess. Confess, go out—and perish.

"Suddenly you stood before me! You alone in all the world to whom I must confess. You fascinated me—you have freed me from the blindness of anger and hate—the truth shining in you drew the truth out of me. Now I have done it; and as I write here, I am in the depths of anguish, but there is air to breathe at last—air! And, by-the-by, that old man sprang up from somewhere as I was speaking to you, and raged at me like a disappointed devil. I suffer horribly, but I am not in despair. There is only one more thing to do for me. After that—if they let me—I shall go away and bury myself in obscure misery. In giving Victor Haldin up, it was myself, after all, whom I have betrayed most basely. You must believe what I say now, you can't refuse to believe this. Most basely. It is through you that I came to feel this so deeply. After all, it is they and not I who have the right on their side!—theirs is the strength of invisible powers. So be it. Only don't be deceived, Natalia Victorovna, I am not converted. Have I then the soul of a slave? No! I am independent—and therefore perdition is my lot."

On these words, he stopped writing, shut the book, and wrapped it in the black veil he had carried off. He then ransacked the drawers for paper and string, made up a parcel which he addressed to Miss Haldin, Boulevard des Philosophes, and then flung the pen away from him into a distant corner.

This done, he sat down with the watch before him. He could have gone out at once, but the hour had not struck yet. The hour would be midnight. There was no reason for that choice except that the facts and the words of a certain evening in his past were timing his conduct in the present. The sudden power Natalia Haldin had gained over him he ascribed to the same cause. "You don't walk with impunity over a phantom's breast," he heard himself mutter. "Thus he saves me," he thought suddenly. "He himself, the betrayed man." The vivid image of Miss Haldin seemed to stand by him, watching him relentlessly. She was not disturbing. He had done with life, and his thought even in her presence tried to take an impartial survey. Now his scorn extended to himself. "I had neither the simplicity nor the courage nor the self-possession to be a scoundrel, or an exceptionally able man. For who, with us in Russia, is to tell a scoundrel from an exceptionally able man? . . ."

He was the puppet of his past, because at the very stroke of midnight he jumped up and ran swiftly downstairs as if confident that, by the power of destiny, the house door would fly open before the absolute necessity of his errand. And as a matter of fact, just as he got to the bottom of the stairs, it was opened for him by some people of the house coming home late—two men and a woman. He slipped out through them into the street, swept then by a fitful gust of wind. They were, of course, very much startled. A flash of lightning enabled them to observe him walking away quickly. One of the men shouted, and was starting in pursuit, but the woman had recognized him. "It's all right. It's only that young Russian from the third floor." The darkness returned with a single clap of thunder, like a gun fired for a warning of his escape from the prison of lies.

He must have heard at some time or other and now remembered unconsciously that there was to be a gathering of revolutionists at the house of Julius Laspara that evening. At any rate, he made straight for the Laspara house, and found himself without surprise ringing at its street door, which, of course, was closed. By that time the thunderstorm had attacked in earnest. The steep incline of the street ran with water, the thick fall of rain enveloped him like a luminous veil in the play of lightning. He was perfectly calm, and between the crashes listened attentively to the delicate tinkling of the doorbell somewhere within the house.

There was some difficulty before he was admitted. His person was not known to that one of the guests who had volunteered to go downstairs and see what was the matter. Razumov argued with him patiently. There could be no harm in admitting a caller. He had something of importance to communicate to the company upstairs.

"Something of importance?"

"That'll be for the hearers to judge."

"Urgent?"

"Without a moment's delay."

Meantime, one of the Laspara daughters descended the stairs, small lamp in hand, in a grimy and crumpled gown, which seemed to hang on her by a miracle, and looking more than ever like an old doll with a dusty brown wig, dragged from under a sofa. She recognized Razumov at once.

"How do you do? Of course you may come in."

Following her light, Razumov climbed two flights of stairs from the lower darkness. Leaving the lamp on a bracket on the landing, she opened a door and went in, accompanied by the skeptical guest. Razumov entered last. He closed the door behind him, and stepping on one side, put his back against the wall.

The three little rooms *en suite*, with low, smoky ceilings and lit by paraffin lamps, were crammed with people. Loud talking was going on in all three, and tea glasses, full, half-full, and empty, stood everywhere, even on the floor. The other Laspara girl sat, disheveled and languid, behind an enormous samovar. In the inner doorway Razumov had a glimpse of the protuberance of a large stomach, which he recognized. Only a few feet from him Julius Laspara was getting down hurriedly from his high stool.

The appearance of the midnight visitor caused no small sensation. Laspara is very summary in his version of that night's happenings. After some words of greeting, disregarded by Razumov, Laspara (ignoring purposely his guest's soaked condition and his extraordinary manner of presenting himself) mentioned something about writing an article. He was growing uneasy, and Razumov appeared absent-minded. "I have written already all I shall ever write," he said at last, with a little laugh.

The whole company's attention was riveted on the newcomer, dripping with water, deadly pale, and keeping his position against the wall. Razumov put Laspara gently aside, as though he wished to be seen from head to foot by everybody. By then the buzz of conversation had died down completely, even in the most distant of the three rooms. The doorway facing Razumov became blocked by men and women, who craned their necks and certainly seemed to expect something startling to happen.

A squeaky, insolent declaration was heard from that group.

"I know this ridiculously conceited individual."

"What individual?" asked Razumov, raising his bowed head, and searching with his eyes all the eyes fixed upon him. An intense surprised silence lasted for a time. "If it's me ..."

He stopped, thinking over the form of his confession, and found it suddenly, unavoidably suggested by the fateful evening of his life.

"I am come here," he began, in a clear voice, "to talk of an individual called Ziemianitch. Sophia Antonovna has informed me that she would make public a certain letter from St. Petersburg ..."

"Sophia Antonovna has left us early in the evening," said Laspara. "It's quite correct. Everybody here has heard ..."

"Very well," Razumov interrupted, with a shade of impatience, for his heart was beating strongly. Then, mastering his voice so far that there was even a touch of irony in his clear, forcible enunciation:

"In justice to that individual, the much ill-used peasant, Ziemianitch, I now declare solemnly that the conclusions of that letter calumniate a man of the people—a bright Russian soul. Ziemianitch had nothing to do with the actual arrest of Victor Haldin."

Razumov dwelt on the name heavily, and then waited till the faint, mournful murmur which greeted it had died out.

"Victor Victorovitch Haldin," he began again, "acting with, no doubt, noble-minded imprudence, took refuge with a certain student of whose opinions he knew nothing but what his own illusions suggested to his generous heart. It was an unwise display of confidence. But I am not here to appreciate the actions of Victor Haldin. Am I to tell you of the feelings of that student, sought out in his obscure solitude, and menaced by the complicity forced upon him? Am I to tell you what he did? It's a rather complicated story. In the end the student went to General T—— himself, and said, 'I have the man who killed de P—— locked up in my room, Victor Haldin, a student like myself.'"

A great buzz arose, in which Razumov raised his voice.

"Observe—that man had certain honest ideals in view. But I didn't come here to explain him."

"No. But you must explain how you know all this," came in grave tones from somebody.

"A vile coward!" This simple cry vibrated with indignation. "Name him!" shouted other voices.

"What are you clamoring for?" said Razumov disdainfully, in the profound silence which fell on the raising of his hand. "Haven't you all understood that I am that man?"

Laspara went away bruskly from his side and climbed upon his stool. In the first forward surge of people towards him, Razumov expected to be torn to pieces, but they fell back without touching him, and nothing came of it but noise. It was bewildering. His head ached terribly. In the confused uproar he made out several times the name of Peter Ivanovitch, the word "judgment," and the phrase, "But this is a confession," uttered by somebody in a desperate shriek. In the midst of the tumult, a young man, younger than himself, approached him with blazing eyes.

"I must beg you," he said, with venomous politeness, "to be good enough not to move from this spot till you are told what you are to do." Razumov shrugged his shoulders.

"I came in voluntarily."

"Maybe. But you won't go out till you are permitted," retorted the other.

He beckoned with his hand, calling out, "Louisa! Louisa! come here, please"; and, presently, one of the Laspara girls (they had been staring at Razumov from behind the samovar) came along, trailing a bedraggled tail of dirty flounces, and dragging with her a chair, which she set against the door, and, sitting down on it, crossed her legs. The young man thanked her effusively, and rejoined a group carrying on an animated discussion in low tones. Razumov lost himself for a moment.

A squeaky voice screamed, "Confession or no confession, you are a police spy!"

The revolutionist Nikita had pushed his way in front of Razumov, and faced him with his big, livid cheeks, his heavy paunch, bull neck, and enormous hands. Razumov looked at the famous slayer of gendarmes in silent disgust.

"And what are you?" he said, very low, then shut his eyes, and rested the back of his head against the wall.

"It would be better for you to depart now." Razumov heard a mild, sad voice, and opened his eyes. The gentle speaker was an elderly man, with a great brush of fine hair making a silvery halo all round his keen, intelligent face. "Peter Ivanovitch shall be informed of your confession—and you shall be directed . . ."

Then, turning to Nikita, nicknamed Necator, standing by, he appealed to him in a murmur:

"What else can we do? After this piece of sincerity he cannot be dangerous any longer."

The other muttered, "Better make sure of that before we let him go. Leave that to me. I know how to deal with such gentlemen."

He exchanged meaning glances with two or three men, who nodded slightly, then turning roughly to Razumov, "You have heard? You are not wanted here. Why don't you get out?"

The Laspara girl on guard rose and pulled the chair out of the way unemotionally. She gave a sleepy stare to Razumov, who started, looked round the room and passed slowly by her as if struck by some sudden thought.

"I beg you to observe," he said, already on the landing, "that I had only to hold my tongue. Today, of all days since I came amongst you, I was made safe, and today I made myself free from falsehood, from remorse—independent of every single human being on this earth."

He turned his back on the room, and walked towards the stairs, but, at the violent crash of the door behind him, he looked over his shoulder and saw that Nikita, with three others, had followed him out. "They are going to kill me, after all," he thought.

Before he had time to turn round and confront them fairly, they set on him with a rush. He was driven headlong against the wall. "I wonder how," he completed his thought.

Nikita cried, with a shrill laugh right in his face, "We shall make you harmless. You wait a bit."

Razumov did not struggle. The three men held him pinned against the wall, while Nikita, taking up a position a little on one side, deliberately swung off his enormous arm. Razumov, looking for a knife in his hand, saw it come at him open, unarmed, and received a tremendous blow on the side of his head over his ear. At the same time he heard a faint, dull, detonating sound, as if someone had fired a pistol on the other side of the wall. A raging fury awoke in him at this outrage. The people in Laspara's rooms, holding their breath, listened to the desperate scuffling of four men all over the landing; thuds against the walls, a terrible crash against the very door, then all of them went down together with a violence which seemed to shake the whole house. Razumov, overpowered, breathless, crushed under the weight of his assailants, saw the monstrous Nikita squatting on his heels near his head, while the others held him down, kneeling on his chest, gripping his throat, lying across his legs.

"Turn his face the other way," the paunchy terrorist directed, in an excited, gleeful squeak.

Razumov could struggle no longer. He was exhausted; he had to watch passively the heavy open hand of the brute descend again in a degrading blow over his other ear. It seemed to split his head in two, and all at once the men holding him became perfectly silent—soundless as shadows. In silence they pulled him brutally to his feet, rushed with him noiselessly down the staircase, and, opening the door, flung him out into the street.

He fell forward, and at once rolled over and over helplessly, going down the short slope together with the rush of running rain water. He came to rest in the roadway of the street at the bottom, lying on his back, with a great flash of lightning over his face—a vivid, silent flash of lightning which blinded him utterly. He picked himself up and put his arm over his eyes to recover his sight. Not a sound reached him from anywhere, and he began to walk, staggering, down a long, empty street. The lightning waved and darted round him its silent flames, the water of the deluge fell, ran, leaped, drove—noiseless like the drift of mist. In this unearthly stillness his footsteps fell silent on the pavement, while a dumb wind drove him on and on, like a lost mortal in a phantom world ravaged by a soundless thunderstorm. God only knows where his noiseless feet took him to that night, here and there, and back again without pause or rest. Of one place, at least, where they did lead him, we heard afterwards; and, in the morning, the driver of the first south-shore tramcar, clanging his bell desperately, saw a bedraggled, soaked man without a hat, and walking in the roadway unsteadily with his head down, step right in front of his car, and go under.

When they picked him up, with two broken limbs and a crushed side, Razumov had not lost consciousness. It was as though he had tumbled, smashing himself, into a world of mutes. Silent men, moving unheard, lifted him up, laid him on the sidewalk, gesticulating and grimacing round him their alarm, horror, and compassion. A red face with moustaches stooped close over him, lips moving, eyes rolling. Razumov tried hard to understand the reason of this dumb show. To those who stood around him, the features of that stranger, so grievously hurt, seemed composed in meditation. Afterwards his eyes sent out at them a look of fear and closed slowly. They stared at him. Razumov made an effort to remember some French words.

"*Je suis sourd*," he had time to utter feebly, before he fainted.

"He is deaf," they exclaimed to each other. "That's why he did not hear the car."

They carried him off in that same car. Before it started on its journey, a woman in a shabby black dress, who had run out of the iron gate of some private grounds up the road, clambered on to the rear platform and would not be put off.

"I am a relation," she insisted, in bad French. "This young man is a Russian, and I am his relation."

On this plea they let her have her way. She sat down calmly, and took his head on her lap; her scared faded eyes avoided looking at his deathlike face. At the corner of a street, on the other side of the town, a stretcher met the car. She followed it to the door of the hospital, where they let her come in and see him laid on a bed. Razumov's new-found relation never shed a tear, but the officials had some difficulty in inducing her to go away. The porter observed her lingering on the opposite pavement for a long time. Suddenly, as though she had remembered something, she ran off.

The ardent hater of all Finance Ministers, the slave of Madame de S——, had made up her mind to offer her resignation as lady companion to the Egeria of Peter Ivanovitch. She had found work to do after her own heart.

But hours before, while the thunderstorm still raged in the night, there had been in the rooms of Julius Laspara a great sensation. The terrible Nikita, coming in from the landing, uplifted his squeaky voice in horrible glee before all the company:

"Razumov! Mr. Razumov! The wonderful Razumov! He shall never be any use as a spy on anyone. He won't talk, because he will never hear anything in his life— not a thing! I have burst the drums of his ears for him. Oh, you may trust me. I know the trick. Ha, ha, ha! I know the trick."

V

It was nearly a fortnight after her mother's funeral that I saw Natalia Haldin for the last time.

In those silent, somber days the doors of the *appartement* on the Boulevard des Philosophes were closed to everyone but myself. I believe I was of some use, if only in this, that I alone was aware of the incredible part of the situation. Miss Haldin nursed her mother alone to the last moment. If Razumov's visit had anything to do with Mrs. Haldin's end (and I cannot help thinking that it hastened it considerably), it is because the man, trusted impulsively by the ill-fated Victor Haldin, had failed to gain the confidence of Victor Haldin's mother. What tale, precisely, he told her cannot be known—at any rate, I do not know it—but to me she seemed to die from the shock of an ultimate disappointment borne in silence. She had not believed him. Perhaps she could no longer believe anyone, and consequently had nothing to say to anyone—not even to her daughter. I suspect that Miss Haldin lived the heaviest hours of her life by that silent deathbed. I confess I was angry with the brokenhearted old woman passing away in the obstinacy of her mute distrust of her daughter.

When it was all over I stood aside. Miss Haldin had her compatriots round her then. A great number of them attended the funeral. I was there too, but afterwards managed to keep away from Miss Haldin, till I received a short note rewarding my self-denial. "It is as you would have it. I am going back to Russia at once. My mind is made up. Come and see me."

Verily, it was a reward of discretion. I went without delay to receive it. The *appartement* of the Boulevard des Philosophes presented the dreary signs of impending abandonment. It looked desolate and as if already empty to my eyes.

Standing, we exchanged a few words about her health, mine, remarks as to some people of the Russian colony, and then Natalia Haldin, establishing me on the sofa, began to talk openly of her future work, of her plans. It was all to be as I had wished it. And it was to be for life. We should never see each other again. Never!

I gathered this success to my breast. Natalia Haldin looked matured by her open and secret experiences. With her arms folded she walked up and down the whole length of the room, talking slowly, smooth-browed, with a resolute profile. She gave me a new view of herself, and I marveled at that something grave and measured in her voice, in her movements, in her manner. It was the perfection of collected independence. The strength of her nature had come to surface because the obscure depths had been stirred.

"We two can talk of it now," she observed, after a silence and stopping short before me. "Have you been to inquire at the hospital lately?"

"Yes, I have." And as she looked at me fixedly, "He will live, the doctors say. But I thought that Tekla . . ."

"Tekla has not been near me for several days," explained Miss Haldin quickly. "As I never offered to go to the hospital with her, she thinks that I have no heart. She is disillusioned about me."

And Miss Haldin smiled faintly.

"Yes. She sits with him as long and as often as they will let her," I said. "She says she must never abandon him—never as long as she lives. He'll need somebody—a hopeless cripple, and stone deaf with that."

"Stone deaf? I didn't know," murmured Natalia Haldin.

"He is. It seems strange. I am told there were no apparent injuries to the head. They say, too, that it is not very likely that he will live so very long for Tekla to take care of him."

Miss Haldin shook her head.

"While there are travelers ready to fall by the way our Tekla will never be idle. She is a good Samaritan by an irresistible vocation. The revolutionists didn't understand her. Fancy a devoted creature like that being employed to carry about documents sewn in her dress, or made to write from dictation."

"There is not much perspicacity in the world."

No sooner uttered, I regretted that observation. Natalia Haldin, looking me straight in the face, assented by a slight movement of her head. She was not offended, but turning away began to pace the room again. To my Western eyes she seemed to be getting farther and farther from me, quite beyond my reach now, but undiminished in the increasing distance. I remained silent as though it were hopeless to raise my voice. The sound of hers, so close to me, made me start a little.

"Tekla saw him picked up after the accident. The good soul never explained to me really how it came about. She affirms that there was some understanding between them—some sort of compact—that in any sore need, in misfortune, or difficulty, or pain, he was to come to her."

"Was there?" I said. "It is lucky for him that there was, then. He'll need all the devotion of the good Samaritan."

It was a fact that Tekla, looking out of her window at five in the morning, for some reason or other, had beheld Razumov in the grounds of the Château Borel, standing stock-still, bareheaded in the rain, at the foot of the terrace. She had screamed out to him, by name, to know what was the matter. He never even raised his head. By the time she had dressed herself sufficiently to run downstairs he was gone. She started in pursuit, and rushing out into the road, came almost directly upon the arrested tramcar and the small knot of people picking up Razumov. That much Tekla had told me herself one afternoon we happened to meet at the door of the hospital, and without any kind of comment. But I did not want to meditate very long on the inwardness of this peculiar episode.

"Yes, Natalia Victorovna, he will need somebody when they dismiss him, on crutches and stone deaf, from the hospital. But I do not think that when he rushed like an escaped madman into the grounds of the Château Borel it was to seek the help of that good Tekla."

"No," said Natalia, stopping short before me, "perhaps not." She sat down and leaned her head on her hand thoughtfully. The silence lasted for several minutes. During that time I remembered the evening of his atrocious confession—the plaint she seemed to have hardly enough life left in her to utter, "It is impossible to be more unhappy. . . ." The recollection would have given me a shudder if I had not been lost in wonder at her force and her tranquillity. There was no longer any Natalia Haldin, because she had completely ceased to think of herself. It was a great victory, a characteristically Russian exploit in self-suppression.

She recalled me to myself by getting up suddenly like a person who has come to a decision. She walked to the writing table, now stripped of all the small objects associated with her by daily use—a mere piece of dead furniture; but it contained something living still, since she took from a recess a flat parcel which she brought to me.

"It's a book," she said rather abruptly. "It was sent to me wrapped up in my veil. I told you nothing at the time, but now I've decided to leave it with you. I have the right to do that. It was sent to me. It is mine. You may preserve it, or destroy it after you have read it. And while you read it, please remember that I *was* defenseless. And that he . . ."

"Defenseless!" I repeated, surprised, looking hard at her.

"You'll find the very word written there," she whispered. "Well, it's true! I *was* defenseless—but perhaps you were able to see that for yourself." Her face colored, then went deadly pale. "In justice to the man, I want you to remember that I was. Oh, I was, I was!"

I rose, a little shakily.

"I am not likely to forget anything you say at this our last parting."

Her hand fell into mine.

"It's difficult to believe that it must be goodbye with us."

She returned my pressure and our hands separated.

"Yes. I am leaving here tomorrow. My eyes are open at last and my hands are free now. As for the rest—which of us can fail to hear the stifled cry of our great distress? It may be nothing to the world."

"The world is more conscious of your discordant voices," I said. "It is the way of the world."

"Yes." She bowed her head in assent, and hesitated for a moment. "I must own to you that I shall never give up looking forward to the day when all discord shall be silenced. Try to imagine its dawn! The tempest of blows and of execrations is over; all is still; the new sun is rising, and the weary men united at last, taking count in their conscience of the ended contest, feel saddened by their victory, because so many ideas have perished for the triumph of one, so many beliefs have abandoned them without support. They feel alone on the earth and gather close together. Yes, there must be many bitter hours! But at last the anguish of hearts shall be extinguished in love."

And on this last word of her wisdom, a word so sweet, so bitter, so cruel sometimes, I said goodbye to Natalia Haldin. It is hard to think I shall never look anymore into the trustful eyes of that girl—wedded to an invincible belief in the advent of loving concord springing like a heavenly flower from the soil of men's earth, soaked in blood, torn by struggles, watered with tears.

•   •   •   •   •   •   •   •

It must be understood that at that time I didn't know anything of Mr. Razumov's confession to the assembled revolutionists. Natalia Haldin might have guessed what was the "one thing more" which remained for him to do; but this my Western eyes had failed to see.

Tekla, the ex-lady companion of Madame de S——, haunted his bedside at the hospital. We met once or twice at the door of that establishment, but on these occasions she was not communicative. She gave me news of Mr. Razumov as concisely as possible. He was making a slow recovery, but would remain a hopeless cripple all his life. Personally, I never went near him: I never saw him again, after the awful evening when I stood by, a watchful but ignored spectator of his scene with Miss Haldin. He was in due course discharged from the hospital, and his "relative"—so I was told—had carried him off somewhere.

My information was completed nearly two years later. The opportunity, certainly, was not of my seeking; it was quite accidentally that I met a much-trusted woman revolutionist at the house of a distinguished Russian gentleman of liberal convictions, who came to live in Geneva for a time.

He was a quite different sort of celebrity from Peter Ivanovitch—a dark-haired man with kind eyes, high-shouldered, courteous, and with something hushed and circumspect in his manner. He approached me, choosing the moment when there was no one near, followed by a gray-haired, alert lady in a crimson blouse.

"Our Sophia Antonovna wishes to be made known to you," he addressed me, in his guarded voice. "And so I leave you two to have a talk together."

"I would never have intruded myself upon your notice," the gray-haired lady began at once, "if I had not been charged with a message for you."

It was a message of a few friendly words from Natalia Haldin. Sophia Antonovna had just returned from a secret excursion into Russia, and had seen Miss Haldin. She lived in a town "in the center," sharing her compassionate labors between the horrors of overcrowded jails and the heartrending misery of bereaved homes. She did not spare herself in good service, Sophia Antonovna assured me.

"She has a faithful soul, an undaunted spirit, and an indefatigable body," the woman revolutionist summed it all up, with a touch of enthusiasm.

A conversation thus engaged was not likely to drop from want of interest on my side. We went to sit apart in a corner where no one interrupted us. In the course of our talk about Miss Haldin, Sophia Antonovna remarked suddenly:

"I suppose you remember seeing me before? That evening when Natalia came to ask Peter Ivanovitch for the address of a certain Razumov, that young man who . . ."

"I remember perfectly," I said. When Sophia Antonovna learned that I had in my possession that young man's journal given me by Miss Haldin she became intensely interested. She did not conceal her curiosity to see the document.

I offered to show it to her, and she at once volunteered to call on me next day for that purpose.

She turned over the pages greedily for an hour or more, and then handed me the book with a faint sigh. While moving about Russia, she had seen Razumov too. He lived, not "in the center," but "in the south." She described to me a little two-roomed wooden house, in the suburb of some very small town, hiding within the high plank-fence of a yard overgrown with nettles. He was crippled, ill, getting weaker every day, and Tekla the Samaritan tended him unweariedly with the pure joy of unselfish devotion. There was nothing in that task to become disillusioned about.

I did not hide from Sophia Antonovna my surprise that she should have visited Mr. Razumov. I did not even understand the motive. But she informed me that she was not the only one.

"Some of *us* always go to see him when passing through. He is intelligent. He has ideas. . . . He talks well, too."

Presently I heard for the first time of Razumov's public confession in Laspara's house. Sophia Antonovna gave me a detailed relation of what had occurred there. Razumov himself had told her all about it, most minutely.

Then, looking hard at me with her brilliant black eyes:

"There are evil moments in every life. A false suggestion enters one's brain, and then fear is born—fear of oneself, fear for oneself. Or else a false courage—who knows? Well, call it what you like; but tell me, how many of them would deliver themselves up deliberately to perdition (as he himself says in that book) rather than go on living, secretly debased in their own eyes? How many? . . . And please mark this—he was safe when he did it. It was just when he believed himself safe and more—infinitely more—when the possibility of being loved by that admirable girl first dawned upon him, that he discovered that his bitterest railings, the worst wickedness, the devil work of his hate and pride, could never cover up the ignominy of the existence before him. There's character in such a discovery."

I accepted her conclusion in silence. Who would care to question the grounds of forgiveness or compassion? However, it appeared later on that there was some compunction, too, in the charity extended by the revolutionary world to Razumov the betrayer. Sophia Antonovna continued uneasily:

"And then, you know, he was the victim of an outrage. It was not authorized. Nothing was decided as to what was to be done with him. He had confessed voluntarily. And that Nikita who burst the drums of his ears purposely, out on the landing, you know, as if carried away by indignation—well, he has turned out to be a scoundrel of the worst kind—a traitor himself, a betrayer—a spy! Razumov told me he had charged him with it by a sort of inspiration . . ."

"I had a glimpse of that brute," I said. "How any of you could have been deceived for half a day passes my comprehension!"

She interrupted me.

"There! There! Don't talk of it. The first time I saw him, I, too, was appalled. They cried me down. We were always telling each other, 'Oh! you mustn't mind his appearance.' And then he was always ready to kill. There was no doubt of it. He killed—yes! in both camps. The fiend . . ."

Then Sophia Antonovna, after mastering the angry trembling of her lips, told me a very queer tale. It went that Councillor Mikulin, traveling in Germany (shortly after Razumov's disappearance from Geneva), happened to meet Peter Ivanovitch in a railway carriage. Being alone in the compartment, these two talked together half the night, and it was then that Mikulin the Police Chief gave a hint to the arch-revolutionist as to the true character of the arch-slayer of gendarmes. It looks as though Mikulin had wanted to get rid of that particular agent of his own! He might have grown tired of him, or frightened of him. It must also be said that Mikulin had inherited the sinister Nikita from his predecessor in office.

And this story, too, I received without comment in my character of a mute witness of things Russian, unrolling their Eastern logic under my Western eyes. But I permitted myself a question:

"Tell me, please, Sophia Antonovna, did Madame de S—— leave all her fortune to Peter Ivanovitch?"

"Not a bit of it." The woman revolutionist shrugged her shoulders in disgust. "She died without making a will. A lot of nephews and nieces came down from St. Petersburg, like a flock of vultures, and fought for her money amongst themselves. All beastly Kammerherrs and Maids of Honor—abominable court flunkeys. Tfui!"

"One does not hear much of Peter Ivanovitch now," I remarked, after a pause.

"Peter Ivanovitch," said Sophia Antonovna gravely, "has united himself to a peasant girl."

I was truly astonished.

"What! On the Riviera?"

"What nonsense! Of course not."

Sophia Antonovna's tone was slightly tart.

"Is he, then, living actually in Russia? It's a tremendous risk—isn't it?" I cried. "And all for the sake of a peasant girl. Don't you think it's very wrong of him?"

Sophia Antonovna preserved a mysterious silence for a while, then made a statement:

"He just simply adores her."

"Does he? Well, then, I hope that she won't hesitate to beat him."

Sophia Antonovna got up and wished me goodbye, as though she had not heard a word of my impious hope; but, in the very doorway, where I attended her, she turned round for an instant, and declared in a firm voice:

"Peter Ivanovitch is an inspired man."

THE END